THE WESTERN

# THE WESTERN

## FOUR CLASSIC NOVELS
## OF THE 1940s & 50s

*The Ox-Bow Incident* • Walter Van Tilburg Clark
*Shane* • Jack Schaefer
*The Searchers* • Alan Le May
*Warlock* • Oakley Hall

Ron Hansen, *editor*

THE LIBRARY OF AMERICA

Published in the United States by Library of America.
Visit our website at www.loa.org.

*The Ox-Bow Incident* copyright © 1940, renewed 1968
by Walter Van Tilburg Clark.
Reprinted with permission from the Estate and ICM Partners.
*The Searchers* copyright © 1954 by Alan LeMay.
Reprinted with permission from Kensington Publishing Corp.
*Shane* copyright © 1949, renewed 1976 by Jack Schaefer.
Reprinted by arrangement with Houghton Mifflin Harcourt
Publishing Company and Orion Publishing Group.
*Warlock* copyright © 1958 by Oakley Hall.
Reprinted with permission from the Estate c/o InkWell Management, LLC.

This paper exceeds the requirements of
ANSI/NISO Z39.48–1992 (Permanence of Paper).

Distributed to the trade in the United States
by Penguin Random House Inc.
and in Canada by Penguin Random House Canada Ltd.

Library of Congress Control Number: 2019952255
ISBN 978–1–59853–661–4

First Printing
The Library of America—331

Manufactured in the United States of America

# Contents

*Introduction* by Ron Hansen . . . . . . . . . . . . . . . . . . . . .    xi

THE OX-BOW INCIDENT
  by Walter Van Tilburg Clark . . . . . . . . . . . . . . . . . .    1

SHANE
  by Jack Schaefer . . . . . . . . . . . . . . . . . . . . . . . . . . .    209

THE SEARCHERS
  by Alan Le May . . . . . . . . . . . . . . . . . . . . . . . . . . .    325

WARLOCK
  by Oakley Hall . . . . . . . . . . . . . . . . . . . . . . . . . . .    561

*Biographical Notes* . . . . . . . . . . . . . . . . . . . . . . . . . . .    1083
*Note on the Texts* . . . . . . . . . . . . . . . . . . . . . . . . . . .    1087
*Notes* . . . . . . . . . . . . . . . . . . . . . . . . . . . . . . . . . . .    1090

# Four Classic Westerns

## INTRODUCTION BY RON HANSEN

M Y FIRST published novel was *Desperadoes*, about the Old
West's Dalton gang—three brothers and a vary-
ing number of reprobates who gave up their ill-paying jobs
as cowhands and deputy marshals to rob banks and trains.
Rather than a paperback shoot-'em-up, I'd hoped it would
be an entertaining but serious, high-class novel based on fact
—Shakespearean histories were my model—but whenever I
mentioned what I was working on, my hearers would offer a
wry, disbelieving smile, as in *You're kidding, right*? And some
seemed to consider it suicidal for me to try to launch my fiction writing career with such a shallow and hayseed form as
*the Western*.

The origin of the disdain may lie in the so-called dime novels of the late nineteenth century when eastern journalists like
Ned Buntline, at one time the highest-paid writer in America,
penned hundreds of fanciful narratives about headline outlaws
that were less indebted to their actual crimes than to earlier
swashbuckling tales of derring-do by the likes of Sinbad, Robin
Hood, and the Three Musketeers.

Yet ever since *The Great Train Robbery* of 1903, Western
movies have been well-established moneymakers at the box
office, and when I was a kid in the fifties *Gunsmoke* was the
highest-rated television show, with copycat variations like
*Rawhide, Maverick, Wyatt Earp, The Rifleman, Wagon Train,
Have Gun—Will Travel, The Lone Ranger, Johnny Ringo,
Sugarfoot*, and more than twenty other series.

The foundations of the attraction are in the brook-no-guff
self-reliance of the hero, his carefree calm in the face of adversity, his old-fashioned chivalry with women and fatherliness
with children, and his overriding sense of justice and the right-
ing of maddening wrongs. And in the egalitarianism of the
frontier those knightly qualities could just as readily be seen in
its more dashing and daredevil outlaws.

The Western's faults as a genre are generally based on its
tendency to over-simplicity and hyperbole, but there have been

a host of exceptions, and some of what can make the form intellectual, literary, and classic can be found in these four differently excellent novels.

***

Walter Van Tilburg Clark was a thirty-one-year-old high school English teacher when his first novel, *The Ox-Bow Incident* (1940), was published. And there's a good deal of English teacher in his class-time themes of innocence and guilt, mob violence and rash lawlessness, and his yoking of the legal thriller with the Old West. You can almost hear the Socratic questions as you read: "What is the novel saying about frontier justice?" "What feelings and fears influenced the posse's decision?" "Is America now any different?"

A rancher is murdered and his cattle stolen, so an outraged twenty-eight men form a posse to haul in and lynch the rustlers, but in their impatience to hang the culprits they finally settle on three random, innocent men whose only crime is that they share the misfortune of being strangers in the region.

Clark's father was the president of the University of Nevada, so the cultivation, refinement, and interest in philosophical ideas in *The Ox-Bow Incident* are perhaps unsurprising from his son. But combined with that was a child of the West's enchantment with the Sierras, the harsh desert landscape, and weather that can be so wildly overbearing that it can seem to have personality. And the year 1885 in which Clark's novel is set would have been vivid, immediate, and easily reconstructed once he was outside of any major town.

Acclaimed almost instantly as a classic, *The Ox-Bow Incident* was made into a 1943 William Wellman film starring Henry Fonda, Harry Morgan, Mary Beth Hughes, and Dana Andrews. The book is better than the movie if only because of its preoccupation with deeply ethical concerns that are fleetingly treated, if at all, in hundreds of other Westerns. Wallace Stegner wrote of his friend Walt Clark that "his theme was civilization and he recorded, indelibly, its first steps in a new country."

It's, so far, one of a kind.

***

I was a freshman in high school in Omaha and had force-marched my way through Nathaniel Hawthorne's *The Scarlet Letter*, which, given its sexual theme, ought to have been captivating to a fourteen-year-old boy but was decidedly not. Then, in a kind of feel-that-refreshing-breeze reprieve we got to the next book on our English class reading list: *Shane* by Jack Schaefer (1949). The faculty may have selected the novel because it was, at 168 pages, winningly short and was narrated by Bob Starrett, recollecting when he was a kid like us but in nineteenth-century Wyoming. And just like more than a few of us, he hero-worshipped, as if he was a cool uncle or a lordly older brother, the stoic and mysterious Shane.

The high school faculty may also have wanted to educate us in genre, for all the old-fashioned typologies of the Western were wedged into the book. Shane is the stranger who rides into town, the gunslinger with a dark past who wants to give up that life and simply work as a humble hired hand, until villainy forces him into what Vladimir Nabokov otherwise called "ox-stunning fisticuffs" and to holster his weapons again and defend the folks he's befriended in a thrilling shoot-out. "He was the man," Schaefer writes, "who rode into our little valley out of the heart of the great glowing West and when his work was done rode back whence he had come."

The historical basis for Schaefer's novel was the Johnson County War of 1889–1893, a conflict in which wealthy cattle companies vied with homesteading farmers and ranchers for grazing and water rights on the formerly unfenced rangelands, and finally hired assorted gunmen to persecute, lynch, and otherwise slaughter those opposing them. *Shane* mythologizes those deadly skirmishes into a good-versus-evil affair that has the grandness of chapters in *The Iliad*.

But what of young Bob Starrett's stolid, aloof, get-the-chores-done father who seems to be so indifferent to his appealing and seemingly lovelorn wife? Much of the psychological interest of *Shane* is its innuendos about sexual irregularities that went completely over this high school freshman's head but are more creepily overt in the 1953 film starring Alan Ladd and directed by George Stevens, an adaptation that Schaefer frankly disliked because he thought the male lead was "a runt."

Hundreds of novels set in the Old West have worked up the same material, but few have had *Shane*'s metaphorical impact and complexity.

*** 

Seeking to preserve their way of life, in 1836 hundreds of fearsome Comanches with some Kiowa and Kichai allies attacked outnumbered Anglo-European settlers in the wild frontier south of Dallas, killing adults and children alike but kidnapping for later ransom six young girls. Among them was the pretty, blue-eyed, nine-year-old Cynthia Ann Parker. Though the other girls were misused and finally returned to their homes in exchange for horses, rifles, and worldly goods, Cynthia was taken in by the squaws, forgot the English language and much about her former life, and eventually married a chief, giving birth to his three children, including a boy, the great Quanah, who would assume his mother's last name and grow up to be the greatest of the Comanche leaders during the so-called Indian Wars. Cynthia's uncle, John Parker, carried out a difficult, fixated, and fruitless quest for his niece until he died of exhaustion, and it was only after a full twenty-four years with the tribe that Cynthia was unwillingly rescued by forces of the Army and the Texas Rangers and was returned to relatives she didn't know and to what she did not think of as civilization.

Alan Le May was a very successful Hollywood screenwriter when he sought to combine various accounts of the long pursuit of Cynthia Parker into his novel *The Searchers* (1954). Just two years later it became John Ford's masterpiece of the same title, voted the Greatest Western Movie of All Time by the American Film Institute. Yet the original novel has been largely ignored of late, though it too is a masterpiece and, for me, even finer than the movie.

In the book, Martin Pauley and Amos Edwards are hunting down maverick cattle in post–Civil War Texas when warlike Comanches slaughter the Edwards family and other homesteaders, and carry off Debbie, Amos's niece. Convinced she's still alive and seeking her deliverance, Amos and Martin (played by John Wayne and Jeffrey Hunter in the movie) join up in a dogged, relentless, wearying six-year search that Le May fills with episodes of terror, aching boredom, prolonged taciturnity, and wry humor.

Le May dedicated his novel to a grandfather who died on the prairie in the mid-nineteenth century, leaving behind his widow and their three sons, each under the age of seven. That grandmother may have fascinated Le May as a child with tales of their hardscrabble life, for there's the hard-to-fake feel of firsthand information in Le May's telling and an idiosyncratic dialogue that's so fresh and authentic-seeming he must have once overheard it.

An old horse wrangler on the movie set for the adaptation of *The Assassination of Jesse James by the Coward Robert Ford* leaned over his creaking saddle to confide to me in near John Wayne fashion that he'd finished reading my novel just a night earlier and offered his highest praise with cowpoke brevity by gruffly saying, "Your book's the real deal."

It's a compliment I'll pass along: *The Searchers* is the real deal.

\*\*\*

*Warlock* was a finalist for the 1958 Pulitzer Prize and book reviews often compared it to *The Ox-Bow Incident*, implying that it was no rip-roaring yarn but worthy of serious attention. Larry McMurtry may have had imitation of Oakley Hall's novel as a goal when constructing his Pulitzer Prize–winning *Lonesome Dove*.

A gunslinger is hired by the upper crust of a southwestern silver-mining town to quell the rampant bloodshed that is impeding commerce and civic progress. His sidekicks are a worshipful political schemer and a quick-on-the-draw hothead versus a manipulative villain overseeing a gang of henchmen. There's even a gunfight in the Acme Corral. It's standard fare for the Western, and those who know something of Wyatt Earp, Doc Holliday, the Clanton gang, and the O.K. Corral in Tombstone, Arizona, will find the contents fetchingly familiar. But there's more: hints of the Lincoln County War in New Mexico, the murderous cattle barons of Wyoming, the later miners' strikes of the Wobblies, and a kitchen sink full of all the blood-soaked, messy ruckus of the West that caused it to be called Wild.

In a prefatory note to *Warlock* Oakley Hall wrote that he appropriated, rearranged, or ignored the accepted facts of those Old West legends, feeling that "the pursuit of truth, not facts, is the business of fiction." And his truth is that the nineteenth-century world, and our own, are fragile places ever at risk of dissolution and destruction. Warlock, of course, means "sorcerer," and a good deal of sly, wicked, jocular conjuring has gone into Hall's examination of the American mythos as it was influenced by the Cold War of the 1950s, with all of its confrontations and slam-bang action periodically worried over in the lucid, conservative, aching-to-be-fair "Journals of Henry Holmes Goodpasture," a straitlaced citizen of the town.

Rarely have I read a book that seemed to so clearly entertain its author in its composition. *Warlock* is epic in scope and rather devastating in its satirical portrait of how the West was won, but the gleefulness of Oakley Hall continually comes through and makes reading him a sheer joy.

So, four very different books, each of the highest quality and an outstanding example of what that seemingly woebegone genre, the Western, can rise to with the right intentions and in skillful hands.

# THE OX-BOW INCIDENT

*Walter Van Tilburg Clark*

# I

GIL AND I crossed the eastern divide about two by the sun. We pulled up for a look at the little town in the big valley and the mountains on the other side, with the crest of the Sierra showing faintly beyond like the rim of a day moon. We didn't look as long as we do sometimes; after winter range, we were excited about getting back to town. When the horses had stopped trembling from the last climb, Gil took off his sombrero, pushed his sweaty hair back with the same hand, and returned the sombrero, the way he did when something was going to happen. We reined to the right and went slowly down the steep stage road. It was a switch-back road, gutted by the run-off of the winter storms, and with brush beginning to grow up in it again since the stage had stopped running. In the pockets under the red earth banks, where the wind was cut off, the spring sun was hot as summer, and the air was full of a hot, melting pine smell. Rivulets of water trickled down shining on the sides of the cuts. The jays screeched in the trees and flashed through the sunlight in the clearings in swift, long dips. Squirrels and chipmunks chittered in the brush and along the tops of snow-sodden logs. On the outside turns, though, the wind got to us and dried the sweat under our shirts and brought up, instead of the hot resin, the smell of the marshy green valley. In the west the heads of a few clouds showed, the kind that come up with the early heat, but they were lying still, and over us the sky was clear and deep.

It was good to be on the loose on that kind of a day, but winter range stores up a lot of things in a man, and spring roundup hadn't worked them all out. Gil and I had been riding together for five years, and had the habit, but just the two of us in that shack in the snow had made us cautious. We didn't dare talk much, and we wanted to feel easy together again. When we came onto the last gentle slope into the valley, we let the horses out and loped across the flat between the marshes where the red-wing blackbirds were bobbing the reeds and twanging. Out in the big meadows on both sides the long grass was

3

bending in rows under the wind and shining, and then being let upright again and darkening, almost as if a cloud shadow had crossed it. With the wind we could hear the cows lowing in the north, a mellow sound at that distance, like little horns.

It was about three when we rode into Bridger's Wells, past the boarded-up church on the right, with its white paint half cracked off, and the houses back under the cottonwoods, or between rows of flickering poplars, every third or fourth one dead and leafless. Most of the yards were just let run to long grass, and the buildings were log or unpainted board, but there were a few brick houses, and a few of painted clapboards with gimcracks around the veranda rails. Around them the grass was cut, and lilac bushes were planted in the shade. There were big purple cones of blossom on them. Already Bridger's Wells was losing its stage-stop look and beginning to settle into a half-empty village of the kind that hangs on sometimes where all the real work is spread out on the land around it, and most of the places take care of themselves.

Besides the houses on the main street and the cross street that ran out into a lane to the ranches at the north and south ends, there wasn't much to Bridger's Wells: Arthur Davies' general store, the land and mining claims office, Canby's saloon, the long, sagging Bridger Inn, with its double-decker porch, and the Union Church, square and bare as a New England meeting house, and set out on the west edge of town, as if it wanted to get as far from the other church as it could without being left alone.

The street was nearly dried, though with wagon ruts hardened in it, so you could see how the teams had slithered and plowed in it. It drummed hard when we touched up to come in right. After all the thinking we'd done about it, the place looked dead as a Piute graveyard. There were a few horses switching at the tie rails in front of the inn and Canby's, but only one man in sight. That was Monty Smith, a big, soft-bellied, dirty fellow, with matted, gray streaked hair down to his shoulders and a gray, half-shaved beard with strawberry patches showing through, sore and itchy. Monty had been a kind of half-hearted rider once, but now he was the town bum, and kept balanced between begging and a conceited, nagging humor that made people afraid of him. Nobody liked him, but he was a tradition they'd have missed. Monty was leaning against a post of the arcade in front of Canby's, picking his teeth with a splinter and spitting. He looked us over out of his small, reddened eyes, nodded as if he was thinking of something else, and looked away again. We didn't see him. We knew that soon enough he'd be in to sponge on us. The notion made Gil sore, I guess, because he pulled in so sudden I had to rein Blue Boy around sharp to keep from climbing him.

"Take it easy," I told him.

He didn't say anything. We swung down, tied up, crossed the boardwalk, our boots knocking loudly, and went up the three steps to the high, narrow double door with the frosted glass panels that had Canby's name on them, inside two wreaths. Smith was watching us, and we went in without looking around.

It was dark and cool inside, and smelled of stale beer and tobacco. There was sawdust on the floor, the bar along one side and four green-covered tables down the other. There were the same old pictures on the wall too. Up back of the bar a big, grimy oil painting in a ponderous gilded frame of fruits and musical instruments showing a woman who was no girl any longer, but had a heavy belly and thighs and breasts, stretched out on a couch pretending to play with an ugly bird on her wrist, but really encouraging a man who was sneaking up on her from a background so dark you could see only his little, white face. The woman had a fold of blue cloth between her legs and up over one hip. I'd been around back once, and knew the picture had a little brass plate which said, dryly, *Woman with Parrot*, but Canby called it "The Bitching Hour." On the other wall was a huge, yellowish print, like a map, of a reception at the Crystal in Virginia City. On it President Grant and a lot of senators, generals, editors and other celebrities were posed around so you could get a good, full-length view of each. The figures were numbered, and underneath was a list, telling you who they all were. Then there was a bright-colored print of a bleached Indian princess in front of a waterfall, a big painting of a stagecoach coming in, the horses all very smooth, round bellied and with little thin legs all in step and all off the ground, and an oval, black and white picture of the heads of three white horses, all wild eyed and their manes flying.

Four men were playing poker at a back table with a lamp over them. I didn't know any of the men. They looked as if they'd been playing a long time, hunched down to their work, with no life showing except in the slits of their eyes or a hand which one of them moved once in a while to pick up his glass or a silver dollar from his pile, or to throw out a card. They were quiet.

Canby was behind his bar, a tall, thin, take-your-time kind of man with seedy gray hair combed to cover a bald spot. All Canby's bones were big and heavy, and those in his wrists were knobby and red. His arms were so long that he could sit on the back counter, where his glasses and bottles were arranged, and mop the bar. It was clean and dry now, but he mopped it while he waited for us. He looked at us, first one and then the other of us, but didn't say anything. He had watery, pale blue eyes, such as alcoholic old men sometimes have, but not weak, but hard and uninterested. They suited the veined, pitted, but tight-to-the-bone look of his face, which always seemed too large, the nose too large, the mouth too large, the cheekbones and black eyebrows too prominent. I wondered again where he'd come from. He looked like a man who knew he'd been somebody. Nobody ever found out, that I know of. He drank a lot, but he didn't talk except to pass the time of day, and he always kept that quiet, who-the-hell-are-you look.

"Well?" he said, when we just stood looking from the Bitch to the bottles.

Gil pushed his hat back so his red, curly hair showed, and folded his arms on the bar, and kept looking up at the Bitch. Gil has a big, pale, freckled face that won't darken and never shows any expression except in the eyes, and then only temper. His nose has been broken three times, and his mouth is thick and straight. He's a quick, but not a grudgy kind of fighter, and always talks as if he had a little edge, which is his kind of humor. It was Canby's kind too.

"That guy," said Gil, still looking at the picture, "is awful slow getting there."

Canby didn't look at the picture, but at Gil. "I feel sorry for him," he said. "Always in reach and never able to make it."

They said something like this every time we came in. It was

a ritual, Gil always taking the side of the woman with the parrot, and Canby always defending the man. Canby could deliver quite a lecture on the mean nature of the woman with the parrot.

"I got a feeling she could do better," Gil said.

"You're boasting," Canby told him, and then said again, "Well?"

"Don't rush me," Gil said.

"Take your time," Canby said.

"It don't look to me," Gil said, "like you was so rushed you couldn't wait!"

"It's not that. I hate to see a man who can't make up his mind."

"What do you care?"

"I either have to put them to bed or listen to their troubles, depending on what they drink," Canby said. His mouth only opened a slit when he talked, and the words came out as if he enjoyed them, but had to lift a weight to get them started.

"I ain't lookin' for either sleep or comfortin'," Gil said. "And if I was, I wouldn't come here for it."

"I feel better," said Canby. "What'll you have? Whisky?"

"What have you got?"

"Whisky."

"Did you ever know such a guy?" Gil said to me. "All this time I'm thinkin', and all he's got's whisky.

"And that's rotten, ain't it?" he asked Canby.

"Rotten," Canby agreed.

"Two glasses and a bottle," Gil said.

Canby set them out in front of us and uncorked the bottle.

"I wouldn't have the heart to open any of this other stuff," Canby said, taking a bottle of wine down and polishing it with his cloth. "I've had it ever since I was a boy; same bottles."

We put our fingers around the tops of the glasses, and Gil poured us one apiece, and we took them down. It was raw, and made the eyes water after being dry so long. We hadn't had a drop since Christmas.

"First time in?" Canby asked.

"Yessir," Gil said with pleasure. Canby shook his head.

"What's the matter?" Gil asked him.

Canby looked at me. "Do you always have this much trouble with him?" You always felt Canby was grinning at you, though his face stayed as set as an old deacon's.

"More, mostly," I said, and told him about the fight we'd had, which Gil had finished by knocking me across the red-hot stove. We drank slowly while we talked, and Gil listened politely, as if I were telling a dull story about somebody else. "It was just being cooped up together so long," I finished, remembering the one-room shack with the snow piled up to the window ledge and more of it coming, blowing against the glass like sand; the lonely sound of the wind, and Gil and I at opposite ends of the room, with two lamps burning, except for a truce at meal times. "It got so he wouldn't even ride with me. We took turns tailing up and feeding."

"He's naturally mean," Canby said. "You can tell that."

"A man needs exercise," Gil said. "He's not much of a fighter, but there wasn't anything else handy." He poured us another. "Besides, he started them all."

"Like hell I did," I said. "Do we look like I'd start them?" I asked Canby. I'm as tall as Gil is, but flat and thin, while Gil is built like a bull; his hands are twice as big as mine. Gil looks like a fighter too, with a long heavy chin and those angular eyes with a challenging stare in them. I could see myself in the mirror under the *Woman with a Parrot*. My face was burned dark as old leather already, but it's thin, with big eyes.

"You should have heard the things he said," Gil told Canby.

"By January," I put in, "he'd only talk about one thing, women. And even then he wouldn't be general. He kept telling the same stories about himself and the same women."

"Well, he wouldn't talk," Gil said, "and somebody had to. He'd sit there reading his old books like he had a lesson to learn, or writing all the time, scratch, scratch, scratch. It got on my nerves. Then I'd try to sing, and he'd get nasty. Once he went to the door, in the middle of a good song too, and stood there like he was listening for something, and all the time the wind blowing in, and thirty below outside. When I asked him what the matter was, he said nothing, he was just listening to the steers bawling; they sounded so good."

"Gil has a fine voice," I said, "but he only knows three songs, all with the same tune."

We kept on talking off our edge, Canby putting in a word now and then to keep us going, until Monty Smith came in. He started to say something to Gil, but Gil just looked at him, and Monty came over on my side and edged up to be friendly, with his back to the bar, as though it didn't mean a thing to him. I can't look a man down the way Gil can, so I just didn't look at him and didn't answer. I put a half dollar out on the bar, Canby poured out a couple of drinks, and Smith took them. He tried to be polite about it, saying, "Here's mud in your eye," and I felt mean to make him feel so much like a beggar. But Gil gave me the elbow, and I didn't say anything. Smith hung around for a minute or two, and then went out, hitching his belt in the doorway to get his conceit back.

When the door was closed Canby said, "Now that you two are peaceable again, what's on your mind?" He was talking to Gil.

"Does something have to be on my mind?" Gil asked.

"When you talk that long just being unsociable," said Canby, filling the glasses again, "yes." Gil turned his glass around and didn't say anything.

"What's he so bashful about?" Canby asked me.

"He wants to know if his girl is still in town," I told him.

"*His* girl?" said Canby, mopping a wet place and stooping to put the empty bottle under the bar.

"Take it easy," Gil said. He stopped turning his glass.

"If you mean Rose Mapen," Canby said, straightening up, "no. She went to Frisco the first stage out this spring."

Gil stood looking at him.

"It's a fact," Canby said.

"Hell," Gil said. He finished his drink in a toss. "Christ, what a town," he said furiously. His eyes were watering, he felt so bad about missing it.

"Have a drink," Canby said, opening another bottle, "but don't get drunk while you're feeling like that. The only unmarried woman I know of in town is eighty-two, blind and a Piute. She's got everything."

He poured another for each of us, and took one himself. You could see it tickled him that Gil had given himself away like that. But Gil was really feeling bad. All winter he'd talked about Rose Mapen, until I'd been sick of her. I thought she was a tart anyway. But Gil had dreamed out loud about buying a ranch and settling.

"It's my guess the married women ran her out," Canby said.

"Yeh?" Gil said.

"Oh, no tar and feathers; no rails. They just righteously made her uncomfortable. Not that she ever did anything; but they couldn't get over being afraid she would. Most of the men were afraid to be seen talking to her, even the unmarried ones. The place is too small."

Gil kept looking at him, but didn't say anything, and didn't look so personal. It's queer how deeply a careless guy like Gil can be cut when he does take anything seriously.

"Anything come of this gold they were talking about last fall?" I asked Canby.

"Do I look it?" he asked.

"No," he went on. "A couple of young fellows from Sacramento found loose gold in Belcher's Creek, up at the north end, and traced it down to a pocket. They got several thousand, I guess, but there was no lode. A lot of claims were staked, but nobody found anything, and it was too near winter for a real boom to get started." He looked at me with that malicious grin in his eyes. "Not even enough to get more than two or three women in, and they left before the pass was closed."

"It's nothing to me," I lied.

"What is there to do in this town, anyway?" Gil demanded.

"Unless you aim to get in line and woo Drew's daughter," Canby began.

"We don't," I informed him.

"No," he agreed. "Well, then, you have five choices: eat, sleep, drink, play poker or fight. Or you can shoot some pool. There's a new table in the back room."

"That's just great," Gil said.

The door opened, and Moore, Drew's foreman, came in. Moore was past forty and getting fat so his belt hung under his belly. He looked even older than he was, his face being heavily lined and sallow and his hair streaked with gray, with one white patch, like ash, on the back of his head. Moore was really a sick man, though he wouldn't stand for having anybody ask how he felt. He was past any fancy riding now, and even an ordinary day's work in the saddle would tire him out so his face got pasty. He had a lot of pain, I guess; his insides were all shot from staying at broncho busting too long. But he'd been a great rider once, one of the best, and he was still worth his salt. He knew horses and cattle and country as he knew his own mind, which was thoroughly. His eyes were still quiet and sure, and he never blew off or got absent-minded, no matter how bad he felt. Only I suspected he hadn't saved any money, any more than the rest of us did, and was really scared he wouldn't be fit to work much longer. He was a way more than average short on those questions about how he felt.

He came over to the bar, said hello to us, and threw a silver dollar onto the bar, nodding at Canby. Canby poured him a glass, finger around, and he downed it. Canby filled him another, which he let sit while he rolled a cigarette and licked it into shape.

"I see Risley's still around," Canby said. Moore nodded.

Risley was the sheriff for this territory, but he wasn't often closer than Reno, except on special call. I could see Moore didn't want to talk about it, hadn't liked Canby's mentioning Risley in front of us. But I was curious.

"There was talk about rustling last fall, wasn't there?" I asked Moore.

"Some," he said. He sucked two little streams of smoke up his nostrils and drank half his whisky before he let the smoke out. When it came out there wasn't much of it, and that thin. He didn't look at me, but at the three rows of dark bottles behind Canby. Canby wiped the dry bar again. He was ashamed. It was all right for Moore, but I didn't like Canby acting as if we were outsiders. Neither did Gil.

"Do they know anything about it?" he asked Moore. "Is that why Risley's out here?"

Moore finished his whisky, and nodded at the glass, which Canby filled up a third time. "No, we don't know anything, and that's why he's here," he said. He put his change in his pocket, and took his whisky over to the table by the front window. He sat down with his back to us, so Canby could talk.

"It's getting touchy, huh?" Gil said.

"They don't like to talk about it," Canby said, "except with fellows they sleep with."

"It's a long way from any border," he said after a minute, "and everybody in the valley would know if there was a stranger around."

"And there isn't?" I asked.

"There hasn't been, that knew cattle," said Canby, sitting back up on the counter, "except you two."

"That's not funny," Gil told him, and set his glass down very quietly.

"Now who's touchy?" Canby asked him. He was really grinning.

"You're talking about my business," Gil said. "Stick to my pleasures."

"Sure," Canby said. "I just thought I'd let you know how you stand."

"Listen," Gil said, taking his hands down from the bar.

"Take a drink of water, Gil," I said. And to Canby, "He's had five whiskies, and he's sore about Rose." I didn't really believe Gil would fight Canby, but I wasn't sure after his disappointment. Whenever Gil gets low in spirit, or confused in his mind, he doesn't feel right again until he's had a fight. It doesn't matter whether he wins or not, if it's a good fight he feels fine again afterward. But he usually wins.

"And you keep your mouth shut about Rose, see?" Gil told me. He had turned around so he was facing right at me, and I could tell by his eyes he was a little drunk already.

"All right, Gil," I reassured him. "All right. But you don't want to go pitching into your best friends on account of a little joke, do you? You can take a joke, can't you, Gil?"

"Sure I can take a joke," he argued. "Who says I can't take a joke?" He stared at us. We kept quiet. "Sure I can take a joke," he said again, but then turned back to his drink. "Some jokes though," he said, after a swallow, but then took another swallow, and let it go at that. I looked at Canby and bent my head a little toward Gil. Canby nodded.

"No offense meant, Carter," he said, and filled Gil's glass again, pouring slowly, as if he were doing it very carefully for somebody he thought a lot of.

"It's all right, it's all right," Gil said; "forget it."

Canby put two plates on the bar, and then got some hard bread and dried beef from under the counter and put them on the plates. Gil looked at them.

"And I don't need any of your leftovers to sober me up, either," he said.

"Just as you like," Canby said. "It's a long time since lunch. I just thought you might be hungry." He put some strong cheese on the plates too, and then took some cheese and a bottle over to Moore at the table. He stood by Moore, talking to him for a while. I was glad neither of them laughed.

I ate some of the dry food and cheese. It tasted good, now that I was wet down. We'd had a long ride, and nothing to eat since before daybreak. Finally Gil began to eat too, at first as though he weren't thinking about it, but just picking at it absent-mindedly, then without pretense.

"Are they sure about this rustling?" I asked Canby when he came back.

"Sure enough," he said. "They thought they'd lost some last fall, but with this range shut in the way it is by the mountains, they'd been kind of careless in the tally, and couldn't be too sure. Only Bartlett was sure. He doesn't run so many anyway, and his count was over a hundred short. He started some talk that might have made trouble at home, but Drew got that straightened out, and had them take another tally, a close one. During the winter they even checked by the head on the cows that were expected to calve this spring. Then, it was about three weeks ago now, more than that, a month, I guess, Kinkaid, who was doing the snow riding for Drew, got suspicious. He thought one of the bunches that had wintered mostly at the south end was thinning out more than the thaw explained. He and Farnley kept an eye out. They even rode nights some. Just before roundup they found a small herd trail, and signs of shod horses, in the south draw. They lost them over in the Antelope, where there'd been a new fall of snow. But in the Antelope, in a ravine west of the draw, they found a kind of lean-to shelter, and the ashes of several fires that had been built under a ledge to keep the smoke down. They figured about thirty head, and four riders."

"And the count came short this spring?"

"Way short," Canby said. "Nearly six hundred head, counting calves."

"Six hundred?" I said, only half believing it.

"That's right," Canby said. "They tallied twice, and with everybody there."

"God," Gil said.

"So they're touchy," said Canby.

"Did everybody lose?" I asked after a minute.

"Drew was heaviest, but everybody lost."

"But they would, wouldn't they, with that kind of a job," Gil said angrily.

"The way you say," Canby agreed.

We could see how it was, now, and we didn't feel too good being off our range. Not when they'd been thinking about it all year.

"What's Risley doing here? Have they got a lead?" Gil asked.

"You want to know a lot," said Canby. "He's down just in case of trouble. It's Judge Tyler's idea, not the cattlemen."

I was going to ask more questions. I didn't want to, and yet I did. But Moore got up and came back to the bar with the partly emptied bottle. He pushed it across to Canby, with another dollar beside it.

"Three out of that," he said.

"Lost any over your way?" he asked us.

"No," I admitted. "No more than winter and the coyotes could account for."

"Got any ideas?" Gil asked him. Canby paused, holding Moore's change in his hand.

"No ideas, except not to have any ideas," Moore said. He reached for his change and put it in his pocket. "Game?" he asked, to show we were all right.

Canby fished a deck out of a back drawer for us, and the three of us sat down at the front table. Moore played his cards close to his vest, and looked up at the ceiling with narrowed eyes every time before he'd discard. We played a twenty-five-cent limit, which was steep enough. Canby sat in with us until others began coming. Then he went back and stood wiping the bar and looking at them; he never liked to speak first. Most of the men who came in were riders and men we knew. I thought they looked at Gil and me curiously and longer than usual, but probably that wasn't so. Each of them nodded, or raised a hand, or said "hi," in the usual manner. They all went to the bar first, and had a drink or two. Then some of them got up a game at the table next to ours, and the rest settled into a row at the bar, elbows up and hats back. The place was full of the gentle vibration of deep voices talking mostly in short sentences with a lot of give and take. Now and then some man would throw his head back and laugh, and then toss off his drink before he leaned over again. Things didn't seem any different than usual, and yet there was a difference underneath. For one thing, nobody, no matter how genially, was calling his neighbor an old horse thief, or a greaser, or a card sharp, or a liar, or anything that had moral implications.

Some of the village men came in too: old Bartlett, who was a rancher, but had his house in the village, Davies, the store owner, and his clerk, Joyce, a tall thin sallow boy with pimples, a loose lower lip which made him look like an idiot, and big hands, which embarrassed him. Even the minister from the one working church, Osgood, came in, though he ostentatiously didn't take a drink. He was a Baptist, bald-headed, with a small nose and close-set eyes, but built like a wrestler. His voice was too enthusiastic and his manner too intimate to be true, and while he kept strolling pompously among the men, with one arm flexed behind him, the fist clenched, like the statue of a great man in meditation, the other hand was constantly and nervously toying with a seal on the heavy gold watch chain across his vest. I noticed that none of the men would be caught alone with him, and that they all became stiff or too much at ease when he approached, though they kept on drinking and playing, and spoke with him readily, but called him Mr. Osgood.

Bartlett came over to the table and watched. He was a tall man, looking very old and tired and cross. The flesh of his face was pasty and hung in loose folds, even his lower lids sagging and showing pools of red, like those of a bloodhound. He breathed audibly through his mouth, and kept blowing his mustache. He had on boots, but a flat Spanish sombrero and a long black frock coat, such as only the old men were wearing then. When Jeff Farnley came over too, Moore invited them to sit in. Farnley had a thin face, burned brick red, stiff yellow hair and pale hostile eyes, but a quick grin on a stiff mouth. He wiped his hands on his red and white cowhide vest and sat. Bartlett sat down slowly, letting himself go the last few inches, and fumbled for a cigar in his vest. When he got to playing he would chew the cigar and forget to draw on it, so that after every hand he had to relight it.

Osgood stood behind Moore and watched Gil and me play-ing. We were new to him, and I had an uneasy feeling, from the way he was sizing us up, that we were due to get our souls worked over a little. There was that about Osgood; he wouldn't know the right time from the wrong. Not that he'd try it here, but we'd have to move sharp when we left.

Then I forgot Osgood because I had something else to worry about. Gil was tight enough so I could see him squint-ing, sometimes two or three times, to make out what he had in his hand, but he was having a big run of luck. I knew he wasn't cheating; Gil didn't. Even if he'd wanted to he couldn't, with hands like his, not even sober. But with his gripe on he wasn't taking his winning right. He wasn't showing any signs of being pleased, not boasting, or bulling the others along about how thin they'd have to live, the way you would in an ordinary game with a bunch of friends. He was just sitting there with a sullen dead-pan and raking in the pots slow and contemptu-ous, like he expected it. The only variation he'd make would be to signal Canby to fill his glass again when he'd made a good haul. Then he'd toss the drink off in one gulp without looking at anybody or saying a "mud," and set the glass down and flick it halfway to the middle of the table with his finger. If there hadn't been anything else in the air you couldn't play long with a man acting like that without getting your chin out, especially when he was winning three hands out of four. I was getting riled myself.

It didn't seem to be bothering Moore. Once when Gil took in the chips three times running on straight poker, Moore looked at him and then at me, and shook his head a little, but that was all. A couple of other riders who'd sat in after Bart-lett and Farnley, started prodding Gil about it, but they stayed good natured and Gil just looked at them and went on playing cold. But that made their jokes sound pretty hollow, and after a little they didn't joke any more, though they didn't seem sore either. Old Bartlett, though, was beginning to mutter at his cards; nothing you could hear, just a constant talking to him-self. And he was throwing his hands in early and exasperated, and not bothering to relight his cigar any more. But it was Farnley I was really worried about. He had a flaring kind of face, and he wasn't letting off steam in any way, not by a look or a word or a move, but staring a long time at his bad hands and then laying the cards down quietly, sliding them onto the table and keeping his fingers on them for a moment, as if he had half a mind to do something else with them.

I hoped Gil's luck would change enough to look reasonable, but it didn't, so I dropped out of the game, saying he'd had enough off me. I thought maybe he'd follow suit, but even if he didn't, it would look better without his buddy in there. He didn't, and he kept winning. I didn't want to get too far from him, so I did the best I could and stood right behind him, where I could see his hand, but nobody else's.

After two more rounds Farnley said, "How about draw?" He said it quietly and watching Gil, as if changing the game would make a real difference. Gil was dealing and Farnley had no business asking for the change; it was picking the worst time he could. I knew by the set of his head that Gil was staring back at him like he'd just noticed he was there and wanted to get a clear impression. He held the cards in his fist for a moment and ruffled the edge of them with his other thumb. Moore was going to say something, and I had my fist all doubled to persuade Gil, but then Gil said,

"Sure. Why not?" So I saw the muscles bunch on Farnley's jaws; and Gil began to deal them out.

"Double draw, for a real change," Farnley said.

That's no poker player's game; draw's bad enough, but double draw's for old ladies playing with matches.

"Wait, Jeff," Moore started. Farnley looked at him quick, like he'd paste him if he said another word.

"Double draw it is," Gil said, without breaking his deal.

"Look 'em over careful, boys," he said, when they were all out. "Maybe somebody has two aces of spades."

Farnley let it go. He picked up his cards, and his face didn't change from its set look, but I could tell from the way he looked them all over again, and then bunched them together with his other hand before fanning them to stay, that he thought he had something this time. He drew two cards out and slid them onto the table face down, and this time didn't keep his fingers on them.

I looked at Gil's hand. He had the queen, jack and ten of spades, the ten of clubs and the four of hearts. He looked at it for a moment, but this was double draw. He threw off the club and the heart.

"How many?" he asked.

They drew around, Gil dropping Farnley's cards where he had to reach for them. Farnley looked at them longer this time. Then he put one down very slowly, like he wasn't sure. Four of a kind played cute, or keeping one for luck, I thought.

"Come again," he said.

"Don't hurry me," Gil said, putting down the deck to look at his own draw. He had the nine of spades and the queen of hearts. He thought again, but threw off the queen.

"Place your bets," he said sharp.

Moore, on his left, tossed his hand in. So did the next man. Farnley bet the limit. Bartlett and the other puncher, a fellow with curly black sideburns like wirehair, stayed, though Bartlett muttered.

Gil threw a half dollar out on top of his quarter so it clinked. "Double," he said.

"There's a limit," Moore said.

"How about it?" Gil asked Farnley, as if the other two weren't in the game.

Farnley put in the quarter, then threw a silver dollar after it. "Again," he said.

Bartlett balked, but I guess he had something too. When they didn't pay any attention to him he stayed. So did the other man, but sheepishly.

Gil matched the dollar.

"How many?" he asked again.

Moore pushed his chair back from the table to get his legs clear. The change in the game had got to the men at the bar. Five or six of them came over to watch, and the others turned around, leaning on the bar with their elbows, and were quiet too. Canby stood in the ring with his towel over his shoulder and that dry look of malicious pleasure on his face, but watching Gil and Farnley just the same.

"One," Farnley said. It was quiet enough so his voice sounded loud, and we could hear Gil slide the card off, and its tap on the table.

"You?" he asked Bartlett.

The old man had changed his mind. He'd taken just one the first time, but now he took two.

Farnley picked up his card slowly and looked at it. Then he put it slowly into the hand, closed the hand up, fanned it again, and sat there waiting for Gil to finish. The man standing behind Farnley couldn't help lifting his eyebrows and looking at Canby, who could see the hand too. Canby didn't appear to notice, but glanced at Gil. Gil was tending to business. He didn't even look up when Bartlett snorted violently and slapped his hand down, face up.

"Cover them cards," Moore said. Bartlett glared at him, but then turned the hand over.

The sheepish man took two.

"I'm taking one," Gil said, and put the deck down away from his hand, and slid one off the top and rubbed it back and forth on the felt for Farnley to see it was only one. Even at that Farnley didn't give any sign. Gil drew the card into his hand and picked them all up. He'd drawn the king of spades.

The sheepish man plucked at his mustache a couple of times and threw in.

"Your bet," Gil told Farnley.

Farnley tossed out another silver dollar. Gil threw out two. Farnley raised it another. Men stirred uneasily, but were careful to be quiet. Only when Farnley made it five Canby said, "Enough's enough. See him, Carter, or I'll close up the game."

Gil put out the dollar to see, and we started to relax, when he counted five more off the top of his pile and shoved them out.

"And five," he said.

That still didn't make it any sky-limit game, but it was mean for the kind of a game this had started out to be. There was plenty left in Gil's stack, but when Farnley had counted out the five there was only one dollar left on the green by his hand.

"Make it six," Gil said, and put in the extra one.

"Pick it up, Gil," I said. "You were seen at five."

There was some muttering from others too. Gil didn't pay any attention. He sat looking at Farnley. Farnley was breathing hard, and his eyes were narrowed, but he looked at his hand, not Gil.

"That's enough," Canby said, and started to pick up. It was Farnley, not Gil, who looked at him.

"Your funeral," Canby said.

"Maybe," Farnley said, and threw in the sixth dollar.

"I'm seeing you," he said, and laid out his hand carefully in a nice fan in front of him but opening toward Gil. We craned to see it. It was a full house, kings and jacks.

Gil tossed his cards into the center so they fell part covered and reached for the pot.

"Hold it," Moore said. Gil leaned back and watched Moore as if he was being patient with a fool. Moore spread the cards out so everybody could see them. One of the watchers whistled.

"Suit you?" Gil asked Moore.

Moore nodded and Gil reached the money in and began to put it in neat stacks, slowly and with pleasure.

Farnley sat staring at Gil's cards for a moment.

"Jesus," he said, "that's damned long luck," and suddenly let off by banging the table with his fist so hard that Gil's stacks slid down again into a loose pile. Gil had the canvas sack out of his jeans and was just ready to scoop the silver into it. He stopped and held the sack in the air. But Farnley wasn't going to start anything. He got up and turned toward the bar. He was doing well, I thought; you could tell by his face he was near crazy mad. Gil was the fool.

"Wouldn't suggest it was anything but luck, would you?" he asked, still holding the sack out in the air.

At first Farnley stood there with his back turned. Then he came back to the table, but slow enough so Moore had time to get to his feet before he spoke.

"I wasn't going to," he said; "but now you mention it."

Gil stood up too, letting the sack drop onto the coins on the table.

"Make it clear," he said, his voice thick and happy.

Gil was taller and a lot more solid than Farnley, and Farnley was so far gone I was scared. He had the look of a kill-fighter, not a man who was happy to rough it up. I saw his hand start for his belt, and I reached too. Gil doesn't think of a gun when he gets like that; he wants to slug. And he was drunk. But Farnley didn't have a gun; no belt on. He remembered it too, before he'd reached all the way, and wiped both hands on his seat to cover.

"There's a lot of things around here aren't clear," he said.

And then Gil had to say, "You're talking about cows now, maybe?"

I got set to hit him. There wasn't any use grabbing. "You're saying it this time too," Farnley told him.

"Come on, boys, the game's over," Canby put in. "The drinks are on you, Carter. You're heavy winner."

He took my mind off what I was doing. I swung, but Gil was already part way round the table. In spite of his weight and all he'd had to drink, he was quick, clumsy quick, like a bear. Canby reached but missed. Gil shoved Moore nearly off his feet and was on Farnley in three jumps, letting go a right that would have broken Farnley's neck. Farnley got under that one, but ducked right into a wild left that caught him on the corner of the mouth. He spun part way around, crashed across two chairs, and folded up under the front window, banging his head against the sill. Gil stood swaying and laughing as if he loved it. Then his face straightened and got that deadly pleased look again.

"Called me a rustler, did he?" he said thickly, as if somebody had just reminded him of it again. I knew the look; he was going to pile Farnley and hammer him. Nobody seemed to move. They were standing back leaving Gil alone by the table. I yelled something and started around, bumping into Moore, who was just getting set on his feet again. But I was too far behind. Canby turned the trick. Without even looking excited, he reached back to the bar, got hold of a bottle, and rapped Gil, not too hard either, right under the base of the skull. He must have done it a thousand times to be that careful about it. For a moment Gil's tension held him up. Then his knees bellied like cloth and he came down in a heap and rolled over onto his back, where he lay with a silly, surprised grin on his face and his eyes rolled up so only the whites showed. He slid against the table when he fell, and jarred it, so some of the coins and one glass of whisky slipped off, while another glass tipped over and the whisky streamed briefly, and then dribbled into a little pool by Gil's head. One of the coins lit on its edge and started rolling away by itself, and a man jumped out of the way of it like it was a snake. There was a little laughing.

"Looks happy, don't he?" Canby said, standing over Gil with the bottle in his hand.

"He'll be all right," he told me. "I just gave him a touch of it."

"It was neat," I said, and laughed. Others laughed too, and the talk began.

I helped Canby with Gil, who was heavy and limp and hard to prop in a chair. When we had him there I turned to the table to get some whisky to throw in his face, and had to laugh again. Bartlett was still sitting there, with a look on his face as if he didn't know yet what had happened, and the edge of the table shoved into him so it creased his big middle.

Canby had already thrown water in Gil's face, and was taking his gun out of the holster.

"He'll be all right," I said. "He always comes out of it nice."

Canby studied me for a moment, then nodded and let the gun slip back.

"How about him, though?" I asked, meaning Farnley.

Canby had hold of Gil's head between his two long hands and was working it around loosely and massaging the back of his neck. Still working, he looked over his shoulder at Farnley, where Moore had him in another chair by the window. Farnley was still out, but he was coming. His face was already beginning to swell, and his mouth was bleeding some from the corner. I didn't like the way he was coming back, slow, and without any chatter or struggle. Canby watched him too, until Farnley got back of his eyes again, and then, as if everything was all at once clear, sat up and shook off the hands working on him, and leaned forward, propping himself with his arms on his knees.

Gil was beginning to come up too. Canby turned back.

"Yeh," he said to me. "That's a different matter. Better pick up his dough," he added.

I got the sack and scooped the winnings from the table into it. Osgood, who had been standing around trying to think of something useful, picked up the coins that had fallen onto the floor, even tracking down the one that had rolled off.

Gil started to talk before he was out of it, muttering and

sort of joking and protesting. He rolled around some on the chair. When he really woke up he pushed us off, but gently, not wanting to jar himself. Then he took hold of his head with both hands and leaned way over.

"Holy cow," he said, and worked his hands in and out from his head to show how it was feeling.

Everybody laughed but Farnley, who looked across slow, and didn't seem to think anything was funny.

Gil got up, testing his legs, and turned his head carefully.

"I must have hit myself," he said. They laughed again.

Farnley got up, and the laughing stopped. But he only walked to the bar and got himself a drink. He didn't talk to anyone or look at anyone.

Gil closed his eyes, then his mouth, and got a queer, strangled look on his face. He put a hand up to his mouth and turned and hurried out through the back room. I followed him with his Indian sack in my hand. He was staggering some, and bumped against the outside kitchen door, but he got out quickly. I could hear the men laughing again behind us. They liked the way Gil took it; he made it all right for them to laugh, and he did look funny, that big, red-headed bear trotting out like a little kid holding his pants.

When I got to him he was standing in a little cleared, black space where Canby burned his rubbish, with his hands on his knees, leaning over some green tumbleweed that was still rooted in. He was pretty well emptied out already, and just getting hold of himself again.

He stood up with his eyes watering and his face red.

"Holy cow," he gulped.

"It must have been Canby," he said. "Now I've got to start all over again."

"Take your time," I advised. "You've got head enough."

Gil stood there breathing in and looking around like he was really starting life again, though doubtfully. The clouds had risen higher in the west, and now and then one blew free across the valley, making a deeper, passing shadow on the shadow of the bending grass.

From somewhere down the side street we caught the sound of a running horse on the hard-pan. By the clatter, he was being pushed.

"Somebody's in a hell of a hurry," Gil said.

We got a glimpse of the rider as he rounded onto the main street. The horse banked around at a considerable angle, and was running hard and heavily. There was white dropping away from his bit. The rider had been bent over with his hat pulled down hard, but even in the little space we could see him, he straightened back and began to rein in strong. Then they were out of sight behind Canby's. There'd be trouble stopping that horse. He looked to me like he'd been run till he couldn't quit.

"I'm not, though," Gil said.

I liked it out there too. It was good after the stale darkness inside. A long roundup makes you restless inside houses for a while. Now and then in the freshening wind we could hear a meadow lark "chink-chink-a-link," and then another, way off and higher, "tink-tink-a-link." I could see how they'd be leaping up out of the grass, fluttering while they just let off for all the spring was worth to them, and then dropping back into the grass again.

Gil, though, was thinking about something.

"He didn't use his fist, did he?"

"What?"

"Canby. He didn't knock me out with his fist, did he?"

"No, a bottle."

"That's all right, then. I thought it must have been that."

And after breathing in a couple of times more, "He shouldn't have stopped me though. I don't feel any better."

"It takes a lot to please you," I told him. "Anyway, lay off Farnley. You were pretty low on that."

"Listen who's giving the orders," he said, but grinning.

"Yeh, I guess I was at that," he said seriously. "Maybe I ought to give him back his money. Say, the money," he said quickly.

"I've got it," I told him, and gave him the sack. He weighed it in his hand and ran his tongue over his lower lip.

"You think I ought to give it back?" he asked unhappily.

"Not all of it," I said. "Most of it was won fair. But not the last pot; that was no poker."

That cheered him up. "Yeh, the last pot," he agreed, "that was the one."

He stared at the sack. "Maybe you'd better give it to him," he said. "How much was it?"

"No, you give it to him," I said. "That will fix it better."

He looked at me, thinking about it.

"You don't need to say anything, just that you were pretty drunk," I advised.

That seemed to satisfy him.

"How much was it?" he asked again.

"Ten dollars is near enough," I said.

"Is that all?" he said, feeling better.

He poured coins out into his hand, counted out ten dollars, dropped the rest back in, drew the sack tight, tied it around the neck and slipped it into his pocket. It still made a big bulge. With the ten dollars in his hand he started for the back door.

"Better kind of sidle up," I said.

He stopped short and looked at me. "The hell I will," he said. He was coming back all right. He had a wonderful strong head when his belly was clean. "Why should I?" he asked, as if he was willing to be reasonable if I didn't expect too much.

"You hit him plenty hard," I said, "and you made him look foolish."

"Did I?" he asked. Then, "Did I get him?"

"You got him. I thought you'd busted his neck."

Gil grinned. "Well, I'll try and go easy," he said.

We went in through the kitchen and the back room where Canby served meals and had a pool table now. But when we got to the bar door I could see right away something was wrong. Farnley was standing at the other end, by the front door, looking like he hadn't come out of his daze yet, and Moore had hold of him by the arm and was talking to him. Davies was trying to say something too. Just when we stopped, Farnley shook Moore off, though still standing there.

"The lousy sons-of-bitches," he said, and then repeated it slowly, each word by itself.

At first I was going to try to get Gil out the back way again. It wouldn't be easy. When he heard Farnley he pulled the sack out of his jeans again and dropped the ten dollars back into it. And it wasn't his drunk fighting face that was coming on now, either.

Then I saw how the men were, all gathered together along the bar there, looking quiet and angry, and not paying any attention to us. When they heard our boots a few glanced at us, but didn't even seem to see us. They'd been watching Farn-ley at first, and now they were looking at a new rider who was talking excitedly, so I couldn't get what he said. He was a young fellow, still in his teens, I thought, and he was out of breath. He was feeling important, but wild too, talking fast and waving his right hand, and then slapping the gun on his thigh, which was tied down like a draw-fighter's. His black sombrero was pushed onto the back of his head, and his open vest was flapping. There was a movement and mutter beginning among the men, but at the end the kid's voice came up so we could hear what he was saying.

"Shot right through the head, I tell you," he cried, like somebody was arguing with him, though nobody was.

Farnley reached out and grabbed the kid by the two sides of his vest in one hand, yanked him close and spoke right in his face. The kid looked scared and said something low. Farnley still held him for a moment, staring at him, then let him go, turned and pushed through to the front door and out onto the walk.

Some of the men followed him, but most of them milled around the kid, trying to get something more out of him, but not being noisy now either.

"Come on," I told Gil, "it's not us."

"It better not be," Gil said, starting slow to come with me.

"It's the kid that was riding so fast," I explained.

They were all beginning to crowd outside now. Only Smith was trying to push in past them, with his eye out for drinks they'd left on the bar. And they'd left a lot, seven or eight that weren't empty. And Canby saw Smith and didn't say anything either, but went and stood in the door behind the others, look-ing out. Something was up.

"What's up?" I asked Canby, trying to see past him. He didn't turn his head.

"Lynching, I'd judge," he said, like it didn't interest him.

"Those rustlers?" I asked.

"Maybe," he said, looking at me kind of funny. "They don't know yet who. But somebody's been in down on Drew's range and killed Kinkaid, and they think there's cattle gone too."

"Killed Kinkaid?" I echoed, and thought that over quick. Kinkaid had been Farnley's buddy. They'd been riding together from the Panhandle to Jackson Hole ever since they were kids. Kinkaid was a little, dark Irishman who liked to be by himself, and never offered to say anything, but only made short answers when he had to, and then you had to be close to hear him. He always seemed halfway sad, and though he had a fine, deep singing voice, he wouldn't often sing when he knew anybody could hear. He was only an ordinary rider, with no flair to give him a reputation, but still there was something about him which made men cotton to him; nothing he did or said, but a gentle, permanent reality that was in him like his bones or his heart, that made him seem like an everlasting part of things. You didn't notice when he was there, but you noticed it a lot when he wasn't. You could no more believe that Kinkaid was dead than you could that a mountain had moved and left a gap in the sky. The men would go a long way, and all together, to get the guy that had killed Kinkaid. And I was remembering Canby's joke about Gil and me.

"When?" Gil asked.

Then Canby looked at him too. "They don't know," he said; "about noon, maybe. They didn't find him till a lot later." And he looked at me again.

I wanted to feel the way the others did about this, but you can feel awful guilty about nothing when the men you're with don't trust you. I knew Gil was feeling the same way when he started to say something, and Canby looked back at him, and he didn't say it. But we couldn't afford to stand in there behind Canby either. I pushed past him and went down onto the walk, Gil right behind me.

# 2

---

F ARNLEY WAS climbing onto his horse. He moved slowly
and deliberately, like a man with his mind made up. A rider
yelled, as if Farnley was half a mile off, "Hey, Jeff. Wait up;
we'll form a posse."

"I can get the sons-of-bitches," Farnley said, and reined
around.

Moore said, "He's crazy," and started out into the street.
But Davies was ahead of him. He came alongside Farnley in
a little, shuffling run, and took hold of his bridle. The horse,
checked, wheeled his stern away from Davies and switched
his tail. The way Farnley looked down, I thought he was
going to let Davies have it in the face with his quirt. But
he didn't. Davies was an old man, short and narrow and so
round-shouldered he was nearly a hunchback, and with very
white, silky hair. His hollow, high-cheeked face, looking up at
Farnley, was white from indoor work, and had deep forehead
lines and two deep, clear lines each side of a wide, thin mouth.
The veins made his hollow temples appear blue. He would
have been a good figure for a miser except for his eyes, which
were a queerly young, bright and shining blue, and usually,
though not now, humorous. Farnley looked at those eyes and
held himself.

"There's no rush, Jeff," Davies said, coaxing him. "They
have a long start of us, anyway."

Farnley said something we couldn't hear.

Davies said, "You don't know how many of them there are,
Jeff. There might be twenty. It won't help Larry to get yourself
killed too."

Farnley didn't say anything, but he didn't pull his horse away.
The horse yanked its head up twice, and Davies let go of the
bridle, and put a hand on Farnley's knee.

"We aren't even certain which way they went, Jeff, or how
long they've had. You just wait till we know what we're doing.
We're all with you about Kinkaid. You know that, son."

He kept his hand on Farnley's knee, and stood there with his
hat off and the sun shining in his white hair. The hair was long,

28

down over his collar. Farnley must have begun to think a little. He waited. Moore went out to them.

Osgood was standing beside me on the walk. "They mustn't do this; they mustn't," he said, waving his hands and looking as if he were going to cry. Then he thrust his hands back into his pockets again.

Gil was behind us. He said to Osgood, "Shut up, gran'ma. Nobody expects you to go."

Osgood turned around quickly and nervously. "I'm not afraid," he asserted. "Not in the least afraid. It is quite another consideration which prevents . . ."

"You can preach later," Gil cut him off without looking at him, but watching Moore talk to Farnley. "There'll be more of us needing it, maybe."

"You ain't even got a gun yet, Jeff," Moore was repeating.

Osgood suddenly went out to the two men by the horse. He went busily, as if he didn't want to, but was making himself. His bald head was pale in the sun. The wind fluttered his coat and the legs of his trousers. He looked helpless and timid. I knew he was trying to do what he thought was right, but he had no heart in his effort. He made me feel ashamed, as disgusted as Gil.

"Farnley," he said, in a voice which was too high from being forced, "Farnley, if such an awful thing has actually occurred, it is the more reason that we should retain our self-possession. In such a position, Farnley, we are likely to lose our reason and our sense of justice.

"Men," he orated to us, "let us not act hastily; let us not do that which we will regret. We must act, certainly, but we must act in a reasoned and legitimate manner, not as a lawless mob. It is not mere blood that we want; we are not Indians, savages to be content with a miserable, sneaking revenge. We desire justice, and justice has never been obtained in haste and strong feeling." I thought he intended to say more, but he stopped there and looked at us pathetically. He talked with no more conviction than he walked.

The men at the edge of the walk stirred and spit and felt of their faces. It was not Osgood, really, who was delaying them, but uncertainty, and perhaps the fear that they were going to hunt somebody they knew. They had been careful a long time.

Davies saw that Osgood had failed. His mouth tightened downward.

Farnley paid no attention, but having admitted he would wait, just sat his saddle rigidly. His horse knew something was wrong, and kept swinging his stern, his heels chopping. Farnley let him pivot. He reared a little and swung his tail back toward the Reverend. Osgood backed away hurriedly. One of the punchers laughed. Osgood did look queer, feinting and wavering out there. Moore looked back at us angrily. Farnley's back had gone stiff under the cowhide vest. The man who had laughed pulled his hat down and muttered.

"We'll organize a posse right here, Jeff," Moore promised. "If we go right, we'll get what we're after." For Moore, that was begging. He waited, looking up at Farnley.

Then Farnley pulled his horse around slowly, so he sat facing us.

"Well, make your posse," he said. He sat watching us as if he hated us all. His cheeks were twitching.

Canby was still leaning in the door behind us, his towel in his hand. "Somebody had better get the sheriff, first thing," he advised. He didn't sound as if it mattered to him whether we got the sheriff or not.

"And Judge Tyler," Osgood said. He was impressed by the suggestion, and came over to stand in front of us, closer. "Judge Tyler must be notified," he said.

"To hell with that," somebody told him. That started others. "We know what that'll mean," yelled another. A third shouted, "We know what that'll mean is right. We don't need no trial for this business. We've heard enough of Tyler and his trials." The disturbance spread. Men began to get on their horses.

The kid, Greene, had been forgotten too long. He pushed through toward Osgood with his fist doubled. But Osgood faced him well enough. Greene stopped at the edge of the walk. "This ain't just rustling," he yelled.

"Rustling is enough," Bartlett told him; then he pulled off his hat and waved it above his head. His head looked big when it was uncovered. There was a pasted-down line around it from the sweat under his hatband. He curled his upper lip when he talked angrily, showing his yellow, gappy teeth and making his mustache jerk.

"I don't know about the rest of you," he cried. He had a big, hollow voice when he was angry enough to lift it. "I don't know about the rest of you, but I've had enough rustling. Do we have rights as men and cattlemen, or don't we? We know what Tyler is. If we wait for Tyler, or any man like Tyler," he added, glaring at Osgood, "if we wait, I tell you, there won't be one head of anybody's cattle left in the meadows by the time we get justice." He ridiculed the word justice by his tone. "For that matter," he called, raising his voice still higher, "what is justice? Is it justice that we sweat ourselves sick and old every damned day in the year to make a handful of honest dollars, and then lose it all in one night to some miserable greaser because Judge Tyler, whatever God made him, says we have to fold our hands and wait for his eternal justice? Waiting for Tyler's kind of justice, we'd all be beggars in a year.

"What led rustlers into this valley in the first place?" he bellowed. "This is no kind of a place for rustlers. I'll tell you what did it. Judge Tyler's kind of justice, that's what did it. They don't wait for that kind of justice in Texas any more, do they? No, they don't. They know they can pick a rustler as quick as any fee-gorging lawyer that ever took his time in any courtroom. They go and get the man, and they string him up. They don't wait for that kind of justice in San Francisco any more, do they? No, they don't. They know they can pick a swindler as well as any overfed judge that ever lined his pockets with bribes. The Vigilance Committee does something—and it doesn't take them six months to get started either, the way it does justice in some places.

"By the Lord God, men, I ask you," he exhorted, "are we going to slink on our own range like a pack of sniveling boys, and wait till we can't buy the boots for our own feet, before we do anything?

"Well, I'm not, for one," he informed us, with hoarse determination. "Maybe if we do one job with our own hands, the law will get a move on. Maybe. And maybe it never will. But one thing is sure. If we do this job ourselves, and now, it will be one that won't have to be done again. Yes, and what's more, I tell you we won't ever have to do any such job again, not here.

"But, by God," he begged, "if we stand here yapping and whining and wagging our tails till Judge Tyler pats us on the head, we'll have every thieving Mex and Indian and runaway Reb in the whole territory eating off our own plates. I say, stretch the bastards," he yelped, "stretch them."

He was sweating, and he stared around at us, rolling his bloodshot eyes.

He had us excited. Gil and I were quiet, because men had moved away from us, but I was excited too. I wanted to say something that would square me, but I couldn't think what. But Bartlett wasn't done. He wiped his face on his sleeve, and when he spoke again his voice went up so high it cracked, but we could understand him. Faces around me were hard and angry, with narrow, shining eyes.

"And that's not all," Bartlett was crying, piping. "Like the boy here says, it's not just a rustler we're after, it's a murderer. Kinkaid's lying out there now, with a hole in his head, a God-damned rustler's bullet hole. Let that go, and I'm telling you, men, there won't be anything safe, not our cattle, not our homes, not our lives, not even our women. I say we've got to get them. I have two sons, and we all know how to shoot; yes, and how to tie a knot in a rope, if that's worrying you, a knot that won't slip.

"I'm for you, Jeff," he shouted at Farnley, waving his hat in a big arc in front of him. "I'm going to get a gun and a rope, and I'll be back. If nobody else will do it, you and I and the boys will do it. We'll do it alone."

Farnley raised one hand, carelessly, in a kind of salute, but his face was still tight, expressionless and twitching. At his salute the men all shouted. They told him loudly that they were with him too. Bartlett stirred us, but Farnley, sitting there in the sun, saying nothing, now stirred us even more. If we couldn't do anything for Kinkaid now, we could for Farnley. We could help Farnley get rid of his lump. He became a hero, just sitting there, the figure which concentrated our purpose.

Thinking about it afterward I was surprised that Bartlett succeeded so easily. None of the men he was talking to owned any cattle or any land. None of them had any property but their horses and their outfits. None of them were even married, and the kind of women they got a chance to know weren't likely to be changed by what a rustler would do to them. Some out of that many were bound to have done a little rustling on their own, and maybe one or two had even killed a man. But they weren't thinking of those things then, any more than I was. Old Bartlett was amazing. It seemed incredible that so much ferocity hadn't killed him, weak and shaky as he appeared. Instead, it had made him appear straighter and stronger.

He turned around and pushed through us in a hurry, not even putting his hat on. I could hear him wheezing when he shoved past me, and his lower lip stuck out, reaching for his mustache.

Osgood called to the men. "Listen, men," he called. Most of them were already on their horses. "Listen, men," he called again. Old Bartlett stopped out in the sun on the walk beyond us. He was going to come back and collar the preacher. "Listen to me, men. This insane violence . . ."

Gil walked over close to Osgood. "You listen to me, preacher," he said. "I thought I told you once to shut up." Osgood couldn't help backing away from him. He backed off the walk, and stumbled in the street. This mortified him so he grasped his forehead with both hands for a moment, as if trying vainly to get himself back together again; or else to protect his skull. When we all laughed, businesslike, contemptuous laughter, in a short chorus, old Bartlett grinned and turned around and went off up the walk again.

Suddenly Osgood uncovered his head and ran to Davies, holding both hands out in front of him, first like a child running to beg for something, then weaving them back and forth while he talked.

"They won't listen to me, Mr. Davies," he babbled. "They won't listen. They never would. Perhaps I'm weak. Any man is weak when nobody cares for the things that mean something to him. But they'll listen to you. You know how to talk to them, Davies. You tell them.

"Oh, men," he cried out, coming back at us, "think, won't you; think. If you were mistaken, if . . ."

He gave up, and stared at us, still moving his hands like birds with their legs caught.

Davies, without moving away from Farnley, said clearly, "Mr. Osgood is right, men. We should wait until . . ."

"What do you know about it?" Gil asked him.

A voice from the door called, "The trouble with Davies is

that he can't see no profit in this. It's hard to move Davies when he can't see no profit. Now, if you'd offer to buy the rope from him . . ." It was Smith. He still had a whisky glass in his hand, and he'd pushed past Canby and was standing on the top step with his legs apart and his other hand in his belt, where it hung under his belly.

Davies did look sharp at that, but Moore acted for him. He reached up and grabbed Smith by the belt, and pulled him down among us.

"If we go, you're going, porky."

"You don't have to tell me," Smith laughed. He pushed Moore off. "I wouldn't miss it," he said. "The only thing would get me out faster, would be your necktie party, Moore." A few men watching them laughed, and this encouraged Smith. "Who knows," he added, "maybe this *is* yours."

They'd all been afraid for months that they'd know the man. This was a hit. Moore, though, just looked Smith in the eye until the big drunk couldn't face him. Then he said, "I'll remember that. I'll see that you get to handle a rope!"

Gil had been pleased, his words to Osgood having made things better for us. Now suddenly he was quieter, and sober.

Canby said, "You're wasting a lot of time. Whoever you're after has made five miles while you argued."

"You gotta get guns," Greene piped. "They shot Kinkaid. They got guns."

Only two or three of the men had guns. Gil and I had ours, because we were on the loose and felt better with them. They called to Farnley they'd be back and went off after guns, some of them riding, some running on the walks.

To the rest of us Davies said, "There are only a few of you now. Will you listen to me?" Moore and Osgood were looking at us too.

"We listened once," Smith said, "listened, and heard nothing. As for me," he grinned, "I think I'll have a couple of drinks on the house. I want to be primed."

Canby blocked the door. "Not here, you don't," he said. "Two more and you'd have to be tied on. If you went."

"It's past talk, Davies," a puncher told him. "You can see that." He didn't sound angry.

"Yes," Davies said. "Yes, I guess you're right."

"I'm going to have a drink," Gil said; "I want a hell of a long drink."

I told him that suited me. There were only a few men left now, talking quietly in the blue shadow of the arcade. Up and down the street you could hear the others, their boots on the boardwalk or their horses trotting. A few called to each other, reminding that it might be a long ride, or to bring a rope, or advising where a gun might be borrowed, since most of them were from ranches outside the village. The sun was still bright in the street, but it was a late-in-the-afternoon light. And the wind had changed. The spring feeling, warm when it was still, chilly when the air stirred, was gone. Even right out in the sun it was pretty cold now. I went out in the street to take a look west. The clouds over the mountains had pushed up still more, and were dark under their bellies.

Davies stood on the walk while I was looking at the sky. I thought he was waiting for me, and took longer than I had to, hoping he would go in. But there's only about so much to look at in one sky; I'm no painter. I gave it up and he came in with me, though not saying anything. He stood up to drink with us too. There were half a dozen of us drinking. Canby had left the door open, and through it I could see Farnley still sitting in his saddle in the sun. Nobody was going to change his mind with Farnley sitting there. Gil kept looking out at him too. Gil felt partly to blame for how hard Farnley was taking this; or maybe it was the ten dollars.

"What made you so hot for a drink?" I asked Gil, to keep ahead of Davies.

"Nothing; I'm thirsty," he said, drinking one and pouring another.

"Yes, there is too," he admitted. "I'd forgot all about it until Moore told Smith he could hold a rope that way. I was layin' up in Montana that winter, stayin' with an old woman who put out good grub. Sittin' right on her front porch I saw them hang three men on one limb."

He took his other drink down. That didn't worry me now. Feeling this way he could drink twenty and not know it. He poured another. He talked low and quick, as if he didn't mind my hearing it, but didn't want anyone else to.

"They kicked a barrel out from under each one of them, and

the poor bastards kept trying to reach them with their toes."
He looked down at his drink. "They didn't tie their legs," he
said, "just their arms."

After a minute he said, "That was an official posse though,
sheriff and all. All the same . . ." He started his third drink,
but slowly, like he didn't want it much.

"Rustlers?" I asked him.

"Held up a stagecoach," he told me. "The driver was shot."

"Well, they had it coming," I said.

"One of them was a boy," he said, "just a kid. He was scared
to death and kept crying, and telling them he hadn't done it.
When they put the rope around his neck his knees gave out.
He fell off the barrel and nearly choked."

I could see how Gil felt. It wasn't a nice thing to remember
with a job of this kind in front of you. But I could tell Davies
was listening to Gil. He wasn't looking at us, but he was just
sipping his drink, and being too quiet.

"We got to watch ourselves, Gil," I told him, very low, and
looking up at the woman with the parrot.

"To hell with them," he said. But he didn't say it loudly.

"Greene was all mixed up," I said, still muttering over my
chin. "He wasn't sure of anything except Kinkaid was shot in
the head. But he thought it was about noon."

"I know," Gil said.

Then he said, "They're gettin' back already. Hot for it, ain't
they?" It sounded like remembering that Montana job had
changed his whole way of looking at things.

I could tell without turning who was coming. There wasn't
a big, flat-footed clop-clop like horses make on hard-pack, but
a kind of edgy clip-clip-clip. There was only one man around
here would ride a mule, at least on this kind of business. That
was Bill Winder, who drove the stage between Reno and Bridger's Wells. A mule is tough all right; a good mule can work two
horses into the ground and not know it. But there's something
about a mule a man can't get fond of. Maybe it's just the way
a mule is, just as you feel it's the end with a man who's that
way. But you can't make a mule part of the way you live, like
your horse is; it's like he had no insides, no soul. Instead of a
partner you've just got something else to work on along with
the steers. Winder didn't like mules either, but that's why he

rode them. It was against his religion to get on a horse; horses
were for driving.

"It's Winder," Gil said, and looked at Davies and grinned.
"The news gets around, don't it?"

I looked at Davies too, in the glass, but he wasn't showing anything, just staring at his drink and minding his own
thoughts.

Winder wouldn't help Davies any; we knew that. He was
edgy the same way Gil was, but angry, not funning, and you
couldn't get at him with an idea.

We saw him stop beside Farnley and say something and,
when he got his answer, shake his head angrily and spit, and
pull his mule into the tie rail with a jerk. Waiting wasn't part
of Winder's plan of life either. He believed in action first and
make your explanation to fit.

Gabe Hart was with him, on another mule. Gabe was his
hostler, a big, ape-built man, stronger than was natural, but
weak-minded; not crazy, but childish, like his mind had never
grown up. He was dirty too; he slept in the stables with his
horses, and his knees and elbows were always out of his clothes,
and his long hair and beard always had bits of hay and a powder of grain chaff in them. Gabe was gentle, though; not a
mean streak in him, like there generally is in stupid, very strong
men. Gabe was the only man I ever knew could really love a
mule, and with horses he was one of them. That's why Winder
kept him. Gabe was no use for anything else, but he could do
everything with horses, making clucking, senseless talk in his
little, high voice and just letting them feel his hands, which
were huge even for a man his size. And Winder liked his horses
hard to handle. Outside of horses there were only two things in
Gabe's life, Winder and sitting. Winder was his god, and sitting
was his way of worshipping. Gabe could sit for hours if there
wasn't something to do to a horse. Sometimes I've thought
Gabe just lived for the times Winder took him on the coach
because he had a really ugly team or had some heavy loading
to do. Riding on the coach got everything into Gabe's life that
mattered, Winder, sitting and horses, and he'd sit up there on
the high seat, holding on like a scared kid, with his hair and
tatters blowing and solemn joy in his huge face with the little,
empty eyes.

Winder had a Winchester with him, but he left it against the tie rail and came in, Gabe behind him, and looked at Davies like a stranger, and ordered a whisky.

Canby offered Gabe a drink too, just to see him refuse it. He looked at Canby and grinned to show he meant to be pleasant and shook his head. Then he stood looking slowly around as if he'd never been in the place before, though he'd followed Winder in, almost every day for years.

Winder winked at Canby. "Gabe don't care nothin' for drinkin' or smokin' or women, do you, Gabe?"

Gabe grinned and shook his head again, and then looked down at the floor like he was going to blush. Winder cackled.

"He's a good boy, Gabe is," he said.

This joke was as old as Canby's and Gil's about the woman in the picture.

Winder drank one down, put his glass out to be filled again, and looked at Davies. He was a short, stringy, blond man, with a freckled face with no beard or mustache but always a short, reddish stubble. He had pale blue eyes with a constant hostile stare, as if he was trying to pick a fight even when he laughed.

"They're takin' their time, ain't they?" he said.

"They might as well," Davies said.

"Yeh?" Winder demanded.

"They haven't much to go on yet," Davies told him.

"They got enough, from what I heard."

"Maybe, but not enough to know what to do."

"How do you mean?"

"Well, for one thing they don't know who did it."

"That's what we aim to find out, ain't it?"

"You can't tell who it might be."

"What the hell does that matter? I'd string any son-of-a-bitchin' rustler like that." He slapped the bar. "If he was my own brother, I would," he said furiously.

Gabe made a little noise like he was clearing his throat.

"You're getting Gabe stirred up," Canby said.

"Yes, suh, if he was mah own brothah," Gabe said in his high voice. He was watching Davies, and swinging his hands back and forth on the ends of the long arms, close to his legs. We all knew there were two things made Gabe angry, seeing Winder angry, and being teased about niggers. Winder could handle him about getting mad himself, which was a good thing, he was mad so much; but Gabe was from Mississippi, and the worst about niggers I ever knew. He wouldn't eat where they'd eaten, sleep where they'd slept, or be seen talking to one. That seemed to be the one idea he'd kept from his earlier days, and it had grown on him.

"Well, there's another thing," Davies said.

"What's that?" Winder wanted to know.

"What's that?" Gabe asked too.

"Shut up, Gabe," Winder told him. "This ain't none of your affair. Go sit down."

Gabe looked at him like he didn't understand.

"Go on, sit down." Winder waved at the chairs along the back wall.

Gabe shuffled back to them and sat down, leaning on his knees and looking at the floor between his feet, so all you could see was the swell of his big shoulders, like the shoulders of a walrus, and the top of his head with the hair matted and straw in it, and those tremendous, thick paws hanging limp between his knees. He made a strong smell of horses and manure in the room, even through the stale beer odor.

"This sorta thing's gotta stop," Winder said, "no matter who's doin' it."

"It has," Davies agreed. "But we don't know how many of them there are; or which way they went, either. There's no use going off half-cocked."

"What the hell way would they go?" Winder asked him. "Out the south end by the draw, wouldn't they? There ain't no other way. They wouldn't head right back up this way, would they, with the whole place layin' for them? You're damn shootin' they wouldn't."

"No," Davies said. He hadn't finished his drink; was just sipping it, but he filled the glass again and asked Winder, "Have one with me?"

"I don't mind," Winder said.

Canby filled Winder's glass again, and then Gil's. He held the bottle at me, but I shook my head.

"We might as well sit down," Davies said. "They're waiting on Bartlett anyway." He included Gil and me in the invitation. I didn't like it, but I didn't see how to get out of it. We sat down at the table where we'd been playing cards. Canby had that want-to-grin look in his eyes.

Winder pushed his hat back. "All the more reason to get going," he said.

"No particular hurry, though. If they're from around here, they aren't going far. If they aren't, they're going a long ways, too long for a few hours to matter when they've already got a big start."

"The sooner we get started, the sooner we get them."

"It looks that way to me, too," Gil said.

I tried to kick him under the table. I had a feeling Davies was working most on us anyway. He knew better than to think he could reach Winder.

"And how do you know they've got a start?" Winder asked.

"That's what young Greene said."

"Oh, him."

"He was tangled, but if he had anything straight it was the time. He figured Kinkaid must have been killed about noon."

"Well?"

"It's four-thirty now. Say they have a four-hour start. You aren't going to ride your head off to pick that up, are you?"

"Maybe not," Winder admitted.

"No," Davies said. "It's a long job at best, and stern chase. And it's more than five hundred miles to the first border that will do them any good. Part of that will be a tracking job too. The same way if they're heading for a hide-out to let things cool. It'll be dark in a couple of hours; three anyway. We won't even get down to the draw in that time."

"It's that much of a start if we get there tonight," Winder said.

"Yes, but there's no hurry. We can take our time, and form this posse right."

"Who the hell said anything about a posse?" Winder flared.

"He did," Gil put in; "but it didn't seem to go down so good."

"Why the hell would it?"

"Risley's here," Davies said.

"Risley's been here all summer," Winder said. "It didn't stop Kinkaid gettin' killed, did it?"

"One man can't be every place," I had to chip in. "This is a big valley."

Gil grinned at me to say now who needed a kick.

"He could be a hell of a lot more places than Risley is," Winder told me, staring across at me so I wanted to get up and let him have one.

"Risley's a good man," Davies said, "and a good sheriff."

"You 'mind me of Tyler and the preacher. What have they got us, your good men? A thousand head of cattle gone and a man killed, that's what they got us. We gotta do this ourselves. One good fast job, without no fiddlin' with legal papers, and that's all there'll be to it."

Davies had his hands out on the table in front of him, knobby fingers extended and fingertips together, and was looking at them. He didn't answer.

"It's like those damn, thievin' railroads," Winder said, staring around at all three of us to dare us to disagree. "They got the law with them; they're a legal business, they are. They killed off men, didn't they? You damn shootin' they did; one for every tie their son-of-a-bitchin' rails is laid on. And they robbed men of honest to God men's jobs from Saint Looey to Frisco, didn't they? And for what? For a lot of plush-bottomed, soft-handed bastards, who couldn't even drive their own wagons, to ride across the country and steal everything they could lay their hands on in Californy the same way they been doin' in the East for a hundred years. That's what for. And they got the law with them, ain't they? Well, it's men like us shoulda taken the law in their own hands right then. By God, I hate the stink of an Injun, but an Injun smells sweet comparin' to a railroad man. If we'd wanted to keep this country for decent people, we'da helped the Injuns bust up the railroad, yes, by God, we woulda. And that's the same law you're tryin' to hold us up for, ain't it?—the kind of law that'll give a murderer plenty of time to get away and cover up, and then help him find his excuses by the book. You and your posses and waitin'. I say get goin' before we're cooled off, and the lily liver that's in half these new dudes gets time to pisen 'em again, so we gotta just set back and listen to Judge Tyler spout his law and order crap. Jesus, it makes me sick."

He spit aside on the floor, and then glared at Davies.

That hatred of the railroad was Winder's only original no-tion, and when he got mad that always came in some way. Everything else was what he'd heard somebody, or most every-body, say, only he always got angry enough to make it sound like a conviction. His trouble was that he was a one-love man, and stagecoaching was his one love. Guard and driver, he'd been in it from the start with Wells Fargo on the Santa Fe, but it had such a short life he'd outlasted it, and by now, 1885, Lincoln dead and Grant out, the railroads had everything but these little sidelines, like Winder's. The driving was still tough enough, but the pay was poor as a puncher's and the driver was no hero any more. Winder took it personally.

Davies knew how he was, and let him cool. Then he said, without looking up, "Legal action's not always just, that's true."

"You're damn shootin' it ain't."

"What would you say real justice was, Bill?"

Winder got cautious. "Whadya mean?" he asked.

"I mean, if you had to say what justice was, how would you put it?"

That wouldn't have been easy for anyone. It made Winder wild. He couldn't stand getting reined down logical.

"It sure as hell ain't lettin' things go till any sneakin' cattle thief can shoot a man down and only get a laugh out of it. It ain't that, anyway," he defended.

"No, it certainly isn't that," Davies agreed.

"It's seein' that everybody gets what's comin' to him, that's what it is," Winder said.

Davies thought that over. "Yes," he said, "that's about it."

"You're damn shootin' it is."

"But according to whom?" Davies asked him.

"Whadya mean, 'according to whom'?" Winder wanted to know, saying "whom" like it tasted bad.

"I mean, who decides what everybody's got coming to him?"

Winder looked at us, daring us to grin. "We do," he said belligerently.

"Who are we?"

"Who the hell would we be? The rest of us. The straight ones."

Gabe was standing up and looking at us again, with his hands working. Winder saw him.

"Sit down, you big ape," he yelled at him. "I told you once this is none of your business." Gabe sat down, but kept watching us, looking worried. Winder felt better. It pleased him to see Gabe mind.

Davies said, "Yes, I guess you're right. It's the rest of us who decide."

"It couldn't be any other way," Winder boasted.

"No; no, it couldn't. Though men have tried."

"They couldn't get away with it."

"Not in the long run," Davies agreed. "Not if you make the 'we' big enough, so it takes in everybody."

"Sure it does."

"But how do we decide?" Davies asked, as if it were troubling him.

"Decide what?"

"Who's got what coming to him?"

"How does anybody? You just know, don't you? You know murder's not right and you know rustlin's not right, don't you?"

"Yes, but what makes us feel so sure they aren't?"

"God, what a fool question," Winder said. "They're against the law. Anybody . . ." Then he saw where he was, and his neck began to get red. But Davies wasn't being just smart. He let his clincher go and made his point, mostly for Gil and me, that it took a bigger "we" than the valley to justify a hanging, and that the only way to get it was to let the law decide.

"If we go out and hang two or three men," he finished, "without doing what the law says, forming a posse and bringing the men in for trial, then, by the same law, we're not officers of justice, but due to be hanged ourselves."

"And who'll hang us?" Winder wanted to know.

"Maybe nobody," Davies admitted. "Then our crime's worse than a murderer's. His act puts him outside the law, but keeps the law intact. Ours would weaken the law."

"That's cuttin' it pretty thin," Gil said.

He'd let himself in. Davies turned to him. "It sounds like it at first," he said earnestly, "but think it over and it isn't." And he went on to prove how the greater "we," as he called it, could absorb a few unpunished criminals, but not unpunished extra-legal justice. He took examples out of history. He proved that it was equally true if the disregard was by a ruler or by a people. "It spreads like a disease," he said. "And it's infinitely more deadly when the law is disregarded by men pretending to act for justice than when it's simply inefficient, or even than when its elected administrators are crooked."

"But what if it don't work at all," Gil said; and Winder grinned.

"Then we have to make it work."

"God," Winder said patiently, "that's what we're tryin' to do." And when Davies repeated they would be if they formed a posse and brought the men in for trial, he said, "Yeah; and then if your law lets them go?"

"They probably ought to be let go. At least there'll be a bigger chance that they ought to be let go than that a lynch gang can decide whether they ought to hang." Then he said a lynch gang always acts in a panic, and has to get angry enough to overcome its panic before it can kill, so it doesn't ever really judge, but just acts on what it's already decided to do, each man afraid to disagree with the rest. He tried to prove to us that lynchers knew they were wrong; that their secrecy proved it, and their sense of guilt afterward.

"Did you ever know a lyncher who wasn't afraid to talk about it afterward?" he asked us.

"How would we know?" Winder asked him. "We never knew a lyncher. We'll tell you later," he added, grinning.

I said that with the law it was still men who had to decide, and sometimes no better men than the rest of us.

"That's true," Davies said, "but the poorest of them is better fitted to judge than we are. He has three big things in his favor: time, precedent, and the consent of the majority that he shall act for them."

I thought about it. "I can see how the time would count," I said.

He explained that precedent and the consent of the majority lessened personal responsibility and gave a man more than his own opinion to go on, so he wasn't so likely to panic or be swung by a mob feeling. He got warmed up like a preacher

with real faith on his favorite sermon, and at the end was pleading with us again, not to go as a lynching party, not to weaken
the conscience of the nation, not to commit this sin against
society.

"Sin against society," Winder said, imitating a woman with
a lisp.

"Just that," Davies said passionately, and suddenly pointed
his finger at Winder so Winder's wry, angry grin faded into a
watchful look. Davies' white, indoor face was hard with his
intensity, his young-looking eyes shining, his big mouth drawn
down to be firm, but trembling a little, as if he were going to
cry. You can think what you want later, but you have to listen
to a man like that.

"Yes," he repeated, "a sin against society. Law is more than
the words that put it on the books; law is more than any decisions that may be made from it; law is more than the particular
code of it stated at any one time or in any one place or nation;
more than any man, lawyer or judge, sheriff or jailer, who may
represent it. True law, the code of justice, the essence of our
sensations of right and wrong, is the conscience of society. It
has taken thousands of years to develop, and it is the greatest,
the most distinguishing quality which has evolved with mankind. None of man's temples, none of his religions, none of his
weapons, his tools, his arts, his sciences, nothing else he has
grown to, is so great a thing as his justice, his sense of justice.
The true law is something in itself; it is the spirit of the moral
nature of man; it is an existence apart, like God, and as worthy
of worship as God. If we can touch God at all, where do we
touch him save in the conscience? And what is the conscience
of any man save his little fragment of the conscience of all men
in all time?"

He stopped, not as if he had finished, but as if he suddenly
saw he was wasting something precious.

"Sin against society," Winder repeated the same way, and
got up.

Gil got up too. "That may be all true," he said, "but it don't
make any difference now."

"No," Winder said, "we're in it now."

Gil asked, "Why didn't you tell them all this out there?"

"Yeah," Winder said.

"I tried to," Davies said, "and Osgood tried. They wouldn't listen. You know that."

"No," Gil said. "Then why tell us?" He included me. "We're just a couple of the boys. We don't count."

Davies said, "Sometimes two or three men will listen."

"Well," Gil said, "we've listened. What can we do?"

Winder grinned like he'd won the argument by a neat point, and he and Gil went back to the bar.

Davies sat staring at the table, with his two hands lying quiet on top of it. Outside we could hear the men beginning to come back, the hoofs and harness and low talk. Finally he turned his head slowly and looked at me. His mouth had a crooked smile that made me sorry for him.

"Why take it so hard?" I asked him. "You did all you could."

He shook his head. "I failed," he said. "I got talking my ideas. It's my greatest failing."

"They had sense," I said.

But I wasn't sure of this myself. I'm slow with a new idea, and want to think it over alone, where I'm sure it's the idea and not the man that's getting me. And there's another thing I've always noticed, that arguments sound a lot different indoors and outdoors. There's a kind of insanity that comes from being between walls and under a roof. You're too cooped up, and don't get a chance to test ideas against the real size of things. That's true about day and night too; night's like a room; it makes the little things in your head too important. A man's not clear-headed at night. Some of what Davies had said I'd thought about before, but the idea I thought was the main one with him, about law expressing the conscience of society, and the individual conscience springing from that mass sense of right and wrong, was a new one to me, and needed work. It went so far and took in so much. Only I could see how, believing that, he could feel strongly about law, like some men do about religion.

When he didn't say anything, I said, "Only it seems to me sometimes you have to change the laws, and sometimes the men who represent them."

Davies looked at me, as if to calculate how much I'd thought about it. I guess he didn't think that was much, because finally he just nodded and said, as though it didn't interest him, "The soul of a nation or a race grows the same way the soul of a man does. And there have always been impure priests."

There was a lot in that, but he didn't give me time to get hold of it.

"Will you do me a favor?" he asked all of a sudden.

"That depends," I said.

"I have to stay here," he said. "I have to stop them if I can, till they know what they're doing. If I can make this regular, that's all I ask."

"Yes?"

"I'm going to send Joyce for Risley and Judge Tyler. I want you to go with him. Will you?"

"You know how Gil and I stand here. We came in at a bad time," I said. I didn't like being put over the fence into the open.

"I know," he said, and waited.

"All right," I said. "But why two?"

"Do you know Mapes?" he asked.

"The one they call Butch?"

"That's the one."

"I've seen him."

"Risley's made him deputy for times he's out of town, and we don't want Mapes."

"No," I said. I could see why, and I could see why he didn't want Joyce to have to go alone if there was a question of keeping Mapes out of it, though I still thought that was chiefly sucking me in. Mapes was a powerful man, and a crack shot with a six-gun, but he was a bully, and like most bullies he was a play-the-crowd man. He wouldn't be any leader.

"Tyler may not help much," Davies said, as if to himself, "but he ought to be here. Risley's the man we want," he told me.

We got up. Gil was looking at me, and so was Winder.

Before we could get out the door, Smith came in. He had on a reefer jacket and a gun belt with two guns, and he had a coil of rope in his hand. When he saw Davies he grinned.

"Well, if it ain't big-business," he said. "It looks like we'd be going after all, big-business."

He held up the rope. "Look," he said. "Moore says I'm head

executioner, so I come all primed." He held the end of the rope up next to his ear, and nudged it a couple of times, as if he was tightening the knot, and then suddenly jerked it up and let his head loll over to the other side. He stuck his tongue out and crossed his eyes. Then he laughed.

"Don't tell me I don't know the trade," he said.

He pretended to be looking at Davies closely, with a worried look. He shook his head and clucked his tongue against his teeth.

"You don't look well, Mr. Davies," he said. "You don't look at all well. Maybe you'd better stay to home and get rested up for the funeral." He laughed again. "Maybe you could get the flowers," he piled it on. "The boys wouldn't begrudge showin' a few flowers, even for a rustler," he said seriously. "A good dead one." And he laughed again.

Osgood had come in in time to see Smith making the hanging motions. He stood in the door watching the act, white and big-eyed, like it was a real stretch he was seeing.

Smith saw me looking at the preacher, I guess, and turned around, and when he saw him laughed again, as if he couldn't stop.

"Oh, Jee-zus," he roared, "look at that. They're all sick. The flower pickers," he bellowed, and then, in a little thin voice, "Girls, shall we lay out the poor dear rustler wustler?" and roared again.

The place was pretty quiet, most of the men not looking at Smith.

"Never see a dead man, preacher?" Smith asked him. "Should, in your trade. But not the ones that was hung, is that it? Well, better not, better not. They get black in the face, and sometimes . . ."

Gil banged his glass down and hitched up his gun belt. Smith turned at the sound, and when he saw Gil walking right at him, he half put up one arm, and wasn't laughing at all. He backed to the side as Gil came closer. But Gil didn't even turn his head to look at him, but went on out and down the steps. Smith stayed quiet, though. Davies and I went out too, Osgood pattering behind us, making a funny, half-crying noise.

"But to go like that," he cried at Davies, waving an arm back at the door. "To go like that," he kept repeating.

"I know," Davies said.

When he saw Joyce he went over and talked to him for a minute. The boy looked scared, and kept nodding his head in little jerks, as if he had the palsy.

"Where you off to?" Gil was asking me, standing beside me.

I rolled a cigarette and took my time to answer. When I'd had a drag I told him. He didn't take it the way I'd thought he would, but looked at me with a lot of questions in his eyes that he didn't ask, the way Canby had looked at both of us in the door. I was getting too many of those looks.

"Davies is right," I said. "Want to come along?"

"Thanks," he said, "but somebody's got to keep this company in good ree-pute." He said it quiet. I guess Smith's act had made him wonder again, in spite of Winder.

The sky was really changing now, fast; it was coming on to storm, or I didn't know signs. Before it had been mostly sunlight, with only a few cloud shadows moving across fast in a wind that didn't get to the ground, and looking like burnt patches on the eastern hills where there was little snow. Now it was mostly shadow, with just gleams of sunlight breaking through and shining for a moment on all the men and horses in the street, making the guns and metal parts of the harness wink and lighting up the big sign on Davies' store and the sagging, white veranda of the inn. And the wind was down to earth and continual, flapping the men's garments and blowing out the horses' tails like plumes. The smoke from houses where supper had been started was lining straight out to the east and flawing down, not up. It was a heavy wind with a damp, chill feel to it, like comes before snow, and strong enough so it wuthered under the arcade and sometimes whistled, the kind of wind that even now makes me think of Nevada quicker than anything else I know. Out at the end of the street, where it merged into the road to the pass, the look of the mountains had changed too. Before they had been big and shining, so you didn't notice the clouds much. Now they were dark and crouched down, looking heavier but not nearly so high, and it was the clouds that did matter, coming up so thick and high you had to look at them instead of the mountains. And they weren't firm, spring clouds, with shapes, or the deep, blue-black kind that mean a quick, hard rain, but thick, shapeless and gray-white, like dense steam, shifting so rapidly and with so little outline that you more felt than saw them changing.

Probably partly because of this sky-change and partly because a lot of them were newcomers who hadn't heard that there were any doubts about this lynching, the temper of the men in the street had changed too. They weren't fired up the way some of them had been after Bartlett's harangue, but they weren't talking much, or joking, and they were all staying on their horses except those that had been in Canby's. Most of them had on reefers or stiff cowhide coats, and some even had scarves tied down around their heads under their hats, like you wear on winter range. They all had gun belts, and had ropes tied to their saddles, and a good many had carbines, generally carried across the saddle, but a few in long holsters by their legs, the shoulder curved, metal heeled, slender stocks showing out at the top. Their roughened faces, strong-fleshy or fine with the hard shape of the bones, good to look at, like the faces of all outdoor, hard-working men, were set, and their eyes were narrowed, partly against the wind, but partly not. I couldn't help thinking about what Davies had said on getting angry enough not to be scared when you knew you were wrong. That's what they were doing, all right. Every new rider that came in, they'd just glance at him out of those narrow eyes, like they hated his guts and figured things were getting too public. And there were new men coming in all the time; about twenty there already. Every minute it was getting harder for Davies to crack. They were going to find it easy to forget any doubts that had been mentioned. It just seemed funny now to think I'd been listening to an argument about what the soul of the law was. Right here and now was all that was going to count. I felt less than ever like going on any missions for Davies.

When Joyce came over for me, I took a look at Davies, and he was feeling it too. When he looked at the men in the street he had a little of the Osgood expression. It was hard for him to shift from the precious idea in which he had just been submerged, to what he really had to handle. Osgood was standing near him, at the edge of the walk, his baggy suit fluttering and his hands making arguing motions in front of him. They made a pair.

But Davies was still going to try. When he saw me looking at him, and Joyce just standing there waiting for me, the muscles came out at the back jaw again, and he made a fierce little motion at us to get going. I started.

"Take it easy, law-and-order," Gil said to me. "This ain't our picnic."

I was getting touchy, and for a second I thought he was still trying to talk me out of lining up with the party that wasn't going to be any too popular, win or lose. I looked around at him a bit hot, I guess, but he just grinned at me, a soft, one-sided grin not like his usual one, and shook his head once, not to say no, but to say it was a tough spot. Then I knew he wasn't thinking of sides right then, but just of me, me and him, the way it was when we were best. I shook my head at him the same way, and had to grin the same way too. I felt a lot better.

Joyce and I crossed the street, picking our way among the riders, which made us step a bit because the horses were restless, not only the way they always are in wind bringing a storm, but because the excitement had got into them too. Any horse but an outlaw will feel with his rider. They were wheeling and backing under the bridles, and tossing their heads so you could hear the clinking of the bits along with the muffled, uneasy thudding. Now and then a rider would turn his horse down the street and let him go a bit away from the gathering, and then turn him back in, like racers waiting for a start. Joyce was horse-shy, and dodged more than he had to, and then went into a little weak-kneed run, like an old man's, to catch up with me again. I knew the men were watching us, and I felt queer myself, walking instead of riding, but Joyce had said it wasn't far, and he didn't have a horse, and I'd have felt still queerer doubling up with him. I didn't look at anybody. I could feel myself tighten up when I passed in front of Farnley's horse, but he held him, and didn't say anything.

Just when we got to the other side of the street I heard Winder calling me by my last name. That can make you mad when it's done right, and I checked, but then had sense enough to keep going.

"Croft," he yelled again, and when I still kept going yelled louder and angrily, "Croft, tell the Judge he'll have to step pronto if he wants to see us start."

Joyce was breathing in little short whistles, and not from dodging either. I knew how he felt. That yell had marked us all right. I thought quickly, in the middle of what I was really thinking, that now I didn't know any of those men; they were strangers and enemies, except Gil. And yet I did know most of them, at least by their faces and outfits, and to talk to, and liked them: quiet, gentle men, and the most independent in the world too, you'd have said, not likely, man for man, to be talked into anything. But now, stirred up or feeling they ought to be, one little yelp about Judge Tyler and I might as well have raped all their sisters, or even their mothers. And the queerest part of it was that there weren't more than two or three, those from Drew's outfit, who really knew Kinkaid; he wasn't easy to know. And the chances were ten to one that a lot more than that among them had, one time or another, done a little quiet brand changing themselves. It wasn't near as uncommon as you'd think; the range was all still pretty well open then, and those riders came from all ends of cow country from the Rio to the Tetons. It wouldn't have been held too much against them either, as long as it wasn't done on a big scale so somebody took a real loss. More than one going outfit had started that way, with a little easy picking up here and there.

"Don't mind that big-mouth," I told Joyce.

I'd underrated the kid. He was scared in the flesh, all right, but that wasn't what he was going to think about.

"Do you think he can hold them?" he asked.

He meant Davies. When Joyce spoke about Davies he said "he" as if it had a capital H.

"Sure he can," I said.

"Risley hang out at the Judge's too?" I asked him.

"When he's here," Joyce said, not looking at me. "We've got to get him, though. We've got to get him, anyway."

"Sure," I pacified, "we'll get him."

He led me onto the cross street and we walked faster. There was no boardwalk here, and the street wasn't used so much, so my bootheels sank into the mud a little. There were only a few people standing in front of their houses or on the edge of the street, looking toward the crossing, men in their shirt-sleeves, hunched against the wind, but more women, wearing aprons and holding shawls over their hair. They looked at us, not knowing whether to be frightened or to ask us their questions. One man, standing on his doorstep, with a pipe in his hand, joked to try us.

"What's going on, a roundup?"

"That's it," I gave him back. "Yessir, a roundup."

Joyce got red, but didn't say anything, or look at me yet. I woke up, and saw the kid was scared of me too. I was just one of those riders to him, and a strange one at that.

"They'll wait," I picked up. "They don't know what they're going to do."

Joyce thought he ought to say something. "Mr. Davies didn't think they'd go. Not if somebody stood up against them."

I wasn't so sure of that. Most men are more afraid of being thought cowards than of anything else, and a lot more afraid of being thought physical cowards than moral ones. There are a lot of loud arguments to cover moral cowardice, but even an animal will know if you're scared. If rarity is worth, then moral courage is a lot higher quality than physical courage; but, excepting diamonds and hard cash, there aren't many who take to anything because of its rarity. Just the other way. Davies was resisting something that had immediacy and a strong animal grip, with something remote and mistrusted. He'd have to make his argument look common sense and hardy, or else humorous, and I wasn't sure he could do either. If he couldn't he was going to find that it was the small but present "we," not the big, misty "we," that shaped men's deeds, no matter what shaped their explanations.

"Maybe," I said.

"He says they have to get a leader; somebody they can blame."

"Scapegoat," I said.

"That's what he calls it too," Joyce said. "He says that's what anything has to have, good or bad, before it can get started, somebody they can blame."

"Sometimes it's just that they can't get anywhere without a boss."

"It's the same thing," he argued. "Only one's when it's dangerous."

We kept moving. Joyce had to trot a little to catch up with me. Finally I said, "Mr. Davies doesn't think we've got a leader, then?"

"No," Joyce said. "That's why he thought they'd wait."

I gave that a turn, and knew he was right. That was half what ailed us; we were waiting for somebody, but didn't know who. Bartlett had done the talking, but talk won't hold. Moore was the only man who could take us, and Moore wouldn't.

"He's not far wrong," I said.

"If we can get Risley," he said, "before they pick some-body . . ."

We passed a house with a white picket fence, and then an-other with four purple lilac trees in the yard. Their sweetness was kind of strange, as if we should have been thinking about something else.

"You know," I said, teasing, "I'm not so sure Davies wants those rustlers brought in at all. You sure he doesn't think even the law's a mite rough and tumble?"

He really looked at me then, and I saw why Davies might talk to him. He was pimply and narrow and gawky, but his eyes weren't boy's eyes.

"Maybe he does," he said, "and maybe he's right. Maybe it would be better if they got away."

"Just because he's gentle," he flared.

"Sure," I said, "it's a good thing to be gentle."

"But he wouldn't let them get away," Joyce said sharply. "Even if he wanted to, he wouldn't let them get away, if he thought they'd get any kind of a show."

"Sure," I said. And then asked him, "How about you? Going, if we form the posse?"

He looked where he was walking again, and swallowed hard.

"If he wants me to go, I'll go," he said. "I don't want to," he told me suddenly, "but it might be my duty."

"Sure," I said again, just to say something.

"That's the place," Joyce said, pointing across the street. I flicked my cigarette away.

Judge Tyler's house was one of the brick ones, with a Man-sard roof and patterns in the shingles. There were dormer win-dows. It was three stories high, with a double-decker veranda, and with white painted stonework around all the windows, which were high and narrow. The whole house looked too high and narrow, and there were a lot of steps up to the front door. There was a lawn, and lilac bushes, and out back a long, white carriage house and stable. It was a new place, and the brick looked very pink and the veranda and stonework very white. It looked more than ever high and narrow because there weren't any big trees around it yet, but only some sapling Lombardies, about twice as high as a man, along the drive. The place looked as if it was meant to be crammed in between two others on a city street, going up because it didn't have room to spread. That made it appear even sillier than that kind of a house naturally does, being in a village where hardly anything was more than one story high, and they all had plenty of room around them. The Judge, having settled on the edge of the village, had the whole valley for a yard, if he'd wanted it. You could see the southwest spread of it, and the snow mountains between his little poplars.

I couldn't help wondering where the Judge got the money for that house. Brick doesn't come for nothing, that far out. But then, of course, the Judge had business in other parts too, and now and then a big stake did come out of some of the mining or water litigation.

On the inside wall of the veranda, where you could see it plain from the road, was the Judge's shingle, a big black one with gold letters. There was a fancy, metal-knobbed pull bell beside the front door.

"Scrape your boots, put your hat on your arm, and straighten your wig," I told Joyce as we went up onto the porch. He grinned like it hurt.

I gave the knob a yank, and it was attached to something all right. Way inside the house there was a little, jingly tinkle that kept on after I let go of the knob. A door opened and closed somewhere inside, and there were slow, heavy steps coming. Then the door opened in front of us. It was a tall big-boned woman with a long, yellow, mistrustful face and gold-rimmed glasses, wearing a frilly house-cap and a purple dress that was all sleeves and skirt. Probably we'd just taken her out of something she was doing, but she acted like we were there to mob the Judge. She stood in the opening with her hands on her hips, so nobody could have squeezed by, and took a hard look at my gun belt and chaps.

"Well?" she wanted to know.

I figured a soft beginning wasn't going to hurt, and took off my hat.

"The Judge in, ma'am?"

"Yes, he is."

I waited for the rest, but it didn't come.

"Could we see him?" I asked.

"You got business?"

I was getting a little sore. "No," I said, "we just dropped over for tea."

"Humph," she said, and didn't crack a bit.

"Mr. Davies sent us, ma'am," Joyce explained. "It's important, ma'am. The Judge would want to know."

"Mr. Davies, eh?" she said. "That's different. But it's not regular office hours," she added.

I started to follow her in, and she stopped.

"You wait here," she told us. "I'll ask the Judge if he'll see you. What's your name?" she asked me without warning.

I told her, and she grunted again, and went about five steps in the dark, red-carpeted hall, and gave a couple of sharp raps on a door, half turning around at the same time to keep an eye on us.

A big voice boomed out, "Come in, come in," like it had been looking forward for hours and with a lot of pleasure to that knock. She gave us another look, and went in and closed the door firmly behind her. We weren't going to get in on any secrets, anyway.

"That the Judge's wife?" I asked.

Joyce shook his head. "She died before I came here. That's his housekeeper, Mrs. Larch."

"How long she been with him?"

"I don't know. Ever since his wife died, I guess."

"Well," I said, "you can see why the Judge has times when he don't seem able to make up his mind."

Joyce grinned again as if he didn't want to. I was making up a little.

The office door opened again, and Mrs. Larch came out. She

closed the door and advanced on us, but this time, when she halted, left us room to squeeze by.

"Go on in," she ordered.

"Is the sheriff here too?" I asked her.

She closed the outside door behind us, so we were trapped in the dark with her, except for a little oil flame burning in a red globe overhead.

"No, he isn't," she said, and started her slow parade toward the back of the house.

Joyce gave me a rabbity look and ran after her a few steps.

"Mrs. Larch . . ."

She stopped and wheeled into a company-front facing him.

"Do you know where he is, Mrs. Larch? The sheriff, I mean?"

"No, I don't," she said, and went on back.

After that I couldn't help knocking at the office door too, and I kept my hat off.

Joyce was whispering at me that we had to find the sheriff, we had to.

The same big voice called, "Come in, come in," again.

When we got inside the big voice kept booming, "Well, well, Croft; how are things out in your neck of the woods?"

"All right, I guess," I said.

But they weren't all right here. The Judge looked the same as I'd always seen him outside, wide and round, in a black frock coat, a white, big-collared shirt and a black string tie, his large face pasty, with folds of fat over the collar, bulging brown eyes, and a mouth with a shape like a woman's mouth, but with a big, pendulous lower lip, like men get who talk a lot without thinking much first. He got up from in front of his roller-top desk in the corner which was full of shelves of thick, pale-brown books with red labels, all pretty new-looking, and came to meet me with his hand out as if he was conferring a special favor. The Judge never missed a chance on that sort of thing. But not only Risley wasn't there, but Mapes was. He was sitting with his chair tilted back right next to the door. His gun belt and sombrero and coat were hanging on the hooks above him.

When he was done shaking hands with me, the Judge smoothed back his thick, black mane, cut off square at the collar, like a senator's, put one hand in his pocket, played with the half-dozen emblems and charms on his watch chain with the other, teetered from his heels to his toes two or three times, lifted his head, smiled at me like I was the biggest pleasure he'd had in years, and drew a great, deep breath, like he was about to start an oration. I'd seen him go through all that when all he finally said was, "How-do-you-do?" to some lady he wasn't sure he hadn't met before. The Judge had a lot of public manner.

"Well, well," he said, "you don't appear to have been pining away, exactly, since I last saw you." He took Joyce in kind of on the side.

"And what can I do for you gentlemen?"

I knew he probably hadn't the faintest notion where he'd seen me before, but I let that go, and nodded at Joyce to show he was doing the talking. But the kid was tangled. He didn't know what to say with Mapes there. I had to risk it.

"We're here for Mr. Davies," I said.

"Yes, yes, so Mrs. Larch said. And how is my good friend Davies these days? Well, I trust?"

"He's all right, I guess," I said. "Could we see you alone for a minute, Judge?"

Mapes let his chair down, but it wasn't to go. He sat looking at us.

The Judge didn't know what to do about that. He cleared his throat and inflated again, grinning more than ever.

"So, so," he said, "matters of a rather private nature, eh?"

"Yes, sir."

Mapes stayed there, though.

Joyce got his breath. "Mr. Davies said particularly, just you and Mr. Risley, sir."

"So, so," said the Judge again, and looked at Mapes.

"Risley ain't here," Mapes said. "I'm actin' sheriff."

"That's right, quite right," the Judge assured us, before I could speak. I tried to pick up the ground we'd lost.

"Where'd he go?" I asked Mapes.

"Down to Drew's, early this mornin'."

"When'll he be back?"

"He didn't say. Maybe not for a couple of days." He grinned like he wanted to see me try to get out of that one.

"I'm acting sheriff," he said, thumbing out the badge on his vest. "Anything you can tell Risley, you can tell me."

Joyce started to speak, and decided not to. I looked at the Judge.

"That's right, quite right," he said, with that damn-fool cheerfulness. "The sheriff deputized Mr. Mapes before me, last night. It's official; entirely official." He cleared his throat and teetered again. He'd argued himself around to suit the way it had to go anyhow.

"If you have business which requires Mr. Risley's services, you may speak quite freely before Mr. Mapes."

"I saw that kid Greene, from down to Drew's, come by here hell-for-leather half an hour ago," Mapes said, standing up. "I thought it didn't look like no pleasure jaunt. What's up?"

I couldn't see any way out of it. It was more than ten miles down to Drew's. Like Davies, I didn't think the Judge would be any help, and I knew Mapes wouldn't. He'd do just what the men wanted him to do. But we couldn't get Risley, and they couldn't make things any worse than they were anyway, from Davies' point of view. If the Judge couldn't change the direction of things, at least with him there Davies wouldn't have to feel that the whole blame was his. And besides, maybe the fact that Risley was down at Drew's meant something itself.

Joyce, though, was sticking to orders.

"Mr. Davies said you and Mr. Risley, sir."

"Quit the stalling," Mapes said, his neck swelling out and his heavy, red face getting redder. "What the hell does Mr. Davies want, anyway?"

"Now, Mapes," the Judge said, "the boy has a mission. He's merely acting on instructions, I presume."

"If it's sheriff's business, I'm sheriff," Mapes said.

"Sure," I said, thinking I'd make one more try. "We know that, Butch. But it's not us. We're here for Mr. Davies. Now if you'd let us have a minute alone, we'll give the Judge our story, and then if he thinks it's your job, he'll tell you."

"Certainly, certainly," the Judge said. "If the matter touches your official capacity, I shall let you know at once, Mapes."

Mapes stood with his feet apart and stared at us, one after the other. He had a huge chest and shoulders, and a small head with a red, fleshy face, small black eyes, thick black eye-brows, and short-cropped, bristly hair and beard. Like Winder, he always looked angry, even when he laughed, but in a more irritated way, as if his blood was up but he wasn't clear what was wrong.

"All right," he said finally, as if he'd decided that whatever we had to say couldn't matter much, anyway.

At the door he turned, his face redder than ever, and told the Judge, "If it's a sheriff's job, you call me. See?"

"Of course, of course," the Judge said, flushing.

When I had closed the door behind Mapes the Judge said, "And now," rubbing his hands together as if he had settled everything without a hitch, "now what seems to be the trouble?"

With Mapes out of the way, Joyce told him rapidly. I went over to the front window, but listened while Joyce told him, and the Judge, all business, asked him questions about who was there, and just what Greene had said, and other things, most of which Joyce couldn't answer very well. But I figured my job, which was bodyguard, was done, and didn't horn in. From the window, which was in a bow, I could see Mapes standing at the top of the porch steps with his thumbs in his belt. The Judge didn't show any signs of doing anything but put more questions. Joyce was getting excited.

"It's not that Mr. Davies doesn't want them to go," he explained for the third or fourth time.

"No, no, of course not," the Judge agreed.

"He just doesn't want it to be a lynching."

"No. Can't let that sort of thing start, of course."

Joyce explained again how he wanted a posse sworn in.

"Assuredly," the Judge said. "Only proper procedure. Anything else inevitably leads to worse lawlessness, violence. I've been telling them that for years," he said angrily, as if he suddenly recognized a personal insult. "For years," he repeated. And then I could hear him striding back and forth and snorting.

"Mr. Davies asks will you come at once, sir. The men are already gathering, and they wouldn't listen to him or Mr. Osgood."

The Judge stopped walking.

I saw a rider coming down the street at a lope. He was one of the men who had been at Canby's when Greene came. He saw

Mapes and yelled something to him. Mapes called out to him, and the rider pulled around, yelling something more.

"Mr. Davies wanted you and Mr. Risley to come, sir," Joyce was pleading.

"Eh? Oh, yes, yes. But Risley isn't here."

He started walking again. "Today of all days," he said angrily.

"If you would come, sir. You could talk to them."

"It's not in my position—" the Judge began. Then he said, even more angrily, "No, no. It's not the place of either a judge or a lawyer. It lies in the sheriff's office. I have no police authority."

The rider had wheeled his horse toward the main street and pushed him up to a lope again. Mapes was coming in. I turned around.

"Risley's at Drew's?" I asked.

"Yes, yes. Thought there might be something . . ." the Judge began.

I cut in. "If you could get the men to promise they'd take orders from Risley. They'll have to go that way, anyhow."

Mapes came in, leaving the door open again. He didn't look at us, or say anything, but took his gun down, and buckled it on, and then took down another little gun in an arm-pit holster and slung it on so it would be between his vest and coat. He had big, thick, stubby-fingered hands, and had trouble with the waist thong on the arm-holster.

"And where are you going, Mapes?" the Judge fumed.

"Rustlers got Kinkaid this morning," Mapes said, still working at the knot. He got it, and looked around at us with that angry grin.

"There's a posse forming, just in case you hadn't heard," he said.

"That's sheriff's work, ain't it, Judge?" he asked, reaching his coat down.

"That's no posse, Mapes," the Judge roared. "It's not a posse," he repeated, "it's a lawless mob, a lynching mob, Mapes."

That seemed to me to be stretching it a little. Those men may have been bent on hanging somebody without the delay of a trial, but there was a lot of difference between the way they were going at it and what I thought of as a mob. I didn't say anything, though.

"It'll be a posse when I get there, won't it, Judge?" Mapes asked.

"It will not," bellowed the Judge, a lot angrier than there was any call for, even with the way Mapes spoke.

Joyce looked from one to the other of them for a moment. His face was white, so the pimples showed in red blotches on it, or rather kind of blue. Then he slipped out the door silently.

"I'll deppitize 'em all proper, Judge," Mapes said. His coat was on, and he put his sombrero on the back of his head.

"You can't do it," the Judge told him. "Risley's the only one empowered to deputize."

Mapes started to answer back. He put one foot upon his chair, and spit over on the corner stove first. He liked it when he had the Judge this way, and didn't want to hurry it too much. There was going to be a wrangle, but I could only see one end of it. I started out after Joyce. We'd give Davies warning, anyhow, though I didn't see what he could do with it.

I stopped in the door and said, loud enough so the Judge could hear over what Mapes was saying, "I'll tell Davies you're coming then, Judge."

"Yes, yes, of course," he said, just glancing away from Mapes for an instant, and giving me a big, fixed smile. I figured that had him hooked the best I could manage, and ducked out quick, not stopping when I heard him call out in a different voice, showing he knew now what I'd said, "Wait, wait a moment . . ." I passed Mrs. Larch in the middle of the hall, her hands folded over her belly and looking at me like she figured I was to blame for the whole disorder. I gave her a wink and went on out without bothering to close the front door. I figured she'd take care of that, and I was right. Before I could get to the road, I heard it slam, and by the time the Judge got my name from her, and opened the door again to call to me, I was far enough toward the main street so I could pretend not to hear him.

Joyce was nearly at the crossing already, running with his coat flapping around him. He could tell Davies all there was to tell. I eased off when I'd got beyond fair cry of the Judge's house. There's better things to run in than high-heeled boots, and it looked like the word had really got around now. I didn't want to make a fool of myself. There were people out in front of every house, craning down toward the corner, and I passed women in the street who were trying to call back their children. One of them looked at me with a scared face. She looked at my gun belt and twisted her apron in her hands. But it wasn't me that scared her.

"The horses," she said, like I knew everything she was thinking.

"Send Tommy home if you see him, please," she begged. She didn't even know she didn't know me.

At the next house a man in chaps was getting on his horse. There was a Winchester on his saddle. A woman, his wife I suppose, was standing right beside the horse and holding onto the man's leg with both hands. She was looking up at him and trying to say something and trying not to cry. The man wasn't answering, but just shaking his head short. His face was set and angry, like so many faces I'd been seeing, and he was trying to get her to let go of him before the horse, which was nervy, stepped on her. He was trying to do it without being rough, but she kept hanging on. A little kid, maybe two or three years old, was standing out in the brush in front of the house and crying hard, with her hands right down at her sides.

More people than before were out in the middle of the street watching the crossing, where now and then they could see one of the riders who had let his horse go that far. The excitement had got through the whole village.

One skinny old man in a blue work shirt, with his galluses out over it, and with a narrow, big-nosed head and his gray hair rumpled up so he looked like a rooster, was peering hard through his spectacles, and exclaiming furiously when a rider showed. A little old woman, as skinny and stooped and chickenlike as he was, was trying to keep him from going any farther. When he saw me he stared at me wildly. He had big eyes, anyway, and they were twice as big through those glasses.

"You goin'?" he rasped at me, shaking his stick at the corner.

"John, John," the old lady clucked, "it don't do for you to go gettin' excited."

"I ain't excited," the old man twittered, pounding his stick on the road, "I ain't excited; I'm jest plumb disgusted."

I'd stopped because he'd caught hold of my shirtsleeve.

"You're goin', ain't you?" he threatened me again.

"It looks like it, dad," I said.

He didn't like my answer.

"Looks like it?" he crowed. "Looks like it? Well, I guess it better look like it. What kinda stuff you boys made of these days?

"You know how long they been dandlin' around down there?" He jabbed his stick at the corner again.

"They got to get information yet," I told him.

"More'n half an hour, that's what, more'n half an hour already. Half an hour since I seen how they was lally-laggin' around and started timin' them," he said triumphantly, hauling a big, thick turnip out of his pocket and rapping it with the forefinger of the hand that had the cane in it. He glared up at me with those big eyes.

"An' God knows how long before that; God only knows. Looks like," he cackled scornfully.

"John," the old woman protested, "the young man don't even know us."

"An' a good job fer him he don't," the old man told her. He was still hanging onto me.

"You know those men that was killed?" he asked me.

"There was only one."

"Only one. There was three. Three of Drew's men was killed. Another one of 'em just told me so. And they gotta get information." He spit off to the side.

My face was getting hot. I didn't like to just yank my arm away from an old man like that, but people along the street were beginning to look at us instead of the show down at the corner. They weren't having any trouble hearing the old man either.

"There's no great rush," I told him, sharp. "They got four or five hours' start already."

"No hurry," he said, but not so loud, and let go of my shirt. "Chee-rist," he boiled again, "five hours' start and no hurry. That's sense now, ain't it? I s'pose if they had ten hours' start you'd jest set to home and wait fer 'em.

"You get on down there," he ordered, when I'd started on anyway. He trotted after me two or three steps, cackling, "Get a move on," and gave me a rap across the seat with his stick.

I didn't look around, but could still hear him, "No hurry, Chee-rist, no hurry," and his wife trying to gentle him down.

I was pretty hot, the way you get when old people or sick people or smart kids talk up to you and make you look foolish because they know you won't do anything, or even say much. I rolled myself a cigarette as I went along, and at the corner stopped and lit it and sucked in a couple to get hold of myself. But one thing I did see. If that old cackler who didn't even have the facts straight could heat me up when I knew he was wrong, then a lot of these men must be fixed so that nothing could turn them off unless it could save their faces. The women were as stirred up as the men, and though a lot of them would have been glad if they could keep their own men out of it, that didn't make any difference. When a man's put on his grim business face, and hauled out a gun he maybe hasn't used for years, except for jack rabbits, he doesn't want to go back without a good excuse. And there were people along the walks now, too, a few old men, and a good many women and excited small boys, some of the women holding smaller children by the hands to keep them from getting out where the horses were. That meant an audience that had to be played up to from the start.

In the edge of the street opposite Canby's, where things were thickest, I saw a little fellow no bigger than the one that had been crying because her mother and father were arguing. He was barefooted, and had on patched overalls, and had a big head of curls bleached nearly white. He was all eyes for what was going on, and stood there squirming his toes on the hard mud without a notion where he was. I didn't see any other kid as small who wasn't attached, so I figured he must be Tommy.

"Young fellow, your mother's looking for you," I told him.

He said for me to look at the horsies, and explained something pretty lengthy, which I couldn't rightly follow, about the guns. It was too bad to spoil his big time, but he was in a bad place. I put on a hard face, and put it right down close to him, and said, "Tommy, you git for home," and switched him around and patted him on the pants, saying, "Git now," again. I guess I overdid it, because he backed as far as the boardwalk, looking at me all the time, and stopped there, and then his face gathered in a pucker toward his nose and he burst out bawling. I started toward him to ease it off a little, but when he saw me coming he let out a still louder wail and lit out for the corner. He slowed down there, and looked back a couple of times, digging at his eyes, but then went on out of sight up the cross street at a little half-jog that I figured was going to take him all the way. Well, I probably wouldn't ever have to see that woman again, anyway.

When I got across the street to Davies, he was done talking to Joyce, and was standing there staring blankly at the men, his face tired as it had been after the talk in the bar, but the jaw muscles still bulging.

"Bartlett not back yet?" I asked him.

He shook his head.

"Wonder what's holding him?" I said.

He shook his head again.

"I'm sorry about Risley," I said, "but I think the Judge will come."

He nodded. Then he brought his eyes back to see me, and smiled a little.

"There wasn't anything else you could do," he said. "Maybe there isn't anything any of us can do. They've made a show out of it now."

I saw I didn't have to tell him anything about that.

"Yeh," I said, looking at the riders in the street too. And there was a change in them. Farnley was still sitting there with no change but a tighter bridle hand, and three or four others, one of them Gil, were still standing at Canby's tie rail. But the rest of them, what with the wait, and the women standing on the walk watching them, looked as grim as ever, but not quite honest. There was a lot of play-acting in it now, passing pretty hard jokes without much point to them, and having more trouble with the horses than they had to.

"They'd be willing to quit if it was dark," I said.

He smiled a little, but shook his head again.

"Well, they'd go orderly pretty easy," I suggested.

"They might do that," he admitted.

I told him what I'd told the Judge about their having to go by Drew's anyway.

"You could get them to promise to pick Risley up, and he'd take care of it."

He considered that and nodded more vigorously. He thought it was a clincher too.

"It's queer what simple things you don't think of when you're excited," he said. "There's a simple little thing, and it's the whole answer."

Then he added, "We'll have to let the Judge tell them, though. They wouldn't dare listen to me."

I looked at him. He shook his head. "Don't worry," he said, "I don't care who does it."

He went on as if he was thinking it farther to himself. "Yes, that will do it."

Then, "Thank you. I know it was a hard place for you."

I didn't see why he felt as sure as all that about it, but I was glad he thought it cleared me.

"That's all right," I said. "Glad to do it. But the way things are, that'll have to be my stake to you."

He looked at me with those eyes full of questions too. I thought maybe he'd get rid of them, that being more his way than Canby's. But he didn't get the chance if he was going to. Smith, being tight and bored, and having a crowd, picked this time to play the clown again. He got everybody's attention, which wasn't on much, by picking on Gabe Hart's one meanness. He called out from the steps to the bar.

"Coming along, Sparks?" he called, so the men grinned, finding that old joke funny about a nigger always being easy to scare. I hadn't noticed Sparks, but I saw him now, standing on the other side of the street with that constant look of his of pleasant but not very happy astonishment.

Sparks was a queer, slow, careful nigger, who got his living as a sort of general handy man to the village, splitting wood, shoveling snow, raking leaves, things like that; even baby tending, and slept around wherever was handiest to the jobs, in sheds or attics, though he had a sort of little shack he called his own out in the tall weeds behind the boarded-up church. He was a tall, stooped, thin, chocolate-colored man, with kinky hair, gray as if powdered, and big, limp hands and feet. When he talked his deep, easy voice always sounded anxious to please, slow but cheerful, but when he sang, which he did about most any work which had a regular rhythm, like sweeping or raking, he sang only slow, unhappy hymn tunes. He was anything but a fast worker, but he did things up thorough and neat, and he was honest to the bone, and the cleanest nigger I ever knew. He wore dungarees and a blue shirt, always like they'd just been washed, and his palms were clean tan, and clean steel-blue where they met the skin from the backs of his hands. He had a dry, clean, powdered look all over all the time. It was said that he'd been a minister back in Ohio before he came west, but he didn't talk about himself, outside of what he was doing right at the time, so nobody really knew anything about him, but they all liked him all right, and there wasn't anything they wouldn't trust him with. They made jokes about him and to him, but friendly ones, the sort they might make to any town character who was gentle and could take joking right.

When the men grinned they all looked across at Sparks. He was embarrassed.

"No, suh, Mistah Smith, ah don't guess so," he said, shaking his head but smiling to show he wasn't offended.

"You better come, Sparks," Smith yelled again. "It ain't every day we get a hanging in a town as dead as this one."

The men stopped grinning. They didn't mind Smith joking Sparks, but that offended their present sense of indecision and secrecy. It seemed wrong to yell about a lynching. I felt it too, that someone might be listening who shouldn't hear; and that in spite of the fact that everybody in town knew.

Smith saw he'd made a mistake. When Sparks continued to look down and smile and shake his head, he yelled, "Yoh ain't afraid, is yoh, Spahks," badly imitating Spark's drawl. "Not of a little thing like this," he cried in his own voice again. "You don't have to do anything, you know. The real work is all signed up. But I thought maybe we ought to have a reverend along. There'll be some praying to do, and maybe we ought to have a hymn or two afterward, to kind of cheer us up. You do know the cheerfullest hymns, Sparks."

The men laughed again, and Smith was emboldened.

"That is," he said loudly, "unless Mr. Osgood here is going along. He has first call, of course, being in practice."

"I'm not going, if it interests you," Osgood said, with

surprising sharpness for him. "If you men choose to act in violence, and with no more recognition of what you're doing than this levity implies, I wash my hands. Willful murderers are not company for a Christian."

That stung, but not usefully. A bawling out from a man like Osgood doesn't sit well. Some of the men still grinned a little, but the sour way.

"I was afraid the shepherd would feel his flock was a bit too far astray for him to risk herding them this time," Smith lamented. Osgood was hit, and looked it. He knew the men tolerated him at best, and the knowledge, even when he could delude himself into believing it private, made it doubly difficult for him to keep trying to win them. Sometimes, as now, he was even pitiable. But he had an incurable gift of robbing himself even of pity. After a moment he answered, "I am sorry for you, all of you."

"Don't cry, parson," Smith warned him. "We'll do the best we can without you."

"I guess it's up to you, Sparks," he yelled.

Sparks surprised us. "Maybe it is, Mistah Smith," he said seriously. "Somebody ought to go along that feels the way Mistah Osgood and ah do; beggin' yoh pahdon, Mistah Osgood. If he don' feel it's raght foh him to go, it looks lahk ah'm the onlay one laift."

This unassuming conviction of duty, and its implication of distinct right and wrong, was not funny.

Quickly Smith struggled. "Maybe Mr. Osgood will lend you his Bible, Sparks, so's we can have the right kind of reading at the burial."

This was partially successful. Osgood was obviously offended to be so freely talked of by Smith, and perhaps even to have his name coupled with Sparks'. And everyone knew Sparks couldn't read.

"You will lend him your Book, won't you, Reverend," Smith asked Osgood. He had no sense for the end of a joke. Osgood had the thick, pale kind of skin that can't get red, so he got whiter, and was trembling a little.

Sparks came across the street in his slow, dragging gait. He didn't swing his arms when he walked, but let them hang down as if he had a pail of water in each hand.

When he was close enough to talk more quietly, he said, "No, thank you, Mistah Osgood," and turning to Smith told him, "Ah knows mah text to pray without the Book, Mistah Smith.

"But ah'm a slow walkah," he said, smiling especially at Winder, "you wouldn't have anothah mule ah could borrow, would you, Mistah Winder?"

Winder didn't know what to say, knowing it was still a joke except to Sparks.

Smith said, "Sure he would, Sparks. Gabe, you just trot back and get the Reverend a good saddle mule, will you? An easy one, mind; he ain't much padded."

The men were quiet.

Finally, Winder said, "Your mouth's too damn loose, Smith."

"I'm talking to Gabe," Smith said, but avoided Winder's stare.

Gabe stared back at Smith, but sat solid and appeared un-moved. He muttered something that nobody could hear.

"What's that you said, Gabe?" Smith prodded him.

Gabe got it out. "I said I ain't waitin' on no nigger," he said.

"Shut up, Smith," Winder said, before Smith could make anything of this.

Smith got red, which was remarkable for him, since he could swallow almost any insult, but with Winder staring at him he couldn't think of a retort.

"It's all right, Mistah Windah," Sparks said, "but if they is a mule at yoh place ah could borrow, ah'd be obliged. Ah can get him mahself, if thayas tahm."

"They're kidding you, Sparks," Canby said from the door. He liked the nigger.

"Ah know that, Mistah Canby," Sparks said, grinning again. "But ah think maybe Mistah Smith was accidentally right when he said ah should go."

"You really want to go?" Winder asked him.

"Yessuh, Mistah Windah, ah do."

Winder studied him, then shrugged and said, "There's a horse in the shed you can use. There's no saddle, but he's got a head-stall on, and there's a rope in the back stall you can use for a bridle.

"You'll have to get him yourself, though. You know how Gabe is," he apologized.

Gabe continued to stare heavily at Smith, but he didn't seem to hold anything against Sparks.

"Yassuh, ah undahstand," Sparks said, and turned to go. Winder felt he'd been too soft.

"Move along, or you'll get left," he said. "We're only waiting for Mr. Bartlett and his boys."

Sparks turned his head back, and grinned and nodded, and then went on down the street toward the stage depot, walking quickly for him. You could tell by his carriage that he was pleased in the way of a man doing what he ought to do.

Smith had missed being funny, and Sparks had given a kind of body, which the men could recognize, to an ideal which Davies' argument hadn't made clear and Osgood's self-doubt had even clouded. I thought it would be a good time for Davies to tackle them again, and looked at him. He saw the chance too, but found it hard to get started in the open, with all those men, and waited too long. A rider called out, "Here comes Ma," and there was as much of a cheering sound as they felt presently fitting, to greet her. Here was a person could head them up.

Ma was up the street quite a ways when they hailed her, but she waved at them, a big, cheerful, unworried gesture. It made me feel good, too, just to see Ma and the way she waved. She was riding, and was dressed like a man, in jeans and a shirt and vest, with a blue bandanna around her neck and an old sombrero on her head. She had a Winchester across her saddle, and after she waved she held it up, and then held part way up, as far as the tie would let it, a coil of rope she had hitched to the flap of the saddle. There was another cheer, stronger than the first, and jokes about Ma and her power that showed how much better the men were feeling. She changed the whole attitude in two moves, and from a quarter mile off.

Jenny Grier was the name of the woman we called Ma. She was middle-aged and massive, with huge, cushiony breasts and rump, great thighs and shoulders, and long, always unkempt, gray hair. Her wide face had fine big gray eyes in it, but was fat and folded, and she always appeared soiled and greasy. She was strong as a wrestler, probably stronger than any man in

the valley except Gabe, and with that and her appearance, if
it hadn't been for the loud good nature she showed most of
the time, people would have been afraid of her. All the women
were, anyway, and hated her too, which was all right with her.
There were lively, and some pretty terrible, stories about her
past, but now she kept a kind of boarding house on the cross
street, and it was always in surprisingly good order, considering
how dirty she was about herself. She was a peculiar mixture of
hard-set ideas too. Though mostly by jokes, she'd been dead
set against Osgood from the first day he came. She had no use
for churches and preaching, and she'd made it hard for him by
starting all kinds of little tales, like her favorite one about being
surprised at how hungry she was when she woke up after the
only sermon of his she ever heard, only to find that was because
he'd gone right on through and it was the second Sunday, and
he hadn't wound up his argument then, but his voice gave out.
And she could imitate him too, his way of talking, his nervous habits with his hands, his Gladstone pose. She always pretended to be friendly, in a hearty way, when she saw him, and
the man was afraid of her. But on the other hand she was a lot
more than ordinarily set against what she thought was wrong-
doing. I missed my guess if she hadn't had a part in driving
Gil's Rose out of town. She didn't like women, wouldn't have
one in her house, not even for one night's sleep. In ways, I
think she was crazy, and that all her hates and loves came out
of thinking too much about her own past. Sometimes I even
wondered if the way she mistreated her own body, with dirt
and more work than she needed to do and long hunts and
rides she didn't want to make and not much rest or sleep, when
about everything else she was a great joker and clean and orderly, wasn't all part of getting even with herself, a self-imposed
penance. The other side of that, I thought, was another little
trait. She was fond to foolishness of mountains and snow, just
of looking at them, but of going up in them too, though snow-
shoeing nearly killed her with her weight. She said she'd settled
in Bridger's just to look at mountains; that they brought out
what little was good in her. Most of the time, though, she was
big and easy, and she had the authority of a person who knew
her own mind and was past caring what anybody else thought
about anything, and a way of talking to us in our own language

so we'd laugh and still listen, the style Judge Tyler would like to have had.

I knew that, at least until she had seen the victims in the flesh, she'd be as much for lynching a rustler as Winder or Bartlett. The only thing that made me wonder how she'd turn was that she liked Davies quite as much as she didn't like Osgood. She wasn't given to thinking very far, but she did a lot of intelligent feeling.

She was greeted right and left when she joined us, and she spoke to Gil and me with the others, calling me "boy" as she had when I'd stayed at her place, and we stood a lot better with the rest just on that. Then she started asking questions, and they told her what they knew, which she saw right off, from the different versions, wasn't straight. She set out to straighten it. It wasn't that she was trying to be boss. She simply wanted things in order in her mind when she had anything to do, and in putting them in order she just naturally took over. When some of them were all for starting without Bartlett she checked that. When they told her about Davies she just looked down at him standing on the walk and grinned and asked him if he wasn't going. Davies said he was if they went right, if anybody really needed to go. Ma looked at him, not grinning now, and he explained that Risley was already down at Drew's, and that Drew had a dozen men down there, and that he thought it would be just good sense not to go unless we were sent for, sent for by Risley, who would really know what was going on. There was muttering around him at that. I was surprised myself. So that was why he'd thought that little fact could do a lot; he believed he could use it to stop them from going at all.

Ma said, "Art, you read too many books," to him, and began to dig into young Greene, calling him son, and acting as if what he thought was just as important as what he knew. At that she boiled it down better than anybody else had. Kinkaid had been killed way down in the southwest corner of the valley, eight miles below the ranch. They didn't know just when, but it must have been noon or earlier, because a couple of the riders had picked up his horse clear over by the ranch road, and at about two o'clock had found Kinkaid lying on his back in the sun in a dry wash over under the mountains. Greene didn't know if there were any more cattle gone; they hadn't been able to distinguish the rustlers' tracks. Too many cattle had been working over the range there, and there were still a lot of horses' prints from the roundup. She kept him toned down except on that one thing, that Kinkaid had been shot through the head. That was the one thing he seemed to have clear without question. He had kept on saying that to the men too. It impressed him that Kinkaid had been shot through the head, as if he could feel it more, as if he would have felt better if Kinkaid had been shot in the belly or in the back, or anywhere but in the head. When Ma asked him, he admitted that he hadn't seen Kinkaid, but that the man who told him had. No, he hadn't seen the sheriff down there; it must have been three o'clock before they sent him to Bridger's and he hadn't seen the sheriff all day.

Ma said to Davies, "I guess we're goin', Art; as quick as Bartlett gets here."

Somebody said, "He's comin' now."

The men who weren't mounted climbed up, Gil and I with them. Only Davies and Osgood and Joyce were left standing on the walk, and Canby on the steps. Sparks was back too, on an old and sick-looking horse with a wheat sack for a saddle.

Davies said to Ma, "At least wait for Judge Tyler. He's coming. I sent word for him." He sounded stubborn and defeated now, nearly as bad as Osgood. Riders looked at him contemptuously, and some started to tell him off, but Ma made them grin at him instead.

"Art, you're gettin' worse every day," she said. "First you let the reverend there give you prayin' faith, and then you let Tyler argue you into drummin' up business for him. It's them books, Art, them books. You better lay off them."

And then, "Not the reverend and you *and* Tyler. I couldn't stand it, Art. I'm only a woman, and I'm gettin' on toward my time." The men laughed.

Bartlett came up at a lope, his son Carl, the blond one, with him. The other one, Nate, was dark, but that was the only difference between them. They were both tall, thin, silent and mean. I wondered if Nate had got too drunk to sit in a saddle, the way he did, and they'd had to leave him. Carl stayed behind his father, away from the men, and after the first glance didn't look at them.

"Carl was riding," Bartlett explained. "We had to get him in."

"Tetley not here?" he asked, looking around. And then, louder, "We'll have to wait for Tetley. Nate's gone for him."

"What do we need with God-Almighty-Tetley," Winder said. But he didn't say it loudly; if I hadn't been right next to him, I wouldn't have heard it at all. All the men were uneasy, but not loud. They were irritated at the further delay, but they were quiet about it, nearly sullen. It was news if Tetley was coming. It would make a difference; even Ma was afraid of Tetley.

Excepting Drew, Tetley was the biggest man in the valley, and he'd been there a lot longer than Drew, the first big rancher in the valley, coming there the year after the Civil War. On the west edge of town he'd built a white, wooden mansion, with pillars like a Southern plantation home, and big grounds around it, fenced with white picket fence. The lawns were always cut, and there were shrubbery and flower beds, a stone fountain where birds drank, and benches set about under the trees. Tetley was like his house, quiet and fenced away; something we never felt natural with, but didn't deride either. Except for the servants, he had only his son Gerald living with him now, and they didn't get on. Tetley had been a Confederate cavalry officer, and the son of a slave owner, and he had that kind of a code, and a sharp, quiet head for management. Gerald was always half sick, kept to himself and the big library as much as his father would let him, hated the ranching life and despised yet feared the kind of men Tetley had to deal with now. Things had been better between them before Mrs. Tetley had died; she had acted as a go-between, and even as a shield for Gerald, and had been such a charming little thing herself, beautiful, intense and cheerful, yet gentle, that nothing could be very unpleasant around her. But when she died each of them had become only more what he was. People who had been there said the house was like it never had the dust-covers off the furniture now, and Tetley, though he wouldn't tolerate a word about the boy from anyone else, was himself ashamed of him, and a hard master. Sparks, who worked there quite often, had said once, when he was more off his guard than usual, that he had seen things between them that made him sure Tetley would have killed the boy if he hadn't looked so much like his mother. He did, too, as much as a sullen, sick boy can look like a woman with all her spirit and knack for being happy.

It looked like Bartlett thought he had talked himself into something when he had to get Tetley. I knew that if Tetley came he'd take over. Wherever he came things always quieted down, and nothing sounded important except what Tetley had to say. Partly, I think, that was because nothing else seemed important to Tetley either. A man so sure of himself can always sound important if he isn't a windbag, and Tetley was no windbag. He didn't talk often, and usually it was short then. When you happened to meet him on the street, which was seldom, he would only nod, and nobody ever started a talk with him. It wasn't that he was impolite or superior acting either. He had more real manner than any other man in the valley, or than any I'd ever met. You just couldn't get close to him. I don't think it would have mattered who you were.

The word that Tetley was coming gave Davies a little more time, if that could do him any good now, but it looked to me like a reprieve for a man that knew he had to swing at the end of it, anyway. Tetley wouldn't be coming to do Bartlett a favor, and if he objected to the lynching on principle, which wasn't likely, he still wouldn't be coming down himself to stop it. There was only one reason that I could see for Tetley's interest, that he wanted that lynching.

Davies must have figured the same way, but he was still going to make a try. I saw him talking hard and quickly to Joyce again, and then Joyce, looking more frightened than ever, went off down the street at a run, and Davies went out, keeping it casual, to talk to Bartlett. Bartlett wasn't so wild any more, just touchy, the way a man is who feels strongly about something, but is a muddy thinker. He answered a bit short, but didn't blow off. He kept looking at his watch, a big silver turnip, and then at the sky, and only paid a fretful half-attention to Davies. Davies knew better than to argue the soul of society with Bartlett, and even held out on his notion of the men not going at all, and just stuck to legal deputation and trying to get a promise Bartlett wouldn't act without Risley. And he stayed friendly while he made his points, always seeming to be making just suggestions, and asking Bartlett's opinion, and Ma's, and even Winder's. The men let him talk because they had to wait, anyhow, though I noticed a few, close to him, seemed to be listening. Bartlett, though, wouldn't hear more than once about bringing prisoners in. Short justice was the kind he wanted. And Ma kept taking the point out of Davies' talk by making jokes. He hadn't got anywhere when the Judge and Mapes appeared, the Judge, by the way his free hand was waving, still arguing it hot and heavy with Mapes, who wasn't even answering now.

When they pulled up, just on the edge of the crowd of riders, everything was silent, even the people on the walks waiting to see what the Judge would say. They didn't have much respect for the Judge, but he was the law, and they waited to see what line he would take. The Judge felt the hostility and was nervous about the quiet; he made a bad start, taking off his hat by habit, like he was starting an oration, and raising his voice more than he had to.

"I understand how it is, men," he began, and went on about their long tolerance, and their losses, and the death of a dear friend, a long apology for what he was working up to.

Mapes, beside him, took off his sombrero solemnly, the way the Judge had taken his off, and began slowly and carefully to improve the crease in it.

The men grinned, and Smith called, "Cut the stumping, Judge," and when the Judge hesitated, "It's all been said for you, Tyler. All we want's your blessing."

Davies didn't want the Judge to get into an oration any more than the rest did. He came over beside the Judge's horse before the Judge could start again, and said something. Osgood trailed out too.

"Certainly, certainly, Mr. Davies," the Judge said, but still in his platform voice, "just the point I was coming to.

"Men," he addressed us, "you cannot flinch from what you believe to be your duty, of course, but certainly you would not wish to act in the very spirit which begot the deed you would punish."

"By the time you got us ready to act, Tyler," Smith shouted, "the rustlers could be over the Rio." There was agreement; others called ribald advice. Ma leaned on her saddle directly in front of the Judge and grinned at him. The Judge's neck and jowls began to swell slowly and turn red.

"One more word out of you, Smith," he bellowed, "and I'll have you up for impeding the course of justice and connivance in an act of violence."

It was a bad move after his weak start. The joking rose to shouting. There were jeers, and men made signs of his insignificance at the Judge. Ma said, still grinning, "Judge, you can't impede what don't move anyway."

"And you, a woman," the Judge shouted at her, "to lend yourself to this . . ." He couldn't describe us, but just waved a hand over us, choking, and then suddenly put his hat back on and yanked it down, and glared at us.

In the general roar you could still hear Farnley's voice, so furious it was high and breaking, "For Christ's sake, Butch, let's get out of this."

Horses began to mill and yank, and the riders chose to let them. A woman, holding onto a post of the arcade with one hand, leaned out and shrieked at us. She was a tall, sallow, sooty-looking woman, with black hair streaming down and blowing across her face, and her sunbonnet fallen back off her head so she looked wild. She kept screaming something about Kinkaid. Smith called out salaciously to know what Kinkaid was to her.

"More than he was to any of you, it looks like," she screamed back at him.

Some of the other women too called out at us then, laughing angrily and jibing. Others, who had men in the street, were quiet and scared-looking. One small boy, being yanked about by his mother, began to cry. This scared others of the children.

Moore rode over, holding his horse close, and spoke to the wild-looking woman. "We can take care of this, Frena," he told her, then said to the others, "Get those kids out of here; this is no place for a kid."

The woman he called Frena ran into the street beside him, as if she'd like to pull him off and throw him around. "Why ain't it?" she shrieked up at him. "There isn't anything going to happen, is there?" Moore didn't say anything, or even look at her, but just waited there until the women with children began to lead them away. Two of them stopped at the corner, though, and watched again.

Davies hadn't paid any attention to the uproar, but talked

up earnestly to the Judge. He got the Judge calmed a little. He
nodded and said something.

"Where's Greene?" Ma Grier called back. Things quieted
a little. "Greene," she called to him, "come on up here. The
Judge wants to talk to you."

The rest of us wanted to hear, and tried to bunch around
the talkers, but the horses kept sidling out, and were blowing
and hammering and making leather squeal. We couldn't hear
much, but only catch glimpses of young Greene on his horse
facing the Judge on his and making answers. They didn't appear to be getting anywhere; the kid grinned sardonically a
couple of times and the Judge, though pompous, was flustered
again. Then, apparently, Davies took over again. They were
both looking down and not saying anything. The kid began
giving answers again, and not looking so sure. The men right
around them had quieted down a lot. Once most of them,
all together, and the Judge, too, looked up at the sky, and
the Judge, when he looked down, nodded. The Judge, then,
was apparently putting in a word here and there for Davies.
Greene looked ready to cry. Only once, when he'd stood
about all he could, we heard him cry out, "Olsen told me so.
I've told you that twenty times already." Mapes ceased pretending to look bored, and began glancing around the circle
of men. Once he said something, but the Judge, a lot surer of
himself now, turned on him and made a quick reply. The only
thing I caught was the word "constituted" which sounded
as if the Judge was in his usual line of blather. But Mapes
didn't say anything further, only stuck out his chin and looked
surly and stared for a moment at his saddle horn. But though
we couldn't hear anything, we could feel that the drift was
changing. Men close in began to look at each other, just quick
glances, or look down. The temper was out of them. When,
after four or five minutes, the woman Frena had waited as long
as she could with her mouth closed, and wanted to know if
they were holding a prayer meeting, one of the men angrily
called to her to shut up.

It became quiet enough to hear the voices, the kid's choky
and stubborn, Davies' easy in short even questions, or sometimes a longer remark, and then the Judge, his voice being
so heavy, we could catch a word here and there from him.

Then the kid was let out of the ring. His face was red, and he wouldn't look at any of us, or answer when Winder asked him a question, only shrug his shoulders. The riders who had heard pulled their horses back so that we had to pull away to give them room. Davies and Osgood came through them toward the arcade. Osgood looked happy, and kept chattering beside Davies in an excited way, Davies just nodding. Under the edge of the arcade Davies climbed up onto the tie rail and stood there, holding onto a post to steady himself. He didn't call out, but just waited until it was quiet. Most of us reined around to listen to him; only Farnley and young Greene stayed clear out, as if they didn't want to hear. Farnley started to curse us for listening to more such talk, which he called lily-livered, but Moore quieted him, saying that Davies didn't want to stop them, and that they had to wait for Tetley anyhow.

"If you guys get careful of yourselves," Farnley told him, as if he meant it, "I'm going myself. Don't forget that." Then he was quiet too, and Davies started to talk. When the woman Frena tried to interrupt him, and twice Smith also, he didn't talk back to them, but just waited, as you would until a door was closed that was letting in too much noise, and then went on the same reasonable way, just loudly enough to be heard.

"We don't know anything about those rustlers, boys," he told us, "or whether they were rustlers, or who shot Kinkaid. Young Greene there wasn't trying to make trouble; he was doing what he thought he ought to do, what he was told to do. But he got excited; he was sent for the sheriff, but on the way up he got excited thinking about it, and forgot what he should do, and did what seemed to him like the quickest thing. Really, he doesn't know anything about it. He didn't see any rustlers or any killer. He didn't even see Kinkaid. He only heard what Olsen told him, and Olsen was in a hurry. All that Olsen actually told him, when we get down to the facts, was that Kinkaid had been shot, that they'd found him in the draw, and that he was to come to town for the sheriff. That's not much to go on.

"Then there's another thing. It's late now. If it was a gang that Kinkaid ran into, they must have gone out by the south pass, as they did before." He went on to show us that it was twenty miles to that pass and would be dark before we got there, that the rustlers had at least a five or six hour start of us. He showed us that the sheriff had been down there since early morning, that there were a dozen men there if he wanted them, and pointed out that it wasn't the sheriff who had sent for us, that nobody had sent for us, that Greene had been sent only for the sheriff, and that if the sheriff had wanted more men we'd have heard from him by now.

He argued that although he could understand our feelings, there certainly was no use in acting in a way that might get us into trouble, or lead us to do something we'd regret for a long while, when the matter was probably being taken care of legally as it was.

"It's my advice, men, for what it's worth," he concluded, "that you all come in and have a drink on me . . ."

"Drinks," said Canby from the door, "on the house. But only one round, by God. I'm not filling any bucket bellies."

"Our friend Canby offers the drinks," Davies said, "and I'll make it two. I guess I owe it. Then, I'd say, we'd all better go home and have supper, and get a good night's sleep. If we're wanted, we'll hear. I sent Joyce down to the ranch to find out what the sheriff has to say. If any of you want to stay in town, Mrs. Grier can put you up, or Canby, or the Inn, if they can still get the doors open."

"I told you the money was all he thought about," Smith cried.

"And I can bed two myself," Davies went on, grinning down at Smith, "and no charge. I'd be glad of the company."

"I can take six," Canby said, "if they don't mind sleeping double. And no charge either; not for those beds, when I know I'm bound to see the guys again."

"I can take care of two, and more than welcome," Osgood said. He sounded really hearty for the first time.

Canby said, "About those drinks, though. The offer don't go for any man that's had more than five free ones already. Monty, I'll stand you to a cup of coffee. It won't make you more than a little sick." There was some grudging laughter.

Ma, feeling defeated, was a bit surly, but she had to offer rooms too. "Only," she told them belligerently, "any lazy puncher that holes up with me is going to pay for his grub. I'm no charity organization." They jeered her more cheerfully, and she seemed to feel better. Still they didn't break up, though, or get off their horses. Neither did I; I didn't want to look like I was anxious to quit; not any more than anybody else.

Sparks really limbered things up. In the hesitation he said, in that mournful voice of his, "I'd ce'tainly admiah to have any gen'lmun that wishes spend the naght at mah qua'tahs too." They laughed. One of them asked, "Where you sleeping to-night, Sparks?"

"In Mistah Davies' shed foh storin' things, but it'll be all raght with him."

"It's not like you were giving up, boys," Davies told us. "It's just good sense. If it's a short chase it's over by now. If it's a long one the sheriff will let you know, and you'll have time to get ready."

"I'm settin' 'em up, boys," Canby called.

The riders closest in began to dismount. They felt foolish, and didn't look at each other much, and made bad jokes about how old they were getting. But I guess they felt chiefly the way I did. I hadn't had much stomach for the business from the beginning. I got down too. Gil tied up beside me.

"Well, the little bastard pulled it," he said. "Jees, and just when I thought for once there'd be something doin'." But he wasn't sore.

We heard the Judge calling, "Going home, Jeff?" We looked. Others who had started in, stopped and looked back too. Farn-ley was riding off down the street. Winder was with him, and of course Gabe. He didn't pay any attention, and the Judge called again. Davies told the Judge to let him alone, he'd have to go to the ranch, anyway, but I guess the Judge was tired of playing second fiddle. He bellowed this time, and wasn't asking, but ordering Jeff to come back.

Jeff came back. When the Judge saw his face he explained, "You might as well have a shot with us, Jeff. It'll be cold rid-ing. You don't need to worry. This business will be taken care of." He explained it heartily, and at a distance. The woman Frena, who was still hanging around, laughed.

Farnley rode his horse straight in until it was shouldering the Judge's. Winder waited where he had stopped down the street, and Gabe with him. In the Judge's face, as if spitting on him, Farnley told him, "Yeh, but I know now who's going to take care of it. The bastard that shot Larry Kinkaid ain't comin' in here for you to fuddle with your damned lawyer's tricks for six months and then let him off because Osgood or Davies, or some other whining women, claim he ain't bad at heart. He ain't comin' in anywhere. Kinkaid didn't have six months to decide if he wanted to die, did he?"

"Now look here, Jeff," the Judge began.

Davies went out and stood by Jeff's horse, as he had before, but didn't, at first, touch him. "Jeff," he said, and then again, "Jeff," until Farnley quit staring at the Judge and slowly looked down at him. Then he said, "Jeff, you know nobody in this country is going to let a thing like this go. Risley is a good man, Jeff; he'll get him. And there aren't twelve men in the West that wouldn't hang him." Then he put his hand on Jeff's knee again. Jeff's face looked to me like he couldn't understand what was being said. But he'd heard it. "You can see that, can't you, Jeff?" Davies asked him.

"No," Farnley said, "when I look at you, any of you," he said, looking around at us slowly, "I can't see anything. Not one damned thing." He knocked Davies' hand off his knee with the back of his own hand, and began to rein around, nearly riding Moore down. Moore was trying to talk to him too.

The rest of us were keeping out of it, except Gil. He was unhitching again. "By God," he told me, with pleasure, "if he goes, I'm going. That won't be no hanging; that'll be a fight." Even Moore was afraid of Farnley, the way he was feeling now, but he ran along beside him, still trying to talk to him.

We'd all been watching this business so close that we hadn't seen Tetley coming until Farnley pulled around to look because Winder was pointing. Even then it didn't seem to matter, except that there'd be more explaining, which we wanted to escape. We'd been pulled back and forth enough. We were already chilled with sitting in the wind; there was a storm coming on, you could feel that definitely now. All I wanted right now was a drink, a meal and a smoke. Most of us were in this mood; there were more men on the walk than mounted, and their attention to Tetley was more curious than anything else. He was so obviously ready to go somewhere. With military rigidity he was riding alone on his tall, thin-legged palomino with the shortened tail and clipped mane like those of a performing horse. He wore a Confederate field coat with the epaulets, collar braid and metal buttons removed, and a Confederate officer's hat, but his gray trousers were tucked into an ordinary pair of cowboy's shin boots. There was a gun belt strapped around his waist, over the coat. It had a flap holster, like a cowboy would never wear, which let show just the butt of a pearl-handled Colt. He didn't have a stock saddle either, but a little, light McLellan.

Behind him, like aides-de-camp, almost abreast, were three riders, his son Gerald, his Mex hand called Amigo, and Nate Bartlett.

When he had drawn up, his three riders stopping behind him too, he looked us over, his small, lean, gray-looking face impassive; no, he reviewed us, and was amused without expression. Irony was the constant expression of Tetley's eyes, dark and maliciously ardent under his thick black eyebrows. His hair, an even gray, was heavy and of senatorial length, cut off straight at his coat collar, and curling up a little. There were neat, thin sideburns of the same gray from under his campaign hat to the lower lobes of his ears, and a still thinner, gray mustache went clear to the corners of his mouth, but didn't cover the upper lip of his mouth, which was long, thin, inflexibly controlled, but as sensitive as a woman's. He was a small, slender man who appeared frail and as if dusted all over, except his eyes and brows, with a fine gray powder. Yet, as he sat quietly, rigidly, his double-reined bridle drawn up snugly in his left hand in a fringed buckskin glove, his right arm hanging straight down, we all sat or stood quietly too. He addressed Tyler as the man who should be in authority.

"Disbanding?"

Tyler avoided the condemnation. "Davies convinced us, Major Tetley."

"So?" Tetley said. "Of what, Mr. Davies?" he asked him.

Even Davies was confused. He began an explanation that sounded more like an excuse than a plea. Nate Bartlett cut him short, drawing up cautiously beside Tetley, and speaking to him cautiously.

"I guess they don't know about their having gone by the pass, sir."

Tetley nodded. Davies looked from one to the other of them uncertainly.

"You were acting on the supposition that the raiders left by the south draw, I take it, Mr. Davies?"

"Yes," Davies said, doubtfully. He didn't know where he stood.

"They didn't," Tetley smiled. "They left by the pass."

We knew what he meant, Bridger's Pass, which went through the mountains to the west; it was part of the stage-road to Pike's Hole, the next grazing range over, which had a little town in it, like Bridger's Wells. It was a high pass, going up to about eight thousand; snow closed it in the winter, and with the first thaws the creek came down beside it like a steep river, roaring and splashing in the narrows, until it bent south in the meadows and went brimming down toward Drew's and through the draw at the south. The west road from Drew's came up along the foothills and joined the stage-road right at the foot of the pass. It was only a little off this west road that Greene thought Kinkaid had been found. If the rustlers had gone by the pass, it changed the whole picture. Then it was the sheriff who was off the track. If he'd gone to the draw, toward that branding camp Kinkaid had found, he'd be twenty miles off. We began to really listen.

"By the pass, from the south end," Davies said, "that would be crazy." He didn't sound convinced. He sounded as if he had a lump in his throat. It wasn't which way they'd gone that mattered to Davies.

Tetley still smiled. "Not so crazy, perhaps," he said, "knowing how crazy it would look; or if you lived in Pike's Hole."

"You seem pretty sure," Ma said.

"Amigo saw them," Tetley said.

A half a dozen of us echoed that, "Saw them?" Farnley came back in, Winder and Gabe with him.

"He was coming back from Pike's, and had trouble getting by them in the pass."

"Trouble?" Mapes asked importantly. The Judge was just sitting in his saddle and staring at Tetley. Osgood, I thought, was going to cry. It was hard, when it had all been won. And Davies was standing there as if somebody had hit him but not quite dropped him.

"Si," Amigo said for himself. He was grinning, and had very white teeth in a face darker than Sparks'. He liked the attention he was getting. Tetley didn't look around, but let him talk.

"Heem not see me, I theenk," Amigo explained. "Eet was low down, where I can steel get out from the road. I take my horse into the hollow place so they can get by. At first I theenk I say hello when they come; I have no to smoke left by me. Then I theenk it funny to drive the cattle then."

"Cattle," Moore said sharply.

"But sure," Amigo said. He grinned at Moore. "Why you theenk I have to get out of hees road?"

"Go on," Moore said.

"Well," Amigo said, "when I theenk that, I be quiet. Then, when I see what marks those cattle have, I be veree quiet; veree slow I take my horse behind the bush, and we be still." He explained his conduct. "See, I have not the gun with me." He slapped his hip.

"What were the marks?" Mapes asked.

"What you theenk? On the throat, sweenging nice, three leetle what-you-call-heems—" He didn't need to say any more. We all knew Drew's dewlap mark.

"Why, the dirty rats," Gil said. It sounded as if he half admired them. "To kill a man," he said, "and still risk a drive."

"I told you, didn't I?" old Bartlett cried. "Let them get away with it a few times, I said, and there's no limit to what they'll try."

Davies was looking at Amigo. "Were they all Drew's?" he asked him.

"You can't get around it that way," Bartlett yelped at him. "With roundup just over they'd still be bunched, wouldn't they? And Drew was branding down his own end; he just cut out at the main camp. Ain't that right, Moore?"

"That's right," Moore said.

"How many of them?" Farnley asked Tetley.

"About forty head," Tetley said.

"That's what you said, isn't it, Amigo?" he asked over his shoulder.

"Si," said Amigo, grinning.

"No; I mean rustlers."

"Three, eh, Amigo?"

"Si, they was three."

"Did you know any of them?" Ma asked Amigo.

The grin disappeared from Amigo's face. But he shook his head. "I not evair see heem before," he said, "not any of heem."

"Well, you can't find a way out of this one, can you?" Farnley asked. But he didn't look at Davies. He seemed to be asking us all. Davies was looking at the Judge, but the Judge couldn't think of anything to say. I thought Davies was going to cry. He looked whipped. Until then I hadn't known how hard he was taking this; I'd felt it was just a kind of contest between his ideas and our feelings. Now I saw he was feeling it too. But I knew that I, for one, wasn't with him. I untied and mounted. Others were doing the same. Some slipped in to claim their drink from Canby, but came right out again.

Davies, without much conviction, tried Tetley. "Major Tetley," he said, "it's late. You can't get them tonight."

"If we can't," Tetley told him, "we can't get them at all. It's going to storm; snow, I think. We have time. They will move slowly with those cattle, and in the pass there is no place for them to branch off."

"Yes," admitted Davies, "yes, that's true." He ran a hand through his hair as if he was puzzled. He was smiling shakily.

"What time did Amigo see them?" Ma asked.

"About four o'clock, I believe. Wasn't it, Amigo?"

"Si."

"In the lower pass at four," said Farnley. "Sure we can get 'em."

"You were a long time bringing the word, Major," the Judge said. I was surprised to hear him still sounding like a friend of Davies.

Tetley looked at him with that same smile. It had a different meaning every time he used it.

"I wanted my son to go along," he said. "He was out on the range."

Young Tetley was sitting with his bridle across the saddle horn, pulled tight between his hands. His face got red, but he gave no other signs of having heard. We all had the same notion, I guess, that young Tetley hadn't been on the range at all. But nobody would have said so, and it didn't matter now.

Davies made one more try. "The sheriff should be here," he protested.

"Isn't he?" Tetley asked. "We must do what we can, then," he said.

"Major Tetley," Davies pleaded, "you mustn't let this be a lynching."

"It's scarcely what I choose, Davies," Tetley said. His voice was dry and disgusted.

"You'll bring them in for trial then?"

"I mean that I am only one of those affected. I will abide by the majority will."

Ma grinned at Davies. "There's your majority stuff right back at you, old man," she said.

Davies didn't argue that. He looked around again, but he didn't find friends. I didn't look at him myself. We knew what we were after now, and where, and it encouraged us to know there were only three rustlers. We'd thought, perhaps, being bold to work right in daylight on a small range, there might be twenty of them.

When Davies tried to speak again, Winder and Farnley told him to shut up.

The Judge expanded and said, "Tetley, you know what's legal in a case like this as well as I do. Davies is only asking what any law-abiding man should choose to do without the asking. He wants the posse to act under a properly constituted officer of the law, and as a posse, not a mob."

"Risley made me deputy," Mapes said loudly.

The Judge went on: "This action is illegal, Major," he blew. Tetley stared at him without any smile. "But in a measure I sympathize with it," the Judge admitted. "Sympathize. The circumstances make action imperative. But a lynching I cannot and will not condone."

"No?" Tetley inquired.

"No, by God. I insist, and that's all Davies asks too, that's all any of us ask, that you bring these men in for a fair trial."

"The Judge ain't had anything bigger to deal with than a drunk and disorderly Indian since he got here, Major," Ma said, with a sympathetic face. "You can see how he'd feel about it."

"That attitude," shouted the Judge, waving a hand at Ma, "that's what I must protest, Major. Levity, levity and prejudice in a matter of life and law."

"Regrettable," said Tetley, smiling at Ma.

"We shall observe order and true justice, Judge," he told him.

"Are we going, or aren't we?" Farnley wanted to know.

Tetley looked at him. "In time," he said.

"Mapes," he said, turning to Butch.

"Yes, sir?"

"You said Risley had made you deputy?"

"Yes, sir," said Butch.

"Then suppose you deputize the rest of us."

"It's not legal," Tyler told him. He appeared infuriated by Tetley's smiling, elusive talk. "No deputy has the right to deputize."

"It'll do for me, Butch; go head and pray," Smith yelled.

Butch looked at Tetley. Tetley didn't say anything or even nod. He just smiled, that thin little smile that barely moved the corners of his mouth.

"How about it, boys?" Butch asked us.

"Mapes," Tyler bellowed at him, "It's ineffective. You're violating the law yourself, in such an act."

Men called out to Mapes: "Go ahead, Butch"; "I guess it will take as well with you as any, Butch"; "Fire away, sheriff."

"Raise your right hands," Butch told us. We did. He recited an oath, which he seemed to have not quite straight. "Say 'I do,'" he told us. We said it together.

Farnley had already ridden out of the press. We began to swing into loose order after him. Davies was standing alone in the middle of the road with a stricken face. When the Judge bellowed after us in a sudden access of fury, "Tetley, you bring those men in alive, or, by God, as I'm justice of this county, you'll pay for it, you and every damned man-jack of your gang," Davies didn't even seem to hear him. Then suddenly he ran down the road, and then was running beside Tetley's horse, talking to him. Then he dropped back and let them go. I called to ask him if he wasn't coming. He looked up at me, and God, I felt sorry for the man. He'd looked funny, an old man running stiffly in the road after armed men on horses who wouldn't pay any attention to him. But now he wasn't funny. He didn't say anything, but nodded after a moment. When I was going to pull up to wait for him, he made a violent gesture to me to go on.

Looking back I saw him standing with Osgood in the street. The Judge had dismounted, and was talking to them, waving his hands rapidly. Canby hadn't come down, but was watching them and us, from the door. I could see the white towel he still had in his hand.

# 3

DAVIES DIDN'T catch up with us until we had passed Tetley's big and secret house behind its picket fence and trees and were out in the road between the meadows. The meadows were really marshes close to the road, and the road was only a kind of ranch lane, with deep wheel ruts in the mud and a high, grassy center and edges. The road had been built up, like a railroad embankment, to keep it out of the spring flood, and every few hundred yards there was a heavy plank bridge where the water flowed under from one part of the marsh to the other, and the chock of the horses in the mud, or the plop-plop on the sod, deepened into a hard, hollow thunder for a moment.

Davies was riding a neat little sorrel with white socks and small feet. His saddle was an old, dark leather which had turned cherry color and shiny. He'd put on a plaid blanket coat to keep warm, but he had no gun. He still looked hard bitten in the matter, but not the way he had in the street.

I asked him, "Still aiming to cure us?" and he shook his head and smiled.

"I guess not," he said.

Davies and I were riding last, and up ahead we could see the whole cavalcade strung out by ones and twos. Right ahead of us was Sparks, slowly singing something about Jordan to himself. We could hear sad bits of it now and then in the wind. He looked queer, elongated and hunched, saddleless astride that tall old mare with joints that projected like a cow's. His pants had inched up on him and showed his brown shanks like dark bones going down without socks into big, flat shoes that bobbed of their own weight when the mare jogged.

Ahead of him young Tetley and the Mex were riding together, Tetley silent and not looking around, Amigo pleased with himself, talking a lot and illustrating with his bridle hand while he rolled a cigarette against his chaps with the other. When he had lit the cigarette he talked with the hand that held it. The smell of his heavy Mex tobacco, stronger than a cigar, was still hot when it got to us. His horse, a red and white

pinto, like Gil's but smaller and neater, had to take two steps
to every one of Tetley's horse, a long-legged, stable-bred black
that picked each foot up with a flick, as if he wanted to dance.

We counted twenty-eight of us in all, with a little bunch riding separately up at the head, Tetley, Mapes, Farnley, Winder,
Bartlett and Ma, with Gabe and Smith not far behind them.

Old Pete Snyder's board shack with one window and one
door, set well out by itself on a high spot among the tules, was
the last place west of town. There was smoke coming out of its
tin chimney with a conical cap, but Pete's horse, with a saddle
on, was baiting on the west side of the shack, and Pete himself
was sitting on the step, his big, bare arms hanging over his
knees, and his short pipe nestled down in his gray club beard.
Pete raised a hand to us as if he didn't care and found it a foolish effort. Pete had had a wife once, but not since he'd lived
here, and he'd been alone so long he'd got to thinking differently from the rest of us. It's queer how clearly I remember the
way Pete just sat there and let us go. To see him just sit and go
on with his own thoughts, made me understand for the first
time what we were really going to do, so my breath and blood
came quicker for a minute.

Beyond Pete's we opened out into a lope. The horses, after
so much standing and fidgeting, were too willing, and kept
straining to gallop, moving up on each other until the riders
had to pull them to escape the mud and clods of soggy turf
they were throwing. Blue Boy was nervy from being with all
those other horses, but tired too, from roundup and two days
of riding, with a lot of climbing. He kept slipping and coming out of it stiff-legged and snorting, but then wanting to
lay out again. Others were having trouble too, and we pulled
to the jog again, and held it, all the hoofs trampling squilch-
squelch, squilch-squelch, and little clods popping gently out to
the side and rolling toward the water. The blackbirds, usually
noisy this time of day, were just taking short flights among the
reeds, and out farther, in the meadows, the cattle weren't feeding, but moving restlessly in small bunches, and the grass they
were plowing through was flattened by the wind. I looked for
a meadow lark. Usually about sunset you can see them playing,
leaping up and fluttering for a moment, and then dropping
again, suddenly, as if they'd been hit; then, after they're down

again, that singing will come to you, thin and sweet, chink-chink-a-link. But there was too much wind. Probably all over the big meadow they were down flat in the grass and ruffled. They could feel the storm coming too. Ahead of us the shadowy mountains, stippled all over by their sparse pelt of trees, and piebald with lingering snow, loomed up higher than they were, right against the moving sky.

"It'll be dark before we're out of the pass," I said to Davies. He looked up at the mountains and at the clouds and nodded. "Snow too," he said. We didn't say anything more. That was enough to show I wasn't unfriendly. He was thick with the same feeling of mortality I had, I guess. We were all feeling it some, out in the great spread of the valley, under the growing mountains, under the storm coming. Even Amigo wasn't talking any more, and had quit trying to smoke in that wind.

We rode that way across half the valley until, right under a steep foothill, we came to the fork where the road bent right to go into the draw, and the west lane from Drew's came into it.

There, while the rest of us jockeyed in a half circle, waiting and watching him, Tetley rode a ways into the lane and pulled up and sat there like he was carefully looking over a field to be fought. Mapes stopped beside him, Ma and Winder behind him. Tetley and Mapes said a few words together; then Mapes got off his horse, and drawing it on the bridle after him, went slowly down one side of the lane, looking down at the lane and at the spongy grass beside it. This lane was even less of a track than the one across the valley. On the valley side of it, perhaps fifty yards down, was the creek winding south, with willows, aspens and alders forming a screen along it; here and there a big, half-leafed cottonwood rose above this serpent of brush. On the other side, quite close in places, began the pine forest of the mountain. Through the trees, black in the shadow, showed patches of snow which hadn't melted yet. The forest rose steeply from there, and when you could no longer see the shape of the mountain leaning away from you, you could feel it rolling on up much higher. On the east side of the valley the tops of the mountains had disappeared above the plane of cloud.

Amigo was saying, in a clear, explanatory voice, "Eet was thees branding, si. What for you theenk I have the eyes, not to

know heem; like thees," and he held up the thumb and forefinger of his right hand, with the second finger curved out and
touching the forefinger at the nail, and placed a finger of his
left hand across the space between the thumb and forefinger
of the right. This made a fair figure of Drew's joined 𝕆 brand.
"I theenk I not mees heem," he said contemptuously, and spit
and started to roll a cigarette to make his hands feel natural
again. The mountain cut off the wind there.

"Look," he said, pointing while he licked the cigarette, "he
have made beeg track all the way, like the army." He seemed to
feel this halt was to test his word. He talked to Gil because Gil
was beside him, but he didn't care who heard.

He was right enough about the tracks; you didn't have to
ride out and scout to see them. The lane was churned with the
sharp marks, fresh, the new grass crushed down into the mud
still.

Mapes went about thirty or forty yards, then crossed the
lane and came back up the other side in the same way. When
he got back to Tetley he said something and mounted. Tetley
nodded. I could guess he was smiling his I-knew-it-all-the-time
smile. They rode back to us and Tetley said, "Amigo's right.
They're fresh tracks, the first made this spring. We can't tell
how many head, of course . . ."

"Forty," Amigo said, looking around at us.

"Possibly," Tetley said. "There were three riders. They left
tracks going both ways." We nodded like that settled it.

Tetley rode around us to get ahead again. Mapes and Ma
Grier and Winder followed him, and Gabe Hart. Farnley had
ridden farther up the main road and waited alone, watching,
below him, Tetley and Mapes playing field officers, but he let
them pass him now, and turned in with the rest of us. I was
nearer the middle of the bunch now, and when we strung out
I was riding with young Tetley.

In the shadow under the mountain we felt hurried because
of the lateness. We stepped up to the jog again until we came
around the bend where the pass opened above us. There the
road began to climb stiffly from the start and we had to walk.
The soft lane of the meadow turned into a mountain track,
hard and bouldery, with loose gravel and deep ruts made by
the water, but already dry. The horses clicked and stumbled,

climbing with a clear, slow, choppy rhythm. Where, at the side of the road, it was still muddy from seepage, the mud was already stiffening for the night.

Behind us Sparks began one of his hymns; it came in lonely fragments through the sounds of the horses and the rushing of the creek below us on the right. When I first heard him, I saw too that young Tetley shivered and bent a little, drawing his shoulders together. But that might have been only the wind. It sucked rapidly and heavily down this draw.

I looked back at Sparks. No one was riding with him, and he was grasping his horse's shoulders and gripping the barrel with his long legs to keep from sliding back off. But he didn't know he was having so much trouble; he was thinking about something else. Behind him were Davies, the two Bartlett boys, Moore and Gil riding together, and two men I didn't know, except that one of them had been playing poker at the back table in Canby's. I believe I looked back to keep from looking too much at young Tetley. But I looked at him again. He was riding easily, but too slumped for a cowboy. He was a thin, very young-looking fellow. In this light his face was a pale daub with big shadows for eyes. His black hair came out over his shirt collar in the back. I'd noticed before, in better light, how heavy and shining it was, as if oiled. He looked lonely and unhappy. I knew he didn't know me.

"Cold wind," I began.

He looked at me as if I'd said something important.

Then he said, "It's more than wind," and stared ahead of him again.

"Maybe," I said. I didn't get his drift, but if he wanted to talk, "maybe" shouldn't stop him.

"It's a lot more," he said, as if I'd contradicted him. "You can't go hunting men like coyotes after rabbits and not feel anything about it. Not without being like any other animal. The worst animal."

"There's a difference; we have reasons."

"Names for the same thing," he said sharply. "Does that make us any better? Worse, I'd say. At least coyotes don't make excuses. We think we can see something better, but we go on doing the same things, hunt in packs like wolves; hole up in warrens like rabbits. All the dirtiest traits."

"There's still a difference," I said. "We've got it over wolves and rabbits."

"Power, you mean," he said bitterly.

"Over your wolves, and bears too."

"Oh, we're smart," he said, the same way. "It's the same thing," he cried; "all we use it for is power. Yes, we've got them scared all right, all of them, except the tame things we've taken the souls out of. We're the cocks of the dungheap, all right; the bullies of the globe."

"We're not hunting rabbits tonight," I reminded him.

"No; our own kind. A wolf wouldn't do that; not a mangy coyote. That's the hunting we like now, our own kind. The rest can't excite us any more."

"We don't have to hunt men often," I told him. "Most people never have. They get along pretty well together."

"Oh, we love each other," he said. "We labor for each other, suffer for each other, admire each other. We have all the pack instincts, all right, and nice names for them."

"All right," I said, "what's the harm in their being pack instincts, if you want to put it that way? They're real."

"They're not. They're just to keep the pack with us. We don't dare hunt each other alone, that's all. There's more ways of hunting than with a gun," he added.

He'd jumped too far for me on that one. I didn't say anything.

"Think I'm stretching it, do you?" he asked furiously. "Well, I'm not. It's too nice a way of putting it, if anything. All any of us really want any more is power. We'd buck the pack if we dared. We don't, so we use it; we trick it to help us in our own little killings. We've mastered the horses and cattle. Now we want to master each other, make cattle of men. Kill them to feed ourselves. The smaller the pack the more we get."

"Most of life's pretty simple and quiet," I said. "You talk like we all had knives out."

"Your simple life," he said. "Your quiet life. All right," he said, "take the simplest, quietest life you know. Take the things that are going on around us all the time, so we don't notice them any more than old furniture. Take women visiting together, next-door neighbors, old friends. What do they talk about? Each other, all the time, don't they? And what are the parts they like, the ones they remember and bring home to tell to the men?"

"I don't know anything about women," I said.

"You don't have to," he said. "You know anyway. Gossip, scandalous gossip, that's what wakes them up, makes them talk faster and all together, or secretively, as if they were stalking enemies in their minds; something about a woman they know, something that can spoil her reputation: the way she was seen to look at a certain man, or that she can't cook, or doesn't keep her parlor clean, or can't have children, or, worse, could but won't. That's what wakes them up. And do you know why?" He turned the white shape of his face toward me sharply.

I didn't like the way the talk was getting to sound like a quarrel. I tried to ease it off.

"No," I said. "Why?" as if I was really curious.

"Because it makes them feel superior; makes them feel they're the wolves, not the rabbits. If each of them had it the way she wants it," he said after a moment, "she'd be the only woman left in the world. They can't manage that, so they do the best they can toward it."

"People can be pretty mean sometimes," I admitted, "picking on the weak ones." It was no good.

"It's not always the weak ones," he said angrily. "They're worse than wolves, I tell you. They don't weed out the unfit, they weed out the best. They band together to keep the best down, the ones who won't share their dirty gossip, the ones who have more beauty or charm or independence, more anything, than they have. They did it right there in Bridger's Wells this spring," he blazed.

"How was that?" I asked, remembering what Canby had said about Rose Mapen.

"They drove a girl out. Made a whore of her with talk."

"Why? What did she do?"

"Nothing. That's what I'm telling you. You know what they had against her? You know what was her intolerable sin against the female pack?"

"How would I know?"

"She was better looking than any of them, and men liked her."

"That can make a whore sometimes," I said.

"She wasn't, and they knew it."

"There must have been something."

"There was when they got done," he said. "Everything. But not before. They were scared of her, that's all."

"Why should they be?"

"Men. They're the biggest part of a woman's power."

I had to grin; this kid talking about women like he'd had the testing of the whole breed. And he the kind that would fall over himself to do anything for any of them if they asked it, or just looked it.

He didn't say anything more for a moment, and I heard the creek far down, and the horses clicking and heaving on the grade.

Then he asked, "Do you know Frena Hundel?"

"No," I said. So far we'd kept it pretty general; anyway, no names.

"The wild-looking woman who was so afraid we wouldn't come out and hunt down these three, the whole heroic thirty of us."

"Yeah," I said. "What about her?"

"You know what's the matter with her?"

"How would I know?" I asked again. It didn't feeze him.

"She wants those men to die."

He'd got beyond me again, chasing his own hate.

"Before you came," I told him, "she was wild because Larry Kinkaid had been killed. That was what she kept yelling about. I thought she was sore about Larry, maybe sweet on him."

"Oh, yes," he said scornfully, "now he's dead, she's sweet on him. She'd take any dead man as her personal grief; it makes her feel important."

"What's the sense in that?" I asked.

"He wasn't anything to her before he was shot. In her heart she's glad he's dead."

That still didn't make sense to me. I waited, twisting a hand in Blue Boy's mane and feeling his big shoulders working under it.

"Frena can't get a man," he explained, "so she wants to see them all die. Yes, all of them. She's glad Kinkaid's dead. She doesn't know these men we're after, doesn't know anything about them, but she's wild to have us kill them. And she's wild to get the rest of us the same way, too, to push us into something that will kill our souls, if we have any; that will make us afraid to face men again, anyhow. Because she can't get a man."

"It's a big project," I said, "to kill us all because she can't get one of us."

"I don't say she can. I say it's what she wants."

I didn't say anything.

"If there were no men, she could do what she pleased with most women, make them her slaves. Men are the part of power she can't get, and Frena wants power. Frena's got a bigger appetite for power than the pack will tolerate because most of them couldn't stand it themselves. It would tear them to pieces in a week to want anything as much as Frena wants everything."

"You don't think much of women, do you?" I said.

"Men are no better," he said. "Men are worse. They're not so sly about their murder, but they don't have to be; they're stronger; they already have the upper hand of half the race, or they think so. They're bullies instead of sneaks, and that's worse. And they're just as careful to keep up their cheap male virtues, their strength, their courage, their good fellowship, to keep the pack from jumping them, as the women are to keep up their modesty and their hominess. They all lie about what they think, hide what they feel, to keep from looking queer to the pack."

"Is there anything so fine about being different?" I asked him.

"Did you ever hear a man tell another man about the dreams he's had that have made him sweat and run his legs in the bed and wake up moaning with fear? Did you?"

"What do you want? Everybody running around telling his dreams, like a little kid?"

"Or any woman tell about the times she's sighed and panted in her sleep for a lover she wasn't married to?"

"For Lord's sake," I said.

"No," he babbled on, "you never did and you never will."

"It's all right with me if I don't."

The white of his face was to me again. "You're like all the rest," he raged. "You've had dreams like that; you know you have. We've all had those dreams. In our hearts we know they're true, truer than anything we ever tell; truer than anything we ever do, even. But nothing could make us tell them, show our weakness, have the pack at our throats.

"Even in dreams," he said, after a bit, as if he was talking to himself, but so I could hear, "even in dreams it's the pack that's worst; it's the pack that we can never quite see but always feel coming, like a cloud, like a shadow, like a fog with our death in it. It's the spies of the pack who are always hidden behind the next pillars of the temples and palaces we dream we're in, watching us go between them. They're behind the trees in the black woods we dream about; they're behind the boulders on the mountains we dream we're climbing, behind the windows on the square of every empty dream city we wander in. We've all heard them breathing; we've all run screaming with fear from the pack that's coming somewhere. We've all waked up in the night and lain there trembling and sweating and staring at the dark for fear they'll come again.

"But we don't tell about it, do we?" he dared me. And said quickly, "No, no, we don't even want to hear anybody else tell. Not because we're afraid for him. No, we're afraid our own eyes will give us away. We're afraid that sitting there hearing him and looking at him we'll let the pack know that our souls have done that too, gone barefoot and gaping with horror, scrambling in the snow of the clearing in the black woods, with the pack in the shadows behind them. That's what makes us sick to hear fear admitted, or lust, or even anger, any of the things that would make the pack believe that we were either weak or dangerous."

He turned his face fully toward me, furious and challenging. "That is what makes you sick now, to hear me," he told me. "That's what makes you so damned superior and cold and quiet." His voice choked him so I thought he was going to cry. "You're just hiding the truth, even from yourself," he babbled.

My hands were twitching, but I didn't say anything.

Then he said more quietly, "You think I'm crazy, don't you? It always seems crazy to tell the truth. We don't like it; we won't admit what we are. So I'm crazy."

I was thinking that. I don't like to hear a man pouring out his insides without shame. And taking it for granted everyone else must be like him. You'd have thought he was God, making everyone in his own pattern. Still, he was a kid and weak and unhappy, and his own father, they said, was his enemy.

"Every man's got a right to his own opinion," I told him.

After a moment he said, "Yes," low and to his saddlehorn.

Having heard myself speak I realized that queerly, weak and bad-tempered as it was, there had been something in the kid's raving which had made the canyon seem to swell out and become immaterial until you could think the whole world, the universe, into the half-darkness around you: millions of souls swarming like fierce, tiny, pale stars, shining hard, winking about cores of minute, mean feelings, thoughts and deeds. To me his idea appeared just the opposite of Davies'. To the kid, what everybody thought was low and wicked, and their hanging together was a mere disguise of their evil. To Davies, what everybody thought became, just because everybody thought it, just and fine, and to act up to what they thought was to elevate oneself. And yet both of them gave you that feeling of thinking outside yourself, in a big place; the kid gave me that feeling even more, if anything, though he was disgusting. You could feel what he meant; you could only think what Davies meant.

I heard him talking again. "Why are we riding up here, twenty-eight of us," he demanded, "when every one of us would rather be doing something else?"

"I thought you said we liked killing?"

"Not so directly as this," he said. "Not so openly. Not many of us, at least. We're doing it because we're in the pack, because we're afraid not to be in the pack. We don't dare show our pack weakness; we don't dare resist the pack."

"What do you want us to do," I asked him, "sit and play a harp and worry about how bad we are while some damned rustler kills a man and cleans out the country?"

"It isn't that," he said. "How many of us do you think are really here because there have been cattle stolen, or because Kinkaid was shot?"

"I'm not wrong about your being here, am I?" I asked him.

Then he was quiet. I felt mean. The thing that made me sorest about this whole talk was that I knew the kid was just scared. I knew he didn't want to quarrel; but he talked so you couldn't do anything else.

"No," he said finally. "I'm here, all right." He had dug himself up by the roots to say that.

"Well?" I said, easier.

"I'm here because I'm weak," he said, "and my father's not."

There wasn't anything a guy could say to that. It made me feel as I had once listening to a man describing just how he'd got to a woman, undressing her, so to speak, right in front of us, even telling us what she'd said; a woman we all knew at that. But at least he'd been drunk.

"That doesn't help, does it?" young Tetley was asking.

"I'm not claiming to be superior to anyone else," he said. "I'm not. I'm not fit to be alive. I know better than to do what I do. I've always known better, and not done it."

He burst out, "And that's hell; can you understand that that's hell?"

"You kind of take it for granted nobody else is as smart as you are, don't you, kid?" I asked him.

He hunched over the saddle, twisting the front of his coat, I thought, with one hand. It was too dusky to be sure. After a while he answered, as if he had forgotten what I'd said, and then remembered it again.

"I didn't mean it that way," he said. He sounded far away and tired; ashamed he'd said so much. It was as if he'd been on a jag, but it was over now and he was feeling sick. He couldn't let it drop, though.

"Maybe I am crazy, in a way," he said very quietly.

"You take it too hard, son," I told him. "You didn't start this."

"But I know this," he said, "if we get those men and hang them, I'll kill myself. I'll hang myself."

Louder he said, "I tell you I won't go on living and remembering I saw a thing like this; was part of it myself. I couldn't. I'd go really crazy."

Then he said, quietly again, "It's better to kill yourself than to kill somebody else. That settles the mess anyway; really settles it."

I'd had enough. I'd heard drunks talk like this and it was half funny, but the kid was cold sober.

"We haven't hung anybody yet," I told him. "You can go home and keep your own hands clean."

"No, I can't," he said.

"I can't," he said again; "and if I could it wouldn't matter. What do I matter?"

"You seem to think you matter a lot," I said.

I could see the pale patch of his face turned toward me in the dusk, then away again.

"It does sound that way, doesn't it?" he asked, as if I was wrong.

I began humming the "Buffalo Gal" to myself. He didn't say anything more, but after a bit dropped back and rode beside Sparks. They didn't talk, because I stopped humming and heard Sparks still singing to himself.

At the first level stretch in the road we stopped to breathe the horses. It was dark now, and really cold, not just chilly. There was frost on my blanket roll when I went to get my sheepskin out. The sheepskin was good, cutting the wind right away, and I swung my arms across my chest to get warm inside it. Others were warming themselves too. I could see them spreading and closing like dark ghosts, and hear the thump of their fists.

Gil came up alongside and peered to make sure who it was. Then he said, "Doing this in the middle of the night is crazy. Moore don't like it much either," he added. We sat there, listening to the horses breathe, and some of the other men talking in low voices.

Gil was still worrying about the dark. "If it hadn't clouded up," he said, "there would have been a full moon tonight, bright as day." Gil knew his sky like the palm of his hand. One place and another I'd read quite a lot about the sun and moon and the constellations, but I could never remember it. Gil had never read anything, but he always knew.

When the horses were breathing quietly again, and beginning to stamp, we started on, Gil and I riding together, which felt more natural. Except right in front of us and right behind us, we couldn't see the riders. We could only hear small sounds of foot and saddle and voice from along the line. The sounds were short, flat and toneless, just bits coming back on the rushing of the creek. Gil was quiet, for him. He didn't talk or hum; he didn't change position in his saddle or play with the quirt end of his bridle. He didn't look around. There wasn't much to see, of course, the broken shadows of the forest against the fainter but rearing and uniform shadow that was the mountain rising across the creek; that and the patches of snow, bigger and more numerous, showing at vague distances through the trees, like huge, changing creatures standing upright and seeming to move. Even so a man will usually look around even more when it's dark, unless he's got saddle-sleepy and dazed. Gil wasn't sleepy; he wasn't sitting his horse like a sleepy man. If I knew him, he was thinking about something he didn't like. I should have let him alone, but I didn't.

"Still seeing those three guys reaching for the barrels, Gil?"

"No," he said, coming out of it. "I'd forgot all about them until you mentioned it. Why should I worry about that now?"

"What's eating you?"

He didn't say anything.

"I thought you liked excitement," I said. "I thought you'd be honing for something to do."

"I've got nothing against hanging a rustler," he said loudly. The riders ahead turned in their saddles and peered back at us. One of them hissed at us angrily. That made me sore on account of Gil; we were like that, fight each other a good part of the time, but be happier to pitch in together on somebody else. Though there was a difference between us. Gil really liked to fight, liked to let his temper slip and to feel the sweat and the hitting. I just fought because Gil got so pigheaded and insulting when he wanted to fight that I had to or feel yellow.

"Why all the secret?" I said, as loud as Gil had. "Afraid the three of them will round us up?"

The man who had hissed pulled his horse in and reined half around. It was old Bartlett. For a minute I thought he was coming for us. But Gil rode right over toward him, like he would love to mix it, and Bartlett turned back into line, though slowly, to show he wasn't afraid of Gil.

When we were straightened out, Gil said, "It ain't that I don't believe in gettin' a killer, any way you have to. But I don't like it in the dark. There's always some fool will get wild and plug anything that moves; like young Greene there, or Smith, or maybe young Tetley."

"He won't do any shooting," I said.

"Maybe not; but he scares easy; he's scared now. And he's got a gun."

He went on, "That ain't what bothers me most, though. I like to pick my bosses. We didn't pick any bosses here, but we got 'em just the same. We was just herded in. So, and who herded us in? That kid Greene, if I remember, with a wild-eyed story he couldn't get straight, and Smith and Bartlett blowing off, and Osgood because he got us sore. That's a sweet outfit to tell you what you're going to do, ain't it?"

"They didn't really get us in," I said.

"They started us, them and Farnley. Not that Farnley's like them; Farnley's got plenty of sand. But when he's mad he's crazy. He's no kind of a guy to have in this business. When he's mad he can't think at all. He don't rile cool.

"I remember once," he began narrating, "I saw Farnley get mad. We was together in Hazey's outfit over on the Humboldt. It was beef roundup. Some wise guy, trying to improve his stock, had got a lot of long-horns in with his reds that spring. They was big as a chuck-wagon, and wild. Some of 'em you couldn't drive; they was fast as a pony, and didn't want to bunch, like a steer. You had to get 'em one at a time with a rope, like you would for branding.

"Well, in the thick of it, all dust and flurry, one of these long-horns, a big gray-splotched fellow with legs like a horse and nine feet of horns, got under Farnley's pony and ripped him open like splitting a fish; the guts sagged right out in a belch of black blood. The steer pulled loose all right, but he'd got in deeper than it looked at first. The pony, stiff-legged, tried to get away from him, but then, all of a sudden, came red blood, a lot of it, and he went over all at once, his legs folding right under him. Farnley got clear, he's quick as a cat and smooth. But then you know what he done? He took one look at the pony, it was his best one, one he'd had four years, and then he went wild-eyed for that steer. Yes he did, on his feet, no gun or anything; like he thought he could break its neck with his hands. Lucky I saw him, and there was another fellow, Cornwall, Corny we called him, not too far off that I yelled to. We got the steer turned off before he'd more than punched one hole under Farnley's ribs; not too deep, a sort of rip along the side. And even then it wasn't enough for Farnley. He fought us like a wildcat to get at the critter again. I was sore enough to let him go ahead and be mashed, but Corny'd known him a long time, and knew how he got. So Corny climbs down, and says to me, 'Let him come,' and when I let Farnley go he went for Corny milling. Corny just stood there cool and knocked him out with one punch. He folded up like an empty sack, and we had to get water from the chuck-wagon to bring him to.

"You'd think that was enough, wouldn't you? Corny'd risked his own neck plenty, gettin' down in the middle of all that. The steer was near as wild as Farnley was, dodging around us, trying to get in another poke. I had all I could do to keep heading him out. He was blood crazy, and I didn't relish the idea of losing my pony the same way. But do you think Farnley said thanks? He did not. Lying there in the shade of the chuck-wagon, while the cook tied up his side the best he could, he kept looking at us like he wanted to take a knife to both of us. By Godfreys, if he had of tried something I'da let him have it fer a nickel. Corny made me come off.

"It was pretty near the end of roundup before Farnley'd even see us when he went by. And he never did mention the thing, not to this day. That's how long he can stay that way."

I thought Gil was off the track, but he wasn't.

"And that's the guy that's going to do something when it comes to doing something," he said.

"He's had a lot of time to think it over," I reminded him. "It's not the same. Tetley can stop him."

"Not Tetley or anybody else," Gil said. "And that's another thing. Who picked Tetley? He's not our man, the damn reb dude."

"It was Tetley brought us, when it came to the showdown," I said.

"I don't like it," Gil said.

"We can quit," I reminded him. "There's no law makes us be part of this posse."

Gil said quickly, "Hell, no. I'll see this thing out as far as any man will.

"You watch yourself," he added, "don't you let Davies and Osgood, or that loose-mouth Tyler, get to you. There's not a damn thing they can do to us as long as we stick together, and they know it."

"I didn't bring this up," I reminded him.

"Neither did I," he said. "I'm just warnin' you we got to keep an eye on some of these guys, Farnley and Bartlett and

Winder and Ma; yes, and Tetley too. No slick-smiling bastard's going to suck me into a job I don't like, that's all."

"Have your own way, whatever way that is."

"Shut up," he ordered.

We rode along saying nothing then, Gil still angry because he couldn't make his feelings agree, and me laughing at him, though not out loud. He'd have ridden right over me if I'd even peeped.

We came to a steeper pitch, where I could feel Blue Boy's shoulders pump under the saddle and hear his breath coming in jerks. Then we came into a narrows and I knew we were nearly at the top of the pass. The road there just hung on the face of a cliff, and the other wall across the creek wasn't more than twenty feet away. On a night as dark as that you wouldn't think it could get any darker, but it did in that narrows. The wall went straight up beside us, probably forty or fifty feet. The clambering of the horses echoed a little against it even with the wind, and with the creek roaring as if we were on the edge of it. The wind was strong in the slot, and smelled like snow again.

We all hugged the cliff side of the road, not being able to see the drop-off side clearly. I was on the inside, and sometimes my foot scraped the wall, and sometimes Gil and I clicked stirrups, he had pulled over so far. His horse sensed the edge and didn't like it, and kept twisting around trying to face it.

"A nice place for a holdup," Gil said, showing he was willing to talk again.

"In here three men could do in a hundred," I agreed.

"But they won't."

"I wouldn't think so."

After a minute I said, "It's going to snow."

He must have been testing the wind himself; then he said, "Hell. Won't that be just lovely! Still," he said, "it can't be much of a storm this time of year."

"I don't know. I remember trying to get through Eagle Pass the first week in June one year. I had to go back; the horse was up to his belly and we weren't half way to the summit. A fellow bringing the mail across on snowshoes said there was nine feet at the summit. He had a stick poked in up there with notches on it."

"Yeh, but that wasn't all new snow."

"Every inch of it. The trail had been clear two days before."

"Eagle Pass is higher, though."

"Some. But this is nearly eight thousand. That's high enough."

"Maybe they'll have to call it off," Gil suggested.

"Depend on how much of a lead they thought the rustlers had."

"Well, it won't be any picnic," Gil said, "but we'll be making a lot better time than they can. This was a fool way to come with cattle. And they'd have to stop when it got dark, too. You can't drive cattle on this road in the dark."

"By the same sign," I said, "we could go right by them and never know it."

Gil thought. Then he said, "Not unless they stopped in the Ox-Bow. There's no place else from here to the Hole where they could get forty head of cattle off the road."

The Ox-Bow was a little valley up in the heart of the range. Gil and I had stayed there a couple of days once, on the loose. It was maybe two or three miles long and half or three quarters of a mile wide. The peaks were stacked up on all sides of it, showing snow most of the summer. The creek in the middle of it wound back on itself like a snake trying to get started on loose sand, and that shape had named the valley. There was sloping meadow on both sides of the creek, and in the late spring millions of purple and gold violets grew there, violets with blossoms as big as the ball of a man's thumb. Beyond the meadow, on each side, there was timber to the tops of the hills. It was a lovely, chill, pine-smelling valley, as lonely as you could want. Scarcely anybody came there unless there was a dry season. Just once in a while, if you passed in the late summer, you'd see a sheepherder small out in the middle, with his burro and dogs and flock. The rest of the time the place belonged to squirrels, chipmunks and mountain jays. They would all be lively in the edge of the wood, scolding and flirting.

Someone had lived there once, though, and tried to ranch the place. In the shelter of a few isolated trees extending from the forest on the west side, he'd built a log cabin with a steep roof to slide the snow off. There'd been a corral too, and a regular barn with a loft to store hay. But whoever he was, he'd

given up years before. The door and windows were out of the
cabin, and the board floor was rotten, seedling pines and sagebrush coming up through it. There were only a few posts of
the corral left, and the snow had flattened the barn, splitting
the sides out and settling the roof right over them. Small circles
of blackened stone showed where short stoppers, like Gil and
me, had burned pieces of the barn and fences.

We discussed the chances of the rustlers using the Ox-Bow.
The road ran right along the edge of it at the south end; there
was good grazing and water and wood to be picked up. But
then, there was only that one way in and out, at least for men
driving cattle. On the other three sides the mountains were
steep, heavily timbered at the base, then grown thick with
manzanita, then covered with frost-split, sliding shale, and they
didn't let you out anywhere except into more mountains. On
the other hand there was no other place on the trail where they
could have stopped. There was a clearing right at the summit, but the road ran through the middle of it and there was
no grass or water. And the road down the other side was like
this one, steep and narrow all the way; a few little washes big
enough for the coach to get off the track and stand, but none
to hold forty head of cattle. We couldn't see anything but the
Ox-Bow or keep going.

On the summit the wind hit full force, as if you'd stepped
out from behind a wall. It was bitter cold and damp. I thought
I felt a few flakes of snow on my face, but my face was already
too numb to be sure. Even the horses ducked their heads into
the wind.

In the clearing Tetley and Mapes stopped us to breathe
the horses again. Also they began arguing what Gil and I had
thought about the trail and the Ox-Bow, and some were for
turning back. With snow beginning to come, and that wind
blowing, they felt sure of a blizzard. Tetley maintained that was
all the more reason for pressing the chase. With their trail covered with snow, and a day or two start, time to switch brands,
what would we have to go on? Davies, and Moore backed him
up this time, was for sending a couple of riders on across to
Pike's Hole, and getting the men there to pick the rustlers up. I
could see what he wanted. Kinkaid was nothing to most of the
Pike's men, and it wasn't their cattle had been rustled. They'd

pick the men up on principle, but they'd be willing to hold them for the sheriff and a trial. Winder and Ma sided with Tetley. Winder was accusing Davies, and even Moore, of being so scared of the job they'd rather let a murderer slip than do it. Davies admitted he'd rather let ten murderers go than have it on his soul that he'd hung an honest man. Tetley said he wasn't going to hang an innocent man; he'd make sure enough of that to suit even Davies. To Farnley, even Tetley's manner smacked of delay. He told them he'd rather see a murderer hanged than shot, it was a dirtier death, but that he'd bush-whack all three of those men before he'd let one of them get out of the mountains free. I tried to shut Gil up when he started, but he went ahead and told Farnley that nobody who wasn't a horse-thief himself would bush-whack any man, let alone three men for one, and the one a man he hadn't seen do it. Farnley was going to climb Gil, for which I couldn't blame him, but they couldn't pick each other out in the dark, and others held them down. I tried to talk Gil quiet, but he said, "Aw, hell," in disgust, and spit as if it was on the whole bunch of us, and rode farther out by himself. It looked as if it might be another long squabble. I'd been walking Blue Boy back and forth along the edge so I could hear some of the talk, but still keep him from cooling too fast. Cold as it was, the climb had sweated him. Other punchers were doing the same.

Now I eased him over to the edge of the clearing where the trees broke the wind a little, and got down and wiped him over with a few handfuls of old, softened, damp pine needles. They pricked him, and he was restless, but he liked it fine when I finished him off with snow from a little drift at the top of the creek bank. The snow was hard and granular, and brought the blood back into my hands. I listened for the talk to end, but took my time. It felt good to be on my feet and moving around; I'd stiffened to the saddle.

Somebody in the middle of the clearing sang out, "Scatter, boys, there's horses coming." Tetley didn't seem to like the order, for I heard him giving others quickly, but not loud enough so I could understand. The group was already scattering to both sides of the clearing. I could see the shadowy huddle in the middle fanning out toward the edges. In the wind I couldn't hear them, any more than I'd heard anything coming.

They were so many shadows floating off slowly, like a cloud breaking up in front of the moon. The middle of the clearing became just a gray, open space waiting for something to come into it. I could see why Tetley hadn't liked that order, besides its being yelled that way. There wasn't a man among us, in the edge of the woods, that could risk a shot into the clearing in the dark and with others right across from him. Four or five riders stayed together and disappeared into the shadow where the road entered the clearing. Tetley was with them, I thought. He kept his head in this sort of thing. I listened hard, but still couldn't hear the running horses I expected from that shout. All I could hear was the wind, roaring on and off in the pines, and higher up booming at intervals, as if clapping in space; and faintly, like a lesser wind, the falling of the creek. Those, and right behind me the trunks of the taller pines complaining.

One of the shadows, on foot and leading his horse, came toward me and disappeared under the trees very near. Then I was listening for him too. A man hates to have somebody near him in the dark when he doesn't know who it is. I felt the animal advantage of being there first.

A voice from the other side of me, Mapes I thought, called out, "Stay where you are till I give you the hail. Then circle out slow if it's anything we want. Don't do any shooting."

It struck me that in that darkness and wind, unless Tetley's bunch stopped him, a rider could be across the clearing and into the narrows before we were sure he was there. And on that down grade, riding alone, he'd have a big advantage on us. I told myself that was none of my worry, but the thought kept me tense.

The man near me was coming closer. I could hear the slow, soft thuds of his horse plodding on the thick blanket of pine needles.

"Who is it?" I asked.

The thudding stopped. "It's jus' me, Spahks," a voice finally said. "Who ah you, suh?"

"Art Croft," I told him.

He seemed to think that over. For some reason I thought of my history since this business had begun; what I found made me feel humble but irritated. Then he asked, "Don't mahnd if ah come ovah a bit closah, do you, Mistah Croft?"

"No, come on. I'm findin' it lonesome myself."

He stopped right beside me. It was black in there though; I still couldn't see him. He reached out and touched me, just light and quick, to make sure I was there.

"Theah you ah," he said.

Then, apologizing, "Ah wasn't quite cleah you was with us, Mistah Croft. Guess ah wasn't noticin' all that was goin' on. Ah did see you fren' Mistah Cahtah."

"I wasn't mixin' in much," I admitted.

"It's mortal cold, ain't it?"

I remembered that he had on only a thin shirt and jeans. He was a heat-loving nigger anyway, not used to this mountain country yet.

"I've got a blanket if you want it."

"Thank you jus' the same, Mistah Croft," he said. He had a sad little chuckle. "It takes all mah hands to keep on this ole hoss."

I'd noticed that Sparks never called me "sir" when he knew who I was. Not that I wanted to be called sir, and not that Sparks was ever anything but polite, but it did nettle me that he wouldn't be as careful of me as he would of a sponge like Smith, or a weak sister like Osgood. And even if you don't believe in them, you pick up feelings about darkies from men you work with. I'd worked in outfits with a lot of Southern boys, mostly Texas. They'd drop a white man who played with a nigger even faster than they would a nigger, and they had a sharp line about niggers. They wouldn't condescend about them, the way some of us did, but they wouldn't eat or drink where black men did, or sleep in blankets a nigger had used, or have anything more to do with a house where a nigger had been let in the front door. They didn't condescend, I thought, just because they never even considered a nigger the same kind of creature enough to make comparisons. I'd picked up just enough of this crude habit to make me feel guilty whenever I had such thoughts. I did now.

"I've got some whisky in my canteen," I said; "better have a couple of shots."

"No, thanks, Mistah Croft, ah guess not."

"Go on," I said, "I've got plenty."

"Ah don't drink it, Mistah Croft." He didn't want to sound

like a temperance lady. "There's devil enough in me bah mah-self," he explained.

"In this cold you could drink the whole canteen," I told him.

"No, thanks."

I shut up, and he felt I was a little stiff, I guess.

"Ah wish we was well out of this business," he said.

"It's a way of spendin' time," I told him.

"It's man takin' upon himself the Lohd's vengeance," he said. "Man, Mistah Croft, is full of error." He said it jokingly, but he wasn't joking.

I suppose I think as much about God as the next man who isn't in the business. I spend a lot of time alone. But I'd seen, yes and done, some things that made me feel that if God was worried about man it was only in large numbers and in the course of time.

"Do you think the Lord cares much about what's happening up here tonight?" I asked him, too sharply.

Sparks took it gently though. "He mahks the sparrow's fall," he said.

"Then He won't miss this, I guess."

"God is in us, Mistah Croft," he pleaded. "He wuhks th'ough us."

"Maybe, then, we're the instruments of the divine vengeance," I suggested.

"Ah can't fahnd that in mah conscience, Mistah Croft," he said after a moment. "Can you?" he asked me.

"I'm not sure I've got a conscience any more."

He persisted, taking another angle. "Mistah Croft, if you had to hold the rope on one of those men with your own hands, could you fohget it raght away aftahwahds?" he asked me.

"I don't suppose I could," I admitted.

"And wouldn't it trouble you to think of it, even a long time aftah?"

"Not with a rustler," I lied.

When Sparks didn't say anything I felt I'd let another good man down, the way I had about Davies.

"I haven't heard anything yet," I said. "Did you hear anything out there?"

"Ah didn't," Sparks said, as if he wasn't interested. "It was Mistah Mapes and Mistah Windah."

"It don't seem to me the rustlers would double back when there's only one trail," I said.

"No, suh." That "sir" had the politeness of a grievance. It annoyed me.

"You seem to be taking this pretty personal."

"It's like ah was sayin', Mistah Croft," he answered after a moment. "There's some things a man don't fohget seein'."

You can't ask a man to talk about such things, so I didn't say anything. Perhaps on account of the darkness Sparks decided to tell me anyway.

"Ah saw mah own brothah lynched, Mistah Croft," he said stiffly. "Ah was just a little fella when I saw that, but sometimes ah still wakes up from dreamin' about it."

There was still nothing for me to say.

"And pahtly ah was to blame," Sparks remembered.

"You were?"

"Ah went to find Jim where he was hidin' and they followed me and got him."

"How old did you say you were?"

"Ah'm not shuah; a little fella, six or seven or eight."

"You couldn't have been much to blame then," I said.

"Ah've ahgued that with mahself, Mistah Croft, but it don't help the feelin'," Sparks said. "That's what ah mean," he added.

"Well, had he done what they picked him up for?"

"Ah don' know; we didn' any of us evah know foh shuah. But it still don' seem lahk anythin' ah evah knew about Jim."

"They wouldn't lynch him without knowing," I said.

He thought for a while before he answered that. "They made him confess," he admitted. "But they would have anyhow," he protested. "It wouldn't have done him any good not to, and confessin' made it shortah. It was still bad, though; awful bad," he added. "Ah wouldn' lahk to see a thing lahk that again, Mistah Croft."

"No," I said.

We were quiet and I could hear his teeth chattering.

"I'll tell you," I said, as if I was joking, "a drop or two more whisky can't do my soul any harm. You take my coat and I'll take the drink."

"No, thanks, Mistah Croft." I was afraid he was going to feel responsible for my drinking too, but he went on, "Ah'm all used to it now, an' you'd catch youah death o' cold takin' that coat off." He wanted that coat, though; it wasn't easy for him to object.

"I've gone in my shirt sleeves when it was colder than this," I said, "and my shirt's flannel."

I took off the coat. He protested, but I talked him down cheerfully and he put it on.

"Sure a fahn coat," he said happily. "Ah'll get me warmed up a mite in it, then you take it. Ah get awful cold around the heart," he said seriously. "Seems like ah always feel it most there. This woolly'll warm me up in no tahm. Then you take it again."

"I don't even feel it," I said, which wasn't true. "You keep the coat, Reverend." I'd been cold again from standing around, even before I'd taken the coat off, and there was more snow in the wind now, blowing in even under the trees. There was no question about its being snow. Still I felt more cheerful than I had since morning, which seemed a long way back now, and like another life.

I found the canteen on my saddle and had two long swallows. It was rotten stuff of Canby's all right, but it was hot in the mouth and warming in the belly. It gave me a good shiver, then settled broadly in my middle and began to spread through my body like a fire creeping in short grass. I stood there and let her spread for a minute; then I had another, corked the canteen, tied it back on the saddle and rolled a cigarette. I offered Sparks the makings, but he didn't smoke either. I turned my back to the clearing to cover the flare I'd make; two or three voices called at me though, low and angry. Having started, I held the flame until my cigarette was going. The smoke was good, drawn in that cold air, and after the whisky in my mouth.

I could hear somebody leading his horse, and stopping close on my right.

"You damn fool," he said in a low, hostile voice, "want to give us away?" I thought it was Winder. I knew I was in wrong, which made me even sorer.

"Who to?" I asked him out loud.

"You guys have been hearing things," I told him, the same way. "Let's get moving before we freeze stiff and can't. Or are we giving this up?"

I heard his hammer click; the sound brought me awake, quick and clear. I kept the cigarette in my mouth, but didn't draw on it, and got hold of my own gun.

"You chuck that butt," he ordered, "or I'll plug you. You've been a lily since this started, Croft." He must have seen my face when I lit up.

"Start something," I told him. "For every hole you make, I'll make two. Anybody who'd ride a mule couldn't hit a barn in the daylight, let alone a man in the dark."

I was scared though. I knew Winder's temper, and he wasn't more than five steps off. When I'd talked the cigarette had bobbed in my mouth too, in spite of my trying to talk stiff-lipped; he'd know where it was. I made a swell target; he could judge every inch of me. When he didn't say anything, my back began to crawl. I wouldn't have thought I could feel any colder, but I did, all under the back of my shirt. Still, after the way he'd put it, I couldn't let that cigarette go either. I drew my own gun slowly, and kept staring hard to see what he was doing, but couldn't. I wanted to squat, but it was no use with that cigarette. The best was to hold still and let the ash form.

I jumped when Sparks spoke behind me, but felt better at once. My mind was beginning to freeze on the situation, and his voice brought me to my senses, though I didn't move after that first start, or look away.

"It looks like you'll have a lot of shootin' to do, Mistah Baht-lett," Sparks said. So he thought it was Bartlett. That idea made me feel a lot happier. I looked along the edge of the woods and saw what Sparks meant. Half a dozen men were lighting up. They felt the same way I did, I guess, foolish about waiting so long. The closest man was Tetley's Amigo. He had his hands cupped around the match, and I could see his brown, grease-shining face before he flipped the match out and drew deeply, making the cigarette glow and fade.

"Damned fools," the man said, whoever he was. Then I heard him let the hammer down again, and his horse following him off.

"Let's go," I said to Sparks. Other shadows were moving out into the clearing again.

It was a thick dark, even out there. You couldn't have told it was snowing except by the feel. I didn't get used to the feel; it kept on being a surprise. I could see shapes moving when they crossed against a snow bank, but that was about all, except the cigarettes. Once in a while one of these made a brief shower of sparks when a man turned across the wind.

In the huddle somebody, Mapes I thought, said, "Reckon we must have been hearing our own ears, boys."

"We heard it, and it warn't no ears," a voice told him. That was Winder I was sure, and I thought again that it must have been Winder under the trees.

"To hell with it," somebody said. "This is no kind of a night for the job." His voice was nervous from waiting blind.

"You're right there," another agreed.

"This snow will be three feet deep by morning," the first man said.

There was a lot of muttering in agreement. After trying to see into the clearing all that time the job did look ridiculous. Also, unseasonable winter takes the heart out of men the same as it does out of animals. You just get used to the sun and the limber feeling, and when they go you want to crawl back into your hole.

Tetley spoke up. You could tell his voice without any question. That superior smile was in the tone of it. "It's either now or not at all," he said. "The entrance to the Ox-Bow is less than a mile from here."

"Let's get at it," Ma said cheerfully. "Boys," she told us, "we'd be the laughing stock of the country if we went home on account of a little snow, and it turned out we'd been right there within a mile of the men we wanted all the time."

"Well, then, let's go," Smith said. His voice was big and hearty and empty as ever. You couldn't mistake it. "This rope will have to be thawed out now, before it's fit to use." He added, "I'm stiff enough myself. Got a drink, anybody?"

"Hey," a man in back of us yelled, "look out!"

"Jesus," said the man next to me. He was scared. So was I. That yelp had been loud. At first I didn't see, the horses milling some, what he was yelping about. Then I saw it. It was the stagecoach. It wasn't coming fast, but it was already close. The trees and bank had hidden it till it was nearly on us. We scattered out to the sides, some of the horses wheeling and acting up.

"Stop him," Mapes yelled.

"He can tell us," Ma called.

Others were shouting too, and some of them rode back toward the coach, calling at the driver to stop.

Caught by surprise, the driver started to pull up; his lead horses reared and the brakes squealed a little. Then he changed his mind. There was a lantern swinging off the seat on the road side. It made a long narrowing shadow of the coach and driver up a snow bank on the far side. By its light I saw the driver stand straight up and let his whip go out over the horses. The tip exploded like a pistol shot. The horses yanked from side to side, then scrambled and dug and got under way. Checked and then yanked forward again like that, the coach rocked on its straps like a cradle, and the lantern banged back and forth. The driver was huddled down as much as he dared with that hill coming. When the lantern swung up I could see over him that there was another man. He was trying to stick with the bucking seat and get himself laid over the top to shoot. There were four horses, and by the middle of the clearing that whip, which the driver kept snaking out the best he could, had them stretching together, bending away right for that grade in the narrows. We all yelled at him then, but there were too many yelling. There were passengers too. A woman screamed, and behind the flapping curtain a light went out. The guard shouted from the roof.

"Keep down," he yelled at the people inside. "Stickup. Keep down, I tell you, they'll shoot."

I saw the driver reaching for the lantern to throw it away, but he couldn't get to it and keep his lines. All the time he was staring ahead, trying to see where the dip started.

A man's voice from inside was yelling at the driver to stop, and the woman was still screaming almost every time the coach lurched.

Several riders had started out to come alongside but, seeing the guard, had pulled away, yelling at him. Winder, though, didn't seem to see him. That was his coach heading for the narrows and the creek below. He kept calling, "Hey, Alec, hey, Alec; hey, Alec, you god-damned fool," but his mule couldn't keep beside the coach. We were all yelling at the driver and at Bill now. I saw it wasn't doing any good, and touched Blue Boy up, intending to turn Winder anyhow, before he was drilled. It was all serious enough, God knows, and yet so crazy, all that commotion suddenly, and the driver and the guard playing hero, that I was nearly laughing too, while I yelled.

I was hit in the shoulder, so unexpectedly it nearly drove me out of the saddle. At once I heard the bang of the guard's carbine, and then somebody scream and keep moaning for a moment while I pulled straight in the saddle. The report was a flat sound in the clearing, but distinct above all the others. The yelling stopped at once, and then, even in the wind, the explosion echoed faintly in the narrows.

Distantly, with the sounds of the coach, I heard Ma Grier's big voice calling her name at the driver; then saw the horses dip suddenly onto the steep down grade and the coach yank over after them. One instant the lantern was there, flying like a comet gone loco, and the next it had winked out. There was a long screeching and wailing of brakes which echoed so I couldn't tell which was brakes and which echo.

Blue Boy was still trying to bolt with the others following the coach, but for some reason I was pulling him. On the edge of the pitch-over I got him stopped. Then I just sat there. I was hanging onto the saddle-horn, and my stomach was sick and I was trembling all over. It wasn't until I reached up and felt of my shoulder because it was hot and tickling, and found my shirt wet, and that it slipped greasily on my flesh, that it got through to me that I'd been shot. The guard had meant to get Winder, but he'd got me behind him. I understood then, with shame, that I'd done the moaning too.

I wondered how bad it was, and started to get down, but couldn't. After trying, I started making a silly little chattering, whining noise, which I couldn't stop. I thought, by God, if he's killed me, what a fool way to die; what a damn fool way to die!

The driver had got the coach stopped at the foot of the first pitch; I don't know how. It was standing on the level-off just before the first turn, which would have put it into the creek. The lantern settling made a big shadow of the coach moving back and forth slowly on the wall of the gorge. The driver was leaning out to look back, and the guard was standing up beside him, watching, over the baggage on the roof, the riders come down in the dark and spit of snow. He wasn't sure yet, and was holding the carbine ready in both hands. Most of the riders passed me and went down to the coach. Those that didn't want to delay any longer hesitated, but then slowly went down too. I felt like crying when they all left me. It was the jolt, I suppose; it hadn't begun to hurt yet, but I felt shaken to pieces, like I'd been hit by a big rock instead of pierced by a little slug. I heard Tetley asking who'd been hit, but couldn't seem to tell him. I wanted to wait until I was steadier before I tried talking. I was holding onto my shoulder with some idea of stopping the bleeding, but I could tell by the warm tickle down my ribs that I didn't have it stopped.

One rider passed me, but turned in the saddle and peered at me, then pulled around and came back. It was Gil.

"That you, Art?" he asked, still peering.

"I guess so," I said, trying to pass it off.

He came alongside, but facing me. "What's the matter?"

I told him.

"Where?" he asked.

"In the shoulder, I think; in the left shoulder." It seemed important to me that he knew it was the left shoulder.

"Lemme see," he said.

"Hell," he said after a moment, "can't tell a thing here. How do you feel?"

"All right."

"Can you make it down to the coach? We can see something there."

When we started down he steadied me in the saddle, but I was already a lot clearer. The shoulder was beginning to hurt, so the dizziness was gone and I didn't feel so much like throwing up. I told him I could make it.

There was a lot of talk around the coach. The driver, who was white, and still trembling in the knees from his close call and standing on the brakes, was hanging onto the edge of the seat and repeating, "I thought it was a stickup. God, there was a lot of you. I thought it was a stickup." He was Alec Small, a little, thin, blond man with a droopy mustache, a nice fellow, but not tough, and not the driver Winder was. Winder was bawling him out and telling him he was lucky by turns, and looking at the horses' ankles between curses. The horses were trembling and restless; they kept turning their heads toward the drop-off and wanting to sidle into the cliff. Gabe was getting down to quiet them. Small didn't seem to hear Winder. He was drunk, and the mob dazed him.

I knew the guard too, Jimmy Carnes, a big, black-bearded man with a slouch hat and a leather coat. He'd been a government hunter for the army and then for the railroad while it was building. It had been a good thing for Winder, if not for me, that it was dark and the coach rocking.

Carnes was saying, "I hope I didn't get him too bad."

"Get who?" Ma asked him.

"I got somebody," he said. "I heard him yell. You know," he went on, "you hadn't ought to have come barging out like that, in the dark especially. It's only lucky if I haven't killed somebody. You hadn't ought to have come barging out like that." He shook his head heavily. He'd been drinking too, and was thick, and his face was worried. "I was pretty near asleep when Alec yelled at me," he said. "I couldn't see who you was, and everybody yelling.

"I didn't kill anybody, did I?" he asked.

Now Winder was wanting to know what the hell the stage was doing on the pass at night anyway. For a minute Gil and I couldn't get through the press; I didn't care if we got through; I felt far away, like watching a picture. Gil was getting angry though, and trying to be heard and to push a way to the light.

The passengers were getting out while everybody watched them. They were two women and a man, and they'd been thrown around, by their looks. Their stylish clothes were askew, and the ladies, after they got down shakily, were trying to straighten themselves without being too obvious about it. They looked around haughtily. They'd been well scared. The man was young, tall and thin, and had red mutton-chop whiskers, and was elegant in the way young Tetley might have been if he had noticed things more. He was laughingly accepting it all as a joke, although his beaver was badly bent. This made the men around them grin too.

When the shorter woman turned around I saw she was Rose Mapen. You could understand why young Tetley was so hot about the hens running her out, and why Gil had talked about her all winter like a boy about his first love. She had dark hair showing out from under her bonnet, which was lacy, a broad-cheeked face with big, dark eyes and a big, full-shaped mouth that was beginning to smile inclusively, and yet personally. She had big, full but firm breasts too, and a round-limbed, strong, fiery figure. Her dress was cut as far down between her breasts as she dared. When she recognized some of the riders she began to charm them at once; it was a habit with her. Right then I wasn't much interested, but I could see how I might have been. Her manner wasn't that of handing out cheap promises though. Nobody but a drunk or a jealous woman would take it for that.

Or a jealous man. When Gil saw her he stopped shoving and sat still on his horse. The man with the red whiskers was holding Rose's elbow to show she was his property. Winder stopped chewing, and we could hear Rose's voice too, a voice such as I thought Ma Grier's must have been once. She was introducing the man to Tetley and Gerald and Davies, and to the rest of us in the pack, as Mr. Swanson of San Francisco, and her husband. Tetley managed a compliment to Swanson and a joke about Rose being in such a hurry to show the women what could be done, all in one. Even Tetley was willing to be delayed further to have a look at Rose and hear her talk. She laughed at his joke, but I don't think it was altogether funny to her; she bridled with an air of purpose. Davies was pleased by her too, and congratulated her and shook hands with Swanson, but chiefly he was watching the men. They were all congratulating Rose too, some, who couldn't get closer, calling out to her, and only Smith was a little bit ribald, asking Swanson had they only been married that day that he was still able to get around. The others went no farther than saying to Rose they thought it was mean of her to do it secretly and where they couldn't interfere, and telling Swanson he could thank his stars it was all done and beyond help before he came to Bridger's Wells. They were all cheerful and lively seeming, as men always were with Rose, but some of them had moments of being a bit stiff too. They were embarrassed at this pleasantry when they thought of the job they were supposed to be on. They didn't know what to say when Rose asked them back to Canby's to have a celebration for the Swansons. They looked at Tetley or at Davies, and just grinned. It was a temptation, in their doubt and on such a night. Only young Tetley didn't offer any congratulations or even smile, but stared at her with big serious eyes and kept swallowing as if about to say something. Rose tried to ignore him to keep cheerful. She was curious about what we were doing up there at night too, but didn't ask, and nobody wanted to tell her.

The other woman was introduced too, but nobody paid any attention to her after the first polite murmur and hat-lifting. She was Swanson's sister, a tall thin woman, older than he was I thought, dressed in dark silk with a cape around her shoulders. Her face was long and thin too, with heavy lines under the eyes, hollow cheeks, and heavy, unhappy grooves down from her mouth. In the lantern-light her complexion was powdery white. She stood there while they talked, playing with the coach door with one hand and looking from face to face, quickly and nervously, as the men spoke, yet not as if she really expected them to do anything. She wanted to get back into the coach and be sheltered from the spit of snow and all the unknown faces.

Then Gil recovered enough to stop glaring at Rose and her red-whiskered man. There was no change of expression on his battered face, but I could tell he was furious. He shouldered his horse through to the lantern without even making a sign to the men, and I followed him. None of the men said anything though; they thought he was going to make trouble about Rose. Tetley must have thought so too, for he stopped talking to Rose and Swanson and watched Gil, and didn't understand him for a minute when he said, "Art's shot. Carnes got him in the shoulder."

But Davies understood right away, and helped me down, telling Gil to get a trunk from the coach for me to sit on. Gil did this without saying anything to Rose or even looking at her, though he passed right in front of her. If he hadn't been too busy about what he was doing, you couldn't have told he knew she was there. Rose watched him, though, and stopped smiling, expecting him to speak. When he didn't she began to smile again at once, and was all worried over what had happened to me. I didn't notice her. Rose and I had never got on, and I wasn't going to help her out now. Swanson noticed this act. He studied Gil while Gil was getting the trunk down, and then looked at Rose and then at Gil again. He was still smiling, but not the same way. I'd figured him for a weak sister at first, something Rose had got hold of because she could handle it, but now I wasn't so sure.

I sat down on the trunk, and Sparks brought the lantern over and held it while Davies began to take my shirt off, being too gentle where it was beginning to stick.

"It's nothing," I told him.

"Do the women have to watch this?" I asked him. I was going to feel sick again, and it made me angry, with everybody watching.

The women offered to help, Rose saying she was good at that sort of thing. I told Davies I didn't want their help, and Rose stopped smiling and encouraging me. She and Gil looked at each other for the first time, and Gil grinned. Rose turned around quickly and got into the coach. Swanson also stopped smiling and stared at Gil at the same time he helped his sister into the coach with Rose. Gil was standing with his legs apart and his thumbs hooked in his gun belt, which was a bad sign. He stared back at Swanson and continued to grin the way he had at Rose. It wouldn't take much to set him off, but when Swanson closed the coach door he leaned in the window and talked to Rose for a moment, and nothing happened.

Carnes climbed down from the box, and came over with that worried look on his face, and kept asking me in his thick voice if I was all right, and telling me that he hadn't meant to get me, that he was sorry, that he was sure sorry it had happened, until I was tired of assuring him, while Davies was picking at the wound, that it was all right and how could he tell who we were. The picking around the edge of the wound made me faint, and I didn't think I could stand much more of Carnes' apology. Gil finally saw how it was, and told Carnes to shut up. Again I thought there'd be a scrap, but Carnes was really feeling so guilty he did shut up, looking as if he were going to cry.

I'd spilled quite a lot of blood already. That side of my jeans, under the chaps, was soaked with it too. But the wound itself wasn't so much. The bullet had just gone through the flesh of my chest, and ripped on out at the back, lower down, Davies told me. He thought maybe it had nicked a rib, but nothing much more. He pressed me along the side to see if it had nicked the rib, and it hurt all right, but I couldn't be sure. Davies was careful, but too slow. I had to go out to the edge of the road and throw up, with Gil holding onto me. Then Moore gave me a stiff drink, and another when Davies was done picking the threads of shirt out of the hole, and I felt strong enough, just light-headed. All that bothered me was that I continued to tremble all over, as if I had a chill or was all nerves, but Davies said that was probably just from the impact; that it would take a long time for the shock to wear off from being hit from a heavy rifle that way. He washed the wound clean with whisky, but told me they'd have to fire it to prevent infection. They took the lantern into the coach to get it out of the wind, and slowly heated a pistol barrel red hot in the flame. Then Gil and Moore held me down while the wound was burned. I got through the front side well enough, just holding my breath and sweating, but on the back I passed out.

When I next knew where I was Davies had me bandaged up tightly with strips of somebody's shirt, my sheepskin was on me again, and Moore was trying to pour another drink into me. I felt shaky and empty, but angry too, because so many people had watched me pass out.

The men pretended they hadn't seen any weakness; they were going about their business, remounting and forming above the coach. Gil lit me a cigarette, and when I looked at the men forming and then at him, he nodded. I felt weak, all washed out, and it was snowing harder than before, a thin cover of snow showing on the ground in the light around the circular shadow of the bottom of the lantern. I wasn't interested any longer, not either way; the voices talking were like those of people in another room, heard through the wall. They didn't concern me. But when Davies told me that "the fools still meant to go on," but there was room for me in the coach, and I'd better go back and rest at Canby's and get some hot food and get out of the wind, I told him hell no, there was nothing the matter with me. He argued a little, and Ma came and joked at me but helped him argue, and I got to feeling stubborn and just sat there smoking my cigarette and saying no, and finally just smoking. When I had to stand up so they could put the trunk back on the coach, Rose got out and came over and took hold of my elbow and tried to charm me into going down with them. Somehow I could tell from her talk that she knew what we were doing now. That only made me all the surer; I didn't want to ride down with her and the spinster sister and red-whiskers all interested and pumping me about it. I liked her hand holding me affectionately by the arm as if I were an old, dear friend she was worried about, but even so it only made me more stubborn, because I knew she didn't mean it. Then Winder came and told me not to be a damned fool, to get in the coach and go on home, where I wouldn't be in the way. Gil told Winder to mind his own business, that he'd look after me himself if I needed any looking after. Winder turned his head slowly and stared at Gil like he couldn't believe he'd heard anyone speak to him that way, but Rose broke it up this time by letting go of my arm and telling Winder to let the idiot, meaning me, go ahead and act like an idiot if he wanted to, it was none of their funeral. That made Gil grin at her again. She stared at him for an instant too, but thought better of what she was going to say, and turned her back on him and got back into the coach with a flourish of her skirts. She slammed the door after her, although her husband wasn't in. He'd been standing by the back wheel of the coach all this time, once in a while brushing the snow from his front, and talking with Tetley, Small and Carnes. Again he hadn't missed anything. He took his part in the talk, so quietly I couldn't hear him, but he watched Gil all the time, very steadily. He didn't even stop watching Gil when Rose slammed into the coach, but kept looking at him like he wanted to remember everything about him.

Out of the corner of my mouth I told Gil, "Red-whiskers is measuring you for a coffin, my friend."

Gil looked at Swanson, and then returned his stare, grinning. "Yeah?" he said to me, and then, still staring at Swanson, "What have I said? I didn't say anything."

"That's his wife, now," I reminded him, "and kind of new."

"It does look that way, don't it?" Gil said, as if it didn't. He said it too loudly, and from the way Swanson stared more intently for just a moment, I thought he'd heard. But then he turned away from Gil and looked at Tetley again, answering a question of Tetley's. Gil relaxed, his little grin changing so it meant he knew he'd won.

Swanson and Carnes and Small had been telling Tetley about some men they'd seen, four, Carnes and Swanson thought, but Small thought three, who had a fire in the mouth of a ravine five miles the other side of the summit. They had seen horses, but no cattle, but Swanson said the ravine was so black they couldn't have told past the fire. Small said, if there'd been any cattle, there couldn't have been many. He knew the ravine, used the mouth of it as a turn-out to rest his horses, and it was too small. No, he was sure they couldn't have got forty head in there; not even ten or fifteen without their showing. Yes, he was sure about the place. He'd had it in his mind to stop there to breathe the horses, but the men were so quiet he hadn't liked it; he'd changed his mind and gone right by and breathed the team at Indian Springs, farther up.

Swanson agreed that the men had not seemed friendly. They'd stood up when the coach came by, and when Alex had hailed them they hadn't said anything, and only one of them had raised a hand. He was sure there'd been a fourth man, just beyond the firelight, and that he'd stood up too. Alec admitted he might have missed him; he'd been busy with the team, to keep them from turning in there, where they expected to. No, neither Small nor Carnes had recognized any of the men. Carnes thought they'd kept their faces out of the light on purpose. He thought also that all the men except the one who had raised his hand had been ready to draw, but Carnes must have been drunk then, and now his imagination was working from the story about Kinkaid. Swanson didn't think they were going to draw; he merely thought they were very watchful and too quiet. But yes, he agreed with Carnes and Small that the men were wearing guns. He couldn't be sure whether the men were really camped for the night. Carnes said they weren't. The fire, he said, was a small one, and the horses weren't hobbled or tethered, but just standing at one side of the fire with their bridles trailing and the saddles still on. When Tetley asked him, Small repeated exactly where the place was and what you came to before you got there. He tried to remember just what marks you could still tell by in the snow, and then Winder, who had joined them, told Tetley he knew the place, and could warn them long enough before they got there, even if the fire was out. There were marks you couldn't miss, he said, and mentioned trees and boulders, and the shape of the road, and Tetley was satisfied.

He thanked Swanson, as if Swanson had told him everything and the other two hadn't even been along. He told Swanson that he and the sheriff were very grateful that Swanson had been so observant, that it let them know more clearly what to expect; they could figure on four men, armed and wary. I looked at Gil and Gil looked at me and grinned just a little. It tickled us, in an ornery way, that even Tetley didn't like the idea of Swanson knowing that this was a lynching party instead of a posse. Then Tetley complimented Swanson again on his fortune in wedding, and hoped he might have the pleasure of entertaining Swanson and his bride and his sister in his own poor way, if they were going to be in Bridger's Wells for a while. From all the anxiety Tetley let show you'd have thought they were two men passing the time of day in a hotel lobby, with nothing coming up but a good night's sleep. Then Tetley turned toward his horse, and Winder with him, and Carnes and Small climbed up onto the high seat.

Gil was just going to help me into the saddle when there was Swanson standing in front of us. It surprised us, and Gil let go of me quickly to get his hands free. It made him sore that he had been surprised into moving quickly.

Swanson smiled a little. He spoke very politely and quietly. "I take it," he said, "that yours was the privilege of knowing Miss Mapen before she became my wife?"

"Yeah," Gil said slowly, "that's right."

"And that possibly you imagined, at the time, that there was something between you?"

"I didn't have to imagine it," Gil said.

"No?" Swanson asked him. "Possibly not," he continued. "My wife is a very impulsive woman, given naturally to regarding everyone as a friend."

He stopped and looked at Gil, still smiling. Gil didn't say anything. He was slow in understanding what to make of that kind of talk.

"Needless to say," Swanson went on, "I am pleased to regard

any friend of my wife as a friend of my own." He smiled at Gil, but didn't offer his hand. Gil still just looked at him.

"However," Swanson said, "I needn't remind you, of course, that the pleasure of such an acquaintance depends somewhat upon the recognition by all parties of the fact that Miss Mapen is now my wife. She must be given a little time," he continued, "to become accustomed to her new responsibilities. As yet, I must confess, I am peculiarly jealous of even her least attentions. You will forgive me, I know. A bridegroom is prone to be overly susceptible for a time.

"Later," he concluded, "when we have had time to become accustomed to our new relations, I will be most anxious, if it is still my wife's desire, to welcome you, and others of my wife's friends, at our home in San Francisco.

"Until then," he nodded pleasantly, still smiling, turned around, walked to the coach, got in, and closed the door quietly. He relighted the lamp inside the coach, and as it started on down we could see him sitting beside Rose. She had her hands joined through his arm and was smiling up at him, but he wasn't smiling any more.

Gil had it all straight by then. "The damned superior son-of-a-bitch," he said softly, looking after the coach. He'd never got a taking down like that in his life before.

He mounted silently, but turned his horse to look after the coach again. I got up too, making more fuss than I had to, so he'd help me. Then I said, "It looks to me like Rose had caught herself a load of trouble."

We started up after the others, just feeling the snow in the dark again.

"Yeah?" Gil said. "Maybe she ain't the only one. Rose is no stable filly."

I didn't answer. I was glad enough we'd come out of it without any more trouble than the talk. We were up in the clearing again before Gil said, "If that bastard's got her all roped and tied the way he talks, what are they doing up here at all? I'll bet a dollar to a doughnut hole that wasn't his idea."

"Forget it," I told him.

"Sure, for now," he said.

Then he said, "If you get to feelin' it, fellow, sound off. This still ain't any of our picnic."

"I will."

"I should have made you go down in the coach," he apologized later, "but with all of them raggin' you, I didn't think."

I told him I was all right. In a way I was, too. The whisky was working good, like I had all the blood back, and somehow being hit like that, now that I was patched up, made me feel like I had a stake in the business.

We rode across the clearing and under the trees on the other side. The snow was right in our faces, and we couldn't tell where we were farther than the rumps of the horses ahead. We went slowly, but even so the procession kept stopping while Tetley and Mapes made sure we were still on the road, and nearly every time we stopped, Blue Boy rammed his nose on the horse ahead and brought up short, throwing his head. My shoulder would jerk then, and finally I got to swearing softly. Just sitting there in the dark, with nothing else to think about, I began to feel that shoulder. It felt hard and drawn together, like it was crusted, and would tear if I moved it. They'd put my shirt back on me too, and it was stiff and scratchy down that side where the blood had dried in it. Twice I had a drink from my canteen to keep my head from getting light. But my head got even lighter, and, besides, it was so much work trying to twist around and get the canteen that I quit that too. Between the whisky and the pain I must have been getting dopey, because at first I didn't hear Gil trying to say something to me. Then the wind was so strong and muffled with snow that I had to ask him twice what he'd said before he heard me.

"I said that damned Small and his free-shootin' friend Carnes were drunk." They were generally a little drunk, and I said so.

"Well," Gil said, "they oughtn'ta be drivin' when they're like that. Winder oughta know better'n to let them on like that." Then I lost a few words in the wind. Then he was saying, "Can you imagine any guy damned fool enough to start down that grade like that? He didn't know where he was, that's all. He just got scared and saw an open place and let drive. He couldn't have known where he was, to drive like that. If his horses hadn't been a sight smarter than he was, that coach would be all piled up at the bottom of the creek right now, and everybody in it with a broken neck."

"What do you care?" I asked him. "There's nobody there

makes any difference to you now, is there?" I didn't like being drawn out of my shell just when I was beginning to forget myself.

"Not a damned bit," he said. And then, "Let her go ahead and break her neck. It's none of my worry. What was she in such a hell of a hurry to get back up here for, anyway? Wouldn't her delicate friend keep overnight?"

"All right," I agreed, "let her break her neck. That's what I say too."

I knew that would make him sore, but it would shut him up about Rose Mapen too.

We rode some distance then without any halt, the trees being even on the two sides so the road was plain. Then there came another, and I knew I'd nearly fallen asleep. I felt unreal and scared. Ahead, men were exclaiming about something in low voices. I saw what they were talking about. To the right, far through the trees through the snow, was a fire burning. It looked very small, and sometimes disappeared when the trees moved in the wind. Then I realized we were at the end of the Ox-Bow valley, and that the fire must be way out toward the center. I judged that when it disappeared it must have been flattening in the wind, and then I decided it was partially concealed by the cabin, and we only saw it when it blew back. But it must have been a big fire at that, because even when it was out of sight I thought I could see a kind of halo of light from around it, like the moon through the thin edges of clouds. It was easy, though, to see how the men on the stage missed it. Having our minds set on those men in the gully on the downgrade, we didn't know quite what to make of it. Then, with a turn of the wind, we heard a steer bellowing. You couldn't trust it, of course. Nobody said anything, or moved, and we heard it a second time.

Word came back along the line that we were turning down into the valley, and then to bunch up for last orders. I recovered the sensation that our business was real, instead of everybody being crazy and just wandering around in the mountains. Previously, in my dozing, I'd been remembering a story I'd heard once about the Flying Dutchman, and wondering vaguely if that was the way we were getting. It made a fine picture, twenty-eight riders you could see through on twenty-six horses and two mules nothing but bones, riding around forever through snowstorms in the mountains, looking for three dead rustlers they had to find before their souls could be at peace.

We had passed the turn-off into the valley, and had to slide and scramble down a bank. Even in the wind you could hear the horses snort about it, and the slap of leather and the jangle of jerked bits. They didn't like it in the dark. By the time I got to the slide it was a long black streak torn down through the snow. Blue Boy smelled the rim, tossed his head two or three times, and pitched over. He descended scraping and stiff-legged, like a dog sitting down, and the wrenching made me sick to my stomach again.

When we were grouped among the cottonwoods in the hollow, Tetley gave us our marching orders. We were underneath the wind, and he didn't have to talk very loudly. First he said maybe the stage men had been mistaken, that this was a better place for men with cattle to hide, and that anyway it was our job to make sure before we went on. He cautioned us about playing safe, and against any shooting or rough work until we were sure.

"They must have an opportunity to tell it their way," he said. "Mapes and I will do the talking, and if there's any shooting to do I'll tell you. The rest of you hold your fire unless they try to break through you. We'll divide to close in on them.

"Where is Croft?" he asked.

"Here," I said.

"How do you feel, Croft?" he asked.

"I'm all right."

"Good. But you stay with my group. We'll go the most direct way."

Farnley said, "The son-of-a-bitch that got Kinkaid is mine, Tetley. Don't forget that."

"He's yours when we're sure," Tetley told him.

"Well, don't forget, that's all."

"I won't forget," was all Tetley said, and that quietly.

Then, like an officer enjoying mapping out a battle plan that pleases him because the surprise element is with him, he directed our attack. But I noticed he put Farnley in his own group, and his son Gerald too. He picked Bartlett and Winder and Ma Grier to lead on the other three sides, and divided the rest among the four parties. Winder's party was to work around through the woods and come down back of the cabin, Bartlett's to circle clear around and come in by the far side, Ma Grier's to come up from the valley side. They were to fan out so they'd contact by the time they got close to the firelight and make a closed circle. He didn't say so, but you could tell by his care that he thought either the rustlers trusted too much to the snow to stop us, or there were a lot more than three of them; others waiting up here maybe, to support them and hurry the branding.

"They're least likely to break for the valley or the side away from this," he continued. "The unarmed men, then, unless they'd rather wait here, had best go, one with Mr. Bartlett and one with Mrs. Grier."

"Give them guns," Winder said; "lots of us have a couple."

"Will you take a gun, Davies?" Tetley asked.

Davies answered from the other side of him, "No, thanks. I'll go with the Bartletts."

"Just as you choose," Tetley said. His voice was even, but the scorn was there.

"Sparks?" he asked.

"No, suh, Cun'l Tetley, thank you jus' the same."

"With Mrs. Grier, then."

"Yessuh."

"Keep your eyes and ears open," Tetley warned us. "They may have pickets out. And if you come on the cattle ride easy, don't disturb them.

"If any party does spring a picket," he added, "and he gets away, shoot into the air once. All of you, if you hear the shot close in as quickly as you can, but keep spread."

"This is no battle, you know," Farnley said. "We're after three rustlers, not an army."

"We don't know what we're after until we see. Unnecessary risk is simply foolish," Tetley told him, still evenly.

"And don't fire," he told the rest of us, "unless they fire first, except if they should break through. Then stop them any way you have to. The quicker and cleaner this job is, the less chance we'll have anything to regret. A surprise is what we want, and no shooting if we can help it.

"All clear?" he asked, like he was getting ready to roll up the maps again.

We said it was.

"All right," Tetley said, "my group will wait here until we judge the rest of you have had time to move into position.

"Good luck, boys," he said.

# 4

WINDER AND his outfit started off, working single file into the woods. In a moment you couldn't tell which was riders and which trees. The snow blurred everything, and blotted up sound too, into a thick, velvety quiet. Ma Grier and Bartlett led off at an angle toward the valley. They were heading for the shallows of the creek, where there weren't any banks but an easy incline, a cross gully worn by sheep and cattle going down to drink. I'd seen deer drinking there too, but only in the early spring, and then warily. It would take time to find that crossing in this kind of a night.

Gil came alongside me.

"How you feeling now, fellow?" he asked.

"Good," I said.

"Take care of yourself," he said. "This still don't have to be our picnic."

"It looks like it was," I said.

"Yeah," he agreed, "but it ain't."

He went away from me, stepping his pinto a little long to catch up with his gang.

The rest of us, in Tetley's outfit, didn't talk much. There was nothing to do but wait, and none of the arguing ones were left with us. Only Mapes tried a little of his cottoning-up, he-man talk on Tetley, but since Tetley didn't want to talk, that stopped too. We weren't a friendly gang anyway; no real friends in the lot. Tetley, I thought, was short with Mapes because he was trying to count in his mind, or some such system, to keep track of the time. Through the trees we watched the fire out by the cabin. Once it began to die down, and then a shadow went across it, and back across, and the fire darkened and flattened completely. At first we thought they had wind of us, but the fire gradually grew up again, brighter than ever. It was just somebody throwing more wood on.

The snowing relaxed for a spell, then started again with a fresh wind that whirled it around us for a minute or two, even in the woods, and veiled the fire, probably with snow scudding up from the open meadow. Then the wind died off and the snow was steady and slanting again, but thinner. It didn't feel any longer as if it might be a real blizzard. The branches rattled around us when the wind blew. Being in the marshy end of the valley they weren't pines, but aspens, and willow grown up as big as trees. When the horses stirred, the ground squelched under them, and you could see the dark shadow of water soaking up around their hoofs through the snow. In places, though, the slush was already getting icy, and split when it was stepped on.

Several times we heard the steers sounding off again, hollow in the wind, and sounding more distant than they could have been.

After a time Tetley led us out to the edge of the aspens to where the wind was directly on us again. We waited there, peering into the snow blowing in the valley, and the dark gulf of the valley itself, but unable to see the other riders, of course, or anything but the fire. It felt to me as if it must be one o'clock at least, but I learned early that I couldn't tell within four hours on a cloudy night unless I was doing some work I did every night, like riding herd in the same valley.

Finally Tetley said, as if he had been holding a watch before him all the time, and had predetermined the exact moment to start, "All right, let's go."

As we started Mapes asked, "Want us to spread out now?"

"No, we'll ride in on them in a bunch, unless they get wind of us. If the fire goes out, or there's any shooting, then spread and work toward the fire. In that case, you on the wings, don't tangle with Mrs. Grier or Winder."

So we went out in a group, plowing a wide track through the half-frozen sponginess. Tetley and Farnley and Mapes rode abreast ahead. They didn't any of them want another to get there ahead of him. Young Tetley and I came behind them, and there were two other riders following us. We all watched toward the fire steadily.

But even when we came much closer there was nothing to see but the fire, beginning to die again, and the little its light revealed of the cabin wall and the trunks of the closest pines on the other side. I got to wondering if they had built the fire up as a blind and had already run out on us, or even were lying up somewhere ready to pick us off. My head came clear again and I didn't even notice my shoulder. Only the snow annoyed me, though it was falling light and far spaced now. It made me feel that my eyes were no good. The four of us in back kept watching out to the sides, feeling that we didn't have our side of the square covered, but the three in front continued abreast and seeming to watch only the fire and the clearing right around it, though I could tell by the way they sat that they were as wide awake as we were.

When we began to climb the little rise the cabin was on, I could see the three silhouetted clearly against the fire. Mapes reached under his arm pit and got a gun out into his hand. Farnley's carbine moved across his saddle, and I thought I heard the hammer click. Tetley, though, just rode right ahead.

I reached my gun out too. There was a twinge in the injured shoulder when I raised the right one, and I didn't want to have to make a fast draw and get sick and dizzy as I had riding down the pitch. My head was clear, all right; I thought of every little thing like that. And my senses were up keen too. Without even looking around I could tell how the men behind me were getting set. I was excited, and peculiarly happy. It seemed to me that if the rustlers were concealed I could pick the trees they'd gone behind. Only young Tetley was wrong. I risked a look, and we were so close to the fire I could see his face. He was staring ahead, but blindly, and he wasn't getting any gun out. Now I can see that he was perhaps still having a struggle with himself that he was here at all, but then it just angered me that one of us failed to be alert; then it just seemed to me that he was too scared to know what to do, and I got furious at him for a moment, the way you will when you think another man's carelessness is risking your neck. I pulled over and jogged him, though jogging him wrenched my shoulder so my breath whistled. He turned his head and looked at me, and I could see he wasn't blanked out. He was awake, all right, but he still didn't look any better.

We were really into the edge of the firelight before Tetley stopped us. I had my mind made up they were laying for us, so what I saw surprised me. Between Tetley and Mapes I could see a man asleep on the ground in a blanket with a big pattern on it. His head was on his saddle and toward the fire, so his face was in the shadow, but when we looked at him he drew an arm up out of his blanket and laid it across his eyes. He had on an orange shirt and the hand and wrist lifted into the light were as dark as an old saddle. Not Indian, either; at least not thick and stubby like the hands of Washoes and Piutes I'd seen, but long and narrow and with prominent knuckles. We were so close that I could see on his middle finger a heavy silver ring with an egg-shaped turquoise, a big one, in it; a Navajo ring. By the bulk of him he was a big man, and heavy.

There were two other men asleep also, one with his side to the fire and his head away from me, the other on the far side with his feet to the fire. I couldn't make out anything but their shapes and that they had dark bluish-gray blankets with a black stripe near each end, the kind of blankets the Union had used during the rebellion.

I guess Tetley figured as I did, that they were strangers, at least, if nothing else, because he only waited long enough to be sure they were not playing possum, and then rode into the light, and right up to the feet of the man with the ring. We followed him, spreading around that edge of the fire as he motioned us to. After looking down at the man for a moment he said sharply and loudly, "Get up."

The other two stirred in their blankets, and began to settle again, but the man with the ring woke immediately and completely, and when he saw us said something short to himself and twisted up out of his blanket in one continuous, smooth movement, trailing one hand into the blanket as he came up.

"Drop it," Farnley ordered. He was holding the carbine at his thigh, the muzzle pointing at the man. The man had heavy black hair and a small black mustache. He looked like a Mex, though his hair was done up in a club at his neck, like an Indian's, and his face was wide, with high, flat cheeks. He looked to me like a Mex playing Navajo.

He looked quickly but not nervously around at all of us, sizing us up, but didn't move the hand which had come up behind him.

"I said drop it," Farnley told him again, and nudged the carbine out toward him, so he wouldn't make any mistake about what was meant.

The Mex suddenly smiled, as if he had just understood, and

dropped a long-barreled, nickel-plated revolver behind him onto the blanket. He was an old hand, and still thinking.

"Now put 'em up," Farnley told him.

The smile died off the Mex's face, and he just stared at Farnley and shrugged his shoulders.

"Put 'em up; reach, you bastard."

The Mex shrugged his shoulders again. "No sabbey," he said.

Farnley grinned now. "No?" he asked. "I said reach," he repeated, and jerked the muzzle of the carbine upward two or three times. The Mex got that, and put his hands up slowly. He was studying Farnley's face all the time.

"That's better," Farnley said, still grinning, "though some ways I'd just as soon you hadn't, you son-of-a-bitch." He was talking as quietly as Tetley usually did, though not so easily. He seemed to be enjoying calling the man a name he couldn't understand, and doing it in a voice like he was making an ordinary remark.

"No sabbey," the Mex said again.

"That's all right, brother," Farnley told him, "you will."

The other two were coming out of their sleep. I was covering the one on the cabin side, and Mapes the other. Mapes' man just sat up, still in his blanket. He was still fumed with sleep; a thick, wide-faced old-timer with long, tangled gray hair and a long, droopy gray mustache. He had eyebrows so thick they made peaked shadows on his forehead. The way he was staring now he didn't appear to be all there.

My man rose quickly enough, though tangling a little with his blanket. He started to come toward us, and I saw he'd been sleeping with his gun on and his boots off.

"Take it easy, friend," I told him. "Stay where you are and put your hands up."

He didn't understand, but stared at me, and then at Tetley, and then back at me. He didn't reach for his gun, didn't even twitch for it, and his face looked scared.

"Put your hands up," I told him again. He did, looking as if he wanted to cry.

"And keep them there."

The old man was out of his blanket now too, and standing with his hands raised.

"Gerald, collect their guns," Tetley said.

"What are you trying to do? What do you want? We haven't got anything." It was my man babbling, half out of breath. He was a tall, thin, dark young fellow, with thick black hair, but no Indian or Mex.

"Shut up," Mapes instructed him. "We'll tell you when we want you to talk."

"This is no stickup, brother," I explained to him. "This is a posse, if that means anything to you."

"But we haven't done anything," he protested. "What have we done?" He wasn't over his first fright yet.

"Shut up," Mapes said, with more emphasis.

Young Tetley was sitting in his saddle, staring at the three men.

"Gerry," Tetley said, in that pistol-shot voice he'd used to wake the men.

The boy dismounted dreamily and picked up the Mex's gun from the blanket. Then, like a sleepwalker, he came over to my man.

"Behind him," said Tetley sharply.

The boy stopped and looked around. "What?" he asked.

"Wake up," Tetley ordered. "I said go behind him. Don't get between him and Croft."

"Yes," Gerald said, and did what he was told. He fumbled around a long time before he found the old man's gun, which was under his saddle.

"Give the guns to Mark," Tetley ordered, jerking his head at one of the two riders I didn't know. Gerald did that, handing them up in a bunch, belts, holsters and all.

It made me ashamed the way Tetley was bossing the kid's every move, like a mother making a three-year-old do something over that he'd messed up the first try.

"Now," he said, "go over them all, from the rear. Then shake out the blankets."

Gerald did as he was told, but he seemed to be waking a little now. His jaw was tight. He found another gun on the Mex, a little pistol like the gamblers carry. It was in an arm-sling under his vest. There was a carbine under the young fellow's blanket. He shrank from patting the men over, the way he was told to, and when he passed me to give Mark the carbine and pistol, I could hear him breathing hard.

Tetley watched Gerald, but spoke to my prisoner while he was working.

"Are there any more of you?"

The young fellow was steadier. He looked angry now, and started to let his arms down, asking, "May I inquire what business . . ."

"Shut up," Mapes said, "and keep them up."

"It's all right now, Mapes," Tetley said. "You can put your hands down now," he said to the young man. "I asked you, are there any others with you?"

"No," the kid said.

I didn't think the kid was lying. Tetley looked at him hard, but I guess he thought it was all right too. He turned his head toward Mark and the other rider I didn't know.

"Tie their hands," he ordered.

The young fellow started to come forward again.

"Stay where you are," Tetley told him quietly, and he stopped. He had a wide, thick-lipped mouth that was nonetheless as sensitive as young Tetley's thin one, and now it was tight down in the corners. Even so you would have said that mouth was beautiful on some women, Rose Mapen for instance, the fiery or promising kind. And his eyes were big and dark in his thin face, like a girl's too. His hands were long and bony and nervous, but hung on big, square wrists.

He spoke in a husky voice. "I trust that at least you'll condescend to tell us what we're being held for."

Mapes was still busy being an authority. "Save your talk till it's asked for," he advised.

Tetley, though, studied the young man all during the time the two punchers were tying the prisoners on one lass rope and pushing them over to the side of the fire away from the cabin. He looked at them still when they were standing there, shoulder to shoulder, the Mex in the middle, their faces to the fire and their backs to the woods and the little snow that was still falling. It was as if he believed he could solve the whole question of their guilt or innocence by just looking at them and thinking his own thoughts; the occupation pleased him. The Mex was stolid now, the old man remained blank, but the kid was humiliated and angry at being tied. He repeated his question in a manner that didn't go well with the spot he was in.

Then Tetley told him, "I'd rather you told us," and smiled that way.

After that he signaled to the parties in the dark in the woods and behind the cabin, dismounted, giving the bridle to his son, and walked over to the fire, where he stood with his legs apart and held out his hands to warm them, rubbing them together. He might have been in front of his own fireplace. Without looking around he ordered more wood put on the fire. All the time he continued to look across the fire at the three men in a row, and continued to smile.

We were all on foot now, walking stiff-legged from sitting the saddle so long in the cold. I got myself a place to sit near the fire, and watched the Mex. He had his chin down on his chest, like he was both guilty and licked, but he was watching everything from under his eyebrows. He looked smart and hard. I'd have guessed he was about thirty, though it was hard to tell, the way it is with an Indian. The lines around his mouth and at the corners of his eyes and across his forehead were deep and exact, as if they were cut in dark wood with a knife. His skin shone in the firelight. There was no expression on his face, but I knew he was still thinking how to get out. Then all at once his face changed, though you couldn't have said what the change was in any part of it. I guess in spite of his watchfulness he'd missed Tetley's signal, and now he saw Ma and her gang coming up behind us. He looked around quickly, and when he saw the other gangs coming in too he turned back and stared at the ground in front of him. He was changed all over then, the fire gone out of him; he was empty, all done.

The old man stood and stared, as he had from his first awakening. He didn't seem to have an idea, or even a distinct emotion, merely a vague dread. He'd look at one of us and then another with the same expression, pop-eyed and stupid, his mouth never quite closed, and the gray stubble sticking out all over his jaws.

When the young fellow saw the crowd he said to Tetley, "It appears we're either important personages or very dangerous. What is this, a vigilance committee?" He shivered before he spoke though. I thought the Mex elbowed him gently.

Tetley kept looking at him and smiling, but didn't reply. It was hard on their nerve. Ma Grier had ridden up right behind us, and said, before she got down, "No, it ain't that you're so difficult, son. It's just that most of the boys has never seen a real triple hangin'."

There wasn't much laughter.

Everybody was in now except the Bartlett boys. Some stayed on their horses, not expecting the business to take much time, and maybe just as glad there were others willing to be more active. Some dismounted and came over to the fire with coils of rope; there was enough rope to hang twenty men with a liberal allowance to each.

As if it had taken all that time for the idea to get through, the young fellow said, "Hanging?"

"That's right," Farnley said.

"But why?" asked the kid, beginning to chatter. "What have we done? We haven't done anything. I told you already we haven't done anything."

Then he got hold of himself and said to Tetley, more slowly, "Aren't you even going to tell us what we're accused of?"

"Of course," Tetley said. "This isn't a mob. We'll make sure first."

He half turned his head toward Mapes. "Sheriff," he said, "tell him."

"Rustling," said Mapes.

"Rustling?" the kid echoed.

"Yup. Ever heard of it?"

"And murder," said Farnley, "maybe he'll have heard of that."

"Murder?" the kid repeated foolishly. I thought he was going to fold, but he didn't. He took a brace and just ran his tongue back and forth along his lips a couple of times, as if his throat and mouth were all dried out. He looked around, and it wasn't encouraging. There was a solid ring of faces, and they were serious.

The old man made a long, low moan like a dog that's going to howl but changes its mind. Then he said, his voice trembling badly, "You wouldn't kill us. No, no, you wouldn't do that, would you?"

Nobody replied. The old man's speech was thick, and he spoke very slowly, as if the words were heavy, and he was considering them with great concentration. They didn't mean anything, but you couldn't get them out of your head when he'd said them. He looked at us so I thought he was going to cry. "Mr. Martin," he said, "what do we do?" He was begging, and seemed to believe he would get a real answer.

The young man tried to make his voice cheerful, but it was hollow. "It's all right, Dad. There's some mistake."

"No mistake, I guess." It was old Bartlett speaking. He was standing beside Tetley, looking at the Mex and idly dusting the snow off his flat sombrero. The wind was blowing his wispy hair up like smoke. When he spoke the Mex looked up for a second. He looked down again quickly, but Bartlett grinned. He had a good many teeth out, and his grin wasn't pretty.

"Know me, eh?" he asked the Mex. The Mex didn't answer. Farnley stepped up to him and slapped him across the belly with the back of his hand.

"He's talking to you, Mister," he said.

The Mex looked wonderfully bewildered. "No sabbey," he repeated.

"He don't speak English," Mapes told Bartlett.

"I got a different notion," Bartlett said.

"I'll make him talk," Farnley offered. He was eager for it; he was so eager for it he disgusted me, and made me feel sorry for the Mex.

The young fellow appeared bewildered. He was looking at them and listening, but he didn't seem to make anything of it. He kept closing his eyes more tightly than was natural, and then opening them again quickly, as if he expected to find the whole scene changed. Even without being in the spot he was in, I could understand how he felt. It didn't look real to me either, the firelight on all the red faces watching in a leaning ring, and the big, long heads of horses peering from behind, and up in the air, detached from it, the quiet men still sitting in the saddles.

When Farnley started to prod the Mex again, Tetley said sharply, "That will do, Farnley."

"Listen, you," Farnley said, turning on him, "I've had enough of your playing God Almighty. Who in hell picked you for this job anyway? Next thing you'll be kissing them, or taking them back for Tyler to reform them. We've got the bastards; well, what are we waiting for? Let them swing, I say."

Smith put in his bit too. "Are you going to freeze us to death, Tetley, waiting for these guys to admit they shot a man and stole a bunch of cattle? Maybe you know somebody who likes to talk his head into a noose."

"There's the fire. Warm yourself," Tetley told him. "And you," he said, looking at Farnley, "control yourself, and we'll get along better."

Farnley's face blanched and stiffened, as it had in the saloon, when he'd heard the news about Kinkaid. I thought he was going to jump Tetley, but Tetley didn't even look at him again. He leaned the other way to listen to something Bartlett was saying privately. When he had heard it he nodded and looked at the young fellow across the fire.

"Who's boss of this outfit?" he asked.

"I am," the young fellow said.

"And your name's Martin?"

"Donald Martin."

"What outfit?"

"My own."

"Where from?"

"Pike's Hole."

The men didn't believe it. The man Tetley called Mark said, "He's not from Pike's, or any place in the Hole, I'll swear to that."

For the first time there was real antagonism instead of just doubt and waiting.

"Mark there lives in Pike's," Tetley told the kid, smiling. "Want to change your story?"

"I just moved in three days ago," the kid said.

"We're wasting time, Willard," Bartlett said.

"We'll get there," Tetley said. "I want this kept regular for the Judge."

Not many appreciated his joking. He was too slow and pleasurable for a job like this. Most of us would have had to do it in a hurry. If you have to hang a man, you have to, but it's not my kind of fun to stand around and watch him keep hoping he may get out of it.

Tetley may have noticed the silence, but he didn't show it. He went on asking Martin questions.

"Where did you come from before that?"

"Ohio," he said angrily, "Sinking Spring, Ohio. But not just before. I was in Los Angeles. I suppose that proves something."

"What way did you come up?"

"By Mono Lake. Look, Mister, this isn't getting us anywhere, is it? We're accused of murder and rustling, you say. Well, we haven't done any rustling, and we haven't killed anybody. You've got the wrong men."

"We'll decide as to that. And I'm asking the questions."

"God," the kid broke out. He stared around wildly at the whole bunch of us. "God, don't anybody here know I came into Pike's Hole? I drove right through the town; I drove a Conestoga wagon with six horses right through the middle of the town. I'm on Phil Baker's place; what they call the Phil Baker place, up at the north end."

Tetley turned to Mark.

"Phil Baker moved out four years ago," Mark said. "The place is a wreck, barns down, sagebrush sticking up through the porch."

Tetley looked back at Martin.

"I met him in Los Angeles," Martin explained. "I bought the place from him there. I paid him four thousand dollars for it."

"Mister, you got robbed," Mark told him. "Even if Baker'd owned the place you'da been robbed, but he didn't. He didn't even stay on it long enough to have squatter's rights." We couldn't help grinning at that one. Mark said to Tetley, "Baker's place is part of Peter Wilde's ranch now."

Martin was nearly crying. "You can't hang me for being a sucker," he said.

"That depends on the kind of sucker you are."

"You haven't got any proof. Just because Baker robbed me, doesn't make me a murderer. You can't hang me without any proof."

"We're getting it," Tetley said.

"Is it so far to Pike's that you can't go over there and look?" Martin cried. "Maybe I don't even own the Baker place; maybe I've been sold out. But I'm living there now. My wife's there now; my wife and two kids."

"Now that's really too bad," Smith said, clucking his tongue in a sound of old-maid sympathy. "That's just too, too bad."

The kid didn't look at him, but his jaw tightened and his eyes were hot. "This is murder, as you're going at it," he told Tetley. "Even in this God-forsaken country I've got a right to be brought to trial, and you know it. I have, and these men have. We have a right to trial before a regular judge."

"You're getting the trial," Tetley said, "with twenty-eight of the only kind of judges a murderer and a rustler gets in what you call this God-forsaken country."

"And so far," Winder put in, "the jury don't much like your story."

The kid looked around slowly at as many of us as he could see, the way he was tied. It was as if he hadn't noticed before that we were there, and wanted to see what we were like. He must have judged Winder was right.

"I won't talk further without a proper hearing," he said slowly.

"Suit yourself, son," Ma said. "This is all the hearing you're likely to get short of the last judgment."

"Have you any cattle up here with you?" Tetley asked him.

The kid looked around at us again. He was breathing hard. One of the men from Bartlett's gang couldn't help grinning a little. The kid started to say something, then shut his mouth hard. We all waited, Tetley holding up a hand when the man who had grinned started to speak. Then he asked the question again in the same quiet way.

The kid looked down at the ground finally, but remained silent.

"I'm not going to ask you again," Tetley said. Smith stepped out with a rope in his hands. He was making a hangman's noose, with half a dozen turns to it. The place was so quiet the tiny crackling of the burned-down wood sounded loud. Martin looked at the rope, sucked in his breath, and looked down again.

After a moment he said, so low we could hardly hear him, "Yes, I have."

"How many?"

"Fifty head."

"You miscounted, Amigo," Tetley remarked. Amigo grinned and spread his hands, palms up, and shrugged his shoulders.

"Where did you get them, Mr. Martin?"

"From Harley Drew, in Bridger's Valley."

When he looked up, there were tears in his eyes. Most of the watchers looked down at their boots for a moment, some of them making wry faces.

"I'm no rustler, though. I didn't steal them, I bought them and paid for them." Then suddenly he wanted to talk a lot. "I bought them this morning; paid cash for them. My own were so bad I didn't dare try to risk bringing them up. I didn't know what the Mono Lake country was like. I sold them off in Salinas. I had to stock up again."

He could see nobody believed him.

"You can wait, can't you?" he pleaded. "I'm not likely to escape from an army like this, am I? You can wait till you see Drew, till you ask about me in Pike's. It's not too much to ask a wait like that, is it, before you hang men?"

Everybody was still just looking at him or at the ground.

"My God," he yelled out suddenly, "you aren't going to hang innocent men without a shred of proof, are you?"

Tetley shook his head very slightly.

"Then why don't you take us in, and stop this damned farce?"

"It would be a waste of time," Farnley said. "The law is almightly slow and careless around here."

The kid appeared to be trying to think fast now.

"Where do you come from?" he asked.

"Bridger's Valley," Farnley told him. There were grins again.

Martin said to Tetley, "You know Drew then?"

"I know him," Tetley said. You wouldn't have gathered it was a pleasure from the way he spoke.

"Well, didn't you even see him? Who sent you up here?"

"Drew," Tetley said.

"That's not true," Davies said. He came out from the ring and closer to the fire. He looked odd among the riders, little and hunched in an old, loose jacket and bareheaded.

"Don't let him get started again," Smith said in a disgusted voice. "It's one o'clock now."

Davies didn't pay any attention to him. "That statement is not true," he repeated. "Drew didn't send us up here. Drew didn't even know we were coming."

Tetley was watching him closely. There was only a remnant of his smile.

"As I've told you a hundred times," Davies told us all, "I'm not trying to obstruct justice. But I do want to see real justice. This is a farce; this is, as Mr. Martin has said, murder if you carry it through. He's perfectly within his rights when he demands trial. And that's all I've asked since we started, that's all I'm asking now, a trial." He sounded truculent, for him, and was breathing heavily as he spoke. "This young man," he said, pointing to Martin and looking around at us, "has said repeatedly that he is innocent. I, for one, believe him."

"Then I guess you're the only one that does, Arthur," Ma told him quietly.

Tetley made a sign to Mapes with his hand. Mapes stepped out and took Davies by the arm and began to shove him back toward the ring of watchers. Davies did not struggle much; even the little he did looked silly in Mapes' big hands. But while he went he called out angrily, "If there's any justice in your proceedings, Tetley, it would be only with the greatest certainty, it would be only after a confession. And they haven't confessed, Tetley. They say they're innocent, and you haven't proved they aren't."

"Keep him there," Mapes told the men around Davies after he'd been pushed back.

"Indirectly, Drew," Tetley said, as if Davies had not spoken.

"Now, if you're done," he went on, "I'd like to ask another question or two." Martin seemed to have taken some hope from Davies' outburst. Now he was looking down again. It was clear enough what most of the men thought.

"First, perhaps you have a bill of sale for those cattle?"

Martin swallowed hard. "No," he said finally. "No, I haven't."

"No?"

"Drew said it was all right. I couldn't find him at the ranch house. He was out on the range when I found him. He didn't have a bill of sale with him. He just said it was all right, not to wait, that he'd mail it to me. He told me it would be all right."

"Moore," Tetley said, without looking away from Martin.

"Yes?" Moore said. He didn't want to talk.

"You ride for Drew, don't you?"

"You know I do."

"In fact you're his foreman, aren't you?"

"Yes, what of it?"

"How long have you been riding for Drew?"

"Six years," Moore said.

"Did you ever know Drew to sell any cattle without a bill of sale?"

"No, I can't say as I ever did. But I can't remember every head he's sold in six years."

"It's customary for Drew to give a bill of sale, though?"

"Yes."

"And Moore, did you ever know Drew to sell any cattle after spring roundup, this year, or any other year?"

"No," Moore admitted, "I don't know that he's ever done that."

"Was there any reason why he should make a change in his regular practice this spring?"

Moore shook his head slowly. Young Greene shouted from over in front of Davies, "I heard him myself, say, just a couple of days ago, that he wouldn't sell a head to God himself this spring."

"Well?" Tetley asked Martin.

"I know it looks bad," the kid said, in a slow tired voice. He didn't expect to be believed any more. "I can't tell you anything else, I guess, except to ask Drew. It was hard to get them from him, all right. We talked a long time, and I had to show him how I was stuck, and how nobody wanted to sell this spring because there were so few calves. He really let me have them just as a favor, I think. That's all I have to tell you; I can't say anything else, I guess, not that would make any difference to you."

"No," Tetley agreed, "I don't believe you can."

"You don't believe me?"

"Would you, in my place?"

"I'd ask," Martin said more boldly. "I'd do a lot of asking before I'd risk hanging three men who might be innocent."

"If it were only rustling," Tetley said, "maybe. With murder, no. I'd rather risk a lot of hanging before too much asking. Law, as the books have it, is slow and full of holes."

In the silence the fire crackled, and hissed when the snow fell into it. The light of it flagged up and down on the men's serious faces, and turned to observe Tetley. The mouths were hard and the eyes bright and nervous. Finally Ma said mildly, "I guess it would be enough, even for Tyler, wouldn't it, Willard?"

"For Martin, perhaps," Tetley said.

"The others are his men, ain't they?" Farnley inquired.

Others quietly said it had been enough for them. Even Moore said, "It's no kindness to keep them waiting."

Still Tetley didn't say anything, and Ma burst out, "What you tryin' to do, play cat and mouse with them, Tetley? You act like you liked it."

"I would prefer a confession," Tetley said. He was talking to Martin, not to us.

Martin swallowed and wet his lips with his tongue, but couldn't speak. Besides Smith, Farnley and Winder were knotting ropes now. Finally Martin groaned something we couldn't understand, and abandoned his struggle with himself. The sweat broke out on his face and began to trickle down; his jaw was shaking. The old man was talking to himself, now and then shaking his head, as if pursuing an earnest and weighty debate. The Mex was standing firmly, with his feet a little apart, like a boxer anticipating his opponent's lunge or jab, saying nothing and showing nothing. It got to Gil even.

"I don't see your game, Tetley," he said. "If you got any doubts let's call off this party and take them in to the Judge, like Davies wants."

This was the first remark that had made any impression on Tetley's cool disregard. He looked directly at Gil and told him, "This is only very slightly any of your business, my friend. Remember that."

Gil got hot. "Hanging is any man's business that's around, I'd say."

"Have you a brief for the innocence of these men?" Tetley asked him. "Or is it merely that your stomach for justice is cooling?"

"Mister, take it easy with that talk," Gil said, swinging out of line and hitching a thumb over his gun belt. A couple of men tried to catch hold of him, but he shook them off short and sharp, without looking at them or using a hand. He was staring at Tetley in a way I knew enough to be scared of. I got up, but I didn't know what I'd do.

"No man," Gil said, standing just across the corner of the fire from Tetley, "no man is going to call me yellow. If that's what you mean, make it plainer."

Tetley was smooth. "Not at all," he said. "But we seem to have a number of men here only too willing to foist the burden of a none too pleasant task onto others, even when those others, as we all know, may well never perform it. I was just wondering how many such men. It would be a kindness, in my estimation, to let them leave before we proceed further. Their interruptions are becoming tiresome."

Gil stood where he was. "Well, I'm not one of them, get that," he said.

"Good," Tetley said, nodding as if he were pleased. "We have no quarrel then, I guess."

"No," Gil admitted, "but I still say I don't see your game. Hanging is one thing. To keep men standing and sweating for it while you talk is another. I don't like it."

Tetley examined him as if to remember him for another time. "Hurry is scarcely to be recommended at a time like this," he said finally. "I am taking, it seems to me, the chief responsibility in this matter, and I do not propose to act prematurely, that's all."

I could see Gil didn't believe this any more than I did, but there wasn't anything to say to it, no clear reason that you could put a finger on, for doubt. Gil stood there, but said nothing more. It was a hard spot for him to retreat from. Martin was watching him, hoping to God something would break. He sagged again, though, and closed his eyes and worked his mouth, when Gil just stood balanced and Tetley said, "Since they will not ease our task directly, we'll get on."

"We've had enough questions," Winder said. "They aren't talking."

Tetley said to Martin, "You called the old man Dad. Is he your father?"

"No," Martin said, and again added something too low to hear.

"Speak up, man," Tetley said sharply, "you're taking it like a woman."

"Everybody's gotta die once, son. Keep your chin up," Ma said. That was bare comfort for him, but I knew Ma wasn't thinking of him so much as of us. His weakness was making us feel as if we were mistreating a dog instead of trying a man.

The kid brought his head up and faced us, but that was

worse. The tears were running down his cheeks and his mouth was working harder than ever.

"God Almighty, he's bawlin'," said Winder, and spit as if it made him sick.

"No," said Martin, thick and blubbery, but loudly, "he works for me."

"What's your name?" Tetley asked, turning to the old man. The old man didn't hear him; he continued to talk to himself. Mapes went and stood in front of him and said loudly in his face, "What's your name?"

"I didn't do it," argued the old man. "No, how could I have done it? You can see I didn't do it, can't you?" He paused, thinking how to make it clear. "I didn't have anything in my gun," he explained. "Mr. Martin won't let me have any bullets for my gun, so how could I do it? I wasn't afraid to, but I didn't have any bullets."

"You didn't do what?" Tetley asked him gently.

"No, I didn't, I tell you. I didn't." Then his wet wreck of a face seemed to light up with an idea. "He done it," he asserted. "He done it."

"Who did it?" said Tetley, still quietly, but slowly and distinctly.

"He did," burbled the old man, "Juan did. He told me so. No, he didn't; I saw him do it. If I saw him do it," he inquired cutely, "I know, don't I? I couldn't have done it if I saw him do it, could I?"

The Mex didn't stir. Farnley was watching the Mex, and even his hard grin was gone. He was holding his breath, and then breathing by snorts.

Martin spoke. "Juan couldn't have done anything. I was with him all the time."

"Yes, he did too do it, Mr. Martin. He was asleep; he didn't mean to tell me, but I was awake and I heard him talking about it. He told me when he was asleep."

"The old man is feeble-minded," Martin said, slowly and quietly, trying to speak so the old man wouldn't hear him. "He doesn't know what he's talking about. He's dreamt something." He looked down; either it hurt him to say this or he was doing a better job of acting than his condition made probable. "You can't trust anything he says. He dreams constantly; when he's awake he invents things. After a little while he really believes they have happened. He's a good old man; you've scared him and he's inventing things he thinks will save him."

Then he flared, "If you've got to go on with your filthy comedy you can let him alone, can't you?"

"You keep out of this," Mapes shouted, stepping quickly past the Mexican and standing in front of Martin. "You've had your say. Now shut up."

Martin stared down at him. "Then let the old man alone," he said.

Mapes suddenly struck him across the face so hard it would have knocked him over if he hadn't been tied to the others. As it was, one knee buckled under him, and he ducked his head down to shake off the sting or block another slap if it was coming.

"Lay off, Mapes," somebody shouted, and Moore said, "You've got no call for that sort of thing, Mapes."

"First he wouldn't talk, and now he talks too damned much," Mapes said, but let Martin alone.

We had closed the circle as much as the fire would let us. Tetley moved closer to Martin, and Mapes made room for him, though strutting because of the yelling at him.

"You mean actually feeble-minded?" Tetley asked.

"Yes."

"What's his name?"

"Alva Hardwick."

"And the other speaks no English?"

Martin didn't reply.

"What's his name?"

"Juan Martinez."

"No, it isn't," old Bartlett said.

Tetley turned and looked at old Bartlett. "You seem to know something about this man?" he asked.

"I've been trying to tell you ever since this fool questioning started," Bartlett told him, "but you've got to be so damned regular."

"All right, all right," Tetley said impatiently. "What is it?"

Bartlett suddenly became cautious. "I don't want to say until I'm sure," he said. He went up to the Mex.

"Remember me?" he asked. "At Driver's, last September?"

The Mex wouldn't know he was being talked to. Bartlett got angry; when he got angry his loose jowls trembled.

"I'm talking to you, greaser," he said.

The Mex looked at him, too quick and narrow for not understanding, but then all he did was shake his head and say, "No sabbey," again.

"The devil you don't," Bartlett told him. "Your name's Francisco Morez, and the vigilantes would still like to get hold of you."

The Mex wouldn't understand.

"He talks English better than I do," Bartlett told Tetley. "He was a gambler, and claimed to be a rancher from down Sonora way somewhere. They wanted him for murder."

"What about that?" Tetley asked Martin.

"I don't know," the kid said hopelessly.

"Does he speak English?"

The kid looked at the Mex and said, "Yes." The Mex didn't bat an eye.

"How long's he been with you?"

"He joined us in Carson." Martin looked up at Tetley again. "I don't know anything about him," he said. "He told me that he was a rider, and that he knew this country, and that he'd like to tie up with me. That's all I know."

"They stick together nice, don't they?" Smith said.

"You picked him up on nothing more than that?" Tetley asked Martin.

"Why don't you come to the point?" Martin asked. "Why ask me all these questions if you don't believe anything I tell you?"

"There's as much truth to be sifted out of lies as anything else," Tetley said, "if you get enough lies. Is his name Morez?" he went on.

"I tell you I don't know. He told me his name was Martinez. That's all I know."

Without warning Tetley shifted his questioning to the old man. "What did he do?" he asked sharply.

"He did," mumbled the old man. "Yes, he did too; I saw him."

"What did he do?"

"He said that—he said." The old man lost what he was trying to tell.

"He said . . ." encouraged Tetley.

"I don't know. I didn't do it. You wouldn't kill an old man, Mister. I'm a very old man, Mister, very old man." He assumed his expression of cunning again. "I wouldn't live very long anyway," he said argumentatively.

"You're a big help," Bartlett said.

"Yeah," said Farnley, grinning at Tetley, "he makes it all clear, don't he?"

"What do you know about the old man?" Tetley asked Martin patiently.

"He's all right; he wouldn't hurt anything if he could help it."

"And he's been with you how long?"

"Three years."

"As a rider?"

"I'd rather not talk about this here," Martin said. "Can't you take me in the cabin, or somewhere?"

"It's a better check on the stories if they don't hear each other, at that," Winder put in.

"What stories?" Farnley asked. "One of them don't talk and the other don't make sense. There's only one story."

"We'll do well enough here," Tetley said. "Does the old man here ride for you?"

"Only ordinary driving. He's not a cowboy. He's a good worker if he understands, but you have to tell him just what to do."

"Not much use in this business, then, is he?" Tetley spoke absent-mindedly, as if just settling the point for himself, but he was watching Martin. Martin didn't slip.

"He's a good worker."

"Why did you take him on, if he's what you say?"

Martin was embarrassed. Finally he said, "You would have too."

Tetley smiled. "What did he do before he came to you?"

"He was in the army. I don't know which army; he doesn't seem to be clear about it himself. Maybe he was in both at different times; I've thought so sometimes, from things he's said.

Or that might be just his way of imagining. You can't always tell what's been real with him."

"I know," said Tetley, still smiling. "You've made a point of that. But you're sure he was in the army?"

"He was in one of them. Something started him thinking that way."

"A half-wit in the army?" Tetley asked, tilting his head to one side.

Martin swallowed and wet his lips again. "He must have been," he insisted.

"Still, you say he wouldn't hurt anything?"

"No," Martin said, "he wouldn't. He's foolish, but he's always gentle."

Tetley just stood and smiled at him and shook his head.

"I believe," Martin persisted, "some experience in the war must have injured his mind. There's one he always talks about, and never finishes. He must have been all right before, and something in the war did it to him."

Tetley considered the old man. Then suddenly he drew himself up stiffly and clicked his heels together, and barked out, "Attention," with all the emphasis on the last syllable.

Old Hardwick just looked around at all of us with a scared face, more nervous and vacant than ever because he knew we were all watching him.

Tetley relaxed. "I don't think so," he said to Martin.

"He's forgotten. He forgets everything."

Tetley shook his head, still smiling. "Not that," he said.

"You still don't talk English?" he asked the Mex. The Mex was silent.

Tetley sent two riders to help the Bartlett boys shag in the cattle they'd been holding. At the edge of the clearing, seeing the fire, and the men and horses, and being wild with this unusual night hazing anyway, they milled. But they didn't have to come any closer. As they turned, with the firelight on them enough, we could see Drew's brand and his notches.

"Anything you haven't said that you want to say?" Tetley asked Martin.

Martin drew a deep breath to steady himself. He could feel the set against him that one look at those cattle had brought on if all the talk hadn't.

"I've told you how I got them," he said.

"We heard that," Tetley agreed.

"You have the steers, haven't you?" Martin asked. He was short of breath. "Well, you haven't lost anything then, have you? You could wait to hang us until you talk to Drew, couldn't you?"

"It's not the first time," Tetley said. "We waited before."

He studied Martin for a moment.

"I'll make you a deal, though," he offered. "Tell us which of you shot Kinkaid, and the other two can wait."

Martin half-way glanced at the Mex, but if he was going to say anything he changed his mind. He shook his head before he spoke, as if at some thought of his own. "None of us killed anybody," he said in that tired voice again. "We were all three together all the time."

"That's all, I guess," Tetley said regretfully. He motioned toward the biggest tree on the edge of the clearing.

"My God," Martin said huskily, "you aren't going to, really! You wouldn't, really! You can't do it," he wailed, and started fighting his bond, jerking the other two prisoners about. The old man stumbled and fell to his knees and got up again as if it were a desperate necessity to be on his feet, but as clumsily as a cow because of his bound wrists.

"Tie them separately, Mapes," Tetley ordered.

Many ropes were offered. Smith and Winder helped Mapes. Only Martin was hard to tie. He'd lost his head, and it took two men to hold him while he was bound. Then the three were standing there separately, each with his arms held flat to his sides by a half-dozen turns of rope. Their feet were left free to walk them into position. Each of them had a noose around his neck too, and a man holding it.

In spite of Mapes trying to hold him up, Martin slumped down to his knees. We couldn't understand what he was babbling. When Mapes pulled him up again he managed to stand, but waving like a tree in a shifting wind. Then we could understand part of what he was saying. "One of them's just a baby," he was saying, "just a baby. They haven't got anything to go on, not a thing. They're alone; they haven't got anything to go on, and they're alone."

"Take them over," Tetley ordered, indicating the tree again.

It was a big pine with its top shot away by lightning. It had a long branch that stuck out straight on the clearing side, about fifteen feet from the ground. We'd all spotted that branch.

"The Mex is mine," Farnley said. Tetley nodded and told some others to get the rustlers' horses.

Martin kept hanging back, and when he was shoved along kept begging, "Give us some time, it's not even decent; give us some time."

Old Hardwick stumbled and buckled, but didn't fall. He was silent, but his mouth hung open, and his eyes were protruding enormously. The Mex, however, walked steadily, showing only a wry grin, as if he had expected nothing else from the first.

When the three of them were lined up in a row under the limb, waiting for their horses, Martin said, "I've got to write a letter. If you're even human you'll give me time for that, any-way." His breath whistled when he talked, but he seemed to know what he was saying again.

"We can't wait all night," Mapes told him, getting ready to throw up the end of the rope, which had a heavy knot tied in it to carry it over.

"He's not asking much, Tetley," Davies said.

Old Hardwick seemed to have caught the idea. He burbled about being afraid of the dark, that he didn't want to die in the dark, that in the dark he saw things.

"He's really afraid of the dark," Martin said. "Can't this wait till sunrise? It's customary anyway, isn't it?"

Men were holding the three horses just off to the side now. Farnley was holding the hang rope on the Mex. He spoke to Tetley angrily.

"Now what are you dreaming about, Tetley? They're trying to put it off, that's all; they're scared, and they're trying to put it off. Do you want Tyler and the sheriff to get us here, and the job not done?" As if he had settled it himself, he threw the end of the Mex's rope over the limb.

"They won't come in this snow," Davies said.

"I believe you're right," Tetley told Davies. "Though I doubt if you want to be." He asked Bartlett, "What time is it?" Bartlett drew a thick silver watch from his waistcoat pocket and looked at it.

"Five minutes after two," he said.

"All right," Tetley said after a moment, "we'll wait till daylight."

Farnley stood holding the end of the rope and glaring at Tetley. Then slowly he grinned up one side of his face and tossed down the rope, like he was all done. "Why not?" he said. "It will give the bastard time to think about it." Then he walked down to the fire and stood there by himself. He was wild inside; you could tell that just by looking at his back.

In a way none of us liked the wait, when we'd have to go through the whole thing over again anyway. But you couldn't refuse men in a spot like that three or four hours if they thought they wanted them.

"Reverend," Tetley said to Sparks, "you can settle your business at leisure."

It was suggested that we put the prisoners into the cabin, but Tetley said it was too cold, and no stove. The fire was fed up again, and the three men put on different sides of it. It was hard to tell where to go yourself. You wanted to stay near the fire, and still not right around those men.

Martin asked to have his hands untied. "I can't write like this," he explained. The Mex said something too, in Spanish.

"He wants to eat," Amigo told us. "He say," he grinned, "he ees mucho hongry from so mooch ride and so mooch mooch of the talk." The Mex grinned at us while Amigo was talking.

"Let him ask for it himself, then," Bartlett said.

"Untie them all," Tetley said, and appointed Smith and Moore and Winder to keep them covered.

When he was freed, Martin moved to sit on a log on his side. He sat there rubbing his wrists. Then he asked for paper and a pencil. Davies had a little leather account book and a pencil in his vest. He gave them to Martin, showing him the blank pages in the back of the book. But Martin's hands were shaking so he couldn't write. Davies offered to write for him, but he said no, he'd be all right in a few minutes; he'd rather write this letter for himself.

"Will the others want to write?" Davies asked him.

"You can ask Juan," Martin said, looking at the Mex. Whenever he looked at the Mex he had that perplexed expression of wanting to say something and deciding not to. "It's no use with the old man, though," he said, looking up at Davies and remembering to smile to show he was grateful. "He wouldn't know what to say, or how to say it. I don't believe he has anybody to write to, for that matter. He forgets people if they're not right around him."

When Amigo asked him, Juan said no, he didn't care to write. For some reason he seemed to think the idea of his writing to anyone was humorous.

Ma was examining the rustlers' packs, which had been propped against the cabin wall. She was going to get a meal for the Mex. She drew articles out, naming them for everybody to hear as she removed them. There was a lot more than three men could want for a meal or two. There was a whole potato sack of very fresh beef, which had been rolled up in paper and then put in the sack, and the sack put in the lee of the cabin, half buried in an old drift. There was coffee too.

When Ma had called off part of her list Smith yelled to her to fix a spread for everybody. He explained loudly that if they had to freeze and lose sleep because somebody was afraid of the dark, they didn't have to starve too, and that it wasn't exactly robbery because by the time it was eaten that food wouldn't belong to anybody anyway. He also hinted that the beef probably belonged to some of us anyhow. He had managed to bring a bottle along, and now that there was no immediate excitement he pulled on it frequently. He was a good deal impressed with how funny he was.

A few men looked around hard at Smith, but most pretended that they were thinking about something and hadn't heard him. Moore spoke up though, and told Ma he didn't want anything; then others of us told her the same thing. Smith called us queasy, but when nobody answered he didn't go any further. He knew what we meant. You can't eat a man's food before him and then hang him.

When Ma set to cooking it, though, with Sparks helping her, many changed their minds. There was a belly-searching odor from that meat propped on forked sticks and dripping and scorching over the coals. None of us had had a real meal since midday, and some not then, and the air was cold and snowy and with a piny edge. It carried the meat smell very richly.

Gil made me drink some of the coffee because my teeth were chattering. I wasn't really so cold as thinned out by the loss of blood. Coffee was better than the whisky had been, and after it I sneaked a bit of the meat too, being careful that Martin didn't see me eat it. I only chewed a little, though, and knew I didn't want it. I took more coffee.

Sparks took meat and bread and coffee on their own plates and in their own cups to the three prisoners. The Mex ate with big mouthfuls, taking his time and enjoying it. The strong muscles in his jaws worked in and out so the firelight shone on them when he chewed. He washed it down with long draughts of coffee too hot for me to have touched, and nodded his head at Ma to show it was all good. When he was done eating he took a pull of whisky from Gil, rolled and lit a cigarette, and sat cross-legged, drawing the smoke in two streams up his nostrils and blowing it out between his lips in strong jets that bellied out into clouds at the end. He watched the fire and the smoke from his cigarette, and sometimes smiled to himself reminiscently.

Old Hardwick ate his meat and bread too, but didn't know he was doing it. He chewed with the food showing out of his mouth, and didn't stop staring. Sometimes he continued to chew when he had already swallowed. Some of the bread he pulled into little pieces and dropped while he was chewing the meat.

Martin drank some coffee, but refused food and whisky. He was holding the notebook and pencil and thinking. It was a hard letter to write. He would stare at the fire with glazed eyes, wake up with a shiver and look around him, put the pencil to the paper, and then relapse into that staring again. It was a long time before he really began to write, and then he twice tore out a page on which there were only a few words, and began again. Finally, he seemed to forget where he was, and what was going to happen to him, and wrote slowly and steadily, occasionally crossing out a line or so with two slow, straight strokes.

Gil made me lie down with a couple of blankets around me and my back against the cabin, but between Ma and Tetley sitting and eating and smoking and not talking much, I could see Martin's face and his hand busy writing.

The young Bartletts were relieved and came in, but they wouldn't eat either, but drank coffee and smoked. It was very quiet, all the men sitting around except the guards. Tetley insisted that the guards stand up. Some of the men talked in low voices, and now and then one of them would laugh, but stop quickly. Tetley kept looking over at Gerald, who hadn't eaten or even taken any coffee, and who wasn't smoking, but sitting there picking up little sticks and digging hard at the ground with them, and then realizing he had them, and tossing them away. When another squall of wind brought the snow down in waves again, men looked up at the sky, where there wasn't anything to see. The wind wasn't steady, however, and shortly the snow thinned out again. Most of it had shaken from its loose lodging on the branches of the pines. I became drowsy, and felt that I was observing a distant picture. After eating, Gabe Hart had rolled up and gone to sleep just beyond me, but all the others were trying to stay awake, though some of them would nod, and then jerk up and stare around as if something had happened or they felt a long time had passed. Only young Tetley kept the scene from going entirely dream-like. Between times of playing with his sticks he would rise abruptly and walk out to the edge of the dark and stand there with his back turned, and then suddenly turn and come back to the fire and stand there for a long time before he sat down again. After the third or fourth time his father leaned toward him when he sat down, and spoke to him. The boy remained seated then, but always with those busy hands.

Then I slept myself, after short broken dozes. I woke suddenly, with my shoulder aching badly, my head light again, and my mouth dry. I was scared about something, and tried to get out of my blanket quickly and stand up, but a weight was holding me under. I thought that if it should stop pressing I'd take off like a leaf in the wind. Only the ache seemed real, and the weight.

The weight was Gil. He had a hand on my ribs beneath the bad arm, and was holding me down as gently as he could, but heavily.

"What's eating on you?" he asked.

I told him nothing was, and he helped me to sit up and lean against the cabin. Having slept, I felt weak and miserable. The shoulder was round and tight as a river boulder and the ache reached to my breastbone in front and my spine in back. In the center of it there was a small and ambitious core of fire.

"You were jabbering," Gil said, "and flopping around like a fish out of water. I thought maybe you was out of your head."

"No, I'm all right," I told him.

"You must have been dreaming," Gil said. "You was scared to death when I took hold of you."

I said I couldn't remember.

"I wouldn'ta woke you up," he apologized, "only I was afraid you'd start that shoulder bleeding again."

"I'm glad you did," I told him. I didn't like the idea of lying there talking in my sleep.

"Have I been asleep long?" I asked him.

"An hour or two, I guess."

"An hour or two?" I felt like a traitor, as if I'd wasted the little time those three men had by sleeping myself.

"You didn't miss anything," Gil said, "except Smith working on Ma."

That was still going on. They were sitting in front of us, and Smith had one arm around her thick middle and was holding a bottle up to her. He wasn't making any headway, though. She was solid as a stump.

Martin had finished his letter, and was sitting hunched over with his forehead in his hands. I saw him stare at Smith and Ma once, and then bend his head again, locking his hands behind it and pulling down hard, like he was stretching his neck and shoulders. Then he relaxed again, and put his arms across his knees and his head down on them. He was having a hard time of it, I judged.

Sparks was busy with old Hardwick, squatting in front of him and exhorting and now and then taking hold of him gently to make him pay attention. But the old man was scared out of what little wits he had and wasn't listening, but still staring and talking to himself. Davies was trying to get Tetley to talk about something he was showing him, but failing. The Mex was sitting there drowsily, with his elbows on his knees and his forearms hanging loosely between his legs.

Only two men were standing, one on guard with a carbine across his arm, and Farnley, who had moved around to put his back against the big tree, and was much more awake than the guard.

There was no wind, and no snow falling, but no stars showing either; just thick, dark cold.

I heard Tetley making a retort to Davies. It was the first time either of them had raised his voice, and Davies nervously motioned him to be quiet, but he finished what he was saying clearly enough so I could hear it. "It may be a fine letter; apparently, from what you say, it's a very fine letter. But if it's an honest letter it's none of my business to read it, and if it isn't I don't want to."

Martin had heard. He lifted his head and looked across at them.

"Is that my letter you're showing?" he asked.

"It's yours," Tetley told him. I knew how he was smiling when he said it.

"What are you doing, showing my letter?" Martin asked Davies. His voice had aroused the whole circle to watch them now. He repeated his question more sharply.

Smith gave up his game with Ma and rose unsteadily and came toward Martin, hitching his belt as he stumbled.

"Don't go to raising your voice like that, rustler," he ordered thickly.

"Never mind, Monty," Davies said. "He's right. I told him I'd keep it for him."

Smith stood waveringly and looked around at Davies. His face was knotted with the effort to look disgusted and hostile and to see straight at the same time. "Well," he said, "if you like to suck the hind tit . . ."

"Sit down before you fall down, Monty," Ma advised him.

"Nobody's gonna fall down," Smith assured her. "But I'll be damned," he said, squaring around on Martin again, "if I'd let any yellow, thievin' rustler raise his voice at me for tryin' to do him a favor. It's a little late to get fussy about privacy when you got the knot under your ear already."

This time Tetley told him to shut up, and he did.

Martin paid no attention to Smith. He stood up and spoke to Davies. "If I remember rightly, all I asked was that you keep that letter and make sure it was delivered."

"I'm sorry," Davies said, "I was just trying to prove . . ."

Martin began to move across toward Davies. The veins were standing out in his neck. Several men scrambled to their feet. Davies rose too, defensively. The guard didn't know what to do. He took a step or two after Martin, but then stood there holding his carbine like it was a live rattler. Farnley came down from his stand against the tree. He had his gun out when he got to the fire.

"Sit down, you, and pipe down," he ordered.

Martin stood still, but he didn't show any signs of retreating or of sitting down. He didn't even look around at Farnley.

Mapes was standing up behind Tetley. He ordered Martin to sit down also, and drew his gun when Martin didn't move or even glance at him.

"It's enough," Martin said in a smothered voice to Davies, "to be hanged by a pack of bullying outlaws without having your private thoughts handed around to them for a joke."

"I've said I'm sorry," Davies reminded him, sharply for him. "I was merely doing . . ."

"I don't give a damn what you were doing. I didn't write that letter to be passed around. I wrote that letter to—well, it's none of your business, and it's none of the business of any of these other murdering bastards."

"Take it easy on that talk," Farnley said behind him.

"I made no promise," Davies told Martin.

"All right, you made no promise. I should have known I'd need a promise. Or would that have done any good? I thought there was one white man among you. Well, I was wrong."

Then he became general in his reference. He waved an arm around to take us all in. "But what good would an oath do, in a pack like this, an oath to do what any decent man would do by instinct? You eat our food in front of us and joke about it. You make love publicly in front of men about to die, and are able to sleep while they wait. What good would an oath do where there's not so much conscience in the lot as a good dog has?

"Give me that letter," he ordered, taking another step toward Davies.

"I'll see that she gets it," Davies said stiffly.

"I wouldn't have her touch it," Martin said.

Tetley stood up. "That's enough," he said. "You've been told to go back and sit down. If I were you, I'd do that. Give him the letter, Davies."

Still holding the letter, Davies said quietly, "Your wife ought to hear from you, son. None of us could be so kind as that letter; and she'd want it to keep."

Martin stared at him. His face changed, the wrath dying out

of it. "Thanks," he said. "I'm sorry. Yes, keep it, please, and see that she gets it."

"Hey, the Mex," Ma yelled. She was pointing up to the edge of the woods, where the horses were tied. There was the Mex, working at the rope on one of the bays, the horse nearest the woods on the road side. There was a general yell and scramble. Somebody yelled to spread, he might have a gun. Several yelled to shoot. They circled out fast, snapping hammers as they ran. They were mad and ashamed at having been caught napping. Tetley was as angry as anyone, but he kept his head.

"Mapes, Winder," he called out, "keep an eye on the other two. You," he said to Davies, "if you're part of this trick—" but didn't finish it, but went around the fire quickly to where he could see better.

Martin stood where he was, and old Hardwick, when he saw the guns come out, put his hands up over his eyes, like a little, scared kid.

The Mex did have a gun. At the first shout he just worked harder on the tie, but when Farnley shot and then two more shots came from off at the side, he yanked the horse around in front of him and shot back. In the shadow you could see the red jet of the gun. I heard the bullet whack into the cabin at the left of me. Everybody broke farther to the sides to get out of the light, and nobody was crowding in very fast. Farnley tried another shot and nicked the horse, which squealed and reared so the Mex lost him. The other horses were scared and wheeled and yanked at the tie ropes, and nobody could see the Mex to shoot again. He must have given up trying to get the horse, though, and made a break for it on foot, because Farnley, who was out in the edge of the woods quit creeping and stood up and shot again. Then he came back running and took the carbine away from the guard, and plunged back into the woods, yelling something as he went. Others fanned out into the woods too.

Then it was quiet for a few minutes, those of us who had stayed behind waiting to hear it happen. Finally it began, somewhere up on the mountain and over toward the road, not too far, from the loudness of the reports. There were three short, flat shots in quick succession, then a deeper one that got an echo from some canyon up among the trees. Then it was quiet again, and we thought it was all over, when there were two more of the flat explosions and after a moment the deeper one again. Then it stayed quiet.

We were all nervous waiting, and nobody talked, just watched around the edge of the woods to see where they'd come out. The wait seemed so long that some of the men, who weren't on guard, began edging cautiously into the woods to see what had happened.

Then we saw the others coming down again. Two of them had the Mex between them, but he wasn't dead; he wasn't even out. They carried him down into the light and set him on the log Martin had been sitting on. He was sweating, but not saying anything, and not moaning.

"Tie the others up again," Tetley ordered.

"That must have been some fine shooting," he said to Farnley. "Where's he hit?"

Farnley flushed. "It was good enough," he retorted. "It was dark in there; you couldn't even see the barrel sometimes, let alone the sights." Then he answered, "I hit him in the leg."

"Saving him for the rope, eh?"

"No, I wasn't. I wanted to kill the bastard bad enough. It was the slope that done it; it's hard to tell shooting uphill."

They were talking like it had been a target shoot, and the Mex right there.

One of the men who had gone in after Farnley came up to Tetley and handed him something. "That's the gun he had," he said, nodding at the Mex. It was a long, blue-barreled Colt six-shooter with an ivory grip. "It's empty," the man said, "he shot 'em all out, I guess."

Farnley was looking at the gun in Tetley's hand. He was staring at it. After a moment, without asking, he reached out and took it away from Tetley.

"Well," he said, after turning it over in his own hands, "I guess we know now, don't we? If there was ever anything to wonder about, there ain't now."

Tetley watched him looking at the gun and waited for his explanation.

"It's Larry's gun," Farnley said. "Look," he said to the rest of us, and pointed to the butt and gave it to us to look at.

Kinkaid's name, all of it, Laurence Liam Kinkaid, was inlaid in tiny letters of gold in the ivory of the butt.

Tetley recovered the gun and took it over and held it for the Mex to see.

"Where did you get this?" he asked. His tone proved he would take only one answer. Sweating from his wound, the Mex grinned at him savagely.

"If somebody will take this bullet out of my leg, I will tell you," he said.

"God, he talks American," Ma said.

"And ten other languages," said the Mex, "but I don't tell anything I don't want to in any of them. My leg, please. I desire I may stand upright when you come to your pleasure."

"What's a slug or two to you now?" Farnley asked.

"If he wants it out, let him have it out," Moore said, "there's time."

The Mex looked around at us all with that angry grin. "If somebody will lend me the knife, I will take it out myself."

"Don't give him no knife," Bartlett said. "He can throw a knife better than most men can shoot."

"Better than these men, it is true," said the Mex. "But if you are afraid, then I solemnly give my promise I will not throw the knife. When I am done, then quietly I will give the knife back to its owner, with the handle first."

Surprisingly, young Tetley volunteered to remove the slug. His face was white, his voice smothered when he said it, but his eyes were bright. In his own mind he was championing his cause still, in the only way left. He felt that doing this, which would be difficult for him, must somehow count in the good score. He crossed to the Mex and knelt beside him, but when he took the knife one of the men offered him, his hand was shaking so he couldn't even start. He put up a hand, as if to clear his eyes, and the Mex took the knife away from him. Farnley quickly turned the carbine on the Mex, but he didn't pay any attention. He made a quick slash through his chaps from the thigh to the boot top. His leg, inside, was muscular and thick and hairless as an Indian's. Just over the knee there was the bullet hole, ragged and dark, but small; dark tendrils of blood had dried down from it, not a great deal of blood.

Young Tetley saw it close to his face, and got up drunkenly and moved away, his face bloodless. The Mex grinned after him.

"The little man is polite," he commented, "but without the stomach for the blood, eh?"

Then he said, while he was feeling from the wound along his leg up to the thigh, "Will someone please to make the fire better? The light is not enough."

Tetley ordered them to throw on more wood. He didn't look to see them do it. He was watching Gerald stagger out toward the dark in the edge of the woods to be sick.

When the fire had blazed up the Mex turned to present his thigh to the light, and went to work. Everybody watched him; it's hard not to watch a thing like that, though you don't want to. The Mex opened the mouth of the wound so it began to bleed again, freely, but then again he traced with his fingers up his thigh. He set his jaw, and high on the thigh made a new incision. His grin froze so it looked more like showing his teeth, and the sweat beads popped out on his forehead. He rested a moment when the first cut had been made, and was bleeding worse than the other.

"That is very bad shooting," he said. He panted from the pain.

Nonetheless, when he began to work again he hummed a Mexican dance tune through his teeth. He halted the song only once, when something he did with the point of the knife made his leg straighten involuntarily, and made him grunt in spite of himself. After that his own hand trembled badly, but he took a breath and began to dig and sweat and hum again. It got so I couldn't watch it either. I turned and looked for young Tetley instead, and saw him standing by a tree, leaning on it with one hand, his back to the fire. His father was watching him too.

There was a murmur, and I looked back, and the Mex had the bloody slug out and was holding it up for us to look at. When we had seen it he tossed it to Farnley.

"You should try again with that one," he said.

Sparks brought some hot water to the Mex, and after propping the knife so the blade was in the coals, he began washing out the two wounds with a purple silk handkerchief he'd had around his neck. He took care of himself as carefully as if he still had a lifetime to go. Then, when the knife blade was hot enough, he drew it out of the fire and clapped it right against the wounds, one after the other. Each time his body stiffened, the muscles of his jaw and the veins of his neck protruded, and the sweat broke out over his face, but still he drew the knife away from the thigh wound slowly, as if it pleased him to take his time. He asked for some of the fat from the steaks, rubbed the grease over the burned cuts, and bound them with the purple kerchief and another from his pocket. Then he lit a cigarette and took it easy.

After inhaling twice, long and slow, he picked up the knife he'd used and tossed it over in front of the man who had lent it. He tossed it so it spun in the air and struck the ground point first with a chuck sound, and dug in halfway to the hilt. It struck within an inch of where the man's boot had been, but he'd drawn off quickly when he saw it coming. The Mex grinned at him.

Martin and old Hardwick were bound again. Tetley told them they needn't tie the Mex, he wouldn't go far for awhile. The Mex thanked him, grinning through the smoke of his cigarette.

But when Tetley began to question him about the gun, all he'd say was that he'd found it; that it was lying right beside the road, and he'd brought it along, thinking to meet somebody he could send it back with. When Tetley called him a liar, and repeated the questions, the Mex at first just said the same thing, and then suddenly became angry and stubborn-looking, called Tetley a blind fool, lit another cigarette, and said no sabbey as he had at first. Martin told the same story about the gun, that they'd found it lying by the west lane when they came out from Drew's place, that all the cartridges had been in it, that he'd told the Mex to leave it because it was too far back to the ranch to take, but that the Mex had thought they might meet somebody who could return it. There wasn't anything else to be had out of either of them.

The Mexican's courage, and even, in a way, young Martin's pride in the matter of the letter, had won them much sympathy, and I think we all believed now that the old man was really a pitiful fool, but whatever we thought, there was an almost universal determination to finish the job now. The gun was a clincher with us.

All but Davies. Davies was trying to get other men to read the letter. He maintained stronger than ever that young Martin was innocent, that Martin was not the kind of a man who could either steal or kill. He worked on those of us who had shown some sympathy with his ideas before. He tried hard not to let Tetley notice what he was doing, to stand naturally when he talked, and not to appear too earnest to a person who couldn't hear him. But he didn't make much headway. Most of the men had made up their minds, or felt that the rest had and that their own sympathy was reprehensible and should be concealed. That was the way I felt. None of us would look at the letter. When he came to us, telling us to read the letter, Gil said, "I don't want to read the letter. It's none of my business. You heard the kid; you ought to remember if anybody does."

"Do you suppose it matters to his wife who sees this letter?" Davies said. "In her place which would you rather have, a live husband with some of his secrets with you revealed, or a dead husband and all your secrets still?

"I don't like to pry any more than you do," he insisted, "but you can't put a life against a scruple. I tell you, if you'll read this letter you'll know he couldn't have done it; not any of it. And if the letter's a fake we have only to wait to know, don't we?"

It wasn't long until daylight, and the men hadn't really settled down again, but were moving around in groups, talking and smoking. Still, I thought Tetley was watching us.

"That must be some letter," Gil was saying.

Davies held it out to him. "Read it," he pleaded.

"You get Martin to ask me to read it and I will," Gil told him, grinning.

"Then you read it," Davies said, turning to me. Gil was watching me, still grinning.

"No," I said, "I'd rather not." I was curious to read that letter, but I couldn't, there, like that.

Davies stood and looked from one to the other of us, despairingly.

"Do you want that kid to hang?" he asked finally.

"You can't change rustlin' and murder," Gil said.

"Never mind that," Davies said. "Don't think about anything but the way you really feel about it. Do you feel that you'd like to have that kid hanged; any of them, for that matter?"

"My feelings haven't got anything to do with it," Gil said.

Davies began to argue to show us that feelings did; that they were the real guide in a thing like this, when Tetley called out to him by name. Everyone looked at Tetley and Davies, and stopped moving around or talking.

"Don't you know a trick when you see one, Davies?" Tetley asked him, for all of us to hear. "Or are you in on this?"

Davies retorted that he knew a trick as well as the next man, and that Tetley himself knew that this wasn't any trick; yes, and that Tetley knew he'd had no part in any such games himself. He was defiant, and stated again, defiantly, his faith in the innocence of the three men. But he talked hurriedly, defensively, and finally stopped of his own accord at a point that was not a conclusion. Whatever else was weakening him, I believe he felt all the time that it was ugly to talk so before the men themselves, that his own defense sounded no prettier there than Tetley's side. Then too, he had little support, and he knew it. He knew it so well that, when he had faltered to silence, and Tetley asked him, "Are you alone in this, Davies?" he said nothing.

"I think we'd better get this settled," Tetley said. "We must act as a unit in a job like this. Then we need fear no mistaken reprisal. Are you content to abide by a majority decision, Davies?"

Davies looked him in the face, but even that seemed to be an effort. He wouldn't say anything.

"How about the rest of you men?" Tetley asked. "Majority rule?"

There were sounds of assent. Nobody spoke out against it.

"It has to," Ma said. "Among a bunch of pigheads like this you'd never get everybody to agree to anything."

"We'll vote," Tetley said. "Everybody who is with Mr. Davies for putting this thing off and turning it over to the courts, step out here." He pointed to a space among us on the south side of the fire.

Davies walked out there and stood. Nobody else came for a moment, and he flushed when Tetley smiled at him. Then

Sparks shambled out too, but smiling apologetically. Then Gerald Tetley joined them. His fists were clenched as he felt the watching, and saw his father's sardonic smile disappear slowly until his face was a stern mask. There was further movement, and some muttering, as Carl Bartlett and Moore stood out with them also. No more came.

"Five," said Tetley. "Not a majority, I believe, Mr. Davies."

He was disappointed that anyone had ventured to support Davies; I'm sure he hadn't expected as many as four others. I know I hadn't. And he was furious that Gerald had been among them. But he spoke quietly and ironically, as if his triumph had been complete.

Davies nodded, and slowly put Martin's letter away in his shirt pocket, under his waistcoat.

It was already getting light; the cabin and the trees could be seen clearly. There was no sunrise, but a slow leaking in of light from all quarters. The firelight no longer colored objects or faces near it. The faces were gray and tired and stern. We knew it was going to happen now, and yet, I believe, most of us still had a feeling it couldn't. It had been delayed so long; we had argued so much. Only Tetley seemed entirely self-possessed; his face showed no signs of weariness or excitement.

He asked Martin if there was any other message he wished to leave. Martin shook his head. In this light his face looked hollow, pale, and without individuality. His mouth was trembling constantly, and he was careful not to talk. I hoped, for our sake as much as his, that he'd make the decent end he now had his will set on.

Sparks was talking to the old fool again, but he, seeing the actual preparations begin, was frightened sick once more, and babbled constantly in a hoarse, worn-out voice, about his innocence, his age and his not wanting to die. Again and again he begged Martin to do something. This, more than anything else, seemed to shake Martin. He wouldn't look at old Hardwick, and pretended not to hear him.

We were surprised that the Mex wanted to make a confession, but he did. There wasn't any priest, so Amigo was to hear the confession, and carry it to a priest the first time he could go himself. There couldn't be any forgiveness, but it was the best they could do. They went down to the place where the sheds had stood, the Mex limping badly, and Amigo half carrying him along. Bartlett was stationed at a respectful distance as sentinel. We saw the Mex try to kneel, but he couldn't, so he stood there confessing with his back to us. Occasionally his hands moved in gestures of apology, which seemed strange from him. Amigo was facing us; but, when he wants, Amigo has a face like a wooden Indian. If the Mex was saying anything we ought to know now, which was what we were all thinking, we couldn't tell it from watching Amigo. He appeared merely to be intent upon remembering, in order that all the Mex's sins might be reported and forgiven.

In his field-officer manner Tetley was directing. Farnley knotted and threw up three ropes, so they hung over the long branch with the three nooses in a row. Then others staked down the ends of the ropes. The three horses were brought up again, and held under the ropes.

Tetley appointed Farnley, Gabe Hart and Gerald to whip the horses out. It was all right with Farnley, but Gabe refused. He gave no excuse, but stood there immovable, shaking his head. I was surprised Tetley had picked him.

"Gabe's not agin us, Mr. Tetley," Winder apologized, "he can't stand to hurt anything. It would work on his mind."

Tetley asked for a volunteer, and when no one else came forward Ma took the job. She was furious about it, though. Moore looked at Smith, and so did Tetley, but Smith pretended to be drunker than he really was. Really he was scared sober now.

When it seemed all settled, young Tetley, nearly choking, refused also.

"You'll do it," was all Tetley told him.

"I can't, I tell you."

"We'll see to it you can."

The boy stood there, very white, still shaking his head.

"It's a necessary task," Tetley told him, evenly. "Someone else must perform it if you fail. I think you owe it to the others, and to yourself, on several scores."

The boy still shook his head stubbornly.

Moore, although he had refused on his own account, came over to Tetley and offered to relieve Gerald. "The boy's seen too much already. You shouldn't press him, man."

Tetley's face abruptly became bloodless; his mouth stretched downward, long and thin and hard, and his eyes glimmered with the fury he restrained. It was the first time I'd ever seen him let that nature show through, though I had felt always that it was there. He still spoke quietly though, and evenly.

"This is not your affair, Moore. Thank you just the same."

Moore shrugged and turned his back on him. He was angry himself.

Tetley said to Gerald, "I'll have no female boys bearing my name. You'll do your part, and say nothing more." He turned away, giving the boy no opportunity to reply.

"That must have been a very busy life," he remarked, looking down where the Mex was still confessing to Amigo.

When at last the Mex was done and they came back up, and the three prisoners were stood in a row with their hands tied down, Martin said,

"I suppose it's no use telling you again that we're innocent?"

"No good," Tetley assured him.

"It's not for myself I'm asking," Martin said.

"Other men have had families and have had to go for this sort of thing," Tetley told him. "It's too bad, but it's not our fault."

"You don't care for justice," Martin flared. "You don't even care whether you've got the right men or not. You want your way, that's all. You've lost something and somebody's got to be punished; that's all you know."

When Tetley just smiled, Martin's control broke again. "There's nobody to take care of them; they're in a strange place, they have nothing, and there's nobody to take care of them. Can't you understand that, you butcher? You've got to let me go; if there's a spot of humanity in you, you've got to let me go. Send men with me if you want to; I'm not asking you to trust me; you wouldn't trust anybody; your kind never will. Send men with me, then, but let me see them, let me arrange for them to go somewhere, for somebody to help them."

Old Hardwick began to whimper and jabber aloud again, and finally buckled in the knees and fell forward on his face. The Mex looked straight ahead of him and spit with contempt. "This is fine company for a man to die with," he said.

Martin started to yell something at the Mex, who was right

beside him, but Mapes walked up to him and slapped him in the face. He slapped him hard, four times, so you could hear it like the crack of a lash. He paid no attention to protests or to Davies trying to hold his arm. After the fourth blow he waited to see if Martin would say anything more. He didn't, but stood there, crying weakly and freely, great sobs heaving his chest up and making him lift his chin to catch his breath because of the bonds.

Others put the old man back on his feet, and a couple of shots of whisky were given to each of the three. Then they walked them over to the horses. The old man went flabby on them, and they had nearly to carry him.

I saw Davies keeping Amigo behind, holding him by the arm and talking. Amigo's face was angry and stubborn, and he kept shaking his head. Tetley saw it too, and guessed what I had. Smiling, he told Davies that a confession was a confession, and not evidence, even in a court.

"He doesn't have to tell us," Davies said. "All he has to do is say whether we'd better wait; then we could find out."

Amigo looked worried.

Tetley said, "Men have been known to lie, even in confession, under pressure less than this." Amigo looked at him as if for the first time he questioned his divinity, but then he said, "It wasn't a priest; I don' know."

"Even if it had been," Tetley said, eying the Mex. "I'll give you two minutes to pray," he told the three. They were standing by the horses now, under the branch with the ropes hanging down from it.

Martin was chewing his mouth to stop crying. He looked around at us quickly. We were in a fairly close circle; nobody would face him, man after man looked down. Finally, like he was choking, he ducked his head, then, awkwardly because of the rope, got to his knees. The Mex was still standing, but had his head bent and was moving his lips rapidly. The old man was down in a groveling heap with Sparks beside him; Sparks was doing the praying for him. Moore took off his hat, and then the rest of us did the same. After a moment Davies and some of the others knelt also. Most of us couldn't bring ourselves to do that, but we all bowed and kept quiet. In the silence, in the gray light slowly increasing, the moaning of the old man,

Sparks' praying and the Mex going again and again through his rapid patter sounded very loud. Still you could hear every movement of the horses, leather creaking, the little clinks of metal.

"Time's up," Tetley said, and the old man wailed once, as if he'd been hit. The Mex lifted his head and glanced around quickly. His face had a new expression, the first we'd seen of it in him. Martin rose slowly to his feet, and looked around slowly. The moments of silence and the crisis had had the reverse effect on him. He no longer appeared desperate or incoherent, but neither did he look peaceful or resigned. I have never seen another face so bitter as his was then, or one that showed its hatred more clearly. He spoke to Davies, but even his voice proved the effort against his pride and detestation.

"Will you find someone you can trust to look out for my wife and children?" he asked. "In time she will repay anything it puts you out."

Davies' eyes were full of tears. "I'll find someone," he promised.

"You'd better take some older woman along," Martin said. "It's not going to be easy."

"Don't worry," Davies said, "your family will be all right."

"Thanks," Martin said. Then he said, "My people are dead, but Miriam's are living. They live in Ohio. And Drew didn't want to sell his cattle; he'll buy them back for enough to cover their travel."

Davies nodded.

"Better not give her my things," Martin said, "just this ring, if you'll get it."

Davies fumbled at the task. He had trouble with the rope, and his hands were shaking, but he got the ring, and held it up for Martin to see. Martin nodded. "Just give her that and my letter first. Don't talk to her until she's read my letter." He didn't seem to want to say any more.

"That all?" Tetley asked.

"That's all, thanks," Martin said.

They asked the Mex, and he suddenly started speaking very rapidly. He was staring around as if he couldn't quite see us. It had got to him finally, all right. Then he stopped speaking just as suddenly and kept shaking his head in little short shakes. He'd been talking in Spanish. They didn't ask the old man.

The three of them were lifted onto the horses and made to stand on them. Two men had to support old Hardwick.

"Tie their ankles," Mapes ordered.

"God," Gil whispered, "I was afraid they weren't going to." He felt it a great relief that their ankles were going to be tied.

Farnley got up on a horse and fixed the noose around each man's neck. Then he and Ma got behind two of the horses with quirts in their hands. Young Tetley had to be told twice to get behind his. Then he moved to his place like a sleepwalker, and didn't even know he had taken the quirt somebody put in his hand.

The old man, on the inside, was silent, staring like a fish, and already hanging on the rope a little in spite of the men holding him up. The Mex had gone to pieces too, buckling nearly as badly as Hardwick, and jabbering rapid and panicky in Spanish. When the horse sidled under him once, tightening the rope, he screamed. In the pinch Martin was taking it the best of the three. He kept his head up, not looking at any of us, and even the bitterness was gone from his face. He had a melancholy expression, such as goes with thinking of an old sorrow.

Tetley moved around behind the horses, and directed Mapes to give the signal. We all moved out of the circle to give the horses room. In the last second even the Mex was quiet. There was no sound save the shifting of the three horses, restless at having been held so long. A feathery, wide-apart snow was beginning to sift down again; the end of a storm, not the beginning of another, though. The sky was becoming transparent, and it was full daylight.

Mapes fired the shot, and we heard it echo in the mountain as Ma and Farnley cut their horses sharply across the haunches and the holders let go and jumped away. The horses jumped away too, and the branch creaked under the jerk. The old man and the Mex were dead at the fall, and just swung and spun slowly. But young Tetley didn't cut. His horse just walked out from under, letting Martin slide off and dangle, choking to death, squirming up and down like an impaled worm, his face bursting with compressed blood. Gerald didn't move even then, but stood there shaking all over and looking up at Martin fighting the rope.

After a second Tetley struck the boy with the butt of his pistol, a back-handed blow that dropped him where he stood.

"Shoot him," he ordered Farnley, pointing at Martin. Farnley shot. Martin's body gave a little leap in the air, then hung slack, spinning slowly around and back, and finally settling into the slowing pendulum swing of the others.

Gil went with Davies to help young Tetley up. Nobody talked much, or looked at anybody else, but scattered and mounted. Winder and Moore caught up the rustlers' ponies. The Bartlett boys and Amigo remained to drive the cattle, and to do the burying before they started. All except Mapes and Smith shied clear of Tetley, but he didn't seem to notice. He untied his big palomino, mounted, swung him about and led off toward the road. His face was set and white; he didn't look back.

Most of the rest of us did, though, turn once or twice to look. I was glad when the last real fall of the snow started, soft and straight and thick. It lasted only a few minutes, but it shut things out.

## 5

G IL CAUGHT up and rode with me after he and Davies had
helped Gerald. I'd thought, seeing him drop, that the kid
had been killed, but Gil said no, it had been a glancing blow,
that snow on his face and a drink had fixed him up enough to
ride.

We rode slowly because of my shoulder, letting the others
disappear ahead of us, and Gerald and Davies come up behind
us. It was difficult to turn in my saddle, but I did, to get a
look at Gerald. His face had a knife-edge, marble-white look,
and the circles under his eyes were big and dark, so that he
appeared to have enormous eyes, or none at all, but empty
sockets, like a skull. He wasn't looking where he was going,
but the trouble wasn't his injury. I don't think he knew now
that he had it. He was gnawing himself inside again. Passionate
and womanish, but with a man's conscience and pride, that boy
kept himself thin and bleached just thinking and feeling.

Davies, riding beside him, kept passing his hand over his face
in a nerveless way unusual to him, rubbing his nose or finger-
ing his mouth or drawing the hand slowly across his eyes and
forehead, as if there were cobwebs on his skin.

We were all tired, even Gil half asleep in his saddle, and we
nearly rode into the horses standing in the clearing before we
saw them. They were quietly bunched under the falling snow.

"It's the sheriff," Gil said. "It's Risley."

Then he said, "Jesus, it's Kinkaid."

It was too, with a bandage on his head, and a bit peaked, but
otherwise as usual, quiet, friendly and ashamed to be there.
The other three men, besides the sheriff, were Tyler, Drew and
Davies' pimply clerk Joyce. The Judge was red in the face and
talking violently, but through the snow his voice came short
and flat.

"It's murder, murder and nothing less. I warned you, Tetley,
I warned you repeatedly, and Davies warned you, and Osgood.
You all heard us; you were all warned. You wanted justice, did
you? Well, by God, you shall have it now, real justice. Every
man of you is under arrest for murder. We'll give you a chance

to see how slow regular justice is when you're in the other chair."

Nobody replied to him, that I could hear.

"My God," Gil said, "I knew it didn't feel right. I knew we should wait. That bastard Tetley," he finished.

Everybody would hang it on Tetley now. I didn't say anything.

The sheriff was stern, but he wasn't the kind to gabble easily, like Tyler. He was a small, stocky man with a gray, walrus mustache and black bushy eyebrows. He had a heavy sheepskin on, with the collar turned up around his ears. His deepset, hard, blue eyes looked at each of us in turn. Nobody but Tetley tried to hold up against his look, and even Tetley failed.

When he'd made us all look down, he said something we couldn't hear to the Judge. The Judge began to sputter, but when Risley looked level at him too the sputter died, and the Judge just stared around at us belligerently again, thrusting his lower lip out and sucking it in and making a hoarse, blowing noise.

Risley sat silent for a moment, as if considering carefully, looking us over all the time. Finally he stared into the snow over us and the milky blue shadows of the trees through it and said, "I haven't recognized anybody here. We passed in a snowstorm, and I was in a hurry."

"That's collusion, Risley," the Judge began loudly, getting redder than ever. "I'll have you understand I won't . . ."

"What do you want to do?" Risley cut in, looking at him.

The Judge tried to say something impressive about the good name of the valley and of the state, and the black mark against his jurisdiction and Risley's, but it was no use. Everybody just waited for him to stop; he couldn't hold out against all of us without Risley.

When he was just blowing again, Risley said, "I'm not even looking for the leaders. Nobody had to go if he didn't want to."

He went on in a changed tone, as if he had finished unimportant preliminaries and was getting down to business.

"I'll want ten men for my posse."

We all volunteered. We were tired, and we'd had plenty of

man hunting and judging to hold us for a long time, but we felt he was giving us a chance to square ourselves. Even Tetley volunteered, but Risley didn't notice him; he passed up Mapes also. But he took Winder, which added Gabe Hart, and he took Moore, and after looking at him for a long time he took Farnley. Kinkaid looked up at that, smiled a little and raised one hand off the horn just enough so Farnley could see it. Farnley straightened as if he'd had half a life given back to him. Farnley was mean with a grudge, but honest. If he didn't like Risley right then, he liked himself a lot less.

When Risley had selected his ten men, he ordered the rest of us to go home. "Go on about your own business," he told us. "Don't hang around in bunches. If you have to tell anybody anything, just tell them I'm taking care of this with a picked posse. You can't stop the talk, but there'll be a lot less fuss if you keep out of it. Nobody knew these men."

He turned to the Judge. "It'll have to be that way," he apologized.

"Perhaps, perhaps," the Judge muttered. "All the same—" and he subsided. Actually, though, he was relieved. We didn't have to worry about him.

Risley and Drew pushed through us, the chosen men falling in behind them. The rest began to drift down toward the valley. Tetley was left to ride by himself this time. But he was iron, that man; his face didn't show anything, not even weariness.

Davies stopped Risley and Drew. Both his manner and his speech were queerly fumbling, as if he were either exhausted or a little mad. While he spoke to them he twisted his bridle, occasionally jerking a length of it between his two hands, and then halting his speech for a moment while he rubbed his forehead and eyes that feeble way. When Drew had questioned him a bit they got it straight. For some obscure reason, connected apparently only with the way he felt, he didn't believe he should take that letter to Martin's wife. He wanted Drew to take it. He wanted Drew to get a woman to help Martin's wife too; he was much impressed by the need of the woman, and repeated it several times, saying it should be an older woman who had had children and wouldn't gush. He insisted that Drew must be able to see why he couldn't take the letter.

You could tell by Drew's face that he couldn't see. He was a

big, fleshy man with gray eyes, a yellow tan and a heavy, chest-
nut beard. He was wearing a gray frock coat and a Spanish
sombrero with silver conches on the band, and was smoking
a thin Mexican cigar. He talked with the cigar in the corner
of his mouth. He was taking the whole thing impatiently, as
business to be done. But then, he hadn't seen what we had.
And he wasn't totally without concern, because, when Davies
asked him, as if, somehow, the answer was very important to
him personally, if he had sold the cattle to Martin, he answered
only after a delay, and then said, "Yes, poor kid. A lot better for
him if I hadn't. It don't do to change your regular ways," he
added. "Men get to banking on them."

You could see he thought there was something queer about
the way Davies was acting, but he took the letter and the ring
from him, assuring him that he would send somebody he
could trust if he couldn't take them himself. He promised he
would send a woman too, a woman who would take care of
things and not be a sympathy monger. When Davies was still
fretful, like a man with a very orderly mind who is dying and
can't remember if everything is arranged, Drew became short
in his answers. But he also thought of the thing which seemed
to relieve Davies most for the moment; he hadn't wanted to
ask about it.

"I'll give his wife the money he paid me for the cattle, of
course," Drew said impatiently. "I have it with me; I haven't
even had a chance to get back to the house yet."

Then he got ready to go, but looked hard at Davies, and
decided to risk an opinion on something which wasn't strictly
any of his business.

"You'd better get some rest," he told Davies. "You're taking
this too hard. From what I've heard, you did all you could;
there's nothing you or anybody else can do about it now."

Davies looked at him as if Drew were the crazy one. But he
didn't say anything, just nodded.

Risley made a come-on motion with his hand to the posse,
and they filed off slowly on the snowy road. When they had
entered the aisle between the big pines they picked up to a
little jog, and finally disappeared, dimming away man by man
through the screen of falling snow. In the clearing there was
already beginning to be sunlight in the snow.

"Must have been that other bunch after all," Gil said.

"What?" Davies asked.

"The bunch Small and Carnes told us about."

"Oh," said Davies. "Yes, I suppose so."

When we reined around, Gil said, "What the hell's going on now?"

There weren't more than half a dozen riders left in the clearing; they were all bunched on the farther edge, where the ravine pitches down to the creek. Among them were two horses without riders; one of them was young Tetley's black.

We rode over to the edge too, and looked down with the others. About half way up the steep bank, scrambling in the snow and among the loose stones, and slipping on the pine needles, were Smith and Gerald. Smith had one arm around the boy, and was grabbing from bush to bush and at saplings to pull himself up. The kid didn't seem to be hurt, though, he just wasn't doing anything to help himself. Sparks dismounted and went part way down to give a hand to the pair. They came up that way, stumbling and sliding to the top, the kid dragging his feet and not even hanging on.

When they got up he stood by himself all right. Sparks kept a hand on his shoulder.

"What you want to try a thing like that foh, Mastah Tetley?" Sparks asked him. He was trying to prod the kid awake, but console him too. He was scared at what the kid had been doing. The others were scared too, but they were tired and they didn't care so much; they were resentful.

"He's crazy," Ma said, looking down at him.

Gerald didn't say anything. He shook Sparks' hand off his shoulder and walked over slowly to his horse and struggled up into the saddle.

"Keep an eye on him," Ma said. "He's crazy. You got the gun?" she asked Smith.

Smith held it up for her to see. "Damned young fool," he said proudly. "I didn't get down there any too soon. Maybe you think that bank isn't steep," he boasted, "and slick. By Godfreys I went down; thought I was gonna dive right in the creek."

"He wouldn't have done it," one of the riders said. He was a thin, middle-aged man with a long, thin nose and a thin, down-turned mouth. He looked sandy, weedy and sour. I didn't know him, or where he came from.

"What was he up to this time?" Gil asked.

Smith was excited and wanted to prove how quick he'd been.

"First thing we just noticed his horse," he said, "and nobody on it." He pointed at the horse, but if young Tetley heard he didn't look at us. "Well, I knew what he was thinking, of course. Who didn't? He hadn't been making any secret about it. Right off I picked the creek canyon as the place. Sure enough, there he was, standing by himself down at the bottom. He was just staring at the water then, but he had this gun in his hand," Smith held the gun up again, "and it didn't take more than one look to know what he was going to do. I tell you, I piled down there in a hurry. Lucky he didn't hear me till I was right on him; noise of the water, I guess. When he did hear me, he was going to do it quick, but I got to him." He looked around at us for admiration.

"He wouldn't have done it," the sour man said again.

"The hell he wouldn't," Smith said, raising his voice.

Young Tetley still didn't look at us, but started his horse for the narrows. Smith didn't notice; he was going right on to prove Gerald would have killed himself.

"We saw it," Ma said. She was watching Gerald.

But Smith had to convince the sour man. He lowered his voice, but went on waving the gun. The sour man was watching the gun; it made him nervous. Smith was going to explain how Tetley had made a fool of his son in front of everybody.

"You're certainly taking a lot of responsibility," the sour man said.

"Somebody had to," Smith yelled at him. "I didn't see you in any hurry."

"He wanted to, maybe," said the sour man, "but he couldn't have done it."

Smith was still going to argue it, but we were all moving away. He stared after the sour man for a minute, then spit and went over to his own horse.

He caught up with us and kept trying to prove Gerald would have shot himself, and on the side that Tetley was responsible for all the trouble. We didn't want to talk, or hear him talk, and finally he gave up and rode on ahead to try it on Ma.

On the way down we just stopped on a few level spots to give me a breather. My shoulder felt stiff and very big. We didn't talk except when I asked Gil for a drink or to light me a cigarette.

By the time we got to the fork at the foot of the grade it had stopped snowing and the sky was beginning to clear, not breaking up, but thinning away everywhere at once and letting pale sunlight through. It was still cold though, and the mountains on both sides of the valley were white to their bases.

On the edge of town Gil asked me, "How do you feel now?"

It seemed to cheer him up when I told him I was coming all right.

"The quicker we get out of this town," he said, "the better I'll feel."

I didn't feel like two days' riding right then. I had my mind set on food and a change of bandage and a bed. I didn't say anything.

He saw what I was thinking, though.

"Still," he said, "I wouldn't mind getting good and drunk and staying that way for a couple of days. We'll lay up at Canby's. Canby's as good as a doctor. And he don't gossip."

"I'll be all set by tomorrow," I told him.

"Sure," he said.

When we went in at Canby's Smith was already there, drinking and arguing. He was working himself up to a fit of righteousness. Canby was standing behind the bar, listening to him, but not showing anything or saying anything. Smith was quiet when he saw us, and began staring down into his drink as if he was thinking hard but keeping his thoughts to himself.

"What'll it be?" Canby asked us, like we'd just come in from work.

"We want a room," Gil said, looking at Smith hunched over his drink.

Canby looked at me. He knew all right. "Go on up," he said, "the front room's empty.

"The whole damn place is empty, for that matter," he continued, looking at Smith, "but the front room's all made up."

Gil put a hand on Smith's shoulder. Smith started to shake it off, but when Gil clinched it he stood still, not even trying to look around.

"Listen, fellow," Gil said, "don't talk so much."

We went up to the front room, which was bare and clean. There was a dresser with a wash bowl and a pitcher of water and a glass on it, a curtain strung across one corner for a closet, one chair, an iron double bed, and a small stove with nickel trimmings. Everything but the stove was painted white, and the curtain was heavy white canvas. The bed had clean but wrinkled linen on it. There was no carpet on the floor and no curtains on the two windows, which made the room seem scrubbed and full of light. Through the eastern window we could see the mountains with the snow on them, and through the other the street, with Davies' store right across from us. But it was cold in there too. While I lay down on the bed Gil built a fire in the stove. There was fresh-cut wood in a heap on the floor beside it. Then he came over and pulled my boots off for me.

"You lay here and take a rest for a while," he said. "I'll take the horses over to Winder's."

When he'd left I could hear Smith talking again downstairs. Then, after a bit, it was quiet. I was half asleep when the door opened and Canby came in. He had another armload of wood for the stove. He dumped it, and started putting some in.

"Monty won't talk for a while," he said, without looking around. "He's back in the poolroom with a whole bottle. Then he'll have to sleep it off."

"It doesn't matter anyway," I said. "Everybody knows."

"Yes," Canby said, straightening up, "but Smith strengthens the facts a bit."

He came over and stood by the bed.

"How's the shoulder?" he asked.

"Not so good," I admitted. "Smith tell you about that too?"

"No," he said, "he was telling me mostly about how he saved young Tetley, and what a first-rate bastard Tetley was, and more about how he saved young Tetley. You didn't walk right," he explained.

"Let me have a look at it," he went on, starting to undo my shirt.

"You a doctor?" I asked him.

"You have to know a little of everything in this business," he said. "Somebody's always getting hurt. They come in to get their courage up, and then they have to prove it."

He peeled me down to my shoulder, and then yanked the rags off. He was neat and quick about it, but they stuck a little before they came away. The shoulder under them was swollen and dark red, the bullet hole looking little and dark in it, like the head of a boil. I had to grind my teeth when he felt around it.

"It could be better," he said. "I'll be back in a minute."

When he came back he had a pitcher of hot water, a jar of some kind of ointment, and some clean strips of white cloth. He squeezed the wound open again, washed it out, and rubbed in the ointment, which burned. Then he bandaged it snugly.

"No," he said while he was finishing up, "Rose Mapen was in for a minute last night, with her new attachment and the duenna. Pretty proper Rose is getting these days. She told me you'd been shot. She said you weren't very polite about their helping either."

"I don't like women around; not the fussy kind anyway," I told him.

"No," he agreed.

"I'll bet Gil was tickled to see them," he said. "I'll bring you up something to eat when Gil gets back."

"I can come down," I said. "There's nothing the matter with my legs."

"No need," he said.

I told him Gil was going to get drunk, and asked him to keep an eye out. He said he would, and went out, closing the door.

I lay there dozing and letting the ointment work. The fire was burning well now, and with that and the sun in the east window the room was getting warm. The sunlight was cheerful too. I didn't feel much connected with anything that had happened, not even my own wound.

I must have fallen asleep, and they didn't want to wake me. The next thing I knew it was afternoon. The room was still warm but there was no sun any more. I forgot about the shoulder and stretched and remembered it. Downstairs I could hear the voices of a number of men. They sounded distant, and didn't interest me. But I was really hungry.

I started to get up to go downstairs and eat, and then I saw Davies. He was sitting on the one chair, looking at the floor. Waking up from a sleep that had freshened me and put the night's business behind me some, I was surprised to see how bad he looked. His hair was tangled from running his hands through it, and he had a little white stubble of beard. He looked tired too, his face slack and really old, with big bruised pouches under the eyes. But that wasn't what made him look so bad. It was his forehead and eyes. His forehead was knotted and his eyes were too steady, like a careful drunk's, but not fogged in that way, but so bright they were mad. The whites of them were bloodshot too, and the rims a raw red, which made that light blue look even crazier. He was so tired he would have keeled over if he'd given up, but he hadn't given up. He was still fighting something.

I sat up as quick as I dared.

"What's wrong?" I asked.

He looked up when he heard the bed creak, but didn't seem to hear me.

"How's the shoulder?" he asked. "You feel better?"

His voice was husky and worn out, as if he'd been arguing for hours.

"It's all right," I said. "Canby fixed it up good."

"You had a long sleep," he said.

"I didn't know you were here."

"It's all right. No hurry. Now or another time; it wouldn't matter."

He wanted to say something, but couldn't get started. I was afraid of it. I didn't want to get mixed up in anything more. But I had to give him a chance to unload.

"You don't look like you'd slept much," I told him.

"I haven't," he said, "any."

I waited.

He got up with slow labor and went to the window where he could look out into the street. Without turning around he said, "Croft, will you listen to me?"

"Sure," I said, but not encouraging him.

"I've got to talk," he protested. "I've got to talk so I can get some sleep."

I didn't say anything.

"I thought about everybody who was up there," he explained, "and I have to talk to you, Art. You're the only one will understand."

Why in hell, I wondered, did everybody have to take me for his father confessor?

"Maybe you'll think I'm crazy," he said, still at the window.

"You sound like you had a confession to make."

He turned around. "That's it," he said, more quickly. "That's it, Croft, a confession."

I still waited.

"Croft," he said, "I killed those three men."

I just stared.

"I told you you'd think I was crazy," he said.

Well, I did, and I didn't like a man twice my age confessing to me.

"As much as if I'd pulled the ropes," he was saying.

"Why blame anybody?" I asked him. "It's done now."

"No, it's not done," he said, "it's just beginning. Every act," he began.

I broke in. "If we have to blame somebody," I said, "then I'd say . . ."

This time he stopped me.

"I know," he said, almost angrily, "you'd say it was Tetley. That's what you all say. Smith's been preaching it was Tetley. He has himself all worked up to lynch Tetley."

"Well, wasn't it?"

"No," he said, and then seemed to be making sure of his thought. "No," he said again, after a moment, "Tetley couldn't help what he did."

"Oh, that way," I said. "If you take it that way, nobody can help it. We're all to blame, and nobody's to blame. It just happened."

"No," he said. "Most of you couldn't help it. Most men can't; they don't really think. They haven't any conception of basic justice. They . . ."

"I got all that," I told him. I thought I had too. It seemed to have ironed out while I slept, so I knew right away what he meant by anything he started.

"Yes," he said, smiling hard, and looking down at my sharpness.

"Most people," he went on slowly, "all of those men, see the sins of commission, but not of omission. They feel guilty now, when it's done, and they want somebody to blame. They've chosen Tetley."

"If it's anybody," I began.

"No," he interrupted, "not any more than the rest of you. He's merely the scapegoat. He recognized only the sin of commission, and he couldn't feel that. Sin doesn't mean anything to Tetley any more."

"That doesn't mean he wasn't wrong," I said.

"No," Davies said, "but not to blame."

"If you look at it that way," I said, "only a saint could be to blame for anything."

"There's some truth in that."

I was mean then, but I wanted to shut him up before he'd talked so much he'd be ashamed of it afterwards. You can hate a man you've talked too much to. He's like a man who's seen you show yellow.

"Meaning you're a saint?" I asked him.

He looked at me, but didn't wait even to make sure how I meant it. He was just following his own trouble.

"Something like that," he said without a smile, "by comparison. Or I was before this," he added after a moment. "Oh, God," he said suddenly. "That boy; all night."

He closed his eyes hard and turned back to the window. Holding onto the window sash, he pressed his forehead against his hand and leaned there, trembling all over, like a woman who's been told pretty bad news too suddenly.

I waited until he wasn't shaking, and then asked him, easy as I could, "Meaning this was a sin of omission?"

He moved his head to say yes, but still keeping it against his hand.

"You're thinking about it too much," I told him. "You're making it all up." I was embarrassed that he could show so much emotion. It wasn't natural. Most old men have their feelings so thinned out they can't be much stirred, or their habits so set they can't show it if they are. He was like a boy, or a woman who hasn't had to work much with her body.

He moved his head again, to say no.

I got up off the bed. "You get some sleep," I said. "You can sleep right here. I'm going down and get some grub. I'll tell Canby not to let anybody bother you."

He shook his head, but then turned around slowly, not looking at me.

"You're cutting it too fine," I told him. "This was a sin of commission if I ever saw one. We hung three men, didn't we? Or was that a nightmare I had?"

He looked up at me so I began to hope I was reaching him. All of a sudden I felt awful sorry for that little, bent, old man, ripping himself up about something most of us wouldn't have known was there.

"And if anybody came out of it clean," I said, "you're the one. You and Sparks, and Sparks was just letting it go."

You'd have thought I was offering him his first water after two days in the dry hills in August. He nearly whispered.

"Do you think so, Croft," he whispered, "really?"

"Sure," I said, "I know so. Now you get some sleep," I said, shaking up the bed to get my own dent out of it.

"You'll see it from the outside when you've slept," I told him.

When I straightened up and looked at him again that light was all gone out of him.

Now what the hell have I said? I wondered.

"Now what's the matter?" I asked him.

He stared at me out of an old and heavy face again, and the eyes dead in it too now. I thought he was going to pass out, and started to give him a hand.

He brushed me off with a short, angry gesture, and stood there swaying like he was drunk.

"For a minute I was going to believe it," he said hoarsely. "Oh, I want to believe it, all right. All day," he went on, "I've been trying to convince myself I was the saint. For a minute," he said, with a little, crazy laugh, "I thought you really knew."

I didn't have anything clear by now.

"If you mean all that about justice," I began.

"Yes, all that about justice," he said.

"I got that," I assured him. "I got that so I could tell what you were thinking every move; like it was me."

"Could you?" he asked.

"Sure. Every move.

"Listen," I argued, "if being able to think of all those things but still not stop it, is all that makes your sin of omission, then I'm as guilty as you are. More, for that matter," I added. "I didn't even try to do anything. Why was it your business any more than mine?"

"You knew what I was thinking?" he insisted.

"Every move. And so did most of the rest, for that matter."

"They couldn't have," he said hopefully.

"They did. They wouldn't have argued it the same way, maybe, but they knew it was there. They could feel it. And they didn't do anything either. Why, if that's all you mean," I burst out when he just kept watching me like I still might say something, "we're all more guilty than you are. You tried. You're the only one that did try. And Tetley's the worst of all. They're right about Tetley."

"Tetley's a beast," Davies said suddenly, with more hatred in his voice than I'd have thought he could have against anybody.

"A depraved, murderous beast," he said, the same way.

"Now," I said, "you're talking sense."

He was quiet at once, as if I had accused him of something, and then said slowly, "But a beast is not to blame."

"He loved it," I said.

Again he searched me, as if to determine how deep my reasons went, and as if it would set him free if they went deep enough.

"Yes," he agreed, "he loved it. He extracted pleasure from every morsel of suffering. He protracted it as long as he could. It was all one to him, the boy's mental torment, the old man's animal fear, the Mex taking that bullet out of his leg. Did you see his face when the Mex was taking that bullet out of his leg?" he asked.

"I saw it. He loved it."

"Yes," he said, "and his son."

"You mean hitting him?"

"And the rest," he said, "clear to the end."

"He's always been like that about Gerald," I said.

"Tetley is a vile man," he said slowly. "That is the only security I have."

I was lost again. He seemed to have some central conception that was the core of the whole thing to him, but to be afraid to get at it, to keep working around it, and losing me all the time.

"Only two things mean anything to Tetley," he said, "power and cruelty. He can't feel quiet or gentle things any more; and he can't feel pity, and he can't feel guilt."

"You know that?" I asked. "Then why be so hard on yourself?"

Davies didn't answer that.

"I keep telling myself," he said, "that I couldn't have changed it; that even though Tetley can't be blamed, I couldn't have made him see."

"That's right," I said.

"And I wouldn't have killed him," Davies said.

"God, no," I said.

"And nothing else would have helped."

"No," I said, "nothing else. Maybe," I said, "that's what made us all feel yellow. We didn't think it that way, but just knew we'd have to kill him, that we couldn't stop him any other way. And you can't do that. He was like a crazy animal," I said, remembering, "cold crazy."

"Yes," Davies said, "cold crazy."

Neither of us said anything for a minute, and I heard the voices downstairs in the bar and knew there was a change in them. At first I couldn't figure out what it was. Then I heard a woman laugh, a deep, throaty, pleased laugh, and then her voice saying something, and her laugh again, and a lot of men joining the laugh. Then it was all quiet but one voice, a man's voice, telling something long, and then the woman's laugh again, and the general laugh, as if they were just a little slower than she was to get the point. At first, thinking about Davies still, I couldn't figure what it was that was bothering me about that talk and laughing. Then the man spoke again, and I knew. It was Rose and her husband down there. And Gil had said he was going to get drunk. I didn't know how long I'd been asleep, or whether Gil had already got drunk and passed out and Canby had put him to bed somewhere else, not to bother me, or what. Only I knew Gil wasn't down there now; not with all that laughing, and I didn't like to think what could happen if he did come in drunk and still spoiling for his fight and feeling mean about last night.

I got to feeling mean myself. They laughed again down there. I didn't see how anybody could find anything to laugh at today. They sounded like fools.

Davies had said something.

"What?" I asked.

"He killed the boy, too," Davies repeated.

"Sure," I said, trying to get back to where I'd been. "All three of them."

"No, Gerald," he said.

"Gerald?" I echoed.

"You haven't heard then?" he asked, and that seemed to be another of those peculiar disappointments to him. "I thought you'd have heard."

"I've been right here, sleeping. What would I have heard?"

"That Gerald did kill himself."

"He didn't," I said. I was like the sour man. I still didn't think he'd try again.

Davies sat down slowly in the chair. Then he sat there twisting his hands.

"You didn't think he would?" he asked finally, with that same big question.

"No," I said. "He couldn't have. He talked too much."

"He did, though," Davies said. "He did." And suddenly he put his head down and clung to it with both hands, passing through another seizure like the one at the window.

Then he was quiet again, and looked up, though not at me, and told me evenly, "When he got home his father had locked the house against him. He went out into the barn and hanged himself from a rafter. The hired man found him about noon. I saw him," he said slowly. His hands stopped twisting and gripped together.

"Jeez, the poor kid," I said.

"Yes," he said, "the poor kid."

And then, "The hired man was afraid to tell Tetley. He saw Sparks and told him, and Sparks came for me."

"Did you have to see Tetley then?"

"I didn't want to. I didn't trust myself. But I saw him."

I didn't ask the question, but he answered it anyway.

"It meant nothing to him; not a flicker. Just thanked me as if I'd delivered a package from the store."

The news was like a home punch to me too. I should have known if anybody should, after the way the kid had opened up to me. Also I could see why that might have put Davies off on this spree of blaming himself. It could have been prevented so easily; just somebody to stay with the kid. The sins of omission.

They laughed again downstairs.

Shut up, you brainless bastards, I thought. I guess I half said it, because Davies looked up at me.

"That's not your fault," I said. "With Tetley what he is, it would have happened sooner or later anyway. There's some things you can't butt in on."

"But you didn't think it would happen?"

"No," I said. "Well, I was wrong."

"I did," he whispered. "I knew."

"You couldn't. *I* should have. He talked to me all the way up. I knew then he wasn't straight. But when he didn't, when he let Smith go down and get him like that, I didn't think he'd make another try. You couldn't know."

He suddenly switched our talk again. He couldn't sit still, tired as he was, but got up and went to the window.

"I'm not making a very clear confession, am I?"

"Listen, Mr. Davies," I started, and stopped because the men were laughing again downstairs and the laugh stopped short. I was listening for Gil's voice. But it must have been just a short laugh, the sort you get when the story has to go on. One voice was talking steadily, and though I couldn't hear the words I could hear the way they were clipped off, and the smooth, level tone. Rose's husband. Then he got his big, final laugh, and somebody else started.

I don't think Davies had even heard them. He thought I just couldn't find anything to say, and turned to face me once more, and there was neither that hope or the blind self-torture showing in his face for the moment. There was more a balance, as though he had finally decided exactly what to say and was intent upon my reply. That look brought me back too, so I was only half listening for Gil.

"You say you know what I was thinking all the time?" he asked.

"I could feel it," I said carefully. "We all could."

"Did you believe Martin was innocent?" he asked. "I mean at the time, before we knew. Did you believe he was innocent when they put the rope up over the limb?" he put it.

I stayed careful. "I felt we were wrong," I said slowly, looking right at him, "I felt that he shouldn't hang."

"That's scarcely the same thing," he said. "Nobody wants to see a man hang."

"You couldn't *know* he was innocent," I said. "None of us would have stood there and seen him hang if we'd known."

"No," Davies said. "So you didn't know." He was very quiet saying that.

"You're twisting it again," I told him sharply.

"No," he said, "you didn't know, but I did."

Then it struck me so it made the blood come to my own face. He'd known something all along, and been afraid to bring it out, because of Tetley. He'd had a proof, perhaps in that letter, and been afraid for his own skin to bring it out. I could see then why he wanted to believe nothing could have turned Tetley.

"How could you know?" I tried to bluff, but my voice didn't sound right and he caught it.

"Yes," he said. "I knew. I'd read that letter."

He got my question again.

"No," he said, "not that way. There was nothing a court would have called a proof. A court won't take the picture of a man's soul for a proof. But I knew then, beyond any question, what he was like. From the first I felt a boy like that couldn't have done it; not the rustling even; certainly not the murder. And when I'd read that letter I knew it."

So I was wrong again.

"Is that all?" I asked.

"He talked about me in the letter," Davies mooned. "He told his wife how kind I was to him, what I risked trying to defend him. And he trusted me; you saw that. He worked so hard to ease it for his wife, too," he went on, lower. "To keep her from breaking herself on grief or hating us. And he reminded her of things they had done together."

He bent his head in a spasm again. "It was a beautiful letter," he whispered.

"Listen," I said, "that may all make you feel bad, sure. It was a rotten deal, sure. But we all knew we should have brought them in like you said, and if we had, it never would have happened."

"Half an hour," Davies mumbled. "Half an hour would have done it."

"I know," I said. "You think I haven't thought of that too? But there wasn't anything you could do."

"I knew," he repeated. His knowing seemed to be what hurt him most.

"You didn't know," I told him, "any more than the rest of us did. You knew what he was like from that letter, you say. Well, maybe. But we all had a chance to see that letter. That kind of an argument can't stand up against branded cattle, no bill of sale, a dead man's gun, and a guy that acts like that Mex did."

"It could have," he said. "You admit yourself you were ready to be stopped. You admit you thought most of them were."

"There wasn't the proof," I said angrily. "You don't get all set for a hanging and stop for some little feeling you have."

"You might," he said, "when you're hanging on a feeling too."

"You tried to stop it, hard enough and often enough," I said.

"That's the point," he said. This calm and reasonable self-denunciation was worse than when he broke a little. "I tried. I took the leadership, and with it I accepted the responsibility. I set myself up as the power of justice, of common pity, even. I set myself up as the light to oppose Tetley's darkness. And in their hearts the men were with me; and the right was with me. Everything was with me."

"Everything," I reminded him, "except what we all took to be the facts."

"They didn't matter then," he maintained. "They didn't matter."

"God," I said, "if you take any pleasure in feeling responsible for three gang hangings and a suicide."

He closed his eyes like I'd slapped him.

"I'm sorry," I said.

"No, you're right," he said. "I was."

"You get some sleep," I ordered. He'd skirted the point again, if he had one. He was just cutting himself up.

"You'll admit I took it on myself to stand up against Tetley," he persisted.

"All right, you did. There were none of us there hog-tied, or tongue-tied either, for that matter."

He looked at me. I was going to say something more, but suddenly the chatter downstairs stopped, and there was one voice, a new one, had it all; and it was loud and thick and angry. It wasn't till then that I realized how much I was worried about Gil. I had my hand out to take my gun belt off the foot of the bed before I knew it wasn't Gil talking, but Smith. Drunk, too, by the sound. He had it to himself for a minute. Then I heard the deep, even rumble that was Canby. Then Smith, louder than before, even, and Canby pretty short, and it was quiet. Finally a subdued general talk started again.

I went over to the table by the east window and poured myself a glass of water. My hand was trembling so I slopped water on the floor. The shoulder burned, and I was dizzy. I drank the water off, and felt better, though it was cold and trickling in my empty gut. I was angry at shaking up so easy. I wished Davies would get done. His conscience was getting too big for me. I was used to confessions, but I was lost in this one.

When I turned around Davies was at the window, staring out again. I crossed and sat down on the bed again, to get the dizziness over. He came and stood by the foot of the bed.

"I won't bother you much longer, Art," he said.

"You're not bothering me."

"A man ought to keep things to himself," he said. "Even guilt, unless there's something can be done about it. Confession's no good except for the one confessing. Only I want to be sure," he finished.

"Sure of what?"

"Art, you say you know what I was thinking—" He stopped.

There it was again; that question. And I knew I didn't have the answer this time either. I just sat and waited and didn't look at him.

"Art, just when they were going to hang them, when the ropes were up, what was it I was thinking?"

"How would I know? A man thinks about funny things at a time like that. Every man's would be different. Maybe a song you heard once. I don't know."

"What would you think?" he insisted.

"Like all of us, I suppose. That you wished it didn't have to be done; at least not there in front of you. Or that it was all over, and the poor bastards were dead and happy."

"You didn't think it could be stopped?" he asked.

"It was too late for that."

"You didn't think of using your gun?"

That surprised me. "On what?" I asked.

"Tetley," he said.

"You mean . . ."

"No, just to force him to take them back for trial."

"No," I said finally, "I don't think I did. It was all settled. I had a kind of wild idea for a moment, but I didn't really think of it. You get those wild ideas, you know, out of nothing, when you have to do something you don't much like. I didn't really think of it, no," I said again.

"Did you have a feeling it would have worked? That you could have turned the whole thing right then? Or that somebody could have?"

I thought. "No," I said, "I guess not. I guess I just thought it was settled. I didn't like it, but it was settled."

"It should have been stopped," he said, "even with a gun."

"I can see that now."

"I could see it then," he said.

"You didn't even *have* a gun."

"No," he said, "no, I didn't," as if admitting the ultimate condemnation of himself.

After a moment I admitted, "I guess you're not twisting it; I guess I am. I don't see what you've got to feel bad about."

"I thought of all that," he said. "Do you see? I knew Tetley could be stopped then. I knew you could all be turned by one man who would face Tetley with a gun. Maybe he wouldn't even have needed a gun, but I told myself he would. I told myself he would to face Tetley, because Tetley couldn't bear to be put down, and because Tetley was mad to see those three men hang, and to see Gerald made to hang one of them. I told myself you'd have to stop him with fear, like any animal from a kill."

"You were right," I said. "I wasn't thinking much then; but you were right."

"It doesn't matter whether I was right or not. Do you know what I felt when I thought that, Croft?"

I thought he was going to answer his own question, and let it go. But he didn't.

"Can't you guess, Croft?" he begged.

"No," I said slowly, "I can't. What?"

"I was glad, Croft, glad I didn't have a gun."

I didn't look up. I felt something rotten in what he was

saying, or maybe just that he was saying it. It was obscure, but I didn't want to look at him.

"Now do you see," he said triumphantly, like all he had wanted to do was make himself out the worst he could. "I knew those men were innocent. I knew it as surely as I do now. And I knew Tetley could be stopped. I knew in that moment you were all ready to be turned. And I was glad I didn't have a gun."

He was silent, except that I could hear him breathing hard over what he seemed to consider an unmerciful triumph, breathing as if he had overcome something tremendous, and could begin to rest now. I could hear the talking downstairs again too. There wasn't much laughing now, though. For some reason I was relieved that there wasn't much laughing, as if, coming at that moment, even from downstairs, it would have been too much.

But he had to rub it in.

"Yes, you see now, don't you?" he said in a low voice. "I had everything, justice, pity, even the backing—and I knew it—and I let those three men hang because I was afraid. The lowest kind of a virtue, the quality dogs have when they need it, the only thing Tetley had, guts, plain guts, and I didn't have it."

"You take it too hard," I said, still looking at the floor. "You take it too much on yourself. There was no reason  . . ."

"Don't trouble yourself," he said hoarsely. "I know what you think. And you're right. Oh, don't you worry," he said, before I could call him, "I've thought of all the excuses. I told myself I was the emissary of peace and truth, and that I must go as such; that I couldn't even wear the symbol of violence. I was righteous and heroic and calm and reasonable."

He paused, and I could feel the bed shaking under his hands.

"All a great, cowardly lie," he said violently. "All pose; empty, gutless pretense. All the time the truth was I didn't take a gun because I didn't want it to come to a showdown. The weakness that was in me all the time set up my sniveling little defense. I didn't even expect to save those men. The most I hoped was that something would do it for me.

"Something," he said bitterly.

Then I thought he was done, but he wasn't. Getting over the hump, the big fact of what he saw as his cowardice, had just unplugged him. He let it all come. He was so tired he was like a blind man in a strange room, always bumping into something, the chair, the wash stand, the foot of the bed, but he couldn't stay anywhere long. Only now and then he'd sit down, or stand briefly in front of one of the windows, looking out, or by the bed, looking at me. It got so I knew from where he was and the tone of his voice when he started, what he was going to talk about. When he was stumbling around, his voice would be hoarse and his words tumultuous, and then it was always self-condemnation or a blast against Tetley, but with the blasts always ending in blaming himself too, more quietly, as if each time he saw anew the injustice of accusing Tetley. When he was sitting in the chair he would be still for a long time, and then begin, in a low, breaking voice, to remember something about Martin, or Martin's wife and children as he saw them from that letter. The letter was an obsession itself. When he came to stand over me, it was to offer another clear proof, as he saw it now, that the flaw had been in him from the start, that he had never really hoped to save those men or force justice.

Once, when he had subsided into the chair and was silent longer than usual, I could hear that Rose and her husband weren't down in the bar any longer, and after that I listened better.

Even so it was hard talk to hear because there wasn't any answer. It was disordered and fragmentary, but if you admitted the big point, his own guilt, it wasn't illogical, and it was impossible to make him see that nobody else could think him guilty. I tried just once to make him see that, and he turned and stared at me till I was done, which didn't take long, and then laughed hard and suddenly, and stopped laughing suddenly and said, oh, yes, he was trying to play the Christ all right, but it wasn't a part for cowards, and it hadn't needed a Christ anyway; all it had needed was a man. And after that he would end each tirade against himself with another sudden laugh about trying to play the Christ. I had to let him go; if anything would help, that would. We couldn't bridge the gap; he was all inside, I was all outside.

Finally, though, he was played out. He'd talked more than an hour; I wasn't sure, maybe two. From where I was sitting on the bed I could see through the window that it was late-afternoon sun on the eastern hills, and that the snow was almost gone from them already. It was a sad light, but lovely and peaceful, glowing as if it burned within the hills themselves. Then Davies just sat there with his head in his hands, now and then bending it so his fingers ran through his hair, but then lifting his head again, as if each time he decided he wouldn't break, but stand it.

"You'd better get that sleep now," I said, as quiet as I could.

He looked at me slowly, bringing his mind back. He appeared nearly dead, the hollows of his face so sunken that his skull showed in startling relief. But his eyes were a lot calmer, and though he was shivering, it wasn't with that tightness any longer, but just as if he were exhausted and cold.

"I might as well, hadn't I?" he said.

He got up slowly and came to stand by the foot of the bed again.

"I'm sorry, Art," he said.

"It's all right," I said. "You had to. You can rest now."

He nodded.

I must have forgotten the voices downstairs, which had grown quieter as it got toward supper time, for I didn't even realize that Gil's was one of them now, until I heard somebody running on the boardwalk under the arcade, and coming in below us, slamming the door so the talk stopped. I stood up quickly, still listening, but there was just the one voice, young and excited, some boy, and then exclamations without anger, and a low murmur. I withdrew my hand from the gun belt again. I'd have to get Gil in sight to feel easy.

Davies said, as though it didn't matter now, "I've even thought—" and paused so long I said, "What?"

"I've even thought," he said, "that I wouldn't have needed a gun, that at the very end Tetley knew he was wrong too, and all I'd have had to do was say so."

I shook my head. "No," I said, "you were right in the first place. He was frozen onto that hanging. You'd have had to hit him over the head to bring him out of it."

"I hold to that," he said, like he was really hanging on hard to something. "I hold to that."

And after a moment, "That he couldn't have been moved, that there was for him no realization of sin."

"There wasn't," I said. "You'd have had to kill him."

There was no talk in the bar now, and I could hear somebody coming up the stairs.

"And I couldn't have done that," Davies said slowly. "And though even that might have been better, it is not altogether a weakness that I couldn't."

"Nobody could have done that," I told him. I was glad he'd come back to that idea. It would be a saver for him.

"No," he said wearily, and nodded.

"If I didn't believe that—" he said.

"You couldn't have stopped him any other way," I assured him.

"No," he said.

The door opened, and it was Gil and Canby.

"Hello," Canby said to both of us, and then to me, "How long have you been awake? I just came up to see if you wanted something to eat."

"I'll come down," I told him and, when he asked, said the shoulder was doing fine.

Gil was drunk, all right, in his steady way.

"Sorry," he said, "didn't know you had company," as if he'd found me with a girl.

"It's all right," Davies said, "I was just going."

"Did he wake you up?" Gil asked, belligerently, looking hard at us, to focus.

"I was awake," I said. "Where did you go to get that drunk without my hearing you?"

"I took the horses over to Winder's," he said, "and he wanted to drink. He felt pretty low about the business."

"*He* did?" I said.

"Bill's not a bad guy, when you get to know him," Gil maintained; "only pig-headed.

"Anyway," he said cheerfully, "we won't have to have another hanging. Tetley took care of himself."

It caught me wide open, and I made a bad cover.

"Oh, Gerald, you mean?" I said, after too long a wait. "Yeah, I heard," and tried to signal him off. He didn't get it.

"No," he said, "his old man too. After he heard about the kid he locked himself in the library and jumped on a sword. They had to break the door open to get him. Saw him through the window, lying on his face in there on the rug, with that big cavalry sword of his sticking up through his back."

Canby saw me glance at Davies, and I guess I looked as funny as I felt. Canby turned quick to look at him too.

"Who would have thought the old bastard had that much feeling left in him?" Gil said.

Davies just stood there for a moment, staring at Gil. Then he made a little crying noise in his throat, a sort of whimper, like a pup, and I thought he was going to cave. He didn't, though. He made that noise again, and then suddenly went out, closing the door behind him. We could hear him on the stairs, whimpering more and more. Once, by the sound, he fell.

"What in hell ails the prophet?" Gil asked.

"Go get him," I told Canby, and when he stood there trying to see what I meant, "you can't leave him alone, I tell you." And then started to go myself. But Canby caught on, and pushed past me, and went out and down the stairs three or four at a time. I went to the window, and saw Davies already out in the street. He was sagging in the knees, but trying to run like he had to get away from something. I saw Canby catch up with him, and Davies try to fight him off, but then give up. They came back together, Davies with his head down and wobbling loose on his neck. Canby was half holding him up.

"What in hell ails him?" Gil asked again, watching over my shoulder.

I heard Canby getting him up the stairs, and went over and closed the door. But we could still hear the shuffle of their feet, and Davies whimpering constantly now, like a woman crazy with grief. We listened while the shuffle and whimper passed the door and went down the hall, and then was shut off by another door closing.

"What's the matter?" Gil asked, scared.

"He had a notion he was to blame," I told him.

"For what?"

"The whole business."

"*He* was?" Gil said. "That's a good one."

"Isn't it?" I said. I didn't want to talk about it. I felt sick for the old man.

We both thought about it for a minute.

"Well," Gil said, "you better eat something. All this time, and losing that blood."

"I'm not hungry," I told him. I wasn't, either.

"You better eat, though," he said. "I gotta eat too," he added. "I can't drink any more till I eat something."

Going down the stairs he said back up at me, "Smith was all for getting up a lynching party for Tetley, till we heard."

"Smith's a great hanger," I said.

"Ain't he," Gil said.

We ate out in the back room, where it was already laid out for us, salt pork, winter rotten potatoes, beans and black coffee. At first it stuck in my throat, but I drank two cups of the coffee, and was hungry again. Canby came in while we were eating, and said Davies would be all right, he'd given him something to make him sleep and sent Sparks up to be with him. There was nobody in the bar, so he stood watching us eat, with his towel in his hand. He said the story was all over town all right, that it took more to pass Smith out than he'd thought. But in one way it was working out good. They were taking up a pot for Martin's wife. There was more than five hundred dollars in it already.

"Even old Bartlett chipped in," Canby said, "but he's not showing his face around much. He sent the money down by Sparks."

"That reminds me," Gil said, as if it hadn't been on his mind, "I put in twenty-five apiece for us."

I squared with him out of my Indian sack.

"She picked a good time for the pot, anyway," Canby said. "Roundup over and none of you guys taken yet.

"It's not a bad price at that," he added, "for a husband that don't know any better than to buy cattle in the spring without a bill of sale."

He went back out to the bar, and we could hear him talking to somebody out there.

After a while, when he wasn't talking any more, we went out, and Gil and Canby had their joke about the "Bitching Hour," and we had a couple of drinks and a smoke. I didn't want any more; what I still wanted was sleep. It seemed as if I hadn't even got started on the sleeping I could do. I've noticed it works that way, when there's something bothering you that you can't do anything about, you always get sleepy. Besides, there were men beginning to come in who hadn't been up there with us. They would look at us, and then stay at the other end of the bar and talk to Canby in low voices, now and then sneaking another look at us. Gil was getting sore about it. He still hadn't had the fight he wanted, and he was drinking like he was just a pipe through the floor. He would stand there, staring at the men, and just waiting for one of them to say something he could start on.

When Rose Mapen came in again, all big smiles and walking like she was at the head of a parade, and the man with the red sideburns right behind her, I was scared. But Gil fooled me. He picked up the bottle and two glasses and said, "Come on, I don't want to fight that guy now. I'd kill him."

Up in the room I stretched out on the bed. Gil put the bottle and glasses on the dresser and went over and looked out of the window into the street. It was about sunset, a clear sky again, and everything still. Gil opened the window, and the cool air came in, full of the smell of the meadows. Way off we could hear the meadow larks. Gil poured himself a drink and lit another cigarette. He blew the smoke hard, and it went out the window in a long, quick stream.

"I gave Winder the ten to give Farnley," he said, like that made up for something.

"That's good," I said.

Downstairs we could hear Rose talking and then laughing and all the men laughing after her, the way they had in the afternoon. She was on show all right.

"If I started a fight with that guy, it would come to shootin'," Gil said.

"We've had enough of that," I told him.

"I know it," he said, "but I don't know how to start a decent fight with that kind of a guy."

And then, like he was giving it a lot of attention, "He's a funny guy. I don't know how you'd start a decent fight with him."

Tink-tink-a-link went the meadow lark. And then another one, even farther off, teenk-teenk-a-leenk.

Then Gil said, "I'll be glad to get out of here," as if he'd let it all go.

"Yeh," I said.

# SHANE

*Jack Schaefer*

TO CARL
for my first son
my first book

# I

H E RODE into our valley in the summer of '89. I was a kid
then, barely topping the backboard of father's old chuck-
wagon. I was on the upper rail of our small corral, soaking
in the late afternoon sun, when I saw him far down the road
where it swung into the valley from the open plain beyond.

In that clear Wyoming air I could see him plainly, though
he was still several miles away. There seemed nothing remarkable about him, just another stray horseman riding up the road
toward the cluster of frame buildings that was our town. Then
I saw a pair of cowhands, loping past him, stop and stare after
him with a curious intentness.

He came steadily on, straight through the town without
slackening pace, until he reached the fork a half-mile below
our place. One branch turned left across the river ford and on
to Luke Fletcher's big spread. The other bore ahead along the
right bank where we homesteaders had pegged our claims in a
row up the valley. He hesitated briefly, studying the choice, and
moved again steadily on our side.

As he came near, what impressed me first was his clothes.
He wore dark trousers of some serge material tucked into tall
boots and held at the waist by a wide belt, both of a soft black
leather tooled in intricate design. A coat of the same dark
material as the trousers was neatly folded and strapped to his
saddle-roll. His shirt was finespun linen, rich brown in color.
The handkerchief knotted loosely around his throat was black
silk. His hat was not the familiar Stetson, not the familiar gray
or muddy tan. It was a plain black, soft in texture, unlike any
hat I had ever seen, with a creased crown and a wide curling
brim swept down in front to shield the face.

All trace of newness was long since gone from these things.
The dust of distance was beaten into them. They were worn
and stained and several neat patches showed on the shirt. Yet
a kind of magnificence remained and with it a hint of men and
manners alien to my limited boy's experience.

Then I forgot the clothes in the impact of the man himself. He was not much above medium height, almost slight in

build. He would have looked frail alongside father's square, solid bulk. But even I could read the endurance in the lines of that dark figure and the quiet power in its effortless, unthinking adjustment to every movement of the tired horse.

He was clean-shaven and his face was lean and hard and burned from high forehead to firm, tapering chin. His eyes seemed hooded in the shadow of the hat's brim. He came closer, and I could see that this was because the brows were drawn in a frown of fixed and habitual alertness. Beneath them the eyes were endlessly searching from side to side and forward, checking off every item in view, missing nothing. As I noticed this, a sudden chill, I could not have told why, struck through me there in the warm and open sun.

He rode easily, relaxed in the saddle, leaning his weight lazily into the stirrups. Yet even in this easiness was a suggestion of tension. It was the easiness of a coiled spring, of a trap set.

He drew rein not twenty feet from me. His glance hit me, dismissed me, flicked over our place. This was not much, if you were thinking in terms of size and scope. But what there was was good. You could trust father for that. The corral, big enough for about thirty head if you crowded them in, was railed right to true sunk posts. The pasture behind, taking in nearly half of our claim, was fenced tight. The barn was small, but it was solid, and we were raising a loft at one end for the alfalfa growing green in the north forty. We had a fair-sized field in potatoes that year and father was trying a new corn he had sent all the way to Washington for and they were showing properly in weedless rows.

Behind the house mother's kitchen garden was a brave sight. The house itself was three rooms—two really, the big kitchen where we spent most of our time indoors and the bedroom beside it. My little lean-to room was added back of the kitchen. Father was planning, when he could get around to it, to build mother the parlor she wanted.

We had wooden floors and a nice porch across the front. The house was painted too, white with green trim, rare thing in all that region, to remind her, mother said when she made father do it, of her native New England. Even rarer, the roof was shingled. I knew what that meant. I had helped father split those shingles. Few places so spruce and well worked could be found so deep in the Territory in those days.

The stranger took it all in, sitting there easily in the saddle. I saw his eyes slow on the flowers mother had planted by the porch steps, then come to rest on our shiny new pump and the trough beside it. They shifted back to me, and again, without knowing why, I felt that sudden chill. But his voice was gentle and he spoke like a man schooled to patience.

"I'd appreciate a chance at the pump for myself and the horse."

I was trying to frame a reply and choking on it, when I realized that he was not speaking to me but past me. Father had come up behind me and was leaning against the gate to the corral.

"Use all the water you want, stranger."

Father and I watched him dismount in a single flowing tilt of his body and lead the horse over to the trough. He pumped it almost full and let the horse sink its nose in the cool water before he picked up the dipper for himself.

He took off his hat and slapped the dust out of it and hung it on a corner of the trough. With his hands he brushed the dust from his clothes. With a piece of rag pulled from his saddle-roll he carefully wiped his boots. He untied the handkerchief from around his neck and rolled his sleeves and dipped his arms in the trough, rubbing thoroughly and splashing water over his face. He shook his hands dry and used the handkerchief to remove the last drops from his face. Taking a comb from his shirt pocket, he smoothed back his long dark hair. All his movements were deft and sure, and with a quick precision he flipped down his sleeves, reknotted the handkerchief, and picked up his hat.

Then, holding it in his hand, he spun about and strode directly toward the house. He bent low and snapped the stem of one of mother's petunias and tucked this into the hatband. In another moment the hat was on his head, brim swept down in swift, unconscious gesture, and he was swinging gracefully into the saddle and starting toward the road.

I was fascinated. None of the men I knew were proud like that about their appearance. In that short time the kind of magnificence I had noticed had emerged into plainer view. It was in the very air of him. Everything about him showed the effects of long use and hard use, but showed too the strength of quality and competence. There was no chill on me now. Already I was imagining myself in hat and belt and boots like those.

He stopped the horse and looked down at us. He was refreshed and I would have sworn the tiny wrinkles around his eyes were what with him would be a smile. His eyes were not restless when he looked at you like this. They were still and steady and you knew the man's whole attention was concentrated on you even in the casual glance.

"Thank you," he said in his gentle voice and was turning into the road, back to us, before father spoke in his slow, deliberate way.

"Don't be in such a hurry, stranger."

I had to hold tight to the rail or I would have fallen backwards into the corral. At the first sound of father's voice, the man and the horse, like a single being, had wheeled to face us, the man's eyes boring at father, bright and deep in the shadow of the hat's brim. I was shivering, struck through once more. Something intangible and cold and terrifying was there in the air between us.

I stared in wonder as father and the stranger looked at each other a long moment, measuring each other in an unspoken fraternity of adult knowledge beyond my reach. Then the warm sunlight was flooding over us, for father was smiling and he was speaking with the drawling emphasis that meant he had made up his mind.

"I said don't be in such a hurry, stranger. Food will be on the table soon and you can bed down here tonight."

The stranger nodded quietly as if he too had made up his mind. "That's mighty thoughtful of you," he said and swung down and came toward us, leading his horse. Father slipped into step beside him and we all headed for the barn.

"My name's Starrett," said father. "Joe Starrett. This here," waving at me, "is Robert MacPherson Starrett. Too much name for a boy. I make it Bob."

The stranger nodded again. "Call me Shane," he said. Then to me: "Bob it is. You were watching me for quite a spell coming up the road."

It was not a question. It was a simple statement. "Yes . . ." I stammered. "Yes. I was."

"Right," he said. "I like that. A man who watches what's going on around him will make his mark."

A man who watches . . . For all his dark appearance and lean, hard look, this Shane knew what would please a boy. The glow of it held me as he took care of his horse, and I fussed around, hanging up his saddle, forking over some hay, getting in his way and my own in my eagerness. He let me slip the bridle off and the horse, bigger and more powerful than I had thought now that I was close beside it, put its head down patiently for me and stood quietly while I helped him curry away the caked dust. Only once did he stop me. That was when I reached for his saddle-roll to put it to one side. In the instant my fingers touched it, he was taking it from me and he put it on a shelf with a finality that indicated no interference.

When the three of us went up to the house, mother was waiting and four places were set at the table. "I saw you through the window," she said and came to shake our visitor's hand. She was a slender, lively woman with a fair complexion even our weather never seemed to affect and a mass of light brown hair she wore piled high to bring her, she used to say, closer to father's size.

"Marian," father said, "I'd like you to meet Mr. Shane."

"Good evening, ma'am," said our visitor. He took her hand and bowed over it. Mother stepped back and, to my surprise, dropped in a dainty curtsy. I had never seen her do that before. She was an unpredictable woman. Father and I would have painted the house three times over and in rainbow colors to please her.

"And a good evening to you, Mr. Shane. If Joe hadn't called you back, I would have done it myself. You'd never find a decent meal up the valley."

She was proud of her cooking, was mother. That was one thing she learned back home, she would often say, that was of some use out in this raw land. As long as she could still prepare a proper dinner, she would tell father when things were not going right, she knew she was still civilized and there was hope of getting ahead. Then she would tighten her lips and whisk together her special most delicious biscuits and father would watch her bustling about and eat them to the last little crumb and stand up and wipe his eyes and stretch his big frame and stomp out to his always unfinished work like daring anything to stop him now.

We sat down to supper and a good one. Mother's eyes sparkled as our visitor kept pace with father and me. Then we all leaned back and while I listened the talk ran on almost like old friends around a familiar table. But I could sense that it was following a pattern. Father was trying, with mother helping and both of them avoiding direct questions, to get hold of facts about this Shane and he was dodging at every turn. He was aware of their purpose and not in the least annoyed by it. He was mild and courteous and spoke readily enough. But always he put them off with words that gave no real information.

He must have been riding many days, for he was full of news from towns along his back trail as far as Cheyenne and even Dodge City and others beyond I had never heard of before. But he had no news about himself. His past was fenced as tightly as our pasture. All they could learn was that he was riding through, taking each day as it came, with nothing particular in mind except maybe seeing a part of the country he had not been in before.

Afterwards mother washed the dishes and I dried and the two men sat on the porch, their voices carrying through the open door. Our visitor was guiding the conversation now and in no time at all he had father talking about his own plans. That was no trick. Father was ever one to argue his ideas whenever he could find a listener. This time he was going strong.

"Yes, Shane, the boys I used to ride with don't see it yet. They will some day. The open range can't last forever. The fence lines are closing in. Running cattle in big lots is good business only for the top ranchers and it's really a poor business at that. Poor in terms of the resources going into it. Too much space for too little results. It's certain to be crowded out."

"Well, now," said Shane, "that's mighty interesting. I've been hearing the same quite a lot lately and from men with pretty clear heads. Maybe there's something to it."

"By Godfrey, there's plenty to it. Listen to me, Shane. The

thing to do is pick your spot, get your land, your own land. Put in enough crops to carry you and make your money play with a small herd, not all horns and bone, but bred for meat and fenced in and fed right. I haven't been at it long, but already I've raised stock that averages three hundred pounds more than that long-legged stuff Fletcher runs on the other side of the river and it's better beef, and that's only a beginning.

"Sure, his outfit sprawls over most of this valley and it looks big. But he's got range rights on a lot more acres than he has cows and he won't even have those acres as more homesteaders move in. His way is wasteful. Too much land for what he gets out of it. He can't see that. He thinks we small fellows are nothing but nuisances."

"You are," said Shane mildly. "From his point of view, you are."

"Yes, I guess you're right. I'll have to admit that. Those of us here now would make it tough for him if he wanted to use the range behind us on this side of the river as he used to. Altogether we cut some pretty good slices out of it. Worse still, we block off part of the river, shut the range off from the water. He's been grumbling about that off and on ever since we've been here. He's worried that more of us will keep coming and settle on the other side too, and then he will be in a fix."

The dishes were done and I was edging to the door. Mother nailed me as she usually did and shunted me off to bed. After she had left me in my little back room and went to join the men on the porch, I tried to catch more of the words. The voices were too low. Then I must have dozed, for with a start I realized that father and mother were again in the kitchen. By now, I gathered, our visitor was out in the barn in the bunk father had built there for the hired man who had been with us for a few weeks in the spring.

"Wasn't it peculiar," I heard mother say, "how he wouldn't talk about himself?"

"Peculiar?" said father. "Well, yes. In a way."

"Everything about him is peculiar." Mother sounded as if she was stirred up and interested. "I never saw a man quite like him before."

"You wouldn't have. Not where you come from. He's a special brand we sometimes get out here in the grass country. I've come across a few. A bad one's poison. A good one's straight grain clear through."

"How can you be so sure about him? Why, he wouldn't even tell where he was raised."

"Born back east a ways would be my guess. And pretty far south. Tennessee maybe. But he's been around plenty."

"I like him." Mother's voice was serious. "He's so nice and polite and sort of gentle. Not like most men I've met out here. But there's something about him. Something underneath the gentleness . . . Something . . ." Her voice trailed away.

"Mysterious?" suggested father.

"Yes, of course. Mysterious. But more than that. Dangerous."

"He's dangerous all right." Father said it in a musing way. Then he chuckled. "But not to us, my dear." And then he said what seemed to me a curious thing. "In fact, I don't think you ever had a safer man in your house."

# 2

I N THE morning I slept late and stumbled into the kitchen to find father and our visitor working their way through piles of mother's flapjacks. She smiled at me from over by the stove. Father slapped my rump by way of greeting. Our visitor nodded at me gravely over his heaped-up plate.

"Good morning, Bob. You'd better dig in fast or I'll do away with your share too. There's magic in your mother's cooking. Eat enough of these flannel cakes and you'll grow a bigger man than your father."

"Flannel cakes! Did you hear that, Joe?" Mother came whisking over to tousle father's hair. "You must be right. Tennessee or some such place. I never heard them called that out here."

Our visitor looked up at her. "A good guess, ma'am. Mighty close to the mark. But you had a husband to help you. My folks came out of Mississippi and settled in Arkansas. Me, though—I was fiddle-footed and left home at fifteen. Haven't had anything worth being called a real flannel cake since." He put his hands on the table edge and leaned back and the little wrinkles at the corners of his eyes were plainer and deeper. "That is, ma'am, till now."

Mother gave what in a girl I would have called a giggle. "If I'm any judge of men," she said, "that means more." And she whisked back to the stove.

That was how it was often in our house, kind of jolly and warm with good feeling. It needed to be this morning because there was a cool grayness in the air and before I had even begun to slow on my second plate of flapjacks the wind was rushing down the valley with the rain of one of our sudden summer storms following fast.

Our visitor had finished his breakfast. He had eaten so many flapjacks that I had begun to wonder whether he really would cut into my share. Now he turned to look out the window and his lips tightened. But he pushed back from the table and started to rise. Mother's voice held him to his chair.

"You'll not be traveling in any such weather. Wait a bit and it'll clear. These rains don't last long. I've another pot of coffee on the stove."

Father was getting his pipe going. He kept his eyes carefully on the smoke drifting upward. "Marian's right. Only she doesn't go far enough. These rains are short. But they sure mess up the road. It's new. Hasn't settled much yet. Mighty soggy when wet. Won't be fit for traveling till it drains. You better stay over till tomorrow."

Our visitor stared down at his empty plate as if it was the most important object in the whole room. You could see he liked the idea. Yet he seemed somehow worried about it.

"Yes," said father. "That's the sensible dodge. That horse of yours was pretty much beat last night. If I was a horse doctor now, I'd order a day's rest right off. Hanged if I don't think the same prescription would do me good too. You stick here the day and I'll follow it. I'd like to take you around, show you what I'm doing with the place."

He looked pleadingly at mother. She was surprised and good reason. Father was usually so set on working every possible minute to catch up on his plans that she would have a tussle making him ease some once a week out of respect for the Sabbath. In bad weather like this he usually would fidget and stomp about the house as if he thought it was a personal insult to him, a trick to keep him from being out and doing things. And here he was talking of a whole day's rest. She was puzzled. But she played right up.

"You'd be doing us a favor, Mr. Shane. We don't get many visitors from outside the valley. It'd be real nice to have you stay. And besides—" She crinkled her nose at him the way she did when she would be teasing father into some new scheme of hers. "And besides—I've been waiting for an excuse to try a deep-dish apple pie I've heard tell of. It would just be wasted on these other two. They eat everything in sight and don't rightly know good from poor."

He was looking up, straight at her. She shook a finger at him. "And another thing. I'm fair bubbling with questions about what the women are wearing back in civilization. You know, hats and such. You're the kind of man would notice them. You're not getting away till you've told me."

Shane sat back in his chair. A faint quizzical expression soft-ened the lean ridges of his face. "Ma'am, I'm not positive I appreciate how you've pegged me. No one else ever wrote me down an expert on ladies' millinery." He reached out and pushed his cup across the table toward her. "You said some-thing about more coffee. But I draw the line on more flannel cakes. I'm plumb full. I'm starting in to conserve space for that pie."

"You'd better!" Father was mighty pleased about some-thing. "When Marian puts her mind to cooking, she makes a man forget he's got any limits to his appetite. Only don't you go giving her fancy notions of new hats so she'll be sending off to the mail-order house and throwing my money away on silly frippery. She's got a hat."

Mother did not even notice that. She knew father was just talking. She knew that whenever she wanted anything real much and said so, father would bust himself trying to get it for her. She whisked over to the table with the coffee pot, poured a fresh round, then set it down within easy reach and sat down herself.

I thought that business about hats was only a joke she made up to help father persuade our visitor to stay. But she began almost at once, pestering him to describe the ladies he had seen in Cheyenne and other towns where the new styles might be. He sat there, easy and friendly, telling her how they were wearing wide floppy-brimmed bonnets with lots of flowers in front on top and slits in the brims for scarves to come through and be tied in bows under their chins.

Talk like that seemed foolish to me to be coming from a grown man. Yet this Shane was not bothered at all. And father listened as if he thought it was all right, only not very inter-esting. He watched them most of the time in a good-natured quiet, trying every so often to break in with his own talk about crops and steers and giving up and trying again and giving up again with a smiling shake of his head at those two. And the rain outside was a far distance away and meaningless because the friendly feeling in our kitchen was enough to warm all our world.

Then Shane was telling about the annual stock show at Dodge City and father was interested and excited, and it was mother who said: "Look, the sun's shining."

It was, so clear and sweet you wanted to run out and breathe the brilliant freshness. Father must have felt that way because he jumped up and fairly shouted, "Come on, Shane. I'll show you what this hop-scotch climate does to my alfalfa. You can almost see the stuff growing."

Shane was only a step behind him, but I beat them to the door. Mother followed and stood watching awhile on the porch as we three started out, picking our path around the puddles and the taller clumps of grass bright with the raindrops. We covered the whole place pretty thoroughly, father talking all the time, more enthusiastic about his plans than he had been for many weeks. He really hit his stride when we were behind the barn where we could have a good view of our little herd spreading out through the pasture. Then he stopped short. He had noticed that Shane was not paying much attention. He was quiet as could be for a moment when he saw that Shane was looking at the stump.

That was the one bad spot on our place. It stuck out like an old scarred sore in the cleared space back of the barn— a big old stump, all jagged across the top, the legacy of some great tree that must have died long before we came into the valley and finally been snapped by a heavy windstorm. It was big enough, I used to think, so that if it was smooth on top you could have served supper to a good-sized family on it.

But you could not have done that because you could not have got them close around it. The huge old roots humped out in every direction, some as big about as my waist, pushing out and twisting down into the ground like they would hold there to eternity and past.

Father had been working at it off and on, gnawing at the roots with an axe, ever since he finished poling the corral. The going was slow, even for him. The wood was so hard that he could not sink the blade much more than a quarter inch at a time. I guess it had been an old burr oak. Not many of those grew that far up in the Territory, but the ones that did grew big and hard. Ironwood we called it.

Father had tried burning brushpiles against it. That old

stump just jeered at fire. The scorching seemed to make the
wood harder than ever. So he was fighting his way around root
by root. He never thought he had much time to spare on it.
The rare occasions he was real mad about something he would
stomp out there and chew into another root.

He went over to the stump now and kicked the nearest root,
a smart kick, the way he did every time he passed it. "Yes," he
said. "That's the millstone round my neck. That's the one fool
thing about this place I haven't licked yet. But I will. There's no
wood ever grew can stand up to a man that's got the strength
and the will to keep hammering at it."

He stared at the stump like it might be a person sprouting
in front of him. "You know, Shane, I've been feuding with
this thing so long I've worked up a spot of affection for it. It's
tough. I can admire toughness. The right kind."

He was running on again, full of words and sort of happy
to be letting them out, when he noticed again that Shane was
not paying much attention, was listening to some sound in the
distance. Sure enough, a horse was coming up the road.

Father and I turned with him to look toward town. In a moment we saw it as it cleared the grove of trees and tall bushes
about a quarter-mile away, a high-necked sorrel drawing a light
buckboard wagon. The mud was splattering from its hooves,
but not bad, and it was stepping free and easy. Shane glanced
sideways at father.

"Not fit for traveling," he said softly. "Starrett, you're poor
shakes as a liar." Then his attention was on the wagon and he
was tense and alert, studying the man upright on the swaying
seat.

Father simply chuckled at Shane's remark. "That's Jake
Ledyard's outfit," he said, taking the lead toward our lane. "I
thought maybe he'd get up this way this week. Hope he has
that cultivator I've been wanting."

Ledyard was a small, thin-featured man, a peddler or trader
who came through every couple of months with things you
could not get at the general store in town. He would pack in
his stock on a mule-team freighter driven by an old, white-
haired Negro who acted like he was afraid even to speak
without permission. Ledyard would make deliveries in his

buckboard, claiming a hard bargain always and picking up orders for articles to bring on the next trip. I did not like him,
and not just because he said nice things about me he did not
mean for father's benefit. He smiled too much and there was
no real friendliness in it.

By the time we were beside the porch, he had swung the
horse into our lane and was pulling it to a stop. He jumped
down, calling greetings. Father went to meet him. Shane
stayed by the porch, leaning against the end post.

"It's here," said Ledyard. "The beauty I told you about." He
yanked away the canvas covering from the body of the wagon
and the sun was bright on a shiny new seven-pronged cultivator lying on its side on the floor boards. "That's the best buy
I've toted this haul."

"Hm-m-m-m," said father. "You've hit it right. That's what
I've been wanting. But when you start chattering about a best
buy that always means big money. What's the tariff?"

"Well, now." Ledyard was slow with his reply. "It cost me
more than I figured when we was talking last time. You might
think it a bit steep. I don't. Not for a new beauty like that
there. You'll make up the difference in no time with the work
you'll save with that. Handles so easy even the boy here will be
using it before long."

"Pin it down," said father. "I've asked you a question."

Ledyard was quick now. "Tell you what, I'll shave the price,
take a loss to please a good customer. I'll let you have it for a
hundred and ten."

I was startled to hear Shane's voice cutting in, quiet and even
and plain. "Let you have it? I reckon he will. There was one like
that in a store in Cheyenne. List price sixty dollars."

Ledyard shifted part way around. For the first time he looked
closely at our visitor. The surface smile left his face. His voice
held an ugly undertone. "Did anyone ask you to push in on
this?"

"No," said Shane, quietly and evenly as before. "I reckon
no one did." He was still leaning against the post. He did not
move and he did not say anything more. Ledyard turned to
father, speaking rapidly.

"Forget what he says, Starrett. I've spotted him now. Heard
of him half a dozen times along the road up here. No one

knows him. No one can figure him. I think I can. Just a stray wandering through, probably chased out of some town and hunting cover. I'm surprised you'd let him hang around."

"You might be surprised at a lot of things," said father, beginning to bite off his words. "Now give it to me straight on the price."

"It's what I said. A hundred and ten. Hell, I'll be out money on the deal anyway, so I'll shave it to a hundred if that'll make you feel any better." Ledyard hesitated, watching father. "Maybe he did see something in Cheyenne. But he's mixed up. Must have been one of those little makes—flimsy and barely half the size. That might match his price."

Father did not say anything. He was looking at Ledyard in a steady, unwavering way. He had not even glanced at Shane. You might have believed he had not even heard what Shane had said. But his lips were folding in to a tight line like he was thinking what was not pleasant to think. Ledyard waited and father did not say anything and the climbing anger in Ledyard broke free.

"Starrett! Are you going to stand there and let that—that tramp nobody knows about call me a liar? Are you going to take his word over mine? Look at him! Look at his clothes! He's just a cheap, tinhorn—"

Ledyard stopped, choking on whatever it was he had meant to say. He fell back a step with a sudden fear showing in his face. I knew why even as I turned my head to see Shane. That same chill I had felt the day before, intangible and terrifying, was in the air again. Shane was no longer leaning against the porch post. He was standing erect, his hands clenched at his sides, his eyes boring at Ledyard, his whole body alert and alive in the leaping instant.

You felt without knowing how that each teetering second could bring a burst of indescribable deadliness. Then the tension passed, fading in the empty silence. Shane's eyes lost their sharp focus on Ledyard and it seemed to me that reflected in them was some pain deep within him.

Father had pivoted so that he could see the two of them in the one sweep. He swung back to Ledyard alone.

"Yes, Ledyard, I'm taking his word. He's my guest. He's here at my invitation. But that's not the reason." Father straightened

a little and his head went up and he gazed into the distance beyond the river. "I can figure men for myself. I'll take his word
on anything he wants to say any day of God's whole year."

Father's head came down and his voice was flat and final.
"Sixty is the price. Add ten for a fair profit, even though you
probably got it wholesale. Another ten for hauling it here. That
tallies to eighty. Take that or leave that. Whatever you do, snap
to it and get off my land."

Ledyard stared down at his hands, rubbing them together as
if they were cold. "Where's your money?" he said.

Father went into the house, into the bedroom where he
kept our money in a little leather bag on the closet shelf. He
came back with the crumpled bills. All this while Shane stood
there, not moving, his face hard, his eyes following father with
a strange wildness in them that I could not understand.

Ledyard helped father heave the cultivator to the ground,
then jumped to the wagon seat and drove off like he was glad
to get away from our place. Father and I turned from watching
him into the road. We looked around for Shane and he was not
in sight. Father shook his head in wonderment. "Now where
do you suppose—" he was saying, when we saw Shane coming
out of the barn.

He was carrying an axe, the one father used for heavy kindling. He went directly around the corner of the building. We
stared after him and we were still staring when we heard it, the
clear ringing sound of steel biting into wood.

I never could have explained what that sound did to me. It
struck through me as no single sound had ever done before.
With it ran a warmth that erased at once and forever the feelings of sudden chill terror that our visitor had evoked in me.
There were sharp hidden hardnesses in him. But these were
not for us. He was dangerous as mother had said. But not to
us as father too had said. And he was no longer a stranger. He
was a man like father in whom a boy could believe in the simple
knowing that what was beyond comprehension was still clean
and solid and right.

I looked up at father to try to see what he was thinking, but
he was starting toward the barn with strides so long that I had
to run to stay close behind him. We went around the far corner

and there was Shane squared away at the biggest uncut root of that big old stump. He was swinging the axe in steady rhythm. He was chewing into that root with bites almost as deep as father could drive.

Father halted, legs wide, hands on hips. "Now lookahere," he began, "there's no call for you—"

Shane broke his rhythm just long enough to level a straight look at us. "A man has to pay his debts," he said and was again swinging the axe. He was really slicing into that root.

He seemed so desperate in his determination that I had to speak. "You don't owe us anything," I said. "Lots of times we have folks in for meals and—"

Father's hand was on my shoulder. "No, Bob. He doesn't mean meals." Father was smiling, but he was having to blink several times together and I would have sworn that his eyes were misty. He stood in silence now, not moving, watching Shane.

It was something worth seeing. When father worked on that old stump, that was worth seeing too. He could handle an axe mighty well and what impressed you was the strength and will of him making it behave and fight for him against the tough old wood. This was different. What impressed you as Shane found what he was up against and settled to it was the easy way the power in him poured smoothly into each stroke. The man and the axe seemed to be partners in the work. The blade would sink into the parallel grooves almost as if it knew itself what to do and the chips from between would come out in firm and thin little blocks.

Father watched him and I watched the two of them and time passed over us, and then the axe sliced through the last strip and the root was cut. I was sure that Shane would stop. But he stepped right around to the next root and squared away again and the blade sank in once more.

As it hit this second root, father winced like it had hit him. Then he stiffened and looked away from Shane and stared at the old stump. He began to fidget, throwing his weight from one foot to the other. In a short while more he was walking around inspecting the stump from different angles as if it was something he had never seen before. Finally he gave the nearest root a kick and hurried away. In a moment he was back with the other axe, the big double-bladed one that I could hardly heft from the ground.

He picked a root on the opposite side from Shane. He was not angry the way he usually was when he confronted one of those roots. There was a kind of serene and contented look on his face. He whirled that big axe as if it was only a kid's tool. The striking blade sank in maybe a whole half-inch. At the sound Shane straightened on his side. Their eyes met over the top of the stump and held and neither one of them said a word. Then they swung up their axes and both of them said plenty to that old stump.

# 3

IT WAS exciting at first watching them. They were hitting a fast pace, making the chips dance. I thought maybe each one would cut through a root now and stop. But Shane finished his and looked over at father working steadily away and with a grim little smile pulling at his mouth he moved on to another root. A few moments later father smashed through his with a blow that sent the axe head into the ground beneath. He wrestled with the handle to yank the head loose and he too tackled another root without even waiting to wipe off the dirt. This began to look like a long session, so I started to wander away. Just as I headed around the corner of the barn, mother came past the corner.

She was the freshest, prettiest thing I had ever seen. She had taken her hat and stripped the old ribbon from it and fixed it as Shane had told her. Some of the flowers by the house were in a small bouquet in front. She had cut slits in the brim and the sash from her best dress came around the crown and through the slits and was tied in a perky bow under her chin. She was stepping along daintily, mighty proud of herself.

She went up close to the stump. Those two choppers were so busy and intent that even if they were aware she was there they did not really notice her.

"Well," she said, "aren't you going to look at me?"

They both stopped and they both stared at her.

"Have I got it right?" she asked Shane. "Is this the way they do it?"

"Yes, ma'am," he said. "About like that. Only their brims are wider." And he swung back to his root.

"Joe Starrett," said mother, "aren't you at least going to tell me whether you like me in this hat?"

"Lookahere, Marian," said father, "you know damned well that whether you have a hat on or whether you don't have a hat on, you're the nicest thing to me that ever happened on God's green earth. Now stop bothering us. Can't you see we're busy?" And he swung back to his root.

Mother's face was a deep pink. She pulled the bow out and

the hat from her head. She held it swinging from her hand by the sash ends. Her hair was mussed and she was really mad.

"Humph," she said. "This is a funny kind of resting you're doing today."

Father set the axe head on the ground and leaned on the handle. "Maybe it seems funny to you, Marian. But this is the best resting I've had for about as long as I can remember."

"Humph," said mother again. "You'll have to quit your resting for a while anyhow and do what I suppose you'll call work. Dinner's hot on the stove and waiting to be served."

She flounced around and went straight back to the house. We all tagged her in and to an uncomfortable meal. Mother always believed you should be decent and polite at mealtime, particularly with company. She was polite enough now. She was being special sweet, talking enough for the whole table of us without once saying a word about her hat lying where she had thrown it on the chair by the stove. The trouble was that she was too polite. She was trying too hard to be sweet.

As far as you could tell, though, the two men were not worried by her at all. They listened absently to her talk, chiming in when she asked them direct questions, but otherwise keeping quiet. Their minds were on that old stump and whatever it was that old stump had come to mean to them and they were in a hurry to get at it again.

After they had gone out and I had been helping mother with the dishes awhile, she began humming low under her breath and I knew she was not mad any more. She was too curious and puzzled to have room for anything else.

"What went on out there, Bob?" she asked me. "What got into those two?"

I did not rightly know. All I could do was try to tell her about Ledyard and how our visitor had called him on the cultivator. I must have used the wrong words, because, when I told her about Ledyard talking mean and the way Shane acted, she got all flushed and excited.

"What do you say, Bob? You were afraid of him? He frightened you? Your father would never let him do that."

"I wasn't frightened of him," I said, struggling to make her see the difference. "I was—well, I was just frightened. I was scared of whatever it was that might happen."

She reached out and rumpled my hair. "I think I understand," she said softly. "He's made me feel a little that way
too." She went to the window and stared toward the barn.
The steady rhythm of double blows, so together they sounded
almost as one, was faint yet clear in the kitchen. "I hope Joe
knows what he's doing," she murmured to herself. Then she
turned to me. "Skip along out, Bob. I'll finish myself."

It was no fun watching them now. They had eased down
to a slow, dogged pace. Father sent me once for the hone, so
they could sharpen the blades, and again for a spade so he
could clear the dirt away from the lowest roots, and I realized
he might keep me running as long as I was handy. I slipped
off by myself to see how mother's garden was doing after the
rain and maybe add to the population in the box of worms I
was collecting for when I would go fishing with the boys in
town.

I took my time about it. I played pretty far afield. But no
matter where I went, always I could hear that chopping in the
distance. You could not help beginning to feel tired just to hear
it, to think how they were working and staying at it.

Along the middle of the afternoon, I wandered into the
barn. There was mother by the rear stall, up on a box peering
through the little window above it. She hopped down as soon
as she heard me and put a finger to her lips.

"I declare," she whispered. "In some ways those two aren't
even as old as you are, Bob. Just the same—" She frowned at
me in such a funny, confiding manner that I felt all warm inside. "Don't you dare tell them I said so. But there's something
splendid in the battle they're giving that old monster." She
went past me and toward the house with such a brisk air that I
followed to see what she was going to do.

She whisked about the kitchen and in almost no time at all
she had a pan of biscuits in the oven. While they were baking,
she took her hat and carefully sewed the old ribbon into its old
place. "Humph," she said, more to herself than to me. "You'd
think I'd learn. This isn't Dodge City. This isn't even a whistle
stop. It's Joe Starrett's farm. It's where I'm proud to be."

Out came the biscuits. She piled as many as she could on a
plate, popping one of the leftovers into her mouth and giving

me the rest. She picked up the plate and marched with it out behind the barn. She stepped over the cut roots and set the plate on a fairly smooth spot on top of the stump. She looked at the two men, first one and then the other. "You're a pair of fools," she said. "But there's no law against me being a fool too." Without looking at either of them again, she marched away, her head high, back toward the house.

The two of them stared after her till she was out of sight. They turned to stare at the biscuits. Father gave a deep sigh, so deep it seemed to come all the way from his heavy work shoes. There was nothing sad or sorrowful about it. There was just something in him too big to be held tight in comfort. He let his axe fall to the ground. He leaned forward and separated the biscuits into two piles beside the plate, counting them even. One was left on the plate. He set this by itself on the stump. He took up his axe and reached it out and let it drop gently on the lone biscuit exactly in the middle. He rested the axe against the stump and took the two halves of the biscuit and put one on each pile.

He did not say a word to Shane. He pitched into one pile and Shane did into the other, and the two of them faced each other over the last uncut roots, munching at those biscuits as if eating them was the most serious business they had ever done.

Father finished his pile and dabbled his fingers on the plate for the last crumbs. He straightened and stretched his arms high and wide. He seemed to stretch and stretch until he was a tremendous tower of strength reaching up into the late afternoon sun. He swooped suddenly to grab the plate and toss it to me. Still in the same movement he seized his axe and swung it in a great arc into the root he was working on. Quick as he was, Shane was right with him, and together they were talking again to that old stump.

I took the plate in to mother. She was peeling apples in the kitchen, humming gaily to herself. "The woodbox, Bob," she said, and went on humming. I carried in stove-lengths till the box would not hold any more. Then I slipped out before she might think of more chores.

I tried to keep myself busy down by the river skipping flat stones across the current all muddy still from the rain. I was able to for a while. But that steady chopping had a peculiar fascination. It was always pulling me toward the barn. I simply could not grasp how they could stick at it hour after hour. It made no sense to me, why they should work so when routing out that old stump was not really so important. I was wavering in front of the barn, when I noticed that the chopping was different. Only one axe was working.

I hurried around back. Shane was still swinging, cutting into the last root. Father was using the spade, was digging under one side of the stump, bringing the dirt out between the cut roots. As I watched, he laid the spade aside and put his shoulder to the stump. He heaved against it. Sweat started to pour down his face. There was a little sucking sound and the stump moved ever so slightly.

That did it. Of a sudden I was so excited that I could hear my own blood pounding past my eardrums. I wanted to dash to that stump and push it and feel it move. Only I knew father would think I was in the way.

Shane finished the root and came to help him. Together they heaved against the stump. It angled up nearly a whole inch. You could begin to see an open space in the dirt where it was ripping loose. But as soon as they released the pressure, it fell back.

Again and again they heaved at it. Each time it would angle up a bit farther. Each time it would fall back. They had it up once about a foot and a half, and that was the limit. They could not get past it.

They stopped, breathing hard, mighty streaked now from the sweat rivulets down their faces. Father peered underneath as best he could. "Must be a taproot," he said. That was the one time either of them had spoken to the other, as far as I knew, the whole afternoon through. Father did not say anything more. And Shane said nothing. He just picked up his axe and looked at father and waited.

Father began to shake his head. There was some unspoken thought between them that bothered him. He looked down at his own big hands and slowly the fingers curled until they were clenched into big fists. Then his head stopped shaking and he stood taller and he drew a deep breath. He turned and backed in between two cut root ends, pressing against the stump. He pushed his feet into the ground for firm footholds. He bent his knees and slid his shoulders down the stump and wrapped his big hands around the root ends. Slowly he began to straighten. Slowly that huge old stump began to rise. Up it came, inch by inch, until the side was all the way up to the limit they had reached before.

Shane stooped to peer under. He poked his axe into the opening and I heard it strike wood. But the only way he could get in position to swing the axe into the opening was to drop on his right knee and extend his left leg and thigh into the opening and lean his weight on them. Then he could bring the axe sweeping in at a low angle close to the ground.

He flashed one quick glance at father beside and behind him, eyes closed, muscles locked in that great sustained effort, and he dropped into position with the whole terrible weight of the stump poised above nearly half of his body and sent the axe sweeping under in swift powerful strokes.

Suddenly father seemed to slip. Only he had not slipped. He had straightened even further. The stump had leaped up a few more inches. Shane jumped out and up and tossed his axe aside. He grabbed one of the root ends and helped father ease the stump down. They both were blowing like they had run a long way. But they would not stay more than a minute before they were heaving again at the stump. It came up more easily now and the dirt was tearing loose all around it.

I ran to the house fast as I could. I dashed into the kitchen and took hold of mother's hand. "Hurry!" I yelled. "You've got to come!" She did not seem to want to come at first and I pulled at her. "You've got to see it! They're getting it out!" Then she was excited as I was and was running right with me.

They had the stump way up at a high angle. They were down in the hole, one on each side of it, pushing up and forward with hands flat on the under part reared before them higher than their heads. You would have thought the stump was ready to topple over clear of its ancient foundation. But there it stuck. They could not quite push it the final inches.

Mother watched them battling with it. "Joe," she called, "why don't you use some sense? Hitch up the team. Horses will have it out in no time at all."

Father braced himself to hold the stump still. He turned his head to look at her. "Horses!" he shouted. All the pent silence of the two of them that long afternoon through was being shattered in the one wonderful shout. "Horses! Great jumping Jehosaphat! No! We started this with manpower and, by Godfrey, we'll finish it with manpower!"

He turned his head to face the stump once more and dropped it lower between his humped shoulders. Shane, opposite him, stiffened, and together they pushed in a fresh assault. The stump quivered and swayed a little—and hung fixed at its crazy high angle.

Father grunted in exasperation. You could see the strength building up in his legs and broad shoulders and big corded arms. His side of the upturned stump rocked forward and Shane's side moved back and the whole stump trembled like it would twist down and into the hole on them at a grotesque new angle.

I wanted to shout a warning. But I could not speak, for Shane had thrown his head in a quick sideways gesture to fling his hair from falling over his face and I had caught a glimpse of his eyes. They were aflame with a concentrated cold fire. Not another separate discernible movement did he make. It was all of him, the whole man, pulsing in the one incredible surge of power. You could fairly feel the fierce energy suddenly burning in him, pouring through him in the single coordinated drive. His side of the stump rocked forward even with father's and the whole mass of the stump tore loose from the last hold and toppled away to sprawl in ungainly defeat beyond them.

Father climbed slowly out of the hole. He walked to the stump and placed a hand on the rounded bole and patted it like it was an old friend and he was perhaps a little sorry for it. Shane was with him, across from him, laying a hand gently on the old hard wood. They both looked up and their eyes met and held as they had so long ago in the morning hours.

The silence should have been complete. It was not because someone was shouting, a high-pitched, wordless shout. I realized that the voice was mine and I closed my mouth. The silence was clean and wholesome, and this was one of the things you could never forget whatever time might do to you in the furrowing of the years, an old stump on its side with root ends making a strange pattern against the glow of the sun sinking behind the far mountains and two men looking over it into each other's eyes.

I thought they should join the hands so close on the bole of the stump. I thought they should at least say something to each other. They stood quiet and motionless. At last father turned and came toward mother. He was so tired that the weariness showed in his walk. But there was no weariness in his voice. "Marian," he said, "I'm rested now. I don't believe any man since the world began was ever more rested."

Shane too was coming toward us. He too spoke only to mother. "Ma'am, I've learned something today. Being a farmer has more to it than I ever thought. Now I'm about ready for some of that pie."

Mother had been watching them in a wide-eyed wonder. At his last words she let out a positive wail. "Oh-h-h—you —you—men! You made me forget about it! It's probably all burned!" And she was running for the house so fast she was tripping over her skirt.

The pie was burned all right. We could smell it when we were in front of the house and the men were scrubbing themselves at the pump-trough. Mother had the door open to let the kitchen air out. The noises from inside sounded as if she might be throwing things around. Kettles were banging and dishes were clattering. When we went in, we saw why. She had the table set and was putting supper on it and she was grabbing the things from their places and putting them down on the table with solid thumps. She would not look at one of us.

We sat down and waited for her to join us. She put her back to us and stood by the low shelf near the stove staring at her big pie tin and the burned stuff in it. Finally father spoke kind of sharply. "Lookahere, Marian. Aren't you ever going to sit down?"

She whirled and glared at him. I thought maybe she had been crying. But there were no tears on her face. It was dry and pinched-looking and there was no color in it. Her voice was sharp like father's. "I was planning to have a deep-dish apple pie. Well, I will. None of your silly man foolishness is going to stop me."

She swept up the big tin and went out the door with it. We heard her on the steps, and a few seconds later the rattle of the cover of the garbage pail. We heard her on the steps again. She came in and went to the side bench where the dishpan was and began to scrub the pie tin. The way she acted, we might not have been in the room.

Father's face was getting red. He picked up his fork to begin eating and let it drop with a little clatter. He squirmed on his chair and kept taking quick side looks at her. She finished scrubbing the tin and went to the apple barrel and filled her wooden bowl with fat round ones. She sat by the stove and started peeling them. Father fished in a pocket and pulled out his old jackknife. He moved over to her, stepping softly. He reached out for an apple to help her.

She did not look up. But her voice caught him like she had flicked him with a whip. "Joe Starrett, don't you dare touch a one of these apples."

He was sheepish as he returned to his chair. Then he was downright mad. He grabbed his knife and fork and dug into the food on his plate, taking big bites and chewing vigorously. There was nothing for our visitor and me to do but follow his example. Maybe it was a good supper. I could not tell. The food was only something to put in your mouth. And when we finished, there was nothing to do but wait because mother was sitting by the stove, arms folded, staring at the wall, waiting herself for her pie to bake.

We three watched her in a quiet so tight that it hurt. We could not help it. We would try to look away and always our eyes would turn back to her. She did not appear to notice us. You might have said she had forgotten we were there.

She had not forgotten because as soon as she sensed that the pie was done, she lifted it out, cut four wide pieces, and put them on plates. The first two she set in front of the two men. The third one she set down for me. The last one she laid at her own place and she sat down in her own chair at the table. Her voice was still sharp.

"I'm sorry to keep you men waiting so long. Your pie is ready now."

Father inspected his portion like he was afraid of it. He needed to make a real effort to take his fork and lift a piece. He chewed on it and swallowed and he flipped his eyes sidewise at mother and back again quickly to look across the table at Shane. "That's prime pie," he said.

Shane raised a piece on his fork. He considered it closely. He put it in his mouth and chewed on it gravely. "Yes," he said. The quizzical expression on his face was so plain you could not possibly miss it. "Yes. That's the best bit of stump I ever tasted."

What could a silly remark like that mean? I had no time to wonder, for father and mother were acting so queer. They both stared at Shane and their mouths were sagging open. Then father snapped his shut and he chuckled and chuckled till he was swaying in his chair.

"By Godfrey, Marian, he's right. You've done it, too."

Mother stared from one to the other of them. Her pinched look faded and her cheeks were flushed and her eyes were soft and warm as they should be, and she was laughing so that the tears came. And all of us were pitching into that pie, and the one thing wrong in the whole world was that there was not enough of it.

# 4

T HE SUN was already well up the sky when I awakened the next morning. I had been a long time getting to sleep because my mind was full of the day's excitement and shifting moods. I could not straighten out in my mind the way the grown folks had behaved, the way things that did not really matter so much had become so important to them.

I had lain in my bed thinking of our visitor out in the bunk in the barn. It scarce seemed possible that he was the same man I had first seen, stern and chilling in his dark solitude, riding up our road. Something in father, something not of words or of actions but of the essential substance of the human spirit, had reached out and spoken to him and he had replied to it and had unlocked a part of himself to us. He was far off and unapproachable at times even when he was right there with you. Yet somehow he was closer, too, than my uncle, mother's brother, had been when he visited us the summer before.

I had been thinking, too, of the effect he had on father and mother. They were more alive, more vibrant, like they wanted to show more what they were, when they were with him. I could appreciate that because I felt the same way myself. But it puzzled me that a man so deep and vital in his own being, so ready to respond to father, should be riding a lone trail out of a closed and guarded past.

I realized with a jolt how late it was. The door to my little room was closed. Mother must have closed it so I could sleep undisturbed. I was frantic that the others might have finished breakfast and that our visitor was gone and I had missed him. I pulled on my clothes, not even bothering with buttons, and ran to the door.

They were still at the table. Father was fussing with his pipe. Mother and Shane were working on a last round of coffee. All three of them were subdued and quiet. They stared at me as I burst out of my room.

"My heavens," said mother. "You came in here like something was after you. What's the matter?"

"I just thought," I blurted out, nodding at our visitor, "that maybe he had ridden off and forgotten me."

Shane shook his head slightly, looking straight at me. "I wouldn't forget you, Bob." He pulled himself up a little in his chair. He turned to mother and his voice took on a bantering tone. "And I wouldn't forget your cooking, ma'am. If you begin having a special lot of people passing by at mealtimes, that'll be because a grateful man has been boasting of your flannel cakes all along the road."

"Now there's an idea," struck in father as if he was glad to find something safe to talk about. "We'll turn this place into a boarding house. Marian'll fill folks full of her meals and I'll fill my pockets full of their money. That hits me as a mighty convenient arrangement."

Mother sniffed at him. But she was pleased at their talk and she was smiling as they kept on playing with the idea while she stirred me up my breakfast. She came right back at them, threatening to take father at his word and make him spend all his time peeling potatoes and washing dishes. They were enjoying themselves even though I could feel a bit of constraint behind the easy joshing. It was remarkable, too, how natural it was to have this Shane sitting there and joining in almost like he was a member of the family. There was none of the awkwardness some visitors always brought with them. You did feel you ought to be on your good behavior with him, a mite extra careful about your manners and your speech. But not stiffly so. Just quiet and friendly about it.

He stood up at last and I knew he was going to ride away from us and I wanted desperately to stop him. Father did it for me.

"You certainly are a man for being in a hurry. Sit down, Shane. I've a question to ask you."

Father was suddenly very serious. Shane, standing there, was as suddenly withdrawn into a distant alertness. But he dropped back into his chair.

Father looked directly at him. "Are you running away from anything?"

Shane stared at the plate in front of him for a long moment. It seemed to me that a shade of sadness passed over him. Then he raised his eyes and looked directly at father.

"No. I'm not running away from anything. Not in the way you mean."

"Good." Father stooped forward and stabbed at the table with a forefinger for emphasis. "Look, Shane. I'm not a rancher. Now you've seen my place, you know that. I'm a farmer. Something of a stockman, maybe. But really a farmer. That's what I decided to be when I quit punching cattle for another man's money. That's what I want to be and I'm proud of it. I've made a fair start. This outfit isn't as big as I hope to have it some day. But there's more work here already than one man can handle if it's to be done right. The young fellow I had ran out on me after he tangled with a couple of Fletcher's boys in town one day." Father was talking fast and he paused to draw breath.

Shane had been watching him intently. He moved his head to look out the window over the valley to the mountains marching along the horizon. "It's always the same," he murmured. He was sort of talking to himself. "The old ways die hard." He looked at mother and then at me, and as his eyes came back to father he seemed to have decided something that had been troubling him. "So Fletcher's crowding you," he said gently.

Father snorted. "I don't crowd easy. But I've got a job to do here and it's too big for one man, even for me. And none of the strays that drift up this way are worth a damn."

"Yes?" Shane said. His eyes were crinkling again, and he was one of us again and waiting.

"Will you stick here awhile and help me get things in shape for the winter?"

Shane rose to his feet. He loomed up taller across the table than I had thought him. "I never figured to be a farmer, Starrett. I would have laughed at the notion a few days ago. All the same, you've hired yourself a hand." He and father were looking at each other in a way that showed they were saying things words could never cover. Shane snapped it by swinging toward mother. "And I'll rate your cooking, ma'am, wages enough."

Father slapped his hands on his knees. "You'll get good wages and you'll earn 'em. First off, now, why don't you drop into town and get some work clothes. Try Sam Grafton's store. Tell him to put it on my bill."

Shane was already at the door. "I'll buy my own," he said, and was gone.

Father was so pleased he could not sit still. He jumped up and whirled mother around. "Marian, the sun's shining mighty bright at last. We've got ourselves a man."

"But, Joe, are you sure what you're doing? What kind of work can a man like that do? Oh, I know he stood right up to you with that stump. But that was something special. He's been used to good living and plenty of money. You can tell that. He said himself he doesn't know anything about farming."

"Neither did I when I started here. What a man knows isn't important. It's what he is that counts. I'll bet you that one was a cowpuncher when he was younger and a tophand too. Anything he does will be done right. You watch. In a week he'll be making even me hump or he'll be bossing the place."

"Perhaps."

"No perhapsing about it. Did you notice how he took it when I told him about Fletcher's boys and young Morley? That's what fetched him. He knows I'm in a spot and he's not the man to leave me there. Nobody'll push him around or scare him away. He's my kind of a man."

"Why, Joe Starrett. He isn't like you at all. He's smaller and he looks different and his clothes are different and he talks different. I know he's lived different."

"Huh?" Father was surprised. "I wasn't talking about things like that."

Shane came back with a pair of dungaree pants, a flannel shirt, stout work shoes, and a good, serviceable Stetson. He disappeared into the barn and emerged a few moments later in his new clothes, leading his horse unsaddled. At the pasture gate he slipped off the halter, turned the horse in with a hearty slap, and tossed the halter to me.

"Take care of a horse, Bob, and it will take care of you. This one now has brought me better than a thousand miles in the last few weeks." And he was striding away to join father, who was ditching the field out past the growing corn where the ground was rich but marshy and would not be worth much till it was properly drained. I watched him swinging through the rows of young corn, no longer a dark stranger but part of the place, a farmer like father and me.

Only he was not a farmer and never really could be. It was not three days before you saw that he could stay right beside father in any kind of work. Show him what needed to be done and he could do it, and like as not would figure out a better way of getting it done. He never shirked the meanest task. He was ever ready to take the hard end of any chore. Yet you always felt in some indefinable fashion that he was a man apart.

There were times when he would stop and look off at the mountains and then down at himself and any tool he happened to have in his hands as if in wry amusement at what he was doing. You had no impression that he thought himself too good for the work or did not like it. He was just different. He was shaped in some firm forging of past circumstance for other things.

For all his slim build he was plenty rugged. His slenderness could fool you at first. But when you saw him close in action, you saw that he was solid, compact, that there was no waste weight on his frame just as there was no waste effort in his smooth, flowing motion. What he lacked alongside father in size and strength, he made up in quickness of movement, in instinctive coordination of mind and muscle, and in that sudden fierce energy that had burned in him when the old stump tried to topple back on him. Mostly this last slept in him, not needed while he went easily through the day's routine. But when a call came, it could flame forward with a driving intensity that never failed to frighten me.

I would be frightened, as I had tried to explain to mother, not at Shane himself, but at the suggestion it always gave me of things in the human equation beyond my comprehension. At such times there would be a concentration in him, a singleness of dedication to the instant need, that seemed to me at once wonderful and disturbing. And then he would be again the quiet, steady man who shared with father my boy's allegiance.

I was beginning to feel my oats about then, proud of myself for being able to lick Ollie Johnson at the next place down the road. Fighting, boy style, was much in my mind.

Once, when father and I were alone, I asked him: "Could you beat Shane? In a fight, I mean."

"Son, that's a tough question. If I had to, I might do it. But, by Godfrey, I'd hate to try it. Some men just plain have dynamite inside them, and he's one. I'll tell you, though. I've never met a man I'd rather have more on my side in any kind of trouble."

I could understand that and it satisfied me. But there were things about Shane I could not understand. When he came in to the first meal after he agreed to stay on with us, he went to the chair that had always been father's and stood beside it waiting for the rest of us to take the other places. Mother was surprised and somewhat annoyed. She started to say something. Father quieted her with a warning glance. He walked to the chair across from Shane and sat down like this was the right and natural spot for him and afterwards he and Shane always used these same places.

I could not see any reason for the shift until the first time one of our homestead neighbors knocked on the door while we were eating and came straight on in as most of them usually did. Then I suddenly realized that Shane was sitting opposite the door where he could directly confront anyone coming through it. I could see that was the way he wanted it to be. But I could not understand why he wanted it that way.

In the evenings after supper when he was talking lazily with us, he would never sit by a window. Out on the porch he would always face the road. He liked to have a wall behind him and not just to lean against. No matter where he was, away from the table, before sitting down he would swing his chair into position, back to the nearest wall, not making any show, simply putting it there and bending into it in one easy motion. He did not even seem to be aware that this was unusual. It was part of his fixed alertness. He always wanted to know everything happening around him.

This alertness could be noted, too, in the watch he kept, without appearing to make any special effort, on every approach to our place. He knew first when anyone was moving along the road and he would stop whatever he was doing to study carefully any passing rider.

We often had company in the evenings, for the other homesteaders regarded father as their leader and would drop in to discuss their affairs with him. They were interesting men in their own fashions, a various assortment. But Shane was not anxious to meet people. He would share little in their talk.

With us he spoke freely enough. We were, in some subtle way, his folks. Though we had taken him in, you had the feeling that he had adopted us. But with others he was reserved; courteous and soft-spoken, yet withdrawn beyond a line of his own making.

These things puzzled me and not me alone. The people in town and those who rode or drove in pretty regularly were all curious about him. It was a wonder how quickly everyone in the valley, and even on the ranches out in the open country, knew that he was working with father.

They were not sure they liked having him in their neighborhood. Ledyard had told some tall tale about what happened at our place that made them stare sharply at Shane whenever they had a chance. But they must have had their own measure of Ledyard, for they did not take his story too straight. They just could not really make up their minds about Shane and it seemed to worry them.

More than once, when I was with Ollie Johnson on the way to our favorite fishing hole the other side of town, I heard men arguing about him in front of Mr. Grafton's store. "He's like one of these here slow-burning fuses," I heard an old muleskinner say one day. "Quiet and no sputtering. So quiet you forget it's burning. Then it sets off one hell of a blow-off of trouble when it touches powder. That's him. And there's been trouble brewing in this valley for a long spell now. Maybe it'll be good when it comes. Maybe it'll be bad. You just can't tell." And that puzzled me too.

What puzzled me most, though, was something it took me nearly two weeks to appreciate. And yet it was the most striking thing of all. Shane carried no gun.

In those days guns were as familiar all through the Territory as boots and saddles. They were not used much in the valley except for occasional hunting. But they were always in evidence. Most men did not feel fully dressed without one.

We homesteaders went in mostly for rifles and shotguns when we had any shooting to do. A pistol slapping on the hip was a nuisance for a farmer. Still every man had his cartridge belt and holstered Colt to be worn when he was not working or loafing around the house. Father buckled his on whenever he rode off on any trip, even just into town, as much out of habit, I guess, as anything else.

But this Shane never carried a gun. And that was a peculiar thing because he had a gun.

I saw it once. I saw it when I was alone in the barn one day and I spotted his saddle-roll lying on his bunk. Usually he kept it carefully put away underneath. He must have forgotten it this time, for it was there in the open by the pillow. I reached to sort of feel it—and I felt the gun inside. No one was near, so I unfastened the straps and unrolled the blankets. There it was, the most beautiful-looking weapon I ever saw. Beautiful and deadly-looking.

The holster and filled cartridge belt were of the same soft black leather as the boots tucked under the bunk, tooled in the same intricate design. I knew enough to know that the gun was a single-action Colt, the same model as the Regular Army issue that was the favorite of all men in those days and that oldtimers used to say was the finest pistol ever made.

This was the same model. But this was no Army gun. It was black, almost due black, with the darkness not in any enamel but in the metal itself. The grip was clear on the outer curve, shaped to the fingers on the inner curve, and two ivory plates were set into it with exquisite skill, one on each side.

The smooth invitation of it tempted your grasp. I took hold and pulled the gun out of the holster. It came so easily that I could hardly believe it was there in my hand. Heavy like father's, it was somehow much easier to handle. You held it up to aiming level and it seemed to balance itself into your hand.

It was clean and polished and oiled. The empty cylinder, when I released the catch and flicked it, spun swiftly and noiselessly. I was surprised to see that the front sight was gone, the barrel smooth right down to the end, and that the hammer had been filed to a sharp point.

Why should a man do that to a gun? Why should a man with a gun like that refuse to wear it and show it off? And then, staring at that dark and deadly efficiency, I was again suddenly chilled, and I quickly put everything back exactly as before and hurried out into the sun.

The first chance I tried to tell father about it. "Father," I said, all excited, "do you know what Shane has rolled up in his blankets?"

"Probably a gun."

"But—but how did you know? Have you seen it?"

"No. That's what he would have."

I was all mixed up. "Well, why doesn't he ever carry it? Do you suppose maybe it's because he doesn't know how to use it very well?"

Father chuckled like I had made a joke. "Son, I wouldn't be surprised if he could take that gun and shoot the buttons off your shirt with you awearing it and all you'd feel would be a breeze."

"Gosh agorry! Why does he keep it hidden in the barn then?"

"I don't know. Not exactly."

"Why don't you ask him?"

Father looked straight at me, very serious. "That's one question I'll never ask him. And don't you ever say anything to him about it. There are some things you don't ask a man. Not if you respect him. He's entitled to stake his claim to what he considers private to himself alone. But you can take my word for it, Bob, that when a man like Shane doesn't want to tote a gun you can bet your shirt, buttons and all, he's got a mighty good reason."

That was that. I was still mixed up. But whenever father gave you his word on something, there was nothing more to be said. He never did that except when he knew he was right. I started to wander off.

"Bob."

"Yes, father."

"Listen to me, son. Don't get to liking Shane too much."

"Why not? Is there anything wrong with him?"

"No-o-o-o. There's nothing wrong about Shane. Nothing you could put that way. There's more right about him than most any man you're ever likely to meet. But—" Father was throwing around for what to say. "But he's fiddle-footed. Remember. He said so himself. He'll be moving on one of these days and then you'll be all upset if you get to liking him too much."

That was not what father really meant. But that was what he wanted me to think. So I did not ask any more questions.

## 5

THE WEEKS went rocking past, and soon it did not seem possible that there ever had been a time when Shane was not with us. He and father worked together more like partners than boss and hired man. The amount they could get through in a day was a marvel. The ditching father had reckoned would take him most of the summer was done in less than a month. The loft was finished and the first cutting of alfalfa stowed away.

We would have enough fodder to carry a few more young steers through the winter for fattening next summer, so father rode out of the valley and all the way to the ranch where he worked once and came back herding a half-dozen more. He was gone two days. He came back to find that Shane, while he was gone, had knocked out the end of the corral and posted a new section making it half again as big.

"Now we can really get going next year," Shane said as father sat on his horse staring at the corral like he could not quite believe what he saw. "We ought to get enough hay off that new field to help us carry forty head."

"Oho!" said father. "So we can get going. And we ought to get enough hay." He was pleased as could be because he was scowling at Shane the way he did at me when he was tickled silly over something I had done and did not want to let on that he was. He jumped off his horse and hurried up to the house where mother was standing on the porch.

"Marian," he demanded right off, waving at the corral, "whose idea was that?"

"Well-l-l," she said, "Shane suggested it." Then she added slyly, "But I told him to go ahead."

"That's right." Shane had come up beside him. "She rode me like she had spurs to get it done by today. Kind of a present. It's your wedding anniversary."

"Well, I'll be damned," said father. "So it is." He stared foolishly at one and then the other of them. With Shane there watching, he hopped on the porch and gave mother a kiss. I was embarrassed for him and I turned away—and hopped about a foot myself.

"Hey! Those steers are running away!"

The grown folks had forgotten about them. All six were wandering up the road, straggling and separating. Shane, that soft-spoken man, let out a whoop you might have heard half-way to town and ran to father's horse, putting his hands on the saddle and vaulting into it. He fairly lifted the horse into a gallop in one leap and that old cowpony of father's lit out after those steers like this was fun. By the time father reached the corral gate, Shane had the runaways in a compact bunch and padding back at a trot. He dropped them through the gateway neat as pie.

He was tall and straight in the saddle the few seconds it took father to close the gate. He and the horse were blowing a bit and both of them were perky and proud.

"It's been ten years," he said, "since I did anything like that."

Father grinned at him. "Shane, if I didn't know better, I'd say you were a faker. There's still a lot of kid in you."

The first real smile I had seen yet flashed across Shane's face. "Maybe. Maybe there is at that."

I think that was the happiest summer of my life.

The only shadow over our valley, the recurrent trouble be-tween Fletcher and us homesteaders, seemed to have faded away. Fletcher himself was gone most of those months. He had gone to Fort Bennett in Dakota and even on East to Wash-ington, so we heard, trying to get a contract to supply beef to the Indian agent at Standing Rock, the big Sioux reservation over beyond the Black Hills. Except for his foreman, Morgan, and several surly older men, his hands were young, easy-going cowboys who made a lot of noise in town once in a while but rarely did any harm and even then only in high spirits. We liked them—when Fletcher was not there driving them into harass-ing us in constant shrewd ways. Now, with him away, they kept to the other side of the river and did not bother us. Sometimes, riding in sight on the other bank, they might even wave to us in their rollicking fashion.

Until Shane came, they had been my heroes. Father, of course, was special all to himself. There could never be anyone quite to match him. I wanted to be like him, just as he was. But first I wanted, as he had done, to ride the range, to have my own string of ponies and take part in an all-brand round-up and in a big cattle drive and dash into strange towns with just such a rollicking crew and with a season's pay jingling in my pockets.

Now I was not so sure. I wanted more and more to be like Shane, like the man I imagined he was in the past fenced off so securely. I had to imagine most of it. He would never speak of it, not in any way at all. Even his name remained mysterious. Just Shane. Nothing else. We never knew whether that was his first name or last name or, indeed, any name that came from his family. "Call me Shane," he said, and that was all he ever said. But I conjured up all manner of adventures for him, not tied to any particular time or place, seeing him as a slim and dark and dashing figure coolly passing through perils that would overcome a lesser man.

I would listen in what was closely akin to worship while my two men, father and Shane, argued long and amiably about the cattle business. They would wrangle over methods of feeding and bringing steers up to top weight. But they were agreed that controlled breeding was better than open range running and that improvement of stock was needed even if that meant spending big money on imported bulls. And they would speculate about the chances of a railroad spur ever reaching the valley, so you could ship direct without thinning good meat off your cattle driving them to market.

It was plain that Shane was beginning to enjoy living with us and working the place. Little by little the tension in him was fading out. He was still alert and watchful, instinct with that unfailing awareness of everything about him. I came to realize that this was inherent in him, not learned or acquired, simply a part of his natural being. But the sharp extra edge of conscious alertness, almost of expectancy of some unknown trouble always waiting, was wearing away.

Yet why was he sometimes so strange and stricken in his own secret bitterness? Like the time I was playing with a gun Mr. Grafton gave me, an old frontier model Colt with a cracked barrel someone had turned in at the store.

I had rigged a holster out of a torn chunk of oilcloth and a belt of rope. I was stalking around near the barn, whirling every few steps to pick off a skulking Indian, when I saw Shane watching me from the barn door. I stopped short, thinking of that beautiful gun under his bunk and afraid he would make fun of me and my sorry old broken pistol. Instead he looked gravely at me.

"How many you knocked over so far, Bob?"

Could I ever repay the man? My gun was a shining new weapon, my hand steady as a rock as I drew a bead on another one.

"That makes seven."

"Indians or timber wolves?"

"Indians. Big ones."

"Better leave a few for the other scouts," he said gently. "It wouldn't do to make them jealous. And look here, Bob. You're not doing that quite right."

He sat down on an upturned crate and beckoned me over. "Your holster's too low. Don't let it drag full arm's length. Have it just below the hip, so the grip is about halfway between your wrist and elbow when the arm's hanging limp. You can take the gun then as your hand's coming up and there's still room to clear the holster without having to lift the gun too high."

"Gosh agorry! Is that the way the real gunfighters do?"

A queer light flickered in his eyes and was gone. "No. Not all of them. Most have their own tricks. One likes a shoulder holster; another packs his gun in his pants belt. Some carry two guns, but that's a show-off stunt and a waste of weight. One's enough, if you know how to use it. I've even seen a man have a tight holster with an open end and fastened on a little swivel to the belt. He didn't have to pull the gun then. Just swung up the barrel and blazed away from the hip. That's mighty fast for close work and a big target. But it's not certain past ten or fifteen paces and no good at all for putting your shot right where you want it. The way I'm telling you is as good as any and better than most. And another thing—"

He reached and took the gun. Suddenly, as for the first time, I was aware of his hands. They were broad and strong, but not heavy and fleshy like father's. The fingers were long and square on the ends. It was funny how, touching the gun, the hands seemed to have an intelligence all their own, a sure movement that needed no guidance of thought.

His right hand closed around the grip and you knew at once

it was doing what it had been created for. He hefted the old gun, letting it lie loosely in the hand. Then the fingers tightened and the thumb toyed with the hammer, testing the play of it.

While I gaped at him, he tossed it swiftly in the air and caught it in his left hand and in the instant of catching, it nestled snugly into this hand too. He tossed it again, high this time and spinning end over end, and as it came down, his right hand flicked forward and took it. The forefinger slipped through the trigger guard and the gun spun, coming up into firing position in the one unbroken motion. With him that old pistol seemed alive, not an inanimate and rusting metal object, but an extension of the man himself.

"If it's speed you're after, Bob, don't split the move into parts. Don't pull, cock, aim, and fire. Slip back the hammer as you bring the gun up and squeeze the trigger the second it's up level."

"How do you aim it, then? How do you get a sight on it?"

"No need to. Learn to hold it so the barrel's right in line with the fingers if they were out straight. You won't have to waste time bringing it high to take a sight. Just point it, low and quick and easy, like pointing a finger."

Like pointing a finger. As the words came, he was doing it. The old gun was bearing on some target over by the corral and the hammer was clicking at the empty cylinder. Then the hand around the gun whitened and the fingers slowly opened and the gun fell to the ground. The hand sank to his side, stiff and awkward. He raised his head and the mouth was a bitter gash in his face. His eyes were fastened on the mountains climbing in the distance.

"Shane! Shane! What's the matter?"

He did not hear me. He was back somewhere along the dark trail of the past.

He took a deep breath, and I could see the effort run through him as he dragged himself into the present and a realization of a boy staring at him. He beckoned to me to pick up the gun. When I did, he leaned forward and spoke earnestly.

"Listen! Bob. A gun is just a tool. No better and no worse than any other tool, a shovel—or an axe or a saddle or a stove or anything. Think of it always that way. A gun is as good—and as bad—as the man who carries it. Remember that."

He stood up and strode off into the fields and I knew he wanted to be alone. I remembered what he said all right, tucked away unforgettably in my mind. But in those days I remembered more the way he handled the gun and the advice he gave me about using it. I would practice with it and think of the time when I could have one that would really shoot.

And then the summer was over. School began again and the days were growing shorter and the first cutting edge of cold was creeping down from the mountains.

# 6

MORE THAN the summer was over. The season of friendship in our valley was fading with the sun's warmth. Fletcher was back and he had his contract. He was talking in town that he would need the whole range again. The homesteaders would have to go.

He was a reasonable man, he was saying in his smooth way, and he would pay a fair price for any improvements they had put in. But we knew what Luke Fletcher would call a fair price. And we had no intention of leaving. The land was ours by right of settlement, guaranteed by the government. Only we knew, too, how faraway the government was from our valley way up there in the Territory.

The nearest marshal was a good hundred miles away. We did not even have a sheriff in our town. There never had been any reason for one. When folks had any lawing to do, they would head for Sheridan, nearly a full day's ride away. Our town was small, not even organized as a town. It was growing, but it was still not much more than a roadside settlement.

The first people there were three or four miners who had come prospecting after the blow-up of the Big Horn Mining Association about twenty years before, and had found gold traces leading to a moderate vein in the jutting rocks that partially closed off the valley where it edged into the plain. You could not have called it a strike, for others that followed were soon disappointed. Those first few, however, had done fairly well and had brought in their families and a number of helpers.

Then a stage and freighting line had picked the site for a relay post. That meant a place where you could get drinks as well as horses, and before long the cowboys from the ranches out on the plain and Fletcher's spread in the valley were drifting in of an evening. With us homesteaders coming now, one or two more almost every season, the town was taking shape. Already there were several stores, a harness and blacksmith shop, and nearly a dozen houses. Just the year before, the men had put together a one-room schoolhouse.

Sam Grafton's place was the biggest. He had a general store with several rooms for living quarters back of it in one half of his rambling building, a saloon with a long bar and tables for cards and the like in the other half. Upstairs he had some rooms he rented to stray drummers or anyone else stranded overnight. He acted as our postmaster, an elderly man, a close bargainer but honest in all his dealings. Sometimes he served as a sort of magistrate in minor disputes. His wife was dead. His daughter Jane kept house for him and was our schoolteacher when school was in session.

Even if we had had a sheriff, he would have been Fletcher's man. Fletcher was the power in the valley in those days. We homesteaders had been around only a few years and the other people still thought of us as there by his sufferance. He had been running cattle through the whole valley at the time the miners arrived, having bought or bulldozed out the few small ranchers there ahead of him. A series of bad years working up to the dry summer and terrible winter of '86 had cut his herds about the time the first of the homesteaders moved in and he had not objected too much. But now there were seven of us in all and the number rising each year.

It was a certain thing, father used to say, that the town would grow and swing our way. Mr. Grafton knew that too, I guess, but he was a careful man who never let thoughts about the future interfere with present business. The others were the kind to veer with the prevailing wind. Fletcher was the big man in the valley, so they looked up to him and tolerated us. Led to it, they probably would have helped him run us out. With him out of the way, they would just as willingly accept us. And Fletcher was back, with a contract in his pocket, wanting his full range again.

There was a hurried counsel in our house soon as the news was around. Our neighbor toward town, Lew Johnson, who heard it in Grafton's store, spread the word and arrived first. He was followed by Henry Shipstead, who had the place next to him, the closest to town. These two had been the original homesteaders, staking out their hundred and eighties two years before the drought and riding out Fletcher's annoyance until the cut in his herds gave him other worries. They were solid, dependable men, old-line farmers who had come West from Iowa.

You could not say quite as much for the rest, straggling in at intervals. James Lewis and Ed Howells were two middle-aged cowhands who had grown dissatisfied and tagged father into the valley, coming pretty much on his example. Lacking his energy and drive, they had not done too well and could be easily discouraged.

Frank Torrey from farther up the valley was a nervous, fidgety man with a querulous wife and a string of dirty kids growing longer every year. He was always talking about pulling up stakes and heading for California. But he had a stubborn streak in him, and he was always saying, too, that he'd be damned if he'd make tracks just because some big-hatted rancher wanted him to.

Ernie Wright, who had the last stand up the valley butting out into the range still used by Fletcher, was probably the weakest of the lot. Not in any physical way. He was a husky, likable man, so dark-complected that there were rumors he was part Indian. He was always singing and telling tall stories. But he would be off hunting when he should be working and he had a quick temper that would trap him into doing fool things without taking thought.

He was as serious as the rest of them that night. Mr. Grafton had said that this time Fletcher meant business. His contract called for all the beef he could drive in the next five years and he was determined to push the chance to the limit.

"But what can he do?" asked Frank Torrey. "The land's ours as long as we live on it and we get title in three years. Some of you fellows have already proved up."

"He won't really make trouble," chimed in James Lewis. "Fletcher's never been the shooting kind. He's a good talker, but talk can't hurt us." Several of the others nodded. Johnson and Shipstead did not seem to be so sure. Father had not said anything yet and they all looked at him.

"Jim's right," he admitted. "Fletcher hasn't ever let his boys get careless thataway. Not yet anyhow. That ain't saying he wouldn't, if there wasn't any other way. There's a hard streak in him. But he won't get real tough for a while. I don't figure he'll start moving cattle in now till spring. My guess is he'll try putting pressure on us this fall and winter, see if he can wear us down. He'll probably start right here. He doesn't like any of us. But he doesn't like me most."

"That's true." Ed Howells was expressing the unspoken verdict that father was their leader. "How do you figure he'll go about it?"

"My guess on that," father said—drawling now and smiling a grim little smile like he knew he was holding a good hole card in a tight game—"my guess on that is that he'll begin by trying to convince Shane here that it isn't healthy to be working with me."

"You mean the way he—" began Ernie Wright.

"Yes." Father cut him short. "I mean the way he did with young Morley."

I was peeping around the door of my little room. I saw Shane sitting off to one side, listening quietly as he had been right along. He did not seem the least bit surprised. He did not seem the least bit interested in finding out what had happened to young Morley. I knew what had. I had seen Morley come back from town, bruised and a beaten man, and gather his things and curse father for hiring him and ride away without once looking back.

Yet Shane sat there quietly as if what had happened to Morley had nothing to do with him. He simply did not care what it was. And then I understood why. It was because he was not Morley. He was Shane.

Father was right. In some strange fashion the feeling was abroad that Shane was a marked man. Attention was on him as a sort of symbol. By taking him on father had accepted in a way a challenge from the big ranch across the river. What had happened to Morley had been a warning and father had deliberately answered it. The long unpleasantness was sharpened now after the summer lull. The issue in our valley was plain and would in time have to be pushed to a showdown. If Shane could be driven out, there would be a break in the homestead ranks, a defeat going beyond the loss of a man into the realm of prestige and morale. It could be the crack in the dam that weakens the whole structure and finally lets through the flood.

The people in town were more curious than ever, not now so

much about Shane's past as about what he might do if Fletcher tried any move against him. They would stop me and ask me questions when I was hurrying to and from school. I knew that father would not want me to say anything and I pretended that I did not know what they were talking about. But I used to watch Shane closely myself and wonder how all the slow-climbing tenseness in our valley could be so focused on one man and he seem to be so indifferent to it.

For of course he was aware of it. He never missed anything. Yet he went about his work as usual, smiling frequently now at me, bantering mother at mealtimes in his courteous manner, arguing amiably as before with father on plans for next year. The only thing that was different was that there appeared to be a lot of new activity across the river. It was surprising how often Fletcher's cowboys were finding jobs to do within view of our place.

Then one afternoon, when we were stowing away the second and last cutting of hay, one fork of the big tongs we were using to haul it up to the loft broke loose. "Have to get it welded in town," father said in disgust and began to hitch up the team.

Shane stared over the river where a cowboy was riding lazily back and forth by a bunch of cattle. "I'll take it in," he said.

Father looked at Shane and he looked across the way and he grinned. "All right. It's as good a time as any." He slapped down the final buckle and started for the house. "Just a minute and I'll be ready."

"Take it easy, Joe." Shane's voice was gentle, but it stopped father in his tracks. "I said I'll take it in."

Father whirled to face him. "Damn it all, man. Do you think I'd let you go alone? Suppose they—" He bit down on his own words. He wiped a hand slowly across his face and he said what I had never heard him say to any man. "I'm sorry," he said. "I should have known better." He stood there silently watching as Shane gathered up the reins and jumped to the wagon seat.

I was afraid father would stop me, so I waited till Shane was driving out of the lane. I ducked behind the barn, around the end of the corral, and hopped into the wagon going past. As I did, I saw the cowboy across the river spin his horse and ride rapidly off in the direction of the ranch-house.

Shane saw it, too, and it seemed to give him a grim amusement. He reached backwards and hauled me over the seat and sat me beside him.

"You Starretts like to mix into things." For a moment I thought he might send me back. Instead he grinned at me. "I'll buy you a jackknife when we hit town."

He did, a dandy big one with two blades and a corkscrew. After we left the tongs with the blacksmith and found the welding would take nearly an hour, I squatted on the steps on the long porch across the front of Grafton's building, busy whittling, while Shane stepped into the saloon side and ordered a drink. Will Atkey, Grafton's thin, sad-faced clerk and bartender, was behind the bar and several other men were loafing at one of the tables.

It was only a few moments before two cowboys came galloping down the road. They slowed to a walk about fifty yards off and with a show of nonchalance ambled the rest of the way to Grafton's, dismounting and looping their reins over the rail in front. One of them I had seen often, a young fellow everyone called Chris, who had worked with Fletcher several years and was known for a gay manner and reckless courage. The other was new to me, a sallow, pinch-cheek man, not much older, who looked like he had crowded a lot of hard living into his years. He must have been one of the new hands Fletcher had been bringing into the valley since he got his contract.

They paid no attention to me. They stepped softly up on the porch and to the window of the saloon part of the building. As they peered through, Chris nodded and jerked his head toward the inside. The new man stiffened. He leaned closer for a better look. Abruptly he turned clear about and came right down past me and went over to his horse.

Chris was startled and hurried after him. They were both so intent they did not realize I was there. The new man was lifting the reins back over his horse's head when Chris caught his arm.

"What the hell?"

"I'm leaving."

"Huh? I don't get it."

"I'm leaving. Now. For good."

"Hey, listen. Do you know that guy?"

"I didn't say that. There ain't nobody can claim I said that.

I'm leaving, that's all. You can tell Fletcher. This is a hell of a country up here anyhow."

Chris was getting mad. "I might have known," he said. "Scared, eh. Yellow."

Color rushed into the new man's sallow face. But he climbed on his horse and swung out from the rail. "You can call it that," he said flatly and started down the road, out of town, out of the valley.

Chris was standing still by the rail, shaking his head in wonderment. "Hell," he said to himself, "I'll brace him myself." He stalked up on the porch, into the saloon.

I dashed into the store side, over to the opening between the two big rooms. I crouched on a box just inside the store where I could hear everything and see most of the other room. It was long and fairly wide. The bar curved out from the opening and ran all the way along the inner wall to the back wall, which closed off a room Grafton used as an office. There was a row of windows on the far side, too high for anyone to look in from outside. A small stairway behind them led up to a balcony-like across the back with doors opening into several little rooms.

Shane was leaning easily with one arm on the bar, his drink in his other hand, when Chris came to perhaps six feet away and called for a whiskey bottle and a glass. Chris pretended he did not notice Shane at first and bobbed his head in greeting to the men at the table. They were a pair of mule-skinners who made regular trips into the valley freighting in goods for Grafton and the other shops. I could have sworn that Shane, studying Chris in his effortless way, was somehow disappointed.

Chris waited until he had his whiskey and had gulped a stiff shot. Then he deliberately looked Shane over like he had just spotted him.

"Hello, farmer," he said. He said it as if he did not like farmers.

Shane regarded him with grave attention. "Speaking to me?" he asked mildly and finished his drink.

"Hell, there ain't nobody else standing there. Here, have a drink of this." Chris shoved his bottle along the bar. Shane poured himself a generous slug and raised it to his lips.

"I'll be damned," flipped Chris. "So you drink whiskey."

Shane tossed off the rest in his glass and set it down. "I've had better," he said, as friendly as could be. "But this will do."

Chris slapped his leather chaps with a loud smack. He turned to take in the other men. "Did you hear that? This farmer drinks whiskey! I didn't think these plow-pushing dirt-grubbers drank anything stronger than soda pop!"

"Some of us do," said Shane, friendly as before. Then he was no longer friendly and his voice was like winter frost. "You've had your fun and it's mighty young fun. Now run home and tell Fletcher to send a grown-up man next time." He turned away and sang out to Will Atkey. "Do you have any soda pop? I'd like a bottle."

Will hesitated, looked kind of funny, and scuttled past me into the store room. He came back right away with a bottle of the pop Grafton kept there for us school kids. Chris was standing quiet, not so much mad, I would have said, as puzzled. It was as though they were playing some queer game and he was not sure of the next move. He sucked on his lower lip for a while. Then he snapped his mouth and began to look elaborately around the room, sniffing loudly.

"Hey, Will!" he called. "What's been happening in here? It smells. That ain't no clean cattleman smell. That's plain dirty barnyard." He stared at Shane. "You, farmer. What are you and Starrett raising out there? Pigs?"

Shane was just taking hold of the bottle Will had fetched him. His hand closed on it and the knuckles showed white. He moved slowly, almost unwillingly, to face Chris. Every line of his body was as taut as stretched whipcord, was alive and somehow rich with an immense eagerness. There was that fierce concentration in him, filling him, blazing in his eyes. In that moment there was nothing in the room for him but that mocking man only a few feet away.

The big room was so quiet the stillness fairly hurt. Chris stepped back involuntarily, one pace, two, then pulled up erect. And still nothing happened. The lean muscles along the sides of Shane's jaw were ridged like rock.

Then the breath, pent in him, broke the stillness with a soft sound as it left his lungs. He looked away from Chris, past him, over the tops of the swinging doors beyond, over the roof of the shed across the road, on into the distance where the mountains loomed in their own unending loneliness. Quietly he walked, the bottle forgotten in his hand, so close by Chris as almost to brush him yet apparently not even seeing him, through the doors and was gone.

I heard a sigh of relief near me. Mr. Grafton had come up from somewhere behind me. He was watching Chris with a strange, ironic quirk at his mouth corners. Chris was trying not to look pleased with himself. But he swaggered as he went to the doors and peered over them.

"You saw it, Will," he called over his shoulder. "He walked out on me." Chris pushed up his hat and rolled back on his heels and laughed. "With a bottle of soda pop too!" He was still laughing as he went out and we heard him ride away.

"That boy's a fool," Mr. Grafton muttered.

Will Atkey came sidling over to Mr. Grafton. "I never pegged Shane for a play like that," he said.

"He was afraid, Will."

"Yeah. That's what was so funny. I would've guessed he could take Chris."

Mr. Grafton looked at Will as he did often, like he was a little sorry for him. "No, Will. He wasn't afraid of Chris. He was afraid of himself." Mr. Grafton was thoughtful and perhaps sad too. "There's trouble ahead, Will. The worst trouble we've ever had."

He noticed me, realizing my presence. "Better skip along, Bob, and find your friend. Do you think he got that bottle for himself?"

True enough, Shane had it waiting for me at the blacksmith shop. Cherry pop, the kind I favored most. But I could not enjoy it much. Shane was so silent and stern. He had slipped back into the dark mood that was on him when he first came riding up our road. I did not dare say anything. Only once did he speak to me and I knew he did not expect me to understand or to answer.

"Why should a man be smashed because he has courage and does what he's told? Life's a dirty business, Bob. I could like that boy." And he turned inward again to his own thoughts and stayed the same until we had loaded the tongs in the wagon and were well started home. Then the closer we came, the more cheerful he was. By the time we swung in toward the barn, he was the way I wanted him again, crinkling his eyes at me and gravely joshing me about the Indians I would scalp with my new knife.

Father popped out the barn door so quick you could tell he had been itching for us to return. He was busting with curiosity, but he would not come straight out with a question to Shane. He tackled me instead.

"See any of your cowboy heroes in town?"

Shane cut in ahead of me. "One of Fletcher's crew chased us in to pay his respects."

"No," I said, proud of my information. "There was two of them."

"Two?" Shane said it. Father was the one who was not surprised. "What did the other one do?"

"He went up on the porch and looked in the window where you were and came right back down and rode off."

"Back to the ranch?"

"The other way. He said he was leaving for good."

Father and Shane looked at each other. Father was smiling. "One down and you didn't even know it. What did you do to the other?"

"Nothing. He passed a few remarks about farmers. I went back to the blacksmith shop."

Father repeated it, spacing the words like there might be meanings between them. "You—went—back—to—the—blacksmith—shop."

I was worried that he must be thinking what Will Atkey did. Then I knew nothing like that had even entered his head. He switched to me. "Who was it?"

"It was Chris."

Father was smiling again. He had not been there but he had the whole thing clear. "Fletcher was right to send two. Young ones like Chris need to hunt in pairs or they might get hurt." He chuckled in a sort of wry amusement. "Chris must have been considerable surprised when the other fellow skipped. And more when you walked out. It was too bad the other one didn't stick around."

"Yes," Shane said, "it was."

The way he said it sobered father. "I hadn't thought of that. Chris is just cocky enough to take it wrong. That can make things plenty unpleasant."

"Yes," Shane said again, "it can."

# 7

I T WAS just as father and Shane had said. The story Chris told was common knowledge all through the valley before the sun set the next day and the story grew in the telling. Fletcher had an advantage now and he was quick to push it. He and his foreman, Morgan, a broad slab of a man with flattened face and head small in proportion to great sloping shoulders, were shrewd at things like this and they kept their men primed to rowel us homesteaders at every chance.

They took to using the upper ford, up above Ernie Wright's stand, and riding down the road past our places every time they had an excuse for going to town. They would go by slowly, looking everything over with insolent interest and passing remarks for our benefit.

The same week, maybe three days later, a covey of them came riding by while father was putting a new hinge on the corral gate. They acted like they were too busy staring over our land to see him there close.

"Wonder where Starrett keeps the critters," said one of them. "I don't see a pig in sight."

"But I can smell 'em!" shouted another one. With that they all began to laugh and whoop and holler and went tearing off, kicking up a lot of dust and leaving father with a tightness around his mouth that was not there before.

They were impartial with attentions like that. They would hand them out anywhere along the line an opportunity offered. But they liked best to catch father within earshot and burn him with their sarcasm.

It was crude. It was coarse. I thought it silly for grown men to act that way. But it was effective. Shane, as self-sufficient as the mountains, could ignore it. Father, while it galled him, could keep it from getting him. The other homesteaders, though, could not help being irritated and showing they felt insulted. It roughed their nerves and made them angry and restless. They did not know Shane as father and I did. They were not sure there might not be some truth in the big talk Chris was making.

264

Things became so bad they could not go into Grafton's store without someone singing out for soda pop. And wherever they went, the conversation near by always snuck around somehow to pigs. You could sense the contempt building up in town, in people who used to be neutral, not taking sides.

The effect showed, too, in the attitude our neighbors now had toward Shane. They were constrained when they called to see father and Shane was there. They resented that he was linked to them. And as a result their opinion of father was changing.

That was what finally drove Shane. He did not mind what they thought of him. Since his session with Chris he seemed to have won a kind of inner peace. He was as alert and watchful as ever, but there was a serenity in him that had erased entirely the old tension. I think he did not care what anyone anywhere thought of him. Except us, his folks. And he knew that with us he was one of us, unchangeable and always.

But he did care what they thought of father. He was standing silently on the porch the night Ernie Wright and Henry Shipstead were arguing with father in the kitchen.

"I can't stomach much more," Ernie Wright was saying. "You know the trouble I've had with those blasted cowboys cutting my fence. Today a couple of them rode over and helped me repair a piece. Helped me, damn them! Waited till we were through, then said Fletcher didn't want any of my pigs getting loose and mixing with his cattle. My pigs! There ain't a pig in this whole valley and they know it. I'm sick of the word."

Father made it worse by chuckling. Grim, maybe, yet still a chuckle. "Sounds like one of Morgan's ideas. He's smart. Mean, but—"

Henry Shipstead would not let him finish. "This is nothing to laugh at, Joe. You least of all. Damn it, man, I'm beginning to doubt your judgment. None of us can keep our heads up around here any more. Just a while ago I was in Grafton's and Chris was there blowing high about your Shane must be thirsty because he's so scared he hasn't been in town lately for his soda pop."

Both of them were hammering at father now. He was sitting back, saying nothing, his face clouding.

"You can't dodge it, Joe." This was Wright. "Your man's

responsible. You can try explaining all night, but you can't change the facts. Chris braced him for a fight and he ducked out—and left us stuck with those stinking pigs."

"You know as well as I do what Fletcher's doing," growled Henry Shipstead. "He's pushing us with this and he won't let up till one of us gets enough and makes a fool play and starts something so he can move in and finish it."

"Fool play or not," said Ernie Wright, "I've had all I can take. The next time one of those—"

Father stopped him with a hand up for silence. "Listen. What's that?"

It was a horse, picking up speed and tearing down our lane into the road. Father was at the door in a single jump, peering out.

The others were close behind him. "Shane?"

Father nodded. He was muttering under his breath. As I watched from the doorway of my little room, I could see that his eyes were bright and dancing. He was calling Shane names, cursing him, softly, fluently. He came back to his chair and grinned at the other two. "That's Shane," he told them and the words meant more than they seemed to say. "All we can do now is wait."

They were a silent crew waiting. Mother got up from her sewing in the bedroom where she had been listening as she always did and came into the kitchen and made up a pot of coffee and they all sat there sipping at the hot stuff and waiting.

It could not have been much more than twenty minutes before we heard the horse again, coming swiftly and slewing around to make the lane without slowing. There were quick steps on the porch and Shane stood in the doorway. He was breathing strongly and his face was hard. His mouth was a thin line in the bleakness of his face and his eyes were deep and dark. He looked at Shipstead and Wright and he made no effort to hide the disgust in his voice.

"Your pigs are dead and buried."

As his gaze shifted to father, his face softened. But the voice was still bitter. "There's another one down. Chris won't be bothering anybody for quite a spell." He turned and disappeared and we could hear him leading the horse into the barn.

In the quiet following, hoofbeats like an echo sounded in

the distance. They swelled louder and this second horse galloped into our lane and pulled to a stop. Ed Howells jumped
to the porch and hurried in.

"Where's Shane?"

"Out in the barn," father said.

"Did he tell you what happened?"

"Not much," father said mildly. "Something about burying
pigs."

Ed Howells slumped into a chair. He seemed a bit dazed.
The words came out of him slowly at first as he tried to make
the others grasp just how he felt. "I never saw anything like it,"
he said, and he told about it.

He had been in Grafton's store buying a few things, not caring about going into the saloon because Chris and Red Marlin, another of Fletcher's cowboys, had hands in the evening
poker game, when he noticed how still the place was. He went
over to sneak a look and there was Shane just moving to the
bar, cool and easy as if the room was empty and he the only
one in it. Neither Chris nor Red Marlin was saying a word,
though you might have thought this was a good chance for
them to cut loose with some of their raw sarcasm. One look
at Shane was enough to tell why. He was cool and easy, right
enough. But there was a curious kind of smooth flow to his
movements that made you realize without being conscious of
thinking about it that being quiet was a mighty sensible way to
be at the moment.

"Two bottles of soda pop," he called to Will Atkey. He
leaned his back to the bar and looked the poker game over
with what seemed a friendly interest while Will fetched the
bottles from the store. Not another person even twitched a
muscle. They were all watching him and wondering what the
play was. He took the two bottles and walked to the table and
set them down, reaching over to put one in front of Chris.

"The last time I was in here you bought me a drink. Now
it's my turn."

The words sort of lingered in the stillness. He got the impression, Ed Howells said, that Shane meant just what the
words said. He wanted to buy Chris a drink. He wanted Chris
to take that bottle and grin at him and drink with him.

You could have heard a bug crawl, I guess, while Chris

carefully laid down the cards in his right hand and stretched it to the bottle. He lifted it in a sudden jerk and flung it across the table at Shane.

So fast Shane moved, Ed Howells said, that the bottle was still in the air when he had dodged, lunged forward, grabbed Chris by the shirtfront and hauled him right out of his chair and over the table. As Chris struggled to get his feet under him, Shane let go the shirt and slapped him, sharp and stinging, three times, the hand flicking back and forth so quick you could hardly see it, the slaps sounding like pistol shots.

Shane stepped back and Chris stood swaying a little and shaking his head to clear it. He was a game one and mad down to his boots. He plunged in, fists smashing, and Shane let him come, slipping inside the flailing arms and jolting a powerful blow low into his stomach. As Chris gasped and his head came down, Shane brought his right hand up, open, and with the heel of it caught Chris full on the mouth, snapping his head back and raking up over the nose and eyes.

The force of it knocked Chris off balance and he staggered badly. His lips were crushed. Blood was dripping over them from his battered nose. His eyes were red and watery and he was having trouble seeing with them. His face, Ed Howells said, and shook a little as he said it, looked like a horse had stomped it. But he drove in again, swinging wildly.

Shane ducked under, caught one of the flying wrists, twisted the arm to lock it and keep it from bending, and swung his shoulder into the armpit. He yanked hard on the wrist and Chris went up and over him. As the body hurtled over, Shane kept hold of the arm and wrenched it sideways and let the weight bear on it and you could hear the bone crack as Chris crashed to the floor.

A long sobbing sigh came from Chris and that died away and there was not a sound in the room. Shane never looked at the crumpled figure. He was straight and deadly and still. Every line of him was alive and eager. But he stood motionless. Only his eyes shifted to search the faces of the others at the table. They stopped on Red Marlin and Red seemed to dwindle lower in his chair.

"Perhaps," Shane said softly, and the very softness of his

voice sent shivers through Ed Howells, "perhaps you have something to say about soda pop or pigs."

Red Marlin sat quiet like he was trying not even to breathe. Tiny drops of sweat appeared on his forehead. He was frightened, maybe for the first time in his life, and the others knew it and he knew they knew and he did not care. And none of them blamed him at all.

Then, as they watched, the fire in Shane smouldered down and out. He seemed to withdraw back within himself. He forgot them all and turned toward Chris unconscious on the floor, and a sort of sadness, Ed Howells said, crept over him and held him. He bent and scooped the sprawling figure up in his arms and carried it to one of the other tables. Gently he set it down, the legs falling limp over the edge. He crossed to the bar and took the rag Will used to wipe it and returned to the table and tenderly cleared the blood from the face. He felt carefully along the broken arm and nodded to himself at what he felt.

All this while no one said a word. Not a one of them would have interfered with that man for a year's top wages. He spoke and his voice rang across the room at Red Marlin. "You'd better tote him home and get that arm fixed. Take right good care of him. He has the makings of a good man." Then he forgot them all again and looked at Chris and went on speaking as if to that limp figure that could not hear him. "There's only one thing really wrong with you. You're young. That's the one thing time can always cure."

The thought hurt him and he strode to the swinging doors and through them into the night.

That was what Ed Howells told. "The whole business," he finished, "didn't take five minutes. It was maybe thirty seconds from the time he grabbed holt of Chris till Chris was out cold on the floor. In my opinion that Shane is the most dangerous man I've ever seen. I'm glad he's working for Joe here and not for Fletcher."

Father leveled a triumphant look at Henry Shipstead. "So I've made a mistake, have I?"

Before anyone else could push in a word, mother was speaking. I was surprised, because she was upset and her voice was a little shrill. "I wouldn't be too sure about that, Joe Starrett. I think you've made a bad mistake."

"Marian, what's got into you?"

"Look what you've done just because you got him to stay on here and get mixed up in this trouble with Fletcher!"

Father was edging toward being peeved himself. "Women never do understand these things. Lookahere, Marian. Chris will be all right. He's young and he's healthy. Soon as that arm is mended, he'll be in as good shape as he ever was."

"Oh, Joe, can't you see what I'm talking about? I don't mean what you've done to Chris. I mean what you've done to Shane."

# 8

THIS TIME mother was right. Shane was changed. He tried to keep things as they had been with us and on the surface nothing was different. But he had lost the serenity that had seeped into him through the summer. He would no longer sit around and talk with us as much as he had. He was restless with some far hidden desperation.

At times, when it rode him worst, he would wander alone about our place, and this was the one thing that seemed to soothe him. I used to see him, when he thought no one was watching, run his hands along the rails of the corral he had fastened, test with a tug the posts he had set, pace out past the barn looking up at the bulging loft and stride out where the tall corn was standing in big shocks to dig his hands in the loose soil and lift some of it and let it run through his fingers.

He would lean on the pasture fence and study our little herd like it meant more to him than lazy steers to be fattened for market. Sometimes he would whistle softly, and his horse, filled out now so you could see the quality of him and moving with a quiet sureness and power that made you think of Shane himself, would trot to the fence and nuzzle at him.

Often he would disappear from the house in the early evening after supper. More than once, the dishes done, when I managed to slip past mother, I found him far back in the pasture alone with the horse. He would be standing there, one arm on the smooth arch of the horse's neck, the fingers gently rubbing around the ears, and he would be looking out over our land where the last light of the sun, now out of sight, would be flaring up the far side of the mountains, capping them with a deep glow and leaving a mystic gloaming in the valley.

Some of the assurance that was in him when he came was gone now. He seemed to feel that he needed to justify himself, even to me, to a boy tagging his heels.

"Could you teach me," I asked him, "to throw somebody the way you threw Chris?"

He waited so long I thought he would not answer. "A man doesn't learn things like that," he said at last. "You know them

271

and that's all." Then he was talking rapidly to me, as close to
pleading as he could ever come. "I tried. You can see that,
can't you, Bob? I let him ride me and I gave him his chance. A
man can keep his self-respect without having to cram it down
another man's throat. Surely you can see that, Bob?"

I could not see it. What he was trying to explain to me was
beyond my comprehension then. And I could think of nothing
to say.

"I left it up to him. He didn't have to jump me that second
time. He could have called it off without crawling. He could
have if he was man enough. Can't you see that, Bob?"

And still I could not. But I said I could. He was so earnest
and he wanted me to so badly. It was a long, long time before I
did see it and then I was a man myself and Shane was not there
for me to tell. . . .

I was not sure whether father and mother were aware of
the change in him. They did not talk about it, not while I was
around anyway. But one afternoon I overheard something that
showed mother knew.

I had hurried home from school and put on my old clothes
and started out to see what father and Shane were doing in the
cornfield, when I thought of a trick that had worked several
times. Mother was firm set against eating between meals. That
was a silly notion. I had my mind set on the cookies she kept in
a tin box on a shelf by the stove. She was settled on the porch
with a batch of potatoes to peel, so I slipped up to the back of
the house, through the window of my little room, and tiptoed
into the kitchen. Just as I was carefully putting a chair under
the shelf, I heard her call to Shane.

He must have come to the barn on some errand, for he was
there by the porch in only a moment. I peeped out the front
window and saw him standing close in, his hat in his hand,
his face tilted up slightly to look at her leaning forward in her
chair.

"I've been wanting to talk to you when Joe wasn't around."

"Yes, Marian." He called her that the same as father did,
familiar yet respectful, just as he always regarded her with a
tenderness in his eyes he had for no one else.

"You've been worrying, haven't you, about what may happen

in this Fletcher business? You thought it would just be a case of not letting him scare you away and of helping us through a hard time. You didn't know it would come to what it has. And now you're worried about what you might do if there's any more fighting."

"You're a discerning woman, Marian."

"You've been worrying about something else too."

"You're a mighty discerning woman, Marian."

"And you've been thinking that maybe you'll be moving on."

"And how did you know that?"

"Because it's what you ought to do. For your own sake. But I'm asking you not to." Mother was intense and serious, as lovely there with the light striking through her hair as I had ever seen her. "Don't go, Shane. Joe needs you. More than ever now. More than he would ever say."

"And you?" Shane's lips barely moved and I was not sure of the words.

Mother hesitated. Then her head went up. "Yes. It's only fair to say it. I need you too."

"So-o-o," he said softly, the word lingering on his lips. He considered her gravely. "Do you know what you're asking, Marian?"

"I know. And I know that you're the man to stand up to it. In some ways it would be easier for me, too, if you rode out of this valley and never came back. But we can't let Joe down. I'm counting on you not ever to make me do that. Because you've got to stay, Shane, no matter how hard it is for us. Joe can't keep this place without you. He can't buck Fletcher alone."

Shane was silent, and it seemed to me that he was troubled and hard pressed in his mind. Mother was talking straight to him, slow and feeling for the words, and her voice was beginning to tremble.

"It would just about kill Joe to lose this place. He's too old to start in again somewhere else. Oh, we would get along and might even do real well. After all, he's Joe Starrett. He's all man and he can do what has to be done. But he promised me this place when we were married. He had it in his mind for all the first years. He did two men's work to get the extra money for the things we would need. When Bob was big enough to walk and help some and he could leave us, he came on here and filed his claim and built this house with his own hands, and when he brought us here it was home. Nothing else would ever be the same."

Shane drew a deep breath and let it ease out slowly. He smiled at her and yet, somehow, as I watched him, my heart ached for him. "Joe should be proud of a wife like you. Don't fret any more, Marian. You'll not lose this place."

Mother dropped back in her chair. Her face, the side I could see from the window, was radiant. Then, woman like, she was talking against herself. "But that Fletcher is a mean and tricky man. Are you sure it will work out all right?"

Shane was already starting toward the barn. He stopped and turned to look at her again. "I said you won't lose this place." You knew he was right because of the way he said it and because he said it.

# 9

Another period of peace had settled over our valley. Since the night Shane rode into town, Fletcher's cowboys had quit using the road past the homesteads. They were not annoying us at all and only once in a while was there a rider in view across the river. They had a good excuse to let us be. They were busy fixing the ranch buildings and poling a big new corral in preparation for the spring drive of new cattle Fletcher was planning.

Just the same, I noticed that father was as watchful as Shane now. The two of them worked always together. They did not split any more to do separate jobs in different parts of the farm. They worked together, rode into town together when anything was needed. And father took to wearing his gun all the time, even in the fields. He strapped it on after breakfast the first morning following the fight with Chris, and I saw him catch Shane's eye with a questioning glance as he buckled the belt. But Shane shook his head and father nodded, accepting the decision, and they went out together without saying a word.

Those were beautiful fall days, clear and stirring, with the coolness in the air just enough to set one atingling, not yet mounting to the bitter cold that soon would come sweeping down out of the mountains. It did not seem possible that in such a harvest season, giving a lift to the spirit to match the wellbeing of the body, violence could flare so suddenly and swiftly.

Saturday evenings all of us would pile into the light work wagon, father and mother on the seat, Shane and I swinging legs at the rear, and go into town. It was the break in routine we looked forward to all week.

There was always a bustle in Grafton's store with people we knew coming and going. Mother would lay in her supplies for the week ahead, taking a long time about it and chatting with the womenfolk. She and the wives of the other homesteaders were great ones for swapping recipes and this was their bartering ground. Father would give Mr. Grafton his order for what he wanted and go direct for the mail. He was always getting catalogues of farm equipment and pamphlets from Washington. He would flip through their pages and skim through any letters, then settle on a barrel and spread out his newspaper. But like as not he would soon be bogged down in an argument with almost any man handy about the best crops for the Territory and it would be Shane who would really work his way into the newspaper.

I used to explore the store, filling myself with crackers from the open barrel at the end of the main counter, playing hide and seek with Mr. Grafton's big and knowing old cat that was a whiz of a mouser. Many a time, turning up boxes, I chased out fat furry ones for her to pounce on. If mother was in the right mood, I would have a bag of candy in my pocket.

This time we had a special reason for staying longer than usual, a reason I did not like. Our schoolteacher, Jane Grafton, had made me take a note home to mother asking her to stop in for a talk. About me. I never was too smart at formal schooling to begin with. Being all excited over the doings at the big ranch and what they might mean to us had not helped any. Miss Grafton, I guess, just sort of endured me under the best of conditions. But what tipped her into being downright annoyed and writing to mother was the weather. No one could expect a boy with any spirit in him to be shut up in a schoolroom in weather like we had been having. Twice that week I had persuaded Ollie Johnson to sneak away with me after the lunch hour to see if the fish were still biting in our favorite pool below town.

Mother finished the last item on her list, looked around at me, sighed a little, and stiffened her shoulders. I knew she was going to the living quarters behind the store and talk to Miss Grafton. I squirmed and pretended I did not notice her. Only a few people were left in the store, though the saloon in the adjoining big room was doing fair business. She went over to where father was leafing through a catalogue and tapped him.

"Come along, Joe. You should hear this, too. I declare, that boy is getting too big for me to handle."

Father glanced quickly over the store and paused, listening to the voices from the next room. We had not seen any of

Fletcher's men all evening and he seemed satisfied. He looked at Shane, who was folding the newspaper.

"This won't take long. We'll be out in a moment."

As they passed through the door at the rear of the store, Shane strolled to the saloon opening. He took in the whole room in his easy, alert way and stepped inside. I followed. But I was supposed not ever to go in there, so I stopped at the entrance. Shane was at the bar, joshing Will Atkey with a grave face that he didn't think he'd have soda pop tonight. It was a scattered group in the room, most of them from around town and familiar to me by sight at least. Those close to Shane moved a little away, eyeing him curiously. He did not appear to notice.

He picked up his drink and savored it, one elbow on the bar, not shoving himself forward into the room's companionship and not withdrawing either, just ready to be friendly if anyone wanted that and unfriendly if anyone wanted that too.

I was letting my eyes wander about, trying to tag names to faces, when I saw that one of the swinging doors was partly open and Red Marlin was peeking in. Shane saw it too. But he could not see that more men were out on the porch, for they were close by the building wall and on the store side. I could sense them through the window near me, hulking shapes in the darkness. I was so frightened I could scarcely move.

But I had to. I had to go against mother's rule. I scrambled into the saloon and to Shane and I gasped: "Shane! There's a lot of them out front!"

I was too late. Red Marlin was inside and the others were hurrying in and fanning out to close off the store opening. Morgan was one of them, his flat face sour and determined, his huge shoulders almost filling the doorway as he came through. Behind him was the cowboy they called Curly because of his shock of unruly hair. He was stupid and slow-moving, but he was thick and powerful, and he had worked in harness with Chris for several years. Two others followed them, new men to me, with the tough, experienced look of old herd hands.

There was still the back office with its outside door opening on a side stoop and the rear alley. My knees were shaking and

I tugged at Shane and tried to say something about it. He stopped me with a sharp gesture. His face was clear, his eyes bright. He was somehow happy, not in the pleased and laughing way, but happy that the waiting was over and what had been ahead was here and seen and realized and he was ready for it. He put one hand on my head and rocked it gently, the fingers feeling through my hair.

"Bobby boy, would you have me run away?"

Love for that man raced through me and the warmth ran down and stiffened my legs and I was so proud of being there with him that I could not keep the tears from my eyes. I could see the rightness of it and I was ready to do as he told me when he said: "Get out of here, Bob. This isn't going to be pretty."

But I would go no farther than my perch just inside the store where I could watch most of the big room. I was so bound in the moment that I did not even think of running for father.

Morgan was in the lead now with his men spread out behind him. He came about half the way to Shane and stopped. The room was quiet except for the shuffling of feet as the men by the bar and the nearest tables hastened over to the far wall and some of them ducked out the front doors. Neither Shane nor Morgan gave any attention to them. They had attention only for each other. They did not look aside even when Mr. Grafton, who could smell trouble in his place from any distance, stalked in from the store, planting his feet down firmly, and pushed past Will Atkey behind the bar. He had a resigned expression on his face and he reached under the counter, his hands reappearing with a short-barreled shotgun. He laid it before him on the bar and he said in a dry, disgusted voice: "There will be no gunplay, gentlemen. And all damages will be paid for."

Morgan nodded curtly, not taking his eyes from Shane. He came closer and stopped again little more than an arm's length away. His head was thrust forward. His big fists were clenched at his sides.

"No one messes up one of my boys and gets away with it. We're riding you out of this valley on a rail, Shane. We're going to rough you a bit and ride you out and you'll stay out."

"So you have it all planned," Shane said softly. Even as he was speaking, he was moving. He flowed into action so swift you could hardly believe what was happening. He scooped up his half-filled glass from the bar, whipped it and its contents into Morgan's face, and when Morgan's hands came up reaching or striking for him, he grasped the wrists and flung himself backwards, dragging Morgan with him. His body rolled to meet the floor and his legs doubled and his feet, catching Morgan just below the belt, sent him flying on and over to fall flat in a grotesque spraddle and slide along the boards in a tangle of chairs and a table.

The other four were on Shane in a rush. As they came, he whirled to his hands and knees and leaped up and behind the nearest table, tipping it in a strong heave among them. They scattered, dodging, and he stepped, fast and light, around the end and drove into the tail man, one of the new men, now nearest to him. He took the blows at him straight on to get in close and I saw his knee surge up and into the man's groin. A high scream was literally torn from the man and he collapsed to the floor and dragged himself toward the doors.

Morgan was on his feet, wavering, rubbing a hand across his face, staring hard as if trying to focus again on the room about him. The other three were battering at Shane, seeking to box him between them. They were piling blows into him, crowding in. Through that blur of movement he was weaving, quick and confident. It was incredible, but they could not hurt him. You could see the blows hit, hear the solid chunk of knuckles on flesh. But they had no effect. They seemed only to feed that fierce energy. He moved like a flame among them. He would burst out of the mêlée and whirl and plunge back, the one man actually pressing the three. He had picked the second new man and was driving always directly at him.

Curly, slow and clumsy, grunting in exasperation, grabbed at Shane to grapple with him and hold down his arms. Shane dropped one shoulder and as Curly hugged tighter brought it up under his jaw with a jolt that knocked him loose and away.

They were wary now and none too eager to let him get close to any one of them. Then Red Marlin came at him from one side, forcing him to turn that way, and at the same time the second new man did a strange thing. He jumped high in the air, like a jack rabbit in a spy hop, and lashed out viciously with one boot at Shane's head. Shane saw it coming, but could not avoid it, so he rolled his head with the kick, taking it along the side. It shook him badly. But it did not block the instant response. His hands shot up and seized the foot and the man crashed down to land on the small of his back. As he hit, Shane twisted the whole leg and threw his weight on it. The man buckled on the floor like a snake when you hit it and groaned sharply and hitched himself away, the leg dragging, the fight gone out of him.

But the swing to bend down on the leg had put Shane's back to Curly and the big man was plowing at him. Curly's arms clamped around him, pinning his arms to his body. Red Marlin leaped to help and the two of them had Shane caught tight between them.

"Hold him!" That was Morgan, coming forward with the hate plain in his eyes. Even then, Shane would have broke away. He stomped one heavy work shoe, heel edged and with all the strength he could get in quick leverage, on Curly's near foot. As Curly winced and pulled it back and was unsteady, Shane strained with his whole body in a powerful arch and you could see their arms slipping and loosening. Morgan, circling in, saw it too. He swept a bottle off the bar and brought it smashing down from behind on Shane's head.

Shane slumped and would have fallen if they had not been holding him. Then, as Morgan stepped around in front of him and watched, the vitality pumped through him and his head came up.

"Hold him!" Morgan said again. He deliberately flung a huge fist to Shane's face. Shane tried to jerk aside and the fist missed the jaw, tearing along the cheek, the heavy ring on one finger slicing deep. Morgan pulled back for another blow. He never made it.

Nothing, I would have said, could have drawn my attention from those men. But I heard a kind of choking sob beside me and it was queer and yet familiar and it turned me instantly.

Father was there in the entranceway!

He was big and terrible and he was looking across the over-turned table and scattered chairs at Shane, at the dark purplish bruise along the side of Shane's head and the blood running down his cheek. I had never seen father like this. He was past anger. He was filled with a fury that was shaking him almost beyond endurance.

I never thought he could move so fast. He was on them before they even knew he was in the room. He hurtled into Morgan with ruthless force, sending that huge man reeling across the room. He reached out one broad hand and grabbed Curly by the shoulder and you could see the fingers sink into the flesh. He took hold of Curly's belt with the other hand and ripped him loose from Shane and his own shirt shredded down the back and the great muscles there knotted and bulged as he lifted Curly right up over his head and hurled the threshing body from him. Curly spun through the air, his limbs waving wildly, and crashed on the top of a table way over by the wall. It cracked under him, collapsing in splintered pieces, and the man and the wreckage smacked against the wall. Curly tried to rise, pushing himself with hands on the floor, and fell back and was still.

Shane must have exploded into action the second father yanked Curly away, for now there was another noise. It was Red Marlin, his face contorted, flung against the bar and catching at it to keep himself from falling. He staggered and caught his balance and ran for the front doorway. His flight was frantic, headlong. He tore through the swinging doors without slowing to push them. They flapped with a swishing sound and my eyes shifted quickly to Shane, for he was laughing.

He was standing there, straight and superb, the blood on his face bright like a badge, and he was laughing.

It was a soft laugh, soft and gentle, not in amusement at Red Marlin or any single thing, but in the joy of being alive and released from long discipline and answering the urge in mind and body. The lithe power in him, so different from father's sheer strength, was singing in every fiber of him.

Morgan was in the rear corner, his face clouded and uncertain. Father, his fury eased by the mighty effort of throwing Curly, had looked around to watch Red Marlin's run and now was starting toward Morgan. Shane's voice stopped him.

"Wait, Joe. The man's mine." He was at father's side and he put a hand on father's arm. "You'd better get them out of here." He nodded in my direction and I noticed with surprise that mother was near and watching. She must have followed father and have been there all this while. Her lips were parted. Her eyes were glowing, looking at the whole room, not at anyone or anything in particular, but at the whole room.

Father was disappointed. "Morgan's more my size," he said, grumbling fashion. He was not worried about Shane. He was thinking of an excuse to take Morgan himself. But he went no further. He looked at the men over by the wall. "This is Shane's play. If a one of you tries to interfere, he'll have me to reckon with." His tone showed that he was not mad at them, that he was not even really warning them. He was simply making the play plain. Then he came to us and looked down at mother. "You wait out at the wagon, Marian. Morgan's had this coming to him for quite a long time now and it's not for a woman to see."

Mother shook her head without moving her eyes now from Shane. "No, Joe. He's one of us. I'll see this through." And the three of us stayed there together and that was right, for he was Shane.

He advanced toward Morgan, as flowing and graceful as the old mouser in the store. He had forgotten us and the battered men on the floor and those withdrawn by the wall and Mr. Grafton and Will Atkey crouched behind the bar. His whole being was concentrated on the big man before him.

Morgan was taller, half again as broad, with a long reputation as a bullying fighter in the valley. But he did not like this and he was desperate. He knew better than to wait. He rushed at Shane to overwhelm the smaller man with his weight. Shane faded from in front of him and as Morgan went past hooked a sharp blow to his stomach and another to the side of his jaw. They were short and quick, flicking in so fast they were just a blur of movement. Yet each time at the instant of impact Morgan's big frame shook and halted in its rush for a fraction of a second before the momentum carried him forward. Again and again he rushed, driving his big fists ahead. Always Shane slipped away, sending in those swift hard punches.

Breathing heavily, Morgan stopped, grasping the futility of straight fighting. He plunged at Shane now, arms wide, trying to get hold of him and wrestle him down. Shane was ready and let him come without dodging, disregarding the arms stretching to encircle him. He brought up his right hand, open, just as Ed Howells had told us, and the force of Morgan's own lunge as the hand met his mouth and raked upwards snapped back his head and sent him staggering.

Morgan's face was puffy and red-mottled. He bellowed some insane sound and swung up a chair. Holding it in front of him, legs forward, he rushed again at Shane, who sidestepped neatly. Morgan was expecting this and halted suddenly, swinging the chair in a swift arc to strike Shane with it full on the side. The chair shattered and Shane faltered, and then, queerly for a man usually so sure on his feet, he seemed to slip and fall to the floor.

Forgetting all caution, Morgan dove at him—and Shane's legs bent and he caught Morgan on his heavy work shoes and sent him flying back and against the bar with a crash that shook the whole length of it.

Shane was up and leaping at Morgan as if there had been springs under him there on the floor. His left hand, palm out, smacked against Morgan's forehead, pushing the head back, and his right fist drove straight to Morgan's throat. You could see the agony twist the man's face and the fear widen his eyes. And Shane, using his right fist now like a club and lining his whole body behind it, struck him on the neck below and back of the ear. It made a sickening, dull sound and Morgan's eyes rolled white and he went limp all over, sagging slowly and forward to the floor.

IN THE hush that followed Morgan's fall, the big barroom was so quiet again that the rustle of Will Atkey straightening from below the bar level was loud and clear and Will stopped moving, embarrassed and a little frightened.

Shane looked neither at him nor at any of the other men staring from the wall. He looked only at us, at father and mother and me, and it seemed to me that it hurt him to see us there.

He breathed deeply and his chest filled and he held it, held it long and achingly, and released it slowly and sighing. Suddenly you were impressed by the fact that he was quiet, that he was still. You saw how battered and bloody he was. In the moments before you saw only the splendor of movement, the flowing brute beauty of line and power in action. The man, you felt, was tireless and indestructible. Now that he was still and the fire in him banked and subsided, you saw, and in the seeing remembered, that he had taken bitter punishment.

His shirt collar was dark and sodden. Blood was soaking into it, and this came only in part from the cut on his cheek. More was oozing from the matted hair where Morgan's bottle had hit. Unconsciously he put up one hand and it came away smeared and sticky. He regarded it grimly and wiped it clean on his shirt. He swayed slightly and when he started toward us, his feet dragged and he almost fell forward.

One of the townsmen, Mr. Weir, a friendly man who kept the stage post, pushed out from the wall, clucking sympathy, as though to help him. Shane pulled himself erect. His eyes blazed refusal. Straight and superb, not a tremor in him, he came to us and you knew that the spirit in him would sustain him thus alone for the farthest distance and forever.

But there was no need. The one man in our valley, the one man, I believe, in all the world whose help he would take, not to whom he would turn but whose help he would take, was there and ready. Father stepped to meet him and put out a big arm reaching for his shoulders. "All right, Joe," Shane said, so softly I doubt whether the others in the room heard. His eyes closed and he leaned against father's arm, his body relaxing and his head dropping sideways. Father bent and fitted his other arm under Shane's knees and picked him up like he did me when I stayed up too late and got all drowsy and had to be carried to bed.

Father held Shane in his arms and looked over him at Mr. Grafton. "I'd consider it a favor, Sam, if you'd figure the damage and put it on my bill."

For a man strict about bills and keen for a bargain, Mr. Grafton surprised me. "I'm marking this to Fletcher's account. I'm seeing that he pays."

Mr. Weir surprised me even more. He spoke promptly and he was emphatic about it. "Listen to me, Starrett. It's about time this town worked up a little pride. Maybe it's time, too, we got to be more neighborly with you homesteaders. I'll take a collection to cover this. I've been ashamed of myself ever since it started tonight, standing here and letting five of them jump that man of yours."

Father was pleased. But he knew what he wanted to do. "That's mighty nice of you, Weir. But this ain't your fight. I wouldn't worry, was I you, about keeping out of it." He looked down at Shane and the pride was plain busting out of him. "Matter of fact, I'd say the odds tonight, without me butting in, too, was mighty close to even." He looked again at Mr. Grafton. "Fletcher ain't getting in on this with a nickel. I'm paying." He tossed back his head. "No, by Godfrey! We're paying. Me and Shane."

He went to the swinging doors, turning sideways to push them open. Mother took my hand and we followed. She always knew when to talk and when not to talk, and she said no word while we watched father lift Shane to the wagon seat, climb beside him, hoist him to sitting position with one arm around him and take the reins in the other hand. Will Atkey trotted out with our things and stowed them away. Mother and I perched on the back of the wagon, father chirruped to the team, and we were started home.

There was not a sound for quite a stretch except the clop of hooves and the little creakings of the wheels. Then I heard a chuckle up front. It was Shane. The cool air was reviving him and he was sitting straight, swaying with the wagon's motion.

"What did you do with the thick one, Joe? I was busy with the redhead."

"Oh, I just kind of tucked him out of the way." Father wanted to let it go at that. Not mother.

"He picked him up like—like a bag of potatoes and threw him clear across the room." She did not say it to Shane, not to any person. She said it to the night, to the sweet darkness around us, and her eyes were shining in the starlight.

We turned in at our place and father shooed the rest of us into the house while he unhitched the team. In the kitchen mother set some water to heat on the stove and chased me to bed. Her back was barely to me after she tucked me in before I was peering around the door jamb. She got several clean rags, took the water from the stove, and went to work on Shane's head. She was tender as could be, crooning like to herself under her breath the while. It pained him plenty as the warm water soaked into the gash under the matted hair and as she washed the clotted blood from his cheek. But it seemed to pain her more, for her hand shook at the worst moments, and she was the one who flinched while he sat there quietly and smiled reassuringly at her.

Father came in and sat by the stove, watching them. He pulled out his pipe and made a very careful business of packing it and lighting it.

She finished. Shane would not let her try a bandage. "This air is the best medicine," he said. She had to be content with cleaning the cuts thoroughly and making certain all bleeding had stopped. Then it was father's turn.

"Get that shirt off, Joe. It's torn all down the back. Let me see what I can do with it." Before he could rise, she had changed her mind. "No. We'll keep it just like it is. To remember tonight by. You were magnificent, Joe, tearing that man away and—"

"Shucks," said father. "I was just peeved. Him holding Shane so Morgan could pound him."

"And you, Shane." Mother was in the middle of the kitchen, looking from one to the other. "You were magnificent, too. Morgan was so big and horrible and yet he didn't have even a chance. You were so cool and quick and—and dangerous and—"

"A woman shouldn't have to see things like that," Shane interrupted her, and he meant it. But she was talking right ahead.

"You think I shouldn't because it's brutal and nasty and not just fighting to see who is better at it, but mean and vicious and to win by any way, but to win. Of course it is. But you didn't start it. You didn't want to do it. Not until they made you anyway. You did it because you had to."

Her voice was climbing and she was looking back and forth and losing control of herself. "Did ever a woman have two such men?" And she turned from them and reached out blindly for a chair and sank into it and dropped her face into her hands and the tears came.

The two men stared at her and then at each other in that adult knowledge beyond my understanding. Shane rose and stepped over by mother. He put a hand gently on her head and I felt again his fingers in my hair and the affection flooding through me. He walked quietly out the door and into the night.

Father drew on his pipe. It was out and absently he lit it. He rose and went to the door and out on the porch. I could see him there dimly in the darkness, gazing across the river.

Gradually mother's sobs died down. She raised her head and wiped away the tears.

"Joe."

He turned and started in and waited then by the door. She stood up. She stretched her hands toward him and he was there and had her in his arms.

"Do you think I don't know, Marian?"

"But you don't. Not really. You can't. Because I don't know myself."

Father was staring over her head at the kitchen wall, not seeing anything there. "Don't fret yourself, Marian. I'm man enough to know a better when his trail meets mine. Whatever happens will be all right."

"Oh, Joe . . . Joe! Kiss me. Hold me tight and don't ever let go."

# II

WHAT HAPPENED in our kitchen that night was beyond me in those days. But it did not worry me because father had said it would be all right, and how could anyone, knowing him, doubt that he would make it so.

And we were not bothered by Fletcher's men any more at all. There might not have been a big ranch on the other side of the river, sprawling up the valley and over on our side above Ernie Wright's place, for all you could tell from our house. They left us strictly alone and were hardly ever seen now even in town. Fletcher himself, I heard from kids at school, was gone again. He went on the stage to Cheyenne and maybe farther, and nobody seemed to know why he went.

Yet father and Shane were more wary than they had been before. They stayed even closer together and they spent no more time than they had to in the fields. There was no more talking on the porch in the evenings, though the nights were so cool and lovely they called you to be out and under the winking stars. We kept to the house, and father insisted on having the lamps well shaded and he polished his rifle and hung it, ready loaded, on a couple of nails by the kitchen door.

All this caution failed to make sense to me. So at dinner about a week later I asked: "Is there something new that's wrong? That stuff about Fletcher is finished, isn't it?"

"Finished?" said Shane, looking at me over his coffee cup. "Bobby boy, it's only begun."

"That's right," said father. "Fletcher's gone too far to back out now. It's a case of now or never with him. If he can make us run, he'll be setting pretty for a long stretch. If he can't, it'll be only a matter o' time before he's shoved smack out of this valley. There's three or four of the men who looked through here last year ready right now to sharpen stakes and move in soon as they think it's safe. I'll bet Fletcher feels he got aholt of a bear by the tail and it'd be nice to be able to let go."

"Why doesn't he do something, then?" I asked. "Seems to me mighty quiet around here lately."

288

"Seems to you, eh?" said father. "Seems to me you're mighty young to be doing much seemsing. Don't you worry, son. Fletcher is fixing to do something. The grass that grows under his feet won't feed any cow. I'd be easier in my mind if I knew what he's up to."

"You see, Bob"—Shane was speaking to me the way I liked, as if maybe I was a man and could understand all he said—"by talking big and playing it rough, Fletcher has made this a straight win or lose deal. It's the same as if he'd kicked loose a stone that starts a rockslide and all he can do is hope to ride it down and hit bottom safe. Maybe he doesn't realize that yet. I think he does. And don't let things being quiet fool you. When there's noise, you know where to look and what's happening. When things are quiet, you've got to be most careful."

Mother sighed. She was looking at Shane's cheek where the cut was healing into a scar like a thin line running back from near the mouth corner. "I suppose you two are right. But does there have to be any more fighting?"

"Like the other night?" asked father. "No, Marian. I don't think so. Fletcher knows better now."

"He knows better," Shane said, "because he knows it won't work. If he's the man I think he is, he's known that since the first time he sicced Chris on me. I doubt that was his move the other night. That was Morgan's. Fletcher'll be watching for some way that has more finesse—and will be more final."

"Hm-m-m," said father, a little surprised. "Some legal trick, eh?"

"Could be. If he can find one. If not—" Shane shrugged and gazed out the window. "There are other ways. You can't call a man like Fletcher on things like that. Depends on how far he's willing to go. But whatever he does, once he's ready, he'll do it speedy and sure."

"Hm-m-m," said father again. "Now you put it thataway, I see you're right. That's Fletcher's way. Bet you've bumped against someone like him before." When Shane did not answer, just kept staring out the window, he went on. "Wish I could be as patient about it as you. I don't like this waiting."

But we did not have to wait long. It was the next day, a Friday, when we were finishing supper, that Lew Johnson and Henry Shipstead brought us the news. Fletcher was back and he had not come back alone. There was another man with him.

Lew Johnson saw them as they got off the stage. He had a good chance to look the stranger over while they waited in front of the post for horses to be brought in from the ranch. Since it was beginning to get dark, he had not been able to make out the stranger's face too well. The light striking through the post window, however, was enough for him to see what kind of man he was.

He was tall, rather broad in the shoulders and slim in the waist. He carried himself with a sort of swagger. He had a mustache that he favored and his eyes, when Johnson saw them reflecting the light from the window, were cold and had a glitter that bothered Johnson.

This stranger was something of a dude about his clothes. Still, that did not mean anything. When he turned, the coat he wore matching his pants flapped open and Johnson could see what had been half-hidden before. He was carrying two guns, big capable forty-fives, in holsters hung fairly low and forward. Those holsters were pegged down at the tips with thin straps fastened around the man's legs. Johnson said he saw the tiny buckles when the light flashed on them.

Wilson was the man's name. That was what Fletcher called him when a cowboy rode up leading a couple of horses. A funny other name. Stark. Stark Wilson. And that was not all.

Lew Johnson was worried and went into Grafton's to find Will Atkey, who always knew more than anyone else about people apt to be coming along the road because he was constantly picking up information from the talk of men drifting in to the bar. Will would not believe it at first when Johnson told him the name. What would he be doing up here, Will kept saying. Then Will blurted out that this Wilson was a bad one, a killer. He was a gunfighter said to be just as good with either hand and as fast on the draw as the best of them. He came to Cheyenne from Kansas, Will claimed he had heard, with a reputation for killing three men there and nobody knew how many more down in the southwest territories where he used to be.

Lew Johnson was rattling on, adding details as he could think of them. Henry Shipstead was slumped in a chair by the stove. Father was frowning at his pipe, absently fishing in a pocket for a match. It was Shane who shut off Johnson with a suddenness that startled the rest of us. His voice was sharp and clear and it seemed to crackle in the air. You could feel him taking charge of that room and all of us in it.

"When did they hit town?"

"Last night."

"And you waited till now to tell it!" There was disgust in Shane's voice. "You're a farmer all right, Johnson. That's all you ever will be." He whirled on father. "Quick, Joe. Which one has the hottest head? Which one's the easiest to prod into being a fool? Torrey is it? Or Wright?"

"Ernie Wright," father said slowly.

"Get moving, Johnson. Get out there on your horse and make it to Wright's in a hurry. Bring him here. Pick up Torrey, too. But get Wright first."

"He'll have to go into town for that," Henry Shipstead said heavily. "We passed them both down the road riding in."

Shane jumped to his feet. Lew Johnson was shuffling reluctantly toward the door. Shane brushed him aside. He strode to the door himself, yanked it open, started out. He stopped, leaning forward and listening.

"Easy, man," Henry Shipstead was grumbling, "what's your hurry? We told them about Wilson. They'll stop here on their way back." His voice ceased. All of us could hear it now, a horse pounding up the road at full gallop.

Shane turned back into the room. "There's your answer," he said bitterly. He swung the nearest chair to the wall and sat down. The fire blazing in him a moment before was gone. He was withdrawn into his own thoughts, and they were dark and not pleasant.

We heard the horse sliding to a stop out front. The sound was so plain you could fairly see the forelegs bracing and the hooves digging into the ground. Frank Torrey burst into the doorway. His hat was gone, his hair blowing wild. His chest heaved like he had been running as hard as the horse. He put his hands on the doorposts to hold himself steady and his voice was a hoarse whisper, though he was trying to shout across the room at father.

"Ernie's shot! They've killed him!"

The words jerked us to our feet and we stood staring. All but Shane. He did not move. You might have thought he was not even interested in what Torrey had said.

Father was the one who took hold of the scene. "Come in, Frank," he said quietly. "I take it we're too late to help Ernie now. Sit down and talk and don't leave anything out." He led Frank Torrey to a chair and pushed him into it. He closed the door and returned to his own chair. He looked older and tired.

It took Frank Torrey quite a while to pull himself together and tell his story straight. He was frightened. The fear was bedded deep in him and he was ashamed of himself for it.

He and Ernie Wright, he told us, had been to the stage office asking for a parcel Ernie was expecting. They dropped into Grafton's for a freshener before starting back. Since things had been so quiet lately, they were not thinking of any trouble even though Fletcher and the new man, Stark Wilson, were in the poker game at the big table. But Fletcher and Wilson must have been watching for a chance like that. They chucked in their hands and came over to the bar.

Fletcher was nice and polite as could be, nodding to Torrey and singling out Ernie for talk. He said he was sorry about it, but he really needed the land Ernie had filed on. It was the right place to put up winter windshelters for the new herd he was bringing in soon. He knew Ernie had not proved up on it yet. Just the same, he was willing to pay a fair price.

"I'll give you three hundred dollars," he said, "and that's more than the lumber in your buildings will be worth to me."

Ernie had more than that of his money in the place already. He had turned Fletcher down three or four times before. He was mad, the way he always was when Fletcher started his smooth talk.

"No," he said shortly. "I'm not selling. Not now or ever."

Fletcher shrugged like he had done all he could and slipped a quick nod at Stark Wilson. This Wilson was half-smiling at Ernie. But his eyes, Frank Torrey said, had nothing like a smile in them.

"I'd change my mind if I were you," he said to Ernie. "That is, if you have a mind to change."

"Keep out of this," snapped Ernie. "It's none of your business."

"I see you haven't heard," Wilson said softly. "I'm Mr. Fletcher's new business agent. I'm handling his business affairs for him. His business with stubborn jackasses like you." Then he said what showed Fletcher had coaxed him to it. "You're a damn fool, Wright. But what can you expect from a breed?"

"That's a lie!" shouted Ernie. "My mother wasn't no Indian!"

"Why, you crossbred squatter," Wilson said, quick and sharp, "are you telling me I'm wrong?"

"I'm telling you you're a God-damned liar!"

The silence that shut down over the saloon was so complete, Frank Torrey told us, that he could hear the ticking of the old alarm clock on the shelf behind the bar. Even Ernie, in the second his voice stopped, saw what he had done. But he was mad clear through and he glared at Wilson, his eyes reckless.

"So-o-o-o," said Wilson, satisfied now and stretching out the word with ominous softness. He flipped back his coat on the right side in front and the holster there was free with the gun grip ready for his hand.

"You'll back that, Wright. Or you'll crawl out of here on your belly."

Ernie moved out a step from the bar, his arms stiff at his sides. The anger in him held him erect as he beat down the terror tearing at him. He knew what this meant, but he met it straight. His hand was firm on his gun and pulling up when Wilson's first bullet hit him and staggered him. The second spun him halfway around and a faint froth appeared on his lips and all expression died from his face and he sagged to the floor.

While Frank Torrey was talking, Jim Lewis and a few minutes later Ed Howells had come in. Bad news travels fast and they seemed to know something was wrong. Perhaps they had heard that frantic galloping, the sound carrying far in the still night air. They were all in our kitchen now and they were more shaken and sober than I had ever seen them.

I was pressed close to mother, grateful for her arms around

me. I noticed that she had little attention for the other men. She was watching Shane, bitter and silent across the room.

"So that's it," father said grimly. "We'll have to face it. We sell and at his price or he slips the leash on his hired killer. Did Wilson make a move toward you, Frank?"

"He looked at me." Simply recalling that made Torrey shiver through. "He looked at me and he said, 'Too bad, isn't it, mister, that Wright didn't change his mind?'"

"Then what?"

"I got out of there quick as I could and came here."

Jim Lewis had been fidgeting on his seat, more nervous every minute. Now he jumped up, almost shouting. "But damn it, Joe! A man can't just go around shooting people!"

"Shut up, Jim," growled Henry Shipstead. "Don't you see the setup? Wilson badgered Ernie into getting himself in a spot where he had to go for his gun. Wilson can claim he shot in self-defense. He'll try the same thing on each of us."

"That's right, Jim," put in Lew Johnson. "Even if we tried to get a marshal in here, he couldn't hold Wilson. It was an even break and the faster man won is the way most people will figure it and plenty of them saw it. A marshal couldn't get here in time anyway."

"But we've got to stop it!" Lewis was really shouting now. "What chance have any of us got against Wilson? We're not gunmen. We're just a bunch of old cowhands and farmers. Call it anything you want. I call it murder."

"Yes!"

The word sliced through the room. Shane was up and his face was hard with the rock ridges running along his jaw. "Yes. It's murder. Trick it out as self-defense or with fancy words about an even break for a fair draw and it's still murder." He looked at father and the pain was deep in his eyes. But there was only contempt in his voice as he turned to the others.

"You five can crawl back in your burrows. You don't have to worry—yet. If the time comes, you can always sell and run. Fletcher won't bother with the likes of you now. He's going the limit and he knows the game. He picked Wright to make the play plain. That's done. Now he'll head straight for the one real man in this valley, the man who's held you here and will go on trying to hold you and keep for you what's yours as long as there's life in him. He's standing between you and Fletcher and Wilson this minute and you ought to be thankful that once in a while this country turns out a man like Joe Starrett."

And a man like Shane. . . . Were those words only in my mind or did I hear mother whisper them? She was looking at him and then at father and she was both frightened and proud at once. Father was fumbling with his pipe, packing it and making a fuss with it like it needed his whole attention.

The others stirred uneasily. They were reassured by what Shane said and yet shamed that they should be. And they did not like the way he said it.

"You seem to know a lot about that kind of dirty business," Ed Howells said, with maybe an edge of malice to his voice.

"I do."

Shane let the words lie there, plain and short and ugly. His face was stern and behind the hard front of his features was a sadness that fought to break through. But he stared levelly at Howells and it was the other man who dropped his eyes and turned away.

Father had his pipe going. "Maybe it's a lucky break for the rest of us," he said mildly, "that Shane here has been around a bit. He can call the cards for us plain. Ernie might still be alive, Johnson, if you had had the sense to tell us about Wilson right off. It's a good thing Ernie wasn't a family man." He turned to Shane. "How do you rate Fletcher now he's shown his hand?"

You could see that the chance to do something, even just to talk at the problem pressing us, eased the bitterness in Shane.

"He'll move in on Wright's place first thing tomorrow. He'll have a lot of men busy on this side of the river from now on, probably push some cattle around behind the homesteads, to keep the pressure plain on all of you. How quick he'll try you, Joe, depends on how he reads you. If he thinks you might crack, he'll wait and let knowing what happened to Wright work on you. If he really knows you, he'll not wait more than a day or two to make sure you've had time to think it over and then he'll grab the first chance to throw Wilson at you. He'll want it, like with Wright, in a public place where there'll be plenty of witnesses. If you don't give him a chance, he'll try to make one."

"Hm-m-m," father said soberly. "I was sure you'd give it to

me straight and that rings right." He pulled on his pipe for a moment. "I reckon, boys, this will be a matter of waiting for the next few days. There's no immediate danger right off anyway. Grafton will take care of Ernie's body tonight. We can meet in town in the morning to fix him a funeral. After that, we'd better stay out of town and stick close home as much as possible. I'd suggest you all study on this and drop in again tomorrow night. Maybe we can figure out something. I'd like to see how the town's taking it before I make up my mind on anything."

They were ready to leave it at that. They were ready to leave it to father. They were decent men and good neighbors. But not a one of them, were the decision his, would have stood up to Fletcher now. They would stay as long as father was there. With him gone, Fletcher would have things his way. That was how they felt as they muttered their goodnights and bunched out to scatter up and down the road.

Father stood in the doorway and watched them go. When he came back to his chair, he walked slowly and he seemed haggard and worn. "Somebody will have to go to Ernie's place tomorrow," he said, "and gather up his things. He's got relatives somewhere in Iowa."

"No." There was finality in Shane's tone. "You'll not go near the place. Fletcher might be counting on that. Grafton can do it."

"But Ernie was my friend," father said simply.

"Ernie's past friendship. Your debt is to the living."

Father looked at Shane and this brought him again into the immediate moment and cheered him. He nodded assent and turned to mother, who was hurrying to argue with him.

"Don't you see, Joe? If you can stay away from any place where you might meet Fletcher and—and that Wilson, things will work out. He can't keep a man like Wilson in this little valley forever."

She was talking rapidly and I knew why. She was not really trying to convince father as much as she was trying to convince herself. Father knew it, too.

"No, Marian. A man can't crawl into a hole somewhere and hide like a rabbit. Not if he has any pride."

"All right, then. But can't you keep quiet and not let him ride you and drive you into any fight?"

"That won't work either." Father was grim, but he was better and facing up to it. "A man can stand for a lot of pushing if he has to. 'Specially when he has his reasons." His glance shifted briefly to me. "But there are some things a man can't take. Not if he's to go on living with himself."

I was startled as Shane suddenly sucked in his breath with a long breaking intake. He was battling something within him, that old hidden desperation, and his eyes were dark and tormented against the paleness of his face. He seemed unable to look at us. He strode to the door and went out. We heard his footsteps fading toward the barn.

I was startled now at father. His breath, too, was coming in long, broken sweeps. He was up and pacing back and forth. When he swung on mother and his voice battered at her, almost fierce in its intensity, I realized that he knew about the change in Shane and that the knowing had been cankering in him all the past weeks.

"That's the one thing I can't stand, Marian. What we're doing to him. What happens to me doesn't matter too much. I talk big and I don't belittle myself. But my weight in any kind of a scale won't match his and I know it. If I understood him then as I do now, I'd never have got him to stay on here. But I didn't figure Fletcher would go this far. Shane won his fight before ever he came riding into this valley. It's been tough enough on him already. Should we let him lose just because of us? Fletcher can have his way. We'll sell out and move on."

I was not thinking. I was only feeling. For some strange reason I was feeling Shane's fingers in my hair, gently rocking my head. I could not help what I was saying, shouting across the room. "Father! Shane wouldn't run away! He wouldn't run away from anything!"

Father stopped pacing, his eyes narrowed in surprise. He stared at me without really seeing me. He was listening to mother.

"Bob's right, Joe. We can't let Shane down." It was queer, hearing her say the same thing to father she had said to Shane, the same thing with only the name different. "He'd never forgive us if we ran away from this. That's what we'd be doing. This isn't just a case of bucking Fletcher any more. It isn't just a case of keeping a piece of ground Fletcher wants for his range. We've got to be the kind of people Shane thinks we are. Bob's right. He wouldn't run away from anything like that. And that's the reason we can't."

"Lookahere, Marian, you don't think I want to do any running? No. You know me better than that. It'd go against everything in me. But what's my fool pride and this place and any plans we've had alongside of a man like that?"

"I know, Joe. But you don't see far enough." They were both talking earnestly, not breaking in, hearing each other out and sort of groping to put their meaning plain. "I can't really explain it, Joe. But I just know that we're bound up in something bigger than any one of us, and that running away is the one thing that would be worse than whatever might happen to us. There wouldn't be anything real ahead for us, any of us, maybe even for Bob, all the rest of our lives."

"Humph," said father. "Torrey could do it. And Johnson. All the rest of them. And it wouldn't bother them too much."

"Joe! Joe Starrett! Are you trying to make me mad? I'm not talking about them. I'm talking about us."

"Hm-m-m," said father softly, musing like to himself. "The salt would be gone. There just wouldn't be any flavor. There wouldn't be much meaning left."

"Oh, Joe! Joe! That's what I've been trying to say. And I know this will work out some way. I don't know how. But it will, if we face it and stand up to it and have faith in each other. It'll work out. Because it's got to."

"That's a woman's reason, Marian. But you're part right anyway. We'll play this game through. It'll need careful watching and close figuring. But maybe we can wait Fletcher out and make him overplay his hand. The town won't take much to this Wilson deal. Men like that fellow Weir have minds of their own."

Father was more cheerful now that he was beginning to get his thoughts straightened out. He and mother talked low in the kitchen for a long time after they sent me to bed, and I lay in my little room and saw through the window the stars wheeling distantly in the far outer darkness until I fell asleep at last.

## 12

T HE MORNING sun brightened our house and everything in the world outside. We had a good breakfast, father and Shane taking their time because they had routed out early to get the chores done and were waiting to go to town. They saddled up presently and rode off, and I moped in front of the house, not able to settle to any kind of playing.

After she bustled through the dishes, mother saw me standing and staring down the road and called me to the porch. She got our tattered old parchesi board and she kept me humping to beat her. She was a grand one for games like that. She would be as excited as a kid, squealing at the big numbers and doubles and counting proudly out loud as she moved her markers ahead.

When I had won three games running, she put the board away and brought out two fat apples and my favorite of the books she had from the time she taught school. Munching on her apple, she read to me and before I knew it the shadows were mighty short and she had to skip in to get dinner and father and Shane were riding up to the barn.

They came in while she was putting the food on the table. We sat down and it was almost like a holiday, not just because it was not a work day, but because the grown folks were talking lightly, were determined not to let this Fletcher business spoil our good times. Father was pleased at what had happened in town.

"Yes, sir," he was saying as we were finishing dinner. "Ernie had a right good funeral. He would have appreciated it. Grafton made a nice speech and, by Godfrey, I believe he meant it. That fellow Weir had his clerk put together a really fine coffin. Wouldn't take a cent for it. And Sims over at the mine is knocking out a good stone. He wouldn't take a cent either. I was surprised at the crowd, too. Not a good word for Fletcher among them. And there must have been thirty people there."

"Thirty-four," said Shane. "I counted 'em. They weren't just paying their respects to Wright, Marian. That wouldn't have brought in some of those I checked. They were showing their

299

opinion of a certain man named Starrett, who made a pretty fair speech himself. This husband of yours is becoming quite a respected citizen in these parts. Soon as the town gets grown up and organized, he's likely to start going places. Give him time and he'll be mayor."

Mother caught her breath with a little sob. "Give . . . him . . . time," she said slowly. She looked at Shane and there was panic in her eyes. The lightness was gone and before anyone could say more, we heard the horses turning into our yard.

I dashed to the window to peer out. It struck me strange that Shane, usually so alert, was not there ahead of me. Instead he pushed back his chair and spoke gently, still sitting in it. "That will be Fletcher, Joe. He's heard how the town is taking this and knows he has to move fast. You take it easy. He's playing against time now, but he won't push anything here."

Father nodded at Shane and went to the door. He had taken off his gunbelt when he came in and now passed it to lift the rifle from its nails on the wall. Holding it in his right hand, barrel down, he opened the door and stepped out on the porch, clear to the front edge. Shane followed quietly and leaned in the doorway, relaxed and watchful. Mother was beside me at the window, staring out, crumpling her apron in her hand.

There were four of them, Fletcher and Wilson in the lead, two cowboys tagging. They had pulled up about twenty feet from the porch. This was the first time I had seen Fletcher for nearly a year. He was a tall man who must once have been a handsome figure in the fine clothes he always wore and with his arrogant air and his finely chiseled face set off by his short-cropped black beard and brilliant eyes. Now a heaviness was setting in about his features and a fatty softness was beginning to show in his body. His face had a shrewd cast and a kind of reckless determination was on him that I did not remember ever noticing before.

Stark Wilson, for all the dude look Frank Torrey had mentioned, seemed lean and fit. He was sitting idly in his saddle, but the pose did not fool you. He was wearing no coat and the two guns were swinging free. He was sure of himself, serene and deadly. The curl of his lip beneath his mustache was a combination of confidence in himself and contempt for us.

Fletcher was smiling and affable. He was certain he held the cards and was going to deal them as he wanted. "Sorry to bother you, Starrett, so soon after that unfortunate affair last night. I wish it could have been avoided. I really do. Shooting is so unnecessary in these things, if only people would show sense. But Wright never should have called Mr. Wilson here a liar. That was a mistake."

"It was," father said curtly. "But then Ernie always did believe in telling the truth." I could see Wilson stiffen and his lips tighten. Father did not look at him. "Speak your piece, Fletcher, and get off my land."

Fletcher was still smiling. "There's no call for us to quarrel, Starrett. What's done is done. Let's hope there's no need for anything like it to be done again. You've worked cattle on a big ranch and you can understand my position. I'll be wanting all the range I can get from now on. Even without that, I can't let a bunch of nesters keep coming in here and choke me off from my water rights."

"We've been over that before," father said. "You know where I stand. If you have more to say, speak up and be done with it."

"All right, Starrett. Here's my proposition. I like the way you do things. You've got some queer notions about the cattle business, but when you tackle a job, you take hold and do it thoroughly. You and that man of yours are a combination I could use. I want you on my side of the fence. I'm getting rid of Morgan and I want you to take over as foreman. From what I hear your man would make one hell of a driving trail boss. The spot's his. Since you've proved up on this place, I'll buy it from you. If you want to go on living here, that can be arranged. If you want to play around with that little herd of yours, that can be arranged too. But I want you working for me."

Father was surprised. He had not expected anything quite like this. He spoke softly to Shane behind him. He did not turn or look away from Fletcher, but his voice carried clearly.

"Can I call the turn for you, Shane?"

"Yes, Joe." Shane's voice was just as soft, but it, too, carried clearly and there was a little note of pride in it.

Father stood taller there on the edge of the porch. He stared straight at Fletcher. "And the others," he said slowly. "Johnson, Shipstead, and the rest. What about them?"

"They'll have to go."

Father did not hesitate. "No."

"I'll give you a thousand dollars for this place as it stands and that's my top offer."

"No."

The fury in Fletcher broke over his face and he started to turn in the saddle toward Wilson. He caught himself and forced again that shrewd smile. "There's no percentage in being hasty, Starrett. I'll boost the ante to twelve hundred. That's a lot better than what might happen if you stick to being stubborn. I'll not take an answer now. I'll give you till tonight to think it over. I'll be waiting at Grafton's to hear you talk sense."

He swung his horse and started away. The two cowboys turned to join him by the road. Wilson did not follow at once. He leaned forward in his saddle and drove a sneering look at father.

"Yes, Starrett. Think it over. You wouldn't like someone else to be enjoying this place of yours—and that woman there in the window."

He was lifting his reins with one hand to pull his horse around and suddenly he dropped them and froze to attention. It must have been what he saw in father's face. We could not see it, mother and I, because father's back was to us. But we could see his hand tightening on the rifle at his side.

"Don't, Joe!"

Shane was beside father. He slipped past, moving smooth and steady, down the steps and over to one side to come at Wilson on his right hand and stop not six feet from him. Wilson was puzzled and his right hand twitched and then was still as Shane stopped and as he saw that Shane carried no gun.

Shane looked up at him and Shane's voice flicked in a whiplash of contempt. "You talk like a man because of that flashy hardware you're wearing. Strip it away and you'd shrivel down to boy size."

The very daring of it held Wilson motionless for an instant and father's voice cut into it. "Shane! Stop it!"

The blackness faded from Wilson's face. He smiled grimly at Shane. "You do need someone to look after you." He whirled his horse and put it to a run to join Fletcher and the others in the road.

It was only then that I realized mother was gripping my shoulders so that they hurt. She dropped on a chair and held me to her. We could hear father and Shane on the porch.

"He'd have drilled you, Joe, before you could have brought the gun up and pumped in a shell."

"But you, you crazy fool!" Father was covering his feelings with a show of exasperation. "You'd have made him plug you just so I'd have a chance to get him."

Mother jumped up. She pushed me aside. She flared at them from the doorway. "And both of you would have acted like fools just because he said that about me. I'll have you two know that if it's got to be done, I can take being insulted just as much as you can."

Peering around her, I saw them gaping at her in astonishment. "But, Marian," father objected mildly, coming to her. "What better reason could a man have?"

"Yes," said Shane gently. "What better reason?" He was not looking just at mother. He was looking at the two of them.

## 13

I DO not know how long they would have stood there on the porch in the warmth of that moment. I shattered it by asking what seemed to me a simple question until after I had asked it and the significance hit me.

"Father, what are you going to tell Fletcher tonight?"

There was no answer. There was no need for one. I guess I was growing up. I knew what he would tell Fletcher. I knew what he would say. I knew, too, that because he was father he would have to go to Grafton's and say it. And I understood why they could no longer bear to look at one another, and the breeze blowing in from the sun-washed fields was suddenly so chill and cheerless.

They did not look at each other. They did not say a word to each other. Yet somehow I realized that they were closer together in the stillness there on the porch than they had ever been. They knew themselves and each of them knew that the other grasped the situation whole. They knew that Fletcher had dealt himself a winning hand, had caught father in the one play that he could not avoid because he would not avoid it. They knew that talk is meaningless when a common knowledge is already there. The silence bound them as no words ever could.

Father sat on the top porch step. He took out his pipe and drew on it as the match flamed and fixed his eyes on the horizon, on the mountains far across the river. Shane took the chair I had used for the games with mother. He swung it to the house wall and bent into it in that familiar unconscious gesture and he, too, looked into the distance. Mother turned into the kitchen and went about clearing the table as if she was not really aware of what she was doing. I helped her with the dishes and the old joy of sharing with her in the work was gone and there was no sound in the kitchen except the drip of the water and the chink of dish on dish.

When we were done, she went to father. She sat beside him on the step, her hand on the wood between them, and his covered hers and the moments merged in the slow, dwindling procession of time.

Loneliness gripped me. I wandered through the house, finding nothing there to do, and out on the porch and past those three and to the barn. I searched around and found an old shovel handle and started to whittle me a play saber with my knife. I had been thinking of this for days. Now the idea held no interest. The wood curls dropped to the barn floor, and after a while I let the shovel handle drop among them. Everything that had happened before seemed far off, almost like another existence. All that mattered was the length of the shadows creeping across the yard as the sun drove down the afternoon sky.

I took a hoe and went into mother's garden where the ground was caked around the turnips, the only things left unharvested. But there was scant work in me. I kept at it for a couple of rows, then the hoe dropped and I let it lie. I went to the front of the house, and there they were sitting, just as before.

I sat on the step below father and mother, between them, and their legs on each side of me made it seem better. I felt father's hand on my head.

"This is kind of tough on you, Bob." He could talk to me because I was only a kid. He was really talking to himself.

"I can't see the full finish. But I can see this. Wilson down and there'll be an end to it. Fletcher'll be done. The town will see to that. I can't beat Wilson on the draw. But there's strength enough in this clumsy body of mine to keep me on my feet till I get him, too." Mother stirred and was still, and his voice went on. "Things could be worse. It helps a man to know that if anything happens to him, his family will be in better hands than his own."

There was a sharp sound behind us on the porch. Shane had risen so swiftly that his chair had knocked against the wall. His hands were clenched tightly and his arms were quivering. His face was pale with the effort shaking him. He was desperate with an inner torment, his eyes tortured by thoughts that he could not escape, and the marks were obvious on him and he did not care. He strode to the steps, down past us and around the corner of the house.

Mother was up and after him, running headlong. She stopped abruptly at the house corner, clutching at the wood, panting and irresolute. Slowly she came back, her hands out-stretched as if to keep from falling. She sank again on the step, close against father, and he gathered her to him with one great arm.

The silence spread and filled the whole valley and the shadows crept across the yard. They touched the road and began to merge in the deeper shading that meant the sun was dipping below the mountains far behind the house. Mother straightened, and as she stood up, father rose, too. He took hold of her two arms and held her in front of him. "I'm counting on you, Marian, to help him win again. You can do it, if anyone can." He smiled a strange little sad smile and he loomed up there above me the biggest man in all the world. "No supper for me now, Marian. A cup of your coffee is all I want." They passed through the doorway together.

Where was Shane? I hurried toward the barn. I was almost to it when I saw him out by the pasture. He was staring over it and the grazing steers at the great lonely mountains tipped with the gold of the sun now rushing down behind them. As I watched, he stretched his arms up, the fingers reaching to their utmost limits, grasping and grasping, it seemed, at the glory glowing in the sky.

He whirled and came straight back, striding with long steady steps, his head held high. There was some subtle, new, unchangeable certainty in him. He came close and I saw that his face was quiet and untroubled and that little lights danced in his eyes.

"Skip into the house, Bobby boy. Put on a smile. Everything is going to be all right." He was past me, without slowing, swinging into the barn.

But I could not go into the house. And I did not dare follow him, not after he had told me to go. A wild excitement was building up in me while I waited by the porch, watching the barn door.

The minutes ticked past and the twilight deepened and a patch of light sprang from the house as the lamp in the kitchen was lit. And still I waited. Then he was coming swiftly toward me and I stared and stared and broke and ran into the house with the blood pounding in my head.

"Father! Father! Shane's got his gun!"

He was close back of me. Father and mother barely had time to look up from the table before he was framed in the doorway. He was dressed as he was that first day when he rode into our lives, in that dark and worn magnificence from the black hat with its wide curling brim to the soft black boots. But what caught your eye was the single flash of white, the outer ivory plate on the grip of the gun, showing sharp and distinct against the dark material of the trousers. The tooled cartridge belt nestled around him, riding above the hip on the left, sweeping down on the right to hold the holster snug along the thigh, just as he had said, the gun handle about halfway between the wrist and elbow of his right arm hanging there relaxed and ready.

Belt and holster and gun . . . These were not things he was wearing or carrying. They were part of him, part of the man, of the full sum of the integrate force that was Shane. You could see now that for the first time this man who had been living with us, who was one of us, was complete, was himself in the final effect of his being.

Now that he was no longer in his crude work clothes, he seemed again slender, almost slight, as he did that first day. The change was more than that. What had been seeming iron was again steel. The slenderness was that of a tempered blade and a razor edge was there. Slim and dark in the doorway, he seemed somehow to fill the whole frame.

This was not our Shane. And yet it was. I remembered Ed Howells' saying that this was the most dangerous man he had ever seen. I remembered in the same rush that father had said he was the safest man we ever had in our house. I realized that both were right and that this, this at last, was Shane.

He was in the room now and he was speaking to them both in that bantering tone he used to have only for mother. "A fine pair of parents you are. Haven't even fed Bob yet. Stack him full of a good supper. Yourselves, too. I have a little business to tend to in town."

Father was looking fixedly at him. The sudden hope that had sprung in his face had as quickly gone. "No, Shane. It won't do. Even your thinking of it is the finest thing any man ever did for me. But I won't let you. It's my stand. Fletcher's making his play against me. There's no dodging. It's my business."

"There's where you're wrong, Joe," Shane said gently. "This is my business. My kind of business. I've had fun being a farmer. You've shown me new meaning in the word, and I'm proud that for a while maybe I qualified. But there are a few things a farmer can't handle."

The strain of the long afternoon was telling on father. He pushed up from the table. "Damn it, Shane, be sensible. Don't make it harder for me. You can't do this."

Shane stepped near, to the side of the table, facing father across a corner. "Easy does it, Joe. I'm making this my business."

"No. I won't let you. Suppose you do put Wilson out of the way. That won't finish anything. It'll only even the score and swing things back worse than ever. Think what it'll mean to you. And where will it leave me? I couldn't hold my head up around here any more. They'd say I ducked and they'd be right. You can't do it and that's that."

"No?" Shane's voice was even more gentle, but it had a quiet, inflexible quality that had never been there before. "There's no man living can tell me what I can't do. Not even you, Joe. You forget there is still a way."

He was talking to hold father's attention. As he spoke the gun was in his hand and before father could move he swung it, swift and sharp, so the barrel lined flush along the side of father's head, back of the temple, above the ear. Strength was in the blow and it thudded dully on the bone and father folded over the table and as it tipped with his weight slid toward the floor. Shane's arm was under him before he hit and Shane pivoted father's loose body up and into his chair and righted the table while the coffee cups rattled on the floor boards. Father's head lolled back and Shane caught it and eased it and the big shoulders forward till they rested on the table, the face down and cradled in the limp arms.

Shane stood erect and looked across the table at mother. She had not moved since he appeared in the doorway, not even when father fell and the table teetered under her hands on its edge. She was watching Shane, her throat curving in a lovely proud line, her eyes wide with a sweet warmth shining in them.

Darkness had shut down over the valley as they looked at each other across the table and the only light now was from the lamp swinging ever so slightly above them, circling them with its steady glow. They were alone in a moment that was all their own. Yet, when they spoke, it was of father.

"I was afraid," Shane murmured, "that he would take it that way. He couldn't do otherwise and be Joe Starrett."

"I know."

"He'll rest easy and come out maybe a little groggy but all right. Tell him, Marian. Tell him no man need be ashamed of being beat by Shane."

The name sounded queer like that, the man speaking of himself. It was the closest he ever came to boasting. And then you understood that there was not the least hint of a boast. He was stating a fact, simple and elemental as the power that dwelled in him.

"I know," she said again. "I don't need to tell him. He knows, too." She was rising, earnest and intent. "But there is something else I must know. We have battered down words that might have been spoken between us and that was as it should be. But I have a right to know now. I am part of this, too. And what I do depends on what you tell me now. Are you doing this just for me?"

Shane hesitated for a long, long moment. "No, Marian." His gaze seemed to widen and encompass us all, mother and the still figure of father and me huddled on a chair by the window, and somehow the room and the house and the whole place. Then he was looking only at mother and she was all that he could see.

"No, Marian. Could I separate you in my mind and afterwards be a man?"

He pulled his eyes from her and stared into the night beyond the open door. His face hardened, his thoughts leaping to what lay ahead in town. So quiet and easy you were scarce aware that he was moving, he was gone into the outer darkness.

# 14

NOTHING COULD have kept me there in the house that night. My mind held nothing but the driving desire to follow Shane. I waited, hardly daring to breathe, while mother watched him go. I waited until she turned to father, bending over him, then I slipped around the doorpost out to the porch. I thought for a moment she had noticed me, but I could not be sure and she did not call to me. I went softly down the steps and into the freedom of the night.

Shane was nowhere in sight. I stayed in the darker shadows, looking about, and at last I saw him emerging once more from the barn. The moon was rising low over the mountains, a clean, bright crescent. Its light was enough for me to see him plainly in outline. He was carrying his saddle and a sudden pain stabbed through me as I saw that with it was his saddle-roll. He went toward the pasture gate, not slow, not fast, just firm and steady. There was a catlike certainty in his every movement, a silent, inevitable deadliness. I heard him, there by the gate, give his low whistle and the horse came out of the shadows at the far end of the pasture, its hooves making no noise in the deep grass, a dark and powerful shape etched in the moonlight drifting across the field straight to the man.

I knew what I would have to do. I crept along the corral fence, keeping tight to it, until I reached the road. As soon as I was around the corner of the corral with it and the barn between me and the pasture, I started to run as rapidly as I could toward town, my feet plumping softly in the thick dust of the road. I walked this every school day and it had never seemed long before. Now the distance stretched ahead, lengthening in my mind as if to mock me.

I could not let him see me. I kept looking back over my shoulder as I ran. When I saw him swinging into the road, I was well past Johnson's, almost past Shipstead's, striking into the last open stretch to the edge of town. I scurried to the side of the road and behind a clump of bullberry bushes. Panting to get my breath, I crouched there and waited for him to pass.

The hoofbeats swelled in my ears, mingled with the pounding beat of my own blood. In my imagination he was galloping furiously and I was positive he was already rushing past me. But when I parted the bushes and pushed forward to peer out, he was moving at a moderate pace and was only almost abreast of me.

He was tall and terrible there in the road, looming up gigantic in the mystic half-light. He was the man I saw that first day, a stranger, dark and forbidding, forging his lone way out of an unknown past in the utter loneliness of his own immovable and instinctive defiance. He was the symbol of all the dim, formless imaginings of danger and terror in the untested realm of human potentialities beyond my understanding. The impact of the menace that marked him was like a physical blow.

I could not help it. I cried out and stumbled and fell. He was off his horse and over me before I could right myself, picking me up, his grasp strong and reassuring. I looked at him, tearful and afraid, and the fear faded from me. He was no stranger. That was some trick of the shadows. He was Shane. He was shaking me gently and smiling at me.

"Bobby boy, this is no time for you to be out. Skip along home and help your mother. I told you everything would be all right."

He let go of me and turned slowly, gazing out across the far sweep of the valley silvered in the moon's glow. "Look at it, Bob. Hold it in your mind like this. It's a lovely land, Bob. A good place to be a boy and grow straight inside as a man should."

My gaze followed his, and I saw our valley as though for the first time and the emotion in me was more than I could stand. I choked and reached out for him and he was not there.

He was rising into the saddle and the two shapes, the man and the horse, became one and moved down the road toward the yellow squares that were the patches of light from the windows of Grafton's building a quarter of a mile away. I wavered a moment, but the call was too strong. I started after him, running frantic in the middle of the road.

Whether he heard me or not, he kept right on. There were several men on the long porch of the building by the saloon doors. Red Marlin's hair made him easy to spot. They were scanning the road intently. As Shane hit the panel of light from the near big front window, the store window, they stiffened to attention. Red Marlin, a startled expression on his face, dived quickly through the doors.

Shane stopped, not by the rail but by the steps on the store side. When he dismounted, he did not slip the reins over the horse's head as the cowboys always did. He left them looped over the pommel of the saddle and the horse seemed to know what this meant. It stood motionless, close by the steps, head up, waiting, ready for whatever swift need.

Shane went along the porch and halted briefly, fronting the two men still there.

"Where's Fletcher?"

They looked at each other and at Shane. One of them started to speak. "He doesn't want—" Shane's voice stopped him. It slapped at them, low and with an edge that cut right into your mind. "Where's Fletcher?"

One of them jerked a hand toward the doors and then, as they moved to shift out of his way, his voice caught them.

"Get inside. Go clear to the bar before you turn."

They stared at him and stirred uneasily and swung together to push through the doors. As the doors came back, Shane grabbed them, one with each hand, and pulled them out and wide open and he disappeared between them.

Clumsy and tripping in my haste, I scrambled up the steps and into the store. Sam Grafton and Mr. Weir were the only persons there and they were both hurrying to the entrance to the saloon, so intent that they failed to notice me. They stopped in the opening. I crept behind them to my familiar perch on my box where I could see past them.

The big room was crowded. Almost everyone who could be seen regularly around town was there, everyone but our homestead neighbors. There were many others who were new to me. They were lined up elbow to elbow nearly the entire length of the bar. The tables were full and more men were lounging along the far wall. The big round poker table at the back between the stairway to the little balcony and the door to Grafton's office was littered with glasses and chips. It seemed strange, for all the men standing, that there should be an empty chair at the far curve of the table. Someone must have been in that chair, because chips were at the place and a half-smoked cigar, a whisp of smoke curling up from it, was by them on the table.

Red Marlin was leaning against the back wall, behind the chair. As I looked, he saw the smoke and appeared to start a little. With a careful show of casualness he slid into the chair and picked up the cigar.

A haze of thinning smoke was by the ceiling over them all, floating in involved streamers around the hanging lamps. This was Grafton's saloon in the flush of a banner evening's business. But something was wrong, was missing. The hum of activity, the whirr of voices, that should have risen from the scene, been part of it, was stilled in a hush more impressive than any noise could be. The attention of everyone in the room, like a single sense, was centered on that dark figure just inside the swinging doors, back to them and touching them.

This was the Shane of the adventures I had dreamed for him, cool and competent, facing that room full of men in the simple solitude of his own invincible completeness.

His eyes searched the room. They halted on a man sitting at a small table in the front corner with his hat on low over his forehead. With a thump of surprise I recognized it was Stark Wilson and he was studying Shane with a puzzled look on his face. Shane's eyes swept on, checking off each person. They stopped again on a figure over by the wall and the beginnings of a smile showed in them and he nodded almost imperceptibly. It was Chris, tall and lanky, his arm in a sling, and as he caught the nod he flushed a little and shifted his weight from one foot to the other. Then he straightened his shoulders and over his face came a slow smile, warm and friendly, the smile of a man who knows his own mind at last.

But Shane's eyes were already moving on. They narrowed as they rested on Red Marlin. Then they jumped to Will Atkey trying to make himself small behind the bar.

"Where's Fletcher?"

Will fumbled with the cloth in his hands. "I—I don't know. He was here awhile ago." Frightened at the sound of his own voice in the stillness, Will dropped the cloth, started to stoop for it, and checked himself, putting his hands to the inside rim of the bar to hold himself steady.

Shane tilted his head slightly so his eyes could clear his hat-brim. He was scanning the balcony across the rear of the room. It was empty and the doors there were closed. He stepped forward, disregarding the men by the bar, and walked quietly past them the long length of the room. He went through the doorway to Grafton's office and into the semi-darkness beyond.

And still the hush held. Then he was in the office doorway again and his eyes bored toward Red Marlin.

"Where's Fletcher?"

The silence was taut and unendurable. It had to break. The sound was that of Stark Wilson coming to his feet in the far front corner. His voice, lazy and insolent, floated down the room.

"Where's Starrett?"

While the words yet seemed to hang in the air, Shane was moving toward the front of the room. But Wilson was moving, too. He was crossing toward the swinging doors and he took his stand just to the left of them, a few feet out from the wall. The position gave him command of the wide aisle running back between the bar and the tables and Shane coming forward in it.

Shane stopped about three quarters of the way forward, about five yards from Wilson. He cocked his head for one quick sidewise glance again at the balcony and then he was looking only at Wilson. He did not like the setup. Wilson had the front wall and he was left in the open of the room. He understood the fact, assessed it, accepted it.

They faced each other in the aisle and the men along the bar jostled one another in their hurry to get to the opposite side of the room. A reckless arrogance was on Wilson, certain of himself and his control of the situation. He was not one to miss the significance of the slim deadliness that was Shane. But even now, I think, he did not believe that anyone in our valley would deliberately stand up to him.

"Where's Starrett?" he said once more, still mocking Shane but making it this time a real question.

The words went past Shane as if they had not been spoken. "I had a few things to say to Fletcher," he said gently. "That can wait. You're a pushing man, Wilson, so I reckon I had better accommodate you."

Wilson's face sobered and his eyes glinted coldly. "I've no quarrel with you," he said flatly, "even if you are Starrett's man. Walk out of here without any fuss and I'll let you go. It's Starrett I want."

"What you want, Wilson, and what you'll get are two different things. Your killing days are done."

Wilson had it now. You could see him grasp the meaning. This quiet man was pushing him just as he had pushed Ernie Wright. As he measured Shane, it was not to his liking. Something that was not fear but a kind of wondering and baffled reluctance showed in his face. And then there was no escape, for that gentle voice was pegging him to the immediate and implacable moment.

"I'm waiting, Wilson. Do I have to crowd you into slapping leather?"

Time stopped and there was nothing in all the world but two men looking into eternity in each other's eyes. And the room rocked in the sudden blur of action indistinct in its incredible swiftness and the roar of their guns was a single sustained blast. And Shane stood, solid on his feet as a rooted oak, and Wilson swayed, his right arm hanging useless, blood beginning to show in a small stream from under the sleeve over the hand, the gun slipping from the numbing fingers.

He backed against the wall, a bitter disbelief twisting his features. His left arm hooked and the second gun was showing and Shane's bullet smashed into his chest and his knees buckled, sliding him slowly down the wall till the lifeless weight of the body toppled it sideways to the floor.

Shane gazed across the space between and he seemed to have forgotten all else as he let his gun ease into the holster. "I gave him his chance," he murmured out of the depths of a great sadness. But the words had no meaning for me, because I noticed on the dark brown of his shirt, low and just above the belt to one side of the buckle, the darker spot gradually widening. Then others noticed, too, and there was a stir in the air and the room was coming to life.

Voices were starting, but no one focused on them. They were snapped short by the roar of a shot from the rear of the room. A wind seemed to whip Shane's shirt at the shoulder and the glass of the front window beyond shattered near the bottom.

Then I saw it.

It was mine alone. The others were turning to stare at the back of the room. My eyes were fixed on Shane and I saw it. I saw the whole man move, all of him, in the single flashing instant. I saw the head lead and the body swing and the driving power of the legs beneath. I saw the arm leap and the hand take the gun in the lightning sweep. I saw the barrel line up like—like a finger pointing—and the flame spurt even as the man himself was still in motion.

And there on the balcony Fletcher, impaled in the act of aiming for a second shot, rocked on his heels and fell back into the open doorway behind him. He clawed at the jambs and pulled himself forward. He staggered to the rail and tried to raise the gun. But the strength was draining out of him and he collapsed over the rail, jarring it loose and falling with it.

Across the stunned and barren silence of the room Shane's voice seemed to come from a great distance. "I expect that finishes it," he said. Unconsciously, without looking down, he broke out the cylinder of his gun and reloaded it. The stain on his shirt was bigger now, spreading fanlike above the belt, but he did not appear to know or care. Only his movements were slow, retarded by an unutterable weariness. The hands were sure and steady, but they moved slowly and the gun dropped into the holster of its own weight.

He backed with dragging steps toward the swinging doors until his shoulders touched them. The light in his eyes was unsteady like the flickering of a candle guttering toward darkness. And then, as he stood there, a strange thing happened.

How could one describe it, the change that came over him? Out of the mysterious resources of his will the vitality came. It came creeping, a tide of strength that crept through him and fought and shook off the weakness. It shone in his eyes and they were alive again and alert. It welled up in him, sending that familiar power surging through him again until it was singing again in every vibrant line of him.

He faced that room full of men and read them all with the one sweeping glance and spoke to them in that gentle voice with that quiet, inflexible quality.

"I'll be riding on now. And there's not a one of you that will follow."

He turned his back on them in the indifference of absolute knowledge they would do as he said. Straight and superb, he was silhouetted against the doors and the patch of night above them. The next moment they were closing with a soft swish of sound.

The room was crowded with action now. Men were clustering around the bodies of Wilson and Fletcher, pressing to the bar, talking excitedly. Not a one of them, though, approached too close to the doors. There was a cleared space by the doorway as if someone had drawn a line marking it off.

I did not care what they were doing or what they were saying. I had to get to Shane. I had to get to him in time. I had to know, and he was the only one who could ever tell me.

I dashed out the store door and I was in time. He was on his horse, already starting away from the steps.

"Shane," I whispered desperately, loud as I dared without the men inside hearing me. "Oh, Shane!"

He heard me and reined around and I hurried to him, standing by a stirrup and looking up.

"Bobby! Bobby boy! What are you doing here?"

"I've been here all along," I blurted out. "You've got to tell me. Was that Wilson—"

He knew what was troubling me. He always knew. "Wilson," he said, "was mighty fast. As fast as I've ever seen."

"I don't care," I said, the tears starting. "I don't care if he was the fastest that ever was. He'd never have been able to shoot you, would he? You'd have got him straight, wouldn't you—if you had been in practice?"

He hesitated a moment. He gazed down at me and into me and he knew. He knew what goes on in a boy's mind and what can help him stay clean inside through the muddled, dirtied years of growing up.

"Sure. Sure, Bob. He'd never even have cleared the holster."

He started to bend down toward me, his hand reaching for my head. But the pain struck him like a whiplash and the hand jumped to his shirt front by the belt, pressing hard, and he reeled a little in the saddle.

The ache in me was more than I could bear. I stared dumbly

at him, and because I was just a boy and helpless I turned away
and hid my face against the firm, warm flank of the horse.

"Bob."

"Yes, Shane."

"A man is what he is, Bob, and there's no breaking the mold.
I tried that and I've lost. But I reckon it was in the cards from
the moment I saw a freckled kid on a rail up the road there and
a real man behind him, the kind that could back him for the
chance another kid never had."

"But—but, Shane, you—"

"There's no going back from a killing, Bob. Right or wrong,
the brand sticks and there's no going back. It's up to you now.
Go home to your mother and father. Grow strong and straight
and take care of them. Both of them."

"Yes, Shane."

"There's only one thing more I can do for them now."

I felt the horse move away from me. Shane was looking
down the road and on to the open plain and the horse was
obeying the silent command of the reins. He was riding away
and I knew that no word or thought could hold him. The
big horse, patient and powerful, was already settling into the
steady pace that had brought him into our valley, and the two,
the man and the horse, were a single dark shape in the road as
they passed beyond the reach of the light from the windows.

I strained my eyes after him, and then in the moonlight I
could make out the inalienable outline of his figure receding
into the distance. Lost in my loneliness, I watched him go, out
of town, far down the road where it curved out to the level
country beyond the valley. There were men on the porch behind me, but I was aware only of that dark shape growing small
and indistinct along the far reach of the road. A cloud passed
over the moon and he merged into the general shadow and I
could not see him and the cloud passed on and the road was a
plain thin ribbon to the horizon and he was gone.

I stumbled back to fall on the steps, my head in my arms to
hide the tears. The voices of the men around me were meaningless noises in a bleak and empty world. It was Mr. Weir who
took me home.

# 15

FATHER AND mother were in the kitchen, almost as I had left them. Mother had hitched her chair close to father's. He was sitting up, his face tired and haggard, the ugly red mark standing out plain along the side of his head. They did not come to meet us. They sat still and watched us move into the doorway.

They did not even scold me. Mother reached and pulled me to her and let me crawl into her lap as I had not done for three years or more. Father just stared at Mr. Weir. He could not trust himself to speak first.

"Your troubles are over, Starrett."

Father nodded. "You've come to tell me," he said wearily, "that he killed Wilson before they got him. I know. He was Shane."

"Wilson," said Mr. Weir. "And Fletcher."

Father started. "Fletcher, too? By Godfrey, yes. He would do it right." Then father sighed and ran a finger along the bruise on his head. "He let me know this was one thing he wanted to handle by himself. I can tell you, Weir, waiting here is the hardest job I ever had."

Mr. Weir looked at the bruise. "I thought so. Listen, Starrett. There's not a man in town doesn't know you didn't stay here of your own will. And there's damn few that aren't glad it was Shane came into the saloon tonight."

The words broke from me. "You should have seen him, father. He was—he was—" I could not find it at first. "He was —beautiful, father. And Wilson wouldn't even have hit him if he'd been in practice. He told me so."

"He told you!" The table was banging over as father drove to his feet. He grabbed Mr. Weir by the coat front. "My God, man! Why didn't you tell me? He's alive?"

"Yes," said Mr. Weir. "He's alive all right. Wilson got to him. But no bullet can kill that man." A puzzled, faraway sort of look flitted across Mr. Weir's face. "Sometimes I wonder whether anything ever could."

Father was shaking him. "Where is he?"

319

"He's gone," said Mr. Weir. "He's gone, alone and unfollowed as he wanted it. Out of the valley and no one knows where."

Father's hands dropped. He slumped again into his chair. He picked up his pipe and it broke in his fingers. He let the pieces fall and stared at them on the floor. He was still staring at them when new footsteps sounded on the porch and a man pushed into our kitchen.

It was Chris. His right arm was tight in the sling, his eyes unnaturally bright and the color high in his face. In his left hand he was carrying a bottle, a bottle of red cherry soda pop. He came straight in and righted the table with the hand holding the bottle. He smacked the bottle on the top boards and seemed startled at the noise he made. He was embarrassed and he was having trouble with his voice. But he spoke up firmly.

"I brought that for Bob. I'm a damned poor substitute, Starrett. But as soon as this arm's healed, I'm asking you to let me work for you."

Father's face twisted and his lips moved, but no words came. Mother was the one who said it. "Shane would like that, Chris."

And still father said nothing. What Chris and Mr. Weir saw as they looked at him must have shown them that nothing they could do or say would help at all. They turned and went out together, walking with long, quick steps.

Mother and I sat there watching father. There was nothing we could do either. This was something he had to wrestle alone. He was so still that he seemed even to have stopped breathing. Then a sudden restlessness hit him and he was up and pacing aimlessly about. He glared at the walls as if they stifled him and strode out the door into the yard. We heard his steps around the house and heading into the fields and then we could hear nothing.

I do not know how long we sat there. I know that the wick in the lamp burned low and sputtered awhile and went out and the darkness was a relief and a comfort. At last mother rose, still holding me, the big boy bulk of me, in her arms. I was surprised at the strength in her. She was holding me tightly to her and she carried me into my little room and helped me undress in the dim shadows of the moonlight through the window. She tucked me in and sat on the edge of the bed, and then, only then, she whispered to me: "Now, Bob. Tell me everything. Just as you saw it happen."

I told her, and when I was done, all she said in a soft little murmur was "Thank you." She looked out the window and murmured the words again and they were not for me and she was still looking out over the land to the great gray mountains when finally I fell asleep.

She must have been there the whole night through, for when I woke with a start, the first streaks of dawn were showing through the window and the bed was warm where she had been. The movement of her leaving must have wakened me. I crept out of bed and peeked into the kitchen. She was standing in the open outside doorway.

I fumbled into my clothes and tiptoed through the kitchen to her. She took my hand and I clung to hers and it was right that we should be together and that together we should go find father.

We found him out by the corral, by the far end where Shane had added to it. The sun was beginning to rise through the cleft in the mountains across the river, not the brilliant glory of midday but the fresh and renewed reddish radiance of early morning. Father's arms were folded on the top rail, his head bowed on them. When he turned to face us, he leaned back against the rail as if he needed the support. His eyes were rimmed and a little wild.

"Marian, I'm sick of the sight of this valley and all that's in it. If I tried to stay here now, my heart wouldn't be in it any more. I know it's hard on you and the boy, but we'll have to pull up stakes and move on. Montana, maybe. I've heard there's good land for the claiming up that way."

Mother heard him through. She had let go my hand and stood erect, so angry that her eyes snapped and her chin quivered. But she heard him through.

"Joe! Joe Starrett!" Her voice fairly crackled and was rich with emotion that was more than anger. "So you'd run out on Shane just when he's really here to stay!"

"But, Marian. You don't understand. He's gone."

"He's not gone. He's here, in this place, in this place he gave us. He's all around us and in us, and he always will be."

She ran to the tall corner post, to the one Shane had set. She beat at it with her hands. "Here, Joe. Quick. Take hold. Pull it down."

Father stared at her in amazement. But he did as she said. No one could have denied her in that moment. He took hold of the post and pulled at it. He shook his head and braced his feet and strained at it with all his strength. The big muscles of his shoulders and back knotted and bulged till I thought this shirt, too, would shred. Creakings ran along the rails and the post moved ever so slightly and the ground at the base showed little cracks fanning out. But the rails held and the post stood.

Father turned from it, beads of sweat breaking on his face, a light creeping up his drawn cheeks.

"See, Joe. See what I mean. We have roots here now that we can never tear loose."

And the morning was in father's face, shining in his eyes, giving him new color and hope and understanding.

## 16

I GUESS that is all there is to tell. The folks in town and the kids at school liked to talk about Shane, to spin tales and speculate about him. I never did. Those nights at Grafton's became legends in the valley and countless details were added as they grew and spread just as the town, too, grew and spread up the river banks. But I never bothered, no matter how strange the tales became in the constant retelling. He belonged to me, to father and mother and me, and nothing could ever spoil that.

For mother was right. He was there. He was there in our place and in us. Whenever I needed him, he was there. I could close my eyes and he would be with me and I would see him plain and hear again that gentle voice.

I would think of him in each of the moments that revealed him to me. I would think of him most vividly in that single flashing instant when he whirled to shoot Fletcher on the balcony at Grafton's saloon. I would see again the power and grace of a coordinate force beautiful beyond comprehension. I would see the man and the weapon wedded in the one indivisible deadliness. I would see the man and the tool, a good man and a good tool, doing what had to be done.

And always my mind would go back at the last to that moment when I saw him from the bushes by the roadside just on the edge of town. I would see him there in the road, tall and terrible in the moonlight, going down to kill or be killed, and stopping to help a stumbling boy and to look out over the land, the lovely land, where that boy had a chance to live out his boyhood and grow straight inside as a man should.

And when I would hear the men in town talking among themselves and trying to pin him down to a definite past, I would smile quietly to myself. For a time they inclined to the notion, spurred by the talk of a passing stranger, that he was a certain Shannon who was famous as a gunman and gambler way down in Arkansas and Texas and dropped from sight without anyone knowing why or where. When that notion dwindled, others followed, pieced together in turn from scraps of information gleaned from stray travelers. But when they talked like that, I simply smiled because I knew he could have been none of these.

He was the man who rode into our little valley out of the heart of the great glowing West and when his work was done rode back whence he had come and he was Shane.

# THE SEARCHERS

*Alan Le May*

TO MY GRANDFATHER, OLIVER LE MAY, WHO DIED ON THE
PRAIRIE; AND TO MY GRANDMOTHER, KAREN JENSEN LE MAY,
TO WHOM HE LEFT THREE SONS UNDER SEVEN.

"*These people had a kind of courage that may be the finest gift of man: the courage of those who simply keep on, and on, doing the next thing, far beyond all reasonable endurance, seldom thinking of themselves as martyred, and never thinking of themselves as brave.*"

# I

S UPPER WAS over by sundown, and Henry Edwards walked out from the house for a last look around. He carried his light shotgun, in hopes the rest of the family would think he meant to pick up a sage hen or two—a highly unlikely prospect anywhere near the house. He had left his gun belt on its peg beside the door, but he had sneaked the heavy six-gun itself into his waistband inside his shirt. Martha was washing dishes in the wooden sink close by, and both their daughters—Lucy, a grown-up seventeen, and Debbie, just coming ten—were drying and putting away. He didn't want to get them all stirred up; not until he could figure out for himself what had brought on his sharpened dread of the coming night.

"Take your pistol, Henry," Martha said clearly. Her hands were busy, but her eyes were on the holster where it hung empty in plain sight, and she was laughing at him. That was the wonderful thing about Martha. At thirty-eight she looked older than she was in some ways, especially her hands. But in other ways she was a lot younger. Her sense of humor did that. She could laugh hard at things other people thought only a little bit funny, or not funny at all; so that often Henry could see the pretty sparkle of the girl he had married twenty years back.

He grunted and went out. Their two sons were on the back gallery as he came out of the kitchen. Hunter Edwards, named after Martha's family, was nineteen, and as tall as his old man. He sat on the floor, his head lolled back against the adobe, and his mind so far away that his mouth hung open. Only his eyes moved as he turned them to the shotgun. He said dutifully, "Help you, Pa?"

"Nope."

Ben, fourteen, was whittling out a butter paddle. He jumped up, brushing shavings off his blue jeans. His father made a Plains-Indian sign—a fist pulled downward from in front of his shoulder, meaning "sit-stay." Ben went back to his whittling.

"Don't you forget to sweep them shavings up," Henry said.

"I won't, Pa."

They watched their father walk off, his long, slow-looking
steps quiet in his flat-heeled boots, until he circled the corrals
and was out of sight.

"What's he up to?" Ben asked. "There ain't any game out
there. Not short of the half mile."

Hunter hesitated. He knew the answer but, like his father,
he didn't want to say anything yet. "I don't know," he said at
last, letting his voice sound puzzled. Within the kitchen he
heard a match strike. With so much clear light left outside,
it was hard to believe how shadowy the kitchen was getting,
within its thick walls. But he knew his mother was lighting a
lamp. He called softly, "Ma . . . Not right now."

His mother came to the door and looked at him oddly, the
blown-out match smoking in her hand. He met her eyes for a
moment, but looked away again without explaining. Martha
Edwards went back into the kitchen, moving thoughtfully; and
no light came on. Hunter saw that his father was in sight again,
very far away for the short time he had been gone. He was
walking toward the top of a gentle hill northwest of the ranch
buildings. Hunter watched him steadily as long as he was in
sight. Henry never did go clear to the top. Instead he climbed
just high enough to see over, then circled the contour to look
all ways, so that he showed himself against the sky no more
than he had to. He was at it a long time.

Ben was staring at Hunter. "Hey. I want to know what——"

"Shut up, will you?"

Ben looked astonished, and obeyed.

From just behind the crest of the little hill, Henry Edwards
could see about a dozen miles, most ways. The evening light
was uncommonly clear, better to see by than the full glare of
the sun. But the faint roll of the prairie was deceptive. A whole
squadron of cavalry could probably hide itself at a thousand
yards, in a place that looked as flat as a parade ground. So he
was looking for little things—a layer of floating dust in the
branches of the mesquite, a wild cow or an antelope disturbed.
He didn't see anything that meant much. Not for a long time.

He looked back at his house. He had other things, the stuff
he worked with—barn, corrals, stacks of wild hay, a shacky
bunkhouse for sleeping extra hands. But it was the house he
was proud of. Its adobe walls were three and four feet thick,

so strong that the first room they had built had for a long time been called the Edwards Fort. They had added on to it since, and made it even more secure. The shake roof looked burnable, but it wasn't, for the shakes were laid upon two feet of sod. The outside doors were massive, and the windows had heavy battle shutters swung inside.

And the house had luxuries. Wooden floors. Galleries—some called them porches, now—both front and back. Eight windows with glass. He had made his family fairly comfortable here, at long last, working patiently with his hands through the years when there was no money, and no market for cows, and nothing to do about it but work and wait.

He could hardly believe there had been eighteen years of that kind of hanging on. But they had come out here that long ago—the same year Hunter had been born—drawn by these miles and miles of good grass, free to anyone who dared expose himself to the Kiowas and Comanches. It hadn't looked so dangerous when they first came, for the Texas Rangers had just punished the Wild Tribes back out of the way. But right after that the Rangers were virtually disbanded, on the thrifty theory that the Federal Government was about to take over the defense. The Federal troops did not come. Henry and Martha held on and prayed. One year more, they told each other again and again . . . just another month . . . only until spring. . . . So the risky years slid by, while no military help appeared. Their nearest neighbors, the Pauleys, were murdered off by a Comanche raid, without survivors except a little boy less than two years old; and they heard of many, many more.

Six years of that. Then, in 1857, Texas gave up waiting, and the Rangers bloomed again. A tough line of forts sprang up —McKavitt, Phantom Hill, Bell's Stockade. The little strongholds were far strung out, all the way from the Salt Fork to the Rio Grande, but they gave reassurance nonetheless. The dark years of danger were over; they had lasted out, won through to years of peace and plenty in which to grow old—or so they thought for a little while. Then the War Between the States drained the fighting men away, and the Kiowas and Comanches rose up singing once more, to take their harvest.

Whole counties were scoured out and set back to wilderness in those war years. But the Edwardses stayed, and the

Mathisons, and a few more far-spread, dug-in families, holding the back door of Texas, driving great herds of longhorns
to Matagordas for the supply of the Confederate troops. And
they waited again, holding on just one year more, then another, and one more yet.

Henry would have given up. He saw no hope that he would
ever get a foothold out here again, once he drew out, but he
would gladly have sacrificed their hopes of a cattle empire to
take Martha and their children to a safer place. It was Martha
who would not quit, and she had a will that could jump and
blaze like a grass fire. How do you take a woman back to the
poverty of the cotton rows against her will? They stayed.

The war's end brought the turn of fortune in which they had
placed their faith. Hiring cowboys on promise, borrowing to
provision them, Henry got a few hundred head into the very
first drive to end-of-track at Abilene. Now, with the war four
years past, two more drives had paid off. And this year he and
Aaron Mathison, pooling together, had sent north more than
three thousand head. But where were the troops that peace
should have released to their defense? Bolder, wilder, stronger
every year, the Comanches and their Kiowa allies punished the
range. Counties that had survived the war were barren now;
the Comanches had struck the outskirts of San Antonio itself.

Once they could have quit and found safety in a milder land.
They couldn't quit now, with fortune beyond belief coming
into their hands. They were as good as rich—and living in the
deadliest danger that had overhung them yet. Looking back
over the years, Henry did not know how they had survived
so long; their strong house and everlasting watchfulness could
not explain it. It must have taken miracles of luck, Henry knew,
and some mysterious quirks of Indian medicine as well, to preserve them here. If he could have seen, in any moment of the
years they had lived here, the endless hazards that lay ahead, he
would have quit that same minute and got Martha out of there
if he had had to tie her.

But you get used to unresting vigilance, and a perpetual danger becomes part of the everyday things around you. After a
long time you probably wouldn't know how to digest right, any
more, if it altogether went away. All that was behind could not
explain, exactly, the way Henry felt tonight. He didn't believe

in hunches, either, or any kind of spirit warnings. He was sure he had heard, or seen, or maybe even smelled some sign so small he couldn't remember it. Sometimes a man's senses picked up dim warnings he didn't even recognize. Like sometimes he had known an Indian was around, without knowing what told him, until a little later the breeze would bring the smell of the Indian a little stronger—a kind of old-buffalo-robe smell—which of course had been the warning before he knew he smelled anything. Or sometimes he knew horses were coming before he could hear their hoofs; he supposed this came by a tremor of the ground so weak you didn't know you felt it, but only knew what it meant.

He became aware that he was biting his mustache. It was a thin blond mustache, trailing downward at the corners of his mouth, so that it gave his face a dour look it didn't have underneath. But it wasn't a chewed mustache, because he didn't chew it. Patiently he studied the long sweep of the prairie, looking steadily at each quadrant for many minutes. He was sorry now that he had let Amos go last night to help the Mathisons chase cow thieves; Amos was Henry's brother and a rock of strength. It should have been enough that he let Martin Pauley go along. Mart was the little boy they had found in the brush, after the Pauley massacre, and raised as their own. He was eighteen now, and given up to be the best shot in the family. The Mathisons hadn't been satisfied anyway. Thought he should send Hunter, too, or else come himself. You can't ever please everybody.

A quarter mile off a bedded-down meadow lark sprang into the air, circled uncertainly, then drifted away. Henry became motionless, except for his eyes, which moved continually, casting the plain. Five hundred yards to the right of the spot where the meadow lark had jumped, a covey of quail went up.

Henry turned and ran for the house.

# 2

Martin Pauley had found this day a strange one almost from the start. Twelve riders had gathered to trail some cow thieves who had bit into the Mathisons'; and the queer thing about it was that five out of the twelve soon disagreed with all the others as to what they were following.

Aaron Mathison, who owned the run-off cattle, was a bearded, calm-eyed man of Quaker extraction. He had not been able to hold onto the part of his father's faith which forswore the bearing of arms, but he still prayed, and read the Bible every day. Everything about the Mathison place was either scrubbed, or raked, or whitewashed, but the house was cramped and sparely furnished compared to the Edwards'. All the money Aaron could scrape went into the quality of his livestock. Lately he had got his Lazy Lightning brand on ten head of blood bulls brought on from Kansas City. These had been held, by the chase-'em-back method, with a small herd on the Salt Crick Flats. This was the herd that was gone.

They picked up the churned trail of the stolen herd shortly after dawn, and followed it briskly, paced by the light-riding Mathison boys on their good horses. Martin Pauley lagged back, dogging it in the early hours. He had a special grouch of his own because he had looked forward to a visit with Laurie Mathison before they set out. Laurie was eighteen, like himself —straight and well boned, he thought, in terms he might have used to judge a filly. Lately he had caught her unwary gray eyes following him, now and then, when he was around the Mathisons'. But not this morning.

Laurie had been flying around, passing out coffee and quick-grab breakfast, with two of the Harper boys and Charlie MacCorry helping her on three sides—all of them clowning, and cutting up, and showing off, till there was no way to get near. Martin Pauley was a quiet boy, dark as an Indian except for his light eyes; he never did feel he cut much of a figure among the blond and easy-laughing people with whom he was raised. So he had hung back, and never did get to talk to Laurie. She ran out to his stirrup, and said, "Hi," hardly looking at

him as she handed him a hunk of hot meat wrapped in bread
—no coffee—and was gone again. And that was the size of it.

For a while Martin kept trying to think of something cute he
might have said. Didn't think of a thing. So he got bored with
himself, and took a wide unneedful swing out on the flank. He
was casting the prairie restlessly, looking for nothing in particular, when presently he found something that puzzled him and
made him uneasy.

Mystified, he crossed the trail and swung wide on the other
flank to take a look at the ground over there; and here he
found Amos, doing the same thing. Amos Edwards was forty,
two years older than his brother Henry, a big burly figure on
a strong but speedless horse. He was some different from the
rest of the Edwards family. His heavy head of hair was darker,
and probably would have been red-brown, except that it was
unbrushed, without any shine to it. And he was liable to be
pulled back into his shell between rare bursts of temper. Just
now he was riding lumpily, hands in his pockets, reins swinging
free from the horn, while he guided his horse by unnoticeable
flankings with the calves of his legs and two-ounce shifts of
weight. Martin cleared his throat a few times, hoping Amos
would speak, but he did not.

"Uncle Amos," Martin said, "you notice something almighty
fishy about this trail?"

"Like what?"

"Well, at the jump-off I counted tracks of twelve, fifteen ponies working this herd. Now I can't find no more than four,
five. First I supposed the rest had pushed on ahead, and their
trails got tromp out by cows———"

"That's shrewd," Amos snubbed him. "I never would have
thunk of it."

"———only, just now I find me a fit-up where two more ponies
forked off—and they sure didn't push on ahead. They turned
back."

"Why?"

"Why? Gosh, Uncle Amos—how the hell should I know?
That's what itches me."

"Do me one thing," Amos said. "Drop this 'Uncle' foolishness."

"Sir?"

"You don't have to call me 'Sir,' neither. Nor 'Grampaw,' neither. Nor 'Methuselah,' neither. I can whup you to a frazzle."

Martin was blanked. "What should I call you?"

"Name's Amos."

"All right. Amos. You want I should mosey round and see what the rest of 'em think?"

"They'll tell you the same." He was pulled back in his shell, fixing to bide his time.

It was straight-up noon, and they had paused to water at a puddle in a coulee, before Amos made his opinion known. "Aaron," he said in tones most could hear, "I'd be relieved to know if all these boys realize what we're following here. Because it ain't cow thieves. Not the species we had in mind."

"How's this, now?"

"What we got here is a split-off from an Indian war party, running wild loose on a raid." He paused a moment, then finished quietly. "Maybe you knowed that already. In case you didn't, you know it now. Because I just told you."

Aaron Mathison rubbed his fingers through his beard and appeared to consider; and some of the others put in while he did that. Old Mose Harper pointed out that none of the thieves had ridden side by side, not once on the trail, as the tracks showed plain. Indians and dudes rode single file— Indians to hide their numbers, and dudes because the horses felt like it—but white men rode abreast in order to gab all the time. So the thieves were either Indians or else not speaking. One t'other. This contribution drew partly hidden smiles from Mose Harper's sons.

Young Charlie MacCorry, a good rough-stock rider whom Martin resented because of his lively attentions to Laurie Mathison, spoke of noticing that the thieves all rode small unshod horses, a whole lot like buffalo ponies. And Lije Powers got in his two cents. Lije was an old-time buffalo hunter, who now lived by wandering from ranch to ranch, "stopping by." He said now that he had "knowed it from the fust," and allowed that what they were up against was a "passel of Caddoes."

Those were all who took any stock in the theory.

Aaron Mathison reasoned in even tones that they had no real reason to think any different than when they had started. The northeasterly trend of the trail said plainly that the thieves were delivering the herd to some beef contractor for one of the Indian Agencies—maybe old Fort Towson. Nothing else made any sense. The thieves had very little start; steady riding should force a stand before sundown tomorrow. They had only to push on, and all questions would soon be answered.

"I hollered for a back track at the start," Amos argued. "Where's the main war party these here forked off from? If they're up ahead, that's one thing. But if they're back where our families be——"

Aaron bowed his head for several moments, as if in prayer; but when his head came up he was looking at Amos Edwards with narrowed eyes. He spoke gently, slipping into Quakerish phrasings; and Martin Pauley, who had heard those same soft tones before, knew the argument was done. "Thee can turn back," Aaron said. "If thee fears what lies ahead or what lies behind, I need thee no more."

He turned his horse and rode on. Two or three hesitated, but ended by following him.

Amos was riding with his hands in his pockets again, letting his animal keep up as it chose; and Martin saw that Amos had fallen into one of his deadlocks. This was a thing that happened to Amos repeatedly, and it seemed to have a close relationship with the shape of his life. He had served two years with the Rangers, and four under Hood, and had twice been up the Chisholm Trail. Earlier he had done other things—bossed a bull train, packed the mail, captained a stage station—and he had done all of them well. Nobody exactly understood why he always drifted back, sooner or later, to work for his younger brother, with never any understanding as to pay.

What he wanted now was to pull out of the pursuit and go back. If he did turn, it could hardly be set down to cowardice. But it would mark him as unreliable and self-interested to an unforgivable degree in the eyes of the other cowmen. A thing like that could reflect on his whole family, and tend to turn the range against them. So Amos sat like a sack of wheat, in motion only because he happened to be sitting on a horse, and the horse was following the others.

His dilemma ended unexpectedly.

Brad Mathison, oldest of Aaron's boys, was ranging far ahead. They saw him disappear over the saddle of a ridge at more than two miles. Immediately he reappeared, stopped against the sky, and held his rifle over his head with both hands. It was the signal for "found." Then he dropped from sight beyond the ridge again.

Far behind him, the others put the squeeze to their horses, and lifted into a hard run. They stormed over the saddle of the ridge, and were looking down into a broad basin. Some scattered bunches of red specks down there were cattle grazing loose on their own. Aaron Mathison, with his cowman's eyes, recognized each speck that could be seen at all as an individual animal of his own. Here was the stolen herd, unaccountably dropped and left.

Brad was only about a mile out on the flats, but running his horse full stretch now toward the hills beyond the plain.

"Call in that damn fool," Amos said. He fired his pistol into the air, so that Brad looked back.

Aaron spun his horse in close circles to call in his son. Brad turned reluctantly, as if disposed to argue with his father, but came trotting back. Now Aaron spotted something fifty yards to one side, and rode to it for a closer look. He stepped down, and the others closed in around him. One of the young blood bulls lay there, spine severed by the whack of an axe. The liver had been ripped out, but no other meat taken. When they had seen this much, most of the riders sat and looked at each other. They barely glanced at the moccasin prints, faint in the dust-film upon the baked ground. Amos, though, not only dismounted, but went to his knees; and Martin Pauley stooped beside him, not to look wise, but trying to find out what Amos was looking for. Amos jabbed the carcass with his thumb. "Only nine, ten hours old," he said. Then, to Lije Powers, "Can you tell what moccasins them be?"

Lije scratched his thin beard. "Injuns," he said owlishly. He meant it for a joke, but nobody laughed. They followed Mathison as he loped out to meet his son.

"I rode past five more beef kills," Brad said when they came together. He spoke soberly, his eyes alert upon his father's face. "All these down here are heifers. And all killed with the lance. Appears like the lance wounds drive deep forward from just under the short ribs, clean through to the heart. I never saw that before."

"I have," Lije Powers said. He wanted to square himself for his misfire joke. "Them's Comanche buffler hunters done that. Ain't no others left can handle a lance no more."

Some of the others, particularly the older men, were looking gray and bleak. The last five minutes had taken them ten years back into the past, when every night of the world was an uncertain thing. The years of watchfulness and struggle had brought them some sense of confidence and security toward the last; but now all that was struck away as if they had their whole lives to do over again. But instead of taking ten years off their ages it put ten years on.

"This here's a murder raid," Amos said, sending his words at Aaron like rocks. "It shapes up to scald out either your place or Henry's. Do you know that now?"

Aaron's beard was sunk on his chest. He said slowly, "I see no other likelihood."

"They drove your cattle to pull us out," Amos hammered it home. "We've give 'em free run for the last sixteen hours!"

"I question if they'll hit before moonrise. Not them Comanch." Lije spoke with the strange detachment of one who has seen too much for too long.

"Moonrise! Ain't a horse here can make it by midnight!"

Brad Mathison said through his teeth, "I'll come almighty close!" He wheeled his pony and put it into a lope.

Aaron bellowed, "Hold in that horse!" and Brad pulled down to a slamming trot.

Most of the others were turning to follow Brad, talking blasphemies to their horses and themselves. Charlie MacCorry had the presence of mind to yell, "Which place first? We'll be strung out twenty mile!"

"Mathison's is this side!" Mose Harper shouted. Then to Amos over his shoulder, "If we don't fight there, we'll come straight on!"

Martin Pauley was scared sick over what they might find back home, and Laurie was in his mind too, so that the people he cared about were in two places. He was crazy to get started, as if haste could get him to both places at once. But he made himself imitate Amos, who unhurriedly pulled off saddle and bridle. They fed grain again, judging carefully how much their animals would do best on, and throwing the rest away. The time taken to rest and feed would get them home quicker in the end.

By the time they crossed the saddleback the rest of the riders were far spaced, according to the judgment of each as to how his horse might best be spent. Amos branched off from the way the others took. Miles were important, now, and they could save a few by passing well west of Mathison's. Amos had already made up his mind that he must kill his horse in this ride; for they had more than eighty miles to go before they would know what had happened—perhaps was happening now—to the people they had left at home.

# 3

H ENRY EDWARDS stood watching the black prairie through a loophole in a batten shutter. The quartering moon would rise late; he wanted to see it coming, for he believed now that all the trouble they could handle would be on them with the moon's first light. The dark kitchen in which the family waited was closed tight except for the loopholes. The powder smoke was going to get pretty thick in here if they had to fight. Yet the house was becoming cold. Any gleam of light would so hurt their chances that they had even drawn the coals from the firebox of the stove and drowned them in a tub.

The house itself was about as secure as a house could be made. The loopholed shutters, strap-hinged on the inside, were heavy enough to stop a 30-30, if not a buffalo slug, and the doors were even better. Nine or ten rifles could hold the place forever against anything but artillery. As few as seven would have their hands full against a strong war party, but should hold.

There lay the trouble and the fear. Henry did not have seven. He had himself, and his two sons, and Martha. Hunter was a deadly shot, and Ben, though only fourteen, would put in a pretty fair job. But Martha couldn't shoot any too well. Most likely she would hold fire until the last scratch, in hopes the enemy would go away. And Lucy . . . Lucy might do for a lookout someplace, but her dread of guns was so great she would be useless even to load. Henry had made her strap on a pistol, but he doubted if she could ever fire it, even to take her own life in event of capture.

And then there was Deborah. The boys had been good shots at eight; but Debbie, though pushing ten, seemed so little to Henry that he hadn't let her touch a weapon yet. You don't see your own children grow unless there's a new one to remind you how tiny they come. In Henry's eyes, Debbie hadn't changed in size since she was brand new, with feet no bigger than a fingertip with toes.

Four rifles, then, or call it three and a half, to hold two doors and eight shuttered windows, all of which could be busted in.

Out in the work-team corral a brood mare gave a long whinny, then another after a moment's pause. Everyone in the kitchen held his breath, waiting for the mare's call to be answered. No answer came, and after a while, when she whinnied again, Henry drew a slow breath. The mare had told him a whole basket of things he didn't want to know. Strange ponies were out there, probably with stud horses among them; the mare's nose had told her, and the insistence of her reaction left no room for doubt. They were Indian ridden, because loose ponies would have answered, and horses ridden by friends would have been let to answer. The Indians were Comanches, for the Comanches were skillful at keeping their ponies quiet. They wove egg-size knots into their rawhide hackamores, so placed that the pony's nostrils could be pinched if he so much as pricked an ear. This was best done from the ground, so Henry judged that the Comanches had dismounted, leaving their ponies with horse holders. They were fixing to close on foot—the most dangerous way there was.

One thing more. They were coming from more than one side, because none would have approached downwind, where the mare could catch their scent, unless they were all around. A big party, then, or it would not have split up. No more hope, either, that the Comanches meant only to break fence on the far side of the corrals to run the stock off. This was a full-scale thing, with all the chips down, tonight.

Lucy's voice came softly out of the dark. "Debbie?" Then more loudly, with a note of panic, "Debbie! Where are you?" Everyone's voice sounded eery coming out of the unseen.

"Here I am." They heard the cover put back on the cookie crock at the far end of the room.

"You get back on your pallet, here! And stay put now, will you?"

Long ago, hide-hunting at the age of eighteen, Henry and two others had fought off more than twenty Kiowas from the shelter of nothing more than a buffalo wallow. They had fought with desperation enough, believing they were done for; but he couldn't remember any such sinking of the heart as he felt now behind these fort-strong walls. Little girls in the house —that's what cut a man's strings, and made a coward of him, every bit as bad as if the Comanches held them hostage already.

His words were steady, though, even casual, as he made his irrevocable decision.

"Martha. Put on Debbie's coat."

A moment of silence; then Martha's single word, breathy and uncertain: "Now?"

"Right now. Moon's fixing to light us up directly." Henry went into a front bedroom, and quietly opened a shutter. The sash was already up to cut down the hazard of splintering glass. He studied the night, then went and found Martha and Debbie in the dark. The child was wearing moccasins, and hugged a piece of buffalo robe.

"We're going to play the sleep-out game," he told Debbie. "The one where you hide out with Grandma. Like you know? Very quiet, like a mouse?" He was sending the little girl to her grandmother's grave.

"I know." Debbie was a shy child, but curiously unafraid of the open prairie or the dark. She had never known her grandmother, or seen death, but she had been raised to think the grave on the hill a friendly thing. Sometimes she left little picnic offerings up there for Grandma.

"You keep down low," Henry said, "and you go quietly, quietly along the ditch. Then up the hill to Grandma, and roll up in your robe, all snug and cozy."

"I remember how." They had practiced this before, and even used it once, under a threat that blew over.

Henry couldn't tell from the child's whisper whether she was frightened or not. He supposed she must be, what with the tension that was on all of them. He picked her up in his arms and carried her to the window he had opened. Though he couldn't see her, it was the same as if he could. She had a little triangular kitty-cat face, with very big green eyes, which you could see would be slanting someday, if her face ever caught up to them. As he kissed her, he found tears on her cheek, and she hugged him around the neck so hard he feared he would have to pull her arms away. But she let go, and he lifted her through the window.

"Quiet, now—stoop low—" he whispered in her ear. And he set her on the ground outside.

# 4

Amos pulled up at the top of a long rise ten miles from home; and here Martin Pauley, with very little horse left under him, presently caught up. On the south horizon a spot of fire was beginning to show. The glow bloomed and brightened; their big stacks of wild hay had caught and were going up in light. The east rim still showed nothing. The raiders had made their choice and left Mathison's alone.

For a moment or two Martin Pauley and Amos Edwards sat in silence. Then Amos drew his knife and cut off the quirt, called a romal, that was braided into his long reins. He hauled up his animal's heavy head; the quirt whistled and snapped hard, and the horse labored into a heavy, rocking run.

Martin stepped down, shaking so hard all over that he almost went to his knees. He reset his saddle, and as he mounted again his beat-out pony staggered, almost pulled over by the rider's weight. Amos was out of sight. Mart got his pony into an uncertain gallop, guiding the placement of its awkwardly slung hoofs by the light of the high moon. It was blowing in a wind-broke roar, and when a patch of foam caught Martin in the teeth he tasted blood in it. Yet the horse came nearer to getting home than Martin could have hoped. Half a mile from the house the animal stumbled in a shallow wash and came down heavily. Twice the long head swung up in an effort to rise, but flailed down again. Martin drew his six-gun and put a bullet in the pony's head, then dragged his carbine from the saddle boot and went on, running hard.

The hay fires and the wooden barn had died down to bright beds of coals, but the house still stood. Its shingles glowed in a dozen smoldering patches where torches had been thrown onto the roof, but the sod beneath them had held. For a moment a great impossible hope possessed Martin, intense as a physical pain. Then, while he was still far out, he saw a light come on in the kitchen as a lamp was lighted inside. Even at the distance he could see that the light came through a broken door, hanging skew-jawed on a single hinge.

Martin slowed to a walk, and went toward the house unwillingly. Little flames still wandered across the embers of the hay stacks and the barn, sending up sparks which hung idly on the quiet air; and the house itself showed against the night in a dull red glow. On the back gallery lay a dead pony, tail to the broken door. Probably it had been backed against the door to break the bar. By the steps Amos' horse was down, knees folded under. The heavy head was nodded lower and lower, the muzzle dipping the dust; it would never get up.

Martin stepped over the legs of the dead Comanche pony and went into the kitchen, walking as though he had never learned to walk, but had to pull each separate string. Near the door a body lay covered by a sheet. Martin drew back the limp muslin, and was looking into Martha's face. Her lips were parted a little, and her open eyes, looking straight up, appeared perfectly clear, as if she were alive. Her light hair was shaken loose, the lamplight picking out the silver in it. Martha had such a lot of hair that it was hardly noticeable, at first, that she had been scalped.

Most of the batten shutters had been smashed in. Hunter Edwards lay in a heap near the splintered hall door, his empty hands still clawed as if grasping the duck gun that was gone. Ben had fallen in a tangled knot by the far window, his gangly legs sprawled. He looked immature and undersized as he lay there, like a skinny small boy.

Martin found the body of Henry Edwards draped on its back across the broad sill of a bedroom window. The Comanche knives had done eery work upon this body. Like Martha, Henry and both boys had been scalped. Martin gently straightened the bodies of Henry, and Hunter, and Ben, then found sheets to put over them, as Amos had done for Martha. Martin's hands were shaking, but he was dry-eyed as Amos came back into the house.

When Martin had got a good look at his foster uncle, he was afraid of him. Amos' face was wooden, but such a dreadful light shone from behind the eyes that Martin thought Amos had gone mad. Amos carried something slim and limp in his arms, clutched against his chest. As Amos passed the lamp, Martin saw that the thing Amos carried had a hand, and that it was Martha's hand. He had not drawn down the sheet that covered Martha far enough to see that the body lacked an arm. The Comanches did things like that. Probably they had tossed the arm from one to another, capering and whooping, until they lost it in the dark.

"No sign of Lucy. Or Deborah," Amos said. "So far as I could find in the lack of light." The words were low and came unevenly, but they did not sound insane.

Martin said, "We used to practice sending Debbie up the hill to Grandma's grave—"

"I been up. They sent her there. I found her bit of buffalo robe. But Debbie's not up there. Not now."

"You suppose Lucy—" Martin let the question trail off, but they had worked so much together that Amos was able to answer.

"Can't tell yet if Lucy went up with Debbie to the grave. Not till daylight comes on."

Amos had got out another sheet and was tearing it into strips. Martin knew Amos was making bandages to fix up their people as decently as he could. His hands moved methodically, going through the motions of doing the next thing he ought to do, little as it mattered. But at the same time Amos was thinking about something else. "I want you to walk to the Mathisons'. Get them to hook their buckboard, and bring their women on. . . . Martha should have clean clothes put on."

Probably Amos would have stripped and bathed the body of his brother's wife, and dressed it properly, if there had been no one else to do it. But not if a walk of fifteen miles would get it done a more proper way. Martin turned toward the door without question.

"Wait. Pull off them boots and get your moccasins on. You got a long way to go." Martin obeyed that, too. "Where's them pegs you whittled out? I figure to make coffins out of the shelves."

"Behind the woodbox. Back of the range." Martin started off into the night.

Martin Pauley was eight miles on the way to Mathisons' when the first riders met him. All ten who had ridden the day before were on their way over, riding fresh Mathison horses and leading spares. A buckboard, some distance back, was bringing Mrs. Mathison and Laurie, who must no longer be left alone with a war party on the loose.

The fore riders had been pressing hard, hoping against hope that someone was left alive over there. When they had got the word from Martin, they pulled up and waited with him for the buckboard. Nobody pestered at him for details. Laurie made a place for him beside her on the buckboard seat, and they rode in silence, the team at a good trot.

After a mile or two Laurie whimpered, "Oh, Martie . . . Oh, Martie . . ." She turned toward him, rested her forehead against the shoulder of his brush jacket, and there cried quietly for a little while. Martin sat slack and still, nothing left in him to move him either toward her or away from her. Pretty soon she straightened up, and rode beside him in silence, not touching him any more.

# 5

Dawn was near when they got to the house. Amos had been hard at work. He had laid out his brother Henry and the two boys in one bedroom, and put their best clothes on them. He had put Martha in another room, and Mrs. Mathison and Laurie took over there. All the men went to work, silently, without having to be told what to do. These were lonely, self-sufficient people, who saw each other only a few times a year, yet they worked together well, each finding for himself the next thing that needed to be done. Some got to work with saw, boxplane, auger, and pegs, to finish the coffins Amos had started, while others made coffee, set up a heavy breakfast, and packed rations for the pursuit. They picked up and sorted out the litter of stuff the Indians had thrown about as they looted, put everything where it had belonged, as nearly as they could guess, scrubbed and sanded away the stains, just as if the life of this house were going to go on.

Two things they found in the litter had a special meaning for Martin Pauley. One was a sheet of paper upon which Debbie had tried to make a calendar a few weeks before. Something about it troubled him, and he couldn't make out what it was. He remembered wishing they had a calendar, and very dimly he recalled Debbie bringing this effort to him. But his mind had been upon something else. He believed he had said, "That's nice," and, "I see," without really seeing what the little girl was showing him. Debbie's calendar had not been hung up; he couldn't remember seeing it again until now. And now he saw why. She had made a mistake, right up at the top, so the whole thing had come out wrong. He turned vaguely to Laurie Mathison, where she was washing her hands at the sink.

"I . . ." he said. "It seems like . . ."

She glanced at the penciled calendar. "I remember that. I was over here that day. But it's all right. I explained to her."

"Explained what? What's all right?"

"She made a mistake up here, so it all—"

"Yes, I see that, but——"

348

"Well, when she saw she had spoiled it, she ran to you. . . ." Her gray eyes looked straight into his. "You and I had a fight that day. Maybe it was that. But—you were always Debbie's hero, Martie. She was—she's still just a baby, you know. She kept saying——" Laurie compressed her lips.

"She kept saying what?"

"Martie, I made her see that——"

He took Laurie by the arms hard. "Tell me."

"All right. I'll tell you. She kept saying, 'He didn't care at all.'"

Martin let his hands drop. "I wasn't listening," he said. "I made her cry, and I never knew."

He let her take the unlucky sheet of paper out of his hand, and he never saw it again. But the lost day when he should have taken Debbie in his arms, and made everything all right, was going to be with him a long time, a peg upon which he hung his grief.

The other thing he found was a miniature of Debbie. Miniatures had been painted of Martha and Lucy, too, once when Henry took the three of them to Fort Worth, but Martin never knew what became of those. Debbie's miniature, gold-framed in a little plush box, was the best of the three. The little triangular face and the green eyes were very true, and suggested the elfin look that went with Debbie's small size. He put the box in his pocket.

# 6

THEY LAID their people deep under the prairie sod beside Grandma. Aaron Mathison read from the Bible and said a prayer, while Martin, Amos, and the six others chosen for the pursuit stood a little way back from the open graves, holding their saddled horses.

It wasn't a long service. Daylight had told them that Lucy must have been carried bodily from the house, for they found no place where she had set foot to the ground. Debbie, the sign showed, had been picked up onto a running horse after a pitifully short chase upon the prairie. There was hope, then, that they still lived, and that one of them, or even both, might be recovered alive. Most of Aaron's amazing vitality seemed to have drained out of him, but he shared the cracking strain that would be upon them all so long as the least hope lasted. He made the ritual as simple and as brief as he decently could. "Man that is born of woman . . ."

Those waiting to ride feared that Aaron would get carried away in the final prayer, but he did not. Martin's mind was already far ahead on the trail, so that he heard only the last few words of the prayer, yet they stirred his hair. "Now may the light of Thy countenance be turned away from the stubborn and the blind. Let darkness fall upon them that will not see, that all Thy glory may light the way of those who seek . . . and all Thy wisdom lead the horses of the brave. . . . Amen."

It seemed to Martin Pauley that old Aaron, by the humility of his prayer, had invited eternal damnation upon himself, if only the search for Lucy and Debbie might succeed. His offer of retribution to his God was the only word that had been spoken in accusation or in blame, for the error of judgment that had led the fighting men away.

Amos must have had his foot in the stirrup before the end of the prayer, for he swung into the saddle with the last "Amen," and led off without a word. With Martin and Amos went Brad Mathison, Ed Newby, Charlie MacCorry, Mose Harper and his son Zack, and Lije Powers, who thought his old-time prairie wisdom had now come into its own, whether anybody else thought so or not. Those left behind would put layers of boulders in the graves against digging varmints, and set up the wooden crosses Martin Pauley had sectioned out of the house timbers in the last hours of the dark.

At the last moment Laurie Mathison ran to Martin where he sat already mounted. She stepped up lightly upon the toe of his stirruped boot, and kissed him hard and quickly on the mouth. A boldness like that would have drawn a blast of wrath at another time, but her parents seemed unable to see. Aaron still stood with bowed head beside the open graves; and Mrs. Mathison's eyes were staring straight ahead into a dreadful loneliness. The Edwardses, Mathisons, and Pauleys had come out here together. The three families had sustained each other while the Pauleys lived, and after their massacre the two remaining families had looked to each other in all things. Now only the Mathisons were left. Mrs. Mathison's usually mild and kindly face was bleak, stony with an insupportable fear. Martin Pauley would not have recognized her, even if he had been in a mood to notice anything at all.

He looked startled as Laurie kissed him, but only for a second. He seemed already to have forgotten her, for the time being, as he turned his horse.

# 7

OUT IN the middle of a vast, flat plain, a day's ride from anything, lay a little bad-smelling marsh without a name. It covered about ten acres and had cat-tails growing in it. Tules, the Mexicans called the cat-tails; but at that time certain Texans were still fighting shy of Mexican ways. Nowhere around was there a river, or a butte, or any landmark at all, except that nameless marsh. So that was how the "Fight at the Cat-tails" got its foolish-sounding name.

Seven men were still with the pursuit as they approached the Cat-tail fight at sundown of their fifth day. Lije Powers had dropped out on the occasion of his thirty-ninth or fortieth argument over interpretation of sign. He had found a headdress, a rather beautiful thing of polished heifer horns on a browband of black and white beads. They were happy to see it, for it told them that some Indian who still rode was wounded and in bad shape, or he would never have left it behind. But Lije chose to make an issue of his opinion that the headdress was Kiowa, and not Comanche—which made no difference at all, for the two tribes were allied. When they got tired of hearing Lije talk about it, they told him so, and Lije branched off in a huff to visit some Mexican hacienda he knew about somewhere to the south.

They had found many other signs of the punishment the Comanches had taken before the destruction of the Edwards family was complete. More important than other dropped belongings—a beaded pouch, a polished ironwood lance with withered scalps on it—were the shallow stone-piled Indian graves. On each lay the carcass of a horse of the Edwards' brand, killed in the belief that its spirit would carry the Comanche ghost. They had found seven of these burials. Four in one place, hidden behind a hill, were probably the graves of Indians killed outright at the ranch; three more, strung out at intervals of half a day, told of wounded who had died in the retreat. In war, no Indian band slacked its pace for the dying. Squaws were known to have given birth on the backs of traveling ponies, with no one to wait for them or give help. The cowmen could not hope that the wounded warriors would slow the flight of the murderers in the slightest.

Amos kept the beaded pouch and the heifer-born headdress in his saddlebags; they might help identify the Comanche killers someday. And for several days he carried the ironwood lance stripped of its trophies. He was using it to probe the depth of the Indian graves, to see if any were shallow enough so that he could open them without falling too far back. Probably he hoped to find something that would give some dead warrior a name, so that someday they might be led to the living by the unwilling dead. Or so Martin supposed at first.

But he could not help seeing that Amos was changing. Or perhaps he was seeing revealed, a little at a time, a change that had come over Amos suddenly upon the night of the disaster. At the start Amos had led them at a horse-killing pace, a full twenty hours of their first twenty-four. That was because of Lucy, of course. Often Comanches cared for and raised captive white children, marrying the girls when they were grown, and taking the boys into their families as brothers. But grown white women were raped unceasingly by every captor in turn until either they died or were "thrown away" to die by the satiated. So the pursuers spent themselves and their horseflesh unsparingly in that first run; yet found no sign, as their ponies failed, that they had gained ground upon the fast-traveling Comanches. After that Amos set the pace cagily at a walk until the horses recovered from that first all-out effort, later at a trot, hour after hour, saving the horses at the expense of the men. Amos rode relaxed now, wasting no motions and no steps. He had the look of a man resigned to follow this trail down the years, as long as he should live.

And then Amos found the body of an Indian not buried in the ground, but protected by stones in a crevice of a sandstone ledge. He got at this one—and took nothing but the scalp. Martin had no idea what Amos believed about life and death; but the Comanches believed that the spirit of a scalped warrior had to wander forever between the winds, denied entrance to the spirit land beyond the sunset. Amos did not keep the scalp, but threw it away on the prairie for the wolves to find.

Another who was showing change was Brad Mathison. He was always the one ranging farthest ahead, the first to start out each morning, the most reluctant to call it a day as the sun went down. His well-grained horses—they had brought four spares and two pack mules—showed it less than Brad himself, who was turning hollow-eyed and losing weight. During the past year Brad had taken to coming over to the Edwardses to set up with Lucy—but only about once every month or two. Martin didn't believe there had been any overpowering attachment there. But now that Lucy was lost, Brad was becoming more involved with every day that diminished hope.

By the third day some of them must have believed Lucy to be dead; but Brad could not let himself think that. "She's alive," he told Martin Pauley. Martin had said nothing either way. "She's got to be alive, Mart." And on the fourth day, dropping back to ride beside Mart, "I'll make it up to her," he promised himself. "No matter what's happened to her, no matter what she's gone through. I'll make her forget." He pushed his horse forward again, far into the lead, disregarding Amos' cussing.

So it was Brad, again, who first sighted the Comanches. Far out in front he brought his horse to the edge of a rimrock cliff; then dropped from the saddle and led his horse back from the edge. And now once more he held his rifle over his head with both hands, signaling "found."

The others came up on the run. Mart took their horses as they dismounted well back from the edge, but Mose Harper took the leads from Mart's hands. "I'm an old man," Mose said. "Whatever's beyond, I've seen it afore—most likely many times. You go on up."

The cliff was a three-hundred-foot limestone wall, dropping off sheer, as if it might be the shoreline of a vanished sea. The trail of the many Comanche ponies went down this precariously by way of a talus break. Twenty miles off, out in the middle of the flats, lay a patch of haze, shimmering redly in the horizontal light of the sunset. Some of them now remembered the cat-tail marsh that stagnated there, serving as a waterhole. A black line, wavering in the ground heat, showed in front of the marsh haze. That was all there was to see.

"Horses," Brad said. "That's horses, there at the water!"

"It's where they ought to be," Mart said. A faint reserve, as of disbelief in his luck, made the words come slowly.

"Could be buffler," Zack Harper said. He was a shag-headed young man, the oldest son of Mose Harper. "Wouldn't look no different."

"If there was buffalo there, you'd see the Comanche runnin' 'em," Amos stepped on the idea.

"If it's horses, it's sure a power of 'em."

"We've been trailin' a power of 'em."

They were silent awhile, studying the distant pen scratch upon the world that must be a band of livestock. The light was failing now as the sunset faded.

"We better feed out," Brad said finally. He was one of the youngest there, and the veteran plainsmen were usually cranky about hearing advice from the young; but lately they seemed to listen to him anyway. "It'll be dark in an hour and a half. No reason we can't jump them long before daylight, with any kind of start."

Ed Newby said, "You right sure you want to jump all them?"

Charlie MacCorry turned to look Ed over. "Just what in hell you think we come here for?"

"They'll be took unawares," Amos said. "They're always took unawares. Ain't an Indian in the world knows how to keep sentries out once the night goes cold."

"It ain't that," Ed answered. "We can whup them all right. I guess. Only thing . . . Comanches are mighty likely to kill any prisoners they've got, if they're jumped hard enough. They've done it again and again."

Mart Pauley chewed a grass blade and watched Amos. Finally Mart said, "There's another way. . . ."

Amos nodded. "Like Mart says. There's another way." Mart Pauley was bewildered to see that Amos looked happy. "I'm talking about their horses. Might be we could set the Comanch' afoot."

Silence again. Nobody wanted to say much now without considering a long while before he spoke.

"Might be we can stampede them ponies, and run off all the whole bunch," Amos went on. "I don't believe it would make 'em murder anybody—that's still alive."

"This thing ain't going to be too easy," Ed Newby said.

"No," Amos agreed. "It ain't easy. And it ain't safe. If we did get it done, the Comanch' should be ready to deal. But I don't say they'll deal. In all my life, I ain't learned but one thing about an Indian: Whatever you know you'd do in his place—he ain't going to do that. Maybe we'd still have to hunt them Comanches down, by bunches, by twos, by ones."

Something like a bitter relish in Amos' tone turned Mart cold. Amos no longer believed they would recover Lucy alive —and wasn't thinking of Debbie at all.

"Of course," Charlie MacCorry said, his eyes on a grass blade he was picking to shreds, "you know, could be every last one of them bucks has his best pony on short lead. Right beside him where he lies."

"That's right," Amos said. "That might very well be. And you know what happens then?"

"We lose our hair. And no good done to nobody."

"That's right."

Brad Mathison said, "In God's name, will you try it, Mr. Edwards?"

"All right."

Immediately Brad pulled back to feed his horses, and the others followed more slowly. Mart Pauley still lay on the edge of the rimrock after the others had pulled back. He was thinking of the change in Amos. No deadlock now, no hesitation in facing the worst answer there could be. No hope, either, visible in Amos' mind that they would ever find their beloved people alive. Only that creepy relish he had heard when Amos spoke of killing Comanches.

And thinking of Amos' face as it was tonight, he remembered it as it was that worst night of the world, when Amos came out of the dark, into the shambles of the Edwards' kitchen, carrying Martha's arm clutched against his chest. The mutilation could not be seen when Martha lay in the box they had made for her. Her face looked young, and serene, and her crossed hands were at rest, one only slightly paler than the other. They were worn hands, betraying Martha's age as her face did not, with little random scars on them. Martha was always hurting her hands. Mart thought, "She wore them out, she hurt them, working for us."

As he thought that, the key to Amos' life suddenly became plain. All his uncertainties, his deadlocks with himself, his labors without pay, his perpetual gravitation back to his brother's ranch—they all fell into line. As he saw what had shaped and twisted Amos' life, Mart felt shaken up; he had lived with Amos most of his life without ever suspecting the truth. But neither had Henry suspected it—and Martha least of all.

Amos was—had always been—in love with his brother's wife.

# 8

Amos held them where they were for an hour after dark. They pulled saddles and packs, fed out the last of their grain, and rubbed down the horses with wads of dry grass. Nobody cooked. The men chewed on cold meat and lumps of hard frying-pan bread left from breakfast. All of them studied the shape of the hills a hundred miles beyond, taking a line on the Comanche camp. That fly speck, so far out upon the plain, would be easy to miss in the dark. When the marsh could no longer be seen they used the hill contours to take sights upon the stars they knew, as each appeared. By the time the hills, too, were swallowed by the night, each had star bearings by which he could find his way.

Mose Harper mapped his course by solemnly cutting notches in the rim of the hat. His son Zack grinned as he watched his father do that, but no one else thought it comical that Mose was growing old. All men grew old unless violence overtook them first; the plains offered no third way out of the predicament a man found himself in, simply by the fact of his existence on the face of the earth.

Amos was still in no hurry as he led off, sliding down the talus break by which the Comanches had descended to the plain. Once down on the flats, Amos held to an easy walk. He wanted to strike the Comanche horse herd before daylight, but when he had attacked he wanted dawn to come soon, so they could tell how they had come out, and make a finish. There must be no long muddle in the dark. Given half a chance to figure out what had happened, the war party would break up into singles and ambushes, becoming almost impossible to root out of the short grass.

When the moon rose, very meager, very late, it showed them each other as black shapes, and they could make out their loose pack and saddle stock following along, grabbing jawfuls of the sparse feed. Not much more. A tiny dolloping whisk of pure movement, without color or form, was a kangaroo rat. A silently vanishing streak was a kit fox. About midnight the coyotes began their clamor, surprisingly near, but not in the key that bothered Mart; and a little later the hoarser, deeper howling of a loafer wolf sounded for a while a great way off. Brad Mathison drifted his pony alongside Mart's.

"That thing sound all right to you?"

Mart was uncertain. One note had sounded a little queer to him at one point, but it did not come again. He said he guessed it sounded like a wolf.

"Seems kind of far from timber for a loafer wolf. This time of year, anyway," Brad worried. "Known 'em to be out here, though," he answered his own complaint. He let his horse drop back, so that he could keep count of the loose stock.

After the loafer wolf shut up, a dwarf owl, such as lives down prairie dog holes, began to give out with a whickering noise about a middle distance off. Half a furlong farther on another took it up, after they had left the first one silent behind, and later another as they came abreast. This went on for half an hour, and it had a spooky feel to it because the owls always sounded one at a time, and always nearby. When Mart couldn't stand it any more he rode up beside Amos.

"What you think?" he asked, as an owl sounded again.

Amos shrugged. He was riding with his hands in his pockets again, as Mart had often seen him ride before, but there was no feel of deadlock or uncertainty about him now. He was leading out very straight, sure of his direction, sure of his pace.

"Hard to say," he answered.

"You mean you don't know if that's a real owl?"

"It's a real something. A noise don't make itself."

"I know, but that there is an easy noise to make. You could make it, or——"

"Well, I ain't."

"——or I could make it. Might be anything."

"Tell you something. Every critter you ever hear out here can sometimes sound like an awful poor mimic of itself. Don't always hardly pay to listen to them things too much."

"Only thing," Mart stuck to it, "these here all sound like just one owl, follering along. Gosh, Amos. I question if them things ever travel ten rods from home in their life."

"Yeah. I know. . . . Tell you what I'll do. I'll make 'em

stop, being's they bother you." Amos pushed his lips out and sounded an owl cry—not the cry of just any owl, but an exact repeat of the one they had just heard.

No more owls whickered that night.

As Mart let his pony drop back, it came almost to a stop, and he realized that he was checking it, unconsciously holding back from what was ahead. He wasn't afraid of the fighting—at least, he didn't think he was afraid of it. He wanted more than anything in the world to come to grips with the Comanches; of that he felt perfectly certain. What he feared was that he might prove to be a coward. He tried to tell himself that he had no earthly reason to doubt himself, but it didn't work. Maybe he had no earthly reason, but he had a couple of unearthly ones, and he knew it. There were some strange quirks inside of him that he couldn't understand at all.

One of them evidenced itself in the form of an eery nightmare that he had had over and over during his childhood. It was a dream of utter darkness, at first, though after a while the darkness seemed to redden with a dim, ugly glow, something like the redness you see through your lids when you look at the sun with closed eyes. But the main thing was the sound— a high, snarling, wailing yammer of a great many voices, repeatedly receding, then rising and swelling again; as if the sound came nearer in search of him, then went past, only to come back. The sound filled him with a hideous, unexplained terror, though he never knew what made it. It seemed the outcry of some weird semihuman horde—perhaps of ghoulish and inimical dead who sought to consume him. This went on and on, while he tried to scream, but could not; until he woke shivering miserably, but wet with sweat. He hadn't had this nightmare in a long time, but sometimes an unnatural fear touched him when the coyotes sung in a certain way far off on the sand hills.

Another loony weakness had to do with a smell. This particularly worried him tonight, for the smell that could bring an unreasoning panic into him was the faintly musky, old-leather-and-fur smell of Indians. The queer thing about this was that he felt no fear of the Indians themselves. He had seen a lot of them, and talked with them in the fragments of sign language he knew; he had even made swaps with some of them—mostly Caddoes, the far-wandering peddlers of the plains. But if he came upon a place where Indians had camped, or caught a faint scent of one down the wind, the same kind of panic could take hold of him as he felt in the dream. If he failed to connect this with the massacre he had survived, it was perhaps because he had no memory of the massacre. He had been carried asleep into the brush, where he had presently wakened lost and alone in the dark; and that was all he knew about it firsthand. Long after, when he had learned to talk, the disaster had been explained to him, but only in a general way. The Edwardses had never been willing to talk about it much.

And there was one more thing that could cut his strings; it had taken him unawares only two or three times in his life, yet worried him most of all, because it seemed totally meaningless. He judged this third thing to be a pure insanity, and wouldn't let himself think about it at all, times it wasn't forced on him without warning.

So now he rode uneasily, dreading the possibility that he might go to pieces in the clutch, and disgrace himself, in spite of all he could do. He began preaching to himself, inaudibly repeating over and over admonishments that unconsciously imitated Biblical forms. "I will go among them. I will prowl among them in the night. I will lay hands upon them; I will destroy them. Though I be cut in a hundred pieces, I will stand against them. . . ." It didn't seem to do any good.

He believed dawn could be no more than an hour off when Brad came up to whisper to him again. "I think we gone past."

Mart searched the east, fearing to see a graying in the sky too soon. But the night was still very dark, in spite of the dying moon. He could feel a faint warm breath of air upon his left cheek. "Wind's shifted to the south," he answered. "What little there is. I think Amos changed his line. Wants to come at 'em up wind."

"I know. I see that. But I think——"

Amos had stopped, and was holding up his hand. The six others closed up on him, stopped their horses and sat silent in their saddles. Mart couldn't hear anything except the loose animals behind, tearing at the grass. Amos rode on, and they traveled another fifteen minutes before he stopped again.

This time, when the shuffle of their ponies' feet had died, a faint sound lay upon the night, hard to be sure of, and even harder to believe. What they were hearing was the trilling of frogs. Now, how did they get way out here? They had to be the little green fellows that can live anywhere the ground is a little damp, but even so—either they had to shower down in the rare rains, like the old folks said, or else this marsh had been here always, while the dry world built up around.

Amos spoke softly. "Spread out some. Keep in line, and guide on me. I'll circle close in as I dare."

They spread out until they could just barely see each other, and rode at the walk, abreast of Amos as he moved on. The frog song came closer, so close that Mart feared they would trample on Indians before Amos turned. And now again, listening hard and straining their eyes, they rode for a long time. The north star was on their right hand for a while. Then it was behind them a long time. Then on their left, then ahead. At last it was on their right again, and Amos stopped. They were back where they started. A faint gray was showing in the east; their timing would have been perfect, if only what they were after had been here. Mose Harper pushed his horse in close. "I rode through the ashes of a farm," he said to Amos. "Did you know that? I thought you was hugging in awful close."

"Hush, now," Amos said. "I'm listening for something."

Mose dropped his tone. "Point is, them ashes showed no spark. Amos, them devils been gone from here all night."

"Catch up the loose stock," Amos said. "Bring 'em in on short lead."

"Waste of time," Mose Harper argued. "The boys are tard, and the Comanches is long gone."

"Get that loose stuff in," Amos ordered again, snapping it this time. "I want hobbles on 'em all—and soon!"

Mart was buckling a hobble on a pack mule when Brad dropped on one knee beside him to fasten the other cuff. "Look out yonder," Brad whispered. "When you get a chance."

Mart stood up, following Brad's eyes. A faint grayness had come evenly over the prairie, as if rising from the ground, but nothing showed a shadow yet. Mart cupped his hands over his eyes for a moment, then looked again, trying to look beside, instead of straight at, an unevenness on the flat land that he could not identify. But now he could not see it at all.

He said, "For a minute I thought—but I guess not."

"I swear something showed itself. Then took down again."

"A wolf, maybe?"

"I don't know. Something funny about this, Mart. The Comanch' ain't been traveling by night nor laying up by day. Not since the first hundred miles."

Now followed an odd aimless period, while they waited, and the light imperceptibly increased. "They're out there," Amos said at last. "They're going to jump us. There's no doubt of it now." Nobody denied it, or made any comment. Mart braced himself, checking his rifle again and again. "I got to hold fast," he kept telling himself. "I got to do my share of the work. No matter what." His ears were beginning to ring. The others stood about in loose meaningless positions, not huddled, not restless, but motionless, and very watchful. When they spoke they held their voices low.

Then Amos' rifle split the silence down the middle, so that behind lay the quiet night, and ahead rose their hour of violence. They saw what Amos had shot at. A single file of ten Comanches on wiry buffalo ponies had come into view at a thousand yards, materializing out of the seemingly flat earth. They came on at a light trot, ignoring Amos' shot. Zack Harper and Brad Mathison fired, but weren't good enough either at the range.

"Throw them horses down!" Amos shouted. "Git your backs to the marsh and tie down!" He snubbed his pony's muzzle back close to the horn, picked up the off fetlock, and threw the horse heavily. He caught one kicking hind foot, then the other, and pig-tied them across the fore cannons. Some of the others were doing the same thing, but Brad was in a fight with his hotblood animal. It reared eleven feet tall, striking with fore hoofs, trying to break away. "Kill that horse!" Amos yelled. Obediently Brad drew his six-gun, put a bullet into the animal's head under the ear, and stepped from under as it came down.

Ed Newby still stood, his rifle resting ready to fire across the saddle of his standing horse. Mart lost his head enough to yell, "Can't you throw him? Shall I shoot him, Ed?"

"Leave be! Let the Comanch' put him down."

Mart went to the aid of Charlie MacCorry, who had tied his

own horse down all right and was wrestling with a mule. They never did get all of the animals down, but Mart felt a whole lot better with something for his hands to do. Three more of the Comanche single-file columns were in sight now, widely spread, trotting well in hand. They had a ghostly look at first, of the same color as the prairie, in the gray light. Then detail picked out, and Mart saw the bows, lances bearing scalps like pennons, an occasional war shield carried for the medicine in its painted symbols as much as for the bullet-deflecting function of its iron-tough hide. Almost half the Comanches had rifles. Some trader, standing on his right to make a living, must have taken a handsome profit putting those in Comanche hands.

Amos' rifle banged again. One of the lead ponies swerved and ran wild as the rider rolled off into the grass. Immediately, without any other discernible signal, the Comanches leaned low on their ponies and came on at a hard run. Two or three more of the cowmen fired, but without effect.

At three hundred yards the four Comanche columns cut hard left, coming into a single loose line that streamed across the front of the defense. The cowmen were as ready as they were going to be; they had got themselves into a ragged semicircle behind their tied-down horses, their backs to the water. Two or three sat casually on their down horses, estimating the enemy.

"May as well hold up," Mose Harper said. His tone was as pressureless as a crackerbox comment. "They'll swing plenty close, before they're done."

"I count thirty-seven," Ed Newby said. He was still on his feet behind his standing horse.

Amos said, "I got me a scalp out there, when I git time to take it."

"Providin'," Mose Harper tried to sound jocular, "they don't leave your carcass here in the dirt."

"I come here to leave Indian carcasses in the dirt. I ain't made no change of plan."

They could see the Comanche war paint now as the warriors rode in plain sight across their front. Faces and naked bodies were striped and splotched in combinations of white, red, and yellow; but whatever the pattern, it was always pointed up with heavy accents of black, the Comanche color for war, for battle, and for death. Each warrior always painted up the same, but it was little use memorizing the paint patterns, because you never saw an Indian in war paint except when you couldn't lay hands on him. No use remembering the medicine shields, either, for these, treated as sacred, were never out of their deerskin cases until the moment of battle. Besides paint the Comanches wore breech clouts and moccasins; a few had horn or bear-claw headdresses. But these were young warriors, without the great eagle-feather war bonnets that were the pride of old war chiefs, who had tallied scores of coups. The ponies had their tails tied up, and were ridden bareback, guided by a single jaw rein.

Zack Harper said, "Ain't that big one Buffalo Hump?"

"No-that-ain't-Buffler-Hump," his father squelched him. "Don't talk so damn much."

The Comanche leader turned again and circled in. He brought his warriors past the defenders within fifty yards, ponies loosely spaced, racing full out. Suddenly, from every Comanche throat burst the screaming war cry; and Mart was paralyzed by the impact of that sound, stunned and sickened as by a blow in the belly with a rock. The war cries rose in a high unearthly yammering, wailing and snarling, piercing to his backbone to cut off every nerve he had. It was not exactly the eery sound of his terror-dream, but it was the spirit of that sound, the essence of its meaning. The muscles of his shoulders clenched as if turned to stone, and his hands so vised upon his rifle that it rattled, useless, against the saddle upon which it rested. And at the same time every other muscle in his body went limp and helpless.

Amos spoke into his ear, his low tone heavy with authority but unexcited. "Leave your shoulders go loose. Make your shoulders slack, and your hands will take care of theirselves. Now help me git a couple!"

That worked. All the rifles were sounding now from behind the tied-down horses. Mart breathed again, picked a target, and took aim. One Comanche after another was dropping from sight behind his pony as he came opposite the waiting rifles; they went down in order, like ducks in a shooting gallery, shamming a slaughter that wasn't happening. Each Comanche hung by one heel and a loop of mane on the far side of his pony and fired under the neck, offering only one arm and part of a painted face for target. A pony somersaulted, its rider springing clear unhurt, as Mart fired.

The circling Comanches kept up a continuous firing, each warrior reloading as he swung away, then coming past to fire again. This was the famous Comanche wheel, moving closer with every turn, chewing into the defense like a racing grindstone, yet never committing its force beyond possibility of a quick withdrawal. Bullets buzzed over, whispering "Cousin," or howled in ricochet from dust-spouts short of the defenders. A lot of whistling noises were arrows going over. Zack Harper's horse screamed, then went into a heavy continuous groaning.

Another Indian pony tumbled end over end; that was Amos' shot. The rider took cover behind his dead pony before he could be killed. Here and there another pony jerked, faltered, then ran on. A single bullet has to be closely placed to bring a horse down clean.

Amos said loud through his teeth, "The horses, you fools! Get them horses!" Another Comanche pony slid on its knees and stayed down, but its rider got behind it without hurt.

Ed Newby was firing carefully and unhurriedly across his standing horse. The buzzbees made the horse switch its tail, but it stood. Ed said, "You got to get the shoulder. No good to gut-shot 'em. You fellers ain't leading enough." He fired again, and a Comanche dropped from behind his running horse with his brains blown out. It wasn't the shot Ed was trying to make, but he said, "See how easy?"

Fifty yards out in front of him Mart Pauley saw a rifle snake across the quarters of a fallen pony. A horn headdress rose cautiously, and the rifle swung to look Mart square in the eye. He took a snap shot, aiming between the horns, which disappeared, and the enemy rifle slid unfired into the short grass.

After that there was a letup, while the Comanches broke circle and drew off. Out in front of the cowmen lay three downed ponies, two dead Comanches, and two live ones, safe and dangerous behind their fallen horses. Amos was swearing softly and steadily to himself. Charlie MacCorry said he thought he goosed one of them up a little bit, maybe, but didn't believe he convinced him.

"Good God almighty," Brad Mathison broke out, "there's got to be some way to do this!"

Mose Harper scratched his beard and said he thought they done just fine that trip. "Oncet when I was a little shaver, with my pa's bull wagons, a couple hundred of 'em circled us all day long. We never did get 'em whittled down very much. They just fin'y went away. . . . You glued to the ground, Zack? Take care that horse!"

Zack got up and took a look at his wounded horse, but didn't seem to know what to do. He stood staring at it, until his father walked across and shot it.

Mart said to Amos, "Tell me one thing. Was they hollering like that the time they killed my folks?"

Amos seemed to have to think that over. "I wasn't there," he said at last. "I suppose so. Hard to get used to, ain't it?"

"I don't know," Mart said shakily, "if I'll ever be able to get used to it."

Amos looked at him oddly for some moments. "Don't you let it stop you," he said.

"It won't stop me."

They came on again, and this time they swept past at no more than ten yards. A number of the wounded Comanche ponies lagged back to the tail of the line, their riders saving them for the final spurt, but they were still in action. The Co-manches made this run in close bunches; the attack became a smother of confusion. Both lead and arrows poured fast into the cowmen's position.

Zack whimpered, "My God—there's a million of 'em!" and ducked down behind his dead horse.

"Git your damn head up!" Mose yelled at his son. "Fire into 'em!" Zack raised up and went to fighting again.

Sometime during this run Ed Newby's horse fell, pinning Ed under it, but they had no time to go to him while this burst of the attack continued. An unhorsed Comanche came screaming at Amos with clubbed rifle, and so found his finish. Another stopped at least five bullets as a compadre tried to rescue him in a flying pickup. There should have been another; a third pony was down out in front of them, but nobody knew where the rider had got to. This time as they finished the run the Comanches pulled off again to talk it over.

All choices lay with the Comanches for the time being. The cowmen got their backs into the job of getting nine hundred pounds of horse off Ed Newby. Mose Harper said, "How come you let him catch you, Ed?"

Ed Newby answered through set teeth. "They got my leg —just as he come down—"

Ed's leg was not only bullet-broken, but had doubled under him, and got smashed again by the killed horse. Amos put the shaft of an arrow between Ed's teeth, and the arrowwood splintered as two men put their weight into pulling the leg straight.

A party of a dozen Comanches, mounted on the fastest of the Indian ponies, split off from the main bunch and circled out for still another sweep.

"Hold your fire," Amos ordered. "You hear me? Take cover —but let 'em be!"

Zack Harper, who had fought none too well, chose this moment to harden. "Hold hell! I aim to get me another!"

"You fire and I'll kill you," Amos promised him; and Zack put his rifle down.

Most took to the ground as the Comanches swept past once more, but Amos stood up, watching from under his heavy brows, like a staring ox. The Indians did not attack. They picked up their dismounted and their dead; then they were gone.

"Get them horses up!" Amos loosed the pigging string and got his own horse to its feet.

"They'll scatter now," Mose Harper said.

"Not till they come up with their horse herd, they won't!"

"Somebody's got to stay with Ed," Mose reminded them. "I suppose I'm the one to do that—old crip that I be. But some of them Comanch' might circle back. You'll have to leave Zack with me."

"That's all right."

"And I need one fast man on a good horse to get me help. I can't move him. Not with what we got here."

"We all ought to be back," Amos objected, "in a couple of days."

"Fellers follering Comanches don't necessarily ever come back. I got to have either Brad Mathison or Charlie MacCorry."

"You get Mathison, then," Charlie said. "I'm going on."

Brad whirled on Charlie in an unexpected blast of temper.

"There's a quick way to decide it," he said, and stood braced, his open hand ready above his holster.

Charlie MacCorry looked Brad in the eye as he spat at Brad's boots and missed. But after that he turned away.

So three rode on, following a plume of dust already distant upon the prairie. "We'll have the answer soon," Amos promised. "Soon. We don't dast let 'em lose us now."

Mart Pauley was silent. He didn't want to ask him what three riders could do when they caught up with the Comanches. He was afraid Amos didn't know.

# 9

THEY KEPT the feather of dust in sight all day, but in the morning, after a night camp without water, they failed to pick it up. The trail of the Comanche war party still led westward, broad and plain, marked at intervals with the carcasses of buffalo ponies wounded at the Cat-tails. They pushed on, getting all they could out of their horses.

This day, the second after the Fight at the Cat-tails, became the strangest day of the pursuit before it was done, because of something unexplained that happened during a period while they were separated.

A line of low hills, many hours away beyond the plain, began to shove up from the horizon as they rode. After a while they knew the Comanches they followed were already into that broken country where pursuit would be slower and more treacherous than before.

"Sometimes it seems to me," Amos said, "them Comanches fly with their elbows, carrying the pony along between their knees. You can nurse a horse along till he falls and dies, and you walk on carrying your saddle. Then a Comanche comes along, and gets that horse up, and rides it twenty miles more. Then eats it."

"Don't we have any chance at all?"

"Yes. . . . We got a chance." Amos went through the motions of spitting, with no moisture in his mouth to spit. "And I'll tell you what it be. An Indian will chase a thing until he thinks he's chased it enough. Then he quits. So the same when he runs. After while he figures we must have quit, and he starts to loaf. Seemingly he never learns there's such a thing as a critter that might just keep coming on."

As he looked at Amos, sitting his saddle like a great lump of rock—yet a lump that was somehow of one piece with the horse—Mart Pauley was willing to believe that to have Amos following you could be a deadly thing with no end to it, ever, until he was dead.

"If only they stay bunched," Amos finished, and it was a

prayer; "if only they don't split and scatter . . . we'll come up to 'em. We're bound to come up."

Late in the morning they came to a shallow sink, where a number of posthole wells had been freshly dug among the dry reeds. Here the trail of the main horse herd freshened, and they found the bones of an eaten horse, polished shiny in a night by the wolves. And there was the Indian smell, giving Mart a senseless dread to fight off during their first minutes in this place.

"Here's where the rest of 'em was all day yesterday," Amos said when he had wet his mouth; "the horse guards, and the stole horses, and maybe some crips Henry shot up. And our people—if they're still alive."

Brad Mathison was prone at a pothole, dipping water into himself with his tin cup, but he dropped the cup to come up with a snap. As he spoke, Mart Pauley heard the same soft tones Brad's father used when he neared an end of words. "I've heard thee say that times enough," Brad said.

"What?" Amos asked, astonished.

"Maybe she's dead," Brad said, his bloodshot blue eyes burning steadily into Amos' face. "Maybe they're both dead. But if I hear it from thee again, thee has chosen me—so help me God!"

Amos stared at Brad mildly, and when he spoke again it was to Mart Pauley. "They've took an awful big lead. Them we fought at the Cat-tails must have got here early last night."

"And the whole bunch pulled out the same hour," Mart finished it.

It meant they were nine or ten hours back—and every one of the Comanches was now riding a rested animal. Only one answer to that—such as it was: They had to rest their own horses, whether they could spare time for it or not. They spent an hour dipping water into their hats; the ponies could not reach the little water in the bottom of the posthole wells. When one hole after another had been dipped dry they could only wait for the slow seepage to bring in another cupful, while the horses stood by. After that they took yet another hour to let the horses crop the scant bunch grass, helping them by piling grass they cut with their knives. A great amount of this work gained only the slightest advantage, but none of them begrudged it.

Then, some hours beyond the posthole wells, they came to a vast sheet of rock, as flat and naked as it had been laid down when the world was made. Here the trail ended, for unshod hoofs left no mark on the barren stone. Amos remembered this reef in the plain. He believed it to be about four miles across by maybe eight or nine miles long, as nearly as he could recall. All they could do was split up and circle the whole ledge to find where the trail came off the rock.

Mart Pauley, whose horse seemed the worst beat out, was sent straight across. On the far side he was to wait, grazing within sight of the ledge, until one of the others came around to him; then both were to ride to meet the third.

Thus they separated. It was while they were apart, each rider alone with his tiring horse, that some strange thing happened to Amos, so that he became a mystery in himself throughout their last twenty-four hours together.

Brad Mathison was first to get around the rock sheet to where Mart Pauley was grazing his horse. Mart had been there many hours, yet they rode south a long way before they sighted Amos, waiting for them far out on the plain.

"Hasn't made much distance, has he?" Brad commented.

"Maybe the rock slick stretches a far piece down this way."

"Don't look like it to me."

Mart didn't say anything more. He could see for himself that the reef ended in a couple of miles.

Amos pointed to a far-off landmark as they came up. "The trail cuts around that hump," he said, and led the way. The trail was where Amos had said it would be, a great welter of horse prints already blurred by the wind. But no other horse had been along here since the Comanches passed long before.

"Kind of thought to see your tracks here," Brad said.

"Didn't come this far."

Then where the hell had he been all this time? If it had been Lije Powers, Mart would have known he had sneaked himself a nap. "You lost a bed blanket," Mart noticed.

"Slipped out of the strings somewhere. I sure ain't going back for it now." Amos was speaking too carefully. He put Mart in mind of a man half stopped in a fist fight, making out he was unhurt so his opponent wouldn't know, and finish him.

"You feel all right?" he asked Amos.

"Sure. I feel fine." Amos forced a smile, and this was a mistake, for he didn't look to be smiling. He looked as if he had been kicked in the face. Mart tried to think of an excuse to lay a hand on him, to see if he had a fever; but before he could think of anything Amos took off his hat and wiped sweat off his forehead with his sleeve. That settled that. A man doesn't sweat with the fever on him.

"You look like you et something," Mart said.

"Don't know what it could have been. Oh, I did come on three-four rattlesnakes." Seemingly the thought made Amos hungry. He got out a leaf of jerky, and tore strips from it with his teeth.

"You sure you feel—"

Amos blew up, and yelled at him. "I'm all right, I tell you!" He quirted his horse, and loped out ahead.

They off-saddled in the shelter of the hump. A northering wind came up when the sun was gone; its bite reminded them that they had been riding deep into the fall of the year. They huddled against their saddles, and chewed corn meal. Brad walked across and stood over Amos. He spoke reasonably.

"Looks like you ought to tell us, Mr. Edwards." He waited, but Amos didn't answer him. "Something happened while you was gone from us today. Was you laid for? We didn't hear no guns, but . . . Be you hiding an arrow hole from us by any chance?"

"No," Amos said. "There wasn't nothing like that."

Brad went back to his saddle and sat down. Mart laid his bedroll flat, hanging on by the upwind edge, and rolled himself up in it, coming out so that his head was on the saddle.

"A man has to learn to forgive himself," Amos said, his voice unnaturally gentle. He seemed to be talking to Brad Mathison. "Or he can't stand to live. It so happens we be Texans. We took a reachin' holt, way far out, past where any man has right or reason to hold on. Or if we didn't, our folks did, so we can't leave off, without giving up that they were fools, wasting their lives, and wasted in the way they died."

The chill striking up through Mart's blankets made him homesick for the Edwards' kitchen, like it was on winter nights, all warm and light, and full of good smells, like baking bread. And their people—Mart had taken them for granted, largely;

just a family, people living alone together, such as you never thought about, especially, unless you got mad at them. He had never known they were dear to him until the whole thing was busted up forever. He wished Amos would shut up.

"This is a rough country," Amos was saying. "It's a country knows how to scour a human man right off the face of itself. A Texan is nothing but a human man way out on a limb. This year, and next year, and maybe for a hundred more. But I don't think it'll be forever. Someday this country will be a fine good place to be. Maybe it needs our bones in the ground before that time can come."

Mart was thinking of Laurie now. He saw her in a bright warm kitchen like the Edwards', and he thought how wonderful it would be living in the same house with Laurie, in the same bed. But he was on the empty prairie without any fire —and he had bedded himself on a sharp rock, he noticed now.

"We've come on a year when things go hard," Amos talked on. "We get this tough combing over because we're Texans. But the feeling we get that we fail, and judge wrong, and go down in guilt and shame—that's because we be human men. So try to remember one thing. It wasn't your fault, no matter how it looks. You got let in for this just by being born. Maybe there never is any way out of it once you're born a human man, except straight across the coals of hell."

Mart rolled out to move his bed. He didn't really need that rock in his ribs all night. Brad Mathison got up, moved out of Amos' line of sight, and beckoned Mart with his head. Mart put his saddle on his bed, so it wouldn't blow away, and walked out a ways with Brad on the dark prairie.

"Mart," Brad said when they were out of hearing, "the old coot is just as crazy as a bedbug fell in the rum."

"Sure sounds so. What in all hell you think happened?"

"God knows. Maybe nothing at all. Might be he just plainly cracked. He was wandering around without rhyme or principle when we come on him today."

"I know."

"This puts it up to you and me," Brad said. "You see that, don't you? We may be closer the end than you think."

"What you want to do?"

"My horse is standing up best. Tomorrow I'll start before light, and scout on out far as I can reach. You come on as you can."

"My horse got a rest today," Mart began.

"Keep saving him. You'll have to take forward when mine gives down."

"All right." Mart judged that tomorrow was going to be a hard day to live far behind on a failing pony. Like Brad, he had a feeling they were a whole lot closer to the Comanches than they had any real reason to believe.

They turned in again. Though they couldn't know it, until they heard about it a long time after, that was the night Ed Newby came out of his delirium, raised himself for a long look at his smashed leg, then put a bullet in his brain.

## 10

B Y DAYLIGHT Brad Mathison was an hour gone. Mart hadn't known how Amos would take it, but there was no fuss at all. They rode on in silence, crossing chains of low hills, with dry valleys between; they were beginning to find a little timber, willow and cottonwood mostly along the dusty streambeds. They were badly in need of water again; they would have to dig for it soon. All day long the big tracks of Brad Mathison's horse led on, on top of the many-horse trample left by the Comanche herd; but he was stirring no dust, and they could only guess how far he must be ahead.

Toward sundown Amos must have begun to worry about him, for he sent Mart on a long swing to the north, where a line of sand hills offered high ground, to see what he could see. He failed to make out any sign of Brad; but, while he was in the hills alone, the third weird thing that could unstring him set itself in front of him again. He had a right to be nerve-raw at this point, perhaps; the vast emptiness of the plains had taken on a haunted, evilly enchanted feel since the massacre. And of course they were on strange ground now, where all things seemed faintly odd and wrong, because unfamiliar. . . .

He had dismounted near the top of a broken swell, led his horse around it to get a distant view without showing himself against the sky. He walked around a ragged shoulder —and suddenly froze at sight of what stood on the crest beyond. It was nothing but a juniper stump; not for an instant did he mistake it for anything else. But it was in the form of similar stumps he had seen two or three times before in his life, and always with the same unexplainable effect. The twisted remains of the juniper, blackened and sand-scoured, had vaguely the shape of a man, or the withered corpse of a man; one arm seemed upraised in a writhing gesture of agony, or perhaps of warning. But nothing about it explained the awful sinking of the heart, the terrible sense of inevitable doom, that overpowered him each of the times he encountered this shape.

An Indian would have turned back, giving up whatever he was about; for he would have known the thing for a medicine tree with a powerful spirit in it, either telling him of a doom or placing a doom upon him. And Mart himself more or less believed that the thing was some kind of a sign. An evil prophecy is always fulfilled, if you put no time limit upon it; fulfilled quite readily, too, if you are a child counting little misfortunes as disasters. So Mart had the impression that this mysteriously upsetting kind of an encounter had always been followed by some dreadful, unforeseeable thing.

He regarded himself as entirely mature now, and was convinced that to be filled with cowardice by the sight of a dead tree was a silly and unworthy thing. He supposed he ought to go and uproot that desolate twist of wood, or whittle it down, and so master the thing forever. But even to move toward it was somehow impossible to him, to a degree that such a move was not even thinkable. He returned to Amos feeling shaken and sickish, unstrung as much by doubt of his own soundness as by the sense of evil prophecy itself.

The sun was setting when they saw Brad again. He came pouring off a long hill at four miles, raising a reckless dust. "I saw her!" he yelled, and hauled up sliding. "I saw Lucy!"

"How far?"

"They're camped by a running crick—they got fires going— look, you can see the smoke!" A thin haze lay flat in the quiet air above the next line of hills.

"Ought to be the Warrior River," Amos said. "Water in it, huh?"

"Didn't you hear what I said?" Brad shouted. "I tell you I saw Lucy—I saw her walking through the camp——"

Amos' tone was bleak. "How far off was you?"

"Not over seventy rod. I bellied up a ridge this side the river, and they was right below me!"

"Did you see Debbie?" Mart got in.

"No, but—they got a bunch of baggage; she might be asleep amongst that. I counted fifty-one Comanch'— What you unsaddling for?"

"Good a place as any," Amos said. "Can't risk no more dust like you just now kicked up. Come dark we'll work south, and water a few miles below. We can take our time."

"*Time?*"

"They're making it easy for us. Must think they turned us back at the Cat-tails, and don't have to split up. All we got to do is foller to their village——"

"Village? You gone out of your mind?"

"Let 'em get back to their old chiefs and their squaws. The old chiefs have gone cagy; a village of families can't run like a war party can. For all they know——"

"Look—look——" Brad hunted desperately for words that would fetch Amos back to reality. "Lucy's there! I saw her—can't you hear? We got to get her out of there!"

"Brad," Amos said, "I want to know what you saw in that camp you thought was Lucy."

"I keep telling you I saw her walk——"

"I heard you!" Amos' voice rose and crackled this time. "*What* did you see walk? Could you see her yellow hair?"

"She had a shawl on her head. But——"

"She ain't there, Brad."

"God damn it, I tell you, I'd know her out of a million——"

"You saw a buck in a woman's dress," Amos said. "They're game to put anything on 'em. You know that."

Brad's sun-punished blue eyes blazed up as they had at the pothole water, and his tone went soft again. "Thee lie," he said. "I've told thee afore——"

"But there's something I ain't told you," Amos said. "I found Lucy yesterday. I buried her in my own saddle blanket. With my own hands, by the rock. I thought best to keep it from you long's I could."

The blood drained from Brad's face, and at first he could not speak. Then he stammered, "Did they—was she——"

"Shut up!" Amos yelled at him. "Never ask me what more I seen!"

Brad stood as if knocked out for half a minute more; then he turned to his horse, stiffly, as if he didn't trust his legs too well, and he tightened his cinch.

Amos said, "Get hold of yourself! Grab him, Mart!" Brad stepped into the saddle, and the gravel jumped from the hoofs of his horse. He leveled out down the Comanche trail again, running his horse as if he would never need it again.

"Go after him! You can handle him better than me."

Mart Pauley had pulled his saddle, vaulted bareback onto the sweaty withers, and in ten jumps opened up all the speed his beat-out horse had left. He gained no ground on Brad, though he used up what horse he had in trying to. He was chasing the better horse—and the better rider, too, Mart supposed. They weighed about the same, and both had been on horses before they could walk. Some small magic that could not be taught or learned, but had been born into Brad's muscles, was what made the difference. Mart was three furlongs back as Brad sifted into the low hills.

Up the slopes Mart followed, around a knob, and onto the down slope, spurring his wheezing horse at every jump. From here he could see the last little ridge, below and beyond as Brad had described it, with the smoke of Comanche campfires plain above it. Mart's horse went to its knees as he jumped it into a steep ravine, but he was able to drag it up.

Near the mouth of the ravine he found Brad's horse tied to a pin-oak scrub; he passed it, and rode on into the open, full stretch. Far up the last ridge he saw Brad climbing strongly. He looked back over his shoulder, watching Mart without slowing his pace. Mart charged through a dry tributary of the Warrior and up the ridge, his horse laboring gamely as it fought the slope. Brad stopped just short of the crest, and Mart saw him tilt his canteen skyward; he drained it unhurriedly, and threw it away. He was already on his belly at the crest as Mart dropped from his horse and scrambled on all fours to his side.

"God damn it, Brad, what you doing?"

"Get the hell out of here. You ain't wanted."

Down below, at perhaps four hundred yards, half a hundred Comanches idled about their business. They had some piled mule packs, a lot of small fires in shallow fire holes, and parts of at least a dozen buffalo down there. The big horse herd grazed unguarded beyond. Most of the bucks were throwing chunks of meat into the fires, to be snatched out and bolted as soon as the meat blackened on the outside. No sign of pickets. The Comanches relied for safety upon their horsemanship and the great empty distances of the prairies. They didn't seem to know what a picket was.

Mart couldn't see any sign of Debbie. And now he heard Brad chamber a cartridge.

"You'll get Debbie killed, you son-of-a-bitch!"

"Get out of here, I said!" Brad had his cheek on the stock; he was aiming into the Comanche camp. He took a deep breath, let it all out, and lay inert, waiting for his head to steady for the squeeze. Mart grabbed the rifle, and wrenched it out of line.

They fought for possession, rolling and sliding down the slope. Brad rammed a knee into Mart's belly, twisted the rifle from his hands, and broke free. Mart came to his feet before Brad, and dived to pin him down. Brad braced himself on one hand, and with the other swung the rifle by the grip of the stock. Blood jumped from the side of Mart's head as the barrel struck. He fell backward, end over end; then went limp, rolled slackly down the hill, and lay still where he came to rest.

Brad swore softly as he settled himself into firing position again. Then he changed his mind and trotted northward, just behind the crest of the ridge.

Mart came to slowly, without memory or any idea of where he was. Sight did not return to him at once. His hands groped, and found the rocky ground on which he lay; and next he recognized a persistent rattle of gunfire and the high snarling of Comanche war cries, seemingly some distance away. His hands went to his head, and he felt clotting blood. He reckoned he had got shot in the head, and was blind, and panic took him. He struggled up, floundered a few yards without any sense of balance, and fell into a dry wash. The fall knocked the wind out of him, and when he had got his breath back his mind had cleared enough so that he lay still.

Some part of his sight was coming back by the time he heard a soft footstep upon sand. He could see a shadowy shape above him, swimming in a general blur. He played possum, staring straight up with unwinking eyes, waiting to lose his scalp.

"Can you hear me, Mart?" Amos said.

He knew Amos dropped to his knees beside him. "I got a bullet in my brain," Mart said. "I'm blind."

Amos struck a match and passed it before one eye and then the other. Mart blinked and rolled his head to the side. "You're all right," Amos said. "Hit your head, that's all. Lie still till I get back!" He left, running.

Amos was gone a long time. The riflery and the war cries stopped, and the prairie became deathly still. For a while Mart believed he could sense a tremor in the ground that might mean the movement of many horses; then this faded, and the night chill began to work upward out of the ground. But Mart was able to see the winking of the first stars when he heard Amos coming back.

"You look all right to me," Amos said.

"Where's Brad?"

Amos was slow in answering. "Brad fit him a one-man war," he said at last. "He skirmished 'em from the woods down yonder. Now, why from there? Was he trying to lead them off you?"

"I don't know."

"Wha'd you do? Get throwed?"

"I guess."

"Comanches took him for a Ranger company, seemingly. They're long gone. Only they took time to finish him first."

"Was he scalped?"

"Now, what do you think?"

After he had found Mart, Amos had backed off behind a hill and built a signal fire. He slung creosote bush on it, raised a good smoke, and took his time sending puff messages with his saddle blanket.

"Messages to who?"

"Nobody, damn it. No message, either, rightly—just a lot of different-size hunks of smoke. Comanches couldn't read it, because it didn't say nothing. So they upped stakes and rode. It's all saved our hair, once they was stirred up."

Mart said, "We better go bury Brad."

"I done that already." Then Amos added one sad, sinister thing. "All of him I could find."

Mart's horse had run off with the Comanche ponies, but they still had Brad's horse and Amos'. And the Comanches had left them plenty of buffalo meat. Amos dug a fire pit, narrow but as deep as he could reach, in the manner of the Wichitas. From the bottom of this, his cooking fire could reflect only upon its own smoke, and he didn't put on stuff that made any. When Mart had filled up on buffalo meat he turned wrong side out, but an hour later he tried again, and this time it stuck.

"Feel like you'll be able to ride come daylight?"

"Sure I'll ride."

"I don't believe we got far to go," Amos said. "The Co-manch' been acting like they're close to home. We'll come up to their village soon. Maybe tomorrow."

Mart felt much better now. "Tomorrow," he repeated.

# II

TOMORROW CAME and went, and showed them they were wrong. Now at last the Comanche war party split up, and little groups carrying two or three horses to the man ranged off in ten directions. Amos and Mart picked one trail at random and followed it with all tenacity as it turned and doubled, leading them in far futile ways. They lost it on rock ledges, in running water, and in blown sand, but always found it again, and kept on.

Another month passed before all trails became one, and the paired scratches of many travois showed they were on the track of the main village at last. They followed it northeast, gaining ground fast as the trail grew fresh.

"Tomorrow," Amos said once more. "All hell can't keep them ahead of us tomorrow."

That night it snowed.

By morning the prairie was a vast white blank; and every day for a week more snow fell. They made some wide, reaching casts and guesses, but the plains were empty. One day they pushed their fading horses in a two-hour climb, toiling through drifts to the top of a towering butte. At its craggy lip they set their gaunted horses in silence, while their eyes swept the plain for a long time. The sky was dark that day, but near the ground the air was clear; they could see about as far as a man could ride through that clogging snow in a week. Neither found anything to say, for they knew they were done. Mart had not wept since the night of the massacre. Then he had suffered a blinding shock, and an inconsolable, aching grief so great he had never expected to cry again. But now as he faced the emptiness of a world that was supposed to have Debbie in it, yet was blank to its farthest horizons, his throat began to knot and hurt. He faced away to hide from Amos the tears he could no longer hold back; and soon after that he started his horse slowly back down that long, long slope, lest Amos hear the convulsive jerking of his breath and the snuffling of tears that ran down inside his nose.

They made an early, snowbound camp, with no call to hurry any more or stretch the short days. "This don't change anything," Amos said doggedly. "Not in the long run. If she's alive, she's safe by now, and they've kept her to raise. They do that time and again with a little child small enough to be raised their own way. So . . . we'll find them in the end; I promise you that. By the Almighty God, I promise you that! We'll catch up to 'em, just as sure as the turning of the earth!"

But now they had to start all over again in another way.

What Mart had noticed was that Amos always spoke of catching up to "them"—never of finding "her." And the cold, banked fires behind Amos' eyes were manifestly the lights of hatred, not of concern for a lost little girl. He wondered uneasily if there might not be a peculiar danger in this. He believed now that Amos, in certain moods, would ride past the child, and let her be lost to them if he saw a chance to kill Comanches.

They were freezing miserably in the lightweight clothes in which they had started out. Their horses were ribby shells, and they were out of flour, grease, block matches, coffee, and salt. Even their ammunition was running dangerously low. They were always having to shoot something to eat—a scrawny antelope, a jackrabbit all bones and fur; nothing they shot seemed to last all day. And it took two cartridges to light a fire—one to yield a pinch of powder to be mixed with tinder, a second to fire into the tinder, lighting it by gun flash. They needed to go home and start again, but they could not; there was much they could do, and must do, before they took time to go back.

President Grant had given the Society of Friends full charge of the Indian Agencies for the Wild Tribes, which in the Southwest Plains included Indians speaking more than twenty languages. Important in strength or activity were the Cheyennes, Arapahoes, and Wichitas; the Osages, a splinter of the Sioux; and, especially, that most murderous and irreconcilable alliance of all, the Comanches and Kiowas. The gentle and unrequiring administration of the Quakers very quickly attracted considerable numbers of these to the Agencies as winter closed. Besides government handouts, this got them a snow-weather amnesty from the trouble stirred up by their summer raids. Traders, Indian Agents, and army officers ransomed captive white children from winter peace-lovers like these every year. Failing this kind of good fortune, the situation still offered the best of opportunities to watch, to listen, and to learn.

Mart and Amos swung south to Fort Concho, where they re-outfitted and traded for fresh horses, taking a bad beating because of the poor shape their own were in. Amos seemed to have adequate money with him. Mart had never known how much money was kept, variously hidden, around the Edwards' place, but during the last two or three years it had probably been a lot; and naturally Amos wouldn't have left any of it in the empty house. The two riders headed up the north fork of the Butterfield Trail, laid out to provide at least one way to El Paso, but abandoned even before the war. Fort Phanton Hill, Fort Griffin, and Fort Belknap—set up to watch the Tonkawas —were in ruins, but still garrisoned by worried little detachments. At these places, and wherever they went, they told their story, pessimistically convinced that information was best come by in unlikely ways, being seldom found where you would reasonably expect it. Amos was posting a reward of a thousand dollars for any clue that would lead to the recovery of Debbie alive. Mart supposed it could be paid out of the family cattle, or something, if the great day ever came when it would be owed.

Laboriously, sweatily, night after night, Mart worked on a letter to the Mathison family, to tell them of the death of Brad and the manner in which he died. For a while he tried to tell the facts in a way that wouldn't make his own part in it look too futile. But he believed that he had failed, perhaps unforgivably, at the Warrior River, and that if he had been any good, Brad would still be alive. So in the end he gave up trying to fix any part of it up, and just told it the way it happened. He finally got the letter "posted" at Fort Richardson—which meant he left it there for some random rider to carry, if any should happen to be going the right way.

At Fort Richardson they struck north and west, clean out of the State of Texas. Deep in Indian Territory they made Camp Wichita, which they were surprised to find renamed Fort Sill —still a bunch of shacks but already heavily garrisoned. They stayed two weeks; then pushed northward again, far beyond Sill to the Anadarko Agency and Old Fort Cobb. By a thousand questions, by walking boldly through the far-strung-out camps of a thousand savages, by piecing together faint implications and guesses, they were trying to find out from what band of Comanches the raiders must have come. But nobody seemed to know much about Comanches—not even how many there were, or how divided. The military at Fort Sill seemed to think there were eight thousand Comanches; the Quaker Agents believed there to be no more than six thousand; some of the old traders believed there to be at least twelve thousand. And so with the bands: there were seven Comanche bands, there were sixteen, there were eleven. When they counted up the names of all the bands and villages they had heard of, the total came to more than thirty.

But none of this proved anything. The Comanches had a custom that forbade speaking the name of a dead person; if a chief died who had given himself the name of his band, the whole outfit had to have a new name. So sometimes a single village had a new name every year, while all the old names still lived on in the speech of Comanches and others who had not got the word. They found reason to think that the River Pony Comanches were the same as the Parka-nowm, or Water-hole People; and the Widyew, Kitsa-Kahna, Titcha-kenna, and Yapa-eena were probably all names for the Root-eaters, or Yampareka. For a time they heard the Way-ah-nay (Hill Falls Down) Band talked about as if it were comparable to the Pen-netecka (Honey-eaters), which some said included six thousand Comanches by itself. And later they discovered that the Way-ah-nay Band was nothing but six or seven families living under a cut-bank.

The Comanches themselves seemed unable, or perhaps unwilling, to explain themselves any more exactly. Various groups had different names for the same village or band. They never used the name "Comanche" among themselves. That name was like the word "squaw"—a sound some early white man thought he heard an Indian make once back in Massachusetts; the only Indians who understood it were those who spoke English. Comanches called themselves "Nemmenna," which meant "The People." Many tribes, such as the Navajo and Cheyenne, had names meaning the same thing. So the Comanches considered themselves to be the total population by simple definition. Nothing else existed but various kinds of

enemies which The People had to get rid of. They were working on it now.

Mart and Amos did learn a few things from the Comanches,
mostly in the way of tricks for survival. They saved themselves
from frozen feet by copying the Comanche snow boots, which
were knee length and made of buffalo hide with the fur turned
inside. And now they always carried small doeskin pouches of
tinder, made of punkwood scrapings and fat drippings—or lint
and kerosene, which worked even better, when they had it.
This stuff could be lighted by boring into dry-rotted wood
with a spinning stick. But what they did not learn of, and did
not recognize until long after, was the mortal danger that had
hung over them as they walked through those Comanche
camps—such danger as turned their bellies cold, later, when
they knew enough to understand it.

Christmas came and went unnoticed, for they spent it in the
saddle; they were into another year. Mart was haunted by no
more crooked stumps in this period, and the terror-dream did
not return. The pain of grief was no longer ever-present; he
was beginning to accept that the people to whom he had been
nearest were not in the world any more, except, perhaps, for
the lost little child who was their reason for being out here. But
they were baffled and all but discouraged, as well as ragged and
winter-gaunted, by the time they headed their horses toward
home, nearly three hundred miles away.

Night was coming on as they raised the lights of the Mathison ranch two hours away. The sunset died, and a dark haze
walled the horizon, making the snow-covered land lighter
than the sky. The far-seen lights of the ranch house held their
warmest promise in this hour, while you could still see the
endless emptiness of the prairie in the dusk. Martin Pauley
judged that men on horseback, of all creatures on the face
of the world, led the loneliest and most frost-blighted lives.
He would have traded places with the lowest sodbuster that
breathed, if only he could have had four walls, a stove, and
people around him.

But as they drew near, Mart began to worry. The Mathi-
sons should have got his letter two months ago, with any luck.
But maybe they hadn't got it at all, and didn't even know that
Brad was dead. Or if they did know, they might very likely be

holding Brad's death against him. Mart turned shy and fearful, and began to dread going in there. The two of them were a sorry sight at best. They had been forced to trade worn-out horses four times, and had taken a worse beating every swap, so now they rode ponies resembling broke-down dogs. Amos didn't look so bad, Mart thought; gaunted though he was, he still had heft and dignity to him. Thick-bearded to the eyes, his hair grown to a great shaggy mane, he looked a little like some wilderness prophet of the Lord. But Mart's beard had come out only a thin and unsightly straggle. When he had shaved with his skinning knife he was left with such a peaked, sore-looking face that all he needed was a running nose to match. His neck was wind-galled to a turkey red, and his hands were so scaly with chap that they looked like vulture's feet. They had no soap in many weeks.

"We're lucky if they don't shoot on sight," he said. "We ain't fitten to set foot in any decent place."

Amos must have agreed, for he gave a long hail from a furlong out, and rode in shouting their names.

The Mathison house was of logs and built in two parts in the manner of the southern frontier. One roof connected what was really two small houses with a wind-swept passage, called a dog-trot, running between. The building on the left of the dog-trot was the kitchen. The family slept in the other, and Mart didn't know what was in there; he had never been in it.

Brad Mathison's two brothers—Abner, who was sixteen, and Tobe, fifteen—ran out from the kitchen to take their horses. As Abner held up his lantern to make sure of them, Mart got a shock. Ab had the same blue eyes as Brad, and the same fair scrubbed-looking skin, to which no dirt ever seemed to stick; so that for a moment Mart thought he saw Brad walking up to him through the dark. The boys didn't ask about their brother, but they didn't mention Mart's letter, either. Go on in, they said, the heck with your saddles, Pa's holding the door.

Nothing in the kitchen had changed. Mart remembered each thing in this room, as if nothing had been moved while he was gone. His eyes ran around the place anyway, afraid to look at the people. A row of shined-up copper pots and pans hung over the wood range, which could feed a lot of cowhands when it needed to; it was about the biggest in the country. Everything else they had here was homemade, planed or whittled, and pegged together. But the house was plastered inside, the whole thing so clean and bright he stood blinking in the light of the kerosene lamps, and feeling dirty. Actually he smelled mainly of juniper smoke, leather, and prairie wind, but he didn't know that. He felt as though he ought to be outside, and stand downwind.

Then Aaron Mathison had Mart by the hand. He looked older than Mart remembered him, and his sight seemed failing as his mild eyes searched Mart's face. "Thank thee for the letter thee wrote," Mathison said.

Mrs. Mathison came and put her arms around him, and for a moment held onto him as if he were her son. She hadn't done that since he was able to walk under a table without cracking his head, and to give him a hug she had to kneel on the floor. He vaguely remembered how beautiful and kind she had seemed to him then. But every year since she had gradually become dumpier, and quieter, and less thought about, until she had no more shape or color than a sack of wheat. She still had an uncommonly sweet smile, though, what times it broke through; and tonight as she smiled at Mart there was such wistfulness in it that he almost kissed her cheek. Only he had not been around people enough to feel as easy as that.

And Laurie . . . she was the one he looked for first, and was most aware of, and most afraid to look at. And she was the only one who did not come toward him at all. She stood at the wood range, pretending to get ready to warm something for them; she flashed Mart one quick smile, but stayed where she was.

"I have a letter for you," Aaron said to Amos. "It was brought on and left here by Joab Wilkes, of the Rangers, as he rode by."

"A what?"

"I have been told the news in this letter," Aaron said gravely. "It is good news, as I hope and believe." Amos followed as Aaron retired to the other end of the kitchen, where he fumbled in a cupboard.

Laurie was still at the stove, her back to the room, but her hands were idle. It occurred to Martin that she didn't know what to say, or do, any more than he did. He moved toward her with no clear object in view. And now Laurie turned at last, ran to him, and gave him a peck of a kiss on the corner of his mouth. "Why, Mart, I believe you're growing again."

"And him on an empty stomach," her mother said. "I wonder he doesn't belt you!"

After that everything was all right.

## 12

THEY HAD fresh pork and the first candied yams Mart had
seen since a year ago Thanksgiving. Tobe asked Amos how
many Comanch' he had converted in the Fight at the Cat-tails.

"Don't know." Amos was at once stolid and uncomfortable
as he answered. "Shot at two-three dozen. But the other varmints carried 'em away. Worse scared than hurt, most like."

Tobe said, "I bet you got plenty scalps in your saddle bags!"

"Not one!"

"He just stomp' 'em in the dirt," Mart explained, and was
surprised to see Amos' eyes widen in a flash of anger.

"Come morning," Amos said to Mart, wrenching clear of
the subject, "I want you borry the buckboard, and run it over
to my place. The boys will show you which team. Round up
such clothes of mine, or yours, as got overlooked."

That "my place" didn't sound just right to Mart. It had always been "Henry's place" or "my brother's place" every time
Amos had ever spoken of it before.

"Load up any food stores that wasn't stole or spoilt. Especially any unbust presarves. And any tools you see. Fetch 'em
here. And if any my horses have come in, feed grain on the tail
gate, so's they foller you back." There was that "my" again.
"My horses" this time. Amos had owned exactly one horse,
and it was dead.

"What about——" Mart had started to ask what he must
do about Debbie's horses. Debbie, not Amos, was heir to the
Edwards' livestock if she lived. "Nothing," he finished.

When they had eaten, Aaron Mathison and Amos got their
heads together again in the far end of the room. Their long
conference partly involved tally books, but Mart couldn't hear
what was said. Laurie took her sewing basket to a kind of settle
that flanked the wood range, and told Mart by a movement of
her eyes that she meant him to sit beside her.

"If you're going over—over home," she said in a near whisper, "maybe I ought to tell you about—something. There's
something over there. . . . I don't know if you'll understand."
She floundered and lost her way.

He said flatly, "You talking about that story, the place is haunted?"

She stared at him.

He told her about the rider they had come on one night, packing up toward the Nations on business unknown. This man had spoken of heading into what he called the "old Edwards place," thinking to bed down for the night in the deserted house. Only, as he came near he saw lights moving around inside. Not like the place was lived in and lighted up. More like a single candle, carried around from room to room. The fellow got the hell out of there, Mart finished, and excuse him, he hadn't meant to say hell.

"What did Amos say?"

"He went in one of his black fits."

"Martie," Laurie said, "you might as well know what he saw. You'll find the burnt-out candle anyway."

"What candle?"

"Well . . . you see . . . it was coming on Christmas Eve. And I had the strongest feeling you were coming home. You know how hard you can know something that isn't so?"

"I sure do," Mart said.

"So . . . I rode over there, and laid a fire in the stove, and dusted up. And I—you're going to laugh at me, Martie."

"No, I ain't."

"Well, I—I made a couple of great gawky bush-holly wreaths, and cluttered up the back windows with them. And I left a cake on the table. A kind of a cake—it got pretty well crumbed riding over. But I reckoned you could see it was meant for a cake. You might as well fetch home the plate."

"I'll remember."

"And I set a candle in a window. It was a whopper—I bet it burned three-four days. That's what your owl-hoot friend saw. I see no doubt of it."

"Oh," said Mart. It was all he could think of to say.

"Later I felt foolish; tried to get over there, and cover my tracks. But Pa locked up my saddle. He didn't like me out so long worrying Ma."

"Well, I should hope!"

"You'd better burn those silly wreaths. Before Amos sees 'em, and goes in a 'black fit.'"

"It wasn't silly," Mart said.

"Just you burn 'em. And don't forget the plate. Ma thinks Tobe busted it and ate the cake."

"It beats me," Mart said honestly. "How come anybody ever to take such trouble. I never see such a thing."

"I guess I was just playing house. Pretty childish. I see that now. But—I just love that old house. I can't bear to think of it all dark and lonely over there."

It came to him that she wanted the old house to be their house to make bright and alive again. This was the best day he had ever had in his life, he supposed, what with the promising way it was ending. So now, of course, it had to be spoiled.

Two rooms opened off the end of the kitchen opposite the dog-trot, the larger being a big wintry storeroom. The other, in the corner nearest the stove, was a cubbyhole with an arrow-slit window and a buffalo rug. This was called the grandmother room, because it was meant for somebody old, or sick, who needed to be kept warm. Nowadays it had a couple of rawhide-strung bunks for putting up visitors without heating the bunk-house where the seasonal hands were housed.

When the family had retired across the dog-trot, Amos and Mart dragged out a wooden tub for a couple of long-postponed baths. They washed what meager change of clothes they had, and hung the stuff on a line back of the stove to dry overnight. Their baggy long-handled underwear and footless socks seemed indecent, hung out in a room where Laurie lived, but they couldn't help it.

"What kind of letter you get?" Mart asked. The average saddle tramp never got a letter in his life.

Amos shook out a pair of wet drawers, with big holes worn on the insides of the thigh, and hung them where they dripped into the woodbin. "Personal kind," he grunted, finally.

"Serves me right, too. Don't know why I never learn."

"Huh?"

"Nothing."

"I been fixing to tell you," Amos began.

"That ain't needful."

"What ain't?"

"I know that letter ain't none of my business. Because

nothing is. I just set on other people's horses. To see they foller along."

"I wasn't studying on no letter. Will you leave a man speak? I say I made a deal with old Mathison."

Mart was silent and waited.

"I got to be pushing on," Amos said, picking his words. Passing out information seemed to hurt Amos worse every day he lived. "I won't be around. So Mathison is going to run my cattle with his own. Being's I can't see to it myself."

"What's he get, the increase?"

"Why?"

"No reason. Seemed the natural thing to ask, that's all. I don't give a God damn what you do with your stock."

"Mathison come out all right," Amos said.

"When do we start?"

"You ain't coming."

Mart thought that over. "It seems to me," he began. His voice sounded thin and distant to himself. He started over too loudly. "It seems to me——"

"What you hollering for?"

"——we started out to look for Debbie," Mart finished.

"I'm still looking for her."

"That's good. Because so am I."

"I just told you—by God, will you listen?" It was Amos' voice raised this time. "I'm leaving you here!"

"No, you ain't."

"What?" Amos stared in disbelief.

"You ain't telling me where I stay!"

"You got to live, ain't you? Mathison's going to leave you stay on. Help out with the work what you can, and you'll know where your grub's coming from."

"I been shooting our grub," Mart said stubbornly. "If I can shoot for two, I can shoot for one."

"That still takes ca-tridges. And a horse."

Mart felt his guts drop from under his heart. All his life he had been virtually surrounded by horses; to ride one, you only had to catch it. Only times he had ever thought whether he owned one or not was when some fine fast animal, like one of Brad's, had made him wish it was his. But Amos was right. Nothing in the world is so helpless as a prairie man afoot.

"I set out looking for Debbie," he said. "I aim to keep on."

"Why?"

Mart was bewildered. "Because she's my—she's——" He had started to say that Debbie was his own little sister. But in the moment he hesitated, Amos cut him down.

"Debbie's my brother's young'n," Amos said. "She's my flesh and blood—not yours. Better you leave these things to the people concerned with 'em, boy. Debbie's no kin to you at all."

"I—I always felt like she was my kin."

"Well, she ain't."

"Our—I mean, her—her folks took me in off the ground. I'd be dead but for them. They even——"

"That don't make 'em any kin."

"All right. I ain't got no kin. Never said I had. I'm going to keep on looking, that's all."

"How?"

Mart didn't answer that. He couldn't answer it. He had his saddle and his gun, because Henry had given him those; but the loads in the gun were Amos', he supposed. Mart realized now that a man can be free as a wolf, yet unable to do what he wants at all.

They went on to bed in silence. Amos spoke out of the dark. "You don't give a man a chance to tell you nothing," he complained. "I want you to know something, Mart——"

"Yeah—you want me to know I got no kin. You told me already. Now shut your God damned head!"

One thing about being in the saddle all day, and every day, you don't get a chance to worry as much as other men do once you lie down at night. You fret, and you fret, and you try to think your way through—for about a minute and a half. Then you go to sleep.

# 13

M ART WOKE up in the blackness before the winter dawn. He pulled on his pants, and started up the fire in the wood range before he finished dressing. As he took down his ragged laundry from behind the stove, he was of a mind to leave Amos' stuff hanging there, but he couldn't quite bring himself to it. He made a bundle of Amos' things, and tossed it into their room. By the time he had wolfed a chunk of bread and some leavings of cold meat, Tobe and Abner were up.

"I got to fetch that stuff Amos wants," he said, "from over —over at his house. You want to show me what team?"

"Better wait while we hot up some breakfast, hadn't you?"

"I et already."

They didn't question it. "Take them little fat bays, there, in the nigh corral—the one with the shelter shed."

"I want you take notice of what a pretty match they be," said Tobe with shining pride. "We call 'em Sis and Bud. And pull? They'll outlug teams twice their heft."

"Sis is about the only filly we ever did bust around here," Abner said. "But they balanced so nice, we just couldn't pass her by. Oh, she might cow-kick a little——"

"A little? She hung Ab on the top bar so clean he just lay there flappin'."

"Feller doesn't mind a bust in the pants from Sis, once he knows her."

"I won't leave nothing happen to 'em," Mart promised.

He took the team shelled corn, and brushed them down while they fed. He limbered the frosty straps of the harness with his gloved hands, and managed to be hooked and out of there before Amos was up.

Even from a distance the Edwards place looked strangely barren. Hard to think why, at first, until you remembered that the house now stood alone, without its barn, sheds, and haystacks. The snow hid the black char and the ash of the burned stuff, as if it never had been. Up on the hill, where Martha, and Henry, and the boys were, the snow had covered even the crosses he had carved.

Up close, as Mart neared the back gallery, the effect of desolation was even worse. You wouldn't think much could happen to a sturdy house like that in just a few months, but it already looked as if it had been unlived in for a hundred years. Snow was drifted on the porch, and slanted deep against the door itself, unbroken by any tracks. In the dust-glazed windows Laurie's wreaths were ghostly against empty black.

When he had forced the door free of the iced sill, he found a still cold inside, more chilling in its way than the searing wind of the prairie. A thin high music that went on forever in the empty house was the keening of the wind in the chimneys. Almost everything he remembered was repaired and in place, but a gray film of dust lay evenly, in spite of Laurie's Christmas dusting. Her cake plate was crumbless, centering a pattern of innumerable pocket-mouse tracks in the dust upon the table.

He remembered something about that homemade table. Underneath it, an inch or so below the top, a random structural member made a little hidden shelf. Once when he and Laurie had been five or six, the Mathisons had come over for a taffy pull. He showed Laurie the secret shelf under the table, and they stored away some little square-cut pieces of taffy there. Afterward, one piece of taffy seemed to be stuck down; he wore out his fingers for months trying to break it loose. Years later he found out that the stubbornly stuck taffy was really the ironhead of a lag screw that you couldn't see where it was, but only feel with your fingers.

He found some winter clothes he sure could use, including some heavy socks Martha and Lucy had knitted for him. Nothing that had belonged to Martha and the girls was in the closets. He supposed some shut trunks standing around held whatever of their stuff the Comanches had left. He went to a little chest that had been Debbie's, with some idea of taking something of hers with him, as if for company; but he stopped himself before he opened the chest. I got these hands she used to hang onto, he told himself. I don't need nothing more. Except to find her.

He was in no hurry to get back. He wanted to miss supper at the Mathisons for fear he would lash out at Amos in front of the others; so, taking his time about everything he did, he managed to fool away most of the day.

A red glow from the embers in the stove was the only light in the Mathison house as he put away the good little team, but a lamp went up in the kitchen before he went in. Laurie was waiting up, and she was put out with him.

"Who gave you the right to lag out till all hours, scaring the range stock?"

"Amos and me always night on the prairie," he reminded her. "It's where we live."

"Not when I'm waiting up for you." She was wrapped twice around in a trade-blanket robe cinched up with a leather belt. Only the little high collar of her flannel nightgown showed, and a bit of blue-veined instep between her moccasins and the hem. Actually she had no more clothes than he had ever seen her wear in her life; there was no reason for the rig to seem as intimate as it somehow did.

He mumbled, "Didn't go to make work," and went to throw his rag-pickings in the grandmother room.

Amos was not in his bunk; his saddle and everything he had was gone.

"Amos rode on," Laurie said unnecessarily.

"Didn't he leave no word for me?"

"Any word," she corrected him. She shook down the grate and dropped fresh wood in the firebox. "He just said, tell you he had to get on." She pushed him gently backward against a bench, so that he sat down. "I mended your stuff," she said. "Such as could be saved."

He thought of the saddle-worn holes in the thighs of his other drawers. "Goddle mighty," he whispered.

"Don't know what your purpose is," she said, "getting so red in the face. I have brothers, haven't I?"

"I know, but——"

"I'm a woman, Martie." He had supposed that was the very point. "We wash and mend your dirty old stuff for you all our lives. When you're little, we even wash you. How a man can make out to get bashful in front of a woman, I'll never know."

He couldn't make any sense out of it. "You talk like a feller might just as leave run around stark nekkid."

"Wouldn't bother me. I wouldn't try it in front of Pa, was I you, so long as you're staying on." She went to the stove to fix his supper.

"I'm not staying, Laurie. I got to catch up with Amos."

She turned to see if he meant it. "Pa was counting on you. He's running your cattle now, you know, along with his own——"

"Amos' cattle."

"He let both winter riders go, thinking you and Amos would be back. Of course, riders aren't too hard to come by. Charlie MacCorry put in for a job."

"MacCorry's a good fast hand," was all he said.

"I don't know what you think you can do about finding Debbie that Amos can't do." She turned to face him solemnly, her eyes very dark in the uneven light. "He'll find her now, Mart. Please believe me. I know."

He waited, but she went back to the skillet without explanation. So now he took a chance and told her the truth. "That's what scares me, Laurie."

"If you're thinking of the property," she said, "the land, the cattle——"

"It isn't that," he told her. "No, no. It isn't that."

"I know Debbie's the heir. And Amos has never had anything in his life. But if you think he'd let harm come to one hair of that child's head on account of all that, then I know you're a fool."

He shook his head. "It's his black fits," he said; and wondered how he could make a mortal danger sound so idiotic.

"What?"

"Laurie, I swear to you, I've seen all the fires of hell come up in his eyes, when he so much as thinks about getting a Comanche in his rifle sights. You haven't seen him like I've seen him. I've known him to take his knife . . ." He let that drop. He didn't want to tell Laurie some of the things he had seen Amos do. "Lord knows I hate Comanches. I hate 'em like I never knew a man could hate nothin'. But you slam into a bunch of 'em, and kill some—you know what happens to any little white captives they got hold of, then? They get their brains knocked out. It's happened over and over again."

He felt she didn't take any stock in what he was saying. He tried again, speaking earnestly to her back. "Amos is a man can go crazy wild. It might come on him when it was the worst thing could be. What I counted on, I hoped I'd be there to stop him, if such thing come."

She said faintly, "You'd have to kill him."

He let that go without answer. "Let's have it now. Where's he gone, where you're so sure he'll find her?"

She became perfectly still for a moment. When she moved again, one hand stirred the skillet, while the other brought a torn-open letter out of the breast of her robe, and held it out to him. He recognized the letter that had been left with Aaron Mathison for Amos. His eyes were on her face, questioning, as he took it.

"We hoped you'd want to stay on," she said. All the liveliness was gone from her voice. "But I guess I knew. Seems to be only one thing in the world you care about any more. So I stole it for you."

He spread out the single sheet of ruled tablet paper the torn envelope contained. It carried a brief scrawl in soft pencil, well smeared.

Laurie said, "Do you believe in second sight? No, of course you don't. There's something I dread about this, Martie."

The message was from a trader Mart knew about, over on the Salt Fork of the Brazos. He called himself Jerem (for Jeremiah) Futterman—an improbable name at best, and not his own. He wasn't supposed to trade with Indians there any more, but he did, covering up by claiming that his real place of business was far to the west in the Arroyo Blanco, outside of Texas. The note said:

> I bougt a small size dress off a
> Injun. If this here is a peece of
> yr chiles dress bring reward, I know
> where they gone.

Pinned to the bottom of the sheet with a horseshoe nail was a two-inch square of calico. The dirt that grayed it was worn evenly into the cloth, as if it had been unwashed for a long time. The little flowers on it didn't stand out much now, but they were there. Laurie was leaning over his shoulder as he held the sample to the light. A strand of her hair was tickling his neck, and her breath was on his cheek, but he didn't even know.

"Is it hers?"

He nodded.

"Poor little dirty dress . . ."

He couldn't look at her. "I've got to get hold of a horse. I just got to get me a horse."

"Is that all that's stopping you?"

"It isn't stopping me. I'll catch up to him. I got to."

"You've got horses, Martie."

"I—what?"

"You've got Brad's horses. Pa said so. He means it, Martie. Amos told us what happened at the Warrior. A lot of things you left out."

Mart couldn't speak for a minute, and when he could he didn't know what to say. The skillet started to smoke, and Laurie went to set it to the back of the range.

"Most of Brad's ponies are turned out. But the Fort Worth stud is up. He's coming twelve, but he'll outgame anything there is. And the good light gelding—the fast one, with the blaze."

"Why, that's Sweet-face," he said. He remembered Laurie naming that colt herself, when she was thirteen years old. "Laurie, that's your own good horse."

"Let's not get choosey, Bub. Those two are the ones Amos wanted to trade for and take. But Pa held them back for you."

"I'll turn Sweet-face loose to come home," he promised, "this side Fiddler's Crick. I ought to cross soon after daylight."

"Soon after— By starting when?"

"Now," he told her.

He was already in the saddle when she ran out through the snow, and lifted her face to be kissed. She ran back into the house abruptly, and the door closed behind her. He jabbed the Fort Worth stud, hard, with one spur. Very promptly he was bucked back to his senses, and all but thrown. The stallion conveyed a hard, unyielding shock like no horse Mart had ever ridden, as if he were made all of rocks and iron bands. Ten seconds of squealing contention cleared Mart's head, though he thought his teeth might be loosened a little; and he was on his way.

# 14

WHEN LAURIE had closed the door, she stood with her forehead against it a little while, listening to the violent hammer of hoofs sometimes muffled by the snow, sometimes ringing upon the frozen ground, as the Fort Worth stud tried to put Mart down. When the stud had straightened out, she heard Mart circle back to pick up Sweet-face's lead and that of the waspish black mule he had packed. Then he was gone, but she still stood against the door, listening to the receding hoofs. They made a crunch in the snow, rather than a beat, but she was able to hear it for a long time. Finally even that sound stopped, and she could hear only the ticking of the clock and the winter's-night pop of a timber twisting in the frost.

She blew out the lamp, crossed the cold dog-trot, and crept softly to her bed. She shivered for a few moments in the chill of the flour-sack-muslin sheets, but she slept between two deep featherbeds, and they warmed quite soon. For several years they had kept a big gaggle of geese, especially for making featherbeds. They had to let the geese range free, and the coyotes had got the last of them now; but the beds would last a lifetime almost.

As soon as she was warm again, Laurie began to cry. This was not like her. The Mathison men had no patience with blubbering women, and gave them no sympathy at all, so Mathison females learned early to do without nervous outlets of this kind. But once she had given way to tears at all, she cried harder and harder. Perhaps she had stored up every kind of cry there is for a long time. She had her own little room, now, with a single rifle-slit window, too narrow for harm to come through; but the matched-fencing partition was too flimsy to be much of a barrier to sound. She pressed her face deep into the feathers, and did her best to let no sound escape. It wasn't good enough. By rights, everybody should have been deep asleep long ago, but her mother heard her anyway, and came in to sit on the side of her bed.

Laurie managed to snuffle, "Get under the covers, Ma. You'll catch you a chill."

Mrs. Mathison got partly into the bed, but remained sitting up. Her work-stiffened fingers were awkward as she tentatively stroked her daughter's hair. "Now, Laurie. . . . Now, Laurie. . . ."

Laurie buried her face deeper in the featherbed. "I'm going to be an old maid!" she announced rebelliously, her words half smothered.

"Why, Laurie!"

"There just aren't any boys—men—in this part of the world. I think this everlasting wind blows 'em away. Scours the whole country plumb clean."

"Come roundup there's generally enough underfoot, seems to me. At least since the peace. Place swarms with 'em. Worse'n ants in a tub of leftover dishes."

"Oh!" Laurie whimpered in bitter exasperation. "Those hoot-owlers!" Her mind wasn't running very straight. She meant owl-hooters, of course—a term applied to hunted men, who liked to travel by night. It was true that the hands who wandered out here to pick up seasonal saddle work were very often wanted. If a Ranger so much as stopped by a chuck wagon, so many hands would disappear that the cattlemen had angrily requested the Rangers to stay away from roundups altogether. But they weren't professional badmen—not bandits or killers; just youngsters, mostly, who had got into some trouble they couldn't bring themselves to face out. Many of the cattlemen preferred this kind, for they drifted on of their own accord, saving you the uncomfortable job of firing good loyal riders who really wanted to stick and work. And they were no hazard to home girls. They didn't even come into the house to eat, once enough of them had gathered to justify hiring a wagon cook. Most of them had joked with Laurie, and made a fuss over her, so long as she was little; but they had stopped this about the time she turned fifteen. Nowadays they steered clear, perhaps figuring they were already in trouble enough. Typically they passed her, eyes down, with a mumbled, "Howdy, Mam," and a sheepish tug at a ducked hat brim. Soon they were off with the wagon, and were paid off and on their way the day they got back.

Actually, Laurie had almost always picked out some one of them to idolize, and imagine she was in love with, from a good safe distance. After he rode on, all unsuspecting, she would sometimes remember him, and spin daydreams about him, for months and months. But she was in no mood to remember all that now.

Mrs. Mathison sighed. She could not, in honesty, say much for the temporary hands as eligible prospects. "There's plenty others. Like—like Zack Harper. Such a nice, clean boy——"

"That nump!"

"And there's Charlie MacCorry——"

"*Him*." A contemptuous rejection.

Her mother didn't press it. Charlie MacCorry hung around a great deal more than Mrs. Mathison wished he would, and she didn't want him encouraged. Charlie was full of high spirits and confidence, and might be considered flashily handsome, at least from a little distance off. Up close his good looks seemed somehow exaggerated, almost as in a caricature. What Mrs. Mathison saw in him, or thought she saw, was nothing but stupidity made noisy by conceit. Mentioning him at all had been a scrape at the bottom of the barrel.

She recognized the upset Laurie was going through as an inevitable thing, that every girl had to go through, somewhere between adolescence and marriage. Mrs. Mathison was of limited imagination, but her observation was sound, and her memory clear, so she could remember having gone through this phase herself. A great restlessness went with it, like the disquiet of a young wild goose at the flight season; as if something said to her, "Now, now or never again! Now, or life will pass you by. . . ." No one who knew Mrs. Mathison now could have guessed that at sixteen she had run away with a tinhorn gambler, having met him, in secret, only twice in her life. She could remember the resulting embarrassments with painful clarity, but not the emotions that had made her do it. She thought of the episode with shame, as an unexplainable insanity, from which she was saved only when her father overtook them and snatched her back.

She had probably felt about the same way when she ran off a second time—this time more successfully, with Aaron Mathison. Her father, a conservative storekeeper and a pillar of the Baptist Church, had regarded the Quakers in the Mathison background as benighted and misled, more to be pitied than anything else. But the young shaggy-headed Aaron he considered a dangerously irresponsible wild man, deserving not a whit more confidence than the staved-off gambler—who at least had the sense to run from danger, not at it. He never spoke to his daughter again. Mrs. Mathison forever after regarded this second escapade as a sound and necessary move, regarding which her parents were peculiarly blind and wrongheaded. Aaron Mathison in truth was a man like a great rooted tree, to which she was as tightly affixed as a lichen; no way of life without him was conceivable to her.

She said now with compassion, "Dear heart, dear little girl—Martin will come back. He's bound to come back." She didn't know whether they would ever see Martin Pauley again or not, but she feared the outrageous things—the runaways, the cheap marriages—which she herself had proved young girls to be capable of at this stage. She wanted to give Laurie some comforting hope, to help her bridge over the dangerous time.

"I don't care what he does," Laurie said miserably. "It isn't that at all."

"I never dreamed," her mother said, thoughtfully, ignoring the manifest untruth. "Why, you two always acted like—more like two tomboys than anything. How long has . . . When did you start thinking of Mart in this way?"

Laurie didn't know that herself. Actually, so far as she was conscious of it, it had been about an hour. Mart had been practically her best friend, outside the family, throughout her childhood. But their friendship had indeed been much the same as that of two boys. Latterly, she recalled with revulsion, she had idiotically thought Charlie MacCorry more fun, and much more interesting. But she had looked forward with a warm, innocent pleasure to having Mart live with them right in the same house. Now that he was suddenly gone—irrecoverably, she felt now—he left an unexpectedly ruinous gap in her world that nothing left to her seemed able to fill. She couldn't explain all that to her mother. Wouldn't know how to begin.

When she didn't answer, her mother patted her shoulder. "It will all seem different in a little while," she said in the futile cliché of parents. "These things have a way of passing off. I know you don't feel that way now; but they do. Time, the great healer . . ." she finished vaguely. She kissed the back of Laurie's head, and went away.

## 15

AFTER DAYS of thinking up blistering things to say, Mart judged he was ready for Amos. He figured Amos would come at him before they were through. Amos was a respected rough-and-tumble scrapper away from home. "I run out of words," Mart had heard him explain many a tangle. "Wasn't nothing left to do but hit him." Let him try.

But when he caught up, far up the Salt Fork, it was all wasted, for Amos wouldn't quarrel with him. "I done my best to free your mind," Amos said. "Mathison was fixing to step you right into Brad's boots. Come to think of it, that's a pair you got on. And Laurie—she wanted you."

"Question never come up," Mart said shortly.

Amos shrugged. "Couldn't say much more than I done."

"No, you sure couldn't. Not without landing flat on your butt!" Mart had always thought of Amos as a huge man, perhaps because he had been about knee high to Amos when he knew him first. But now, as Amos for a moment looked him steadily in the eye, Mart noticed for the first time that their eyes were on the same level. Mrs. Mathison had been right about Mart having taken a final spurt of growth.

"I guess I must have left Jerem's letter lying around."

"Yeah. You left it lying around." Mart had meant to ball up the letter and throw it in Amos' face, but found he couldn't now. He just handed it over.

"This here's another thing I tried to leave you out of," Amos said. "Martha put herself out for fifteen years bringing you up. I'll feel low in my mind if I get you done away with now."

"Ain't studying on getting done away with."

"'Bring the reward,' he says here. From what I know of Jerem, he ain't the man to trust getting paid when he's earned it. More liable to try to make sure."

"Now, he ought to know you ain't carrying the thousand around with you!"

"Ain't I?"

So he was. Amos did have the money with him. Now there's a damn fool thing, Mart considered. Aloud he said, "If he's

406

got robbery in mind, I suppose he won't tell the truth anyway."

"I think he will. So he'll have a claim later in case we slip
through his claws."

"You talk like we're fixing to steal bait from a snap trap!"

Amos shrugged. "I'll admit one thing. In a case like this, two
guns got about ten times the chance of one."

Mart was flattered. He couldn't work himself up to picking a fight with Amos after that. Things dropped back to
what they had been before they went home at all. The snow
melted off, and they traveled in mud. Then the weather went
cold again, and the wet earth froze to iron. More snow was
threatening as they came to Jerem Futterman's stockade,
where Lost Mule Creek ran into the Salt Fork. The creek
had not always been called the Lost Mule. Once it had been
known as Murder River. They didn't know why, nor how
the name got changed, but maybe it was a good thing to
remember now.

Jerem Futterman was lightly built, but well knit, and moved
with a look of handiness. Had he been a cow-horse you might
have bought him, if you liked them mean, and later shot him,
if you didn't like them treacherous. He faced them across a
plank-and-barrel counter in the murk of his low-beamed log
trading room, seeming to feel easier with a barrier between
himself and strangers. Once he had had another name. Some
thought he called himself Futterman because few were likely
to suspect a man of fitting such a handle to himself, if it wasn't
his right one.

"Knew you'd be along," he said. "Have a drink."

"Have one yourself." Amos refused the jug, but rang a four-
bit piece on the planks.

Futterman hesitated, but ended by taking a swig and pocket-
ing the half dollar. This was watched by four squaws hunkered
down against the wall and a flat-faced breed who snoozed in a
corner. Mart had spotted four or five other people around the
place on their way in, mostly knock-about packers and bull-
team men, who made up a sort of transient garrison.

The jug lowered, and they went into the conventional exchange of insults that passed for good humor out here. "Wasn't
sure I'd know you standing up," Futterman said. "Last I saw,

you were flat on your back on the floor of a saloon at Painted Post."

"You don't change much. See you ain't washed or had that shirt off," Amos said; and decided that was enough politeness. "Let's see the dress!"

A moment of total stillness filled the room before Futterman spoke. "You got the money?"

"I ain't paying the money for the dress. I pay when the child is found—alive, you hear me?"

The trader had a trick of dropping his lids and holding motionless with cocked head, as if listening. The silence drew out to the cracking point; then Futterman left the room without explanation. Mart and Amos exchanged a glance. What might happen next was anybody's guess; the place had an evil, trappy feel. But Futterman came back in a few moments, carrying a rolled-up bit of cloth.

It was Debbie's dress, all right. Amos went over it, inch by inch, and Mart knew he was looking for blood stains. It was singular how often people west of the Cross Timbers found themselves searching for things they dreaded to find. The dress was made with tiny stitches that Amos must be remembering as the work of Martha's fingers. But now the pocket was half torn away, and the square hole where the sample had been knifed out of the front seemed an Indian kind of mutilation, as if the little dress were dead.

"Talk," Amos said.

"A man's got a right to expect some kind of payment."

"You're wasting time!"

"I paid twenty dollars for this here. You lead a man to put out, and put out, but when it comes to——"

Amos threw down a gold piece, and Mart saw Futterman regret that he hadn't asked more.

"I had a lot of other expense, you realize, before——"

"Bull shit," Amos said. "Where'd you get this?"

One more long moment passed while Jerem Futterman gave that odd appearance of listening. This man is careful, Mart thought; he schemes, and he holds back the aces—but he's got worms in his craw where the sand should be.

"A young buck fetched it in. Filched it, naturally. He said it belonged off a young'n——"

"*Is she alive?*"

"He claimed so. Said she was catched by Chief Scar the tail end of last summer."

"Take care, Jerem! I never heard of no Chief Scar!"

"Me neither." Futterman shrugged. "He's supposed to be a war chief with the Nawyecky Comanches."

"War chief," Amos repeated with disgust. Among the Comanches any warrior with a good string of coups was called a war chief.

"You want me to shut up, say so," Futterman said testily. "Don't be standing there giving me the lie every minute!"

"Keep talking," Amos said, relaxing a little.

"Scar was heading north. He was supposed to cross the Red, and winter-in at Fort Sill. According to this buck. Maybe he lied."

"And maybe you lie," Amos said.

"In that case, you won't find her, will you? And I won't get the thousand."

"You sure as hell won't," Amos agreed. He stuffed Debbie's dress into the pocket of his sheepskin.

"Stay the night, if you want. You can have your pick of them squaws."

The squaws sat stolidly with lowered eyes. Mart saw that a couple of them, with the light color of mixed blood, were as pretty as any he had seen. Amos ignored the offer, however. He bought a skimpy mule load of corn for another twenty dollars, with only a token argument over the outrageous price.

"I expect you back when you find her," Futterman reminded him, "to pay the money into this here hand." He showed the dirty hand he meant.

"I'll be back if I find her," Amos said. "And if I don't."

Little daylight was left as they struck northward along Lost Mule Creek. The overcast broke, and a full moon rose, huge and red at first, dwindling and paling as it climbed. And within two hours they knew that the lonely prairie was not half lonely enough, from the standpoint of any safety in this night. Mart's stud horse told them first. He began to prick his ears and show interest in something unseen and unheard, off on their flank beyond the Lost Mule. When he set himself to whinny they knew there were horses over there. Mart picked him up sharply, taking up short on the curb, so the uproar the stud was planning on never come out. But the horse fussed and fretted from then on.

Though the stud could be stopped from hollering, their pack mule could not. A little farther on he upped his tail, lifted his head, and whipsawed the night with a bray fit to rouse the world.

"That fool leatherhead is waking up people in Kansas," Mart said. "You want I should tie down his tail? I heard they can't yell at all, failin' they get their tail up."

Amos had never seen it tried, but he figured he could throw off on that one by percentage alone. "That's what I like about you," he said. "Man can tell you any fur-fetched thing comes in his head, and you'll cleave to it for solemn fact from then on."

"Well, then—why don't we split his pack, and stick a prickle pear under his tail, and fog him loose?"

"He'd foller anyway."

"We can tie him. Shoot him even. This here's the same as traveling with a brass band."

Amos looked at him with disbelief. "Give up a fifteen-dollar mule for the likes of Jerem? I guess you don't know me very well. Leave the brute sing."

The thing was that nothing answered the mule from beyond the creek. The stud might have scented a band of mustangs, but mustangs will answer a mule same as a horse. Their animals were trying to call to ridden horses, probably Spanish curbed.

"I see no least reason," Mart said, "why they can't gallop ahead and dry-gulch us any time they want to try."

"How do you know they haven't tried?"

"Because we ain't been fired on. They could pick any time or place they want."

"I ain't led you any kind of place they want. Why you think I swung so far out back there a few miles? That's our big advantage—they got to use a place I pick."

They rode on and on, while the moon shrunk to a pale dime, and crossed the zenith. The mule lost interest, but the stud still fretted, and tried to trumpet. The unseen, unheard stalkers who dogged them were still there.

"This can't run on forever," Mart said.

"Can't it?"

"We got to lose 'em or outrun 'em. Or——"

"What for? So's they can come on us some far place, when we least expect?"

"I can't see 'em giving up," Mart argued. "If this kind of haunting has to go on for days and weeks——"

"I mean to end it tonight," Amos said.

They off-saddled at last in the rough ground from which the Lost Mule rose. Amos picked a dry gully, and they built a big tenderfoot fire on a patch of dry sand. Mart did what Amos told him up to here.

"I figure I got a right to know what you aim to do," he said at last.

"Well, we might make up a couple of dummies out o'——"

Mart rebelled. "If I heard one story about a feller stuffed grass in his blanket and crawled off in the buck brush, I heard a million! Come morning, the blanket is always stuck full of arrows. Dozens of 'em. Never just one arrow, like a thrifty Indian would make do. Now, you know how hard arrows is to make!"

"Ain't studyin' on Indians."

"No, I guess not. I guess it must be crazy people."

"In poker, in war," Amos said, "what you want is a simple, stupid plan. Reason you hear about the old flim-flams so much is they always work. Never try no deep, tricky plan. The other feller can't foller it; it throws him back on his common sense —which is the last thing you want."

"But this here is childish!"

Amos declared that what you plan out never helps much any; more liable to work against you than anything else. What the other fellow had in mind was the thing you wanted to figure on. It was the way you used *his* plan that decided which of you got added to the list of the late lamented. But he said no more of dummies. "You hungry? I believe they'll stand off and wait for us to settle down. We got time to eat, if you want to cook."

"I don't care if I never eat. Not with what's out there in the dark."

Only precaution they took was to withdraw from the ember-lighted gully, and take cover under a low-hung spruce on the bank. About the first place a killer would look, Mart thought, once he found their camp. Mart rolled up in his blankets, leaving Amos sitting against the stem of the spruce, his rifle in his hands.

"You see, Martie," Amos went back to it, "a man is very liable to see what he's come expecting to see. Almost always, he'll picture it all out in his mind beforehand. So you need give him but very little help, and he'll swindle hisself. Like one time in the Rangers, Cap Harker offered five hundred dollars reward for a feller——"

"Now who ever give the Rangers five hundred dollars? Not the Texas legislature, I guarandamtee."

"——for taking a feller alive, name of Morton C. Pettigrew. Cap got the description printed up on a handbill. Middling size; average weight; hair-colored hair; eye-colored eyes——"

"Now wait a minute!"

"Shut up. Temperment sociable and stand-offish; quiet, peaceable, and always making trouble."

"Never see such a damn man."

"Well, you know, that thing got us more than forty wanted men? Near every settlement in Texas slung some stranger in the calabozo and nailed up the door. We gathered in every size and shape, without paying a cent. A little short red-head Irishman, and a walking skeleton a head taller'n me, and a Chinaman, and any number of renegade Mex. Near every one of 'em worth hanging for something, too, except the Chinaman; we had to leave him go. Cap Harker was strutting up and down Texas, singing 'Bringing home the sheaves,' and speaking of running for governor. But it finished him."

"How?"

"Marshal down at Castlerock grobe a feller said he *was* Morton C. Pettigrew. We sent a man all the way back to Rhode Island, trying to break his story. But it was his right name, sure enough. Finally we had to make up the reward out of our own pants."

Mart asked nervously, "You think they'll try guns, or knives?"

"What? Who? Oh. My guess would be knives. But you let them make the choice. We'll handle whichever, when it comes. Go'n to sleep. I got hold of everything."

All they really knew was that it would come. No doubt of that now. The stud was trumpeting again, and stammering with his feet. Mart was not happy with the probability of the knives. Most Americans would rather be blown to bits than face up to the stab and slice of whetted steel—nobody seems to know just why. Mart was no different. Sleep, the man says. Fine chance, knowing your next act must be to kill a man, or get a blade in the gizzard. And he knew Amos was a whole lot more strung-up than he was willing to let on. Amos hadn't talked so much in a month of Sundays.

Mart settled himself as comfortably as he could for the sleepless wait that was ahead; and was asleep in the next half minute.

The blast of a rifle wakened him to the most confusing ten minutes of his life. The sound had not been the bang that makes your ears ring when a shot is fired beside you, but the explosive howl, like a snarl, that you hear when it is fired toward you from a little distance off. He was rolling to shift his probably spotted position when the second shot sounded. Somebody coughed as the bullet hit, made a brief strangling noise, and was quiet. Amos was not under the spruce; Mart's first thought was that he had heard him killed.

Down in the gully the embers of their fire still glowed. Nothing was going on down there at all; the action had been behind the spruce on the uphill side. He wormed on his belly to the place where he had heard the man hit. Two bodies were there, instead of one, the nearer within twenty feet of the spot where he had slept. Neither dead man was Amos. And now Mart could hear the hoof-drum of a running horse.

From a little ridge a hundred feet away a rifle now spoke twice. The second flash marked for him the spot where a man stood straight up, firing deliberately down their back trail. Mart leveled his rifle, but in the moment he took to make sure of his sights in the bad light, the figure disappeared. The sound of the running horse faded out, and the night was quiet.

Mart took cover and waited; he waited a long time before he heard a soft footfall near him. As his rifle swung, Amos' voice said, "Hold it, Mart. Shootin's over."

"What in all hell is happening here?"

"Futterman held back. He sent these two creeping in. They was an easy shot from where I was. Futterman, though—it took an awful lucky hunk of lead to catch up with that one. He was leaving like a scalded goat."

"What the devil was you doing out there?"

"Walked out to see if he had my forty dollars on him." It wasn't the explanation Mart was after, and Amos knew it. "Got the gold pieces all right. Still in his pants. I don't know what become of my four bits."

"But how come—how did you make out to nail 'em?"

What can you say to a man so sure of himself, so belittling of chance, that he uses you for bait? Mart could have told him something. There had been a moment when he had held Amos clean in his sights, without knowing him. One more pulse-beat of pressure on the hair-set trigger, and Amos would have got his head blown off for his smartness. But he let it go.

"We got through it, anyway," Amos said.

"I ain't so sure we're through it. A thing like this can make trouble for a long, long time."

Amos did not answer that.

As they rode on, a heavy cloud bank came over the face of the lowering moon. Within the hour, snow began to fall, coming down in flakes so big they must have hissed in the last embers of the fire they had left behind. Sunrise would find only three low white mounds back there, scarcely recognizable for what they were under the blanketing snow.

# 16

WINTER WAS breaking up into slush and sleet, with the usual freezing setbacks, as they reached Fort Sill again. The Indians would begin to scatter as soon as the first pony grass turned green, but for the present there were many more here than had come in with the early snows. Apparently the Wild Tribes who had taken the Quaker Peace Policy humorously at first were fast learning to take advantage of it. Three hundred lodges of Wichitas in their grass beehive houses, four hundred of Comanches in hide tepees, and more Kiowas than both together, were strung out for miles up Cache Creek and down the Medicine Bluff, well past the mouth of Wolf Creek.

Nothing had been seen of the Queherenna, or Antelope Comanches, under Bull Bear, Black Horse, and Wolf-Lying-Down, or the Kotsetaka (Buffalo-followers) under Shaking Hand, all of whom stayed in or close to the Staked Plains. The famous war chief Tabananica, whose name was variously translated as Sound-of-Morning, Hears-the-Sunrise, and Talks-with-Dawn-Spirits, was not seen, but he was heard from: He sent word to the fort urging the soldiers to come out and fight. Still, those in charge were not heard to complain that they hadn't accumulated Indians enough. A far-sighted chief named Kicking Bird was holding the Kiowas fairly well in check, and the Wichitas were quiet, as if suspicious of their luck; but the Comanches gleefully repaid the kindness of the Friends with arrogance, insult, and disorderly mischief.

Mart and Amos were unlikely to forget Agent Hiram Appleby. This Quaker, a graying man in his fifties, looked like a small-town storekeeper, and talked like one, with never a "thee" nor "thou"; a quiet, unimpressive man, with mild short-sighted eyes, stains on his crumpled black suit, and the patience of the eternal rocks. He had watched the Comanches kill his milch cows, and barbecue them in his dooryard. They had stolen all his red flannel underwear off the line, and paraded it before him as the outer uniform of an improvised society of young bucks. And none of this changed his attitude toward them by the width of a whistle.

Once they watched a Comanche buck put a knife point to Appleby's throat in a demand for free ammunition, and spit in the Agent's face when it didn't work. Appleby simply stood there, mild, fusty looking, and immovable, showing no sign of affront. Amos stared in disbelief, and his gun whipped out.

"If you harm this Indian," Appleby said, "you will be seized and tried for murder, just as soon as the proper authorities can be reached." Amos put away his gun. The Comanche spat in an open coffee bin, and walked out. "Have to make a cover for that," Appleby said.

They would never understand this man, but they could not disbelieve him, either. He did all he could, questioning hundreds of Indians in more than one tribal tongue, to find out what Mart and Amos wanted to know. They were around the Agency through what was left of the winter, while Comanches, Kiowas, and Kiowa Apaches came and went. When at last Appleby told them that he thought Chief Scar had been on the Washita, but had slipped away, they did not doubt him.

"Used to be twelve main bands of Comanches, in place of only nine, like now," Appleby said, with the customary divergence from everything they had been told before. "Scar seems to run with the Wolf Brothers; a Comanche peace chief, name of Bluebonnet, heads them up."

They knew by now what a peace chief was. Among Comanches, some old man in each family group was boss of his descendants and relatives, and was a peace chief because he decided things like when to move and where to camp—anything that did not concern war. When a number of families traveled together, their peace chiefs made up the council—which meant they talked things over, sometimes. There was always one of the lot that the others came to look up to, and follow more or less—kind of tacitly, never by formal election—and this one was *the* peace chief. A war chief was just any warrior of any age who could plan a raid and get others to follow him. Comanche government was weak, loose, and informal; their ideas of acceptable behavior were enforced almost entirely by popular opinion among their kind.

"Putting two and two together, and getting five," Appleby told them, "I get the idea Bluebonnet kind of tags along with different bunches of Nawyeckies. Sometimes one bunch of 'em, sometimes another. Too bad. Ain't any kind of Comanche moves around so shifty as the Nawyecky. One of the names the other Comanches has for 'em means 'Them As Never Gets Where They're Going.' Don't you believe it. What it is, they like to lie about where they're going, and start that way, then double back, and fork off. As a habit; no reason needed. I wouldn't look for 'em in Indian Territory, was I you; nor anyplace else they should rightfully be. I'd look in Texas. I kind of get the notion, more from what ain't said than what they tell me, they wintered in the Pease River breaks. So no use to look there—they'll move out, with the thaw. I believe I'd look up around the different headwaters of the Brazos, if I was doing it."

"You're talking about a hundred-mile spread, cutting crosswise—you know that, don't you? Comes to tracing out all them branches, nobody's going to do that in any one year!"

"I know. Kind of unencouraging, ain't it? But what's a man to say? Why don't you take a quick look at twenty-thirty miles of the Upper Salt? I know you just been there, or nigh to it, but that was months ago. Poke around in Canyon Blanco a little. Then cut across and try the Double Mountain Fork. And Yellow House Crick after, so long as you're up there. If you don't come on some kind of Nawyeckies, some place around, I'll put in with you!"

He was talking about the most remote, troublesome country in the length of Texas, from the standpoint of trying to find an Indian.

Amos bought two more mules and a small stock of trade goods, which Appleby helped them to select. They took a couple of bolts of cotton cloth, one bright red and one bright blue, a lot of fancy buttons, spools of ribbon, and junk like that. No knives, because the quality of cheap ones is too easily detected, and no axe heads because of the weight. Appleby encouraged them to take half a gross of surplus stock-show ribbons that somebody had got stuck with, and shipped out to him. These were flamboyant sateen rosettes, as big as your hand, with flowing blue, red, or white ribbons. The gold lettering on the ribbons mostly identified winners in various classes of hogs. They were pretty sure the Indians would prize these highly, and wear them on their war bonnets. No notions of comedy or fraud occurred either to Appleby or the greenhorn traders in connection with the hog prizes. A newcomer might think it funny to see a grim-faced war chief wearing a First Award ribbon, Lard-Type Boar, at the temple of his headdress. But those who lived out there very early got used to the stubbornness of Indian follies, and accepted them as commonplace. They gave the savage credit for knowing what he wanted, and let it go at that.

And they took a great quantity of sheet-iron arrowheads, the most sure-fire merchandise ever taken onto the plains. These were made in New England, and cost the traders seven cents a dozen. As few as six of them would sometimes fetch a buffalo robe worth two and a half to four dollars.

So now they set out through the rains and muck of spring, practicing their sign language, and learning their business as they went along. They were traveling now in a guise of peace; yet they trotted the long prairies for many weeks without seeing an Indian of any kind. Sometimes they found Indian signs —warm ashes in a shallow, bowl-like Comanche firepit, the fresh tracks of an unshod pony—but no trail that they could follow out. Searching the empty plains, it was easy to understand why you could never find a village when you came armed and in numbers to destroy it. Space itself was the Comanche's fortress. He seemed to live out his life immune to discovery, invisible beyond the rim of the world; as if he could disappear at will into the Spirit Land he described as lying beyond the sunset.

Then their luck changed, and for a while they found Comanches around every bend of every creek. Mart learned, without ever quite believing, the difference between Comanches on raid and Comanches among their own lodges. Given the security of great space, these wildest of horsemen became amiable and merry, quick with their hospitality. Generosity was the key to prestige in their communal life, just as merciless ferocity was their standard in the field. They made the change from one extreme to the other effortlessly, so that warriors returning with the loot of a ravaged frontier settlement immediately became the poorest men in their village through giving everything away.

Their trading went almost too well for their purposes. Comanche detachments that had wintered in the mountains, on the borders of Piute and Shoshone country, were rich in furs, particularly fox and otter, far more valuable now than beaver plews since the passing of the beaver hat. A general swap, big enough to clean out a village, took several days, the first of which was spent in long silences and casual conversations pretending disinterest in trade. But by the second day the Comanche minds had been made up; and though Mart and Amos raised their prices past the ridiculous, their mules were soon so loaded that they had to cache their loot precariously to keep an excuse for continuing their search.

Once the first day's silences were over, the Indians loved to talk. Caught short of facts they made up stories to suit—that was the main trouble when you wanted information from them. The searchers heard that Debbie was with Woman's Heart, of the Kiowas; with Red Hog, with Wolves-talk-to-him, with Lost Pony in the Palo Duro Canyon. They heard, in a face-blackened ritual of mourning, that she had died a full year before. Later they heard that she had been dead one month. Many Indians spoke of knowing Scar. Though they never knew just where he was, he was most often said to ride with Bluebonnet—a name sometimes translated as "the Flower." Mart and Amos both felt certain that they were closing in.

That was the summer a sub-chief of the Nocona Comanches, named Double Bird, tried to sell them a gaggle of squaws. They didn't know what he was driving at, to begin with. He signed that he had something to show them, and walked them out of his squalid ten-lodge village to the banks of the Rabbit Ear. Suddenly they were looking down at a covey of eight or nine mother-naked Indian girls, bathing in a shallow pool. The girls yipped and sat down in the water as the strangers appeared. Double Bird spoke; slowly the girls stood up again, and went on washing themselves in a self-conscious silence, lathering their short-cropped hair with bear grass.

Double Bird explained in sign language that he found himself long on women, but short of most everything else—especially gunpowder. How did they like these? Fat ones. Thin ones. Take and try. Amos told the chief that they didn't have his price with them, but Double Bird saw no obstacle in that. Try now. You like, go get gunpowder, lead; he would like a few dozen breech-loading rifles. Squaw wait.

Some of the young squaws were slim and pretty, and one or two were light-skinned, betraying white blood. Amos looked at Mart, and saw that he was staring with glassy eyes.

"Wake up," Amos said, jabbing him with a thumb like the butt of a lance. "You going to pick some, or not?"

"I know one thing," Mart said, "I got to give up. Either give up and go back, or give up and stay out."

"That's just the trouble. Pretty soon it's too late. Longer you're out, the more you want to go back—only you don't know how. Until you don't fit any place any more. You'll end up a squaw man—you can mark my word. You see why I tried to leave you home?"

During this time Mart had one recurrence of the terror-dream. He had supposed he would never have it any more, now that he had a pretty fair idea of how it had been caused. But the dream was as strong as ever, and in no way changed. The deathly dream voices in the reddish dark were as weird and un-earthly as ever, only vaguely like the yammering war cries he had heard at the Cat-tails. Amos shook him out of it, on the theory he must be choking on something, since he made no sound. But he slept no more that night.

Nevertheless, he was steadying, and changing. His grief for his lost people had forked, and now came to him in two ways, neither one as dreadful as the agony of loss he had felt at first. One way was in the form of a lot of little guilt-memories of unkindnesses that he now could never redress. Times when he had talked back to Martha, hadn't had time to read to Debbie, failed to thank Henry for fixing him up a saddle—sometimes these things came back in cruelly sharp detail.

The other way in which his grief returned was in spells of homesickness. Usually these came on him when things were uncomfortable, or went wrong; while they lasted, nothing ahead seemed to offer any hope. He had no home to which he could ever go back. No such thing was in existence any more on this earth. This homesickness, though, was gradually being replaced by a loneliness for Laurie, who could give him worries of another kind, but who at least was alive and real, however far away.

A more immediate frustration was that he could not seem to catch up with Amos in learning Comanche. He believed this to be of the utmost importance. Sign language was adequate, of course, for talking with Indians, but they wanted to understand the remarks not meant for their ears. Maybe Mart was trying too hard. Few Comanche syllables had anything like the sound of anything in English. But Amos substituted any crude approximate, whereas Mart was trying to get it right and could not.

Then Mart accidentally bought a squaw.

He had set out to buy a fox cape she was wearing, but ran into difficulty. His stubbornness took hold, and he dickered with her whole family for hours. At one point, Amos came and stood watching him curiously, until the stare got on Mart's nerves. "What the devil you gawkin' at? Y'see somepin' green?"

"Kind of branching out, ain't you?"

"Caught holt of a good hunk o' fur—that's all!"

Amos shrugged. "Guess that's one thing to call it." He went away.

Mart fingered the fox skins again. They still looked like prime winter stuff to him. He closed the deal abruptly by paying far too much, impatient to get it over with. And next he was unable to get possession. Amos had already diamond-hitched the mule packs, and it was time to go. But the squaw would only clutch the cape around her, chattering at him. When finally she signed that she would be back at once, and ran off among the lodges, Mart noticed that an uncomfortable number of Comanches were pressed close around him, looking at him very strangely. Bewildered and furious, he gave up, and pushed through them to his horse.

By the time he was set to ride, the young squaw had unexpectedly reappeared, exactly as she had promised. She was mounted bareback on an old crowbait that evidently belonged to her, and she carried her squaw bag, packed to bulging, before her on the withers. Behind her massed a whole phalanx of her people, their weapons in their hands. Mart sign-talked at the scowling bucks, "Big happy present from me to you," in rude gestures dangerously close to insult; and he led out, wanting only to be away from there.

The Comanche girl and her old plug fell in behind. He ignored her for a mile, but presently was forced to face it: She thought she was going with them. Brusquely he signed to her to turn her pony. She wheeled it obediently in one complete revolution, and fell in behind them again. He signaled more elaborately, unmistakably this time, telling her she must go back. She sat and stared at him.

Amos spoke sharply. "What the hell you doing?"

"Sending her home, naturally! Can't leave her tag along with——"

"What for God's sake you buy her for, if you didn't want her?"

"*Buy her?*"

"Mean to tell me——" Amos pulled up short and glared at him with disbelief—"You got the guts to set there and say you didn't even know it?"

"Course I didn't know it! You think I——" He didn't finish it. Comprehension of his ridiculous situation overwhelmed him, and he forgot what he had had in mind.

Amos blew up. "You God damned chunkhead!" he yelled. "When in the name of the sweet Christ you going to learn to watch what you're doing?"

"Well, she's got to go back," Mart said sullenly.

"She sure as hell is not going back! Them bastards would snatch our hair off before sundown, you flout 'em like that!"

"Oh, bloody murder," Mart moaned. "I just as lief give up and——"

"Shut up! Fetch your God damned wife and come along! What we need is distance!"

*Wife.* This here can't be happening, Mart thought. Man with luck like mine could never last. Not even this far. Should been killed long ago. And maybe I was—that's just what's happened. This horse ain't carrying a thing but a haunted saddle. . . .

He paid no more attention to her, but when they camped by starlight she was there, watering and picketing their animals, building their fire, fetching water. They wouldn't let her cook that night, but she watched them attentively as they fried beans and antelope steak, then made coffee in the same frying pan. Mart saw she was memorizing their motions, so that she would someday be able to please them. He furtively looked her over. She was quite young, a stocky little woman, inches less than five feet tall. Her face was broad and flat, set woodenly, for the time being, in a vaguely pleasant expression. Like most Comanche women, her skin was yellowish, of a lighter color than that of the males, and her hair was cropped short, in accordance with Comanche custom. Her long, entirely unlearnable name, when Amos questioned her about it, sounded like T'sala-ta-komal-ta-nama. "Wants you to call her Mama," Amos interpreted it, and guffawed as Mart answered obscenely. Now that he was over his mad, Amos was having more fun out of this than anything Mart could remember. She tried to tell them in sign language what her name meant without much success. Apparently she was called something like "Wild-Geese-Fly-Over-in-the-Night-Going-Honk," or, maybe, "Ducks-Talk-All-Night-in-the-Sky." In the time that she was with them Mart never once pronounced her name so that she recognized it; he usually began remarks to her with "Look——" which she came to accept as her new name. Amos, of course, insisted on calling her Mrs. Pauley.

Time came to turn in, in spite of Mart's efforts to push it off as long as he could. Amos rolled into his blankets, but showed no sign of dozing; he lay there as bright-eyed as a sparrow, awaiting Mart's next embarrassment with relish. Mart ignored the little Comanche woman as he finally spread out his blankets, hoping that she would let well enough alone if he would. No such a thing. Her movements were shy, deferential, yet completely matter-of-fact, as she laid her own blankets on top of his. He had braced himself against this, and made up his mind what he must do, lest he arm Amos with a hilarious story about him, such as he would never live down. He did not want this Comanche woman in the least, and dreaded the night with her; but he was determined to sleep with her if it killed him.

He pulled his boots, and slowly, gingerly, doubled the blankets over him. The Comanche girl showed neither eagerness nor hesitation, but only an acceptance of the inevitable, as she crept under the blankets, and snuggled in beside him. She was very clean—a good deal cleaner than he was, for the matter of that. The Comanche women bathed a lot when they had any water—they would break ice to get into the river. And often steeped themselves in sage smoke, particularly following menstruation, when this kind of cleansing was a required ritual. She seemed very small, and a little scared, and he felt sorry for her. For a moment he thought the night was going to be all right. Then, faint, but living, and unmistakable, the smell of Indian. . . . It was not an offensive odor; it had to do, rather, with the smoke of their fires, with the fur and wild-tanned leather they wore, and with the buffalo, without which they did not know how to live. He had supposed he had got used to the smoky air of lodges, and outgrown the senseless fear that had haunted his childhood. But now he struck away the blankets and came to his feet.

"Need water," he said in Comanche. She got up at once, and brought him some. A choking sound came from where Amos lay; Mart had a glimpse of Amos' compressed mouth and reddening face before Amos covered his head, burying the laughter he could not repress. Anger snatched Mart, so violent that he stood shaking for a moment, unable to turn away. When he could, he walked off into the dark in his sock feet; he was afraid he would kill Amos if he stood there listening to that smothered laughter.

He had figured out an excuse to give her by the time he came back. He explained in signs that his power-medicine was mixed up with a taboo, such that he must sleep alone for a period of time that he left indefinite. She accepted this tale readily; it was the kind of thing that would seem logical, and reasonable, to her. He thought she looked mildly relieved.

At their noon stop on the third day, Amos believed they had come far enough to be safe. "You can get rid of her, now, if you want."

"How?"

"You can knock her on the head, can't you? Though, now I think of it, I never seen you show much stomick for anything as practical as that."

Mart looked at him a moment. He decided to assume Amos was fooling, and let it pass without answer. Amos doubled a lead rope, weighted it with a couple of big knots, and tested it with a whistling snap. "Show you another way," he said; and started toward the Comanche girl.

Suddenly Mart was standing in front of him. "Put that thing down before I take it away from you!"

Amos stared. "What the hell's got into you now?"

"It's my fault she's here—not hers. She's done all she possibly could to try to be nice, and make herself helpful, and wanted. I never seen no critter try harder to do right. You want to rough something—I'm in reach, ain't I?"

Amos angered. "I ought to wrap this here around your gullet!"

"Go ahead. But when you pick yourself up, you better be running!"

Amos walked away.

The Comanche girl was with them eleven days, waiting on them, doing their work, watching them to foresee their needs. At the end of the eleventh day, in the twilight, the girl went after water, and did not come back. They found their bucket grounded in the shallows of the creek, and traced out the sign to discover what they were up against. A single Indian had crossed to her through the water; his buffalo pony had stood in the damp sand while the girl mounted behind the rider. The Indian had been the girl's lover most likely. They were glad to have him take her, but it made their scalps crawl to consider that he must have followed them, without their at all suspecting it, for all that time.

Though he was relieved to be rid of her, Mart found that he missed her, and was annoyed with himself for missing her, for many weeks. After a while he could not remember what had made him leap up, the night she had crept into the blankets with him; he regretted it, and thought of himself as a fool. They never saw her again. Years later Mart thought he heard of her, but he could not be sure. A Comanche woman who died a captive had told the soldiers her name was "Look." Mart felt a strange twinge, as of remorse without reason for remorse, as he remembered how a sad-eyed little Comanche woman had once got that name.

He had realized she had been trying to teach him Comanche, though without letting him notice it any more than she could help. When she talked to him in sign language she pronounced the words that went with the signs, but softly, so that he could ignore the spoken speech, if he wished. She responded to his

questions with a spark of hidden eagerness, and with the least
encouragement told hour-long stories of wars and heroes, miracles and sorceries, in this way. He wouldn't have supposed he
could learn anything in so short a time after beating his skull
against the stubborn language for so long. But actually it was
a turning point; the weird compounds of Comanche speech
began to break apart for him at last. When next he sat among
Comanches he became aware that he was able to follow almost
everything they said. Amos presently began to turn to him for
translations; and before the end of that summer, he was inter-
preter for them both.

Understanding the Comanches better, Mart began to pick
up news, or at least rumors filtered through Indian minds, of
what was happening upon the frontier. Most of the Comanches didn't care whether the white men understood their tales
of misdeeds or not. The Wild Tribes had as yet been given little
reason to think in terms of reprisals. Returning raiders boasted
openly of the bloodiest things they had done.

There were enough to tell. Tabananica, having again chal-
lenged the cavalry without obtaining satisfaction, crept upon
Fort Sill in the night, and got off with twenty head of horses
and mules out of the Agency corral. White Horse, of the
Kiowas, not to be outdone, took more than seventy head from
the temporary stake-and-rider corral at the Fort itself. Kicking
Bird, bidding to regain prestige lost in days of peace, went into
Texas with a hundred warriors, fought a cavalry troop, and
whipped it, himself killing the first trooper with his short lance.
Wolf-Lying-Down walked into Sill in all insolence, and sold
the Quaker agent a little red-haired boy for a hundred dollars. Fast Bear's young men got similar prices for six children,
and the mothers of some of them, taken in a murderous Texas
raid. The captives could testify to the wholesale murder of their
men, yet saw the killers pick up their money and ride free. The
Peace Policy was taking effect with a vengeance—though not
quite in the way intended.

Often and often, as that summer grew old, the searchers believed they were close to Debbie; but Bluebonnet somehow
still eluded them, and War Chief Scar seemed a fading ghost.
They saw reason to hope, though, in another way. The Comanches held the Peace Policy in contempt, but now leaned

on it boldly, since it had proved able to bear their weight. Surely, surely all of them would come in this time, when winter clamped down, to enjoy sanctuary and government rations in the shadow of Fort Sill. For the first time in history, perhaps, the far-scattered bands would be gathered in a single area—and fixed there, too, long enough for you to sort through them all.

So this year they made no plans to go home. As the great buffalo herds turned back from their summer pastures in the lands of the Sioux and the Blackfeet, drifting down-country before the sharpening northers, the two pointed their horses toward Fort Sill. Soon they fell into the trail of a small village —twenty-five or thirty lodges—obviously going to the same place that they were. They followed the double pole scratches of the many travois lazily, for though they were many weeks away from Fort Sill, they were in no great hurry to get there. It took time for the Indians to accumulate around the Agency, and the kind they were looking for came late. Some would not appear until they felt the pinch of the Starving Moons—if they came at all.

Almost at once the fire pits they rode over, and the short, squarish shape of dim moccasin tracks, told them they were following Comanches. A little later, coming to a place where the tracks showed better detail, they were able to narrow that down. Most Comanches wore trailing heel fringes that left faint, long marks in the dust. But one bunch of the Kotsetakas —the so-called Upriver branch—sewed weasel tails to the heels of their moccasins, leaving broader and even fainter marks. That was what they had here, and it interested them, for they had seen no such village in the fourteen months that they had searched.

But still they didn't realize what they were following, until they came upon a lone-hunting Osage, a long way from the range where he belonged. This Indian had an evil face, and seemingly no fear at all. He rode up to them boldly, and as he demanded tobacco they could see him estimating the readiness of their weapons, no doubt wondering whether he could do the two of them in before they could shoot him. Evidently he decided this to be impractical. In place of tobacco he settled for a handful of salt, and a red stock-prize ribbon placing him second in the class for Aged Sows. He repaid them with a cogent and hard-hitting piece of information, conveyed in crisp sign language, since he spoke no Comanche.

The village they were following, he said, was two sleeps ahead. Twenty-four lodges; six hundred horses and mules; forty-six battle-rated warriors. Tribe, Kotsetaka Comanche, of the Upriver Band (which they knew, so that the Osage's statements were given a color of truth); Peace Chief, Bluebonnet; War Chiefs, Gold Concho, Scar; also Stone Wold, Pacing Bear; others.

Amos' signs were steady, casual, as he asked if the village had white captives. The Osage said there were four. One woman, two little girls. One little boy. And two Mexican boys, he added as an afterthought. As for himself, he volunteered, he was entirely alone, and rode in peace. He walked the White Man's Way, and had never robbed anybody in his life.

He rode off abruptly after that, without ceremony; and the two riders went into council. The temptation was to ride hard, stopping for nothing, until they overtook the village. But that was not the sensible way. They would be far better off with troops close at hand, however tied-down they might be. And the gentle Quakers were the logical ones to intercede for the child's release, for they could handle it with less risk of a flare-up that might result in hurt to the child herself. No harm in closing the interval, though. They could just as well pick up a day and a half, and follow the Indians a few hours back to cut down chance of losing them in a mix with other Indians, or even a total change of plans. Anyway, they had to put distance between themselves and that Osage, whose last remarks had convinced both of them that he was a scout from a war party, and would ambush them if they let him.

They made a pretense of going into camp, but set off again in the first starlight, and rode all night. At sunrise they rested four hours for the benefit of their livestock, then made a wide cast, picked up the trail of the village again, and went on. The weather was looking very ugly. Brutal winds screamed across the prairie, and at midday a blue-black wall was beginning to rise, obscuring the northern sky.

Suddenly the broad trail they were following turned south at a right angle, as if broken square in two by the increasing weight of the wind.

"Are they onto us?" Mart asked; then repeated it in a yell, for the wind so snatched his words away that he couldn't hear them himself.

"I don't think that's it," Amos shouted back. "What they got to fear from us?"

"Well, something turned 'em awful short!"

"They know something! That's for damn sure!"

Mart considered the possibility that the Osages had thrown in with the Cheyennes and Arapahoes, and gone to war in great force. Forty-six warriors could only put their village on the run, and try to get it out of the path of that kind of a combination. He wanted to ask Amos what he thought about this, but speech was becoming so difficult that he let it go. And he was already beginning to suspect something else. This time the apprehension with which he watched developments was a reasoned one, with no childhood ghosts about it. The sky and the wind were starting to tell them that a deadly danger might be coming down on them, of a kind they had no means to withstand.

By mid-afternoon they knew. Swinging low to look closely at the trail they followed, they saw that it was now the trail of a village moving at a smart lope, almost a dead run. The sky above them had blackened, and was filled with a deep-toned wailing. The power of the wind made the prairie seem more vast, so that they were turned to crawling specks on the face of a shelterless world. Amos leaned close to shout in Mart's ear. "They seen it coming! They've run for the Wichita breaks—that's what they done!"

"We'll never make it by dark! We got to hole up shorter than that!"

Amos tied his hat down hard over his ears with his wool muffler. Mart's muffler snapped itself and struggled to get away, like a fear-crazed thing, as he tried to do the same. He saw Amos twisting in the saddle to look all ways, his eyes squeezed tight against the sear of the wind. He looked like a man hunting desperately for a way of escape, but actually he was looking for their pack mules. Horses drift before a storm, but mules head into it, and keep their hair. For some time their pack animals had shown a tendency to swivel into the wind, then come on again, trying to stay with the ridden horses. They were far back now, small dark marks in the unnatural dusk. Amos mouthed unheard curses. He turned his horse, whipping hard, and forced it back the way they had come.

Mart tried to follow, but the Fort Worth stud reared and fought, all but going over on him. He spurred deep, and as the stud came down, reined high and short with all his strength. "Red, you son-of-a-bitch——" Both man and horse might very easily die out here if the stallion began having his way. The great neck had no more bend to it than a log. And now the stud got his head down, and went into his hard, skull-jarring buck.

Far back, Amos passed the first mule he came to, and the second. When he turned downwind, it was their commissary mule, the one with their grub in his packs, that he dragged along by a death-grip on its cheek strap. The Fort Worth stud was standing immovable in his sull as Amos got back. Both Mart and the stud horse were blowing hard, and looked beat out. Mart's nose had started to bleed, and a bright trickle had frozen on his upper lip.

"We got to run for it!" Amos yelled at him. "For God's sake, get a rope on this!"

With his tail to the wind, the stud went back to work, grudgingly answering the rein. Mart got a lead rope on the mule, to the halter first, then back to a standing loop around the neck, and through the halter again. Once the lead rope was snubbed to the stud's saddle horn the mule came along, sometimes sitting down, sometimes at a sort of bounding trot, but with them just the same.

It was not yet four o'clock, but night was already closing; or rather a blackness deeper than any natural night seemed to be lowering from above, pressing downward implacably to blot out the prairie. For a time a band of yellow sky showed upon the southern horizon, but this narrowed, then disappeared, pushed below the edge of the world by the darkness. Amos pointed to a dark scratch near the horizon, hardly more visible than a bit of thread laid flat. You couldn't tell just what it was, or how far away; in that treacherous and failing light you couldn't be sure whether you were seeing half a mile or fifteen. The dark mark on the land had better be willows, footed in the gulch of a creek—or at least in a dry run-off gully. If it was nothing but a patch of buckbrush, their chances were going to be very poor. They angled toward it, putting their horses into a high lope.

Now came the first of the snow, a thin lacing of ice needles, heard and felt before they could be seen. The ice particles were traveling horizontally, parallel to the ground, with an enormous velocity. They made a sharp whispering against leather, drove deep into cloth, and filled the air with hissing. This thin bombardment swiftly increased, coming in puffs and clouds, then in a rushing stream. And at the same time the wind increased; they would not have supposed a harder blow to be possible, but it was. It tore at them, snatching their breaths from their mouths, and its gusts buffeted their backs as solidly as thrown sacks of grain. The galloping horses sat back against the power of the wind as into breechings, yet were made to yaw and stumble as they ran. The long hair of their tails whipped their flanks, and wisps of it were snatched away.

In the last moments before they were blinded by the snow and the dark, Mart got a brief glimpse of Amos' face. It was a bloodless gray-green, and didn't look like Amos' face. Some element of force and strength had gone out of it. Most of the time Amos' face had a wooden look, seemingly without expression, but this was an illusion. Actually the muscles were habitually set in a grim confidence, an almost built-in certainty, that now was gone. They pushed their horses closer together, leaning them toward each other so that they continually bumped knees. It was the only way they could stay together, sightless and deafened in the howling chaos.

They rode for a long time, beaten downwind like driven leaves. They gave no thought to direction; the storm itself was taking care of that. It was only when the winded horses began to falter that Mart believed they had gone past whatever they had seen. His saddle was slipping back, dragged toward the stud's kidneys by the resistance of the mule. He fumbled at the latigo tie, to draw up the cinch, but found his hands so stiff with cold he was afraid to loosen it, lest he slip his grip, and lose mule, saddle, horse, and himself, all in one dump. This thing will end soon, he was thinking. This rig isn't liable to stay together long. Nor the horses last, if it does. Nor us either, if it comes to that. . . . His windpipe was raw; crackles of ice were forming up his nose. And his feet were becoming numb. They had thrown away their worn-out buffalo boots last spring, and had made no more, because of their expectations of wintering snugly at Fort Sill.

No sense to spook it, he told himself, as breathing came hard. Nothing more a man can do. We'll fall into something directly. Or else we won't. What the horses can't do for us won't get done. . . .

Fall into it was what they did. They came full stride, without warning, upon a drop of unknown depth. Seemingly they struck it at a slant, for Amos went over first. His horse dropped a shoulder as the ground fell from under, then was gone. Even in the roar of the storm, Mart heard the crack of the pony's broken neck. He pulled hard, and in the same split second tried first to sheer off, and next to turn the stud's head to the drop—neither with the least effect, for the rim crumbled, and they plunged.

Not that the drop was much. The gully was no more than twelve-feet deep, a scarcely noticeable step down, had either horse or man been able to see. The stud horse twisted like a cat, got his legs under him, and went hard to his knees. The mule came piling down on top of the whole thing, with an impact of enormous weight, and a great thrashing of legs, then floundered clear. And how that was done without important damage Mart never knew.

He got their two remaining animals under control, and groped for Amos. They hung onto each other, blind in the darkness and the snow, leading the stud and the mule up the gully in search of better shelter. Within a few yards they blundered upon a good-sized willow, newly downed by the wind; and from that moment they knew they were going to come through. They knew it, but they had a hard time remembering it, in the weary time before they got out of there. They were pinned in that gully more than sixty hours.

In some ways the first night was the worst. The air was dense with the dry snow, but the wind, rushing with hurricane force down a thousand miles of prairie, would not let the snow settle, or drift, even in the crevice where they had taken refuge. No fire was possible. The wind so cycloned between the walls of the gulch that the wood they lighted in the shelter of their coats immediately vanished in a shatter of white sparks. Mart chopped a tub-sized cave into the frozen earth at the side, but the fire couldn't last there, either. Their canteens were frozen solid, and neither dry cornmeal nor their iron-hard jerky would go down without water. They improvised parkas and foot wrappings out of the few furs they had happened to stuff into the commissary pack, and stamped their feet all night long.

Sometime during that night the Fort Worth stud broke loose, and went with the storm. In the howling of the blizzard they didn't even hear him go.

During the next day the snow began rolling in billows across the prairie, and their gully filled. They were better off by then. They had got foot wrappings on their mule, lest his hoofs freeze off as he stood, and had fed him on gatherings of willow twigs. With pack sheet and braced branches they improved their bivouac under the downed willow, so that as the snow covered them they had a place in which a fire would burn at last. They melted snow and stewed horse meat, and took turns staying awake to keep each other from sleeping too long. The interminable periods in which they lay buried alive were broken by sorties after wood, or willow twigs, or to rub the legs of the mule.

But the third night was in some ways the worst of all. They had made snowshoes of willow hoops and frozen horsehide, tied with thongs warmed at the fire; but Mart no longer believed they would ever use them. He had been beaten against the frozen ground by that murderous uproar for too long; he could not hear the imperceptible change in the roar of the churning sky as the blizzard began to die. This nightmare had gone on forever, and he accepted that it would always go on, until death brought the only possible peace.

He lay stiffened and inert in their pocket under the snow, moving sluggishly once an hour, by habit, to prevent Amos from sleeping himself to death. He was trying to imagine what it would be like to be dead. They were so near it, in this refuge so like a grave, he no longer felt that death could make any unwelcome difference. Their bodies would never be found, of course, nor properly laid away. Come thaw, the crows would pick their bones clean. Presently the freshets would carry their skeletons tumbling down the gulch, breaking them up, strewing them piecemeal until they hung in the driftwood, a thighbone here, a rib there, a skull full of gravel half buried in the drying streambed.

People who knew them would probably figure out they had died in the blizzard, though no one would know just where. Mart Pauley? Lost last year in the blizzard . . . Mart Pauley's been dead four years . . . ten years . . . forty years. No—not even his name would be in existence in anybody's mind, anywhere, as long as that.

Amos brought him out of that in a weird way. Mart was in a doze that was dangerously near a coma, when he became aware that Amos was singing—if you could call it that. More of a groaning, in long-held, hoarse tones, from deep in the galled throat. Mart lifted his head and listened, wondering, with a desolation near indifference, if Amos had gone crazy, or into a delirium. As he came wider awake he recognized Comanche words. The eery sound was a chant.

> The sun will pour life on the earth forever . . .
>     (I rode my horse till it died.)
> The earth will send up new grass forever . . .
>     (I thrust with my lance while I bled.)
> The stars will walk in the sky forever . . .
>     (Leave my pony's bones on my grave.)

It was a Comanche death song. The members of some warrior society—the Snow Wolf Brotherhood?—were supposed to sing it as they died.

"God damn it, you stop that!" Mart shouted, and beat at Amos with numbed hands.

Amos was not in delirium. He sat up grumpily, and began testing his creaky joints. He grunted, "No ear for music, huh?"

Suddenly Mart realized that the world beyond their prison was silent. He floundered out through the great depth of snow. The sky was gray, but the surface of the snow itself almost blinded him with its glare. And from horizon to horizon, nothing on the white earth moved. The mule stood in a sort of well it had tromped for itself, six feet deep in the snow. It had chewed the bark off every piece of wood in reach, but its hoofs were all right. Mart dragged Amos out, and they took a look at each other.

Their lips were blackened and cracked, and their eyes blood-shot. Amos' beard had frost in it now that was going to stay there as long as he lived. But they were able-bodied, and they were free, and had a mule between them.

All they had to do now was to get through a hundred and ten miles of snow to Fort Sill; and they could figure they had put the blizzard behind them.

## 17

THEY TOOK so many weeks to make Fort Sill that they were sure Bluebonnet's village would be there ahead of them; but it was not. They were in weakened, beat-down shape, and they knew it. They slept much, and ate all the time. When they went among the Indians they moved slowly, in short hauls, with long rests between. Hard for them to believe that only a year and a half had passed in their search for Debbie. Many thought they had already made a long, hard, incredibly faithful search. But in terms of what they had got done, it wasn't anything, yet.

Living things on the prairie had been punished very hard. The buffalo came through well, even the youngest calves; only the oldest buffalo were winter killed. Things that lived down holes, like badgers, prairie dogs, and foxes, should have been safe. Actually, animals of this habit were noticeably scarcer for the next few years, so perhaps many froze deep in the ground as they slept. The range cattle were hit very hard, and those of improved breeding stood it the worst. Where fences had come into use, whole herds piled up, and died where they stood. Hundreds had their feet frozen off, and were seen walking around on the stumps for weeks before the last of them were dead.

After the blizzard, a period of melt and freeze put an iron crust on the deep snow. A lot of the cattle that had survived the storm itself now starved, unable to paw down to the feed with their cloven hoofs. Horses did considerably better, for their hoofs could smash the crust. But even these were fewer for a long time, so many were strewn bones upon the prairie before spring.

Yet all this devastation had come unseasonably early. After the first of the year the winter turned mild, as if it had shot its wad. Once travel was practicable, more Indians streamed into the sanctuary of Fort Sill than ever before. Their deceptively rugged tepees, cunningly placed, and anchored by crossed stakes driven five feet into the ground, had stood without a single reported loss; and the villages seemed to have plenty of pemmican to feed them until spring. Perhaps they had been awed by the power of the warring wind spirits, so that they felt their own medicine to be at a low ebb.

They were anything but awed, however, by the soldiers, whom the Peace Policy tied down in helplessness, or by the Society of Friends, whose gentle pacifism the Wild Tribes held in contempt, even while they sheltered behind it. Appears-in-the-Sky, Medicine Chief of the Kiowas, who claimed a spirit owl as his familiar, in January moved out a short distance through the snow to murder four Negro teamsters. Two cowboys were killed at Sill's beef corral, barely half a mile from the fort, and a night wrangler was murdered and scalped closer than that. Half a dozen Queherenna, or Antelope Comanches—the military were calling them Quohadas—stole seventy mules out of Fort Sill's new stone corral, and complacently camped twenty miles away, just as safe as upon their mothers' backboards.

Both Kiowas and Comanches were convinced now of the integrity of the Quakers. They pushed into the Quakers' houses, yanked buttons off the Agent's clothes; helped themselves to anything that caught the eye, then stoned the windows as they left. Those Quakers with families were ordered to safety, but few obeyed. Resolute in their faith, they stood implacably between their Indian charges and the troops. It was going to be a hard, rough, chancy year down below in Texas.

Meanwhile Mart and Amos searched and waited, and still Bluebonnet did not come in. As spring came on they bought new horses and mules, replenished their packs and once more went looking for Indians who forever marched and shuffled themselves in the far lost wastes of their range.

# 18

MOST OF that second trading summer was like the first. Being able to understand what the Indians said among themselves had proved of very little use, so far as their search was concerned. They did hear more, though, of what was happening back home, upon the frontier their wanderings had put so far behind. Mart, particularly, listened sharply for some clue as to whether the Mathisons still held, but heard nothing he could pin down.

In Texas the outlying settlers were going through the most dreadful year in memory. At least fourteen people were dead, and nine children captive, before the middle of May. Only a stubbornness amounting to desperation could explain why any of the pioneers held on. Bloody narratives were to be heard in every Comanche camp the searchers found. A party of surveyors were killed upon the Red River, and their bodies left to spoil in a drying pool. The corpses of three men, a woman and a child were reduced to char in a burning ranch house, cheating the raiders of the scalps. Oliver Loving's foreman was killed beside his own corral. By early summer, Wolf-Lying-Down had stolen horses within sight of San Antonio; and Kiowas under Big Bow, crossing into Mexico near Laredo, had killed seventeen vaqueros, and got back across Texas with a hundred and fifty horses and a number of Mexican children.

General Sherman, who habitually took Texan complaints with a grain of salt, finally had a look for himself. He appeared in Texas along about the middle of the summer, with an escort of only fifteen troopers—and at once nearly added himself to a massacre. Near Cox Mountain a raiding party of a hundred and fifty Comanches and Kiowas destroyed a wagon train, killing seven, some by torture. Unfortunately, for it would have been the highlight of his trip, General Sherman missed riding into this event by about an hour and a half. Proceeding to Fort Sill, Sherman supervised the arrest of Satanta, Satank, and Big Tree, showing a cool personal courage, hardly distinguishable from indifference, in the face of immediate mortal danger.

He presented the three war chiefs in handcuffs to the State of Texas; and after went away again.

All this, the two riders recognized, was building up to such a deadly, all-annihilating showdown as would be their finish, if they couldn't get their job done first. But for the present they found the Comanches in high and celebrative mood, unable to imagine the whirlwind that was to come. The warriors were arrogant, boastful, full of the high-and-mighty. Yet, luckily, they remained patronizingly tolerant, for the time, of the white men who dared come among them in their own far fastnesses.

During this time the terror-dream of the red night and the unearthly voices came to Mart only once, and he saw no copy of the unexplained death tree at all. Yet the attitudes of the Indians toward such things were beginning to influence him, so that he more than half believed they carried a valid prophecy. The Comanches were supposed to be the most literal-minded of all tribes. There are Indians who live in a poetic world, half of the spirit, but the Comanches were a tough-minded, practical people, who laughed at the religious ceremonies of other tribes as crazy-Indian foolishness. They had no official medicine men, no pantheon of named gods, no ordered theology. Yet they lived very close to the objects of the earth around them, and sensed in rocks, and winds, and rivers, spirits as living as their own. They saw themselves as of one piece with a world in which nothing was without a spirit.

In this atmosphere, almost every Comanche had a special spirit medicine that had come to him in a dream, usually the gift of some wild animal, such as an otter, a buffalo, or a wolf —never a dog or horse. By the time a Comanche was old, he was either a medicine man, believed to know specific magics against certain ills or disasters, or a black-magic sorcerer, feared because he could maim or kill from far away.

You could never learn to understand an Indian's way of thinking, or guess what he was about to think next. If you saw an Indian looking at the sky, you might know why you would be looking at the sky in his place—and be sure the Indian had some different reason. Yet sometimes they ran into a Comanche, usually an old one, who knew something there was no possible way for him to know.

"You speak Nemenna very well," an old Nocona said to Mart once. (The names of the bands were turning themselves over again; in a single year the name "Nawyecky" had fallen into almost total disuse.) Mart supposed the old man had heard of him, for he had not opened his mouth. He pretended not to understand, hoping to discredit a rumor of that kind. But the old Comanche went on, smiling at Mart's effort to dissimulate. "Sometimes you come upon a spirit in the form of a dead tree," he said. "It is blackened; it looks like a withered corpse, struggling to free itself from the earth."

Mart stared, startled into acknowledgment that he understood the old man's speech. At this the Comanche grinned derisively, but went on in grave tones. "You do not fear death very much, I think. Last year, maybe; not this year any more. But you will do well to fear the evil tree. Death is a kind and happy thing beside the nameless things beyond the tree."

He sat back. "I tell you this as a friend," he finished. "Not because I expect any kind of gift. I wish you well, and nothing more. I want no gift at all." Which of course meant that he did.

By middle fall the mood of the Comanches had begun to change. Raids were lacing into Texas at an unprecedented pace; Colorado was heavily scourged, and Kansas hurt to the very borders of Nebraska. Almost every village they came to was waiting in brooding quiet for a great war party to return, if it were not whooping up a scalp dance to celebrate a victory, or a glory dance for sending a party out. But now both Texas and the United States Army were fighting back. The Texas Rangers were in the saddle again, losing men in every skirmish, but making the Indians pay three and four lives for one. The Fort Sill garrison was still immobilized, but Fort Richardson, down on the West Fork of the Trinity, was beyond the authority of the Friends. From Richardson rode Colonel Mackenzie with a regiment and a half of yellowlegs; his forced marches drove deep into the land of the Quohadas. Shaking Hand's Kotsetakas got out of his way, and the great Bull Bear of the Antelopes, with such war chiefs under him as Black Horse, Wolf Tail, Little Crow, and the brilliant young Quanah, threatened briefly in force but drew back.

Old chiefs were losing favorite sons, and you could see black death behind their eyes when they looked at white men.

Warrior societies who scalp-danced for victory after victory counted their strength, and found that in the harvest season of their greatest success they were becoming few. The searchers learned to scout a village carefully, to see if it were in mourning for a raiding party decimated or destroyed, before they took a chance on going in. Over and over, white captives were murdered by torture in revenge for losses sustained upon the savage raids. Mart and Amos rode harder, longer, turning hollow-eyed and gaunted. Their time was running out, and very fast; already they might be too late.

Yet their goal, while it still eluded them, seemed always just ahead. They never had come to any point where either one of them could have brought himself to turn back, from the first day their quest had begun.

Then, as the snow came again, they struck the trail they had hunted for so long. It was that of twenty-two lodges led by Bluebonnet himself, and he had a captive white girl in his village, beyond any reasonable doubt. The horse-trampled parallel lines left by the many travois led south and eastward, crossing the high ground between the Beaver and the Canadian; they followed it fast and easily.

"Tomorrow," Amos said once more as they rode. The captive girl had been described to them as smallish, with yellow hair and light eyes. As they went into camp at twilight he said it again, and now for the last time: "Tomorrow. . . ."

# 19

MART PAULEY woke abruptly, with no notion of what had roused him. Amos breathed regularly beside him. Each slept rolled in his own blankets, but they shared the wagon sheet into which they folded themselves, heads and all, for shelter from the weather. The cold air stiffened the slight moisture in Mart's nostrils as he stuck his head out. Only the lightest of winds whispered across the surface of the snow. The embers of their fire pulsed faintly in the moving air, and by these he judged the time to be after midnight.

At first he heard nothing; but as he held his breath a trick of the wind brought again the sound that must have come to him in his sleep, so faint, so far off, it might have been a whispering of frost in his own ears.

He closed his grip slowly on Amos' arm until he waked. "Whazzamatter?"

"I swear I heard fighting," Mart said, "a long way off."

"Leave the best man win." Amos settled himself to go back to sleep.

"I mean big fighting—an Indian fight. . . . There! . . . Ain't that a bugle way off down the river?"

A few small flakes of snow touched their faces, but the night turned soundless again as soon as Amos sat up. "I don't hear nothing."

Neither did Mart any more. "It's snowing again."

"That's all right. We'll come up with Bluebonnet. Snow can never hide him from us now! It'll only pin him down for us!"

Mart lay awake for a while, listening hard; but no more sound found its way through the increasing snowfall.

Long before daylight he stewed up a frying-pan breakfast of shredded buffalo jerky, and fed the horses. "Today," Amos said, as they settled, joint-stiff, into their icy saddles. It was the first time they had ever said that after all the many, many times they had said "Tomorrow." Yet the word came gruffly, without exultation. The day was cold, and the snow still fell, as they pushed on through darkness toward a dull dawn.

By mid-morning they reached the Canadian, and forded its unfrozen shallows. They turned downstream, and at noon found Bluebonnet's village—or the place it had seen its last of earth.

They came to the dead horses first. In a great bend of the river, scattered over a mile of open ground, lay nearly a hundred head of buffalo ponies, their lips drawing back from their long teeth as they froze. The snow had stopped, but not before it had sifted over the horses, and the blood, and the fresh tracks that must have been made in the first hours of the dawn. No study of sign was needed, however; what had happened here was plain. The cavalry had learned long ago that it couldn't hold Comanche ponies.

Beyond the shoulder of a ridge they came upon the site of the village itself. A smudge, and a heavy stench of burning buffalo hair, still rose from the wreckage of twenty-two lodges. A few more dead horses were scattered here, some of them the heavier carcasses of cavalry mounts. But here, too, the snow had covered the blood, and the story of the fight, and all the strewn trash that clutters a field of battle. There were no bodies. The soldiers had withdrawn early enough so that the Comanche survivors had been able to return for their dead, and be gone, before the snow stopped.

Mart and Amos rode slowly across the scene of massacre. Nothing meaningful to their purpose was left in the burnt-out remains of the lodges. They could make out that the cavalry had ridden off down the Canadian, and that was about all.

"We don't know yet," Mart said.

"No," Amos agreed. He spoke without expression, allowing himself neither discouragement nor hope. "But we know where the answer is to be found."

It was not too far away. They came upon the bivouacked cavalry a scant eight miles below.

## 20

AYLIGHT STILL held as Mart and Amos approached the cavalry camp, but it was getting dark by the time they were all the way in. The troopers on duty were red-eyed, but with a harsh edge on their manners, after the night they had spent. An outlying vedette passed them into a dismounted sentry, who called the corporal of the guard, who delivered them to the sergeant of the guard, who questioned them with more length than point before digging up a second lieutenant who was Officer of the Day. The lieutenant also questioned them, though more briefly. He left them standing outside a supply tent for some time, while he explained them to a Major Kinsman, Adjutant.

The major stuck a shaggy head out between the tent flaps, looked them over with the blank stare of fatigue, and spat tobacco juice into the snow.

"My name," Amos began again, patiently, "is——"

"Huntin' captives, huh?" The shaggy head was followed into the open by a huge frame in a tightly buttoned uniform. "Let's see if we got any you know." Major Kinsman led the way, not to another tent, but to the wagon park. They followed him as he climbed into the wagonbed of a covered ambulance.

Under a wagon sheet, which the adjutant drew back, several bodies lay straight and neatly aligned, ice-rigid in the cold. In the thickening dark inside the ambulance, Mart could see little more than that they were there, and that one or two seemed to be children.

"Have a light here in a minute," Major Kinsman said. "Orderly's filling a lantern."

Mart Pauley could hear Amos' heavy breathing, but not his own; he did not seem able to breathe in here at all. A dreadful conviction came over him, increasing as they waited, that they had come to the end of their search. It seemed a long time before a lighted lantern was thrust inside.

The bodies were those of two women and two little boys. The older of the women was in rags, but the younger and smaller one wore clean clothes that had certainly belonged to her, and shoes that were scuffed but not much worn. She appeared to have been about twenty, and was quite beautiful in a carved-snow sort of way. The little boys were perhaps three and seven.

"Both women shot in the back of the head," Major Kinsman said, objectively. "Flash-burn range. Light charge of powder, as you see. The little boys got their skulls cracked. We think this woman here is one taken from a Santa Fe stagecoach not many days back. . . . Know any of them?"

"Never saw them before," Amos said.

Major Kinsman looked at Mart for a separate reply, and Mart shook his head.

They went back to the supply tent, and the adjutant took them inside. The commanding officer was there, sorting through a great mass of loot with the aid of two sergeants and a company clerk. The adjutant identified his superior as Colonel Russell M. Hannon. They had heard of him, but never seen him before; he hadn't been out here very long. Just now he looked tired, but in high spirits.

"Too bad there wasn't more of 'em," Colonel Hannon said. "That's the only disappointing thing. We were following the river, not their trail. Wichita scouts brought word there must be a million of 'em. What with the snow, and the night march, an immediate attack was the only course permissible."

He said his troops had killed thirty-eight hostiles, with the loss of two men. Comanches, at that. A ratio of nineteen to one, as compared to Colonel Custer's ratio of fourteen to one against Black Kettle at the Battle of the Washita. "Not a bad little victory. Not bad at all."

Mart saw Amos stir, and worried for a moment. But Amos held his tongue.

"Four hundred ninety-two ponies," said Hannon. "Had to shoot 'em, of course. Wild as antelope—no way to hold onto them. Four captives recovered. Unfortunately, the hostiles murdered them, as we developed the village. Now, if some of this junk will only show *what* Comanches we defeated, we'll be in fair shape to write a report. Those Wichita scouts know nothing whatever about anything; most ignorant savages on earth. However——"

"What you had there," said Amos wearily, "was Chief

Bluebonnet, with what's left of the Wolf Brothers, along with a few Nawyecky. Or maybe you call 'em Noconas."

"Get this down," the colonel told the clerk.

It was going to take a long time to find out just who had fought and died at the riverbend—and who had got away into the night and the snow, and so still lived, somewhere upon the winter plain. Even allowing for the great number of dead and dying the Comanches had carried away uncounted, somewhere between a third and a half of Bluebonnet's people must have escaped.

They were glad to help sort through the wagonload of stuff hastily snatched up in the gloom of the dawn before the lodges were set on fire. Some of the pouches, quivers, and squill breastplates were decorated with symbols Mart or Amos could connect with Indian names; they found insignia belonging to Stone Wolf, Curly Horn, Pacing Bear, and Hears-the-Wind-Talk. The patterns they didn't know they tried to memorize, in hopes of seeing them again someday.

Especially valued by Colonel Hannon, as exonerating his attack in the dark, was certain stuff that had to be the loot from raided homesteads: a worn sewing basket, an embroidered pillow cover, a home-carved wooden spoon. Hard to see what the Comanches would want with a store-bought paper lamp shade, a wooden seat for a chamber pot, or an album of pressed flowers. But if someone recognized these poor lost things someday, they would become evidence connecting the massacred Comanches with particular crimes. One incriminating bit was a mail pouch known to have been carried by a murdered express rider. The contents were only half rifled; some Comanche had been taking his time about opening all the letters—no man would ever know what for.

But the thing Mart found that hit him hard, and started his search all over again, was in a little heap of jewelry—Indian stuff mostly: carved amulets, Mexican and Navajo silver work, sometimes set with turquoise; but with a sprinkling of pathetic imitation things, such as frontiersmen could afford to buy for their women. Only thing of interest, at first sight, seemed to be a severed finger wearing a ring which would not pull off. Mart cynically supposed that any stuff of cash value had stayed with the troopers who collected it.

Then Mart found Debbie's locket.

It was the cheapest kind of a gilt-washed metal heart on a broken chain. Mart himself had given it to Debbie on the Christmas when she was three. It wasn't even a real locket, for it didn't open, and had embarrassed him by making a green spot on her throat every time she wore it. But Debbie had hung on to it. On the back it said "Debbie from M," painfully scratched with the point of his knife.

Both officers showed vigorous disinterest as Mart pressed for the circumstances in which the locket had been found. These were professionals, and recognized the question as of the sort leading to full-dress investigations, and other chancy outcomes, if allowed to develop. But Amos came to Mart's support, and presently they found the answer simply by walking down the mess line with the locket in hand.

The locket had been taken from the body of a very old squaw found in the river along with an ancient buck. No, damn it, the colonel explained, of course they had not meant to kill women and children, and watch your damn tongue. All you could see was a bunch of shapeless figures firing on you—nothing to do but cut them down, and save questions for later. But one of the sergeants remembered how these two bodies had come there. The squaw, recognizable in hindsight as the fatter one, had tried to escape through the river on a pony, and got sabered down. The old man had rushed in trying to save the squaw, and got sabered in turn. Nothing was in hand to tell who these people were.

Colonel Hannon saw to it that the locket was properly tagged and returned to the collection as evidence of a solved child stealing. Restitution would be made to the heirs, upon proper application to the Department, with proof of loss.

"She was there," Mart said to Amos. "She was there in that camp. She's gone with them that got away."

Amos did not comment. They had to follow and find the survivors—perhaps close at hand, if they were lucky; otherwise by tracing them to whatever far places they might scatter. This time neither one of them said "Tomorrow."

## 21

THEY HAD been winter-driven that first time they went home, all but out of horseflesh, and everything else besides. But after the "Battle" of Deadhorse Bend they went home only because all leads very soon staled and petered out in the part of the country where they were. Otherwise, they probably would have stayed out and kept on. They had lived on the wild land so long that they needed nothing, not even money, that they did not know how to scratch out of it. It never occurred to them that their search was stretching out into a great extraordinary feat of endurance; an epic of hope without faith, of fortitude without reward, of stubbornness past all limits of reason. They simply kept on, doing the next thing, because they always had one more place to go, following out one more forlorn-hope try.

And they had one more idea now. It had been spelled out for them in the loot Colonel Hannon's troopers had picked up in the wreckage of Bluebonnet's destroyed village. Clear and plain, once you thought of it, though it had taken them weeks of thinking back over the whole thing before they recognized it. Amos, at least, believed that this time they could not fail. They would find Debbie now—if only she still lived.

Their new plan would carry them far into the southwest, into country hundreds of miles from any they had ever worked before. And so long as they had to go south, home was not too far out of the way. Home? What was that? Well, it was the place they used to live; where the Mathisons still lived—so far as they knew—and kept an eye on the cattle that now belonged to Debbie. Mart would always think of that stretch of country as home, though nothing of his own was there, nor anybody waiting for him.

As they rode, a sad, dark thing began to force itself upon their attention. When they came to the country where the farthest-west fringe of ranches had been, the ranches were no longer there. Often only a ghostly chimney stood, solitary upon the endless prairie, where once had been a warm and friendly place with people living in it. Then they would remember the time they had stopped by, and things they had eaten there, and the little jokes the people had made. If you hunted around in the brush that ran wild over all, you could usually find the graves. The remembered people were still there, under the barren ground.

More often you had to remember landmarks to locate where a place had been at all. Generally your horse stumbled over an old footing or something before you saw the flat place where the little house had been. Sometimes you found graves here, too, but more usually the people had simply pulled their house down and hauled the lumber away, retreating from a place the Peace Policy had let become too deadly, coming on top of the war. You got the impression that Texas had seen its high tide, becoming little again as its frontier thinned away. Sundown seemed to have come for the high hopes of the Lone Star Republic to which Union had brought only war, weakening blood losses, and the perhaps inevitable neglect of a defeated people.

On the morning of the last day, with Mathison's layout only twenty-odd miles away, they came upon one more crumbling chimney, lonely beside a little stream. Mart's eyes rested upon it contemplatively across the brush at five hundred yards without recognizing it. He was thinking what a dreadful thing it would be if they came to the Mathisons, and found no more than this left of the place, or the people. Then he saw Amos looking at him strangely, and he knew what he was looking at. Surprising that he had not known it, even though he had not been here in a long time. The chimney marked the site of the old Pauley homestead; the place where he had been born. Here the people who had brought him into the world had loved him, and cared for him; here they had built their hopes, and here they had died. How swiftly fade the dead from people's minds, if he could look at this place and not even know it! He turned his horse and rode toward it, Amos following without question.

He had no memory of his own of how this homestead had looked, and no faintest images of his people's faces. He had been taken over this ground, and had all explained to him when he was about eight years old, but no one had ever been willing to talk to him about it, else. And now, except for the chimney, he couldn't locate where anything had been at all. The snow had gone off, but the ground was frozen hard, so

that their heels rang metallically upon it as they dismounted
to walk around. The little stream ran all year, and it had a fast
ripple in it that never froze, where it passed this place; so that
the water seemed to talk forever to the dead. This creek was
called the Beanblossom; Mart knew that much. And that was
about all.

Amos saw his bewilderment. "Your old m— your father wag-
oned the Santa Fe Trail a couple of times," he said, "before he
settled down. Them Santa Fe traders, if any amongst 'em died,
they buried 'em ahead in the trail; so every dang ox in the train
tromped over the graves. Didn't want the Indians to catch on
they were doing poorly. Or maybe dig 'em up. So your father
was against markers on graves. Out here, anyways. Knowing
that, and after some argument, we never set none up."

Mart had supposed he knew where the graves were anyway. They had been plainly visible when he had been shown,
but now neither mound nor depression showed where they
were. The brush had advanced, and under the brush the wind
and the rain of the years had filled and packed and planed and
sanded the sterile earth until no trace showed anywhere of anything having crumbled to dust beneath.

Amos picked a twig and chewed it as he waded into the
brush, taking cross-sightings here and there, trying to remember. "Right here," he said finally. "This is where your mother
lies." He scraped a line with the toe of his boot, the frozen
ground barely taking the mark. "Here's the foot of the grave."
He stepped aside, and walked around an undefined space, and
made another mark. "And here's the head, here."

A great gawky bunch of chaparral grew in the middle of
what must be the side line of the grave. Mart stood staring
at the bit of earth, in no way distinguishable from any other
part of the prairie surface. He was trying to remember, or to
imagine, the woman whose dust was there. Amos seemed to
understand that, too.

"Your mother was a beautiful girl," he said. Mart felt
ashamed as he shoved out of his mind the thought that whatever she looked like, Amos would have said that same thing of
the dead. "Real thin," Amos said, mouthing his twig, "but real
pretty just the same. Brown eyes, almost what you'd call black.
But her hair. Red-brown, and a lot of it. With a shine in it, like

a gold kind of red, when the light struck through it right. I never seen no prettier hair."

He was silent a few moments, as if to let Mart think for a decent interval about the mother he did not remember. Then Amos got restless, and measured off a long step to the side. "And this here's Ethan—your father," he said. "You favor him, right smart. He had a black-Welsh streak; marked his whole side of the family. It's from him you got your black look and them mighty-near crockery eyes. He was just as dark, with the same light eyes."

Amos turned a little, and chewed the twig, but didn't bother to pace off the locations of the others. "Alongside lies my brother—mine and Henry's brother. The William you've heard tell of so many, many times. I don't know why, but in the family, we never once did call him Bill. . . . William was the best of us. The best by far. Good looking as Henry, and strong as me. And the brains of the family—there they lie, right there. He could been governor, or anything. Except he was less than your age—just eighteen. . . ." Mart didn't let himself question the description, even in his mind. You could assume that the first killed in a family of boys was the one who would have been great. It was what they told you always.

"Beyond, the three more—next to William lies Cash Dennison, a young rider, helping out Ethan; then them two bullwhackers that lived out the wagon-train killing, and made it to here. One's name was Caruthers, from a letter in his pocket; I forget the other. Some blamed them for the whole thing—thought the Comanches come down on this place a-chasing them two. But I never thought that. Seems more like the Comanch' was coming here; and it was the wagon train they fell on by accident on their way."

"You got any notion—does anybody know—did they get many of the Comanches? Here, the night of this thing?"

Amos shook his head. "A summer storm come up. A regular cloudburst—you don't see the like twice in twenty year. It washed out the varmints' trail. And naturally they carried off their dead—such as there was. Nobody knows how many. Maybe none."

Waste, thought Mart. Useless, senseless, heartbreaking waste. All these good, fine, happy lives just thrown away. . . .

Once more Amos seemed to answer his thought. "Mart, I don't know as I ever said this to anybody. But it's been a long time; and I'll tell you now what I think. My family's gone now, too—unless and until we find our one last little girl. But we lived free of harm, and the Mathisons too, for full eighteen years before they struck our bunch again. You want to know what I think why? I think your people here bought that time for us. They paid for it with their lives."

"Wha-at?" No matter what losses his people had inflicted on the raiders, Comanches would never be stopped by that. They would come back to even the score, and thus the tragic border war went on forever. But that wasn't what Amos meant.

"I think this was a revenge raid," Amos said. "It was right here the Rangers come through, trailing old Iron Shirt's band. They cut that bunch down from the strongest there was to something trifling, and killed Iron Shirt himself. So the trail the Rangers followed that time had a black history for Comanches. They come down it just once in revenge for their dead—and Ethan's little place was the farthest out on this trail. And it was a whole Indian generation before they come again. That's why I say—your people bought them years the rest of us lived in peace. . . ."

Mart said, "It's been a long time. Do you think my father would mind now if I come and put markers on them graves? Would that be a foolishness after all this while?"

Amos chewed, eating his twig. "I don't believe he'd mind. Not now. Even could he know. I think it would be a right nice thing to do. I'll help you soon's we have a mite of time." He turned toward the horses, but Mart wanted to know one thing more that no one had ever told him.

"I don't suppose——" he said—"well, maybe you might know. Could you show me where I was when Pa found me in the brush?"

"Your Pa? When?"

"I mean Henry. He always stood in place of my own. I heard tell he found me, and picked me up. . . ."

Amos looked all around, and walked into the brush, chewing slowly, and taking sights again. "Here," he said at last. "I'm sure now. Right—exactly—here." The frost in the earth crackled as he ground a heel into the spot he meant. "Of course, then, the brush was cleared back. To almost this far from the house." He stood around a moment to see if Mart wanted to ask anything more, then walked off out of the brush toward the horses.

This place, this very spot he stood on, Mart thought, was where he once awoke alone in such terror as locked his throat, seemingly; they had told him he made no sound. Queer to stand here, in this very spot where he had so nearly perished before he even got started; queer, because he felt nothing. It was the same as when he had stood looking at the graves, knowing that what was there should have meant so much, yet had no meaning for him at all. He couldn't see anything from here that looked familiar, or reminded him of anything.

Of course, that night of the massacre, he hadn't been standing up better than six feet tall in his boots. He had been down in the roots of the scrub, not much bigger than his own foot was now. On an impulse, Mart lay down in the tangle, pressing his cheek against the ground, to bring his eyes close to the roots.

A bitter chill crept along the whole length of his body. The frozen ground seemed to drain the heat from his blood, and the blood from his heart itself. Perhaps it was that, and knowing where he was, that accounted for what happened next. Or maybe scars, almost as old as he was, were still in existence down at the bottom of his mind, long buried under everything that had happened in between. The sky seemed to darken, while a ringing, buzzing sound came into his ears, and when the sky was completely black it began to redden with a bloody glow. His stomach dropped from under his heart, and a horrible fear filled him—the fear of a small helpless child, abandoned and alone in the night. He tried to spring up and out of that, and he could not move; he lay there rigid, seemingly frozen to the ground. Behind the ringing in his ears began to rise the unearthly yammer of the terror-dream—not heard, not even remembered, but coming to him like an awareness of something happening in some unknown dimension not of the living world.

He fought it grimly, and slowly got hold of himself; his eyes cleared, and the unearthly voices died, until he heard only the hammering of his heart. He saw, close to his eyes, the stems of the chaparral; and he was able to move again, stiffly, with his muscles shaking. He turned his head, getting a look at the actual world around him again. Then, through a rift in the brush that showed the creek bank, he saw the death tree.

Its base was almost on a level with his eyes, at perhaps a hundred feet; and for one brief moment it seemed to swell and tower, writhing its corpse-withered arms. His eyes stayed fixed upon it as he slowly got up and walked toward it without volition, as if it were the only thing possible to do. The thing shrunk as he approached it, no longer towering over him twice his size as it had seemed to do wherever he had seen it before. Finally he stood within arm's length; and now it was only a piece of weather-silvered wood in a tormented shape, a foot and a half shorter than himself.

An elongated knot at the top no longer looked like a distorted head, but only a symbol representing the hideous thing he had imagined there. He lashed out and struck it, hard, with the heel of his right hand. The long-rotted roots broke beneath the surface of the soil; and a twisted old stump tottered, splashed in the creek, and went spinning away.

Mart shuddered, shaking himself back together; and he spoke aloud. "I'll be a son-of-a-bitch," he said; and rejoined Amos. If he still looked shaken up, Amos pretended not to notice as they mounted up.

# 22

MARTIN PAULEY was taken by another fit of shyness as they approached the Mathison ranch. He was a plainsman now, a good hunter, and a first-class Indian scout. But the saddle in which he lived had polished nothing about him but the seat of his leather pants.

"I tried to leave you back," Amos reminded him. "A couple of burr-matted, sore-backed critters we be. You got a lingo on you like a Caddo whiskey runner. You know that, don't you?"

Mart said he knew it.

"Our people never did have much shine," Amos said. "Salt of the earth, mind you; no better anywhere. But no book learning, like is born right into them Mathisons. To us, grammar is nothing but grampaw's wife."

Mart remembered the times Laurie had corrected his speech, and knew he didn't fit with civilized people. Not even as well as before, when he was merely a failure at it. But someway he was finally herded into the Mathison kitchen.

Laurie ran to him and took both his hands. "Where on earth have you been?"

"We been north," he answered her literally. "Looking around among the Kiowas."

"Why up there?"

"Well . . ." he answered lamely, "she might have been up there."

She said wonderingly, "Martie, do you realize how long you've been on this search? This is the third winter you've been out."

He hadn't thought of the time in terms of years. It had piled up in little pieces—always just one more place to go that would take just a few weeks more. He made a labored calculation, and decided Laurie was twenty-one. That explained why she seemed so lighted up; probably looked the best she ever would in her life. She was at an age when most girls light up, if they're going to; Mexicans and Indians earlier. A look at their mothers, or their older sisters, reminded you of what you knew for certain: All that bright glow would soon go out again. But you couldn't ever make yourself believe it.

Laurie made him follow her around, dealing out facts and figures about Kiowas, while she helped her mother get dinner. He didn't believe she cared a hoot about Kiowas, but he was glad for the chance to have a look at her.

There was this Indian called Scar, he explained to her. Seemed he actually had one on his face. They kept hearing that Scar had taken a little white girl captive. He showed her how the Indians described the scar, tracing a finger in a sweeping curve from hairline to jaw. A well-marked man. Only they couldn't find him. They couldn't even find any reliable person —no trader, soldier, or black hat—who had ever seen an Indian with such a scar. Then Mart had happened to think that the sign describing the scar was a whole lot like the Plains-Indian sign for sheep. The Kiowas had a warrior society called the Sheep, and he got to wondering if all those rumors were hitting around the fact that the Kiowa Sheep Society had Debbie. So they went to see. . . .

"A pure waste of time, and nobody to blame but me. It was me thought of it."

"It was I," she corrected him.

"You?" he fumbled it; then caught it on the bounce. "No, I meant—the blame was on I."

"There's going to be a barn party," she told him. "Mose Harper built a barn."

"At his age?"

"The State of Texas paid for it, mainly; they're going to put a Ranger stopover in part of it, and store their feed there next year—or the year after, when they get around to it. But the party is right away. I bet you knew!"

"No, I didn't."

"Bet you did. Only reason you came home."

He thought it over, and guessed he would give her some real comical answer later; soon as he thought of one.

After supper Aaron Mathison and Amos Edwards got out the herd books and ledgers, as upon their visit before. Aaron's head bent low, eyes close to the pages, so that Mart noticed again the old man's failing sight, much worse than it had been the last time.

And now Mart made his next mistake, rounding out his tally for the day. He set up camp, all uninvited, on the settle flanking the stove where he had sat with Laurie before; and here, while Laurie finished picking up the supper things, he waited hopefully for her to come and sit beside him. He had a notion that all the time he had been gone would melt away, once they sat there again.

But she didn't come and sit there. Had to get her beauty sleep, she said. Great long drive tomorrow; probably no sleep at all tomorrow night, what with the long drive home.

"Harper's is seven miles," Mart said. "Scarcely a real good spit."

"Don't be coarse." She said good night, respectfully to Amos and briskly to Mart, and went off across the dog-trot into that unknown world in the other section of the house, which he had never entered.

Mart wandered to the other end of the room, intending to join Amos and Aaron Mathison. But "G'night" Amos said to him. And Mathison gravely stood up to shake hands.

"It comes to me," Mart said, "I've been a long time away."

"And if we stayed for the damn barn burning," Amos said, "we'd be a long time off the road." Amos believed he knew where he was going now. All that great jackstraw pile of Indian nonsense was straightening itself in his mind. He could add up the hundreds of lies and half truths they had ridden so far to gather, and make them come out to a certain answer at last.

"You be stubborn men," Aaron Mathison said, "both of you."

Mart tried to share Amos' fire of conviction, but he could not. "Man has to live some place," he said, and slung on his coat, for they were to sleep in the bunkhouse this time. The coat was a long-skirted bearskin, slit high for the saddle; it was big enough to keep his horse warm, and smelled like a hog. "The prairie's all I know any more, I guess." He went out through the cold dark to his bed.

# 23

Mart was up long before daylight. Some internal clock-work always broke him out early nowadays. In summer the first dawn might be coming on, but in the short days he woke in the dark at exactly half-past four. He started a fire in the bunkhouse stove, and set coffee on. Then he went out to the breaking corral into which they had thrown the horses and mules Amos had picked for the next leg of their perpetual trip.

He grained them all, then went back to the bunkhouse. He set the coffee off the fire, and studied Amos for signs of arisal. He saw none, so he went out to the corral again. They carried three mules now, on account of the trading, and a spare saddle horse, in case one should pull up lame when they were in a hurry. Mart picked himself a stocky buckskin, with zebra stripes on his cannons and one down his back. He snubbed down, saddled, and bucked out this horse with his bearskin coat on; all horses took outrage at this coat, and had to be broke to it fresh every day for a while, until they got used to it.

He laid aside the bearskin to top off the great heavy stock horse he supposed Amos would ride. Its pitch was straight, and easy to sit, but had such a shock to it that his nose bled a little. Finally he got the pack saddles on the mules, and left them standing hump-backed in a sull. By this time the gray bitter dawn was on the prairie, but the white vapor from the lungs of the animals was the only sign of life around the place as yet.

Amos was sitting up on the edge of his bunk in his long-handled underwear, peering at the world through bleary lids and scratching himself.

"Well," Mart said, "we're saddled."

"Huh?"

"I say I uncorked the ponies, and slung the mule forks on."

"What did you do that for?"

"Because it's morning, I suppose—why the hell did you think? I don't see no smoke from the kitchen. You want I should stir up a snack?"

"We're held up," Amos said. "We got to go to that roof raising."

"Thought you said we had to flog on. Jesus, will you make up your mind?"

"I just done so. By God, will you clean out your ears?"

"Oh, hell," Mart said, and went out to unsaddle.

THE BARN party was just a rough-and-ready gathering of frontier cattle people, such as Mart knew perfectly well. He knew exactly how these people spent every hour of their lives, and he could do everything they knew how to do better than most of them. What bothered him was to see such a raft of them in one place. They filled the big new barn when they all got there. Where had these dozens of scrubbed-looking girls come from, in all shapes and sizes? All this swarming of strangers gave Mart an uncomfortable feeling that the country had filled up solid while he was gone, leaving no room for him here.

Mart had got stuck with the job of bringing along the pack mules, for Amos wanted to get started directly from Harper's without going back. In consequence, Mart hadn't seen any of the Mathison family after they got dressed up until they appeared at the party. Aaron Mathison was patriarchal in high collar and black suit, across his vest the massive gold chain indispensable to men of substance; and Mrs. Mathison was a proper counterpart in a high-necked black dress that rustled when she so much as turned her eyes. They joined a row of other old-timers, a sort of windbreak of respectability along the wall, suggestive of mysteriously inherited book learning and deals with distant banks.

But it was Laurie who took him by shock, and for whom he was unprepared. She had made her own dress, of no prouder material than starched gingham, but it was full-skirted and tight at the waist, and left her shoulders bare, what time she wasn't shawled up against the cold. He would have been better off if he could have seen this rig at the house, and had time to get used to it. He had never seen her bare shoulders before, nor given thought to how white they must naturally be; and now he had trouble keeping his eyes off them. A wicked gleam showed in her eyes as she caught him staring.

"Honestly, Mart—you act as though you came from so far back in the hills the sun must *never* shine!"

"Listen here," he said, judging it was time to take her down a peg. "When I first rode with you, you was about so high, and round as a punkin. And you wore all-overs made of flour sack. I know because I seen a yearling calf stack you wrong end up in a doodle of wild hay, and you said 'Steamboat Mills' right across the bottom."

She giggled. "How do you know I still don't?" she asked him. But her eyes were searching the crowd for somebody else.

He drew off, to remuster according to plan; and when next he tried to go near her, she was surrounded. The whole place was curdled up with lashings of objectionable young jaybirds he had never seen before in his life, and Laurie had rings in the noses of them all. Some of them wore borrowed-looking store clothes, generally either too long in the sleeves or fixing to split out someplace. But more had come in their saddle outfits, like Mart, with clean handkerchiefs on their necks and their shirts washed out by way of celebration. He took them to be common saddle pounders, mostly. But he imagined a knowingness behind their eyes, as if they were all onto something he did not suspect. Maybe they knew what they were doing here—which was more than he could say for himself. Tobe and Abner knew everybody and mixed everywhere, leaving Mart on his own. Brad had been his best friend, but these younger brothers seemed of a different generation altogether; he had nothing in common with them any more.

Some of the boys kept sliding out the back way to the horse lines, and Mart knew jugs were cached out there. He had taken very few drinks in his life, but this seemed a good time for one. He started to follow a group who spoke owlishly of "seeing to the blankets on the team," but Amos cut him off at the door.

"Huh uh. Not this time." Amos had not had a drop, which was odd in the time and place. Mart knew he could punish a jug until its friends cried out in pain, once he started.

"What's the matter now?"

"I got special reasons."

"Something going to bust?"

"Don't know yet. I'm waiting for something."

That was all he would say. Mart went off and holed up in a corner with old Mose Harper, who asked him questions about "present day" Indians, and listened respectfully to his answers —or the first few words of them, anyway. Mose got the bit in his teeth in less than half a minute, and went into the way things used to be, in full detail. Mart let his eyes wander past Mose to follow Laurie, flushed and whirling merrily, all over the place. The country-dance figures kept people changing partners, and Laurie always had a few quick words for each new one, making him laugh, usually, before they were separated again. Mart wondered what on earth she ever found to say.

"In my day," Mose was telling Mart, "when them Tonkawas killed an enemy, they just ate the heart and liver. Either raw or fussy prepared—didn't make no difference. What they wanted was his medicine. Only they never ate a white man's vitals; feared our medicine wouldn't mix with theirs, seemingly, though they respected our weapons. . . ."

Mart more than half expected that Laurie would come around and try to pull him into a dance, and he was determined he wasn't going to let her do it. He was making up speeches to fend her off with, while he pretended to listen to Mose.

"Nowadays," Mose explained, "they've took to eating the whole corpse, as a food. 'Tain't a ceremony, any more, so much as a saving of meat. But they still won't eat a white man. 'Tain't traditional."

Laurie never did come looking for Mart. She made a face at him once, as she happened to whirl close by, and that was all. Holding back became tiresome pretty fast, with no one to insist on anything different. He got into the dance, picking whatever girls caught his eye, regardless of whom they thought they belonged to. He was perversely half hoping for the fight you can sometimes get into that way, but none started.

He had been afraid of the dancing itself, but actually there wasn't anything to it. These people didn't party often enough to learn any very complicated dances. Just simple reels, and stuff like that. Sashay forward, sashay back, swing your lady, drop her slack. You swing mine, and I'll swing yours, and back to your own, and everybody swing. At these family parties, out here on civilization's brittle edge, they didn't even swing their girls by the waist—a dissolute practice to be seen mainly in saloons. Man grabbed his lady by the arms, and they kind of skittered around each other, any way they could. He got hold of Laurie only about once every two hours, but there were plenty of others. The fiddles and the banjos whanged out a rhythm that shook the barn, and the time flew by, romping and stomping.

Through all this Amos stood by, withdrawn into the background and into himself. Sometimes men he had known came to shake hands with him, greeting him with a heartiness Amos did not return. They were full of the questions to be expected of them, but the answers they got were as short as they could civilly be, and conveyed nothing. No conversation was allowed to develop. Amos remained apart, neither alone nor with anybody. Small use speculating on what he might be waiting for. Mart presently forgot him.

It was long after midnight, though nobody but the nodding old folks along the wall seemed to have noticed it, when the Rangers came in. There were three of them, and they made their arrival inconspicuous. They wore no uniforms—the Rangers had none—and their badges were in their pockets. Nobody was turned nervous, and nobody made a fuss over them, either. Rangers were a good thing, and there ought to be more of them. Sometimes you needed a company of them badly. Didn't need any just now. So long as no robbery or bloody murder was in immediate view, Rangers ranked as people. And that was it.

That, and one thing more: Everyone knew at once that they were there. Within less than a minute, people who had never seen any of these three before knew that Rangers had come in, and which men they were. Mart Pauley heard of them from a girl he swung but once, and had them pointed out to him by the next girl to whom he was handed on. "Who? *Him?*" The youngest of the three Rangers was Charlie MacCorry.

"He enlisted last year sometime."

As they finished the set, Mart was trying to make up his mind if he should go shake hands with Charlie MacCorry, or leave him be. He never had liked him much. Too much flash, too much swagger, too much to say. But now he saw something else. Amos and one of the older Rangers had walked toward each other on sight. They had drawn off, and were talking secretly and intently, apart from anyone else. Whatever Amos had waited for was here. Mart went over to them.

"This here is Sol Clinton," Amos told Mart. "Lieutenant in the Rangers. I side-rode him once. But that was long ago. I don't know if he remembers."

Sol Clinton looked Mart over without to-do, or any move to shake hands. This Ranger appeared to be in his forties, but he was so heavily weathered that he perhaps looked older than he was. He had a drooping sandy mustache and deep grin lines that seemed to have been carved there, for he certainly wasn't smiling.

"I'm that found boy the Edwards family raised," Mart explained, "name of——"

"Know all about you," Sol Clinton said. His stare lay on Mart with a sort of tired candor. "You look something like a breed," he decided.

"And you," Mart answered, "look something like you don't know what you're talking about."

"Stop that," Amos snapped.

"He's full of snakehead," Mart stood his ground. "I can smell it on him."

"Why, sure," the Ranger conceded mildly. "I've had a snort or two. This is a dance, isn't it? Man can't haul off and dance in cold blood."

"Mind your manners anyway," Amos advised Mart.

"That's all right," Sol said. "You know a trader calls himself Jerem Futterman up the Salt Fork of the Brazos?"

Mart looked at Amos, and Amos answered him. "He knows him, and he knows he's dead."

"Might let him answer for himself, Amos."

"Sol was speaking of us riding to Austin with him," Amos went on stolidly, "to talk it over."

Mart said sharply, "We got no time for——"

"I explained him that," Amos said. "Will you get this through your damn head? This is an invite to a neck-tie party! Now stop butting in."

"Not quite that bad," Clinton said. "Not yet. We hope. No great hurry, either, right this minute. Best of our witnesses broke loose on us; got to catch him again before we put anything together. Most likely, all we'll want of you fellers is to pad out a good long report. Show zeal, you know." He dropped into a weary drawl. "Show we're unrestin'. Get our pay raised—like hell."

"I guarantee Mart Pauley will come back to answer," Amos said, "same as me."

"I guess the same bond will stretch to cover you both," Sol Clinton said. "I'll scratch down a few lines for you to sign."

"It's a wonderful thing to be a former Ranger," Amos said. "It's the way everybody trusts you—that's what gets to a man."

"Especially if you're also a man of property," Clinton agreed in that same mild way. "Amos put up a thousand head of cattle," he explained to Mart, "that says you and him will come on into Austin, soon as you finish this next one trip."

"Aaron Mathison told me about this," Amos said. "I couldn't believe he had it right. I got to believe it now."

"They know about this, then. They knew it all the time. . . ."

"I stayed on to make sure. There's nothing more to wait on now. Go and tell the Mathisons we're leaving."

"Stay on awhile," Sol Clinton suggested. "Have a good time if you want."

Martin Pauley said, "No, thanks," as he turned away.

He went looking for Laurie first. She wasn't dancing, or anywhere in the barn. He went out to the barbecue pit, where some people were still poking around what was left of a steer, but she wasn't there. He wandered down the horse line, where the saddle stock was tied along the length of a hundred-foot rope. He knew some of the women had gone over to Mose Harper's house; a passel of young children had been bedded down over there, for one thing. He had about decided to go butt in there when he found her.

A couple stood in the shadows of a feed shelter. The man was Charlie MacCorry; and the girl in his arms was Laurie Mathison, as Mart somehow knew without needing to look.

Martin Pauley just stood there staring at them, his head down a little bit, like some witless cow-critter half knocked in the head. He stood there as long as they did. Charlie Mac-Corry finally let the girl go, slowly, and turned.

"Just what the hell do *you* want?"

A weakness came into Mart's belly muscles, and then a

knotting up; and he began to laugh, foolishly, sagging against the feed rack. He never did know what he was laughing at.

Charlie blew up. "Now you look here!" He grabbed Mart by the front of the jacket, straightened him up, and slapped his face fit to break his neck. Mart lashed out by reflex, and Charlie MacCorry was flat on his back in the same tenth of a second.

He was up on the bounce, and they went at it. They were at it for some time.

They had no prize ring out in that country; fights were many but unrehearsed. These men were leathery and hard to hurt, but their knuckle brawls were fought by instinct, without the skill they showed with other weapons. Mart Pauley never ducked, blocked, nor gave ground; he came straight in, very fast at first, later more slowly, plodding and following. He swung workmanlike, slugging blows, one hand and then the other, putting his back into it. Charlie MacCorry fought standing straight up, circling and sidestepping, watching his chances. He threw long-armed, lacing blows, mostly to the face. Gradually, over a period of time, he beat Mart's head off.

They never knew when Laurie left them. A close circle of men packed in around them, shouting advice, roaring when either one was staggered. Amos Edwards was there, and both of MacCorry's fellow Rangers. These three stood watching critically but impassively in the inner circle, the only silent members of the crowd. Neither fighter noticed them, or heard the yelling. Somewhere along the way Mart took a slam on the side of the face with his mouth open, and the inside of his cheek opened on his own teeth. Daylight later showed frozen splotches of bright red over a surprising area, as if a shoat had been slaughtered. Mart kept on moving in, one eye puffed shut and the other closing; and suddenly this thing was over.

The blow that ended it was no different than a hundred others, except in its luck. Mart had no idea which hand had landed, let alone how he did it. Charlie MacCorry went down without notice, as if all strings were cut at once. He fell forward on his face, and every muscle was slack as they turned him over. For a couple of moments Mart stood looking down at him with a stupid surprise, wondering what had happened.

He turned away, and found himself facing Sol Clinton. He spit blood, and said, "You next?"

The Ranger stared at him. "Who? Me? What for?" He stood aside.

A dawn as cheerless as a drunkard's awakening was making a line of gray on the eastern horizon. Mart walked to their mules after passing them once and having to turn back. Any number of hands helped him, and took over from him, as he went about feeding their animals, so he took time to take the handkerchief from his neck, and stuff it into his cheek. The sweat with which it was soaked stung the big cut inside his cheek, but his mouth stopped filling up.

Charlie MacCorry came to him. "You all right?" His nose showed a bright blaze where it had hit the frozen ground as he fell.

"I'm ready to go on with it if you are."

"Well—all right—if you say. Just tell me one thing. What was you laughing at?"

"Charlie, I'll be damned if I know."

Watching him narrowly, Charlie said, "You don't?"

"Don't rightly recall what we was fighting about, when it comes to that."

"Thought maybe you figured I cross-branded your girl."

"I got no girl. Never had."

Charlie moved closer, but his hands were in his pockets. He looked at the ground, and at the cold streak of light in the east, before he looked at Mart. "I'd be a fool not to take your word," he decided. Charlie stuck out his hand, then drew it back, for it was swollen to double size around broken bones. He offered his left hand instead. "God damn, you got a hard head."

"Need one, slow as I move." He gave Charlie's left hand the least possible shake, and pulled back.

"You don't move slow," Charlie said. "See you in Austin." He walked away.

Amos came along. "Stock's ready."

"Good." Mart tightened his cinch, and they rode. Neither had anything to say. As the sun came up, Amos began to sing to himself. It was an old song from the Mexican War, though scarcely recognizable as Amos sang it. A good many cowboys had replaced forgotten words and turns of tune with whatever came into their heads before the song got to Amos.

> Green grow the rushes, oh,
>     Green grow the rushes, oh,
> Only thing I ever want to know
>     Is where is the girl I left behind. . . .

Well, it had been sung a good many thousand times before by men who hadn't left anything behind, because they had nothing to leave.

## 25

T<sup>HEY</sup> ANGLED southwest at a good swinging pace, their animals fresh and well grained. At Fort Phantom Hill they
found the garrison greatly strengthened and full of aggressive
confidence for a change. This was surprising enough, but at
Fort Concho they saw troop after troop of newly mustered
cavalry; and were told that Fort Richardson was swarming
with a concentration of much greater strength. Southwest
Texas was going to have a real striking force at last. They had
prayed for this for a long time, and they welcomed it no less
because of a sardonic bitterness in it for those to whom help
had come too late.

Beyond the Colorado they turned toward the setting sun,
through a country with nothing man-made to be seen in it.
So well were they moving that they outrode the winter in a
couple of weeks. For once, instead of heading into the teeth
of the worst weather they could find, they were riding to meet
the spring. By the time they rounded the southern end of the
Staked Plains the sun blazed hot by day, while yet the dry-
country cold bit very hard at night. The surface of the land
was strewn with flints and black lava float; it grew little besides
creosote bush, chaparral, and bear grass, and the many, many
kinds of cactus. Waterholes were far apart, and you had better
know where they were, once you left the wagon tracks behind.

Beyond Horsehead Crossing they rode northwest and across
the Pecos, skirting the far flank of the Staked Plains—called
Los Llanos Estacados over here. They were reaching for New
Mexico Territory, some hundred and fifty miles above, as a
horse jogs; a vulture could make it shorter, if he would stop
his uncomplimentary circling over the two riders, and line out.
Their time for this distance was much worse than a week, for
half of which they pushed into a wind so thick with dust that
they wore their neckerchiefs up to their eyes.

When finally they crossed the Territory line, they didn't even
know it, being unable to tell Delaware Creek from any other
dry wash unfed by snows. Dead reckoning persuaded them
they must be in New Mexico, but they wouldn't have known

it. Where were the señoritas and cantinas, the guitars and tequila, Amos had talked about? He may have confused this
lately Mexican country he had never seen with the Old Mexico
he knew beyond the lower Rio Grande. Without meaning to,
probably, he had made the Southwest sound like a never-never
country of song and illicit love, with a streak of wicked bloody
murder interestingly hidden just under a surface of ease and
mañana. The territory didn't look like that. Nor like anything
else, either, at the point where they entered it. There wasn't
anything there at all.

But now the wind rested, and the air cleared. The country
recovered its characteristic black and white of hard sun and
sharp shadows. Mart dug Debbie's miniature out of his saddle
bags to see how it had come through the dust. He carried the
little velvet box wrapped in doeskin now, and he hadn't opened
it for a long time. The soft leather had protected it well; the little portrait looked brighter and fresher in the white desert light
than he had ever seen it. The small kitty-cat face looked out
of the frame with a life of its own, bright-eyed, eager, happy
with the young new world. He felt a twinge he had almost
forgotten—she seemed so dear, so precious, and so lost. From
this point on he began to pull free from the backward drag of
his bad days back home. No, not back home; he had no home.
His hopes once more led out down the trail.

For now they were in the land of the Comancheros, toward
which they had been pointed by the loot of Deadhorse Bend.
Here Bluebonnet must have traded for the silverwork and turquoise in the spoils; here surely he would now seek refuge from
the evil that had come upon him in the north.

That name, Comanchero, was a hated one among Texans.
Actually the Comancheros were nothing but some people who
traded with Comanches, much as Mart and Amos themselves
had often done. If you were an American, and traded with Comanches from the United States side, basing upon the forts of
West Texas and Indian Territory, you were a trader. But if you
were a Mexican, basing in Mexico, and made trading contact
with Comanches on the southwest flank of the Staked Plains,
you were not called a trader, but a Comanchero.

During the years of armed disagreement with Mexico,
the Comancheros had given Texans plenty of reasons for

complaint. When thousands of head of Texas horses, mules, and cattle disappeared into the Staked Plains every year, it was the Comancheros who took all that livestock off Indian hands, and spirited it into deep Mexico. And when great numbers of breech-loading carbines appeared in the hands of Comanche raiders, it was the Comancheros who put them there.

Of course, Amos had once traded some split-blocks of sulphur matches and a bottle of Epsom salts (for making water boil magically by passing your hand over it) for some ornaments of pure Mexican gold no Indian ever got by trading. But that was different.

Mart had always heard the Comancheros described as a vicious, slinking, cowardly breed, living like varmints in unbelievable filth. These were the people who now seemed to hold their last great hope of finding Debbie. The great war chiefs of the Staked Plains Comanches, like Bull Bear, Wild Horse, Black Duck, Shaking Hand, and the young Quanah, never came near the Agencies at all. Well armed, always on the fight, they struck deep and vanished. Amos was certain now that these irreconcilables did business only with the Comancheros—and that the Flower had to be with them.

Somewhere there must be Comancheros who knew every one of them well. Somewhere must be one who knew where Debbie was. Or maybe there isn't, Mart sometimes thought. But they're the best bet we got left. We'll find her now. Or never at all.

First they had to find the Comancheros. Find Comancheros? Hell, first you had to find a human being. That wasn't easy in this country they didn't know. Over and over they followed trails which should have forked together, and led some place, but only petered out like the dry rivers into blown sand. There had to be people here someplace, though, and eventually they began to find some. Some small bunches of Apaches, seen at a great distance, were the first, but these shied off. Then finally they found a village.

This was a cluster of two-dozen, mud-and-wattle huts called jacals, around a mud hole and the ruins of a mission, and its name was Esperanza. Here lived some merry, friendly, singing people in possession of almost nothing. They had some little corn patches, and a few sheep, and understood sign language.

How did they keep the Apaches out of the sheep? A spreading of the hands. It was not possible. But the Apaches never took all the sheep. Always left some for seed, so there would be something to steal another year. So all was well, thanks to the goodness of God. Here were some guitars at last, and someone singing someplace at any hour of day or night. Also some warm pulque, which could bring on a sweaty lassitude followed by a headache. No señoritas in evidence, though. Just a lot of fat squawlike women, with big grins and no shoes.

Once they had found one village, the others were much more easily discoverable—never exactly where they were said to be, nor at anything like the distance which was always described either as "Not far" or "Whoo!" But landmarked, so you found them eventually. They made their way to little places called Derecho, Una Vaca, Gallo, San Pascual, San Marco, Plata Negra, and San Philipe. Some of these centered on fortified ranchos, some on churches, others just on waterholes. The two riders learned the provincial Spanish more easily than they had expected; the vocabulary used out here was not very large. And they became fond of these sun-sleepy people who were always singing, always making jokes. They had voluble good manners and an open-handed hospitality. They didn't seem to wash very much, but actually it didn't seem necessary in this dry air. The villages and the people had a sort of friendly, sun-baked smell.

They looked much happier, Mart thought, than Americans ever seem to be. A man built a one-room jacal, or maybe an adobe, if mud was in good supply when he was married. Though he bred a double-dozen children, he never built onto that one room again. As each day warmed up, the master of the house was to be found squatting against the outer wall. All day long he moved around it, following the shade when the day was hot, the sun when the day was cool; and thus painlessly passed his life, untroubled. Mart could envy them, but he couldn't learn from them. Why is it a man can never seem to buckle down and train himself to indolence and stupidity when he can see what sanctuary they offer from toil and pain?

But they found no Comancheros. They had expected a spring burst of fur trading, but spring ran into summer without any sign of anything like that going on. They were in the wrong place for it, obviously. And the real Comanchero rendezvous would be made in the fall at the end of the summer-raiding season. They worked hard to make sure of their Comancheros by the end of the summer—and they didn't learn a thing. The paisanos could retreat into a know-nothing shell that neither cunning nor bribery could break down. A stranger could see their eyes become placidly impenetrable, black and surface-lighted like obsidian; and when he saw that he might as well quit.

Then, at Potrero, they ran into Lije Powers. They remembered him as an old fool; and now he seemed immeasurably older and more foolish than he had been before. But he set them on the right track.

Lije greeted them with whoops and exaggerated grimaces of delight, in the manner of old men who have led rough and lonely lives. He pumped their hands, and stretched eyes and jaws wide in great meaningless guffaws. When that was over, though, they saw that there wasn't so very much of the old man left. His eyes were sunken, his cheeks had fallen in; and his worn clothes hung on a rack of bones.

"You look like holy hell," Amos told him.

"I ain't been too well," Lije admitted. "I been looking for you fellers. I got to talk to you."

"You heard we came out here?"

"Why, sure. Everybody I seen in the last six months knows all about you. Come on in the shade."

Lije took them to a two-by-four cantina without even a sign on it where whiskey was to be had, for a new thing and a wonder.

"I been looking for Debbie Edwards," he told them.

"So have we. We never have quit since we seen you last."

"Me neither," Lije said. He had turned abstemious, sipping his whiskey slowly, as if with care. When it came time to re-fill the glasses, his was always still more than half full, and he wouldn't toss it off, as others did, but just let the glass be filled up. He didn't seem much interested in hearing what they had tried, or where they had been, or even if they had ever found any clues. Just wanted to tell at great length, with all the detail he could get them to stand for, the entire history of his own long search. He droned on and on, while Mart grew restless, then drunk, then sober again. But Amos seemed to want to listen.

"Guess you heard about the reward I put up," Amos said.

"I don't want the money, Amos," Lije said.

"Just been doing this out of the goodness of your heart, huh?"

"No . . . I'll tell you what I want. I want a job. Not a good job, nor one with too much riding. Bull cook, or like that, without no pay, neither, to speak of. Just a bunk, and a little grub, and a chai' by a stove. A place. But one where I don't never get throwed out. Time comes for me to haul off and die up, I want to be let die in that bunk. Not be throwed out for lack of the space I take up, or because a man on the die don't do much work."

There you had it—the end a prairie man could look forward to. Reaching out to accomplish some one great impossible thing at the last—as your only hope of securing just a place to lie down and die. Mart expected to hear Amos say that Lije was welcome to the bunk in any case.

"All right, Lije," Amos said. But he added, "If you find her."

Lije looked pleased; he hadn't expected anything more, nor been sure of this much. "So now lately, I been talking to these here Comancheros," he said.

"*Talking* to 'em?" Amos butted in.

"What's wrong with that? Ain't you been?"

"I ain't even seen one!"

Lije looked at him with disbelief, then with wonder; and finally with pity. "Son, son. In all this time you been in the Territory, I don't believe you've seen one other dang thing else!"

Not that these peons knew much about what they were doing, he admitted. They hired on as trail drivers, or packers, or bullwhackers, when the work was shoved at them. Probably wouldn't want to name their bosses, either, to a stranger who didn't seem to know any of them. You had to find los ricos —the men who ran the long drives down into Old Mexico, too deep for anything ever to be recovered. He named about a dozen of these, and Amos made him go back over some of the names to be sure he would remember them all.

"Old Jaime Rosas—he's the one I'd talk to, was I you." (He pronounced it "Hymie Rosies.") "I swear he knows where Bluebonnet is. And the girl."

"You think she's alive?"

"I figure *he* thinks so. I figure he's seen her. I all but had it out of him. Then I was stopped."

"How stopped? Who stopped you?"

"You did. . . . Jaime got word you was in the territory. He wouldn't deal no more with me. I figure he believed he could do better for himself letting you come to him. Direct."

Find Jaime Rosas. It was all they had to do, and it shouldn't be too hard with the Comanchero willing to deal. He was around this border someplace for a part of every year. Most years, anyway. Find him, and this search is licked. Out of the rattle-brained old fraud of a broke-down buffalo hunter had come the only straight, direct lead they had ever had.

Amos gave Lije forty dollars, and Lije rode off in a different direction than Amos took. Said he wanted to check on some Caddoes he heard was running whiskey in. He always had seemed to have Caddoes on the brain. And Amos and Mart went looking for Jaime Rosas.

## 26

THEY DID find old Jaime Rosas; or perhaps he had to find them in the end. It was the heartbreaking distances that held them back from coming up with him for so long. You were never in the wrong place without being about a week and a half away from the right one. That country seemed to have some kind of weird spell upon it, so that you could travel in one spot all day long, and never gain a mile. You might start out in the morning with a notched butte far off on your left; and when you camped at nightfall the same notched butte would be right there, in the same place. Maybe it was a good thing that a man and his plodding horse could not see that country from the sky, as the vultures saw it. If a man could have seen the vastness in which he was a speck, the heart would have gone out of him; and if his horse could have seen it, the animal would have died.

Now that they knew the names of the boss Comancheros, the people were more willing to help them, relaying news of the movements of Jaime Rosas. If they had no news they made up some, and this could prove a costly thing. If a peon wanted to please you he would give you a tale of some kind—never hesitating to send you ninety miles out of your way, rather than disappoint you by telling you he didn't know.

While they were hunting for Jaime Rosas, Martin Pauley's nights became haunted for a while by a peculiar form of dream. The source of the dream was obvious. One blazing day in Los Gatos, where they were held up through the heat of the siesta hours, Mart had wandered into a church, because it looked cool and pleasantly dark within the deep adobe walls. Little candles grouped in several places stood out in bright pinpoints, some of them red where they had burned down in their ruby glasses. Mart sat down, and as his eyes adjusted he began to see the images, life-size and dark-complected mostly, of saints and martyrs, all around him in the gloom. Painted in natural colors, with polished stones for eyes, they looked a lot like people, here in the dark. Except that they were unnaturally still. Not even the candle flames wavered in the quiet air. Mart sat there, fascinated, for a long time.

About a week after that, Mart dreamed of Debbie. In all this time he had never seen her in a dream before; perhaps because he rarely dreamed at all. But this dream was very real and clear. He seemed to be standing in the dark church. The images around him again, like living people, but holding unnaturally still. He could feel their presence strongly, but they seemed neither friendly nor hostile—just there. Directly in front of him a candlelighted shrine began to brighten, and there was Debbie, in the middle of a soft white light. She was littler than when she was lost, littler than in the miniature even, and with a different look and pose than the miniature had—more of a side-face position. She didn't look out at him, or move, any more than the images did, but she was alive—he knew she was alive; she fairly glowed with life, as if made of the light itself.

He stood holding his breath, waiting for her to turn and see him. He could feel the moment when she would turn to him coming nearer, and nearer, until the strain was unbearable, and woke him up just too soon.

The same dream returned to him on other nights, sometimes close together, sometimes many days apart, perhaps a dozen times. The whole thing was always as real and clear as it had been the first time; and he always woke up just before Debbie turned. Then, for no reason, he quit having that dream, and he couldn't make it come back.

Rumors found their way to them from Texas, most of them fourth- or fifth-hand tales of things that had happened months before. Yet there was enough substance to what they heard to tell that the smoldering frontier was blazing up into open war. A chief usually called Big Red Food, but whose name Mart translated as Raw Meat, charged a company of infantry close to Fort Sill, broke clean through it, and rode away. Wolf Tail drummed up a great gathering of warriors from many bands, dragging Quanah into it. For three days they pressed home an attack upon a party of buffalo hunters at Adobe Walls, charge after charge, but were beaten off with heavy loss. Every war chief they had ever known seemed to be up; but now Washington at last had had enough. The Friends were out of the

Agencies, and the military was in the saddle. A finish fight seemed cocked and primed. . . .

But they had had no news for weeks, the night they found Jaime Rosas.

They had come after dark into Puerto del Sol, a village with more people in it than most. It had no hacienda and no church, but it did have a two-acre corral with high adobe walls, loopholed, so that the corral could be fought as a fort. Several unnecessarily large adobe stores, with almost nothing for sale in them, looked a lot like warehouses. A Comanchero base, sure enough, Mart thought.

The place had two cantinas, each with more volunteer guitar singers than it needed, cadging for drinks. Amos picked the smaller and better of the two, and as they went in, Mart saw that in Puerta del Sol the cantinas actually did have señoritas, for a rarity. They had been overanticipated for a long time, due to Amos' original confusion of this country with a part of Old Mexico that was the whole length of Texas away. The territory dance girls had been disappointing, what few times they had seen any—just stolid-faced little women like squaws, either too fat or with a half-grown look. These of Puerto del Sol didn't look much better, at first.

Amos fell in at once with a smart-looking vaquero with leather lace on his hat. A haciendado, or the son of one—if he wasn't one of the boss Comancheros. Mart bought a short glass of tequila and a tall glass of tepid water clouded with New Mexico Territory, and took them to a table in a corner. Amos didn't seem to like Mart standing by when he was angling for information. Sooner or later he was likely to include Mart in the conversation by some remark such as: "What the devil you haunting me for?" Or: "What in all hell you want now?" Since the dreams of Debbie had stopped, Mart was beginning to have a hard time remembering why he was still riding with Amos. Most days it was a matter of habit. He kept on because he had no plans of his own, nor any idea of where to head for if he split off.

The vaquero with the expensive hat went away, and came back with a shabby old man. Amos sat with these two, buying them drinks, but he seemed to have lost interest. All three seemed bored with the whole thing. They sat gazing idly about, with the placid vacuity common to the country, seeming to be trying to forget each other, as much as anything. Mart saw Amos make a Spanish joke he had worked out, something about the many flies drinking his liquor up, and the other two laughed politely. Amos wasn't finding out anything, Mart judged.

Mart's attention went back to the girls. There were five or six of them in here, but not the same ones all the time. They flirted with the vaqueros, and danced for them, and with them; and now and then a girl disappeared with one, whereupon another wandered in to take her place. They drank wine, but smelled mostly of vanilla-bean perfume and musk. These girls carried a sudden danger with them, as if death must be a he-goat, and liked to follow them around. Mart himself had seen one case of knife-in-the-belly, and had heard of a good many more. A girl let her eyes wander once too often, and the knives jumped with no warning at all. In the next two seconds there was liable to be a man on the dirt floor, and a surprised new face in hell. The girl screamed, and yammered, and had to be dragged away in a hollering tizzy; but was back the next night, with her eyes wandering just as much. Mart wondered if a girl got famous, and had songs made about her, if people pointed her out and said, "Five men are dead for that little one."

So he was watching for it, and able to handle it, when it almost happened to him. The tequila had an unpleasant taste, hard to get used to, as if somebody had washed his sox in it, but it hid a flame. As it warmed his brain, everything looked a lot prettier; and a new girl who came in looked different from all the others he had seen out here—or anywhere, maybe.

This girl was pert and trim, and her skirts flared in a whirl of color when she turned. Her Spanish-heeled shoes must have been a gift brought a long way, perhaps from Mexico City. The shoes set her apart from the others, who wore moccasins, at best, when they weren't barefoot altogether. She had a nose-shaped nose, instead of a flat one, and carried her head with defiance. Or anyhow, that was the way Mart saw her now, and always remembered her.

A lot of eyes looked this one up and down with appreciation, as if her dress were no more barrier to appraisal than harness on a filly. Martin Pauley dropped his eyes to his hands. He had a tall glass in one hand and a short glass in the other, and he studied this situation stupidly for a few moments before he swallowed a slug of warmish chalky water, and tossed off the rest of his tequila. He had drunk slowly, but a good many. And now the tequila looked up, fastened eyes upon the girl, and held without self-consciousness, wherever she went. There is a great independence, and a confident immunity to risk, in all drinks made out of cactus.

An old saying said itself in his mind. "Indian takes drink; drink takes drink; drink takes Indian; all chase squaw." It had a plausible, thoughtful sound, but no practical meaning. Presently the girl noticed him, and looked at him steadily for some moments, trying to make up her mind about him in the bad light. Nothing came of this immediately; a peonish fellow, dressed like a vaquero, but not a good one, took hold of her and made her dance with him. Mart sucked his teeth and thought nothing of it. He had no plans.

The girl had, though, and steered her partner toward Mart's table. She fixed her eyes on Mart, swung close, and kicked him in the shin. One way to do it, Mart thought. And here it comes. He drained a last drop from his tequila glass, and let his right hand come to rest on his leg under the table. Sure enough. The vaquero turned and looked him over across the table. His shirt was open to the waist, showing the brown chest to be smooth and hairless.

"Your eye is of a nasty color," the vaquero said poetically in Chihuahua Spanish. "Of a sameness to the belly of a carp."

Mart leaned forward with a smile, eyebrows up, as if in response to a greeting he had not quite caught. "And you?" he returned courteously, also in Spanish. "We have a drink, no?"

"No," said the vaquero, looking puzzled.

"We have a drink, yes," the girl changed his mind. "You know why? The gun of this man is in his right hand under the table. He blows your bowels out the door in one moment. This is necessary."

She extended an imperious palm, and Mart slid a silver dollar across the table to her. The vaquero was looking thoughtful as she led him away. Mart never knew what manner of drink she got into the fellow, but she was back almost at once. The vaquero was already to be seen snoring on the mud floor. A compadre dragged him out by the feet, and laid him tenderly in the road.

She said her name was Estrellita, which he did not believe; it had a picked-out sound to him. She sat beside him and sang at him with a guitar. The tequila was thinking in Spanish now, so that the words of the sad, sad song made sense without having to be translated in his head.

> I see a stranger passing,
>> His heart is dark with sorrows,
> Another such as I am,
>> Behind him his tomorrows . . .

This song was a great epic tragedy in about a hundred stanzas, each ending on a suspended note, to keep the listener on the hook. But she hadn't got through more than half a dozen when she stopped and leaned forward to peer into his eyes. Perhaps she saw signs of his bursting into tears, for she got him up and danced with him. A whole battery of guitars had begun whaling out a *baile* as soon as she stopped singing, and the tequila was just as ready to romp and stomp as to bawl into the empty glasses. As she came close to him, her musk-heavy perfume wrapped around him, strong enough to lift him off his feet with one hand. The tequila thought it was wonderful. No grabbing of arms in dancing with this one—you swung the girl by taking hold of the girl. The round neckline of her dress was quite modest, almost up to her throat, and her sleeves were tied at her elbows. But what he found out was that this was a very thin dress.

"I think it is time to go home now," she said.

"I have no home," he said blankly.

"My house is your house," she told him.

He remembered to speak to Amos about it. The young well-dressed vaquero was gone, and Amos sat head to head with the shabby old man, talking softly and earnestly. "All right if I take a walk?" Mart interrupted them.

"Where you going to be?" Amos asked the girl in Spanish.

She described a turn or two and counted doors on her fingers. Amos went back to his powwow, and Mart guessed he was dismissed. "Wait a minute," Amos called him back. He gave Mart a handful of silver dollars without looking up. Good thing he did. Running out of *dinero* is another first-class way to get in trouble around a cantina señorita.

Her *casa* turned out to be the scrubbiest horse stall of a jacal he had seen yet. She lighted a candle, and the place looked a little better inside, mostly because of a striped serape on the dirt floor and a couple tied on the walls to cover holes where the mud had fallen out of the woven twigs. The candle stood in a little shrine sheltering a pottery Virgin of Tiburon, and this reminded Mart of something, but he couldn't remember what. He blinked as he watched Estrellita cross herself and kneel briefly in obeisance. Then she came to him and presented her back to be unbuttoned.

All through this whole thing, Mart showed the dexterity and finesse of a hog in a sand boil, and even the tequila knew it. It was very young tequila at best, as its raw bite had attested, and it couldn't help him much after a point. One moment he was afraid to touch her, and in the next, when he did take her in his arms, he almost broke her in two. The girl was first astonished, then angry; but finally her sense of humor returned, and she felt sorry for him. She turned patient, soothing and gentling him; and when at last he slept he was in such a state of relaxation that even his toe nails must have been limp.

So now, of course, he had to get up again.

Amos came striding down the narrow *calle*, banging his heels on the hard dirt. One of his spurs had a loose wheel; it had always been that way. It never whispered when he rode, but afoot this spur made some different complaint at every step. Thug, ding, thug, clank, thug, bingle, went Amos as he walked; and the familiar sound woke Mart from a hundred feet away.

"Get your clothes on," Amos said, as soon as the door was open. "We're on our way."

Except for a slight queerness of balance as he first stood up, Mart felt fine. There is no cleaner liquor than tequila when it is made right, however awful it may taste. "Right now? In the middle of the night?"

"Look at the sky."

Mart saw that the east was turning light. "I suppose that old man seen Jaime Rosas some far-fetched place. Maybe last year, or the year before."

"That old man is Jaime Rosas."

Mart stared at Amos' silhouette, then stamped into his boots.

"He says Bluebonnet has a young white girl," Amos told him. "One with yaller hair and green eyes."

"Where at?"

"Rosas is taking us to him. We'll be there before night."

They had been in New Mexico more than two years and a half.

# 27

THEY SAT in a circle in the shade of a tepee eighteen feet across, three white men and seven war chiefs around a charred spot that would have been a council fire if a fire had been tolerable that day. The scraped buffalo hide of the tepee had been rolled up for a couple of feet, and the hot wind crept under, sometimes raising miniature dust devils on the hard dirt floor.

Bluebonnet, the elusive ghost they had followed for so long, sat opposite the entrance flap. Mart had long since stopped trying to believe there was any Comanche named Bluebonnet, or the Flower, or whatever his damned name meant in words. He judged Bluebonnet to be a myth, the work of an all-Indian conspiracy. Every savage in creation had probably heard of the two searchers by this time, and stood ready to join in the sport of sending them hither and yon in chase of a chief who did not exist. Yet there he was; and on the outside of the tepee, large as a shield, the oft-described, never-seen symbol of the Flower was drawn in faded antelope blood.

An oddly shimmering light, a reflection from the sun-blasted surface of the earth outside, played over the old chief's face. It was the broad, flat face common to one type of Comanche, round and yellow as a moon. Age was crinkling its surface in fine-lined patterns, into which the opaque eyes were set flush, without hollows.

The other six war chiefs weren't needed here. Bluebonnet had them as a courtesy—and to reassure his village that he wasn't making foolish trades behind the backs of his people. It wasn't much of a village. It numbered only fourteen lodges, able to turn out perhaps thirty or forty warriors by counting all boys over twelve. But it was what he had. His pride and his special notion of his honor were still very great, far though he was on his road to oblivion.

Jaime Rosas had four vaqueros with him, but he hadn't brought them into council. They were tall Indian-looking men, good prairie Comancheros, but he owed them no courtesies.

The vaqueros had pitched a shade-fly of their own a little way off. Three of them slept most of the time, but one was always awake, day or night, whatever the time might be. Whenever several were awake at once they were to be heard laughing a good deal, or else singing a sad long song that might last a couple of hours; then all but one would go back to sleep again.

What was going on in the tepee was in the nature of a horse trade. The evening of their arrival had been devoted to a meager feast without dancing, the atmosphere considerably dampened by the fact that Rosas had brought no rum. The council began the next morning. It was a slow thing, with long stillnesses between irrelevant remarks conveyed in sign language. One thing about it, no one was likely to go off half cocked in a session like that. From time to time the pipe, furnished by Bluebonnet, was filled with a pinch of tobacco, furnished by Rosas, and passed from hand to hand, as a sort of punctuation.

They were in that tepee three days, the councils running from forenoon to sundown. Even a cowboy's back can get busted, sitting cross-legged as long as that. Jaime Rosas did all the talking done on the white men's side. This old man's face was weathered much darker than Bluebonnet's; his dirty gray mustache looked whiter than it was against that skin. His eyes had brown veins in the whites and red-rimmed lids. All day long he chewed slowly on a grass stem with teeth worn to brown stubs; by night he would have a foot-long stem eaten down to an inch or two. He could sit quiet as long as Bluebonnet could, and maybe a little longer; and when he unlimbered his sign language it ran as smoothly as Bluebonnet's, though this chief prided himself on the grace of his sign talk. The unpunctuated flow of compound signs made the conversation all but impossible to follow.

Rosas' hands might say, "Horse-dig-hole-slow-buffalo-chase-catch-no-enemy-run-chase-catch-no-sad." Mart read that to mean, "The horse is worthless—too slow for hunting or for war; it's too bad."

And Bluebonnet's answer, in signs of smooth speed and great delicacy: "Stiff-neck-beat-enemy-far-run-still-neck-horse-ride-leave-tepee-warriors-pile-up." They had him there, Mart admitted to himself. He believed Bluebonnet had said, "When a chief has run his enemies out of the country, he wants a horse he can ride with pride, like to a council." But he didn't know. Here came the pipe again.

"I'll never get no place in this dang country," he said to Amos. "It's a good thing we'll soon be heading home."

"Shut up." It was the first remark Amos had made that day.

Toward sundown of the first day Bluebonnet admitted he had a young white girl, blonde and blue-eyed, in his lodge.

"May not be the one," Amos said in Spanish.

"Who knows?" Rosas answered. "Man is the hands of God."

Around noon of the second day, Rosas presented Bluebonnet with the horse they had talked about most of the first day. It was a show-off palomino, with a stud-horse neck and ripples in its silver mane and tail. About what the old dons would have called a palfrey once. Mart wouldn't have wanted it. But the saddle on it, sheltered under a tied-down canvas until the moment of presentation, was heavily crusted with silver, and probably worth two hundred dollars. Rosas gave the old chief horse and rig upon condition that no present would be accepted in return. Bluebonnet turned wary for a while after that, as if the gift might have done more harm than good; but his eyes showed a gleam toward the end of the day, for what they talked about all afternoon was rifles.

Sundown was near on the third day when they came to the end at last. The abruptness of the finish caught Mart off guard. Rosas and Bluebonnet had been going through an interminable discussion of percussion caps, as near as Mart could make out. He had given up trying to follow it, and had let his eyes lose focus in the glow of the leveling sun upon the dust. He took a brief puff as the pipe passed him again, and was aware that one of the warriors got up and went out.

Amos said, "He's sent for her, Mart."

The desert air seemed to press inward upon the tepee with an unbelievable weight. His head swam, and he could not recognize a single familiar symbol among the next posturings of Bluebonnet's hands.

"He says she's well and strong," Amos told him.

Mart returned his eyes to Bluebonnet's hands. His head cleared, and he saw plainly the next thing the hands said. He turned to Amos in appeal, unwilling to believe he had properly understood.

"The girl is his wife," Amos interpreted.

"It doesn't matter." His mouth was so dry that the thick words were not understandable at all. Mart cleared his throat, and tried to spit, but could not. "It doesn't matter," he said again.

The warrior who had left the lodge now returned. As he entered, he spoke a Comanche phrase over his shoulder, and a young woman appeared. Her form was not that of a little girl; it hardly could have been after the lost years. This was a woman, thin, and not very tall, but grown. Her face and the color of her hair were hidden by a shawl that must once have been red, but now was dulled by the perpetually blowing dust.

His eyes dropped. She wore heel-fringed moccasins, a prerogative of warriors, permitted to squaws only as a high honor. But her feet were narrow and high-arched, unlike the short, splayed feet of Comanches. The ankles were tanned, and speckles of the everlasting dust clung to them, too, as if they were sprinkled with cinnamon; yet he could see the blue veins under the thin skin. She followed the warrior into the lodge with a step as light and tense as that of a stalking wolf. He realized with a sinking of the heart that the girl was afraid —not of the Flower, or his warriors, but of her own people.

Bluebonnet said in the Comanche tongue, "Come stand beside me."

The young woman obeyed. Beside Bluebonnet she turned reluctantly toward the council circle, still clutching the shawl that hid her face so that nothing was visible but the whitened knuckles of one hand. On one side of Mart, Amos sat, an immovable lump. On his other side, Rosas had thrown down his grass stem. His eyes were slitted, but his glance flickered back and forth between the girl and Amos' face, while he moved no other muscle. Over and over, white girls captured as children and raised by the Comanches have been ashamed to look white men in the face.

"Show them your head," Bluebonnet said in Comanche, Mart thought; though perhaps he had said "hair" instead of "head."

The white girl's head bowed lower, and she uncovered the top of it, to let them see the color of her hair. It was cropped short in the manner of the Comanches, among whom only the men wore long hair, but it was blonde. Not a bright blonde; a mousy shade. But blonde.

"Show your face," came Bluebonnet's Comanche words, and the girl let the shawl fall, though her face remained averted. The old chief spoke sharply at last. "Hold up your head! Obey!"

The girl's head raised. For a full minute the silence held while Mart stared, praying, trying to persuade himself of —what? The tanned but once white face was broad and flat, the forehead low, the nose shapeless, the mouth pinched yet loose. The eyes were green, all right, but small and set close together; they darted like an animal's, craving escape. Mart's mind moved again. Stare an hour, he told himself. Stare a year. You'll never get any different answer. Nor find room for any possible mistake.

This girl was not Debbie.

Mart got up, and blundered out into the reddening horizontal rays of the sunset. Behind him he heard Amos say harshly, "You speak English?" The girl did not answer. Mart never asked Amos what else was said. He walked away from the tepee of the Flower, out of the village, a long way out onto the thin-grassed flats. Finally he just stood, alone in the twilight.

# 28

Once more they went around the Staked Plains, passing to the south; but this time as they turned north they were headed home. They traveled by listless stages, feeling nothing much ahead to reach for now. Home, for them, was more of a direction than a place. It was like a surveyor's marker that is on the map but not on the ground: You're south of it, and you ride toward it, and after a while you're north of it, but you're never exactly there, because there isn't any such thing, except in the mind. They were nothing more than beaten men, straggling back down the long, long way they had traveled to their final defeat.

Fort Concho was deserted as they came to it, except for a token guard. But for once the emptiness had a difference. This was one garrison that had not been withdrawn by the fat-headed wishfulness that had disarmed more American troops than any other enemy. Three regiments under the colonel were on the march, riding northwest into the heart of the Comanche country. And these were part of a broad campaign, planned with thoroughness, and activated by a total resolution. For General Sheridan was in the saddle again, this time with a latitude of action that would let him put an end to rewarded murder once and for all.

North of Mackenzie's column, Colonel Buell was advancing; Colonel Nelson A. Miles was marching south from Fort Supply; Major William Price was coming into it from Fort Union beyond the Staked Plains. And at Fort Sill, Colonel Davidson, with perhaps the strongest force of all, to judge by the rumors they heard, hung poised until the other columns should be advantageously advanced. Under Sheridan there would be no more of the old chase, charge, scatter 'em and go home. These troops would dog and follow, fighting if the Indians stood, but always coming on again. Once a column fastened upon a Comanche band, that band would be followed without turn-off, regardless of what more tempting quarry crossed between. And this would go on until no hostile could find a way to stay out and live.

When they had learned the scope of what was happening, Mart knew without need of words what Amos, with all his heart, would want to do now. It was the same thing he himself wanted, more than women, more than love, more than food or drink. They made a close study of their horses—a study about as needful as a close count of the fingers on their hands. Each horse had served as his rider's very muscles, day in and day out, for months. The two men were trying to persuade themselves that their horses were wiry, and wise in tricks for saving their strength, instead of just gaunted and low of head. But it couldn't be done, and not a horse was left at Fort Concho worth saddling.

Finally the two rode out and sat looking at the trail, stale and all but effaced, that the cavalry had made as it rode away. Up that trail hundreds of men were riding to what seemed a final kill—yet riding virtually blind for lack of just such scouts as Mart and Amos had become. But the column had so great a start it might as well have been on another world. Amos was first to shrug and turn away. Mart still sat a little while more, staring up that vacant trail; but at last drew a deep breath, let it all out again, and followed Amos.

They plodded north and east through a desolate land, for this year the country looked the worst they had ever seen it. The summer had been wickedly hot and totally dry; and on top of the drought great swarms of grasshoppers had come to chop what feed there was into blowing dust. The few bands of cattle they saw were all bones, and wild as deer. Only the aged cattle showed brands, for no one had worked the border ranges in a long time. Yet, if above all you wanted the cavalry to succeed, you had to look at the drought-ravaged range with a grim satisfaction. The cavalry carried horse corn, something no Indian would ever do, and the drought had given the grain-fed mounts an advantage that not even Comanche horsemanship could overcome this one year.

Toward noon of a colorless November day they raised the Edwards layout—"the old Edwards place," people called it now, if they knew what it was at all. And now came an experience worth forgetting altogether, except for the way it blew up on them later on. A thread of smoke rose straight up in the dead air from the central chimney of the house. They saw it from a great way off, and Mart looked at Amos, but they did not change the pace of their horses. Riding nearer, they saw a scratched-up half acre in front of the house, where Martha had meant to have a lawn and a garden someday. Here a bony rack of a mule was working on some runty corn stalks. It lifted its head and stood motionless, a rag of fodder hanging from its jaws, as it watched them steadily all the way in.

They saw other things to resent. Most of the corral poles were gone for firewood, along with a good many boards from the floors of the galleries. The whole homestead had the trashy look of a place where nothing is ever taken care of.

"Got a sodbuster in here," Amos said as they came up.

"Or a Mex," Mart suggested.

"Sodbuster," Amos repeated.

"I guess I'll ride on," Mart said. "I got no craving to see how the house looks now."

"If you hear shots," Amos said, "tell the Mathisons I ain't coming."

"Looking for trouble?"

"Fixing to make some."

That settled that. They tied their ponies to the gallery posts. The latch string whipped out of sight into its little hole in the door as Amos crossed the gallery. He kicked the door twice, once to test it, and once to drive it in. The bar brackets never had been repaired very well since the dreadful night when they were broken.

By the woodbox, as if he wanted to take cover behind the stove, a gaunt turkey-necked man was trying to load a shotgun with rattling hands. Automatically Mart and Amos moved apart, and their six-guns came out. "Put that thing down," Amos said.

"You got no right bustin' in on——"

Amos fired, and splinters jumped at the squatter's feet. The shotgun clattered on the floor, and they had time to take a look at what else was in the room. Five dirty children stood goggle-eyed as far back as they could get, and a malarial woman was frying jack rabbit; the strong grease smelled as if fur had got into it. A dress that had been Martha's dress hung loose on the woman's frame, and some of the children's clothes were Debbie's. He might have been sorry for all these saucer eyes except for that.

"You're in my house," Amos said.

"Wasn't nobody using it. We ain't hurting your——"

"Shut up!" Amos said. There was quiet, and Mart noticed the dirt, and some big holes in the chimney, the walls, the window reveals, where adobe bricks had been prized out.

"Been looking for something, I see," Amos said. "Let's see if you found it. Hold 'em steady, Mart." Amos picked up a mattock, and went into a bedroom, where he could be heard chunking a hole in the adobe with heavy strokes. He came back with an adobe-dusted tin box, and let them watch him pour gold pieces from it into a side pocket; Mart guessed there must be about four hundred dollars.

"I'll be back in a week," Amos said. "I want this place scrubbed out, and the walls patched and whitewashed. Fix them gallery floors out there, and start hauling poles for them corrals. Make all as it was, and might be I'll leave you stay till spring."

"I got no time for——"

"Then you better be long gone when I come!"

They walked out of there and rode on.

# 29

NOTHING EVER changed much at the Mathisons. The old, well-made things never wore out; if they broke they were mended stronger than they were before. Pump handles wore down to a high polish, door sills showed deeper hollows. But nothing was allowed to gather the slow grime of age. Only when you had been gone a couple of years could you see that the place was growing old. Then it looked smaller than you remembered it, and kind of rounded at the corners everywhere. Mart rode toward it this time with a feeling that the whole place belonged to the past that he was done with, like the long search that had seemed to have no end, but had finally run out anyway.

They didn't mean to be here long. Amos meant to ride on to Austin at once, to clear up the killings at Lost Mule Creek; and if he got held up, Mart meant to go there alone, and get it over. He didn't know what he was going to do after that, but it sure would be someplace else. He believed that he was approaching the Mathisons for the last time. Maybe when he looked over his shoulder at this place, knowing he would never see it again, then he would feel something about it, but he felt nothing now. None of it was a part of him any more.

The people had aged like the house, except a little faster and a little plainer to be seen. Mart saw at first glance that Aaron was almost totally blind. Tobe and Abner were grown men. And Mrs. Mathison was a little old lady, who came out of the kitchen into the cold to take him by both hands. "My, my, Martie! It's been so long! You've been gone five—no, it's more. Why, it's coming on six years! Did you know that?" No; he hadn't known that. Not to count it all up together that way. Seemingly she didn't remember they had been home twice in the meantime.

But the surprise was that Laurie was still here. He had assumed she would have gone off and married Charlie MacCorry long ago, and she had quit haunting him once he swallowed that. She didn't come out of the house as he unsaddled, but as he came into the kitchen she crossed to him, drying her hands.

Why did she always have to be at either the stove or the sink? Well, because it was always coming time to eat again, actually. They were close onto suppertime right now.

She didn't kiss him, or take hold of him in any way. "Did you—have you ever——" Resignation showed in her eyes, but they were widened by an awareness of tragedy, as if she knew the answer before she spoke. And his face confirmed it for her. "Not anything? No least trace of her at all?"

He drew a deep breath, wondering what part of their long try needed to be told. "Nothing," he said, finally, and judged that covered it all.

"You've been out so long," she said slowly, marveling. "I suppose you talk Comanche like an Indian. Do they call you Indian names?"

"I sure wouldn't dast interpret the most of the names they call us," he answered automatically. But he added, "Amos is known to 'em as 'Bull Shoulders.'"

"And you?"

"Oh—I'm just the 'Other.'"

"I suppose you'll be going right out again, Other?"

"No. I think now she was dead from the first week we rode."

"I'm sorry, Martie." She turned away, and for a few minutes went through slow motions, changing the setting of the table, moving things that didn't need to be moved. Something besides what she was doing was going through her mind, so plainly you could almost hear it tick. Abruptly, she left her work and got her coat, spinning it over her shoulders like a cape.

Her mother said, "Supper's almost on. Won't be but a few minutes."

"All right, Ma." Laurie gave Mart one expressionless glance, and he followed her, putting his sheepskin on, as she went out the door to the dog-trot.

"Where's Charlie?" he asked, flat-footed, once they were outside.

"He's still in the Rangers. He's stationed over at Harper's, now; he's done well enough so he could politic that. But we don't see him too much. Seems like Rangers live on the hard run nowadays." She met his eyes directly, without shyness, but without lighting up much, either.

A small wind was stirring now, shifting the high overcast. At the horizon a line of blood-bright sunset light broke through, turning the whole prairie red. They walked in silence, well apart, until they had crossed a rise and were out of sight of the house. Laurie said, "I suppose you'll be going on to Austin soon."

"We've got to. Amos put up a thousand head— Of course, the Rangers can't collect until a judge or somebody declares Debbie dead. But they'll do that now. We got to go there, and straighten it out."

"Are you coming back, Martie?"

The direct question took him off guard. He had thought some of working his way up toward Montana, if the Rangers didn't lock him up, or anything. They were having big Indian trouble up there, and Mart believed himself well qualified to scout against the Sioux. But it didn't make much sense to head north into the teeth of winter, and spring was far away. So he said something he hadn't meant to say. "Do you want me to come back, Laurie?"

"I won't be here."

He thought he understood that. "I figured you'd be married long before now."

"It might have happened. Once. But Pa never could stand Charlie. Pa's had so much trouble come down on him—he always blamed himself for what happened to your folks. Did you know that? I didn't want to bring on one thing more, and break his heart. Not then. If I had it to do over—I don't know. But I don't want to stay here now. I know that. I'm going to get out of Texas, Mart."

He looked stupid, and said, "Oh?"

"This is a dreadful country. I've come to hate these prairies, every inch of 'em—and I bet they stretch a million miles. Nothing to look forward to—or back at, either—I want to go to Memphis. Or Vicksburg, or New Orleans."

"You got kinfolk back there?"

"No. I don't know anybody."

"Now, you know you can't do that! You never been in a settlement bigger'n Fort Worth in your life. Any gol dang awful thing is liable to happen to you in a place like them!"

"I'm twenty-four years old," she said bitterly. "Time something happened."

He searched for something to say, and came up with the most stilted remark he had ever heard. "I wouldn't want anything untoward to happen to you, Laurie," he said.

"Wouldn't you?"

"I've been long gone. But I was doing what I had to do, Laurie. You know that."

"For five long years," she reminded him.

He wanted to let her know it wasn't true that he hadn't cared what happened to her. But he couldn't explain the way hope had led him on, dancing down the prairie like a fox fire, always just ahead. It didn't seem real any more. So finally he just put an arm around her waist as they walked, pulling her closer to his side.

The result astonished him. Laurie stopped short, and for a moment stood rigid; then she turned toward him, and came into his arms. "Martie, Martie, Martie," she whispered, her mouth against his. She had on a lot of winter clothes, but the girl was there inside them, solider than Estrellita, but slim and warm. And now somebody began hammering on a triangle back at the house, calling them in.

"Oh, damn," he said, "damn, damn——"

She put her fingers on his lips to make him listen. "Start coughing soon's we go in the house. Make out you're coming down with a lung chill."

"Me? What for?"

"The boys put your stuff in the bunkhouse. But I'll work it out so you're moved to the grandmother room. Just you, by yourself. Late tonight, when they're all settled in, I'll come to you there."

Jingle-jangle-bang went the triangle again.

# 30

THAT NIGHT Lije Powers came back.

They were still at the supper table as they heard his horse; and the men glanced at each other, for the plodding hoofs seemed to wander instead of coming straight on up to the door. And next they heard his curiously weak hail. Abner and Tobe Mathison went out. Lije swayed in the saddle, then lost balance and buckled as he tried to dismount, so that Tobe had to catch him in his arms.

"Drunker than a spinner wolf," Tobe announced.

"Drunk, hell," Abner disagreed. "The man's got a bullet in him!"

"No, I ain't," Lije said, and went into a coughing fit that made a fool of Mart's effort to fake a bad chest. Tobe and Abner were both wrong; Lije was as ill a man as had ever got where he was going on a horse. At the door he tottered against the jamb, and clung to it feebly, preventing them from closing it against the rising wind, until the coughing fit passed off.

"I found her," Lije said, still blocking the door. "I found Deb'rie Edwards." He slid down the side of the door and collapsed.

They carried him into the grandmother room and put him to bed. "He's out of his head," Aaron Mathison said, pulling off Lije Powers' boots.

"I got a bad cold," Lije wheezed at them. He was glassy-eyed, and his skin burned their fingers. "But I'm no more out of my mind than you. I talked to her. She spoke her name. I seen her as close as from here to you. . . ."

"Where?" Amos demanded.

"She's with a chief named Yellow Buckle. Amos—you mind the Seven Fingers?"

Amos looked blank. The names meant nothing to him.

Aaron Mathison said, "Will you leave the man be? He's in delirium!"

"Be still!" Mart snapped at Aaron.

"I got a cold," Lije repeated, and his voice turned pleading. "Ain't anybody ever heard of the Seven Fingers?"

497

"Seems like there's a bunch of cricks," Mart said, groping for a memory, "west of the Wichita Mountains. . . . No, farther —beyond the Little Rainies. I think they run into the North Fork of the Red. Lije, ain't Seven Fingers the Kiowa name for them little rivers?"

"That's it! That's it!" Lije cried out eagerly. "Do this get me my rocking chai', Amos?"

"Sure, Lije. Now take it easy."

They piled blankets on him, and wrapped a hot stove lid to put at his feet, then spooned a little soup into him. It was what Mrs. Mathison called her "apron-string soup," because it had noodles in it. But Lije kept on talking, as if he feared he might lose hold and never be able to tell them once he let down.

"Yellow Buckle's squaws was feeding us. One comes behind me and she puts this calabash in my lap. Full of stewed gut tripe. . . . She bends down, and makes out like she picks a stick out of it with her fingers. And she whispers in my ear. 'I'm Deb'rie,' she says. 'I'm Deb'rie Edwards.'"

"Couldn't you get a look at her?"

"I snuck a quick look over my shoulder. Her head was covered. But I seen these here green eyes. Greener'n a wild grape peeled out . . ."

"Was that all?" Amos asked as the old man trailed off.

"I didn't see her no more. And I didn't dast say nothing, or ask."

"Who's Yellow Buckle with?" The answer was so long in coming that Mart started to repeat, but the sick man had heard him.

"I seen . . . Fox Moon . . . and Bull Eagle . . . Singin' Dog . . . Hunts-His-Horse—I think it was him. Some more'll come back to me. Do it get me my chai' by the stove?"

"You're never going to want for anything," Amos said.

Lije Powers rolled to the edge of the bunk in a spasm of coughing, and the blood he brought up dribbled on the floor.

"Lije," Mart raised his voice, "do you know if——"

"Leave be now," Aaron Mathison commanded them. "Get out of this room, and leave be! Or I put you out!"

"Just one more thing," Mart persisted. "Is Yellow Buckle ever called any other name?"

Aaron took a step toward him, but the thin voice spoke once more. "I think—" Lije said, "I think—some call him Cut-face."

"Get out!" Aaron roared, and moved upon them. This time they obeyed. Mrs. Mathison stayed with the very ill old man, while Laurie fetched and carried for her.

"It upsets a man," Aaron said, all quietness again, when the door had closed upon the grandmother room. "But I find no word in it to believe."

Mart spoke up sharply. "I think he's telling the truth!"

"There's a whole lot wrong with it, Mart," Amos said. "Like: 'I'm Deb'rie,' she says. Nobody in our family ever called her 'Deb'rie' in her life. She never heard the word."

"Lije says 'Debrie' for the same reason he says 'prairuh,'" Mart disputed him. "He'd talk the same if he was telling what you said, or me."

"And them Indians. Fox Moon is a Kotsetaka, and so is Singing Dog. But Bull Eagle is a Quohada, and never run with no Kotsetakas. I question if he ever seen one!"

"Can't a sick old man get one name wrong without you knock apart everything he done?"

"We was all through them Kotsetakas——"

"And maybe passed her within twenty feet!"

"All right. But how come we never heard of any Yellow Buckle?"

"We sure as hell heard of Scar!"

"Sure," Amos said wearily. "Lije was the same places we been, Martie. And heard the same things. That's all."

"But he saw her," Mart insisted, circling back to where they had begun.

"Old Lije has been a liar all his life," Amos said with finality. "You know that well as me."

Mart fell silent.

"You see, Martin," Aaron Mathison said gently, "yon lies a foolish old man. When you've said that, you've said all; and there's the end on it."

"Except for one thing," Amos said, and his low voice sounded very tired. They looked at him, and waited, while for several moments he seemed lost in thought. "We've made some far casts, looking for a chief called Scar. We never found him. And

Aaron, I believe like you: We never will. But suppose there's just one chance in a million that Lije is right, and I am wrong? That one slim shadow of a doubt would give me no rest forever; not even in my grave." He turned his head, and rested heavy eyes on Mart. "Better go make up the packs. Then catch the horses up. We got a long way more to go."

Mart ran for the bunkhouse.

# 31

In the bunkhouse Mart lighted a lamp. They had cracked their bedrolls open to get out clean shirts, and some of their stuff had got spread around. He started throwing their things together. Then he heard a scamper of light boots, and a whisk of wind made the lamp flutter as the door was thrown open. Laurie appeared against the dark, and she showed a tension that promised trouble.

"Shut the door," he told her.

She pressed it shut and stood against it. "I want the truth," she said. "If you start off again, after all this time— Oh, Mart, what's it supposed to mean?"

"It means, I see a chance she's there."

"Well, you're not going!"

"Who isn't?"

"I've dallied around this god-forsaken wind-scour for nearly six long years—waiting for you to see fit to come back! You're not going gallivanting off again now!"

It was the wrong tone to take with him. He no more than glanced at her. "I sure don't know who can stop me."

"You're a wanted man," she reminded him. "And Charlie MacCorry is less than half an hour away. If it takes all the Rangers in Texas to put handcuffs on you—they'll come when he hollers!"

He had no time to fool with this kind of an ambuscade, but he took time. He was clawing for a way to make her see what he was up against, why he had no choice. Uncertainly he dug out the doeskin packet in which he carried Debbie's miniature. The once-white leather was stained to the color of burlap, and its stiffened folds cracked as he unwrapped it; he had not dug it out for a long time. Laurie came to look as he opened the little plush case and held it to the light. Debbie's portrait was very dim. The dust had worked into it finally, and the colors had faded to shades of brown stain. No effect of life, or pertness, looked out from it any more. The little kitty-cat face had receded from him, losing itself behind the years.

Laurie hardened. "That's no picture of her," she said.

He looked up, appalled by the bitterness of her tone.

"It might have been once," she conceded. "But now it's nothing but a chromo of a small child. Can't you count up time at all?"

"She was coming ten," Mart said. "This was made before."

"She was eleven," Laurie said with certainty. "We've got the Edwards' family Bible, and I looked it up. Eleven—and it's been more than five years! She's sixteen and coming seventeen right now."

He had known that Debbie was growing up during all the long time they had hunted for her; but he had never been able to realize it, or picture it. No matter what counting on his fingers told him, he had always been hunting for a little child. But he had no reason to doubt Laurie. He could easily have lost a year in the reckoning some way, so that she had been a year older than he had supposed all the time.

"Deborah Edwards is a woman grown," Laurie said. "If she's alive at all."

He said, "If she's alive, I've got to fetch her home."

"Fetch what home? She won't come with you if you find her. They never do."

Her face was dead white; he stared at it with disbelief. He still thought it to be a good face, finely made, with beautiful eyes. But now the face was hard as quartz, and the eyes were lighted with the same fires of war he had seen in Amos' eyes the times he had stomped Comanche scalps into the dirt.

"She's had time to be with half the Comanche bucks in creation by now." Laurie's voice was cold, but not so brutal as her words. "Sold time and again to the highest bidder—and you know it! She's got savage brats of her own, most like. What are you going to do with them—fetch them home, too? Well, you won't. Because she won't let you. She'll kill herself before she'll even look you in the face. If you knew anything at all about a woman, you'd know that much!"

"Why, Laurie——" he faltered. "Why, Laurie——"

"You're not bringing anything back," she said, and her contempt whipped him across the face. "It's too late by many years. If they've got anything left to sell you, it's nothing but a—a rag of a female—the leavings of Comanche bucks——"

He turned on her with such a blaze in his eyes that she

moved back half a step. But she stood her ground then, and faced up to him; and after a while he looked away. He had hold of himself before he answered her. "I'll have to see what Amos wants to do."

"You know what he wants to do. He wants to lead the yellowlegs down on 'em, and punish 'em off the face of creation. He's never wanted anything else, no matter how he's held back or pretended. Amos has leaned way backwards for love of his brother's dead wife—and not from regard for anything else on this earth or beyond it!"

He knew that was true. "That's why I've stayed with him. I told you that a long time ago."

"Amos has had enough of all this. I knew it the minute he stepped in the house. He's very patiently gone through all the motions Martha could have asked of him—and way over and beyond. But he's done."

"I know that, too," he said.

She heard the fight go out of his voice, and she changed, softening, but without taking hope. "I wanted you, Mart. I tried to give you everything I've got to give. It's not my fault it wasn't any good."

She had shaken him up, so that he felt sick. He couldn't lay hands on the purposes by which he had lived for so long, or any purpose instead. His eyes ran along the walls, looking for escape from the blind end that had trapped him.

A calendar was there on the wall. It had a strange look, because it picked up beyond the lost years his life had skipped. But as he looked at it he remembered another calendar that hadn't looked just right. It was a calendar a little child had made for him with a mistake in it, so that her work was wasted; only he hadn't noticed that then. And he heard the little girl's voice, saying again the words that he had never really heard her say, but only had been told, and imagined: "He didn't care. . . . He didn't care at all. . . ."

"Do you know," Laurie said, "what Amos will do if he finds Deborah Edwards? It will be a right thing, a good thing—and I tell you Martha would want it now. He'll put a bullet in her brain."

He said, "Only if I'm dead."

"You think you can outride the yellowlegs—and Amos,

too," she read his mind again. "I suppose you can. And get to Yellow Buckle with a warning. But you can't outride the Rangers! You've been on their list anyway for a long time! Charlie MacCorry is only seven miles away. And I'm going to fetch him—now!"

"You so much as reach down a saddle," he told her, "and I'll be on my way in the same half minute. You think there's a man alive can give me a fourteen-mile start? Get back in that house!"

She stared at him a moment more, then slammed her way out. When she was gone Mart put Debbie's miniature in his pocket, then retied his packs to be ready for a fast departure in case Laurie carried out her threat; and he left the lamp burning in the bunkhouse as he went back to the kitchen.

Laurie did not ride for Charlie MacCorry. As it turned out, she didn't need to. MacCorry arrived at the Mathisons in the next fifteen minutes, stirred up by the squatter to whom Amos had laid down the law in the Edwards house.

# 32

"I<small>F</small> <small>YOU'D</small> come in and faced it out, like you said," Charlie MacCorry told them, "I don't believe there'd ever been any case against you at all."

Four years in the Rangers had done Charlie good. He seemed to know his limitations better now, and accepted them, instead of noisily spreading himself over all creation. Within those limits, which he no longer tried to overreach, he was very sure of himself, and quietly so, which was a new thing for Charlie.

"I said I'd come in when I could. I was on my way to Austin now. Until I run into Lije as I stopped over."

"He spoke of that," Aaron Mathison confirmed.

Resentment kept thickening Amos' neck. He shouldn't have been asked to put up with this in front of the whole Mathison family. Mrs. Mathison came and went, staying with Lije Powers mostly. But there had been no way to get rid of Tobe and Abner, who kept their mouths shut in the background, but were there, as was Laurie, making herself as inconspicuous as she could.

"And you had my bond of a thousand head of cattle, in token I'd come back," Amos said. "Or did you pick them up?"

"We couldn't, very well, because you didn't own them. Not until the courts declared Deborah Edwards dead, which hasn't been done. I don't think Captain Clinton ever meant to pick them up. He was satisfied with your word. Then."

"Captain, huh?" Amos took note of the promotion. "What are you—a colonel?"

"Sergeant," MacCorry said without annoyance. "You've been close to three years. Had to come and find you on a tip. Your reputation hasn't improved any in that time, Mr. Edwards."

"What's the matter with my reputation?" Amos was angering again.

"I'll answer that if you want. So you can see what us fellers is up against. Mark you, I don't say it's true." No rancor could be heard in MacCorry's tone. He sat relaxed, elbows on the table, and looked Amos in the eye. "They say it's funny you leave a good ranch, well stocked, to be worked by other men, while you sky-hoot the country from the Nations to Mexico on no reasonable business so far as known. They say you're almighty free with the scalping knife, and that's a thing brings costly trouble on Texas. They say you're a squaw man, who'd sooner booger around with the Wild Tribes than work your own stock; and an owlhoot that will murder to rob."

"You dare set there and say——"

"I do not. I tell you what's said. But all that builds up pressure on us. Half the Indian trouble we get nowadays is stirred up by quick-trigger thieves and squaw men poking around where they don't belong. And your name—names—are a couple that come up when the citizens holler to know why we don't do nothing. I tell you all this in hopes you'll see why I got to do my job. After all, this is a murder case."

"There ain't any such murder case," Amos said flatly.

"I hope you're right. But that's not my business. All I know, you stand charged with the robbery and murder of Walker Finch, alias Jerem Futterman. And two other deceased——"

"What's supposed to become of Yellow Buckle, while——"

"That's up to Captain Clinton. Maybe he wants to throw the Rangers at Yellow Buckle, with you for guide. You'll have to talk to him."

Watching Amos, Mart saw his mind lock, slowly turning him into the inert lump Mart remembered from long ago. He couldn't believe it at first, it was so long since he had seen Amos look like that.

"I'll ride there with you, Amos," Aaron Mathison said. "Sol Clinton will listen to me. We'll clear this thing once and for all."

Amos' eyes were on his empty hands, and he seemed incapable of speech.

"I'm not going in," Mart said to Charlie MacCorry.

"What?" The young Ranger looked startled.

"I don't know what Amos is of a mind to do," Mart said. "I'm going to Yellow Buckle."

"That there's maybe the worst thing I could hear you say!"

"All I want to do is get her out of there," Mart said, "before you hit him, or the cavalry hits. Once you jump him, it'll be too late."

"Allowing she's alive," Charlie MacCorry said, "which I don't—you haven't got a chance in a million to buy her, or steal her, either!"

"I've seen a white girl I could buy from an Indian."

"This one can talk. Letting her go would be like suicide for half a tribe!"

"I got to try, Charlie. You see that."

"I see no such thing. Damn it, Mart, will you get it through your head—you're under arrest!"

"What if I walk out that door?"

Charlie glanced past Aaron at Laurie Mathison before he answered. "Now, you ought to know the answer to that."

Laurie said distinctly, "He means he'll put a bullet in your back."

Charlie MacCorry thought about that a moment. "If he's particular about getting his bullets in front," he said to her, "he can walk out backwards, can't he?"

A heavy silence held for some moments before Amos spoke. "It's up to Sol Clinton, Mart."

"That's what I told you," Charlie said.

Amos asked, "You want to get started?"

"We'll wait for daylight. Seeing there's two of you. And allowing for the attitude you take." He spoke to Aaron. "I'll take 'em out to the bunkhouse; they can get some sleep if they want. I'll set up with 'em. And don't get a gleam in your eye," he finished to Mart. "I was in the bunkhouse before I come in here—and I put your guns where they won't be fell over. Now stand up, and walk ahead of me slow."

The lamp was still burning in the bunkhouse, but the fire in the stove was cold. Charlie watched them, quietly wary but without tension, while he lighted a lantern for a second light, and set it on the floor well out of the way. He wasn't going to be left in the dark with a fight on his hands by one of them throwing his hat at the lamp. Amos sat heavily on his bunk; he looked tired and old.

"Pull your boots if you want," Charlie MacCorry said. "I ain't going to stamp on your feet, or nothing. I only come for you by myself because we been neighbors from a long way back. I want this as friendly as you'll let it be." He found a chair with the back broken off, moved it nearer the stove with his foot, and sat down facing the bunks.

"Mind if I build the fire up?" Mart asked.

"Good idea."

Mart pawed in the woodbox, stirring the split wood so that a piece he could get a grip on came to the top.

Charlie spoke sharply to Amos. "What you doing with that stick?"

From the corner of his eye, Mart saw that Amos was working an arm under the mattress on his bunk. "Thought I heard a mouse," Amos said.

Charlie stood up suddenly, so that the broken chair overturned. His gun came out, but it was not cocked or pointed. "Move slow," he said to Amos, "and bring that hand out empty." For that one moment, while Amos drew his hand slowly from under the tick, Charlie MacCorry was turned three-quarters away from Mart, his attention undivided upon Amos.

Mart's piece of cordwood swung, and caught MacCorry hard behind the ear. He rattled to the floor bonily, and lay limp. Amos was kneeling beside him instantly, empty-handed; he hadn't had anything under the mattress. He rolled Charlie over, got his gun from under him, and had a look at his eyes.

"You like to tore his noggin' off," he said. "Lucky he ain't dead."

"Guess I got excited."

"Fetch something to make a gag. And my light *reata*."

# 33

THEY DIDN'T know where the Seven Fingers were as well as they thought they did. West of the Rainy Mountains lay any number of watersheds, according to how far west you went. No creek had exactly seven tributaries. Mart had hoped to get hold of an Indian or two as they drew near. With luck they would have found a guide to take them within sight of Yellow Buckle's Camp. But Sheridan's long-awaited campaign had cleared the prairies; the country beyond the North Fork of the Red was deserted. They judged, though, that the Seven Fingers had to be one of two systems of creeks.

Leaving the North Fork they tried the Little Horsethief first. It had nine tributaries, but who could tell how many a Kiowa medicine man would count? This whole thing drained only seventy or eighty square miles; a few long swings, cutting for sign, disposed of it in two days.

They crossed the Walking Wolf Ridge to the Elkhorn. This was their other bet—a system of creeks draining an area perhaps thirty miles square. On the maps it looks like a tree. You could say it has thirty or forty run-ins if you followed all the branches out to their ends; or you could say it has eight, or four, or two. You could say it has seven.

The country had the right feel as they came into it; they believed this to be the place Lije had meant. But now both time and country were running out, and very fast. The murder charge against them might be a silly one, and liable to be laughed out of court. But they had resisted arrest by violence, in the course of which Mart had assaulted an officer with a deadly weapon, intending great bodily harm. Actually all he had done was to swing on that damn fool Charlie MacCorry, but such things take time to cool off, and they didn't have it. No question now whether they wanted to quit this long search; the search was quitting them. One way or the other, it would end here, and this time forever.

Sometimes they had sighted a distant dust far back on their trail, losing them when they changed direction, picking them up again when they straightened out. They hadn't seen it now for four days, but they didn't fool themselves. Their destination was known, within limits, and they would be come for. Not that they had any thought of escape; they would turn on their accusers when their work was done—if they got it done. But they must work fast now with what horseflesh they had left.

The Elkhorn Country is a land of low ridges between its many dust-and-flood-water streams. You can't see far, and what is worse, it is known as a medicine country full of dust drifts and sudden hazes. You can ride toward what looks like the smoke of many fires, and follow it as it recedes across the ridges, and finally lose it without finding any fire at all. Under war conditions this was a very slow-going job of riding indeed. Each swale had to be scouted from its high borders before you dared cut for sign; while you yourself could be scouted very easily, at any time or all the time, if the Indians you sought were at all wary of your approach.

Yet this whole complex was within three days military march from Fort Sill itself, at the pace the yellowlegs would ride now. No commander alive was likely to search his own doorstep with painful care, endlessly cordoning close to home, while the other columns were striking hundreds of miles into the fastnesses of the Staked Plains. Yellow Buckle had shown an unexampled craftiness in picking this hole-up in which to lie low, while the military storm blew over. Here he was almost certain to be by-passed in the first hours of the campaign, and thereafter could sit out the war unmolested, until the exhaustion of both sides brought peace. When the yellowlegs eventually went home, as they always did, his warriors and his ponies would be fresh and strong, ready for such a year of raids and victories as would make him legendary. By shrewdly setting aside the Comanche reliance upon speed and space, he had opened himself a way to become the all-time greatest war chief of the Comanches.

Would it have worked, except for a wobbly old man, whose dimming eyes saw no more glorious vision than that of a chair by a hot stove?

"We need a week there," Mart said.

"We're lucky if we've got two days."

They didn't like it. Like most prairie men, they had great belief in their abilities, but a total faith in their bad luck.

Then one day at daylight they got their break. It came as the result of a mistake, though of a kind no plainsman would own to; it could happen to anybody, and most it had happened to were dead. They had camped after dark, a long way past the place where they had built their cooking fire. Before that, though, they had studied the little valley very carefully in the last light, making sure they would bed down in the security of emptiness and space. They slept only after all reasonable precautions had been taken, with the skill of long-practiced men.

But as they broke out in the darkness before dawn, they rode at once upon the warm ashes of a fire where a single Indian had camped. They had been within less than a furlong of him all night.

He must have been a very tired Indian. Though they caught no glimpse of him, they knew they almost stepped on him, for they accidentally cut him off from his hobbled horse. They chased and roped the Indian pony, catching him very easily in so short a distance that Mart's back was full of prickles in expectation of an arrow in it. None came, however. They retired to a bald swell commanding the situation, and lay flat to wait for better light.

Slowly the sun came up, cleared the horizon haze, and leveled clean sunlight across the uneven land.

"You think he's took out on us?"

"I hope not," Amos answered. "We need the bugger. We need him bad."

An hour passed. "I figured he'd stalk us," Mart said. "He must be stalking us. Some long way round. I can't see him leaving without any try for the horses."

"We got to wait him out."

"Might be he figures to foller and try us tonight."

"We got to wait him out anyway," Amos said.

Still another hour, and the sun was high.

"I think it's the odds," Mart believed now. "We're two to one. Till he gets one clean shot. Then it's even."

Amos said with sarcasm, "One of us can go away."

"Yes," Mart said. He got his boots from the aparejos, and changed them for the worn moccasins in which he had been scouting for many days.

"What's that for?" Amos demanded.

"So's he'll hear me."

"Hear you doing what? Kicking yourself in the head?"

"Look where I say." Mart flattened to the ground beside Amos again. "Straight ahead, down by the crick, you see a little willer."

"He ain't under that. Boughs don't touch down."

"No, and he ain't up it neither—I can see through the leaves. Left of the willer, you see a hundred-foot strip of saw grass about knee high. Left of that, a great long slew of buckbrush against the water. About belt deep. No way out of there without yielding a shot. I figure we got him pinned in there."

"No way to comb him out if that's where he is," Amos said; but he studied the buckbrush a long time.

Mart got up, and took the canteens from the saddles.

"He'll put an arrow through you so fast it'll fall free on the far side, you go down to that crick!"

"Not without raising up, he won't."

"That's a seventy-five yard shot from here—maybe more. I ain't using you for bait on no such——"

"You never drew back from it before!" Mart went jauntily down the slope to the creek, swinging the canteens. Behind him he could hear Amos rumbling curses to himself for a while; then the morning was quiet except for the sound of his own boots.

He walked directly, unhurrying, to the point where the firm ground under the buckbrush mushed off into the shallow water at the saw-grass roots. He sloshed through ten yards of this muck, skirting the brush; and now his hackles crawled at the back of his neck, for he smelled Indian—a faint sunburnt smell of woodfires, of sage smoke, of long-used buffalo robes.

He came to the water, and stopped. Still standing straight up he floated the two canteens, letting them fill themselves at the end of their long slings. This was the time, as he stood motionless here, pretending to look at the water. He dared not look at the buckbrush, lest his own purpose be spoiled. But he let his head turn a little bit downstream, so that he could hold the buckbrush in the corner of his eye. He was certain nothing moved.

Amos' bullet yowled so close to him it seemed Amos must have fired at his back, and a spout of water jumped in the river straight beyond. Mart threw himself backward, turning as he fell, so that he came down on his belly in the muck. He didn't know how his six-gun came cocked into his hand, but it was there.

"Stay down!" Amos bellowed. "Hold still, damn it! I don't think I got him!" Mart could hear him running down the slope, chambering a fresh cartridge with a metallic clank. He flattened, trying to suck himself into the mud, and for a few moments lay quiet, all things out of his hands.

Amos came splashing into the saw grass so close by that Mart thought he was coming directly to where Mart lay.

"Yes, I did," Amos said. "Come looky this here!"

"Watch out for him!" Mart yelled. "Your bullet went in the crick!"

"I creased him across the back. Prettiest shot you ever see in your life!"

Mart got up then. Amos was standing less than six yards away, looking down into the grass. Two steps toward him and Mart could see part of the dark, naked body, prone in the saw grass. He stopped, and moved backward a little; he had no desire to see anything more. Amos reached for the Indian's knife, and spun it into the creek.

"Get his bow," Mart said.

"Bow, hell! This here's a Spencer he's got here." Amos picked it up. "He threw down on you from fifteen feet!"

"I never even heard the safety click———"

"That's what saved you. It's still on."

Amos threw the rifle after the knife, far out into the water.

"Is he in shape to talk?"

"He'll talk, all right. Now get your horse, quick!"

"What?"

"There's two Rangers coming up the crick. I got one quick sight of 'em at a mile—down by the far bend. Get on down there, and hold 'em off!"

"You mean fight?"

"No-no-no! Talk to 'em—say anything that comes in your head———"

"What if they try to arrest me?"

"Let 'em! Only keep 'em off me while I question this Comanch'!"

Mart ran for his horse.

## 34

NO RANGERS were in sight a mile down the creek when Mart got there. None at two miles, either. By this time he knew what had happened. He had been sent on a fool's errand because Amos wanted to work on the Indian alone. He turned back, letting his horse loiter; and Amos met him at the half mile, coming downstream at a brisk trot. He looked grim, and very ugly, but satisfied with his results.

"He talked," Mart assumed.

"Yeah. We know how to get to Yellow Buckle now. He's got the girl Lije Powers saw, all right."

"Far?"

"We'll be there against night. And it's a good thing. There's a party of more than forty Rangers, with sixty-seventy Tonkawas along with 'em, on 'the hill by the Beaver' —that'll be old Camp Radziminski—and two companies of yellowlegs, by God, more'n a hundred of 'em, camped right alongside!"

"That's no way possible! Your Indian lied."

"He didn't lie." Amos seemed entirely certain. Mart saw now that a drop of fresh blood had trickled down the outside of Amos' scalping-knife sheath.

"Where is he now?"

"In the crick. I weighted him down good with rocks."

"I don't understand this," Mart said. He had learned to guess the general nature of the truth behind some kinds of Indian lies, but he couldn't see through this story. "I never heard of Rangers and cavalry working together before. Not in Indian territory, anyway. My guess is Sill sent out a patrol to chase the Rangers back."

Amos shrugged. "Maybe so. But the Rangers will make a deal now—they'll have to. Give the soldiers Yellow Buckle on a plate in return for not getting run back to Texas."

"Bound to," Mart said glumly, "I suppose."

"Them yellowlegs come within an ace of leaving a big fat pocket of Comanch' in their rear. Why, Yellow Buckle could have moved right into Fort Sill soon as Davidson marches!

They'll blow sky high once they see what they nearly done. They can hit that village in two days—tomorrow, if the Rangers set the pace. And no more Yellow Buckle! We got to get over there."

They reset their saddles, and pressed on at a good long trot, loping one mile in three.

"There's something I got to say," Mart told Amos as they rode. "I want to ask one thing. If we find the village——"

"We'll find it. And it'll still be there. That one Comanche was the only scout they had out between them and Fort Sill."

"I want to ask one thing——"

"Finding Yellow Buckle isn't the hard part. Not now." Amos seemed to sense a reason for putting Mart off from what he wanted to say. "Digging the girl out of that village is going to be the hard thing in what little time we got."

"I know. Amos, will you do me one favor? When we find the village— Now, don't go off half cocked. I want to walk in there alone."

"You want—what?"

"I want to go in and talk to Yellow Buckle by myself."

Amos did not speak for so long that Mart thought he was not going to answer him at all. "I had it in mind," he said at last, "the other way round. Leave you stay back, so set you can get clear, if worst goes wrong. Whilst I walk in and test what their temper be."

Mart shook his head. "I'm asking you. This one time—will you do it my way?"

Another silence before Amos asked, "Why?"

Mart had foreseen this moment, and worked it over in his mind a hundred times without thinking of any story that had a chance to work. "I got to tell you the truth. I see no other way."

"You mean," Amos said sardonically, "you'd come up with a lie now if you had one to suit."

"That's right. But I got no lie for this. It's because I'm scared of something. Suppose this. Suppose some one Comanche stood in front of you. And you knew for certain in your own mind—he was the one killed Martha?"

Mart watched Amos' face gray, then darken. "Well?" Amos said.

"You'd kill him. And right there'd be the end of Debbie, and all hunting for Debbie. I know that as well as you."

Amos said thickly, "Forget all this. And you best lay clear like I tell you, too—if you don't want Yellow Buckle to get away clean! Because I'm going in."

"I got to be with you, then. In hopes I can stop you when that minute comes."

"You know what that would take?"

"Yes; I do know. I've known for a long time."

Amos turned in the saddle to look at him. "I believe you'd do it," he decided. "I believe you'd kill me in the bat of an eye if it come to that."

Mart said nothing. They rode in silence for a furlong more.

"Oh, by the way," Amos said. "I got something for you here. I believe you better have it now. If so happens you feel I got to be gunned down, you might's well have some practical reason. One everybody's liable to understand."

He rummaged in various pockets, and finally found a bit of paper, grease-marked and worn at the folds. He opened it to see if it was the right one; and the wind whipped at it as he handed it to Mart. The writing upon it was in ink.

> Now know all men: I, Amos Edwards, being of sound mind, and without any known blood kin, do will that upon my death my just debts do first be paid. Whereafter, all else I own, be it in property, money, livestock, or rights to range, shall go to my foster nephew Martin Pauley, in rightful token of the help he has been to me, in these the last days of my life.
>
> AMOS EDWARDS

Beside the signature was a squiggle representing a seal, and the signatures of the witnesses, Aaron Mathison and Laura E. Mathison. He didn't know what the "E" stood for; he had never even known Laurie had a middle name. But he knew Amos had fixed him. This act of kindness, with living witnesses to it, could be Mart's damnation if he had to turn on Amos. He held out the paper to Amos for him to take back.

"Keep hold of it," Amos said. "Come in handy if the Comanches go through my pockets before you."

"It don't change anything," Mart said bleakly. "I'll do what I have to do."

"I know."

They rode four hours more. At mid-afternoon Amos held up his hand, and they stopped. The rolling ground hid whatever was ahead but now they heard the far-off barking of dogs.

## 35

Yellow Buckle's village was strung out for a considerable distance along a shallow river as yet unnamed by white men, but called by Indians the Wild Dog. The village was a lot bigger than the Texans had expected. Counting at a glance, as cattle are counted, Mart believed he saw sixty-two lodges. Probably it would be able to turn out somewhere between a hundred fifty and two hundred warriors, counting old men and youths.

They were seen at a great distance, and the usual scurrying about resulted all down the length of the village. Soon a party of warriors began to build up just outside. They rode bareback, with single-rope war bridles on the jaws of their ponies, and their weapons were in their hands. A few headdresses and medicine shields showed among them, but none had tied up the tails of their ponies, as they did when a fight was expected. This group milled about, but not excitedly, until twenty or so had assembled, then flowed into a fairly well-dressed line, and advanced at a walk to meet the white men. Meanwhile three or four scouts on fast ponies swung wide, and streaked in the direction from which Mart and Amos had come to make sure that the two riders were alone.

"Seem kind of easy spooked," Mart said, "don't they?"

"I wouldn't say so. Times have changed. They're getting fought back at now. Seems to me they act right cocky, and sure."

The mounted line halted fifty yards in front of them. A warrior in a buffalo-horn headdress drew out two lengths, and questioned them in sign language: "Where have you come from? What do you want? What do you bring?" The conventional things.

And Amos gave conventional answers. "I come very far, from beyond the Staked Plains. I want to make talk. I have a message for Yellow Buckle. I have gifts."

A Comanche raced his pony back into the village, and the spokesman faked other questions, meaninglessly, while he waited for instructions. By the time his runner was back from the village, the scouts had signaled from far out that the strangers appeared to be alone, and all was well up to here. The two riders were escorted into the village through a clamoring horde of cur dogs, all with small heads and the souls of gad-flies; and halted before a tepee with the black smoke flaps of a chief's lodge.

Presently a stocky, middle-aged Comanche came out, wrapped himself in a blanket, and stood looking them over. He was weaponless, but had put on no headdress or decoration of any kind. This was a bad sign, and the slouchy way he stood was another. Amos' gestures were brusque as he asked if this man called himself Yellow Buckle and the chief gave the least possible acknowledgment.

Visitors were supposed to stay in the saddle until invited to dismount, but Yellow Buckle did not give the sign. He's making this too plain, Mart thought. He wants us out of here, and in a hurry, but he ought to cover up better than this. Mart felt Amos anger. The tension increased until it seemed to ring as Amos dismounted without invitation, walked within two paces of the chief, and looked him up and down.

Yellow Buckle looked undersized with Amos looming over him. He had the short bandy legs that made most Comanches unimpressive on the ground, however effective they might be when once they put hands to their horses. He remained expressionless, and met Amos' eyes steadily. Mart stepped down and stood a little in back of Amos, and to the side. Getting a closer look at this chief, Mart felt his scalp stir. A thin line, like a crease, ran from the corner of the Comanche's left eye to the line of the jaw, where no natural wrinkle would be. They were standing before the mythical, the long-hunted, the forever elusive Chief Scar!

The Indian freed one arm, and made an abrupt sign that asked what they wanted. Amos' short answer was all but contemptuous. "I do not stand talking in the wind," his hands said.

For a moment more the Comanche chief stood like a post. Amos had taken a serious gamble in that he had left himself no alternatives. If Yellow Buckle—Scar—told him to get out, Amos would have no way to stay, and no excuse for coming back. After that he could only ride to meet the Rangers, and

guide them to the battle that would destroy Scar and most of
the people with him. It's what he wants, Mart thought. I have
to stay if Amos rides out of here. I have to make what try I can,
never mind what Amos does.

But now Scar smiled faintly, with a gleam in his eye that
Mart neither understood nor liked, but which might have contained derision. He motioned Amos to follow him, and went
into the tepee.

"See they keep their hands off the mule packs," Amos said,
tossing Mart his reins.

Mart let the split reins fall. "Guard these," he said in Comanche to the warrior who had been spokesman. The Comanche
looked blank but Mart turned his back on him, and followed
Amos. The door flap dropped in his face; he struck it aside with
annoyance, and went inside.

A flicker of fire in the middle of the lodge, plus a seepage of
daylight from the smoke flap at the peak, left the lodge shadowy. The close air carried a sting of wood smoke, scented with
wild-game stew, buffalo hides, and the faintly musky robe smell
of Indians. Two chunky squaws and three younger females had
been stirred into a flurry by Amos' entrance, but they were
settling down as Mart came in. Mart gave the smallest of these,
a half-grown girl, a brief flick of attention, without looking
directly at her but even out of the corner of his eye he could
see that her shingled thatch was black, and as coarse as a pony's
tail.

Women were supposed to keep out of the councils of warriors, unless called to wait on the men. But the two squaws
now squatted on their piled robes on the honor side of the
lodge, where Scar's grown sons should have been, and the
three younger ones huddled deep in the shadows opposite.
Mart realized that they must have jumped up to get out of
there, and that Scar had told them to stay. This was pretty close
to insult, the more so since Scar did not invite the white men
to sit down.

Scar himself stood opposite the door beyond the fire. He
shifted his blanket, wrapping it skirtlike around his waist; and
his open buckskin shirt exposed a gold brooch in the form
of a bow of ribbon, hung around his neck on a chain. In all
likelihood his present name, assumed midway of his career,

commemorated some exploit with which this brooch was associated.

Amos waited stolidly, and finally Scar was forced to address them. He knew them now, he told them in smooth-running sign language. "You," he said, indicating Amos, "are called Bull Shoulders. And this boy," he dismissed Mart, "is The Other."

Amos' hands lied fluently in answer. He had heard of a white man called Bull Shoulders, but the Chickasaws said Bull Shoulders was dead. He himself was called Plenty Mules. His friends, the Quohadas, so named him. He was a subchief among the Comanchero traders beyond the Staked Plains. His boss was called the Rich One. Real name—"Jaime Rosas," Amos used his voice for the first time.

"You are Plenty Mules," Yellow Buckle's hands conceded, while his smile expressed a contrary opinion. "A Comanchero. This—" he indicated Mart—"is still The Other. His eyes are made of mussel shells, and he sees in the dark."

"This—" Amos contradicted him again—"is my son. His Indian name is No-Speak."

Mart supposed this last was meant to convey an order.

The Rich One, Amos went on in sign language, had many-heap rifles. (It was that sign itself, descriptive of piles and piles, that gave Indians the word "heap" for any big quantity, when they picked up white men's words.) He wanted horses, mules, horned stock, for his rifles. He had heard of Yellow Buckle. He had been told—here Amos descended to flattery—that Yellow Buckle was a great horse thief, a great cow thief—a fine sneak thief of every kind. Yellow Buckle's friend had said that.

"What friend?" Scar's hands demanded.

"The Flower," Amos signed.

"The Flower," Scar said, "has a white wife."

No change of pace or mood showed in the movement of Scar's hands, drawing classically accurate pictographs in the air, as he said that. But Mart's hair stirred and all but crackled; the smoky air in the lodge had suddenly become charged, like a thunderhead. Out of the corner of his eye Mart watched the squaws to see if Scar's remark meant anything to them in their own lives, here. But the eyes of the Comanche women were on the ground; he could not see their down-turned faces, and they had not seen the sign.

White wife. Amos made the throw-away sign. The Rich One did not trade for squaws. If the Yellow Buckle wanted rifles, he must bring horses. Many-heaps horses. No small deals. Or maybe—and this was sarcasm—Yellow Buckle did not need rifles. Plenty Mules could go find somebody else. . . . Amos was giving a very poor imitation of a man trying to make a trade with an Indian. But perhaps it was a good imitation of a man who had been sent with this offer, but who would prefer to make his deal elsewhere to his own purposes.

Scar seemed puzzled; he did not at once reply. Behind the Comanche, Mart could see the details of trophies and accoutrements, now that his eyes were accustomed to the gloom. Scar's medicine shield was there. Mart wondered if it bore, under its masking cover, a design he had seen at the Fight at the Cat-tails long ago. Above the shield hung Scar's short lance, slung horizontally from the lodgepoles. Almost a dozen scalps were displayed upon it, and less than half of them looked like the scalps of Indians. The third scalp from the tip of the lance had long wavy hair of a deep red-bronze. It was a white woman's scalp, and the woman it had belonged to must have been beautiful. The squaws had kept this scalp brushed and oiled, so that it caught red glints from the wavering fire. But Scar's lance bore none of the pale fine hair that had been Martha's, nor the bright gold that had been Lucy's hair.

Scar turned his back on them while he took two slow, thoughtful steps toward the back of the lodge and in that moment, while Scar was turned away from them, Mart felt eyes upon his face, as definitely as if a finger touched his cheek. His glance flicked to the younger squaws on the women's side of the lodge.

He saw her then. One of the young squaws wore a black head cloth, covering all of her hair and tied under her chin; it was a commonplace thing for a squaw to wear, but it had sufficed to make her look black-headed like the others in the uncertain light. Now this one had looked up, and her eyes were on his face in an unwavering stare, as a cat stares; and the eyes were green and slanted, lighter than the deeply tanned face. They were the most startling eyes he had ever seen in his life, strangely cold, impersonal yet inimical, and as hard as glass. But this girl was Debbie.

The green eyes dropped as Scar turned toward the strangers again and Mart's own eyes were straight ahead when the Comanche chief looked toward them.

Where were the rifles? Scar's question came at last.

Beyond the Staked Plains, Amos answered him. Trading must be there.

Another wait, while Mart listened to the ringing in his ears.

Too far, Scar said. Let the Rich One bring his rifles here.

Amos filled his lungs, stood tall, and laughed in Scar's face. Mart saw the Comanche's eyes narrow but after a moment he seated himself cross-legged on his buffalo robes under the dangling scalps and the shield. "Sit down," he said in Comanche, combining the words with the sign.

Amos ignored the invitation. "I speak no more now," he said, using his voice for the second time. His Comanche phrasings were slow and awkward but easily understood. "Below this village I saw a spring. I camp there, close by the Wild Dog River. Tomorrow, if you wish to talk, find me there. I sleep one night wait one day. Then I go."

"You spoke of gifts," Yellow Buckle reminded him.

"They will be there." He turned and, without concession to courtesy, he said in English, "Come on, No-Speak." And Mart followed him out.

## 36

PRINGLES RAN up and down Mart's back as they rode out of that village with the cur dogs bawling and blaspheming again all around them, just beyond kick-range of their horses' feet. But until they were out of there they had to move unhurriedly, as if at peace and expecting peace. Even their eyes held straight ahead, lest so much as an exchange of glances be misread as a trigger for trouble.

Amos spoke first, well past the last of the lodges. "Did you see her? . . . Yeah," he answered himself. "I see you did." His reaction to the sudden climax of their search seemed to be the opposite of what Mart had expected. Amos seemed steadied, and turned cool.

"She's alive," Mart said. It seemed about the only thing his mind was able to think. "Can you realize it? Can you believe it? We found her, Amos!"

"Better start figuring how to stay alive yourself. Or finding her won't do anybody much good."

That was what was taking all the glory, all the exultation, out of their victory. They had walked into a hundred camps where they could have handled this situation, dangerous though it must always be. White captives had been bought and sold before time and again. Any Indian on earth but Scar would have concealed the girl, and played for time, until they found a way to deal.

"How in God's name," Mart asked him, "can this thing be? How could he let us walk into the lodge where she was? And keep her there before our eyes?"

"He meant for us to see her, that's all!"

"This is a strange Comanche," Mart said.

"This whole hunt has been a strange thing. And now we know why. Mart, did you see—there's scarce a Comanch' in that whole village we haven't seen before."

"I know."

"We've even stood in that same one lodge before. Do you know where?"

"When we talked to Singing Dog on the Little Boggy."

"That's right. We talked to Singing Dog in Scar's own lodge —while Scar took the girl and hid out. That's how they've kept us on a wild-goose chase five years long. They've covered up, and decoyed for him, every time we come near."

"We've caught up to him now!"

"Because he let us. Scar's learned something few Indians ever know: He's learned there's such a thing as a critter that never quits follering or gives up. So he's had enough. If we stood in the same lodge with her, and didn't know her, well and good. But if we were going to find her, he wanted to see us do it."

"So he saw—I suppose."

"I think so. He has to kill us, Mart."

"Bluebonnet didn't think he had to kill us."

"He never owned to having a white girl until Jaime Rosas made him a safe deal. And down there below the Llanos we was two men alone. Up here, we got Rangers, we got yellow-legs, to pull down on Scar. We rode square into the pocket where he was figuring to set until Davidson marched, and all soldiers was long gone. Scar don't dast let us ride loose with the word."

"Why'd he let us walk out of there at all?"

"I don't know," Amos said honestly. "Something tied his hands. If we knew what it was we could stretch it. But we don't know." Amos bent low over the horn to look back at the village under his arm. "They're holding fast so far. Might even let us make a pass at settling down at the spring. . . ."

But neither believed the Comanches would wait for night. Scar was a smart Indian, and a bitter one. The reason his squaws were on the honor side of the lodge where his sons should be was that Scar's sons were dead, killed in war raids upon the likes of Mart and Amos. He would take no chances of a slip-up in the dark.

"We'll make no two mistakes," Amos said, and his tone was thoughtful. "They got some fast horses there. You saw them scouts whip up when they took a look at our back trail. Them's racing ponies. And they got nigh two hours of daylight left."

They reached the spring without sign of pursuit, and dismounted. Here they had a good three-furlong start, and would be able to see horses start from the village when the Comanches made their move. They would not, of course, be able to see warriors who ran crouching on foot, snaking on their bellies across open ground. But the Comanches hated action afoot. More probably they would try to close for the kill under pretense of bringing fresh meat, perhaps with squaws along as a blind. Or the Comanches might simply make a horse race of it. The fast war ponies would close their three-eighths-mile lead very easily, with even half an hour of daylight left. Some Indians were going to be killed but there could hardly be but one end.

They set to work on the one thin ruse they could think of. Mart kicked a fire together first—about the least token of a fire that would pass for one at all—and set it alight. Then they stripped saddles and packs. They would have to abandon these, in order to look as though they were not going any place. Bridles were left on the horses, and halters on the mules.

"We'll lead out," Amos said, "like hunting for the best grass. Try to get as much more lead as we can without stirring 'em up. First minute any leave the village, we'll ease over a ridge, mount bareback—stampede the mules. Split up, of course—ride two ways———"

"We'll put up a better fight if we stay together," Mart objected.

"Yeah. We'd kill more Indians that way. There's no doubt of it. But a whole lot more than that will be killed if one of us stays alive until dark—and makes Camp Radziminski."

"Wait a minute," Mart said. "If we lead the yellowlegs on 'em—or even the Rangers, with the Tonkawas they got—there'll be a massacre, Amos! This village will be gutted out."

"Yes," Amos said.

"They'll kill her—you know that! You saw it at Deadhorse Bend!"

"If I didn't think so," Amos said, "I'd have killed her myself."

There was the substance of their victory after all this long time: One bitter taste of death, and then nothing more, forever.

"I won't do this," Mart said.

"What?"

"She's alive. That means everything to me. Better she's alive and living with Indians than her brains bashed out."

A blaze of hatred lighted Amos' eyes, while his face was still a mask of disbelief. "I can't believe my own ears," he said.

"I say there'll be no massacre while she's in that village! Not while I can stop it, or put it off!"

Amos got control of his voice. "What do you want to do?"

"First we got to live out the night. That I know and agree to. Beyond that, I don't know. Maybe we got to come at Scar some far way round. But we stay together. Because I'm not running to the troops, Amos. And neither are you."

Amos' voice was half choked by the congestion of blood in his neck. "You think the likes of you could stop me?"

Mart pulled out the bit of paper upon which the will was written, in which Amos left Mart all he had. He tore it slowly into shreds, and laid them on the fire. "Yes," he said, "I'll stop you."

Amos was silent for a long time. He stood with his shoulders slack, and his big hands hanging loose by his thighs, and he stared into space. When finally he spoke his voice was tired. "All right. We'll stay together through the night. After that, we'll see. I can't promise no more."

"That's better. Now let's get at it!"

"I'm going to tell you something," Amos said. "I wasn't going to speak of it. But if we fight, you got to murder all of 'em you can. So I'll tell you now. Did you notice them scalps strung on Scar's lance?"

"I was in there, wasn't I?"

"They ain't there," Mart said. "Not Martha's. Not Lucy's. Not even Brad's. Let's——"

"Did you see the third scalp from the point of the lance?"

"I saw it."

"Long, wavy. A red shine to it——"

"I saw it, I told you! You're wasting——"

"You didn't remember it. But I remember." Amos' voice was harsh, and his eyes bored into Mart's eyes, as if to drive the words into his brain. "That was your mother's scalp!"

No reason for Mart to doubt him. His mother's scalp was somewhere in a Comanche lodge, if a living Indian still possessed it. Certainly it was not in her grave. Amos let him stand there a moment, while his unremembered people became real to him—his mother, with the pretty hair, his father, from whom he got his light eyes, his young sisters, Ethel and Becky, who were just names. He knew what kind of thing their massacre had been, because he had seen the Edwards place, and the people who had raised him, after the same thing happened there.

"Let's lead off," Amos said.

But before they had gone a rod, the unexpected stopped them. A figure slipped out the willows by the creek, and a voice spoke. Debbie was there—alone, so far as they could see she had materialized as an Indian does, without telltale sound of approach.

She moved a few halting steps out of the willow scrub, but stopped as Mart came toward her. He walked carefully, watchful for movement in the thicket behind her. Behind him he heard the metallic crash as Amos chambered a cartridge. Amos had sprung onto a hummock, exposing himself recklessly while his eyes swept the terrain.

Mart was at four paces when Debbie spoke, urgently, in Comanche. "Don't come too close. Don't touch me! I have warriors with me."

He had remembered the voice of a child, but what he was hearing was the soft-husky voice of a grown woman. Her Comanche was fluent, indistinguishable from that of the Indians, yet he thought he had never heard that harsh and ugly tongue sound uglier. He stopped six feet from her; one more inch, he felt, and she would have bolted. "Where are they, then?" he demanded. "Let 'em stand up and be counted, if they're not afraid!"

Mystification came into her face; she stared at him with blank eyes. Suddenly he realized that he had spoken in a rush of English—and she no longer understood. The lost years had left an invisible mutilation as definite as if fingers were missing from her hand. "How many warriors?" he asked in gruff Comanche; and everything they said to each other was in Comanche after that.

"Four men are with me."

His eyes jumped then, and swept wide; and though he saw nothing at all, he knew she might be telling the truth. If she had not come alone, he had to find out what was happening here, and quick. Their lives might easily depend upon their next guess. "What are you doing here?" he asked harshly.

"My——" He heard a wary hesitancy, a testing of words before they were spoken. "My—father—told me come."

"Your *what*?"

"Yellow Buckle is my father."

While he stared at her, sure he must have misunderstood the Comanche words, Amos put in. "Keep at her! Scar sent her all right. We got to know why!"

Watching her, Mart was sure Debbie had understood none of Amos' Texan English. She tried to hurry her stumbling tale. "My father—he believes you. But some others—they know. They tell him—you were my people once."

"What did *you* tell him?"

"I tell him I don't know. I must come here. Make sure. I tell him I must come."

"You told him nothing like that," he contradicted her in Comanche. "He smash your mouth, you say 'must' to him!"

She shook her head. "No. No. You don't know my father."

"We know him. We call him Scar."

"My father—Scar—" she accepted his name for the chief— "He believes you. He says you are Comancheros. Like you say. But soon—" she faltered—"soon he knows."

"He knows now," he contradicted her again. "You are lying to me!"

Her eyes dropped, and her hands hid themselves in her ragged wash-leather sleeves. "He says you are Comancheros," she repeated. "He believes you. He told me. He———"

He had an exasperated impulse to grab her and shake her; but he saw her body tense. If he made a move toward her she would be gone in the same instant. "*Debbie*, listen to me! I'm *Mart*! Don't you remember me?" He spoke just the names in English, and it was obvious that these two words were familiar to her.

"I remember you," she said gravely, slowly, across the gulf between them. "I remember. From always."

"Then stop lying to me! You got Comanches with you—so you say. What do you want here if you're not alone?"

"I come to tell you, go away! Go tonight. As soon as dark. They can stop you. They can kill you. But this one night— I make him let you go."

"Make him?" He was so furious he stammered. "*You* make him? No squaw alive can move Scar a hand span—you least of all!"

"I can," she said evenly, meeting his eyes. "I am—bought. I am bought for—to be—for marriage. My—man—he pays sixty ponies. Nobody ever paid so much. I'm worth sixty ponies."

"We'll overcall that," he said. "Sixty ponies! We'll pay a hundred for you—a hundred and a half——"

She shook her head.

"My man—his family——"

"You own five times that many ponies yourself—you know that? We can bring them—many as he wants—and enough cattle to feed the whole tribe from here to——"

"My man would fight. His people would fight. They are very many. Scar would lose—lose everything."

Comanche thoughts, Comanche words—a white woman's voice and form . . . the meeting toward which he had worked for years had turned into a nightmare. Her face was Debbie's face, delicately made, and now in the first bloom of maturity; but all expression was locked away from it. She held it wooden, facing him impassively, as an Indian faces a stranger. Behind the surface of this long-loved face was a Comanche squaw.

He spoke savagely, trying to break through to the Debbie of long ago. "Sixty ponies," he said with contempt. "What good is that? One sleep with Indians—you're a mare—a sow—they take what they want of you. Nothing you can do would turn Scar!"

"I can kill myself," she said.

In the moment of silence, Amos spoke again. "String it out. No move from the village yet. Every minute helps."

Mart looked into the hard green eyes that should have been lovely and dear to him; and he believed her. She was capable of killing herself, and would do it if she said she would. And Scar must know that. Was this the mysterious thing that had tied Scar's hands when he let them walk away? An accident to a sold but undelivered squaw could cost Scar more than sixty ponies. It could cost him his chiefship, and perhaps his life.

"That is why you can go now," she said, "and be safe. I have told him—my father——"

His temper flared up, "Stop calling that brute your father!"

"You must get away from here," she said again, monotonously, almost dropping into a ritual Comanche singsong. "You must go away quick. Soon he will know. You will be killed——"

"You bet I'm getting out of here," he said, breaking into English. "And I got no notion of getting killed, neither! Amos! Grab holt that black mule! She's got to ride that!"

He heard leather creak as Amos swung up a saddle. No chance of deception now, from here on; they had to take her and run.

Debbie said, "What———?"

He returned to Comanche. "You're going with us now! You hear me?"

"No," Debbie said. "Not now. Not ever."

"I don't know what they have done to you. But it makes no difference!" He wouldn't have wasted time fumbling Comanche words if he had seen half a chance of taking her by main force. "You must come with me. I take you to———"

"They have done nothing to me. They take care of me. These are my people."

"Debbie, Debbie—these—these Nemenna murdered our family!"

"You lie." A flash of heat-lightning in her eyes let him see an underlying hatred, unexpected and dreadful.

"These are the ones! They killed your mother, cut her arm off—killed your own real father, slit his belly open—killed Hunter, killed Ben———"

"Wichitas killed them! Wichitas and white men! To steal cows———"

"*What?*"

"These people saved me. They drove off the whites and the Wichitas. I ran in the brush. Scar picked me up on his pony. They have told me it all many times!" He was blanked again, helpless against lies drilled into her over the years.

Amos had both saddles cinched up. "Watch your chance," he said. "You know now what we got to do."

Debbie's eyes went to Amos in quick suspicion, but Mart was still trying. "Lucy was with you. You know what happened to her!"

"Lucy—went mad. They—we—gave her a pony———"

"Pony! They—they———" He could not think of the word for rape. "They cut her up! Amos—Bull Shoulders—he found her, buried her———"

"You lie," she answered, her tone monotonous again, without heat. "All white men lie. Always."

"Listen! Listen to me! I saw my own mother's scalp on Scar's lance—there in the lodge where you live!"

"Lies," she said, and looked at him sullenly, untouched. "You Long Knives—you are the evil ones. You came in the night, and started killing us. There by the river."

At first he didn't know what she was talking about; then he remembered Deadhorse Bend and Debbie's locket that had seemed to tell them she had been there. He wondered if she had seen the old woman cut down, who wore her locket, and the old man sabered, as he tried to save his squaw.

"I saw it all," she said, as if answering his thought.

Mart changed his tone. "I found your locket," he said gently. "Do you remember your little locket? Do you remember who gave it to you? So long ago. . . ."

Her eyes faltered for the first time; and for a moment he saw in this alien woman the little girl of the miniature, the child of the shrine in the dream.

"At first—I prayed to you," she said.

"You what?"

"At first—I cried. Every night. For a long time. I cried to you—come and get me. Take me home. You didn't come." Her voice was dead, all feeling washed out of it.

"I've come now," he said.

She shook her head. "These are my people. You—you are Long Knives. We hate you—fight you—always, till we die."

Amos said sharply, "They're mounting up now, up there. We got to go." He came over to them in long, quick strides, and spoke in Comanche, but loudly, as some people speak to foreigners. "You know Yellow Buckle thing?" he demanded, backing his words with signs. "Buckle, Scar wear?"

"The medicine buckle," she said clearly.

"Get your hands on it. Turn it over. Can you still read? On the back it says white man's words 'Ethan to Judith.' Scratched in the gold. Because Scar tore it off Mart's mother when he killed and scalped her!"

"Lies," Debbie repeated in Comanche.

"Look and see for yourself!"

Amos had been trying to work around Debbie, to cut her off from the willows and the river, but she was watching him, moving enough to keep clear. "I go back now," she said. "To my father's lodge. I can do nothing here." Her movements brought her no closer to Mart, but suddenly his nostrils caught the distinct, unmistakable Indian odor, alive, immediate, near. For an instant the unreasoning fear that this smell had brought him, all through his early years, came back with a sickening chill of revulsion. He looked at the girl with horror.

Amos brought him out of it. "Keep your rifle on her, Mart! If she breaks, stun her with the butt!" He swayed forward, then lunged to grab her.

She wasn't there. She cried out a brief phrase in Comanche as she dodged him, then was into the brush, running like a fox. "Git down!" Amos yelled, and fired his rifle from belt level, though not at her; while simultaneously another rifle fired through the space in which Debbie had stood. Its bullet whipped past Mart's ear as he flung himself to the ground. The Comanche who had fired on him sprang up, face to the sky, surprisingly close to them, then fell back into the thin grass in which he had hidden.

Dirt jumped in Mart's face, and a ricochet yowled over. He swiveled on his belt buckle, and snap-fired at a wisp of gunsmoke sixty yards away in the brush. He saw a rifle fall and slide clear of the cover. Amos was standing straight up, trading shots with a third sniper. "Got him," he said, and instantly spun half around, his right leg knocked from under him. A Comanche sprang from an invisible depression less than thirty yards away, and rushed with drawn knife. Mart fired, and the Indian's legs pumped grotesquely as he fell, sliding him on his face another two yards before he was still. All guns were silent then; and Mart went to Amos.

"Go on, God damn it!" Blood pumped in spurts from a wound just above Amos' knee. "Ride, you fool! They're coming down on us!"

The deep thrumming of numberless hoofs upon the prairie turf came to them plainly from a quarter mile away. Mart sliced off a pack strap, and twisted it into a tourniquet. Amos cuffed him heavily alongside the head, pleading desperately. "For God's sake, Mart, will you ride? Go on! Go on!"

The Comanches weren't yelling yet, perhaps wouldn't until they struck. Of all the Wild Tribes, the Comanches were the last to start whooping, the first to come to close grips. Mart took precious seconds more to make an excuse for a bandage. "Get up here!" he grunted, stubborn to the bitter last; and he lifted Amos.

One of the mules was down, back broken by a bullet never meant for it. It made continual groaning, whistling noises as it clawed out with its fore hoofs, trying to drag up its dead hind-quarters. The other mules had stampeded, but the horses still stood, snorting and sidestepping, tied to the ground by their long reins. Mart got Amos across his shoulders, and heaved him bodily into the saddle. "Get your foot in the stirrup! Gimme that!" He took Amos' rifle, and slung it into the brush. "See can you tie yourself on with the saddle strings as we ride!"

He grabbed his own pony, and made a flying mount as both animals bolted. Sweat ran down Amos' face; the bullet shock was wearing off, but he rode straight up, his wounded leg dan-gling free. Mart leaned low on the neck, and his spurs raked deep. Both horses stretched their bellies low to the ground, and dug out for their lives, as the first bullets from the pursuit buzzed over. The slow dusk was closing now. If they could have had another half hour, night would have covered them before they were overtaken.

They didn't have it. But now the Comanches did another unpredictable, Indian kind of a thing. With their quarry in full view, certain to be flanked and forced to a stand within the mile, the Comanches stopped. Repeated signals passed for-ward, calling the leaders in; the long straggle of running ponies lost momentum, and sucked back upon itself. The Comanches bunched up, and sat their bareback ponies in a close mass—seemingly in argument.

Things like that had happened before that Mart knew about, though never twice quite the same. Sometimes the horse Indi-ans would fight a brilliant battle, using the fast-breaking cavalry tactics at which they were the best on earth—and seem to be winning; then unexpectedly turn and run. If you asked them later why they ran, they would say they ran because they had fought enough. Pursued, they might turn abruptly and fight again as tenaciously as before—and explain they fought then because they had run enough. . . .

This time they came on again after another twenty-five min-utes; or, at least, a picked party of them did. Looking back as he topped a ridge, Mart saw what looked like a string of perhaps ten warriors, barely visible in the last of the light, coming on fast at three miles. He turned at a right angle, covered by the ridge, and loped in the new direction for two miles more. The dusk had blackened to almost solid dark when he dismounted to see what he could do for Amos.

"Never try to guess an Indian," Amos said thickly, and slumped unconscious. He hung to the side of the horse by the saddle strings he had tied into his belt, until Mart cut him down.

Camp Radziminski was twenty miles away.

## 37

MARTIN PAULEY sprawled on a pile of sacked grain in Ranger Captain Sol Clinton's tent, and waited. With Amos safe under medical care, of sorts, Mart saw a good chance to get some sleep; but the fits and starts of a wakeful doze seemed to be the best he could make of it. The Ranger was still wrangling with Brevet-Colonel Chester C. Greenhill over what they were about to do, if anything at all. He had been over there for two hours, and it ought to be almost enough. When he got back, Mart would hear whether or not five years' search could succeed, and yet be altogether wasted.

Camp Radziminski was a flattish sag in the hills looking down upon Otter Creek—a place, not an installation. It had been a cavalry outpost, briefly, long ago; and an outfit of Rangers had wintered here once after that. In the deep grass you could still fall over the crumbling footings of mud-and-wattle walls and the precise rows of stones that had bordered military pathways; but the stockaded defenses were long gone.

Mart had been forced to transport Amos on a travois. This contraption was nothing but two long poles dragged from the saddle. The attached horse had shown confusion and some tendency to kick Amos' head off, but it hadn't happened. Mart found Radziminski before noon to his own considerable surprise. And the dead Comanche scout was proved to have told the truth with considerable exactness under Amos' peculiarly effective methods of questioning.

Here were the "more than forty" Rangers, their wagon-sheet beds scattered haphazardly over the best of the flat ground, with a single tent to serve every form of administration and supply. Here, too, were the two short-handed companies of cavalry—about a hundred and twenty men—with a wagon train, an officer's tent, a noncom's tent, a supply tent, and a complement of pup tents sheltering two men each. This part of the encampment was inconveniently placed, the Rangers having been here first; but the lines of tents ran perfectly straight anyway, defying the broken terrain.

And here, scattered up and down the slopes at random, were the brush wickiups of the "sixty or seventy" Tonkawas, almost the last of their breed. These were tall, clean, good-looking Indians, but said to be cannibals, and trusted by few; now come to fight beside the Rangers in a last doomed, expiring effort to win the good will of the white men who had conquered them.

As Mart had suspected, the Army and the Rangers were not working together at all. Colonel Greenhill had not, actually, come out to intercept the Rangers. Hadn't known they were there. But, having run smack into them, he conceived his next duty to be that of sending them back where they belonged. He had been trying to get this done without too much untowardness for several days; and all concerned were now fit to be tied.

In consequence, Mart found Captain Sol Clinton in no mood to discuss the murder charge hanging over Mart and Amos, by reason of the killings at Lost Mule Creek. From this standpoint, Clinton told Mart, he had been frankly hopeful of never seeing either one of them again. Seeing's they saw fit to thrust themselves upon him, he supposed he would have to do something technical about them later. But now he had other fish to fry—and by God, they seemed to have brought him the skillet! Come along here, and if you can't walk any faster than that you can run, can't you?

He took Mart to Colonel Greenhill who spent an hour questioning him in what seemed a lot like an effort to break his story; and sent him to wait in Clinton's tent after. Sol Clinton had spoken with restraint while Mart was with them, but as Mart walked away he heard the opening guns of Sol's argument roar like a blue norther, shaking the tent walls. "I'm sick and tired of war parties murdering the be-Jesus out of Texas families, then skedaddling to hide behind you yellowlegs! What are you fellers running, a damn Wild Indian sanctuary up here? The chief purpose of this here Union is to protect Texas —that's how *we* understood it! Yonder's a passel of murderers, complete with Texican scalps and white girl captive! I say it's up to you to protect us from them varmints by stepping the hell to one side while I——"

They had been at it for a long time, and they were still at it, though with reduced carrying power. Mart dozed a little, but was broad awake instantly as Sergeant Charlie MacCorry came in. Charlie seemed to have worked up to the position of right-hand man, or something, for he had stood around while Captain Clinton first talked to Mart, and he had been in Colonel Greenhill's tent during Mart's session there as well. His attitude toward Mart had seemed noncommittal—neither friendly nor stand-offish but quiet, rather, and abstracted. It seemed to Mart an odd and overkindly attitude for a Ranger sergeant to take toward a former prisoner who had slugged him down and got away. And now Charlie seemed to have something he wanted to say to Mart, without knowing how to bring it up. He warmed up by offering his views on the military situation.

"Trouble with the Army," Charlie had it figured, "there's always some damn fool don't get the word. A fort sends some colonel chasing all over creation after a bunch of hostiles; and he finds 'em, and jumps 'em, and makes *that* bunch a thing of the past; and what does he find out then? Them hostiles was already coming into a different fort under full-agreed truce. Picked 'em off right on the doorstep, by God. Done away with them peaceful Indians all unawares. Well! Now what you got? Investigations—boards—court-martials—and wham! Back goes the colonel so many files he's virtually in short pants. Happens every time."

He paced the tent a few moments, two steps one way, two steps back, watching Mart covertly, as if expecting him to speak.

"Yeah," Mart said at last.

Charlie seemed freed to say what he had on his mind. "Mart . . . I got a piece of news."

"Oh?"

"Me and Laurie—we got married. Just before I left."

Mart let his eyes drop while he thought it over. There had been a time, and it had gone on for years, when Laurie was always in his mind. She was the only girl he had ever known very well except those in the family. Or perhaps he had never known her, or any girl, at all. He reached for memories that would bring back her meaning to him. Laurie in a pretty dress, with her shoulders bare. Laurie joking about her flour-sack all-overs that had once read "Steamboat Mills" across her little bottom. Laurie in his arms, promising to come to him in the night . . .

All that should have mattered to him, but he couldn't seem

to feel it. The whole thing seemed empty, and dried out, without any real substance for him any more. As if it never could have come to anything, no matter what.

"Did you hear me?" Charlie asked. "I say, I married Laurie."

"Yeah. Good for you. Got yourself a great girl."

"No hard feelings?"

"No."

They shook hands, briefly, as they always did; and Charlie changed the subject briskly. "You sure fooled me, scouting up this attack on Scar. I'd have swore that was the last thing you wanted. Unless you got Debbie out of there first. Being's they're so liable to brain their captives when they're jumped. You think they won't now?"

"Might not," Mart said dully. He stirred restlessly. "What's happened to them king-pins over there? They both died, or something?"

Charlie looked at him thoughtfully, unwilling to be diverted. "Is she— Have they——" He didn't know how to put it, so that Mart would not be riled. "What I'm driving at—has she been with the bucks?"

Mart said, "Charlie, I don't know. I don't think so. It's more like—like they've done something to her mind."

"You mean she's crazy?"

"No—that isn't it, rightly. Only—she takes their part now. She believes them, not us. Like as if they took out her brain, and put in an Indian brain instead. So that she's an Indian now inside."

Charlie believed he saw it now. "Doesn't want to leave 'em, huh?"

"Almost seems like she's an Indian herself now. Inside."

"I see." Charlie was satisfied. If she wanted to stay, she'd been with the bucks all right. Had Comanche brats of her own most likely.

"I see something now," Mart said, "I never used to understand. I see now why the Comanches murder our women when they raid—brain our babies even—what ones they don't pick to steal. It's so we won't breed. They want us off the earth. I understand that, because that's what I want for them. I want them dead. All of them. I want them cleaned off the face of the world."

Charlie shut up. Mart sounded touched in the head, and maybe dangerous. He wouldn't have slapped Mart's face again for thirty-seven dollars.

Sol Clinton came in, now, at last. He looked angry, yet satisfied and triumphant all at once. "I had to put us under his command," the Ranger captain said. "I don't even know if I legally can—but it's done. Won't matter, once we're out ahead. We're going to tie into 'em, boys!"

"The Tonks, too?"

"Tonkawas and all. Mart, you're on pay as civilian guide. Can you find 'em again in the dark? Can you, hell—you've got to! I want to hit before sunrise—leave Greenhill come up as he can. You going to get us there?"

"That I am," Mart said; and smiled for the first time that day.

## 38

S COUTING AHEAD, Mart Pauley found Scar's village still where he had seen it last. Its swarming cur dogs yammered a great part of every night, and their noise placed the village for him now. The Comanches claimed they could always tell what the dogs were barking at—wolves, Indians, white men, or spooks—and though Mart only partly believed this he reconnoitered the place from a great way out, taking no chances. He galloped back, and met Captain Sol Clinton's fast-traveling Rangers less than an hour before dawn.

"We're coming in," he said to Captain Clinton, turning his horse alongside. "I should judge we're within——" He hesitated. He had started to say they were within three to five miles, but he had been to very few measured horse races, and had only a vague idea of a mile. "Within twenty minutes trot and ten minutes walk," he put it. "There you top a low hogback, looking across flat ground; and the village is in sight beyond."

"In sight from how far?"

There it was again. Mart thought the hogback was about a mile from the village, but what's a mile? "Close enough to see trees, too far to see branches," he described it.

That was good enough. "Just about what we want," Sol accepted it. Everything else had been where Mart had said it would be throughout the long night's ride. The captain halted his forty-two Rangers, passing the word back quietly along the loose column of twos.

His men dismounted without further command, loosened cinches, and relieved themselves without military precision. They looked unhurried, but wasted no motions. These men supplied their own clothes, saddles, and weapons, and very often their own horses; what you had here was a bunch of individuals, each a tough and weathered fighting man in his own right, but also in his own manner.

Behind them the sixty-odd Tonkawas pulled up at an orderly interval, a body of riders even more quiet than the

Rangers. They stepped down and looked to their saddles, which included every form of museum piece from discarded McClellans to Indian-craft rigs with elkhorn trees. Each dug a little hole in which to urinate, and covered it over when he was done.

A word from Clinton sent a young Ranger lacing forward to halt the point, riding a furlong or so ahead in the dark. They were in their last hour before action, but the Ranger captain made no inspection. He had inspected these men to their roots when he signed them on, and straightened them out from time to time after, as needed; they knew their business if they were ever going to.

Clinton sharpened a twig, picked his teeth with it, and looked smug. He had made a good march, and he knew it, and judged that the yellowlegs would be along in about a week. He cast an eye about him for the two cavalry troopers who had ridden with them as runner-links with Colonel Greenhill. They didn't seem to be in earshot. Captain Clinton spoke to Lieutenant Bart Lester, a shadowy figure in the last of the night. "Looks like we might get this thing cleaned up by breakfast," he said, "against something different goes wrong." Before Colonel Greenhill comes up, he meant. "Of course, when's breakfast is largely up to Scar. You can't— Who's this?"

Charlie MacCorry had come galloping up from the rear, where he had been riding tail. Now he pulled up, leaning low to peer at individuals, looking for Captain Clinton.

"Here, Charlie," Sol spoke.

"Hey, they're on top of us!"

"Who is?"

"The yellowlegs! They're not more than seven minutes behind!"

The toothpick broke between Sol Clinton's teeth, and he spit it out explosively as he jumped for his horse. "Damn you, Charlie, if you've let——"

"Heck, Sol, we didn't hear a thing until the halt. It's only just this minute we——"

"Bart!" Clinton snapped. "Take 'em on forward, and quick! Lope 'em out a little—but a lope, you hear me, not a run! I'll be up in a couple of minutes!" He went into his loose-cinched saddle with a vault, like a Comanche. He was cussing smokily, and tightening the cinch with one hand as he started hell-for-leather to the rear. The word had run fast down the column, without any shouting, and some of the Rangers were already stepping into their saddles. Charlie ducked his head between his shoulders. "Knew I'd never git far in the Rangers." Mart followed as Charlie spurred after Clinton who was riding to the Tonkawas.

"We can run for it," Charlie offered hopefully as Sol pulled up. "I believe if we hold the Tonks at a slow gait behind us——"

"Oh, shut up," Clinton said. He had to send the Tonkawas on, so that his own men would be between the Tonkawas and the cavalry when they went into action. The Cavalry couldn't be expected to tell one Indian from another, Clinton supposed, in the heat of action. The Tonks would race forward, anyway, pretty soon. No power on earth could hold those fools once the enemy was sighted.

"Hey, Spots!" Clinton called. "Where are you?"

Spotted Hog, the war chief commanding the Tonkawas, sprang onto his pony to ride the twenty yards to Clinton. "Yes, sir," he said in English of a strong Texan accent.

"Tell you what you do," Clinton said. "We're pretty close now; I'm sending you on in. I want——"

Spotted Hog whistled softly, a complicated phrase, and they heard it repeated and answered some distance to the rear.

"Wait a minute, will you? Damn it, Spots, I'm telling you what I want—and nothing no different!"

"Sure, Captain—I'm listening."

"The village is still there, right where it was supposed to be. So——"

"I know," Spotted Hog said.

"—so swing wide, and find out which side the crick they're holding their horses. Soon as you know——"

"The west side," the Tonkawa said. "The ponies are on the west side. Across from the village."

"Who told you to put your own scouts out? Damnation, if you've waked up that village— Well, never mind. You go hit that horse herd. The hell with scalps—run off that herd, and you can have the horses."

"We'll run 'em!"

"All right—get ahead with it."

"Yes, sir!" Spotted Hog jumped his pony off into the dark where a brisk stir of preparation could be heard among the Tonkawas.

"I got to send Greenhill some damn word," Clinton began; and one of the cavalry troopers was beside him instantly.

"You want me, sir?"

"God forbid!" Clinton exploded. "Git forward where you belong!" The trooper scampered, and Clinton turned to Mac-Corry. "Charlie . . . No. No. What we need's a civilian—and we got one. Here, Mart! You go tell Greenhill where he's at."

"What when he asks where you are?"

"I'm up ahead. That's all. I'm up ahead. And make this stupid, will you? If he gives you orders for me, don't try to get loose without hearing 'em; he'll only send somebody else. But you can lose your way, can't you? You're the one found it!"

"Yes, sir," Mart said with mental reservations.

"Go on and meet him. Come on, Charlie." They were gone from there, and in a hurry.

Galloping to the rear, past the Tonkawas, Mart saw that they were throwing aside their saddles, and all gear but their weapons, and tying up the tails of their ponies. No war paint had been seen on them until now, but as they stripped their shirts their torsos proved to be prepainted with big circles and stripes of raw colors. Great, many-couped war bonnets were flowering like turkey tails among them. Each set off, bareback, as soon as he was ready, moving up at the lope; there would be no semblance of formation. The Tonkawas rode well, and would fight well. Only they would fight from the backs of their horses, while the Comanches would be all over their ponies, fighting from under the necks, under the bellies—and still would run their horses the harder.

Once clear of the Tonkawas, Mart could hear the cavalry plainly. The noise they made came to him as a steady metallic whispering, made up of innumerable clinks, rattles, and squeaks of leather, perhaps five minutes away. Darkness still held as he reached them, and described the position of the enemy to Colonel Greenhill. The hundred and twenty cavalrymen wheeled twos into line.

"Has Clinton halted?" Greenhill asked.

"Yes, sir." Well . . . he had.

Some restrained shouting went on in the dark. The cavalry prepared to dismount, bringing even numbers forward one horse length; dismounted; reset saddles; and dressed the line. Colonel Greenhill observed that he remembered this country now; he had been over every foot of it, and would have recognized it to begin with, had he been booned with any decent kind of description. He would be glad to bet a barrel of forty-rod that he could fix the co-ordinates of that village within a dozen miles. If he had had so much as a single artillery piece, he would have shown them how to scatter that village before Scar knew they were in the country.

Mart was glad he didn't have one, scattering the Comanches being the last thing wanted. In his belief, the pony herd was the key. A Comanche afoot was a beaten critter; but let him get to a horse and he was a long gone Comanche—and a deadly threat besides. He felt no call, however, to expound these views to a brevet-colonel.

"Tell Captain Clinton I'll be up directly," Greenhill ordered him; and went briskly about his inspection.

Mart started on, but made a U-turn, and loped to the rear, behind the cavalry lines. At the far end of the dismounted formation stood four narrow-bowed covered wagons, their drivers at attention by the bridles of the nigh leaders. Second wagon was the ambulance; a single trooper, at attention by a front wheel, was the present sanitary detail. Martin Pauley rode to the tail gate, stepped over it from the saddle, and struck a shielded match. Amos lay heavily blanketed, his body looking to be of great length but little substance, upon a narrow litter. By his heavy breathing he seemed asleep, but his eyes opened to the light of the match.

"Mart? Where are we?"

"Pretty close on Scar's village. I was to it. Within dogbark, anyway. Sol sent the Tonks to make a try at their horses, and took the Rangers on up. He wants to hit before Greenhill finds what he's up to. How you feel?"

Amos stared straight upward, his eyes bleak and unforgiving upon the unseen night above the canvas; but the question brought a glint of irony into them, so that Mart was ashamed of having asked it.

"My stuff's rolled up down there by my feet," Amos said. "Get me my gun from it."

If he had been supposed to have it, the sanitary detail would have given it to him, but it was a long time since they had gone by what other people supposed for them. Mart brought Amos his six-gun, and his cartridge belt, and checked the loading. Amos lifted a shaking hand, and hid the gun under his blankets. Outside they heard the "Prepare to mount!"

"I got to get on up there." Mart groped for Amos' hand. He felt a tremor in its grip, but considerable strength.

"Get my share of 'em," Amos whispered.

"You want scalps, Amos?"

"Yeah . . . No. Just stomp 'em—like I always done——"

Men and horses were beginning to show, black and solid against a general grayness. You could see them now without stooping to outline them against the stars, as Mart stepped from the wagon bed into the saddle. The cavalry had wheeled into column of twos and was in motion at the walk. Mart cleared the head of the column, and lifted his horse into a run.

# 39

Sol Clinton's forty-two Rangers were dismounted behind the last ridge below Scar's village as Mart came up. They had plenty of light now—more than they had wanted or intended. Captain Clinton lay on the crest of the ridge, studying the view without visible delight. Mart went up there, but Clinton turned on him before he got a look beyond.

"God damn you, Pauley, I——"

"Greenhill says, tell you he's coming," Mart got in hastily. "And that's all he says."

But Clinton was thinking about something else. "Take a look at this thing here!"

Mart crawled up beside Clinton, and got a shock. The fresh light of approaching sunrise showed Scar's village in clear detail, a scant mile from where they lay. Half the lodges were down, and between them swarmed great numbers of horses and people, the whole thing busy as a hoof-busted ant hill. This village was packing to march.

A hundred yards in front of the village a few dozen mounted warriors had interposed themselves. They sat about in idle groups, blanket-wrapped upon their standing ponies. They looked a little like the Comanche idea of vedettes, but more were riding out from the village as Mart and Sol Clinton watched. What they had here was the start of a battle build-up. Clinton seemed unsurprised by Scar's readiness. You could expect to find a war chief paying attention to his business once in a while, and you had to allow for it. But—"What the hell's the matter with you people? Can't you count? That band will mount close to three hundred bucks!"

"I told you he might want this fight. So he's got himself reinforced, that's all."

A rise of dust beyond the village and west of the Wild Dog showed where the Comanche horse herd had been put in motion. All animals not in use as travois horses or battle ponies —the main wealth of the village—were being driven upstream and away. But the movement was orderly. Where were the Tonkawas? They might be waiting upstream, to take the horses away from the small-boy herders; they might have gone home. One thing they certainly were not doing was what they had been told. Captain Clinton had no comment to waste on that, either.

He pulled back down the hill, moving slowly, to give himself time to think. Lieutenant Bart Lester came forward, dogged by the two uniformed orderlies. "Flog on back, boy," Clinton told one of them. "Tell Colonel Greenhill I am now demonstrating in front of the village to develop the enemy strength, and expedite his commitment. . . . Guess that ought to hold him. Mount 'em up, Bart."

The Rangers mounted and drifted into line casually, but once they were formed the line was a good one. These men might shun precision of movement for themselves, but they habitually exacted it from their horses, whether the horses agreed to it or not. Mart placed himself near the middle of the line and watched Clinton stoically. He knew the Ranger would be justified in ordering a retreat.

Clinton stepped aboard his horse, looked up and down the line of Rangers, and addressed them conversationally. "Well, us boys was lucky again," he said. "For once we got enough Comanches to go around. Might run as high as a dozen apiece, if we don't lose too many. I trust you boys will be glad to hear this is a fight, not a surprise. They're forming in front of the village, at about a mile. I should judge we won't have to go all the way; they'll come to meet us. What I'd like to do is bust through their middle, and on into the village; give Greenhill a chance to hit 'em behind, as they turn after us. This is liable to be prevented. In which case we'll handle the situation after we see what it is."

Some of the youngsters—and most of the Rangers were young—must have been fretting over the time Clinton was taking. The Cavalry would be up pretty quick, and Colonel Greenhill would take over; probably order a retirement according to plan, they supposed, without a dead Comanche to show. Clinton knew what he was doing, however. In broad daylight, lacking surprise, and with unexpected odds against him, he wanted the cavalry as close as it could get without telling him what to do. And he did not believe Greenhill would consider retreat for a second.

"In case you wonder what become of them antic Tonks," Clinton said, "I don't know. And don't pay them Comanches no mind, neither—just keep your eye on me. I'm the hard case you're up against around here—not them childish savages. If you don't hear me first time I holler, you better by God read my mind—I don't aim to raise no two hollers on any one subject in hand."

He pretended to look them over, but actually he was listening. The line stood steady and perfectly straight. Fidgety horses moved no muscle, and tired old nags gathered themselves to spring like lions upon demand, before a worse thing happened. And now they heard the first faint, far-off rustle of the bell-metal scabbards as the cavalry came on.

"I guess this sloppy-looking row of hay-doodles is what you fellers call a line," Sol criticized them. "Guide center! On Joe, here. Joe, you just follow me." Deliberately he got out a plug of tobacco, bit off a chew, and rolled it into his cheek. It was the first tobacco Mart had ever seen him use. "Leave us go amongst them," the captain said.

He wheeled his horse, and moved up the slope at a walk. The first direct rays of the sun were striking across the rolling ground as they breasted the crest, bringing Scar's village into full view a mile away. A curious sound of breathing could be heard briefly along the line of Rangers as they got their first look at what they were going against. A good two hundred mounted Comanches were now strung out in front of the village, where only the vedettes had stood before; and more were coming from the village in a stream. The war ponies milled a bit, and an increased stir built up in the village beyond, in reaction to the Ranger advance.

Clinton turned in his saddle. "Hey, you—orderly!"

"Yes, sir!"

"Ride back and tell Colonel Greenhill: Captain Clinton, of the Texas Rangers, presents his respects——"

"Yes, sir!" The rattled trooper whirled his horse.

"Come back here! Where the hell you going? Tell him the Comanches are in battle line east of the crick, facing south— and don't say you seen a million of 'em! Tell him I say there's a couple hundred. If he wants to know what I'm doing, I'm keeping an eye on 'em. All right, go find him."

They were at a thousand yards, and the stream of Comanches from the village had dwindled to a straggle. It was about time; their number was going to break three hundred easily. A line was forming in a practiced manner, without confusion, and it was going to be a straight one. It looked about a mile long, but it wasn't; it wouldn't be much longer than a quarter of a mile if the Comanches rode knee to knee. Still, Mart expected a quarter mile of Comanches to be enough for forty-two men.

Clinton waved an arm, and stepped up the pace to a sharp trot. He was riding directly toward the village itself, which would bring them against the Comanche center. A single stocky warrior, wearing a horn headdress, loped slowly across the front of the Comanche line. Mart recognized Scar first by his short lance, stripped of its trophy scalps for combat. Incredibly, in the face of advancing Rangers, Scar was having himself an inspection! At the end of the line he turned, and loped back toward the center, unhurrying. When he reached the center he would bring the Comanche line to meet them, and all this spooky orderliness would be over.

Captain Clinton let his horse break into a hand-lope, and the forty behind him followed suit in the same stride. Their speed was little increased, but the line moved in an easier rhythm. Scar's line still stood quiet, unfretting. The beef-up from the village had stopped at last; Scar's force stood at more than three hundred and fifty Comanches.

They were within the half mile. They could see the tall fan-feathered bonnets of the war chiefs, now, and the clubbed tails of the battle ponies. The warriors were in full paint; individual patterns could not yet be made out, but the bright stripes and splotches on the naked bodies gave the Comanche line an oddly broken color.

Now Scar turned in front of his center; the line moved, advancing evenly at a walk. Some of the veteran Indian fighters among the Rangers must have felt a chill down their backs as they saw that. This Indian was too cool, held his people in too hard a grip; his battle would lack the helter-skelter horse-race quality that gave a smaller and better disciplined force its best opportunities. And he wasn't using a Comanche plan of attack at all. The famous Comanche grinding-wheel attack made use of horsemanship and mobility, and preserved the option to

disengage intact. The head-on smash for which Scar was forming was all but unknown among Comanches. Scar would never
have elected close grips to a finish if he had not been sure of
what he had. And he had reason. Coolly led, this many hostiles
could mass five deep in front of Clinton, yet still wrap round
his flanks, roll him up, enfold him. The Rangers watched Sol,
but he gave no order, and the easy rating of his horse did not
change.

They were at the quarter mile. A great swarm of squaws,
children, and old people had come out from the village.
They stood motionless, on foot, a long, dense line of them
—spectators, waiting to see the Rangers eaten alive. Scar's line
still walked, unflustered, and Clinton still came on, loping easily. Surely he must have been expecting some break, some turn
in his favor; perhaps he had supposed the cavalry would show
itself by this time, but it had not. What he would have done
without any break, whether he would have galloped steadily
into that engulfing destruction, was something they were
never going to know. For now the break came.

Out of the ground across the river the Tonkawas appeared,
as if rising out of the earth. Nothing over there, not a ridge,
not an arroyo, looked as though it would hide a mounted
man, let alone seventy; yet, by some medicine of wits and
skill, they appeared with no warning at all. The tall Tonkawas
came in no semblance of a line; they rode singly, and in loose
bunches, a rabble. But they moved fast, and as if they knew
what they were doing, as they poured over the low swell that
had somehow hidden them on the flank of the Comanches.
A sudden gabble ran along Scar's line, and his right bunched
upon itself in a confused effort to regroup.

And now the Tonkawas did another unpredictable thing that
no Comanche could have expected because he never would
have done it. On the open slope to the river the Tonkawas
pulled up sliding, and dropped from their horses. They turned
the animals broadside, rested their firearms across the withers, and opened fire. In enfilade, at four hundred yards, the
effect was murderous. Ragged gaps opened in the Comanche
right where riderless ponies bolted. Some of the bonneted war
chiefs—Hungry Horse, Stiff Leg, Standing Elk, Many Trees—
were among the first to go down, as crack shots picked off the

marked leaders. A few great buffalo guns slammed, and these killed horses. Scar shouted unheard as his whole right, a third of his force, broke ranks to charge splashing through the river.

The Tonkawas disintegrated at once. Some faded upstream after the horse herd, but scattered shots and war cries could be heard among the lodges as others filtered into the village itself. More gaps opened in Scar's line as small groups turned back to defend the village and the horses.

"I'll be a son-of-a-bitch," Clinton said.

He gave the long yell, and they charged; and Scar, rallying his hundreds, rode hard to meet them. The converging lines were at a hundred feet when Clinton fired. Forty carbines crashed behind him, ripping the Comanche center. The Rangers shifted their carbines to their rein hands, drew their pistols. Immediately the horses cannoned together.

It was Mart's first mounted close action, and what he saw of it was all hell coming at him, personally. A war pony went down under his horse at the first bone-cracking shock; his horse tripped, but got over the fallen pony with a floundering leap, and Comanches were all around him. Both lines disappeared in a yelling mix, into which Comanches seemed to lace endlessly from all directions. They rode low on the sides of their ponies, stabbing upward with their lances, and once within reach they never missed. If a man side-slipped in the saddle to avoid being gutted, a deep groin thrust lifted him, and dropped him to be trampled. Only chance was to pistol your enemy before his lance could reach you. The gun reached farther than the lance, and hit with a shock that was final; but every shot was a snapshot, and nobody missed twice. You had five bullets, and only five—the hammer being carried on an empty cylinder—to get you through it all.

A horse screamed, close by, through the war whoops and the gun blasting. Beside Mart a Ranger's horse gave a great whistling cough as it stumbled, and another as its knees buckled, then broke its neck as it overended. The shoulder of a riderless pony smashed Mart's knee. Struggling to hold up his staggered horse, he pistol-whipped a lance at his throat; the splintered shaft gashed his neck, but he fired into a painted face. A whipping stirrup somehow caught him on the temple. An unearthly, inhuman sound was cidered out of a Ranger as his knocked-down horse rolled over him, crushing his chest with the saddle horn.

The Comanches became a mass, a horde, seeming to cover the prairie like a buffalo run. Then abruptly he was clear of it, popped out of it like a seed. The battle had broken up into running fights, and he saw that most of the Rangers were ahead of him into the village. One last Comanche overtook him. Mart turned without knowing what warned him, and fired so late that the lance fell across his back, where it balanced weirdly, teetering, before it fell off.

He looked back, letting his horse run free as he reloaded; and now he saw the stroke that finished the battle, and won his respect for the cavalry forever. Greenhill was coming in at the quarter mile, charging like all hell-fire, in so tight a line the horses might have been lashed together. Scar massed his Comanches, and he outnumbered his enemies still; he struck hard, and with all he had. Into the packed war ponies the cavalry smashed head on, in as hard a blow as cavalry ever struck, perhaps. A score of the light war ponies went down under the impact of the solid line, and the rest reeled, floundered backward, and broke. Into the unbalanced wreckage the cavalry plowed close-locked, sabering and trampling.

Most of the village had emptied, but at the far end a great number of Comanche people—squaws, children, and old folks, mostly—ran like wind-driven leaves in a bobbing scatter. The Rangers were riding through to join the Tonkawas in the running fight that could be heard far up the Wild Dog; but they made it their business to stamp out resistance as they went. The dreadful thing was that the fleeing people were armed, and fought as they ran, as dangerous as a torrent of rattlesnakes. Here and there lay the body of an old man, a squaw, or a half-grown boy, who had died rather than let an enemy pass unmolested; and sometimes there was a fallen Ranger. Mart had to go through these people; he had to hunt through them all, and keep on hunting through them, until he found Debbie, or they got him.

A squaw as broad as a horse's rump, with a doll-size papoose on her back, whirled on him at his stirrup. Her trade gun blasted so close that the powder burned his hand, yet somehow she missed him. And now he saw Amos.

He couldn't believe it, at first, and went through a moment of fright in which he thought his own mind had come apart. Amos looked like a dead man riding, his face ash-bloodless, but with a fever-craze burning in his eyes. It seemed a physical impossibility that he should have stayed on a horse to get here, even if some bribed soldier had lifted him into the saddle.

Actually, witnesses swore later, there had been no bribed soldier. Amos had pistol-whipped one guard, and had taken a horse at gunpoint from another . . .

He must have seen Mart, but he swept past with eyes ahead, picking his targets coolly, marking his path with Comanche dead. Mart called his name, but got no response. Mart's blown horse was beginning to wobble, so that Amos pulled away, gaining yards at every jump; and though Mart tried to overtake him, he could not.

Then, ahead of Amos, Mart believed he saw Debbie again. A young squaw, slim and shawl-headed, ran like a deer, dodging among the horses. She might have got away, but she checked, and retraced two steps, to snatch up a dead man's pistol; and in that moment Amos saw her. The whole set of his laboring body changed, and he pointed like a bird dog as he charged his horse upon her. The lithe figure twisted from under the hoofs, and ran between the lodges. Amos whirled his horse at the top of its stride, turning it as it did not know how to turn; it lost footing, almost went down, but he dragged it up by the same strength with which he rode. Its long bounds closed upon the slim runner, and Amos leaned low, his pistol reaching.

Mart yelled, "Amos—no!" He fired wild at Amos' back, missing from a distance at which he never missed. Then, unexpectedly, Amos raised his pistol without firing, and shifted it to his rein hand. He reached down to grab the girl as if to lift her onto his saddle.

The girl turned upon the rider, and Mart saw the broad brown face of a young Comanche woman, who could never possibly have been Debbie. Her teeth showed as she fired upward at Amos, the muzzle of her pistol almost against his jacket. He fell heavily; his body crumpled as it hit, and rolled over once, as shot game rolls, before it lay still.

# 40

O<small>NLY A</small> handful of squaws, mostly with small children on their backs, had been taken prisoner. Mart talked to them, in their own tongue and in sign language, until the night grew old, without learning much that seemed of any value. Those who would talk at all admitted having known Debbie Edwards; they called her by a Comanche name meaning "Dry-Grass-Hair." But they said she had run away, or at least disappeared, three nights before—during the night following Mart and Amos' escape.

They supposed, or claimed to suppose, that she had run to the soldiers' camp on the Otter. Or maybe she had tried to follow Bull Shoulders and the Other, for she had gone the same way he himself had taken. Trackers had followed her for some distance in that direction, they said, before losing trace. They didn't know why she had gone. She had taken no pony nor anything else with her. If she hadn't found somebody to help her, they assumed she was dead; they didn't believe she would last long, alone and afoot, upon the prairie. Evidently they didn't think much of Dry-Grass-Hair in the role of an Indian.

"They're lying," Sol Clinton thought. "They've murdered her, is about the size of it."

"I don't think so," Mart said.

"Why?"

"I don't know. Maybe I just can't face up to it. Maybe I've forgot how after all this time."

"Well, then," Clinton humored him, "she must be between here and Camp Radziminski. On the way back we'll throw out a cordon. . . ."

Mart saw no hope in that, either, though he didn't say so, for he had nothing to suggest instead. He slept two hours, and when he awoke in the darkness before dawn he knew what he had to do. He got out of camp unnoticed, and rode northwest in a direction roughly opposite to that in which Camp Radziminski lay.

He had no real reason for doubting Clinton's conclusion that Debbie was dead. Of course, if it was true she was worth sixty horses, Scar might have sent her off to be hidden; but this did not jibe with Scar's bid for victory or destruction in open battle. The squaws' story didn't mean anything, either, even if they had tried to tell the truth, for they couldn't know what it was. The bucks never told them anything. His only excuse, actually, for assuming that Debbie had in truth run away, and perhaps still lived, was that only this assumption left him any course of action.

If she had run away it was on the spur of the moment, without plan, since she had taken nothing with her that would enable her to survive. This suggested that she had found herself under pressure of some sudden and deadly threat—as if she had been accused, for instance, of treachery in connection with his own escape. In such a case she might indeed have started after Mart and Amos, as the squaws claimed. But he had a feeling she wouldn't have gone far that way without recoiling; he didn't believe she would have wanted to come to him. Therefore, she must have wanted only to get away from Comanches; and, knowing them, she would perhaps choose a way, a direction, in which Comanches would be unlikely to follow. . . .

He recalled that the Comanches believed that the mutilated, whether in mind or body, never entered the land beyond the sunset, but wandered forever in an emptiness "between the winds." They seemed to place this emptiness to the northwest, in a general way; as if long-forgotten disasters or defeats in some ancient time had made this direction which Debbie, thinking like an Indian, might choose if she was trying to leave the world of the living behind her. He had it all figured out —or thought he did.

This way took him into a land of high barrens, without much game, grass, or water. About a million square miles of broken, empty country lay ahead of him, without trails, and he headed into the heart of the worst of it. "I went where no Comanche would go," he explained it a long time after. He thought by that time that he had really worked it out in this way, but he had not. All he actually had to go on was one more vagueness put together out of information unnoticed or forgotten, such as sometimes adds itself up to a hunch.

He drifted northwest almost aimlessly, letting his weariness, and sometimes his horse, follow lines of least resistance—which was what a fugitive, traveling blindly and afoot, would almost inevitably have done. After a few miles the country itself began to make the decisions. The terrain could be counted on to herd and funnel the fugitive as she tired.

Toward the end of that first day, he saw vultures circling, no more than specks in the sky over a range of hills many hours ahead. He picked up the pace of his pony, pushing as hard as he dared, while he watched them circling lower, their numbers increasing. They were still far off as night closed down, but in the first daylight he saw them again, and rode toward them. There were more of them now, and their circles were lower; but he was certain they were a little way farther on than they had been when first seen. What they were watching still moved, then, however slowly; or at least was still alive, for they had not yet landed. He loped his stumbling pony, willing to kill it now, and go on afoot, if only he could come to the end before daylight failed him.

Early in the afternoon he found her moccasin tracks, wavering pitifully across a sand patch for a little way, and he put the horse full out, its lungs laboring. The vultures were settling low, and though they were of little danger to a living thing, he could wait no longer for his answer.

And so he found her. She lay in a place of rocks and dust; the wind had swept her tracks away, and sifted the dust over her, making her nearly invisible. He overrode, passing within a few yards, and would have lost her forever without the vultures. He had always hated those carrion birds of gruesome prophecy, but he never hated them again. It was Mart who picked—or blundered into—the right quarter of the compass; but it was the vultures that found her with their hundred-mile eyes, and unwillingly guided him to her by their far-seen circles in the sky.

She was asleep, rather than unconscious, but the sleep was one of total exhaustion. He knew she would never have wakened from it of herself. Even so, there was a moment in which her eyes stared, and saw him with terror; she made a feeble effort to get up, as to escape him, but could not. She dropped into lethargy after that, unresisting as he worked over her. He gave her water first, slowly, in dribbles that ran down her chin from her parched lips. She went into a prolonged chill, during which he wrapped her in all his blankets, chafed her feet, and

built a fire near them. Finally he stewed up shredded jerky,
scraped the fibers to make a pulp, and fed it to her by slow
spoonfuls. It was not true she smelled like a Comanche, any
more than Mart, who had lived the same kind of life that she
had.

When she was able to talk to him, the story of her runaway
came out very slowly and in pieces, at first; then less haltingly,
as she found he understood her better than she had expected.
He kept questioning her as gently as he could, feeling he had
to know what dreadful thing had frightened her, or what they
had done to her. It no longer seemed unnatural to talk to her
in Comanche.

They hadn't done anything to her. It wasn't that. It was the
medicine buckle—the ornament, like a gold ribbon tied in a
bow, that Scar always wore, and that had given him his change
of name. She had believed Amos lied about its having belonged
to Mart Pauley's mother. But the words that he had said were
written on the back stayed in her mind. Ethan to Judith . . .
The words were there or they weren't. If they were there, then
Amos' whole story was true, and Scar had taken the medicine
buckle from Mart's mother as she died under his knife.

That night she couldn't sleep; and when she had lain awake
a long time she knew that somehow she was going to have
to see the medicine buckle's back. Scar had been in council
most of the night, but he slept at last. Mart had to imagine for
himself, from her halting phrases, most of what had happened
then. The slanting green eyes in the dark-tanned face were not
cat's eyes as she told him, nor Indian's eyes, but the eyes of a
small girl.

She had crawled out from between the squaws, where she
always slept. With two twigs she picked a live coal out of the
embers of the fire. Carrying this, she crept to the deep pile of
buffalo robes that was Scar's bed. The chief lay sprawled on
his back. His chest was bare, and the medicine buckle gleamed
upon it in the light of the single ember. Horribly afraid, she
got trembling fingers upon the bit of gold, and turned it over.

How had she been able to do that? It was a question he
came back to more than once without entirely understanding
her answer. She said that Mart himself had made her do it; he

had forced her by his medicine. That was the part he didn't get. Long ago, in another world, he had been her dearest brother; he must have known that once. The truth was somewhere in that, if he could have got hold of it. Perhaps he should have known by this time that what the Indians call medicine is three-fourths the compelling ghosts of early associations, long forgotten. . . .

She had to lean close over the Comanche, so close that his breath was upon her face, before she could see the writing on the back of the medicine buckle. And then—she couldn't read it. Once, for a while, she had tried to teach Comanche children the white man's writing; but that was long ago, and now she herself had forgotten. But Amos had told her what the words were; so that presently the words seemed to fit the scratches on the gold: "Ethan to Judith . . ." Actually, the Rangers were able to tell Mart later, Amos had lied. The inscription said, "Made in England."

Then, as she drew back, she saw Scar's terrible eyes, wide open and upon her face, only inches away. For an instant she was unable to move. Then the coal dropped upon Scar's naked chest, and he sprang up with a snarl, grabbing for her.

After that she ran; in the direction Mart and Amos had gone, at first, as the squaws had said—but this was chance. She didn't know where she was going. Then, when they almost caught her, she had doubled back, like any hunted creature. Not in any chosen direction, but blindly, running away from everything, seeking space and emptiness. No thought of the limbo "between the winds" had occurred to her.

"But you caught me. I don't know how. I was better off with them. There, where I was. If only I never looked—behind the buckle——"

Sometime, and perhaps better soon than late, he would have to tell her what had happened to Scar's village after she left it. But not now.

"Now I have no place," Debbie said. "No place to go, ever. I want to die now."

"I'm taking you back. Can't you understand that?"

"Back? Back where?"

"Home, Debbie—to our own people!"

"I have no people. They are dead. I have no place———"

"There's the ranch. It belongs to you now. Don't you want to———"

"It is empty. Nobody is there."

"I'll be there, Debbie."

She lifted her head to stare at him—wildly, he thought. He was frightened by what he took to be a light of madness in her eyes, before she lowered them. He said, "You used to like the ranch. Don't you remember it?"

She was perfectly still.

He said desperately, "Have you forgotten? Don't you remember anything about when you were a little girl, at all?"

Tears squeezed from her shut eyes, and she began to shiver again, hard, in the racking shake they called the ague. He had no doubt she was taking one of the dangerous fevers; perhaps pneumonia, or if the chill was from weakness alone, he feared that the most. The open prairie had ways to bite down hard and sure on any warm-blooded thing when its strength failed. Panic touched him as he realized he could lose her yet.

He knew only one more way to bring warmth to her, and that was to give her his own. He lay close beside her, and wrapped the blankets around them both, covering their heads, so that even his breath would warm her. Held tight against him she seemed terribly thin, as if worked to the very bone; he wondered despairingly if there was enough of her left ever to be warmed again. But the chill moderated as his body heat reached her; her breathing steadied, and finally became regular.

He thought she was asleep, until she spoke, a whisper against his chest. "I remember," she said in a strangely mixed tongue of Indian-English. "I remember it all. But you the most. I remember how hard I loved you." She held onto him with what strength she had left; but she seemed all right, he thought, as she went to sleep.

# WARLOCK

*Oakley Hall*

*This book is for my son Tad*

## Prefatory Note

THIS BOOK is a novel. The town of Warlock and the territory in which it is located are fabrications. But any relation of the characters to real persons, living or dead, is not always coincidental, for many are composites of figures who live still on a frontier between history and legend.

The fabric of the story, too, is made up of actual events interwoven with invented ones; by combining what did happen with what might have happened, I have tried to show what should have happened. Devotees of Western legend may consequently complain that I have used familiar elements to construct a fanciful design, and that I have rearranged or ignored the accepted facts. So I will reiterate that this work is a novel. The pursuit of truth, not of facts, is the business of fiction.

—OAKLEY HALL

# Contents

Prefatory Note. . . . . . . . . . . . . . . . . . . . . . . . . . . . .  563

BOOK ONE. THE FIGHT IN THE ACME CORRAL
 1. Journals of Henry Holmes Goodpasture . . . . . .  569
 2. Gannon Comes Back. . . . . . . . . . . . . . . . . . .  580
 3. The Jail . . . . . . . . . . . . . . . . . . . . . . . . . . . .  585
 4. Morgan and Friend . . . . . . . . . . . . . . . . . . . .  591
 5. Gannon Sees a Showdown. . . . . . . . . . . . . . . .  599
 6. The Doctor and Miss Jessie . . . . . . . . . . . . . . .  607
 7. Curley Burne Plays His Mouth Organ . . . . . . . .  616
 8. Journals of Henry Holmes Goodpasture . . . . . .  624
 9. Gannon Calls the Turn . . . . . . . . . . . . . . . . . .  636
 10. Morgan Doubles His Bets . . . . . . . . . . . . . . . .  646
 11. Main Street . . . . . . . . . . . . . . . . . . . . . . . . . .  653
 12. Gannon Meets Kate Dollar . . . . . . . . . . . . . . .  656
 13. Morgan Has Callers. . . . . . . . . . . . . . . . . . . . .  660
 14. Gannon Watches a Man among Men . . . . . . . . .  667
 15. Boot Hill. . . . . . . . . . . . . . . . . . . . . . . . . . . .  681
 16. Curley Burne Tries to Mediate. . . . . . . . . . . . .  685
 17. Journals of Henry Holmes Goodpasture . . . . . .  693
 18. The Doctor Arranges Matters . . . . . . . . . . . . . .  697
 19. A Warning. . . . . . . . . . . . . . . . . . . . . . . . . . . .  702
 20. Gannon Has a Nightmare . . . . . . . . . . . . . . . . .  709
 21. The Acme Corral. . . . . . . . . . . . . . . . . . . . . . .  713
 22. Morgan Sees It Pass. . . . . . . . . . . . . . . . . . . . .  722
 23. Gannon Witnesses an Assault. . . . . . . . . . . . . .  729
 24. Journals of Henry Holmes Goodpasture . . . . . .  733
 25. Gannon Goes to a Housewarming. . . . . . . . . . .  738
 26. Journals of Henry Holmes Goodpasture . . . . . .  752
 27. Curley Burne and the Dog Killer . . . . . . . . . . .  755
 28. Journals of Henry Holmes Goodpasture . . . . . .  760

BOOK TWO. THE REGULATORS
 29. Gannon Looks for Trouble . . . . . . . . . . . . . . .  767
 30. The Doctor Considers the Ends of Men . . . . . .  769
 31. Morgan Uses His Knife . . . . . . . . . . . . . . . . . .  780

| | | |
|---|---|---|
| 32. | Gannon Takes a Trick | 790 |
| 33. | A Buggy Ride | 800 |
| 34. | Gannon Puts Down His Name | 810 |
| 35. | Curley Burne Loses His Mouth Organ | 822 |
| 36. | Journals of Henry Holmes Goodpasture | 830 |
| 37. | Gannon Answers a Question | 839 |
| 38. | The Doctor Attends a Meeting | 847 |
| 39. | Morgan Looks at the Deadwood | 861 |
| 40. | Bright's City | 867 |
| 41. | Journals of Henry Holmes Goodpasture | 874 |
| 42. | Morgan Is Dealt Out | 880 |
| 43. | Journals of Henry Holmes Goodpasture | 887 |
| 44. | The New Sign | 888 |
| 45. | Gannon Visits San Pablo | 890 |
| 46. | Journals of Henry Holmes Goodpasture | 901 |
| 47. | Dad McQuown | 910 |
| 48. | Gannon Takes a Walk | 921 |

BOOK THREE. THE ANTAGONISTS

| | | |
|---|---|---|
| 49. | Gannon Walks on the Right | 937 |
| 50. | Journals of Henry Holmes Goodpasture | 942 |
| 51. | The Doctor Hears Threats and Gunfire | 947 |
| 52. | Gannon Backs Off | 952 |
| 53. | At the General Peach | 958 |
| 54. | Morgan Makes a Bargain | 961 |
| 55. | Judge Holloway | 966 |
| 56. | Morgan Looks at the Cards | 972 |
| 57. | Journals of Henry Holmes Goodpasture | 987 |
| 58. | Gannon Speaks of Love | 992 |
| 59. | Morgan Shows His Hand | 998 |
| 60. | Gannon Sits It Out | 1004 |
| 61. | General Peach | 1014 |
| 62. | Journals of Henry Holmes Goodpasture | 1029 |
| 63. | The Doctor Chooses His Potion | 1034 |
| 64. | Morgan Cashes His Chips | 1043 |
| 65. | The Wake at the Lucky Dollar | 1052 |
| 66. | Gannon Takes Off His Star | 1058 |
| 67. | Journals of Henry Holmes Goodpasture | 1064 |
| 68. | Gannon Sees the Gold Handles | 1067 |

| | |
|---|---|
| Afterword | 1076 |

# BOOK ONE

# THE FIGHT IN THE ACME CORRAL

# I. *Journals of Henry Holmes Goodpasture*

August 25, 1880

DEPUTY CANNING had been Warlock's hope. During his re-
gime we had come to think, in man's eternal optimism, that
progress was being made toward at least some mild form of
Law & Order in Warlock. Certainly he was by far the best of
the motley flow of deputies who have manned our jail.

Canning was a good man, a decent man, an understand-
ably prudent man, but an honorable one. He coped with our
daily and nightly problems, with brawling, drunken miners,
and with Cowboys who have an especial craving to ride a horse
into a saloon, a Cyprian's cubicle, or the billiard parlor, and
shoot the chimneys out of the chandeliers.

Writing of Canning now, I wonder again how we manage
to obtain deputies at all, who must occupy a dangerous and
frequently fatal position for miserly pay. We do not manage
to keep them long. They collect their pittance for a month or
two, and die, or depart, or do not remain long enough even
to collect it at all. One, indeed, fled upon the first day of his
employment, leaving his star of office awaiting his successor
on the table in the jail. We have had bad ones, too; Brown,
the man before Canning, was an insolent, drunken bully, and
Billy-the-kid Gannon gained a measure of fame and gratitude
by ventilating him in a saloon brawl down valley in San Pablo.

Canning, too, must have known that some day he would be
thrown up against one of that San Pablo crew, incur, prudent
as he was, the enmity, or merely displeasure, of Curley Burne
or Billy Gannon, of Jack Cade or Calhoun or Pony Benner, of
one of the Haggin brothers, or even of Abe McQuown himself. I wonder if, in his worst dreams, it ever occurred to him
that the whole down valley gang of badmen would come in
against him at once.

There is no unanimity of opinion even now amongst those
of us who believe them at least to be a regrettable element in
Warlock. There are those who will say that of the lot only Cade
is truly "bad," and possibly Calhoun when in his cups; who will
say that Luke Friendly may be something of a bully, and Pony

Benner scratchy at times, but that Billy Gannon is, if you know him, a fine boy, Curley Burne a happy-go-lucky, loyal friend, and McQuown not actually an outlaw, since his forays after stock into Mexico are not really rustling.

However many good men die at their hands, or are driven out for fear of them, there will, it seems, always be their defenders to say they are only high-spirited, mischievous, fun-loving, perhaps a little careless—and even I will admit that there are likeable young fellows among them. Yet however many Saturday evenings are turned into wild carnivals of violence and bloodshed, however many cattle are rustled and stages held up, there will always be their champions to claim that they steal very little from their neighbors (I must admit, too, that Matt Burbage, whose range adjoins McQuown's, does not blame McQuown for depredations upon his stock); that they confine their rustling raids to below the border; that the stages are robbed not by them, but by lonesomers hiding out here from true-bills further east; that, indeed, matters would be much worse if it were not for Abe McQuown to keep the San Pablo hardcases in hand, and so forth and so forth. And it may be so, in part.

McQuown is an enigmatic figure, certainly. He and his father possess a range as large and fertile as that of Matt Burbage, and, it would seem, could be ranchers as eminent and respected. Certainly they seem no more prosperous, in their lawlessness. Abe McQuown is a red-bearded, lean, brooding fellow, who has about him an explosive aura of power and directionless determination. He has protruding green eyes, which, it is said, can spit fire, or freeze a man at fifty feet; is of medium height, almost slight, with long arms, and walks with a curious, backward-leaning gait, like a young cadet, with hands resting upon his concho belt, his beard tipped down against his chest, and his green eyes darting glances right and left. Yet there is about him a certain paradoxical shyness, and a certain charm, and in conversation with the man it is difficult not to think him a fine fellow. His father, old Ike, was shot through the hips six months or so ago on a rustling expedition, is paralyzed from the hips down, and is, reportedly, a dying man. Good riddance it will be; he is unequivocably a mean and ugly old brute.

I say, Deputy Canning must have known the clash would come. In retrospect I suffer for him, and at the same time I wonder what went on in McQuown's cunning and ruthless mind. What kind of challenge to himself did he see in Canning? Merely that of one strong man as a threat to the supremacy of another? The two were, to all appearances, friendly. Certainly Canning never interfered with McQuown, or with McQuown's. He was too prudent for that. Canning was widely liked and respected, and a man as intelligent as McQuown must have had to take that into consideration, for is there a man of stature anywhere who does not wish to be the more admired? And will any such man commit a despicable act without attempting to color it in his own favor?

I will put down, then, what I think: that McQuown carefully chose the time, the place, the occasion; that this was deeply premeditated; that McQuown is not merely high-spirited, mischievous, careless, that he is not simply a spoiled and willful youth; that, further and specifically, McQuown was jealous of what his henchman Billy Gannon had won for himself by dispatching an obnoxious bully of a deputy, and sought to repeat a winning trick.

About a month ago, Canning buffaloed a young Cowboy named Harms. It was a Saturday night and Harms was in town with a month's pay, which he promptly lost over Taliaferro's faro layout. With whisky under his belt and no more money in his pocket, and so nothing to do for excitement, Harms vented his feelings by proceeding to the center of Main Street and firing off his six-shooter at the moon—for which he is not much to be blamed. Canning, however, accosted him, for which the deputy was not to be blamed either, and, at some danger to his person, grappled with Harms in order to relieve him of the offending Colt's. In the end he had to clout the boy over the ear with the weapon to quiet him, which is acceptable practice. Canning then bore Harms off to see Judge Holloway, who presented him with a night's accommodation in the jail. Released the next morning, Harms started back down valley, but was thrown from his horse en route, was dragged, and died. No doubt his death was in good part brought about by the buffaloing he had received.

It was too bad. We felt badly, those who thought of it at all, and I am sure Canning was as sorrowful as anyone. Still, in this rough-and-tumble corner of creation, such things will happen, and are usually considered no more than too bad.

I think there is some East Indian doctrine to the effect that our fate is shaped in the most inconsequential of our acts, and so it was with poor Canning. Enter, then, a further minister of providence, a week or ten days later, in the person of Lige Harrington, a braggart, blowhard fellow more ridiculous than dangerous, but a minor hanger-on of McQuown's. Harrington announced himself a bosom friend of Harms, and his avenger. Harrington was patently seeking to make himself a reputation at Canning's expense, and to give himself prestige among the San Pabloites. Well primed with liquid courage, Harrington sought Canning's demise, but was dispatched in short order, crated, and immured upon Boot Hill.

Again, I think, no one was much concerned. This sort of asinine bravado must be the bane of any peace officer's existence. Yet I wonder if Canning did not have a fearful vision of how Right carries the seeds of Wrong within it, and Wrong its particular precariousness for a man in his position. For what are Right & Wrong in the end, but opinion held to? Certainly there were men who said that Canning had murdered the unfortunate Harms, and so had murdered Harrington his avenger, bad rubbish or not. Is not the semblance of guilt, however slight the tinge, already a corruption?

And I wonder if Canning did not feel the web beginning to encase him and the red spider gently shaking the strands. For soon rumors started. Canning had better get out of town. The threat was nameless at first, but after a time it was joined with McQuown's name. What other name would do?

I had heard rumors of impending trouble between Canning and McQuown, and dismissed them as idle gossip. At some point, I cannot say when, I realized they were not; I realized it as Warlock itself did, with a jerk to deadly anxiety as of a rope pulled suddenly tight and singing with strain. I have said that Canning was a prudent man. Had he been prudent enough he would have left town as soon as these rumors started, while still he could have done so without too great a loss of face. Yet he had come too far along the course. He had his own reputation as man and gunman now. He was caught in his own web as well as in McQuown's. He did not get out in time, and McQuown came in from San Pablo day before yesterday with all his men.

They hurrahed the town that night. Not so wildly, though, as to be much out of the ordinary, and I see that, too, as cunning upon McQuown's part: there was cause, but perhaps not urgent or completely justifiable cause (by our standards!), for Deputy Canning to step in. But Canning made no trouble; we did not see him abroad that night.

By then, however, the handwriting was etched upon the wall for all to see, and early yesterday men were loitering in the street, and Canning was early at the jail. I watched from my window as avidly as the rest of Warlock, in that crackling deadly tension, waiting for the trouble to start.

It was noon before McQuown came down the center of Main Street in his shining sugar-loaf hat and his buckskin shirt, stepping with disdain through the powdery dust. He fired into the air and shouted his taunts, such as, "Come out into the street, for you have murdered too many good men!" etc. Canning came out of the jail and I retreated—no more cowardly, I say in defense of myself, than any other citizen of Warlock —from my store to my rooms upstairs where I could watch from a more protected coign of vantage. There I watched Canning advance unfalteringly down the street toward McQuown. Once he looked back, and I saw behind him, almost hidden in the shadows under the arcade—two men. One from his short stature I knew to be Pony Benner, the other I have heard since was Jack Cade, both henchmen of McQuown's.

Canning came on still, but a few yards more and his steps slowed. They quickened again, but not with courage. He ran down Southend Street and got his horse from the Skinner Bros. Acme Corral, and fled Warlock.

My eyes smarted with rage and shame that there was not a man in Warlock to get out in the street with a Winchester and face down those devils behind him, and to see McQuown tip his white hat back on his head and laugh, as though he had won a trick at cards. My eyes smart still.

Last night honest men barricaded their doors, and no lights were left burning for fear they would be shot at. The Cowboys roamed the street and quarreled, and loudly joked, and shot at the moon to their hearts' content. They only quieted, like stallions, when they trooped off to the French Palace and the cribs along Peach Street. After a brief respite their unholy din began again, and lasted until morning, when the wagons that transport the miners out to the mines were held up, and the mules set loose and chased out of town. The doctor's buggy was commandeered and put to a wild race down Main Street against the water wagon, and many other pranks were played. Before noon they had departed for San Pablo with much hilarity, leaving our poor barber dying at the General Peach with a bullet through his lungs. Pony Benner shot him, evidently because he cut Pony's cheek while shaving him.

So the wild boys have had their fun, and played their mischievous games, driving a good man from this town, and murdering a poor, harmless fellow whose razor slipped because he was deadly afraid.

I think we would have done nothing about Canning, for his shame was ours. McQuown must know our cowardice well, and count on it, and despise us for it. So he should, and so should we despise ourselves. Yet, as with Canning, an inconsequential act may have set in train forces of adversity against McQuown. Our little barber's death has caused a congealing of feeling and determination here such as I have never seen before. If we cannot give voice to our indignation over Canning's shame, since it is too much our own, we can cry out in righteous wrath against the murder of the barber.

The Citizens' Committee meets tonight, called upon to defend Warlock's Peace & Safety, not righteously, only sensibly, for as this town is affected adversely by anarchy, violence, and murder, so are we, its merchants. Furthermore, Warlock has no other possible protector. It is to be hoped that the Citizens' Committee can, on this occasion, pull itself together and gain for itself, at last, the name of action.

The original organization, from which the Citizens' Committee sprang, was perhaps more fittingly titled the Merchants of Warlock Committee, including Dr. Wagner in his capacity as proprietor of the Assay Office, Miss Jessie in hers as boarding-house mistress, and the judge as the operator of a commercial enterprise in his judgeship.* Some time ago, however, when it became obvious that the granting of a town patent, and so of some measure of government, to Warlock, was not imminent, it was resolved that the original committee be expanded into something more. Since we were the only organization that existed, except for the Mine Superintendents Assn., we, the merchants, seemed the ones to initiate some sort of pro-tem governing assembly.

The old town-meeting style of government was immediately proposed. The suggestion was met with high democratic enthusiasm, which, however, waned rapidly. I, who made this proposal myself, immediately came to regard it as patently unworkable here, in a place where passions in all things run high, and men go armed as they wear hats against the sun, and where such a large proportion of the inhabitants is of the ignorant and unwashed class, if not actual renegades from the law elsewhere.

There are, for instance, the miners, the bulk of the town's population. Are they intelligent and responsible enough to be entrusted with the vote? They are not, we feel, perhaps a little guiltily. Then there are the brothel, gambling, and saloon interests; it is true that Taliaferro and Hake belonged to the Merchants Committee, but could we afford to give them and their disreputable employees proportionate power over the more decent citizenry? The question also arose as to how extensive the city-state should be. If it were to include ranchers from the San Pablo valley, what of such as Abe McQuown, not to speak of the Haggins, Cade, and Earnshaw, all of them landholders at least in a small way, and at the same time Warlock's scourges?

Our projected state was thus gradually whittled down, to become a kind of club restricted to the decent people, the

---

*The Citizens' Committee at this time consisted of the following members: Dr. Wagner, Miss Jessie Marlow, Judge Holloway, Goodpasture (the General Store), Petrix (Warlock and Western Bank), Slavin (the Warlock Stage Co.), Pike Skinner (the Acme Corral), Hart, Winters (Hart and Winters Gunshop), MacDonald, Godbold (superintendents, respectively, of the Medusa and Sister Fan mines), Egan (the Feed and Grain Barn), Brown (the Billiard Parlor), Pugh (Western Star Hotel), Kennon (Kennon's Livery Stable), Rolfe (Frontier Fast Freight), Swartze (the Boston Café), Robinson (lumber yard, carpenter shop, and Bowen's Sawmill), Hake (the Glass Slipper), and Taliaferro (owner of the Lucky Dollar and the French Palace).

right-thinking people, the better class of citizens; became, ultimately, restricted to the merchants of Warlock—ourselves; with a few additions, for Warlock had grown meanwhile; and a new name: The Citizens' Committee of Warlock. Now we must act, or abandon all claim to that name.

The situation is indeed fantastic. Keller* never appears here. We are none of his concern, he says firmly. When given argument by various volunteers passing through Bright's City, or by any of the numerous subcommittees that have been assigned to plead with him and General Peach† himself on the subject of law enforcement here, Keller gives it as his opinion that the country beyond the Bucksaws is not properly Bright's County at all, and that General Peach and his aides are presently working on boundaries of the new county, which will soon be established. Warlock will then be given a town patent, and will, of course, be the county seat. This will be any day, he says; any day, he repeats, and again repeats—but it has not been yet. Keller points out, when badgered further, that he did not campaign for our votes when running for his office, and promised us nothing, which is true; and that he has given us deputies, when they could be hired, which also is true enough.

Despairing, consequently, of aid from above, savaged beyond patience by McQuown and his San Pablo crew, some of us of the Citizens' Committee have decided that we must put it strongly in meeting tonight that our only solution is to hire a Peace Officer on a commercial basis. This is common enough practice, and there are a number of renowned gunmen available for such positions if the pay is high enough. They are hired by groups such as we are, or by town councils in luckier and more legitimate localities, and paid either a monthly fee or on a bounty system.

Something must be done, and there is no one to do it but the Citizens' Committee. It will be seen tonight whether the determined among us outnumber the timid. I think not a man of us has not been badly frightened by Canning's flight, and fear can engender its own determination.

---

*Sheriff Keller of Bright's County.
†General G. O. Peach, the military governor in Bright's City.

August 26, 1880

At last, it seems, Something Has Been Done. The meeting last night was quiet and brief; we were of one mind, except for Judge Holloway. We have sent for a man, a Marshal, and have obliged ourselves to open our pocketbooks in order to offer him a very large sum of money monthly. He is Clay Blaisedell, at present Marshal in Fort James. I know little of his deeds, except that it was he who shot the Texas badman, Big Ben Nicholson, and that his name at present is renowned—names such as his flash up meteor-like from time to time, attaching to themselves all manner of wild tales of courage and prowess.

We have made him a peerless offer, for what we hope will be a peerless man. Such, at least, is our prospective Marshal's reputation, that he was one of the five famous law officers to whom Caleb Bane, the writer, recently presented braces of gold-handled Colt's Frontier Models, as being most eminent in their field, and so, no doubt, most lucrative to Bane as a chronicler of deeds of derring-do. A fine act of gratitude on Bane's part, certainly, although it is cynically rumored that he asked for their own many-notched pacifiers in return, and from the sale of these to collectors of such grim mementoes realized a very tidy profit on the transaction.

So Clay Blaisedell has been sent for—not to be Marshal of Warlock, for there is no such place, and no such position, legally; but to be Marshal acting for the Citizens' Committee of an official limbo.* This is our third, and most presumptuous, action as the government-by-default of this place—the local government "on acceptance," a term Judge Holloway often uses to refer to himself as a judge, who has no legal status either. Our first act was to build Warlock's little jail by subscription

---

*Warlock's situation was much as Goodpasture has described it. General Peach was a notoriously inept administrator, sulking because he felt his fame and services to the nation justified a more exalted position than military governor of the territory. Despite repeated pleas and demands, no town patent had been issued Warlock, which had a population almost as large as that of Bright's City, both the county seat and territorial capital; and the rumor was so strong that the western half of Bright's County was to be formed into a new county, that Sheriff Keller was able to ignore almost completely, and evidently thankfully, the Warlock and San Pablo Valley area. There was, however, provision for a deputy sheriff in Warlock.

among ourselves, in the hope that the presence of such a structure might have a steadying influence upon the populace. It
has had no such effect, although it has proved useful on at least
two occasions as a fortress in which deputies were able to seek
refuge from murderously-inclined miscreants. Our second was
to purchase a pumping wagon, and to guarantee a part of the
salary of Peter Bacon as jointly the driver of Kennon's water
wagon and as Fireman in Chief. Taxes are no less painful under
another guise.

I write with levity of what have been serious decisions for
small men to make, but I am elated and hopeful, and the members of the Citizens' Committee, if I am representative, feel
a great pride in having overcome our fears of offending the
Cowboys, and our natural reluctance to part with any of the
profits we extract from them, from the miners, and from each
other, and at last having made an attempt to hire ourselves a
Man. It will be the luck of the camp to have its savior venti-
lated by road agents en route, and arrive here boots before
hardware.

He is to be hired, as we said last night, to enforce Law &
Order in Warlock. He is actually to be hired, as no one said
aloud, against the San Pabloites. What one man is to do against
the legion of wild Cowboys of McQuown's kin or persuasion,
we have, of course, asked ourselves. The question being unan-
swerable, like sensible men we have stopped asking it. We do
not demand Law & Order so much as Peace & Safety, and a
town in which men can go about their affairs without the fear
of being shot down by an errant bullet from a gun battle no
concern of theirs, or of incurring in a trifling manner the murderous dislike of some drunken Cowboy. Warlock's Marshal
will have to be a Warlock indeed.*

---

*The town took its name from the Warlock mine, which was inoperative by
this time. One story of the naming of the Warlock mine is as follows: Richelin,
who made the silver strike, had been prospecting in the Bucksaws under exceedingly dangerous conditions. The inhabitants of Bright's City, to which he
returned from time to time for supplies and with specimens for assay, viewed
him as mad, and his continued existence, in close proximity to Espirato's band
of marauding Apaches, as miraculous. On the occasion of his actual strike, he
had, on his journey into Bright's City, an encounter with some Apaches in
which his burro was killed. He managed to reach town, however, and, when

It is not known when Blaisedell will arrive here, if he accepts our offer, which we are certain he will. At any rate we pray he will. He is our hope now. I think we must have, in him, not so much a man of pure, daredevil courage, but a man who can impart courage to this town, which is, in the end, no more than the sum of every one of us.

September 1, 1880

Evidently Canning managed to pass on some of *his* limited portion. Carl Schroeder, who was, I understand, Canning's closest friend, has given up his position as shotgun messenger for Buck Slavin's stage line, to undertake the post of deputy here at one-third the pay. He is a fool. God protect such fools, for we will not.

September 8, 1880

Blaisedell has accepted our offer! He will be here in about six weeks. This delay is unfortunate, but presumably Fort James must be possessed of a suitable substitute before he departs. On the other hand, McQuown and his gang are reported in Mexico on a rustling expedition, so Warlock may still be inhabited when our new Marshal arrives.

September 21, 1880

A gambler named Morgan has arrived, and purchased the Glass Slipper from Bill Hake, who has departed for California. The new proprietor of Warlock's oldest gambling and drinking establishment has brought with him two attendants; a huge, wall-eyed fellow who serves as lookout and general factotum; and a tiny, bright, birdlike man of whose function I was uncertain until it developed that Morgan had imported for his shabby and run-down establishment (besides a fine chandelier, which much enhances the interior of the Glass Slipper), a

---

news of his escape was heard, someone remarked to him that he must have flown back, riding the handle of his shovel like a witch. Richelin is supposed to have made an obscene gesture in reply to this, and cried, "Warlock, damn you!" Be that as it may, he named his first mine the Warlock, his second the Medusa. The Warlock, after producing over a million dollars' worth of ore, played out, and was closed down in 1878, shortly after the Porphyrion & Western Mining Company had purchased Richelin's holdings.

piano, and the Little Man is its "professor." It is Warlock's first such instrument, and the music issuing from the saloon is a wonder and joy to Warlock, and a despair to Taliaferro and the Lucky Dollar. It is rumored that Taliaferro will now bring in a piano himself, either for the Lucky Dollar or the French Palace on the Row, to meet the competition.

Morgan is a handsome, prematurely gray fellow, of a sardonic aspect and reserved nature. His deportment, as a newcomer, has been subject to much comment, and his manner with his customers seems bad business practice, in a place where men are apt to be friends or enemies. But his "professor's" music remains much admired.

October 11, 1880

McQuown and several of his comrades have been back in town twice now—not including Benner, the barber-killer. They have been very much on their good behavior, as though ashamed of their last excesses here, and aware of the hostile attitude toward them that now generally obtains. Or else McQuown may be aware that we have hired a Nemesis.

## 2. *Gannon Comes Back*

WARLOCK lay on a flat, white alkali step, half encircled by the Bucksaw Mountains to the east, beneath a metallic sky. With the afternoon sun slanting down on it from over the distant peaks of the Dinosaurs, the adobe and weathered plank-and-batten, false-fronted buildings were smoothly glazed with yellow light, and sharp-cut black shadows lay like pits in the angles out of the sun.

The heat of the sun was like a blanket; it had dimension and weight. The town was dust- and heat-hazed, blurred out of focus. A water wagon with a round, rust-red tank moved slowly along Main Street, spraying water in a narrow, shining strip behind it. But Warlock's dust was laid only briefly. Soon again it was churned as light as air by iron-bound wheels, by hoofs and bootheels. The dust rose and hung in the air and drifted down in a continuous fall, onto the jail and Goodpasture's General Store, onto the Lucky Dollar and the Glass Slipper and the smaller saloons, onto the Billiard Parlor, the Western Star Hotel, the Boston Café and the Warlock and Western Bank, onto the houses in the Row, the cribs along Peach Street, Kennon's Livery Stable and the freight yard, onto Buck Slavin's stage yard and the Skinner Brothers Acme Corral in Southend Street, onto the Feed and Grain Barn and the General Peach boardinghouse in Grant Street, onto the tarpaper shacks of the miners and the wagons and the riders passing through and the men in the street. It got into men's eyes and irritated their dry throats, it dusted them all over with a whitish sheen, and turned to mud in the sweat of their faces.

Trails, and stage and wagon roads, led into the town like twisted spokes to a dusty hub—from the silver mines in the nearer Bucksaws: the Medusa, Sister Fan, Thetis, Pig's Eye, and Redgold: from the hamlet of Redgold and the stamp mill there; from the more distant hamlet of San Pablo in the valley and on the river of that name; from Welltown to the northwest, where the railroad was; from Bright's City, the territorial capital.

Dust rose, too, where there were travelers along the roads: a prospector with his burro; a group of riders coming in from San Pablo; great, high-wheeled, heavy-laden ore wagons descending from the mines; loads of lagging timbers for the stopes being hauled from the forests in the northern Bucksaws; a stage inbound from Bright's City; and, close in on the Welltown road, a single horseman slowly making his way up through the huge, strewn boulders toward Warlock's rim.

John Gannon rode bent tiredly forward against the slope, his hand on the dusty, sweated shoulder of the gray he had bought in Welltown, urging her up this last hill out of the malpais and over the rim, where she increased her gait at the sight of town. He glanced down the rutted trail to his right that led out to the cemetery called Boot Hill, and to the dump, where he could see the sun glinting on whisky bottles and a skirl of papers blown up by a wind gust.

The mare plodded heavy-footed past the miners' shacks on the edge of town. Beyond, and looming above them, was the tall, narrow-windowed rear of the French Palace. A woman waved a hand at him from one of the windows and called something lost in the wind. He looked quickly straight ahead of him, and laid his hand on the mare's shoulder once more. At

Main Street he swung to the left and the mare's hoofs sucked
and plopped in thicker dust.

The sign over the jail swung and creaked in a gust of wind as
he passed it. The sign was barely legible; weathered, thick with
dust, dotted with clusters of perforations, it humbly located
the law in Warlock:

DEP. SHERIFF

JAIL

Gannon reined left into Southend Street and turned at last
into the Acme Corral. Nate Bush, the Skinner brothers' hostler, came out to meet him. Bush took the reins as he dismounted, spat sideways, wiped his mustache, and, without
looking at Gannon directly, said, "Back, huh?"

"Back," he said.

"McQuown pulling them back in from all around, I guess,"
Bush said, in a flat, hostile voice, and immediately turned away
and led the mare clop-hoofing toward the water trough.

Gannon stood looking after him. He felt heavy and tired
after a day in the murderous sun, heavy and tired with coming
back to the valley as he watched Nate Bush's back carefully
held toward him. He had tried to hope he was not coming
back to trouble, but he had heard in Rincon that Warlock
had hired Clay Blaisedell as town marshal, had known without hearing it that the Fort James man had been hired against
Abe McQuown; and he knew Abe McQuown. He had ridden
for McQuown—even in Rincon they had known it—and in
Warlock they would never forget it. Billy, his brother, rode for
McQuown still.

He spat into his bandanna and closed his eyes as he tried to
scrub some of the dust from his face. Then he walked slowly up
to Main Street, stopping on the corner before Goodpasture's
store as a wagon rolled by in the street, dust rising beneath
the mules' hoofs in clouds and streaming from the wheels like
liquid. He turned his face away and blew his breath out against
Warlock's dust, remembering its smell and prickly taste; as it
settled behind the wagon he saw a thin figure appear and lean
against the arcade post before the jail. It was Carl Schroeder;
in his depression at the hostler's greeting he had forgotten that
there were a few men in Warlock he would be glad to see. He

started catercornered across the street as Carl stared, and then raised a hand.

"Well, Johnny Gee!" Carl said, as Gannon came down toward him along the boardwalk. Carl's lean, hard-calloused hand wrung his. "How's the trains running over in Rincon, Johnny?"

"Coming and going. What's that on your vest there, Carl?"

Carl Schroeder glanced down and thumbed the star out where he could see it. He did not smile. His plain, sad-mustached face was older than Gannon had remembered it, tired and strained. He said, "Bill Canning got run out and I kind of fell into the hole he left. You knew Bill, didn't you?"

"I didn't know him."

"I guess you have been gone a good while at that." Carl's eyes flickered at him, not quite casually, and then away. "Canning come in after Jim Brown got shot."

He nodded. His brother Billy had shot Jim Brown. The only letter he had had from Billy during the six months he had been in Rincon had been a strange mixture of brag and apology for having shot a deputy. "Dirty-mouth, bull-ragging son of a bitch," Billy had written. "He had it coming bad. Everybody says he had it coming. Abe says he'd choose him himself if I didn't choose him out first, Bud."

"Come on in and sit," Carl said, turning and moving into the jail. As he followed Carl inside he read the legend neatly lettered on the square of paper fastened to the adobe beside the door:

2ND DEPUTY WANTED
SEE SCHROEDER

The sign above his head creaked in another gust of wind. Judge Holloway was staring up at him from the shadow inside the jail, his sick face darker, thinner, more closely hatched with red veins than ever, on one cheek the wart or mole like a peg driven into the flesh, his bloated body hunched over the battered pine table that was his bench. The crutch that substituted for the leg he had lost at Shiloh leaned against the wall behind him with his hard-hat hung from its armrest. Peter Bacon, the water-wagon driver, sat at the back, beside the alley door, with a knife and a bit of gray wood in his hands.

"Well, Bud Gannon," Peter said, raising an eyebrow.

"Peter," he said. "Judge."

The judge didn't reply. Peter said, "How's the telegraphing going, Bud?"

No one had called him "Bud" for a long time now, but the name was as familiar and disagreeable as Warlock's dust. He felt a silly, apologetic grin cramp his face. "Well, I gave it up," he said.

"Come back for good, then?" Carl asked, turning toward him. He hitched at his shell belt. "Here or San Pablo, Johnny?" he asked quietly.

Gannon rubbed his hands on the dusty thighs of his store pants. "Why—" he said, and paused as he saw something very hard, very sharp, show for an instant in Carl's eyes. "Why, San Pablo, I guess. The only thing I know besides telegraphing's running a branding iron."

Peter bent to his whittling. The judge stared, darkly brooding, at the line of late sunlight that came a little way into the jail. Carl propped a boot up on the chair beside the cell door. "How come you to give it up, Johnny?" he asked. "Looked like you was going to make something of yourself."

"Laid off," he said. He could feel their unspoken questions. Although there was no call to answer them, he said, "Fellow I was apprentice to went and died, and they brought in another had his own apprentice." And he was pretty sure they had brought in another because it was known he had once run with McQuown, which was what Carl and Peter were surmising. But he had said enough, and he watched them both nod, almost in unison, apparently without interest.

Carl turned away from him to gaze at the wall where former deputies of Warlock had scratched their names brown in the whitewash. Carl's name had been added at the bottom. Above it was WM. CANNING, above that, in big, crooked letters, JAMES BROWN, above that, B. EGSTROM. Higher on the list was ED. SMITHERS, whom Jack Cade had shot in a cruel fuss at the Lucky Dollar. Gannon had seen that.

"Matt Burbage might be needing some hands," Peter Bacon said, without looking up from his whittling. "Usually comes in town Saturday nights, too."

"Thanks," he said gratefully. "Well, I guess I'll go have

myself a drink of whisky." No one volunteered to accompany him. The judge's fingers drummed on the table top.

"Got ourself a marshal now," Peter said.

"I heard. Did Peach come around to giving Warlock a town patent?"

Carl shook his head. "No, the Citizens' Committee hired him."

"Gunman from Fort James," Peter said. "Name of Clay Blaisedell."

Gannon nodded. A gunman from Fort James hired against Abe McQuown, against McQuown's people, against Billy, who was one of them. The town had turned against McQuown. The taste and smell of Warlock was not merely that of its dust, but the taste of apprehension, the smell of fear and anger like a dangerous animal snarling and stinking in its cage. He had come back to it, that had changed only for the worse since he had run from it. And now the town was waiting. He said quietly to Carl, "Trouble?"

"Not yet," Carl said, quietly too, his hand rising to pick at the dull five-pointed star limply hanging from his vest, his face, in profile as he still stared at the names on the wall, showing clearly anger and fear, determination and dread.

As Gannon started out the judge's hot, bloodshot eyes with their yellow whites slanted up to meet his own. No one spoke behind him. Outside, in the sun that came in under the arcade, his bootheels resounded on the planks as he started down toward the central block.

He would look up Matt Burbage tonight, he thought, doggedly. He knew it was useless. He had been one of McQuown's, and he would have to go back to McQuown, in San Pablo. Once he had thought he was quit of them.

## 3. *The Jail*

THE SUN, misshapen and red, was resting on the jagged spine of the Dinosaurs when Pike Skinner turned into the jail. Halting in the thick arch of the doorway, he cleared his throat and said, "I guess McQuown's coming in tonight."

Inside were Judge Holloway and Peter Bacon, Carl Schroeder, leaning back in the chair beside the cell door, with a hand grasping one of the bars to balance himself, and old Owen Parsons, the wheelwright at Kennon's Livery Stable, squatting against the wall at the back.

Schroeder nodded once, gently let his chair down, and stretched one leg out with a slow, careful motion. "Heard about it," he said. Then he said, "Bound to come in some time."

Peter Bacon said, "We was just saying it was none of Carl's worry." He bent down to sweep his whittlings into a neat pile between his boots.

"It's sure none of your put-in, Carl," Skinner said quickly.

No one looked at Schroeder. At a sound of hoofs and wheels in the street Parsons spat. The spittoon rang deeply. Bacon glanced up at the door, and Skinner turned to watch a buggy roll by in the street, its yellow and red striped wheels bright with motion in the last of the sun.

Skinner hooked his thumbs into the sweat-stained shell belt that hung over his broad hips, and teetered on his bootheels. He was a tall, heavy, slope-shouldered man and he filled the doorway. The others watched him remove his hat and slap it once against his leg. He scowled sideways at the square of paper tacked to the wall before he turned back inside. He had a clean-shaven, red, ugly face, and great protruding ears.

"Blaisedell buggy-riding Miss Jessie again," he said.

Peter Bacon nodded. "Fine-looking man."

"Him and Morgan is friendly," Old Owen Parsons said disapprovingly. "Heard they are partners in the Glass Slipper, and was before in a place in Fort James."

"Signifies what, if they are?" said Skinner, who was a member of the Citizens' Committee, scowling.

He stood aside as Arnold Mosbie, the freight-line mule skinner, came in. Mosbie's handsome, blackly-sunburnt face was marred by a great scar running down his right cheek.

"Heard Dechine was in town saying McQuown and them was maybe coming in tonight," he said, to no one in particular.

Schroeder said nothing. The judge raised his eyes to the round, dented bowl of the lamp suspended above his head. Peter Bacon sighed and said, "What Owen here was saying."

"Abe's been a while making up his mind to come," Mosbie said.

Skinner said to Parsons, "What's it to you if Blaisedell is friendly with Morgan, old man?"

Parsons spat, rang the spittoon, and jerked his fingers through his tobacco-stained beard. "Morgan is a damned high-rolling son of a bitch."

"It don't make Blaisedell one."

"Maybe it don't."

"A man has got a right to a friend," Bacon said.

"Why, what if it does make Blaisedell one?" Mosbie said, in his heavy, rasping voice. "What he is here for is against sons of bitches, and maybe a man has got to be one himself to make it. A real son of a bitch that shot Ben Nicholson loose from his boots and chased those wild Texas men out of Fort James till they are running yet, I hear—that's the kind we need here bad."

The judge folded his hands over his belly and turned his muddy-looking eyes to watch Schroeder plucking at the star on his vest. Milky dust drifted into the jail as riders passed in the street.

"Five hundred dollars a month, I hear the Citizens' Committee is paying him," Parsons said. "Five *hundred*, and what's Carl here—"

"Four hundred, God damn it!" Skinner broke in. "By God, how the talk in this town makes everything something it isn't. Old man, you'd set yourself where he sets for four hundred a month?"

Tim French, who worked at the Feed and Grain Barn, squeezed inside past Skinner. He had a round, cheerful, bright-eyed face, like a boy's. "Heard the news, Carl?"

Schroeder nodded tightly, and, with the same slow, careful movement, tipped his chair back again. "Heard it. Some fellow named McQuown's coming in."

There was a silence. Then French said, "Saw Bud Gannon down the street. I thought he was over at Rincon."

"Come back," Schroeder said. "Just came in an hour ago."

"Expect McQuown figures he needs all the help he can get," Mosbie said. "Pleasant to see Abe with the nerves."

"If Bud Gannon's any shakes of a gunhand I never heard anything about it," Skinner said scornfully.

"Johnny's all right," Schroeder said. "I don't care he's Billy's brother or whose. He quit them down there."

"Come back, though," Parsons said, grinning sourly.

"He got laid off over at Rincon," Bacon said.

"I wait and see," Parsons said. "Looks like he come back at the right time for McQuown." He grunted and said, "I wait and see on Blaisedell, too. Maybe he's no son of a bitch, but all I've seen so far is him hanging over a faro layout or whisky-drinking with Morgan. Or buggy-riding Miss Jessie Marlow. He—"

He broke off, for the judge was speaking. "Any man," the judge said, and paused for their attention. "Any man," he went on, "who has got himself set over others and don't have any responsibility to something bigger than him, is a son of a bitch." He stared from face to face, his cheek twisting around the great wart, his mouth drawn out flat and contemptuous. "Bigger than all men," he said, "which is the law."

Then he looked at Schroeder again. "And those the same that take the law for a fraud. For the law is for all, not just against some you hate their livers."

Schroeder had flushed, but he said without heat, "Can't see everybody's livers from where I sit, Judge."

"See just toward San Pablo from where you sit," the Judge said. "So where is the law?"

"In a book, Judge," Tim French said gravely.

"Never been a man yet to know what it was he swore when he put on that badge," the judge said. "Maybe you thought you swore blood on Abe McQuown and his people, Deputy. But that wasn't what you swore."

The front legs of Schroeder's chair tapped to the floor; his hand, where it still clutched a bar of the cell door beside him, was white with strain. In the easy voice he said, "Judge, I went up to Sheriff Keller and told him I'd come in here because Bill Canning got run and not a man to stand up for him. I come in here against Abe McQuown and people getting run or else burnt down by sons of bitches like him and Cade and Benner and Billy Gannon and Curley Burne. That's what I swore to, and your law for Warlock's in a book still, the way Tim said, if you don't like it." Then he laughed a little and said, "Though I have kind of got this ice water in my bowels right now."

The others silently avoided his eyes, except for Peter Bacon, who was watching his friend steadily. Bacon said, "I guess you could leave things up to Blaisedell, Horse."

"None of your put-in, Carl," Tim French said.

"Never said it was," Schroeder said. "Only—" He was silent for a time, and the others stirred nervously. He drew a long breath and said, "Only if they run him. If they run him and think they are going to whoop this town like they did before." He paused again and his face stiffened. "I guess that'd be my put-in. I guess you'd say I was looking the right way if I took that for my put-in, wouldn't you, Judge?"

The judge moved his head in what might have been a nod, but he didn't speak. Skinner said, in an embarrassed, too-loud voice, "Well, now, I expect you can count on Clay Blaisedell not running, Carl."

"There was Texas men tried to run him out of Fort James," French said. "I expect maybe Abe is going to bust a few teeth on Blaisedell, and choke on them too."

"I just wait and see," Parsons said.

"Every man is waiting to see, Owen," Bacon said.

"Well, Blaisedell looks a decent one to me," Mosbie said. "Don't look to be holding himself above a man, being what he is and all. I expect he will make out tonight. I expect he will make a fine marshal here, and Carl an easy job out of it."

Schroeder's lips twitched beneath his colorless mustache as he glanced up at the names of predecessors scratched in the whitewash. The judge was shaking his head.

"No," the judge said. "Not an easy job for Carl if he does his job. No, and not enough for Blaisedell to look decent either. For he has set himself to kill men and judge men to kill. And the Citizens' Committee has." He glared up at Skinner as Skinner started to interrupt. "No, not enough!" he said.

"Blow!" Skinner said. "By God, you are on the Citizens' Committee the same as me. It seems like you could go along with what the rest of us decided had to be done or shut up about it. Blaisedell isn't costing you nothing."

"He costs me," the judge said hoarsely.

"You damned drunken old fraud!" Skinner cried. "Nobody ever got any money out of you for anything yet but whisky. I am sick of your damned blowing! You are no more judge than I am, anyhow!"

"On acceptance," the judge said. He looked flustered. Clumsily he opened the table drawer against his belly, took out a bottle of whisky and started to pry the cork out with his thumbnail. Then, as he saw the others all watching him, he changed his mind and only set the bottle down before him. "On acceptance only, in this law-forsaken place," he said.

Tim French said suddenly, "Well, I will sure say this, Carl. How you ought to let Blaisedell take on what he is paid good money for. It is his showdown tonight and none of yours."

"Surely," Schroeder said.

Mosbie, his dark face flushing more darkly, said, "There is others but you have come hard against McQuown now, Carl."

"Not a man here that isn't with you," Pike Skinner said heavily. "Me included. And not a man here that won't back off when it comes time to scratch, I guess. That has been proved on us hard."

No one spoke. The judge sat staring at the whisky bottle before him.

"But with you all the same," Skinner said. He slapped his hat against his leg and turned to leave, but stopped.

"Got a help-wanted sign outside there," Schroeder said, with an edge to his voice. "Keller says I can have another deputy in here, can I hire one."

Skinner grunted explosively and flung on outside. His heels hammered away on the boardwalk. Owen Parsons rose and stretched, and Peter Bacon bent forward to sweep up his shavings. His face hidden, he said, "People have been shamed, Horse. I expect next time a man needs help, there'll be help."

"Uh-huh," Schroeder said. His mustache twitched again, but his voice still held the bitter edge. "There'll maybe be help, but I haven't heard much about anybody offering it to Blaisedell tonight. That might need it bad." He rubbed his hand over his mouth. "Me included," he said.

## 4. *Morgan and Friend*

IN HIS office at the rear of the Glass Slipper, Tom Morgan changed into a clean linen shirt and tied his tie by the dim last dregs of daylight. From the mirror the image of his pale face with the silver-white sleek hair and the black slash of mustache gazed back at him, expressionless and shadowy. He put on a bed-of-flowers vest, his shoulder harness, and short holster that carried his Banker's Special flat against his side, and his fine black broadcloth coat.

Then he poured a quarter of an inch of whisky into a glass from the decanter on his desk, and rinsed it through his mouth, gazing up now at the dull painting of the nude woman sprawled lushly on a maroon coverlet that hung, slanting sharply, on the wall over the door into the Glass Slipper. He raised his empty glass to her in a formal salute, and swallowed the whisky in his mouth. As though it had been a signal, the piano began to fret and tinkle beyond the door, the notes muted sourly in the increasing busy hum of evening.

He went out into the Glass Slipper. The big chandelier was still unlighted. To his right the long bar was lined with men's backs, the mirror behind it lined with their faces, but the miners had not started coming in yet and only one faro layout was going. Two barkeeps were hustling whisky and beer. The professor sat erect and narrow-shouldered at the piano, his hands prancing along the keys, a glass of whisky before him. He turned and smiled nervously at Morgan, the little tuft of whiskers on his chin popping up. Murch, brooding over the faro layout, his shotgun lying across the slots in the arms of his highchair, nodded down at him. Morgan nodded back, and, as he passed on, nodded to Basine, and to the case keeper, and to the dealer, shadowy-eyed in his green eyeshade; to Matt Burbage and Doctor Wagner. He sat down at an empty table in the corner to the left of the louvre doors, and raised two fingers to one of the barkeepers.

There was a deck of cards on the table, and he began to sort the cards by suit and number, his pale, long hands moving rapidly. When he had finished the sorting he quickly cut, recut, and shuffled. He frowned as he examined the result. The barkeeper arrived with a bottle and two glasses, but he did not look up, sorting, cutting and shuffling as before. This time the cards had reformed in proper order. He regarded them more with boredom than with pleasure. He was thirty-five, he thought suddenly, for no reason; half done. He poured a little whisky in his glass and touched it to his lips, but only to taste it, and his eyes glanced around the Glass Slipper. It was the same, here as in Fort James, here as anywhere. He had been pleased to sell out there and come ahead when Clay had told him he was going to take the place as marshal in Warlock; he had been eager to move on, eager for a change, but there was no change. It was the same, and he was only half done.

The batwing doors swung inward and Curley Burne and one of the Haggins came in. They did not see him, and he watched them go down along the bar, Curley Burne with his sombrero hanging against his back from the cord around his neck. They shouldered their way up to the bar, McQuown's first lieutenant and McQuown's cousin. And McQuown himself was coming in tonight, Dechine had said. He felt an anticipatory pleasure, and, almost, excitement.

He sat regarding the slight nervousness within himself as though it were some organic peculiarity, watching the heads turning covertly toward the newcomers and listening to the heavy conglomerate noise of men drinking, quarreling, whispering, gossiping, and to the little silences from the nearby layout when a card was turned and then the sudden click of chips and counters. The piano notes flickered through the noise like shards of bright glass. The sounds of money, he thought, and raised his glass again.

"Here's to money," he said, not quite aloud. After a time you discovered that it was all that was important, because with it you could buy liquor and food, clothes and women, and make more money. Then, after a further time, you went on to discover that liquor was unnecessary and food unimportant, that you had all the clothes you could use and had had all the women you wanted, and there was only money left. After which there was still another discovery to be made. He had made that by now, too.

Still, though, he thought, putting his glass down untouched

and turning again to gaze at the two at the bar, there was a thing or two worth watching yet. The eyes that chanced to meet his in the mirrors behind the bar glanced away; they all disliked him already, as always, and he could enjoy that, and enjoy, too, their displeasure and surprise that Clay should associate with him, that Clay was his friend. There were a few things yet.

Basine had lowered the chandelier and was lighting the wicks with the long-handled spill. As each flame climbed and spread, the room lightened perceptibly. He noticed that the piano notes no longer filtered through the sounds around him; the professor was coming toward him, in his shiny black suit.

"Well, sir!" the professor said, sitting down opposite him. "Place should be filling up pretty soon now, shouldn't it?" His eyes were like bright beads.

"Why, yes, sir, Professor. I believe it should."

"Well, now, this place has done fine here, Mr. Morgan. I wouldn't have believed it, coming in here cold like we did. Nice town too, but noisy." He leaned forward, conspiratorially. "However, I see that a couple of McQuown's people are in tonight. Expecting trouble, sir?"

"Always expect trouble, Professor," he said, conspiratorially too. "That's my practice."

The professor cackled, but he seemed distressed. The professor leaned toward him again as he shuffled the cards once more and dealt them out for patience.

"I've been thinking, Mr. Morgan."

"Now, why is that, Professor?"

"You know me, Mr. Morgan. I have worked for you for two years now, here and Fort James, and I'm an honest man. You know, I have to speak my mind when I see a thing that's wrong. Well, sir, money is being wasted here. By you, Mr. Morgan, on me!"

The professor had spoken dramatically, but Morgan did not look up from his cards. "How is that, Professor?"

"Mr. Morgan, I am an honest, outspoken man, and I have to say it. No one can hear that piano going, with the runkus in here. It is a waste of money, sir, and I made up my mind I was just going to say it to you."

"Play louder," he said; now he saw, and was bored. Taliaferro, who owned the Lucky Dollar and the French Palace, had been after the professor again. He flipped the cards rapidly, red onto black, black onto red, the aces coming out one by one; cheating yourself, he thought, as the kings appeared, queen to king, and jack to queen, and ten to jack—what use to play it out? But he continued to turn and place the cards, cheat himself, and laugh at himself for it. The last day, he thought, would be the day when he could laugh at himself no longer.

The professor was staring at him with his face askew as though he were about to cry. "Why, I play as loud as I can, sir!" the professor said, in an aggrieved and trembling voice.

Morgan said, "Taliaferro?"

The professor licked his lips. "Well, sir, it is that fellow Wax that works for Mr. Taliaferro. You know that Mr. Taliaferro went and got a piano for the French Palace, but there is no one around can play one but me. Well, they have been after me, Mr. Morgan, and you know I wouldn't leave working for you for double pay, but— Well, I was thinking, like I said, since it is a waste of your good money me playing here with nobody can hear it, so much runkus going on—I thought I might go up there to the French Palace and waste Mr. Taliaferro's money."

"You are too good to play a piano in a whorehouse, Professor," he said, and sat staring steadily at the other until the professor left him and went slowly back over to the piano.

Morgan watched a man he had never seen before enter and move over to the faro layout to stand behind Matt Burbage. The newcomer wore dusty store pants and a dust- and sweat-stained shirt. He was not heeled, was thin, not quite tall, with a narrow, clean-shaven face and a prominent bent nose. He bent over to speak to Burbage, and straightened suddenly, his lips bent into a strained grin. As he turned away and moved toward the bar, somebody cried, "Hey, Bud!"

Haggin flung himself upon the newcomer, and Curley Burne came up to slap him on the back. "Why, Bud Gannon!" Burne said. One on either side of him, they dragged him to the bar.

Morgan watched the three of them in the mirror. He had heard that Billy Gannon had a brother off somewhere. A group of miners came in, in their wool hats and faded blue clothes and heavy boots, two of them sporting red sashes—heavy, pale, bearded men. It was difficult to tell one from the other among them, but they were trade. Clay appeared behind them in his black frock coat.

Clay held the batwing doors apart as he halted for a fraction of a second, and in that fraction glanced, without even appearing to turn his head, right and left with that blue, intense and comprehensive gaze. Then, removing his black hat, he came over and sat down on the far side of the table and placed his hat on the chair beside him. "Evening," he said.

Morgan grinned. "Is, isn't it? And a couple or three San Pablo boys over there at the bar, too."

"Is that so?" Clay said, with interest. "McQuown?"

"He's supposed to show tonight."

"Is that so?" Clay said again. He stuck out his lower lip a little, raised his eyebrows a little. "Hadn't heard. I guess I ought to be tending to business instead of buggy-riding around."

Now the professor's piano playing carried well enough. Morgan could see the eyes watching Clay in the mirror. Murch had shifted the shotgun slightly, so that the muzzle was directed toward the three at the bar.

"Been a hot day," Clay said. He propped a boot up on the chair where he had laid his hat. Beneath the black broadcloth of his coat his shirt was wilted.

"Hot," Morgan said, nodding. As he poured whisky into the second glass he watched Clay's pursed, half-smiling mouth beneath the thick, blond crescent of mustache. "And it looks like a hot night," he said.

Clay grinned crookedly at him and they raised their glasses together. "How?" Clay said.

"How," he replied, and drank. "Look at them," he said, and indicated the people in the Glass Slipper with a nod of his head. "They are all in a twitch. If they stay around they might see a man shot dead—you or one of McQuown's. Only there might be stray lead slung and bad for their hides. But the money's been paid and time for the show to begin. You like this town, Clay?"

"Why, it's just a town," Clay said, and shrugged.

"Just a town," Morgan said, grinning again as Jack Cade came in. "Smaller than most and about as dull. Hotter than most, and dustier, but it has got a fine pack of bad men. Not just tourists like those *Tejanos* in Fort James, either."

"Who's that one?" Clay said thoughtfully, as Cade swung on down the bar, dark-faced with a stubble of beard, his round-crowned hat exactly centered on his head, his holstered Colt swung low.

"Jack Cade," Morgan said; he had made it his business to know who McQuown's people were. Cade joined the others at the bar, elbowing a miner out of the way. "Next to him is Curley Burne—number two to McQuown. That'll be Billy Gannon's brother in the store pants, and the other is one of the Haggin twins, cousins of McQuown's. One's right-handed and one left. This's the left-handed one, but I forget his name."

Clay nodded, watching them with a slight shine now in his blue eyes, a little more color showing in his cheeks. The room had quieted again, and there was traffic moving toward the door. The doctor and Burbage left the faro layout. As they went out they encountered another bunch of miners entering. "Doc," each miner said, as he passed the doctor. "Doc." "Evening, Doc." "You'll be needed later, I hear, Doc."

Clay grinned again. Luke Friendly came in. With him was a cocky, mean-faced little man who swaggered like a sailor walking the deck in rough weather. They joined the others, where the little man turned to glance at Clay, and spat on the floor.

"I expect that might be Pony Benner, that shot the barber a while back," Morgan said. "I haven't seen him in before. The big one is Friendly. By name, not nature. But watch out for Cade. He is a bad one."

"So I hear."

"McQuown is sitting off to let you chew your fingernails up a while. He won't play it your way, Clay. He will play it with a backshooter, which is his style. Watch out for Cade."

"Why, I will play it my own way, Morg. And see if they don't have to, too."

Morgan shrugged and raised his glass. "How?"

"How," Clay said, nodding, and they drank.

"I hope you have got on your gold-handled pair. There will be a lot disappointed here if they don't get to see them flash."

He laughed, and Clay laughed too, easily. Clay said, "Why, they are for Sunday-go-to-meeting. This is a work day."

Carl Schroeder was approaching, and Clay got politely to his feet. "Evening, Deputy," he said, and put out his hand.

Schroeder shook it, said, "Evening, Marshal," nodded tightly to Morgan, and sat down, pushing his hat back on his head. Above the brown of his face his forehead was a moist, pasty white. Little muscles stood out along his jaw, like the heads of upholstery tacks.

"I will stick by tonight, Marshal," Schroeder said, in a strained voice that was almost a stutter. "I am no shakes of a gunhand, but it'll maybe help to have me by."

"Why, I kind of thought I could count on you, Deputy," Clay said. He paused a moment, frowning. "But when it comes right down to it, this is no trouble of yours. You are not paid for it and I am—no offense meant."

"Pay is not the only reason for a thing, Marshal," Schroeder said. He looked down, scrubbing his hands together as though they itched.

Clay said, "Morg, would you call for another glass, and—"

"No, not for me. No, thanks," the deputy said. He looked sick with dread. His back was to the bar and he tried awkwardly to glance around, and then he said, "Is Johnny Gannon with them over there, can you see, Morgan?"

"He's there," Morgan said, and picked up the cards again. Schroeder bared his teeth in some kind of grimace. Clay got to his feet. His Colt was out of sight beneath the skirt of his black frock coat.

"Might take a little *pasear* around town, Deputy," he said. "There is no reason to sit in here and give ourselves the nerves." Schroeder scrambled up quickly, and Clay took up his hat.

"I'll probably clean them out myself," Morgan said, "if they get noisy." Schroeder stared, and Clay grinned at him. Morgan watched them leave, taking a cigar from his breast pocket and clamping his teeth down on it. Schroeder kept close as a shadow to Clay's heels.

As soon as they had gone, Murch signaled to Basine to replace him as lookout. Murch clambered ponderously down and came over toward Morgan. He looked like a carp, with his wall eye and his great slit of a mouth.

"Something going to come off in here?" Murch said, in his gravelly voice.

"Yes."

"How you want to handle it?"

"Tell Basine I want him behind the bar. You on the stand.

They'll play one behind him. It'll probably be Cade. You hold on whoever it is with the shotgun and let go if he moves."

"Holy Jumping H. Jupiter!" Murch muttered. "I can't let that thing off, it's crowded in here! It'll mash half the place full. I'll—"

"You'll let it off if one of them makes a move at Clay's back," he said, through his teeth. He stared into Murch's straight-on eye. "I don't care who you mash."

Murch said, "All right," unemotionally. The piano began to play again. Murch poured whisky into the glass Clay had left; his throat worked as he drank.

"What's chewing the professor?" he asked.

"Taliaferro wants him to play that new piano at the French Palace. That Wax's been scaring him."

"That's poor of Wax," Murch said.

"He just works for Taliaferro, and Taliaferro's got a new piano and nobody to run it."

Murch nodded stolidly. "What'll we do about it, Tom?"

"I'll see," Morgan said. "Get back up on that stand. I meant what I said about backshooters, Al."

Murch nodded again. Sweat showed on his forehead in a delicate fringe beneath his receding hair. He went back over to the faro layout.

Morgan poured himself another quarter-inch of whisky, leaned back, and waited.

It was dark outside when McQuown came in, wearing a pale buckskin shirt, smiling pleasantly, his face slanted down and his red beard against his chest, the lamplight catching glints off the big silver conchos on his belt. With him were Billy Gannon and Calhoun. Billy looked like his brother, Morgan thought, except that he was six or eight years younger and had a sparse young mustache sprouting on his lip, and his nose was straight, his eyes narrower and warier. His walk was a copy of Curley Burne's slow-gaited, cocky stride.

Morgan nodded to McQuown as the three of them went on down the bar. Billy yelled with surprise and jumped forward to embrace his brother, while McQuown glanced casually around the room. Now there was a steadier exodus. When McQuown's eyes met his for a moment, Morgan grinned back. "All right, McQuown," he whispered, hardly aloud. "Clay Blaisedell won't play your game, but I can, and better than you."

## 5. *Gannon Sees a Showdown*

STANDING beside his brother at the bar of the Glass Slipper, John Gannon looked from one to another around him—at Pony Benner's mean, twisted little face; at Luke Friendly, who could, at least, be dismissed as a blowhard and braggart; at the sour, cruel, dark features of Jack Cade, whom he had always feared; at Calhoun, with whom he had learned to be merely careful, as with a rattlesnake out of striking distance; at Curley Burne, who, with Wash Haggin, had been his friend, whose droll, easy manner of speech he had once tried to copy, and whose easy gait he had seen that Billy was copying now. He looked at Abe McQuown's keen, cold, red-bearded face. Once, when he had been Billy's age, he had admired Abe more than he ever had any other man.

Now he was back among them, and he tried to smile at Billy, his brother. Billy looked thinner and taller in his double-breasted flannel shirt and his narrow-legged jeans pants. It was like seeing a photograph of himself taken five years ago—same height, same weight, the same quick, not quite sure movements that he recognized as having been his own, but surer than his own had been; the same narrow, intent, deep-eyed face, with the only differences the mustache Billy was trying to grow, and Billy's nose straight still, whereas his own slanted off to one side, broken-bridged and ugly. Billy was watching Abe McQuown.

"Blaisedell'll be about halfway to Bright's by now," Pony said, in his shrill voice, and Luke Friendly laughed and glanced toward the batwing doors.

"Don't you wish it, Shorty," Wash Haggin said, and winked at Gannon. He had a big mustache, whereas his twin was—or had been—clean-shaven, silent, and reserved. Chet was home, Wash had said, disgustedly, when Gannon had asked.

"Blaisedell'll be around," Wash went on, to Pony. "This one is a different breed of horse."

Abe smiled and bent his head forward as he lit a cheroot. In the brightness of the match flame, his skin looked clear and fine as oiled parchment. Long, harshly cut wrinkles ran down his cheeks into his beard. He shook the match out, blew smoke, glanced up to meet Gannon's gaze, and smiled again.

"It is surely nice to see you back, Bud," he said. His eyes were bright as wet green stones. Casually he turned his buckskin back, and Cade leaned forward to whisper to him. Abe nodded in reply.

Gannon saw the big, flat-faced lookout staring down at them. "What's going on?" he said to Billy.

"New marshal," Billy said. "Clay Blaisedell, that's a gunman from Fort James. Citizens' Committee hired him to run us out of town. We'll see who's going to run tonight."

"Well, I expect he won't run," Wash said cheerfully. "He's the one that shot Big Ben Nicholson," he told Gannon. "And got a pair of gold-handled Colts from some Wild West writer for it."

Gannon nodded, watching Billy's stony young profile. "Pretty bad odds against him, isn't it?" he said, more drily than he intended.

Billy's face turned sullen. "Why, we'll make a play in here," he said.

"Not so bad odds in here," Wash explained. He jerked a thumb and whispered, "Morgan over there is kin to him, I heard; anyway they are partners here. And a charge of buckshot up there," he went on, indicating the lookout. "Only I hope to God it is birdshot. And count up Morgan's dealers and barkeeps and who knows what the hell else besides. Morgan is supposed to've cut plenty score himself. It is a fair enough shake."

Cade finished his conversation with Abe and turned to the bar with his back to the others. Calhoun was watching the door, scraping a thumbnail along his boneless nose.

"Billy," Abe said. "Maybe you and me and Curley and Wash could have a hand of cards over there."

Billy nodded tautly, and, with Wash and Curley, moved off after Abe. As they sat down in the rear, beyond the piano, a group of miners hurriedly vacated a nearby table. The piano player banged his hands down in a sour chord, and got up too, bumping, in his departure, against Calhoun and Friendly as they moved down to the end of the bar, and apologizing profusely. Pony Benner swaggered over toward the lookout's stand. Men were crowding out the door.

Gannon felt leaden as he stood alone against the bar, watching, in the mirror, McQuown's disposition of his men. At the table Billy sat facing the bar, with Abe and Wash on either side of him, Curley across from him, back to the room. So it would be Billy. He remembered that his father, dying, had charged him with watching out for Billy until Billy was grown. But Billy had grown too fast for him, and already Deputy Jim Brown was dead by Billy's six-shooter. His responsibility had been long ago dissolved in incapacity, and now the dread he felt as he stared into the mirror was more disgust and hopelessness than fear. He had fled this hard and aimless callousness where a human life was only a part of a game, and never, so far as he had seen, a fair game. He had thought he could escape it by fleeing it. But he could not escape having been one of McQuown's, nor the nightmare-crowded memory of what they had done, himself as much as any of them, one day six months ago, in Rattlesnake Canyon just over the border; and he could not escape himself.

The Glass Slipper continued to empty, men abandoning the bar and the gambling layouts without apparent haste, but steadily, clotting together as they thrust their way out the doors. The gambler, Morgan, came down along the bar against the traffic, his hair gleaming smoothly silver under the light of the chandelier, his face dead pale with the black bar of the mustache across it. Icy eyes touched his briefly. Morgan disappeared through the door at the back, beyond where Calhoun and Friendly stood.

Then Gannon was aware of the congealing silence. He saw the men crowded at the louvre doors pushing back out of someone's way. Among them appeared a man in black broadcloth, wearing a black hat. A step behind him was Carl Schroeder.

Carl halted there, among the others, but the man who must be Blaisedell came on, a tall, broad man with long arms, and a way of carrying himself that was halfway between proud and arrogant. His faintly smiling mouth was framed between a thick, fair curve of mustache and a prominent, rounded chin. For an instant the most intensely blue eyes Gannon had ever seen glanced directly into his. The marshal halted at a vacant stretch of bar between him and Jack Cade, who was bent forward over his glass.

"Whisky," the marshal said. A reluctant barkeep brought it. The sound as he set the bottle down on the bar was very loud, as was the slap of a coin on wood. The bartender, his hands in his apron, glided rapidly backward. Then there was no sound at all.

In the mirror Gannon saw that Curley Burne had risen and turned, and was standing to the right of McQuown, facing the room now. So it was not to be Billy; but he felt no relief.

Curley was grinning. Glints of light flickered in his black curls. Billy and Wash were sitting with their hands on the table before them. McQuown shuffled the deck of cards with a sound like tearing cloth.

"Oh, Mister Marshal!" Curley said.

Out of the corners of his eyes Gannon watched the marshal raise his glass to his lips and toss down the whisky. Then he set the glass down, and turned.

Curley's face wore a mock sheepish expression. "Marshal," Curley said. "I wonder could I make a little complaint?"

Blaisedell inclined his head once, politely.

"I guess it is up to me, Marshal," Curley went on. "There is a lot of complaint around about it—but folks have just kind of gone and left it up to me. Those gold-handles of yours, Marshal. They are awful hard on a fellow's eyes."

Someone laughed shrilly.

The door through which Morgan had disappeared stood open now, and Morgan leaned there casually.

"I mean, speaking for myself now, Marshal," Curley said. "I would surely hate to get a case of eyestrain from those gold-handles. They are so bright in the sun and all. A fellow is not much use without his good eyes. I hear they have been strained bad in Warlock lately."

"You could close your eyes," Blaisedell said, in his deep voice, but pleasantly still.

With a deprecating gesture Curley said, "Aw, Marshal. I'd just be bumping and wumping all over the place, trying to get around with my eyes closed. And look foolish! Marshal, *por favor*, couldn't you just not polish them handles so bright, hand-rubbing on them like they say you do?"

"Why, I guess I could do that. If things fell right in town here."

Curley nodded seriously, but long dimples cut his cheeks. Blaisedell stood with his boots set apart, his arms hanging loosely. Beyond him Gannon saw Jack Cade's head half turned, his lips drawn tight and bloodless over his teeth. Carl Schroeder stood alone just inside the batwing doors; he looked as though he were in pain.

"Marshal," Curley said loudly. "What if somebody painted them handles black for you?"

"It might do," Blaisedell said. He walked forward, not directly toward Curley, but at a slant to the right, and Gannon knew the marshal had not moved until he had worked out the geometry involved. Gannon found himself sidling doorward along the bar. He stepped past Jack Cade, but Cade's hand caught his arm and held him there, between Jack and the lookout on the stand. He stared up into the lookout's sweating face and the round huge muzzle of the shotgun.

"But who is to do it?" Blaisedell said. He moved another step toward Curley.

Gannon felt the movement of Cade's arm behind him. Instinctively he jerked his elbow back, and slammed his hand down on Cade's Colt, gasping as the sharp point of the hammer tore into the web of flesh between his thumb and forefinger, and staring up at the shotgun barrel. He fought the Colt down, looking wildly toward the table now, and saw, past Blaisedell's broad back, Curley's hand snatch for his six-shooter; and saw the swifter flick of the bottom of Blaisedell's coat. Curley's hand halted, the gleaming barrel of his Colt not quite level, and his left hand held spread-fingered and protective before his belly. His face was twisted into a grimace that was half grin still, half shock and horror as he stared at Blaisedell's hand, which was hidden from Gannon. In that same frozen instant McQuown flinched forward away from Curley, Wash straightened stiffly, and Billy sat perfectly still with his hands held six inches above the table top. Gannon saw him glance to his right, where Morgan had produced a short-barreled shotgun, which he held trained on Calhoun and Friendly. Then, as Gannon turned back to face the lookout again, he had a glimpse, behind and below the stand, of Pony Benner's baffled, furious face gaping at Blaisedell.

"Whoooo-eee!" he heard Curley whisper. Jack Cade's breath was scalding on the back of his neck. The upward pressure on the gun beneath his hand was released, the hammer drew loose from his flesh. He saw Blaisedell make a peremptory motion with his head at Curley.

Curley gave his hand a little shake and his Colt fell with a thump shockingly loud. Blaisedell returned his own piece to the holster hidden by the skirt of his coat. It was not gold-handled, Gannon saw.

He felt blood sticky and warm in the palm of his hand; he pressed it hard against his pants leg, his back to Cade still. Sweat stung in his eyes, and above him he saw sweat dripping from the lookout's chin. The muzzle of the shotgun was drawn back a little. Glancing toward the door he saw that Carl Schroeder had disappeared.

"McQuown," Blaisedell said. McQuown sat in profile, his head bent forward, deep shadows caught in the lines in his cheeks. He acted as though he had not heard. "McQuown," Blaisedell said, again.

Billy's hot eyes swung toward his chief, and Abe McQuown slowly pushed his chair back and rose. He slowly turned, one hand braced on the back of his chair, his eyes moving jerkily from side to side, his nostrils flaring and slackening with his breathing. His beard twitched as though he were trying to smile. Morgan was leaning casually in the doorway again, the short-barreled shotgun under his arm.

"McQuown," Blaisedell said, for the third time. Then he said, his deep voice without expression, "My name is Blaisedell and I am marshal here. I am hired to keep the peace here," he said, and stopped, and waited, just long enough for McQuown to speak if he wished, but not so long that he had to.

Then Blaisedell glanced around as though he were talking to all now, in the breathless silence. "Since there is no law for this town I will have to keep the peace as best I can. And as fair as I can. But there is two things I am going to lay down right now and back up all the way. The first one is this." His voice took on an edge. "Any man that starts a shooting scrape in a place where there is others around to get hurt by it, I will kill him unless he kills me first."

Gannon saw the furious tears in Billy's eyes. Billy got to his feet, and McQuown glanced nervously at him. Morgan shifted his shotgun around. McQuown's face was deep red.

Blaisedell continued. "Number two is what the Citizens' Committee has agreed to. I will say it again in case it hasn't got around yet. If a man makes trouble, or looks to make it and go on making it, he is going to see himself posted out of town. That is what they call some places a white affidavit. It is backed by me. Any man that comes in here when he has got himself posted comes in against me."

Again he paused, and again McQuown did not speak.

"That's all I've got to say, McQuown," Blaisedell said. "Except that you and your people are welcome here so long as you can keep them in order."

"Hear, hear!" someone yelled from the doorway. It was the only utterance. McQuown suddenly started forward. He came at a slow, steady walk along the bar. As he passed Friendly and Calhoun he nodded to them; they fell in behind him. Blaisedell half turned to watch, and Gannon could see the line of his face, calm and sure; and proud.

"Blaisedell!" Billy yelled. His voice broke. "Go for your iron, Blaisedell!" He leaned forward in a crouch, his hands hovering at his waist.

Billy, Gannon whispered, not even aloud; he tried to shake his head. He saw Morgan raise the shotgun.

Blaisedell didn't move. "Go along, son," he said gently.

Billy stood there with his upper lip working over his teeth; he twisted away as Wash put out a hand toward him. Then McQuown said, over his shoulder, "Let's go, Billy," and Billy let his hands fall to his sides.

The men who had crowded back in through the batwing doors now squeezed apart to let McQuown through, and Friendly, Calhoun, and Pony Benner behind him. Wash and Billy came down past Gannon, and Curley stooped to retrieve his gun, holstering it with a flourish. Billy stared at Blaisedell as he passed, and Wash, walking heavy-footed behind him, rolled his eyes exaggeratedly at Gannon. Curley came last, and made a little saluting gesture to Blaisedell. He looked pale, but unconcerned now.

Then Blaisedell turned squarely to face him, John Gannon. The lookout gazed down at him still from the stand, and Morgan watched him from the doorway at the end of the bar.

Everyone was looking at him; he felt it like a blow in the stomach, and slowly he too started out after the rest. Behind him there was the sudden whispering of the Glass Slipper coming back to life.

They stood on the boardwalk in the near-darkness. As he came outside, slipping his still-bleeding hand into his pocket, he saw Curley standing close to Abe. He heard Curley laugh nervously. "Whooooo-eee, Abe! Fast, I *mean*!"

Gannon let the batwing doors swing closed behind him. They struck against his back on their outswing, without force. Jack Cade was sitting on the rail, his head in his round-crowned hat bent down. He rose and came forward, his face featureless in the darkness.

"You God damned yellow-livered son of a bitch!" Cade whispered. "By God, I will cut your damned throw-down interfering hand right—"

Gannon backed up a step. Billy sprang forward toward Cade. "Shut your face!" he cried, almost hysterically. "You was supposed to hold on that lookout! I saw you making for Blaisedell, you backshooting son—"

"Here!" Curley said, and Wash stepped between Cade and Billy. "Abe's going, boys," Curley said. "Let's go along now, and not stand around squawling at each other." He started after McQuown, his sombrero swinging across his back from the cord around his neck. Abe was already a half-block away, heading toward the Acme Corral.

The group before Gannon dissolved as Billy and Wash moved aside. Gannon stared into Jack Cade's face—without judgment, for he had known what Cade was for a long time; and now he knew, too, that McQuown had put Cade to the backshooting which had just failed. With a slow, upward movement of his hand, Cade hooked his thumb behind his front teeth and snapped it out viciously.

"I'll shoot that thumb off, one day, Jack," Billy said, in a quieter voice. "Come on, Bud," he said to Gannon.

Gannon stepped past Cade, and ducked under the tie rail to join the others in the street. Billy laid an arm over his shoulders; it felt like wire rope.

"Back to old San Pablo with our tails between our legs," Wash said.

"Did you see that damned Morgan?" Luke Friendly said, in an aggrieved voice. "Brought that God damned short-barreled out of somewhere and had it on us before you could say spit."

Cade caught up and fell into step with Benner. "Who is going to get hisself posted first?" he said, and there were curses.

"He had it his way this time!" Pony said shrilly. "But there'll be another time!"

"We should've known better than to make a play in that damned place," Friendly said. "Too bad odds."

Gannon trudged through the dust between his brother and Wash Haggin, Billy's arm heavy on his shoulders. He had never felt so tired, and his dread of Cade was lost in his revulsion against them all. Ahead, alone, Abe McQuown disappeared in the shadows on the corner before Goodpasture's store. He heard muffled laughter behind them, and Billy cursed under his breath. Someone called, "Say, did you see those gold-handles good enough, Curley Burne?"

"Ah, sons of bitches!" Calhoun muttered. Curley, strolling ahead of the rest, began to hum a mournful tune on his mouth organ. Gannon remembered that mouth organ, and Curley playing it on quiet evenings in the bunkhouse—that had been one of the pleasant things. There had not been many.

And suddenly he knew he was not going with them back to San Pablo. He slowed his steps; he felt the strain of stubbornness in him that was as strong as the same strain in Billy, tighten and halt him like a snubbed rope caught around his waist. Billy's arm slipped off his shoulders.

Gannon turned to face his brother. "I guess I will be staying in town, Billy," he said.

## 6. *The Doctor and Miss Jessie*

DOCTOR WAGNER, bag in hand, watched the riders appear against the whitish dust of the street and the night sky. They turned west toward the rim, one of them riding well ahead, the others bunched behind. The suspirant music of Curley Burne's mouth organ was mingled with the confused pad of hoofs as they disappeared into the darkness.

Clearly they were leaving town. There had been no shooting, no need for his bag of medicines and his small skill. He
heard a man near him sigh with relief.

He turned and pushed his way through the crowd of men
along the boardwalk. "Doc," one said, in greeting. Others took
it up: "Doc!" "Evening, Doc." Behind him the piano in the
Glass Slipper began tinkling brightly. A man caught his arm.
"What happened, Doc?" Buck Slavin cried excitedly.

"The marshal got the drop on Curley Burne in the Glass
Slipper. The cowboys have all gone out of town."

Slavin let out an amazed and pleased ejaculation. The doctor
disengaged his arm and hurried on, for he must go and tell
Jessie, who would be waiting.

He crossed Broadway. Several men were standing on the veranda of the Western Star Hotel, outlined against the yellow
windows there.

"What happened, Wagner?" MacDonald called, in his harsh
voice.

A burst of whooping from the men back in the central block
gave the doctor an excuse not to hear the superintendent of the
Medusa mine. He hurried away across Main Street. There was
no reason not to be civil, he thought, and he was irritated with
himself. When the miners came to him with their complaints
and wrongs, he could patiently explain that MacDonald's ways
were only company policy, common practice—yet it was hy-
pocrisy, for he shared their hatred of MacDonald.

He turned down Grant Street toward the high, narrow bulk
of the General Peach. A lamp was burning in the window of
Jessie's room, on the ground floor to the right of the doorway.
All the other windows were dark, the boarders in town to watch
trouble, to see one of the gun fights that were at the same time
Warlock's chief source of entertainment and Warlock's curse.
They had been disappointed this time, he thought.

Panting a little, he mounted the plank steps to the porch,
opened the door, and set his bag down inside the dense block
of darkness of the entryway.

"Jessie!" he called, but before her name was spoken the darkness paled and she was standing in the doorway of her room.

"I haven't heard anything," she said quietly.

"There was no shooting."

She smiled a flickering, tentative smile. He followed her into her room and sat down in the red plush chair just inside the door. Jessie stood facing him, slight and straight in her best black dress with its lace collar and cuffs. Her hands were clasped at her waist. Her hair, parted neatly in the middle, fell almost to her shoulders in cylindrical brown ringlets that slid forward along her cheeks when she inclined her head toward him. Her triangular face was strained with anxiety. It was a face that some thought plain; they did not see the light behind it.

"Tell me," she said pleadingly.

"I didn't see it, Jessie. I had gone to get my bag. But from what I heard, the marshal got the drop on Curley Burne, and took the occasion to announce to McQuown his intentions here. There was no trouble, and McQuown and his people have gone."

The tip of her tongue appeared, to touch her upper lip. When she smiled, tiny muscles pulled at the corners of her mouth. "Oh, that's good," she said, in a curiously flat voice. She turned half away from him, and laid a hand on the edge of the table. "Was he—" She paused, and then she said, "Did he look very fine, David?"

"I'm sure he did," he said. "Although I didn't see him, as I have said."

"Oh, that's good," she said again.

He glanced away from her, at the bookcase with the set of Scott gleaming with gold titling; at the lithographs and mezzotints upon the walls—Bonnie Prince Charlie in heroic pose, Cuchulain battling the waves, The Grave at St. Helena; at the curved-fronted bureau next to the bed, on top of which were two daguerreotypes, one of Jessie as a girl, with the same ringleted hair and her eyes cast demurely down at a little book held lovingly in her hands. The other was of her father, sad-faced with his neat triangle of mustache and beard, seated against a manufactured backdrop that spread away behind him to dreamy distance.

"Are you angry, David?" Jessie asked.

"Why would I be angry?"

She sat down on the black horsehair sofa, her hands still clasped at her lap. He was, he thought, only angry that she should have seen so easily that he was jealous. "Don't be angry with me, David," she said, and he was moved despite himself, by the girlishness that was her manner whenever she was alone with him; by her sympathy and her sweet guilelessness that were her stock in trade, and, at the same time, her armor against rough men. She smiled at him, with the incisive understanding that always surprised him. Then her eyes wandered from his face, and, though she smiled still, he knew that she was thinking about Clay Blaisedell, who had come riding to her one day out of the half-calf and gilt-titled set of Waverley Novels.

She cocked her head a little, to something he could not hear. "Cassady is coughing again," she said.

"There is nothing more I can do for him, Jessie. There never was anything. I don't know how he is still alive."

Her face saddened. He knew that sympathy was as real as anything about her, and the tears when Cassady died would be real, and yet he wondered if any of it really touched her. He had always the feeling that death could not touch her, as rough men could not. He himself had always hated disease and death, and all the other outrages of nature upon man. But he himself became always less removed; hating them, he had, slowly, come intensely to hate Warlock, where death was so commonplace as to be a sort of rude joke, and especially to hate the mines that were the real destroyers of men. Most of all he hated the Medusa, the worst destroyer; and so he had come to hate its superintendent, MacDonald.

Yet Jessie, too, had seen much of death. She had spent her girlhood nursing her father to his slow demise, and now she had nursed more dying men in Warlock than he could count any more, holding their hands as they departed quietly and bravely —as they usually did if she was with them, for they knew it was what she wanted, though others wept, or fought and cursed death, as though they could drive death off or shout it down. And now in the last week or so he had come to see that she was in love with Clay Blaisedell, had fallen in love with him immediately, was in love as obviously and unaffectedly as she was Angel of Warlock. He wondered if *that* could touch her, either.

Maybe it depended upon Clay Blaisedell, he thought, and felt a stricture knot his throat.

She was listening again. This time he heard it too, the heavy, helpless, muffled coughing. Footsteps came hurrying down the hall, and Jessie lifted the brass lamp from the bright-colored yarn lamp mat on the table.

"Miss Jessie!" Ben Tittle cried, from the doorway. "He has gone and started it again!"

"Yes, I'm coming, Ben. And Doctor Wagner's here now." She hurried out with the lamp, and he retrieved his bag and followed her down the hall, reluctantly; Cassady only made him feel his helplessness the more. Shadows swung and tilted in the hallway as Jessie hurried along it with the lamp, toward the room at the back that she had converted into a hospital. Tittle hobbled after her on the crippled, twisted foot. They had not taken him back on at the Medusa because of that foot, and now he worked for Jessie as an errand boy and orderly.

When he entered the hospital, Jessie was already bending over Cassady's cot. Tittle was holding the lamp for her. Rows of cots extended into the shadows, and men were sitting up watching as Jessie poured water from an olla into a glass, and tipped the glass to Cassady's lips. The coughing continued, fleshy-sounding and murderous in the man's crushed chest.

"He sounds like a goner, Doc," Buell said softly from his cot nearest the door. "We sure thought he was going about three times tonight, and a blessed relief it would be, God help me for saying it."

The doctor nodded, watching Jessie lay her hand on Cassady's chest; he had never known another woman who would have done that, except a hardened professional nurse. "Drink it!" Jessie said. "Drink it, please, Tom. Drink as much as you can!" She spoke urgently, she sounded almost angry; and Cassady drank, and choked. Beneath a fringe of curly beard his face was drawn tight over the bone, and freckles stood out on the clean, gray flesh like bee stings on an apple. Water streamed down his beard.

"You can stop, Tom," Jessie said. "Try now. *David!*" she called, as Cassady began to gasp, horribly. The water might choke and kill him as easily as the coughing fit, the doctor thought, but he did not move. Cassady would not die simply because Jessie commanded him not to.

The gasping ceased, and the coughing. Jessie straightened. "There, Tom!" she said, as though she had merely talked a child out of a willful pet. "Now, that's better, isn't it?"

The doctor picked up Cassady's limp wrist. The pulse was almost imperceptible. Cassady was staring up at Jessie with worship in his eyes. The man could not possibly live for more than a day or two, and, heaven knew, there would be another along soon to need his cot. The cots were always needed, for the men were continually being broken and crushed in rock falls, in the collapse of a stope or the failure of a lift, or were poisoned at the stamp mill, or knife-slashed or shot, or got broken jaws or heads in saloon fights.

It would be merciful to let Cassady die, but Jessie adhered to a sterner philosophy than his. It was not that she considered death a sin, as he had once; she considered it a failure, and could not believe that there were wills less strong than her own. He knew her persuasion to duty, too, and he wondered if she did not also refuse to let Cassady die because her duty as the Miners' Angel, the Angel of Warlock, was to be just that, to the limit of her powers, and of her will. Perhaps, he thought, almost guiltily, in this singlemindedness she was incapable of any interest in Cassady, or any other, as a person at all, but saw them only as objects for her ministrations and as proofs of her office.

He shook his head at her, as Cassady tried to speak.

"Hush now, Tom," Jessie whispered, smiling down at the dying man. "You mustn't try to talk, the doctor says. It is time you tried to sleep."

Cassady's pale tongue appeared, to swipe at pale, dry lips. He closed his eyes. In the lamplight spilled water shone like jewels in his beard.

Jessie handed the olla to Ben Tittle and took back the lamp. She raised it so that its light spread farther, and smiled around the hospital room at the others. "Now you boys try to be quiet, won't you? We must let Tom get some sleep."

"Surely, Miss Jessie," young Fitzsimmons said, cradling his thickly bandaged hands to his chest. "Yes, Miss Jessie," the others said, in hushed voices. "We sure will, Miss Jessie."

"Good night, Miss Jessie. Doc."

"Good night, boys." She started toward the door. Her skirts rustled as she walked. They all stared after her.

"Doc," MacGinty whispered, as Jessie went out. MacGinty's thin, pocked face was raised to him; it did not look so feverish tonight, and he pressed the back of his hand to the dry forehead and nodded with satisfaction.

MacGinty said, "I guess you heard how Frank tried to get a contrib from MacDonald for—" He rolled his eyes toward Cassady. "But MacDonald said how if he gave anything we'd think the Medusa owed us something when we hurt ourself."

"Frank was stupid to ask."

"Lumber's too high to run in enough laggings," Dill said. "But it don't cost them nothing when we get busted up."

The doctor only nodded, curtly. It was difficult to meet their eyes. Sometimes that was even harder than trying to excuse MacDonald and the mine owners. "I'll come in in the morning," he said. "Good night."

"Good night, Doc."

He took up his bag, went out, and closed the door behind him. Halfway along the hall, Jessie was standing in conversation with Frank Brunk, a miner whom MacDonald had fired a month ago.

"He won't last long," Brunk was saying, in his heavy voice. "Not busted up the way he is. He can't."

"He can if he will," Jessie said. She raised the lamp, and Brunk drew back a little, as though to avoid the light. He was a huge, almost square man, with a square, red, clean-shaven face. He wore a bowie knife slung from his broad belt.

"Hello, Doc," he said. "Well, I went to MacDonald and I asked him straight out to—"

"You knew there was no use asking."

"Maybe I did," Brunk said. "Maybe I just wanted it clear what a son— Pardon me, Miss Jessie."

"Asked him what, Frank?" Jessie said.

"Well, told him. How the Medusa ought to pay part of Tom Cassady's keep."

"Tom doesn't have to worry about his keep, Frank."

Brunk nodded a little; his eyes were pits of shadow. "No, I guess it won't run to much, either," he said. "But *I* worry about it, Miss Jessie. And it was the Medusa smashed him."

"You are beginning to talk like Lathrop," Jessie said.

"And maybe MacDonald will put Jack Cade to run me out

of town, too?" Brunk said. "Well, I am just saying there is going to be trouble when Tom dies, is all."

The doctor said, "Do you need him to die? So you can have your trouble?"

Brunk looked at him reproachfully. "That kind of hurts, Doc." He leaned against the wall. "Do you think I want that? I only know what all of us want, and that's help."

"I have tried to talk to Charlie MacDonald about the laggings," Jessie said. She put a hand on Brunk's arm. "But he is no easier for me to talk to. He—"

"I think maybe he is, if you'll pardon me, Miss Jessie," Brunk said. "Doc, it is a fact. I am a miserable no-account miner. We all are. We are dirty, ignorant bullprod drillers and muckers, as everybody knows. No one will listen when the animals try to talk. We will have to have a union."

"Have it, then," the doctor said, with an irritation he did not understand. "If you break your heads fighting for a union or in the stope it is the same broken head."

"It is not the same," Brunk said.

Jessie said in her quiet voice, "Frank, my father used to say that men could do anything they wanted if they wanted it enough. Just to look at history to see what they have done, because they wanted it with all their hearts. He was going to write a book about it and he had collected pieces for the book —the impossible things that men have accomplished because it is in them to do anything if—"

"It's not so," Brunk broke in, roughly.

The doctor saw Jessie's eyes widen. "You can be civil, Brunk," he said.

Brunk rubbed a hand over his mouth. "Sorry. But it is not so, Miss Jessie. We can't have a union because we are not strong enough to make it and never will be, and what we want's nothing to do with it. That's all," he said bitterly. "Jim Lathrop was a good man and he did his best, and all he got was run out by a hired hardcase for his pains. Wanted enough!" he said, with scorn.

"Jim Lathrop did not have courage enough," Jessie said.

"Jesus Christ!" Brunk cried. "I will not hear that from anybody, Miss Jessie!"

Jessie's face was stiff as she gazed back at Brunk, the lamp steady in her hand, her breast rising and falling, and all the power of her will in her eyes.

And Brunk sighed and said in a humble voice, "I am sorry, Miss Jessie. I guess I have got the nerves tonight."

"All right, Frank," Jessie said. "I know Tom Cassady is your friend. And I know Jim Lathrop was." Footsteps sounded in the entryway, and she excused herself and hurried away down the hall, carrying the light with her.

The doctor said to Brunk, "Don't you know how to be civil? Don't you ever consider what she has done for you?"

"Christ knows she helps us enough," Brunk said, in his heavy, tired voice. "And Christ knows you do, Doc. But—" Brunk stopped.

"But what?" He put his bag down and stepped closer to the miner. He could not see Brunk's features now in the darkness.

"But Christ knows we shouldn't ought to be dirty charity cases," Brunk groaned. "We are people like anybody else. When we are charity cases it just makes it worse what everybody thinks of us. We—"

"Just a moment," the doctor said. "Let me tell you something. Who will you blame for the fact that you are charity cases? Jessie? Is it MacDonald's fault that Cassady has saved no money and must become a charity case? You make more money by far than any other laboring men in Warlock. Have any of you ever thought of saving any of it? I will grant you that the saloons, gambling halls, and the Row are snares constructed to relieve you of your earnings. But must all of you fall into those snares payday after payday? Saving is good for the moral fiber—a quality extremely rare among you. Saving your pay might also keep you from becoming charity cases, since you resent that status so much."

Brunk said, "If we had a union we could—"

"There is not moral fiber enough among you to make a union."

Brunk was silent for a time. Then he said, "Doc, I'm not saying what you just said isn't so. But it isn't all there is to it. We have got to have help to have a union, Doc. And the help we have to have is from respectable people. Like you."

He had told Brunk many times he would not engage himself in trying to form a miners' union; he had told himself, as many times, that there was no reason why he should. He said with finality, "I am a doctor, Frank. That's all I am."

"That's a funny way to be. For I am a miner, but I am a man too."

He didn't answer; he picked up his bag.

Brunk said bitterly, "Well, don't worry—they won't fight when a man dies, not having any of that moral fiber you said. But maybe they will try to cut wages one of these days. I have never seen a man yet that wouldn't fight for money."

Brunk moved away from him, down toward the hospital room. Carrying his bag, the doctor walked rapidly to the entryway, and the stairs that led to the rooms on the second story of the General Peach. Outside the open front door a group of boarders on the porch were talking together in the darkness.

As he started up the stairs he could see through Jessie's door, which she always left open, when she had company, for the sake of propriety. She was sitting stiffly on the horsehair sofa, with her hands clasped in her lap and her face alight. Just past the edge of the door a black strip of Blaisedell's coat sleeve was visible, on the arm of the red plush chair.

"They were reasonable enough," Blaisedell was saying. "Most men are, when you can talk to them straight. I don't know as McQuown is one I'd trust far, but then I don't know him."

Blaisedell's voice ceased for a moment, and Jessie glanced toward the door. The doctor went on up the stairs. Below him they began talking again, but now he couldn't hear the words. In his room, as he poured a glass of water, and, into the water, the carefully measured drops of laudanum, he could not hear them at all.

## 7. *Curley Burne Plays His Mouth Organ*

IN THE night Curley let Spot pick his own way, only pushing on him when he began to fritter. By day it was a six-hour ride from Warlock to San Pablo, but by night it was slow. The stars were out and a burnt quarter-moon hung in the west, but the darkness was thick, and shapes came suddenly out of it to make his heart start and pound. From time to time he brought out the mouth organ that hung on a cord inside his shirt, and blew a tune through it.

He had dropped the others behind, but Abe had dropped him, too. Still, it was pleasant riding alone in the night, hearing now the wind whispering through trees he couldn't even see. He reined up a moment to locate himself by the sound; he must be on the slope where, below, the river made a bend around a thick stand of cottonwoods. He turned downhill toward the river, Spot picking his way along with care. He heard the river itself and immediately, as he always did when he first heard it, he reined up again and dismounted to make water.

He rode on alongside the river, with its trembling rapid sheen under the moon and the trees soaring against the black sky, light-streaked where the wind turned the leaves. He listened for the thick rush of the rapids, and saw before him the outline of a horseman. He raised his mouth organ and blew into it, tunelessly. Spot scrambled down a rocky ledge, striking hoof-sparks.

"Curley?" Abe said.

"Ho," he replied, and Spot whinnied at Abe's black. They were on the northwest corner of the spread now, and Abe always stopped and watered here.

"Pretty night for a ride," Curley said, dismounting and giving Spot a slap on the flank. "But I sure don't own night eyes like you do. It is lucky Spot knows the route."

"Where's the others?" Abe asked.

"Back somewhere, bickering and whickering."

Abe said nothing, and Curley waited to see if he would start off or wait. If he started off he would let him go in alone. But Abe waited until he remounted, and together they rode on down along the river beneath the cottonwoods.

After a time Curley said, "Quite a one, the marshal!"

"Yes," Abe said. "He is quite a one." Abe didn't pick it up any more than that, nor, although his voice had seemed short, quite cut him off either.

Curley was silent for a time, thinking that it was still all right between the two of them, but thinking painfully now, too, that if he, Curley Burne, left San Pablo and moved west, or north, or down to Sonora somewhere, the way he had been considering lately, Abe would turn into pure son of a bitch. Like Jack Cade, only a bigger one; and that would be too bad. Abe had

been knocking at it close for a good while now—he knew well
enough that Abe had put Jack there to backshoot Blaisedell if
it came to it—and it seemed to him more and more that but
for him, and some kind of decency Abe owed him, Abe would
go all the way over.

And the old man, he thought, shaking his head. The old
man was a trial and a terror, and born unholy mean.

"Let's go on along the river instead of cutting in," Abe said.

"Sounds nice tonight, don't it?" He reined right as Abe cut
back down under the deep shadow of the cottonwoods. He
spat, scraped his hand over his face, and braced himself to try
again. Once he and Abe had been able to talk things out.

"Well," he said loudly. "Looks like I am some beholden to
him. He could've burned me down there as well as not."

"No," Abe said.

"Surely," he insisted. "I was looking right down it, six feet
long and six deep. And lonely!"

"No," Abe said again. "It looks better for him like this."

He grimaced to think of having to try to figure everything
that way. "Well, he is greased lightning, sure enough," he went
on. "I never saw a man get unhooked that fast and have himself
in hand enough so he didn't have the trigger on the pull. I am
some pleased to be with us here, tonight."

Abe didn't turn, didn't speak.

"Well, it was coming anyhow," Curley said. "Warlock was
about due to get fed up with folks. There's been things done
that would make *me* mad, I know. Pony, now; Pony is an aggravating kind of man. Sometimes I think he don't have good
sense. Looks like Warlock was due for somebody like this
Blaisedell."

"I was here before he was," Abe said, in a stifled voice. "But
now he is set up to say who comes and goes in Warlock."

"Aw, Abe," he said. He didn't know how to go on, but he
was filled with it now and he had to try to say it out. "What's
got into you, Abe?" he asked.

"Meaning what?" Abe said.

He couldn't bring himself to reproach Abe for setting Jack
Cade to backshoot Blaisedell. He said, "Well, it used to be
you'd come out and shoot tomato cans off fence posts with the
rest of us. And mostly you'd win, but sometimes you'd lose out

—that will happen to any man. And Indian wrestle and hand wrestle with us when we got to fooling, and that the same. But you have stopped it."

The black cantered ahead, but when Curley caught up again he kept at it.

"Like you had got to be too big a man to lose any more." His voice felt thick in his throat. "Like if you lost even one time at anything now you lost face, or some damned foolish thing. Like—" He cleared his throat. "Like I kind of think you couldn't stand to lose tonight."

This time Abe glanced back at him, and Curley turned in his spurs in order to draw up even.

"Abe," he said. "Anything where you stand to win, you have got to be able to stand to lose, too. For that's the way things go. Abe," he said. "Maybe I know how you feel some. But say you kept on being the biggest man in the San Pablo valley and Warlock too. You still wouldn't be the biggest man in the territory by a damn sight. And say you called out old Peach and the cavalry, and massacreed them and took Peach's scalp—where'd you go then? What'd you have to be the biggest of then?"

It sounded as though Abe laughed, and his spirits rose.

"Why, Curley," Abe said. "The last time I saw that scalp of Peach's there wasn't a hell of a lot of hair to take. Come to think of it, maybe that's why Espirato took his Paches out of here—when he saw old Time had beat him to Peach's hair."

He laughed too. It sounded like the old Abe.

"Bud Gannon coming along with the others?" Abe asked.

"He stayed in town."

"He did?" Abe said. When he spoke again his voice had turned somber. "I know there is some that's turned against me."

"That's not so, Abe!" he protested.

"It's so. Like Bud. And Chet—you see how he has been staying clear. And I felt it hard in Warlock tonight. But you can't back off."

"Nothing ever stopped me from it." Curley tried to say it lightly. "I surely backed tonight, and glad to."

"I couldn't have done that," Abe said. "I guess you know that's why I let you take it."

He nodded sickly. He thought again of Cade, and he

thought of how it had been worked when they had run Canning; he had tried to shut that from his mind, but it had been as clear as this tonight. He felt sick for Abe. "Surely I knew it," he said. "But what the hell? Abe—I am damned if I think poor of myself for backing off tonight. Or why you—"

"There gets a time when it don't matter what you think of yourself," Abe broke in. "That's it, you see. Maybe it is what everybody else thinks instead." The black cantered on ahead again. "Let's get on in," Abe called back to him.

Curley spurred Spot to a half-trot, but he stayed behind Abe all the way.

As they walked up from the horse corral, the dogs barked and jumped around their legs. Curley sighed as he looked up at the squat ranch house, where a little light showed in a window. Behind it soared the monolith of the chimney of the old house, which had burned down. The lonely chimney seemed incredibly high and narrow against the night sky, pointing its stone and crumbling mortar height at the stars. He wondered if that chimney would not fall some day, despite the poles that propped it up, and mash them all to smithereens.

He said to Abe, "Well, I'll be going over to the bunkhouse."

"Come inside and take a glass of whisky," Abe said. His voice was bleak. One of the dogs sprawled away in front of him, yelping. They mounted the slanting steps to the porch, and Abe jerked on the latch-string and shouldered the door open. "What the hell are you doing out here, Daddy?" he said.

Following him in, Curley saw the old man on his pallet on the floor. He was raised on one elbow, his skinny neck corded with strain. There was a Winchester across his legs, a jug and lamp on the floor beside him. His beard was thick, pure-white wool in the lamplight, and his mouth was round and pink as a kitten's button.

"Didn't stay long, did you?" Dad McQuown said. "Think I'm going to stay in that bedroom and burn?"

"Burn?" Abe said. He picked up the lamp and set it atop the potbelly stove. With the lamplight on it the stovepipe looked red. "You're not dead yet. Burn?"

"Burn is what I said," the old man said. "Don Ignacio is going to hear some time you have left me all alone. You think he won't send some of his dirty, murdering greasers up here to burn me in my bed?"

It was strange, Curley thought, that those Mexicans, killed six months ago in Rattlesnake Canyon, had turned almost every man of them into a greaser-hater—afterward. It was a strange thing.

"There's three men out in the bunkhouse," Abe said. He picked up the jug, hooked it to his mouth, and took a long draught. He handed it to Curley and went to sit on the old buggy-seat sofa against the wall.

"Burn them too," the old man said. "Sneakier than Paches. Those sons of bitches out in the bunkhouse'd sleep through a stampede coming over them anyhow." His eyes glittered at Curley. "What happened up there?"

From the buggy seat Curley heard a clack and metallic singing. He turned to see Abe bend to pull his bowie knife loose, where it was stuck in the floor. Abe spun it down again, the blade shining fiery in the light.

"Let me tell you," Curley said to the old man. "Bold as brass I went in there against him. In the Glass Slipper, that was packed with guns to back the bastard up. 'Let's see the color of your belly, Marshal!' I said to him."

The old man said, "Son, how come you let Curley—"

"Hush now, Dad McQuown. I am telling this. How come he let me? Why, he knows I am the coolest head in San Pablo, and that saloon stacked hard against us." Feeling a fool, he bent his knees into a crouch and heard Abe spin the knife into the floor again. The old man stared as Curley jerked out his Colt and took a bead on the potbelly stove. "I don't mind saying that was the fastest draw human eye ever did see," he said. "Fast, and—" He stopped, straightened, sighed, and holstered his Colt.

"Kill him clean off?" the old man demanded.

"He was way ahead of me," he said, and glanced toward the buggy seat. He had hoped for a laugh from Abe, to clear things a little; he knew what Abe was going to have to take from the old man. But Abe only flung the knife down again. This time the point didn't stick and it clattered across the floor and rang against a leg of the stove. Abe made no move to retrieve it.

"Run you out of town," the old man breathed.

"He surely did."

The old man lay back on his pallet, and sucked noisily at his teeth. "Son of mine running," he said.

"Yep," Abe said, tightly.

"That all you can say?" the old man yelled.

"Yep," Abe said.

"Go in myself," the old man said. "See anybody run me out."

"Walk in," Abe said.

"I will drag in, by God!" Dad McQuown said, straining his head up again. "See anybody run me out. I have been through Warlock when it wasn't but a place in the road where me and Blaikie and old man Gannon used to meet and go into Bright's together. Went together because of Paches in the Bucksaws, thick as fleas. Many's the time we fought them off, too, before Peach was ever heard of. Took my son with me sometimes that I thought was going to amount to something, and not get run out of—"

"Say, now, speaking of Gannons," Curley broke in. "Bud's come back from Rincon. We saw him in town."

"Bud Gannon," the old man said, lying back again, "never was worth nothing at all. Billy, now; there is a boy any man'd be glad for a son. Proud."

"Well, Dad McQuown, he run with the rest of us. Maybe not so fast as me, but he run all right."

"How fast did my boy run?" the old man whispered, and Abe cursed him.

Curley took a long pull on the jug, watching the old man's fingers plucking at the Winchester while Abe cursed him, harshly and at length.

"You will answer to the Lord for that cussing some day, boy," Dad McQuown said, at last. "Cussing your daddy when he is crippled so he can't beat your teeth down your throat for it. Well, it is sire and dam in a man like a horse, and no way to get yourself a boy without there is half woman in him."

"One way," Abe said, in a dead, strained voice. "Breed one mule on another like did for you."

"Cuss your father, and his ma and pa before him, do you? You will answer for that, too."

"Not to you," Abe said.

"You will answer to another Father than me."

"I'll answer maybe for killing a pack of greasers for what they did to you. I won't answer for calling you what every man knows you are, and the Lord too."

Standing there listening to them, trying to grin as though they were just joking each other, it came on Curley strongly that he had to move on. He had been here too long now; he had seen the beginning, which he had not even known was the beginning, and he did not want to see the end. Abe was a man he had respected and loved as he had no other man, and did still, but lately he could not bear to see where Abe was heading. Or maybe he had to stay, and watch, he thought, and felt a kind of panic.

The dogs set up another clamor outside, and hoofbeats came in through the yard. The old man said, "They didn't run so fast as you."

"That is some greasers of Don Ignacio's come up to burn you in your bed," Abe said savagely. "By God, how you would burn and stink!"

The hoofbeats and the barking and yelping diminished, going down toward the horse corral. "Well, I will be getting over to the bunkhouse," Curley said, pretending to yawn. "Good night, Dad McQuown. Abe."

"We'll be going down tomorrow after supper," Abe said.

"Down where?" the old man demanded. "What you going to do now?"

Abe ignored him. "That will put us through Rattlesnake Canyon after dark," he said. "Tell the boys."

Curley tipped his hat back and scratched his fingers through his hair, grimacing. "Hacienda Puerto?" he said. "I thought you figured we ought to lay off that awhile, Abe. They followed us a good way last time and we didn't make off with hardly enough head to count. It is getting tight."

"We will take more people this time."

"Well, there is talk Don Ignacio's got himself an army down there now, Abe. They are going to be waiting for us, one of these times. If they catch us—"

Abe swung toward him. "God damn it, there will be nothing

happen because I will be along! You only get caught when I am not there. One shot through and another one dead, and then run home to me to back them off you!"

Curley had brought the old man back that time, leaving Hank Miller dead; and he had refused to go back with Abe and the rest to the ambush in Rattlesnake Canyon. Abe had not forgiven him that, and had not forgiven Bud Gannon, who had left San Pablo afterward. And Abe had not, he thought, forgiven himself either. Rattlesnake Canyon still ate at them all.

"All right, I'll tell them, Abe," he said, and went outside and closed the door behind him. He stood on the porch looking up at the stars past the old chimney. He should go, he thought; he should get out now. As he walked tiredly down the steps and over toward the bunkhouse, he took out his mouth organ and began to blow into it. The music he made was sad in the night.

## 8. *Journals of Henry Holmes Goodpasture*

November 16, 1880

*Venit, Vidit, Vicit.* The recent dramatics at the Glass Slipper were eminently satisfactory to all, except, no doubt, McQuown and his men, and Clay Blaisedell has succeeded almost past our wildest hopes in subduing the Cowboys. We have been most marvelously impressed with his demeanor here so far.

A man in his position is, of course, handicapped, but he is evidently experienced with makeshift arrangements. A tiny, one-cell jail, no court, no proper judge this side of Bright's City —except for a J.P. who is only that on his own mandate and general tolerance, have not fazed our Marshal at all. Thus he has for weapons only his reputation and his own six-shooters, with which to threaten, to buffalo, to maim, or to kill. The first, the inherent threat of his reputation, we hope will serve our purposes.

Blaisedell had various suggestions to make. One was that we set up a deadline; no firearms to be carried past a certain part of town. We were uneasy about this, and Blaisedell readily agreed

that the edict might cause more trouble than it prevented. Another suggestion of his was met with more enthusiasm: this is
what is known as a "white affidavit." If it is felt that the peace
of this town or the safety of its inhabitants are threatened by
any man, or if a criminal is transported to Bright's City for trial
for a major crime, and the Bright's City jurymen fail to render
a true judgment (as is often the case), a white affidavit is to be
issued. This is no more than an order on the part of the Citizens' Committee that an offender is to be forbidden entry to
the town by the Marshal. If such a one disregards this posting,
he then enters under pain of death—which is to say, he must
face Blaisedell's six-shooter prowess, which, we are hopeful,
will strike fear into the bravest hearts.

We are most pleased with ourselves, and with our Marshal,
so far. As Buck Slavin points out, Warlock's bad reputation
has long stood in the paths of Commerce and Population. If
Blaisedell can effect order here we may expect both to increase,
for the peaceable and the timid must certainly shy away from
the violence well known to have ruled here. Thus, with an in-
flux of citizens of finer stamp, in time the better element of the
population will come to overbalance by far that of the violent
and irresponsible, peace will come to enforce itself, and Commerce will flourish. To the good fortune of the members of the
Citizens' Committee of Warlock.

Still, there are doubts. I have been troubled in wondering
whether we of the Citizens' Committee have fully realized
the responsibility we have assumed. We have hired a gunman
whose only recommendation is a certain notoriety. We are responsible for this man of whom we know, actually, nothing. I
suppose our troubled consciences are assuaged by the thought
that we have assumed a makeshift authority for a makeshift
situation, and a temporary one.

The question of our status remains frozen in suspension.
Are we in Bright's County, or in a new, yet-to-be-surveyed
county? What keeps us from being granted a town patent before this matter is settled? Is there more to it than merely General Peach's carelessness and senility? Is there, as Buck Slavin
hints in his darker moods, some official feeling that Warlock is
not worth troubling with, since it will soon fade away with its
subterranean wealth exhausted, or its mines gradually closing

down as the market price of silver continues to fall, or becoming flooded and unworkable?*

Poor and makeshift our efforts may be, yet there would seem proof in them that a society of sorts is possible in an anarchistic state. We feel we are ultimately in the Republic, separated from her only by an incredibly inept and laggard territorial government, and so obedience to the forms is necessary. Or are those forms themselves so ineradicably imbedded in men's minds that we cannot think but in terms of them? The general passive acceptance of Judge Holloway's fines (which everyone knows he pockets), and his imposition of sentences to our little jail or to unpaid community tasks, would seem to indicate this.

Be that as it may, I think the Citizens' Committee has been most lucky in their employment of Blaisedell. He might have begun his action here in Warlock against the lesser fry. Instead he waited (and incurred some initial criticism for his inaction), and made his play against McQuown himself. I understand that his handling of McQuown, Burne, et al. in the Glass Slipper was masterful. He could have shed blood, but correctly chose not to do so. It is said that Curley Burne actually saluted Blaisedell in tribute to his gentlemanliness and forbearance, as he departed.

We have not seen McQuown since, nor any of his men. There has been no bloodshed since Blaisedell's arrival. Blaisedell has had to buffalo a few recalcitrants, and has escorted some Cowboys and drunken miners to the jail, but violent death has removed itself from our midst temporarily.

Blaisedell is an imposing figure of a man, with a leonine fair head, an erect and powerful carriage, and eyes of an astonishing concentration. He seems guileless and straightforward, very dignified, yet I have seen him laughing and joking like a boy with his friend Morgan in the Glass Slipper. It is rumored that Blaisedell has an interest in that gambling hall. He spends much time there in company with Morgan, and on several occasions has engaged himself in dealing faro there. From what we have seen of Blaisedell thus far, he seems to have no excesses; he is not given to whoring, drunkenness, or profanity. I

*The Sister Fan and Pig's Eye were already at this time having difficulty disposing of the water encountered at the lower levels.

think he must needs be a blessedly simple man, in his position, for does not the capacity to deal in violence without excesses, to deal actually in men's lives as he must do, denote an almost appalling simplicity?

Or is he, in the end, only a merchant like myself, with his goods for sale as I have mine, knowing, as I know, that the better the goods the better price they will command, and the price variable as well with the Need? I see my mind must seek to bring this man to my terms, or perhaps it is to my level.

November 27, 1880

Pranksters have poured cement into the new piano at the French Palace. The piano, which Taliaferro had brought here at what I am sure must have been enormous expense, is ruined, the culprits unknown. It was a mean and thoughtless trick, in that coarse vein of frontier humor of which I have seen far too much. I have offered my sympathy to Taliaferro, who merely glowered. I suppose he suspects that since I mentioned it, I may be the guilty one.

There has also been another rash of rumors about the presence of Apaches in the Dinosaurs, that Espirato has returned from Mexico and is gathering his band again, preparatory to going on the warpath. This is not given much credence, since it has been several years since Espirato was last heard from. He is widely believed dead, and the bulk of his warriors secretly returned to the reservation at Granite.

In consequence of these rumors, however, we have had the pleasure of again seeing General Peach, who is always sensitive to news of his old adversary. He came through Warlock last Sunday with one troop of horse, another having swept up the far side of the valley. It was a shock to see him, for he has grown incredibly gross, and, viewing him, it is easy to believe that his mind is eaten away with paresis. Still, there is something inherently heroic about him; it is like watching an equestrian statue of the Cid or George Washington wrapped in a cloak of heroic deeds, to the accompaniment of stirring martial music. The man has had the capacity throughout his career for giving miserable and inexcusable fiasco the semblance of a thrilling victory. He rode down Main Street at the head of his troop as in a Fourth of July Parade, wearing his huge hat, his white beard blowing back, his strange, pale eyes fixed straight ahead while he saluted right and left with the leather-covered shaft which is supposed to be that of an arrow that almost ended his days at the battle of Bloody Fork. We watched him fresh from a fool's errand to the border, and reminded ourselves that he has a harem of Apache and Mexican women out of which he has produced (supposedly) a get of half-breed bastards numerous enough to increase by a good percentage the population of this territory; that, in his senility, he wets his trousers like a child, and must have his hand guided by Colonel Whiteside when he writes his name; and still we could not forbear to applaud his passage—badly as he has treated us here.

There have been rumors that silver will drop again on the market, and there is unrest among the miners, who fear a cut in their wages. Especially those of the Medusa. Some weeks ago, in the collapse of a stope at that unlucky mine, two miners were killed outright, and a third horribly crushed—the doctor says the man, Cassady by name, did not die the same night only because he seemed to feel it would put Miss Jessie out, and so clung to his life until early this week, when he finally gave up the ghost. The Medusa miners are incensed about these deaths, and I understand that talk of the Miners' Union has begun again. They claim that insufficient lagging-timbers are furnished to support their burrowings. This MacDonald denies heatedly, and calls them overpaid and pampered as it is. The price of lumber is certainly fantastic. There are trees of any size only in the northernmost Bucksaws, Bowen's Sawmill is small, the water power to run it often insufficient, and breakdowns frequent.

There is this time more sympathy than usual with the miners, of whom a large number have been killed and maimed in mine accidents this year. The doctor is quite beside himself about it, a man rarely given to shows of anger. Still, as I said to him, the fellows do make wages of $4.50 a day, and are free to take themselves elsewhere and to other work, if they choose.

December 14, 1880

A death of note has been that of the little professor, whose piano playing at the Glass Slipper all of Warlock had enjoyed.

Poor fellow, apparently, while in his cups, he fell insensible into the street at night, where his skull was crushed by a hoof or wagon wheel; not found until morning. God rest his soul, his passing so tragically has saddened us all.

December 28, 1880

Christmas has come and gone and a New Year is almost upon us. The cold spell has broken, and in this the peaceful season there is peace, but perhaps no more than the usual amount of good will. I have a crèche in my store window, Mary and Joseph bending over the Infant in the manger, attended by kings and shepherds. It is surprising how men stop and stare. I think they are not enraptured at the old story; the star of Bethlehem interests them not, nor do the shepherds and the kings. The baby fascinates them, a hideous little piece, out of scale to the rest of the figures, pink plaster with daubs of deeper pink upon the cheeks. It is not that there are no babies here, for the miners beget them upon their Mexican "wives" in some quantity. But they are not proper babies, being illegitimate; and not pink, being half-breed tan to begin with, which soon becomes a deeper hue due to the lack of frequent applications of soap and water. Most important, I think, is that the Babe is surrounded by His family. For there are no proper families here, and pitifully few proper women. There are Cyprians in quantity (more attentive to my crèche even than the men), there are a few ranch women whom we see from time to time, shapeless and bonneted against the sun and rude eyes. There are, in town, besides Miss Jessie, Mrs. Maple and Mrs. Sturges, the one, as is said, twice the man Dick Maples is and as tough as bootsole leather, the other ancient, huge, and a reformed harlot from the look of her.

The reigning queen is Myra Burbage, to court whom, of a Sunday, a great procession of Warlock's most affluent young bachelors rides down valley to irritate Matt Burbage. Men are made slaves to women by a cunning nature, who designed lust as the means to the continuation of our kind; we are made slaves as well by a trap of our own devising, whereby we desire to stand, as it were, for one of those stiff and smug photographer's portraits, as man and wife amid our offspring in that proud and self-contained protective society, a family.

A Christmas party at the General Peach, and all were invited to sip a cup of Christmas cheer—paying two dollars to the miners' fund for the privilege. Myra Burbage distributing her favors among her admirers, and, wonder of wonders, Miss Jessie apparently much interested and amused in conversation with the Marshal! She looked very pretty with her face flushed by the warmth of her labors—or was it something else that had caused her color to rise? There will be much surmise about this, I have no doubt. The Marshal and Miss Jessie have been observed, before this, buggy-riding together, and now, I am sure, more notice will be taken of their activities.

January 2, 1881

I suppose we should have realized that if the infection were only thrust down here, it would crop up elsewhere. There have been a great number of rustling raids in the lower valley, and stage hold-ups on the San Pablo and Welltown roads—so many, in fact, that Buck Slavin has instructed his stage drivers not to resist road agents, and is refusing to transport any shipments of value, as well as warning his passengers to carry none. The Welltown stage was robbed day before yesterday. This is laid at McQuown's door by some, while others claim that worthy has merely relaxed his control over the San Pablo hardcases, who are consequently running wild.

Road agents are none of Blaisedell's affair, unless a coach were to be assaulted within the limits of Warlock. Schroeder, however, is showing signs of life. There is another deputy with him now: I understand that one of his conditions to Sheriff Keller for taking up the post was that he be allowed an assistant. The other is John Gannon, elder brother to Billy Gannon and at one time a rider for McQuown himself. He seems an odd choice for an assistant on the part of Schroeder (an honest man, although heretofore exceedingly timid), but there has been a sign attached to the wall of the jail for some time now, advertising the need of another deputy, and no doubt Gannon has been the only one to apply. There has been some talk about this, and some suspect darkly that Gannon has come at McQuown's bidding to corrupt the Warlock branch of the law in some kind of plot against Blaisedell.

Gannon and Schroeder did collaborate to capture a road

agent when an attempt was made on the Bright's City stage a week or ten days ago. The stage, although under fire, ran for it and gained the town quickly, where Schroeder immediately organized a posse including Gannon and a number of Schroeder's friends, who happened to be passing the time of day at the jail. The posse lost one of the bandits, but captured the other, one Nat Earnshaw. Schroeder then took Earnshaw to Bright's City for trial, where he now resides, awaiting court session. Great praise has been heaped upon Schroeder for his quick action, and his courage—for Earnshaw, although not actually a member of McQuown's band, is a San Pabloite, a rustler, and a badman of some repute.

Possibly Schroeder's triumph has been made the more of because Blaisedell has had a failure of sorts. Wax, one of Taliaferro's dealers, was shot in the alley behind the Lucky Dollar, and his murderer has not been apprehended. It could have been almost anyone, since the victim was a gunman himself, quarrelsome and overbearing. Wax is not widely mourned. There has been some hint, however, that Morgan was the murderer, in some unnoticed and growing feud between the Lucky Dollar and the Glass Slipper, whose rear doors both open upon the same fatal alley. Morgan has made a great number of enemies here. He can be most unpleasant, brusque and rude, and has a way of looking at a person that expresses all too explicitly an almost unbounded contempt for his fellow man.

January 10, 1881

There has been a Social Event, a Wedding, and we are stuffed with punch and wedding cake, and, perhaps, with envy. Ralph Egan* has married Myra Burbage, and the happy couple is by now entrained from Welltown to a honeymoon in San Francisco at Matt's expense, the bride's fondest wish having been to see the ocean before she settled down in Warlock.

I wonder how many of us have realized the change inherent in this event, the first such a one that we have had. Civilization is stalking Warlock.

The bride was very attractive indeed, particularly, I am sure, to the unsuccessful swains, Jos. Kennon, Pike Skinner, and Ben

* Proprietor of the Feed and Grain Barn.

Hutchinson. There have been a horde of others along the way, including Chet Haggin, but these were the ones who galloped cheek by jowl down to the finish line, with Ralph, in the opinion of the pretty judge, the winner.

Curley Burne was on hand, as pleasant, humorous, and eminently likable as always; with him the Haggin twins, the bantering Wash and the silent Chet—alike as two peas, they are commonly identified by the side upon which they wear their six-shooters, Wash being left-handed, his brother right. All three were very much upon their good behavior, and Curley in particular went out of his way to ingratiate himself to one and all. It is difficult to think badly of the fellow. As Blaikie puts it, who is something of a philosopher, McQuown is like a coin, with Curley Burne imprinted upon one side, and the evil physiognomy of Jack Cade upon the other. A man's attitude toward McQuown depends upon which side of the coin he has seen.

Matt Burbage fixed me with his glittering eye; I was the wedding guest in fact. He tells me not only of the dangers he has passed, but of those that beset him on every hand. He has lost much stock, he says, but is not inclined to hold McQuown responsible. He says he has never known McQuown to steal from his neighbors, and that he has heard that McQuown recently brought back from Mexico nearly a thousand head, which he will fatten and drive up to sell to the reservation at Granite. He has seen McQuown very little of late. He thinks —this in a most discreet whisper—that Benner, Calhoun, and possibly Friendly have been responsible for a good part of the road-agentry.

Matt is worried about squatters coming in, a good proportion of downright outlaws among them. San Pablo, he says, has grown, and has become even more tough-town, calky, and dangerous than ever. He intends to do all his purchasing in Warlock now, a much longer trip for him, but good news for me. I think Matt longs for the peaceful past (he was one of the first to settle along the San Pablo River) when he had only Apaches to worry about. He has heard that Bright's City is about to unleash hordes of tax collectors upon us; on the other hand he bewails the lack of law officers to pursue his lost stock. Some of us love Freedom not so much as Safety, but are given pause by Safety's Cost.

Miss Jessie attended as bridesmaid, and afterward played on the melodeon, which tended to wheeze and rattle under her ministrations but still produced most pleasant harmonies. She has a high, sweet soprano, and it was wonderful to hear her render such favorites as: "She Wore A Wreath of Roses"; "Days of Absence"; and "Long, Long Ago." All joined in with a will on "Tenting Tonight" and "A Life on the Ocean Wave," etc.

It is rare to see her without Blaisedell these days. (I should imagine that Matt did not wish to offend his neighbor McQuown by inviting the Marshal.) The occasion of Myra Burbage's wedding was a romantic one to a populace of bachelors, for Ralph is a well-liked young fellow, and his spouse has long been the belle of the valley. Still, they are as nothing compared to Miss Jessie and the Marshal, who are as romantic a match as Tristram and Isolde.

The Angel of Warlock is a fascinating woman, not beautiful certainly, although she has a wealth of ringleted brown hair and fine eyes. She arrived in Warlock during the first boom, perhaps six months after I did. She was preceded by a lawyer, who purchased the old Quimby boardinghouse from the crippled prospector who was the proprietor of that riotous and unsavory place. The lawyer remained to have it refurbished into a decent boardinghouse, repainted, and rechristened in honor of the governor, upon which Miss Jessie herself arrived, in a clamor of speculation. She quickly won our hearts, as much by her gentle demeanor and apparent defenselessness, as by her actions during the typhoid epidemic of that summer, when she converted a part of her establishment to a hospital, which she has maintained as such ever since on what must be some regular and not inconsiderable income which she receives from elsewhere, for surely the money paid by her boarders cannot support the General Peach.

The doctor, who knows her best, says she comes from St. Louis, and that her father was a wealthy sickly man, whom she nursed until he died, which was shortly before she came to Warlock. This is all the information the doctor will give, and is perhaps all he possesses. Beyond this I have only my own speculations.

I would deduce, for instance, that she began nursing her father on an intensive basis, so that she was completely occupied with him, before she reached her twentieth year. Her girlish mannerisms and dress, which at first I thought affected, now seem to me to indicate that before this age she was removed from the normal social contacts of feminine society, to become so preoccupied with her duties to her parent that many of her habits of dress, speech, etc., remain those of a young girl.

Beneath her gentleness is a great strength of character. We have had occasion to see this in Citizens' Committee meeting, where she often locks horns with MacDonald, a bullheaded and rude man, over matters pertaining to the miners. Indeed, upon occasion she can don an almost repellent schoolmarmish attitude. To continue with my deductions about her, however: she has a strong will, she is a romantic, she is also quite plain. I think she came to Warlock in order to be Someone. Possibly she came, too, because this is the Frontier, which term I understand is a romantic one to those not there residing. I imagine she had been a nonentity in her own locality and society. If this is true, she has achieved entirely her object in coming here. She is certainly unique, a Personality, and her stature here is immense.

Her reputation is spotless, which is, in itself, astonishing in this place where foul rumor is a favorite pastime, and gossip vicious and pervasive. Indeed, I think one of the quickest ways to commit suicide in Warlock would be to cast aspersion against her good name. She lives with one fat Mexican maid in a house full of the roughest kind of ignorant, crude, dishonorable fellows, with only the doctor in one of her rooms as, I suppose, a sort of duenna. She walks streets which rock with catcalls when such an old harridan as Mrs. Sturges passes by, and where women from the Row are all but physically assaulted if they dare to promenade, and is greeted always in the most polite and gentlemanly manner. She can nurse miners mouthing dreadful obscenities in their pain, and yet find men completely tongue-tied before her for fear they will utter some slight impropriety of speech that might offend her ears. She is a miracle without being in the least miraculous.

She is also, now that I find myself thinking of her, a lonely and slightly pitiful figure, and I am pleased by Blaisedell's attentions to her, and by her reception of them.

The Marshal has, very recently, taken up residence at the General Peach, takes tea with Miss Jessie in the afternoon, and, the doctor says, submits amiably to having poetry read him. All in all, Blaisedell's courtship of her is fitting, and I think there will be few to resent it. This romance is an ennobling thing for this foul-minded, whore-ridden town, a showing-forth to limited minds that there can be more to the conjunction of men and women than a befouled and sweating purchased trick in bed.

January 15, 1881

Blaisedell has posted a man from town. We knew it must come eventually, and I have dreaded it. For if he posts a man out, and that man comes in, he comes under threat of death. If it is carried out are not we of the Citizens' Committee, who have hired Blaisedell and directed the posting, executioners? So I have waited in dread for this to happen, and waited in more dread still to see if the edict would be honored. Earnshaw, however, has reportedly left the territory.

Earnshaw had been acquitted by a jury of supposedly good men and true in Bright's City. I suppose there is no reason to damn the jurors, who were bound to abide by the evidence; and ten witnesses had ridden in from San Pablo to swear that Nat Earnshaw was seen by all of them in San Pablo on the day that the prosecution claimed he had tried to rob the Bright's City stage, and that he had been mistakenly apprehended by the posse while innocently riding into Warlock. It was not stated why he sought to flee the posse with his accomplice, who was not named.

Unfortunately, no one on the stage could identify Earnshaw as one of the bandits, for both had been masked, and the only witnesses for the prosecution were Schroeder and the possemen, whose evidence that they had followed the tracks of Earnshaw's horse from the scene of the assault upon the stage to the point of capture, was not given as much credence as that of the San Pablo hardcases, whose threatening demeanor was no doubt more effective than their verbal testimony.

The Citizens' Committee met upon the subject of Earnshaw, and discussed posting him with a considerable lack of resolution. Blaisedell spoke to the effect that if we ever intended to post anyone, Earnshaw was a good place to begin. Upon which we entrusted our consciences to the Marshal's capable hands. There was no dissent, although Miss Jessie was not present, nor Judge Holloway, who, I am sure, would have loudly damned the illegality of our action. Luckily the judge had drunk himself into insensibility that day, and was not heard from for several days thereafter.

We would have heard from him had Blaisedell been forced to ventilate Earnshaw, I am sure. He can be as nettlesome as various of the wild-eyed Jewish prophets must have been to their rulers. But thank God the fatal day when we must look at each other and try to shrug off some stubborn fellow's death as being only his own doing, is put off a little longer.

## 9. *Gannon Calls the Turn*

IT HAD turned chilly with the sun gone down and some quality in the atmosphere did not hold the dust, so that the air was clear and sweet now as Gannon walked back from supper at the Boston Café. The stars were already showing in the soft, violet darkness that shaded off to a pale yellow above the peaks of the Dinosaurs, where the sun had disappeared. Men lounged in groups along the boardwalk in the central block, leaning against the saloon fronts or seated on the tie rail, where a number of horses were tied. They talked in quiet voices and here and there among them was the orange glow of a cheroot or a match flame—wool-hatted miners, and cowboys in flannel shirts and shell belts, striped pants or jeans, and star boots, with the shadows cast by their sombreros making of their faces only pale ovals. They fell silent as Gannon passed. No one spoke to him, or spoke at all; there was only the stamp and snort of a horse at the rail, the hollow clumping of his bootheels.

He walked through the thin stripes of light thrown out by the louvre doors of the Glass Slipper. Other groups of men fell silent before him. Unwillingly he felt his steps hasten a little, his wrist brushed against the butt of his Colt, and his stomach twisted with its own cold colic. He glanced down to see a little light glitter on the star pinned to his vest.

It was quiet tonight, he told himself calmly, quiet for a Saturday night; the concentrated jumble of sound from the Lucky Dollar faded behind him.

When he descended into Southend Street dust prickled in his nostrils. To his right were the brightly lit houses of the Row; to his left, across Main Street, the second-story window above Goodpasture's darkened store was a dim yellow rectangle. Light from the jail spread out across the planks of the boardwalk, beneath the hanging sign.

Carl sat alone at the table, one hand on the shotgun. "Seen the marshal?" he asked.

"I expect he's in at the Glass Slipper."

"Pony and Calhoun and Friendly's in town," Carl said. He leaned back in his chair, stiffly. "See them?"

"No."

"And your brother," Carl said.

Gannon went over and sat down in the chair beside the cell door. The key was in the lock and he withdrew it, and hung the ring on the peg above his head.

"They are in the Lucky Dollar, I heard," Carl said. He chewed on the end of his mustache; he stretched. "Well," he said, in a shaky voice. "He handled the whole bunch at once, I don't know why he can't four of them."

"I expect he can," Gannon said. At least Cade was not in, he thought, and despised himself.

"I don't know," Carl said, rubbing a hand over his face. "Seems like I face up to it every night as soon as I close my eyes. But damn if I can—" He shook his head, and said, "When you see a real man it surely shames you for what you are, don't it?"

"Meaning Blaisedell?"

"Meaning Blaisedell. You know, I had got to thinking that if I didn't go up against McQuown sometime I would know I was dirt. But maybe that's wrong. Maybe *he* is the one— I don't know, maybe I mean big enough or clean enough or something—to do it. My God *damn* how I have chewed myself to ribbons over that bunch. But maybe McQuown is Blaisedell's by rights."

Gannon said nothing. It seemed to him that hate was a disease, and that he did not know a man who didn't have it, turned inward or outward. He had felt the hate when he had walked along Main Street tonight, hate for him because he was suspected of being friendly with McQuown; he wondered if McQuown, in San Pablo, could not feel the hate all the more.

Maybe McQuown had gotten used to it long ago. Carl hated both McQuown and his own self, and that was the worst kind, the pitiful kind.

"Dirt," Carl said. "Me"—he laughed breathlessly—"that thought I was the finest thing to walk the earth when I put this star on here. Not because of Bill Canning exactly, either," he said. "But because I was ashamed of every damned man in Warlock. And hating that red-bearded son of a bitch so much. And Curley."

Gannon looked down to examine the little scar in the fold of flesh stretched between his thumb and forefinger. It had healed quickly. "Why, Carl, I believe you have the Saturday night jim-jams!"

"Something awful," Carl said, laughing and stretching again. "Well, I have never seen one yet that didn't pass on by come Sunday morning. And a damned comfort when they do."

After a long time Carl spoke again. "Had a delegation from the Citizens' Committee come to call this afternoon. Buck and Will Hart."

"What did they want?"

"Wanted some action about all this road-agenting. I told them there'd been some starch took out of us running any more posses, since Keller hadn't got pay sent down yet for those boys that run the last one for me. It turned out they had a proposition, which was the Citizens' Committee guaranteeing posse pay."

"That will make things easier," Gannon said. "It is good to know we can jump if we get another clear shot."

"It is," Carl said. He leaned back in his chair again. "I told them it was fine and public-spirited and all, but Buck is hard to get along with sometimes. We got along better when I rode shotgun for him; he was always afraid I was going to quit. We had some words."

Gannon saw that Carl had flushed; Carl avoided his eyes, and he thought that Carl and Buck Slavin might have had words over him.

"Well, I told him if he didn't like the way I did my job he could hang this star on himself and welcome," Carl went on. "I told him and Will to look at those names over there," he said, nodding toward the scratchings in the whitewash. He glanced toward Gannon now, and his deep-set eyes looked very hot. "Like I have to every time I turn around in here. See if they could count a man on there didn't turn in his star and run, or get shot out from behind it. And I told them they wouldn't see me run. I might not maybe go out on the prod for Curley Burne or any of them, but I won't ever run. Made a damned fool of myself," he said, flushing more darkly.

"Curley?" Gannon said carefully.

"Well, there is a lot that thinks high of Curley. Will Hart is one. Said he didn't think Curley ever robbed a coach in his life. We had some words on that, too." Carl scrubbed his hands up over his face. "I don't know—I am pretty down on Curley, Johnny," he said, in a washed-out voice. "I guess it is a laughing backshooter makes me madder than any other kind. I don't know. Or maybe it is McQuown is Blaisedell's size, but maybe Curley is mine."

Speaking very carefully again, Gannon said, "Like you said, there are a lot that don't think bad of Curley."

Carl nodded jerkily. "Part of it, too. For he is what the rest is and can fool folks to think he is not. And so he is worse." He glanced at Gannon again with his hot eyes, and Gannon knew enough had been said.

He nodded noncommittally.

Carl sighed and said, careful-voiced now in his turn, "Well, it was sure a surprise to me when it was you come in here with me, Johnny. I guess you know there is some that won't take to you kindly, right off."

"Surely," he said, and he felt the questions Carl wanted to ask, but hadn't yet.

"Well, you come in and that's the main thing," Carl said. "But I guess you don't really hate San Pablo the way I do, do you?"

"I guess not, Carl."

"Don't mean anything by mentioning it," Carl said apologetically. "But I remember there was some talk at the time— I guess it was Burbage. How what happened to that bunch of greasers down in Rattlesnake Canyon that time wasn't Apaches' doing."

Gannon didn't reply as footsteps came along the planks outside. Carl stiffened in his chair, slapped his hands on the shotgun, started to rise. Pony Benner came in, with the marshal a step behind him.

"This one is getting a little bit quarrelsome," Blaisedell said, putting Pony's Colt down on the table before Carl. "Maybe he'd better cool off overnight, Deputy."

Carl got to his feet. The Colt rattled as he slid it into the table drawer and closed the drawer with a slap. Pony looked past Carl to meet Gannon's eyes. He spat on the floor.

Blaisedell said, "If the judge comes in tell him this one was picking away at Chick Hasty in the Lucky Dollar. It looked like trouble so I took him out of circulation."

"Surely, Marshal," Carl said. Blaisedell nodded to Gannon, turned, and went out, tall in the doorway before he disappeared.

"Well, Mister run-chicken, pee-on-your-own, Deputy Bud Gannon," Pony said, his small, mean face contorted with fury and contempt. "Why didn't you get down and kiss his boots for him?" he cried, swinging toward Carl. "Gimme that damned hogleg back, Carl!"

Carl straightened his shoulders, hitched at his shell belt, and, with a swift motion, picked up the shotgun and slammed the muzzle against Pony's belly. Pony yelped and jumped back. Carl said, "G-get in there before I blow you in!"

Pony retreated into the cell before the shotgun, and Carl slammed the door. His face, when he turned to take the key Gannon handed him, was blotched with color.

In the cell Pony was cursing.

"Hear anything?" Carl said, winking at Gannon. "I believe it is those rats moaning in there again. One of these days we are going to have to clean them out, I expect."

"All right!" Pony cried. "All right, Carl, you have chose the way you are going to choke yourself. All right, Bud Gannon, God damn you to hell—we'll see, God damn you all!"

"Damned if that one rat don't squeak just like old Pony Benner," Carl said.

"You will chew dust, you stringy, washed-up old bastard!" Pony yelled. His face disappeared. Immediately it returned. "And that gold-handled, muckering, God-damned long-haired son too!" Pony shouted. "He has threw his weight around for the last time, the last God-damned rotten time. We give him his chance and now he'll eat dust, too. You hear I said it, you kiss-boot sons of bitches!"

He retreated into the cell, and the cot creaked.

"Quieted down," Carl commented. "Sounds like somebody set a cat after those rats." There was a triumphant flush to his face, but Gannon saw the flicker of fear in it, and was embarrassed to see it there. He went to lean in the doorway and stare out into the street.

"No reason to bother the judge, I guess," Carl said, behind him. "Judge was taking on freight heavy this afternoon, and he would need a lot of sobering up by now. We'll just leave this one wait the night, and sweep him out with the cockroaches in the morning."

Gannon watched Billy coming down the boardwalk. "Billy," he said.

"Bud," Billy said, casually. Gannon stepped back inside and Billy followed him in. Pony's face reappeared between the bars.

"Some day you will get just too feisty," Billy said to Pony. He would not look at Gannon. He said to Carl, "What's the fine, Schroeder? I guess I can make it up."

"Judge hasn't been in," Carl said. "I'm holding him for disturbing the peace till he comes, or morning, one."

"He wasn't disturbing it that much," Billy said. "Let him out and we'll settle when the judge shows."

"I guess not, son."

"Kiss-boot bastards!" Pony cried, and kicked the door. Gannon stood watching his brother's face. It was sullen and hard, with only the shadowy mustache to show the youth in it.

"Let him out," Billy said to Carl. He dropped his hands to his shell belt, as though to hitch at it; in an instant his Colt was in his hand, and trained on Carl behind the table.

Gannon heard Carl's sudden ragged breathing, and Pony's laugh, but he stared still at Billy's face. Those cut-steel eyes might have been Jack Cade's, and they were eyes that had looked at Deputy Jim Brown with the same expression in the San Pablo saloon, just before Billy had shot him dead for making too much fun of his youth and his claim to being the best marksman in San Pablo.

But it was a copy of Abe McQuown's shy grin that twisted the corners of Billy's mouth, and a copy of Curley Burne's bantering tone in which he said, "*Por favor*, Carl. *Por favor*."

"Go to hell," Carl whispered.

"Listen to the rats squeaking now!" Pony crowed. "Squeaking awful quiet, seems like."

Billy said, "Get the keys, Bud."

Gannon stepped between Billy and Carl, as though he were going for the key. He stopped there, blocking Billy's Colt. Billy started to jump sideways and Pony yelled, "*Watch the shotgun!*"

Gannon stepped out of the way. Pony was cursing again.

"Buckshot," Carl said.

"Birdshot," Billy said, and again there was a reflection of Curley Burne in his tone. He grinned slightly. "I know what you carry in that piece."

"Buckshot," Carl said. "On Saturday nights." His voice was stronger. "Son," he said. "Buckshot beats a Colt's just like a full house does a pair."

Billy slipped his Colt back into its scabbard. He gave Gannon a blank look, not so much of anger as appraisal.

"You threw me, Bud," he said. "And took kind of a chance too."

"You wasn't going to go to shooting. Whoever it was."

"Maybe I wasn't, but it wasn't a bluff you had to call. I had you and Carl covered fair enough."

"Get out of here," Carl said. "Before I decide to chuck you in there with Mister Squeaky."

Billy said, "The marshal doesn't run this town."

"Looks like he does tonight," Carl said.

"Nah, he doesn't. Just some cowardy-cats in it." Billy inclined his head almost imperceptibly at Gannon, and went out.

Pony yelled, "You, Mister throw-your-brother! I guess maybe next time he won't be so quick to take big Jack off you!"

Carl slammed the barrel of the shotgun against the wooden bars, just as Pony leaped back away from the door.

Gannon cleared his throat. "Well, I guess I will take a walk around town, Carl."

"Feel easy," Carl said, grinning at him hugely. "It is a quiet night after all."

Gannon went out along the boardwalk. Billy was a lean shadow slanted against the wall just around the corner on Southend Street. "We had better talk some, Bud," Billy said.

He stepped down off the boardwalk into the dust. Up the street behind Billy were the lighted windows of the French Palace, and there were men passing on the far side of the street, laughing and talking. He heard Pony's name, and Blaisedell's.

Billy had turned to face the adobe wall beside him; he kicked a boot against it. "What's gone and got into you, Bud? Went off to Rincon to be a telegrapher and then come back, only not going back to Pablo, you said. Warlock is no kind of place to come back to. And deputying. What's got into you, Bud?"

Gannon shrugged.

Billy kicked the wall again. "Well, maybe I know why you lit out. But what the hell, Bud! What would you have done else, let them shoot us down and run that stock back?"

"I guess if you steal stock you have got to shoot to keep it sometimes. But not the way it was done, Billy."

"You've stole before that."

"I never saw it run all the way through like that before, though."

"So you come back and went to deputying to stop it, huh?" Billy sneered. "Well, you have changed, Bud. Got religion or something."

"I guess you have changed, too, Billy, since you made your score. People change."

"Ah, Christ, Bud!" Billy said, and now for the first time in the darkness it sounded like his brother again, and not some awkward and snarling boy-man out of San Pablo. "Well, I wanted to say I didn't blame you for what you did just now, which was slick, and— Hell, I knew it was what you had to do in there! But this is the bad thing, this God-damned marshal that thinks he is Lord God of Creation here. Where does he think he gets off, posting Nat out like that and running Pony into jail?"

"I don't know what Pony was doing, Billy," he said. "I didn't see what happened. But I know Pony—so do you."

"Christ, you have sure gone over, haven't you?" Billy said. He leaned back against the wall. "Like Blaisedell pretty good now, do you? Think he is pretty fine?"

"I don't know him, except to say hello to."

"Well, sometime when you get real good sucked up to him, ask him something for me! Ask him who the hell he thinks he is. Lording it over everybody. Running everybody around and telling them when they can come and go and all. This is a free country, isn't it? God damn it!"

"Billy," he said. "It's been free the way you mean, maybe, but it is going to have to be free the other way. So people are free to live peaceable, and free of being hurrahed and their property busted up, and their stock run off, and stages robbed. And killed for no more—"

"Who's the killer?" Billy broke in. "It is him! He got those gold-handled guns for the grand turkey-shoot prize for killing, didn't he?"

"I guess he is what we have to have here, then. For people like I am afraid you have got to be."

He had meant to say the people Billy has got to be like, but he didn't try to correct himself, and Billy whispered, "Jesus!" A group of horsemen turned into Southend Street and rode up toward the Row. They were laughing, and without even listening to what they were saying he knew they were laughing about Pony Benner.

"I don't mean to take up preaching," he said. "But I guess if I have changed it's because I've seen there has got to be law. It seems like you were always quicker and smarter to see a thing than I was. Can't you see it, Billy?"

"I can see this much," Billy said, in a contemptuous voice. "Who your law is for. Petrix at the bank and Goodpasture's store, and Buck's God-damned stages and Kennon's livery stable and all."

"Not just them. It is decent people running things, not rustlers and road agents and hardcase killers."

"Blaisedell isn't a hardcase killer? I heard he killed ten men in Fort James. Ten!"

"You can hear anything you want to hear. But there is something I saw, and got a hammer pin through my hand to prove it. Jack would have shot him in the back if I hadn't stopped it."

"Oh, I know Jack is a son of a bitch," Billy said. "Everybody knows that."

"Do you think Abe didn't put him to it?"

"Abe didn't have anything to do with it! God damn it, Bud, there is not another man but my own brother I'd let say a thing like that about Abe! Damn, you are wrong! Damn, I don't know how you turned so fast. You have got so damned holier-than-anybody because of us rustling a few old mossy-horns they never get around to rounding up even, they have got so many down at Hacienda Puerto. And a few sons-of-bitching greasers killed." Billy's voice ceased abruptly.

"Did they get to be sons-of-bitching greasers when they came after their stock, Billy? And got shot down by a bunch dressed like Apaches—and worse than Apaches. Is that when they got to be sons of bitches?"

Billy didn't answer, and Gannon leaned against the wall too, and looked up at the cold stars, shivering in the wind that had come up. A newspaper rolled slow and ghostly across the street and flattened itself against the wall beyond Billy.

Billy said in a low voice, "Listen, Bud, you don't want to get Abe thinking you have gone over to Blaisedell's side against him."

"Why not?" he said quickly.

"Well, you couldn't blame Abe for being down on some-body that's trying to throw him!"

Billy would not see, he knew. There had never been any use arguing with Billy. He laughed a little and said, "I was thinking how Daddy told me once I was to watch out for you. But I guess it got so you had to watch out for me—with Jack any-how. That wasn't the only time I thought he'd drink my blood, but for you."

He reached over and slapped Billy's shoulder, awkwardly, and Billy punched him in the ribs. "*That* son of a bitch. I hate that dirty, cold-hearted, mean son of a bitch. I'd drink his blood, but it would probably poison a toad." He went on in a rush. "Christ, Bud, Christ, how things get muckered up! Why, here we are— I mean, there is never going to be any real trou-ble between you and me, is there, Bud? It seems like we had trouble enough when I was a pup."

"I guess we didn't have enough," he said, and tried to laugh again. Billy's fist punched into his ribs again; then Billy stepped away from him, to stand flat and faceless against the lights up the street.

"Well, see you, damn it all, Bud."

"See you, Billy," he said wearily.

Billy backed up another step. He seemed about to speak again, but he did not, and turned and walked up Southend toward the Row.

Gannon did not watch him go, but moved slowly over toward the boardwalk that ran along before the saloons and gambling houses. It was time he took a turn around Warlock. Carl did not leave the jail much on Saturday nights.

## 10. *Morgan Doubles His Bets*

### I

STRIPPED TO the waist, Morgan was leaning over the basin with his face close to the mirror and the razor sliding smoothly over his cheek, when there was a knock on the alley door.

"Who is that?"

"It's Phin Jiggs, Morgan. Ed sent me down from Bright's."

He dropped the razor into the soapy water, went around the desk to the alley door, and slid the bolt back. Jiggs, who did odd jobs for Ed Hamilton who had been Morgan's partner for a time in Texas and now had a place in Bright's City, slipped inside, caked with dust from head to foot except for the part of his face his bandanna had covered. His eyes were muddy around inflamed whites, and there were sweat-tracks on his forehead and cheeks. He swiped at his face with his neckerchief.

"Ed said you might be pleased to know there is a woman named Kate Dollar coming down here."

He stared at Jiggs. At least he was pleased to *know* she was coming.

"She put her name down as Mrs. Cletus at the Jim Bright Hotel there," Jiggs said. "But Ed said to tell you it was Kate Dollar, all right."

"Mrs. Cletus?" he said, and felt stupid as he watched Jiggs nod. He turned uncertainly and went back to the basin, where he fished the razor out of the water. Mrs. Cletus. "Did you see her?" he asked, and stared at his face in the mirror.

"I saw her. Tall woman. Black hair and eyes and a fair-sized nose. About as tall as you, I'd say."

He nodded and raised the razor to his cheek again. Mrs. Cletus. Pleased. "She is on the stage now," Jiggs said. The stage would come in a little after four; Jiggs had ridden through the Bucksaws, instead of going around them as the stage had to do.

"Anybody with her?" he asked casually.

"I guess it is this Cletus she was down as Missus of."

He contemplated the razor with which he might have removed an ear to hear that, while Jiggs continued. "He is a big feller. Heavy-set with a kind of chewed-up looking face. They was down as Mr. and Mrs. Pat Cletus at the hotel there, Ed said to tell you."

Morgan sighed, and his mind began to function again. It was no ghost; she had found kin of some kind, a brother maybe. God damn you, Kate, he thought, without anger. He should have known she would not let it alone. In the mirror he saw Jiggs staring up at the painting over the door.

"Handsome woman," Jiggs said. It was not clear whether he was talking about the nude in the painting, or Kate.

"How many on the stage?"

"There's four of them. Her and him and a drummer, and the little sawed-off from the bank down here."

Money in the box then, he thought. He finished shaving, rinsed the lather from his face, and toweled it dry. He slipped his money belt up where he could get to it and drew out a hundred dollars in greenbacks, which he gave to Jiggs.

"Oh, my!" Jiggs said, in awe.

"Forget about the whole thing and tell Ed thanks. Going right back?"

"Well, I—"

"Surely, I guess you might as well. You know Basine's place, out on the north end of town? Tell him to give you a fresh horse. He'll be there still if you hurry."

Jiggs stuffed the money down into his jeans pocket. "Well, thanks, Morgan! Ed said you'd be pleased to hear it."

"Pleased," he said. When Jiggs had gone he put on his shirt, whistling softly to himself. He opened the door; the Glass Slipper was empty still, and a barkeep was dispiritedly sweeping Saturday night's clutter along in front of the bar.

"Go find Murch," he called, and went back to his desk and poured himself a larger portion of whisky than usual. He raised it before him, squinting up at the painting of the woman over the tilted flat plane of the liquor. "Here's to you, Kate," he whispered. "Did you find one after all that had the guts to come after him? You damned bitch," he said, and drained the glass. Then he remembered that Calhoun and Benner, Friendly and Billy Gannon had been in town last night, and he laughed out loud at this continuing evidence of his luck.

II

Two hours later he was five miles out of Warlock on the Bright's City road, riding slowly, not hurrying. He was hot and uncomfortable with jeans on beneath his trousers, and a canvas jacket was tied in an inconspicuous bundle behind the saddle. A few torn bits of cloud floated in the sky, and their shadows moved swiftly across the yellowish-red earth and the sparse, bristling patches of brush. His horse flung her head back and danced sideways as a tarantula scurried across the stage tracks, heavy-bodied and tan-furred in the dust.

Now he kept off the stage road on the hard-packed earth, and, fifty yards from the rim, dismounted, ground-tied his horse, and went the rest of the way on foot. He grinned as he watched the column of dust moving east along the valley bottom. He could see the riders, two of them, very small in the distance below him. Crouching on his heels beside a staghorn cactus he watched them threading their way through one of the mesquite thickets that grew in patches over the valley bottom, until they were out of sight. The dust they had been raising also ceased. They had stopped at Road Agent Rock, a stony ridge through which the stage road threaded its way before starting up the long grade from the valley floor.

Presently he saw another plume of dust; horse and rider appeared, gradually enlarging, coming up the slope toward him. It was Murch, whom he'd sent up the valley. He stood up and waved his hat. Murch's horse was blowing and heaving as he spurred up the last steep piece. Murch dismounted, sweating and dusty in shotgun chaps and a flannel shirt.

"It is Benner and Calhoun," he said, mouthing the words over a cheekful of tobacco. His left eye studied Morgan's face, his right roving toward the flanks of the Bucksaws. "Them and the other two went on down toward Pablo a couple of miles in the malapai. Then they split, and Billy and Luke went on down valley, and these two come around up here."

"Now what do you suppose they are up to?"

"Couldn't guess," Murch said.

"Well, if I were you I would get on back to town quick where everybody could see me. In case the Bright's City stage runs into trouble. You wouldn't want to get taken for a road agent."

"No," Murch said, and spat.

"Let me have the Winchester."

Murch drew it from the saddle boot and handed it to him, mounted, and started back along the stage road at a fast trot. He looked like a gallon jug in the saddle.

Morgan walked back to his horse, remounted, and, leaving the stage road, headed east to meet the lower slopes of the Bucksaws. He crossed the first ridge and swung downhill in the barren canyon behind it. To his right now was the upper end of the rock outcrop that slanted like the edge of a long, curved knife to the valley floor.

He tied his horse in a mesquite thicket, removed his suit, and in jeans and the canvas jacket, a bandanna tied around his neck and Winchester in hand, scrambled up the ridge. Just on the other side of it, hidden by the crest, he began to work his way down.

Once he stopped to rest, breathing deeply of the clear air, and looked about him. He could see the valley for many miles east from here, with the cloud shadows moving across it. He could make out the cut of the stage road through the low brush for a long distance too. He felt a growing excitement. He accepted it with reluctance at first, cynically, but more and more fully as he made his way on down the ridge. He chuckled to himself from time to time, and paused more often to breathe great sucks of the sweet air and gaze out on the colors of the valley. His senses felt alive, as they had not for a long time; he felt unburdened, young, and larking, but still the dark cynicism in himself kept careful watch, nagging and sneering at him. Once, as he edged his way around a steep rock, he whispered, "Well, Clay, I have never crawled on my belly for any other man."

Finally he heard the sound of voices, and he crawled to the crest of the ridge, where, hidden between two rocks, he could look down to the west side. The stage road cut in close to the ridge below him, swung to the right through a narrow defile, and angled to the left again. He could see the two of them not fifty yards away.

They were sitting on a low ledge just beyond the defile, which was called Road Agent Rock—it was said that so many stages had been stopped there that Buck Slavin had had to send out a crew to fill the rut made by the dropping strongboxes. They were in the full sun and Pony had his hat off and was mopping his face with a blue bandanna. Their horses weren't in sight.

"Just like the bitching coach to run late today," one of them said. The words came to him clearly. He edged the Winchester up beside him, and rested his cheek against the warm stock.

From time to time Calhoun would move into the defile to gaze east along the stage road. Then Benner, a head shorter, would go. They muttered back and forth. Once they both went out together. They sat and quarreled in the sun. Then Calhoun went out to look for the stage.

"Here it comes!" he cried, and ran back. They both tied neckerchiefs over their faces and jammed their hats down to their ears. They arranged themselves on either side of the stage road just beyond the cleft in the rock, facing each other tense and motionless like firedogs of unequal size.

Morgan glanced back to see the dust the stage was raising; it would be ten minutes yet. He watched an ant edging its way along the perpendicular side of one of the rocks that concealed him. It was carrying something white many times its own size. He watched the ant struggling; often it almost fell, but it never let go of its burden.

He whispered to it, "When you get home you'll find it wasn't worth the trouble, you damned fool!"

At last he heard the stage, the squeal of wheels, the whip crack and shout from the driver. It occurred to him suddenly that Kate was there, not a hundred yards away. He heard a steel rim scrape on rock. The lead team came into his field of vision, then the coach itself, Foss holding the reins with a boot up on the brake, Hutchinson, the messenger, with one hand braced behind him for balance and the shotgun ready in the other, leaning forward to try to see around the bend.

"Pull up and reach!" Calhoun bellowed, and fired into the air. Pony leaped out before the leaders, who bucked and plunged sideways. Hutchinson half rose as Pony ran around toward him, a six-shooter in either hand; Calhoun laid the Winchester on Foss.

"Throw it down, God damn you!" Pony shrilled, and Hutchinson pitched the shotgun away from him.

"Box down!" Calhoun said.

Foss had his hands raised shoulder-high, his foot on the brake, his eyes squinted against the sun. Hutchinson dragged the strongbox out. Morgan heard him grunt as he lifted and dropped it at Calhoun's feet.

"Let's see what the passengers got," Calhoun said. He flung the door open, and jumped back with his rifle leveled. Pony dragged the box away from the coach.

Morgan eased his own Winchester forward a little and grimaced as the sun caught fire along the barrel. He framed the door of the coach in the cleft of the rear sight, and gently raised the front sight blade beneath it. The blade danced, suddenly, as he saw Kate's face sharply outlined in the window. A man in a black hat squeezed out the door and dropped lightly to the ground, raising his hands.

Morgan stared at the man's face down his sights. It was a Cletus clearly enough, a tougher, meaner, harder version of Bob Cletus; he felt a weakening run through him and tensed his body against it as though he were clenching a fist. He lowered the sights to the man's shirt front. Kate appeared, a white hand on the door frame, her head bent down so that her hat hid her face.

He stroked the trigger. The rifle jarred in his hands; the coach was obscured in smoke. Ragged and shrill through the crash of the Winchester came the scream, and through the smoke he saw Cletus pitch forward with his broad-brimmed hat rolling free like a cartwheel. A Colt fell from his outstretched hand. Kate jerked back inside the coach. One of the leaders bucked up, hoofs boxing the air, and there was a chorus of yells. Then suddenly the coach was moving, and Foss was thrown back hard upon the seat. Hutchinson ducked down and turned, and, a Colt appearing in his hand, fired at Pony—smoke drifting from the muzzle an instant before the sound of the report. Calhoun raised his rifle and fired, levered and fired again, and Hutchinson slumped. Now Foss was standing and his long whip cracked out alongside the leaders. The stage fled, the door slamming open and shut and Kate's face showing once again in the window as the coach ran out of Morgan's view, with a loose tarpaulin flapping over the boot.

Calhoun fired again, and then he and Benner stood gazing after the coach. Presently Pony went over to where Cletus lay, and, thrusting at his shoulder with a boot, turned him on his back. Neither of them glanced up to where Morgan lay hidden. They bickered over Cletus's body for a while, went through his pockets, and then Pony went out of sight at a run. He reappeared, leading the horses. In a flurry of activity they raised and lashed the strongbox to the saddle of one, mounted, and started down the valley at speed.

Morgan sighed. The sun felt very warm on his back; his face was wet. He rose, stretched, untied the bandanna and wiped his face with it, staring down at the body sprawled on the ground below him, boots twisted together, arms outstretched and the glisten of red on the white shirt front. He felt the excitement slipping away.

He leaned on one of the rocks that had concealed him, and watched the high, tan plume run down the valley. Now he could also see the coach rolling slowly up the long grade toward the rim—the driver still standing and his whip arm working mechanically. Then he looked down at the dead man again. He wondered where Kate had had to go to find him.

"Damn you, Kate," he said aloud. "Why can't you leave a thing alone? It is done." He said it as though he were pleading with her, but half-humorously; it caught in his throat. "It is done," he said again, as though saying it could make it so.

Finally he turned away from the man he had killed. He made his way without haste back along the ridge and down the canyon where he had tied his horse. He buried the Winchester and the canvas jacket, and, in his black broadcloth, rode back along the stage road to Warlock. Before he reached town he cut over to the north side, where he left the horse in Basine's little corral, and walked to the Glass Slipper.

As he entered through the alley he saw Lew Taliaferro's dark, mole-spotted face watching him from the alley door of the Lucky Dollar. He tipped his hat and grinned, and would have spoken, but Taliaferro's face disappeared and the door closed. He was still grinning when he went in through the back door of the Glass Slipper, and stripped off his dusty clothes and began to wash. But he should, he thought, have been more careful, especially since Taliaferro was down one faro dealer named Wax to him. Still, he knew, his luck was good. His luck would stand as long as he believed in it.

## II. *Main Street*

THE BRIGHT'S CITY coach turned into Main Street with its body swinging far over on the thoroughbraces, the team running scared, and the coach sucking a whirlwind of dust behind it. It came fast down the street with the driver yelling, the popper of the whip snapping out alongside the lead team, and the shotgun messenger swaying on his seat with a hand clasped to his shoulder.

Schroeder, walking along before the Glass Slipper, stopped and stared. Then he spat his chew of tobacco into the street and vaulted the rail, coming down hard in the dust with his knees buckling. He cupped his hands to his mouth and shouted at Chick Hasty, who was standing in his dirty canvas apron before Goodpasture's store, "Chick! Get the posse together! Get Pike!"

Hasty went around the corner toward the Acme Corral at a run. "*The Doc!*" Foss, the driver, yelled, standing now as he set the brake. The coach skidded and slowed, and came to a stop before the Assay Office, the lathered, muddy horses crowding and shifting together. Foss leaped down, and, with Schroeder's assistance, helped down Hutchinson, whose sleeve was soaked with blood. They sat him on the rail; holding him, Foss said, "Threw down on us at Road Agent Rock. Shot a passenger, and the team took out, so we run for it."

A crowd began to collect, men running up from all directions. Old Man Parsons halted his team of mules at the corner of Southend Street and Carl yelled at him, "Old Man, you are deputized. We are going out instanter!"

"One of them was Pony Benner, I hope to spit!" Hutchinson said, leaning limply against a post. The doctor came up, panting, his valise slapping against his leg as he ran; he and Sam Brown helped Hutchinson into the Assay Office.

The door of the coach opened and the pale face of a drummer appeared, his sidewhiskers standing out like the fur of a scared cat. He descended, followed by Pusey, the bank clerk, and they both turned to hand a woman down. She looked like a sporting woman, in her fancy clothes, but she did not carry herself like one, and the men on the boardwalk greeted her politely. Her face was chalk white beneath a hat covered with black cherries. Her eyes were black, her nose long and straight, her mouth reddened with rouge. There was a crescent-shaped court-plaster beauty mark at the corner of her mouth.

"The little one was Pony, all right," Foss said to Schroeder.

"Two of them," little Pusey broke in. "They got the strongbox."

"More than two," Foss said. "Couple up on top the ridge. It was one of them killed that big feller."

"I only saw two," the drummer said.

"There were three," the woman said. She looked at Schroeder's star, and up into his face with her hard black eyes. Her face was stiff with shock. "There was one on top of the ridge."

"Shot what big feller?" Schroeder said to Foss.

"Passenger that was with this lady here," Foss said. "We had to leave him lay, for the team took out wild when he got shot. He was dead, miss," he said, apologetically. "You going after them, Carl?"

"Surely am," Schroeder said.

"Went down valley. We could see them raising dust coming up the grade to town."

John Gannon forced his way in through the crowd. There was a lull in the excited talk around them.

"Stage got run, Johnny," Schroeder said. "Hutch shot and a passenger killed and still out there at Road Agent Rock."

"Pony and Calhoun and Friendly and Billy Gannon," someone in the crowd said. "Headed out of here like they was going back to Pablo, and went up valley to agent the coach instead."

"By God if it wasn't!"

Gannon licked his lips. He looked from Foss to Schroeder with his deep-set eyes in his bone-thin face. "Are we going after them, Carl?"

"Well, I thought maybe I'd ask you to ride out after that passenger." Gannon flushed, and Schroeder went on quickly, his voice loud in the hush. "What was his name? Anybody know?"

Everyone looked at the woman, who said, "I think it was Cletus."

"Thought I heard you calling him Pat, ma'am," the drummer said politely. The woman did not reply.

"What'd they kill him for?" someone asked.

"He drawed, looked like," Foss said.

"Fool thing to do," Schroeder said.

The woman said, "He didn't draw till he'd been shot."

Tim French and Chick Hasty, mounted, came into Main Street. Then Peter Bacon appeared, leading an extra horse, and, a moment later, Pike Skinner, Buchanan, and Phlater. Each of them had a rifle in his saddle boot, and Pike Skinner had belts of rifle and shotgun cartridges slung over his saddlehorn, and a shotgun hanging from a saddle strap. Old Owen Parsons came after them in a hurry, on a rat-tailed bay, his hat brim blown back flat against the crown.

"Come on, Carl!" Skinner shouted.

"You go bring the dead one in, Johnny," Schroeder said. "And watch things here." He clapped Gannon on the shoulder. Buck Slavin came through the crowd crying, "Foss! God damn it, Foss!"

"Out of my way fellows," Schroeder said. The crowd parted before him as he hurried out into the street to mount the extra horse.

"Looks like one we're after's Billy," Tim French said.

"Maybe," Schroeder said. "Chick, you ride out with Johnny and track back down valley after them. So we'll have that squarer in court this time. Watch for them shedding the strong-box, too."

Hasty nodded, and Schroeder surveyed the others. He grinned suddenly. "Well, boys," he said. "We will ride to hit the river low down, and try to head them."

They all nodded. Schroeder set his spurs and his horse leaped forward. The posse fell in behind him and went out of War-lock at a fast trot. There were cheers from the crowd standing around the dusty coach in Main Street.

## 12. *Gannon Meets Kate Dollar*

It was after dark when Gannon brought back the body of the big man whose name seemed to be Pat Cletus, and left it, covered with a tarpaulin, at the *carpintería*, where old Eladio would make a coffin for it in the morning.

He went home to Birch's roominghouse to wash, and stopped at the jail to sit at the table in the dark for a while; then he went up to the Western Star for dinner, carefully oblivious under the silent stares of the men he passed upon the way.

But his eyes felt hot and gritty as he listened to them whispering behind him. They were sure that Billy had been one of the road agents, and probably they were right.

In the lobby of the hotel Ben Gough, Pugh's clerk, nodded distantly to him from behind the counter. It was late and the dining room was deserted except for the woman who had come in on the Bright's City stage. She sat at a table near the window, and he moved uncertainly over toward her.

He took off his hat. "Mind if I sit here, ma'am?"

She looked up at him through long lashes that were very black against her white skin. She glanced around at the empty tables, then at the star pinned to his shirt. She said nothing, and he sat down opposite her. Obsidian eyes watched him over her cup as she drank coffee.

"Catch them?" she said finally, setting her cup down in its saucer with a small clatter.

"No, ma'am. At least the posse's not back yet."

"Do they catch them here?"

"I expect they might this time. They got off fast."

She nodded, uninterested. She was a handsome woman, except that her nose was too big. The black cherries on her hat shone overripe with red tints in them in the lamplight.

The waiter wandered over, switching a cloth at the flies and crumbs on the tables he passed.

"Supper," Gannon said. When the waiter had gone switching away again, he said, "Maybe you wouldn't mind answering a few questions?"

"All right."

"Well, I'll ask your name to start off with."

"It's Kate Dollar."

Her eyes regarded him hostilely, and he hesitated. He had hardly talked to a woman before he had gone to Rincon, and very few there except in the course of his duties. He didn't know whether to call her Mrs. Dollar or Miss. You said Mrs. to a sporting woman, if you wanted to be polite, but he was uncertain whether this one was or not. It was not that she was better dressed than a whore, for some of them wore finery to put your eye out, but her dress was expensive looking without being flashy and eye-catching, and there was a certain dignity about her. She was young, but her face was wary and there were bitter lines at the corners of her eyes.

"And yours?" she said.

"Gannon," he said, and added, "John Gannon."

"Oh," she said. "One of them was supposed to be your brother."

He felt his face burn painfully. He looked down quickly and nodded.

"What was it you wanted to ask, besides my name?"

"Why, there seems to be some mix-up, miss. About how many road agents there was. The driver—"

"I saw three of them," she said. "But there might've been four."

"There was one up on top of the ridge there, you mean? You are sure? I mean—" He stopped.

"I saw a rifle barrel up there clear enough," she said. "And gunsmoke." She raised a finger and pressed it to the beauty mark at the corner of her mouth. "When I heard the shot I didn't know who had fired, because I could see the other two road agents, and it wasn't either of them. Then I happened to look up at the top of the ridge and saw the smoke. And I saw the rifle barrel pull back out of sight."

"You didn't see the man?"

"No."

The waiter brought a plate of steak, fried potatoes, and beans. He pushed at the potatoes with his fork. His eyes were burning again. Kate Dollar patted at the corners of her mouth with her handkerchief.

"The driver said you got on with this Cletus at Bright's City."

"So did that little bank clerk, and the drummer."

"I heard the drummer say you called him Pat."

"Maybe I did."

"You wouldn't want to say, then?"

"Say what?"

"Whether you'd been coming out here with this Pat Cletus, or what for. Or who he was."

"What difference does it make?"

"I don't know," he said, hopelessly. He forked a mouthful of potatoes, chewed, and tried to swallow; they were at the same time greasy and dry as dust.

"What do you want me to say?" Kate Dollar asked, in a different voice. "That there were only two of them? Because then one might not have been your brother?"

"I don't know," he said. "The driver and the shotgun seem pretty sure it was Pony Benner and Calhoun. But the third one could've been Friendly. Or— I don't know," he said again. "I just thought you might've got mixed up—with everything happening so sudden and all. I guess you didn't."

"What were you trying to blackguard me into, asking about the man that was killed?"

"I don't know," he said dully. "Just—deputies're supposed to ask questions about a thing. I was just trying to find out what happened," he said. He put his fork down.

"Aren't you going to eat?"

"I guess not," he said, and pushed the plate away from him. Kate Dollar said, "From what I've heard, it sounds like nobody gets convicted of anything at the Bright's City court. Why are you so worried? Because of being deputy?"

"It's not that. I guess they would probably get off in Bright's, all right. If they get caught."

Kate Dollar was frowning a little; she looked at him questioningly.

"Well," he said, "that's it, you see, miss. I expect they will get off all right. But then they'll get posted out of town."

There was a slow tightening around her mouth. Suddenly her face seemed filled with hate, but the expression was gone so quickly that he could not be sure what he had seen. She said, in a curiously flat voice, "I knew Clay Blaisedell in Fort James."

"Did you?" he said.

"So you are worried about him posting your brother out of town," she said. "He is just a boy, I heard somebody say." He saw that she looked very tired.

"He is eighteen. No, he's not a boy." He was embarrassed that he had let the subject of Billy come up. But it was big in him and there was, it seemed, no one else he could speak to like this. He said, "Have you ever seen a gambler in a game of cards and you can tell he knows just where every card is?"

She nodded, as though immediately she had caught his thought; and he went on. "Well, I guess I am like that right now. Cards have been dealt out and they are face down yet, but I know what they are."

Kate Dollar continued to regard him with her black eyes, her expression one of expectant interest. But now he was confused and jarred by the thought that she was estimating him, and was not interested in Billy at all. He thrust his chair back and got to his feet.

"Well, I didn't mean to bother you with all that, Miss Dollar. I just came to ask you some things, and I thank you."

"You are welcome, Deputy."

Halfway to the lobby he realized he had forgotten his hat, and he had to return for it, apologizing to her again. She did not speak this time, although she smiled a little; he noticed that her eyes looked pink and swollen in her tired face, and he thought, as he started back to the jail to begin the long night's wait, that the man Cletus must have been more to her than she wanted to admit.

## 13. *Morgan Has Callers*

### I

MORGAN HAD been waiting for her to come all evening, but still he started at the knock on the alley door, which he knew was her knock. He rose and smoothed his hands back along the sides of his head, pulled down the tabs of his vest, buttoned his coat. He slid back the bar and opened the door; at first he could see nothing, and he didn't speak, waiting for his eyes to accustom themselves to the dark.

She was standing back and a little to one side, where the light did not touch her.

"I've told you tommies to quit bothering me," he said, and made as though to slam the door.

"Tom," she said, and moved closer. "It's Kate."

He was supposed to blow to pieces at the sight of her. "Well, I'll be damned," he said. "Now they are following me out from all over."

"Yes," Kate said. She sounded disappointed, which pleased him. He moved aside and she entered, tall, all in black; black hat with black cherries on it, black skirt draped in thick folds over her hips, black sacque jacket—with only the white ruffled front of her shirtwaist to relieve it.

She clutched her hands, in black mesh mitts, to her waist, watching him close the door. Her dead white face was controlled, and stiff, but filled with hate.

"Couldn't you get along without me, Kate?" he asked, and managed to meet her black eyes and grin. But, when she did not answer, against his will he retreated to his desk and took a cheroot from the silver box there, and lit it. "You should have let me know you were coming."

"Didn't you know?"

"I'd've had a brass band out."

"Didn't you?" she said.

He frowned, as though he'd been struck by a thought. Then he burst out laughing. "I guess you came in on the stage this afternoon," he said. "Well, you had a little excitement at that, didn't you?"

"You don't know who it was that was killed?" Kate said. She was staring at him not quite so intently, and he thought he had got past her. If not, in the end he had only to tell her the truth and she would not believe it, either, from him. She looked very tired, he thought; she looked older than he had remembered, who was not even two years older.

"Somebody said he looked like a high-roller." He paused, frowned again, grinned again. "Why, was he with you? I thought you had had enough of high-rollers, Kate."

"It was Bob Cletus's brother."

He stared at her as if incredulous. He began to laugh again. He put down his cheroot and laughed and watched her upper lip twitching, with hate of him, or as though she were going to cry. "My God, how you run through those Cletuses!" he said.

She made a humming sound in her throat. She said, in a shaky voice, "You knew I would come, Tom. I told you—I would!"

He turned the laughter off like a tap. He stared back into her black eyes that were glazed with tears now, and said, "If I'd known you were coming out here with some cheap gunman you spaded up somewhere, you'd have never got here either. You damned vulture."

"Oh, I don't think *you* shot him," Kate said. "I think you hired Clay to do it. The way you did with Bob."

That was supposed to pin him to the wall. But she could not keep her voice from shaking, and he almost felt sorry for her.

He said, "Or I might've just done nothing and let him choose Clay out and commit suicide. The way it was before."

She turned half away from him, dropping her hands tiredly to her sides. He saw her glance up at the painting over the door. He felt an almost savage relief that she had not got to Fort James with Pat Cletus during the time when he, Morgan, had come on ahead to Warlock, and Clay had remained in Fort James.

"So you went out and hunted up his brother to do Clay down for you. It took you a good while."

"I couldn't find him," Kate said, in a dead voice. "So I gave up. But then I ran onto him." She stopped, as though there were nothing more to say.

"And all for nothing, too. Well, bad luck, Kate. But maybe there is another brother, or cousins. In Australia or somewhere."

She shook her head a little. She reminded him of a clock-work figure running down.

"Haven't you got the fare? Why, there is money I owe you, at that." He put his hands to his money belt, and saw her face come back to life.

"Would you pay me to go? I hope you would pay a lot, for I won't go!"

"Come back to me after all?"

He shouldn't have said it. He saw the revulsion show clearly in her face, and the strain of maintaining the grin that painfully stretched his lips became immense. But he continued. "I have got a nice place out front, and a nice apartment back here. I could set you up in style. You might have to work your trade from time to time if I ran short of cash, but . . ."

She only stared at him.

"Leaving then?" he asked. He had better not underestimate her, he knew, tired as she was now, and shocked. He felt enormously tired himself. He had thought hate did not affect him. He had thought he was used to it.

"No," she said. "No, I will stay and watch Clay Blaisedell shot down like he shot Bob down."

"Do it yourself?"

"Are you afraid I would? No, I won't do that."

He sat down in his chair, inhaled on his cheroot, blew smoke. "Maybe you can get somebody to go after him here. Like the one you just lost." His voice rasped in his throat. "There are some that might be hard up enough to try it for a chance to sleep free with a hydro-phoby skunk bitch."

He felt a lift of pleasure to see her face dissolve. But she quickly regained control of it. She only shook her head.

"Why, you have gone soft, Kate."

"No," she said, and again he saw how exhausted she was. "No, not soft. I went all over looking for Pat Cletus," she said, in the dead voice. "I went more than five thousand miles looking for him—different places I had heard he might be. I couldn't find him so I thought I would give it up. Then a month ago I met him in Denver, and we came out here and he was killed. I don't know whether you did it or not

—except—except I should've known he would be killed. Like I should've known Bob would be killed if he went to tell you he was going to marry me."

"I told you once before he didn't ever come to see me."

She didn't seem to hear him. "So that was my fault too. I should have seen you dead before I thought of wanting to marry Bob Cletus. Or we should have run—to Australia. But I killed him when I let him go to you. And killed Pat when I made him come out here. I have had enough of killing."

He nodded sympathetically, and saw the despair crumple her face again.

"But I will see Clay Blaisedell shot down!" she said. "I will see that, I'll follow him wherever he goes to see it." She took a deep breath, and her lips tightened as though she were trying to smile. "I saw him tonight," she went on. "He looked at me as though he'd seen a ghost, and I thought how fine it would be to be a ghost and haunt and torture somebody who—who" —her voice began to shake again—"who took away the only chance I ever had!" she cried. "Who killed the only decent man I ever knew! And you had Clay shoot him down!" Tears shone suddenly on her cheeks.

"Why, then you should look for somebody to shoot me down."

"No! Because you don't care about yourself—I know you that well. But I know you care about Clay. I think I might've let it alone if I thought you didn't care what happened to him. But I will follow him and haunt him. And you."

"And yourself too, isn't it?"

"Maybe so," she said, with a tired lift of her shoulders. "Haunt myself too for not knowing you would always do the foulest thing you could do. To me or anyone." Her voice rose shrilly, "But I'll stay here and wait it out, and watch! Whenever you see me you will know I am waiting to see him die like Bob died. Or wherever he is when somebody finally shoots him down, I will be there too. And then I'll come and laugh at you!"

"We will have a good laugh together, Kate."

She sobbed. She raised a hand to her eyes and then dropped it, as though she were too proud to hide that she was crying. She was ugly when she cried; he remembered that.

"Come in any time and we will have a good laugh," he

added, pleasantly. She did not answer, moving toward the door. He watched the swing of the thick pleats of her skirt, her hair, blue-black in the light, where it showed beneath her hat. Her white, lined face turned toward him once, and then she was gone and the door slapped shut behind her.

Her scent of lavender water was strong in his nostrils. He was shivering a little, and he stretched, hugely. He had done well enough tonight, he thought; he had given her nothing. He had never given her anything. He saw, indelible in his mind's eye, her tired, hate-filled face. Once there had been good times.

II

Kate had not been gone ten minutes when Clay came in from the Glass Slipper. Clay took off his hat, brushed his fingers back through his thick, fair hair, and sat down on the other side of the desk. He placed his hat on the desk before him and then moved it a little to one side, as though it were of great importance where it was placed.

"Posse back?" Morgan asked.

Clay shook his head. His eyes were deeply shadowed, his mouth a thin shadow beneath the sweep of his mustache. He had been doing some drinking, from the look of him.

"Whisky, Clay?" Morgan asked, and his hand caught the neck of the decanter as though to strangle it. But Clay shook his head again.

"I've just found out something to shake a man," Clay said.

"What's that?"

"The passenger those road agents shot. I heard his name and I didn't believe it. But I went over to the carpenter shop for a look."

"Somebody you knew?" Morgan said, and put the decanter down.

"Knew of. I'd heard Bob Cletus had a brother up in the Dakotas somewhere."

Denver, he commented to himself. "Cletus?" he said aloud.

"Pat Cletus," Clay said, looking down at his hat. "This one's name was Pat Cletus. You would know it was his brother, looking at him."

Morgan whistled.

"Come after me, I guess," Clay said.

"I don't know. Looks like he might just have happened out this way."

Clay shook his head again, and Morgan leaned back in his chair and hooked his thumbs in his vest pockets. He said easily, "What would you have done?"

"Run."

"If he'd come after you like you think, I expect he'd've followed if you'd run."

After a time Clay nodded. "Why, yes," he said. "That's so, isn't it?"

"Then it seems like those San Pablo boys that shot him down did you a favor," Morgan said. He tried to grin, and felt his lips slide dry over his teeth.

"Yes," Clay said. His elbows on the desk, he made a steeple of his hands and gazed through, as though he were shading his eyes to sight at something a long way off.

"Foolishness!" Morgan said suddenly, savagely. "I don't know how you managed to settle it in your mind that Bob Cletus wasn't on the prod for you. You heard he was. It looks to me like you just chose he wasn't so you could chew yourself forever. Foolishness. God damn it, Clay!"

"What is foolish to one man maybe isn't to another, every time," Clay said. "It is different with you. If you lose a stack at your trade you can push out another and win it back. If I lose a stack like that one I can't."

"If you lose at your trade they leave your boots on," Morgan said. He tried to grin, and saw Clay try to grin back. But Clay only shook his head; that wasn't what he had meant.

Morgan said, "Let one Cletus shoot you down because you shot down another—what kind of trade is that?"

"Fair trade," Clay said, and his lips twisted again, more weakly still.

Damned fool, Morgan thought, not even angrily any more; oh, you damned fool! "Why, then it is a funny kind of trade and a funny kind of fair," he said carefully. "It is a trade where you will have to kill a man sometimes. But any time their kin come after you, there is nothing for it but throw down your hardware and go to praying."

"Only Cletus's kin," Clay said. "You know what I mean. Don't try to make a fool of me, Morg." Clay carefully moved his hat two inches to the right. "There's more to it than Pat Cletus," he said.

"I know."

"You've seen her?"

"I heard there was a woman came in on the stage with him. So if it was a Cletus—"

"I guess she went looking for him when she left Fort James."

"There are people I'd rather see in Warlock than Kate."

"You didn't use to feel that way."

"There was a time when I could eat hot chiles too. That was when I was younger."

"I can't look her in the face," Clay said, in an expressionless voice. "I think I could look any Cletus in the face, but I can't her."

Morgan reached for the decanter again. Clay did not take on this way very much, and when he did Morgan was angry, first at Clay, and then at himself; and part of the time it would seem a foolish joke, and part of the time it would sit his back heavy as pig lead because it sat Clay's so. He had not yet discovered how he must act with Clay when Clay was like this. "A little whisky, Clay?" he said.

"*Por favor.*"

He poured whisky into the two glasses, and wondered if Clay had any idea that the man drinking with him had done it to him. "How?" he said.

"How," Clay said. He drank the whisky off at a swallow and got to his feet, putting his hat on. Standing, his face remote and calm, Clay said, "There was a time when I used to pray it wasn't so, what I'd done. It is hard to blame a person for what he does when he is scared, but you can blame yourself. Trigger-nervous and edgy like I was, and seeing a *Tejano* coming at me around every corner. But maybe a man has to have something like that on him." Abruptly he stopped, and turned away from the desk.

"Why, Clay?" Morgan said.

"Why, just so he'll know, I guess," Clay said distantly. He went out. The sounds of gambling and drinking and monotonous

talking were loud for a moment before Clay shut the door behind him.

Morgan took a cheroot from the box. He lit it with steady
fingers, and inhaled deeply until he felt the smoke gripe his
lungs. "How?" he said, raising his glass to the fuzzy, fat nude
on her red couch. She smirked back at him, flat-faced, and he
said, "Don't smile at me, for I would hire you out in a minute
if I needed a stake."

He brought the cheroot up close before his slitted eyes, until all he could see in the world was the hoared cherry ember.
Inverting the cigar, he mashed it out against the back of his
hand, curling his lips back against the fierce, searing pain, and
breathing deep of the stink of burning hair and flesh.

Then he sat grinning idiotically at the red spot on the back
of his hand, thinking of Clay saying that he had prayed.


## 14. *Gannon Watches a Man among Men*

### I

GANNON WAITED alone at the jail. About ten o'clock the judge
appeared, coming in the doorway with his hard hat cocked
over his eye, a bottle under one arm and his crutch under the
other, his left trouser leg neatly turned up and sewed like a
sack across the bottom. Heavy and awkward on the crutch he
moved around to the chair behind the table, which Gannon
vacated, and sank into it, grunting. He put the bottle down
before him, and leaned the crutch against the table.

"Left you behind, did they?" he said, swinging around with
difficulty to confront Gannon, who had seated himself in the
chair beside the cell door. The judge's face was the color of
unfresh liver.

Gannon nodded.

"You see any reason why they should have?" the judge demanded, continuing to regard him with his muddy eyes.

"Yes."

"What reason?"

"I expect you know, Judge."

"I asked you," the judge snapped.

"Well, one they are after is maybe my brother."

"By God, if you are the law you arrest your own brother if he breaks it, don't you?"

"Yes."

"But maybe you lean a little toward McQuown's people," the judge said, squinting at him. "Or Carl is afraid you do. Do you?"

"No."

"Lean toward Blaisedell then, like most here? Seeing he is against McQuown?"

"I don't guess I lean either way. I don't take it as my place to lean any way."

Footsteps came along the boardwalk and Blaisedell turned into the doorway. "Judge," he said, nodding in greeting. "Deputy."

"Marshal," Gannon said. The judge turned slowly toward Blaisedell.

"Any word from the posse?" Blaisedell asked. He leaned in the doorway, the brim of his black hat slanting down to hide his eyes.

"Not yet," he said. He felt Blaisedell's stare. Then Blaisedell inclined his head to glance down at the judge, who had muttered something.

"Pardon, Judge?" Blaisedell said.

"I said, who are you?" the judge said, in a muffled voice.

"Why, we have met, Judge, I believe."

"Who are you?" the judge said again. "Just tell me, so I will know. I don't think it's come out yet, who you are."

Gannon stirred nervously in his chair. Blaisedell stood a little straighter, frowning.

"Something a man's got a right to know," the judge went on. His voice had grown stronger. "Who are you? Are you Clay Blaisedell or are you the marshal of this town?"

"Why, both, Judge," Blaisedell said.

"A man is bound by what he is," the judge said. "An honest man, I mean. I am asking whether you are bound by being marshal, or being Clay Blaisedell."

"Both, I expect. Judge, I don't just know for sure what you are—"

"Which first?" the judge snapped.

This time Blaisedell didn't answer.

"Oh, I know what you are thinking. You think I am a drunk, one-legged old galoot pestering you, and you are too polite to say so. Well, I know what I am, Mister Marshal Blaisedell, or Mister Clay Blaisedell that is incidentally marshal of Warlock. But I want to know *which* you are."

"Why?" Blaisedell said.

"Why? Well, I got to thinking and it seems to me the trouble in a thing like law and order is, there is people working every which way at it, or against it. Like it or not, there has got to be *people* in it. But the trouble is, you never know what a man *is*, so how can you know what he is going to *do*? So I thought, why not ask straight out? I asked Johnny Gannon here just now what he was and where he stood, and he told me. Are you any better than another that you shouldn't?"

Blaisedell still did not speak. He looked as though he had dismissed the judge's words as idle, and was thinking of something else.

The judge went on. "Let me tell you another thing then. Schroeder has gone after those that robbed the stage and killed a passenger. I expect him and that posse would just as soon shoot them down *ley fuga* as bring them back. But say he will catch them, and say he gets them back whole. Well, there will be a lynch mob on hand, like as not, from what I've heard around tonight. But say the lynch mob doesn't pan out, or Schroeder sort of remembers what he is here for and stops them. Then those road agents will go up to Bright's City to trial, and likely get off just the way Earnshaw did.

"Then it is your turn, Mister Marshal, or whatever you are. Which is why I am asking you now beforehand if you know what you are, and what you stand for. If a man don't know that himself, why, nobody does except God almighty, and He is a long way off just now."

"Judge," Blaisedell said. "I guess you don't much like what you think I stand for."

"I don't *know* what you stand for, and it don't look like you are going to tell me, either!" Gannon heard the judge draw a ragged breath. "Well, maybe you can tell me this, then. Why shouldn't the Citizens' Committee have gone out and made itself a vigilante committee like some damned fools wanted to do, instead of bringing you here?"

Blaisedell spread his legs, folded his arms on his chest, and frowned. "Might have done," he said, in his deep voice. "I don't always hold with vigilantes, but sometimes it is the only thing."

"Don't hold with them why?"

"Well, now, Judge, I expect for the same reason you don't. Most times they start out fine, but most times, too, they go bad. Mostly they end up just a mob of stranglers because they don't know when to break up."

"Wait!" the judge said. "You are right, but do you know why they go bad? Because there is nothing they are responsible to. Now! Any man that is set over other men somehow has to be responsible to something. Has to be *accountable*. You—"

Blaisedell said, "If you are talking about me, I am responsible to the Citizens' Committee here."

"Ah!" the judge said. He sat up very straight; he pointed a finger at the marshal. "Well, most ways it is a bad thing, and it is not even much of a thing, but it is an important thing and I warrant you to hang onto it!"

"All right," Blaisedell said, and looked amused.

"I am telling you something for your own good and everybody's good," the judge whispered. "I am telling you a man like you has to be always right, and no poor human can ever be that. So you have got to be accountable somehow. To someone or everybody or—"

"To you, you mean, Judge?" Blaisedell said.

Gannon looked away. His eyes caught the names scratched on the wall opposite him, that were illegible now in the dim light. He wondered to whom those men, each in their turn, had thought they were responsible. Not to Sheriff Keller certainly, nor to General Peach.

The judge had not spoken, and after a moment Blaisedell went on. "Judge, a man will say too often that he is responsible to something because he is afraid to face up alone. That is just putting off on another man or on the law or whatever. A man who has to always think like that is a crippled man."

"No," the judge said; his voice was muffled again. "No, just

a man among men." He drank again, the brown bottle slanting
up toward the base of the hanging lamp above him.

Blaisedell stood with his long legs still spread and his hands
upon his shell belt beneath his black frock coat. Standing there
in the doorway he seemed as big a man as Gannon had ever
seen. When he examined Blaisedell closely, height and girth, he
was not so tall nor yet so broad-chested as some he knew, yet
the impression remained. Blaisedell's blue gaze encased him for
a moment; then he turned back to the judge again.

"Maybe where you've been the law was enough of a thing
there so people went the way the law said," he said. "You
ought to know there's places where it is different than that. It
is different here, and maybe the best that can be done is a man
that is handy with a Colt's—to keep the peace until the law can
do it. That is what I am, Judge. Don't mix me with your law,
for I don't claim to be it."

"You are a prideful man, Marshal," Judge Holloway said. He
sat with his head bent down, staring at his clasped hands.

"I am," Blaisedell said. "And so are you. So is any decent
man."

"You set yourself as always right. Only the law is that and it
is above all men. Always right is too much pride for a man."

"I didn't say I am always right," Blaisedell said. His voice
sounded deeper. "I have been wrong, and dead wrong. And
may be wrong again. But—"

"But then you stand naked before the rest in your wrong,
Marshal," the judge said. "It is what I am trying to say. And
what then?"

"When I have worn out my use, you mean? Why, then I will
move along, Judge."

"You won't know when it is time. In your pridefulness."

"I'll know. It is something I'll know." Gannon thought the
marshal smiled, but he could not be sure. "There'll be ones to
tell me."

"Maybe they will be afraid to tell you," the judge said.

Blaisedell's face grew paler, colder; he looked suddenly furious. But he said in a polite voice, "I expect I'll know when the
time comes, Judge," and abruptly turned and disappeared. His
bootheels cracked away to silence outside.

The judge raised his bottle to drain the last of the whisky in it. With a limp arm he reached down to set it beside his chair, and knocked it over with a drunken hand. It rolled noisily until it brought up against the cell door, while the judge leaned forward with his face in his hands and his fingers working and scraping in his hair.

After a long time he rose and clapped his hat on his head, staggering as he fitted the crutch under his arm. Gannon had a glimpse of his face as he swung out the door. Hectically flushed, it was filled with a sagging mixture of pride and shame, dread and grief.

## 11

It was well after midnight when the posse returned. Gannon stared at the doorway with aching eyes as he heard the tramp of hoofs and shouting. Men began running in the street past the jail, and he felt his heart swell in his chest as though it would smother him. He thrust down hard on the table with his hand, forcing himself to his feet, and went outside.

The street seemed filled solid with horsemen and men on foot milling around the horses. Someone was swinging a lantern to illuminate the faces of the riders—he saw Carl's face, Peter Bacon's, Chick Hasty's; the lantern showed Pony Benner's scowling, frightened face, and the men in the street howled his name. The pale light revealed Calhoun, and another shout went up. Then Gannon saw Billy sitting straight and hatless in the saddle, with his hands tied behind him.

The lantern swung again to show a riderless horse; but not riderless, he saw, for there was a body tied over the saddle.

"Ted Phlater!" someone said, in a sudden silence.

Immediately a roar went up. "Hang them!" a drunken voice screamed. "Oh, hang the sons of bitches! Hang them, boys!"

"Shut that up!" Carl shouted. Gannon swung off the boardwalk and made his way through the crowd as Carl dismounted. Carl looked into his face and gripped his arm for a moment.

"Got Ted Phlater shot and lost Friendly, damn all," he said.

Another drunken voice was raised. "Where's Big Luke, Carl?"

"Where is McQuown? You went and forgot Abe and Curley, boys!"

"They got the barber-killer!"

There was laughter, more shouting. "Hang them, boys! Hang them!" the first voice continued, shrill and mechanical, like a parrot.

"Horse!" Carl called to Peter Bacon. "You and Pike bring them inside." He started for the jail, and Gannon made his way toward Phlater's horse, to help Owen Parsons with the body. Men surged and shouted, mocked and joked and threatened as Pony, Calhoun, and Billy were dismounted. The crowd pressed toward the jail now, as the prisoners came up on the boardwalk, where a man held a lantern high as they moved past him.

"Hang them! Hang them!"

Gannon and Parsons lifted Phlater down and tried to make their way to the jail. "Get the God-damned jumping hell out of the way!" Parsons cried hoarsely. "Got any respect for the dead?"

Inside they put Ted Phlater's stiffening body on the floor at the rear of the jail, and Peter appeared unfolding a blanket, with which he covered it. Pike Skinner was untying Calhoun's arms; he thrust him roughly into the cell with Billy and Pony, and Carl slammed and locked the door.

Chick Hasty and Tim French came inside with the strongbox from the stage, which they shoved under the table. The hanging lamp swung like a pendulum when one of them brushed against it, and shadows swung more wildly still. The dusty window was crowded with bloated, featureless faces pressed against the glass, and men were pushing in at the door

"Out of here!" Carl shouted. His face was lined with fatigue and gray with dust. "Isn't any damned assembly hall. Out of here before I get mad! You!" Pike Skinner swung around and with his arms outstretched forced the men back.

"Hang the murdering sons of bitches!" someone yelled from outside. Pony's scared face appeared at the cell door, and Calhoun's lantern-jawed, cadaverous one; Gannon could see Billy's hand on Calhoun's shoulder.

"Expect they mean to try something, from the sound of them," Peter Bacon said calmly.

"No they won't," Carl said. He stretched and rubbed his back, and grinned suddenly. "Well, three out of four," he said. "That is better than one out of two like we made last time, anyhow."

"You going to want some of us here tonight, Carl?" Parsons said, and Gannon saw that he tilted his grizzled head in his direction. He looked quickly away, to meet Calhoun's eyes. Calhoun pursed his slack mouth, hawked, and spat.

"Go home and get some sleep," Carl said, and slumped down in the chair at the table. "We are all right here."

"I'm staying," Pike Skinner said.

"Stay then. Chick, you and Pete go get some sleep. We'll be taking them into Bright's in the morning."

There was muttering among the men bunched in the doorway. A muffled shout went up outside. The possemen pushed out the door, spurs clinking and scraping.

When they had gone, Pike Skinner swung the door closed and slid the bar through the iron keepers. The goblin faces still pressed against the window glass. There was another burst of shouting and hurrahing outside. Pike Skinner walked heavily to the rear, let himself fall into the chair there, and stared hostilely at Gannon. At the table Carl sighed and rubbed his knuckles into his eyes.

"Didn't take you long," Gannon said.

Carl laughed. "We ran onto them just before they hit the river. Pony and Calhoun, that is. They separated but we rode them down easy. Ted and Pike here kind of flushed Billy out of some trees down there and—"

Pike said abruptly, "It was Billy shot Ted."

"He was shooting at me," Billy said, in a harsh voice, from the cell. "What was I supposed to do, sit and let him do it?"

"Carl," Pony said. "You are not going to let those bastards take us out of here, are you, Carl?"

"Shut your face," Pike said. "You chicken-livered ugly little son of a bitch."

"Thought you wanted me to let you go," Carl said. "Thought you told me I might as well, for a jury up at Bright's would do it anyhow. Save me trouble, you said."

"I got something to tell you, Bud Gannon," Calhoun said. "Come over here so's I can whisper it."

"Never mind," Billy said. "Never mind, Bud."

Gannon didn't look toward the cell, leaning against the wall where the names were scratched, and watching within himself the slow turn of the cards, knowing each one as it turned. He stared at the goblin faces at the window and listened to the shouting and muttering outside. It was the only card he had not foreseen.

"You are so God-damn sure you caught your road agents!" Pony yelled.

"Hush!" Carl said.

"Be damned if I do! You got the wrong people! You—"

Carl got up, swung swiftly and hit Pony in the face through the bars. Pony fell backward, cursing.

"Wrong people!" Carl said, rubbing his knuckles. "You just happened to pick up that strongbox where somebody else dropped it, I guess."

"One wrong, though," Calhoun said quietly, and laughed; he moved back as Carl raised his fist again. Gannon stared in the cell at Billy and he felt his heart swell and choke him again; he had almost missed another card. Billy just looked back at him, scornfully.

"Listen to those boys yell out there," Pike said.

Gannon started and Carl reached for the shotgun as there was a knock. Carl motioned to Gannon to unbolt the door. It was the Mexican cook from the Boston Café; he slipped in, carrying a tray covered with a cloth. The men outside set up a steady whooping, and the Mexican looked very frightened as he put the tray down and departed. As Gannon swung the door closed behind him he had a glimpse of the vast, dark mass in the street, and groups of pale, whiskered faces showing here and there by lanternlight. Someone was haranguing them from the tie rail at the corner. He bolted the door again.

Carl passed bowls of meat and potatoes into Calhoun. Pony threw his to the floor. "Go hungry then," Carl said.

Pike took a steak in his hand and wolfed it down, and Carl attacked his hungrily too. Gannon set his plate on the floor beside him. There was another round of shouting outside, with one voice rising above the rest. The words were lost in the up-roar. The faces at the window had vanished.

"Bud," Billy said. Pony and Calhoun had retreated into the

darkness. Gannon felt Pike Skinner watching him. "What the hell would you do, Bud?" Billy said. "People after you and throwing lead all over the landscape. What the hell would you've done?"

"I don't know," he said. Carl was pretending not to listen.

Pike said, "You might've thought how come there was a posse after you in the first place."

Gannon saw Billy's face twist, and something in him twisted with it. Another yell went up outside, and Pony appeared at the cell door again.

"Sit there and lap your supper!" he shrilled at Carl. "They are coming! Can't you hear them coming?"

"We'll stop them," Carl said, "if they come. You can quit wetting your pants."

"Bud," Billy said again.

"Never mind it now, Billy," Gannon said tightly. Pike glowered at him from the chair beside the alley door. Carl sat humpbacked at the table, forking food into his mouth.

"Long ride to Bright's," Carl said, over a mouthful. "You boys in there better get some sleep."

"We'll never get to Bright's!" Pony cried.

"Oh, hush that!" Calhoun said.

*Bud*—Gannon could hear it, repeated and repeated, although Billy hadn't spoken again. Reluctantly he turned his head to look at Billy again, and he saw Billy's lips tilt beneath the pitiful young mustache. "Go ahead and say you told me what I was heading for," Billy whispered. "Go ahead, Bud."

"What good would that do?"

"No good," Billy said, and disappeared. The cot springs creaked. Gannon could hear them whispering in the cell. "Why don't you tell him?" he heard Calhoun say; then the tumult outside grew suddenly louder, and faces were pressed against the window again.

Someone beat on the door with the flat of his hand. "*Carl!*"

Carl grunted and rose. He wiped his mustache, hitched at his shell belt, and glanced significantly at Gannon and Skinner. He took up the shotgun and nodded at Gannon to unbar the door.

Gannon did so, and leaped back, jerking his Colt free as the door burst inward. Two men hurtled in, to stop suddenly as they saw Carl's shotgun. There was a knot of others jammed in the doorway, and behind them Gannon could feel the whole huge and violent thrust of the mob. Pike leaped forward with his Winchester in his hands. Outside they were whooping steadily again.

"You are going to have to give them up, Carl," Red Slator said loudly, as he and Fat Vint backed up to join the others in the doorway. Close behind these two, Gannon could see Jed Smith, a foreman at the Thetis, Nate Bush, Hap Peters, Charlie Grace, who was one of Dick Maples' bakers, Kinkaid, a cowboy from up the valley, several miners, and Simpson and Parks, who were both macs for some of the crib girls. Their faces were grim. Fat Vint looked drunker than usual.

"Get out of here, you miserable sons of bitches!" Carl said.

"You can't stop us!" Charlie Grace shouted, and cheers went up from the dark, featureless mass behind them.

"See if I don't," Carl said. "If you think a bunch of pimps and drunk bullprods is going to bust this jail, you are mistaken. Get out of here!"

"We will tramp you down!" Vint yelled blusteringly. "You hear, Pike?" He looked at Gannon with his bloodshot pig-eyes, and sneered, "And you'll keep out of it if you know what's good for you, Johnny Gannon."

"Get out of here!" Carl said, in a level voice.

"We'll get out of here taking them with us!" Slator said. "We are going to hang the murdering bastards and bust over you if we have to, Carl Schroeder. You know what'll happen at Bright's; by God, everybody knows. They'll get off sure as hell, with McQuown to send up lying hardcases by the dozen and scare the jury green too. You know that, Carl!" The men in the doorway began all to shout at once, and the shouting gathered power outside until the whole world seemed to be shouting.

Carl waited until the noise had subsided a little; then he said, "Red, I'd like to see them hang as much as you. I caught them and lost Ted Phlater doing it." His voice rose. "And we went out and caught them while you and this bunch was sitting on your slat-asses drinking whisky. So I will be damned if you will take them off us now the hard work is done! Now get!"

He jammed the shotgun against Slator's chest and Slator

backed up. Vint grabbed at the shotgun and Gannon slammed the barrel down on the fat hand. Vint yelped. Pike started forward, and, feinting blows with the butt of the Winchester, drove them all back through the doorway.

"Tromp them down! Tromp them down, fellows!"

"Christ, give us something to help stand them off with, Bud!" Calhoun cried.

They pushed the mob leaders before them out the door, and the crowd in the street gave way. Then it surged forward again with a wild yelling. Hands caught Carl's shotgun and pulled him forward. He stumbled to his knees, then fought and scrambled back away from the men crowding in on him. Gannon fired twice into the air. Someone yelled in terror and the mob fell back again.

The three of them stood close together before the jail door. Carl was panting.

"They won't shoot!" a hoarse voice yelled from the rear of the mob. "They know better than to shoot!"

"Give us a God-damned iron, Carl!" Calhoun shouted.

"Good Christ, Carl, for Christ's sake, give us a gun to hold them off with! Bud!"

"Don't be a damned fool, Carl!" Slator said.

"Get the hell out of the way, Johnny Gannon! You two-way son of a bitch!"

"What the hell are you doing, Pike? Leave us take them!"

Slator, Vint, and Simpson started forward again; Vint was grinning. "You dassn't shoot, Carl!"

"One step more," Carl panted.

"Give us a chance, Carl!" Pony screamed.

"One step more, you bastards!" Pike said, and Gannon started to swing his Colt at Simpson's head.

There were three shots in rapid succession from Southend Street, and then silence, sudden and profound. Craning his neck, Gannon saw men hurrying to get off the boardwalk, and Blaisedell appeared, walking rapidly, the Colt in his hand glittering by lanternlight. A whisper ran through the crowd. "The marshal!" "Blaisedell!" "Here comes the marshal!" "It is Blaisedell!"

Blaisedell joined them before the jail. "Need another man?" he said.

"Surely do," Carl said, and let out his breath in a long, shaking, whispering laugh. "We surely do, Marshal."

"We are taking those road agents out to hang, Marshal!" someone cried from across the street.

"You are not going to stop us, Marshal!" Fat Vint blustered. "We will tromp you with the rest. We are—"

"Come here and tromp me," Blaisedell said.

Vint stepped back. Those around him retreated further.

"Come here," Blaisedell said. "Come here!" Vint came a step forward. His face looked like gray dough.

"This is none of your put-in, Marshal!" someone yelled, but the rest of the mob was silent.

"Come here!" Blaisedell said once more, dangerously. Vint sobbed with fear, but he came on another step. Blaisedell's hand shot up suddenly, the Colt's barrel gleaming as he clubbed it down. The fat man cried out as he fell. There was silence again.

"Damn you, Marshal!" Slator cried. "This is none of your—"

"Come here!" Blaisedell said. When Slator didn't move he fired into the planks at his feet. Slator jumped and yelled. "Come here!" Slator moved forward, trying to cover his head with his hands. Blaisedell slashed the gun barrel down and he staggered back. Hands caught him and he disappeared into the crowd.

"Take that one off, too," Blaisedell said, and the same men hurriedly dragged Vint off the boardwalk.

"You have done McQuown's work tonight, Blaisedell!" a man yelled.

"If you have got something to say, step up here and say it," Blaisedell said, not loudly. "Otherwise skedaddle." No one spoke. There was a movement away down Main Street. "Then all of you skedaddle," Blaisedell said, raising his voice. "And while you are doing it think how being in a lynch mob is as low a thing as a man can be."

There was bitter muttering in the street, but the mob began to disperse. Blaisedell holstered his Colt. Gannon could see his face in profile, stern and contemptuous, and thought how they must hate him for this. But he had saved shooting; he had probably saved lives.

Carl was mopping his face with his bandanna. "Well, thank

you kindly, Marshal," he said. "I expect there isn't a one in there worth any man's trouble. But damned if you don't hate to be run by a bunch of whisky-primed, braying fools like that."

Blaisedell nodded. Pike Skinner, Gannon saw, was looking at the marshal with a reluctant awe on his face.

"Prisoners get a scare?" Blaisedell asked.

"Caterwauling like a bunch of tomcats in there," Carl said, and chuckled breathlessly.

Blaisedell nodded again. Suddenly he said, with anger in his voice, "A person surely dislikes a mob like that. They are men pretending they are brave and hard, but every one so scared of the man beside him he can't do anything but the same." He glanced from Pike to Gannon. "Well, I didn't go to butt in so," he said, as though apologizing. "I expect you boys could've handled it. It is just I surely dislike a mob of men like that."

"I guess we couldn't't've handled it, Marshal," Pike said. "Things had got tight."

Gannon said, "I guess we would've had to go to shooting," and Blaisedell smiled with a brief, white show of teeth below his mustache. He made a curt gesture of salute, as though acknowledging that as the proper compliment.

The four of them stood in awkward silence, watching the men drifting away before them in the darkness. Then Carl turned and went inside, and Pike followed him. When the others had gone, Blaisedell said to Gannon, "Your brother was with them, I heard."

"Yes," he said.

"Too bad," Blaisedell said. "Young fellow like that." Blaisedell stood with him a moment longer, as though waiting for him to speak, but he could think of nothing to say and after a time the marshal said, "Well, I'll be going." With long strides he faded off into the darkness.

Gannon slowly turned back inside the jail. His clothes were soaked with sweat. Billy stood alone at the cell door. "Well," Carl was saying to Pike, leaning against a corner of the table with his arms folded over his chest, "good lesson on how to run off a mob. Haul them out and knock their heads loose one at a time."

"More lesson than that," Pike said ruefully. "For it takes a man to do it." He nodded toward the door.

Gannon looked down at the blanket-wrapped body that was Phlater, whom Billy had shot. So the cards he had missed had not mattered. The lynch mob was gone. He knew that Billy had not been at the stage, but with Phlater dead and Billy's stubborn pride, that would not matter either. So the rest of the cards would continue to play themselves out.

Pony said savagely, "Shut up about that gold-hanneled son of a bitch and leave us get some sleep in here."

Carl's face stiffened. Pike said hoarsely, "Gold-handled son of a bitch that just saved your rotten lives for you!"

"Sleep good on that," Carl said.

Billy's voice was bitter as gall. "Bring his boots and we'll kiss them for him. Like he wants. Like you all do. Bring us his damned boots."

Pike took a step toward the cell door and Billy retreated. Now none of them were visible in the deep shadow of the cell, but it was as though Gannon could see through it, and beyond it, and beyond Bright's City even, see all the massive irrevocable shadows with only the details not clear.

He went out to the Boston Café, after a while, for a pot of coffee to take back to the jail, and sat the night, sleepless himself, watching Carl and Pike fighting sleep. In the morning Buck Slavin furnished a special coach, and Carl, Peter Bacon, Chick Hasty, and Tim French took the prisoners into Bright's City for trial.

## 15. *Boot Hill*

WARLOCK'S BOOT HILL was not a hill at all, but a knoll protruding from the plateau next to the town dump, where flies hovered in great black swarms. From Boot Hill itself the valley all the way to the Dinosaurs was visible: near at hand the jumble of great rocks of the malpais, farther down the cottonwoods lining the river in irregular stretches, the greasy-green mesquite thickets, and the drier green of the grama grass along the bottoms. To the south were the barren, tan sides of the Bucksaws, marked here and there with winding mine roads, the neat ugly smears of tailings below the gallows of the

shafthead frames. Farther to the west were the chimneys of the
stamp mill at Redgold, with the smoke blowing southwest in
gray chunks.

Today there were two open graves, two pine coffins resting
on the stony ground beside them. It was windy among the
mounded graves. Men stood hatless and their hair blew askew
and their trouser bottoms flapped—groups of townsmen, a few
cowboys, two women in deep bonnets, and a number of curious Mexicans standing close by. A little apart stood Miss Jessie
Marlow, with her hand on Marshal Clay Blaisedell's arm, and,
on the other side of her, Dr. Wagner in his old black suit. Further along, all in black and standing alone, was the new woman,
who, it was rumored, had paid for the coffins. Beyond her were
six women from the Row, bunched close together as though
for protection, from time to time one painted, powdered face
or another glancing curiously sideways at the strange woman.
Morgan was also alone, his hat in his hands like the rest of the
men, his sleek hair shining in the sun and undisturbed by the
wind, standing with one foot up on a rock and brooding down
at the first coffin.

The four gravediggers, who had been assigned a month's
duty as such by Judge Holloway in penance for being drunk
and disorderly on various occasions, leaned on their shovels
while Bill Wolters, one of Taliaferro's barkeepers, recited the
service from memory in a loud, sing-song, former-Baptist-
preacher's voice, that was broken into snatches of sound by
the wind. The coffin was let down into the first grave with
new yellow ropes, and Wolters moved to the second grave
and recited again. The second coffin was lowered, and the
gravediggers began shoveling dirt and rocks into the holes.
The Mexicans, the strange woman, and one of the women
from the Row crossed themselves. Morgan brought a cheroot
from his pocket and chewed on it. Some of the other men
took turns with the shovels. Dick Maples produced the two
crosses he had fashioned and painted—it was his hobby. On
the first was:

> PATRICK CLETUS
> *Murdered by Bandits*
> *January 23, 1881*
> *"How long, oh Lord?"*

On the second:

THEODORE PHLATER
*Shot by Billy Gannon*
*January 23, 1881*
*"A time of war—"*

A group of Citizens' Committee members began moving away from the graves together. "Who is the tall woman?" asked Joseph Kennon.

"Came in on the stage yesterday," Buck Slavin said. He nodded back at the first grave. "With that one. Somebody said they were going to put up a dance hall here."

"Married?" Fred Winters inquired.

"I don't know."

"Her name is Kate Dollar," said Paul Skinner, Pike Skinner's brother, as he limped up to join them. "That's how she's got it down at the hotel, anyhow."

The doctor joined them and Winters said, "That is a good arm Miss Jessie is walking on, Doc. Did you see him in action last night?"

The doctor shook his head.

"I saw him," Henry Goodpasture said. "He made fifty or sixty men run with their tails between their legs."

"Who were they?" the doctor asked.

"The usual no-accounts. Slator and Grace among them. A bunch of drunken miners."

"I see you will blame the miners for everything, too," the doctor said.

Goodpasture rolled his eyes heavenward, and Kennon and Winters laughed. The new woman had moved away from Morgan to join Deputy Gannon. Slavin informed the others of this in a whisper, and each found occasion to glance back and confirm the fact.

"It seems Gannon has a friend after all," Winters said.

Morgan passed and one or two of them nodded to him, but no one spoke. Morgan glanced from face to face with his contemptuous eyes, and nodded back with a kind of insulting deference.

"Damned hound," Will Hart said, when Morgan was out of earshot. "There's a man I wouldn't trust my back to."

"There's talk Taliaferro's man Wax trusted his to him," Slavin said. "Damned if I don't believe it, too."

"Blaisedell seems to trust him well enough," Goodpasture said.

"It does not say much for Blaisedell, I'm afraid," Winters said. "Which is too bad."

They all fell silent as the deputy and Kate Dollar caught up with them. The deputy's eyes flickered at them as he passed. The woman walked with him, but separately too. Her face was pale and set.

No one spoke until these had gone on past, and they all stopped when they reached the doctor's buggy. The fat bay mare swung her head from side to side, cropping stubble. Goodpasture and the doctor climbed into the buggy. "Is there a Citizens' Committee meeting, Buck?" the doctor asked.

"Why, I hadn't heard," Slavin said. "Is there, Joe?"

"I don't know," Kennon said, glancing quickly away.

The doctor took up his whip, shook it, and clucked to the mare. They waited while the buggy rolled off. Hart looked at Kennon, who flushed. Hart said to Slavin, "You know damned well there is a meeting, Buck! MacDonald called it."

"You know why he called it?" Kennon said. "He wants to vote Blaisedell to post some troublemaker at the Medusa out of town."

"I don't like that!" Hart said swiftly.

"Cheap," Winters said. "Cheaper than hiring Jack Cade to do it, the way he did with that man Lathrop. This way we all foot the bill."

"Well, I will go along with him," Slavin said. "It's that one called Brunk, Will. You have one man like that and he stirs everybody up. I think Doc is pretty friendly with him, is why I didn't want to say anything."

"Isn't that pretty?" Paul Skinner said, pointing. Ahead of them, cutting across toward the Row, the whores with their pastel clothing fluttering in the wind looked like bright-colored birds.

"I wish Doc would leave those damned jacks alone," Kennon said. "My God, he has got touchy about them."

"Well," Winters said, "in my opinion the troublemaker at the Medusa is Charlie MacDonald himself. Maybe he is the one that should be posted, and I don't know that I wouldn't vote for it."

"I don't like anything about this," Hart said.

"I expect we'll want the marshal to post those three of McQuown's, won't we?" Kennon said. "If they get off at Bright's, I mean."

"They will. They will."

"Four of them," Slavin said. "Friendly was with them, that's for sure. Maybe it'd be better to post that Brunk then, come to think of it. I'll tell Charlie."

Hart was shaking his head worriedly. Winters slapped him on the shoulder. "Do you know what Warlock's second industry is, Will? Coffin manufacture," he said, and laughed. But no one else joined him in his joke, and now they all walked in silence back along the dusty track to Warlock, returning from the burial of yesterday's dead.

## 16. *Curley Burne Tries to Mediate*

CURLEY BURNE rode beside Abe up into Warlock from the rim. As they entered Main Street he could feel Abe's tenseness ten feet away, see him sitting up straighter, his left hand stiff with the reins and his right braced upon his thigh, his green eyes flickering right and left at the almost empty street. Up in the central block there were a few horses tied before the saloons, and, beyond, two teams and wagons stood before Egan's Feed and Grain Barn. Peter Bacon drove the water wagon across on Broadway, water slopping from the top of the tank.

"Got quiet in Warlock," Abe said, in a flat voice.

"Surely has," Curley said, nodding. He pulled his mouth organ from inside his shirt and started to blow on it—and saw Abe frown. He let it drop back. "Chunk of them gone to Bright's for trial tomorrow, I expect," he said. "I hear there's a lot of feeling."

Abe's lips tightened in his red beard. He glanced toward the jail as they passed. The morning sun brightened the east face of the bullet-perforated, weather-beaten sign.

"Bud in there?" Abe asked.

"Didn't see."

"Probably gone up to witness against Billy," Abe said bitterly. He swung his black into Southend Street, so evidently he meant to stop in Warlock instead of just riding through. Curley supposed he felt he had had to come through, and had to stop, just to show himself.

Goodpasture's *mozo* was sweeping the boardwalk in front of the store; when he saw them he began to swing his broom in a burst of animation. A high, battered old Concord stood in the stageyard and a hostler was backing a wheeler into harness. He stared at them as they turned into the Acme Corral. Lame Paul Skinner came out to meet them, silent and hostile. Nate Bush spat on his hands and rammed the tines of his hayfork into the hay as though he were killing snakes.

Abe stood watching Paul Skinner lead Prince and the black off to water with his eyes cold and color burning in his cheeks. "Now, easy, Abe," Curley whispered.

They moved out of the corral, Abe very straight in his buckskin shirt, his shell belt riding his hips low beneath his concho belt. "Easy, now, Abe," Curley said sadly, again, and said it still again but not aloud.

"Sons of bitches!" Abe hissed, as they went along past the buckled, leaning plank fence toward Goodpasture's corner. "They will turn on a man as soon as spit. They will lick up to a new dog and turn on the old every time."

At the corner he started cater-cornered across Main Street toward the jail, and Curley followed a step behind him.

Inside the jail Bud Gannon sat behind the table. His stiff, dark brown hair was neatly combed and his hat lay on the table between his hands. Beside the alley door was a rusty, dented bucket with a mop handle leaning out of it, and the floor was still damp in spots.

Bud nodded to them. He looked tired, and thinner than ever. His star was pinned to the breast of his blue flannel shirt. Abe stopped just inside the door, and, standing at ease, glanced around the jail with careful attention. The cell was unoccupied, the door standing open.

"Well, how's the apprentice deputy?" Curley said, squeezing in past Abe. He had liked Bud Gannon as well as anyone at San Pablo, quiet and sober as he had always been. He had been a top hand with the stock, and he was missed. The killing in

Rattlesnake Canyon had hit Bud the worst, he knew; immediately after it he had left for Rincon. He knew Abe hated Bud for that, and for not coming back to San Pablo now.

"All right," Bud said, nodding. "How are you, Curley?"

"Fine as paint."

"We are going up to Bright's," Abe said.

Bud nodded again.

"Where's your big-chief deputy?"

"Bright's City."

"Looks like half Warlock's gone up." Curley flipped his hat off, so that it hung down his back by its cord. Whistling through his teeth, he stepped over to the cell door and batted it back and forth between his hands.

"Lot of yours going up, Abe?" Bud asked.

"Some," Abe said gravely. "Some people down there are interested pretty good."

"Be jam-packed up there," Curley said, pushing the door in faster, shorter arcs. "People all squunched together in court there and everybody calling everybody else a liar." He laughed to think of it, and to think of the fat, sweaty-faced townsmen in the jury box.

Abe leaned back against the wall and crossed his legs. "You look worried, Bud," he said. "Don't worry about Billy. It'll come right."

"Will it?" Bud said, and he sounded hoarse. "I'm glad to hear that." His thin face had paled. "How will it?" he said.

"Because I will see it does," Abe said. "Because they are friends of mine and I intend to see they are not blackguarded and false-sworn into hanging for something they didn't do— by people that's after me. I will stand up for my own, Bud."

Curley looked down as Bud's eyes turned toward him; he knew Abe had meant what he said, not just about Billy, but about Pony and Calhoun as well. But Luke had told them that Pony and Calhoun had planned to stop the stage. It was all right to stand up for your own, it was the first principle; but there was no need to throw up a dust cloud about what they had or had not done. It was as though Abe were trying to fool himself as well as the rest.

"You wouldn't see what you are doing to your own," Bud said, in the hoarse voice.

"Doing!" Abe said. With a lithe movement he leaned his

hands on the table and stared into Bud's face. "What would you do, let them hang? Let your own brother hang? By God, I think you would do it, just so Blaisedell would pat you on the head and call you a good boy."

"I'd let them have a fair trial," Bud said.

"Fair trial!" Abe said, and straightened and grinned. "I hear Buck is running passengers up free so everybody in Warlock can go swear against them. Fair trial?"

Bud said nothing, and it came over Curley with a sickening shock that Bud would *not* do anything, that he would let Billy hang and not make a move. "Holy smoke, Bud!" he said. "I believe you— What the hell has happened to you?"

Bud swung toward him. "Do you think I want—"

"I know what's happened to him," Abe broke in. "Clay Blaisedell is what's happened to him."

He went on, but Curley didn't listen, staring at Bud who was, in turn, watching Abe. It came on him strongly, all at once, that Bud did not hate Abe, that maybe Bud felt something of the way he did toward Abe. Yet there was some cold lack in him, where friends didn't matter, or even his brother.

"Whose town is it?" Abe was saying. "I mean, who was here to begin with? You know who, when Warlock was nothing but Cousins' store and Bill Hake's saloon. But then Richelin got his silver strike and everybody comes crowding in, and now it's beginning to look like there is no more room for the ones that was here first."

"There is room, Abe," Bud said.

"Just if I make room, it looks like. Bud, I was friendly with people and took care of my own and got along, and people looked up to me some. But not any more. Because there is someone come in that is trying to run me off like you would a dirty, stinking dog. Turning people against me—" His voice began to shake, and he stopped.

Bud said, "So now you are going up to Bright's City and have your own lied free, or the jury scared off, one. Or both. You will trick and mess the law around like you want it until—" He hesitated. "Until you get Clay Blaisedell brought in against you, and then you can't understand it."

"I understand it," Abe said. "I understand he has got people thinking he is Jesus Christ, so that makes me a black devil from hell. I understand it, and you too, Bud. I put you and Billy on when your Daddy died, Bud, but I guess you have surely forgot that."

"No," Bud said. "I haven't forgot it. But there is other things I can't forget either."

Curley said quickly, "There is some things better forgot."

"You son of a bitch!" Abe whispered. Curley saw that he had his hand on the haft of his knife. His lips were pulled back white against his teeth, and the long wrinkles in his cheeks were etched deep. "You son of a bitch!"

Bud licked his lips. When he spoke his voice was dead and dry. "I've come against things like that, is all," he said. "A thing happened there at Rattlesnake Canyon that I guess had to happen because of what'd gone before. So what went before was wrong, and I will try to see— Do you think it is easy?" he said loudly. "Because you think I am for Blaisedell against you, when I am not. And people here think the other way around, when I am not. But I am come against what we did in Rattlesnake Canyon, Abe. And against what was tried that night in the Glass Slipper when Jack would have shot a man in the back like you'd kill a fly. One fly, or seventeen flies."

Abe sucked his breath in; he cried, "If you say I fixed it to backshoot Blaisedell you are a liar!"

Curley tried to say jokingly, "Why, Bud, that kind of hits at me, don't it? I thought that was my fight. My back-off, anyhow." But he felt sick all the way down. He sighed and said, "Where you've gone wrong, Bud. You know where you went wrong? There's been bad things done, surely, but you went wrong lining up against your own instead of trying to change them. Against your friends, Bud; against your brother! That's no good! They are the most important people there is to a man; why, nobody else counts. Your friends and kin—Billy. You know that's wrong!"

"He doesn't think so," Abe said, easily now. "You can see that."

Curley said, "Do you think Billy run that stage and killed that passenger, Bud?" He watched Bud look down at his hat, and crease the top with the edge of his hand.

"Happen to know he didn't," Abe said.

"Luke says he didn't, Bud."

"But you'd have him hang," Abe said.

"He killed a posseman," Bud said tiredly.

"Oh, that's right," Abe said, mockingly. "Banging away at him and he was supposed to just let himself get shot up. Hang for just trying to defend himself."

"Let him plead it then," Bud said. "He wouldn't hang if he got a fair trial. But he will be lied off for what he didn't do in the first place, and stuck with it. No, he won't hang and he won't even go to the territorial, for you will get him off. And I don't guess you will ever see how you killed him by it."

Curley stared at him, uncomprehending, and Abe laughed and said, "My, you are a real worrier, aren't you?" His voice tightened as he went on. "Well, I know what you want—you want us all to hang for that in Rattlesnake Canyon. Don't you? You are like a hellfire-and-damnation preacher gone loco on bad whisky. All for a bunch of stinking, murdering greasers that wasn't worth the lead it cost to burn them down!" He stopped and rubbed a hand across his mouth, and Curley thought of Dad McQuown in one of his fits as he saw the shine of spit in Abe's beard. "But you were there!" Abe cried. "Shooting and hollering with the rest!"

Then Abe said softly, "Well, I am warning you, Bud."

Bud got to his feet and stood, stoop-shouldered, facing Abe. All at once he looked angry. "Warning me what?"

"Why, how Cade knows you have been making talk he was out to backshoot Blaisedell." Abe swiped at his mouth again, and Curley saw his eyes waver from Bud's; they would not meet his, either. Then Abe grinned and said, "But maybe Billy will keep him off you, if he doesn't get hung."

"Cade must be scared I'll tell Blaisedell," Bud said slowly. "Are you, Abe?"

Abe grunted as though he'd been hit in the belly, and snatched for his knife. Curley leaped toward him and caught his wrist. It took all his strength to thrust that steel wrist down, and the knife down, while Abe glared past him at Bud, panting, his teeth bared and beads of sweat on his forehead. "You are to quit this, Abe!" Curley whispered. "I mean right now directly! You are making a damned fool of yourself!" And Abe's hand relaxed against his. Abe resheathed the knife.

"Because I won't," Bud said. "And haven't. That's done. You

can get out of here now. We have said all we have to say, I guess."

Abe's eyes glittered as Curley stepped back away from him. "Why, Bud," Abe said. "I'll take almost anything off you, and have today—because we've been friends. But I won't take you telling me to get out."

"Let's go get some whisky and get along to Bright's, Abe," Curley said. "I mean! I'm not going to hang around here if I'm not wanted."

"Go, if you want," Abe said. Footsteps came along the planks outside, a shadow fell in the door. Abe swung around with his hand jerking back.

Pike Skinner came in, and Curley almost laughed with relief. Pike looked uncomfortable in a tight-fitting suit; he wore a new black, broad-brimmed hat and his shell belt under his sack coat. He halted as he saw them, and scowled. His flap ears turned red.

"Well, howdy, Pike," Curley said. "That is a mighty fine-looking suit of clothes you have got on there."

"Friends come in to see you, did they?" Pike said to Bud, in a rasping voice.

"Anything wrong with it?" Abe said.

"Yes!" Pike said, his face going as red as his ears. He squinted suddenly as though he had a tic. "Looks like something going on to me. There is two sides clear now, Gannon. You've got your pick!"

"You've picked, have you?" Abe said. "It was clear enough brother Paul already did."

"I surely have," Pike said. He stood with his hands held waist-high, as though he didn't really want to make a move, but thought he'd better have them handy in case his mouth got away from him.

"Boo!" Curley said, and laughed to see him start.

Pike flushed redder still. He said to Gannon, "If you are with these people, say so. And get out of here. You have got your pick now, and I will—"

"What if I don't pick?" Bud said.

Pike's eyes kept moving, watching Abe's hands, and Curley's. Curley heard Abe laugh softly. "Nobody sits the rail any more!" Pike said.

Grinning, Curley rested his hands on his shell belt and stretched his shoulders. "Why, give me a good rail to sit for comfort. I will do it every time."

Bud said nothing, and Curley realized that Bud could have made to please Pike, who was on the Citizens' Committee, and decent enough for a townsman, by repeating the order to get out. Bud didn't, and he respected him for it. Bud looked as though he didn't give a good God damn about anything right now.

"Let's move along, Abe. I can't stand this being picked against. Hurts my feelings."

"Going to Bright's City, Pike?" Abe asked.

"God-damned right I am!"

"See you there." Abe moved sideways toward the door. "See you, Bud," he said. "See you when we all hang together."

Abe went on out. Curley tipped his hat back onto his head, saluted Pike, and followed Abe out. He didn't look at Bud. Silently he walked back along the boardwalk beside Abe.

"Let's get riding to Bright's," Abe said in a stifled voice. "I hate this rotten town."

"Sure is down on you," he said. He felt for Abe. It was hard when everybody turned against you. It would be hard on any man, but it was a terrible thing on Abe.

"Sons of dirty whore bitches," Abe said. "Damn them to burning hell and Bud Gannon the first of them!"

Reluctantly Curley said, "Abe, you shouldn't have gone at him so. He is a cold one and no mistake, and I couldn't see it the way he does and ever look at myself shaving again, but—" He broke off as Abe halted and swung toward him. Abe's face was fierce again, his eyes like green ice. "—but you have got to hand it to a man that's doing what he thinks is right," he went on, staring straight back. "Whatever."

"I'll hand him what he handed me," Abe said. "Which is shit."

"Abe—" he started again, but Abe moved off across the street toward Goodpasture's store. Following him, he felt a dull anguish, for Abe, for Bud, for everyone. He wondered how everything had got so messed up; worse, it seemed, all the time. Maybe it was Blaisedell after all.

He glanced down toward where Mosbie stood. He and

Mosbie had drunk together many a time; now he felt the anguish sharpen to see the carefully blank expression on Mosbie's face, and the same expressions on the faces of the other men watching. Why, they all hated Abe, he thought; and they hated him, too.

As he followed Abe through the dust to Goodpasture's corner, and then down the boardwalk toward the Acme Corral, he felt anger begin to stir in him, and a retaliation of hate. What had done it to them all, he wondered? It must, he thought again, have been Blaisedell, after all.

## 17. *Journals of Henry Holmes Goodpasture*

February 1, 1881

THE LATEST bag of road agents has been acquitted by a Bright's City jury. There is high feeling here, and those who journeyed to Bright's City to give evidence or as spectators are exceedingly violent in their anger against judge, jury, lawyers, Bright's City in general, and Abraham McQuown in particular. Since Benner was the only bandit positively identified by his victims, the defense mounted the outrageous presumption that the other two were consequently innocent, and, that since both of these swore that Benner had been with them all day and that they had engaged in no crimes whatsoever, then Benner was also innocent. The witnesses who identified Benner were tricked into admitting that the main factor in their identification was his small stature, which was made to seem ridiculous. The posse itself, it was claimed, was responsible for Phlater's death, since it had begun firing wildly at the "innocent cowboys" as soon as they were within range, and the Cowboys plainly could not be blamed for defending themselves from such a vicious assault. It was implied even further that the whole affair was staged by "certain parties," and the strongbox carefully disposed where it would implicate the poor Cowboys most foully.

It is said that the prosecution was pursued with less than diligence. It is also said that judge and jury were bribed, and that the courtroom was crowded with McQuown's men brandishing six-shooters and muttering threats. Along the way my credulity begins to fail, amongst all this evidence of perfidy, but the fact remains that the three men have been freed. They rode through here yesterday on their way back to San Pablo. They encountered a sullen and most unfriendly Warlock, and had sense enough not to linger here in their triumph.

I think next time it may be very difficult to discourage a lynching party from its objective.

Still, certain good has come out of the affair. Public opinion, as it did when our poor barber was killed and Deputy Canning driven out of town, has again congealed, so that the Citizens' Committee feels itself in not so exposed and arbitrary a position in trying to administer some kind of law in Warlock.

The Citizens' Committee has not met yet. We are not in a hurry to face the situation, and feel it best to move slowly. The question foremost in everyone's mind is, of course, whether or not Blaisedell should be called upon to post the "innocent Cowboys" out of town, and, insofar as I can see, the great majority of the Citizens' Committee, and of Warlock itself, is for this. There is much talk of a Vigilante Army convened to ride upon San Pablo and "clean the rascals out." There is also talk of posting McQuown and *all* his men, and backing up Blaisedell in whatever action might ensue with a vigilante troop, which would be only operative within Warlock and for this one purpose.

As to the wholesale posting, you may hear it being argued on every hand, but with qualifications almost as numerous as the arguers. l think some of us are obsessed with the pleasure and presumption of dictating Life & Death.

There are also some who seem to be having grave second thoughts about the whole system of posting. Will Hart, I notice, is beginning to sound remarkably like the judge in his arguments. True, these say, posting worked in the case of Earnshaw, who is definitely reported to have left the territory—but is it not asking for trouble? Does not posting actually make it a point of honor that a man come in to fight our Marshal? What if a number come in against him at once and he is killed—are we not then still more at the mercy of the outlaws? What, if this be carried too far, is to prevent the enemies of each among us from seeing that he himself is posted?

I must face the fact, of course, that Public Opinion is not so unanimous as I would like to think. There are issues at stake, but as too often happens, we are apt to look to men as symbols rather than to the issues themselves. There are two sides here; one is Blaisedell, the other McQuown. So, alas, have the people chosen to see it. Blaisedell is, at the moment, the favored one by far; the *profanum vulgus* is solidly for him, and, as evinced by the lynch mob (which, curiously, Blaisedell had a large hand in putting down), against McQuown and the "innocents." The Citizens' Committee, of course, is behind Blaisedell too, but, as is usual when some are more violently partisan than we are, we edge away a little and restrain our own enthusiasms.

Still, McQuown retains some of his adherents. Grain, the beef butcher, who, I am sure, buys stolen beef from McQuown, remains loyal to him. Ranchers, such as Blaikie, Quaintance, and Burbage, view the outlaw as a necessary evil, point out that their problems would be greatly increased without the presence of a controlling hand, and in any case are apt to view Blaisedell, possibly because he is a townsman and an agent of townsmen, with suspicion.

I do not think the Citizens' Committee intends to do more than post the three road agents (or more probably four, including Friendly) out of town, but that remains to be seen. There is some talk of posting at the same time a chronic malcontent and agitator among the miners, but I feel this would confuse the present issue. I presume a meeting will be called by this week's end, at the latest.

February 2, 1881

I am sorry for Deputy Gannon. He must know that his brother's fate is being decided, all around him, by the jury this town has become, and he looks gaunt and haunted, and as though he has not slept in days. He, Schroeder, and the Marshal have not had much to occupy their time of late. Warlock is in a fit of righteousness, and men are exceedingly careful in their actions. The presence of Death does not make us feel pity for the dead or the condemned, but only a keen awareness of our own ultimate end and a determination to circumvent it for as long as possible.

February 3, 1881

A despicable rumor is being circulated, to the effect that the Cowboys are truly innocent, and that the bandits actually were Morgan and one or more of his employees from the Glass Slipper; that Morgan was seen riding furtively back to town not long after the stage arrived here, etc. This is an obvious tactic of McQuown's adherents here to backhandedly attack Blaisedell, as well as of Morgan's enemies, of whom there are a great number. Why Morgan should have taken up road-agentry, when he has a most lucrative business in his gambling establishment, has not been stated.

Morgan is certainly roundly hated here, with good reason and bad. I might venture to say that unanimity of opinion comes closest to obtaining in Warlock as regards dislike of him. Personally, I think I would choose him over his competitor, Taliaferro, and I am sure that Taliaferro relieves his customers of their earnings no less rapidly or crookedly than Morgan. Yet Morgan does it with a completely unconcealed disdain of his victims and their manner of play. His contempt of his fellows is always visible, and his habitual expression is that of one who has seen all the world and found none of it worth while, least of all its inhabitants. He has evidently acted viciously enough upon occasion too. There was the instance of a Cowboy who worked for Quaintance, a handsome and well-liked young fellow named Newman, who, unfortunately, had larcenous tendencies. He stole three hundred dollars from his employer, which he promptly lost over Morgan's faro layout. Quaintance learned of this and applied to Morgan for the return of the money. Morgan did return it, possibly under pressure from Blaisedell, but dispatched one of his hirelings, a fellow named Murch, after young Newman. Murch caught him in Bright's City and, following Morgan's instructions, beat the boy half to death.

Like others of prominence here Morgan has been the object of many foul, and, I am sure, untrue tales. Unlike others, he seems pleased and flattered by this attention (I suppose this furnishes further evidence to him in support of his opinions of his fellow man), and has even sometimes hinted that the most incredible accusations of him may be true.

Because of all this, however, Blaisedell, in his fast friendship with Morgan, is rendered most vulnerable. I hope Morgan does not become the Marshal's Achilles' heel.

## 18. *The Doctor Arranges Matters*

THE DOCTOR hurried panting up the steps of the General Peach and into the thicker darkness of the entryway. He rapped on Jessie's door; his knuckles stung. "Jessie!"

He heard her steps. Her face appeared, pale with the light on it, framed in curls. "What's the matter, David?" she said as she opened the door wider for him. He moved in past her. A book lay open on the table, a blue ribbon across the page for a bookmark. "What's the matter?" she said again.

"They have instructed him to post five men out," he said, and sat down abruptly in the chair beside the door. He held up his hand, spread-fingered, and watched it shake with the sickening rage in him. "Benner, Billy Gannon, Calhoun, and Friendly. *And* he is to post Frank Brunk."

She cried out, "Oh, they have not done that!"

"They have indeed."

She looked frightened. He watched her close the book over the blue ribbon. She stood beside the table with her head bent forward and her ringleted hair sliding forward along her cheeks. Then she sank down onto the sofa opposite him.

"I have talked myself dry to the bone," he said. "It did no good. It was not even a close vote. Henry and Will Hart and myself—and Taliaferro, of course, who would not want to offend the miners' trade. The judge had already left in a rage."

"But it is a mistake, David!"

"They did it very well," he went on. "I will admit myself that Brunk is a troublemaker. His activities could easily lead to bloodshed. Lathrop's did. Brunk has been posted to protect the miners from themselves—that is the way Godbold put it. And to protect Warlock from another mob of crazed muckers running wild and smashing everything—that is the way Slavin put it. What if they fired the Medusa stope? Or all the stopes, for that matter? I think the only thing Charlie MacDonald had to say in the matter was what would happen to Warlock if the miners, led by Brunk, succeeded in closing all the mines out of spite? Evidently they are thought entirely capable of it."

He beat his fist down on the arm of the chair. And so we fell into the trap we had set for ourselves when we brought Blaisedell here, he thought. "It was so well done!" he cried.

"But Jessie, if you had been at the meeting, they could not have done it."

"Posting men from Warlock is nothing I can—"

"You should have gone!"

"I will go to see every one of them now."

"It will do no good. Each one will lay it on the rest." He slumped back in the chair; he told himself firmly that he would not hate Godbold, Buck Slavin, Jared Robinson, Kennon, or any of the others; he would only try to understand their fears. What angered him most was the knowledge that they were, in part, right about Frank Brunk. But he knew, too, that he himself was now inescapably on the side of the miners. Heaven knew that a blundering, stupid leader such as Brunk was no good to them; but Brunk was all, at present, that they had. It was as though he had, at last, come face to face with himself, and, at the same moment, saw that the man who was his own mortal enemy was Charles MacDonald of the Medusa mine.

"Poor Clay," he heard Jessie whisper.

"Poor *Clay*! Not poor Frank? Not those poor fellows—" He stopped. She had said it was a mistake, and he saw now what she meant. The miners' angel had become the guardian of Blaisedell's reputation. All at once he could regard her more coldly than he had ever done before.

"Yes," he said. "It is a terrible mistake. Do you think you can persuade Blaisedell that he must do no such a thing?"

"I must try," she said, nodding as though Clay Blaisedell were the object of both their concerns.

"Yes," he said. "For if he does this to Brunk, how is he any better than Jack Cade, who was hired to do it to Lathrop? And you know what Frank is like as well as I do. I think he would not go if ordered to, and how would Clay deal with him then? Frank is no gunman."

He glanced at her from under his brows. She was sitting very stiffly, with her hands clasped white in her lap. Her great eyes seemed to fill the frail triangle of her face. "Oh, no," she said, with a start, as though she had not been listening but knew some reply was called for. "No, he can't be allowed to do it. Of course he can't. It would be terribly wrong."

"I'm glad we agree, Jessie."

She frowned severely. "But if I can't persuade him to—to disobey the Citizens' Committee, then Frank will have to go. That's all there is to it. He will go if I ask him to, won't he, David?"

He did not know, and said so. She announced decisively that she wished to speak with Brunk first, and he left her to find him. In the entryway, with her door closed behind him, he stood with a hand to his chest and his eyes blind in the solid dark. He had thought she was in love with a man, but now he saw, with almost a pity for Blaisedell, that she was in love merely with a name, like a silly schoolgirl.

The doctor moved slowly along the tunnel of darkness toward the lighted hospital room. The faces in the cots turned toward him as he entered. Four men were playing cards on Buell's cot—Buell, Dill, MacGinty, and Ben Tittle. The boy Fitzsimmons stood watching them, with the thick wads of his bandaged hands crossed over his chest.

There was a chorus of greetings. "What about the road agents, Doc?" someone called to him.

"Did Blaisedell post those cowboys yet?"

He nodded curtly, and asked if anyone had seen Brunk.

"Him and Frenchy's up in old man Heck's room, I think," MacGinty said.

"You want him, Doc?" Fitzsimmons said. "I'll go tell him." He went out, his bandaged hands held protectively before him.

"Hey, Doc, how many got posted?" a man called.

"Four," he said. Someone laughed; there was a swell of excited speculation. He said. "Ben, could I see you for a minute?"

He stepped back out into the dark hall. When Tittle came out, he told him to go find Blaisedell in half an hour. Then he went back down to Jessie's room; she glanced up at him and apprehensively smiled when he entered, and he went over and put out a hand to touch her shoulder. But he did not quite touch it, and, as he stared down at the curve of her cheek and the warm brown glow of the lamplight in her hair, his throat swelled with pain, for her. He turned away and his eye caught the dark mezzotint of Bonnie Prince Charlie, kilted, beribboned, gripping his sword in noble and silly bravado.

He heard heavy footsteps descending the stairs. "Come in, Frank," he said, as Brunk appeared in the doorway.

Brunk came inside. "Miss Jessie," he said. "Doc. What was it, Doc?"

"The Citizens' Committee has voted to have you posted out as a troublemaker," he said, and saw Brunk's eyes narrow, his scar of a mouth tighten whitely.

"Did they now?" Brunk said, in a hoarse voice. All at once he grinned. "Is the marshal going to kill me, Miss Jessie?"

"Don't be silly, Frank."

Brunk held out his hands and looked down at them. Then, with a ponderous, triumphant lift of his head Brunk looked up at the doctor and said, "Why, I expect he is going to have to, Doc. Do you know? The boys wouldn't move for Tom Cassady, but maybe they will if—"

"Don't be a fool!" he said.

"Now, Frank, you are to listen to me," Jessie said, in a crisp, sure voice, and she rose and approached Brunk. "I am going to ask him not to do this thing, whatever the Citizens' Committee has decided. But if I—"

"Ah!" Brunk broke in. "The miners' angel!"

"You will be civil, Brunk!"

A flush darkened Brunk's face. He took hold of his forelock and pulled his head down, as though in obeisance. "Bless you, Miss Jessie," he said. "I am beholden to you again."

"I have promised to try," Jessie went on. "But as I was saying when you interrupted me—if I cannot, then you must promise to leave."

"Run for it?" Brunk said. "Run?"

"Do you have to go out of your way to be offensive, Brunk?"

"Doc, I am trying to go out of my way to be a man! But she won't let me, will she? She will nurse me off this. She is too heavy an angel! She wouldn't let Tom Cassady die when he was begging to. She won't let me—" He stopped, and his mouth drew sharply down at the corners. "If I had courage enough," he said. "But maybe I don't."

"I don't know what you are talking about, Frank."

"I don't know what I am talking about either. Because they would not move even for me, and I would be a fool. But what would *you* do, Doc?"

"I think I would do as she asks," he said, and could not meet Brunk's eyes.

"Why, I have to, don't I?" Brunk said. "She has kept me since I was fired at the Medusa. Put up with me, and fed me. But, Miss Jessie—you said Jim Lathrop didn't have courage enough. Why won't you let me have it? Maybe I have got enough."

"I'm sure I don't know what you are talking about," Jessie said. "But if you will not do this for your own sake—and I understand that men must have their pride, Frank—then you must do it for mine. I hope it will not be necessary."

Brunk stared at her. "Why, I would be a fool, wouldn't I?" he said in his heavy, infinitely bitter voice. "And ungrateful too, since it is for your sake, Miss Jessie. But don't you see, Doc?"

The doctor could say nothing, and Jessie put a sympathetic hand on Brunk's arm. But Brunk drew away from her touch and backed out the door. His heavy tread slowly remounted the stairs.

"I don't understand," Jessie said, in a shaky voice.

"Don't you?" he said. "Brunk was just wishing he might be a hero, and knows he cannot be. It is difficult for a man to bring himself to be a martyr when he is afraid he might look a fool instead. Do you think you can persuade Blaisedell?"

She did not answer. She was staring at him strangely, tugging at the little locket that hung around her throat.

"It is very important that you do," he went on. "Because of what the miners would think of you if Blaisedell went through with this. Whether Brunk fled, or not. And because of what everyone would think of Blaisedell."

He felt a blackguard; he turned so as to confront himself in her glass, and saw there a short, gray man with bowed shoulders in a shabby black suit, undistinguished looking, not handsome, not heroic in any way, almost old. The eyes that gazed back at him from the glass looked like those of a man with a dangerous fever.

"There is Clay," Jessie whispered, as footsteps came along the boardwalk outside her window.

"I wish you luck with him, Jessie," he said. He went out into the entryway just as Blaisedell entered; a little light from Jessie's open door gleamed in the marshal's hair as he took off his hat.

"Evening, Doc," he said gravely.

"Pardon me," the doctor said, and Blaisedell stepped aside so that he could pass.

Outside he stood on the porch for a moment, breathing deeply of the fresh, cool air, and gazing up at the stars bright and cold over Warlock. Behind him he heard Blaisedell say, "Did you want to see me, Jessie?" Quickly the doctor descended the steps to get out of earshot. He went up the boardwalk, across Main Street, and on up toward Peach Street and the Row.


## 19. *A Warning*


IN THE jail Carl Schroeder, Peter Bacon, Chick Hasty, and Pike Skinner were talking about the posting, while at the cell door Al Bates, from up valley, watched them with his whiskered chin resting on one of the crossbars.

"You suppose the news got down to Pablo yet?" Hasty asked.

"Dechine was in," Bacon said, from his chair at the rear. "And went back down valley yesterday. I expect he'd take it as neighborly to stop in and tell McQuown the news on his way home."

"They won't come," Schroeder said, hunched over the table, scowling, gouging the point of a pencil into the table top.

Hasty said, "I guess Johnny's plenty worried Billy'll show."

"Worried of getting in bad with McQuown, mostly," Skinner said. "He—"

"You!" Schroeder said. "I am sick of hearing you picking at Johnny Gannon!" He flung the pencil down. "He come in here and put on that star, *you* didn't! You quit fretting at him, Mister Citizens' Committee Skinner!"

Peering up at Skinner from under his hat brim, Hasty said, "Is MacDonald going to see the Committee fires Blaisedell for saying them no on that jack, Pike?"

"He did right," Skinner said, with a sour face. "Nobody's thought of firing him. MacDonald fired that son of a bitch Brunk how long ago, but he still hangs around trying to drum up a fuss. It's the Committee's business to post out troublemakers, but Blaisedell can't go against a dumb jack that doesn't know one end of a Colt from the other."

"Old Owen was saying he heard some muckers talking that if the Committee fired Blaisedell over it, the miners would get together and hire him themself," Schroeder said. "And put him to post MacDonald first thing."

The others laughed.

"There is talk Miss Jessie had a hand in the marshal changing his mind about Brunk," Hasty said.

"Lot of talk up our way them two is going to come to matrimony right quick," Bates said from the cell. "Make a fine-looking couple."

Nobody spoke for a time, and finally Bacon sighed and said, "You suppose the four of them is going to come against him? Or not?"

"They won't come," Schroeder said again, grimly. He began to jab his pencil at the table top once more.

Standing in the doorway Skinner worriedly shook his head. He turned as there was an approaching cracking sound on the boardwalk.

"Here comes old Judge," Bates said. "Charging along on that crutch of his to give everybody pure hell again."

The judge entered past Skinner. With his shoulders hunched up by the crutch and his claw-hammer coat hanging loose, the judge looked like a big, awkward, black bird. He halted and his bloodshot eyes glared fiercely around the jail. "Where's the deputy?"

"Here!" Schroeder said. He raised himself reluctantly from the judge's chair, and leaned against the cell door.

"Not you. The other one."

"Sleeping, I guess. He was on late last night."

"There's no sleep any more," the judge said. He shifted his weight from the crutch to a hand braced on the table, and sat down with a grunt. His crutch clattered to the floor.

"Aw, please, Judge," Hasty said. "Leave us sleep sometimes. We got little enough else."

The judge scraped his chair around to face the others. "You would sleep through the roof of the world caving in and not even know it," he said. He removed his hat, using both hands, and set it before him. He glared around the room.

"By God, you stink, Judge," Skinner said. "Why don't you come down to the Acme and me and Paul and Nate'll scrape you down in the horse trough?"

"I don't stink like you all stink." The judge rubbed at his eyes, muttering to himself. "Where is Blaisedell?" he said suddenly. "He is running from me!"

Everyone laughed. "Laugh!" the judge cried. "Why, you poor, ignorant pus-and-corruption sons of bitches, he is afraid of me!"

"He's went for his gold-handles, Judge," Schroeder said. "Then he'll show."

They laughed again, but the laughter broke off abruptly as a shadow fell in the door. Blaisedell came in, bowing his head a little as he stepped through the doorway. He was coatless, wearing a clean linen shirt and a broad, scrolled-leather shell belt, with a single cedar-handled Colt holstered on his right thigh.

"Judge," he said. He nodded to each of them. "Deputy. Boys. Looking for me, Judge?"

"I was," the judge said, and Bates snickered. The judge said, "I am warning you, Marshal. You are now standing naked and all alone. The Citizens' Committee has gone and disqualified itself plain to everyone from pretending to run any kind of law in this town. Ordering you to something that wasn't only illegal and bad but was pure damned outrage besides. And you have gone and disqualified yourself from them by refusing to do it. Now!" he said, triumphantly.

Blaisedell took off his hat and idly slapped it against his knee. He looked at once amused and arrogant. "You are speaking for who, Judge?" he asked politely.

"I am speaking—" the judge said. His voice turned shrill. "I'm speaking for— I'm just warning you, Marshal!"

"Listen to him go at it!" Bates whispered. "By God, he is a real Turk, that old Judge."

Blaisedell glanced at him and he looked abashed.

"For what you have done," the judge went on, more calmly, "you have run up a ukase on those four boys all by yourself now."

"Pardon?" Blaisedell said.

"Now, hold on, Judge—" Schroeder began.

"Ukase!" the judge said. "That is a kind of imperial king I-want. What the king does when he makes the rules as he goes along. You have run one up the flagstaff and yourself with it. For what was behind you has blown itself out to nothing, and you have walked off away from it anyhow. I told you it was the only thing you had! And a poor thing, but even it gone now."

"Don't listen to the old cowpat, Marshal," Skinner said placatingly. "He has got a load on and raving. He is not talking for anybody. He is surely not talking for the Citizens' Committee."

"I am talking for his conscience," the judge said. "If he can hear it talking in his pride!"

"Why, I can hear you, Judge," Blaisedell said. He stood looking down at the judge with his eyebrows hooked up, and his mouth, beneath the fair mustache, flat and grave. "But saying what?"

"Saying there is nothing you are accountable to any more," the judge said. "You have got no status, you have chucked it away. No blame to you for that, Marshal, but it is gone. What I am saying is you can't post those four fellers out. You are no law-making body. You can't make laws against four men. Neither could the Citizens' Committee, but they had a better claim than you. Mister Blaisedell, you are running up a banishment-or-death ukase and it is illegal and outlaw and pure murder. There is no law behind you!"

"Fry your head in your God-damned law!" Skinner said. "We saw enough of it, up in Bright's City."

The judge massaged his eyes with his hands again. Then he squinted cunningly up at Skinner. "You saw lynch law here in town just before that," he said. "You didn't like that either, did you? Liked that some less, didn't you?" he cried. Pressing down on the table top, he half-raised his thick body, and cords stood out on the sides of his neck. "Did you like that mob? I tell you he is a one-man lynch mob if he goes on like he is headed!"

"By God!" Bates whispered, admiringly. "I bet he could beller a brick wall down."

The judge sank back into his seat. Blaisedell's intense blue stare inspected, one by one, the men in the room. They fastened last upon the judge again, and he said, coldly, "One man is a different thing from a mob. If a man runs with a pack like that he is only a part of the pack and the whole thing hasn't got a brain or anything. I say what you said just now is foolishness, and I think you know it. I am not scared of myself so I have to look around every second to make sure the Citizens' Committee is standing right behind, nodding to me. Or the town either," he said, glancing at Hasty. "Because in a thing like this I know best and can do best by myself."

"You have said it out loud!" the judge whispered. "You have said it. You have set yourself above the rest in your pride!"

Blaisedell's face tightened. "If I am hired to keep the peace in this town," he said, slowly and distinctly, "why, I will do it and the best I can. Judge, I would keep those four birds out of town whether anyone told me to or not."

"You are not going to keep them out! You are going to kill them! You are going to shoot them down dog-dead in the street, or them you. Keep the peace! Why, if that don't make somebody a murderer and somebody dead that didn't need to be then I can't see across my nose! Keep the peace! Why, you will bust it wide open with your hail-to-the-king ukase!"

"Maybe," Blaisedell said. "But most likely they won't come in."

"They will come!" the judge said. "I'll tell you why they will come. Because now they are guilty-as-sin road agents to every man, and they know it. They are that if they stay out, and yellow-bellies besides. If they come in they will think they are honest-to-genuine, gilt-edged heroes proving they are innocent to all, and striking a blow for freedom too. Men have died for that many's the time, and God bless them for it!"

"They know better than to come," Skinner said.

"They will have to come. And you, Mister Marshal of Warlock Blaisedell, have made it so. There is no way out of it. So you will have to kill them. And that will put you wrong. You will fall by it, son."

"Don't call me son, Judge," Blaisedell said, very quietly. A vein began to beat in his temple.

The judge said in a blurred voice, "Marshal, if you understand me and go your way anyhow, God help you. You will be killing men out of pride. You will be doing foul murder before the law, and you will stand trial in Bright's City for it or these deputies here ought to throw their badges in the river. For you will be an illegal black criminal and outlaw and murderer with the blood fresh on you as bad as any of McQuown's and worse, and every man's hand should be against you. Murder for pride, Marshal; it is an ancient and awful crime to go to book for."

Blaisedell backed up a step, to stand in the patch of sunlight just inside the door. He put his hat back on and tapped it once, and glanced around the jail again. This time no one met his eyes.

Blaisedell said gravely, "Maybe somebody will get killed, Judge. But that is between them and me, for who else is hurt by it?"

"Every man is," the judge whispered.

Blaisedell flushed, and the arrogant, masklike expression came over his face again. But his voice remained pleasant. "You have been going on about pride like it was a bad thing, and I disagree with you. A man's pride is about the only thing he has that's worth having, and is what sets him apart from the pack. We have argued this before, Judge, and I guess I will say this time that a man that doesn't have it is a pretty poor specimen and apt to take to whisky for the lack. For all whisky is, is pride you can pour in your belly."

The judge flushed too, as Bates snickered and Schroeder grinned. "That was a mean thing you said, Marshal," the judge said. "But I won't say it isn't so, so maybe I am honester than you. And I don't have to be scared of you, either, Marshal."

Skinner said disgustedly, "You a poor, one-legged, loud-mouthed old—"

The judge raised a finger toward Blaisedell's face. "Being decent like you are—and I didn't say you wasn't!—I think you can brace no man that has got right on you; I think you know that. It is what I am warning you. What you are working toward in your pride is some day meeting a man that has got to kill you or you him, only he is righter and you know it. Because you have gone wrong. And what are you going to do then?" His voice sank until it was almost inaudible. "That is the box, Clay Blaisedell. What are you going to do then?"

There was a taut silence. Blaisedell's face had paled, except for the spots of color on his cheeks. "Judge Holloway," he said, in his deep voice. "I think you haven't only been drinking." He paused ominously. "I think you have been drinking out in the hot sun."

Everyone laughed explosively in the sudden release of tension, and Blaisedell himself grinned. "Well, I guess I will go have a glass of whisky for my bruised-up pride," he said, and turned to go out.

"Marshal," Pike Skinner said. "I just want to say—" His angular, ugly face reddened furiously. "I just wanted to say the judge wasn't speaking for me just now, and I know he wasn't speaking for Carl Schroeder. I expect he wasn't speaking for anybody but Taliaferro's bad whisky."

"That's right, Marshal," Schroeder said.

"That goes for me, Marshal," Hasty said, and got to his feet.

Peter Bacon said nothing. His brown, lined face was sad. The marshal glanced at him. Then he nodded silently to the others and went on outside.

The judge rubbed his hands over his face. Then he turned to Schroeder; his dark face was drawn and puckered around the wart on his cheek. "You mark what I have said, Carl Schroeder. He is going to kill men and it will be on you to arrest him for it. Hear?"

"I don't hear," Schroeder said. "You are acting like a damned virgin, Judge. Like you have never known a man to be shot down before. It'll be a day when I try to arrest Blaisedell."

The judge bent, grunting, to recover his crutch, and then, red-faced with effort, thrust himself upright and hooked the crutch under his armpit. He set his hat, which was too small for him, on his head. He said contemptuously, "Maybe you will see, some day, how if you are bound to arrest some of McQuown's people for a thing, you are bound to arrest another man the same. So if Blaisedell goes out and murders—"

"Great God, Judge!" Schroeder cried. "You are getting it all switched around who is murderers here!"

The judge hobbled toward the door, his crutch tip racketing. Pike Skinner glared at him. At the door the judge turned again, the hat slipping forward over one eye. "We all are, boys," he said. He swung on outside on his crutch and his one good leg.

## 20. *Gannon Has a Nightmare*

It is a dream, he told himself; it is only a dream. Sweating, naked, daubed with mud, he crouched behind a crag upon the canyon wall and watched against the curtain of his memory the sandy river bottom of Rattlesnake Canyon, listening in the waiting silence to the pad of hoof irons in the sand and the sharper, urgent sound as a hoof struck stone, and, nearer, the musical clink of harness, and nearer still, voices soft-mouthed with Spanish; his heart turning over on itself as the first one came around the far bend upon a narrow-faced white horse, looking very tall at first in his high, peaked sombrero, but small, compact, brown, watchful-eyed, with pointed mustachios, behind him another and another, some with striped serapes hung over their shoulders and all with rifles carried underarm; seven, eight, and more and more, until there were seventeen in all, and Abe's Colt crashed the signal. The echo was instantaneous and continuous. Smoke drifted up from all around the canyon where the other mud-daubed figures were concealed, and it was as though an invisible flash flood had in that instant swept down the canyon: horses reared and screamed, swept backward in the flood, and died; men were thrown tumbling, a rifle flung up in a wide arc turning end over end with weird slowness, and there were gobbling Apache cries mixed with the screams of dying men. There was the white horse lying on the reddening sand, there was the leader in his high, silver-chased hat crawling in the stream; then the hat gone, then a part of his head gone, and he lay still in the channel with his jacket shiny and bloated in the water that ran red over him. And now the half-naked, muddy Apache figures stood all around the canyon, yelling as they fired into the mass of dying men and horses below them, the faces magnified and slowly revolving before his eyes—Abe, and Pony and Calhoun and Wash and Chet, and on the far side Billy and Jack Cade, Whitby and Friendly, Mitchell, Harrison, and Hennessey.

And at the end there came the Mexican running and scrambling up the steep bank toward him, hatless, screaming hoarsely, brown eyes huge and rimmed with white like those

of a terrified stallion, and the long gleam of the six-shooter
in his hand, slipping and sliding but coming with unbelievable rapidity up the canyonside toward him, John Gannon. He
changed as he came. Now he came more slowly; now it was a
tall, black-hatted figure walking toward him through the dust,
slow-striding with the massive and ponderous dignity not of
retribution but of justice, with great eyes fixed on him, John
Gannon, like ropes securing him, as he cried out and snatched
in helpless weakness at his sides, and died screaming mercy,
screaming acceptance, screaming protest in the clamorous and
horrible silence.

It is only a dream, he told himself, calmly; it is only the
dream. But there was another reverberating clap of a shot still.
He died again, in peace, and waked with a jolt, as though he
had fallen. There was another knock in the darkness of his
room.

"Who is it?" he called.

"It's me, Bud," came a whisper. He swung off his cot in his
underwear and went to open the door. Billy came in, stealthily.
A little moonlight entered through the window, and Billy was
visible as he moved past it, wearing a jacket and jeans, his hat-
brim pulled low over his face.

"What are you doing in town?"

"Come to see you, Bud." Billy laughed shakily. "Sneaked in.
Tomorrow I don't sneak in."

Billy took off his hat and flung it down on the table. He
swung the chair around and sat down facing Gannon over its
back. The moonlight was white as mother-of-pearl on Billy's
face.

Gannon slumped down on the edge of the bed, shivering.
"Just you?" he said.

"Pony and Luke and me. Calhoun weaseled."

"Why Pony?"

"What do you mean, why Pony?"

"He hasn't any right to come—he was at the stage. Was
Luke in on it, or not?"

"Not," Billy said shortly. Then he said, "It doesn't matter
who was at the stage or not."

"No, it doesn't matter now. They were lied off and you with
them, so it is too late to tell the truth."

"I don't know what you mean," Billy said. Gannon could see that he was shivering too. "But I have got to do it, Bud."

"Got to get yourself killed?" He had not meant to speak so harshly.

"Don't be so damned sure about that!"

"Got to kill Blaisedell then?"

"Well, somebody's got to, for Christ's sake!"

Gannon closed his eyes. It might be the last time he saw Billy; probably it was; he knew it was. And they would wrangle meaninglessly over who was the son of a bitch, Blaisedell or Abe McQuown. It seemed to him that if he was any kind of man at all he could let Billy have his way tonight.

"Listen, Bud!" Billy said. "I know what you think of Abe."

"Let's not talk about it, Billy. It's no good."

"No, listen. I mean, what is different about him? He goes along the way he always did that used to be all right with everybody, but everybody's got down on him. He gets blamed for everything! He—"

"Like the Apaches used to," he said, and despised himself for saying it.

Billy said in a husky voice, "I know that was a piss-poor thing. Do you think I liked that? But you make too much of it."

"I know I do."

"Well, like the Paches; surely," Billy went on. "But you know what it's like all around here. Every son with a true-bill out against him ends up here, and he has got to eat so he swings a wide loop or tries to agent a coach or something. And Abe gets blamed for it all! But you know damned well—"

"Billy, you are not coming in tomorrow because of Abe."

"Coming in because a man has to stand up and be a man!" Billy said. "That suit you? Because it is a free country and sons of bitches like Blaisedell is trying to make it not."

He looked at Billy's taut, proud young face with the glaze of moonlight on it, and slowly lowered his head and massaged his own face with his hands. Billy's voice had been filled with righteousness and it tore him to hear it, and to hear Abe McQuown behind it furnishing the words that were true enough when Billy spoke them and yet were lies because they came from Abe McQuown.

"But I guess you don't think that way," Billy said.

Gannon shook his head.

"He is after Abe," Billy went on. "He is after all of us! A person can't stand it when there is somebody on the prod for him all the time. Trying to run him out or kill him. A man has got to stand up and—"

"Billy, Blaisedell saved your life when he backed off that lynch party. And Pony's, and Cal's, and maybe mine. And he could have killed Curley that night in the Glass Slipper, if that was what he was after. And you too. And Abe."

"He just wanted to look good, was all. And us to look bad. I know how it would've been if he'd had us alone and nobody to see."

"What if he kills you tomorrow?" he whispered.

"I've got to die some day, Christ's sake!" Billy said, with pitiful bravado. "Anyway he won't. I figure Pony and Luke can stand off Morgan and Carl, or that Murch or whoever he's got to back him. I figure I can outpull him and outshoot him too. I'm not scared of him!"

"What if he kills you?" he said again.

"You keep saying that! You're trying to scare me. You want me to run from him?"

"Yes," he said, and Billy snorted. "Billy—" he said, but he knew it was useless even before he said it. "You weren't at the stage and you shot Ted Phlater in self-defense, but not the way it looked in court. Billy, I can't see you die a damned fool. I—"

"Don't you ever say a thing to anybody about any of that," Billy said coldly. "I am with them, whatever way it happened. That is gone past now. You hear? That's all I ask of you, Bud."

That hurt him, as part of the long hurt that Billy had never been able to think much of him. He sat shivering on the edge of the bed, and now, when he didn't look at his brother, Billy seemed to him already to have become just another name on Blaisedell's score, and just another mound on Boot Hill marked with one of Dick Maples' crosses. With horror he looked back to Billy's moonlit face.

"Billy, I don't mean it any way and you don't have to say if you don't want to, but—do you want to die?"

Billy was silent for a long time. He leaned back and his face was lost in shadow. Then he laughed scornfully, and one of his bootheels thumped on the floor. But his voice was not scornful: "No, I am afraid of dying as any man, I guess, Bud." He rose abruptly. "Well, I'll be going. Pony and Luke are camped out in the malapai a way." He started toward the door, pushing his hat down hard on his head.

"Sleep here if you want. I'm not going to try to argue with you any more. I know you are going to do what you are set on doing."

"Surely am," Billy said. He sounded childishly pleased. "No, I'll go on out there, I guess. Thanks." At the door he said, "Going to wish me luck?"

Gannon didn't answer.

"Or Blaisedell?" Billy said.

"Not him because you are my brother. Not you because you are wrong."

"Thanks." Billy pulled the door open.

"Wait," he said, getting to his feet. "Billy—I know if somebody shot me down you would take after them. I guess I had better tell you I won't do it. Because you are wrong."

"I don't expect anything of you," Billy said, and was gone. He left the door open behind him.

Gannon crossed to the door. He couldn't see Billy in the darkness of the hallway, but after a moment he heard the slow, stealthy descent of bootheels in the stairwell. He waited in the darkness until the sounds had ceased, and then he closed the door and returned to his cot, where he flung himself down with his face buried in the pillow and grief tearing at his mind like a dagger.

## 21. *The Acme Corral*

### I

(*From the sworn testimony of Nathan Bush, hostler in the Acme Corral, as reprinted in the* Bright's City Star-Democrat.)

NATE BUSH was alone in the Acme Corral when Billy Gannon, Luke Friendly, and Pony Benner rode in. Calhoun wasn't with them. They had come in up Southend from Medusa Street. It was about nine o'clock in the morning, maybe a little later.

"Go tell Blaisedell we have come in," Billy Gannon said to him. Billy Gannon was wearing two guns. Pony Benner did some fancy swearing about what they were going to do to Blaisedell and Morgan. Friendly didn't have anything to say.

When Bush left the corral they were dismounting. He went to find Blaisedell, and met Carl Schroeder and Paul Skinner coming out of the Boston Café. Schroeder told him to go on and tell Blaisedell. Blaisedell was shaving in his room at the General Peach. Bush told him, and the marshal only asked where they were and said he would be along directly, and went on shaving.

Bush went back then, and told some others he met that the cowboys had come in. There was already a good-sized crowd of people collected at the corner of Southend and Main, by Goodpasture's store.


II

(*From the testimony of Deputy Carl Schroeder.*)


It was a little after nine o'clock when Deputy Schroeder saw the marshal come around the corner from the General Peach. Blaisedell wasn't wearing a coat and he had on his pair of gold-handled Colts. It was the first time, so far as Schroeder knew, that anybody had seen them in Warlock.

He told Blaisedell that there were three of them, and said he stood ready to help any way he could, but Blaisedell said, "Why, thank you, Deputy, but I guess it is my fight."

Schroeder wanted to help, but it did not seem strange to him that the marshal did not accept him. He was no gunman, he knew that.

Blaisedell went on up the center of Main Street toward Southend. There were four or five horses tied to the rail along by the Lucky Dollar, and some men there. A few of them called out to Blaisedell as he passed, warning him to watch out and wishing him well. A wind had come up and dust was blowing, which was worrisome. Schroeder didn't see Morgan till Morgan was out in the street and buckling on his shell belt as he ran after the marshal.

### III

(*From the testimony of S. W. Brown, proprietor of the Billiard Parlor.*)

Sam Brown was standing before the Lucky Dollar with some others when he saw Morgan run out of the Glass Slipper, vault the rail, and, with his vest flapping and buckling his shell belt on, run after Marshal Blaisedell.

The marshal was walking straight up the street toward the corner, and men were calling out to him such things as, "Don't give those cowboys any break this time, Marshal" and "Watch out for some trick of McQuown's, now," "We are holding for you, Blaisedell," and "Good luck, Marshal!"

The marshal didn't act like he heard any of it. He didn't look worried, though. He had on his gold-handled pair everybody had heard about, and they looked fine in the sunshine. His shirt sleeves were gartered up like a bank clerk's. He was a sight to see, plowing toward the corner of Southend Street. Morgan caught up with him before he got there.

Brown heard Morgan say, "Hey, wait for a man!" Morgan fell into step beside the marshal. He had his shell belt hooked on now, and he was coatless like Blaisedell. Usually Morgan wore a shoulder gun, but it seemed more proper to see him this way, and he and the marshal looked pair enough to go against any three cowboys.

He heard Morgan say, "I am always one for a shooting match." Blaisedell said, "It is none of your fight, Morg," and Morgan said, as though he was hurt, "That is a hell of a thing to say to me, Clay!"

They went on up the street to the corner and Morgan was still talking, but by then they were out of Brown's hearing.

### IV

(*From the testimony of Oliver Foss, driver for the Warlock Stage Co.*)

Oliver Foss was on the corner by Goodpasture's store, along with Buck Slavin, Pike and Paul Skinner, Goodpasture, Wolters, and some others, when the marshal and Morgan walked

up Main Street. There was a wagon coming up Southend, Hap
Peters driving a team of mules. Dust was blowing from the
team and wagon and there was a dog running and yelping at
an offside wheel. Foss called to Hap to hurry it along because
the dust was bad and it had better have time to clear before the
marshal went down to the Skinner Brothers' corral.

Foss couldn't see into the Acme, where Billy Gannon, Pony
Benner, and Luke Friendly were supposed to be. He heard
Morgan say to the marshal, "Maybe there are only three, or
maybe there is a nigger in the woodpile." Morgan was grinning
in that way of his, like he didn't think much of anybody but
Tom Morgan and didn't mind rubbing it in either. They both
stopped when Deputy John Gannon came at a run across from
the jail, calling to the marshal.

John Gannon said to the marshal, "Can you give me five
minutes to try and get them out?" He didn't say it like he
expected anything to come of it, and a man had to feel sorry
for him.

Blaisedell said he had warned the road agents they weren't to
come into Warlock any more, but he didn't move on right away
and it sounded to Foss as though he were willing to listen to
reason. Gannon said, "Marshal, give me five minutes and I will
go down there and—" He didn't finish saying what he would
do; he talked in fits and starts, and he looked like he was chewing on something that had got gummed in his mouth. A man
had to feel sorry for him. Finally he said to the marshal how he
might disarm them, but by then his voice had got so low you
could hardly hear it.

Blaisedell asked him if he thought he could disarm them but
John Gannon didn't answer, and Morgan nudged the marshal
with his elbow. Then Gannon looked about to say something
more, but he never did, and the marshal and Morgan went on
down Southend Street, past the old, bowed-out corral fence
there. Morgan walked spread out from the marshal a little, so
when they came up even with the corral gate he and the marshal were about ten feet apart; and Morgan went on a few steps
after the marshal had turned toward the corral gate, so he was a
little behind and maybe ten or fifteen feet beyond the marshal
when the two of them stood facing into the Acme.

It was a little while yet before the shooting started.

V

(*From the testimony of Clay Blaisedell and of Thomas Morgan.*)

When Clay Blaisedell and Thomas Morgan faced the gate of the Acme Corral, halfway across the street from it, they both saw Luke Friendly first. He stood on the south side of the corral about twenty feet inside. There were three horses tied behind him, and the one nearest him had a rifle in the boot on the near side. Friendly was bent forward so he looked smaller than he really was, and had his hands held out at his waist for a fast draw. Crouched like that, with his hands like that, he looked to be backing away, though he didn't move. He looked to both Blaisedell and Morgan as though he didn't much want a fight, now that he had stopped to think about it.

Billy Gannon stood in the center and Pony Benner on the north side, close by the gate. Billy Gannon was wearing two guns, Benner one. They were both outlined against the wall of the Billiard Parlor at the back of the corral. Dust was blowing straight out of the corral in gusts of wind, but both Blaisedell and Morgan noticed that a door to the Billiard Parlor there stood a little way open.

Blaisedell considered Billy Gannon to be the leader, though Benner might be the more dangerous one. Friendly was not much to worry about unless he went for the rifle in the saddle boot. Blaisedell called to Billy Gannon by name and said, "You don't have to fight me, Billy."

Billy didn't answer. They could hear Benner cursing to himself. Morgan saw Friendly look toward the door to the Billiard Parlor and he said to Blaisedell behind his hand, "I will hold on that door. Don't you worry about it."

Blaisedell tried to talk to Billy Gannon again. "You don't have to fight me, Billy. You and your partners just mount up and ride out."

Billy said, "Go for your guns, you son of a b—!"

Blaisedell started moving forward then. He still thought the road agents might be backed out. This time he spoke to Benner. "Don't make us kill you, boys. Clear on out of here."

Billy Gannon yelled at them again to go for their guns, but did not start to draw his own yet, and Blaisedell kept moving forward. He thought he might get close enough to buffalo the boy, and then the others might fold. He had seen they had no stomach for it.

Morgan saw the door of the Billiard Parlor flung open, and yelled to Blaisedell. Blaisedell had seen it too, and he stepped sideways as a man with a Winchester showed there. He didn't know that it was Calhoun till later. The man let fly with the rifle and Morgan fired back, three times. Those were the only times that Morgan fired. The man yelled and fell sprawled out into the corral. Morgan swung around to cover Friendly, in case Friendly thought of going for the rifle in the boot, but he could see that Friendly had lost interest in the whole business.

When Calhoun had fired from the back, Benner had started for his Colt, and Blaisedell drew and fired. Pony went back hard with his hat rolling off, and didn't move again. Billy Gannon had looked back over his shoulder and seemed to be trying to dodge when the rifle went off. It sounded to Blaisedell as though he yelled, "No! No!" and when Billy turned back to face him he thought that Billy was going to put his hands up. But then Billy changed his mind, or else it had been a trick, and made his move. Blaisedell called his name again, but Billy was too close to count on his missing, and Blaisedell fired just as Billy got his six-gun clear of the holster. Billy spun around and dropped his Colt. His right arm was hanging broken, but he grabbed for his left-hand Colt and got a shot off.

Morgan saw Blaisedell stumble back, and jumped forward to try to get out from behind Blaisedell for a shot at Billy. But then Blaisedell fired again and Billy went down.

Friendly came running and yelling toward them with his hands held up. He caught hold of Blaisedell, crying out that he hadn't had anything to do with Calhoun being there and hadn't wanted anything to do with any of it. He was crying like a baby. They had made him come, he said, and he hadn't had anything to do with robbing the stage.

Blaisedell shook him off and said, "Get to shooting or get out of town!"

Friendly went running back toward the horses, still holding his hands up. Morgan thought he looked like he was going to dive into the horse trough. He could see that Blaisedell had been shot in the shoulder, but it looked no more than a crease. He saw Billy trying to get his six-shooter out, where he had fallen on top of it.

Blaisedell walked over to Billy and took the Colt away just as he pulled it free. Billy said to him, "I could have killed you if they hadn't done that." And he said, "I didn't know they was going to do that. Oh, the dirty sons of b----es!"

Morgan went over to the man who had fallen out the door of the Billiard Parlor and turned him over. He called to Blaisedell that it was Calhoun. Calhoun was already dead, and so was Benner. Friendly took out on his horse and went down Southend Street at a run.

Men were starting to come into the corral now, and Blaisedell called to them to get the doctor.

VI

(*From the testimony of Deputy Carl Schroeder.*)

Deputy Schroeder was one of the first into the Acme Corral after the shooting stopped. He saw Luke Friendly light out on his horse as though the fiends were after him. Pony Benner was dead just inside the corral gate and Blaisedell was standing by Billy Gannon, who was still alive. Blaisedell handed Schroeder Billy's Colt, and pointed out another where Billy had dropped it. Blaisedell had been creased on the right shoulder and it was bleeding some.

Billy Gannon was gasping and choking, and Johnny Gannon ran in and knelt beside him. Blaisedell moved off then. Morgan was over toward the back of the corral, where Calhoun was lying dead on a little adobe walkway outside the open side door of Sam Brown's Billiard Parlor. There was a rifle beside Calhoun. He was shot three times, once through the throat and the other two not a finger apart on the left side of his chest.

Schroeder asked Morgan if Calhoun had tried to ambush them from there, and Morgan said he had, and pushed Calhoun back over on his face with his foot.

Some others came over to look at Calhoun and congratulate Morgan, who moved off. A good lot of others were standing around Blaisedell. Dr. Wagner had shown up and was bending down over Billy Gannon, but anybody could see there wasn't anything to do.

After a while the doctor went to bind up Blaisedell's shoulder, and Johnny Gannon laid Billy flat on the ground. Then Gannon went up to Blaisedell, and some seemed to think there was going to be trouble, for they backed away. But Gannon only said to Blaisedell that Billy hadn't known about Calhoun, and Blaisedell answered that he was sure of it.

Schroeder busied himself asking if anybody had seen Calhoun come in, or hiding in the Billiard Parlor or anything. The Billiard Parlor didn't open till eleven o'clock, except Sundays, but Sam Brown told him the corral door was open sometimes in the mornings. Nobody had seen Calhoun at all, which didn't particularly mean anything as far as he, Schroeder, was concerned; because the fact was that Calhoun had been in the Billiard Parlor to try to dry-gulch Blaisedell, and it didn't have to be proved how he had got in there.

Maybe Billy Gannon and the rest of them hadn't known about Calhoun being there in the Billiard Parlor; he didn't see that it made any difference. For it was all McQuown's doing, any man could tell that.


VII

(*From the testimony of Lucas Friendly, cowboy.*)


Lucas Friendly had come into town with William Gannon, Thaddeus Benner, and Edward Calhoun, to protest to Marshal Clay Blaisedell that they had been unfairly and illegally posted from Warlock.

They had not come in to make trouble. They had only wanted to reason with the marshal. There had been no cause for posting them out of Warlock, which everybody knew was illegal anyway, except that some people had got down on them and their friends. They had heard that the marshal was a reasonable man, and had felt they could convince him that they had had no part in the stage robbery of which they had been so foully accused, and justly acquitted by a Bright's City jury. There had been some talk among them on the way up that their entrance into Warlock might be dangerous, but they had felt they had to talk it over with the marshal man to man.

Calhoun's horse had gone lame just before they reached Warlock, so the rest of them had got into town ahead of him. They told Nate Bush to go for the marshal and ask him to come to the Acme Corral so they could talk. They had not wanted to go abroad in Warlock, fearing trouble with certain townsmen who were unjustly set against them, and edgy toward them.

Calhoun had arrived while Bush was gone. They waited a long time, but the marshal did not appear, so, fearing that Bush had gone astray, Calhoun had gone into the Billiard Parlor to try to find someone there to send for the marshal.

But just then the marshal came down Southend Street. When they saw Morgan with him they knew it looked bad, and he, Lucas Friendly, was sick to see the marshal with that high-roller and both clearly coming after trouble.

Both he and Billy Gannon tried to reason with Blaisedell, but the marshal only shouted at them to go for their guns, and called them foul names.

Billy was a hot-headed boy, and Friendly was afraid that he and Benner would not stand for being called names like that. He had cautioned them to hold steady, while he tried to argue with the marshal some more. But he could see it was no use, and that the marshal and Morgan had murder in their hearts. Morgan began to curse them for being yellow—trying to get them to draw so it would be on them for starting the trouble.

Unluckily it was just then that Calhoun came back out of the Billiard Parlor, and right away Morgan started shooting, and Blaisedell drew and shot at Billy and Pony Benner. Billy and Pony started shooting back, but Blaisedell and Morgan had got first draw and shot them down as they had already shot Calhoun.

He, Friendly, kept yelling at Blaisedell that they had not come to make trouble, and trying to stop the shooting. But it was too late. They had killed the others by then, and he could not draw himself for both Blaisedell and Morgan had their six-shooters aimed at him. So he ran for his horse because he could see they were going to shoot him down whatever he did. He heard them arguing behind him which one was going to shoot him. Luckily for him, a lot of people came down Southend

Street toward the corral just then, thinking the shooting was over, and the marshal could not backshoot him for all these others to see it.

There had been nothing for him to do but jump his horse and ride for his life. They would have found some way to kill him if he hadn't.

He thought they would find some way to kill him yet. He had heard that both of them had sworn to do it. He knew they would try to shoot him down in cold blood as they had three fine young fellows with nothing in the world against them except that they had somehow got the marshal of Warlock down on them.

## 22. *Morgan Sees It Pass*

MORGAN SAT at the table in the front corner of the Glass Slipper that was always reserved for Clay and himself. What the Professor had called a "runkus" was in full bloom. The barkeepers were hustling whisky and beer and the conversation along the bar was shrill and reverberating; men called to each other over the heads of those around them, contended for attention, showed hands shaped into six-shooters in illustration, gesticulated with vehemence; in the mirrors behind the bar their eyes were bright and their faces excited. They were hashing over the fight in the Acme Corral. He could hear his own name coupled with Clay's, and the names of the cowboys, repeated and repeated.

Three men came in together. "Morgan," each said, in turn, and nodded to him, friendly and respectful. "That was a good piece of shooting, Morgan," one said. He nodded in reply, and grinned at himself that he should enjoy this. Others came in, and each one had a greeting for him.

"Put two in Calhoun about a finger apart and from clean across the street, I heard," someone said at the bar. Laughter wrenched at him that he should be a hero to them now. They were jackasses and schoolboys; either they saw that the men who had been killed might have been themselves, which made their own miserable lives more precious and engendered gratitude for the increase of value, or else they imagined themselves doing the shooting—and killing made a fellow quite a man, it made his whisky taste better and gave him a brag with the tommies at the French Palace.

Buck Slavin entered and approached him, with a hand out and his jaw shot out grimly; he was one of the second kind. "Morgan," Slavin said. "This town ought to thank you and the marshal. I thank you."

He shook the proffered hand, without rising. "I thank you for thanking me, Buck. But it was nothing."

"That was fine shooting."

"I was lucky, Buck," he said, solemnly, and shot his jaw out too.

Slavin clapped him on the shoulder and swaggered over to the bar. Morgan laughed to himself, as much at himself as at Slavin and the rest. Oh, I am lucky by trade, he thought. More men came in and congratulated him, and he folded his arms on his chest and looked stern, or grinned boyishly, and tried to keep his contempt from showing, the better to enjoy it. Someone sent over a bottle of whisky, which he raised in thanks.

"It will pass," he said to himself, as he poured a little whisky into his glass. He listened to his name coupled with Clay's, proud with the old pride of being counted with Clay. But it would pass. All things would pass, even the passing itself. But for once the pleasure and excitement drowned the sourness in him, and he was very pleased that it had worked so well for Clay. They would produce a brass band for Clay if they would send him a bottle of whisky.

"*Billy was the wrong man, though.*" He heard it, sharp-edged, from the bar. He did not even look to see who had said it, for immediately frozen in his mind's eye was the deeply etched track that led from Bob Cletus to Pat Cletus, from Pat Cletus to Billy Gannon. But it was all right, he reassured himself, so long as Clay did not see the track, see the wrong man again, see him, Tom Morgan— Yet abruptly his mood was broken. All things passed, he thought, except for that one thing.

There was a sudden hush in the Glass Slipper as Clay came in through the batwing doors. Then there was a chorus of greetings and congratulations, and men crowded around Clay to shake his hand, ask about his shoulder, praise him, curse McQuown for him, offer him drinks. Morgan poured whisky into the other glass and looked at nothing until finally Clay made his way over to him, dropped his hat on the table, and sat down with a long leg propped up on an empty chair. He had put on his coat, which would be a disappointment to those watching in the mirrors. Seeing his blood was something they could have told their grandchildren about.

"How?" he said to Clay.

"How," Clay said. His face was drawn and tired-looking. He drank his whisky and set his glass down. "Thanks for coming along, Morg."

"I'd like to have seen you try to stop me."

His heart pumped sickeningly when Clay said, "I was wrong about that boy." Then he sighed with relief as Clay continued. "I thought I could back him down."

"A wild-eyed gunboy trying to be a man."

"Man enough," Clay said. He raised a hand toward his shoulder but didn't touch it.

"McQuown ought to get a better sniper. That one wasn't much good."

Clay frowned, and said, in his deep voice, "Looks like it might've been McQuown behind it, sure enough. I guess I am going to have to have it out with him after all."

"You won't," Morgan said, and Clay glanced at him questioningly. "You won't have it out with him. He is not going to play your game when all he has got to do is use his own rules."

Clay shook his head.

"McQuown is right, too," Morgan went on. "If you are out to kill a man, kill him. It is war, not a silly game with rules."

"There are rules, Morg," Clay said.

"Why?"

"Because of the others—I mean the people not in it."

"Oh, you have started worrying about the people watching, have you?"

"No," Clay said. "But it is just so."

"You are in damned poor shape then against someone that doesn't think it is so. Or care a damn if it is or not. I say you can't beat McQuown for he won't play your rules."

"Why, Morg, I will beat him either way. I will beat him *by* playing the rules, if he won't. Because he will have to pretend there are rules whether he thinks there are or not, just like he had to today. And if he has to pretend, it means he is worrying about the others pretty hard." The corners of Clay's lips tilted up. "See if I'm not right," he said.

Morgan pushed at his glass with a forefinger. He did not know anyone else like Clay who would observe the rules to the end, live or die by them. There were some who would observe them insofar as they were a benefit, and, beyond that, would not, and there were those like McQuown who would make a fraud of the rules. That was the danger, but he did not see that Clay could do anything but ignore it. Clay had to, to be what he was, and Clay was the only man he had ever known, except for himself, who knew exactly what he was. It was the basis of his admiration for Clay. He had never understood their friendship on Clay's side. He only knew that Clay liked and trusted him, and it was the only thing that had become more precious to him than money, which, at the same time, he had come to realize was worth nothing, for it bought nothing. And so, somewhere along the line, his friendship for Clay had become all there was.

Clay's chin jerked up as the batwing doors swung in, and the number two deputy came in. There was a deeper hush than before, and a longer one, as Gannon came over toward them. Gannon's face was gray, his bent nose too big for his thin face; his hair was rumpled when he took off his hat. "Have a seat, Deputy," Clay said gently.

Gannon sat down and put his hat on the floor beside him, folded his hands on the table before him.

"Whisky?" Morgan asked.

"Yes," Gannon said, without looking at him. "Thanks."

Morgan beckoned for a glass. Gannon did not speak until it had been brought, and Clay was silent too. The faces still stared in the mirrors, but the noise began again.

Gannon said suddenly, "I guess I had better tell you, Marshal. Before it comes out another way. Billy wasn't with them when they stopped the stage. I don't know whether Luke was or not, but Billy wasn't."

Carefully Morgan did not look at Clay; he felt the sickening rapid pump of his heart again.

"What good does this do, Deputy?" Clay said harshly.

Gannon shook his head, as though that were not the point. "He wasn't there," he said. "He held with them because he was caught with them and I guess it was all—he thought he could do. And came in because of being posted out, I guess, Marshal."

"There was three of them at the stage at least," Clay said.

"Not him," Gannon said stubbornly. He cleared his throat. "Marshal, I know. Billy said so, and—"

"You could have told me," Clay said.

"What good would that have done?" Gannon said. He sounded almost angry now, and he brushed his fingers back nervously through his hair. "What could you have done different than you did?" he said. "He would have come in against you whatever. He was that kind."

"What difference does it make?" Morgan said, staring at the deputy. "He shot that posseman, didn't he?"

Gannon looked back at him with his deep-set, hot eyes. "That is nothing to do with it." He said to Clay, "Marshal, I am just saying there is probably others than me that know. So I thought you better had."

Clay sat with his head bent down and his mouth drawn tight. He nodded his head once, as though in thanks, and in dismissal. Gannon pushed his chair back and rose. He hesitated a moment, and then, since Clay did not speak again, plucked up his hat and went outside.

Morgan leaned forward toward Clay and said, "What the hell difference does it make? He killed that posseman and was out to kill you. Everybody knows that!"

Clay nodded a little, but when he raised his head the flesh of his face looked eroded, and his eyes were shuttered. He said in a quiet voice, "One time wrong and then every time wrong after it."

To himself Morgan cursed Clay and his rules, his scruples and his conscience. He cursed the Cletus brothers, the Gannon brothers, and himself. He said through his teeth, "You did everything but beg him to get the hell out of town!"

Clay did not reply; Morgan refilled Clay's glass, and filled his own. "How?" he said.

"I guess I had better do it," Clay said, and got to his feet.

"Where are you going?"

"Bright's City," Clay said. He put on his hat and patted the crown.

"What for?"

"Stand trial," Clay said, and went outside. The batwing doors swung through their arcs and came to rest behind him.

Morgan rinsed whisky through his mouth, and finally swallowed it. He smoothed his hands back over his hair, and halted them midway to press his head hard between them. "Damn you, Clay!" he whispered. Yet he should have foreseen, as soon as Gannon had spoken his piece, that Clay would feel he had to do this. One time wrong and every time wrong after it; Bob Cletus to Pat Cletus, and Pat Cletus to Billy Gannon; and not a one of them worth a minute's bother.

He rose and started down along the bar. Men were standing there two-deep now, and thick around Basine's layout. He caught Murch's eye and nodded to the other layout. Men greeted him cordially as he passed; he ignored them, listening to the names dropping out of the loud whine of talk—Billy Gannon, Pony, Calhoun, Curley Burne, Cade, McQuown, Johnny Gannon, Schroeder, and his own name and Clay's. Eyes watched him in the mirror and the talk died a little. He heard his name again, and halted.

A short, heavy-set miner with an arm in a dirty muslin sling was talking to McKittrick and another up-valley cowboy. "Why, this fellow I knew was up there at the trial and he said there wasn't anything but smoke blown against those poor boys there. They wasn't within fifty miles of that stage! So I say it is clear enough who stopped that stage if they didn't, and they didn't. Oh, there is plenty knows how come the marshal and Morgan had to shoot those poor boys down dead crack-out-of-the-box like they did, and you can bet they are sick Friendly got away. For what's dead is dead and don't talk back, and what's dead's forgotten about too. If the marshal and Morgan didn't throw down on that stage, I'll eat—"

His voice faltered as one of the cowboys nudged him, and he broke off. Slowly he raised his eyes to meet Morgan's in the mirror. The cowboys edged away.

"Eat what?" Morgan said.

The miner turned toward him. His mouth was pursed as though he had been sucking on a lemon. With his left hand he shifted the sling around before him. McKittrick moved farther away from him, with disclaiming gestures.

"Eat what?" Morgan said again. "I want to know what you are thinking of eating."

"Sneak around listening you will hear a lot of things," the miner said. He glanced around to see if he was getting any support. Then he said, "I just don't aim on ruckusing with anybody, Mr. Morgan, with this smash elbow I got."

"I want you to get started eating whatever it was you were fixing to eat," Morgan said. He stared into the miner's frightened eyes until the miner shifted the slinged arm again, with a fraud of a grimace of pain as he did it. "Because," Morgan said, "you are a dirty-mouth, stinking, lying, buggering, pissant, yellow-belly, mule-diddling, coyote-bred son of a nigger whore. Which is to say a mucker."

The miner's Adam's apple bounced once. He wiped his free hand across his mouth. "Why, I guess you wouldn't talk like that and still be standing if I had the use of my right arm here," he said. "I said what I said, Mr. Morgan."

"You said it in the wrong place."

The miner said stubbornly, "I guess a man can still talk—"

"Eat this, then," Morgan said, and hit the miner in the mouth. He kicked him in the crotch and the miner screamed and doubled up, clutching himself, and fell. Morgan kicked him in the face as he fell.

The miner lay face down by the rail at the base of the bar, his slinged arm beneath his body, one leg stretching and pulling up rhythmically. He groaned in a hoarse monotone. Murch came stumping up with the toothpick sticking out of the corner of his mouth.

"Get him out of here."

Murch picked the miner up by his belt and carried him like a suitcase toward the louvre doors.

Morgan swung around and went over to the second faro layout, and seated himself in the dealer's chair. He held his hands out over the box. His right knuckle was torn whitely and a trickle of blood showed, but his hands were as steady and motionless as though they were a part of the painted layout beneath them.

When he looked up to meet the eyes that watched him from the glass behind the bar, no longer friendly, he saw that what had been bound to pass had already quickly passed.

## 23. *Gannon Witnesses an Assault*

GANNON stood in the doorway of the *carpintería* staring at the greasy tarpaulin furred with sawdust and fine curls of wood. It was so stiff that the separate shapes beneath it were not discernible. He could not even tell which of the three pairs of boots that protruded beyond its edge was Billy's.

Old Eladio, with a maul and chisel, was cutting dovetails in a yellow pine board, and beyond him the other carpenter pushed his long plane along the edge of another board, freeing crisp curls of wood, which he shook from the plane from time to time. One of the coffins was already finished, and Gannon seated himself upon it. He tried to keep his eyes from those three pairs of narrow-toed boots. Eladio fitted an end and a side together, and meshed the dovetails with sharp raps of his maul.

"*Va bien?*" Gannon said, just to be saying something.

"*Si, bien,*" Eladio said. He bowed his bald, wrinkled brown head for a moment. "*Que lástima, joven.*"

Gannon nodded and closed his eyes, listening to the clean scuff of the plane and the tapping of the maul. Then abruptly he went out into the hot sunlight, and started up Broadway toward the jail. His Colt felt very heavy upon his thigh, his star heavy where it was pinned to his vest; his boots scuffed and tapped along the boardwalk. The men he passed watched him with carefully indifferent side glances.

In the thick shadow of the arcade on Main Street a knot of them, standing before the Billiard Parlor, moved aside to let him by, and he saw a horseman swing out of Southend Street, turning east. It was the marshal, riding a big-barreled black with white face and stockings. Blaisedell rode stiff-backed and heavy in his black broadcloth, trouser legs tucked into his boots, black hat tipped forward against the sun. The black's hoofs danced in the dust. Blaisedell glanced toward Gannon briefly, and he felt the intense blue stare like a physical push. The horse broke into a trot. He heard the men before the Billiard Parlor whispering as the black danced on down Main Street, horse and horseman gradually smaller and more and more dimly seen in the dust, until they disappeared on the Bright's City stage road.

As he went on again, toward the jail, he felt relieved; he had not been sure that Blaisedell had believed him.

The judge sat at the table, his crutch leaning beside him, before him his hard hat, his pen, bottle of ink, Bible, rusty derringer, and a half-empty pint of whisky—all the accoutrements of his office, which he brought out when he sat to fine or jail an evening's transgressors. He frowned when he saw Gannon; he had not shaved, and there was a thick gray stubble on his cheeks and chin. Carl sat on his heels against the wall, teasing a scorpion with a broomstraw. His jaw was shot out and he looked sullen and stubborn.

"Deputy Schroeder has resigned," the judge said.

"I haven't either, you old fool!" Carl got up and smashed the scorpion with his heel. "Damn, how you badger a man!"

"Badger you to do your duty like you are sworn to," the judge said. "You won't, so you have resigned." He looked up at Gannon and said, "Will you do your duty, Deputy?"

"Damned old bastard!" Carl cried. "Murderer, hell!" Then he said apologetically, "Johnny, I am sorry talking this way now, but he has drove me to it. What kind of judge are you?" he said to the judge. "Four hardcases trying to burn down a peace officer and it isn't self-defense? I never heard—"

"Not for you to judge what it is," the judge said.

"Or you!"

Gannon sat down beside the cell door and leaned back. Watching the two angry faces, his eyes felt as though they were bleeding.

"Warned him!" the judge said. "Warned him what he was doing. Making a murderer out of himself, issuing ukases and banishments like a duke. Now he has to stand trial like any ordinary mortal man and poor sinner, and I will witness against him if I have to crutch it into Bright's City."

"You couldn't," Carl said. "There is no place to buy whisky on the way."

"I'll witness against you for malfeasance of duty while I am at it. Will you arrest Blaisedell, Deputy Gannon?"

"He's gone," Gannon said.

The judge stared at him.

"Gone where?" Carl said.

"He rode out toward Bright's City. I expect he's gone up to court."

"What the hell would he do that for?"

"To be shriven," the judge said. He smiled and stretched, smugly. "Ah, he listened after all, did he? Yes, to get it off himself."

"Nothing on him, Christ's sake." Carl swung toward Gannon. "He only did what he had to do. Johnny, you heard him trying to talk Billy out of it!"

Gannon nodded with an incomplete and qualified assent. Carl was right to the boundaries of what he had said; Blaisedell had done what he had to do, given the circumstances. Yet the judge was right when he said that Blaisedell must be accountable. Billy would not have died had the Citizens' Committee not decided to post him, and had Blaisedell not decided to honor their decision, as he had not in the case of the miner Brunk. But on the other hand Billy would not have been posted had McQuown not loaded the court in Bright's City with perjured witnesses, tricked it with a clever lawyer, menaced it with gunmen and the threat inherent in his name. And, in the end, Billy would not have died had he not set himself to kill Blaisedell.

Carl furiously scraped his bootheel over the shredded stain that had been the scorpion. "By God!" he said thickly. He sounded as though he were in pain. "Johnny, what the hell did he think he had to go for?"

"The law is the law, Mister Malfeasor of Duty," the judge said smugly. "And no good getting hysterical—"

Carl took a long stride toward him, swung an arm, and slapped him on the side of the head. The judge screamed and toppled; Carl caught him by the shirt front and set him upright, slapped him again, forehand and backhand. The judge snatched for his derringer and Carl knocked it aside. The judge screamed and tried to cover his face. Gannon leaped out of his chair, caught Carl around the waist, and pulled him away.

"Witness!" the judge cried. "Assault and battery and—"

"Shut up!" Carl shouted. He stopped struggling in Gannon's grip, but when Gannon released him Carl darted for the judge again.

This time he only bent down close to the judge's blotched face. "The law is the law!" he panted. "But there isn't enough of it to go around out here. So when we get a good man protecting this town from hell with its door open I am not going to see him choused and badgered and false-sworn and yawped at fit to puke by a one-legged old son of a bitch like you!

"Until he gets fed up and rides the hell somewheres else and this town left pie on the table again for those San Pablo cowboys to pick it clean and kill anybody fool or awkward enough to get in their way. A good man, God damn you! That gives some of us here some pride and gets our peckers up for a change. God damn you, if by God because of you he has went up there to court and gets frazzled out of patience by it and sets his back against us here I will tear your other leg off and bust it around your God-damned neck for a God-damned necktie and run your God-damned crutch through it for a God-damned stickpin!" He stopped, panting.

"Witness!" the judge said hoarsely, covering his face with his hands.

"Shut up!" Carl yelled. "You don't know what assault and battery is yet, and by God I want witness to what I am saying! Because that's the word with the bark on it—if you have got him turned against us here with your law's-the-law bellywash, I swear to God people will walk ten miles out of their way around what happened to you, so as not to see the mess!"

Carl stepped back from the table. The judge snatched up his whisky bottle and tilted it to his mouth; whisky trickled over his chin.

Carl leaned back against the wall, chewing furiously on a mustache end. "By God, Johnny, it is a shameful thing," he said, in a shaky voice. "Here I am making a damned yelling fool of myself, and you with your brother killed. I am sorry."

"That Blaisedell killed," the judge whispered.

"It wasn't Blaisedell killed him," Gannon said, and Carl gave him a confused look.

Bootheels racketed on the planks outside and Pike Skinner came in. "Where the hell's Blaisedell gone to?"

"Bright's, it looks like," Carl said.

The judge said, in a loud, trumpeting voice, "He knew he had to go, because no man can set himself above the law!" He turned toward Gannon suddenly. Red marks showed on his pale, stubbled cheeks. "That's why, isn't it, Deputy?"

"I guess so," Gannon said.

"You two have been drinking out of the same bottle," Carl said, disgustedly.

"It is the only bottle there is," the judge said.

Pike stared at Gannon with wide eyes in his red face. Pike came forward around the table. "I don't know," he said, with difficulty. "I don't know what's happened or what's going to happen. But Johnny Gannon, I know if you throw Blaisedell down some way because of Billy I will—"

Carl caught Pike by the shoulder and jerked him around. "Shut your face!" Carl drew and jammed his Colt into Pike's side. His face was contorted with fury. "You have shot your mouth one too many times!"

Pike backed up a step and Carl moved after him. "Johnny, I will hold on him and you can beat the holy piss out of him for that if you want."

"Never mind it, Carl," Gannon said.

"Take it back then!" Carl said, through his teeth. "I say back down, you bat-eared ignoramus! You don't know what you are talking about even!"

"I'll not!" Pike said stiffly.

"It doesn't matter, Carl," Gannon said, and Carl cursed and holstered his Colt.

"Pus and corruption," the judge said, in the smug voice. "Small men bickering and quarreling and killing at each other, a whole world full and not one worth the trouble it is to law them. But there is one did a right thing one time in his life."

"Shut up!" Carl cried. He hit his fist back against the wall. "Just shut that up. I'm warning you! Just shut up about it!"

## 24. *Journals of Henry Holmes Goodpasture*

February 10, 1881

THE pipers play "The World Turned Upside Down." Clay Blaisedell is in Bright's City awaiting trial. He took himself there upon his own warrant, evidently preferring not to present himself to the deputies here for arrest, as is fitting his Dignity & Station.

The rumors fly. His action has astounded everyone. We cry that there is no need for him to seek justification in court, and further that he puts himself in grave danger by thus surrendering himself to the mercies of a judge and jury too often proved weak creatures of McQuown's will. Yet perhaps I do see a need. Blaisedell must have come to suspect immediately after the fight what is being more and more widely bruited about here—that Billy Gannon was not one of the road agents. And he must have felt that the fact that Billy Gannon had killed a posseman and had joined with those who were actually and clearly the road agents in order to ambush him (Blaisedell), does not alter this original case. If this is true, I must feel that he has acted correctly and honorably.

I wonder if Blaisedell realizes that he will stand trial for us of the Citizens' Committee as well as for himself.

February 15, 1881

It is too bad that Blaisedell left so soon for Bright's City and was not here to enjoy the luster of his feat in the Acme Corral while that luster remained intact. For within a week his triumph has become somewhat tarnished. Ah, the pure shine of a few moments of heroism, high courage, and derring-do! In its light we genuflect before the Hero, we bask in the warmth of his Deeds, we tout him, shout his praises, deify him, and, in short, make of him what no mortal man could ever be. We are a race of tradition-lovers in a new land, of king-reverers in a Republic, of hero-worshipers in a society of mundane get-and-spend. It is a Country and a Time where any bank clerk or common laborer can become a famous outlaw, where an outlaw can in a very short time be sainted in song and story into a Robin Hood, where a Frontier Model Excalibur can be drawn from the block at any gunshop for twenty dollars.

Yet it is only one side of us, and we are cynical and envious too. As one half of our nature seeks to create heroes to worship, the other must ceaselessly attempt to cast them down and discover evidence of feet of clay, in order to label them as mere lucky fellows, or as villains-were-the-facts-but-known, and the eminent and great are ground between the millstones of envy, and reduced again to common size.

So, quickly, as I have said, Blaisedell's luster has been dimmed.

As if ashamed of our original exuberance, we begin to qualify our praises, and smile a little at the extravagant recountings of the affair. For would we not look fools, were facts to arise that showed Blaisedell's part in the Acme Corral shooting to have been despicable? What cowards we are!

Still, it is a reaction against his having at first been made too much over. The pendulum inevitably swings, and, I hope, may come to rest dead center. But at the moment some scoffing has replaced the adulation, as I will now recount:

Blaisedell had, after all, Morgan with him—a gunman of no small accomplishments.

Blaisedell's antagonists are reconsidered. We realize that there were only four of them, and one did not even participate in the shooting. Pity is felt for their ineffectuality.

I feel some pity for them myself, but I am infuriated when I hear attitudes expounded that go beyond mere pity. For instance, I have heard Pony Benner remembered as a kindly albeit rough-cut spirit, who had unfortunately incurred general displeasure when he killed our poor barber in *self-defense*! Now it seems that the barber insulted a nice woman in Pony's presence, Pony called him down for it, whereupon the barber flew at him brandishing a razor! Who this nice woman could possibly have been, I have no idea.

Even Calhoun's good lives after him, while the evil has been interred with his bones. The fact that he was indisputably trying to shoot down Blaisedell from ambush is glossed over by the claim that he was trying to protect his friend Billy Gannon.

Poor Billy, too, becomes no longer "Billy-the-kid," who shot down Deputy Brown in the San Pablo saloon for trying to force a glass of whisky upon him, but has changed into a lad forced into a fight he did not want. He has grown younger after death, and I have heard him spoken of as a mere sixteen, instead of eighteen or nineteen as formerly.

How the tide of sentiment can swing, and how it has changed in many since the night when a good portion of this town attempted to lynch these same three "innocents," and only the presence of Blaisedell saved them. Men are wild, not wicked, said Rousseau, who knew not Warlock.

There is one wicked rumor that sets me in a rage. It has obviously sprung from another that was current here before the

Acme Corral fight. This was that it was not the "innocents" who robbed the stage at all, but Morgan in company with unnamed accomplices. Now the accomplices have been named. They were Morgan's lookout, Murch, and Blaisedell! It seems that the Cowboys became, somehow, advised of this, had definite proof, and came into Warlock to establish their innocence by broadcasting it. Consequently they had to be shot down immediately by Blaisedell and Morgan, so that the truth would not be known.

Oh, foul! I have not, as a matter of fact, heard it uttered, I have only heard men say they disbelieve it completely. It is said that the original rumor came from Taliaferro, Morgan's competitor, and a vile blotch of a man. The new one can only come from someone who hates Blaisedell completely and ruthlessly. I suspect McQuown, who must hate Blaisedell thus—as one must hate a man he has tried foully to wrong, and failed.

February 18, 1881

Blaisedell will go on trial to determine whether the deaths of Billy Gannon and Pony Benner were acts of murder or of self-defense.* If guilty, we of the Citizens' Committee cannot be punished for our Crime, while Blaisedell can.

My thoughts are much occupied with Blaisedell now, as, of course, are those of everyone in Warlock. I find myself thinking of him with sadness, because of the canards visited upon him *in absentia*, that surely will in some degree and over the years stick to his name in the minds of men. Sadness, too, because he is, I am convinced, a good man, a fair, temperate, and reasonable man, a decent man and an honorable one; and, in the end, of course, he must die. Probably he will die by just the sort of foul trickery that was attempted upon his person in the Acme Corral. If not here, elsewhere. He is, after all, a killer; living by the six-shooter, he will no doubt perish by it. Other killers or would-be killers will be moved from time to time to try his mettle or to usurp his fame, and one day, even if he is not removed by treachery, his hand will lack the necessary swiftness.

It is curious that a man like Blaisedell, no less than outlaws such as Calhoun, Benner, Curley Burne, and McQuown, is

---

*It should be noted that the question seems never to have arisen as to whether or not Morgan should have been tried for the death of Calhoun.

referred to as a "Badman." This describes more a man who is dangerous to meddle with than one murderously inclined, and yet the term has unhappy connotations, and I am more and more displeased to hear it applied to our Marshal.

Obviously Blaisedell must enjoy his role as angel with a sword or he would not undertake so dangerous a role, but can he endure to be called devil? Surely he will be acquitted and his name cleared in court. There are many men here who would walk to Bright's City to testify in his behalf, were it necessary.

February 22, 1881

The trial is to begin tomorrow. Buck has gone in with the doctor, Morgan, the Skinner brothers, Sam Brown, and a number of others. I did not choose to make the onerous journey into Bright's City myself since there is nothing except my high opinion of Blaisedell that I could offer the court. Nor do I wish to see our Marshal being questioned before a jury box full of Bright's City fools. Those of the Citizens' Committee who went in to attend the trial are to carry another appeal to General Peach that he legalize our situation in Warlock. I wish I had counted how many of these appeals have already been made. Doubtless this will meet the same fate as the others, although some hope is felt that General Peach will be forced to see, because of the trial, the extremes we have been brought to by his neglect. Those who are witnesses have been cautioned to mention this in court whenever possible.

A prospector has been reported murdered in the Dinosaurs, and in consequence there has been another rash of Apache rumors. It is embittering to think that Peach will no doubt get wind of this and bring the cavalry down to investigate, but will not hear our appeals for law. Not all Apaches are dark-skinned.

There are also reports of Mexican troops along the border again, probably on watch against rustlers crossing. One of Blaikie's hands was wounded in an encounter with rustlers, and Deputy Gannon, I hear, has gone down to investigate. I wonder why he did not go up for trial. He roams the streets by night, while Schroeder has kept the jail by day; more morose than ever, cadaverously thin, his eyes like holes burnt in his skull. Poor fellow, he is condemned by some for having attempted to shield a villain of a brother, by others for not having attempted to avenge an heroic one.

February 25, 1881

The trial has been put off another week, and the witnesses have returned, grumbling. It appears that Friendly, who was thought to have fled the territory, is in Bright's City where he will give evidence against Blaisedell. He is a fellow whom anyone but a fool would know on sight as a born liar. Blaisedell is not in jail, but resides at the Jim Bright Hotel and spends his days gambling. There is some talk about his not returning here to await the trial, but I can understand his not wishing to do so.

## 25. *Gannon Goes to a Housewarming*

I

FROM THE doorway of the jail, Gannon saw her coming across the street from Goodpasture's corner, her hands lifting her skirts as she waded through the dust, the cord of her reticule twisted around her wrist. Buck Slavin, walking up from the stageyard, tipped his hat and she stopped briefly to talk to him. But then she came on, and it was clear that she was coming to the jail.

He stepped back inside and sat down on a corner of the table. He had seen her many times in the last few weeks; always she would smile at him and more and more often stop to pass a few moments with him, which moments were always difficult ones, because he could think of nothing to say to her and always he had the feeling, after she had gone on, that he had disappointed her in some way.

He heard her steps. Then she was framed in the doorway, smiling at him, with the little court-plaster beauty mark very black against her pale face. "Good morning, Deputy."

"Good morning, Miss Dollar," he said, standing quickly upright. She glanced at the empty cell and took a handkerchief from her reticule and daubed at her temples. The bottom of her skirt was white with dust. Still, perspiring and dusty as she was, she was a handsome woman, and, standing before her, incapable of easy conversation, he felt intensely his own awkwardness, his own inadequacy and ugliness.

"It's cool in here," she said, and came a little farther inside.

"Yes, ma'am. And hot out."

"I've rented a house."

"You are lucky to find a house. Are you—I mean, I guess you are going to stay in Warlock awhile, then."

"I've been here a month. I guess I am staying." She was looking at the names scratched in the whitewashed wall. "It's a pretty fair house," she went on. "I rented it from a miner. Some boys from the livery stable are bringing my trunks around this afternoon." She smiled at him with a mechanical tilt of her reddened lips. "I wondered if you would help me move in."

"Why—" he said. "Why, I would surely appreciate to help, Miss Dollar. What time would you—"

"Toward five. I will try a hand at cooking some supper for us." Then she smiled again, not so mechanically. "You don't have to look worried. I can cook, Deputy."

"I am sure!" he protested. "I will surely be pleased to come."

Her eyes examined him in that way she had that was both careless and intense, as though she could see right through him, but at the same time as though she were searching for something. He had felt it most intensely when, after Billy's death, he had met her on the street and she had stopped to say she was sorry about his brother.

She remained and chatted a little longer, but he became more and more tongue-tied and stupid, as he always did, and finally she left. From the doorway he watched her cross South-end and walk past the loungers in front of the saloons. They did not bother her, he noticed.

He saw the lead mules of a freighter swinging wide into Main Street from the Welltown road, and he moved back inside the jail to get out of the dust. The mules plodded past, almost invisible in the dust they raised, with Earl Posten trotting alongside the swing team, and Mosbie standing and cracking his long whip from the lead wagon. Carl came in and sailed his hat toward the peg on which the key ring hung.

"Damn!" Carl said, and went to pick up his hat, where it had fallen. He sat down at the table and said, in a gloomy voice, "I've been up at the stable talking to Joe Kennon. You don't suppose they are going to find against Blaisedell, do you?"

Gannon shook his head, while Carl guardedly watched his face. "I don't see how they can, Carl."

"Well, I don't like them putting it off a week like this. Like they think if they keep putting it off there'll nobody go in to witness for him. By God, if that's what they think they're trying to do, I'll set up camp on the courthouse steps!"

"Do you think I ought to go in?"

Carl sat scowling down at his hands. He sighed and said, "No, I guess I don't know what good it'd do. I don't know— I have just got the nerves, I guess."

Gannon watched a bluefly circle past Carl's head, to strike and buzz angrily against the window glass. Hoofs clopped by in the street—two of Blaikie's riders. One waved in to him, and he raised a hand in reply.

Carl said, "Saw that Kate Dollar woman coming out of here. What did she want?"

He found himself grinning foolishly. "Well, she wants me to come and help her move her things for her. She has rented herself a house."

"You!" Carl said, in an awed voice.

"Me, sure enough."

"You!" Carl said. "By God, a lady-killer underneath all. I never thought it of you."

"Well, she said she had picked the handsomest man in town here to help her."

"Thought I was," Carl said. He squinted at Gannon. "Well, I'll just pass on what my Daddy said to me. 'Look out for women!' he said, and I have done it all my life. But not a one went and looked back." He laughed a little. "Well, now, that's fine," he said. "She is a handsome-looking woman. What is she doing out here, did she ever say to you, Johnny?"

"Looking for me," he said, and felt himself flush. He grinned at Carl, who snorted.

"A lady-killer underneath," Carl said. "Well, if that don't beat all."

II

At four o'clock Gannon went to the Mexican barber on Medusa Street for a haircut and shave, and, reeking of toilet water, hurried back to his room at Birch's roominghouse and washed off the stink and put on his best shirt and his store suit.

Surveying himself in the shard of mirror over the washstand he thought there had never been a face so ugly, and the suit did not look like anything but what it was, a cheap store-bought, with the jacket pinch-waisted and short and the store creases still in the trousers.

He took off the suit and put on clean moleskin pants; anyway he was going to help her move her things, not to a soiree. He dusted and oiled his shell belt, put on his new star boots that were too small for him, and spent some time brushing his hat and adjusting it upon his head. Then he limped out. He looked in at the jail, where Carl was poring over a Wild West magazine.

"In a pure sweat, aren't you?" Carl said. "I was betting on that store suit of yours, though."

"It's that red-trim house over on Grant Street. If you need me for anything."

"I'm too soft-hearted a man to pull you out of there short of McQuown coming in to burn the town down," Carl said. "Then I guess you'd hear the shooting anyway."

Gannon grinned and went on east along Main Street, walking pigeon-toed and wincing in his star boots. He turned into the Lucky Dollar for a glass of whisky, taking a place at the bar where he could watch the thin hands of the Seth Thomas clock.

He had finished his whisky and was marveling at the incredibly slow movement of the minute hand, when there was a sudden silence in the Lucky Dollar, and then a scuff of boot-heels and clink of spurs. In the mirror he saw Abe and Curley entering. They walked past him, unnoticing, and he watched them find a table and seat themselves.

A barkeeper took them a bottle and two glasses; the hum of conversation was resumed, in a lower, sibilant key. In the mirror Gannon watched Curley whispering to Abe behind his hand, and Abe glancing around him continually with little nervous movements of his head, the lines in his cheeks deeply cut, his face bitter, watchful, and—Gannon thought with a shock —almost fearful.

When the minute hand stood two minutes away from straight up, Gannon turned to go. He nodded to Abe, who stared back without recognition; he nodded to Curley, who wrinkled his nose a little, as though he had smelled something bad. Gannon went on outside. He did not think there was going to be any trouble. Probably they were on their way into Bright's City and Abe had felt he had to show himself in War-lock on the way. The red-bearded face with the clawed-looking lines in the cheeks remained in his mind's eye as he went on east toward Grant Street. He had never thought that he would see Abe McQuown frightened.

The house Kate Dollar had rented was of tarpaper and wooden battens, with red trim around the door and a single narrow window at the front. The door stood open and he knocked on the red frame and waited, hat in hands. Inside he could see two scuffed leather trunks with curved lids, one with a valise on top of it, the other standing open. In the room were three rawhide straight chairs, a love seat with one corner propped up on some bricks, an oilcloth-covered table beneath the pulley lamp, and, on the wall opposite him, a painting in a chipped gilt frame of a shepherd tending some sheep. The glass over it was cracked.

Kate Dollar came out of the doorway beyond the trunks. She had on a soiled apron and a white frilled shirt with a high collar. Her black hair was tied up in a scarf, and her face, clean and scrubbed-looking, seemed strangely different until he noticed that the beauty mark was missing. She did not look so tall, either, as she came across the creaking plank floor toward him. "Come in, Deputy," she said.

He entered, and she stepped past him to close the door with a slap. "How do you like my house?"

"It's a fine house."

She looked at him in the almost rude way she had. "I see you didn't know whether to come dressed for work or supper. There'll be no supper till there's some work done. I want you to slide those trunks into the bedroom for me, and then I want these walls washed down. Can you bring yourself to do that kind of work?"

"If nobody catches me at it."

She raised an eyebrow at him, and raised a finger to touch the place where the beauty mark usually was. She smiled a different kind of smile. "I will have something on you, won't I?"

She stood aside as he lifted the valise to the table, and slid the larger trunk into the bedroom. In the bedroom was a brass bed and an unpainted crate with dirty muslin curtains covering the front. On the crate, on a purple scarf, was a glass-covered picture of the Virgin. There was a wire stretched across one corner of the room, on which hung the clothes she had been wearing when she had come to the jail.

When he returned to the living room he could hear her in the kitchen, and a bucket of water and some cactus-fiber wads were on the table. He went to work on the tarpaper walls.

While he scrubbed the walls Kate Dollar worked in the kitchen and the bedroom, occasionally talking to him from whatever room she happened to be in, and once or twice, as she passed him, pointing out places he had missed. He thought it was as pleasant a time as he had ever spent.

Finished with the front room, he took his bucket into the bedroom. Now the wire in the corner was sagging with clothes. One of the trunks was empty and stood open; there was a mirror in the lid with red roses and blue stars painted around it. The top of the crate had been heaped with her things—a little black book, a silver cross on a beaded chain, a silver-chased box, a derringer, a tinted photograph in a gold frame. The picture of the Virgin stood apart from the clutter. She had a sad, sweet face, full of pity.

He moved closer to the crate. His hand hesitated, as his eyes had hesitated, to pry into her personal things there. But he picked up the tinted photograph. It showed a man with a reddish walrus mustache—a smiling, well-dressed, plump, handsome, touchy-looking man; at first the face seemed familiar and he thought it must be that of the dead man, Cletus, who had come to Warlock with her. Yet he decided it was not. He heard the slap of Kate Dollar's slippers in the front room, and guiltily he put the photograph down and moved quickly away from the crate. Through the door he saw her pull down the lamp and light the wick with a paper spill. The room brightened around her, and she turned and smiled at him, but some essential part of the pleasantness had vanished, and he felt uncomfortable in the bedroom with the brass scrolled bed, and her private things.

He was nearly done when he began to smell the damp, sweet smell of cornbread, and cooking meat. She called to him that it was time to wash up, and he finished quickly. The oilcloth table was set with dented metal plates and thick white mugs. Kate Dollar had put out a crockery bowl of water and a cake of Pears soap for him, and he washed his hands carefully and wiped them dry on his trouser legs. He could see Kate Dollar in the little kitchen, before a charcoal fire set into a brick counter; her face was pink and prettily beaded with perspiration.

"You can sit down, Deputy," she called. He did so, and continued to watch her working. She seemed very slim, and it occurred to him that she must not be wearing certain of her usual undergarments. She brought in a dish of cornbread, with a cloth over it, and he rose hurriedly, and seated himself again when she had returned to the kitchen—to rise again when she brought in the meat and greens. Finally she sat down opposite him.

"We'll have to eat the cornbread dry," she said. "I haven't got anything to put on it."

"Everything certainly smells fine," he said. He watched her hands to see how she would use her knife and fork, and followed her example. He remembered that his mother had switched her fork to her right hand after she had cut her meat, and he was glad to see that Kate did it that way. In the lamplight he watched the dark down on her bare arms. Her knife scraped painfully on the metal plate.

"Eat your greens, Deputy."

He grinned and said, "I remember my mother saying that."

"It is a thing women say." She had taken off her head scarf and her hair gleamed blue-black. Her teeth were very straight and white, and there was a fine down also on her upper lip. "Where is she?" she asked.

"Well, she's dead, Miss Dollar."

"Kate," she said. "Just Kate."

"Kate," he said. "Well, she died, I don't know—twelve years ago. That was back in Nebraska. She and the baby died of the influenza."

"And your father?"

"Apaches shot him. That was in the early days here."

"And Blaisedell killed your brother," Kate said.

He looked down at his plate. Kate didn't speak again, and the silence was heavy. He finished his meat and greens and took a piece of cornbread from under the cloth. It was warm still, but it was dry in his mouth. He knew he was not being very good company. With an effort he laughed and said, "Well, there's not many men in Warlock tonight, I guess, eating home-cooked food. And good, too. I mean with white women," he added, thinking of the miners' Mexican women.

"I'm not all white," Kate said. "I'm a quarter Cherokee."

"That's good blood to have."

"Why, I've thought so," she said. "My grandmother was Cherokee. She was the finest woman I ever knew." She looked at him intently, and then she said, "When my father was killed in the war she was going to go after the Yankee that did it, except she didn't have any way of knowing what Yankee. I was five or six then and the first thing I remember was Grandma getting ready to go with her scalping knife. The only thing that held her back was not knowing how to find out who the Yankee was. Then when I was ten she just died. It always made me think the Yankee'd died too, and she knew it some way, and had gone off to get him where she knew she could find him."

She smiled a little, but the way she had told it made him uncomfortable. It seemed to him they had talked only of death since they had sat down. He said, "I guess I would have known you for part Cherokee. With those black eyes."

"My nose. I think I might've given up a little Cherokee blood for a decent-sized nose."

He protested, and put his hand to his own nose, laughing; it was the first time he had ever been pleased with it.

"How did you break it?" Kate asked.

"Fight," he said. "Well, Billy did it," he said reluctantly. "We got in a fight and he hit me with a piece of kindling. He had a temper."

Silently she rose and went into the kitchen. She brought back the coffee pot and poured steaming coffee into the two cups. When she had seated herself again, she said, "The first time you talked to me you knew he was going to kill your brother. Didn't you?"

"I guess I did."

When she seemed to change the subject he was grateful: "Where were you from before Nebraska?"

"From Pennsylvania to begin with. I don't remember it much."

"Yankee," she said.

"I guess I am. Where are you from, Kate?"

"Texas." She sat very stiffly, not looking at him now but attentive, as though she were listening to something within herself. She said, "I don't know about Yankees. In Texas if a man killed your brother you went after him."

He picked up his cup. The coffee burned his tongue but he drank it anyway, and when he put the cup down he spilled coffee in a thin brown stain on the oilcloth.

"But you're not going after Blaisedell," Kate said, in a flat voice.

He shook his head. "No."

"Afraid of him?"

"I have got no reason to be afraid of him."

She shrugged her shoulders. All at once she seemed very cold, and bored.

"Men brace people they are afraid of," he said. "That's nothing to do with it. I just don't expect I have to set out to kill a man because some people think I ought to."

"Who?" Kate said.

"Some people here. But I am not going to go against Blaisedell just because I don't want people to think I am yellow. I don't care that much what they think of me." He felt himself flushing, as though he had been caught in a brag. Kate was looking at the star on his shirt, her mouth tucked in at the corners.

"Meaning what I think?" she said.

"Why, no. Anyhow all that is nothing to do with it. It's that I don't see how any blame is due Blaisedell. Or not—not much."

"You have called him not guilty before the jury in Bright's City got around to it, have you?"

"Well, it was self-defense clear enough, when you come down to it. They'd come in to kill him. Billy told me that."

Kate drank her coffee. Her eyelashes made delicate shadows upon her white cheeks. He finished his own coffee, disappointed and ill at ease in this silence. Finally he said, "Well, I had better be going now, Miss Dollar."

"Kate," she said. "No, don't go yet. There might be somebody coming by and I think I had better have a man here."

"Who?"

"The jack I rented this house from. I thought he might be planning on paying a call."

He nodded, and he felt better. She poured another cup of coffee, and he said, "You said you knew Blaisedell in Fort James?"

"I knew Tom Morgan. If you knew him you knew Blaisedell."

"What did they think of Blaisedell in Fort James, Kate?"

She didn't answer right away, and he saw the tightening in her face. She said, "About the same as they do here. The way they feel about a badman anywhere. Some like him because they think if they show they like him he'll like them. Others don't like him and stay out of his way. People are the same most places."

Her black eyes met his expressionlessly as she went on. "He dealt faro for Morgan and people knew he was a gunman from the start. Though nobody knew anything about him. Then one day a man named Ben Nicholson came in. A real bad rattlesnake of a man. He was shooting things up. Drunk and cursing everybody and trying to get a fight. He was trying to get the marshal to fight. So Blaisedell went to the marshal and said he'd brace Nicholson, and the mayor heard him and fired the marshal and made Blaisedell marshal. So Blaisedell went out in the street and told Nicholson to get out of town. Nicholson drew on him so Blaisedell killed him."

She stopped, but it didn't sound as though she was finished, and he waited for her to go on.

"So he was marshal but he still worked for Morgan," she said. "Morgan had given him a quarter interest in the place he had there."

"A lot of marshals do that."

"I didn't say there was anything wrong with it."

"I'm sorry. I didn't mean to bust in."

"That's all I was going to say. He killed four or five others —badmen mostly. That writer came and gave him those gold-handled guns. I guess you've seen them. I was gone by then.

I left pretty soon after he killed—Nicholson. Fort James was dying off by then and everybody was beginning to move on."

"What did you mean," he said slowly, "that the four or five others was badmen *mostly?*"

She said, in a voice so thick he could hardly understand her, "I am sick and tired of talking about Clay Blaisedell and who he killed."

"I'm sorry. I guess it's not a thing women are interested in much." He tried desperately to think of something to say that would interest her, but it seemed to him that he didn't know anything that would interest anybody. He wondered why she had gotten so angry.

"I've heard people saying you'd come out here to start up a dance hall," he said, tentatively. "Seems like it would be a good thing."

She shrugged. Then she sighed and said, "I don't know. Maybe I am waiting to see if this town is dying off too." Something in the way she said it made him think it was a kind of apology for her anger, and after that it was almost all right again. They discussed the rumors that wages were going to be dropped at the mines, and she told him of the strike she had seen at Silver Mountain. She regarded him brightly now when he spoke, and so he found himself not so tongue-tied, although he marveled at how much more she knew, and had seen, than he. It was almost like talking to a man, and almost he could forget he was having supper with Kate Dollar in her house and alone, and that they were man and woman. But he would be brought back to it sharply from time to time, by something she said, or by some movement, and it was a very intense thing to him, except that it always made him begin to wonder again what had brought her to Warlock, who she was and what she was; but now he did not want to know. And he marveled too at how fine-looking she was in the lamplight, and at how soft her sharp black eyes could be sometimes, and the crooked way her mouth twisted when she smiled the smile he liked. He could not keep his eyes from the soft shadows her lashes made upon her cheeks.

Then she asked about McQuown. "What sort is he? I've heard a lot about him since I've been here, but I don't think I've ever seen him in town."

"He and Curley are in tonight. I guess on their way up to Bright's for the trial." He paused, to see if she was really interested; she was watching him intently. "Well, he is a rustler, mostly," he went on. "I know him pretty well. He took Billy and me on to work for him after our father died—the Apaches'd run off all our stock."

"How bad is he?"

He laughed shakily and said, "Why, Kate, I guess I don't like to talk about him sort of the way you don't about Blaisedell."

She touched a finger to the corner of her mouth. She looked wary, suddenly. "I see," she said. "You are against McQuown. So you are for Blaisedell."

"No, that's not so. Not like Carl is; not—" He stopped and looked down at his hands. "Maybe I am in a way," he said. "For Abe is bad. Worse than he ought to be, and worse all the time, it seems like. I used to think pretty high of him."

"But you left," she said. "You left and your brother stayed on there."

He stared down at his hands. He was going to tell her; it surprised him that he was. It seemed to him that Kate was gathering information not because she was interested in him, but for some purpose of her own that he had no way of deciphering. Yet, he thought, he would tell her, and only waited to get it calm and in proportion in his mind, so that he could tell it correctly.

"It was eight or ten months ago," he said. "Maybe you've heard about it. Some Mexicans that was supposed to have been shot by Apaches in Rattlesnake Canyon. Peach came down with the cavalry. I guess everybody thought it was Apaches."

"I've heard about it. Somebody said it was McQuown's men dressed like Apaches."

He nodded, and wet his lips. "We'd rustled more than a thousand head down at Hacienda Puerto," he said. "But Abe wasn't along. Abe always ran things like that pretty well, but he wasn't along that time. He was sick, I guess it was, and Curley and Dad McQuown was running it, but there was nobody so clever as Abe. Anyway, they just about caught us, and Hank Miller was shot dead, and Dad McQuown shot and crippled. We lost all the stock, and they trailed us pretty close all the way.

"We got across the border all right, but then we found out they were coming right on after us. Abe was there by then, for Curley had rode the old man back to San Pablo. So a bunch of us stripped down and smeared ourselves with mud and boxed those Mexicans of Don Ignacio's in Rattlesnake Canyon. We killed them all. I guess maybe one or two got away down the south end, but all the others. Seventeen of them."

He picked up his coffee cup; his hand was steady. The coffee was cold, and he set the cup down again.

"That's when you left?" Kate said; she didn't sound shocked.

"I had some money and I went up to Rincon and paid a telegrapher to apprentice me. I thought it would be a good trade. But he died and I got laid off. So I came back here."

It struck him that he had been able to tell her all there was to know about him in a few minutes. He shifted his position in his chair and his scabbarded Colt thumped noisily against the wood. He went on. "I can't say I didn't know what Abe aimed to do there in Rattlesnake Canyon. I knew, and I was against it, but everybody else was for it and I was afraid to go against them. I guess because I was afraid they'd think I was yellow. Curley wouldn't go, though; he wouldn't do it. There was some others that didn't like it. I know Chet Haggin didn't. And Billy was sick—to his stomach, afterwards. But he stuck down there. I guess he figured it out some way inside himself so it was all right, afterwards. But I couldn't."

"If you don't like to see men shot down you are in the wrong business, Deputy," Kate said.

"No, I'm in the right business. I was wrong when I went up to Rincon—that was just running away. There is only one way to stop men from killing each other like that."

He looked up to see her black eyes glittering at him. She smiled and it was the smile he did not like. She started to speak, but then she stopped, and her eyes turned toward the door. He heard quiet footsteps on the porch.

He rose as a key rattled in the lock and the door swung inward. A short, fat, clean-shaven miner stood in the doorway, in clean blue shirt and trousers. His hair gleamed with grease.

"Oh, hello, Mr. Benson," Kate said. "Meet Mr. Gannon, the deputy. Did you want something, Mr. Benson?"

The miner shuffled his feet. He backed up a step, out of the light. "I just come by, miss."

"I guess you came by to give me the other key," Kate said. "Just give it to Johnny, will you? He's been asking for it, but I'd thought there was only one."

"That's it," the miner said. "Remembered I had this other key here and I thought I'd just better bring it by before I went and forgot, the way a man does."

Gannon stepped toward him, and the miner dropped the heavy key into his hand. The miner watched it all the way as Gannon put it in his pocket.

Kate laughed as he fled, and Gannon closed the door again. He couldn't look at Kate as he returned to the table.

"He's sorry he rented it so cheap," Kate said.

"I guess I'd better talk to him tomorrow."

"Don't bother."

He stood leaning on the back of his chair. "Anytime anybody fusses you, Kate. I mean, there's some wild ones here and not much on manners. You could let me know."

"Why, thank you," she said. She got to her feet. "Are you going now?" she said. Dismissing him, he thought; she had just asked him for supper because of the miner.

"Why, yes, I guess I had better go. It was certainly an enjoyable supper. I surely thank you."

"I surely thank you," she said, as though she were mocking him.

He started to put the key down on the table.

"Keep it," she said, and his hand pulled it back, quickly. It was clear enough, he thought. He tried to grin, but he felt a disappointment that worked deeper and deeper until it was a kind of pain.

He started around the table toward her. But something in her stiff face halted him, a kind of shame that touched the shame he felt and yet was a different thing. And there was something cruel, too, in her face, that repelled him. Uncertainly he turned away.

"Well, good night, Miss Dollar," he said thickly.

"Good night, Deputy."

"Good night," he said again, and took his hat from the hook and opened the door. The blue-black sky was full of stars. There was a wind that seemed cold after the warmth inside.

"Good night," Kate said again, and he tipped his hat, without looking back, and closed the door behind him.

Walking back toward Main Street he could feel the weight of the key in his pocket. He wondered what she had meant by it, and thought he had been right about it at first. He wondered what had happened inside her that had showed so in her face at the end; he wondered what she was and what she wanted until his mind ached with it.

## 26. *Journals of Henry Holmes Goodpasture*

March 2, 1881

JED ROLFE in on the stage this afternoon, and everyone gathered around him to hear about the first day of the trial. Evidently the delay came about because at the last moment General Peach decided he would hear the case himself, as Military Governor, from which illegal and senile idiocy he was finally dissuaded. General Peach, however, did sit in at the trial and interrupted frequently to the harrassment of everyone and the baffled rage of Judge Alcock. Peach is evidently inimical to Blaisedell, for what reason I cannot imagine. My God, surely Blaisedell cannot be found guilty of anything! Yet I must remind myself that anything is possible in the Bright's City court.

If Blaisedell were to be found guilty I think this town would rise almost to a man and ride into Bright's City in armed rebellion to free him. Opinion has swung violently back to his behalf in light of this newest report, and his critics are silent. Miss Jessie Marlow in my store this afternoon ostensibly to purchase some ribbon, actually to learn if I had heard anything beyond the news Rolfe had brought. I had not, and could only try to reassure her that Blaisedell would be speedily acquitted. She was sadly pale, ill-looking, and far from her usual cheerful self, but she thanked me for my pitiful offering as though it were of value.

McQuown's absence from Bright's City's courthouse has been remarked upon. He and Burne passed through Warlock on Sunday, and it was presumed they were en route to the trial. But only Burne was there; indeed, he seems to have been the only other San Pabloite other than Luke Friendly to appear. Rolfe said he heard that Burne and Deputy Schroeder exchanged hot words upon the courthouse steps, and would have exchanged more than words had not Sheriff Keller intervened. McQuown is no doubt more frightened that Blaisedell will be acquitted and return, than we are that he will not.

March 4, 1881

Buck Slavin, the doctor, Schroeder, et al. back. The jury is deliberating. They had waited over a day after the jury had left the box, but it was still out. They seem certain Blaisedell will be acquitted, and that the jury's delay is only to enjoy as many meals upon the county as possible. Still, I notice that they seem worried that Luke Friendly's outrageous lies may have told heavily against Blaisedell. Buck is bitter about the prosecuting attorney, Pierce, and that Judge Alcock did not cut him short more often than he did.

Evidently Pierce sought to inflame the jury with Billy Gannon's youth, with the fact that less than a month ago the three Cowboys had been declared innocent in the same court, and with Blaisedell's "murderous presumption" in setting aside the court's decision and declaring himself "Judge and Executioner." Buck says that the same rumor we have had here —that Morgan and Blaisedell were actually the road agents themselves, and murdered the "innocents" in an effort both to silence and permanently affix the blame on them—has been sown in Bright's City, and, although not much believed there (Bright's City has not seen as much of McQuown as we have, but they have seen enough) had evidently been heard by Pierce, and it was Pierce's hints and implications along these lines that Buck felt Judge Alcock should have dealt with more firmly. As all agree that Friendly was a poor witness against Blaisedell, so do they agree that Morgan was the best witness in Blaisedell's behalf; that he was cool and convincing, and gave as good as he got from Pierce, several times calling forth peals of laughter from the courtroom at the prosecutor's expense.

From all I have heard I am glad I did not attend the trial. Poor Blaisedell; I pity him what he has gone through. Yet it was at his own instigation, and I am certain no charges would have been brought against him had he not wished it. Buck says, however, that he has been most calm throughout, and apparently took no umbrage at Pierce's blackguardly accusations.

"What stronger breastplate than a heart untainted?
Thrice is he armed that hath his quarrel just;
And he but naked, though locked up in steel,
Whose conscience with injustice is corrupted."

March 5, 1881

Blaisedell was acquitted yesterday. Peter Bacon arrived this morning with the news, having ridden all night. I sent a note around immediately to Miss Jessie, expressing my pleasure at hearing it, but there was no reply other than her verbal thanks to my *mozo*.

Now that Blaisedell is free and absolved, I am neither pleased nor relieved. The blackguardly statements with which Pierce harangued the jury, the jury's inexcusable delay, Friendly's damnable lies about what happened in the Acme Corral, and General Peach's actions throughout*—how must these have affected him? He must have gone to court wishing absolution, and received only a poor, grudging, and besmudged verdict in his behalf. The official verdict, however, will not affect the verdict here, and I think in days to come there will be bad blood between Warlock men and Bright's City men. Although I will say that the Bright's City paper has treated Blaisedell with great respect in its columns and especially in its editorials, and I will congratulate Editor Jim Askew on these when next I see him.

I find myself deeply emotionally subscribed to all this. It seems to me that I, and all of us here, have a stake and an investment in the Marshal. He has produced, and, looking back, I see that he did from the beginning produce, an intense division for or against him. But Clay Blaisedell is not the rock upon which we are divided, he is only a symptom. We do not break so simply as some think into the two camps of townsmen and

---

*General Peach evidently, upon one occasion, shouted down the judge to say that Blaisedell should properly have been tried by a military tribunal, and that he, General Peach, would have had him shot. Why the military governor was not declared in contempt of court for his interference is perhaps understandable, and references to his peculiar actions, most delicately handled, are contained in the *Bright's City Star-Democrat*'s reports of the trial.

Cowboys. We break into the camps of those wildly inclined, and those soberly, those irresponsible and those responsible, those peace-loving and those outlaw and riotous by nature; further, into the camps of respect, and of fear—I mean for oneself, and for all decent things besides. These are the poles between which we vibrate, and Blaisedell has only emphasized the distance between them. It is too simple perhaps to say that those who fear themselves and fear their fellow men, fear and hate Blaisedell, while those who respect themselves, and Man, respect him. Yet I hold that this is true in a broad sense.

For the arguments continue, what happened in the Acme Corral compounded by the Bright's City court and those who spoke there. I feel strongly that not merely I, but everyone here, sees himself affected personally by all this, and that, somehow, the truth or falsity of the whole affair reflects through and upon each of us. Fine points are argued as heatedly as the whole—how many shots, how many paces, who was stationed in exactly what position, and so on *ad infinitum*. So must the schoolmen have argued in their day, in their own saloons, the number of angels who could dance on the head of a pin.

## 27. Curley Burne and the Dog Killer

CURLEY RODE in from the river on his way back to San Pablo from Bright's City, blowing on his mouth organ. The music was pleasant to his ears in the silence around him, and the sun was pleasant upon his back as the gelding Dick plodded over the bare brown ridges and down the grassy draws. The Dinosaurs towered to the southwest with the sun on their slopes like honey, and from the elevation of the ridges he could see the irregular line of cottonwoods marking the river's course toward Rattlesnake Canyon.

His cheerful mood vanished as he saw the chimney of the long-gone old house, and the windmill on the pump house. He was not bringing good news from Bright's City.

Finally he came in sight of the ranch house, low to the ground and weathered gray as a horned toad; and now he could see the bunkhouse, cook shack, horse corral—the porch of the ranch house. There were two figures seated there.

Going down the last slope Dick quickened his pace expectantly. Curley dropped the mouth organ back inside his shirt, flicked Dick with his spurs, and went down toward the house at a run, bending low in the saddle with his hat flying off and its cord cutting against his throat. He drew up with a yell before the porch, dismounted in a whirl of dust and barking dogs, and went up the steps. The other man he had seen was Dechine, Abe's neighbor to the south, dropped in to pay a call. Dad McQuown was lying on a cot in the sun.

Abe sat staring at the mountains with his hat tipped forward to shade his face, scratching a thumb through his beard. He was leaning back with his boots crossed up on the porch rail.

Curley said, "Well, howdy, Dechine. How's it?"

"Fine-a-lee," Dechine said, fanning dust away with his hat. He was a short, pot-bellied fellow with little reddened eyes and a nose like half a red pear stuck to his face.

The old man propped himself up on one elbow. "Well, what happened, Curley? They set him loose?"

"They did," he said. Abe sat there silently, staring off at the Dinosaurs with the long creases in his cheeks like scars. All the starch had gone out of him since the boys had got killed in the Acme Corral; sometimes he acted as though there were nothing left in him at all.

The old man spat tobacco juice in a puddle beside his pallet, swiped at his little red mouth, and said, "Buggers."

"I was just telling Abe, here," Dechine said, "how people has got down on Blaisedell in Warlock there, over murdering those poor boys."

"One of them's not Carl," Curley said. "I don't know what's got into Carl. Used to be a man could get along with him."

"You have trouble with Schroeder?" the old man said eagerly.

"We went and scratched some. He is taking lawing pretty hard."

"He is one of those thinks Blaisedell is probably Jesus Christ there," Dechine said. "I've been telling Abe they are not all like that, though."

Still Abe didn't move, didn't speak. Curley took out his mouth organ, then put it back. He didn't know what had happened to everybody but it had begun to seem to him more and more that it was time to move on. Everything was nasty now, except when he was off by himself. Dad McQuown scraped his nerves like a rasp, and it was poor to see a man scared loose from himself, which was the case with Abe, who was the best friend he had ever had. He had got Abe to come as far as Warlock with him on his way up to Bright's City, and Abe hadn't said as much as two words the whole time and had acted as though he were madder at him, Curley, than at anybody else. He had stayed in the Lucky Dollar about an hour and then headed on back without an aye, yes, or no, except to say Warlock turned his stomach now. Everything had turned bad because of Blaisedell sitting in Warlock like a poison spider in its dirty web.

"Where's Luke?" Abe asked.

"Well, he decided he'd go over toward Rincon and see what the country's like there. Said he was tired of the territory."

Abe made a sound that was a fair try at a laugh. The old man yelled, "Hollow pure yellow son of a bitch!" He began fretting and cursing to himself, and scratching viciously at his legs. They itched all the time now, he said.

"Well, now," Dechine said. "I didn't get up to the trial there, but I heard Blaisedell had himself an awful hard time up there." His little red eyes sought Curley's. "Isn't that right, Curley?"

"Joy to see it. I wished you'd been there, Abe."

Abe said nothing.

"Well, I mean," Dechine said. "What I come by to tell you, Abe. I was talking to Tom Morgan, kind of talking around it to him there, and he sounded like Blaisedell wasn't going to stand for being pissed on up there at Bright's like he was. Sounded like he thought Blaisedell might move on."

"He won't move on," Abe said. "He's got work to do still." Curley watched him stretch, and knew it was a fraud. "Killing to do yet," Abe said.

Curley averted his eyes to see Dechine scowling down at his knees, and the old man grimacing horribly.

Dechine said, "There is this new woman up in Warlock. Kate Dollar her name is, and high-toned as that madam they used to have at the French Palace there. Won't have anything to do with anybody, but I see her passing the time there with Johnny Gannon the other day. Never thought of him much as being a long-boy, before."

"Hope she gives him the dirty con," the old man said. "Any son of a bitch that would stand by and see his brother burnt down by that hog butcher."

"Dog killer," Abe said, in that way he had, as though he were talking to no one. "He will come back because he didn't get all the dogs killed yet."

"I swear!" Dad McQuown cried. "It makes a man want to puke to hear a son of mine talk like you do!"

Abe didn't even appear to hear. Dechine was studying his knees some more.

"Son, what's got into you?" the old man said. "I never heard such fool talk."

Curley heard snarling beneath the porch. One of the dogs dashed off around the corner; it was the big black bitch, with the little feisty brown one after her. Abe stirred a little, and moved his shoulders in his grease-stained buckskin shirt.

"Why, they make you out a dog," Abe said. "Run everything onto you. Then they put the dog killer after you and it crosses out everything. I see how it works," he said, nodding like that, to himself.

Curley said, "Maybe they will take it far enough back so they can make out it was you all the time, instead of Apaches out here."

Abe looked at him with his green marbles of eyes. "Do you think you are joking, Curley? They could do it if they tried. Because time was when every foul thing any man did it was Paches did it. And so old Peach came dog-killing down and cleaned them out. And so start all over clean. It is like a woman every month. Now it's Abe McQuown is the dog and Blaisedell dog killer so they can start clean again. I see how it works."

"*Jesus!*" the old man said.

"Watch I'm not right, Daddy," Abe said. "They have piled all the foul on me now. Then they will bleed it out and start clean. A man'd been educated he could follow it all the way back through history, I expect. How it's worked just like that. You can't blame them. Can't blame Blaisedell even."

"*Jesus Christ!*" Dad McQuown said. Curley looked at Dechine and shook his head a little, and Dechine found a place on the back of his hand that needed studying more than his knees.

Curley said, "Abe, I guess I never knew a man with as many friends as you. And talking this crazy stuff."

Abe blinked and stared off at the mountains. After a long time he said, "You think I have gone yellow. But I'm not scared. I just feel like one of those calves in the Bible that's going to get its throat cut by a bunch of wild Jews set on it. Only those calves never knew what was happening to them."

"Holy Jesus Christ, son!" the old man yelled. "You have been chewing on the wrong weed. Son—"

But Abe continued, not even raising his voice. "Can't blame Blaisedell even. He is just doing what all the rest want. He is just the one with the knife to do the cutting."

Dechine said, "I never heard about Blaisedell being any shakes with a knife."

Abe's eyes glittered with anger as he glared at Dechine. But he did not speak, and Curley sighed to see him.

"Son," the old man said. "Now listen here, son. Why, God-damned right it looks like Blaisedell is itching to kill you. But the thing you have to do is kill him first."

"He'll kill me if he gets a chance," Abe said. "I'd be a fool to give him the chance."

Curley said slowly, "Blaikie would surely like to buy this spread, Abe." He met Abe's eyes that blazed at him, sorrier for Abe than he had ever been for anyone else; Abe's eyes wavered away from his, and he was sorry for that, too.

"Do you think I would run out like Luke?" Abe said hoarsely.

"What're you going to do, Abe?" Dechine asked.

"Only one thing for a man to do," Dad McQuown said, "that's being chased out of his own country."

"Wait it out," Abe said.

"Why, son, there's them that fought your fight for you moldering on Boot Hill in Warlock! Why, if I was anything but half a man myself I'd—"

"You're not," Abe snapped.

Curley said, "I've been thinking of moving on myself, Abe."

"Run then."

"I wouldn't look at it I was running. Things have gone bad here, is all. I wouldn't look at it that you was running either."

"I don't run," Abe said. He shook his head, his face in shadow beneath his hatbrim, the sun red-gold in his beard.

"Or fight," the old man said contemptuously. "Or anything."

"Wait it out, that's the best thing, Abe," Dechine said. Curley saw Abe's face twist again, as though with pain, and Curley stood up a little straighter, where he leaned against the rail. He could feel the strangled violence in Abe and he was afraid that if Dechine said one more stupid thing Abe would jump him.

But Abe only shrugged and said, "Can't go against what everybody thinks of you." Then, after a time, he said, "Can't run and I can't go against him. He is fast. He is faster than anybody in the country. He's— He'd—"

He stopped, staring, and Curley turned to see the brown dog trotting around the corner of the house, his dark-spotted tongue lolling from his mouth. Abe leaned back stiffly. His hand flicked down, and up; his Colt crashed with a spit of fire and smoke and the dog was knocked rolling in the dirt with about a half a yelp. The Colt crashed and spat again and again, and with each shot the brown, bloody, dusty body was pushed farther away as though it were being jerked along on the end of a rope.

"Like that!" Abe whispered, as the gunsmoke blew away around him. He holstered his Colt. "Like that," he said again.

## 28. *Journals of Henry Holmes Goodpasture*

March 12, 1881

I HAD thought this affair of only local importance. It did not occur to me that it had spread beyond the territory. I was surprised to read a long account of it in a San Antonio paper which someone brought here, and now I have come into possession of a magazine called the *Western Gazette*. This so-called journal combines cheapjack writing with smudged print upon coarse paper, and is devoted almost entirely to an affair vaguely resembling, and called, "The Battle in the Acme Corral." It is a strange experience to read an account such as this, where an occurrence one is closely acquainted with is transformed into something wild, woolly, and improbable, with only the names true, and not all of *them* by any means.

There is a crude illustration upon the cover, depicting a huge St. George of a man whose six-shooter is almost as long as a sword, confronting a host of sombreroed dragons. The execrably written text might be the more infuriating if Blaisedell were held to be the villain of the piece, but possibly nothing could be more intolerable than the fulsome praise, the impossible prowess and nobility, and the heroic speeches that make the gorge rise. The author listed nine dead, of whom Morgan was credited with three. It is fantastic to think of people reading, and believing, this vile fiction, which is solemnly presented as Truth. Buck says there were a number of newspapermen at the trial, however, some of whom had come from great distances to attend it. Presumably Warlock will now go down in History as the site of "The Battle in the Acme Corral," as well as of the Medusa Mine. Blood is as stirring to the human imagination as silver.

I was struck by the artist's depiction of Blaisedell as a huge man. Since the corral shown has nothing to do with the original, other than its name, and the representation of Blaisedell the same, I find myself wondering why the artist chose to draw a great brute of a fellow. A rough-and-tumble Hero for a rough-and-tumble people? Feats of strength being more appealing than feats of finesse? No doubt the artist knows better than I the correct heroic image to present to a republican mentality.

This magazine has affected me more deeply than merely with the contempt and anger I felt upon first examining it. For are we not, perhaps, here in Warlock, sitting in upon the childbed of a Legend? Are we watching such a momentous birth all unknowingly, and, unknowing too, this one or that one of us helping it along, acting as midwife, boiling the water, holding the swaddling clothes, etc? As time goes on and if the infant does not die (literally!), and continues to grow, will not this cheap and fabulous account in this poor excuse for a magazine become, on its terms, a version much more acceptable than ours, the true one? It is a curious thought; how much do these legends, as they outstrip and supersede their originals, rest upon Truth, and how much upon some dark and impenetrable design within Man himself?

March 18, 1881

A most pleasant evening last night, spent with Buck, Joe Kennon, Jed Rolfe, Will Hart, Fred Winters, and the doctor. I held forth mightily, I talked my mouth dry, and my listeners' ears to tatters; but I must hold that Blaisedell is a virtuous man (against no opposition in that company), and that the Acme Corral was a tragedy for him since it was not a clear-cut victory. For he deserves no other kind.

We speculated on the fact that Blaisedell has not yet returned to Warlock, although it has been two weeks since his acquittal. Morgan has been to Bright's City, undoubtedly to see him, but has made no comment or explanation that I have heard. My fear is that Blaisedell will not return at all. This would be a blow to us, for I fear our uneasy peace is coming to an end. A miner was killed by one of his fellows in a quarrel at the French Palace last Thursday night. The survivor was arrested and has been sent to Bright's City for trial, but it is felt that this would not have happened had Blaisedell been here. Will Hart has heard he is riding a tiger in a Bright's City gambling hall and does not wish to quit while he is winning. Buck is irritated with him; after all, there were no provisions made for long vacations in the terms of his employment. We all, of course, fear that Warlock will revert to her former state of violence and lawlessness in his absence, temporary or permanent.

Will, I think, feels that Blaisedell would do better not to return. That, for instance, he might take offense at talk and be forced into petty quarrels. This has occurred to me too. Yet I myself want Blaisedell to return, not merely for the sake of peace here, but in order that he may in some way redeem himself in a further and completely unambiguous action. Joe Kennon, a straightforward man, wishes Blaisedell to return and kill McQuown. Buck Slavin, not so straightforward, fears that McQuown may be feeling vengeful toward him because he has sided with Blaisedell, and wishes devoutly for the same consummation. Buck proclaims that all disorder and lawlessness would die with the San Pabloite, peace would reign, and commerce flourish forever after.

McQuown's death by gunplay, I am afraid, is the climax I also desire. Blaisedell's reputation is important to me. It is as though, through him, I can see a bit of myself immortalized, and the others of this town, and even the whole of this western country. For how can this be done but through those men who, because of their stature among us, we raise still further in tall tales and legends that denote our respect, and which are taken by the world and the generations, from us, as standing for us?

                                                    March 20, 1881

It is said that Blaisedell's decision to go to Bright's City and endure trial was to a large degree brought about by Judge Holloway's righteous rantings at him. I have heard the judge cursed for this often of late. Pike Skinner is especially bitter toward him, and there is a rumor that when Schroeder heard that Blaisedell had departed for Bright's City, he physically assaulted the judge as being the cause. The old story, that arises whenever the judge is in an unpopular phase, is also current again: that he was run out of Dade County, Texas, where he was a J.P., for drunkenness and other more sinister vices. But I must defend him, and counter with the story which seems to me at least complementary to the other: that he was run out of Dade County because he tried to expose a criminally inclined sheriff who was, unfortunately, much better liked by the Texans than Judge Holloway and Rectitude.

I have also heard that he was at one time judge on a bench of some importance in Kansas, where people became so inflamed against him because of a series of unpopular decisions—I have no doubt that these were righteous ones, righteously delivered —that they tarred, feathered, and rode him out of town on a rail.

Certainly he is a bitter man, and one impossible to know, but if there are kernels of truth in these two tales of him, the outlines of his bitterness begin to show; nor will I condemn a man for trying to drown an abysmal bitterness in alcohol. He is a lonely man, too; he has no friends, nor even any regular drinking companions. He is uncomfortable company.

He can be awesome enough on occasion, in his wrath, although he usually ends by making a fool of himself, when he is pitiable. Yet he is, to me at least, more often than not an admirable man, and Warlock owes a debt of gratitude to him. As judge "on acceptance" he has long dealt successfully with our minor disputes and misdemeanors, and he has, almost singlehandedly, as the deputies have come and gone and Sheriff Keller has done neither, maintained at least an awareness of the law here, where there has been no law.

March 28, 1881

Blaisedell has returned. He has resigned his position as Marshal and is dealing faro at the Glass Slipper. Disappointed and heartsick as I am at this turn of events, I cannot find it in my heart to blame him.

# BOOK TWO

# THE REGULATORS

## 29. *Gannon Looks for Trouble*

GANNON WAS alone in the jail when he heard the pound of bootheels on the boardwalk, and Carl hurried in. Carl sailed his hat toward the peg and grunted with satisfaction when it caught and swung there. But he said, "Trouble," as he sat down at the table.

"What?"

"They are dropping wages at the Medusa and the Sister Fan," Carl said. One end of his mustache was wet where he had been chewing on it. "They are going to do it," he said. "And the others'll follow what the Porphyrion and Western Mining Company does, sure as shooting. MacDonald just told me. He is worried about it; he by God ought to be!"

"They knew it was coming."

"Not by a dollar a day, they didn't!"

Gannon whistled.

"Cutting them a dollar a day. MacDonald says it's got to be that much because the price of silver's went down, partly, and partly because they are getting all that water down on the thousand-foot level. Unprofitable labor, getting rid of water, he says. There is going to be hell broke loose when they hear about it."

"They don't know about it yet?"

"He'll tell them payday." Carl took a dirty, irregularly bitten piece of plug out of his pocket, and wrenched a corner off with his teeth.

"That's almost twenty-five per cent."

"It is, and there is going to be hell. MacDonald's not likely to step out of his way to miss any trouble, either. Well, and easy enough to wreck a mine, to give him his due. Charge of giant powder somewhere, or a fire in the stope. There was that one on the Comstock burned for three years and then had to be all retimbered before they could work it again. So MacDonald is getting ready to bust them before they bust him."

"Bust them how? Did he say?"

"He has got his mind set on running out that Brunk he fired a while back, the one he tried to get Blaisedell to post.

767

And Frenchy Martin and old Heck, and some others he says're agitators too. Wants us to run them out for him." Carl looked up at him and grinned a little.

"No," Gannon said.

"What I told him," Carl said. The lump of tobacco moved in his cheek like a mouse. "So Mister Mac is down on me; he is a man that doesn't take kindly to anybody saying him no. I told him we would come out to the Medusa Saturday when they announced it—try to stop trouble. But he'd got other ideas by then."

Carl sighed and said, "And I think what he's got in mind now is rounding up a crew of hardcases to do his dirty work for him. Regulators was what he said, and I thought he meant some Citizens' Committee people he'd get together. But now I wonder if he wasn't thinking San Pablo."

"It's what he did before."

"Cade," Carl said. "By God, I forgot about that. Damn it to hell!" he burst out. "I wish we could count on Blaisedell if MacDonald intends on pulling something like that. By God if I want to see Warlock run by MacDonald and a bunch of San Pablo hardcases any more than McQuown and Curley and the same. What the hell's got into Blaisedell, you suppose, anyhow?"

Gannon went over to sit down beside the alley door, and Carl scraped his chair around to face him. "Maybe he is just waiting for McQuown to come in," Carl went on. "Maybe that's what he is doing. Except why'd he quit marshaling?"

"Maybe he is sick of killing."

Carl stared at him; he licked his lips. "Johnny, you haven't gone and turned against him because of Billy? I thought you hadn't."

Gannon shook his head, patiently. He had prayed that he could remain patient. Always he could feel the accusations, from both sides, picking at him like knives whenever he walked the streets. He had ignored them so far, but he was afraid he was not always going to be able to.

"Well, somebody's got to be peace officers," Carl said. "And killing is part of it. I don't see—" He stopped, and shook his head and said, "I wonder if it wasn't that Miss Jessie went and turned against him. That'd sour a man. He is not rooming

"Oh, no! Oh, I don't think everyone does. Most of them just live along. But there are a few who can do—I suppose I mean *be* something. Something that can go on even after them. And shouldn't those people be trying every moment to *be* that? I mean, God gave it to them to do or be, and if they didn't try I should think they would be very afraid of God."

"It is your move, Jessie," he said.

She was leaning forward with her hand on the locket that hung at her throat, a vertical frown line creasing her forehead, and her eyes were far removed from him. She said, "How terrible for a person to know what he could have been. How he could have gone on. But instead having to live along being nothing, and know he is just going to die and that's the end of it."

She was talking about Blaisedell, and he did not know what to say to her. He removed the checker she had dropped upon the board. Her eyes turned toward the door again; Brunk appeared there, with his cap pulled low upon his forehead and one big hand grasping the door frame. He was grinning, and his face was flushed with liquor.

"Miss Jessie," he said thickly. "And the good doctor Wagner. Good night." He said it with a peculiar inflection.

"Oh, good night, Frank!" Jessie said.

"Good night, Brunk."

"No," Brunk said, with a solemn shake of his head. "I mean, it *is* a good night. Mostly, just before payday, it's not. But this payday—" Brunk grinned again.

"Looking forward to it, are you?" the doctor said grimly.

"Am," Brunk said. He glanced around with exaggerated caution. "Because you know what?" he whispered. "It is going to go down to *three*-fifty a day and they are not going to stand for it." He raised a thick finger to his lips. "Oh, but I won't tell them! Let them hear it from Mister Mac. Then they will bust!"

"And then we can try to patch the bloody heads they bring here."

"Bloody heads to you, but men to me!" Brunk said proudly. "For some'll have to get bloody heads so the others can hold theirs up. It's what I've been waiting for." He turned to Jessie. "Well, Miss Jessie, maybe Lathrop hadn't courage enough. But *I* have. *I* have!" he said, and hit his fist upon his chest.

"That's fine, Frank," Jessie said, in a colorless voice. "But I wish you wouldn't shout so."

Brunk stared at Jessie and his face was at once shocked, hurt, and furious. "You don't think I am good enough, do you, Miss Jessie?"

"Of course I do, Frank!"

"No, you don't," Brunk said. He glanced at the mezzotint of Bonnie Prince Charlie on the wall behind Jessie's head, and his face twisted. "Because I am no *gentleman*," he said. "Because I am no—no long-haired, white-handed gunman. Oh, I know I am not good enough and it is only a bunch of dirty miners anyhow."

The doctor thrust his chair back and rose. "You are drunk," he said. "Get out of here, you drunken fool!"

"Not so drunken as her fair-haired boy-killer!" Brunk cried. "That is so drunk his high-rolling friend's got to half carry him away from the French Pal—"

The doctor darted forward and slapped Brunk's face. Brunk staggered a step back. The doctor slapped him again. "Get out of here!" he cried, in a voice that tore in his throat.

Brunk put his hand to his cheek. He turned slowly away. He moved toward the foot of the stairs, where he leaned against the newel post, a thick, dejected figure in the darkness of the entryway.

Jessie was sitting up very straight, her mouth tightly pursed in her stiff face, her eyes glancing sideways at the checkerboard as though she were considering her next move. Her hand plucked nervously at the locket at her throat.

There was a scuffling sound outside on the stoop, a low cursing. More drunken miners, the doctor thought; he was tired of drunken miners beyond patience. He stepped out toward them just as they came in through the door—two men who were not miners. Clay Blaisedell had come back to the General Peach.

Morgan edged his way inside with an arm around Blaisedell, who was hatless, sagging, stumbling—not wounded in brave battle, merely drunk to helplessness. Brunk had turned and was watching them.

"Come on, Clay boy," Morgan was saying. "Sort those feet out. Almost home now—where you were bound to go." He was panting, his white planter's hat pushed back on his head.

"Evening, Doc," he said. Then Morgan said, "Evening, Miss Marlow," and the doctor felt Jessie's fingers grip his arm.

Blaisedell pulled away from Morgan and stood swaying, his boots set apart and his great, fair head hanging as he faced Jessie. Jessie moved a step forward to confront her drunken hero. He had thought she would be shocked and disgusted but she was smiling and looked, he thought, with a painful wrench at his heart, triumphant.

But she did not speak, and after a moment Blaisedell started for the stairs, holding himself very straight. He stopped at the foot, as though realizing his incapacity to mount them, and leaned upon the newel post as Brunk backed away.

Morgan said to Brunk, "You look like you have a strong back, Jack. How about a hand upstairs?"

"Let him lay in the gutter for all of me!" Brunk said. "One that would shoot down a sixteen-year-old boy in—"

"Don't say that, bullprod!" Morgan said; his voice was like metal scratching metal. Blaisedell clumsily tried to turn, and Morgan caught his arm as he staggered.

"Help you either!" Brunk said. "That would kick a broken-arm fellow's teeth in!" His voice rose hysterically. "High-rollers and road agents and murdering pimps and worse! Well, I am not afraid to talk out, and there's things—"

"Stop it!" Morgan snapped, just as the doctor heard Jessie utter the same words, her fingers tightening on his arm again. Brunk stopped and looked from Morgan to Jessie with his tortured red face.

"I have been looking for coyotes howling that tune," Morgan said, in the metallic voice. His eyes, glinting in the light from Jessie's room, looked as cold as murder.

"You will have a lot of teeth to kick in then!" Brunk cried.

"I'll know where to start!"

"Never mind it, Morg," Blaisedell said. He started up the stairs, and Morgan grasped his arm again and helped him upward, grunting with the effort and glancing back over his shoulder once at Brunk. The two men disappeared into the darkness of the stairwell, laboring and bumping against the railing.

"Frank," Jessie said. Slowly Brunk turned, his scar of a mouth strained wide, his fists clenched at his sides. "You are to get out of my house."

"Miss Jessie, can't you see—"

"Get out of my house!" Jessie said. Her fingers left the doctor's arm; he heard her go back into her room. Brunk stood gazing after her with dumb pain on his face.

"You had better leave, Frank," the doctor said, with difficulty. He knew now that he was not the only man who had been jealous of Clay Blaisedell. He followed Jessie into her room, and heard, behind him, Brunk's slow departing footsteps; above him, shuffling ones.

Jessie was staring up at the ceiling with round eyes. "Are they saying things like that about him?" she whispered.

"I suppose there are a few that—"

"Frank said it," she broke in. "Oh, the fools! Oh—" She put her hands to her face. "Oh, they are!" she whispered through her hands. "It is Morgan's fault! It is because of Morgan! Isn't it, David?"

"I suppose in a way it is," he said, nodding. He could not say more, and he was sorry now for Brunk, who had tried to.

"It is!" Jessie said, and he heard Morgan coming back down the stairs.

Morgan stopped and looked in the doorway, taking off his hat. His figure was slim and youthful, and his face, too, seemed young, except for his prematurely gray hair, which looked like polished pewter in the light. Slanting hoods of flesh at the corners of his eyes gave his face a half-humorous, half-contemptuous expression.

"I am sorry to bring him home in a state like this, Miss Marlow," he said, with a mock humility. "But he would come. And sorry for the fuss with the jack."

The doctor said, "You will have to excuse Brunk, Morgan. Stacey is a friend of his."

"Stacey?" Morgan said, with a lift of his eyebrows.

"Whose teeth you kicked in, at your place. That was a cruel thing."

"Was it?" Morgan said, politely.

"Mr. Morgan," Jessie said in a stiff voice. "Possibly you could tell me what's the matter with him. I mean, what has happened to him since he came back to Warlock."

"What's happened to him is for the best," Morgan said. "Though I don't expect you will agree with me."

"What do you mean?" Jessie said.

Morgan smiled thinly, and said, with the polite and infuriating contempt, "Well, Miss Marlow, he is a man with some good in him. I don't much like to see him broken down under things. He is better off out of marshaling."

"Dealing faro in a saloon!" Jessie cried. The doctor was shocked at the venom in her voice, but Morgan only grinned again.

"Or anything. But that's handy and pays well. Good night, Miss Marlow. Good night, Doc."

"Just a moment, please!" Jessie said. "You didn't want him to come back here, did you, Mr. Morgan?"

"It is hard to argue with him sometimes."

"You don't like me, do you?"

Morgan put his tongue in his cheek and cocked his head a little. "Why, ma'am, I am very respectful of you, like everybody else here in town." He made as though to leave again, but seemed to change his mind. "Well, let me put it this way, Miss Marlow. I am suspicious by nature. I know what sporting women are after, which is money. But I am never quite sure what nice women are after. No offense meant, Miss Marlow."

Again he started to leave, and again Jessie said, "Just a moment, please!" The doctor could hear her ragged breathing. She said to Morgan, "You said you didn't like seeing him broken down under things."

Morgan inclined his head, warily.

"So how you must *hate* yourself, Mr. Morgan!"

Morgan's face looked for an instant as it had when he had confronted Brunk; then it was composed again, like a door being shut, and he bowed once again, silently, and took his leave.

Jessie put her hand down on the checkerboard and with a quick motion swept the checkers off onto the floor. "I hate him!" she whispered. "No one can blame me for hating him!" She raised her face toward the ceiling. He saw it soften and she whispered something inaudible—that must, he thought, have been addressed to Blaisedell, who had come back to her.

She seemed to become aware of him again; she smiled, and it lit her whole face. "Oh, good night, David," she said. "Thank you for playing checkers with me."

It was a dismissal, he knew, not merely for this evening, but of a companion with whom she had passed the time while she waited for Blaisedell to return. He nodded and said, "Good night, Jessie," and backed out the door. She came after him, to close it, the opening narrowing into a thin slice of lamplight that framed her face. The door shut with a gentle sound.

He went up the steps to his room, and sat down on his bed. He felt as though he were smothering in the thick darkness. He felt old, and drained of all emotion except loneliness. Through the window he could see the bright stars and a narrow shaving of moon, and from here he could hear the sounds of laughter and drinking from the saloons on Main Street. He rose and fumbled on the table for the bowl of spills and matches. He lit the lamp, the darkness paled around him; he stood with his hands on the edge of the table, staring into the bright mystery of the flame. He had taken the bottle of laudanum from his bag when there was a soft knock.

"Who is it?"

"It's Jimmy, Doc. Can I come in a minute?"

"All right," he said.

"You'll have to open the door for me, I guess."

He put down the bottle and went to open the door. Young Fitzsimmons came in, carrying his bandaged hands before him as though they were parcels. He had dark wavy hair and thick eyebrows that met over the bridge of his nose. His long, young face was grave.

"Some things bothering, Doc."

"Worried about those hands, Jimmy? Here, let me cut the bandages off and have a look." The boy's hands had been burned so terribly he had told him he might lose them. But miraculously they were healing, although it would be a long time yet.

"No, it's not that," Fitzsimmons said. He held out his hands and grinned at them. "They are coming fine—they don't stink like they used to, do they?" He sat down on the end of the bed and his face turned grave again. "No, it's I am kind of worried about Frank, Doc."

"Are you?" he said, without interest.

"My daddy was a miner," Fitzsimmons said. "And his before him and on back. I know about mines, and I know what you can do and can't do when there is trouble with the company.

They had troubles back in the old country my grandaddy used to tell about. I know one thing you don't do is fire a stope."

"Are they talking about that?"

"Plenty. They won't listen to me because I am only twenty, but I know rock-drilling better than most of them, and union and company too. I know you don't wreck a mine; because there may be trouble, but there is always a time when trouble is over for a while."

"I know, Jimmy," he said. He watched the boy's brows knit up; they looked like black caterpillars. The boy shook his head and sighed, then held up his bandaged hands again.

"It's been kind of good for me to be this way awhile, Doc," he said. "It is fine to be quick with your hands, and hell not to be able to even button your fly or open a door the way I can't. But it makes you understand, too, how you can be too quick with them. Now I have got to think every time before I reach out for anything. That's a caution these others would be better off with."

"But they won't listen to you," he said, and smiled.

Fitzsimmons grimaced. "There's not three of them could beat me single-jacking before I got burnt—Brunk couldn't. But there's not three of them will listen to me, either. All they'll listen to is Frank and Frenchy and old Heck. But they'll listen to me some day!

"Frank's all right in a way," he went on. "He didn't want nothing for himself, and I expect he would jump down a shaft if it would help get a union. Except he would just as soon jump everybody else downshaft too, and then look back and find there wasn't anybody to make a union with."

"I have noticed that in Brunk," the doctor said.

"He is that way, all right. They are all too wrapped up in how they hate MacDonald's guts. Well, I do too, but it doesn't do anybody much good—hating Mister Mac. He is not the only super there'll ever be. The way they are thinking, union now is only something against MacDonald. If the company was smart enough to fire MacDonald the whole union idea'd blow up in Brunk's face."

"Yes, I suppose that's true, Jimmy," he said. Fitzsimmons looked pleased.

"I've tried to tell them MacDonald is nothing but company

policy, and policy will change a good deal faster if the company sees it is good sense to change. Burning the stope or the rest of it'll just bring in a harder man than MacDonald. But they won't listen."

He sat there frowning. This was the most serious the doctor had ever seen Jimmy Fitzsimmons; even when he had warned him about his hands he had been cheerful. He was a strange boy, though not a boy. He wondered if there was not more iron in him than there was in Brunk. There was certainly better sense.

"Well, Jimmy," he said. "I would vote for you for president of the union rather than Brunk, I'll say that."

He had meant it jokingly; he saw that Fitzsimmons had not taken it so. "No," the boy said, very seriously. "I'm too young yet." He looked up from under his thick eyebrows and grinned again. "But I would vote for you, Doc."

"Don't be silly," he said; his heart began to labor, as though he had been running.

"No, I'd vote for you," Fitzsimmons said. "There's others that would too. There's a lot that's sensible but just get carried along by the wild ones like Brunk because they're loudest. Doc, what we need is somebody that can talk straight with MacDonald and Godbold and the rest of them and not be made a fool of. Somebody that is quick and smart, but somebody that is respectable too. It's true what Frank says. But because we are not respectable don't mean a man doesn't have pride in being a miner. My grandaddy and my dad had pride in it, and me too. Brunk doesn't much, underneath all. That is his trouble trying to deal with MacDonald—so that all he can think to do is things like stope-burning. But there is talking and dealing has to be done too, and that is where you would do for us, Doc. Some of us have talked of it already."

"I'm no miner, Jimmy."

"You are *for* us, Doc. Everybody knows that. That's the main thing."

He wondered if he really was; he knew he was against the things that destroyed and maimed them.

Fitzsimmons said quickly, "Well, I guess there is no use talking about it just yet. I guess they are going to have to bust loose this time again, and maybe they will learn from it." Then he said, "I thought of even going to tell Schroeder they was thinking of firing the Medusa, but I couldn't do that. That would bust me with them if they ever found out."

The doctor was surprised at the calculation in Fitzsimmons' voice; it was a side he hadn't seen before.

Fitzsimmons gazed back at him boldly, as though aware of what he was thinking. He grinned again, not quite so boyishly. "What's wrong with that?" he said. "Sometimes if you know better than a bunch what has to be done you have to undercut them a little. You have to be careful, though, for they are hard when they think a man is against them. They will listen to me some day," he said, and rose. Then he laughed. "And don't think you are out of it, Doc. I have got plans for you."

The doctor rose to open the door for Fitzsimmons, who now thanked him for his time and said good night very formally. He went back to the table and took up the bottle of laudanum and held it until his hand warmed the glass. But finally he put it back into his bag, and undressed and went to bed.

In bed he could not sleep, not merely because he had not taken his evening potion, but because always, in the darkness, Jessie's face hung in his eyes. He saw Blaisedell drunken and sagging, and yet, try as he would, he could not look upon him with contempt. He saw Brunk's face, with the jealousy as pitiful and hopeless as his own behind the hate. He saw Morgan's face, full of murder, and yet it was the face of a man much more than the mere unscrupulous and violent gambler he had seemed. He remembered Jessie and Morgan crying at the same instant to Brunk to stop, in their different voices that were as one voice, and remembered them only minutes later facing each other as deadly enemies.

It seemed to him that in this night he had seen many symptoms of the obsession which he had already known in Jessie. He had seen that both Jessie and Morgan accepted the importance of Blaisedell's name and all that it implied even in their antipathy for one another. He had seen the same obsession, though not for Blaisedell, in possession of Brunk, and even stronger in Jimmy Fitzsimmons. It seemed to him, as he considered it, more than an obsession, a disease of the spirit; and yet he wondered if this disease, this obsession, this struggle to preeminence, was not the reason for mankind's triumph on the earth—the complex brain developed to plot for it, the opposing thumb to grasp at it—if it was not what set mankind apart from the animals. No animal cared what was its name.

He stared out at the bright stars over Warlock, regarding, now, himself, and what Fitzsimmons had said about his leading the miners. He felt no call within himself. He felt no urge to strive to be anything more than what, long ago, he had been content to be. He considered his freedom and his bondage, his own soul's sickness and his own particular health, and wondered at the will he did not possess.


## 31. *Morgan Uses His Knife*

ACROSS from Morgan at the desk in the office of the Glass Slipper, Clay sat with his fair head canted forward, his lips pouting a little. He looked white and ill, Morgan thought; Clay had had a bellyful of whisky last night, but he looked sicker than that.

"What do you hear from Porphyry City, Morg?" he said. "I hear it is booming some."

"It is booming right here."

"Not for me," Clay said.

"Why, Porphyry City sounds fine, from what I hear. You thinking of going there?"

"I don't know," Clay said. "I suppose it wouldn't be much different."

Morgan laughed and said, "You were surely bound and determined to go back to the General Peach last night. See the lady today?"

Clay glanced up at him and nodded tersely. Then he leaned back in his chair and said, "I shouldn't have gone back there."

He nodded too.

"It is not her, Morg," Clay said, as though to answer what he, Morgan, had not wanted to ask. "It is everybody. I can feel it walking down the street or anywhere. Even if there is nobody around I can feel it. I can't do what they want. They don't even know what they want, and I can't do anything, for anything I do is either all the way wrong or not right enough."

"Eat your guts out!" Morgan said, and all at once he was angrier at Clay than he had ever been before. "You are either a peace officer eating your guts up, or you are a faro banker. God damn it, Clay, wherever you go you are going to have to not give a damn what people want of you. You can quit marshaling and make it stick here as well as anywhere."

"I should have quit before I started."

"Chew on yourself!"

Clay said, "Abe McQuown is sitting bad on their stomachs and I am supposed to give them a purge. I want no part of it. For it is me that is poisoned every time. Every time now. Who am I to do their killing for them? I just want shut of it, but I can feel them at me all the time. And Jessie—" He did not go on.

"Well, you have quit," Morgan said. "You did the right thing, Clay."

Clay's mustache lifted, as though he were grinning, and his eyes crinkled a little. He said, "There was a time when I thought I could do the right thing."

Morgan poured himself a quarter of an inch of whisky, and, turning it in his hand, frowned carefully at the flat tilt of the liquor. "You were going to say something about Miss Jessie."

"What she says," Clay said heavily. "She says there is a thing a man needs to be—" Morgan saw something uncertain and almost frightened cloud his eyes. "It is hard to say, Morg," Clay said, and sighed and shook his head.

So it was Miss Jessie pushing Clay; his mind closed down on it like a trap. It was as though in a card game with strangers he had picked on sight the one he must play against as most dangerous, and had seen himself proved right on the first hand.

"But she is wrong," Clay said. "For it has gone past and the rest is poison."

"And you have quit."

Clay nodded; Clay's clouded eyes met his for a moment. "But it is not so easy here, Morg. With Kate to see every time I turn around. I see she has taken up with Billy Gannon's brother. Came out with Cletus's brother, and now she has taken up with Gannon. It is a thing to scare me screaming, isn't it?"

"Scare you?" Morgan said, and didn't know if he should laugh at that or not.

"Why, yes. If every man I shot down wrong had a brother, and every one came after me, I would have to die that many times."

"Hard to do," he said, and still he did not know. Anxiously he watched Clay's face. He felt a quickening lift as he saw the rueful smile starting.

"Surely," Clay said. "But I could do it the way I feel now. Like a cat."

"Listen to me now," he said to Clay. "For a change. First thing where you have gone wrong is worrying over what everybody wants of you, or thinks. To hell with them! That is the nugget of it, Clay. And look at it like this—like a hand of cards. It is like throwing in your hand because you made one bad play."

"No, not one," Clay said. "Take your card game another way. The stakes are too high now, it has got too big for me. It was jacks to open once, now it is kings."

Queens, he thought; he felt as though Clay were arguing with Jessie Marlow, through him. "Clay, I don't know what we are quarreling over," he said. "You have quit it."

"That's so," Clay said, and sighed again.

A racket was starting up in the Glass Slipper. It was time for the miners to be coming in, but it sounded to Morgan as though every one of them in Warlock were crowding into the Glass Slipper at once. He heard their raised voices and the confused tramp and scuffle of boots on the floor. Clay turned to glance at the door. "What the hell is going on?" Morgan said, and rose just as the door opened.

Al Murch looked inside; behind him the racket was louder. "There is some jacks here to see you, Blaisedell," Murch said. He stood barring the door with his broad frame, but behind him Morgan could see the big miner, Brunk, and another one with a red welt along the side of his head.

"What about?" he said, as Clay rose.

"Proposition to put to Blaisedell, Morgan!" someone called.

"Let us in, Morgan," Brunk said, and Morgan nodded to Murch, who let four of them in.

"That's enough, Al," he said, and Murch fought the door closed against the rest.

Brunk looked as though he would rather be somewhere else. With him was an old miner with a goat beard, another heavy-set one with a black waxed and pointed mustache, and a fourth, the one with the bruise on his head, who was bald and had an Adam's apple like a billiard ball.

"You do the talking, Frank," Goat-beard said. He said to Clay, "We have went out at the Medusa, Marshal."

"He is not marshal any more," Morgan said, and Goat-beard looked at him with dislike.

Brunk, who had a rough-cut, square face and hands the size of shovels, pointed to Bald-head's bruise. "Wash Haggin did that," he said. "They have dropped wages at the Medusa a dollar a day, and MacDonald's hired himself about fifteen hardcases in case there was any complaint about it. Wash Haggin did that to Bobby Patch."

"Don't do to complain," Bald-head said, and grinned toothily. But he looked scared.

"Winchesters and shotguns around to fit out an army," Waxed-mustache said. "Both Haggins was there, and Jack Cade and that one Quint Whitby."

Morgan said, "McQuown?"

Brunk shook his head. "Not him or Curley Burne."

"Put it to him, Frank," Goat-beard said, and nudged Brunk.

"Well, MacDonald's got these people up there to try to scare everybody to going back to work," Brunk said. "We kind of think they will do more, too. We think MacDonald is going to send them in here to run some of us out of town. Like he did with Lathrop last year."

"Run *you* out, you mean?" Morgan said, and Brunk's big, red face twisted angrily.

"What did you want to see me for?" Clay asked. "It sounds like you had better see the deputies."

Waxed-mustache said, "They are no good for us, Marshal." He spread his hands out. "You are the man for us."

"We've got to keep those hardcases off us some way," Brunk said stolidly. "They've got too much artillery. We need a gunman." He stopped and swallowed; it looked, Morgan thought, as though it swallowed hard.

"You are the one that could do it," Brunk went on. "Schroeder is not much friendly with us, and him and Gannon couldn't do anything against that bunch even if they wanted to. We are having a meeting tonight as soon as we see what's happened at the Sister Fan and the rest." He licked his lips. "And we'll get organized and the union will collect dues. We can pay you for kind of marshaling for us," he said. "That's our proposition, Marshal."

"I guess not, boys," Clay said. "Sorry."

"Told you," Bald-head said. "Told you he wouldn't."

"I guess MacDonald got to him first," Goat-beard said. "MacDonald is a step ahead of us all the way, looks like."

Morgan watched Clay shake his head, apparently without anger. "Nobody's got to me, old man. I am not against you or for you either. I'm just not in it."

Morgan nodded to Murch, who caught hold of Brunk's arm. "Let's skin out, fellows," Murch said, in his rasping voice. "Mr. Morgan and Mr. Blaisedell's busy."

"Told you he wouldn't," Bald-head said, starting for the door.

"Why should he?" Brunk said, and jerked his arm away from Murch.

"What do you mean by that?" Clay said.

"Well, why should you?" Brunk said loudly. "We can't pay you like any rich-man's Citizens' Committee, with MacDonald sitting on it. We don't want killing done to hire you for. Only killers kept off us. So why would you be interested?"

"Al!" Morgan said, and Murch caught hold of Brunk's arm again. Waxed-mustache was grimacing violently.

"Let him be," Clay said. More color showed in his pale face. "Let him have his say out."

Brunk glanced down at Clay's shell belt, which showed beneath his coat; he glanced quickly at Morgan. He said in a stifled voice, "I'm not saying anything but that we need help, Blaisedell."

"Let me tell you," Clay said. "So there is no misunderstanding here. I was hired marshal here, and I have quit it. I'm not hiring out again to the Citizens' Committee, or MacDonald, or you, or anybody. What more is there to say than that?"

"Nothing, by damn!" Goat-beard said. "Let's get out of here, Frank!"

"No, wait a minute," Clay said to Brunk. "There is something you are choking on yet, and was last night. Go ahead and spit it out."

"Do you think I am scared to?" Brunk said.

"Who asked you to be?" Clay said.

"Get him out of here, Al," Morgan said, but Clay looked at him angrily.

"I want to hear what he has to say, Morg."

"Never mind it, Frank!" Waxed-mustache said. "Let be, can't you?"

Clay stared steadily at Brunk, and Brunk took a step back away from him. His face working, he said, "I was just saying—I mean, rich men can have themselves a marshal, but no dirty, ignorant muckers can. Surely; that's all. It's clear enough."

"That wasn't what you was going to say," Clay said. It was as though he were calling Brunk a liar. "That wasn't what you was saying last night, either. Say it out. Say it clear out, Brunk. I would rather a man said a thing to my face than behind my back."

Brunk just stood there facing him with his hands at his sides and his thick shoulders hunched a little. Murch moved toward him and Brunk snatched a hand to the haft of his bowie knife. Suddenly he said, "All right, I will say it to your face! I say you would have shot me down like your Citizens' Committee told you to, only Miss Jessie begged me off." Brunk stopped and his head swung sideways, as Morgan moved to lean forward with his hands on the desk top.

Then Brunk's voice rose. "But even your respectable friends threw you down when you and your high-roller partner went to robbing stages!"

"Holy Christ, Frank!" Bald-head whispered.

Brunk sucked his breath in, and then cried explosively, "And when you and him went to killing cowboys to make like it was them had done it! And Morgan kicks out a broken-arm fellow's teeth for saying it! Well, I say if your high-toned Citizens' Committee don't want you any more, then the damned miners don't either!"

Morgan slowly turned toward Clay. Nothing showed in Clay's face. He reached for his hat, and Brunk drew back at the movement. Brunk shifted his feet to keep facing Clay as Clay slowly came out around the desk. Bald-head and Waxed-mustache backed out of his way. Clay put on his hat, and, without a word, went out the alley door and pulled it closed behind him.

In the silence the noise of the crowd of miners in the Glass

Slipper was very loud. Murch started to slide the bar back and open the door.

"Keep it shut," Morgan said, in a voice he could hardly recognize as his own.

"Here, now!" Bald-head said fearfully.

Morgan stripped off his coat, unbuckled his shoulder holster, and dropped Colt and harness on the desk with a thump. He opened the drawer and brought his knife out. Brunk's scarlet face swam in his eyes. "Do you know how to use that sticker of yours, mucker?" he said.

"Now hold on, now!" Waxed-mustache said. "Now, listen, Morgan; Frank here said things he had no cause to say and didn't mean. Now let's not—"

"Get it out, if you know how to use it," he said to Brunk. He pricked the palm of his hand with the knife's point. "You had better know," he said. He came out from behind his desk, and the others moved away from Brunk.

"He is big, Tom," Murch said. "You had better leave me—"

"This is mine. Get it out!" he said. Brunk was hesitating with his hand on the haft of his bowie. "Why, I am giving you a fair shake, aren't I?" Morgan said, grinning. "Prove you are right by sticking me. Or I'll prove you are an over-grown, yellow-livered lying hog that's not fit to lick his boots you just pissed all over. Get it out and talk like that to me!"

Brunk pulled his bowie loose. He held it waist-high, his left hand out and spread-fingered, his thick forearm blocking.

"Fair fight now, boys!" Goat-beard shrilled. "We are here to see it is fair, Frank!"

"Come on, then, Mister high-roller," Brunk said hoarsely, moving sideways to get his back away from Murch and toward his partners. He swung the bowie blade in a circle before him.

Morgan did not move now, watching Brunk's guard and holding his own knife low in his right hand, with his left close to it. He met Brunk's eyes, and saw, in their black pupils, his own image. He heard the quickened breathing of the men watching as he thrust his right hand up, the knife cutting out. Brunk leaped back, and then immediately pressed forward, feinting with the bowie. Morgan exposed his neck, hoping that Brunk would make a high stroke.

The bowie swept toward his throat, and he dodged to the

left and shifted his knife to his left hand. He thrust it up and felt it catch home, and tear away; Brunk's arm was too long.

He heard the gasp, not from Brunk but from the others. He had drawn blood that darkened the breast of Brunk's dirty blue shirt, but he had wasted his best stroke. For the first time it occurred to him that he might die.

The knife in his right hand again, he raised the blade to touch his forehead, dropped it low once more, feinted left, feinted right. The blood spread on Brunk's chest. Brunk lunged toward him.

Brunk's wrist crashed against his, the bowie blade passing over it. His own knife snubbed into the bone of Brunk's fore-arm, and immediately Brunk's big hand caught his wrist. With a wrench he freed it and dodged aside, but he had felt the power in those hands and arms, and their quickness. Brunk's arm was bleeding now too, but he saw a light of confidence in the miner's eyes.

Morgan swung in to the right to get under Brunk's guard, and the elbow crashed down against his hand. He feinted right again and drove straight in, but had to leap back again as the long arm swept around. He felt the slight tug at his shoulder, and heard the gasp again. He didn't look.

His breath began to tear at his lungs. There had been too many cigars, too many women, too much whisky; he laughed out loud and saw Brunk disconcerted by it. He drove in once more and this time slashed Brunk's upper arm; he jumped back as the bowie flashed past, and immediately thrust up and in and this time his knife ripped into flesh and caught, and Brunk gasped a harsh cough. But his knife did not pull free as he re-treated, and Brunk's left hand clutched down on his. In turn he caught Brunk's wrist as the bowie swung down. Brunk's weight forced him back, and Brunk's height bore him over. He tried to wrench back away, and tripped; he fell and Brunk fell with him. Brunk's grip loosened on his knife hand and he rammed the knife farther into Brunk's belly as he crashed to the floor with Brunk sprawled on top of him. Brunk cried out once.

Brunk's hand caught his wrist again between their bodies, but still he could move his hand a little, to twist and turn the knife blade in Brunk's flesh. He felt the warm wet flow of blood on his own belly, as, grunting and straining, his elbow set and bruised against the floor, he fought to keep Brunk's bowie from his throat.

Brunk's hand bore down impossibly hard. What was the use? he thought suddenly; he did not love life enough to bother to fight this to its end. What was the use? He grinned into Brunk's crazed face and replied to himself: because he would not let a clumsy, stupid mucker beat him; or any man. He twisted the knife in Brunk's body, to kill Brunk before the bowie pierced him, and knew he could not as the huge weight of Brunk's arm came down against his own. Brunk's sweat fell into his face and the muscles in Brunk's neck were spread out like batwings; there was no sound in the world but Brunk's grunting and his own.

He strained his own blade from side to side and Brunk gasped. But he felt his wrist begin to tilt. He had to bend his arm to retain his grip, and so the post he had made of his forearm was gone and there remained only the inadequate strap of his muscles, and his will—not to be beaten. He could feel his arm bending as the blood flowed from Brunk's belly.

He laughed and panted up into Brunk's contorted face, and smelled the stink of him, and watched the bowie that was not a foot from his throat. He worked his own blade up toward Brunk's vitals, up toward Brunk's heart; for Brunk must die too. Why? he thought. What did it matter? There seemed no reason, but his hand needed none. He grinned up at the bowie's point, not six inches from his throat now. Now three, as his arm gave like a rusty ratchet, pure pain now, and caught somehow again; now two inches, as it gave again.

Then out of the corners of his eyes he saw Murch move suddenly, and saw the little double-barreled derringer in Murch's hand. "*No, Al!*" he grunted, and his words were lost in the crash. Brunk's head fell on him, and Brunk did not move again. "No!" he panted.

Weakly he struggled to slide the heavy body off himself, and to his feet. His vest was soaked with blood. He stood there swaying. Murch had the derringer trained on the three miners. Someone was hammering on the door and shouting, "Frank! Hey, Frenchy!"

"Shut up!" Murch whispered to Bald-head. He turned white-rimmed eyes to Morgan. "Christ, what the hell was I supposed to do, Tom?"

"Fair shake!" old Goat-beard cried. "Son-of-a-bitching gambling man, never gave anybody a fair shake in your life!"

Bald-head was leaning back against the wall with a hand in front of him as though to keep the derringer off. The door creaked as the miners in the Glass Slipper tried to force it.

Morgan took up his shoulder holster and Colt, and could not think for a moment. He glanced at his bleeding shoulder.

"Christ, what'll we do, Tom?" Murch said desperately. "Christ, Tom!"

"Sons of bitches!" Waxed-mustache said. "Play fair so long as you win. He had you by the—"

"Shut up!" Murch cried. "Christ, Tom!"

Morgan looked down at Brunk on the floor, with one arm under him and the other flung out, the blood beneath his head and much more blood spreading on the floor beneath his body. He sighed and said, "You had better make tracks, Al."

Murch started for the alley door. The inner door creaked and strained again, and there was another volley of shouting and cursing. Murch turned and the straight-on eye regarded him worriedly. "What about you, Tom?"

Morgan didn't answer, and Murch went out. Morgan stood facing the three miners, trying to get his breath back. As they would not think of blaming the derringer that had put the bullet through Brunk's head, so they would not think either of blaming merely Murch. The bar on the door began to squeal as a more concerted weight crashed against it. He drew the Colt from its holster as Waxed-mustache took a step toward him.

"Bust that door in, boys!" Goat-beard yelled. "For there is rats in here need cleaning out!"

One of the iron keepers sprang loose from the door and flew like an arrow to smack against Waxed-mustache's shoulder. Morgan grinned suddenly to watch Waxed-mustache rubbing his arm, and unhurriedly went to the door and stepped out into the alley. Murch was nowhere in sight. He started to the left. When he heard the crash as the door burst open, he broke into a run. He had reached the end of the alley before he saw, over his shoulder, a flock of them come out of the Glass Slipper and start after him. He laughed as he ran down Southend Street toward Main. It would be quite a run, he thought, if neither Schroeder nor Gannon were at the jail.

## 32. *Gannon Takes a Trick*

GANNON WAS in the jail with Carl when Tom Morgan ran in, panting, covered with blood, hatless, a holstered Colt in his hand. "Lock me up, boys!" he panted. "Or there's a lynching coming off!" He ran into the cell and slammed the door on himself.

Carl sprang up, knocking his chair over backward. There was a roar outside; it came down Main Street like a flood, and Gannon snatched the shotgun down from its pegs. "What the hell?" Carl cried.

"Lock the damned door!" Morgan said, and Carl leaped to do it, and flung the key inside the cell. Gannon ran to the door. Behind him he heard Morgan laughing like an idiot.

Miners were streaming around the corner out of Southend Street, more were coming out of the Glass Slipper to join them, and all of them were yelling.

Gannon held the shotgun out before him with his finger tight on the trigger and felt the sweat starting from his face. "Hold off!" he shouted, "Hold off!" the words lost in the tumult. Beside him Carl was shouting too. Then the leaders halted.

Gradually the whole mass came to a halt, forming a broad semicircle on the boardwalk and in the street around the front of the jail, all of them yelling still, until Carl raised his Colt and fired into the air.

"Now, what the hell?" Carl said, in the silence.

There was a disturbance in the front rank and Frenchy Martin stepped forward through the settling dust; then old man Heck came out.

"Now you turn over that son of a bitch in there, Deputy!" Frenchy Martin cried.

"He is our meat and no business of yours at all!" old man Heck shouted. "Dirty dog killed Frank Brunk and we are—"

The clamor began again and the miners crowded forward. Gannon thrust the muzzle of the shotgun against the belly of the one nearest him. Slowly the shouting died.

"—fair fight," Frenchy Martin was saying. "And then Frank got him down and that lookout of his shot Frank through the head!"

"Where's Murch?" someone yelled. "Somebody'd better get that wall-eyed son too!"

"He lit out on a horse!" another replied. "He was moving!"

"You turn over that bloody-bellied gambler, hear!" old Heck said. "I mean, we will tromp you down, Schroeder!"

Gannon swung the shotgun toward Heck. Another miner made a grab for it and he slammed the barrel against the man's elbow. "Get back!" he said.

Somebody was singing, "We'll hang Tom Morgan to a sour apple tree!"

Frenchy Martin jumped up on the tie rail, and, clinging to a post, motioned for silence. "Boys, are we going to let them stop us? Are we going to take out that murdering bastard or not? Good old Frank was a friend to us all, and MacDonald set Morgan to kill him, most likely." The miners roared.

Gannon looked toward Carl, for this had better be stopped, and Carl leaped forward and clubbed the barrel of his Colt down behind Martin's ear. Martin fell forward into the street, where the miners caught him; the yelling increased in volume and violence. Old man Heck was shaking his fist. Carl fired into the air again. Gannon began edging toward old Heck again, to buffalo him next. He was only worried that it would get dark before they could run the mob off. Already the light was fading with the sun gone.

"Listen!" Carl shouted. "There's been men took out of here and hung but not while I was here and by God there won't be, either! Because I can play hell with a good lot of you and Johnny will just make pure mincemeat with that shotgun. Now; if you want Morgan that bad maybe you can get him, but it's going to cost you dear. You hear now!"

The solid roar went up again, the shoving back and forth. Old man Heck turned and cupped his hands to his mouth to yell, and Gannon slammed the shotgun barrel against the side of his head. He fell to his knees.

"Watch that bull moose over there!" Carl cried, and Gannon swung the shotgun toward a big bearded miner who was moving toward him.

"Back off!"

The miner retreated a step, grinning. Past him, over the heads of the men in the street, Gannon saw riders coming down Main Street from the direction of the rim. They were riding abreast, two ranks of them, and they filled the street. Heads began turning toward them. Abruptly the miners fell silent.

"It's MacDonald!" Carl said.

MacDonald was in the lead, on a white-faced horse, wearing a checked suit and his hard-hat. In the gathering dust Gannon began to recognize the other riders: Chet and Wash Haggin, and Jack Cade, Walt Harrison, Quint Whitby, Jock Hennessey, Pecos Mitchell, and more, and still more in the second rank. Some of them had Winchesters over their arms, and belts of cartridges hung from their saddlehorns.

Abe McQuown was not with them, Gannon saw, straining his eyes; nor Curley. The big miner near him was now flattened against the wall as though he wished he could push back on through it.

"He has brought his Regulators in to do us all down!" Gannon heard someone say. The miners in the street began to retreat, some, on the fringes of the crowd, fading back into Southend Street. Now there was no sound but the pad of oncoming hoofs in the dust.

"MacDonald's come to run his agitators out himself," Carl said. "Damned if he isn't, and damned if it is pleasant to be bailed out by such a bunch."

Someone yelled, "Morgan already did your dirty work for you, Mister Mac!"

"Hold together, fellows!"

"Damned if we will run before a pack of rustlers, MacDonald!"

Carl said mournfully, "What the hell are we going to do, Johnny?" and Gannon took a deep breath and then ducked under the tie rail and jumped down into the street. He moved through the miners as rapidly as he could, pushing right and left with the shotgun butt as though it were an oar. Sweating, dusty faces turned to stare at him. There was muttering behind him. A hand reached out to grasp his shotgun.

"Let me by," he said, and the hand fell away.

"Let the deputy through, boys," a voice said, and the miners began to move more rapidly aside before him. He came out of the mob not fifty feet from the riders, and he walked on through the dust straight toward MacDonald.

"Pull up!" he said, bringing the shotgun muzzle up to bear on the white-faced horse. MacDonald reined in and the horse stood steady, swinging his head around to feign a bite at MacDonald's leg. The others reined up also. Wash Haggin gazed contemptuously down at him, Chet Haggin grinned a little, Jack Cade lifted his round-crowned hat and ran his fingers through his hair, his dark, whiskered face sullen. Gannon looked from face to face. Those in the rear rank were the kind of San Pablo scum that even Abe McQuown was too proud to ride with. Except for the Haggins they were all bad ones, but after the first glance around he looked only at MacDonald. He felt calm enough.

"What's going on here, Mr. MacDonald?" he said.

"This has nothing to do with you, Deputy," MacDonald said coldly. "We have constituted ourselves a regulation committee and we know our objectives. It is none of your business. Stand aside."

"It is my business. You are not coming in here with these people."

"You caught this posting people out from the marshal, Bud?" Chet Haggin asked.

Gannon saw Cade casually draw his Colt and rest it on his thigh. He kept the shotgun trained on MacDonald. "Take them out, Mr. MacDonald."

"You fool!" MacDonald said. His mouth looked like a trap in his ascetic, coldly handsome face. "We intend to round up some agitators who are bent on making trouble at the Medusa. You won't stop us. You—"

"Take them out," he said again. His ribs ached where the

butt of the shotgun was clamped against his side, his hand sweated on the barrel. "Out," he said.

"We'll come through shooting if we have to, Bud," Wash said.

Gannon heard the iron snap as Cade cocked his Colt; he tried not to flinch, not to look. He stared straight at MacDonald over the muzzle of the shotgun, and MacDonald licked his lips.

"Morgan already killed Frank for you, Mister Mac!" a miner yelled, and MacDonald scowled.

"Take your people out of town, Mr. MacDonald," Gannon said once more. "There will be no rounding up done in Warlock."

"Schroeder!" MacDonald cried. "Tell this idiot to get out of the way."

"Do like he says, Mister Mac!" Carl called back. His voice was shrill. "And Jack Cade, you had better hang up that hog leg, for I am laid in on your belt buckle."

Gannon stood watching MacDonald and he thought he had won.

"What do you say, Mister Mac?" Cade said, in his flat, harsh voice. "Shoot in or crawl out?"

Wash said, "You had better back off and let us handle it, MacDonald."

"He doesn't go unless you all go," Gannon said.

"Very well!" MacDonald said. "Your piece there speaks with more authority than you do. I'm forced to honor it, since I want no bloodshed. You will hear more about this from Sheriff Keller." He stood in his stirrups and called to Carl, "This is not the end of this, Schroeder!" He sawed viciously with the reins, and the white-faced horse bucked, scaring Chet's mare sideways. Gannon swung the shotgun toward Wash and Jack Cade. Cade nodded once, thumbed his teeth, nodded again. The Regulators became, for a moment, a milling mass of horsemen, cursing and muttering among themselves as they turned away. Then they sorted themselves out into the same two ranks, and, with MacDonald again at the head, faded into hazy shapes in the twilight as they retreated. A roar went up from the miners; taunts were shouted after them. Gannon made his way back to the boardwalk and mounted it once more. Pike Skinner was standing with Carl; Pike watched him come up with his mouth pursed, and his hat brim shadowing his eyes. Carl was laughing.

"They'll be back, deputy!" someone yelled from among the miners in the street. "Don't think they won't be back!"

Gannon leaned against the adobe wall. The sign above his head creaked a little. He let the shotgun barrel droop.

"Why, I guess you had better clear out of the street then," Carl said. "So they won't ride you down."

"We want Morgan!" someone shouted. A few took it up, but soon the cry died away. Gannon leaned against the wall and watched the miners drift off. A tension had gone out of the air. "Meeting!" somebody was yelling. "Meeting!" The crowd began to break up into small clots of men. A wagon came across on Southend, breaking it up still further.

"You had better go scratch your name on the wall in there, Johnny," Carl said. "You have done smart work tonight. I thought we was due for two falls at once, but damned if you didn't take them both instead. What's that you say, Pike?" he said, turning toward Pike Skinner, who had said nothing.

"It isn't done with yet," Pike said grouchily.

"Well, I expect you are right," Carl said. "And you are deputized, you and Pete and Chick and Tim. Hunt them up for me, will you? There's a good fellow."

Pike went off along the boardwalk. Carl slapped Gannon on the back as he followed him into the jail. Morgan was leaning against the cell door, almost invisible in the darkness.

"Hanging off?" he said.

"For a spell anyway," Carl said. He pulled down the pulley lamp and lit it. Now Gannon could see Morgan's face; it looked as gray and tired as he himself felt. "I wouldn't say clear off, no," Carl went on. "Well, you surely went and roused things up. What'd you want to kill this Brunk for?"

"Bled his dirty blood all over me," Morgan said, distantly. Gannon sat on the table edge with the shotgun leaning against his leg and his arms folded, watching the gambler's face. For all the expression that was there Morgan might have meant what he said.

"I suppose you might call that a reason," Carl said. "You taken up fighting jacks as a steady thing now, Morgan. Knife fight, was it? What was all that yelling how it was supposed to be a fair fight?"

Morgan said in a disgusted voice, "Brunk had me in a little trouble so Murch shot him."

"Heard them saying Murch's lit out, but damned if I think I had better take after him the way things stand. You put Murch to shooting him?"

"He thought of it before I did."

"Get me to believe you didn't put him to it."

"Believe it or don't!"

"Now don't go scratchy, Morgan," Carl said mournfully. "If a hardcase that works for you kills a man that's got you in trouble, maybe it is on your back some."

"Nothing's on my back," Morgan said, and withdrew into the shadows.

Gannon said to Carl, "Maybe somebody'd better get the judge."

"Time enough. You're not in any hurry, are you, Morgan?"

"I'm patient by nature," Morgan said.

Peter Bacon appeared in the doorway; he nodded at Gannon, and raised an eyebrow.

"Witnesses?" Carl said to Morgan.

"All muckers," Morgan replied. "Old Goat-beard and that one with the waxed mustaches, and another one called Patch."

"Old Heck and Frenchy," Carl said. "They seemed kind of maddest, all right. You sure you didn't tell Murch to blow him loose from you?"

There was a crash and splatter of glass and a rock rebounded from the far wall, and came to rest among the shards of glass beneath the broken window. Peter Bacon disappeared out the door, and Gannon ran to look. He could see no one in the darkness, and after a moment Peter returned along the board-walk, shaking his head. Gannon went back inside, where Carl was cursing and trying to push the broken glass into a pile with the side of his boot.

"Oh, hello, miss," Peter said from the doorway, and Kate Dollar came in.

"Good evening, Deputy," Kate said to Carl. "Deputy," she said to Gannon. She wore a tight jacket, a long, thickly pleated black skirt, and her black hat with the cherries on it. She smiled her harsh, unpleasant smile as Morgan appeared at the cell door again.

"Is that Tom Morgan?" Kate said, and her voice was as unpleasant as the smile. "I heard the miners had him on the run."

Gannon backed up uncertainly to lean against the wall, and Carl said, "It sure is him, Miss Dollar. And he sure was running. Not much of a lead on the pack, either."

"You running, Tom?" she said, and laughed.

"Oh, I can run with the best of them," Morgan said. His voice was as harsh as Kate's, his face, framed in the thick, hand-smoothed bars, was blank. "I have run before this. There was a place called Grand Fork I ran and got caught."

"Did they hang you?" Kate asked, and Gannon felt that he was witnessing something he did not want to see, or know.

"Maybe they did," Morgan said. He frowned with thought. "No, come to remember, a friend I had there set fire to the hotel where those vigilantes had me, and during the whoop-de-do I got out some way. No, I didn't hang that time."

"But no friends here?" Kate said.

"Well, now, miss, we made out all right," Carl said uncomfortably. "Johnny and me didn't need any help."

Gannon saw Peter Bacon grimacing painfully as Kate spoke to Morgan again. "But I understand you didn't kill him yourself, Tom. Was he a good man, Tom? That you had your gunman kill for you?"

"Just a big, stupid mucker, Kate," Morgan said. "But you probably would have liked him, at that."

"But what was the matter with Clay?" Kate cried. Now she sounded hysterical, and now, Gannon thought, he must stop this.

He put a hand out toward her and said, "Kate!" just as Morgan said loudly, "What kind of jail is this, where anybody can drift in off the street and bedevil the prisoners?"

"Bedevil!" Kate cried.

Gannon touched her arm. "Now, Miss Dollar," he said.

"Well, now, yes, miss," Carl said. "I don't expect you ought to be in here with a bunch of wild jacks around throwing rocks through the window and all. I guess you had better—"

"I just came down to tell you they are throwing rocks through the windows of the Glass Slipper, too," Kate said, calmly now. "There are some people trying to stop them, but I don't know if they will."

"Durn!" Carl said. "I should've thought of that. I'd better go, Johnny." He took up the shotgun and hurried out. "Come on, Pete!"

Morgan disappeared again and Kate stood facing the cell for a moment longer. Then she bowed her head and turned away. Without looking at Gannon, she said, "Will they try again?"

"I don't know."

"Don't try to save him," she said in the ugly voice. "Don't try to do anything for him. He doesn't want you to, and anybody that ever did has been sorry for it the rest of their lives." She stopped and he saw that she looked almost ashamed; then her face tightened again, and she swept on out of the jail.

In the cell Morgan was laughing softly.

Gannon went outside to stand beneath the gently creaking sign in the cool night breeze. He could hear shouts and see the dark shapes of men against the whitish dust of the street up before the Glass Slipper.

He heard the sad, suspirant music of a mouth organ. A thin figure was coming toward him.

"Well, howdy, Deputy Bud Gannon."

"Hello, Curley," he said. "Did you come in with MacDonald?"

"No, just rode in to watch the fun," Curley said. "Should have; Mister Mac is giving six dollars a day and expenses. There is going to be a lot of expenses, too, up at the French Palace and around."

"No, there's not. They're not coming in here."

Curley looked at him with his eyebrows crawling up. He ran his fingers back through his black curls, and took a step back, raising his hands in mock terror. "By God, posted out of town by Bud Gannon! Not me too, Bud? Say it isn't so!"

Gannon shook his head and tried to grin.

"Whuff!" Curley said. "I was ready to fork it and crawl. Well, I guess I'll have the French Palace to myself then." He looked at Gannon sharply, and his clownish expression vanished. "What're you going to do if some of them come back anyway, Bud?" he said quietly. "Brace a man?"

"They haven't come back in."

"Might, though," Curley said. He pried at a crack in the boardwalk with the toe of his boot. "You know, people don't take to posting so good. Billy didn't."

"I'm not posting anybody," he said tightly. "We are just not going to have MacDonald and that crew in here chasing miners around."

"Strikers," Curley said. "Agitators, what MacDonald said. Bunch of damned, over-paid—"

"Why didn't you hire out with the rest, then?"

Curley laughed cheerfully. "Well, I just don't like Mister Mac much, Bud. One of a few I don't."

"Including me. Are you down on me too, Curley?"

"Yep," Curley said.

"All right," he said, and felt his eyes burning.

Curley sighed and said, "Well, I kind of am and kind of not. I see you think you did right and maybe I see how you could think it honest. But I can't think that way. How a man is brought up, I guess, and you are a cold one, Johnny Gee."

"Maybe I am."

"That was your brother, Bud. The only kin you had."

Gannon said in a shaky voice, "Most people here think Blaisedell only did what he had to."

"You think that way, don't you?" Curley said. His boot toe scuffed at the planks again. "No, I am not all the way down on you, Bud. But I am about the only one. You sure ought to think about putting distance between you and here—when you get a chance."

"Thanks."

"*Por nada*," Curley said.

A group of men was coming across Southend Street and onto the boardwalk. Gannon heard the crack of the judge's crutch; with him were Carl, Pike, Peter Bacon, and some others. Carl stopped while the rest went on into the jail.

"You ride in with the Haggins, Curley?" Carl said, in a rasping voice.

"Oh, no!" Curley said. "No, sir, I am separate. I just swore it in blood to your partner here. I'm just having a little chin with Bud about this posting fellows out of town. You boys have come pretty hard against us cowboys, haven't you?"

"Yeh," Carl said, in a kind of grunt. "Hard."

"The Acme Corral for you boys, huh? Big medicine. Run up a score, maybe they'll make you marshal, Carl, now Blaisedell has quit. Money in it, I hear. Scalp money for—"

"D-don't you say anything against Blaisedell to me!" Carl said.

Gannon could feel the hate. "Carl," he said. But Carl didn't look at him.

"Don't even say his name to me," Carl said hoarsely. "You God-damned picayune rustler."

"You have rewrote the laws, have you?" Curley whispered, dangerously. "A man can still talk, I guess."

"Not to me," Carl said. "Not here or Bright's City either. You or any other rustler."

Gannon took out his Colt and held it pointed down before him. Curley glanced toward him, only his eyes moving in his rigid face. "Better move along, Curley," Gannon said.

Curley shrugged and sauntered off into the darkness. The sound of the mouth organ drifted back. Carl stood staring after him, rubbing his right hand on his pants leg.

"Schroeder!" the judge shouted from the jail, and Pike Skinner appeared in the doorway: "Come on, Carl!"

"Let's go in, Carl," Gannon said.

"Kind of pleasant not to be scared of a man for a change," Carl said in the hoarse voice. "Sure, let's go in and get the hearing started."

## 33. *A Buggy Ride*

THE STRIKERS from the Medusa and the sympathetic miners from the other mines held their meeting on the vacant ground next to Robinson's wood yard on Peach Street. Torches made an orange glow there and smoke from the torches overlay the meeting like a milky sheet illuminated from below. There was a steady roar of shouting and clapping as they listened to various of their number harangue them, or broke up into smaller groups to attend half a dozen different speakers at once.

The town had fortified itself against riot. Shopkeepers sat

inside their stores with shotguns close to hand. Horses were kept off Main Street. The Glass Slipper was dark, its front windows broken and a frame of timbers nailed up before the batwing doors. Men stood along the arcades listening to the sounds of the miners' meeting. Inside the Lucky Dollar the gambling layouts were packed and townsmen stood three deep along the bar. Among them were Arnold Mosbie, the freight-line mule skinner, Fred Wheeler, who worked at the Feed and Grain Barn, Nick Grain, the beef butcher, and Oscar Thompson, Kennon's blacksmith. These four were sharing a bottle of whisky, Mosbie and Wheeler squeezed against a narrow strip of bar, while the others stood behind them.

"Listen to those sons of bitches yell up there!" Mosbie said.

"Think they're going after Morgan again?" Thompson said, glancing worriedly toward the doors.

"Working themselves up to it?" Wheeler commented. "I'll bet Carl and Gannon's wetting their pants."

"Looks like they might've done better not to let out the judge wasn't holding Morgan for Murch killing that jack," Thompson said. "Just keeping him in jail for his own good."

"I heard old Owen wouldn't go stand by the jail with the rest," Grain said, reaching past Wheeler for the bottle. "I sure agree with him about Morgan. I don't hold with miners much, but I'll whistle when they set out to hang Morgan." He glanced at the others from beneath his colorless lashes. "Blaise-dell is going to let him hang, too. See I'm not right."

"Sure been scarce today," Wheeler said, shaking his head.

"What's wrong with Morgan?" Mosbie asked.

"Well, you heard about him and that little Professor of his, didn't you?" Grain said. "Morgan wasn't paying him enough so he was going to go to work for Lew Taliaferro, playing that new piano Lew got for the French Palace. So Morgan had that Murch of his fill Lew's piano with lime mortar, and the Professor knew about it and was going to tell—you know what happened to him. Looked like he got tramped by a horse out here, but it wasn't any horse."

Wheeler snorted. "I heard it," he said. "I didn't have to believe it, though."

Mosbie had turned to face Grain. "That is Lew's story, Nick," he said. "And bull piss just like his whisky."

"Well, it is just hard for a man to like Morgan, Moss," Thompson said.

Someone near them said, "Whooo, listen to them crazy muckers!"

Mosbie turned to face Thompson. "Listen," he said. "I have said it, and you have said it too—hooray for Blaisedell for going against those sons of bitches of McQuown's. He has made McQuown eat it till it comes out of Abe's ears, and hooray for him, I say. So I say hooray for Morgan too, that is the only man in Warlock that ever helped another out against those backshooting bastards." He looked back at Grain again, "And I say piss on those that piss on Morgan, for he is a better man than them, whatever he's supposed to've done."

Grain flushed. "Now, listen, Moss—"

"I'm not through," Mosbie said. "Now it is funny how all of a sudden McQuown and Curley and them is smelling sweeter and sweeter to people again, I don't say who, the mealy-mouthed sons of bitches. And all of a sudden it is clear somehow that it is Morgan that's done everything mean and rotten that ever happened around Warlock, killing piano players and such. And in the whole valley besides, it looks like—riding around dropping off strongboxes to make it look bad for poor, innocent murdering rustlers. It surely is nice for Abe McQuown."

"Now, see here, Moss," Grain said. "I don't hold with McQuown, but—"

"That's good," Mosbie said, turning back to the bar again. "I am glad to hear you don't."

"They're coming!" somebody cried. The Lucky Dollar fell abruptly silent. The yelling of the miners was louder.

"Jesus, here they come," Thompson said, and he and Grain were borne along by the men crowding toward the batwing doors. There was a tramping and a rhythmical shouting now in the street, a burst of singing. The bankers at the layouts were swiftly cashing in the chips. Wheeler tossed his whisky down and looked at Mosbie.

"Want to go watch the hanging, Moss?"

"Hanging, hell," Mosbie said. "Let's go watch Blaisedell." They shouldered their way into the press of men moving toward the doors.

The miners came along Main Street, marching in what must have been ranks when they started, and with a semblance of the martial in their blue shirts and trousers and red sashes. Many of them carried torches or lanterns, and their bearded faces shone sweaty and orange-red in the torchlight. They sang in ponderous unison:

"Oh, my sweetheart's a burro named Jine!
We work at the old Great Hope mine!
On the dashboard I sit,
And tobacco I spit
All over my sweetheart's behind!

Good-by, good-by, good-by, Tom Morgan, good-by . . ."

The singing broke off in a ragged yell. Some tried to continue the tune, while others merely shouted as they went on down Main Street toward the jail, with the dust rising beneath their marching feet and hanging like fog in the darkness. There was a crash of glass as a rock was thrown through Goodpasture's store window, followed by an outcry of argument and laughter. There were other crashes. Torches were swung from side to side, shedding sparks like Catherine wheels.

"Christ, they will burn the town down!" someone exclaimed, as the men streamed out of the Lucky Dollar in their wake. The street began to fill behind the miners as townsmen came out of the saloons and the Billiard Parlor, and, with the sidewalk loungers, drifted along after the marchers. Outlined against the front of the jail, in the light of the torches, stood a small group of men.

Mosbie and Wheeler crossed Main Street and made their way down to Goodpasture's corner, where their bootheels grated on broken glass. Goodpasture stood within the darkened store with a shotgun in his hands. "*Morgan!*" the miners were shouting, all together. "*Morgan! Morgan!*" They approached the boardwalk before the jail in a broad semicircle, the near end of which moved slowly, the far more rapidly. Carl Schroeder shouted something that was lost in the yelling.

"My God!" Wheeler said. "Look at them go! They're going right on in!"

The miners advanced steadily toward the six who opposed

them: the two deputies, Pike Skinner, Peter Bacon, Tim French, and Chick Hasty. Three of them had shotguns, Bacon a rifle, Gannon and Hasty only handguns. The miners in the front rank began swinging their torches and sending up great arcs of sparks.

Finally they halted and Schroeder's voice was heard: "First one across this rail gets shot!"

"Tromp them down!" the miners cried. "Morgan! We want Morgan!"

"Give him up, Schroeder! We'll tramp you down!"

Mosbie said to Wheeler, "By Christ, it looks to be two hundred of them there!"

"Where the hell's Blaisedell?" a man near them said. "He had better damn well hurry!"

"He'll be along and back them off," said another.

"Hell he will," a third said, with a snicker. "He is soaking it over at Miss Jessie's. She'll keep him there, being for those stinking jacks—" He cried out as someone hit him in the mouth.

Mosbie struggled to free himself from those who pressed around him, and flung himself at the man who had spoken; they went down in a cursing pile. Others tried to separate them. "Foul-mouthed son of a bitch!" Mosbie yelled.

On the far corner a miner was haranguing Schroeder. He tried to climb over the rail and Schroeder swung the shotgun barrel down on him. Instantly a wave of miners poured forward over the tie rail. "Moss!" Wheeler shouted. "There they go!"

The boardwalk before the jail was a mass of fighting men. A shotgun was discharged; there was a scream, and the blue-clad figures fled back into the street, leaving one crumpled and shrieking on the boardwalk, with Carl Schroeder standing over him.

"Shot one, by God!" Wheeler said, as Mosbie rejoined him, panting. "Best thing for it, too."

"Who did it?"

"Carl, looked like."

"Hey, Carl shot one!"

The miners began to roar with one voice, and the tightly packed mass of them in the street weaved and swayed, the torches waving wildly above them. "*Kill them! Kill them! Hang them with Morgan!*"

"Boys, they have killed Benny Connors!"

Mosbie leaned against one of the posts that held up the arcade, with Wheeler pressed tightly against him by the men around them. "Oh, Jesus!" a man near them said, over and over, like a prayer. The weaving, uncertain movement of the mob changed, section by section, into a single forward thrust forcing the men in the front rank against the railing. One of the deputies raised his six-shooter and discharged it with a flat shock of sound; still the miners pressed forward, almost in silence now.

"Here he comes!"

"It's Blaisedell, all right. Here he comes!"

"Thank the good Lord!" Wheeler said.

"Look at the buggy!" someone said, but no one paid any attention to him.

Mosbie clambered up on the tie rail and clung to the post. "You ought to see him!" he called down to Wheeler.

Blaisedell came down the center of Main Street, with the townsmen moving quickly aside before him. He came at a swift, certain, long-legged stride, with his black hat showing above the heads of the men he passed. He did not pause as he came to the edge of the mob of miners, forging straight ahead through them like a knife splitting its way through a pine board. Torchlight gleamed on the barrel of his Colt as he knocked a miner aside with it.

"Kill him too!" someone among the miners cried suddenly. "Don't let him get up there, boys!"

But Blaisedell went on, unhindered, and finally he stood before the jail among the deputies, taller than any of them. His voice was sudden and loud. "Back off, boys. There'll be no hanging tonight."

"I believe he could stand off the U.S. Cavalry," Wheeler said. The miners in the street remained silent.

"You had better get this one to Doc Wagner," Blaisedell said, motioning to the miner still groaning on the boardwalk.

Still there was silence. The torches flared and smoked. The front rank had drawn back from the rail.

Then someone shouted, "*He won't shoot!*"

Others took it up. "He won't shoot to save that murdering high-roller! He's bluffing! Run him down!"

The yelling mass began swaying forward once more, compressing those who tried to hold back away from the rail. Then the railing went down and miners leaped and crowded onto the boardwalk. Blaisedell and the deputies were swamped by the blue-clad bodies in a melee of flailing arms and gun barrels. There were two shots, two furry spurts of flame reaching upward. Again the miners retreated. Gannon and Schroeder appeared, and Blaisedell with his hat gone. One of the deputies was down; Pike Skinner and Tim French helped him inside the jail.

"Who was that, Moss?" Wheeler cried.

"Chick Hasty."

"*He won't shoot!*" the same voice shouted again, and again the miners took up the cry.

"They are going to run him," Mosbie said hoarsely.

Blaisedell stood before the jail door with a lock of hair fallen over one eye, his chest heaving, and both his Colts out. Schroeder, shouting unheard, stood on one side of him, Gannon on the other. Skinner and French came out of the jail again and took up their posts. Once more the torches began to swing, and sparks flew upward in the wind.

"They are going to bust over him," Mosbie said.

"There they go again!"

The miners flung themselves forward and Blaisedell and the deputies were thrown back before them. Blaisedell went down; there was a yell as the watchers saw it, and a groan; the other deputies went down. One retreated inside the jail, dragging another with him, and slammed the door. The miners crashed against it, drew back, and crashed against it again.

"Look at that! Look!" cried the man beside Mosbie on the railing.

But no one noticed him as the jail door broke and the miners streamed inside, yelling in triumph. Almost immediately they began thrusting themselves back out again, while others still fought to enter. The deputies began to appear among them.

"What the hell happened?" Wheeler demanded.

"Look! It's Miss Jessie!"

A buggy was coming out of Southend Street. Miss Jessie Marlow was in it, and there was a man on the seat beside her. She was trying to turn the bay horse that drew the buggy east into Main Street and the horse was scaring in the crowd. Miss Jessie sat very straight with a bonnet on, and a white frilled blouse with a black necktie. The man lounging on the seat beside her was Morgan.

"It's Morgan with her!"

"It is Morgan, for Christ's sake!"

Miss Jessie flicked the buggy whip down once, and the bay pranced ahead. Men moved out of the way. The lighted tip of a cigar glowed in Morgan's hand. The two of them looked as though they had been out for a pleasant ride.

"She took him out of the back!" a man cried. "I saw that buggy turning in the alley there a while ago. Look at that, will you?"

"She won't get away with it," Mosbie said, in the hoarse voice.

"Hurry up!" Wheeler whispered, hitting his fist against the tie rail. "Hurry up, ma'am! Bust that bay again!"

The buggy continued its slow progress through the men in the street. The miners had fallen silent, and now the main traffic was away from the jail. Some of them appeared out of the alley in Southend. "He's gone!" a miner shouted. "Got out the back!"

"There he is! In the buggy!"

Miners surged around the buggy, the whole mass of them changing direction now, and pressing back up Main Street. But the miners who surrounded the buggy began to drop away from it. Others ran after it, looked in, and dropped back too. Mosbie began to laugh.

"Did it!" he said. "They are going to make it, by God! Came right through them, and the best thing she could've done, too."

The buggy began moving more swiftly now, out of the press; it disappeared into the darkness up Main Street.

"Taking him to the General Peach," someone commented calmly. "Well, they'll never bust over her."

"Where's Blaisedell?"

"He just went inside the jail. He's all right, looked like."

"He held them long enough for her to get Morgan out. Slick!"

"I'd a lot rather seen him cut a few of them down."

Miners stood in uncertain groups in the street. The deputies were shooing them off the boardwalk. Two of them carried off the miner who had been shot. Schroeder had a long, bloody cut over one eye. Gannon retrieved Blaisedell's black hat from a miner who had picked it up.

Mosbie climbed down from the tie rail. "What the hell did Blaisedell let those sons of bitches run over him for?" he said to Wheeler. "That's what I don't see. God damn it to hell."

Nick Grain appeared beside Wheeler. "Did you see him get run over, Fred?" he cried, in an excited voice. "They sure called his bluff."

"Shut up!" Mosbie said. He caught Grain by his shirt collar. "Shut up! You push-face cow-turd of a butcher! Shut up!" He flung Grain away from him, and Grain disappeared hurriedly into the crowd.

"I hate that stupid asinine flap-mouth son of a bitch," Mosbie said. He and Wheeler started back along the boardwalk with the others. The men around them were talking in low tones; one of them laughed and Mosbie glared at him.

Groups of men stood in the street, looking toward the jail, or up toward the General Peach where the buggy had gone. The miners were heading into the saloons, or congregating along the boardwalks.

Wheeler and Mosbie walked on east in the deep shadow under the arcade, crossed Broadway, and continued up to Grant Street, where they joined a group standing by the side of the Feed and Grain Barn. All the windows were lighted in the General Peach. The buggy stood in front, the fat bay scratching her neck against the hitching post. Eight or ten miners stood near the buggy, and the crippled miner, Tittle, was watching them from the porch with a rifle in his hands.

"The Doc's buggy," someone commented.

"Not a one to try and stop her!" Paul Skinner said. "Not a one!"

"There's a woman with more guts than any man I know."

"Shame to see them bust over Blaisedell," said another.

"Should've shot one for himself like Carl did."

"I heard Carl didn't go to. The stupid muck got hold of his shotgun and yanked on it, and Carl's finger on the trigger."

"Looks like maybe Blaisedell's a human being like the rest of us though," another man said. Mosbie started toward him, but Wheeler grasped his arm.

"There comes Curley Burne," someone whispered.

Curley Burne came across Grant Street toward them with the light from the General Peach gleaming on his black curls.

"Curley," someone said, and several others also greeted him.

"Big night, boys," Curley said. "You boys fun it like this every night in Warlock?"

There was some laughter. "Where's those Regulators of MacDonald's, Curley?" a man drawled from the shadow of the adobe wall. "Just when we needed those Regulators bad they didn't show for beans."

"Warlock's too calky for them," Curley said. "Curl a man's hair just to walk down the street here." He indicated his own head with a sweep of his hand, and there was more laughter.

"There's Blaisedell."

They all fell silent. Blaisedell rounded the corner; he limped a little as he walked down toward the General Peach. As he mounted the porch past Tittle he held to the hand rail, and, in the light there, he did not look so tall. The front door closed behind him with a hollow whack.

"The marshal got himself some chewed up tonight," Curley Burne said.

Wheeler gripped Mosbie's arm, but Mosbie pulled away with a curse. "Go tell it to Abe McQuown, Curley!" he said thickly. "Maybe it will bring him out of his hole."

"Who said that?" Curley said.

Mosbie crouched a little. "I said it!"

"Hold off now!" Paul Skinner said. "Hold off! Curley, you leave be! Moss!" Wheeler stepped between Curley and Mosbie.

"You shouldn't have said it, Moss," Curley said, and his voice was as thick as Mosbie's.

"I'll say it again!"

"Take it and forget it, Curley," a voice said from the darkness. "He has got friends here and you haven't."

"We are pretty sick of cowboys up here," another man said.

Curley glanced toward the two who had spoken, looked past Wheeler at Mosbie, shrugged, and turned away. His hat swung across his back as he disappeared into the darkness.

"Soooooo-boy!" Wheeler said. "He is no man to mess with, Moss!"

"I am no man to mess with tonight either," Mosbie said.

Behind him someone laughed a little, relievedly.

"God damn it to hell!" Mosbie said, and kicked in fury and frustration at the dust.

## 34. *Gannon Puts Down His Name*

I

GANNON LEANED limply against the cell door, pressing a hand to his ribs. Pike Skinner and Peter Bacon were hunkered down with their backs to the wall opposite him, Pike with a bloody ear over which he kept cupping the palm of his hand, Peter supporting himself on the shotgun. Tim French had helped Hasty, who had been badly shaken up, home to bed.

"Nothing to do now," Carl said. He sat at the table brushing his hand back over his graying, thinning, sweat-tangled hair. "It is off our back anyhow. Blaisedell is probably right, there is less chance of trouble if we stay away from the General Peach." He sat looking down at the crooked trigger finger of his right hand.

Gannon slowly seated himself in the chair beside the cell door, holding his breath at the sudden ache in his ribs.

"Damn them," Carl said, without heat. "Looked like they might've saved that one I shot. But they had to let him bleed it out and then tramp what was left of him. Course, any man that's fool enough to give a jerk on a gun barrel when it's pointed right at him and cocked, and your finger—"

"Sure, Horse," Peter said. "None of your doing."

"Well, he held them off long enough for Miss Jessie to get Morgan out the back," Carl said. "What we was after, after all —save a lynching."

"Yes," Gannon said, and Peter Bacon glanced up at him and nodded.

"I guess he did pure right not shooting," Peter said. "But that didn't make it a better thing to see."

"I admire to see a woman cool as Miss Jessie was," Carl said. He straightened and stretched. "You boys go home and get some sleep. This deputy's office is just about to close up for the night."

Pike said, "I'm going out and drink some of the meanness out of me."

"You stay out of scrapes with jacks, now!" Carl said. "I don't want anything more to mess with tonight. If I don't get some rest for my old bones I am going to have to lay right down and die."

"'Night," Peter said, rising; he nodded to Carl and Gannon, and he and Pike went outside into the darkness.

Carl went over and kicked at the broken glass on the floor, and inspected the broken latch of the door. "You suppose the Citizens' Committee'll pay for fixing these? Place could fall down for all of Keller. All I asked him for here was a new sign, but I guess I am not going to get it unless I pay for it myself." Blood had scabbed over the long scratch above his right eye, and run and crusted on his cheek. "Bad night," he said, in a sad voice. "Let's close up, Johnny."

Gannon pulled down the lamp and blew out the flame, and followed Carl out. Outside, in the thick dark, the town seemed very still.

"Quiet," Carl said, and sighed. "I guess I'll have a whisky before I go home. You, Johnny?"

"I guess not; thanks." He watched Carl go off along the boardwalk, frail-looking and limping a little, his bootheels cracking unevenly on the planks.


II

Gannon went along past the wood yard to Grant Street and turned down toward Kate's house. He could see a light burning at the back.

He mounted the two steps, knocked, and waited. He felt for the key in his jeans pocket, and his face prickled; he knocked again. He heard her footsteps inside, and the door was opened a crack.

"It's me," he said.

The crack widened and he was aware of her close to him, although he could not see her yet in the darkness. "Oh, it's my gentleman caller," she said.

"I just came by to tell you Morgan is all right now."

"Come in, Deputy," Kate said. He went inside; Kate was outlined for a moment against the lighted bedroom doorway, but she moved aside to become invisible again. Something thumped on the oilcloth-covered table and he realized that she had had the derringer in her hand.

"Blaisedell?" she said.

"He showed up, but he couldn't stop them either. It was Miss Jessie got him out. She came in the doctor's buggy and took him out through the alley. He's at the General Peach now."

"Is he?" Kate said, as though she were not interested. She was silent for a long time, and he felt like a prying fool. He turned to go.

"Well, I'll be going. I just—"

"The angel of Warlock," Kate said. He couldn't make out her tone. "Is she Blaisedell's sweetheart?"

He nodded, and realized that she could not see him nod. But before he could speak, she said, "I'd heard of her before I came here. She is what you hear of when you hear of Warlock. And I've seen her on the street. What's she like?"

"Why, she is a fine woman, Kate. It took some doing what she did tonight."

"She is a nice woman," Kate said, in the tone he could not make out.

"She is. She—"

"I hate nice women," Kate said. It shocked him to hear her. Again he turned to go; he felt strangely angry.

"Anxious to go, Deputy?"

"It's not that. But I just came by to tell you about Morgan."

"Did you think I cared what happened to Morgan?"

He licked his lips. He could see her now, standing across the table from him. There was some kind of shawl draped over her shoulders. "Well, I couldn't help hearing what you was saying to him earlier tonight," he said. "When you came in the jail. And I thought—"

"Is it any of your business?"

He nodded, and the anger ached in him like the savage ache in his ribs where the miner had kicked him.

"Is it?" Kate said.

"Yes."

"All right. I saved him like that once."

"In Grand Fork."

"He'd killed a man that called him for cheating. That was when he still let himself get caught cheating once in a while. The vigilantes took him to the hotel to hold him till they could hang him. I started a fire and—"

"I understood what he was saying."

"Did you?" Kate said, in a flat voice. "And you want it your business? If you don't want it, say so now." She sounded as though she were warning him. "Maybe you don't," she said.

"I want to know." He leaned on the back of a chair.

"I was Tom Morgan's girl for four years," she said. His fingers tightened on the chair back, not to hear her telling him what he had already sensed, but to hear her say it as though it were no different than telling him where she was born, or how old she was, or who her parents were.

"Most of the time he was flush," she continued. "There were scrapes and sometimes we'd have to run, and sometimes he would bust; but mostly he was flush. He is a real high-roller. He has owned places here and there, the way he does now, but he would always sell out sooner or later and go back to playing against the bank. He did that best. He liked that best. He will get tired of running the Glass Slipper here and sell out and go somewhere else to buck the tiger. That's all he really wants to do. But he has to have a stake to start.

"After we'd run from Grand Fork we went to Fort James. He didn't have a dollar—except me." She laughed a little. Then her voice went flat again as she said, "So he wanted me to make a stake for him. Going back to what I'd been doing when he took me up. Back," she said, as though he might not have understood.

"I did, and I made him his stake. But I told him I was through with him. I didn't even see him for a long time—but I should have known I wasn't through with him. Anyway, Bob Cletus was going to marry me. He had a ranch near Fort James." Her voice began to shake. "Maybe I did know, for

I told Bob he had better tell Morgan. And see if it was—all right." She stopped then.

"Cletus?" he said. "The one you came out here with?"

"That was his brother. Blaisedell killed Bob in Fort James that day."

"Oh," he said.

"So you see," she said, her voice so low he could hardly hear her. "Did you want to know?"

"Why, yes," he lied.

He could smell the perfume she wore; she had moved closer to him. She said, "I looked for his brother for a while —Blaisedell shot Bob in Seventy-nine. Then I just happened to run onto Pat in Denver, and I—he came out here with me. And they killed Pat, too."

He was aware again of the shape of the key in his pocket, and of its weight. He cleared his throat. "You got his brother to come out here with you to try to—"

"Yes," she broke in, curtly, as though he had been stupid even to ask. Then she said, "I want to see Blaisedell shot down like that. It is all I want."

He heard the scrape of her slippers and the creak of the floor as she moved again. She halted so close to him that he could have touched her, and he could see the shape of her face and the rounded pits of her eyes. But all at once she said, "No," and drew back a little. Her voice began to shake once more as she said, "I don't know. Maybe I only want to see it happen and not—do anything. Maybe it is enough. Maybe I have done too much already. But I would like to know the man who was to do it. Beforehand. I thought it might be you."

"No," he said hoarsely.

"After he killed your brother I was almost glad. For I thought there would be reason enough. . . ."

"It won't be me. I couldn't anyway."

"I think you could. But I won't ask you, Deputy. Are you afraid I am going to ask you?"

"Why *him?*" he cried. "I should think it would be Morgan you are after!"

He saw her turn away. When she spoke her voice was clear and small, and she sounded as though she were reasoning with herself as much as with him. "Because I should have known what Tom would do. So maybe it was part my fault. Because it was just the sort of rotten, dog-in-the-manger thing Tom would do. But Blaisedell—"

Her voice ceased, but he saw, and was sick with jealousy and pain at what he saw. How much those four years must have been to her, and Morgan; she must have loved Morgan very much.

He raised a sour, damp hand to rub it over his face. He tried to speak calmly. "Kate, maybe Blaisedell did that. But I don't believe he is bad. He has done good here, killed my brother or not. Kate, do you think it will be someone decent who will kill him? It will not be!"

"Decent to me."

"Do you know who will kill him? Someone like Abe McQuown, or some kid after score like Billy. No, not even that. It will be some backshooter, like Calhoun. Or Cade. It will be somebody like Jack Cade, somebody worse than you think *he* is even. Somebody all bad. Don't you see?"

"It doesn't matter."

"It matters! Don't you see he is a man for men to look up to? There are not many good ones like that, and it will be an all bad one that will kill him, and then the bad one looked up to for it. Don't you see that?"

"Maybe not a bad one," Kate said. She sounded almost indifferent. "Maybe a better one. Someone like you, I mean."

"Don't say that."

"I think it is so."

"That's foolishness, Kate!"

"Why, then it is none of your business after all," she said. There was an edge of anger to her voice, and as she went on it was more and more angry, and filled with hate. "You look up to him, don't you?" she said. "You should know how men look up to him, since you do yourself. Because he is so *fine*. He is quick on the draw—does that make him fine? He has killed I don't even know any more how many men—does that make him fine? He is a hired killer! Morgan hired him to kill a man and Fort James hired him to kill men, and Warlock has. It must be fine and brave and *manly* to be a hired killer, but you can't expect a woman to understand why men will worship him like a saint because he—"

"Stop it!"

"All right, I will stop it. And you get out of here. You are not a *man*. Not the man I want."

"More man than you are woman, I guess, Miss Dollar." He spoke in anger; instantly he was sorry. "I am sorry," he said quickly. "I didn't go to say a thing like that. I'll ask you to forgive me, Kate."

But she didn't speak, and he could feel the hate. It was as though he were in a cage with an animal. He turned and moved toward the door.

He heard a shot. It came from the direction of Main Street, and there was a yell, and a chorus of yells. But still he did not leave. "Kate——" he said.

"Maybe they have killed him for me," Kate said, viciously, and he went outside. He ran down toward the corner of Main Street with his ribs aching and the scabbarded Colt slapping against his leg.

It was some time before he could find out what had happened; no one seemed to know. Someone said that Blaisedell had shot Curley Burne, who had been taken dying to the General Peach; another thought that some of the Regulators had come in and scared up a Medusa miner. He crossed the street finally, to another group of men before the Billiard Parlor. Hutchinson, Foss, and Kennon were there.

"Carl got shot," Foss told him. "It was Curley."

"Dirty hound!" Kennon said, in a cracked voice.

"Where is he?"

"Forked a horse and lit out running," someone said. "There is a bunch going to take out after him. They're down at——"

"No—*Carl*!" he said.

"They took him over to the General Peach," Hutchinson said. "He was bleeding bad."

As Gannon ran back down Main Street, Kennon shouted after him, "You had better start getting a posse together, Gannon!"

There was another bunch before the General Peach, and a number of horses. "It's Gannon," someone said. "Here comes Johnny Gannon." He made his way through them and up the steps, where Miss Jessie's man Tittle barred his way with a Winchester.

"Listen, nobody else comes—"

He shouldered past, and Tittle stumbled back clumsily, banging his rifle butt against the door. "Where is he?" Gannon panted, starting back toward the hospital room. Then he saw Pike Skinner and Mosbie through Miss Jessie's open door. Buck Slavin was there, and Sam Brown and Fred Wheeler. Morgan leaned on the foot of the bed, with the doctor beside him, and Blaisedell stood apart. Miss Jessie was sitting beside the bed, where Carl was.

"Well, hello, Johnny," Carl said, in a breathless voice. He looked like a scared, white-faced boy with a pasted-on, graying mustache. Gannon hadn't realized how gray Carl was. He moved over to kneel beside the bed, next to Miss Jessie's chair. Carl wet his lips and carefully turned his head toward him.

"You will have to deputy alone awhile, Johnny."

"Sure," he panted. "Surely, Carl. We'll make out."

Behind him Pike Skinner said roughly, "We will help him till you are up and around again, Carl."

Carl grinned thinly; he turned his head a little farther toward Gannon, and winked. "Sure," he whispered. "There is some good boys to help. They have been rallying round. You'll be all right, Johnny."

"Hush, now, Carl," Miss Jessie said, and patted his hand. She wore the high-necked, frilled blouse with the black necktie she had worn when she had come to the jail, and she smelled cleanly of sachet and starched linen. "You mustn't talk so much, Carl," she said.

"It's all right," the doctor said, in his clipped, curt voice.

"I have always been a talker, ma'am," Carl said. "It is hard to quit being one now."

Leaning on the brass foot of the bed in a clean shirt and trousers, his cigar bobbing in the corner of his mouth as he spoke, Morgan said gently, "A man needs a little rest after fighting those wild-eyed jacks off my neck half the night."

Carl grinned again. Behind Morgan, Blaisedell stood with his arms folded over his chest, and only his blue eyes alive in his cold, bruised and scraped face. There was a tramp of hoofs outside the window, and Gannon could hear the men talking there. "Let's get moving," one said. "Where's Gannon. He going to weasel on this?"

"What happened?" Gannon said quickly, to Carl.

"Just stupid," Carl said, in an embarrassed voice. "Curley and me had some more words. That was there by the Billiard Parlor and I kind of surprised myself and him too getting drawed before he did." He laughed shakily. "Durned if I didn't! Well, I kind of cooled off, seeing I'd got the drop; so I thought I'd camp him in jail for the night. So I called for his piece—" His voice trailed off.

"Curley went to let him take it and then spun it on him," Mosbie said. "I saw him do it, and a good lot of others standing there saw it. Run the road-agent spin on him, by God— pardon me, Miss Jessie. I should have chose him myself, I just about did earlier."

"We'll see he is caught, Carl," Buck Slavin said solemnly.

Gannon saw a little cluster of bluish veins at Carl's temple, and the slow beat of blood in them. He had never seen those veins there before. The flesh of Carl's face looked as though it had been waxed.

"Better get a posse riding, Johnny," Pike said. "There is a good lot gathered outside already."

"Not much use till morning," Carl said. "If I was doing it I'd wait. Nobody could follow sign till light."

Miss Jessie patted Carl's hand. Her hand was white and small beneath the long cuff of her sleeve, the nails cut shorter than Kate's. Carl's brows knit together beneath the long, crusted scratch on his forehead, and Carl's eyes took on an inward expression.

"Feels like something's broke loose again, Doc," Carl said easily. "I don't want to bleed up Miss Jessie's nice bed."

"It will stop," the doctor said.

"Let's go on outside," Pike whispered, and he left the room, followed by Buck, Wheeler, Mosbie, and Sam Brown.

Gannon could hear more horses in the street now. He saw Carl's eyes close and he quickly looked up at the doctor, who had on his nightshirt beneath his rusty black suit. The doctor shook his head.

Gannon saw that Blaisedell was watching him expressionlessly. Above Blaisedell's head was a mezzotint of a man thrashing at some ocean waves with a long sword.

Carl opened his eyes again. "You know?" he said. "It makes

a person sort of mad—I mean I was just watching it go by in
my head here. Say you catch him, Johnny, and the judge binds
him over to trial in Bright's. He will just get off." He laughed
a little and said, "Are you going to post him out of town for
me, Marshal?"

Gannon heard Miss Jessie draw in her breath; he saw Morgan's face harden. Blaisedell didn't give any sign that he had
heard.

Miss Jessie said, "David, I think he ought to rest a little now.
I think everybody ought to leave and let him rest." She said it
as though she were talking to the doctor, but it sounded like a
command. Gannon started to get to his feet.

"Except Johnny," Carl said. "Leave Johnny stay."

Miss Jessie rose with a quick movement, brushing her hands
together in her skirt. Her eyes looked tired, but very bright;
her brown ringlets swung as she turned toward Blaisedell. She
went over to take Blaisedell's arm, as though she must lead him
out, and Morgan's cold eyes followed her all the way. They all
left the room.

Gannon knelt uncomfortably beside the bed, watching Carl's
face, in profile to him, and the steady throb of the little cluster
of veins. Carl whispered, "I'm going, old horse."

Gannon shook his head.

"It is like big gray curtains coming down. You can kind of
see them trailing down—like the bottom of a tornado cloud
coming down. Getting black like that too, but slow."

"I'm sorry, Carl," he said.

"Surely," Carl said, as though to comfort him. "We have
been friends and got along, haven't we? I was a good enough
deputy, wasn't I? Whatever old Judge had to say about it."

Gannon tried to speak and choked on it.

Carl laughed soundlessly. "Well, I don't know what I am
crying about now. I knew one of those cowboys was going to
score me, and I guess I'd just as soon it was Curley.

"Ah, I came in all big medicine brave on account of Bill
Canning," he went on. "And saw what I was into, and caved
in for a while. Pure fright. But I come up again, I'll say that
for myself. I picked up there toward the last. Why, I was right
proud of myself standing up to Curley like I did. I just wish I
didn't have to go out on killing that poor, stupid jack, though;

that was no kind of thing. And sorry to leave you right in the middle of all hell, Johnny. With Curley to get, and I suppose somebody ought to get word in to Bright's City on Murch, in case he went that way. And muckers and Regulators." He began to chuckle again, his shirt trembling over his chest with it. "Maybe I picked the best time after all," he said. "But damn Curley Burne anyhow."

Carl looked exhausted now, and his eyes seemed suddenly sunken. After a moment he said, "Me and Curley scrapped over Blaisedell mostly. I guess you figured that."

"I thought it'd been that, Carl."

Carl's eyes flared in their sockets, like candles guttering. "Once in a while—once in a long while there's a man—Blaisedell made a man of me, Johnny. But now—"

"I know," he said quickly.

"Things getting him down," Carl whispered. "Bringing him low. Like those jacks tonight, and nothing for a man to do to help him back. Then somebody comes along and you can speak up for him. And maybe because it is the only thing you can do—you push it too hard. Maybe I pushed Curley too hard."

"Never mind it now, Carl." Gannon could hear now, in the street outside, the pad of hoofs and the jingle of spurs and harness, and voices, diminishing as the men rode away.

"I always was a talker," Carl said. His eyes drooped closed. His hands moved slowly to fold themselves upon his chest. He looked as though he were aging at tremendous speed.

Gannon rose from his knees and sank into the chair. He saw Miss Jessie standing in the doorway behind him, one hand to her throat and her round eyes fixed on him steadily.

Carl whispered something and he had to bend forward to hear it.

"—post him out," Carl was saying, smiling a little, his eyes still closed. "And right down the middle of the street with no two ways about it, like that in the Acme was." His voice came more strongly. "Why, that'd be epitaph enough for a man! Carl Schroeder that was deputy in Warlock, shot by Curley Burne. And right next to me: Curley Burne, killed for it by Clay Blaisedell, Marshal. Cut that in stone! That'd be—" His words became a kind of soft rustling Gannon could no longer understand.

Gannon sat watching with fascination the slow movement in the little veins, knowing he should be both with the posse, which was not a posse without him, and here with Carl.

"That stupid jack!" Carl said suddenly. His eyes opened and all at once fright was written with cruel marks upon his face. He reached for Gannon's hand and gripped it tightly. "Johnny! Bring out your Colt's and hand it here!"

"Carl, you—"

"Quick! There is not much time!"

Gannon drew his six-shooter and held it out where Carl could see it, which seemed to be what Carl wanted.

"Hold it right," Carl said. "Finger on the trigger." Carl caught hold of the barrel and gave it a jerk. Then he groaned. "Yes!" he whispered, as Gannon withdrew the Colt. "I pulled on it the same as that damned, stupid jack did to me with the shotgun. *No*, not the *same*! But by God it was!"

Carl turned his head from side to side with a tortured movement. "Oh, God Almighty, there is no way to know! But maybe he didn't go to do it, Johnny."

"But he ran—" he started.

"Because there was half a dozen there would've cut him down! Johnny—" Carl stopped, his throat working as though he could not swallow. Finally he got his breath; he lay there panting. "Forgive as you would be forgiven," he whispered. "And I will be going to that judgment seat directly. Oh, God!" he whispered, dully.

Tears squeezed from beneath his eyelids. His throat worked again. He whispered, "Johnny—I guess you had better tell them that Curley didn't go to do it."

That was all. Still a faint flicker of life showed in the blue veins. Gannon stared at them, slowly thrusting the muzzle of his Colt toward its scabbard, until the barrel finally slid in; he sat hunched and aching, watching the little veins, and at no given instant could he have said that the movement in them ceased. There was only, after a time, the realization that Carl's life was gone, and he rose and disengaged the counterpane from beneath Carl's arms, folded the hands together on the thin chest, and drew the counterpane up over all.

He backed away, upsetting the chair in his clumsiness, and catching it as it fell. Jessie Marlow still stood in the doorway.

She nodded, just as he said, "He's gone," and raised her finger to her lips in a curious, straitened, intense gesture he did not understand.

He moved out past her into the dark entryway. Blaisedell stood across from him, his legs apart, hands behind his back, his head bent down—as still as a statue. Morgan sat on the bottom step, smoking.

"He's gone," he said again. Still Blaisedell didn't move. The doctor came out of the shadows near the front door and followed Miss Jessie into her room. Gannon knew these out here had not heard Carl's last words; he wondered if even Miss Jessie had.

"They went on down toward San Pablo," Morgan told him. "Skinner said he thought you would just as soon not go anyway."

He nodded dumbly, and went on outside. There was no one now in the street before the General Peach. He walked to the jail and in the darkness there sank down in the chair at the table, with his head in his hands. He did not know if he could face telling them what Carl had said. They would say he lied, with utter condemnation and contempt, and the lie thrown in his face until he would have to fight back. But how would he be able to blame them for thinking that he lied? He could only pray that the posse would not catch Curley. Surely they would not catch Curley Burne.

He groaned. Finally he rose, with broken glass scraping beneath his boots, and lit the lamp, staring, in the gathering light, at the names scratched on the wall. He slid open the table drawer and took out Carl's pencil. With his ribs aching, he squatted before the list of the deputies of Warlock, and, carefully, in small, neat lettering, he added, beneath Carl's name, the name of John Gannon.

## 35. *Curley Burne Loses His Mouth Organ*

CURLEY WAS half asleep in the saddle when the sun came up, sudden and painfully bright just above the peaks of the Bucksaws. As he cut in from the river his eyes felt sandy and his spine jarred into the shape of a buttonhook. The gelding he had taken plodded along, stiff-legged, and he was grimacing now at every jolt.

"That is some gait you got, horse," he complained, leaning both hands on the pommel to ease his seat. "I never heard of a horse without knee joints before." He reached for his mouth organ inside his shirt; somehow the cord had got broken, and he had to dig for the mouth organ inside his shell belt. He blew into it to wake himself up, and now he began to feel a growing elation. For now he could go, now he must move on, and there was good news for Abe about Blaisedell's comedown for him to leave on.

The elation faded when he thought of Carl Schroeder. Carl had been an aggravating man, and more and more aggravating and scratchy lately, but he had not wanted to see Carl dead. He wondered if there was a posse out yet, and he looked back for dust; he could see none.

"Poor old Carl," he said aloud. "Damned scratchy old son of a bitch." In his mind's eye he saw Carl go down with the front of his pants afire, and he winced at the sight. He knew that Carl was dead by now.

The gelding went grunting pole-legged down a draw, and labored up the rise beyond it. He had a glimpse of the windmill on the pump house with the blades wheeling slowly in the sun, and the tall chimney of the old house. He pricked the gelding's flanks with his spurs. "Let's run in there with our peckers up, you!" The gelding maintained the same pace. "Gait like banging an ax handle on a fence post," he said.

By dint of jabbing in his spurs, yelling, and flapping his hat right and left, he got the gelding into a shambling, wheezing run down the last slope. He fired his Colt into the air and whooped. The gelding fell back into a trot. Joe Lacey and the breed came out of the bunkhouse and waved to him. Abe appeared on the porch of the ranch house in an old hat and a flannel shirt, and no pants on. The legs of his long-handled underwear were dirty and baggy at the knees.

Curley gave one last half-hearted whoop and jumped off the gelding; his knees gave beneath his weight and he almost fell. Abe leaned on the porch rail, sleepy and cross-looking, as Curley mounted the steps.

"Where'd you get that bottlehead?"

"Stole him, and a bad deal too." He leaned against the porch rail beside Abe. "I'm leaving, Abe," he said. "Things look like they'll be getting hot for me here."

Abe said incuriously, "Blaisedell?"

"Carl and me come to it."

A shadow came down over Abe's red-bearded face, and he blew out his breath in a whisper like a snake hissing.

"Abe!" the old man called from inside. "Abe, who is that rode in? Is that you, Curley?"

"It surely is," he called back. "Coming and going, Dad McQuown. I'm on the run."

"Killed him?" Abe said sharply.

"Looked like it. I didn't stay to see." When he flipped his hat off, the jerk of the cord against his throat made his heart pump sickly.

"Killed who?" Dad McQuown cried. "Son, bring me out so's I can see Curley, will you? Killed who, Curley?"

"Carl," Curley said. He tried to grin at Abe. He said loudly, for the old man's benefit, "Run the road-agent spin on him. Neat!"

The old man's laughter grated on him insupportably, and Abe cried, "Shut up, Daddy!" One of Abe's eyes was slitted now, while the other was wide; he looked as though he were sighting down a Winchester. Curley saw Joe Lacey coming toward the porch.

"You are not needed here!" Abe snapped, and Joe quickly retreated. "What happened?" Abe said.

"Why, it seems like they get a new set of laws up there every time a man comes in. Now you can't even talk any more. And scratchy! Well, I was there by Sam Brown's billiard place, minding my own business and talking to some boys, and Carl comes butting in and didn't like what I was saying. We cussed back and forth some, and—"

"God damn you!" Abe whispered.

Curley stiffened, his hands clenching on the rail on either side of him as he stared back at Abe.

"You did it now," Abe said. He didn't sound angry any more, only washed-up and bitter.

"What's the matter, Abe?"

Abe shrugged and scratched at his leg in the dirty longjohns. "Where you going?" he asked.

"I guess up toward Welltown, and then—*quién sabe?*"

"In a hurry?"

"I don't expect they got a posse off till sun-up. But it's not something I better count on. Why'd you get so mad, Abe?"

"People liked Carl," Abe said. He hit his fist, without force, down on the porch rail, and shook his head as though there were nothing that was any use. "They'll hang this on me too," he went on. "That I put you to killing Carl. But you'll be gone. It's nothing to you."

"Ah, for Christ's sake, Abe!"

"They have got me again," Abe said.

"Sonny, you shut that crazy talk!" the old man shrilled. "Now, you bring me out there with you boys. Abe!"

"I'll get him," Curley said. He went inside to where the old man lay, on his pallet on the floor by the stove, and picked him up pallet and all. The old man clung to his neck, breathing hard. He didn't weigh over a hundred pounds any more, and the smell of him was the hardest part of carrying him.

"Got the deputy, did you, Curley?" the old man said, blinking and scowling in the sun as Curley put the pallet down on the porch. "Well, now; I always thought high of you, Curley Burne!" His mouth was red and wet through his white beard. "Well now," he went on, glancing sideways at Abe. "That's all there is to it. Man's pushing on you, all you do is ride in there—"

"By God, you talk," Abe said, in a strained voice. "Daddy, I've told you I don't mind dying, if that's what you want of me. I just mind dying a damned fool!"

"Abe," Curley said. "I guess I had better be moving."

Abe didn't even hear him. "I mind dying a damned fool, and I mind dying one for every man to spit on," he went on. He began to laugh, shrilly. "Pile everything on me! By God, they will have a torchlight parade and fireworks when I am dead! They will carry him around Warlock on their shoulders and make speeches and set off giant powder, for him; that never did a sin in his life. And tramp me in the dust for the dogs to chew on—that never did anything else but!"

The old man gazed at his son in horror, at Curley in shame. There was an iron clamor from Cookie's triangle, and the dogs began to bark out by the cook shack.

"Well, there is breakfast now," the old man said in a soothing voice. "You boys'll feel better after some chuck."

"Blaisedell don't stand so high now, Abe," Curley said. "I heard a thing or two about Blaisedell, and saw a pack of miners tramp over him too." He told about the miners storming over Blaisedell to try to lynch Morgan. Abe looked barely interested.

"And maybe things're getting stacked against him some, for a change," Curley went on. "There is plenty talk it was Morgan stopped that stage, and maybe Blaisedell with him."

"That's stupid," Abe said, but he stood a little straighter.

"And that those boys was killed in the Acme Corral to cover it over."

"That's a stupid lie," Abe said. He grinned a little.

"No, there is something there. Pony and Cal stopped that stage, surely. But you remember Cal and Pony being kind of suspicious back and forth about who it was shot that passenger, and then they finally decided it must've been Hutchinson trying to sneak a shot at Cal and the passenger jumped out and got hit instead. But maybe it wasn't Hutchinson, either."

Abe was nervously running his fingers through his beard.

"There is something there," Curley said again. "Taliaferro had some news might interest you, and it is spreading around Warlock pretty good, I hear. There is some whore named Violet at the French Palace that was in Fort James when Morgan and Blaisedell was. And this Kate Dollar woman that Bud Gannon is chasing after now. Lew says this Violet says the Dollar woman was Morgan's sweetie in Fort James, and she took up with another fellow and Morgan paid Blaisedell money to burn him dead. How a lot of people knew about it in Fort James— Wait a minute, now!" he said, as Abe started to interrupt. "And then this Dollar woman was married to the passenger that got shot on that stage. Now if Pony or Cal didn't shoot him, who did? Lew likes it it was Morgan—he is down on Morgan something fierce—but there is talk that if Blaisedell hired out to Morgan for that kind of job once, why not twice? There is all kind of things being said around Warlock, Abe."

"Boys, what is this hen-scratch low gossip you are talking here?" the old man said indignantly.

"Shut up," Abe said, but he began to grin again.

He had better go, Curley thought. There was more than he had told Abe, but he did not like to hear himself saying all this. Lew Taliaferro was a man he could stand only if the wind was right; and what Taliaferro had told him, part of which he had just repeated to Abe, had made as poor hearing as telling, medicine though it was to Abe.

"So I expect you will be going into Warlock one of these days yourself," he said, and tried to grin back at Abe's grin. "There is a time coming. I wish I could go in with you when you go, but you won't need me, Abe."

"By God!" the old man whispered.

"I'd sure like to stay to see it," Curley went on. "But it has come time for me to make tracks. Like you said, people liked old Carl." He took a deep breath. "I'm telling you things are running the other way, Abe. You have done right, staying down here till they started changing. And it was the smartest thing you ever did, too, telling MacDonald you wouldn't have nothing to do with his Regulators. Just wait it out. It won't be long. Abe, Blaisedell is starting to come down like a pile of bricks."

He felt exhausted watching the life and sharpness coming back into Abe's face. He had given Abe what he had to give, and he would do it again, but he had lied when he had said he wished he could see the end. He could stomach no more of it.

"Thanks, Curley," Abe said, softly. "You've been a friend." With a lithe swing of his body he turned to gaze off at the mountains. His face, in profile, looked younger. He said, "Well, you will hear one way or other when the time comes."

"I'll drink a bottle of whisky to you, Abe."

"Do that for me. One way or the other."

"One way," Curley said, grinning falsely.

"You have sure bucked him like a dose of kerosene," the old man said, in a breathless voice. The clanging of the iron triangle sounded again.

"Better eat before you go," Abe said.

"I'll grab something and say so long to the boys."

"What do you want to move on for, Curley?" the old man complained. "How'll we make out? Have to break in a new hand on that mouth organ of yours."

"You'll never get one as good as me."

"Wait a minute till I get my pants on," Abe said, and disappeared inside.

Curley took the mouth organ out of his shirt and began to play the old man a tune. "Curley," Dad McQuown said, scrounging up on one elbow. "Tell me how it was you popped that deputy before you go. Ran him the road-agent spin, did you?"

It was sour music he was making. He wiped the spit from the mouth organ, and put it down on the rail beside him. "No, it wasn't that," he said.

"You said—"

"It wasn't so," he said. "The whole thing was poor all around. He had the drop on me and I went to give him my Colt's like a good boy. But he grabbed hold of the barrel—" He stopped, for Abe was standing in the doorway with his hands frozen where he'd been buckling his shell belt on. Abe's eyes were blazing.

"You always was a God-damned liar, Curley Burne," the old man said disgustedly, and lay back again.

"You didn't mean to do it?" Abe whispered, and his face was crafty and cruel as Curley had not seen it since Abe had heard the Hacienda Puerto vaqueros were coming after them through Rattlesnake Canyon.

He shook his head.

"Carl went and did it himself? Pulling on the barrel with your finger on the trigger. Like that?"

"That was it." The expression on Abe's face frightened him a little, but then it was gone and Abe bent to attend to buckling his belt on. "It was poor," Curley said. "It don't set so good either, but it is done. I kind of thought I'd better not stick around and try and explain it to folks, what with five or six of them getting ready to pop away at me. Well, I guess I'll go get some breakfast."

Abe nodded. "I'll go down and saddle up for you," he said, in a strange voice. "You send the breed around and I'll put him on that you rode out here on, and send him on down

Rattlesnake Canyon in case they have got somebody following sign. You head for Welltown and I'll get a herd run over your track." Abe nodded again, to himself.

"Well, that's fine of you, Abe."

"So long, Curley," the old man said. "You take care of yourself, hear?"

Curley hurried down the steps. "So long, Dad McQuown!" he called back over his shoulder. At the cook shack he shook hands around with the boys who hadn't gone with MacDonald, and told them to say so long for him to the rest when they got back from Warlock. He sent the breed to Abe, and got some bread and bacon and a canteen of water from Cookie. Hurrying, he went on out to the horse corral, where Abe had saddled a long-legged, big-barreled, steady-standing gray he had not seen before. "He'll take you in a hurry," Abe said, and slapped the gray on the shoulder. Curley swung into the saddle, and Abe reached up to wring his hand.

"Curley," he said.

"So long, boy, *Suerte*."

"*Suerte*," Abe said, grinning, but not quite meeting his eyes. Something had gone wrong again, but now Curley was only in a hurry to get out. He swung the big gray out of the corral on the hard-packed red earth. He could see the dust the breed was making, heading south. The big gray moved powerfully; he drew up as Abe yelled something after him, and cupped a hand to his ear.

"I say!" Abe yelled. "They catch you all you do is see you get to Bright's City for trial all in one piece. No worry then!"

Curley waved and spurred on again. When he had crossed the river that was the border of the ranch, he had never felt so free. He reached for his mouth organ. But he had left it on the porch rail.

His mood was not affected; he began to sing to himself. The gray loped steadily along. The land stretched board-flat away to Welltown, the gray-brown desert marbled with brush. The sun burned higher in the sky. He glanced back from time to time—at first he thought it was only a dust-devil.

Then he whistled. "We had better stop loafing, boy," he said. "Look at them come!" But he was not worried, for the big gray was strong and fresh, and the posse must have been riding hard from Warlock. The gray broke into a long, swinging stride that ate up the ground, and he laughed to see the dust cloud fading behind him.

Then the gray grunted and went lame.

He dismounted to examine the hoof; carefully he looked over the leg for something wrong, but he could see nothing. The gray stood with the lame leg held off the ground, looking at him with unconcerned brown eyes. "Boy, why would you do such a thing?" he complained, and remounted and dug his spurs in. The gray limped along, grunting, more and more slowly; he bucked half-heartedly at the spurs.

Curley looked back at the oncoming dust. It was a big posse. The gray stopped and would go no more, and he sighed and dismounted, shot the horse through the head, and sat down on the slack, warm haunch to wait in the sun. "Boy," he said again, "why would you do such a thing?" His hand fumbled once more after his mouth organ which he had left behind him.

## 36. *Journals of Henry Holmes Goodpasture*

April 10, 1881

IT IS impossible to watch these things happening and feel nothing. Each of us is involved to some degree, inwardly or outwardly. Nerves are scraped raw by courses of events, passions are aroused and rearoused in partisanships that, even in myself, transcend rationality.

It must be a wracking experience to stand before a mob as Schroeder and Gannon did last night; to do it not once, but twice, and to be trampled at the last by men no more than crazed beasts. I write this trying to understand Carl Schroeder, as well as in memoriam to him. I see now that his office had served to ennoble him, as it had done with Canning before him. We gave him not enough credit while he lived, and I think we did not because he was too much one of us. God bless his soul; he deserves some small and humble bit of heaven, which is all he would have asked for himself.

He was an equable and friendly man. Perhaps he was inadequate to his position here. Yet who would have been wholly

adequate except, perhaps, Blaisedell himself? I think a part of
Schroeder's increasing strength (has it not been a part of all
our increasing strength?) was Blaisedell's presence and example
here. I think he must have been badly shaken by Blaisedell's
decline from Grace. As he drew his strength from Blaisedell, so
must he have been all too rawly aware of the cruel vicissitudes
of error, or rumored error, or of mere foul lies, to which such
dispensers of rough-and-ready law as Blaisedell, and himself,
were prey.

Poor Schroeder, to die not only in an undignified street
scrape, but in one of the multitudinous arguments over Blaisedell and McQuown. Buck Slavin heard the quarrel, and saw it
at the end; he says it seems to him that Carl was as much at
fault in it as Curley Burne. He says there was a deeper grudge
there than the mere quarrel, but I think of my own feelings
of that time last night, and know it would have taken little to
rouse me to a deadly rage.

Buck was present at the General Peach almost until Schroeder's death, and says that Schroeder chided himself bitterly for
being tricked with what is called the "road agent's spin." This
is a device whereby the pistol is proffered butt foremost, and
then spun rapidly upon the trigger finger and discharged when
the muzzle is level. It is a foul trick. Curley Burne has had
more friends in this town by far than any other creature of
McQuown's. He has only sworn enemies now.

Gannon did not accompany the posse that went out after
Burne, perhaps, as Buck suggests, because Curley has been an
especial friend of his, or perhaps, as the doctor says, because
Carl expressed a wish that Gannon remain with him in his final hour. The miners set fire to the Glass Slipper shortly after
Schroeder's death and Gannon has been much occupied in
putting out the fire. The feeling is that he was too much occupied with it, and that his proper business lay with the posse. It
is to be hoped that his office will be as ennobling to Gannon as
it has been to his last two predecessors.

I think that Carl Schroeder would have been pleased to
know that his death has taken men's minds away from Blaisedell's failure before the jail, and concentrated hate upon one
man. I fervently hope that the posse will catch Curley Burne
and hang him to the nearest tree.

I burn the midnight oil, I bleed myself upon this page in inky blots and scratchings. How can I know men's hearts without knowing my own? I peel back the layers one by one, like an onion, and find only more layers, smaller and meaner each than the last. What dissemblers we are, how we seek to conceal from our innermost beings our motives, to call the meanest of them virtue, to label that which in another we can plainly see as devilish, in ourselves angelic, what in another is greed, in ourselves righteousness, etc. Observe. The Glass Slipper is burned, gutted to char and stink, and the pharmacy beside it saved by a miracle. The fire was set by the miners; they have got back at Morgan. They are devils, I say, to so endanger a town as tinder-dry as this. But is that it? No, they have endangered my property. I will forgive being shamed, discountenanced, and insulted; threaten my property and I will never forgive. Take everything from me but my money. With money I can buy back what I need, the rest is worthless.

Poor devils, I suppose they had to destroy something. Men rise to the heights of courage and ingenuity when they avenge their slights or frustrations. It has always been so. It is comforting to some to see men work together with a good will against catastrophe. Humanity at its best, they say. Yet *against*, as I have written. When will humanity work with all its strength, its courage and ingenuity, and all its heart, *for*?

Morgan is burnt out. Will he rebuild, or accept this as earnest of the widespread sentiment against him here and depart our valley of Concord and Happiness? And in that case what of Blaisedell, who has been banking faro for him? Will he go too, or will he undertake the position of Marshal here again? I am sure the Citizens' Committee intends to ask, or beg, him to reassume his office, next time it meets.

Blaisedell and Morgan: it is said that Blaisedell did not shoot his assailants before the jail because he would not kill for the sake of Morgan, who had wrongfully murdered Brunk (if not a number of others!). Yet Blaisedell's prestige would have been even more grievously damaged had Morgan actually been taken out and hanged, and so I see Miss Jessie's part in this.

Blaisedell is obviously very much her concern, and, with the friendship of Blaisedell and Morgan an established fact, did she not realize that Morgan had to be saved at all costs, distasteful as the object of her salvage must have been to her?

There has been some talk to the effect that Blaisedell began his career as a gunman in a position similiar to that of the now-departed Murch, as pistolero-in-chief for Morgan's gambling hall in Fort James, and that he killed at Morgan's behest various and sundry whom Morgan found bothersome in his affairs of the heart, as well as in his business. Morgan once saved Blaisedell's life, it is further said, so Blaisedell is sworn to protect Morgan forever and serve whatever purpose Morgan assigns him. Morgan becomes possessed of horns, trident, a spiky tail, and Blaisedell's soul locked up in a pillbox.

Morgan is replacing McQuown as general scapegoat and what might be called whipping-devil. McQuown has remained in San Pablo and out of our ken for so long that he is becoming only a name, like Espirato, and someone readier to hand is needed. So are the witches burned, like coal, to warm us.

April 11, 1881

The posse has returned with Curley Burne, and Deputy Gannon has shown his true colors.

Burne has gone free on Gannon's oath that Schroeder's death-bed words were that his shooting was accidental, caused by his pulling on the barrel of Burne's six-shooter and thus forcing Burne's finger against the trigger. Judge Holloway, whatever his feelings in the matter, could not under these circumstances remand Burne to Bright's City for proper trial; there would be no point in it with Gannon prepared to swear such a thing. Joe Kennon, who was at the hearing, says he thought Pike Skinner would shoot Gannon then and there, and called him a liar to his face.

It is fortunate for Gannon that this town has had a bellyful of lynch gangs lately, or he and Burne would hang together tonight. Oh, damnable! Gannon must have been eager indeed to please McQuown, for in all probability Burne would have been discharged by the Bright's City court, as is their pleasure. Certainly Gannon is in danger here now, and, if he is here to serve McQuown in any way he can, has destroyed any further usefulness he might have had to the San Pabloite by this infuriating, and, it would seem, foolish, action. It is presumed that he will sneak out of town at the first opportunity, and that will be the last Warlock will see of him. Good riddance!

The posse was evidently divided to begin with as to whether they should capture Curley Burne at all, a number of them feeling he should be shot down on sight. His horse had gone lame, however, and, luckily for him, he offered no resistance. Opportunities were evidently made for him to try to escape, so *ley fuga* could be practiced, but Burne craftily did not attempt to take advantage of them. No doubt he was already counting on Gannon's aid.

It must have taken a strange, perverted sort of courage for Gannon to stand up with such a brazen lie before so partisan a group as there was at Burne's hearing. Evidently he tried to claim that Miss Jessie had also heard Schroeder's last words. Several men promptly ran to ask her if this was so, but she only increased Gannon's shame by replying, in her gentle way, that she had been unable to hear what Schroeder was saying at the end, since his voice had become inaudible to her. Buck says now that he knew all the time that Gannon was trying to play both ends, and was just biding his time to pull one coup for McQuown such as this. I must say I cannot myself view Gannon as a villain, but only as a contemptible fool.

Burne has promptly and sensibly made himself scarce. Some say he has joined the Regulators, who are encamped at the Medusa mine. If Blaisedell will resume his duties as Marshal here, and this town has its say, Curley Burne will become his most urgent project.

Toward this end the Citizens' Committee is meeting tomorrow morning, at the bank.

April 12, 1881

Blaisedell has resumed his position, and Curley Burne has been posted from Warlock. I have never felt the temper of this place in such a unanimously cruel mood. It is fervently hoped that Curley Burne, wherever he is, will take the posting process as what we have never before considered it to be—a summons, instead of a dismissal.

April 13, 1881

Word seems to have come, I'm sure I don't know how—perhaps it is some kind of emanation in the air—that Burne will come in. It seems to me that at one moment there was not a man in Warlock who believed he could be fool enough to come, and at the next it was somehow fixed and certain that he would. He is expected at sun-up tomorrow, but I still cannot believe that he will come.

April 14, 1881

I saw it, not an hour ago, and I will put down exactly what I saw. I will then have this record so that, in time to come, if what others perceived is changed by their passions or the years, I may look back at this and remind myself.

Before sun-up I was on the roof of my store, sitting behind the parapet. Others came up a ladder placed against the South-end Street wall, made apologetic gestures to me for invading my premises, and squatted silently near me in the first gray light. There were men to be seen in the street, too, occupying doorways and windows, and a number of them established within the burnt-out shell of the Glass Slipper. From time to time whispering could be heard, and there were frequent coughs and a continual rustle of movement, as in a theater when the curtain is about to rise.

Some of our eyes were trained east, for the sun, or for Blaisedell, who would presumably appear from the direction of the General Peach; some west, as the proper direction for Curley Burne's entry upon the stage.

There came the rhythmic creaking of wheels; it was the wagons taking the miners out to the Thetis, the Pig's Eye, and the farther mines, ten or twelve of them, with the miners seated in them knee to knee. Their bearded faces glanced from side to side as the wagons passed down Main Street, with, from time to time, a hand raised in greeting to a fellow, but none of the cheerful, disgruntled, or profane calling back and forth we are so used to hearing of a work-day morning. The water wagon, driven by Peter Bacon, crossed Main Street on its morning journey to the river. It was seen that the harness of the mules glittered, and all eyes turned to see the sun.

It climbed visibly over the Bucksaws, a huge sun, not that which Bonaparte saw through the mists of Austerlitz, but the sun of Warlock. I felt its warmth half gratefully, half reluctantly. There was an increasing stirring and rustling in the street. I saw Tom Morgan come out of the hotel, and, cigar between his teeth, seat himself upon the veranda. He leaned back in his rocking chair and stretched, for all the world as though it were a bore but he would make the best of what poor entertainment Warlock had to offer. I saw Buck Slavin with Taliaferro in the upstairs window of the Lucky Dollar, Will Hart in the doorway of the gunshop, Gannon leaning in the doorway of the jail, a part of the shadow there, appearing as tiredly and patiently permanent as though he had spent the night in that position, in that place.

"Blaisedell." Someone said it quite loudly, or else many whispered it in chorus. Blaisedell debouched from Grant Street into Main. He waited there a moment, almost uncertainly, with his shadow lying long and narrow before him. He wore black broadcloth with white linen, a string tie; beneath his open coat the broad buckle of his belt was visible, his weapons were not. With almost a twinge of fear I watched him start forward. He carried his arms most casually at his sides, walked slowly but with long, steady strides. Dust plumed about his feet and whitened his boots and his trouser bottoms. Morgan nodded to him as he passed, but I saw no answering nod.

"He'll just have a little walk and then we'll go home," someone near me whispered.

Blaisedell crossed the intersection of Broadway, and from all around I heard a concerted sigh of relief. Perhaps I sighed myself, with the surety that Curley Burne was not going to appear after all. Hate can burn itself out in the first light of day as readily as love can. I could see Blaisedell's face now very clearly, his broad mouth framed in the curve of his mustache, one of his eyebrows cocked up almost humorously, as though he, too, felt he would only have a little walk and then go home.

The sun had separated itself from the peaks of the Bucksaws by now; it glinted brilliantly upon the brass kick-plate on the hotel door. I saw Morgan, slouched in his rocking chair, raise his hand to take the cheroot from his mouth, then hold cigar and hand arrested. He leaned forward intently, and I heard a swift intake of breath from all around me, and knew that Curley Burne had appeared. I was reluctant to turn and see that this was so.

He was a hundred yards or so down Main Street. I saw Gannon, without changing his position, turn with that same slow reluctance I had felt in myself, to watch him. I found in myself, too, a grudging admiration for Burne, that he managed even now to accomplish that saunter of his we in Warlock knew so well. His shoulders were thrown back at a jaunty angle, his sombrero hung, familiarly, down his back, his flannel shirt was unbuttoned halfway to his cartridge belt as though in contempt of the morning chill, his striped pants were thrust into his boot tops. He looked very much a Cowboy. He was grinning, but even from where I was I could see his struggle to maintain that grin; it was exhausting to see it. I had to remind myself that he had murdered Carl Schroeder by a filthy trick, that he was a rustler, road agent, henchman of McQuown's. "Dirty son of a b - - - -!" growled one of my companions, and summed up what I had to feel, then, for Curley Burne.

He and Blaisedell were not a block apart when there was another gasp around me, as Burne broke stride. He halted, and cried out, "I have got as much right to walk this street as you, Blaisedell!" I felt ashamed for him, and, all at once, pity. Blaisedell did not stop. I saw Burne raise a hand to his shirt and wrench it open further, so that his chest and belly were exposed.

"What color?" he cried out. "What color is it?" He glanced up and around at us, the watchers, with quick, proud movements of his head. The skull-like grin never left his face. Then he started forward toward Blaisedell again. He sauntered no longer, and his hand was poised above the butt of his six-shooter. My eyes were held in awful fascination to that hand, knowing that Blaisedell would give him first draw.

It flashed down, incredibly swift; his six-shooter spat flame and smoke and my ears were shocked by the blast despite my anticipation of it—three shots in such rapid succession they were almost one report, and Burne and his weapon were obscured in smoke. Blaisedell's own hand seemed very slow, in its turn. He fired only once.

Burne was flung back into the dust and did not move again.

He had a depthless look as he lay there, as though he were now only a facsimile of himself laid like a painted cloth upon the uneven surface of the street. Blood stained his bare chest, his right arm was flung out, his smoking Colt still in his hand.

Blaisedell turned away, and as he retraced his steps I watched that marble face for—what? Some sign, I do not even know what. I saw his cheek twitch convulsively, I noticed that he had to thrust twice for his holster before he was able to reseat his Colt there. I could not see whether it was gold-handled or not.

The doctor appeared in the street, to walk through the dust to where Burne lay, carrying his black bag. A short, stocky, bowed figure in his black suit, he looked sad and weary. Gannon did not move from his position in the jail doorway. His eyes, from where I watched, looked like burnt holes in his head. Other men were coming out along the far boardwalk, and there was no longer silence.

"Center-shotted the b------ as neat as you please," a man near me said, as he got to his feet and spat tobacco juice over the parapet.

"Give him three shots," said another. "Couldn't give a man any more than that. I call that fair."

"Give him all the time in the world," agreed a third.

But I could feel in their voices what I myself felt, and feel more strongly now. For all that Blaisedell had given Burne three shots, for all he had given him all the time in the world, we knew we had not witnessed a gunfight but an execution. I leaned upon the parapet and looked down upon the men who had surrounded the mortal remains of Curley Burne, and I saw, when one of them moved aside, a little patch of bloody flesh. I thought of that gesture he had made, opening his shirt and confronting us with the color of his belly; showing us, more than Blaisedell.

It had been an execution, and at our order. Perhaps we had changed our mind at the last moment, but there was no reprieve, no way, before the end, to turn our thumbs up instead of down, and save the gladiator. And I think we felt cheated. There should have been some catharsis, for Carl Schroeder had been avenged, and an evil man had received his just deserts. There was no catharsis, there was only revulsion and each man afraid, suddenly, to look into the face of the one next to him.

And there was the realization that Curley Burne had not been an evil man, the remembrance that we had once, all of us, liked and enjoyed him to some degree; and there was the cancerous suspicion spreading among us that Gannon might not, after all, have been lying.

I feel drained by an over-violent purge to my emotions, that has taken from me part of my manhood, or my humanity. I feel scraped raw in some inner and most precious part. The earth is an ugly place, senseless, brutal, cruel, and ruthlessly bent only upon the destruction of men's souls. The God of the Old Testament rules a world not worth His trouble, and He is more violent, more jealous, more terrible with the years. We are only those poor, bare, forked animals Lear saw upon his dismal heath, in pursuit of death, pursued by death.

I am ashamed not only of this execution I myself have in part ordered, but of being a man. I think the climax to my shame for all of us came when Blaisedell was walking back up the street, dragging his arrow-thin, arrow-long shadow behind him, and Morgan came down from the veranda of the Western Star to put a hand on his shoulder, no doubt to congratulate his friend. At that moment I heard someone near me on my rooftop whisper—I did not see who, but if I believed in devils I would have been sure it was the voice of one come to yet more hideously corrupt our souls than we have ourselves corrupted them this day—whisper, "There is the dirty dog he ought to kill."

## 37. *Gannon Answers a Question*

"COME IN, Deputy," Kate said. She was tall in her white shirt with a velvet band around the collar, and her thickly pleated black skirt. Her hair hung loose around her head, softening the angular lines of her face. She looked neither pleased nor displeased to see him. "Haven't left town yet?" she said.

"No," he said, and sat down at the table, as she indicated he was to do. The oilcloth was cool and cleanly greasy to his touch. He felt something in him relax suddenly, here, for the first time since the posse had returned with Curley. He had become used to men falling silent as he passed them, and whispering behind his back, but now all his strength and will were spent staying out of quarrels, or worse. They no longer whispered behind his back.

"Well, they haven't got a lynch party after you yet," Kate said.

He tried to smile. "I'm not so worried about lynch parties as I am a shooting scrape."

Kate seated herself opposite him, and, regarding him steadily, said, "What did you expect when you swore him out of it?"

"What I said was so." His voice took on an edge he had not meant to have, here.

"Was it?" Kate said. The corners of her mouth pulled in deeply; with contempt, he thought. "Not because he was a friend of yours?"

"No."

"That doesn't signify? No, I thought what you swore was probably so, Deputy. The rest of this town hates you because they think you lied, but I don't think much better of you because I know you didn't. Because you would have sworn it the other way just as well if it had been the other way, friend or not—just what is true out of your cold head. But nothing out of hate or love or anything."

He said roughly, "I don't have any friends."

"No, you wouldn't have. Nor anything." She put out her hand and laid it cool against his for a moment, and then withdrew it. "Why, it's warm!" she said.

Even here, he thought, and he felt as though he had gone blind. He had tried to tell himself it did not matter what everyone thought of him; but it mattered, and he did not know how much longer he could stand under it.

But Kate continued, mercilessly. "You had a brother. Didn't you love your brother?"

"I knew what he was."

"God!" Kate said. "Isn't there anything—haven't there been any people you loved? That you'd do things for because you loved them even if you saw in your cold head it was wrong, or bad?" Her chair scraped back as she rose suddenly; she stood staring down at him with her hands held spread-fingered to her breast. "What do you see here?" she said hoarsely. "Just a bitch, and you know all I want is Blaisedell dead and that's wrong? Well, it may be wrong, but it comes out of *here*!"

"Stop it, Kate!"

"I want to know what you see! Have you got eyes to see just exactly what is there and no more—no blur or warmth in them ever? Then what do you come here for?"

He couldn't answer, for he did not know. Today, he thought, he had only wanted a respite. He shook his head mutely.

"Just to talk?" Kate said, more quietly. "To unload a little. And you have picked me to unload on?"

He nodded again, for maybe that was it.

"You need me?" she said, as though it were a condition she insisted upon.

"Yes; I guess."

"Holy Mary!" Kate said. "There is something to shake the world—that you need anything but your cast-iron conscience." She sat down again, and he heard the drowsy buzzing of flies against her window, and found himself listening for the distant crack of Eladio's maul in the *carpintería*. He could not hear it from here.

"Are you afraid of Blaisedell now?" Kate said.

He shook his head.

"Every other man here is. Or ought to be."

"No, Kate."

"Don't you know why he went back to marshaling and posted Burne out of town?"

"He didn't post him, Kate. The Citizens' Committee did."

"Wait!" she said. "Deputy, there are some people who might kill a man because they hated him. And there are some that might because they thought it was right; cold, like you. And then there is Blaisedell. Do you know why he killed Burne?"

"Because the Cit—"

"He killed him because his reputation was slipping. Do you know why he took the job as marshal again?"

He didn't answer.

"Because he knew the Citizens' Committee would tell him to post Burne out of town. Because he knew that was what everybody wanted, and so he could be the Great Man again. It is like a gambler starting to double his bets because he is losing. Recouping like that. Not hating Curley Burne, or not even thinking of the right or wrong of it. Just his reputation to keep. And where is your brassbound conscience now, when Schroeder told you Burne hadn't done it on purpose?"

"Blaisedell thinks I was lying. Everybody does. They knew I'd been friends with Curley and Abe, and they think I lied because—"

Kate said, "Do you know that the Citizens' Committee almost asked him to post *you* out with Burne? Buck Slavin told me. And Blaisedell would have done it. And killed you, too."

"I don't believe he would have done it. He wouldn't with Brunk."

"He would have posted you and killed you just to feed the kitty. Because people hated you and it would make him a bigger man."

"Stop it!" he said, as anger rose sudden and sickening in him. "Don't do it any more. Trying to pimp a man into going against Blaisedell."

Kate's mouth fell half open; then she closed it tightly, but not, it seemed to him, in the fury he had expected. He watched the rims of her nostrils whiten and slacken with the rhythm of her breathing. Her black eyes stared back into his. Then, at last, she shook her head. "No. No, I don't mean that, Deputy. Not any more."

She was silent for a long time, and all at once it came to him what he must do. Ride to Bright's City to see Keller, to see Peach himself if he could. He could go now, for the Regulators were disbanded and gone, and maybe if he himself were absent for a few days it would not be so bad when he returned. He would go and see Keller and even Peach himself and seek the means of warding off more tragedy, even knowing that those means would be whimsically or ruthlessly withheld, as they had always been.

"What kind of man was Curley Burne?" Kate asked.

"Why, I guess about everybody liked him, even though he rode for McQuown. He was pleasant to talk to, and friendly, and there was no scratch to him. Though he could be hard enough if he wanted to be, and he was man enough to go as he pleased. I told you he wouldn't go along on that in Rattlesnake

Canyon." He scraped his fingernails along the oilcloth in little wrinkled tracks.

"He was strong on kin and friends and that," he went on. "We argued that after Billy got killed. He was always Abe's best friend." He looked up at Kate. "I guess you would have liked him."

"Why did he do it?"

"Come in against Blaisedell? Why, you heard about what he said. Just to show the color of his belly. Just to show he had as much right to walk the street as Blaisedell."

It was not enough, he knew. He sighed and said, "I don't know, Kate. I have been thinking maybe it was for McQuown."

"I guess I would have liked him," Kate said. Then she frowned and said, "Why for McQuown?"

"Well, he said something funny when he was let go and he knew he'd better get out in a hurry. He said he guessed he had been chosen to clear the air. But that he guessed he just couldn't oblige. I didn't know what he meant exactly, but—"

"Blaisedell," Kate said scornfully.

"No, I thought he meant McQuown some way. But then he came in after all. I don't know—probably it was just what he said; how he wanted to show he wasn't yellow."

"Or just being a man," Kate said, in her most contemptuous voice. "I have seen men bucking cards they knew were stacked against them and losing their stake and borrowing more and losing that. All the time knowing they couldn't win."

"I don't know," he said. He tried to formulate what was disturbing him more and more. "I've tried to think it through. Why Billy came in, and why Curley did, when it looked at first as though he wasn't going to. I'm afraid—what I'm afraid is that there is something about Blaisedell so they—"

He stopped as Kate cried, as though she had won something from him, "So they have to! Yes, so they have to; like flies that can't stay out of a spider web."

"Maybe it is something like that," he said. "Well, part that and part different things. For instance, I was thinking about Billy, and how my father used to whip him. He had to whip Billy a lot, for Billy was always wild. And he'd never cover up a thing he'd done." He touched his nose, remembering that time. "He would always tell right off, like he was proud of it. And it seemed like he got whipped for things he hadn't done when he could have got off by speaking up.

"So I've got to wondering if he wasn't just taking the whippings to clear off things he'd done, inside himself. I mean things he felt guilty about. So that if he got whipped it paid him up for a while. I wonder— I wonder if—" He could not quite say it.

"Killed?" Kate said.

"Maybe it would pay for everything."

"*Killed?*" Kate whispered.

"Why, yes." He tried painfully to grin. "Maybe you haven't ever felt that way, being a religious woman. If a person hasn't got any religion there's some things he can't get forgiven for because he can't forgive himself. I wondered if it wasn't partly that with Billy."

"*Killed* for it?" Kate said, and he was pleased to see there were things about men she did not know, after all her bragging that she knew them so well.

"Even that. Though I think it was more than that with Curley. He and Abe was close, and I think he was maybe trying to prove something to everybody about Abe. Or else he couldn't admit he was wrong about Abe and was trying to prove to himself he wasn't. It is hard to see in a man's heart."

"It's not for you to do, Deputy," Kate said. She was staring at him with a curious concern.

He nodded. "But what I was thinking was all the reasons there might be for going against Blaisedell. To prove yourself some way, or cancel something out. Or he is somebody and you are nobody and even if he kills you, you get to be somebody because of it; I have known men to think backwards like that. Or see him a devil, so you are good and fine if you go against him. Or—or just what it would make of you if by luck you managed to kill him. I think of all the reasons and—"

"You had better stop this," Kate said.

"—and I think it is pretty terrible. I hope it isn't so, but I can see how it might be to some, and it is a terrible thing. I think Blaisedell couldn't stand it if he knew."

He gazed back into her eyes and was sorry for what he saw there. He got quickly to his feet. "Oh, I was just talking foolishness," he said. "Just unloading foolishness. I thank you for listening to me. Now I have got to ride up to—"

He heard a sound of heels outside; they thumped on the steps. There was a knock. Kate came around the table and opened the door. Past her, Gannon saw Blaisedell standing on the porch, his black hat in his hands. His fair hair was matted where the hat had compressed it, in a circle around his head.

"Hello, Kate," Blaisedell said, in his deep voice. "I thought the deputy might be here. I wanted to talk to him."

Kate's hand tightened into a claw, gripping the edge of the door. She moved aside; she looked as though she had grown faint. "Talk?" she whispered.

"I wanted to ask him something," Blaisedell said. He stepped inside past Kate, who still clung to the door, her head turning slowly as Blaisedell passed her, until she was staring into Gannon's eyes, and he could feel the fear and hate in her so strongly that it seemed to fill the room.

"What is it, Marshal?" he asked, resting a hand on the back of his chair.

Blaisedell said almost casually, "What Schroeder told you."

"He has already sworn what Schroeder told him!" Kate cried.

"I asked *him*, Kate," Blaisedell said, and did not look at her.

"I told the truth, Marshal," Gannon said.

"Now kill him for saying it!"

"You think badly of me, don't you, Kate?" Blaisedell said. Still Blaisedell's eyes remained fixed on him, and he had the sensation of being examined completely. "Jessie has decided she might have been wrong," Blaisedell went on, after a time. "So I thought I would ask you face to face."

Then Blaisedell nodded as though he was satisfied. "Why, I guess it has been hard, then, Deputy," he said, "with every man down on you for it. You will understand it would be hard for her to come out now and say she has changed her mind, though. Because of what's happened," he said.

"Surely," Gannon said, stiffly. It occurred to him that Miss Jessie might not have admitted willingly even to Blaisedell that she had changed her mind, or that she had lied. "That doesn't matter, Marshal," he said, and Blaisedell started to turn away.

"Marshal," Gannon said. "Carl didn't know for sure. You know he killed that miner that way, when the jack pulled on his shotgun. That was on his mind at the end. And he said—that a man ought to forgive if he wanted to be forgiven, and that he was going to judgment directly. He—" He stopped, and Blaisedell nodded to him again.

Blaisedell turned to face Kate, who drew back away from him. "I have killed another one, being too quick on the draw, Kate," he said. "I had swore I would never do that again."

Then he moved on outside and down the steps in the sunlight, replacing his hat. He walked with his head tipped back a little, as though he were watching something above him. Kate leaned on the door staring after him.

When she flung the door shut the tarpaper walls shivered with the shock. She swung around to face Gannon and there was a kind of wonder in her face. "I thought you had never *felt* anything in your life," she said, in a stifled voice. "But you pity him."

"I guess I do, Kate," he said, and bent to pick up his hat.

"Him!" Kate said, as though she could not believe it. She made a sound that was halfway between a laugh and a sob. "Pity *him*! Why, you were suffering because you had to tell the truth. You would have backed down except that it would have been a lie, and a lie is wrong." She said it not angrily, as he had expected, but as though she was trying to understand.

He strained his ears for the crack of Eladio's maul knocking Curley Burne's coffin together. He could hear it in his mind, and hear the scrape of shovels on the rocky ground of Boot Hill, and the rustle of the wind blowing through the brush and rocky mounds and the grave-markers there. The retreating slow crack of Blaisedell's bootheels had been a sound as lonely, and as fatal.

"What did he mean, too quick?" Kate said, in a breathless whisper, but he did not know what Blaisedell had meant, nor did Kate seem to be speaking to him or even aware of his presence any more. She did not appear to hear when he said good-by and told her he would be going up to Bright's City. He walked slowly back to the jail the long way around, by Peach Street, so he would not have to pass so many men on his way.

## 38. *The Doctor Attends a Meeting*

AFTER THE Citizens' Committee meeting the doctor walked with Jessie and some of the others to the stage yard to see Goodpasture, Slavin, and Will Hart depart for Bright's City. Buck waved from the window as the coach swung out of the yard, carrying another frantic delegation to General Peach, with another series of demands and pleas. And with threats this time.

With Jessie's hand on his arm, he moved on to Goodpasture's corner. The coach was already almost lost to sight in the dust that followed its rapid progress east along Main Street. Jessie, beside him, was silent; it had been a difficult meeting for her, he knew. She had hardly spoken a word throughout, and she seemed listless and tired. There were unhealthy-looking smudges beneath her eyes.

"And how is the miners' angel today?" MacDonald said, coming up behind them. His hands were thrust down into the pockets of his jacket; his derby hat was cocked over one eye. His pale, petulant, handsome face was coldly hateful. He inclined his head to the doctor. "And the miners' sawbones?"

Jessie did not speak, peering at MacDonald past the edge of her bonnet. Her hand tightened on the doctor's arm, and he said, "Idle. There have not been many broken men to try to put back together now that the Medusa is shut down."

MacDonald's upper lip drew up tautly as he sneered. "I'd heard you had taken up *other* work."

"Have you put me on the list of men your Regulators are to deal with?"

"Please stop this!" Jessie said.

Pike Skinner had come up beside MacDonald. "He hasn't got any Regulators any more," Skinner said. "Why'd they quit on you, Charlie? Did you drop their pay?"

MacDonald said hoarsely, "I see you have all turned against me. I know that lies are being told about me. I know who is telling them, and who is plotting against me, and in what boardinghouse." He pointed a finger suddenly, his upper lip twitching up again. "And I know who is the chief troublemaker now!"

The doctor looked from the finger, pointed at him, into MacDonald's face. It was plain enough that the man was half mad with fear of losing his position. MacDonald was in a pitiable condition, but he felt no pity. He would be pleased to see him completely broken. Biting his words off sharply to keep his voice from shaking, he said, "Charlie, I am very proud that you count me among your enemies."

"Oh, please stop it!" Jessie cried. "Aren't there more important things than this silly bickering over the Medusa mine? I wish there were no Medusa mine!"

"I'm sure that everything will be done to see that you get your wish, Jessie!" MacDonald retorted. "I'm sure—" He stopped as Pike Skinner caught his shoulder and wrenched him around.

"Watch who you are talking to! She asked you to stop it; you stop it!"

MacDonald's face reddened in hectic blotches; he pulled away from Skinner's grasp, readjusted the hang of his coat, and silently marched away around the corner.

Watching him go, the doctor saw Taliaferro crossing Main Street, followed closely by the half-breed pistolero, who, it seemed, accompanied him everywhere of late. He saw the deputy coming down Southend Street toward the jail. "Poor Charlie is unhinged," he said, and patted Jessie's hand.

"Gannon keeps off Main Street, I notice," Skinner was saying bitterly to Fred Winters. The doctor felt Jessie's fingers bite into his arm as Skinner continued his denunciation of Gannon.

"I have an errand, David," she said, and left abruptly. Her errand, he saw, involved Gannon, whose dismissal from his position had been one of the objectives of the delegation that had just left for Bright's City. He himself had not voted for it, and he knew the majority had hoped that firing Gannon would somehow be proof that he had lied.

He waited until he saw Jessie enter the jail, and then he started alone for the General Peach, where there was to be a meeting of the miners. Strikers from the Medusa greeted him as he walked along under the arcade, and Morgan was watching him from his rocking chair on the veranda of the Western Star. Morgan inclined his head to him, but he ignored the greeting.

There were a few miners loitering on the porch of the General Peach, but the dining room, where the meeting was to be held, was empty yet, and he went on down the hall to the hospital. As he had said to MacDonald, with the Medusa closed down there had been almost a moratorium on mine accidents, and, in addition, a number of sick men had moved out in what they must have thought was a protest against Jessie's saving Morgan from the mob. There were not many beds occupied now.

The curtains were drawn back on the tall, narrow window, and a long block of sunlight streamed in over the empty cots. Barnes, Dill, and Buell sat on Barnes' cot, engaged in their endless game of red dog, and Ben Tittle and Fitzsimmons stood watching them. Nearby, Stacey, with his bandaged head and jaw, lay on his side reading a tattered newspaper.

Dill flung a card down. "What's happened?" he said, in a flat voice. "Who's shot now?"

"What's the news, Doc?" Barnes asked.

"Is it so the Regulators have gone home?"

"They've gone," he said.

"Who's murdered now?" Dill said, to no one, staring sullenly down at the cards on the bedclothes before him.

"Where is Miss Jessie these days, Doc?" Buell said, and would not meet his eyes. "She has kind of went and forgot us in here, hasn't she?"

"You can shut your face!" Ben Tittle said.

"Good lot of quarreling going on in here today," Fitzsimmons said. Then he said, "I don't know what to make of the Regulators going, do you, Doc?"

The doctor shook his head, and knew that Fitzsimmons was worried that now there would be more definite talk of burning the Medusa stope, since it was unguarded; it was what had terrified MacDonald. Fitzsimmons brushed his hands together worriedly. The fingers of the right one looked like bent sausages where they rested on the left, which was still bandaged.

"Got tired is all," Dill said. "Nobody to shoot. Well, I say it is plain dull myself, no shooting for about twenty minutes, I guess it is now—nobody new killed?" He threw down another card. "Well, it's come fine, I guess," he said, "though not quite even yet. Schroeder kills Benny Connors and Curley Burne kills him, and Blaisedell him. But when Morgan kills Brunk there is Miss Jessie to—"

"I say shut your face!" Tittle cried. He swung his arm and the flat of his hand cracked against Dill's cheek. Dill sprawled on top of Barnes, cursing, and awkwardly got to his feet to face Tittle. The long scar on his forehead was red and shiny. Watching them brawl, the doctor wondered if they were worth anyone's trouble; he was ashamed to realize that he cared nothing for any one of them, except, perhaps, Fitzsimmons. He only hated what oppressed them, and sometimes he was afraid it was not enough.

"You shut that talk, Ira!" Tittle said. "Damn you, Ira! I'll not hear it!"

Dill cursed him, and Fitzsimmons propped a foot on the rail of the cot between them.

"We've been talking, Doc," Buell said apologetically. "And worked up a little heat before you came in. Ira and me was holding that Frank Brunk was right, and it bears hard on a man to be a poor-house case. You can see that, Doc."

"Pay for your keep then!" Tittle said. "I say if you can pay, pay. Or shut up about it. Damned if I see why she'd keep such ungrateful, dirty-mouth bastards anyhow."

"And what have you and Ira decided, Buell?" the doctor said.

"Well, this is a boardinghouse and she has got to make a living of it," Buell said. "And on the other side it is poor to be on somebody's charity. So we was just saying that those that can pay her ought to do it."

"All right, do it."

"Not a one of them's got anything saved to do it," Fitzsimmons said disgustedly. "They are talking gas. Mostly what they are worrying on is some way to make her feel bad because she did for Morgan."

"You talk too much for a young squit," Dill said, and Fitzsimmons grinned at the doctor.

"Yes, it is all right for her to save their lives. But not that of anyone they don't like."

"That's all right, Doc," Dill said. "We know who she likes. I guess her long-hair gunman smells sweeter than we do."

"I'll kill you, Ira!" Tittle cried, starting forward.

"Stop it, Ben!" the doctor said; he was struck by the fury

in Tittle's face. He nodded his head toward the door, and Tittle obediently turned away. He hobbled toward the door, his clothing hanging loosely on his stick of a body.

The doctor turned to Dill, whose eyes reluctantly met his. "I take it you are the one who can't pay, Dill," he said. "What do you want her to do, dun you so you can insult her?"

Dill said nothing.

"Others who seem to have felt the way you do have had the decency to leave here," he went on, still staring into Dill's ugly face. "I suggest that you do so. You are not worth her care, nor my trouble. You are not worth anyone's trouble."

"Oh, I'll be moving out," Dill said. "I know when I'm not wanted."

"I suggest that you buy a stock of pencils from Mr. Goodpasture and sell them on the street. That way you will not be a charity case."

"I'd rather. Don't think I wouldn't."

The doctor took a step toward Dill, who backed away. He saw Jimmy Fitzsimmons watching him worriedly and he fought to keep his voice level. "Let me tell you something, Dill. I don't know what you have been saying here, but if you manage to cause her any pain in your stupid spite, I will do my best to break that head I mended for you."

"Easy, Doc," Fitzsimmons whispered.

"I mean exactly what I say!" he said, and Dill retreated before him. "Did you hear me, Dill?"

"Like Morgan busting Stacey, huh, Doc?" Dill said.

"Exactly."

Dill shrugged cockily, and moved over to his own cot; he stood there glancing back out of the corners of his eyes.

"Go on!" the doctor said. "Get out, Dill!"

He heard Ben Tittle call him from the doorway, and he swung around. "Miss Jessie wants to see you, Doc."

Abruptly his rage died. Almost he could feel sorry for Dill and the others, each of whom fought his own lonely battle to maintain a semblance of pride. He walked out past Tittle and went down the hall. There were a number of miners standing inside the entryway now, worried-looking, stern-faced men in clean blue clothing, several with six-shooters stuck inside their belts. All greeted him gravely. There were some, he knew, who were responsible men, men with dignity who could act for themselves if they were shown the way. He wondered why he must always be so short with them.

He knocked on Jessie's door, and entered when she called to him. She stood facing him with her fists clenched at her sides, and tears showing in her round eyes. He had never seen her look so angry.

"What is it, Jessie?" he asked, closing the door behind him.

"That hateful little man! Oh, that hateful, jealous little man!"

"Who?"

"The deputy!" she said, as though he had been stupid not to know. "I don't see why he couldn't do it! It is just that he is so jealous. So *little*! He—"

"I don't know what you are talking about, Jessie. Gannon wouldn't do what?"

She made an effort to compose herself. The little muscles tugged at the corners of her mouth, and it was, he thought, as if those same muscles were connected to his heart. "What is it, Jessie?" he said, more gently.

"I went to tell him that Henry, Buck, and Will had gone to Bright's City to see that he was removed," she said. "I told him I—that I didn't know whether they would succeed or not. And I— Well, I thought he would leave if I asked him, David."

"Did you?" he said, and wondered how she could presume such a thing, and what she hoped to gain by it.

"I thought if *I* asked him," she said. The tears shone in her eyes again; she daubed at them with her handkerchief. "I thought if I made him understand—" Then she said furiously, "Do you know what he said? He said that Clay could not do it!"

"You asked him to quit so that Blaisedell could be deputy," he said, and, although he nodded, he knew that Gannon was right. There were many reasons why Blaisedell could not do it, but he would rather have slapped her face than try to reason with her.

"Hateful, jealous, *smug* little man!" Jessie said. She put her handkerchief to her mouth in what seemed an unwarranted degree of grief.

"What is it, Jessie?" he said again, and put an arm around her straining shoulders.

"Oh, it is Clay," she whispered. "Clay told him I had lied, and he was so *smug*. Oh, I hate him so!" She drew away from him, and threw herself down on her bed. She sobbed into the pillow. He thought he heard her say, "If he would leave no one would know!"

He went to sit beside her, and after a time she took hold of his hand with her tight hand, and held it against her damp cheek. "Oh, David," she whispered. "You are so kind to me, and I have been such a terrible person."

"You are not terrible, Jessie."

"I lied to him. And he found it out."

"Blaisedell?" he asked, for it was not clear.

She nodded; he felt her tears warm and wet on his hand. "I lied to him about what Carl Schroeder said."

He said nothing, staring down at her tumbled ringlets; gently, awkwardly, he stroked his left hand over them. She sobbed again.

"I told him I had even *lied* for him. That's how he knew. But I did it for *him*! I thought if I could just ask the deputy to—"

"Hush!" he said. "Not so loudly, Jessie. It will be all right."

"Clay hates me, he must hate me!"

"No one could hate you, Jessie."

There was a knock at the door. "Doc, it's time for the meeting." It was Fitzsimmons' voice.

"Just a moment," he called. He stroked his hand over Jessie's hair, and said, "It will be all right, Jessie," without even thinking what he was saying. He looked down at the brown head beneath his hand. She had done something that had been unworthy of her—for Clay Blaisedell. She had dedicated herself to him. He prayed with a sudden fury for a return of the days when there had been no Clay Blaisedell in Warlock.

"But what am I going to do now?" Jessie said. "David, if Gannon would only leave no one would believe him!"

He did not answer, for Fitzsimmons was knocking again. "Doc, they are starting! You had better come."

Jessie was sobbing quietly when he left her, and Fitzsimmons looked relieved to see him. "Come on! Daley is saving us a place!"

There were about thirty men in the dining room. The plank tables and benches had been pushed back against the walls, and men sat on them and on two ranks of chairs at the far end of the room beyond which were Frenchy Martin and old man Heck, at Jessie's table. There were a number of miners standing. The doctor noticed that although most of the men were from the Medusa, there was also a contingent from the Sister Fan, and, it seemed, at least one from each of the other mines. This was the skeleton of the Miners' Union that had been set up under Lathrop's leadership, had lapsed since, but had not been forgotten.

Daley had saved two chairs for them in the front row. Fitzsimmons sat down stiffly, adjusting his hands before him, and the doctor was aware that Fitzsimmons' habit of holding them so, was, in part, to call attention to them—like a soldier's wounds, as some kind of proof of adulthood and initiation before the rest.

Old man Heck waved at the rear of the dining room, and the door there was shut and latched. Heck was scowling beneath his wiry gray eyebrows as he slapped his hand on the table for order. There was a nasty bruise along the side of his head, and a scraped place on his forehead that gave him a fierce expression. Martin, beside him, had a bruised eye, and, with his long, waxed mustaches, looked equally fierce.

Old man Heck said, "The Regulators have gone for sure. We have been up to see for ourself. There is a pack of foremen there and a barricade they put up on the road, but that's all. Now; everybody knows what's the question here."

"I'm for it," someone said quietly, and the doctor swung around to see that it was Bigge who had spoken. He had thought better of Bill Bigge, who flushed to meet his gaze.

"I am for it," Frenchy Martin said. "They have pushed it down our throat long enough. Now we bite it off, eh?"

Fitzsimmons got to his feet.

"Who let *him* in?" someone growled.

Fitzsimmons stood holding his burnt hands before him. He said, "I'd like to ask Doc what he thinks, if everybody is agreeable."

There was a burst of clapping. They called his name, apparently with good grace, although they must know what he would say to them. He rose and glanced around at Daley, Patch, and Andrews, who had asked him to come.

"Very well," he said. "I will say what you all know I will say. Shall I?"

"Go ahead, Doc," Daley said.

"Give them hell!" Fitzsimmons whispered.

"I will say that you had better think before you act, which you already should know. I will say that you have a much greater chance of achieving what you want by sensible means rather than by violent ones. Unless what you want is merely senseless violence, in which case you have proceeded correctly at every turn, and I congratulate you."

There was laughter, and catcalls mixed with it. As the noise ceased he went on more grimly. "I know the reason for this meeting, and I refuse even to discuss the subject. There has been too much lynch-mobbing and burning already, all of it stupid. I hope that whoever it was among you that took it upon himself to fire the Glass Slipper realizes by now how he has hurt you all. For what you need is friends in Warlock, who will help you with your cause. If you feel you do not need friends, you do not need me. I should like to know if this is the prevailing attitude, for if it is there is no reason for me to waste my breath further."

"We sure do need you, Doc!" Fitzsimmons said loudly.

"Hear! Hear!" Patch called, from the back of the room. Martin was chewing on a thumb knuckle, and Heck wore a look of sour disapproval.

"Very well," the doctor said. "I will say again that you need all the friends you can get. MacDonald has made you friends by stupidly trying to bring his Regulators into Warlock. You will just as stupidly lose them by your disgraceful behavior. If I were you I would see to it that there is no more playing with fire, or hurling of rocks through store windows, and the like. In particular, you will throw away every advantage you now possess in the instant it takes to light another match—do you understand me?"

"By God, Doc—" old man Heck cried, but a voice from the rear drowned him out: "We have to do something, Doc! We can't just sit and wait till MacDonald starves us back."

"You can't eat fire!" another broke in, and the dining room resounded with cries and argument. Old man Heck pounded for silence, and the doctor waited patiently with his arms crossed on his chest.

Finally he said, "You will remember a thing that Brunk had to say—that people look down on you miners. I think Brunk never saw why this should be; he only resented the fact. I will tell you why. I know, for it is the reason I am out of patience with you a good part of the time myself. They look down on you because of the wild and irresponsible vandalism you have indulged in all too often. Some idiot among you might have burned this town down. Do you wonder that such things might make you unappealing to the decent citizens?

"As I have said before, MacDonald is a stupid man. Because of his stupidity there is a certain sympathy for you now, despite your own actions. It is your business to see that in the future you are not more stupid than MacDonald, so that this sympathy for your plight may continue to grow. There is a force in public opinion that even MacDonald will have to feel. He—"

"MacDonald wouldn't feel a shafthead frame if it fell on him!" Bull Johnson said, and there was laughter.

"MacDonald has already felt it. The deputies may have stopped the Regulators the first time they tried to come in, but have none of you wondered why he didn't bring them in again? He did not because he knew this town was solidly against such a thing. The marshal—"

There was another outcry at the word, and suddenly he was furious. He sat down. "Now, Doc!" Fitzsimmons said. "You don't want to get mad!" Daley leaned toward him to try to get his attention. The shouting slowly died.

"All right, Doc," Frenchy Martin said. Old man Heck only scowled. "No offense, Doc!" a voice called. They began to chant his name in unison, and he felt a surprised exultation that he could speak to them as he had and make them accept it.

But when he rose again he looked from face to face with contempt. "Why should I take no offense? You yourselves are quick enough to take it, it seems. Anything done in this town that is not exactly what you wish, you feel is traitorous. If you are going to turn on Miss Jessie like sulky boys, or on the marshal or poor Schroeder who defended you as well as Morgan in defending the law—"

There was a louder outcry; the names were shouted— Blaisedell, Morgan, Brunk, Benny Connors, Schroeder, Curley Burne. This time he shouted back at them until he made himself heard. "You contemptible fools! What is the use of trying to help you? Who cares for your piddling dollar a day?

I do not. I hoped there might be some decency and common sense somewhere among you, but I see there is none. Have your damned violence and arson and see where it will get you. You will burn that stope and cut off all your noses to spite one face you hate!"

He sat down again, and again they pleaded with him to go on, but he did not rise. He thought that he could sway them in the end, he was not even particularly angry, but he thought it best to let them whistle for his advice for a while. They would covet it the more if he withheld it.

Fitzsimmons rose, to be met with catcalls. He cried in return, cheerfully, "Cut away, boys! Cut those noses!" He held his burned hands out before him and waited for silence.

"You can laugh at me because I am younger than you," Fitzsimmons went on. "But I am more a miner than three-quarters of the ragtag and bobtail around here. I've been underground since I was twelve, and I know some things about a strike it looks like you don't know. I know when there is a strike the mine don't produce and the miners don't eat. But a mine can go a long time without producing."

Fitzsimmons seemed a little surprised that he had not been shouted down yet, and, watching the boy, the doctor was aware again of the iron in him, and more and more, too, he was aware that Fitzsimmons was as patient, calculating, and ruthless as any gambler.

"And I know another thing it looks like you don't," Fitzsimmons went on. "I know if a stope gets burnt it stays burnt a long time, and you don't eat during that time either. Or after."

"There are other mines, boy," old man Heck said. "There is other camps besides Warlock."

"Not for those that burnt a stope, there isn't!"

"The kid is right on that, old man!"

Again everyone began to talk at once. Fitzsimmons tried to make himself heard, but the others quieted only when Bull Johnson got to his feet, grinning and waving his arms.

"I say we can bust Mister Mac," Johnson said, in his great, deep voice. "Him and the Haggins and Morgan and Blaisedell and the Citizens' Committee and any other sons of bitches in league with him. I say we have got stronger arms than they got, and all we have to do is get guns and—"

"Dig silver ourself then?" Patch broke in. "Do you think Peach wouldn't be down here with the cavalry?"

"Ah, you couldn't get Peach out of Bright's City with a pry-bar."

"Better Peach than a bunch of hardcase Regulators!"

Old man Heck pounded on the table. Fitzsimmons shook his head despairingly and dropped into his chair.

"Doc!" They began chanting his name again. As soon as he got to his feet again they fell respectfully silent.

"I understand your fear." He spoke quietly now, so they would have to be silent in order to hear him. "Now that you have begun this strike, you must get something for your efforts or look like fools. I would hate to see MacDonald's satisfaction, if you were able to gain nothing, as much as any of you. But what do you want in the end? Your wages raised, or the Miners' Union established?"

He looked from face to worried face, and no one answered him. "I think you will get neither of those things," he said. "Lathrop made the Miners' Union too much of a bugbear here for MacDonald even to tolerate the notion, and MacDonald has put himself into a position where to save his face he cannot put wages back to where they were. They were due to come down in any case, and I am sure he was ordered by the company to lower them, though possibly not so much as he did.

"My advice to you is to accept these two facts. Make no issue of the Miners' Union as yet, and let MacDonald have his way about the wages. Then what can you hope for? I know you must save your own faces, and I think you must try to save your lives as well—by which I mean the timbering in the stopes.

"I think you should prepare a series of demands to present to MacDonald. He will refuse them, and then you should submit slightly different ones. If he goes on refusing them, he will come to look more and more unreasonable to everyone —including the Porphyrion and Western Mining Company. I think that is the way you can beat him."

He saw that he had most of them with him. He took a deep breath. "Some of your demands should be these: Demand above all proper timbering, especially in that number two shaft. And demand that the number two lift be made safe.

Demand ventilation at the lower levels. There are a great many more items that concern your personal safety which you know much more about than I. People are going to sympathize with demands of this nature, as they will not sympathize with the drop in your wages, or with the Miners' Union as yet.

"You have every right to demand these things, but I would demand much more at first so that you can bargain downward. I would—" He paused a moment; what he was going to say seemed, in a way, a betrayal of Jessie, but he could see that they must, one day, have it. And, he though bitterly, Jessie had Blaisedell now. He said, "I would demand some kind of hospital for the injured, the cost to be shared between you and the mine owners." He held up a hand for silence, and raised his voice above the muttering. "And there is to be a committee of miners established to supervise that, and to advise on what is to be done about safety in the Medusa. This is the most important thing. A committee," he said, and paused again so as to catch their full attention, "that will be the basis for your Miners' Union!"

They cheered in one voice, and he could not help smiling. He sat down quickly, amid the prolonged yelling and clapping. Fitzsimmons sprang to his feet.

"Listen!" he cried. "The Doc has told us the right way, I guess we all know; but there is something else to bring up. What we are waiting for is the day Peach gives this town a patent. Stop and think how the vote'll run when *we* have got a vote. We—"

"Sit down! Young one—sit!"

"Listen! Why won't you listen to me? I am telling you we can elect the mayor and council and all—and sheriff! We—"

"Sit down, boy!" Bull Johnson growled.

"Peach's forgot us here. He thinks we are in Mexico."

"Brunk was after MacDonald about that retimbering too, Doc. He never got anywhere but fired."

"I say burn the Medusa for Frank's sake!" Bull Johnson shouted. "Then they'll *have* to retimber."

"Hear! Hear!"

Old man Heck pounded on the table. Fitzsimmons sank into his chair again, and turned to grin bitterly at the doctor. "They won't listen. Damn them, they just won't."

"Well, I guess Bull has got us back to what we come here to vote on," old man Heck said. "All this other is interesting and maybe edifying, Doc, but we are here to vote on the first thing. All right, all for it!" Old man Heck got to his feet to count the hands.

The doctor did not turn to see how many had gone up, watching old man Heck's face. Fitzsimmons, who had looked around, grinned and winked at him.

"Seven for," old man Heck said sourly. "Well, all right; against."

"No fire tonight," Frenchy Martin said.

"Yellow-belly bastards!" Bull Johnson said. All around the room men began to stir and rise. There would be no fire tonight.

The doctor sighed and got to his feet; he had better get back to Jessie. He excused himself and hurried from the dining room, waving a hand and nodding to the men who tried to talk to him.

He crossed the hall and entered Jessie's room without knocking.

Blaisedell was there, sitting where he had sat, and Jessie's head was against his chest. It did not appear that Blaisedell hated her, as she had feared. They both stared at him, Blaisedell with the color flushing to his cheeks, Jessie with her eyes round and bright. She smiled at him, and Blaisedell started to his feet.

"You had better keep your door locked, Jessie," the doctor said, and backed out and pulled the door quickly closed behind him. The entryway was full of miners, but he thought no one had seen.

Someone called to him, and he went to join Fitzsimmons, Daley, and Patch, and the two or three others who seemed to make up Fitzsimmons' clique. Fitzsimmons asked if he would like to come to the Billiard Parlor for a game with them, and they all seemed surprised and pleased when he said that he would.

"You can hold my cue for me, Doc," Fitzsimmons said, as they left the General Peach together. "But maybe you could let me call the shots."

## 39. *Morgan Looks at the Deadwood*

TOM MORGAN sat in the sun on the porch of the Western Star Hotel in his only suit of clothes, his only boots, his only hat. He rocked, smoked a good Havana cheroot, and watched the activity of Warlock in the afternoon—the bustle down the street of horsemen and wagons and men afoot, the loungers along the arcades, the groups of Medusa strikers standing along the far side of Main Street. There was a racket of whistling and catcalls as three whores in their finery promenaded down Southend Street and stopped to look into Goodpasture's store window.

As he leaned forward in his chair to try to see down to the ruin of the Glass Slipper, his money belt pressed into his flesh. Quickly he leaned back. In it was his stake; his place was burned, and he had long been sick to death of Warlock. His mind began to poke pleasureably at place names, at things he had heard of this town or that one.

He spun his cigar out into the dust of the street, where it disappeared as into water. He rocked back and stared up at the sun past his hatbrim, and grinned—a painful stretch of flesh over his teeth. He could not go. Clay would not because of Miss Jessie Marlow, and he could not because Clay would not, and because of McQuown, and because he did not know what Kate was up to with the deputy.

At that moment the deputy came into sight, mounted, from Southend Street. He came jogging down Main Street on a shabby buckskin horse, his hat pulled low on his forehead, his face turned aside against the wind. He nodded gravely as he passed, and Morgan turned to see that he took the Bright's City road.

As he watched the deputy ride out of town he saw Kate coming toward him with her skirt blowing and one hand holding her feathered hat on her head. He rose as she came up the steps to the veranda.

"I want to talk to you," she said.

"Fine. Sit and talk."

"Not here."

"Your deputy rides out of town and first thing you are out hunting a tomcat," he said, as he took her arm. They started back toward Grant Street to her house. "You will get yourself a bad name walking with me," he went on. "I am a devil, as everybody knows. What's this about you and Buck Slavin going to build a dance hall?"

"We've talked about it," Kate said shortly. "He'll put up the money if I'll run it."

"Just Buck?" He grinned at her.

"No, I think there is somebody else in it, Tom," she said, in an uninterested voice. He noticed that she was very pale. "I don't know who."

"It is Lew Taliaferro, and if you think I am going to let what's left of the Glass Slipper go to *him* for nothing you can have another think."

But she shook her head; that was not what she wanted to talk about. She unlocked the door of her house and let him in, watching him with her black eyes as he entered. Then she moved to stand across the table from him, as though it were necessary to have something between them.

"What's bothering, Kate?"

"Clay was here. He said he had killed another one being too quick on the draw. I want to know what—"

"He said *what*?"

She repeated it. He stared back at her and slowly he took off his hat and dropped it on the table, and brushed a hand back over his head. "Why did he come here?" he asked.

"He came to ask the deputy if he had lied about what Schroeder told him—there was something about Miss Jessie Marlow being mistaken. But I want to know what he meant about Bob Cletus! Tom, what did he *mean*, he'd been too quick on the draw?"

He hardly listened; he felt a rage at Jessie Marlow that filled him until he thought he would burst with it, then pity and rage for Clay, who had killed Curley Burne wrongfully now by his lights—one time wrong, and every time wrong after it, Clay had said. More and more, it seemed, everyone looked upon Clay as only a name, a thing, a machine to which they fed their pennies and out of him came the same trick which they could then class good or bad for their amusement. Even Miss Jessie

Marlow; he knew she had done it to Clay without even wondering how she had. Talked him into going back to marshaling, for one thing. God damn her to hell! There was no one but Tom Morgan to see the man inside the machine any more.

But Kate was not interested in Curley Burne or Miss Jessie Marlow; she was interested in Bob Cletus.

"I don't know what he meant, Kate," he said. "Why didn't you ask him?"

"What did he mean, Tom?" She hit her fist on the table, and then she leaned on it heavily and the feather swayed on her hat. She looked suddenly as though she were going to break apart. "Now I don't *know*! Don't you see? Now I—" She got control of herself with an effort. "Tom," she said. "Tell me the truth about what happened!"

"Told you and told you, but you won't believe me. Cletus called out Clay over Nicholson."

"Bob didn't care anything for Nicholson! I *know* that!"

He shrugged. "You are going to believe Clay shot him down because I asked him to, whatever I say."

He watched her face crumple. He could smile as he told the truth; "I didn't tell Clay to shoot him down. I wouldn't have if I'd *wanted* him shot down, for Clay wouldn't have done it." And he leaned toward her and said, "Kate, I wish you had gone and married Bob Cletus and that I'd given you away to the happy bridegroom. And that you were fat as a pig and worn out right now cooking chuck for him and all his hands on that spread he had, and a couple of dozen children. Don't you believe I wish it?"

He heard her make a high sound in her throat. "What did Clay mean by that, Tom?" she whispered hopelessly.

"Ask him. But let me ask *you* something. What are you up to with the deputy, Kate? A person would think you had a thing on about somebody whose brother Clay shot. Are you trying to make something out of it?"

She shook her head a little; her eyes were swollen. "No. Nothing. I can't make anything with anybody, for you would just have him killed. Wouldn't you?"

"I don't know which way you mean that. One way I might." He sat down and leaned his chair back and crossed his boots up on the table. She was staring at him with her red lips half open.

"Let me tell you something straight and for all, Kate," he said, and he spoke as seriously as he had ever spoken in his life. He pointed a finger at her. "There have been damned few people I have ever thought anything of. Maybe only two, when it comes down to it. And those I have never thrown down and never will."

"Two!" she cried. "Do you mean *me*? You crucified me!"

"Why, Kate, you'd been a whore and it was your own doing. No mac brought you to it. I thought you figured the way I did, and whoring is a way to make a stake like any other. I didn't know you were going to be so damned delicate about it. A person is what they are and what's there to be ashamed of?"

"I didn't mean that!"

"Oh, you meant Cletus. Well, there is no point talking if you are going to hold I put Clay to that."

"You can't even look at me and say you didn't!"

He looked at her and said he hadn't. He wondered suddenly if he would have done it any differently if he had known he was never going to have Kate back, whatever. "I was saying," he said, "that there have been a couple I held high like that. One was you, the other is Clay. I suppose you wouldn't understand that, being a quarter-breed bitch, but it is so."

He paused and gazed back into her wide eyes and saw her mouth open again, as though she would speak again. But she did not, and he went on. "And I am talking about Clay now, for you have gone your way and it's not mine. I call Clay friend and I don't know that I've ever had another. Do you know what a friend means? I don't expect you do, for all you've known is a bunch of other whores you thought poorly of, and said so. I call Clay friend, and I don't give a damn that some go around holding him up as God's salvation to this country, and others call him a dirty dog of a killer. And I don't expect it makes much of a damn to him either what everybody thinks of me."

He pointed his finger at her again. "Now, that is a thing that is just so, whether you understand it or not, which I expect you don't. But that holds strong with me. Now let me tell you some more. There are people who are trying to throw him down. I am speaking in particular of you, and maybe your deputy. And McQuown. And there are others, like Miss Jessie

Marlow, though I don't expect she thinks she is. Now: I think I will see Clay Blaisedell die, like I told you once. For that is the trade he is in. But I intend to see that he dies decently, and his name held good, and honor to him. Though not the same way some others want it. Listen to me: I will stick with him and try to do in every backshooter there is, and I mean you among them, and Gannon, if you two are up to something. And McQuown; and *all*. You want to see him die, in your woman-meanness, but I will fight you down the line. Maybe you will think you have won when he is dead, but I will win too, for I will see he goes down in the end like he wants to."

Again she started to speak, again he leveled the finger at her. "There is nothing I have ever set myself to do yet I haven't done. Hear me and think if it isn't so. And this is what I have set myself to. I will see it through in spite of every son of a bitch in the world against it. I will kill anybody I think is dangerous to him that way. Or get killed for it either without giving one good God damn, if it would do any good. Do you understand me, Kate?"

"Tom," she said shakily. "I don't want to hear anything more about it. I don't—"

"Just one more thing," he said. His throat felt very dry. "Listen. There is going to come a day when I cash in. When I get up to the Gate they will look at the records, like they do. They will scream to see mine. But I will say to them that I was made the way I was, but I did a decent thing in my life. And I don't know that there are so many decent things done that they can sniff at it. I can say I did this, and by God I did my best, and it was a good thing. I can say I had a reason to *be*, and I don't see many around me that have. I can say I had a reason for being alive that was mine, and that was worth something, and—"

"I have got my reason to be!" Kate cried, but he felt a vast triumph as her voice broke.

"Why, it isn't worth anything and you know it. Two bits' worth of forgiveness would cancel it out. To see a man that never *meant* to do you or yours any harm brought low! You a Catholic, with your Virgin to pray to and your candles and all—do you think you can go up there and when they ask you what reason you had for being alive, say it was to see a man dishonored and killed? It won't pass, Kate." He began to laugh.

"They will send you to a lower part of hell than me. Wouldn't that gripe your everlasting soul!"

He shouted with laughter and beat his hand upon his leg. He tried to suck the laughter back at the sight of her face, but he could not. "Oh, that *would* be hell!"

"Stop it!"

He stopped. He put his feet down and leaned toward her, and said, seriously again, "Kate, do you think I would give a rap for Clay if I could tell him to go out and shoot down a randy son of a bitch that was after my girl?"

He watched her fighting uncertainty. She shook her head and the feather on her hat swooped and swung; he could make her believe the truth a lie, he knew, but not a lie the truth.

"Wait!" he said, as she started to speak. "Let's try to work it out. Maybe I see how it went, come to think of it. You had a few rolls in bed with Clay, didn't you?"

"I did not!"

"Are you sure, now?" he said, grinning, feeling hate of himself like black bile rising in his veins. "Because *I* thought you did, Kate. Wait now! I was just wondering if Cletus might've got wind of it too. Was he a jealous kind? Maybe that was why."

She clutched her hands to her face and he thought he had won; he wondered what he thought he had won. He said softly, "Maybe that was why Cletus called out Clay, Kate. Do you think that might've been why? You knew him better than I did."

"It's not so!" she said, through her hands. "That I— Tom, I knew he was your friend. I—"

"Well, lots of things that aren't so get fought over all the same."

She leaned forward, her hands on the table, her swollen eyes fastened to his. "You—" she whispered. "You—"

"I'm just saying that somebody could have told him that," he said easily. "And if he was a jealous fellow. I've heard—"

"I don't believe you!" she cried. "You didn't. You are just trying to— I can't believe you, I can't ever believe you! Get out of here, Tom!"

All at once he was very shaken by the sight of her face, and he picked up his hat and started for the door. He had only meant to try to take her off Clay's back a little and let her sit his own. He thought of the times he had seen her in anger, the times in grief; it occurred to him, now, that he had never felt sorry for her before. He turned and said, "Kate—"

"Oh, *please* get out!"

He went on outside, where his eyes recoiled from the brightness of the sun. He could hear her sobbing behind him. Why couldn't he tell her the truth? Why wouldn't it be easy? He almost turned to go back to her, but, after a moment's reflection, he did not. He could not, he thought, ever go back.

## 40. *Bright's City*

BRIGHT'S CITY lay just to the east of the Bucksaws, along Bright's Creek. There was a heavy traffic of wagons across the rumbling wooden bridge over the creek, where, straight ahead, on Main Street, lay the Plaza. To the right, half a mile down Fort Street, was Fort Jacob Collins, with its flag rippling and colorful in the wind, and, to the left, the three-storied red-brick courthouse, its tall windows shuttered against the sun, its copper-sheathed cupola raised like a helmeted dragoon's head.

Soldiers from the fort paced the streets or stood upon corners. There were many women in Bright's City, and many men in store suits among the more roughly dressed ranchers and cowboys. Townsmen and housewives kept to the north side of Bright's City's Main Street, while sporting women in their finery passed in promenade on the south side, accompanied by the whistling of cowboys and soldiers.

The delegation from the Warlock Citizens' Committee exited from the Jim Bright Hotel. A Bright's City deputy, chewing on a toothpick, greeted them pleasantly as he sauntered on his rounds.

"How enviable it is," Will Hart said, "to see the same deputies on hand every time you come in here."

"I wish we'd see a different sheriff," Buck Slavin said irritably.

"Well, let's go see what sheriff there is," Goodpasture said, and they proceeded to the sheriff's office, which adjoined the courthouse. Sheriff Keller was visible through the dusty glass of the window. He sat at ease with his scrolled boots propped up on his pigeon-holed desk, his fine, white, sugar-loaf hat tipped over his eyes.

Keller rose ponderously as they entered, a bull-necked, heavy man with the face of a jolly bloodhound, a tobacco-stained mustache, and a gold watch chain with links like barbed wire strung across his massive midsection. Behind him the cell doors stood open, and in one of them a number of prisoners were playing cards.

"Why, it's some gentlemen from Warlock," Keller said, removing his hat and smiling in greeting. Then his face turned sad as he said, "I certainly was distressed to hear about old Carl Schroeder. A good man." He shook his head sadly, and clucked.

The prisoners dropped their cards and crowded into the door of the cell. "What's happened?" one cried.

"Blaisedell throw down on McQuown yet?"

"You boys hush, now!" the sheriff roared. "You! Get back in there!" The prisoners moved back inside, and Keller went over to slam the door on them. "I'll have a little peace and quiet in here!" he said severely, and turned back to the delegation again. Another deputy came in.

"Branch, you run for Jim Askew," the sheriff said. "Here is some more news from Warlock and he'll apoplexy sure if he gets gone to press before he hears it. Now; what's up now, gentlemen?"

"We want some law in Warlock, Sheriff!" Slavin said. "The Citizens' Committee has sent us up here to insist—"

"Well, now, hold on," Keller said. "You people are all right. That young Gannon come up here ahead of you people, and told me he was going to *re*sign, but I have talked him out of it. Anyway, you have got Blaisedell still, haven't you?"

"Damn," Slavin said.

"Well, we wanted to get rid of Gannon, Sheriff," Will Hart said. "I must say we are a little sorry to hear you talked him out of resigning."

The sheriff sat down, frowning heavily. "Well, now, gentlemen; he said people was kind of down on him, thinking he had swore false over Curley Burne. Maybe he did too, but it come right in the end, now, didn't it?" He eyed them each in turn. "You people down there have got to realize it is hard to get a decent man to deputy in Warlock. You don't just chuck one out when he does something you don't like once or twice; no, sir." He scowled at the deputy, who had not left yet. "Run along now, Branch. Get Jim Askew here, boy." The prisoners were whispering together excitedly.

"Like I say," Keller went on. "It came right anyway what with Blaisedell cutting down Curley Burne, so I can't see what you people are so excited about."

"We insist that you fire Gannon!" Slavin said. "The Citizens' Committee has sent us up here to tell you—"

"Huh!" Keller said. "Now, I mean! Who is the Warlock Citizens' Committee to tell me who I am to fire? I mean, I like to get along with you folks, but it is hard to hire a man for that place down there."

"What did he want here, Sheriff?" Goodpasture asked.

The sheriff leaned back in his chair, his face crinkling with amusement. "Why, he didn't really want to resign. He was just trying to blackguard me with it. He wanted four more deputies down there. Four!" He held up four fat fingers. Well, he's young, but he is all right. I promised him if he'd wait over a day or so, I'd get him a new sign made for that jail down there, though."

"That will be an improvement," Goodpasture said.

"Now, see here, Sheriff!" Slavin said heatedly, and then he stopped and sighed.

Keller sat rubbing his red-veined nose and glancing from face to face again. "You gentlemen ought to try to get on with your deputies down there. Down on him, are you? Well, let me tell you. Either he went and lied to get Curley Burne off, or else he didn't lie. You gentlemen know for sure he went and lied?"

"Everybody knows he lied," Slavin said.

"Well, now, I meant proof, Mr. Slavin. No, now, you don't know for sure. You have got to look at it this way, anyhow. I mean, say he did lie; what're you going to do if a man lies for an old partner of his? You'd do it; maybe I'd do it, though I won't admit it straight out. I mean, that is a poor place to be down there, terrible bad pay, and a man doesn't live long enough to take much of it home, either. Look at poor old Carl. And he lasted a coon's age compared with most. I mean, you have got to give a man with a job like that a little leeway."

"There's another way of looking at it, too," Hart said. "Burne probably would have gone free anyway if he'd come up here to trial."

The prisoners broke out laughing. Keller scowled and scratched his nose. "Well, now!" he said. "You know what the man said when he saw the black-headed Swede, don't you? That's a Norse of a different color!" He roared with laughter, amid a further chorus from the cell. The delegation from Warlock looked at each other despairingly.

Then Keller's face assumed a serious expression, and he said, "Well, now, about McQuown's boys getting off up here. I might doubt it some. Things've gone and changed in people's eyes up here a little. I don't expect no jury here is going to let those Pablo 'cases run quite so pecker-up any more. What I mean—it looks like Abe's just about run his string. People used to take a fright you just creep up behind them and whisper '*McQuown!*' It's not so any more, not with Clay Blaisedell salting his tail for him and lopping his gun hands off like he is doing. It is like when the old general got after Espirato and made him run for cover."

Hart said, "You make it sound almost safe enough for you to come down and be a proper sheriff, Sheriff."

"Now it is not going to do any good for you to get insulting, Mr. Hart. I swear, you people come up here and play me the same tune every time, and all I can tell you is just any day now there is going to be a separate county set up down there. Peach County, I expect it'll be called. You will have your own sheriff to pick at then. I was talking to Whiteside just last week, and he was saying any day now that—"

"I do hate to remind you, Sheriff," Goodpasture said. "But it has been any day now for over a year."

"Two years," Hart said.

"Well, it is any day *now* for sure. I'd put money on it—not more than a month, for sure."

"Bellywash!" Slavin cried. "I'll tell you this, Keller. If we don't get some satisfaction from you this time, we will see Peach himself!"

"See him!" Keller said, smiling, nodding. "Do that."

"And if we don't get any satisfaction from him we will by God go to Washington, if we have to!"

"Go," Keller said. "You will probably have to. I'd sure like to go back there myself. I hear it is pleasant this time of year, back there."

"We are asking for your help, Sheriff," Goodpasture said. "The situation in Warlock is much more difficult than you realize."

Keller's eyes flickered a little. He hunkered forward in his chair, and spread his hands. "But what would you want me to do, Mr. Goodpasture? I mean! I'd be all my time riding back and forth between here and Warlock, and I am too old for that foolishness. And don't mind saying I am scared. Mr. Goodpasture, I just don't claim to be anything I'm not. I run for sheriff here, surely, but to my mind this county stops at the Bucksaws there and that is all I run for. That is so, now; you know I didn't come down there beforehand, either. Now, I like this big belly here as it is and not all shot full of holes. Like Carl, and that feller Brown and how many others before that? I am not sheriff down there, that's all. If it was put to me hard I had to be, why, I'd quit. What's the matter with Blaisedell all of a sudden you are so dissatisfied again? Sounds from here like everything is going nice as pie."

Will Hart said, "It has not worked out, Sheriff. He has had to kill too many men."

"Why, my stars! You fellows aren't shedding tears for those rustlers he is popping off, are you?"

"Sheriff," Goodpasture said. "He has no authority. And we had none when we hired him. He and the Citizens' Committee have had to take too much upon themselves."

"It looks from here like it is going nicely. He has got McQuown tramped down and Pablo thinned out some. Those cowboys will stop getting their fingers burnt pretty quick, and settle down. I will give you gentlemen the same advice I gave Gannon. Let Blaisedell work it out. There is no better man nowhere, from what I have heard. I told Gannon to quit worrying, and you too. The time to worry's when things is in bad shape, not—"

"They are in bad shape," Hart said.

"You are an officer of the court!" Slavin cried.

"Not down there."

Hart said, "Well, maybe if we had three or four more deputies, as Gannon suggested—"

Keller shook his head. "You would have to collect taxes down there to have your three or four, and that would take a dozen. And fighting men! Now, maybe you gentlemen wouldn't mind paying taxes, and maybe Mr. Slavin wouldn't even mind having it run into his franchise about transporting prisoners up here, but you gentlemen ought to know those ranchers down that way never even heard of taxes. They'd think a tax collector was a road agent! Why, it'd take Peach and the whole shooting match from the fort to collect taxes down there. All that for some deputies? Why, Blaisedell is serving you better than ten deputies could in a month of Sundays. Now, isn't that so, Mr. Goodpasture?"

"Blaisedell is a very fine man," Goodpasture said. "We have had no cause to be anything but highly satisfied with him. It is a matter of authority. We are in a position of ordering him to kill men. We are in a position of trying to administer severe laws that do not exist, when the responsibility is yours."

"No, sir! It is not mine either. No, sir, you just take all the authority you need."

Goodpasture sighed and said, "And the kind of thing that Blaisedell can deal with is necessarily limited. You should be able to understand that."

"You mean those Cousin Jacks running wild and tearing things up? MacDonald was up here complaining about that just lately, but I thought you people had worked up some sort of regulation committee to deal with those wild men."

"MacDonald has," Hart said. "Please don't connect us with that pack of mongrels."

"I thought it was a Citizens' Committee thing," Keller said. "So did everybody. Well, it goes to show you."

"Say!" one of the prisoners called. "Does it look like McQuown is going to make a play against Blaisedell? There is betting here he won't."

The sheriff regarded them questioningly too, but, sunk in gloom, no one of the delegation answered. The sheriff chuckled and said, "I'd ride down to see that."

"Let's get out of here and see Peach," Slavin said. "I knew there was no damned use in our coming here."

"See him," Keller said, approvingly.

"We are going to! Right now!"

"Let me tell you something first," Keller said, in a confidential tone. "Just like I told Gannon, that's bound and determined he is going to see him too. Don't mention about Blaisedell if you see him. Old Peach doesn't like anything to do with Blaisedell for beans." He winked hugely. "Jealous! Jealous as a lap dog. For you know what used to be the biggest thing in this territory? Peach cleaning out the Apaches. Now it's been so long people's forgotten there ever was Apaches, and new people coming in all the time that's never even seen one. Why, now the biggest thing out here is Blaisedell. By a mile! Jim Askew is coining money from newspapers all over the country.

"He sends out stories by telegraph, for heaven's sake! And those papers back east of here pay for it and beg for more, he says. Nothing new on Blaisedell, he writes about some fool gossip or other, anything. Back East Peach is only some has-been of a general, maybe he is dead by now, it's been so long since anybody heard anything about him. But Blaisedell! Why, Jim got rich on that Acme Corral shoot-up alone, and never stopped a minute since. Jump, when he heard about Curley Burne! You should have seen him!

"Oh, Blaisedell has got to be the biggest thing that ever happened out here, and you remember what I say and keep kind of quiet if you have to mention him to the general. Or talk him down. Here comes Jim right now," he said, nodding toward the window.

Jim Askew, editor and publisher of the *Bright's City Star-Democrat*, came hurrying in. He was a little, wrinkled, side-whiskered man with a green vizor over his eyes, ink-smeared paper cuffs, and a canvas apron. The deputy was a step behind him, and the other deputy, whom the delegation had seen before the hotel, appeared also.

"What's happened now? What's happened now?" Askew demanded, taking a newsprint pad from beneath his apron, a pencil from behind his ear. He stared from one to the other of them with his eyes enlarged and rolling behind his steel-rimmed spectacles. "What's happened in Warlock, fellows?"

"Warlock is gone, Jim," Hart said. "It was a terrible thing. The old Warlock mine opened right up and the whole town fell in. Nobody left but the few miserable survivors you see before you."

"Now, now, fellows," the editor said reprovingly. "Now, seriously, what's been going on lately? What's Blaisedell been up to now?"

## 41. *Journals of Henry Holmes Goodpasture*

April 15, 1881

It has been said, with the exaggeration by which truth is memorialized in a kernel, that the reason people remain in Warlock is that death is preferable to a journey to Bright's City, and damnation better than the stage to Welltown. It is not quite so bad as that, although the trip is a long day's horror, and upon arrival at Bright's City the spine feels like a rock drill that has lost its temper.

This morning, then, to see Sheriff Keller. He is a shameful excuse for a sheriff, venal, cynical, and cowardly, and yet it is difficult to dislike him. Gannon, we found, had preceded us to Bright's City—having ridden through the Bucksaws, a shorter route by half than the stage road—and Keller out-argued our demands for his dismissal, I think more from force of habit than from loyalty to his deputy. His reasoning was: 1) deputies for Warlock are hard to come by, good or bad; 2) Gannon is willing to be deputy in Warlock; ergo, 3) Gannon remains deputy in Warlock.

We are so used to being defeated and thwarted by Sheriff Keller that we no longer feel animus against him. Still, we were depressed by our encounter with him, and when we were kept from seeing General Peach by Whiteside at his most obstructionistic. We will try again tomorrow with renewed determination, revived by a night's rest at the Jim Bright Hotel.

It is curious to talk to the inhabitants here about recent events in Warlock. Bright's Citizens are defenders of Blaisedell to a man, and they are, indeed, surprised and insulted that we should feel there are two sides to the matter. They will not

accept the fact that there are things in heaven, earth, and Warlock undreamt of in their philosophy. To them, Blaisedell is an
uncompromised and untainted Hero, battling a Villain named
McQuown. There are none of the shadows and underbrush
that have so haunted us in Warlock. Morgan is Blaisedell's right
bower, and is somewhat revered himself. The miners and their
quarrel with MacDonald are of no interest, although it is disturbing to hear the Regulators described as a band of eminent
Warlockians convened in aid of Blaisedell.

April 16, 1881

Colonel Whiteside guards his lord like a lion. He is a colorless little man, thin, worried-looking, and nervous to infect
the most placid. He is uneasy with civilians, and his manner
alternates between chill command and an inept cajolery. He
routed us again this morning. This afternoon we won through
to the Presence.

I had not seen the General since November, when he passed
through Warlock en route back from the border after one of
his idiotic dashes after a rumor of Espirato. Since then, I think,
he has not been out of Bright's City. That he is insane, I have
now no doubt.

Whiteside was fending us off again, although with increasing desperation, when the General himself stormed down the
corridor of the courthouse where we were seeking to obtain
an audience, shouting incoherently in his great blown voice.
He was followed by a company of aides, orderlies, and sergeants, all in dress uniform, and was in dress uniform himself, although his blouse hung open and some kind of liquid
had been spilled upon his shirt front. He waved his gauntleted
hands and shouted something at Whiteside which seemed to
have to do with the presence of dogs upon the post, and how
they were to be dealt with. With him chaos came, as he roared
meaningless sounds, and all his company sought to speak at
once, while Colonel Whiteside, with pad and pencil in hand,
called simultaneously for silence, sought to make sense of what
his chief was saying, and watched us nervously for evidences of
a flank attack.

Then, out of the uproar he himself had brought into the
corridor, or out of the decay of his brain slipping into senility

or worse, or because of our unaccustomed presence, General
Peach fell silent and confusion spread over his face. It was pitiful to see it. The little blue eyes, fierce and determined a moment past, wandered distraitly around, all but lost in the fat,
red folds of his face. He stripped his gauntlets off hands as fat
as sofa cushions, and, as soon as he had them off, struggled to
put them on again, while all the time his eyes worried from face
to face as though he did not know where he was, nodding from
time to time as poor Whiteside tried to prompt and question
him into repeating what the order, so urgent a minute before,
was about—with a desperation that called forth pity not only
for his master but for Whiteside himself, who must be the one
to govern this territory under a madman while trying to conceal that madness from the world.

At last Peach's eyes fixed themselves upon me with an en-
raged and defiant glare, and he cried, "Has headquarters sent
out some more damned politicians to try to run my brigade
for me, sir?"

I stammered that we were a deputation from Warlock with
urgent business for his attention, to which he retorted even
more forcibly that I was to tell them that the damned devil had
hidden himself in the Sierra Madre and he could do nothing
unless he was given permission to cross the border in pursuit.
"Nothing, damn his red eyes!" he cried, while Will, Buck, and
I tried to explain where we were from and something of our
mission. Finally either some sense broke through or we were
mistaken for still other emissaries, for all of a sudden we
were swept into the inner temple beyond Whiteside's desk.

It is a great room with westward-looking windows, crowded
with the mementos of his career: an umbrella stand in which are
tattered banners, bullet-torn regimental colors, a pair of confederate standards; on the wall a large painting of the Battle of
the Snake River Crossing, with Peach leading his men through
Lame Deer's painted ranks and the teepees beyond them; on
the wall also a varnished plaque on which was the scalp of some
vanquished foe, with long, dusty braids; and there were quivers
of arrows, moth-eaten war bonnets, Apache shields, war clubs,
peace pipes, and framed photographs of Peach shaking hands
with various chieftains. Upon his desk was the leather-wrapped
stick he often carries, which is supposed to be the shaft of an
arrow that almost killed him. The whole room seems a dusty

and unkempt museum, or perhaps it is only a facsimile of his mind—a vacant space, inhabited by heroic memories.

Peach seated himself behind his desk, swept off his hat and flung it over the inkstand, stripped off his gauntlets again, transfixed us with his glittering, pale eyes, and said that he sympathized with our position, but that he could only fight a defensive campaign until those damned, do-nothing politicians in Washington decided to put it up to the Mexican government, and that there was no way, at present, he could go after the "murdering red rascal."

I was, I remember, terrified lest Buck or Will blurt out that Espirato is presumably dead, and any threat from his renegades extremely improbable. They did not, however, and stood as stupefied as I, while Peach arose and paced the floor in an agitated manner. His actions are a series of mechanical and fustian gestures, each one anticipated by a slight pause, as though, inside him, gears and levers prepare the proper muscles for their roles—almost you can hear the whirr of the aged and imperfect clockwork. Then he will toss his head as though flinging back from his eyes the mane of white hair he no longer possesses (he is quite bald except for a matted ruff that gives his head the broad, flattened look of a badger's), fold his arms with massive dignity, and stare down his nose; or fling himself into his chair with a crash that seems sure to smash it, or rise out of it with labored gruntings. He paces the floor with his hands locked behind his back like a man in a prison cell, or stands glaring at nothing with his great boots spread splay-footed apart and a hand held Bonaparte-like within his blouse, or strokes his beard with the expression of one giving birth to an infinitely cunning stratagem. Now, I find, I am able to sort out these various poses and attitudes one by one; yet, at the time, accompanied by the steely glare of his small, bright, mad eyes, there was a kind of majesty about them.

But it is a variety of dumb-show. The words that accompany these postures and gestures have no relation to them. The mildest words may be set to the most violent gesticulation, and conversely. His speech, gushing from the rusted pipes within him, is of the most monumental and dreadful nonsense.

From time to time poor Whiteside appeared at the door, to be waved away with irritable condescension. At least, when I was able to get a word in edgewise, I sought to tell the General of the plight of Warlock. He let me speak, flinging himself down in his chair again and studying me the while with his bearded chin propped upon his fist, and on his face an expression of terrible dismay, as though I were relaying to him news of some dreadful defeat and rout. But presently his attention wavered, and his eyes began to flicker confusedly around the room—and I to falter in my speech as the impression grew stronger that not a word of what I said was understood, and, moreover, if it had been, would be of no more import to him than reports of injustices among the sparrows to a Zeus brooding over Troy. Buck was of no assistance, paralyzed into dumbness, and Will has confessed that all his energies were taken with stifling a fit of giggles which had smitten him as though he were a schoolboy in church.

I was reduced, in the end, to stammering like a schoolboy myself. Peach made interjection only once. He reared back in his chair, frowning at something I said, took up his hat from the inkwell and cast it to the floor, snatched up a pen and scribbled furiously upon a piece of paper, and stared down at what he had written with an awesome concentration. Then he threw down the pen also, and muttered, "By God, if they come around that way, Miller and half a company could—"

It finished me. Buck gave me a wild, desperate glance. Will had already turned to go, and I retreated also, uttering apologies, statements that perhaps we should return another time, etc., that must have sounded as eccentric and irrational as what we had heard from him. But he spoke calmly behind us, saying, "Warlock," as though my explanations had won through at last.

He was standing behind his desk now, glowering at us from under the white bushes of his eyebrows with eyes that looked sane at last. "Tell him he is getting too big for his boots," he said. "Tell the scoundrel I am governor here. Tell—" he said, and once again confusion showed in his eyes and he was lost. But still he made an effort to recover his train of thought. He slapped a hand down on his desk and said we were to tell Whiteside we were to have fresh mounts and the best Indian Scouts he could furnish us!

We left the room. Before Whiteside's desk there was still the clutter of aides and orderlies. Whiteside, writing busily, took no notice whatever of our exit, and we had nothing to say to him, nor to John Gannon, whom we met outside the court-house and who seemed anxious to ingratiate himself with us. We ignored his overtures and walked back to the hotel more in awe than in black depression. "Mad as a hatter," was all Buck could say, and it has seemed to me an understatement of shat-tering proportions.

We determined to send our telegrams to Washington, as we had been directed to do, all else failing. The wording had been set down, and we engaged ourselves in copying them out, and, further, in making up a statement in the form of a letter which Askew had offered to print for us, to be sent by mail to follow our telegrams, expanding upon our grievances. Whereupon Whiteside burst in on us (for we had made our threats to him before we had seen the General), seized a copy of the telegram, read it, and burst out with the most astonishing threats against us should we send them. He said he would hale us into military court and prosecute us to the full extent of his power, which he hinted was substantial; he said further that he would have us arrested immediately, that he would have the telegraph of-fice closed down, etc. We were in no mood to be frightened, however, and said we knew perfectly well he could not arrest us, and that, if the telegraph office was closed to us, we would travel on to Rincon to send our telegrams.

Threats failing, he turned to pleading; his motivation was plain, and, indeed, he stated it. Obviously he is insanely loyal to his insane chief. The General is old, he said; a famous man, a great man, but failing now, obviously dying. Could we not see that he was a dying man? Could we not wait a little while? Will said that it looked to him as though Peach might live for-ever, and that we would not, Warlock remaining in its present state. Whiteside is not much impressed with the importance of Warlock or its inhabitants, but sought our sympathy and strove desperately not to offend us. He turned to procrasti-nation. Give him a little time; a month or six weeks. General Peach was failing rapidly, he could see it day by day. The Gen-eral had certain prejudices against Warlock, but if we gave him, Whiteside, six weeks, he would see that the necessary orders were given for the issuance of a town patent, and, indeed, the establishment of another county with Warlock, of course, the county seat (here I saw Buck's eyes light up). He would do his utmost to bring the General to these dispositions, but, that failing, would forge the General's name as he has evidently already done on various minor administrative documents.

I think we were all moved with pity for Whiteside. At any rate we promised to wait six weeks, after which, if he failed us, we would bombard Washington with letters and telegrams detailing All. Whiteside thanked us most gratefully, and retired, and we drank a bottle of whisky together, most grim and depressed, wondering how many men we might have condemned to death in this delay and subjection of the public good to one man's already engorged reputation. And I found myself wondering what we might be doing to Blaisedell's reputation, which is precious to us, by making this concession to Peach's, which is not.

We could comfort ourselves only in the hope, and I pray it is a legitimate one, that we had more to gain by enlisting Whiteside's aid than by offending him, and that, though our telegrams could easily become lost among bureaucratic desks and wastebaskets, unsent they became a spur to hasten Whiteside to action.

Will and Buck have gone off to their own rooms, to their own dreams or nightmares. Bright's City is gay tonight outside my window. I can feel strongly a difference in the atmosphere here, the presence of order and of the knowledge of, and trust in, order. Is it too much to hope that Warlock will be like this one day? Or will our mines play out and our town dissolve to an abandoned ruin before it has even come to peace?

We will return to Warlock, I am afraid, despite Whiteside's promises, with heavy hearts and guilty ones, and with little appetite for the explanations we will have to give our fellows.

## 42. *Morgan Is Dealt Out*

SITTING ON the bed in his room in the hotel, Morgan unfolded the piece of stiff paper with steady fingers. He glanced up once at the frightened face of Dechine, in from San Pablo, and then held the paper under the lamp. The words were printed in large, carefully shaped letters:

3–7–77

CLAY BLAISEDELL

FOR THE FOUL MURDER

OF WILLIAM GANNON

AND CHARLES BURNE

3–7–77

BY THE HAND OF

ABRAHAM MCQUOWN

CHIEF OF REGULATORS

"What am I going to do, Tom?" Dechine whined. "Jesus, what am I going to do?"

Morgan refolded the paper carefully. Then, holding it with his thumb and forefinger at one end, snapped it open again with a loud pop. Dechine flinched.

"How many have you got?"

"Ten of them," Dechine said. He rubbed his red nose. "Jesus! Three or four of them I'm supposed to post up somewheres— by the stage depot there, and by the Lucky Dollar and Good- pasture's store. The rest's for him, and you, and Buck, and some others—I got a list here." He made motions toward a vest pocket. "I am supposed to see *he* gets one, for sure. Jesus, what am I going to do, Tom?"

Morgan studied the paper again. It was neatly done. He felt a kind of admiration for McQuown, that he had listed only Billy Gannon and Curley Burne. McQuown had known the cards that were high in Warlock; they were higher still with Clay, though McQuown could not have known that. McQuown had been smart enough not to overload a thing. Well, Clay, what do we do now? he said to himself.

Dechine's voice rattled in his ears. "I was going to chuck them off somewheres and just make tracks. Give *him* one! Then I thought I'd bring them up here for you to see, Tom. I—"

"Who spelled them out like this for McQuown?"

"Joe Lacey. He can write good. Jesus, Tom! What am I going to do?"

"Like you were told. If you don't, Joe Lacey will just have to run up another batch."

"Oh, no! I am getting right on out of the territory. I know God-*damn* well I'm not going to give one of these to Blaisedell." Dechine's shoulders were hunched as though he were afraid someone was standing behind him; gingerly he placed the stack of papers on top of Morgan's bureau. "I told Abe straight out that I wasn't going to do it, but there's no talking to him. He has got a look on him like he's been chewing peyote berry. So I thought I'd just make like I was going to, and get scarce fast and far. I know I—"

"When are they coming in?"

"Not right away, I don't expect. There was everybody there drinking and jawing when I left, but they was laughing there how they would let Warlock stew awhile. I guess not right off. They are all coming, though; that bunch the Haggins rounded up for MacDonald, and all Abe's people this time. The old man even—they are going to bring him in the wagon to see the sport. You should have heard the old son of a bitch! But not me, no sir! Tom, I am not going to post up those damned things!"

"Put them out. If you don't they'll just have to send somebody else to do it." He folded the paper again. His hands remained steady, but there was a taste of copper in his mouth as he wondered what Clay would do. But there was no way of stopping these, or others like them, from showing up.

"I don't know whether I am scareder of Blaisedell or Abe, which," Dechine went on. "Abe is on the prod for a caution!" He hesitated and licked his lips, his eyes flickering. "Well, I guess I ought to tell you, Tom. They almost put you down there too. But Abe said not. They was thinking of putting you and Blaisedell down for killing that Cletus—"

"Who?" Morgan said, raising an eyebrow.

"Well, he was that passenger that got killed that time Pony and Cal shot up the Bright's City stage there. Abe was trying to figure on some way to make like you and Blaisedell did it, or just him. But finally Abe decided this was all he'd put there. I tell you he has gone crazy wild down there, and it's not just over Curley either. Jesus, Tom, I will be glad to get out of this country. This country has went to hell. I'll say this straight out,

Tom, even knowing Blaisedell is a friend to you. And even if I have known Abe and liked him too. There's times I've hoped to God they would come to it and burn each other dead so a man could get his breath out here again!"

Dechine jammed his hat on his head, and said, "I wonder if you couldn't give me a little stake, Tom?"

"Why, surely. How much do you owe me—five or six hundred? Take that."

"Tom, I—" Dechine swung around to face the door as footsteps sounded, on the stairs, in the corridor. There was a knock.

"Tom?" Clay said.

"Come on in," Morgan said, and grinned at Dechine.

Dechine backed into the corner and took off his hat and began wrenching it between his hands. Clay glanced toward him as he entered.

Morgan handed Clay the piece of paper.

"I was nothing to do with it, Marshal!" Dechine cried. "They would have cold-cocked me there if I didn't bring these in! But I brought them straight to Tom here!"

"I thought you were in a hurry to get moving, Dechine."

Dechine made a sound like a leaky pump. He edged toward the door, nodding ingratiatingly; he went down the stairs at a heavy-footed run.

Clay stood reading the paper for what seemed a very long time. Finally he said, "The old vigilante sign. Three feet wide by seven long, by seventy-seven inches deep." And then he said, "Chief of Regulators." He folded the paper carefully.

"They are all coming in," Morgan said. "Those that were Regulators for MacDonald and more besides."

"Fair enough," Clay said.

"What are you going to do?" Morgan said evenly. "Run for it?"

"Not for McQuown."

"What are you going to do?" he repeated, not so evenly. "Lie down and die?"

"Not for McQuown," Clay said. Suddenly he grinned. He looked like a boy when he grinned like that, and he said, "Have you got any whisky, Morg?"

"Have," Morgan said. He got it and poured two glasses. "How?" he said, and chuckled with excitement.

"How," Clay said, nodding, and they drank together.

"Remember that time in Fort James when Hynes and that bunch got the drop on you?"

"Well enough," Clay said. He sat down, taking off his hat and dropping it on the floor beside him. His fair hair looked gold in the lamplight. "I swear, Morg, you were a sight coming out through those batwing doors. It looked like you had about six arms going like a windmill and a gun in every hand. I thought they would tramp each other to pieces getting out of there, and you and me yelling and shooting up the air behind them."

Clay sounded excited, and reenforced his own excitement; he had never felt so pleased, or proud. But then Clay looked down at his lap, and frowned as he said, in a different voice, "There was some good times in Fort James."

"Well, it looks like you will need some help again this time."

He saw Clay's hand tighten around the glass of whisky he had not finished. "No," Clay said. "I won't need help, Morg."

Morgan swung away to face the window. The full moon hung in it like a jack-o'-lantern. All the pocks showed on the round, gold, blind face. He felt as though he could not get his breath as he stood there, following through Clay's thoughts, trying to understand Clay's judgment. It seemed a judgment on him, and it was something he had never known Clay to do before.

His voice sounded very flat when he spoke. "Clay, do you think it is just McQuown coming in? It is all San Pablo."

"It is between McQuown and me."

"Surely. The rest will faint at the sight of those gold-handles."

He heard the paper rustle behind him. "I won't need help this time, Morg," Clay said.

Damned fool, he thought, not even angrily; damned fool. But there was no use in calling Clay a damned fool, no use arguing. He saw what he must do. He had told Kate he would not throw Clay down, but he must throw him down this time.

"Are you moving on, Morg?" Clay asked, in an expressionless voice.

Thank you, but no thanks, and why don't you move on while you are at it? It must be Miss Jessie Marlow speaking. You used to be yourself, Clay Blaisedell, he thought bitterly, staring out at the moonlight pale as milk in Warlock. Now they have talked you into being Clay Blaisedell instead. "You don't mind if I stay and watch, do you?" he said. "Buy you a drink of whisky after, to settle your nerves. Or pall-bear."

"You understand about it, don't you, Morg?"

"Surely. I can't hurt you if I'm not in it, and I have hurt you enough here."

Clay made a disgusted sound. "That's foolishness. Don't pretend you don't understand about this. This is on me alone."

Morgan did not turn from the window. The stars were lost in the moonlight; he could make out only a few dull specks of them. "Well, you won't mind if I don't move on right away, will you?" he said. "I have got business here still."

"What's that, Morg?"

He did not know why he should feel so ugly now. He turned to face Clay, and grinned and said, "It wasn't jacks that burnt the Lucky Dollar, you know."

"It wasn't?"

"Haven't you noticed Taliaferro lately? He has got that pistolero from the French Palace tied on his heels like a shadow."

Clay nodded almost imperceptibly. "Did you shoot that dealer of his, Morg?"

"You mean Wax? That beat my Professor's head in for him?"

Clay picked up his hat and held it in his lap while he dented the crown with blows from the heel of his hand, crosswise and then back to front, continuing it with a kind of abstracted attention as though there were nothing else in the world to do. But at last he said, without looking up, "I have never asked you a thing like this before."

"Like what?"

"Leave it alone about Taliaferro."

"All right."

"For a favor," Clay said. He got to his feet and put his hat on. He held the paper in his hand, and glanced toward the others on the bureau. "That's a silly thing," he said. "For me to be putting those up against myself. Do you know anybody you can get to do it?"

"I'll get Basine."

"Might as well get it over with," Clay said. He moved toward the door.

"For a favor?"

Clay stopped. "Don't go sour, Morg. This is nothing between you and me. I thought you would understand that."

"Why, I suppose I do," he said. He went to the bureau and
took up the whisky bottle again. Standing with his back to Clay
he poured whisky into his glass in a slow trickle until he heard
the door close and Clay's footsteps departing.

He stepped to the window then, and, in the darkness,
watched the tall figure appear below him. He raised his glass
and whispered, "How?" and drank deeply. "Why, Clay, I understand well enough," he said. "But I won't let you do it. Or
McQuown."

Abruptly he sat down on the edge of the bed. "Why, you
damned sanctimonious school marm virgin bitch!" he said, to
Miss Jessie Marlow. It was time he had a talk with her, and he
addressed himself to her and to the whisky in his glass.

You, he said; *you* put Curley Burne on that list to crucify
him, and I suppose you would let him stand alone against that
pack of cowboys because he would look so fine? Don't you
know that McQuown has been sitting down there as patient
and tricky as a hostile waiting for the right time to move? You
handed him Curley Burne to move on.

"How you must *hate* yourself, Miss Jessie Marlow," he mim-
icked, aloud. "Do you think they will curl up and die at the
sight of him because he is so fine? *He* would curl up and die,
they would blast him loose from his boots, backshot, sideshot,
and frontshot too.

"Well, you saved my life, and with damned bad grace. And
you wish I was gone, don't you, and you have told him so,
haven't you? Are you satisfied with what you are making of
him? You have got him so he doesn't know himself any more.
And I am the ugly toad whose life you saved because there
wasn't any way you could get out of it, and I will save his from
McQuown. I suppose it would turn you to screaming to think
of me doing it, and how, wouldn't it? But what do you say,
Miss Jessie Marlow?"

He laughed at her horrified face in his mind's eye.

But damn you to hell, can you let him be, afterward? Can
you ever let him be? You will have him alive. "Can you let
him deal faro in a saloon?" he said aloud, mimicking her scorn
again. Let be, Miss Jessie Marlow, before you have killed him
dead trying to make him into a damned marble statue!

## 43. *Journals of Henry Holmes Goodpasture*

April 17, 1881

WE HAVE returned this night to a Warlock seething with sur-mise. Posters appeared mysteriously this morning in several places about the town—one of them upon my wall!—to the effect that Blaisedell is condemned to death for foul mur-der, his victims listed as Curley Burne and Billy Gannon, and the posters signed by Abraham McQuown as Chief of Regulators!

I did not see any of these, for they have been torn down, but there are tack holes in the adobe to the right of my door, and Kennon says he saw the one upon the Feed and Grain Barn. Dechine, a small rancher and neighbor of McQuown's, was seen in town last night, and it is presumed that he was the one who affixed the posters. It is not known who tore them down, possibly they were merely wanted for keepsakes; it is variously rumored, though, that either Morgan is responsible for their disappearance, or the lamed miner who works for Miss Jessie, or Blaisedell himself.

The name of McQuown, springing to everyone's lips again, is like the reappearance of a ghost long thought laid. Many think it is all only a practical joke, perpetrated by some towns-men, but for most of us the phrase "Chief of Regulators" rings most ominously. If it is a joke, it is a cruel one; it strikes too close to our fears, the names of Billy Gannon and Curley Burne are too aptly chosen.

There has been talk of nothing else since we returned early this evening. The town is crowded; somehow news of this na-ture is disseminated instantaneously throughout the valley. We, the delegation, returned full of defense and explanation of our defeat in Bright's City; what happened to us there is of no in-terest to anyone.

The feeling among the more intelligent here is that these posters are probably more than a joke, but less than an open declaration of war—that it may be a gambit, a bluff, a theatrical gesture of righteousness. They have certainly done their work in arousing and confirming suspicions over the Curley Burne tragedy. The seeds they may have been intended to broadcast have fallen on rich soil. On the other hand can McQuown afford to make such a bluff if it is to be an empty one? Or is this an attempt to rouse Warlock against Blaisedell so that we ourselves will run him out, thus saving McQuown the trouble and the danger? If so, McQuown has woefully misjudged our tempers.

The miners, I understand, feel this is some trick of Mac-Donald's, since MacDonald was the proprietor of the original Regulators. They feel that McQuown may have been won over by MacDonald, but that they, the Medusa strikers, are the actual quarry, and Blaisedell only a ruse.

The town seethes with argument, speculation, and fearful expectation. Yet many in Warlock are eager for a showdown, and, in their minds, this can only satisfactorily be a street duel between Blaisedell and McQuown. McQuown would surely not be such a fool (ah, but I said this of Curley Burne!), and yet McQuown may feel he has some moral advantage now.

There will be a Citizens' Committee meeting in the morning.

## 44. *The New Sign*

PIKE SKINNER swung into the jail doorway and stopped there, with his red face set into a scowl. Inside, Peter Bacon sat at the table spooning juice from a can of peaches into his mouth, and Tim French sat beside the cell door, just outside the circle of light cast by the lamp. A flat, square, newspaper-wrapped package leaned against the wall.

"Gannon back yet?" Skinner demanded.

"Come and gone," French said.

"I am deputying tonight," Bacon said, wiping his mouth with his shirt sleeve. "But I don't want to hear about any trouble. I am just what you might say sitting here so nobody can look in and see nobody's sitting here."

"Where the hell'd he go now?"

"Pablo," French said.

"Threw us again, did he?" Skinner cried. "Gone down there so's he can come in with those Regulators—"

"Hold on!" French said.

"You get down on a man he can't do nothing right, can he?"

Bacon said. "He went down there to stop them from coming in here."

"He told you that, did he?"

"Did," Bacon said.

"You believed it, huh?"

"Did."

"There was a time before I didn't believe him," French said. "But it looks like I was wrong about it."

"I still say he was lying in his damned teeth!" Skinner said.

Bacon shrugged. "Well, anyway, I told him I'd sit it out till he got back. Or till somebody brought his poor, shot-up, hacked-on, chewed-to-pieces corpse back to bury."

"How's he think he's going to stop them?" Skinner sneered.

"Didn't say. He come in blown from riding it down from Bright's, and when he heard the news he just said he'd better go stop them, and borrowed Tim's mare and went." Bacon began spooning peach juice into his mouth again.

Skinner kicked the door jamb. "Buck and them just got back from Bright's," he said. "Buck said Johnny got Keller to half-believing what Carl was supposed to've told him."

"Some do," Bacon said.

"God damn it, Pete; I thought Carl was a friend of yours! God damn it, it played right to McQuown, didn't it?"

"That don't make it not so, Pike," French said.

Skinner shook his head and said, "You mean to say Gannon went down there all by *himself* to tell them not to come in here?"

"Bound to go he was bound to go by himself, I guess," Bacon said. He looked at Skinner with his pale eyes.

"Catch *me* going down there," Skinner said. He glanced almost furtively down the wall to where the names were scratched in the whitewash. "What's that wrapped up there?"

"New sign Keller gave him," Bacon said. He stared down into the empty can. "Would've pleased Carl."

Skinner went over to where the package leaned, picked it up, and stripped off the string and newspaper. The sign was square, with black letters on a white ground within a black border:

WARLOCK JAIL
DEPUTY SHERIFF

Skinner turned it over; it was the same on the reverse. "Nice piece of work," he said. "The old one's got so you can't hardly make it out any more."

"Looks like we might hang it for Johnny tomorrow," French said. "While we're waiting."

Skinner set the sign back where it had been. "I see Gannon got his name scratched on the wall there," he said, straightening and turning away.

"He's deputy," French said. "Deputies get to set their names down there. Why shouldn't he?"

"I just noticed he had it down there, was all."

"You had better quit looking at them names there, Pike," Bacon said, not quite humorously. "Or they will reach out and grab you one of these times."


## 45. *Gannon Visits San Pablo*

GANNON COUNTED the horses as he reined up before the ranch house—ten, eleven, twelve of them. Light shone out on the glossy sweep of manes and rolling eyewhites. The dogs began to bark down by the horse corral.

In the lamplit windows he could see the shadows of the men. He heard the sour, thin chording of a guitar. A voice was raised in drunken song, and was lost in laughter.

He dismounted slowly, leaden with fatigue. He tethered Tim's mare to the rail with the others, sighed, hitched on his shell belt, and started up the steps. On the porch he paused to wipe the palms of his hands on his jeans; then with anxious haste he knocked on the door. It swung inward under the pressure of his knuckles, and the voices died. The guitar chorded on for a moment longer; then it too ceased, in a strum of strings.

The faces were all turned toward him, pale and oily-looking in the lamplight. Abe was leaning on the pot-belly stove with his hand gripped around the neck of the whisky jug. Old man McQuown lay on his pallet on the floor. Chet Haggin was slumped, spread-legged, on the buggy-seat sofa beside Joe Lacey, and Wash sat on the floor before them with a crockery cup in his hand. Beyond Abe were Pecos Mitchell, hunched over the guitar, Quint Whitby, with his fat face and cavalry mustaches, the breed Marko cleaning his nails with a knife, Walt Harrison, Ed Greer, Jock Hennessey, and five or six others he did not know—all staring at him. Standing behind Chet was Jack Cade, his round-crowned, leather-banded hat pulled low upon his forehead, his prune of a mouth bent into a disagreeable smile.

"Why, it's Bud Gannon come back to San Pablo," Abe said, and put the whisky jug down.

"Bud," Joe Lacey said. No one else spoke. Mitchell began to strum the guitar again, humming to himself and watching Gannon with an eyebrow cocked in his smallpox-pitted face. The old man hunched himself up on his pallet.

"Well, come on in, Bud," Abe said. "Don't stand there acting like you mightn't be welcome." He wore a buckskin shirt that reached below his hips and was belted with a concho belt from which hung his knife, in a silver-chased scabbard. He looked drunk, but bright-eyed, keen, young—Abe looked as he had when he had first known him.

"Blaisedell run him out!" the old man said suddenly.

Gannon shook his head. He met Jack Cade's eyes and nodded. He nodded to the others. "Joe," he said. "Chet. Wash. Pecos. Quint. Dad McQuown." He knew them better than he knew anyone in Warlock, he thought; he had known them to get drunk with, work with, rustle with, play cards with. He had fought and whipped Walt Harrison, fought and been whipped by Whitby, had had for his special friends Chet and Wash Haggin, for his enemy Jack Cade; with his brother Billy, and perhaps with all of them, he had hero-worshiped Curley Burne and held Abe McQuown in awe. With all of these except the new ones he did not know, he had killed Mexicans in Rattlesnake Canyon.

Now, he knew, every one of them was contemptuous of him, and more than Jack Cade hated him.

"Where is that big old shotgun, Bud?" Wash said, and laughed.

"Where's Billy, Bud?" someone said, behind him.

Dad McQuown said, "It is kind of bad manners coming in here with that star hanging on you, Bud Gannon."

"Whisky, Bud?" Abe said.

"Thanks," he said, and shook his head.

"Didn't come to drink? Nor talk either? Just come to stand there tongue-tied?"

Mitchell strummed on the guitar, and Joe Lacey glanced at it and then significantly back at Gannon. "Always favored a mouth organ myself," he said. Jack Cade folded his arms and grinned, and Abe grinned too, his teeth showing in his red beard.

"Nothing to say, Bud?"

"Are these your Regulators?"

Abe nodded curtly. "Regulators."

"You are all coming into Warlock?"

"Planned to," Abe said. He raised an eyebrow. "Why? Any objection, Deputy?"

Gannon nodded, and watched the color rise in Abe's cheeks.

"Why, you pissant son of a bitch!" Cade cried.

"Rip that star off him, boys!" the old man said.

"Are we posted out already, Bud?" Wash said, in a mock whining voice. Cade continued to curse.

"If there's names to be called I'll call them," Abe said, and Cade stopped. "Objection, Bud?" he said, grinning again. "Are we posted?"

"Nobody's posted. But no wild bunch calling themselves Regulators is coming in to make trouble, Abe. Not so long as I've got power to deputize every man in Warlock against them."

"That's the way it is?" Abe said, in a level voice. "That way, Bud?"

Gannon nodded, and there was a rising muttering around him.

"But I can come alone, you mean?" Abe said. "Surely, that would be fine, with Blaisedell and Morgan and half a dozen other gun-slinging pimps to burn me down. No; not likely. I am coming in with some friends to back my play, is all. Like he has got them to back his." Abe rubbed a hand over his bearded chin. "I am going to kill him for murdering your brother, Bud," he said, more quietly. "And kill him for murdering Curley down." His voice began to shake. "What the hell do you mean?" he cried. "Coming down on my place and telling me I'm not to go in there?"

Gannon stood very stiffly facing Abe McQuown, and said, "I say you are not to come, Abe."

"You damned snot pup!" the old man yelled.

"Run and hide, Abe," Whitby said. "Look out! Bud is getting mad!"

"You know the trouble with you, Bud?" Abe said easily. "You are so yellow of him you can't bear it for everybody not to be yellow of him too. It makes you look too bad if they aren't. Shot down Billy and all you did was lick his boots for him. Shot down Curley," he said, his voice rising. "After you had swore Curley didn't go to kill Carl. And what'd you do, that'd sworn to it? Licked his boots some more. You are a fine deputy."

Abe took a step toward him. "A whole town-full of them like you. Your hats shy off in the wind when he blows a breath. You can't call yourself men so you can't let anybody else be one either. But there won't be a *man* left anywhere unless somebody kills that black foul devil out of hell! You damned—"

"You are not bringing a bunch of Regulators into Warlock, Abe," he said, raising his voice over Abe's. "I came down to warn you I will have to deputize every man jack in Warlock against you."

"You have sure turned hard against us, Bud," Chet Haggin said.

"I'm deputy, Chet. There's things I'm bound to do."

"For Blaisedell," Chet said.

He shook his head.

"Yeah, for Blaisedell!" Wash Haggin cried, and everyone began to talk at once until Abe shouted angrily for quiet.

But Chet went on. "Just one more thing I want to ask him, Abe. Bud, you think Blaisedell isn't going to choose us out and cut us down one by one unless we go in there against him all together?"

"He's got nothing against you. That'd be a thing I'd be bound to stop too, I expect."

Chet grinned contemptuously and Wash shouted with laughter. They all laughed.

Abe leaned his hands on his concho belt and tilted back on his heels. "Like you stopped him from cutting Curley down, Deputy?"

Gannon felt himself flush painfully. "It was a fair fight, Abe. But you don't mean to fight him fair. You are going in to—"

"Why, you are a liar," Abe broke in. "Fair fight."

"There will be no fight. You are not to bring these people in."

"Be damned to you!" Walt Harrison said.

"Stop us, Bud!" Whitby said.

"I will stop you."

"Let me talk to him a minute, Abe," Jack Cade said, in his grating voice. Cade came forward toward Gannon, his thumbs in his shell belt. Gannon stared back into his hard eyes.

"*You*," Cade said, and paused for a long time. His dirty teeth scraped on his lower lip. "You are," he said, "a yellow-belly suck-up." He grinned and hitched at his belt. "You are a *pure* yellow, pissant, chicken-livered, coyote-bred, no-*cojones* son of a bitch. I say that's what you are. I say—"

Gannon stood listening to the level, grating voice taunting him, mouthing increasing foulness. He was not especially frightened of being forced into a fight, for he did not think it was Abe's wish. He hardly heard the words, for they did not matter to him, but he realized that they would have to be stopped because where the law was merely a man there had to be some respect for that man or the law did not exist and so his journey down here had been worse than useless. He glanced from face to face around him and his heart sank to see them not merely contemptuous, but pleased and crudely eager. Only Wash Haggin looked a little ashamed, and Joe Lacey embarrassed. Chet had turned his face away. Abe was grinning faintly, watching out of the corners of his eyes.

The vile words droned on, without meaning. He unhooked the star from his jacket, and reached over to hand it to Chet Haggin. "Hold it," he said. "I don't want him to be able to say he killed another deputy."

"I'll say it!" Cade said, triumphantly. "Outside, Deputy!"

"Here," Gannon said. "So it will be a fair fight." He untied the bandanna from around his neck, and rapidly fixed a knot in either end. "You count for us," he said to Chet. "We will draw on three." He bit down on one knotted end of the bandanna, and held the other out; he saw immediately that Cade would not do it.

"I'm no God-damned fool for a handkerchief fight!" Cade said hoarsely.

It was enough, Gannon thought, and quickly he stuffed the bandanna into his pocket and took his star back. No one spoke.

It had meant nothing, and yet he hoped he had recovered something in their eyes. But he knew that Abe saw his bluff and the necessity for it, and with dread he realized that in backing Cade down he had challenged Abe himself. Now he wondered if Abe was sure enough of his own authority to let his recovery stand.

"Man doesn't have to be a damned fool!" Cade said. "Come on outside and fight decent!"

"Pure iron," Abe said. "Why, a man with iron in him like that deserves a medal." He swung toward the breed. "Where's the medal, Marko?" The breed looked confused. Abe made a gesture toward his mouth and Marko produced something from his pocket. Abe took it, and, with a swift movement, plucked off Gannon's hat and dropped a cord around his neck. From it was suspended a mouth organ. "Curley won't be needing this any more," Abe said loudly. "How is that for a medal for Bud, boys?"

He recognized the release of tension in their laughter; what had passed between him and Jack Cade was set at nothing and he was a fool to them again as well as a traitor. He stripped the cord from around his neck and handed the mouth organ back to Abe, and took his hat back. "I think you'd better have it," he said, and saw Abe's eyes narrow dangerously.

"I'll be going," he said. "Abe, you have heard me about the Regulators. That's the word with the bark on it." It gave him a start to hear Carl's phrase on his own lips.

"Abe!" the old man cried. "Are you going to let the son of a bitch walk out like that?"

"Just a minute," Abe said. The others leaned forward, attentive and expectant. They were all afraid, Gannon thought suddenly. Maybe they felt, as Chet had said, that Blaisedell would destroy them one by one if they did not destroy him.

"What right have you to stop us?" Abe said quietly. "When

you didn't stop Blaisedell from killing Curley? Tell me that, Bud. How are you going to tell me I can't post Blaisedell and kill him if he don't run, when you didn't stop him with Curley? That was my friend," he said, more quietly still.

"Mine too, by God!" Wash said.

"He ought to be shot down on Billy's grave, what he ought," Dad McQuown said. "Billy was a fine boy, and him nothing."

"I am talking about Curley," Abe said. He waited, his face a bearded, furrowed mask, his eyes hooded. Then he said, "You ought to be riding in with us, Bud."

He shook his head.

"But you swore to it, didn't you?" Abe went on. "You swore Carl told you he'd done it himself, didn't you? Or did you crawfish on that?"

"Not yet," he said, and instantly he knew that what he had meant as only a passing threat was too much more than that. He heard the whistling suck of Abe's breath, and saw Abe's right eye widen while his left remained a slit.

"What do you think you mean by that?" Abe whispered.

He didn't answer right away. But he had not, he thought, come here merely so he could get away without trouble. He had come to tell them they must not come into Warlock as Regulators. He said tiredly, "There is going to be peace and law in Warlock, Abe. Or there is going to be Blaisedell. If you will let be, he will go. He knows he has to go now, for he has been wrong."

"Let him go, then."

"You will have to let be for him to go. And I will see that you let be, and Warlock will. I have more ways than deputizing people for stopping you."

"I am sure scared of that pack of fat-butt bank clerks he is going to round up in there," Whitby said. "Whoooo! I—"

"Shut up!" Abe snapped. He stared at Gannon with his head tipped forward so that his beard brushed his chest, and his green eyes were wild. "What other ways, Bud?"

"I would crawfish to stop you."

"What the hell are you talking about?" the old man said. "I can't make out what—"

"Shut up!" Abe put a hand on top of the stove and leaned on it heavily. "Damn your dirty soul to hell!" he cried. "God damn you, coming down here mealy-mouthing what you are bound to do. I will tell you what you are bound to do! You damned lick-spittle, you will swear here and now to what Carl said to you and what is true!" Abe took a step toward him. "Swear it, damn you!"

"I guess I'll not—" he started, and tried to dodge as Abe's hand swung up against his cheek. He staggered sideways with the blow; his cheek burned maddeningly, and his eyes watered. He heard a murmur of approval from the others, whom, for a moment, he could not see.

"Swear it! You will swear to the truth or I'll kill you!"

He shook his head; he saw the buckskin arm swing again. He did not dodge this time, but only jerked his head back to try to soften the blow. There was pain and the taste of blood in his mouth.

"Hit him all night," the old man said.

"Cut him, Abe!"

"Say it!" Abe said.

He shook his head, and swallowed salt blood.

"*Say it!*"

The fist he hadn't even seen coming this time exploded in his face once more, and he stumbled back in a wild shouting with the room spinning around him. Abruptly the shouting stopped as he caught his balance, and felt in his hand, with horror, the hard rounded shape of the Colt he had drawn. In his clearing eyes he saw Abe McQuown twisted slightly with his right fist down in the uncompleted recovery of the blow. Abe straightened slowly, his chest heaving in the buckskin shirt as he panted, his left hand massaging the knuckles of the right, his eyes glancing from the Colt to Gannon's face. A grin made sharp indentations in his beard.

Gannon spat blood. The Colt felt unsupportably heavy in his hand. Abe grinned more widely. "Uh-uh, Bud," he said, and came a step forward. He came another; his moccasins lisped upon the floor. "Uh-uh, Bud."

Abe's hand snapped down over his hand as sharp and tight as a talon, and wrenched the Colt away. Abe flung it to the floor behind him, and laughed. Abe swung his arm again.

He hunched his shoulder up to catch the blow. He brought his right hand up to catch the next on his forearm. With a sudden wild elation he swung back, and his fist met hair and bone. Abe staggered back and he jumped in pursuit.

A foot tripped him. He fell heavily past Abe, who dodged aside. A fist slammed against his back as he caught himself on his hands and tried to scramble up. He cried out in pain as a boot smashed into his ribs, and fell back again. Beneath him he felt the hard shape of his Colt where Abe had dropped it.

He fumbled it free with his left hand, still trying to rise with his right hand braced on the table beside the buggy seat, dodging aside as Whitby aimed another kick at him, and the men on the buggy seat leaped out of the way. Then he had the Colt free and he swung it desperately to cover Cade, who had drawn. He saw only the long flash of the knife blade in the lamplight.

He screamed, frozen half up, with his right hand pinned to the table top by a white-hot shaft.

Whitby kicked the Colt from his left hand.

"Get up!" Abe panted.

He struggled to stand, with his shoulder cocked down so that his hand lay flat upon the table. He could hardly see for the sweat pouring into his eyes. Abe was leaning on the shaft of the knife with both hands, not forcing it down but merely holding it there. "Move and I'll cut it off, Bud," he said.

He didn't move.

"Geld him, son," the old man said calmly.

Now his hand merely felt numb and the faintness began to leave him. Leaning on the knife still, Abe disengaged his right hand, and, with a careful, measured movement, slapped him, not hard.

"Don't move, Bud," Abe said, grinning. The hand slapped his cheek harder. It came again and again, each time harder. The faintness bore down on him again as the knife edge tore his flesh. He felt only the sensation of tearing, rather than the pain. "Don't move, Bud," Abe warned, and slapped him. The faintness began to crush him.

"Swear it for us, Bud!"

He shook his head. He could feel the blood beneath his hand now, so that it seemed glued to the table as well as nailed there. "Swear it, damn you to hell!" Abe cried, and there was hysteria in his voice.

"Lever that handle a little, son. Let's hear him squeak."

"This isn't doing any good, for Christ's sake, Abe!" Chet Haggin said.

"Let me take that knife to him!" Cade said.

Abe pressed downward on the handle, and Gannon closed his eyes. The pressure ceased and he opened them. He could see the shine of spittle at the corners of the mouth in the red beard. He gazed around at the others, dimly pleased that he could stare each one of them down.

"Hold off, Abe!" Chet said.

"Swear it, Bud!" Abe whispered. "Or I swear to God I will cut your hand off! I'll kill you!"

"You had better kill me if you want to take your Regulators into Warlock," he said. "For I will stop you otherwise."

It was a way out if Abe wanted to take it, and he knew Abe did. Abe turned his face in profile, his long jaw set wolfishly and sweat showing on his cheeks. He looked pale. Wash said quickly, "I would surely like to see him trying to stop us!"

"I'd like to see that," Walt Harrison said.

Abe jerked the knife free, and he gasped as the air got into the wound like another knife. He left his hand on the table to support himself now, as he watched Abe wipe the knife blade on his trouser leg. The old man was muttering.

"Get that neckerchief out and bind that hand up," Chet said roughly. "There may be some that like the stink of blood, but damned if I do."

"Kind of surprised to see he's got any in him," Whitby said.

Gannon fumbled the cloth from his pocket and tried to bind it around his bleeding hand. Joe Lacey came forward to help him, pulling the bandage tight and tying the ends together.

"Stop us then," Abe said, in a cold voice. "We'll be in tomorrow."

"He'll just ride back and warn Blaisedell out of town, God damn it, son!" Dad McQuown cried. "I say kill him or hold him down here!"

"Let me settle my account with him, Abe," Cade said.

McQuown grinned mockingly. "Well, move along, Bud. Before my mind gets changed."

Gannon looked around for his Colt. "Give it to him," Abe said. "He can't do anything with it."

Walt Harrison handed him the Colt. He took it with his wounded hand. It slipped through his fingers and he caught it by slapping it against his leg. Awkwardly he slid it into his holster. Whitby thrust his hat on his head. He walked slowly through them toward the door. There he turned. Abe was still standing at the table, jabbing the point of his knife into the wood with a kind of listless viciousness.

"I've warned you," Gannon said. "You are not to come into Warlock like you are set to do." This time no one laughed.

He went outside into the buzzing darkness. Carefully he descended the steps. A dog began to bark, and the others joined in a chorus. They would be locked up, he remembered; they always were when men were coming and going at night.

In the saddle he sat motionless for a time, his eyes closed, his left hand clutching the pommel. One by one, gingerly, he sought to move the fingers of his right hand; his little finger, ring finger, middle finger, trigger finger. He sighed with relief when he realized that nothing had been severed, and swung the reins. Gripping the pommel, sitting stiff, heavy, and unsteady in the saddle, he touched in his spurs and whispered, "Let's go home, girl."

The mare mounted the first ridge in the pale moonlight, went down the draw, up the second ridge—he didn't look back. A falling star crossed the far flank of the sky, fading, as it fell, to nothing. There was a cold wind. He shivered in it, but drew himself up straighter, released his grip on the pommel, and raised a hand to set his hat on straight. Lowering his hand, he brushed his thumb past the star pinned to his jacket, as though to reassure himself he had not lost it.

He felt a fury that was pain like a tooth beginning to ache. He said aloud, "I am the law!" The fury mounted in him. They had insulted him, cursed him, threatened him. They had beaten and stabbed him, and deliberated his death. They had presumed to judge him, and, finally, to release him in contempt of his warning. The fury filled him cleanly, at their presumption and their ignorance.

But how would they know differently? They had never known differently. He had tried to show them courage to make them see. Once, at least, they had known courage and had respected it. Maybe they would simply not respect it in him, or maybe they knew it no longer, knew now only fear and hate and violence. The clean fury drained from him; he had been able to show them nothing. And now he could almost pity Abe McQuown, remembering the desperation he had seen in Abe's eyes as he leaned upon the knife, Abe fighting and torturing for the Right as though it were something that could be taken by force. For Right had been embodied in Curley's death, and perhaps Blaisedell was as desperate in his way for Right as McQuown was. But he knew that Blaisedell would not cold-bloodedly kill for it, would not plot to take it by trick or treachery—not yet.

He had been riding for an hour or so in the heavier darkness under the cottonwoods along the river when he heard the shot. It was a faint, flat, far-off sound, but unmistakable. There was a silence then in which even the liquid rattle of the river seemed stilled, and then a ragged volley of shots. After another pause there were two more, and, after them, silence again.

He rode looking back over his shoulder. He could see nothing, hear nothing but the riffling of the river and the wind in the trees, the steady pad of the mare's hoofs with the occasional crack of shoes against a rock outcrop. Finally he settled himself in the saddle again and into the weary rhythm of the ride back to Warlock, dozing, snapping awake, and dozing again.

Much later he thought he heard, off to the east, the clatter of fast-moving hoofs, but, coming awake with that unpleasant, harsh grasping at consciousness, he could not be sure. Awake, he did not hear it, and he thought the sound must have been only something he had dreamed.

## 46. *Journals of Henry Holmes Goodpasture*

April 18, 1881

IN VIEW of the importance of this morning's Citizens' Committee meeting, I will set down what happened there in some detail.

One of Blaikie's hands arrived last night with the information that a great number of San Pabloites were gathered at the McQuown ranch, and, with this proof of McQuown's intentions, all the members of the Citizens' Committee with whom I spoke prior to the meeting were resigned to the conclusion that we were forced to undertake the formation of a Vigilance Committee at last. Obviously Blaisedell could not be expected to face alone this force of Regulators patently assembled to bring about his destruction, or his flight. The parallel with poor Canning's fate was all too clear, and we would not be shamed again. Some were eager for war, and some were frightened, but almost all seemed firm in their resolve to back Blaisedell to the hilt.

The meeting was at the bank. All but Taliaferro attended: Dr. Wagner, Slavin, Skinner, Judge Holloway, Hart, Winters, MacDonald, Godbold, Pugh, Rolfe, Petrix, Kennon, Brown, Robinson, Egan, Swartze, Miss Jessie Marlow, and myself. And Clay Blaisedell, not a member, but our instrument.

The Marshal has not been looking well lately. Yet he seemed himself again in Petrix's bank, as though he had recovered from an illness, and he had an air of ease and confidence about him that reassured us all. He did not, however, join us at the table—usually he sits to the right of Miss Jessie when she attends—but remained standing outside the counter while Petrix brought the meeting to order.

Jed Rolfe stated the premise: that we had, many times in the past, rejected the idea of a Vigilance Committee, but now, in his opinion, it was unavoidable.

Pike Skinner moved that a Vigilance Committee be established, he was seconded by Kennon, and the meeting was thrown open to discussion.

The doctor rose to state that it was obvious that the true mission of the Regulators was to punish, murder, or drive from Warlock the leaders of the Medusa strike; this had been their original purpose and was still their purpose, although now they saw that the Marshal would have to be disposed of before they could accomplish it, since he would most certainly stand in their way. MacDonald replied that the Regulators had been originally engaged to defend mine property, but that they were no longer in his employ, that he had no understanding with them whatsoever, nor did he hold patent to the title of Regulators. MacDonald then claimed, in his turn, that the doctor was responsible for a miners' conspiracy against him, MacDonald, and was responsible for an outrageous and threatening set of terms upon which, a delegation of strikers had informed him, they would end the strike.

The doctor responded to this violently, and it was with some difficulty that Petrix restored order. Blaisedell was asked if he wished to speak, but he replied that he would rather hear us out before he expressed his own sentiments.

Will Hart obtained the floor and said with great seriousness that he knew what he was about to say would be unpopular, but that he must, in all honesty, speak out. He felt, he said, that it was the duty of the Citizens' Committee to prevent blood-shed and not to form Vigilante Committees. The whole system of posting had, in his opinion, proved a failure, and had only led to the bloodshed it had been intended to prevent. He felt strongly that a battle with the Regulators should be avoided if it was humanly possible. This could be accomplished, although he was sorry to be the one to suggest such a thing, by Blaise-dell quitting Warlock. The Regulators could then be sent word of this, and they would be deprived of their purpose, which now they could endow with a certain degree of righteousness.

He was afraid, he went on rather nervously, that this might be interpreted as cowardice on Blaisedell's part. He, of course, knew that Blaisedell had no fear of McQuown—quite the opposite. As for himself, he would regard it as a much greater, and nobler, courage upon Blaisedell's part were he to go and leave us in peace.

There was an instantaneous and outraged protest to this on every side. Miss Jessie cried out that Will wanted to drive Blaisedell out, and berated him with a violence that embarrassed us all. "After what he has done for Warlock!" she cried. "For everyone here! When all of us used to be afraid of being murdered on the street by a drunken Cowboy, and you speak of his leaving us in peace!" and so forth. She was out of order, but Petrix, usually the strictest of parliamentarians, was too dumbfounded to call her to order. She desisted only when Blaisedell called her name, and the doctor spoke quietly to her.

Jared Robinson stated loudly that he considered Will Hart's idea a bad one and in bad taste, and that the rest of us apologized to Blaisedell for it. If Blaisedell departed, he said, Warlock would be thrown into chaos again, McQuown would be in the

saddle, and any here who had been friendly with Blaisedell—
and especially we of the Citizens' Committee—would be in
deadly danger. Succeeding speakers agreed with, and expanded
upon, this, until MacDonald reiterated his former statement
within this context: that chaos had already descended upon us,
and had done so as soon as Blaisedell had permitted the miners
to overrun him at the jail, in the attempt to lynch Morgan.

Miss Jessie promptly called him a liar, to which rebuke
MacDonald knew better than to retort, although he was
plainly infuriated by it. The doctor then said, with what was
obviously a stern attempt to control his temper, that it took
considerably more of a man to let himself be overrun by momentarily crazed (and with good reason, he added) creatures,
than to fire among them as MacDonald no doubt would have
preferred. But, he pointed out, Blaisedell, at the time of the
attempt on Morgan's life, had not been in our employ with the
status of Marshal, and in any case, his object, which had been
to save Morgan from a lynching rather than to preserve his
own dignity, had been accomplished.

Judge Holloway, who had been sitting in a gloomy and
alcoholic trance, now seemed to have accumulated enough
strength to deliver one of his harangues. He rose, was recognized, and beat his crutch upon the floor for silence. He clung
to the edge of the table, as fierce of mien (and as noisome of
breath) as a vulture, and glared about him. He can be awesome
enough, even when falling down drunk. He called us fools and
said there was a man to deal with the present situation and
it was not Blaisedell. There was a sheriff's deputy in Warlock
to uphold the law. There were, he said, always bloodthirsty
fools to cry for a Vigilance Committee or a hired Vigilante,
but Deputy Gannon was the one to deal with the Regulators.

His voice was drowned in a sudden burst of speculation as
to Gannon's whereabouts, and condemnation of him. Some
thought him fled, some still in Bright's City (as I did), others
claimed he had gone to join McQuown's forces. Pike Skinner
informed us that Gannon had indeed gone to San Pablo, but
with the announced intention of warning McQuown that he
was not to come into Warlock; at which there were hoots of
disbelief.

When order was restored, the Judge reiterated that the

situation was the Deputy's responsibility. Then, as is his custom, he began to rack us for our sins and presumptions. He accused us of inciting Blaisedell to the murder of an innocent man—to our considerable discomfiture, with Blaisedell present; he called us fools and mortal fools, idiots and monstrous idiots. He shouted down, in his wrath, all interruptions, and was, in short, magnificent in his fashion. I think I might have applauded him had not what he was saying been so painful.

He said to us, more temperately, that if we had not been blind we might have seen that we had almost had a man in Carl Schroeder, and that we unmistakably had one now, in Gannon. He expounded with painful sarcasm the complete illegality of Blaisedell's position as Marshal, a point all too sore with the Citizens' Committee. Not one of us had the temerity even to glance Blaisedell's way while this diatribe continued, but at last Miss Jessie jumped to her feet and cried that he was no more a real Judge than Blaisedell was a real Marshal, and that he was a hypocrite to speak as he had.

The Judge replied that he was well aware of the fact that he was a hypocrite, and that he considered himself something worse than that for even belonging to the Citizens' Committee. He added, "But I do not presume to send men to hang, Miss Jessie Marlow."

Then, as Miss Jessie started to speak again, he gave her an awkward but courtly bow and said he refused to listen to her, for she was a special pleader, as everyone knew; and, finally, with the look of a man who has collected his courage to approach a rattlesnake, he turned to Blaisedell himself.

The Judge addressed Blaisedell deferentially at first, saying he had intended nothing personal by his remarks, and that his criticism was not so much of Blaisedell as of all of us. Soon, however, he recovered his hectoring style, and he raised his voice, lifted his crutch and shook it, and cried that Blaisedell was a crutch like the one he held, had been useful, and we should be grateful to him. But it was only an idiot who continued to use a crutch when the limb had grown whole. Including us all in his glare, he informed us that we no longer needed the crutch of an illegal gunman, that we had better begin properly using the law or it would wither away, and now we had a man to uphold the law, who was the deputy.

Petrix asked Blaisedell, who had been showing signs of wishing to speak, if he desired the floor. Blaisedell replied that he would like to answer some of the things the Judge had had to say. As he spoke I saw Miss Jessie watching him with her great eyes, tugging a little handkerchief between her hands, and if ever I saw a woman's heart in her eyes I saw it then.

Blaisedell's face was very stern as he proceeded upon a track that surprised us. He said that he thought it would be a shame to put too much on the Deputy too soon. He said a new horse should not be racked too hard. "You will bust him to running, or kill him, putting too much on him," he said, to the Judge. And he said, "He has stood up to every man here calling him a liar when he was not, but I don't think he is able yet to stand off a wild bunch from San Pablo."

He went on in this vein. But after we had grasped the fact that he believed that Gannon had not lied, and seemed to favor him—even though he did not feel he was qualified to stop McQuown yet—our comprehension of what he was saying ceased and we stared at him in confusion. I saw Buck Slavin's jaw hanging open like that of a dull-witted boy, and Pike Skinner's face grow fiery red. Miss Jessie had put her handkerchief to her mouth, and her eyes were round as dollars.

"Gentlemen," Blaisedell said. "I have done some service here and I think you know it. But I think a good many of you are beginning to wish I would move along, and not just Mr. Hart." He smiled a little then. "I had better, before you all start thinking of me like the Judge here does."

Skinner and Sam Brown protested emotionally, as did Buck, but Blaisedell only smiled and went on to thank the Citizens' Committee for having paid him well, and backed him as well as he could have wished. "But," he said, "there is value in knowing when to move on. For the Judge is right in more ways than one, though I have argued with him and got as mad at him as the rest of you do."

Blaisedell said, however, that he had one thing which he would ask of us. "I will ask you to let me handle McQuown and his Regulators my own way." He said this in such a way that it was clearly a command for us to stay out of his affair. "It is my job," he went on. "And he is coming after me, so it is my job two ways. If there are going to be Vigilantes I'll ask that they stay out of it unless *I* go down." He looked straight at MacDonald and said, "For I have been known to go down."

There was a general gasp as it was realized that Blaisedell meant to stand alone, or perhaps only with Morgan, against the San Pabloites. A storm of exclamations and protests broke out, to which Blaisedell did not even attempt to reply, while Petrix exercised his gavel violently.

It was at this moment that Gannon made his entrance. He was freshly shaven, his hair neatly combed, but his upper lip was bruised and swollen and his face was drawn with exhaustion. I noticed that his right hand was bound up in a white cloth. He said, in a truculent tone, that there would be no Vigilantes in Warlock.

We were all as shocked at the arrogance of his first words as we had been at the implication of Blaisedell's last ones. I had the impression, however, that Gannon had been steeling and rehearsing himself to his statement for some time, and was prepared, too, for a violent response to it. When there was none he seemed suddenly timid in our august presence.

In a more reasonable voice he said that he was sorry to butt in upon us, but that he had heard the Citizens' Committee intended to form a Vigilante Troop, and he had come to inform us that there would be none of that in Warlock.

Jed Rolfe asked him if those had been his orders from McQuown.

Gannon replied without heat that he did not take orders from McQuown. Neither did he take them from the Citizens' Committee. He had just come back from San Pablo, he said, whence he had ridden to tell McQuown there would be no Regulators. He was now telling us there would be no Vigilantes either. I felt a certain respect for the fellow then, thinking that he must not have pleased McQuown any more than he was pleasing us.

Skinner sneered that he would bet Gannon had scared McQuown out of his foolishness, and it was certainly nice that Warlock, and Blaisedell, had nothing to worry about. At this Gannon looked childishly angered and hurt. He said, however, that if McQuown did come in he would deputize whoever was needed to meet him, and reiterated his statement that there were to be no Vigilantes. I noticed that he studiously avoided Blaisedell's eye.

Joe Kennon cried out that no one trusted Gannon enough to be deputized by him, to which Gannon replied that whoever he deputized would be deputized or go to Bright's City to explain why not to the court. This exchange was followed by other angry statements, until Blaisedell interceded to say that it was his part to make a play against McQuown and whoever came in with him. "It is against me," he said. "So it is me against them, Deputy."

He spoke in a firm voice, and Gannon blanched noticeably. He stood still not facing Blaisedell, with his bandaged hand upon the counter and his forehead creased with what must have been painful thought. To our surprise he shook his head with determination.

"If it was just you against McQuown, I would keep out, Marshal," he said. "I can't when it is the whole bunch coming in and calling themselves Regulators."

"Yes, you can," Blaisedell said. It did not seem to me he said it particularly threateningly, but he drew himself up to his full height as he looked down at the Deputy.

Gannon, however, stood his ground. He said in an emotional voice, "I have told McQuown he is not to come in here with those people. I told him I will stop him if he does. I mean to stop them."

With that he swung around to depart, and, although we waited breathlessly for Blaisedell's reply, he made none. It was the Judge who broke the silence. "Hear! Hear!" he cried, in obnoxious triumph. His voice was drowned in the ensuing outcry, and Gannon was verbally flayed, drawn and quartered, and otherwise disposed of.

In the end, however, nothing was done about the Vigilance Committee.

April 19, 1881

I will confess that for a time I subscribed to a higher opinion of our Deputy than I had previously held. That was yesterday. Today the mercury of my esteem has sunk quite out of sight, for Gannon, in claiming he would stop McQuown from coming into Warlock, has perpetrated one of the most monstrous, grotesque, and completely senseless frauds of which I have ever heard.

Gannon is, in short, accused of murder. McQuown will not bring his Regulators into Warlock because he is dead, shot in the back, and Gannon is named by a host of witnesses as his murderer.

The Regulators have, indeed, arrived, but not in that role. They are pall-bearers, and Abraham McQuown is their charge. The story I have from Joe Lacey, who swears he was witness to it all.

As he informed the Citizens' Committee yesterday, Gannon had ridden down to San Pablo the night before. He accosted the Regulators, who were gathered at McQuown's, with the same brusquerie he showed the Citizens' Committee at the bank. Hot words passed, and shortly, Lacey claims, Gannon drew his six-shooter on McQuown. Here I become a little dubious as to whether I am hearing the whole story, since drawing upon McQuown in the bosom of his friends sounds an act of incredible asininity. Be that as it may, McQuown then closed and tussled with Gannon, and, defending himself, stabbed Gannon through the hand, which accounts for the bandage we saw yesterday. Gannon was then allowed to depart, which he did ungraciously, calling back that he and Blaisedell would "get even."

Lacey claims he thought Gannon might still be skulking about, for the dogs, which were locked up, had started barking when he first left the ranch house and were never entirely quiet thereafter, as though sensing a sinister presence. About an hour later the door was flung open and Gannon fired upon McQuown, who was standing with his back to the door, killing him instantly. He then fled, but not before he was recognized by old Ike McQuown, Whitby, and several others.

All crowded outside to fire after him in his flight, but pursuit was impossible, for he had unhitched the horses and these were stampeded by the shooting. By the time the mounts were recovered it was clearly useless to try to follow him, and some were afraid that Gannon had been accompanied by a whole party of murderers from Warlock, and that he desired to be pursued so that he could lead the Cowboys into an ambush. There is no doubt in Lacey's mind that Gannon was the assassin, for, although he did not see him himself, a number of others did.

The funeral party arrived not two hours ago. It was well known that the Regulators were coming, since they could be seen a long way off from the rim. Gannon had deputized, without the difficulty some had foreseen, more than twenty good men, whom he had stationed up and down Main Street and on the rooftops. He rode out alone to meet the Regulators and their funeral wagon as they came up the rim. I have not heard what transpired there, and am surprised they did not shoot him down on the spot, but he immediately returned to the jail and surrendered himself to Judge Holloway. He is to have a hearing shortly and will have another chance to appear and swear before the judge, this time not as a witness but as a defendant; Ike McQuown being plaintiff, a curious role for him.

This turn of events has staggered us all.

## 47. *Dad McQuown*

JUDGE HOLLOWAY poked right and left with his crutch to clear a path for himself through the jail doorway. "Out of my way! Out of my way, damn you, boys!"

Inside, he glanced worriedly at Gannon, who leaned against the cell door looking listless, exhausted, and profoundly dejected. The judge glared around at Skinner, Bacon, Mosbie, and the others inside the jail. "Turn that table around for me," he said.

It was done and the judge sat down with his back to the door. His crutch fell with a clatter as he moved his chair, and, grunting, opened the drawer against his belly and took out his Bible, derringer, and spectacles. There was a continual mutter of talk from the men crowded into the doorway.

"I will have some order here!" the judge said, and slammed his hand down on the table top. "Or I will clear you people out into the street. Now, I am not going to have that whole bunch from San Pablo in here cluttering, either. Anybody hear who was witnesses in particular?"

"Looks like all of them," Bacon said, in an unhappy voice.

"Send out and tell old Ike he and three others can come in."

Bacon went outside, and the judge drummed his fingers on the table top. Skinner glanced covertly at Gannon with mixed anxiety and disapproval. Mosbie chewed on a cheekful of tobacco and leaned on his shotgun. French and Hasty stood together against the rear wall. There was a silence outside, and a shuffling of feet. The top of a woman's hat appeared among the sombreros, and men moved aside to let Kate Dollar through. She entered the jail, tall and richly curved in a black jacket and pleated skirt. There was a string of jet beads around her neck.

"Here now, Miss Dollar!" the judge said. "This won't do! This is no place for a lady. Now, see here!" he said, as she came on in. Gannon looked up.

"Why not?" Kate Dollar said. "Aren't ladies allowed in a court of law?"

"Well, now—this isn't any real court of law."

"Well, I am not a real lady, Judge," Kate Dollar said, with a tight smile. There were titters behind her, and the judge pointed a finger at the men in the doorway.

"Miss Dollar, it just won't do. Dirty, stinking, foul-mouthed men—"

"I don't mind. Pretend I'm not here."

"Well, get a chair for her. You, Pike!" Skinner hurriedly set out a chair and she sat down, carefully spreading out her skirt and folding her hands in her lap. She looked once at Gannon, without interest.

There was another disturbance outside and the men in the doorway parted again, this time to let through Wash Haggin and Quint Whitby, who were carrying old man McQuown on his pallet. Chet Haggin entered behind them, his face grave; the others were angry and wary. They set the pallet down and the old man raised himself on an elbow and gazed around him with venomous, grief-filled eyes that settled finally upon Gannon.

"Well, Ike," the judge said. "Lost your son."

Old man McQuown nodded curtly. His white beard had been brushed until it looked as fine and light as silk. "Never thought I would live to see it," he said in his harsh voice.

"Backshot by one he'd took in an orphan and befriended too. God damn your black Blaisedell-bought soul, Bud Gannon!"

"Johnny says he didn't shoot your boy. You prepared to swear he did?"

"I God damn am!" old McQuown cried. "And how Blaisedell sent him to—"

"We'll have no cussing in here!" the judge said. "There is a lady present and this may not be any court of justice but we will pretend it is. All right now! Hearing's in session and you are to show cause why Johnny Gannon ought to be sent up to Bright's City to proper court, Ike McQuown. Now: I am nothing here but judge on acceptance, like I have said in here about three thousand times already. Johnny, are you going to accept me here?"

"Yes," Gannon said.

"You, Ike?" the judge asked. "Being plaintiff?"

Old McQuown nodded again.

"Pike, you are appointed sergeant-at-arms. I'll have the artillery collected and put by."

Skinner, moving as stiff-legged and cautious as a dog among unfriendly dogs, took six-shooters from the Haggins and Whitby, and then from the others inside the jail. He stacked the Colts on the table before the judge and hung Mosbie's shotgun on the pegs on the wall. The judge had donned the steel-rimmed spectacles, from which an earpiece was missing. He held out the Bible to Skinner and nodded toward Gannon. "Swear to tell the truth and nothing but the truth, Johnny. Put your hand on the book and swear."

"I swear," Gannon said, and Skinner turned with the Bible to old McQuown.

"I swear," old McQuown said contemptuously, and Skinner moved along to the others, who also swore.

"All right," the judge said. "Did you shoot Abe McQuown, Johnny Gannon?"

"No," Gannon said.

"Who says he did?"

"I say so," old McQuown said. The judge looked at the others.

"I say so!" Whitby and Wash Haggin said, at the same moment.

"Tell me about it then, one of you," the judge said, and leaned back in his chair. Old McQuown told how it had happened, in his harsh, fierce, old voice. "You saw him, huh?" the judge said, when he had finished. "You and these boys saw Johnny clear in the door there, did you?"

"Said I saw him and swore to it," old McQuown said.

"I saw him clear, Judge," Whitby put in.

"All right. Now you tell it your way, Johnny."

Gannon told his version of what had happened, while old McQuown stirred and muttered and cursed to himself upon his pallet, Wash Haggin and Whitby scowled, and Chet Haggin bit his lip.

"You drawed on Abe McQuown twice then, like Ike said?" the judge asked. "But you claim you didn't go back there after leaving. Heard shots, though?"

Gannon nodded. Pike Skinner was watching him closely, while Mosbie scowled back at Wash Haggin.

"Did you say how you and Blaisedell was going to get even?"

"No."

"He said it!" old McQuown cried. "Didn't he, Quint?"

"He said it all right," Whitby said. There was a stirring and whispering among the spectators in the doorway. Kate Dollar stared at Whitby, and, when she caught his eye, shook her head a little. Whitby flushed.

"You?" the judge said, to Wash Haggin.

"Oh, he said it all right," Wash Haggin said, evading Kate Dollar's gaze.

The judge shifted his attention to Chet Haggin.

"I didn't hear him say it," Chet Haggin said.

"You are saying he didn't say it, then?"

"I didn't say that. I just didn't hear it. He might've said it without me hearing it."

"Uh-huh," the judge said. "Now," he said to old McQuown. "You are not claiming Blaisedell was with him, are you?"

"Might've been. I claim Blaisedell put him up to it."

"Swear it, you mean?" the judge said. "You can't—"

"Damned right I swear it!" old McQuown yelled. "And these boys'll swear it too! It stands to reason, don't it?"

"Ike, I have told you once I'm not going to have any cussing in here. There is a lady present."

"What's she doing here, anyhow?" Whitby growled.

Kate Dollar smiled, and said in a clear voice, "I am trying to see if any of you boys will look me in the eye when you lie."

The judge slapped his hand down on the table. "Ma'am, you will keep hushed or I will clear *you* out of here!"

Chet Haggin said, "Cousin Ike, I don't see how you are going to swear to a thing like that. We don't—"

His brother swung around toward him angrily. "Chet, you know well enough Blaisedell put him up to it!"

Old McQuown raised himself on his elbow again. "There is not a man in the territory that don't know Blaisedell was out to kill my boy, and was out for it ever since he came here. Abe a peaceable, law-abiding boy that—"

Someone in the doorway snickered loudly. The judge swung around and pointed a finger at the offender. "You! Get!"

Old McQuown's breathing sounded very loud in the silent room. He rubbed a hand roughly over his eyes. His voice shook as he continued. "Abe wouldn't give him cause to pick a fight, not wanting to kill a man that was marshal even if he was pure devil. So Blaisedell couldn't get at him, and he had to send a dirty, rotten, nose-picking backshooter of a—"

"Never mind that," the judge said. "That's irrelevant and a matter of opinion too. Now, you say every man knows Blaisedell put Johnny Gannon to it?"

"Said so."

"Well, now, Ike, maybe everybody knows it. But I will put it to you that everybody knows too how you and these same boys here, and your son, has gone up to Bright's City to court and swore false I don't know how many times to keep some of yours from prison or hanging for what they did and what everybody knew they did. Now what do you say to that?"

"By God!" old McQuown whispered. "By God, George Holloway, you are calling us liars!"

"I am," the judge said calmly. "Maybe not this time, but I say you have been other times. You just swore to me on the Bible to tell the whole truth, and I am asking you on your oath if you people haven't been liars in court before this time."

Old McQuown didn't speak.

"You going to answer, Ike, or not?"

"Be damned to you!" old McQuown said hoarsely.

"Judge," Chet Haggin said. "If you make us out liars it don't make Bud there not one."

"No, it don't. But the point I am making is that it don't signify that the bunch of you is swearing one way, and him another." The judge took off his glasses and tapped the earpiece against the Bible. Carefully he pushed the stack of six-shooters farther along the table. "Now, the next thing," he said, "is how you all saw Johnny firing in through the door. Kicked it open, you said? And went right to shooting? He was seen clear?"

"Swore to that already," old McQuown said, in the hoarse voice.

"You don't mind if we run through it again, though—since I wasn't there. Now there was light enough to see by, was there?"

"Three lamps burning. Ought to've been."

"It was light enough, all right," Whitby said.

"But he didn't come inside, did he? Thought you said he stayed outside and just kicked the door open."

"Said he was outside."

"Dark outside, though, wasn't it?"

Old McQuown did not reply. He looked from face to face around him, twisting his head so as to look Kate Dollar in the eye. He grunted scornfully, and lay back on his pallet, panting from the exertion.

"Now, what I am trying to get at here," the judge said, "isn't just that every man knows how a man outside can see fine into a lit-up room, but a man in a lit-up room can't see outside when it's dark anywhere near as good. That's not what I'm getting at." He scowled and held up a hand as Whitby started to speak.

"I am just trying to make certain you are sure of your man, is all," he went on. "Now I am asking you to think back hard, Ike, and you, boys—in view of the fact there's been some talk that Blaisedell rode down there himself the night Abe McQuown got murdered. I am asking you if you are absolutely dead certain sure that the man you saw shoot Abe McQuown down was Johnny Gannon here. I mean, since everybody knows Blaisedell was out to kill Abe by hook or crook, like you say. Now!"

There was a sudden excited rustle of comment in the doorway. Whitby whispered triumphantly, "Why, by God, maybe it was at that! Say! Neckerchief pulled up over his face, but—"

His eyes narrowed cunningly as he swung toward the old man. "Say, what do you think, Dad McQuown? By God if it wasn't Blaisedell himself, come to think of it!"

"You was closer to the door than the rest, huh, Quint?" the judge said.

"Cousin Ike!" Wash Haggin said. "It is a trick!"

"Hold on there!" old McQuown shouted. Pike Skinner grinned suddenly, and there was laughter from the men in the doorway. Whitby's brown, fat face paled.

The judge said mildly, "It is hard to see a man clear when he is out in the dark and you in the light."

"I say it was Bud Gannon!" old McQuown cried. "By God, if you have threw us down with this fool—"

"Hush up, now," the judge said. They shouted back and forth at each other until old McQuown gave up and lay back on his pallet in exhaustion again.

"You just listen to me," the judge said. "I am going to sum things up now, and I will have quiet in here to do it. Now, here is Johnny Gannon to swear one thing, and four to swear against him—and more outside that'll do the same, I guess. But—"

"Damned right they'll swear the same!" Wash Haggin cried.

"—but as I said before, it doesn't signify. So now I'll take up things brought in against Johnny Gannon. First how he and Blaisedell planned to kill Abe McQuown in a conspiracy. Dismissed. No evidence whatsoever, except everybody's supposed to know it's so.

"Then there is that Johnny Gannon went down there and tried to pick a fight with Abe McQuown spang in front of fifteen or so of his friends and kin, drew on him, and all that. I just can't believe it. No man with a speck of sense would do such a thing. Say he killed Abe like that, it'd been pure suicide in front of all those. It doesn't stand to reason and I just don't believe it is so."

"He did it!" old McQuown shouted.

"Hush. Now the next thing, that he got stabbed through the hand somehow and went out swearing he would get even for it —that sounds reasonable, and I might believe it. And he might have said that he and Blaisedell was going to get even, knowing the people he was talking to was edgy about Blaisedell.

"But this don't get him to killing Abe McQuown, which is what is primary here. Whitby, and you, Ike, swear you saw him and it was Gannon. Only Whitby went and changed his mind a little—and I will admit I tried to fuddle him saying that about Blaisedell, who was in town that night for all to see, whatever rumors have got started about him. But now it turns out Whitby didn't see quite so clear as he first made out, and now it turns out that the killer had a neckerchief over his face, as would be natural. Only the neckerchief got forgot about, first time you told it. So now it looks to me that since Whitby thinks it might be nice if it was Blaisedell after all, it must be he didn't really see *who* it was, Gannon and Blaisedell not being two that look much alike. And so I figure that if Whitby didn't see who it was at all, then nobody did, and I think you people have accused Johnny Gannon wrong and I think you know it!"

He slapped his hand down on the table top with a report like a revolver shot. "Dismissed!" he said. "I say there is no evidence Johnny Gannon did it what-so-ever that would stand up in proper court, and I just don't believe it!"

Old McQuown spat on the floor. Whitby, red-faced still, laughed harshly, and Wash Haggin stared hard at Gannon.

"Hearing's adjourned," Judge Holloway said hastily. He took off his spectacles and put them, the derringer, and the Bible away in the drawer. "So now you can tell me what you think of me without offending the court, Ike."

Old McQuown glared around the jail with eyes full of tears and hate. "My son is killed," he said. "My son is backshot before my eyes, and not a man anywhere to do anything about it."

"There is plenty to do something, Cousin Ike," Wash Haggin said.

"I guess that is my place, Dad McQuown," Gannon said suddenly. "I will be trying to find out who did it."

Old McQuown grunted as though in pain. He didn't look at the deputy. "I reckon you won't be doing anything if there is a man anywhere," he said. He looked back at the judge. "Come here after justice, George Holloway, even knowing you was a Yankee."

"Ike," the judge said gently. "You said you'd accept what I decided. Are you going to crawfish now?"

"I am! Because I see my son shot down and the cowardly bugger that did it walk free!"

"How many walked free because your son and his people went up to Bright's City and perjured them off?" the judge said.

"I trusted you, George Holloway," the old man said, shaking his head. "And you have tricked and thrown us down today, and mocked an old man with his son dead. I come in here against my inclination, and these boys too. I thought soon or late we was going to have to face up to a change in things, but I see it is dog eat dog like always, and justice only what you make yourself."

"Bud," Wash Haggin said to Gannon. "A man could say you did Curley a disservice swearing what turned him loose for Blaisedell to kill. The judge did you a disfavor the same just now, Bud. You are a dead man."

Kate Dollar sat up very stiffly. All eyes turned on Gannon.

"Wash," Gannon said. "You have known me—what did I ever do you'd think I'd do a thing like this?"

"Know what you turned into," Wash Haggin said.

"Chet," Gannon said. "Maybe you will see that if every man is to think the worst he can think of every other man, then there is going to be no man finally better than that."

The muscles on Chet Haggin's jaw stood out, but he did not answer. Wash Haggin said in a flat voice, "You won't be around to see it get much worse, Bud."

"George Holloway," said old McQuown, "I have known you awhile and you me. I tell you it is a shame on you. You have thrown me hard and by a poor trick. You don't know what it is to lose your son and have it laughed in your face, and the bugger that did it tricked free."

"It's not laughed in your face, Ike."

"Was, and right here. I say he was a good boy and peaceable, and they laugh and scorn me for saying it. He was sitting down there how long with every man to think him yellow for it—because he didn't want to go against Blaisedell that was marshal here. Not a yellow bone in his poor dead body. Oh, I was as bad as the rest, I'll say that right out; his own daddy was as bad as the rest, that was every one of them badgering at him to go against Blaisedell. When he knew it wasn't the thing to do. Knew it better than me, God rest his soul, for I cared too much in my pride about what some coyotes thought of him. Blaisedell pushing on him and pushing on him, that only wanted to be left in peace and to do right, till finally he was pushed too far and his own best friend murdered by that murdering fiend out of hell. And he had to come then, there was nothing else for it.

"And then Blaisedell sends his lick-spittle Judas down to gulch him rather than fight it fair down the street here. But there is no justice to be had. It is bitter, George Holloway, but I will swear something else I didn't swear before because it would've only been laughed to scorn. I swear my boy will go to heaven and that foul devil to hell where he belongs and Bud Gannon along with him."

"And soon," Whitby said, in a low voice.

"That's pled to another judge than me, Ike," the judge said.

"Already been. Abe is looking down on us from heaven right now, and pitying us for poor miserable mortal men."

"He'll be happier before tonight," Wash Haggin said, looking down at his hands.

Old McQuown lay back on his pallet and gazed up at the ceiling. "What have we come to?" he said quietly. "Every man out here used to be a man and decent, and took care of himself and never had to ask for help, for always there was people to give it without it was asked. Fighting murdering Pache devils and fighting greasers, and real men around, then. Murder done there was kin to take it up and cut down the murdering dog, or friends to take it up. Those days when there was friends still. When a man was free to come in town and laugh and jollify with his friends, and friends could meet in town and enjoy towning it, and there was pleasure then. Drink whisky, and gamble some, and fight it stomp and gouge sometimes when there was differences, but afterwards friends again. No one to say a man no, in those days, and kill him if he didn't run for cover and shiver in his boots. Life was worth the living of it in those days."

"And men killed sixteen to the dozen in those days," the judge said, quietly too. "And not by murdering Apaches, either. Rustling and road-agenting all around and this town treated as though it was a shooting gallery on Saturday nights, for the cowboys' pleasure. Miners killed like there was a bounty on them, and a harmless barber shot dead because his razor slipped a little. Yes, things were free in those days."

"Better than these! Maybe men was killed, but killed fair and chance for chance, and not butchered down and backshot. And no man proud enough to raise a hand to stop it!

"But there is some left to raise a hand! There is some of us down valley not eat up with being townfolk and silver-crazy and afraid to breathe. When there is a man killed foul and un-righteous in the sight of God, there will be some to avenge his name. There is some left!"

"Every man's hand will be against you, Ike," the judge said. "It is a battle you poor, dumb, ignorant, misled, die-hard fools have fought a million times and never won in the end, and I lost this leg beating you of it once before. Because times change, and will change, and are changing, Ike. If you will let them change like they are bound to do, why, they will change easy. But fight them like you do every time and they will change hard and grind you to dust like a millstone grinding."

"We'll see who the grinder is!" old man McQuown cried.

"Blaisedell is who it is, Ike. You pull him down on you hard and harder, and on us too who maybe don't like what he stands for a whole lot better than you do. But we will have him, or you, and rather him; and *you* will have him for you will not have law and order."

"We will not have it when it is Blaisedell," Chet Haggin said.

"Blaisedell has run his string," Wash Haggin said grimly.

"Thought he had," the judge said. "But he hasn't if you are going to go on taking law and order as set pure against you every time. Ike, where I was a young fellow there was a statue out before the courthouse that was meant to represent justice. She had a sword that didn't point at nobody, and a blindfold over her eyes, and scales that balanced. Maybe it was different with you Confederates. A good many of you I've seen I've thought it must've been a different statue of her you had down south. One that her sword always poked at *you*. One with no blindfold on her eyes, so you always thought she was looking straight at *you*. And her scales tipped against *you*, every time. For I have never seen such men to take her on and try to fight her.

"And maybe with a fraud like that one you could win. But this here, now, is the United States of America, and it is *my* statue of justice that stands for here. You can cross swords with her till you die doing it, and you are always going to lose. Because back of her, standing right there behind her—or maybe pretty far back, like here in the territory—there is all the people. *All* the people, and when you set yourself against her, you are set against every one of us."

"Get me out of here, boys," old McQuown said. "It is too close in here. Let's get out and bury my son, and then tend to our business."

"Just a minute now!" Pike Skinner said. "I have heard you threatening Johnny Gannon. That is deputy sheriff in this town. I am warning you there are a deal of people watching for you damned rustlers to start trouble."

"There surely are," French said. "You count them when you go out of here."

"Get me outside, boys!" old McQuown cried. "Get me out of here where I can see some decent faces of my own kind, that's not all crooked and mean-scared and town-yellow." The Haggin brothers lifted the pallet, and the old man was borne outside through the men standing in the doorway, who respectfully made a passage for him.

## 48. *Gannon Takes a Walk*

GANNON SAT with his chair tilted back against the wall and his boot-tips just touching the floor, pushing the oily rag through the barrel of his Colt with the cleaning rod. He forced it through time after time, and held the muzzle to his eye to peer up the dark mirror-shine of the barrel. He tested the action and placed the piece, awkward with his bandaged hand, in its holster, and looked up to see Pike Skinner watching him with an almost ludicrous grimace of anxiety. The judge sat at his table with his face averted and his whisky bottle cradled against his chest.

Gannon tapped the wounded hand once against his thigh, then shot it for the Colt. His hand wrapped the butt gingerly,

his forefinger slipping through the trigger guard as he pulled
it free, his thumb joint clamping down on the reluctant cock
of the hammer spring. He did not raise it, holding it pointed
toward the floor.

"Christ!" Pike said.

It had not been as slow as all that, Gannon thought. He
had never been fast, but he could shoot well enough. He felt
very strange; he remembered feeling like this when he had
had the typhoid and had waked finally with the fever broken.
Then, too, all the outer things had seemed removed and unimportant, and as though slowed somehow, so there was much
time to examine all that went on around him, and especially
any movement seen in its entirety, component by component.
Then, as now, there had been a very close connection between
the willed act, and the arm, and hand and fingers that were
the objects of the will; so that, too, his life and breathing had
become conscious acts, and he could almost feel the shape of
his beating heart, and watch the slow expansion and collapse
of his lungs.

The judge drank, spluttered, and went into a coughing fit.
Pike pounded him upon the back until he stopped. "They
must be about through burying by now," Pike said, scowling.

Gannon nodded.

"You just sit, son," the judge said, in a choked voice. His
eyes were watering, and he drank again and wiped his mouth.
"You just let them go on out if they see fit, now, you hear?"
he said feebly. "There is nothing gained anywhere if you are
shot dead."

"You let us handle them if they are calky," Pike said. In a
placating tone he said, "No, now, not vigilantes either, Johnny.
There is Blaisedell down there and no reason for him not to
be, and just some of the rest of us around. Now you hear,
Johnny?"

"Why, I'm not going to hide in here," Gannon said, and felt
the necessity to grin, and, after it, the grin itself. He looked
at the judge, whose face sagged in dark, ugly, bloated lines.
"Nothing is gained if I sit it out in here, either."

"You don't have to prove anything," Pike said. "You leave it
to us, now. There is some of us got to stand now like we never
did for Bill Canning. You leave us that."

Gannon didn't answer, for there was no point in arguing it further. Pike said, "They ought to be about through out there. I am going down." He hitched at his shell belt, loosened his Colt in its holster, gave Gannon another of his confused and accusing glances, and disappeared.

When Pike was gone Gannon took out his own Colt again, and began to replace the heavy, vicious, pleasingly shaped cartridges in the cylinder.

"Blaisedell was right," the judge said. "He said I would put too much on you and I have done it."

"You put nothing on me, Judge. There is just a time and a place for a show. You know that."

"But what place, and what time? Who is to know that?" The judge swung a hand clumsily to try to capture a fly that planed past his head. He contemplated his empty hand with bloodshot eyes, and made a contemptuous sound. "I saw you draw just now, son. Time you got that piece out, Jack Cade or either of the Haggins or any fumble-handed plowboy would have shot you through like a colander and had a drink to celebrate and rode halfway back to San Pablo." He sighed heavily and said, "I thank you for saying I didn't put it on you. Are you scared?"

Gannon shrugged. He felt not so much fright as a curious, flat anxiety. He was only afraid that it would be Jack Cade.

"I'm scared for you," the judge said. "I don't think you have got a Chinaman's chance unless you let Pike and the marshal and those give you a chance. You too proud for that?"

"Proud's nothing to do with it," he said. It touched him that the judge felt responsible for this. "Well, maybe a little," he said. "But if a deputy is going to be worth anything he can't hole up when there is trouble."

"All men are the same in the end," the judge said. "Afraider to be thought a coward than afraid to die."

Gannon rubbed his itching palm on the thigh of his pants, grimacing at the almost pleasant pain. The judge held the bottle up before him and squinted at it.

"Some men drink to warm themselves," he said. "I drink to cool the brain. I drink to get the people out of it. You are nothing to me, boy. You are only a badge and an office, is all you are. Get yourself killed, it is nothing to me."

"All right," he said.

The judge nodded. "Just a process," he said. "That's all you are. What are men to me?" He rubbed his hand over his face as though he were trying to scrape his features off. "I told them they had put Blaisedell there, and put him there for the rest of us. I talk, and it makes me puke to hear myself talking. For Blaisedell is a man too. I wish to God I didn't feel for him, or you, or any man. But do you know what whoever it was that shot down McQuown took away from Blaisedell? Who was it, do you suppose?"

Gannon shook his head.

"What they took away from him," the judge went on. "Ah, I can't stand to see what they will make of him. They will turn him into a mad dog in the end. And I can't stand to see what they will do to you now, just when you—" He drank again. "Whisky used to take the people out of it," he said, after a long time.

Footsteps came along the planks outside. Buck Slavin appeared in the doorway, carrying a shotgun. Kate entered a step behind him. "They are coming," Kate said.

Gannon heard it now, the dry, protesting creak of a wagon wheel and the muffled pad of many hoofs in the dust. He got to his feet, and as he did, Buck raised the shotgun and pointed it at him.

"Now, you are not going out there, Deputy," Buck said patronizingly. "There are people to deal with this. You just sit."

"What the devil is this?" the judge cried.

Gannon began to shake with rage; for they had thought he would be glad of an excuse, and Kate had begged it and Buck furnished it. Kate stood there staring at him with her hands clutched together at her waist.

He started forward. "Get out of my way, Buck Slavin!"

Buck thrust the shotgun muzzle at him. "You will just camp in that cell awhile, Deputy!"

Gannon caught hold of the muzzle with both hands and shoved it back so that the butt slammed into Buck's groin. Buck yelled with pain and Gannon wrenched the shotgun away and reversed it. Buck was bent over with his hands to his crotch.

"*You* march in there!" he said hoarsely. He grasped Buck's shoulder and propelled him into the cell, locked the door, and tossed the key ring onto the peg. He leaned the shotgun against the wall. He didn't look at Kate. The hoofs and the squealing wagon wheel sounded more loudly in the street.

"Now see here, Gannon!" Buck said in an agonized voice.

"Shut up!"

"Oh, you are brave!" Kate cried. "Oh, you will show the world you are as brave as Blaisedell, won't you? I thought you had more sense than the rest behind that ugly, beak-nosed face. But go ahead and *die*!"

"That was a fool trick, Buck!" the judge said. "Interfering with an officer in the performance of his duty. And you ought to be jailed with him, ma'am, only it wouldn't be decent!"

"Shut up, you drunken old fraud!" Kate said. Her eyes caught Gannon's at last, and he saw that she had come to save him, almost as she had once saved Morgan; he felt awed and strangely ashamed for her, and for himself. He started out.

"We'll send flowers," Buck said.

"Why?" Kate whispered, as Gannon passed her. "*Why?*"

"Because if a deputy can't walk around this town when he wants, then nobody can."

Outside, the sun was warm and painfully bright in his eyes as he gazed up at the new sign hanging motionless above his head. The sound of the wagon had ceased. He remembered to compose his face into the mask of wooden fearlessness, that was the proper mask, before he turned to the east.

The wagon had stopped before the gunshop in the central block. The San Pablo men had dismounted and there was a cluster of them around the wagon, and a few were entering the Lucky Dollar. Faces turned toward him. Some of the men, who had been moving toward the saloon, stopped, others moved quickly away from the wagon; they glanced his way and then across Main Street.

Blaisedell was there, he saw, standing coatless under the shadow of the arcade before the Billiard Parlor, one booted foot braced up on the tie rail; it was where he often stood to survey Main Street. His sleeves were gartered up on his long arms, a dark leather shell belt rode his hips. He stood as motionless as one of the posts that supported the roof of the arcade. Farther down were Mosbie and Tim French, and, on the corner of Broadway, Peter Bacon, with a Winchester over his arm. Pike Skinner stood before Goodpasture's store, and in a group in Southend Street were Wheeler, Thompson, Hasty, and little Pusey, Petrix's clerk, with a shotgun. His throat tightened as he saw them watching him; Peter, who was no gunman; Mosbie, who had railed at him most violently over Curley Burne; Pike, who he had begun to think was his sworn enemy, until today; Blaisedell, who had wanted to make this his own play; and a bank clerk, after all.

He started forward down the boardwalk. He flexed his shoulders a little to relieve the tight strain there. He stretched his wounded, aching, sweating hand to try to loosen it. His skin prickled. He wondered, suddenly, that he had no plan. But he had only to walk the streets of Warlock as a deputy must do, as was his duty and his right.

He crossed Southend Street with the Warlock dust itching on his face and teasing in his nostrils. Wash Haggin was standing spread-legged in the center of the boardwalk before the Lucky Dollar, facing him.

Old man McQuown was still in the wagon, beneath a shade rigged from a serape draped over four sticks. There was no one else in view on this side of the street.

"Dad McQuown," he said, in greeting, to the wild eyes that stared at him over the plank side of the wagon. He halted and said, "I will do my best to find out who did it, Dad McQuown."

He started on, and now Wash's face was fixed in his eyes, Wash's hat pushed back a little to show a dark sweep of hair across his forehead, Wash's face set in a wooden expression that must be a reflection of his own face. Wash instead of Jack Cade because Wash was kin to Abe, he thought. He had a glimpse of Chet Haggin's face above the batwing doors of the Lucky Dollar, and Cade, and Whitby and Hennessey shadowy behind them.

"I'll trouble you to let me by, Wash," he said.

Wash's eyes widened a little as he spoke, and he felt a thrill of triumph as Wash sidled a step closer to the tie rail. There was the scuffing of his boots, then an enormous silence that now contained a kind of ticking in it, as of a huge and distant clock. He saw Wash's face twist as he passed him and walked steadily on. Now the prickling of his skin was centered in the small of his back and the nape of his neck. Peter Bacon, across the street, was holding the Winchester higher; Morgan sat in his rocking chair on the veranda of the Western Star. He could see Blaisedell, too, now, as he came past wagon and team.

"Bud!" Wash cried, behind him.

He halted. The ticking seemed closer and louder. He turned. Wash was facing him again, crouching, his hand hovering. Wash cried shrilly, "Go for your gun, you murdering son of a bitch!"

"I won't unless you make me, Wash."

"Go for it, you murdering backshooting—"

"Kill him!" Dad McQuown screamed.

Wash's hand dove down. Someone yelled; instantly there was a chorus of warning yells. They echoed in his ears as he twisted around in profile and his wounded hand slammed down on his own Colt; much too slow, he thought, and saw Wash's gun barrel come up, and the smoke. Gannon stumbled a step forward as though someone had pushed him from behind, and his own Colt jarred in his hand. He was deafened then, but he saw Wash fall, hazed in gunsmoke. Wash fell on his back. He tried to roll over, his arm flopped helplessly across his body, and his six-shooter dropped to the planks. He shuddered once, and then lay still.

Gannon glanced at the doors of the Lucky Dollar; the faces there had disappeared. Then he had a glimpse of the long gleam of the rifle barrel leveled over the side of the wagon. He jumped back, just as a man vaulted into the wagon. It was Blaisedell, and old McQuown screamed as Blaisedell kicked out as though he were killing a snake—and kicked again and the rifle dropped over the edge of the wagon to the boardwalk.

He could see the old man's fist beating against Blaisedell's leg as Blaisedell stood in the wagon, facing the doors of the Lucky Dollar. No one appeared there for a moment, and Gannon started back to where Wash lay. But then Chet Haggin came out and knelt down beside his brother's body, and Gannon turned away. The old man had stopped screaming.

He walked on down toward the corner. After a moment he remembered the Colt in his hand, and replaced it in its holster. There was the same silence as before, but it buzzed in his shocked ears. His hand felt hot and sticky, and, looking down, he saw blood leaking dark red from beneath the bandage. At the corner he turned and crossed Main Street, and mounted the boardwalk on the far side in the shadow. Peter didn't look at him, standing stiffly with the rifle in his white-clenched hands. Tim's eyes slid sideways toward him and Tim nodded once. He heard Mosbie whistle between his teeth. Blaisedell had returned to this side of the street, and leaned against a post, watching the wagon. Now Gannon could hear the old man's pitiable cursing and sobbing, and he could see Chet still bent over Wash.

"I thank you," he said, to Blaisedell's back, and walked on. He looked neither right nor left now but kept his eyes fixed on the black and white sign over the jail doorway. Kate's face appeared there briefly. He had made his turn through Warlock, as was his right, as was his duty; but his knees felt weak and the sign over the jail seemed very distant. He could feel the blood dripping from his fingers, and his wrist brushed the butt of his Colt as his arm swung.

"Hallelujah!" Pike Skinner whispered, as he came to the corner. He did not reply, and crossed Southend Street, feeling the stares of the men—not vigilantes—who were stationed there. Again he saw Kate appear in the jail doorway, but when he approached she disappeared back inside, and, when he entered, she stood with her back to him.

The judge sat hunch-shouldered at the table, his crutch leaning beside him, his bottle and hard-hat before him, his hands clasped between them. Buck's face was framed in the bars.

"Got you in the hand, did he?" Buck said, in a matter-of-fact voice.

"I just broke it open again."

The judge didn't speak as he moved in past the table. He heard Kate gasp. "Your belt!" she cried. He reached back to feel a long gap in the leather and some cartridge loops gone. He sat down abruptly in the chair beside the cell door.

Kate stood facing him. He saw her stocking as she pulled up her skirt. She tore at the hem of her petticoat and then stooped to bite on the hem and pull loose a long strip. She took his hand and roughly bound the strip of smooth, soft cloth around it, and tore it again and tied the ends.

Then she stepped back away from him. "Well, now you are a killer," she said, with her lips flattened whitely over her teeth.

"Who was it, Johnny?" Buck said.

"Wash."

"What're they going to do now?"

"I expect they'll go out."

"He's got a brother, hasn't he?" Kate said. The judge was regarding the whisky bottle, his face a mottled, grayish red, his hands still clasped before him.

Buck cleared his throat and said, "Well, you have made some friends this day, Gannon."

"Friends!" Kate cried. "You mean men to think he is a wonder because he killed a man? Friends!" she said hoarsely. "A friend is someone who will say he did right and what he had to do, and hold to it. They will stew on this until they have figured he murdered this one like he murdered McQuown. I have seen it done too many times. Friends! They will—"

"Now, Kate," Buck said.

"I didn't murder Abe McQuown, Kate."

"What difference does that make?" she cried at him. "Friends! A friend lasts like snow on a hot griddle and enemies like—"

"You are bitter for a young woman, miss," the judge said.

Gannon hung his head suddenly, and bent down still farther. He felt faint and his stomach kept rising and swelling against his laboring heart, and he could taste bile in his throat. In his mind's eye he saw not Wash Haggin's wooden face, but the frantic dark face of the Mexican sweeping up the bank toward him still. "Bitter?" he heard Kate say, above the humming in his ears. "Why, yes, I am bitter! Because men have found some way to crucify every decent man, starting with Our Lord. No, it is not even bitter—it is just common sense. They will admire him for a wonder because he killed a man they wouldn't've had the guts to go against. But they will hate him for it, because of that. So they will say he murdered him like he murdered McQuown. Or they will say it was nothing, with Blaisedell there to back him, and those others. They will say it for they are men. Don't you know they will, Judge?"

"You are bitter," the judge said, in the same dull voice. "And scared for him too. But I know men better than you, I think, Miss Dollar. They are not so bad as that."

"Show me one that isn't! Show me one. But don't show *them*. Or they will kill him for it!"

"There are men that love their fellow men and suffer for their suffering," the judge said. "But you wouldn't see them for hatefulness, it looks like, miss."

Gannon raised his head to look at Kate's face, which was turned toward the judge—and it was hard and hateful, as he had said.

"I would show you Blaisedell for one," the judge said.

"Blaisedell," Kate whispered. "No, not Blaisedell!"

"Blaisedell. Hard as I have judged him, he is a good man. That knew better than you, miss, what had to be done just now. That let Johnny take his play and glory just now, for he needed them, with McQuown took from him. He is a good man. And I will show you Pike Skinner that thought Johnny threw this town down with Curley Burne, but backed him now all the same. And the rest of them out there. Good men, Miss Dollar! The milk of kindness is thick in them, and thicker all the time!"

"Thick as blood!"

"Thicker than blood. And will win in the end, miss—for all your sneering at a man that says it to you. So this old world remakes itself time and time again, each time in labor and in pain and the best men crucified for it. People like you will not see it, being bitter; as I have been myself, and so I know. So they can say a town like this one has its man for breakfast every morning—" He slammed his hand down on the table top, his voice rose. "But not killed to eat for breakfast any more! Not burnt on crosses to the glory of God any more! Not butchered up—"

The judge stopped and swung around in his chair as footsteps sounded outside. Gannon rose as Chet Haggin came into the doorway. Chet wore no shell belt, and there was a smear of blood on the breast of his blue shirt. He stood in the doorway staring at Gannon with burnt, dark eyes in his carefully composed face.

"I'm sorry, Chet," Gannon said.

Chet nodded curtly. He glanced from Gannon to Kate, to Buck, to the judge, and then his burnt eyes returned. "I never thought you come back and shot Abe," he said, in a harsh, flat voice. "I have known you some, Bud. So I know just now you killed Wash because there wasn't anything else you could do, the way it was put. I come up here to tell you I knew that."

Chet made as though to hook his thumbs in his belt, and grimaced and looked down. "Thought I'd better not start up here heeled," he said, in an apologetic tone. "Things are scratchy out."

The judge sat motionless with his chin on his hands. Kate stood tall and straight with her hands clasped before her and her eyes cast down.

Chet said, "Bud, we thought pretty low of you when Billy got killed. And said low things. Now I guess I know how you felt, for when you press to kill a man and he kills you to keep you from it, who is to blame? Anyway, I guess I know how you wouldn't go against Blaisedell, and scared nothing to do with it." His eyes filled suddenly. "For I won't brace you, Bud. And I'm not scared of you!"

"I know you're not, Chet."

"They will say it. Be damned to them. I won't come against you, Bud. But they will try to kill you, Bud. Jack— They won't rest till they do it now. I won't go against you, but I can't go against what's my own kin and kind! I can't go against my own and side with Blaisedell like you have done. I can't!" he cried, and then he stumbled back outside and was gone.

"Always said he was the white one," Buck commented, and the judge gave him a disgusted look.

Gannon stood staring at the dusty sunlight streaming in the door. Presently he heard the creaking of the wagon wheels. He moved slowly past Kate to stand in the doorway. The team and wagon were coming down Main Street toward him, and the riders following in the dust it raised. Pike Skinner, who was still standing before Goodpasture's store, waved to him to get back inside.

"Going out?" the judge asked.

"Looks like it."

"You had better get out of that door, Johnny!" Buck said.

But he didn't move, watching them come down Main Street, Joe Lacey and the breed Marko on the seat of the wagon, and the serape shading the old man in the bed behind them. The horsemen fanned out to fill the street. He watched for Jack Cade.

Cade had dropped a little behind the others. He rode with his shoulders hunched. His round-crowned hat was white with dust, his leather vest hung open; his purple and black striped pants were stuffed into his high boots. A fringed rifle scabbard hung slanting forward along his bay's neck. He reined the bay toward the boardwalk, and behind him on the corner Gannon saw Pike Skinner lower his hand to his Colt.

The wagon rolled past him, the men on the seat staring steadily ahead. The old man's eyes gazed at him over the side of the wagon, white-rimmed, sightless-looking, and insane. The riders had drawn their neckerchiefs up over their faces, and it was difficult to tell one from the other. They turned their faces toward him, like cavalrymen passing in review, but Jack Cade was riding toward him.

"*I'll* kill you, Bud!" Cade said in a voice that was almost a whisper and yet enormously loud in the silence. Then he nodded, and set his spurs, and the bay trotted swiftly on to catch up with the others.

They rode on down the street behind the wagon, fading shapes in the powdery drifting dust, their passage almost soundless except for the occasional eccentric creak of the dry wheel. When they had almost gained the rim, he saw one of the horses rear and a shot rang out; and at once all the horses began to rear in a confused and antic mass, and all the riders fired into the air and yipped and whooped in thin and meaningless defiance.

There was a flat loud whack above his head and the sign swung suddenly. The shooting and whooping ceased as suddenly as it had begun, and, as though team, wagon, and horsemen had fallen through a trapdoor, they disappeared over the rim on the road back to San Pablo.

He looked up at the bullet hole in the lower corner of the new, still swinging sign, and went back inside.

"Was that Cade?" Kate whispered.

He nodded and heard her sigh, and she raised a fist and, like a tired child, rubbed at her eyes. There was a new and closer whooping in the street, and suddenly Kate moved to lean on the table and stare down at the judge.

"Everything is fine now, isn't it?" she said. "Nothing to worry about now, is there? Oh, the good ones always win out in the end and it is all right if they get crucified for it, because—"

"Now, Kate," Buck said. "I don't know why you're taking on so. It's all over now, and he'll have a lot to back him from now on."

"But who is to stand in front of him?" she said, just as Pike Skinner ran in.

Pike leaped on Gannon, laughing and yelling and hugging him; then the others came until the jail was filled with them, all of them talking at once and coming up to slap his shoulder or shake his good hand, to examine and exclaim over the bullet scar on his belt, and ask what Chet had had to say. He didn't see Kate leave, he was just aware suddenly that she was gone, and the judge gone. Someone had brought a bottle of whisky and was passing it around, and others were singing, "Good-by! Good-by! Good-by, Regulators, Good-by! . . ."

He thanked Pike, and thanked the others one by one as they came up to him. "Surely, Horse, surely," Peter Bacon said. "It was a pleasure to see you and worth more than just standing there holding my boots down with a Winchester for ballast." The whisky bottle was forced upon him time and again. Someone had let Buck out of the cell. He thought, with a sinking twisting at his heart, that there had not been such jollity and merriment as this in Warlock for a long time now.

He heard someone ask where Blaisedell was and French replied that he had not come up with them. He had wanted to thank Blaisedell. He flinched as someone slapped him on the shoulder, and in the process brushed against his hand. Hap Peters stuck a finger through the hole in his shell belt. "Drink!" Mosbie was shouting, waving the bottle at him. "Drink to the rootingest-tootingest-shootingest-beatingest deputy this side of Timbuctoo!"

Mosbie forced the bottle on him, but he gagged on the sour whisky. Suddenly he could not stand it any more, and he made his way outside, and almost ran along the boardwalk to his room in Birch's roominghouse.

# BOOK THREE
# THE ANTAGONISTS

been standing by if you hadn't done what you've done in this town.

"But there is that point, Marshal," he went on. He managed to meet the impassive blue stare. "It is like a kid with a big brother to run the bad kids off him. Some time the big brother is going to have to let the kid fight for himself. I mean even if he gets whipped—"

"That is you you are talking about," Blaisedell broke in.

"No, it is the deputy here. Which only happens to be me."

"Do you think you are ready to take it on, Deputy?"

He almost groaned, for it was the question. He shook his head tiredly and said, "I don't know."

"I don't think you are ready yet," Blaisedell said. "But then I didn't think you were before the Regulators came in, either."

He saw Blaisedell smile a little, and he supposed it had been a compliment. "I think I will stay on awhile," Blaisedell said. "It is not time yet." He said it with a certain inflection and Gannon thought he might be talking of himself now.

He remembered Blaisedell's telling the judge that he would know when it was time to go, but now he wondered what time Blaisedell had meant, Warlock's or his own. "Surely," he said quickly. "I don't think it is time yet, either. But I have got to be ready sometime. I couldn't ever have been ready at all if you hadn't been here."

Blaisedell blinked. After a long time he said, "I see you have taken up with Kate Dollar."

Gannon felt himself blushing, and Blaisedell continued, still gazing at the names on the wall. "She is a fine woman. I knew her back awhile."

"She said."

"Down on me," Blaisedell said. "I killed a friend of hers in Fort James."

She said; this time he did not say it aloud.

"It was shoot or get shot," Blaisedell said. "Or I thought it was. I had been edgy about things." He was silent for a time, and Gannon remembered what Kate had told him about it. He had thought she must be telling the truth because she had sounded so certain; but now he wondered about it just because Blaisedell sounded so uncertain.

Then Blaisedell said, "I remember when I killed a man the way you did the other day. And it was clear and had to be done, though I went home afterwards and puked my insides out. The way you did." His voice sounded removed and musing, and, after another pause he went on again. "But there was a lesson I learned. It is that a man can't ever be careful enough. Even careful as a person can be is not enough. For there will be a man you don't want to come against you, and that shouldn't, but all the same he will—"

He stopped and shook his head a little, and Gannon thought he had been speaking of Curley Burne.

Blaisedell said, "I knew a man once who said it was all foolishness—that if you want to kill a man, why, kill him. Shoot him down from behind in the dark if you want to kill him. But don't make a game with rules out of it."

This time it was Morgan; it hit Gannon like a picture slapped across his sight and then drawn back into focus so he could study it: Morgan standing masked in the doorway in the dark, and Abe McQuown with his back turned.

"But he doesn't understand," Blaisedell said. "It is not that at all, for you don't want to kill a man. It is only the rules that matter. It is holding strict to the rules that counts."

Blaisedell let his chair down suddenly, and the legs cracked upon the floor; he leaned forward with his face intent and strained, and Gannon felt the full force of his eyes. "Hold to them like you are walking on eggs," he said. "So you know yourself you have played it fair and as best you could. As right as you could. Like you did with Haggin. I admired that, Deputy, for you did just what it was put on you to do, and did it well."

Then the muscles along the edges of his jaw tightened. "So it was all clear for you," he said, with the bitter edge to his voice again. "But there are things to watch for. Watch yourself, I mean. Don't be too fast. I have been too fast two times in different ways, and it is why I asked you about Cade. For after the first time, there are people out after you, and you know it and worry it, unless you are not the worrying kind. So then, you think, if you don't get drawn first and them killed first—do you see what I mean?"

Gannon nodded. He was being instructed, he knew, and this was a very precious thing to Blaisedell. He felt embarrassed as he had been once when his father had tried to instruct him about women. And he saw that Blaisedell was embarrassed, as his father had been.

"Well, I came in to try to tell you a couple of things, Deputy," he said, in a different tone. "And a long time getting to it. A little thing I noticed watching you draw, for one."

"What was that, Marshal?"

"Well, you lose a little time and your aim, too, flapping your hand out when you pull your piece free. I would put in a little practice bringing it up straight. Down straight with your hand, up straight with your piece. I saw you flapped your hand out a little, and though you center-shot him clean, you lost time. He lost aim. He flapped out so far he didn't get the barrel back in line, was the reason he missed you."

"I'll remember. I hadn't thought of that, Marshal." He waited, tensely.

Blaisedell frowned. "The other thing," he said. "It is something you ought to know, but I don't know quite— Well, it is just something you have got to tell yourself every time. It is a kind of pride a man has to have, and it has got to be genuine. *Has* to. You will see when another man hasn't got it. I mean, when a man thinks maybe you are faster and better than him, he is already through. You can see that, and those times you don't have to hurry a shot, for he will more than likely miss. Like Curley missed," he said, in a flat voice. "I knew he would miss.

"But it is more than that," he said, frowning more deeply. "I don't—I—"

"More than just that you are faster," Gannon said.

Blaisedell looked relieved. "That's it. It is just that you *are* better. A man has to be proud, but he has to have the reason to be proud to hold him. Genuine, like I said." Blaisedell grinned fleetingly. "I guess you will understand me. It is a close thing out there, you and the other. But I mean it is like two parts of something are fighting it out inside—before there is ever a Colt's pulled. Inside you. And you have to know that you are the part that has to win. I mean *know* it."

"Yes," Gannon said, for he saw that.

"There is no play-acting with yourself," Blaisedell said. He got quickly to his feet, and stretched, and put on his hat and patted it. "Why, just some things I thought I could pass along, Deputy," he said.

"Thank you, Marshal." He rose too.

"Have you figured who killed McQuown yet?"

"There are a lot of people who could have done it."

Blaisedell nodded gravely. Then he said, "Maybe you would have a whisky with me?"

"Why, yes, Marshal—I would like to." He took up his own hat, and stood turning it in his hands. He had a feeling that Blaisedell knew exactly what he was going to say. "I've been wondering what Morgan is going to do, with the Glass Slipper burnt down."

"I guess he is thinking of moving along," Blaisedell said. "There is nothing to hold him here, with his place burned. He is one that likes a change."

"Well, maybe it is better."

Blaisedell's eyes were cold as deep ice, and his voice was cold. "Maybe it is," he said, and moved on outside.

Gannon took a deep breath and followed Blaisedell, who waited on the boardwalk. They started down toward the Lucky Dollar together, in silence. They had almost reached the corner when he realized that he was walking on Blaisedell's right, when the gunman always walked to the right in order to keep his gun hand free; and then he knew that Blaisedell had chosen to have it that way.

## 50. *Journals of Henry Holmes Goodpasture*

May 14, 1881

MCQUOWN'S DEATH, which would have been wildly celebrated here a few months ago, has set upon us a pall that is mitigated only in part by the pride we have felt in the emergence of a home-grown hero. The means of his death, for one thing —cowardly murder—and, for another, the meaninglessness of it. There should have been some meaning, some lesson, some sense of triumph. There was none.

Moreover, in the past weeks, it has been brought home to us that perhaps his champions were in part right, and that it was

McQuown, who, although himself a rustler, kept order among the outlaws down valley, and confined their depredations to certain channels. He was not called the Red Fox for nothing. Control was necessary, organization brings control; therefore McQuown.

There has been a rash of petty rustling, and both the Redgold and Welltown stages were stopped by road agents within the last week alone. Blaikie has lost over a hundred head of stock, and one of his hands was wounded, not dangerously, by a crew of thieves he encountered. Burbage is incensed; McQuown was at least a man of honor, says he, indignantly. I, however, refuse to join in the general sainting of the outlaw. The border seems to be very tightly watched now, both by elements of the Mexican Army and Don Ignacio's own vaqueros—it is said that he has declared war upon the rustlers who have harried him for so long, and will deal ruthlessly with any he can catch. Perhaps, in view of the border situation, McQuown died at the right time, or else, like those who have survived him, he might have had to turn to robbing his neighbors.

Gannon, resting on his laurels, has done nothing whatever since he dispatched Wash Haggin. Kennon does not like him, says he is a born coward and main-chancer, and only had the courage to fight Haggin because he knew Blaisedell would protect him. Buck Slavin defends him, but is losing patience. The judge, however, points out that Gannon is helpless to deal with a series of small and scattered raids in a hostile countryside, for he would have to be in constant motion with a posse increasingly difficult to assemble. The judge says that the situation will be alleviated only when backing is received from Sheriff Keller, and this will take place when outrage or notoriety have forced that worthy, or the General, to action. Perhaps Whiteside is seeing that wheels are being turned even now in our behalf; I doubt it to the bottom of my soul.

Pike Skinner, for his part, seems to have swung over to the deputy's side, and defends him wholeheartedly. He points out that Gannon, in enemy territory, puts himself in grave danger of assassination, since to all appearances the Cowboys remain convinced that it was Gannon who murdered their chief; also that the stalwarts who would have enthusiastically formed the Vigilantes to protect Warlock from the Regulators, are not

enthusiastic at all about riding down valley to face the Cowboys whose deadly mien and ready weapons were so much in
evidence on their last appearance here.

 Gannon is looked upon with distrust by a good many members of the Citizens' Committee—or perhaps it is with jealousy.
He remains, however, a hero to the unwashed elements. There
is great interest on every hand in his future actions, and he is at
the moment more a center of interest than is Blaisedell.

> The present eye praises the present object.
> Then marvel not, thou great and complete man,
> That all the Greeks begin to worship Ajax,
> Since things in motion sooner catch the eye
> Than what not stirs.

But Hector is dead, and what is there left for Achilles to do?

                                               May 16, 1881
 It is thought here now that McQuown must have been murdered by Mexicans in the employ of Don Ignacio, in revenge,
and as assurance against further rustling of Hacienda Puerto
stock.

 I am sure there would be some to accuse Blaisedell of the
crime, had not Blaisedell been in evidence here that night. I
have heard it said, though, that Morgan was clearly seen (by
whom?) riding back into Warlock the following dawn upon a
winded horse, as he was also seen (by whom?) riding back from
the scene of the Bright's City stage robbery, etc. No doubt
Morgan is capable of such a murder, as no doubt he is capable
of road-agentry, but I am unable to believe him capable of
such strenuous diabolism merely for its own sake.

 Yet more and more I see the conspiracy to bring Blaisedell
low by gossip and canard, since it cannot be done by gunfire. They will strike at him through Morgan, against whose
name is piled a higher and higher stack of guilt and sin, in the
hope that this will topple over onto the Marshal. Very probably Morgan has no more moral code than a rhinoceros, and
certainly he does nothing to make himself popular. He spends
his time viewing and sneering at our activities from the veranda
of the Western Star, and, afternoons and evenings, gambles

at the Lucky Dollar, where he is having a phenomenal run of luck at the faro table, to Lew Taliaferro's great discomfiture. Morgan was attacked there the other night by two miners, but, although he is not large in stature, he is a powerful and active man, and acquitted himself well. When he had had enough of the brawl he drew his six-shooter and put his attackers to flight, and then returned to his game, Will Hart said, as calmly as though nothing had happened.

The town itself is quiet and well behaved. Our population is growing. Among others, a man named Train and his wife, a faded but indomitable-looking woman, have arrived, with the prospect of building an eating establishment, which they claim will be of high quality. They are having great difficulty obtaining lumber, but Mrs. Train says firmly that she will not have adobe, which is dirty and repellent to white people. There has also been another marriage. Slator has taken to wife a Cyprian from the French Palace. The judge performed the ceremony, the validity of which might consequently be suspect, and Taliaferro, fittingly enough, gave the bride away. The happy couple has rented a cabin from one of the Medusa strikers, who was no doubt badly in need of money. Slator, formerly an irresponsible and drunken odd-jobman, has been given steady employment by Kennon at the livery stable, and shows every sign of having become a reformed character, this being attributed to his new responsibilities. I should think it might be difficult to possess a wife whom almost every other man in town has known so intimately, but no doubt True Love Conquers All.

So peace and civilization are encroaching upon Warlock. Yet it is not a pleasant peace. There is concern as to whether the strikers will accept their defeat, or will break out in some new violence. Miss Jessie has set up a breadline at the General Peach. They stand in the street at meal times, waiting their turn to be fed by her generosity, and are silent and sullen. MacDonald must fume at her feeding them, and yet I am sure that in the end he will win, and they will silently and sullenly go back to work at the Medusa.

It is a Saturday night, and very quiet outside my window. I remember when a Saturday night was a matter of dread in Warlock—I remember the wildness, the shouts and laughter, the brawling, the shooting that would all too often punctuate and bring a bloody climax to the night. Is not this what we wanted? McQuown is dead; I have to remind myself of that. Is not that too what we wanted? Yet I am aware of the dissatisfaction on every hand. It is finished, but not finished. It is not right, but I cannot express what I feel. It is an uneasy peace in Warlock.

May 22, 1881

I have noticed that we are seeing more of Blaisedell these days. He spends much of his time on Main Street, standing at his ease beneath one or the other of the arcades. His leonine head is in continual but almost imperceptible movement—as he glances up the street, then down the street. He gives the impression of intently watching and waiting. He is a part of the furniture of Main Street, a kind of black-suited eminence—a colossus there, or is it astride the town itself?

For what does he watch and wait? The question depresses me greatly, for is not his use gone? He is like a machine primed and ready for instant service with its function no longer of value. Was not his ultimate purpose to fight, and kill, Abe McQuown? So is his use buried with McQuown? I know there is an increasing sentiment in the Citizens' Committee that he should be released. As yet this has hardly been voiced, but I know it is so. I wonder who will tell Blaisedell when, and if, it is agreed upon.

He must then go on to some other Warlock and some other McQuown. There are no more McQuowns or Curley Burnes here, and he is like a heavyweight champion awaiting a challenger where there are only lightweights. I pity him that everything has gone so wrong for him. Is not all, from now on, anticlimax?

I have seen him once or twice in converse with Gannon, more often sitting upon the veranda of the Western Star with Morgan. They sit side by side, uncomfortably similar in black broadcloth suits, black hats. It strikes me that I have no impression of them speaking together. Then Blaisedell makes a round of the town, and Morgan goes to resume his bout with Taliaferro.

The quiet nights pass, and, a little after noon each day, Blaisedell reappears at one of his three or four central posts. You do
not see him come and go, he is only there, or not. Once in a
while you are more conscious of him. A couple of miners tumble out of the Billiard Parlor, fighting and cursing. Calmly he
separates them. Upon seeing him they are at once sober and
out of their fighting mood, and slink away. Or Ash Bredon
rides in from up valley and thinks to do a little shooting into
the air to enliven the atmosphere of Warlock. Blaisedell speaks
to him from across the street, and Bredon changes his mind.

He stands and waits, and the days pass, and I wonder what
will become of him. What he waits and watches for does not
exist; I cannot help but feel he knows this himself. In a very
brief time he has turned, almost, into a monument.


## 51. *The Doctor Hears Threats and Gunfire*

THE DOCTOR stood in the entryway watching the miners file
in through the door of the General Peach for their noon meal.
As usual, they were quiet and orderly. There were more than a
hundred of them now, and each one nodded to him as he came
in the door, and then, carefully, did not look at him again.

The queue bent in through the dining-room doorway and
past the tables where Jessie, Myra Egan, Mrs. Sturges, Mrs.
Train, and Mrs. Maples served them soup, salt pork, bread,
and black coffee in a rattle of plates and cutlery. Jessie looked
faded and tired beside Myra Egan's pink-cheeked freshness.
Those who had been served stood in the middle of the room
and wolfed down their food, more, he knew, from an urge to
get out than from hunger. Finished, they joined another line,
where Lupe, the fat Mexican cook, watched them drop their
plates into a cauldron of hot water, after which they filed outside past those who still entered.

The hot, wet smell of soup that permeated the General
Peach seemed to him the stench of defeat. They were almost
defeated, and he raged at it, and at his presumption in thinking
he could help them, and, most of all, at MacDonald, who had

beaten them so easily. They did not even send MacDonald the
revised demands any more, for MacDonald only threw them
away as soon as they were presented to him. More than a dozen
of the strikers had left Warlock, and he knew most of the rest
were only waiting for some excuse to go back to the Medusa.
Leaning against the newel post, he watched their leaders, old
man Heck and Frenchy Martin, filing out with the rest. Their
faces were resolute still, but he knew it was only for show. Each
day he stood here to watch the strikers and feel their temper,
and each day he could see them weakening.

He stayed to watch the last of the miners leave before he went
into Jessie's room and sat down in the chair beside the door.
He rose when Jessie came in. Myra Egan stood outside in the
entryway, and smiled at him as she tucked her hair up under
her bonnet. Myra's face was plumper, and her breasts looked
swollen in her crisp gingham dress; before many months had
passed she would bear Warlock's first legitimate child.

"My goodness, I am feeling the heat these days, Doc!" she
said, fanning her flushed face with her hand.

"It is natural that you should, Myra."

She flushed still more, prettily. Jessie thanked her, and
thanked the other ladies, whom he could not see from where
he stood. Disparate types though they were, they were beginning to form a women's organization, now dedicating their energies to the welfare of the strikers. He had heard Mrs. Maples
indignantly informing Myra Egan that Kate Dollar had offered
to help them; a club existed as soon as there was someone to
be excluded.

Jessie closed the door and went to stand listlessly by the table. "It is very tiring," she said.

"I don't expect it will need to be done much longer."

She shrugged. He knew she did not really care, yet it was
what she had chosen for her role and she would fulfill that role
to the limit of her strength, and probably better than someone
who cared more. She bent her head as she leafed through the
pages of a little book of poems on the table. The nape of her
neck under the curls was white, downed with fair hair, and
heartbreakingly thin.

He heard the sound of boots mounting the porch. "Jessie!"
a voice called.

She moved to the door and opened it.

"The hogs are all fed, I see." It was MacDonald's voice, and the doctor went to join her in the doorway. "How long are you going to go on feeding this herd?"

"As long as they are hungry," Jessie said. MacDonald stood facing her, his derby hat in his hand. His pale, small-featured face was savage. With him was one of his foremen, Lafe Dawson, with a shotgun over his arm.

"Well, they are going to stay hungry as long as you are going to feed them," MacDonald said. "Why should they work when they can line up at your trough for every meal? You may think you are being quite the little angel of mercy, but let me tell—"

"Maybe you had better not talk so loud, Mr. MacDonald," Dawson said, rolling his eyes toward the stairs.

"I will talk as loudly as I wish! I am talking to you, too, Wagner. You are doing them a disservice. You are going to regret this; and they are."

"There are no Regulators any more, Charlie," the doctor said. It pleased him to see how frightened MacDonald was behind his mask of anger.

"I have heard from the company," MacDonald said. "They are backing me completely—completely! There is no pressure upon me to settle this strike, whatever lying rumors have been circulated to the contrary."

"Then why are you threatening us, Charlie?" Jessie said; she said it calmly and without guile, only as though she were puzzled.

"For your own good!" MacDonald tried to smile, and failed. "I have come to tell you that I have heard from Mr. Willingham. Mr. Arthur Willingham." He folded his arms, as though in triumph. "Mr. Willingham is in Bright's City today, to confer with General Peach. You may know that Mr. Willingham, besides being president of the Porphyrion and Western Mining Company, has very important connections in Washington. I think that General Peach will not ignore what is going on down here any longer. If these men do not go back to work immediately, or if there is any more trouble down here whatsoever, you can be sure we will have martial law down here in every sense of the word, and a Mexican crew will then be brought in to work the Medusa. That," MacDonald said, "was my communication from Mr. Willingham." He waited, as though for some attempt at rebuttal.

Tittle and Fitzsimmons had appeared at the head of the hallway, and Dawson shifted his shotgun around to point at them.

"Have you had orders to settle the strike, Charlie?" Jessie asked.

"Are you calling me a liar?" MacDonald cried. "I tell you that Mr. Willingham is backing me one hundred per cent! The mining companies cannot allow a pack of ignorant, filthy foreigners to dictate to them how stopes are to be constructed, and what wages are to be paid!" MacDonald advanced a step, pointing a finger at the doctor as though it were a weapon. "Committees interfering with the work, and all the rest of this asininity you have put into their heads, Wagner. I see well enough that your *committees* are to be the Miners' Union in fact. It was *you*— the two of you! Well, I will not be blackguarded by a pack of strong-backed louts, nor by a couple of conspiring—criminally conspiring!—busybodies! I swear to you that I will fight this until they come creeping back begging for work!"

"Charlie," the doctor said. "I swear to you that I will do my best to see that they do not!"

MacDonald bared his teeth in the facsimile of a smile again, as though he had cunningly extracted a confession. "Remember that, Dawson," he said. "When General Peach comes down here we will have things to tell him about Doctor David Wagner. And about this house. A disorderly house," he said, and Jessie gasped.

"Watch your tongue, MacDonald!" the doctor cried. Dawson was grimacing horribly; Tittle started forward and Dawson swung the shotgun toward him again.

"I said a disorderly house!" MacDonald said. "A damnable mare's nest of criminal conspiracy against the mining companies. Conspiracy to commit arson! And murder, for all I know!" He stopped, panting, his eyes flickering insanely; and then he cried, "And a disorderly house in more ways than that! This house and you are a scandal to this town, Jessie. I can ruin you!"

"Shut up!" Tittle screamed. Fitzsimmons was trying to hold him, and Dawson nervously threatened him with the shotgun.

"Shut up! You lying, dirty dog!" Tittle screamed, in a mechanical voice.

"That's enough, Ben," Jessie said.

"Shoot that man if he tries to attack me!" MacDonald said to his foreman, but Tittle had quieted.

Dawson was motioning toward the stairs. "Mr. MacDonald, you had better hush!"

MacDonald sneered. "And do not think I am frightened of your adulterous scandal of a marshal, either! You may be sure he will be—"

"Charlie, I will kill you myself!" the doctor cried. He could feel his heart pounding dangerously in his chest as he started forward. Dawson turned the shotgun toward him. Tittle's eyes were glaring from his contorted face, as insane as MacDonald's; as murderous, he thought suddenly, as his own face must look. Jessie put a hand on his arm and he halted.

"Charlie—" Jessie said. She spoke in a clear, loud voice, and her tone was condescending; she might have been speaking to an obstreperous boarder. "Charlie, you must be terribly afraid of losing your position. To speak to me like this."

MacDonald made a shrill sound. "The miners' angel!" he cried. "The gunman's whore, is better; and her eunuch!"

Tittle cried out, and Dawson clutched MacDonald's arm. MacDonald glanced frantically from face to face. "You—have been warned," he said, in a voice so hoarse his words were barely understandable. He backed away, then swung around, and, with Dawson close to his heels, hurried outside.

The doctor stared at Tittle's wild eyes in his gaunt, bony face. Tittle's mouth hung half open and he did not struggle now, in Fitzsimmons' grasp. He looked as though he were in agony as he glanced at Jessie, wordlessly; abruptly he hobbled away down the hall.

Jessie turned back into her room. The doctor had thought she would be shattered, but her face was only a little pink. He wanted to cry out to her to deny it, swear to him that it was not true. He knew that she could not deny it, for, although she had lied that once to Blaisedell, she would not lie to him. The gunman's whore, and her eunuch; he stood staring at her and in his mind's eye saw his heart swelling and stretching until he thought he must faint with it. Motionless, hardly breathing, he waited for the tight pain to recede.

"He was very frightened, Jessie," he said, surprised at the calmness of his voice, "or he would not have spoken as he did."

"Yes," Jessie said, nodding, her face pink still. "Charlie was very foolish to say those things."

In the hall he heard the uneven crack of Tittle's footsteps return and break into a run. With a steady, anguished grunting Tittle hurried outside; the doctor stepped out into the entry-way just as Fitzsimmons came down the hall.

Then in the street he heard the shots, and the cry, and the answering deeper blast of Dawson's shotgun. "Why didn't you stop him?" he cried, as he ran for the door.

"He got away from me, Doc," Fitzsimmons said blandly, behind him.

## 52. *Gannon Backs Off*

GANNON HAD just come back from lunch at the Boston Café when he heard the shots—four of them in rapid succession, and the harsh cough of what sounded like a shotgun. He went out of the jail at a run, vaulted the tie rail, and ran down the street. The hot wind plucked at his hat. Morgan sat in his rocking chair on the veranda of the hotel, and, beyond, figures milled in the haze of heat and dust.

As he approached he saw that two men were supporting a third, while a fourth with a shotgun stood in the middle of the intersection facing into Grant Street. Men were running along with him on the boardwalk. He saw Pike Skinner join the group around the wounded man, and Ralph Egan come out of the Feed and Grain Barn.

It was Lafe Dawson, one of MacDonald's foremen, pointing the shotgun toward a group of miners on the corner of Grant Street. Oscar Thompson and Fred Wheeler set the wounded man down on the hotel steps. Blood spurted from his arm as Wheeler released it, and Wheeler quickly stripped off his belt and cinched it around the arm. The man was white with dust, as though he had been rolled in flour. As Gannon ran up someone tossed a hard-hat onto the boardwalk, where it thumped and rolled erratically.

"MacDonald, for Christ's sake!" Egan said.

MacDonald wiped his left hand over his dusty forehead, and turned his head with a reluctant movement to look at his arm. "Deputy!" he cried, in a stifled voice, as he saw Gannon. His mouth hung open and his lower lip was pulled down to show pale gums; his breath was so rapid it sounded as though he were whistling. He stared at Gannon with terrified eyes.

"Somebody'd better run for the doctor," Gannon said.

"Doc took the other one back to Miss Jessie's," Wheeler said. "He'll be along."

"What other one?"

"Murder!" MacDonald shouted explosively.

"Who the hell shot him?" Sam Brown demanded.

Lafe Dawson was backing toward them, still holding the shotgun pointed at the miners. Pike Skinner said, "Who was it, Lafe?"

"It was that crippled one that works for Miss Jessie," Dawson said shakily. "He was popping away from out of range. I couldn't—"

"Oh, you hit him," Oscar Thompson said.

"Tittle?" Gannon said.

"They put him to it!" MacDonald said. His tongue appeared to mop limply at his lips. "I know they put him to it!"

"Here comes Doc now," Wheeler said, and Gannon glanced around to see the doctor hurrying toward them from Grant Street. There was a good-sized crowd now, and more miners had collected. He saw Blaisedell's back as Blaisedell walked away toward the General Peach.

Men moved aside to let the doctor through. His face was as white as MacDonald's. "This is your work, Wagner!" MacDonald cried, and his eyes rolled toward Gannon again. "He is responsible, Gannon! He put him to it!"

"Hush now," the doctor said. He put down his bag and bent to look at the wound in MacDonald's upper arm.

"Get him away from me! Lafe!"

"You had better wait until I've dressed this arm, hadn't you?" the doctor said, straightening. "Or would it serve you better if you bled to death?"

MacDonald swayed faintly, and Thompson caught his shoulder.

From the hotel porch Morgan's voice was raised tauntingly. "You muckers over there! How come you send a cripple to do a mob's work?"

"You are going to open your flap one too many times yet, Morgan!" a rough voice retorted.

"Is that you, Brunk?" Morgan called, and laughed.

"Brunk's not here. He is keeping company with McQuown and they will hang you yet!"

The doctor said, "Can a couple of you bring him over to the Assay Office?"

"Surely, Doc," Thompson said, and he and Wheeler picked up MacDonald in a cradle-carry. The crowd parted as they carried MacDonald off down the street, with Lafe Dawson and the doctor following them.

Gannon saw Pike Skinner looking at him worriedly. Then, in the silence, he felt all the eyes on him. With an effort he kept himself from glancing down toward the General Peach, where Tittle was, where Blaisedell had gone. He heard whispering, and heard Blaisedell's name. Peter Bacon, chewing upon a toothpick, was watching him with an expression of elaborate unconcern. Someone said, loud in the silence, "Never heard a man make such a fuss over getting shot."

Gannon took a long breath, and, as though he were preparing to dive into very deep, cold, dark waters, slowly turned toward the corner of Grant Street. He started forward and heard the sudden stir of whispering around him. He walked steadily on and the miners on the corner parted before him; there were more before the General Peach, and these also moved silently aside for him. A curtain twitched in the window of Miss Jessie's room, where Carl had died.

The door opened before he reached it, and Miss Jessie confronted him. She wore one of her white schoolgirl's blouses and a black neckerchief, a black skirt. In her face was superiority and dislike, determination and contempt. Behind her, in the dimness of the entryway, he could sense, rather than see, Blaisedell standing.

"Yes, Deputy?" Miss Jessie said.

"I've come for Tittle, Miss Jessie."

She merely shook her head at him, and the brown ringlets slid like live things along the sides of her head.

"He has shot and hurt MacDonald. I will have to take him up to jail for the judge to hear him."

"He is hurt himself. I will not let him be taken anywhere."

Gannon could see Blaisedell now, standing far back beside the newel post at the bottom of the stairs. "I guess I will have to see him, then, Miss Jessie."

"Will you force my house?" she said, very quietly, and she caught hold of the edge of the door as though to slam it in his face.

"Leave him in her custody, Deputy," Blaisedell said, in his deep voice. "He'll not be leaving here."

Gannon tapped his hat against his leg. This was not right, he thought; it did not matter that this was Miss Jessie Marlow, and Blaisedell behind her; it did not matter that it was MacDonald who was hurt, or that it was the crippled fellow who worked for Miss Jessie that had shot him. With growing anger he gazed back into Miss Jessie's contemptuous face. But he wished it had not happened this way.

Someone called his name. The judge came hurrying through the miners on the boardwalk, his crutch flying out and his body lurching so that he looked as though he would fall at every step. The judge waved a hand at him, and, panting, made his way up onto the porch. His hat had slipped forward over one eye. "Miss Jessie Marlow!" he panted. "The prisoner is released on your recognizance. Is that all right with you, ma'am? Fine!" he said, without waiting for an answer. He turned his sweating red face to Gannon. "Fine!" he said, more loudly, as though it were a command. "Now you help me down these steps, Deputy, before I break my neck!"

The judge swung around and tottered; Gannon caught his arm. "Come on!" the judge whispered. Gannon helped him down the stairs, and immediately the judge set out back along the boardwalk with his lurching, pounding gait. The miners stared at them expressionlessly as they passed.

They turned up Main Street under the arcade. "Come on, you damned fool!" the judge said. When they were alone and out of earshot of the men in the street he slowed his pace a little, panting again. "You will leave well enough alone!" he

said savagely. "Or I will take this crutch and club you senseless
—which you already are. Son, any kind of a damned fool ought
to know not to snatch at gnats when there's camels to be swallowed still!"

"I know what I have to snatch at. What am I supposed to
do, let any wild mucker that wants to shoot at MacDonald just
because nobody likes MacDonald?"

"Right now you are going to."

"You damned old fraud!"

"I am," the judge said. "I have admitted it a hundred times.
It is a time for fraud and not for bullheadedness. Son, I didn't
ever think it of you. Did MacDonald make a complaint against
him?"

"Not yet."

"You will anyhow wait till he does. And what will you do
then? Tittle has got a load of buckshot in him; will you haul
him to jail regardless?"

"She wouldn't let me see him even," Gannon said. His rage
was running out, but it did not change anything. He had
stood in the street where MacDonald had been shot and felt
the eyes upon him, and had known they thought to a man that
he would not go after Tittle because of Blaisedell. He would
not let it matter what they thought of him, John Gannon, but
it was time that it mattered what they thought of the deputy
sheriff in Warlock.

"Son," the judge said, almost gently. "Have you been watching Blaisedell these days? I thought you saw things. He will
step back so you can come forward, and God bless him for it.
But he is not going to step back *because* you have come forward. Don't you even think of trying to push on him."

"I was trying to arrest a man that assaulted another with a
deadly weapon in this town I am deputy in."

"Son, son," the judge said, in a tired voice. "It is like hearing
myself talk when I was young and thought there was nothing
but two ways about a thing. Do you know what I learned in
the war besides that a minie ball can take a leg off? I learned it
is better to swing around a flank than charge straight up a hill."

"Judge," he said. "I am going to stand up or I'm not. If I
did not go there after Tittle I backed down in every man's eyes.
And it was not just me that backed down."

"There is a time when a man does best to back down," the judge said, and evaded his eyes.

Gannon started on down toward the Assay Office, where there was another knot of men watching him come. The Judge crutched along beside him, grunting with the effort. Gannon knocked on the door of the doctor's office. It opened a crack and Dawson's scared face appeared. "What do you want?"

"I want to see MacDonald." Past Dawson he could see the doctor washing his hands in a crockery bowl. The doctor shook his head.

"Not now, Deputy. He's resting now. He has lost some blood."

"I want to see him as soon as he is able," he said, and Dawson nodded and closed the door. As he started on back to the jail Pike Skinner caught up with him and caught his arm, and he heard the crack of the judge's crutch behind him.

"Johnny, for Christ's sake!" Pike whispered. "Are you trying to get Blaisedell in a brace?"

"He has caught pride like a dose," the judge said.

Gannon swung around to face them. "It is not so, Judge," he said thickly.

"Listen!" Pike whispered. "Do you know what MacDonald did, Johnny? Went in the General Peach there and called Miss Jessie a whore to her face, and it a whorehouse! Johnny, any man'd done what that crippled one did. MacDonald is lucky Blaisedell wasn't there!"

Gannon looked from Pike's face to the judge's. His mind felt as though it would burst. It did not signify, he told himself. He walked slowly away from them, past Goodpasture's store, and across Main Street to the jail. He sat down heavily in the chair behind the table and stared at the sunlight that came through the door. Nothing was ever clear, everything was incredibly difficult, complex, and suspect; there was no right way. He sat in miserable loneliness contemplating himself and his deputyship. It was a long time before he heard footsteps on the boardwalk outside, and he supposed that it was Dawson coming.

Pike Skinner came inside, grinning. "MacDonald has skedaddled," he said. "Dawson went and got his buggy and brought it around just now, and they have lit out on the Bright's City road." He grinned more widely. "The judge said you might be pleased to hear it."

He didn't answer, and Pike's face stiffened. "What are you going to do, Johnny?"

He shook his head; relief made him feel giddy. "Why, nothing I guess. I guess there is nothing to do."

## 53. *At the General Peach*

### I

UPSTAIRS IN the General Peach a group of miners had collected in old man Heck's room. Heck was standing; his skinny neck stuck out as he spoke. "If there is any trouble we will stand behind Blaisedell," he said. "That's what we have to do, every man jack of us. He said to me there wasn't going to be any trouble and no reason looking for any, and how the deputy'd just left Ben in Miss Jessie's custody. But I notice Miss Jessie didn't look so sure. I told him we would stand right behind him all the way. It is something we got now."

"That deputy's gone and got too big for his britches," Bull Johnson said.

"Jimmy said MacDonald called Miss Jessie a whore," Frenchy Martin said.

They all looked at Fitzsimmons, who stood before the door. He placed one disfigured hand in the other and nodded.

"Why, God damn him!" Bull Johnson said, with awe in his voice. "He did? Did you hear him, Jimmy?"

Fitzsimmons told them what he and Ben Tittle had heard MacDonald say to Miss Jessie and the doctor.

"Dirty God-damned buggering rotten son of a bitch!" Bardaman cried. Patch added his curses, and each man cursed MacDonald in turn, formally, as though it were a kind of ritual.

"We should've burnt the Medusa long since!" old man Heck said. "And run MacDonald right out of the territory."

"It's not too late," Bull Johnson said. "There's matches still."

"Is Ben hurt bad, Jimmy?" Patch asked.

They all looked to Fitzsimmons again. "He has got some shot in him. In his legs mostly." Fitzsimmons looked as though he could hardly restrain a smile.

"I'll break Lafe Dawson in half!" Bull Johnson said.

Fitzsimmons laughed, then, and said, "Do you know what is funny? MacDonald thinks he is way ahead of us now."

"How's that, Jimmy?" Daley asked.

"Why, because Ben shot him. He thinks he can hold it up to everybody now how we are a bunch of wild men."

"What's so funny about that?"

"I believe," Bull Johnson said, squinting at Fitzsimmons. "I do believe that sonny-boy here is going to lecture the grownups again, and going around the barn to do it."

Fitzsimmons flushed. "Well, MacDonald does, and he is wrong. You fellows should have seen him downstairs. Miss Jessie asked him to his face if he'd got orders to settle, and you should have heard him yell. He yelled too much," he said, and grinned. "I would just make a bet he *had* got orders to settle, and he is scared to death we can sit him out. But now he thinks he is way ahead of us, on account of getting shot. Do you know the best thing that could happen to us? If Ben got taken to the judge and heard. And better yet if he got sent up to Bright's City to court. We would be the worst kind of tomfools to try to stop them from taking him out of here. Because then it would come out in court what MacDonald said to Miss Jessie. Threatening her like he did, and calling her what he did. You see?"

"I see we ought to cut his balls for him," Bardaman said uncertainly.

Fitzsimmons shook his head and leaned easily against the door. "No, for if we just tread soft for a while he has ruined himself for good. There'll be others to cut his balls for us when this gets out. And if it came to trial at Bright's! I expect Mister Mac might hear more from Willingham. People think high of Miss Jessie, and not just here. MacDonald is gone out in the bucket if we just play it right. If we can just last it out."

"I think maybe Jimmy is talking sense," Bardaman said.

"Good sense," Daley added quietly.

"By God, maybe we are not plowed under yet!" Patch cried.

Frenchy Martin leaned forward. "You think we might pull it off yet, eh, Jimmy?"

"I know so."

"What about the union, Jimmy?" Bardaman said. He leaned forward too. Old man Heck was scowling a little, and Bull

Johnson gnawed on a knuckle, but he was watching Jimmy Fitzsimmons too. They all watched him, waiting to hear what he had to say, and he smiled triumphantly from face to face, and began to speak.

II

In the hospital room, Ben Tittle lay on his cot like a bas-relief figure beneath the bedclothes. The whisky bottle the doctor had left was on the floor beside him. When Miss Jessie and Blaisedell appeared Tittle raised his head and grinned, showing crooked yellow teeth. The flesh on his bony face was an unhealthy, tender-looking white. "They going to hang me, Miss Jessie?" he said.

"No, they are not going to hang you, Ben," Miss Jessie said. She came forward to sit on the edge of his cot, while the marshal remained in the doorway.

"Why, heck, and I was just in the mood for a hanging, too," Tittle said. "Hello, Mr. Blaisedell." The drunken grin looked pasted to his face. He said in a quieter voice, "Mister Mac cashed in yet?"

"Nobody's heard," Blaisedell said.

"You are to quiet down, Ben," Miss Jessie said. "You have been drinking too much of that whisky. The doctor left it to stop the pain."

"What did you want to take a shot at MacDonald for, fellow?" Blaisedell asked gravely. "That didn't do anybody any good."

The pasted smile disappeared. Tittle pouted. "Well, I know what is owed around here, Mr. Blaisedell. Even if no other ungrateful mutts don't. I can pay my debts as well as any man."

Blaisedell frowned. Miss Jessie, however, patted Tittle's hand, and he seemed relieved. He lay back on his pillow with the smile returning.

"Why, I don't like to make trouble for nobody, Marshal," he said. "Excepting for a man who would talk to a lady like that. Said dirty things," he said, and his voice fell with embarrassment. Then his voice grated as he said, "I hope he goes out painful, if I get lawed for it or not."

"Said what things?" Blaisedell said.

"He threatened me, Clay," Miss Jessie said quickly. "For feeding them here."

"I know that. Said what dirty things, fellow?"

Cords drew tight in Tittle's neck as he raised his head again. "Why, I guess—I guess I knew it was your place, Marshal," he said. "But it come on me so, you see. But I guess you would have got him square, and finished him." He looked pleadingly at Miss Jessie. "Did I do wrong, ma'am?"

She patted his hand. "No, Ben."

"I did it for you. The only thing I ever found to show—" He stopped, and drew a deep breath and said, angrily now, "For all of us! And if I hang for it that is fine too, and little enough."

"We won't let them hang you, Ben," Miss Jessie said. She gazed at Blaisedell with her great eyes. Blaisedell moved aside as footsteps hurried down the hall and the doctor appeared. His gray, crop-bearded face was grim.

"MacDonald?" Blaisedell asked.

"He is all right," the doctor said. He stood frowning down at Tittle. "As a matter of fact he has left for Bright's City. Ben, you have not done the Medusa strikers much good today."

Ben Tittle laughed shrilly. "I run him out!"

"Maybe you did," the doctor said, but he shook his head at Miss Jessie, and strain showed suddenly in her face. "Well, I will give you a little laudanum, Ben," the doctor said. "And start picking the lead out of your hide." He put his bag down and rummaged through it. "Jessie, you had better leave."

Miss Jessie rose quickly. She went over to join Blaisedell, and took his arm as Tittle cried happily, "Go ahead and dig, Doc. A man can stand a lot to know that he has run Mister Mac out of Warlock!"

## 54. *Morgan Makes a Bargain*

MORGAN SAT in his chair in his room at the hotel, reading the magazine by the late sunlight that came in the window. From time to time he chuckled, and frequently he turned back to the cover where, on the cheap gray paper, there was a crude woodcut of a face that was meant to be his face. Beneath it was the inscription: *The Black Rattlesnake of Warlock.*

It was a narrow, dark face with Chinese-slanted eyes, a drooping mustache, and lank black hair combed like a bartender's. There was a wart high on the right cheek, close to the nose. Maybe it was only an ink smear, he thought, and brought the face closer to his eyes; it was a wart. He raised a hand to touch his own mustache, his own hair, his own cheek where the wart was shown. "Why, you devil!" he said, with awed hilarity. "The Black Rattlesnake of Warlock!" He whooped and beat his hand on his thigh.

He skipped rapidly through the account of the Acme Corral shooting again, grinning, shaking his head. "Well, that will teach them to stand around with their backs to the Black Rattlesnake," he said. There was a knock, and he rose and stuffed the magazine under his pillow. "Who's that?"

"It's Kate, Tom."

He stretched and yawned, and went to open the door. Kate came in. She closed the door behind her and he nodded approvingly. "Dangerous," he said. "Dangerous for anybody to know you are creeping in to see Tom Morgan. That's a handsome bonnet, Kate."

"Are you going?" she asked abruptly. Her eyes were very black in her white face, her jaw seemed set crookedly.

"Why, one of these days," he said. "When I get through bleeding Taliaferro. I will have the price of the Glass Slipper back from him before long."

"Where are you going?"

"North, or east. I might go west, though, or south. Or up, or down."

She seated herself on the edge of the bed. She said, "I know you killed McQuown."

"Do you? Well, you don't miss much, do you, Kate?"

"You did it so they would blame the deputy for it."

"Here! I don't give a damn about—"

"I know you did!" she said. She bit her lip, breathing deeply. "But it went wrong. People know you did it and they are saying Blaisedell sent you. It is so wonderful when some dirty thing you do goes wrong."

He sat down again, and propped his boots up on the bed beside her. "I know I am everything bad that's ever happened in this town. I've just been reading about it. Look under the pillow there."

She felt under the pillow as though there might be a rattle-snake there, which, in fact, there was. She looked at the picture on the cover without interest. After a moment she let the magazine drop to the floor.

"I'm famous, Kate!" he went on. "I'm probably the evilest man in the West." He felt his finger touch his cheek, where the picture had showed the wart. "Women will use me to scare their babies with."

"I know you killed McQuown," Kate said. "You did it for Clay, too, didn't you?"

"I forget *why* I did it, Kate. Sometimes I just can't keep track of why I do things." He took out a cheroot and scratched a match. He blew smoke between them and regarded her through the smoke as she slowly inclined her face down away from his eyes, to stare at her clasped hands in her lap.

"Tom," she said. "I will ask you to do something for me for once."

"What do you want? The Glass Slipper for you and Buck and Taliaferro to turn into a dance hall? It is in pretty poor shape."

"No, I don't want anything to do with a dance hall. I want you to do something for me. I am asking you a favor, Tom."

"Ask it."

She spoke rapidly now, and her voice sounded frail and thin. "You've heard about this afternoon. I don't know what happened exactly but—but all of a sudden everybody seems to know there is going to be trouble between the deputy and Clay."

He leaned back and blew more smoke between them.

"Not only that," Kate went on. "But there *is* talk you killed McQuown. Whether you did or not, there is talk."

"You are back on that again."

"Because I think—I think he has an idea you did it. He—"

"Who?"

"The deputy! I think he thinks you did it. I think he will be after you about it. Tom, don't you see that sets him against Clay *again*?" He watched her eyes begin to redden, and her nose. He took the cigar from his mouth and examined it. "I am not going to let Clay Blaisedell kill him!" Kate continued. Now she sounded as though she had a cold in her head.

"Another Bob Cletus," he said. "Well, I am nothing to do with it this time, Kate."

"You can stop Clay." Her eyes glistened with tears, and the tears made little tracks in the powder on her cheeks.

"Why, Kate, you have gone and got yourself in love with that ugly clodhopping farmer of a deputy. Again. What do you want to do, marry him and raise a brood?"

She didn't answer.

"Why, you pitiful old whore," he said, and it twisted within him like a big wrench forcing a rusty bolt.

"There is no word for you!" she whispered.

"Black rattlesnake?" he suggested. "Evilest man in the West?" He stopped; he did not know why he should suddenly feel so angry at her.

"Tom," she begged. "You could ask Clay the way I am asking you. How would it hurt you to do something for me? Make Clay go with you."

"He has got Miss Jessie Marlow to hold him. And she won't go; she is prime angel here."

"You could do something!"

"I might make a bargain with you."

"What?"

"Since your deputy is the only one that matters. If *you* went with me I might be able to do something."

He saw her close her eyes.

"I know you would like to marry up with a famous hardcase-killer, now that your deputy has got to be one. Like Miss Angel Marlow with Clay. But I have got to come out of it with *something*, so you and me is the bargain. Why, you would be a mistress to the evilest man in the West and famous in your own right. We will go around in sideshows and charge admission to see the worst old horrors there are, make a fortune at it. We'd make a pair."

She did not speak, and he went on. "If I can figure some way to get Clay out of line toward killing your deputy, this is. I might as well set it all out for you to agree to, or not. For instance, things might get bad from time to time so that we needed a stake. It would be up to you to apply yourself to your line of work and make us one. Now and then."

"Yes," Kate whispered.

His voice hurt in his throat; his grin hurt his face. "Well, and you would be party to my evil schemes. Murder people together, you and me. Rob stages. Corrupt innocent people to our evil ways—all that sort of thing."

She did not speak, but she was looking up at him. He rose to stand before her, and put a hand on her shoulder. "Why, Kate," he said shakily. "You act like you don't believe what I'm saying."

She shook her head a little.

"You have gone and got yourself in terrible shape over that deputy, haven't you? Pretty decent, is he, Kate?"

"I don't want to talk about him."

He took his hand from her shoulder. He felt as though he had been poisoned. "Not to me?" he said viciously. "Pretty good in your bed, is he? That lean, hungry-looking kind."

Slowly, silently, she bent her head still farther until all he could see was the top of her hat. "Tell me what you want, Tom."

"We'll make our bargain right here and now, then. You are sitting in the right place."

Sour laughter coiled and wrenched inside him as he watched one of her hands rise to her throat. It fumbled at the top cut-steel button of her dress. The button came open and her hand dropped to the second one. Her shoulders were shaking. "Oh, stop it," he said. "I don't want you."

He stooped and picked up the magazine, where she had dropped it. He rolled it and slapped it hard against his leg as he sat down in the chair again. Kate had not moved. Her hand fumbled at the top button again; then she folded her hands in her lap.

"You have touched my black heart," he said. When he re-leased his grip on the magazine it sprang open, but he did not want to see the picture again and he brushed it off onto the floor. He touched the place on his cheek. It occurred to him that he was making a mannerism of this, and it seemed strange that it should be like the one of Kate's he knew so well.

"So I have to give you Johnny Gannon for Bob Cletus," he said.

Her head jerked up, her wet eyes slid toward his. He said harshly, "Clay would no sooner go after him than—" He stopped.

"I am afraid Johnny will make him," Kate said. "Or—they will make him."

"They?"

She shrugged, but he nodded.

"*She*," he said. "More likely. Miss Angel," he said, nodding matter-of-factly. That would be it, although that was a part of it that Kate didn't know enough to worry about yet.

He said, "Well, Gannon for Cletus and square," and laughed a little. "All right, Kate."

"Thanks, Tom."

"Get out of here now. People will think you are not a lady."

Obediently she rose and moved to the door. She was very tall; with her hat on she was taller than he was. She looked back at him as she started to pull the door closed, and he said, "You don't need to worry, Kate. I expect Clay would rather shoot himself than your deputy."

The door shut her face from him. He sat slumped in the chair, chewing on his cigar and listening to her retreating footsteps. He was tired of it all, he told himself. He had no interest in Kate, less in her deputy; what did he care what happened to Clay? He did not care to see how it would all come out. Nothing ever ended anyway. He sat there brooding at the sun-lit window, sometimes raising a finger to his cheek with an exploratory touch. He was the evilest man in the West, he told himself, and tried to laugh. This time it would not come.

After a while he rose reluctantly. It was time to go and try himself against Lew Taliaferro again. Last night he had let Taliaferro beat him. But no one could beat him if he did not want it, and he was tired of that, too.


## 55. *Judge Holloway*

IN THE jail Judge Holloway sat at the table with his arms crossed on his chest and his whisky bottle before him, his crutch leaning against his chair. Mosbie sat with his hat tipped forward over his eyes. In the cell a Mexican snored upon the floor, and Jack Jameson, from Bowen's Sawmill, waited out his twenty-four hours looking through the bars. Peter Bacon whittled on a crooked stick in his chair beside the alley door.

Pike Skinner, standing with his hands on his hips, turned as Buck Slavin came into the doorway. Slavin was in his shirt-sleeves and wore a bed-of-flowers vest with a gold watch chain across it.

"Where is the deputy?" Slavin demanded.

"Rid out somewhere," Bacon said, without looking up from his whittling.

"Run with his tail between his legs," Jack Jameson said, from the cell. Everyone looked at him, and he winked dramatically, stooping to thrust his narrow, lantern-jawed face between the bars. "Run from the pure hypocritter of it," he said. "To see a man hoicked in the lock-up for drunk and disorderly by a judge with a whisky bottle tied on his face."

"You will have another twenty-four hours for contempt before you are through," the judge said mildly.

"Scaring all those poor girls at the French Palace with a mean old six-shooter," Mosbie said. "You ought to be ashamed, Jack."

"'Twasn't any six-shooter that scared them," Jameson said. "It was a dommed big gatling gun. By God, what's things come to when a man hasn't seen hide nor hair of a woman for two months and comes busting into town for it, and then has to spend the night with a puking dommed greaser."

"Rode out where?" Slavin said.

"What's fretting *you*?" Skinner said. "Somebody pop another stage?"

"They've popped enough, and I'm sick of it. It's God-damn time Gannon got out of town and did something about it!"

"Tell it to him to his face!" Skinner said angrily.

"I've told him to his face! I've told him he doesn't earn his keep here. He thinks he did his job forever, shooting Wash Haggin!"

The judge sighed and said, "Buck, let me tell you the sad, sad facts of life. There will be no justice for you or for those poor ranchers weeping over their lost stock, without cash paid on the barrelhead for it. You wail and gnash your teeth for policing, but are you willing to pay for it yet? Are those ranchers I hear screaming down there willing yet? How much louder will they wail and gnash when they see the tax collector coming?

Let me tell you, Buck; the deputy is doing his job exactly right. Those Philistines down there are going to be cleaned out when the sheriff is forced to do it, and that will be when the belly-aching gets so loud it hurts General Peach's ears."

"Seven stages thrown down on since McQuown got killed!" Slavin said. "When McQuown was—"

"McQuown!" Mosbie broke in, and, in a rasping voice, he cursed McQuown at length.

Jameson said, "By God if it don't look like everybody is escared of old Abe yet."

"Let him stay buried," Bacon said gloomily. "If he gets dug up he will stink to heaven."

"Morgan'll stink," Slavin said.

Skinner said uncomfortably, "I just don't see how everybody got so certain all at once it was Morgan did it."

"Johnny rode out to see Charlie Leagle," Bacon said.

"He supposed to've seen Morgan?" Slavin asked, and Bacon nodded.

"Supposed to be more than Leagle saw him," Mosbie said.

Skinner paced the floor with his hands locked behind his back. He glared at the names scratched on the wall; he swung around and glared at the judge, who had picked up the whisky bottle. "Well, tell us about it, you righteous old son of a bitch!" Skinner cried. "I remember how you used to blister Carl, and you are blistering kind of different lately. Tell us how Johnny has to go after Morgan if it looks like Morgan was the one! Tell us how Johnny has to yank Tittle out of Miss Jessie's place under Blaisedell's nose, if a warrant comes down. I saw you charging down to get him out of dutch with Blaisedell like you was trying to bust the pole-vault champeenship, you damned drunken fraud. Come on, tell us, Judge! You won't, will you? You are as sick as any man here, that used to preach at us till it came out our ears. Let's hear you preach now!"

The judge tipped his whisky bottle to his lips and drank.

"Has to pour whisky in itself before it can talk," Jameson commented.

"Shut up!" Skinner said. He leaned back against the wall with his arms folded.

But the judge did not speak, and Mosbie said, "Surely Johnny has got sense enough not to buck up against Blaisedell."

"Hasn't," Skinner said, "is the trouble." He glared at the judge. "Well, what do you say? Preach us about how he is only doing his damned duty!"

The judge nodded, and glanced up at Skinner from under his eyebrows.

"I noticed you stopping him from it the other day fast enough."

"Wheels within wheels," the judge said.

Skinner snorted. He swung around to face Slavin. "And you'd like to see him kiting off down valley so they could snipe him off from behind some rock. I suppose you can't see around a Concord far enough to see it is just what *they* want him to do."

"What they are doing," Bacon said. "They are using McQuown getting killed for an excuse for hell-roaring all over the place. So I expect Johnny figures maybe he can quiet them by sticking who did it."

"Which is Morgan," Mosbie said.

"It's a cleft stick for you," Bacon said, and shook his head.

"It is a cleft stick for Johnny Gannon," Skinner said. "Well, what do you say now?" he said to the judge. "Maybe you like all this?"

"No," the judge said thickly. "I don't like it, and don't you scorn me, you great lumbering lout! I wasn't liking it before you ever saw it."

"Say Morgan did it," Mosbie said, in his rasping voice. "Say he did and he is a dirty dog, and I won't deny it. But he is Blaisedell's friend, and I say this town owes Blaisedell one or two things, or two hundred—what he has done here. I say we can give him Morgan."

"Blaisedell has to go," Slavin said firmly. "Not just because of the friends he picks, either."

"Buck!" Mosbie said. "I want to hear you say out loud that Blaisedell has done no good here. I want to hear you say it."

"Why, I don't deny he has, fellows," Slavin said. "Nobody does. It is just time for him to move on, and mostly it is time because of Morgan."

"Tell you what you do, Buck," Skinner said. "Next meeting you make a motion he is to post Morgan out. Since you are starting to speak up so bold."

Slavin stood there biting his lip and frowning. "One thing," he said. "One thing I have got against Blaisedell that isn't Morgan. He makes people take sides hard against him or for him. He makes bad contention." He nodded to the others, turned, and departed.

"Well, I am for the marshal," Bacon said sadly. "But it certainly makes a man sick and tired—and makes him think. How Johnny is coming against him. Want it or not, looks like."

"Johnny can go his way and Blaisedell his," Skinner said. "I can't see why they can't go along and not scratch each other. Blaisedell has never made a move to set himself against Johnny. Not one!"

"I guess Johnny hasn't gone and made any move against Blaisedell, for that," Bacon said. "I guess it just looks like he is going to have to, one of these days."

"Over Morgan," Mosbie said.

"You boys are starting to make me feel real sorrowful over the deputy," Jameson said. "It looks like he is in dommed bad shape."

They all watched a fly circling in flat, eccentric planes over the judge's head. The judge waved it away. "It is the awkward time," he said. "It is where this town don't know yet whether it still needs a daddy to protect it, or not."

"You don't have to kick your daddy in the face when you have got your growth," Bacon said.

Jameson said, "You know what my old dad did to me once? I—"

"Shut up!" Skinner yelled at him.

Mosbie stirred in his chair. "There's some things I wish I knew about Johnny," he said. "I wish I knew how he felt about it when Blaisedell shot Billy. I wouldn't want to think—"

"He don't hold it against Blaisedell," Skinner said. "I can say that for sure."

Mosbie nodded.

Then Bacon spoke. "Man doesn't like to talk about him when he is not here," he said, in an embarrassed voice. "But there's something been bothering me too I'd better speak up about. Maybe somebody can—" He paused, and his wrinkled face turned pink. "Well, that Kate Dollar he is seeing pretty good. There is that talk how she is down on Blaisedell, and why, from Fort James. And Johnny seeing so much of her, you know."

"Set Johnny against the marshal, you think?" Skinner said worriedly. He began to shake his head. "I don't think—"

The judge slapped the palm of his hand down on the table. "If you boys would accept my judgment," he said. "I would say that Johnny Gannon wouldn't do anything any of you wouldn't, nor hold to a reason you wouldn't. And I would say he is more honest with himself than most, too."

Skinner was scowling. "Only—" he said, in a husky voice. "Only, God damn it to hell, if it comes to it, and pray God it don't, Blaisedell is the one I would have to side with. Because—"

"That's where you are wrong," the judge broke in. "Thinking you can put it so you are choosing between two men."

"Well, Judge," Skinner said. "Maybe us poor, simple, stupid common folks has to look at it that way. Us that sees more trees than forest."

"Yes, I suppose so," the judge said. He let his head hang forward; he gripped the neck of his whisky bottle. "But maybe you have to see by now that the deputy here is only doing what the deputy here is going to have to do."

Skinner's red gargoyle's face grew redder still, and deep corrugations showed in his forehead. He took a deep breath. Then he shouted, "Yes, I can see it! But damned if I want to!" He swung around and stamped out the door.

"He's one for getting upset," Jameson commented. "That one."

"You know what I get to thinking about?" Bacon said. "I get to thinking back on the old days in Texas droving cattle up to the railroad. Didn't own a thing in the world but the clothes I had on and the saddle I sat. So nothing to worry about, and nothing but hard work day in and day out sort of purifies a man. No forests there," he said, smiling faintly at the judge. "It is the forests that wear a man down dead inside, Judge."

"It is the lot of the human race," the judge said. He raised his bottle and shook it. Staring at the bottle he said, "And it is terrible past the standing of it. But I have here the universal solvent. For wine is the color of blood and the texture of tears, and you can drink it to warm your belly and piss it out to get rid of it. And forget the whole damned mess that is too much for any man to face."

"That's not wine," Jameson said. "That's raw whisky."

The judge looked at him with a bleared eye. "I will sleep in a cask of raw whisky," he went on. "Wake me up and pump me out when everyone is dead." His voice shook, and his hand shook, holding the bottle. "What are deputies to me?" he said hoarsely. "Deputies or marshals. They are nothing, and I will not be a hypocrite to sentimentality when I can drink myself above it all. Wake me up when they have killed each other off! Miner and superintendent, vigilante and regulator, deputy and marshal. They are as dead leaves falling and nothing to me. Nothing!" he shouted. He banged the whisky bottle down on the table top, raising it high and crashing it down again, his face twisting and twitching in drunken horror. "Nothing!" he shouted. "Nothing! Nothing!"

They watched him in awe at his grief, as he continued to cry "Nothing!" and bang the bottle. The Mexican's swollen, sleepy face appeared, a square below and to the right of that of Jameson, who whispered, "Listen to the dommed old bastard go!"

## 56. *Morgan Looks at the Cards*

I

SITTING IN the cane-bottomed rocker in the shade on the hotel veranda, Morgan sat watching Warlock in the morning. There were not many people on the street: a prospector with a beard like a bird's nest sat on the bench before the Assay Office; a white-aproned barkeep swept the boardwalk before the Billiard Parlor; a Cross-Bit wagon was pulled up alongside the Feed and Grain Barn, and Wheeler and a Mexican carried out plump bags which one of Burbage's sons stacked into the wagon-bed. To the southwest the Dinosaurs shimmered in the sun. They seemed very close in the clear air, but improbably jagged and the shadows sharply cut, so that they had a painted look, like a fanciful theater backdrop. The Bucksaws, nearer, were smooth and brown, and he watched a wagon train mounting the circuitous road to the Sister Fan mine.

He stretched hugely, sighed hugely. Inside the dining room behind him he could hear the tinny clink and clatter of dishes and cutlery; it was a pleasant sound. He watched Mrs. Egan bustling down Broadway with her market basket, neat and crisp in starched light-blue gingham, her face hidden in a scoop bonnet. He could tell from the way she carried herself that she was daring any man to make a remark to *her*.

He smiled, strangely moved by the fresh, light color of her dress. He had found himself thus susceptible to colors for the last several days. He had admired the smooth, dark, smoked tan of the burnt-out Glass Slipper yesterday, and the velvet sudden black of the charred timbers in it. Now on the faded front of the Billiard Parlor, where Sam Brown had taken his sign down to have it repainted, there was a rectangle of yellow where the paint had been hidden from the sun; yellow was a fine color. He had begun remembering colors, too; in his mind's eye he could see very vividly the color of the grass in the meadows of North Carolina, and the variety of colors of the trees in autumn—a thousand different shades; he remembered, too, the trees in Louisiana, the sleek, warm, blackish, glistening green of the trunks after it had rained and the sun had come out; and the trees in Wyoming after an ice storm in the sun, when all the world was made of crystal, and all seemed fragile and still; and he remembered the sudden red slashes of earth in west Texas where the dull plains began to turn into desert country.

"Pardon me if I take this other chair here, sir." It was the drummer who had come to town yesterday, and had the room across the hall from his. He sat down. He wore a hard-hat, and a tight, cheap, checked suit. He was smooth-shaven, with heavy, pink dewlaps.

"Fine morning," the drummer said heartily, and offered him a cigar, which he took, smelled, and flung out into the dust of the street. He took one of his own from his breast pocket, and turned and stared the drummer in the eye until he lit it for him.

"I wonder if you could point out Blaisedell for me, if he comes by," the drummer said, not so heartily. "I've never been in Warlock before and we've heard so much of Blaisedell. I swore to Sally—that's my wife—I'd be sure I saw Blaisedell so I could tell her—"

"Blaisedell?"

"Yes, sir, the gunman," the drummer said. He lisped a little. "The fellow that runs things here. That killed all those outlaws in the corral there by the stage depot. I stopped in there yesterday when I got in for a look around."

"Blaisedell doesn't run things here." He stared the drummer in the eye again. "*I* do."

The drummer looked as though he were sucking on the inside of his mouth.

"You can tell your wife Sally you saw Tom Morgan," he said. He felt pleased, watching the fright in the drummer's face, but his stomach contracted almost in a cramp. He flicked his cigar toward the drummer's checked trousers. "Don't go around here saying Clay Blaisedell runs Warlock."

"Yes, sir," the drummer whispered.

The water wagon passed on Broadway, Bacon sitting hunched on the seat, his whip nodding over the team. The rust on the tank shone red with spilled water. The red of rust was a fine color. When the water wagon had passed he saw Gannon coming toward him under the arcade.

"Get out of here," he said to the drummer. "Here comes another one that thinks he runs Warlock."

The drummer rose and fled; Morgan laughed to hear the clatter of his boots diminishing, watching Gannon coming on across Broadway. The sun caught the star on his vest in a momentarily brilliant shard of light. He came on up on the veranda and sat down in the chair the drummer had vacated.

"Morning, Morgan," he said, and nervously rubbed his bandaged hand upon his leg.

"Is, isn't it?" He crossed his legs and yawned.

Gannon was frowning. "Going to be hot," he said, as though he had just thought it out.

"Good bet." He nodded and looked sideways at Gannon's lean, strained face, his bent nose and hollow cheeks. He touched a finger gently to his own cheek, waiting for Gannon to get his nerve up.

"I've found two of them saw you coming back," Gannon said finally, "the morning after McQuown was killed."

He didn't say anything. He flicked the gray ash from his cigar.

"I heard you when you went by me," Gannon said, staring straight ahead. "Off to the east of me a way. I couldn't say I saw you, though."

"No?"

"I'd like to know why you did it," Gannon said, almost as though he were asking a favor.

"Did what?"

Gannon sighed, grimaced, rubbed the palm of his hand on his leg. The butt of his Colt hung out, lop-eared, past the seat of his chair; if he wanted to draw it he would have to fight the chair like a boa constrictor. "I think I know why," he went on. "But it would sound pretty silly in court."

"Just leave it alone, Deputy," Morgan said gently.

Gannon looked at him. One of his eyes was larger than the other, or, rather, differently shaped, and his nose looked like something that had been chewed out of hard wood with a dull knife. It was, in fact, very like the face of one of those rude *Christos* carved by a Mexican Indio with more passion than talent. It was a face only a mother could love, or Kate.

"Deputy," he said. "You don't hold any cards. You found two men that saw me riding into town, but I know, and you know, that as much as those people down the valley would be pleased if it turned out I had shot McQuown, they have jerked the carpet out from underneath it by all of them swearing up and down it was you that did it. They can't do anything but make damned fools of themselves, and you can't. So just sit back out of the game and rest while the people that have the cards play this one out. It is none of your business."

"It is my business," Gannon said.

"It is not. It's something so far off from you you will only hear it go by. Off to the east a way. You probably won't even hear it."

They sat in silence for a while. He rocked. Finally Gannon said, "You leaving here, Morgan?"

He gazed at the bright yellow patch over the Billiard Parlor.

"One of these days," he said. "A few things to tend to first. Like seeing to a thing for Kate."

He waited, but Gannon didn't ask what it was, which was polite of him. So he said, "She thinks you are about to choose Clay out. I promised I'd watch over you like a baby."

Gannon cleared his throat. "Why would you do that?"

Why, for one thing, he thought, because I saw you get that hand punctured by a hammer pin one night; but aloud he said, "You mean why would I do it for her?" He turned and looked Gannon in the eye. "Because she was mine for about six years. All mine, except what I rented out sometimes." He was ashamed of saying it, and then he was angry at himself as he saw Gannon's eyes narrow as though he had caught on to something.

"That's no reason," Gannon said calmly. "Though it might be a reason for you to kill Cletus."

It shook him that Kate should have told her deputy. Or maybe she hadn't, since it was something anybody could pick up at the French Palace, along with a dose. "That wasn't in your territory, Deputy," he said. "Leave that alone too."

Gannon looked puzzled, and Morgan realized he had been speaking of Pat Cletus. He felt a stirring of anxiety, and he thought he had better set Gannon back on his haunches. He stretched and said, "Are you going to make an honest woman of Kate, Deputy?"

Gannon's face turned boiled red.

Morgan grinned. "Why, fine," he said. "I'll sign over all rights to you, surface and mining. And give the bride away too. Or don't you want me to stay that long?"

Gannon turned away. "No," he said. "I don't want you to stay, since you asked."

"Running me out?"

"No, but if you don't get out I will have to take this I came to ask you about as far as it goes."

"And you don't want to do that."

"I don't want to, no," Gannon said, shaking his head. "And like you say I don't expect I'll get much of anywhere. But I will have to go after it."

"You could leave it alone, Deputy," he said. "Just stand back out of the way awhile. Things will happen and things will come to pass, and none of it concerns you or much of anybody else. I will be going in my own time."

Gannon got to his feet, splinter-thin and a little bent-shouldered. "A couple of days?" Gannon said doggedly.

"In my own good time."

Gannon started away.

"Don't post me out of town, Deputy," Morgan whispered. "That's not for *you* to do."

He regarded what he had just said. He had not even thought of it before he had said it; or maybe he had, and had just decided it.

But it was the answer, wasn't it? he thought excitedly. And maybe he could still keep the cake intact, and let the others think they saw crumbs and icing all over Clay's face. He began to check it through, calculating it as though it were a poker hand whose contents he knew, but which was held by an opponent who did not play by the same rules he did, or even the same game.

II

Later he sat waiting for Clay at a table near the door of the Lucky Dollar. He watched the thin slants of sun that fell in through the louvre doors, destroyed, each time a man entered or departed, in a confusion of shifting, jumbled light and shadow as the doors swung and reswung in decreasing arcs. Then they would stand stationary again, and the barred pattern of light would reform. During the afternoon the light would creep farther in over Taliaferro's oiled wood floor, and finally would die out as the sun went down, and another day gone.

He did not think he would do more today than test the water with his foot, to see how cold it was.

The pattern of light was broken again; he glanced up and nodded to Buck Slavin, who had come in. Slavin nodded back, hostilely. Look out, he thought, with contempt; I will turn you to stone. "Afternoon," Slavin said, and went on down the bar. Look out, I will corrupt you if you even speak to me. He could see the faces of the men along the bar watching him in the glass; he could feel the hate like dust itching beneath his collar.

From time to time Taliaferro would appear from his office—to see if he had begun to ride the faro game yet, and Haskins, the half-breed pistolero from the French Palace, watched him from the bar, in profile to him, with his thin mustache and the scar across his brown chin like a shoemaker's seam, his Colt thrust into his belt.

He nodded with exaggerated courtesy to Haskins, poured a little more whisky in his glass, and sipped it as he watched the patterns of light. He heard the rumble of hoofs and wheels in the street as a freighter rolled by, the whip-cracks and shouts. The sun strips showed milky with dust.

Clay came in and his bowels turned coldly upon themselves. He pushed out the chair beside him with a foot and Clay sat down. The bartender came around the end of the bar in a hurry with another glass. Morgan poured whisky into Clay's glass and lifted his own, watching Clay's face, which was grave. "How?" he said.

"How," Clay said, and nodded and drank. Clay grinned a little, as though he thought it was the thing to do, and then glanced around the Lucky Dollar. Morgan saw the faces in the mirror turn away. He listened to the quiet, multiple click of chips. "It is quiet these days," Clay said.

Morgan nodded and said, "Dull with McQuown dead." He supposed Clay knew, although there was no way of telling. Clay was turning his glass in his hands; the bottom made a small scraping sound on the table top.

"Yes," Clay said, and did not look at him.

"Look at scarface over there," he said. "Lew can't make up his mind whether to throw him at me or not."

Clay looked, and Haskins saw him looking. His brown face turned red.

"Before I go after Lew," Morgan said.

"I asked you to leave that alone, Morg."

He sighed. "Well, it is hard when a son of a bitch burns your place down. And hard to see the jacks so pleased because they think one of them did it."

Clay chuckled.

Well, he had backed off that, he thought. He said, "I saw Kate last night. She is gone on that deputy—Kate and her damned puppy-dogs. This one kind of reminds me of Cletus, too."

"I don't see it," Clay said.

"Just the way it sets up, I guess it is."

Clay's face darkened. "I guess I don't know what you mean, Morg. It seems like a lot lately I don't know what you are talking about. What's the matter, Morg?"

I have got a belly ache, he observed to himself, and my feet are freezing off besides. He did not think that he could do it now. "Why, I get to thinking back on things that have happened," he said. "Sitting around without much to do. I guess I talk about things without letting the other fellow in on what I've been thinking."

He leaned back easily. "For instance, I was just remembering way back about that old *Tejano* in Fort James I skinned in a poker game. Won all his clothes, and there he was, stamping around town in his lousy, dirty long-handles with his shell belt and his boots on—he wouldn't put those in the pot. Remember that? I forget his name."

"Hurst," Clay said.

"Hurst. The sheriff got on him about going around that way. 'Indecent!' he yelled. 'Why, shurf, I've been sewed inside these old longjohns for three years now and I'm not even sure I have got any skin underneath. Or I'd had them in the pot too, and then where'd we be?'

"Remember that?" he said, and laughed, and it hurt him to see Clay laughing with him. "Remember that?" he said again. "I was thinking about that. And how people get sewed up into things even lousier and dirtier than those long-handles of Hurst's."

He went on hurriedly, before Clay could speak. "And I was remembering back of that to that time in Grand Fork when those stranglers had me. They had me in a hotel room with a guard while they were trying to catch George Diamond and hang him with me. Kate splashed a can of kerosene around in the back and lit up, and came running upstairs yelling fire and got everybody milling and running down to see, and then she laid a little derringer of hers on the vigilante watching me. She got me out of that one. Like you did here, you and Jessie Marlow. I have never liked the idea of getting hung, and I owe Kate one, and you and Miss Jessie one."

"What is this talk of owing?" Clay said roughly. He poured himself more whisky. "You can take it the other way too, Morg

—that time Hynes and those got the drop on me. But I hadn't thought there was any owing between us."

No? he thought. It would have pleased him once to know that there was no owing between them; it did not please him now, for debts could be canceled, but if there were no debts then nothing could be canceled at all.

"Why, there are things owed," he said slowly. And then he said, "I mean to Kate."

Clay's cheeks turned hectically red. Clay said in an uncertain voice, "Morg, I used to feel like I knew you. But I don't know you now. What—"

"I meant about the deputy," he said. He could not do it. "She is scared," he said, and despised himself. "She is scared you and the deputy are going to come to it."

"Is that what you have been working around to asking me?"

"I'm not asking you. I'm just telling you what Kate asked me."

"There is going to be no trouble between the deputy and me," Clay said stiffly. "You can tell Kate that."

"I already told her that."

Clay nodded; the color faded from his cheeks. The flat line of his mouth bent a little. "Foolishness," he said.

"Foolishness," Morgan agreed. "My, I have a time saying anything straight out, don't I?"

Clay's face relaxed. He finished the whisky in his glass. Then he said abruptly, "Jessie and me are getting married, Morg. If you are staying maybe you would stand up for me?"

It seemed to him it had been a long time coming, what he knew was coming. But he would not stand up for Clay this time. "When?" he said.

"Why, in about a week, she said. I have to get a preacher down from Bright's City."

"I guess I won't be staying that long."

"Won't you?" Clay said, and he sounded disappointed.

He could not stay and stand up for Clay, and give the proper wedding gift to him and to his bride; not both. "No, I guess I can't wait," he said. "You will be married half a dozen times before you are through—a wonder like you. I will stand up for you at one of the others. Besides, there's an old saying—gain a wife and lose your friend. What a man I used to travel with said. He said he had been married twice and it was the same both times. First wife ran off with his partner, and number two got him worked into a fuss with another one—shot him and had to make tracks himself."

Clay was looking the other way. "I know she is not your kind of woman, Morg. But I'll ask you to like her because I do."

"I admire the lady!" he protested. "It is not every man that gets a crack at a real angel. It's fine, Clay," he said. "She is quite a lady."

"She is a lady. I guess I have never known one like her before."

"Not many like her. She is one to make the most of a man."

"I'm sorry you can't stay to stand for me."

"Not in Warlock," he said. "I'm sorry too, Clay." He wondered what Clay thought he wanted, married to Miss Jessie Marlow—to be some kind of solid citizen, with all the marshaling and killing behind him and his guns locked away in a trunk? He wondered if Clay knew Miss Jessie would not allow it, or, if she would, that the others would not. And what was he, Clay's friend, going to do? I will put you far enough ahead of the game, Clay, so you can quit, he thought. I can do that, and I will do it yet.

"Morg," Clay said, looking at him and frowning. "What got into you just now?"

Morgan picked up his glass with almost frantic hurry. "How!" he said loudly, and grinned like an idiot at his friend. "We had better drink to love and marriage, Clay. I almost forgot."

Grief gnawed behind his eyes and clawed in his thoat as he watched Clay's face turned reserved and sad. Clay nodded in acceptance and grasped his own glass. "How, Morg," he said.

III

When he returned to his room at the hotel it was like walking into a furnace. He threw the window up and opened the door to try to get a breeze to blow the heat out. He had started to strip off his coat when Ben Gough, the clerk, appeared.

"Some miner just brought this by and wanted to know was you here." Gough handed him a small envelope and departed. The envelope smelled of sachet, and was addressed in a thin, spidery script: *Mr. Thomas Morgan.* He tore open the flap and read the note inside.

June 1, 1881

Dear Mr. Morgan,

Will you please meet me as soon as possible in the little corral in back of "The General Peach," to discuss a matter of great importance.

Jessie Marlow

He put his coat back on, and the note in his pocket. He was pleased that she had sent for him—the Angel of Warlock summoning the Black Rattlesnake of Warlock. Probably she would tell him that what she wanted for a wedding present was his departure.

He went outside, across Main Street, and down Broadway. The sun burned his shoulders through his coat. It was the hottest day yet, and it showed no signs of cooling off now in the late afternoon. There were a number of puffy, ragged-edged clouds to the east over the Bucksaws, some with gray bottoms. When he reached the corner of Medusa Street he saw that one was fastened to the brown slopes by a gray membrane. It was rain, he thought, in amazement. He walked on down past the *carpintería* and turned in the rutted tracks that led to the rear of the General Peach.

There was a small corral there, roofed with red tile. He entered, removing his hat and striking a cobweb aside with it. There was a loud, metallic drone of flies. The June-bride-to-be was sitting on a bale of straw, wearing a black skirt, a white schoolgirl's blouse, and a black neckerchief. She sat primly, with her hands in her lap and her feet close together, her pale, big-eyed, triangular face shining with perspiration.

"It was good of you to come, Mr. Morgan."

"I was pleased to be summoned, Miss Marlow." He moved toward her and propped a boot on the bale upon which she sat; she was a little afraid he would get too close, he saw. "What can I do for you, ma'am?"

"For Clay."

"For Clay," he said, and nodded. "My, it is hot, isn't it? The kind of day where you think what is there to stop it from just getting hotter and hotter? Till we start stewing in our own blood and end up like burnt bacon." He fanned himself with his hat, and saw the ends of her hair moving in the breeze he had created. "Clay has told me you are being married," he said. "I certainly wish you every happiness, Miss Marlow."

"Thank you, Mr. Morgan." She smiled at him, but severely, as though he were to be pardoned for changing the subject since he was observing the amenities. Each time he talked to her she seemed to him a slightly different person; this time she reminded him of his Aunt Eleanor, who had been strict about manners among gentlefolk.

"Mr. Morgan, I am very disturbed by some talk that I have heard."

"What can that be, Miss Marlow?"

"You are suspected of murdering McQuown," she said, staring at him with her great, deep-set eyes. He saw in them how she had steeled herself to this.

"Am I?" he said.

He watched her maiden-aunt pose shatter. "Don't—" she said shakily. "Don't you see how terrible that is for Clay?"

"There is always talk going around Warlock."

"Oh, you must see!" she cried. "Don't you see that it is bad enough that people should think he had something to do with your going down there and—and— Well, and even worse, that—"

"Why, I don't know about that, Miss Marlow. I am inclined to think that whoever killed McQuown did Clay a favor. And you."

"That is a terrible thing to say!"

"Is it? Well, Clay might be terrible dead otherwise."

She opened her mouth as though to cry out again, but she did not. She closed it like a fish with a mouthful to mull on. He nodded to her. "McQuown was coming in here with everything Clay would have had a hard time turning a hand against. I don't mean a bunch of cowboys dressed up to be Regulators, either. I mean Billy Gannon and most of all I mean Curley Burne."

"They were dead," she whispered, but she flinched back as he stared at her and he knew he had been right about Curley Burne.

"Dead pure as driven snow," he said. "Curley Burne, that is, and Billy Gannon not quite so pure but maybe pure enough because of the talk going around Warlock. McQuown was coming in with that and he could have come alone, only he didn't know enough to see it. Clay would have been running yet. But since he wasn't coming alone Clay didn't have to run, and he may be the greatest nonesuch wonder gunman of all time but he wouldn't have lasted the front end of a minute against that crew. The man who shot McQuown did him a favor. And you."

He heard her draw a deep breath. "Then you did kill McQuown," she said, and now she was severe again, as though she had gotten back on track.

He shrugged. Sweat stung in his eyes.

"Well, that is past," she said, in a stilted, girlishly high voice. "It cannot be undone. But I hope I can persuade you—" Her voice ran down and stopped; it was as though she had memorized what she was going to say to him in advance, and now she realized it did not follow properly.

"What do you want, Miss Marlow?"

She didn't answer.

"What do you want of him?" he said. "I think you want to make a stone statue of him."

She looked down at her hands clasped in her lap. "You cannot think me strange if I want everyone to think as highly of him as I do."

It was fair enough, he thought. It was more than that. She had cut the ground right out from beneath him with the first genuine thing she had said. She smiled up at him. "We are on the same side, aren't we, Mr. Morgan?"

"I don't know."

"We are!" Still she smiled, and her eyes looked alight. She was not so plain as he had thought, but she was a curious piece, with her face not so young as the dress she affected and the style of her hair. But her eyes were young. Maybe he could understand why Clay was taken with her.

"What if we are?"

"Mr. Morgan, you must know what people think of you. Whether it is just or not. And don't you see—"

He broke in. "People don't think as highly of him as they should. Because of me."

"Yes," she said firmly, as though at last they had come to terms and understood one another. "And everyone is too ready to criticize him," she went on. "Condemn him, I mean. For men are jealous of him. Too many of them see him as what they should be. I don't mean bad men—I—I mean little men. Like the deputy. Ugly, weak, cowardly little men—they have to see all their own weaknesses when they see him, and they are jealous—and spiteful." She was breathing rapidly, staring down at her clasped hands. Then she said, "Maybe I understand what you meant when you implied he would have been helpless against McQuown, Mr. Morgan. But he is helpless against the deputy, too, because you killed McQuown for *him*, and the deputy is in the right pursuing it."

Her eyes shone more brightly now. There were tears there, and he turned his face away. He had thought he could be contemptuous of her because of the different poses she affected —the faded lady, the maiden aunt, the innocent schoolgirl, the schoolmarm. What she was herself was lost among the poses, and must have been lost years ago. It did not matter to him that there was something piteous in all this, but he was shaken by the sincerity that shone through it all. He had not stopped to think before that she must love Clay.

"He will attack Clay through you," she went on. "He will do it so that Clay will either have to defend you or— Oh, I don't know what!"

He did not speak and after a moment she said, as though she were pleading with him, "I think we are on the same side, Mr. Morgan. I can see it in your face."

What she had seen in his face was the thought that he would rather have someone like Kate scratch his eyes out than Miss Jessie Marlow kiss them. But he could not scorn her concern for Clay. He sighed, removed his foot from the bale, and stood upright to light a cigar. He frowned at the match flame close to his eyes. She must think she was handling him as she would a bad actor among her boarders. "Well," he said finally. "I guess I have a lien to pay off on that buggy ride, don't I? What do you want? Me to pack on out?"

She hesitated a moment. She licked her lips again with a darting movement of her tongue. "Yes," she said, but he had seen from her hesitation that there was more to it and it angered him that she might be one step ahead of him. But he nodded.

"So, since I am going anyway . . ." he said. He drew on the cigar and blew out a gush of smoke. She was working up one of her inadequate little smiles.

He finished it. "He might as well post me out."

"Yes," she said, in a low voice. She took a handkerchief from her sleeve and touched it to her temples. Then she wound it around her hand.

"I'd already thought of that. There is only one thing wrong with it."

"What, Mr. Morgan?"

"Why, I don't expect he'd want to. I don't know if you'd understand why he wouldn't want to, but I am afraid it would take some doing. What am I supposed to do?"

"Oh, I don't know! I—"

"It would have to be something pretty bad," he broke in. He eyed her with an up-and-down movement of his head. She flushed scarlet, but she was watching him closely nevertheless. There was no sound but the buzzing of the flies, and a creaking of buggy wheels in Grant Street.

Finally she said, "Will you try to do something, Mr. Morgan? For my sake?"

"No," he said.

She looked shocked. She flushed again. "I mean for his sake."

"If I can think of something." All of a sudden rain splattered on the tile roof, with a dry, harsh sound like a fire crackling. He glanced up at the roof; a fine mist filtered through the cracks, cool upon his face. Miss Jessie Marlow was still staring at him as though she hadn't noticed the rain.

"Just one thing," he said. "Saying I can think of something and they post me, and I run from him like the yellow dog I am. Afterwards can you let him be?" His voice sounded hoarse. "Can you let him bank faro in a saloon or whatever it is he wants to do? Can *you* let him be? There'll be others that won't, but if you—"

"Why, of course," she said impatiently. "Do you think I would try to force—" She stopped, as though she had decided he had insulted her.

"Did you hear Curley Burne turning in his grave just now?" he said, and she flinched back from him once again as though he had slapped her. He saw the tears return to her eyes. But he said roughly, "You have been telling me a lot of things I ought to see—but you had better see this will be a place he can stop. If he wants to stop I will put it on you to let him. Understand me now!"

Her expression showed that she was not going to quarrel with him, and, more than that, that she thought she had cleverly brought him to the idea of getting himself posted. He had been considering it all day, but it cost nothing to let her think there was no man she couldn't get around.

The rain rattled more sharply on the tiles, and she seemed to become aware of it for the first time. "Why, it's raining!" she cried. She clapped her hands together. Then she got to her feet and put out a hand to him. He took it and she gripped his hand tightly for a moment. "I can promise you that, Mr. Morgan!" she said gaily. "I knew we were on the same side. Thank you, Mr. Morgan. I know you will do your part beautifully!"

He gaped at her. She sounded as though he had promised to play the organ at her wedding and did not know how, but would learn, for her. He laughed out loud and she looked momentarily confused. But then she gathered up her skirts and ran out of the corral and through the pelting rain toward the back steps of the General Peach. She ran as a young girl runs, lightly but awkwardly.

He put on his hat and went out into the rain, and his cigar sizzled and died. The rain beat viciously down on his hat and back from an oyster-colored sky. It made craters in the dust where it fell, and muddy puddles spread in the ruts. He walked back to the Western Star Hotel in the rain.

## 57. *Journals of Henry Holmes Goodpasture*

June 3, 1881

IT HAS been most oppressively hot this last week or ten days, as though the sun were burning each day a little closer to the earth. Then this afternoon it rained, a brief and heavy downpour that turned the streets to mud. By tomorrow the mud will be gone, and the dust as fine and dry as ever. Yet we will have a spring: here there is a miniature spring of green leaves and blossoms appearing after any rain. This should cheer us, for all have been tense, or listless.

Six weeks have passed since Whiteside made his promise to us. Buck feels we should set out immediately to put our threats into effect, but I have instead written a strong letter to Whiteside saying that in one more week we will do so. I am sure my further threats are worthless, but it allows me to procrastinate. Hart, more honest than I, readily admits he has no stomach for another journey to Bright's City.

The Sister Fan has had to put on a night crew. The water struck there at the lower levels has become a problem of increasing dimensions. They have a fifty-gallon bucket to bail out the excess and men must be kept working night and day to stay abreast of the flow. Godbold, the superintendent, says it looks as though expensive pumping machinery will have to be brought in. The Medusa strikers are, the doctor says, in despair over this (as they were previously over a rumor that Mexicans were to be brought in to work the idle Medusa), feeling that the Porphyrion and Western Mining Co. will not attempt to settle the strike until it is seen how grave is the water problem at the Sister Fan.

All is quiet in the valley. The Cowboys, now apparently led by Cade and Whitby, have, according to report, descended into Mexico on a rustling and pillaging expedition. This is looked upon as foolhardy at the present time, since the border is supposedly under close surveillance.

It is whispered that a board cross appeared briefly upon McQuown's grave, with the inscription "murdered by Morgan." In a way, I think, people have come to fear Morgan as they once feared McQuown. It is an unreasonable thing, and I suppose it is closely akin to the passions aroused in a lynch mob. Somehow he stands convicted of the murder of McQuown, and other murders as well, by some purblind emotionality for which there seems little basis in fact.

There is talk of bad blood between Gannon and Blaisedell, this stemming, evidently, from the encounter they had when the miner who shot MacDonald took refuge, himself wounded, in the General Peach. No one seems to know what actually passed between them, but I have found from long experience that much smoke can be generated here from no fire at all.

The human animal is set apart from other beasts by his infinite capacity for creating fictions.

I must say that I myself have felt it necessary to change my own opinions of the deputy to a degree. I feel he is an honorable, though slow-moving man—a plodder. He has taken on a certain stature here—proof of which lies in the pudding of the speculation and of contention regarding him. He has become what none of the other deputies here has ever been—except possibly, and briefly, for Canning—a man to reckon with.

MacDonald is in Bright's City. I suspect he will soon return, and I suspect that he is plotting reprisal. He is indeed hot-headed enough to seek illegal means of punishing the strikers, who I am sure he feels conspired to take his life by means of a hired assassin. If he is fool enough, however, to attempt to convene his erstwhile Regulators again to this purpose, he will find an angry town solidly aligned against him. MacDonald has no friends in Warlock.

So life in Warlock, with terrors more shadows at play upon the wall than actuality. The atmosphere remains a charged one, yet I wonder if it is not merely something that will go on and on without ever breaking into violence; if it is not, indeed, merely part of the atmosphere of Warlock, with the dust and heat—

I spoke too soon. Another drought is ended. A gunshot; I think from the Lucky Dollar.

June 4, 1881

It is uncertain yet what provoked the shooting last night in the Lucky Dollar. Will Hart, who was present, says that Morgan suddenly accused Taliaferro of cheating, and, in an instant, had swung around and shot a half-breed gunman named Haskins through the head, and swung back evidently with every intention of shooting Taliaferro, who, instead of drawing his own pistol, sought to flee, and, on his hands and knees, was crawling to safety through the legs of the onlookers. Morgan, instead of pursuing him, had immediately to face the lookout, who had brought his shotgun to bear. All this, says Hart, took place in an instant, and Morgan was cursing wildly at Taliaferro for his flight and calling upon the lookout to drop his weapon, which order the lookout had the courage to ignore, or more probably, Hart says, was too paralyzed to comply with. The situation remained in this deadlock while Taliaferro made good his escape, and until Blaisedell, who had previously been present but had absented himself for a stroll along Main Street, burst back in.

Blaisedell immediately commanded Morgan to drop his six-shooter, although, Hart says, Blaisedell did not draw his own. Morgan refused and abused Blaisedell in vile terms. Blaisedell then leaped upon his erstwhile friend and wrested his weapon from him, upon which, Morgan, evidently surprised by Blaisedell's quick action and further infuriated by it, closed with the Marshal and a violent brawl ensued. Evidently Morgan sought to cripple Blaisedell a dozen times by some villainous trick or blow, but Blaisedell at last sent him sprawling senseless to the floor, and then carted him off for deposit in the jail as though he had been any drunken troublemaker.

Last night the town was in part aghast, in part wildly jubilant, and the rumor sprang up immediate and full-blown that Blaisedell had posted Morgan out of town—people here are apt to forget that it is the Citizens' Committee who posts the unworthy, not Blaisedell himself. The judge, however, was promptly summoned to hear Morgan on the murder of Haskins. Morgan claimed he had caught Taliaferro using a stacked deck. This is a strange argument. No doubt it is true, but in these engagements between master gamblers, such as the one that has been in progress for some time between Taliaferro and Morgan, it is clear to all that stacked decks are being used and the whole basis of the game becomes Taliaferro's cunning in arranging a deck against Morgan's cunning at ferreting out the system used. It has been said that Morgan was surpassingly clever at guessing Taliaferro's machinations previous to this, but that for the last two days he has been losing heavily. Morgan also claimed that Haskins had, as Taliaferro's gunman, attempted to shoot him in the back. Will says he could not have known this without eyes in the back of his head, but Morgan's statement in this regard was supported by Fred Wheeler and Ed Secord, who swore that Haskins had indeed drawn his six-shooter as soon as Morgan had accused Taliaferro of cheating, and showed every sign of aiming a shot at Morgan. The judge could do nothing but absolve Morgan for the death of

Haskins, and although Morgan had clearly been bent upon Taliaferro's speedy demise, he had been thwarted in this, and was culpable of nothing by our standards of justice, except creating a disturbance, for which he was given a night in jail.

Gannon seems to have arrived in the Lucky Dollar while Morgan and Blaisedell were seeking to maim each other, but was fittingly non-participant throughout. I think it can be said of him that he knows his place.

The hearing over, members of the Citizens' Committee met stealthily to discuss the situation, and to remind ourselves that on the occasion of Blaisedell's first encounter with McQuown and Burne, Blaisedell had warned the outlaws in violent terms against starting gunplay in a crowded place, where there was danger to innocent bystanders; the parallel was clear. Still in cowardly secrecy, a general meeting was called at Kennon's livery stable. The secrecy was necessitated by the fact that we were not sure what Blaisedell's attitude toward his friend now was, but we were one and all determined to seize the occasion at its flood and post Morgan out of Warlock, if possible. All were present except for Taliaferro, who was not sought, and the doctor and Miss Jessie, who, it was felt, would make us uncomfortable in our plotting.

It was speedily and unanimously decided that Morgan should be posted. His actions had constituted, we told ourselves, exactly the sort of threat and menace to the public safety with which the white affidavit was meant to deal. The problem lay only in advising Blaisedell of our decision. It might suit him exactly, some felt, while others were afraid it would not suit him at all. Still, there are members of the Citizens' Committee, whose names I shall not mention here, who, in the past weeks and even months, have become restive over Blaisedell's high salary, or wish him gone for other reasons. They now began to speak up, each giving another courage, or so it seemed—I will not say more about them than that Pike Skinner had to be forcibly restrained from striking one of the more outspoken. Their attitude in general was that if Blaisedell refused to honor our instructions to post Morgan out, as he had done in the case of the miner Brunk, then he should resign his post. In the end their view carried, and I am sorry to say that I, in all conscience, felt I had to agree with them. Blaisedell is our instrument. If he will not accept our authority, then he must not accept our money.

The meeting was adjourned, to be reconvened this morning with Blaisedell instructed to attend. He came, much bruised around the face, but he was not told he was to post Morgan out of Warlock. It was he who did the speaking. He said he was resigning his position. He thanked us gravely for the confidence we had previously reposed in him, said that he hoped his fulfillment of his duties had been satisfactory, and left us.

Warlock, since this morning, has been as silent as was the Citizens' Committee when we heard his statement. I think I am, ashamedly, as disappointed as the rest, but I know I think better of Blaisedell than I have ever before. It was clear that he knew exactly what was our intention at the meeting, and, since he did not wish to do it, saw that he must resign. There was no reproach evident in his demeanor. We will reproach ourselves, however, for what was said of him the night before. And I respect him for not wishing to post his friend from Warlock; I think he has acted with honor and with dignity, and I have cause to wonder now if this town, and the Citizens' Committee, has ever been worthy of the former Marshal of Warlock.

## 58. *Gannon Speaks of Love*

GANNON LAY fully clothed on his bed and contemplated the darkness that enclosed him, the barely visible square of vertical planes that were the walls marred here and there by huddled hanging bunches of his clothing, and the high ceiling that was not visible at all, so that the column of darkness beneath which he lay sprawled seemed topless and infinitely soaring. He had been forced out of the jail tonight not by any danger, but only because there were too many people there endlessly and repetitiously talking about Morgan and Blaisedell, Blaisedell and Morgan, and he did not want to hear any more of it.

Yet even now he could hear the excited murmur of voices from one of the rooms down the hall, and he knew that throughout Warlock it was the same, everyone talking it over and over and over, changing and fitting and rearranging it to suit themselves, or rather making it into something they could accept, angrily or puzzledly or sadly. Each time they would come to the conclusion that Blaisedell had better move on, but, having reached that conclusion, they would only start over again. He, the deputy, he thought, must not enter their minds at all; nor could he see in the black blank of his own mind what his part was. He had come, finally, almost to accept what Morgan had said to him—that it was not his business.

He heard the upward creaking of the stairs, and then Birch's high voice: "Now watch your step, ma'am. It is kind of dark here on these steps."

He started up, and groped his way to the table. His hand encountered the glass shade of the lamp; he caught it as it fell. He lit a match and the darkness retreated a little from the sulphur's flame, retreated farther as the bright wedge mounted from the wick. As he replaced the chimney there was a knock. "Deputy!" Birch said.

He opened the door. Kate stood there in the thick shadows; he could smell the violet water she wore. "Here is Miss Dollar to see you," Birch said, in an oily voice.

"Come in," he said, and Kate entered. Birch faded into the darkness, and the steps creaked downward. The voices in the room down the hall were still. Kate closed the door and glanced around; at his cartridge belt hanging like a snakeskin from the peg beside the door, at the clothes hanging on their nails, at the pine table and chair and the cot with its sagging springs. Lamplight glowed in a warm streak upon her cheek. "Sit down, Kate," he said.

She moved toward the chair, but instead of seating herself she put her hands on the back and leaned there. He saw her looking around a second time, with her chin lifted and her face as impassive as an Indian's. "This is where you live," she said finally.

"It isn't much."

She did not speak again for a long time, and he backed up and sat down on the edge of the bed. She turned a little to watch him; one side of her face was rosy from the lamp and the other half in shadow, so that it looked like only half a face. "I'm leaving tomorrow," she said.

"You are?" he said numbly. "Why—why are you, Kate?"

"There is nothing here for me."

He didn't know what she meant, but he nodded. He felt relief and pain in equal portions as he watched her face, which he thought very beautiful with the light giving life to it. He had never known what she was, but he had known she was not for him. He had dreamed of her, but he had not even known how to do that; his dreams of her had just been a continuation of the sweet, vapid day and night dreams embodied once in Myra Burbage, not so much because Myra had been attractive to him as because she was the only girl there was near at hand; knowing then, as he knew now, that there would be no woman for him. He was too ugly, too poor, and there were too few women ever to reach down the list of unmarried men to his name.

"You're going with Morgan?" he asked.

Her face looked suddenly angry, but her voice was not. "No, not Morgan. Or anybody."

He almost asked her about Buck, but he had once and she had acted as though he were stupid. "By yourself?" he asked.

"By myself."

She said that, too, as though it should mean something. But he felt numb. What had been said was only words, but now the realization of the actuality of her leaving came over him, and he began to grasp at the remembrance of those times he had seen her, as though he must hold them preciously to him so that they would not disappear with her. He had, he thought, the key to remember her by.

"When?" he said.

"Tomorrow or— Tomorrow."

He nodded again, as though it were nothing. He could hear the roomers talking down the hall again. He rubbed his bandaged hand upon his thigh and nodded, and felt again, more intensely than he had ever felt it, his ineptness, his inadequacy, his incapacity with the words which should be spoken.

"I guess I didn't expect anything," Kate said harshly. "I guess you are sulking with the rest tonight."

"Sulking?"

"About Blaisedell," she said, and went on before he could speak. "I was the only one that thought it was wonderful to see," she said in a bitter voice. "For I saw Tom Morgan try to do a decent thing. I think it must have been the first decent thing he had ever tried to do, and did it like he was doing a dirty trick. And had it fall apart on him. Because Blaisedell was too—" Her voice caught. "Too—" she said, and shook her head, and did not go on. Then she said, as though she were trying to hit him, "I'm sorry you feel cheated."

"You think if Blaisedell had posted him he would have gone?"

"Of course he would have gone. He was trying to give Blaisedell that—so people would think Blaisedell had scared him out. I think it's funny," she said, but she did not sound as though she did.

They were talking about Blaisedell and Morgan like everyone else, and he knew she did not want to, and he did not want to.

He looked down at his hands in his lap and said, "I'd thought you might be going with Morgan."

"Why?"

"Well, I talked to him. He said you'd been his girl but that you were through with each other. But I thought you might have—"

"*I* told you I'd been his girl," Kate said. Then she said, "Did he tell you more? I told you more, too. I told you what I'd been."

He closed his eyes; the darkness behind his eyes ached.

"I guess I am still," her voice continued. "Though I don't have to work at it any more, since I've got money. That came from men." Again she spoke as though she were hitting him. She said, "I'm damned if I am ashamed of it. It is honest work and kills no one. What are you waiting for, a little country girl virgin?"

Now he tried to shake his head.

"Why, men marry whores," she said. "Even here. But not you. And not me. There is nothing here at all for me, is there?" Her voice began to shake and he looked up at her and tried to speak, but she rushed on. "So I have been a whore by trade," she said. "But I can love, and I can hate by nature. But you can't. You just sit and stare in at yourself and worry everything every way so there is no time nor place for any of that. Is there?"

"Kate," he said in a voice he could hardly recognize. "That is not so. You know well enough I have loved—"

"Don't say that!" she broke in fiercely. Her face looked very red in the lamplight, and her black eyes glittered. "I have never heard you lie before and don't start for me. I know you haven't been to the French Palace," she said, "because I asked." She said it cruelly. "I wanted to know if you were waiting for a little country virgin or not. And I—"

"That's not so, Kate!" he cried in anguish.

Slowly the lines of her face relaxed until it was as gentle and full of pity as that of the little madonna in her room. He had never seen it this way before. "No," she said gently. "No, I guess it isn't. I guess you thought going to a whore wasn't right. And I guess you thought that about me, too."

"Kate—I guess I knew you felt—kindly toward me. I kind of presumed you did. I'm not a fool. But Kate—" he said, and couldn't go on.

"But Kate?" she said.

"Well, this is where I live."

He waited for a long time, but she did not speak. When he looked up he saw the harsh lines around her mouth again. He heard the rustle of her garments as she moved; she clasped her hands before her, staring down at him, her eyes in shadow.

"Another thing," he said. "You have been in the jail and seen those names scratched on the wall there." He took a deep breath. "There was something Carl used to say," he went on. "That there wasn't a man with his name on there that didn't either run or get killed. And Carl used to say who was he to think he was any different? And that he wouldn't run. I think he even knew who was going to kill him."

"I've got money, Deputy," Kate said. "Do you want to come with me? Deputy, this town is going to die and there is no reason for anybody to die with it. I am asking you to take the stage to Bright's City with me tomorrow. Out of here, out of the territory."

"Kate—" he groaned.

"Do you want to, or not?"

"Yes, but Kate—I can't, now."

"Killed or run!" she cried. "Deputy, you can run with me. I have got six thousand dollars in the bank in Denver. We can—"

She stopped, and her face twisted in anger and contempt, or grief. "What kind of a fool am I?" she said, more quietly. "To beg *you*. Deputy, you can't give me anything I haven't had a thousand times and better. I can give you what you've never had. But you will lie down and die instead. Do you want to die more?"

"I don't want to die at all. I only have to stay here." He beat his bandaged hand upon his knee. "Anyway till there is a proper sheriff down here, and all that."

"Why?" she cried at him. "Why? To show you are a man? I can show you you are more a man than that."

"No." He got to his feet; he rubbed his sweating hands on his jeans. "No, Kate, a man is not just a man that way. I—"

"Because you killed a Mexican once," she broke in. Her tear-shining eyes were fastened to him. "Is that why?"

"No, not that either any more. Kate, I have set out to do a thing." He did not know how to say it any better. "Well, I guess I have been lucky. That's part of it, surely. But I have made something of the deputy in this town, and I can't leave it go back down again. Not till things are—better. I didn't drop it a while back when I was afraid, and, Kate, I can't now because I would rather go off with you"—he groped helplessly for a phrase—"than anything else in the world."

He wet his dry lips. "Maybe to you Warlock is not worth anything. But it is, and I am deputy here and it is something I am proud of. There are things to do here yet that I think I can do. Kate, I can't quit till it is done."

He saw her nod once, her face caught halfway between cruel contempt and pity. He moved toward her and put out a hand to touch her.

"Don't touch me!" she said. "I am tired of dead men!" She stepped to the door and jerked it open. The bottom of her skirt flipped around the door as she disappeared, pulling it half closed behind her.

He took up the lamp and followed her, stopping in the hall-way and holding the lamp high to give her a little light as she hurried down the stairs away from him, and, when she was gone, stared steadily at the faces that peered out at him from the other doorways until the faces were drawn back and the doors closed to leave him alone.

## 59. *Morgan Shows His Hand*

MORGAN STOOD at the open window with his tongue mourning after a lost tooth and the night wind blowing cool on his bruised face. The night was a soft, purplish black, like the back of an old fireplace, the stars like jewels embedded in the soot. He stood tensely waiting until he saw the dark figure outlined against the dust of the street, crossing toward the hotel. Then he cursed and flung his aching body down into the chair, and took out a cigar. His hand shook with the match and he felt his face twisting with a kind of rhythmic tic as he listened to the footsteps coming up the stairs, coming along the hall. Knuckles cracked against the panel of his door. "Morg."

He waited until Clay rapped again. Then he said, "Come on in."

Clay entered, taking off his hat and bowing his head as he passed through the doorway. There was a strip of court plaster on his cheek, and his face was knuckle-marked enough. Morgan looked straight into his eyes and said, "You damned fool!"

"What was I supposed to do?" Clay said, closing the door behind him. "Post you out because you were going anyhow?"

The blue, violent stare pierced him, and his own eyes were forced down before it. "Why not?"

"Would you kill two men to serve a trick like that, Morg?"

"Why not?" he said again. His tongue probed and poked at the torn, pulpy socket. "One," he said. "I had to take scarface first and Lew crawled for it." With an effort he looked back to meet the blue gaze. "I told you I couldn't let a man get away with burning me out!"

"I asked you to leave that alone."

"Post me then, damn you!"

Clay moved over to sit on the edge of the bed, with his shoulders slumped and his face sagging in spare, flat planes. He shook his head. "I couldn't anyhow. I am not marshal any more."

"Well, I will back a play I have made. I don't go unless you post me."

Clay shrugged.

"What would it cost you? It might win you something."

"No."

"What does Miss Jessie Marlow say?"

Clay frowned a little. He said in a level voice, "What would you try to do this for, Morg?"

Because I never liked to look a fool, he thought. He had never hated it so much as he did now. "God damn it, Clay! A whole town full of clodhopping idiots aching for you to play the plaster hero for them one time again, and post out the Black Rattlesnake of Warlock. Which is me. And why not? It would have pleased every damned person I know of here except maybe you. Maybe you are yellow, though—a damned hollow, yellow Yankee. I hate to see you show it for these here!"

"They can have it that way if they want it. I have quit."

"You could have posted me and quit after the big pot when I'd run."

"It wasn't a game to cheat and make a fraud of," Clay said. His face looked pasty pale beneath the bruises. He shrugged again, tiredly. "Or maybe it was and it took a thing like this to show me. And maybe if it could be that, it is time and past time to quit."

"Clay, listen. I am sick to death of this town! I am sick of sitting in the Lucky Dollar taking Lew's money away, I am dead sick of watching the gawps from the chair on the veranda. I want to get out of here! It was a good reason for me to get out of here. I am trying to tell you it would have pleased everybody, me included. Now you are a damned has-been and a fool besides." And you have not quit, he added, to himself; now you have not, whatever you think.

"Why, I have pleased myself then," Clay said. He said, quietly, "What are you so mad about, Morg?"

He sat slumped down in his chair with his cold cigar clenched between his teeth. For whom was he doing this, after all? To please himself, was it? At least he wanted a live plaster saint rather than a dead one, and for that he had done what he had done, and for that he would do more. For whom? he wondered. It stuck now to try to say it was for Clay.

"Mad?" he said. "Why, I am mad because I have looked a fool. I am mad because I am used to having my way. I will have my way this time. If you won't post me for that, I will—" He stopped suddenly, and grinned, and said, "I will ask you for it for a favor."

Clay looked at him as though he were crazy.

"For a favor, Clay," he said.

Clay shook his head.

"Then I will see what it takes. Do you think I can't make you do it?"

"Why would you?" Clay said.

"I said I will have my way!" He felt his fingers touch his cheek, and the tic convulsed his face again.

"I have quit," Clay said. "I will post no man again, nor marshal again." He held his hand up before his face and stared at it as though he had never seen it before. "What is all this worth?" he said, in a shaky voice. "What is all this foolish talk? What's my posting you out of Warlock worth to anybody?"

"It is worth something to me," he said, under his breath.

"What are you trying to make of me?" Clay went on. His voice thickened. "You too, Morg! Not a human being at all, but a damned unholy *thing*—and a fraud of a thing in the end. No, I have quit it!"

"Do it for me, Clay," he said. "For a God-damned favor. Post me out and turn me loose. I am sick to death of it here. I am sick of you."

He saw Clay close his eyes; Clay shook his head, almost imperceptibly. He continued to shake it like that for a long time. He said, "Go then. I don't have to post you so you can go. I—"

"You have to post me!"

"As soon as I did you would walk the street against me."

"I've told you I wasn't a stupid boy to play stupid boys' games!"

"I don't know that many of them was stupid boys," Clay said. "But every time now it is that way. If I posted you out for whatever reason you made me—no sooner it was done than you would come against me. No, God, no!" he groaned, and slapped his hand hard against his forehead. "No, no more! What have I done that I was made to shoot pieces off myself forever? No, I have done with it, Morg!"

"Clay—" he started. "Clay, what are you taking on like this

for? All I am asking is post me and I will get out of town on the first stage or before it. Good Christ! Do you think I am fool enough to—"

"I will not!" Clay said. His lips were stretched tight over his teeth, and his face looked pitted, as though with some skin disease.

Morgan got up and stood with his back to him. He could not look at that face. He said, "If you had been any kind of marshal here you would have posted me before this. But I guess you couldn't see the hand in front of your nose. That everybody else saw."

"What?" Clay asked.

"You should have posted me for killing McQuown, for one. If you had been any kind of marshal."

Clay said nothing, and he felt a dart of hope. "If you had been any kind of marshal," he said again, "which was supposed to be your trade, but I guess you did not think so much of your trade as you liked to make out. And before that. Those cowboys that stopped the Bright's City stage didn't kill Pat Cletus."

"I don't believe that, Morg," Clay said, almost inaudibly. Then he cleared his throat. "Why?"

Morgan swung around. "Because Kate was bringing him out here to show me she had another Cletus to bed her, as big and ugly as the first one. I am tired of watching that parade. Do you think I like her throwing every trick she has rutted with in my face?" His heart beat high and suffocating in his throat as Clay raised his head, and the blue stare was colder than he had ever seen it before. Then, almost in the same instant, it seemed to turn inward upon itself, and Clay only looked gray and old once more.

Do you have to have more? he cried, to himself. For maybe the curse upon him was that now even the truth itself would not be enough. He said calmly, "Why, then, if you will have more I will tell you why Bob Cletus came after you in Fort James."

Clay's head jerked up, and Morgan laughed out loud, proud that he could laugh.

"Are you listening, Clay?" he said. "For I will tell you a bedtime story. Do you know why he came after you? Because he wanted to marry Kate, the son of a bitch. And the bitch—she told him I might make trouble, and he had better see me. So he came to see me. You didn't know you killed Cletus over Kate, did you?"

"Kate?" Clay said; his eyes had a pale, milky look.

"I told him it wasn't me he had to worry about, it was you. You. For you had been rutting Kate and you were jealous by nature and no man to fool with. He was mad because she hadn't told him about you, so I told him if he wanted Kate he had better get you before you got him, and sent word round-about to you that he was out—"

His breath stopped in his throat as Clay got to his feet. But Clay only went to stand at the window. He leaned one hand upon the sash, staring out.

When Morgan spoke again his voice had gone hoarse. "By God, it was the best trick I ever pulled," he said. "It made you a jackass and him a dead jackass—and Kate—" He stopped to catch his breath again. "Do you know what has always eaten on me? That nobody knew how I had served you all. It was a shame nobody knew. But how I laughed to think of Cletus jerking for that hogleg like it was a fence-post stuck in his belt. And you—"

Clay faced him. "He never did draw," Clay said. "I don't think he ever meant to. You are lying, Morg." There was a little pink in his face and his expression was strangely gentle. "Why, Morg, are you trying to give me that, too? I don't need that any more." Then his eyes narrowed suddenly, and he said, "No, it is not even that, is it? You are telling me something to kill you for, not post you."

"I told you I don't play boys' games!"

"Stop playing this one."

"It is so, God damn you to hell!"

"Why, I expect part of it is," Clay said. "I knew you had been in on it, for I have seen you chewing yourself. I expect you told him something like that to scare him so he would let Kate be. Not thinking he would come to me, though maybe you fixed it so that cowboy told me he'd heard Cletus was after me on account of Nicholson and I had better watch out—just in case Cletus did decide to make trouble. But I don't believe he meant to draw on me; he just wanted to find out about Kate when he called after me. I was just edgy about any friends of

Nicholson's, was all, and thought he was out for blood." He stopped, and his throat worked as he shook his head. "It is not so, Morg."

Morgan stared back at him. Strangely it did not shake him that Clay had known, or guessed; he only felt dazed because he could not see what he could do next. He had chewed the end of his cigar to shreds, and with an uncertain movement he took it from his lips. He flung it on the floor. Clay said, "Once I would've wanted pretty bad to think what you just told me was so. But it was more my fault than it was yours. Whatever you did."

"I served you up!" Morgan cried. He could feel the sweat on his face. "Hollow!" he cried. "Hollow as a damned plaster statue."

"It doesn't matter any more," Clay said. "If it hadn't been Bob Cletus dead to teach me a lesson, it would have been another. I learned that day a man could be too fast. I thought I had learned it," he said.

"Damn you, Clay!" he whispered. All at once there was nothing in the world to hold to except this one thing. "Damn you! I will have my way!"

Clay shook his head almost absently. "Do you know what I wish?" he said. "I wish I was some measly deputy in some measly town a thousand miles away. I wish I was not Clay Blaisedell. Morg, you have killed men for my sake—Pat Cletus and McQuown that I know of. But I can't thank you for it. It is the worst thing you have done to me, because it was *for* me, and I am more of a fraud of a thing than I knew. Morg—we think different ways, I guess." He took up his hat; he turned his face away. When he went out he pulled the door quietly but firmly closed behind him.

"Don't you have the dirty rotten gall to forgive me, damn you to hell!" Morgan whispered, as though Clay were still present. "You didn't take that away too, did you? You didn't take that!" He put his hands to his face; his mouth felt stretched like a knife wound. A burst of laughter caught and froze in his bowels like a cramp. "Well, I am sorry, Miss Jessie Marlow," he said aloud. "But he was iron-mouthed beyond me." You took me to the last chip, Clay, and won my pants and shirt too, and my longjohns are riveted on and too foul to bear. He shook his head in his hands. He would rather Clay had shot him through the liver than say what he had said, as he had said it, meaning what he had meant by it: *We think different ways, I guess.*

He pressed his hands harder to his aching face, suffocating in the sour, dead stench of himself. It was a long time before he remembered that he was lucky by trade, and that no one had ever beaten him.

## 60. *Gannon Sits It Out*

THE SUN was standing above the Bucksaws in the first pale green light of morning as Gannon came like a sleepwalker along the echoing planks of the boardwalk, along the empty white street. The inside of the jail was like an icehouse, and he sat at the table shivering and massaging his unwashed, beard-stubbled face. He felt sluggish and unrested, and his blood as slow and cold in the morning chill of the adobe as a lizard's blood.

He sat staring out through the doorway at the thin sunlight in the street, waiting for the sounds of Warlock waking and going about its Sunday business, and waiting especially for the sound of the early stage leaving town. Today, like every other day, the sun would traverse its turquoise and copper arch of sky; a particular sun for a particular place, it seemed to him, this sun for this place bounded by the Bucksaws and the Dinosaurs, illuminating indiscriminately the righteous and the unrighteous, the just and the unjust, the wise and the foolish. Shivering in the cold he waited for Warlock to waken, and for Kate Dollar to leave, examining the righteousness that both moved and paralyzed him, the injustice he had performed upon himself because of his love of justice. He called himself a fool and prayed for wisdom, and saw only that he could not change his mind, for nothing was changed. He felt as though he were a monk bound to this barren cell by some vow he had never even formulated to himself. He thought of the end of the vow that Carl had known, and accepted. Maybe the only thing changed now was that that end was so much harder to accept.

The first sound he heard was a horn blowing a military call. It was faint, but clear and precise in the thin air—as out of place and improbable as though a forest with stream, moss, and ferns had showed itself suddenly in the white dust of the street. He did not move, holding his breath, as though he had mistaken the sound of his breathing for that other sound. After a while it came again, a bugle call signifying what, rallying or commanding what, he did not know. The brassy notes hung in the air after the call had ended. He rose and moved to the doorway. A Mexican woman with a black *rebozo* over her head came down Southend Street, and Goodpasture's *mozo* appeared, broom in hand, to speak to her as she passed, and then turned and leaned on the broom and stared east up Main Street.

He went back inside the jail and sat down again. Once he thought he heard the sound of hoofbeats, but it was faint, and, when he listened for it, inaudible, as though it had only been some kind of ghostly reverberation along his nerves. He began to think he had heard the bugle only in a half-dream, too. Immediately the brassy, shivering call came again, close now, a different call this time, and now when he hurried out the door there were many people up and down the street, all staring east.

Back of the Western Star he could see the cloud of tan dust rising, and he could hear the hoofs clearly as the dust rolled nearer. Preceding it, riders wheeled into Main Street on the road from Bright's City. There were ten or twelve of them, in dusty blue and forage caps, one with the fork-tailed pennon on a staff. They came down Main Street at a pounding trot, looking neither right nor left as men hurried out of the street before them, the leader with three yellow Vs on the sleeve of his dark blue shirt, and a dusty-dark, mustachioed face beneath the vicious-looking, flat-vizored cap; the second man holding the pennon staff, and, next to him, the bugler with rows of braid upon his chest. He watched them pass him, and another group appeared, far up the street. The first group trotted to the end of town, wheeled about, and halted. The second turned south down Broadway. A third did not come into Main Street at all, but trotted dustily on past it. Another bugle sounded and more cavalry appeared, this time a much larger body and a mixed one, for there were civilian riders in it. Frozen into his eye for an instant was the image of a huge, uniformed man in a wide, flat hat with one side pinned up, and a white beard blown back against his chest.

Pike Skinner came running across Main Street toward him, shoving his shirttails down into his pants. "What the hell is this, Johnny?"

He could only shake his head. The main body came slowly down Main Street, to halt before the burnt shell of the Glass Slipper. One of the civilians rode on toward him; it was Sheriff Keller. He reined up and dismounted, heavily, and dropped his reins in the dust. Grunting, he mounted the boardwalk, and with a sideways glance at Gannon stamped on into the dimness of the jail. There he slumped down into the chair at the table as Gannon followed him inside. The sheriff wiped his face and the back of his neck with a blue handkerchief and squinted at Pike, who stood in the doorway.

"Glad to've seen you, *hombre*," he said blandly, and made a slight movement with his head.

Pike started to speak, but changed his mind and went out. Down the street someone was yelling in a brass voice that was drowned in another sudden pad of hoofs.

Gannon felt a sudden wild and rising hope that this was to be some kind of ceremony investing a new county. "What's the cavalry down here for, Sheriff?"

The sheriff rubbed his coarse-veined red nose. The plating was worn from his sheriff's star and the brass showed through. "What we forget," he said slowly, staring at Gannon with his flat eyes. "We get to thinking the general runs things. But there is people to run him too."

The hope burst in him more wildly still; but then the sheriff said, "Gent named Willingham. Porphyrion and Western Mining Company, or some such. There is a flock of wagons coming down."

"Wagons?"

"Wagons for miners to ride in."

"Miners?" he said, stupidly.

"Over to Welltown to the railroad," the sheriff said. He sucked on his teeth. "And out," he said, jerking his thumb east. "Out of the territory. Troublemaking miners," he said, nodding, pursing his lips, scowling. "Ignorant, agitating, murdering foreigners, and a criminal conspiracy, what the general's general says. Willingham, that is." He sighed, then he scowled at Gannon. "This Tittle a friend of yours too, son? That was what tore it."

A crutch-tip cracked on the planks. Judge Holloway came in, red-faced and panting. "Oh, it's you, Keller!" the judge said. "Oh, you have come down to Warlock at last, have you?"

"Uh-huh," Keller said. "Sit," he said, vacating the chair grudgingly, and moving his bulk to the other. The judge sat down. His crutch got away from him, and clattered to the floor.

"Will you tell me what damned dirty devilment is going on here, Keller?"

"Run out of Apaches," the sheriff said. His fat face looked tired and disgruntled. In the street Gannon saw a man running, looking back over his shoulder. He started out. "Here!" Keller barked. "Come back here, boy! You are going to have to pay this no mind."

"Pay what no mind?"

"What are you saying about Apaches, Keller?" the judge said.

"Why, they are all cleaned out, so now it is Cousin Jacks to take out after. New flag; it has got Porphyrion and Western wrote on it. Wagons coming. All those striking ones are going to get hauled up to Welltown and a special train is going to haul them back east somewheres and dump them."

"MacDonald," the judge whispered.

"Why, surely, MacDonald. Only he has got his big brother along, name of Willingham. Out from Frisco. Willingham has thrown a scare into old Peach something terrible."

The judge began to hawk as though he would strangle. The sheriff rose and pounded him on the back. "Son," he said to Gannon. "You should have snatched down on that Tittle, what you should have done. You let me down, boy, and I got ordered down here the same as some tight-britches trooper." He pounded the judge on the back once more, and then reseated himself. Gannon leaned back against the wall.

"They can't do it!" the judge cried. "He is crazy!"

"Didn't you people down here in Warlock know that? But he can surely do it. Colonel Whiteside was arguing and stamping

around, how he couldn't do it; and Willingham giving it to him he had damned well better. I heard Whiteside telling him Washington'd have his ears for it. But when Peach gets a bee in his bonnet he moves and if you think he can't do it, you just watch him."

Keller took off his hat, ran a hand back over his head, sighed, and said, "Whiteside is a nice old feller for a colonel, and thinks high of Peach too. He says all he wants is for Peach to go out well thought of, which he is near to doing—and this will ruin him for sure. But Peach thinks how Willingham can do him some good in Washington some way, and anyway Willingham is claiming this is armed rebellion against the U.S. down here, and up to Peach to stop it. Why, they are going to round up these jacks like a herd of longhorns and ship them out in cattle cars, and it is a crying shame." He extended a long, spatulate finger. "But judge," he said, "and boy: there is nothing to do about it."

The judge slid the drawer open against his belly and worked his bottle of whisky out of it. He cracked it down on the table before him. He said, "We are overrun with Philistines!"

"Save some of that for me," the sheriff said. "I rid drag all the way down here."

Gannon leaned against the wall and stared at the sheriff's face. "What are you here for, Sheriff?"

The sheriff took the bottle the judge handed him, and drank. His belly began to shake; he was laughing silently. He handed the bottle back and winked. "Why, I am to clean things out down here," he said. "You and me, son. Why, we are to fill up one of those wagons ourself. Road agents, rustlers, murderers, and such trash; we are to round up a bagful. Old Peach heard somewhere that things've got a little out of hand down here."

Gannon turned to watch a squad of cavalry ride slowly by, spaced to fill the street from side to side, carbines held at the ready. "Blaisedell," the sheriff said, and laughed.

Gannon's head swung back. He heard the judge draw in a sharp breath. The sheriff's belly shook again with silent laughter. "Shoot him down like a dog if he don't go peaceable," the sheriff said. "And that's when I unpinned this wore-out old badge here and handed it in. And said I had just *re*tired, being too old for the job."

"Great God!" the judge said.

"MacDonald said how Blaisedell went and interfered with Johnny here in the performance of his duty, which was Tittle," Keller went on. "Only that's not all of it. Peach don't like anything about Blaisedell. Blaisedell's been stealing his thunder. There is a lot of bad things being said about Blaisedell now, too, to give the crazy old horse his due. Some talk he went down and settled McQuown kind of backside-to."

"It is a lie!" the judge said, wearily. "Well, what happened? I see you have your badge back. Did you decide to shoot him down?"

"Worked out so I don't have to," Keller said, grinning. "Whiteside talked him some turkey on that one. Told him how Blaisedell was held innocent up in court, and how Peach would just make him more of a thing down here than he is already if he tried to run him out, and Blaisedell got shot or *I* got shot. What he said to do was, since the Citizens' Committee down here had hired Blaisedell and they wanted a town patent pretty bad, was tell them they could have it if they got rid of Blaisedell. It was slick to see Whiteside getting around him on that, and it worked too. Except—" He looked suddenly depressed. "Except if he don't go, it is back to me again. But I can always resign," he said, brightening. "Pass over that bottle again, will you, Judge?"

The judge handed it to him. "We are a bunch of vile sinners," he said in a blurred voice. "But I am damned if we deserve this. What about Doc Wagner, Keller? Does Peach mean to have him transported too?"

"Yep," the sheriff said. "Now, you just sit down, Judge. There is not a thing in the world you can do. Johnny!" he snapped. "Don't sneak that hand up there to be unpinning that star, or I will load you on my wagon first off and you will wait it out in the hot sun till I catch the rest, which might be a while. Now you just calm yourself. All the arguing and maneuvering to be done's been done already. I have seen Peach take out after Whiteside with that sword of his, fit to take his head off. Don't go trying to interfere with him."

"He can't do that to those poor damned—"

"He can," the sheriff said. "What was you going to do to stop it, son?"

Peter Bacon stuck his head in the door. "Johnny, are you going to stand by and let those blue-leg sons of bitches—" He stopped, staring at the sheriff. "My God, are you here, Keller?" he said, incredulously.

"I'm here," the sheriff said. "And how's things going out there?"

Peter's brown face wrinkled up as though he were going to cry. "Sheriff, they are rounding up those poor fellows from the Medusa like—"

"Going well, huh?" the sheriff said. "Well, drop in some later and see us again, Bacon. Pass me that bottle, Judge."

Peter stared at the sheriff, and turned and looked Gannon up and down. Then he withdrew. Keller tilted the bottle to his lips. Gannon saw the sheriff's hand, lying on the table before him, clench into a fist as there was a burst of shrill shouting down the street.

Gannon started toward the door.

"Don't even look, boy," the sheriff said heavily. "You might turn into a pillar of salt or something."

"Salt's not what I'm worth. Or you."

"I know it, boy. I never said otherwise. But you can't interfere with the cavalry, and the military governor. During maneuvers," he added. "That's what they are calling it; maneuvers."

"And you are supposed to maneuver down to San Pablo?" the judge asked.

"Supposed to. I guess I won't rush things, though."

"You might do well to rush. From what we hear they are all down raiding the Hacienda Puerto range right now."

"Rush," the sheriff said, nodding. Then Keller looked at Gannon again with his sad eyes. "Nothing you can do, boy," he said. "Nor any man. Just stand steady and let it go by. He's put his big foot in it now, and who knows but things might change, maybe, because of this."

"I have thought," the judge said bitterly, "that things were so bad they couldn't get any worse. But they have got worse today like I wouldn't believe if I didn't hear it going on. And maybe there is no bottom to it."

"Bottom to everything," the sheriff said, holding up the bottle and shaking it. Through the door Gannon watched a young lieutenant cantering past on a fine-looking sorrel, followed by a sergeant. He slammed his hand against his leg.

"Hold steady now," the sheriff said.

"Yes, learn your lessons as they come your way," the judge said. "And when you have learned them all they can stick red-hot pokers in your wife and babies and you will only laugh to see it. Because you will know by then that people don't matter a damn. Men are like corn growing. The sun burns them up and the rain washes them out and the winter freezes them, and the cavalry tramps them down, but somehow they keep growing. And none of it matters a damn so long as the whisky holds out."

"This here's gone," the sheriff said. "Go cut some of that corn and stir up some more mash, Judge. Say, did you people get any rain down this way?"

A rumble of bootheels came along the boardwalk. Old man Heck came in the door, his chin whiskers bristling with outrage, and Frenchy Martin and four others, of whom Gannon recognized only one named Daley, a tall, mild, likeable miner. Then he saw the doctor, with a trooper holding his arm. The doctor's face was grayer than ever, but his eyes were bright. There followed two other troopers, a sergeant, and Willard Newman, MacDonald's assistant at the Medusa, who shouldered his way inside past troopers and miners.

"Deputy, these men are to be locked up until the wagons get here."

"Lick-spittles, all of you!" the doctor said.

"Now, Doc, that don't do no good," Daley said.

"MacDonald is afraid to look me in the face so he sends his lick-spittles!"

Daley thrust himself between the doctor and Newman, as Newman cursed and raised a hand. "You!" the sergeant said, to Newman. "You mistreat the prisoners and I'll drink your blood, Mister!"

"That's the sheriff!" one of the miners said, and Gannon saw Keller's face redden. The doctor moved stiffly inside the cell, and the others followed him.

"I hope you soldiers are proud of your uniforms today!" the judge said, raising his voice above the shuffling of boots.

"You should be in here with me, George Holloway!" the doctor called, standing with the miners in the cell. "This is a thing every man who likes to think himself of a liberal persuasion should know for himself. We belong—"

"I will stay out and drink myself to death instead," the judge said, with his head bent down.

"Lock them up, Johnny," the sheriff said. He held the bottle up, studied it, and then handed it back to the judge.

Newman kicked the door shut.

"I'll not!" Gannon said, through his teeth.

The sergeant turned to look at him; he had a sour, weather-beaten face and thick graying sideburns. Newman glared at him. "Lock them up, Deputy!"

"By whose orders?"

"General Peach's order, you fool!" Newman cried. "Will you lock these sons of bitches up before I—"

"Not in my jail!" He thrust between the sergeant and New-man, snatched the key ring from its peg, and retreated to stand against the wall where the names were scratched. He put his hand on the butt of his Colt. The sheriff stared at him; the judge averted his face.

The sergeant sighed and said, "Mick!" One of the troopers raised his carbine and started forward. Someone burst in the door behind him.

It was a miner Gannon didn't know; he had gnarled, dis-colored hands and a stubble of beard on his long, young face. He stopped for a moment, panting; then he thrust one of the troopers aside and leaped forward to hit Newman in the face with a long, awkward sweep of his arm. Newman yelled and fell back the length of the room, while the sheriff came to his feet with surprising swiftness and slammed the barrel of his Colt down above the young miner's ear. The miner crumpled and fell, just as Newman, cursing, regained his balance and pulled the six-shooter from his belt. "Here!" the sergeant bellowed, and there was an outcry from the cell. Gannon jerked his Colt free and stepped toward Newman. The trooper named Mick caught the miner by the collar as he scrambled to his feet, and, with the sheriff's help, thrust him into the cell with the others.

Newman backed up, staring at Gannon's Colt. The sheriff came toward Gannon, pushed the gun barrel down with his fat hand, and took the key ring. The sheriff shook his head at him reprovingly. Newman's nose was bleeding.

"Let's get on, Mr. Newman," the sergeant said, and New-man cursed and replaced his own six-shooter in his belt. He stamped on outside, holding a handkerchief to his nose. Gannon leaned against the wall and watched in silence and despair as the sergeant detailed one of the troopers to guard the cell, and, with the others, followed Newman outside. The one who remained stood before the cell door, scowling uneasily. The sheriff put the key ring on the table, and the judge hung it over the neck of the whisky bottle and brooded down at it.

The miners were whispering together in the cell as Gannon returned his Colt to its scabbard. "That was a foolish thing, Jimmy," he heard the doctor say.

"It was not," the young miner said shakily. He laughed, shakily. "Sheep up in the livery stable, goats in here. I'll not be cheated now."

The doctor said, "I thought you had learned to be careful with those hands."

"Why, I guess there might be a day when having been in Warlock jail will be a big thing, Doc. There is more than one way to grow a goat's beard."

"You young pipsqueak," old man Heck growled. "We are all goats today."

"We are cossacks or peasants," the doctor said, in a strong, clear voice. "How do you like it out there with the cossacks, George Holloway?"

The judge said nothing, and Gannon heard him sigh.

"Have they got Tittle yet, anybody heard?" one of the miners demanded. No one answered him. Another began to sing:

> "Good-by, good-by,
> Good-by to Warlock, good-by.
> Here comes the cavalry, lickety-split,
> Here comes MacDonald to give us a fit,
> Oh, good-by, good-by,
> Good-by, old Warlock, good-by!"

There was laughter. "Hush that up!" the trooper growled. The others immediately began to sing it, and the doctor's voice was loudest among them.

"Looks like a fiesta down by Miss Jessie's boarding house," the sheriff commented, and Gannon joined him in the doorway. There was a huge crowd at the corner of Grant Street, extending out of sight down toward the General Peach.

Then there was a shot. He started out past the sheriff, but Keller grasped his arm tightly. "We'll just stay here and wait it out, boy," the sheriff said. "That is cavalry work down there and nothing to do with us. You and me will just sit it out right here, Johnny Gannon."

## 61. *General Peach*

### I

THE TROOPERS turned into Grant Street at a trot, eight of them, with a sergeant riding ahead beside the ninth horseman, who was Lafe Dawson. Townsmen watched them from the corner of Main Street as the dust slowly settled in their wake. The troopers carried carbines; they wore dark blue shirts, web cartridge belts, and lighter blue trousers. Beneath their flat caps their faces were bronzed, clean-shaven, and expressionless. A bugle sang off toward the west end of town.

The troopers reined to a halt in a semicircle before the porch of the General Peach boardinghouse. The sergeant dismounted, and, on short calipers of legs, started for the steps. He stopped as Miss Jessie Marlow appeared on the porch. He and Lafe Dawson, who had also dismounted, removed their hats.

"Miss Jessie," Dawson said. "We are sorry to trouble you, but that Tittle is wanted. These fellows have come after him, and—"

"He is not here any more," Miss Jessie said. She stood very straight before the thick shadow of the doorway, with her brown ringlets shining in the sun, her hands clasped before her.

"Well, now, not to be doubting you, ma'am—but these men have orders to look everywhere for him."

The sergeant said politely, "Why, you'll not mind if we look around in there for him, will you, lady?" He had a wizened, dark, Irish face like a dried apple.

"Yes, I mind. There are sick men in here and I will not have your soldiers tramping around disturbing them. You will have to take my word that Tittle is no longer here."

Dawson muttered to himself. The sergeant scratched his head and said, "Well, we can't do that, lady, you see," but he did not move forward.

"Now, see here, Miss Jessie," Dawson said impatiently. "I am sure he isn't here if you say so. Except it's General Peach's orders we are to round up all the strikers from the Medusa, and I *know* there's some of them in there. Now you don't want to interfere with these men trying to do their duty, do you?"

The sergeant signaled with his hand and the troopers dismounted. At the corner of Main the crowd filled the street now, watching silently.

"Will you use force on a woman, Sergeant?" Miss Jessie said.

The sergeant carefully did not look at her as the troopers came forward to join him. Dawson moved toward the steps. Then he stopped, and his hands rose shoulder high as he stared past Miss Jessie. The sergeant and the troopers stared. Blaisedell stood in the shadow just inside the entryway.

"Now, see here, Marshal," Dawson whispered, as though to himself. He dropped his hands slowly to his sides. The sergeant glanced sideways at him. One of the troopers tilted the muzzle of his carbine up; the man beside him struck it down. There was a rustle of whispering from the townsmen at the corner, and titters. Miss Jessie stood gazing down at Dawson and the troopers, her mouth a pinched, severe line.

The sergeant looked at Dawson with one grizzled eyebrow hooked up interrogatively, and a ghost of a smile.

"Well, let's leave this for now, Sergeant," Dawson said, and swung up onto his horse again. The sergeant replaced his cap and waved the troopers back. In silence, they all remounted and rode back up Grant Street the way they had come. The crowd at the corner parted to let them pass through, and, when they had disappeared into Main Street, someone uttered a low, tentative Apache war cry.

Miss Jessie Marlow went back inside the General Peach.

II

The miners stood in silent, stolid groups, in the dining room, in the hall, on the stairs, watching Miss Jessie as she closed the door behind her and put her hand on Blaisedell's arm.

"God bless you and the marshal for that, Miss Jessie!" Ben Tittle said, leaning on the newel post at the bottom of the stairs.

"Looks like they might be back, though," another miner said.

Blaisedell and Miss Jessie stood at right angles to each other in curiously stiff attitudes; she facing him with her great eyes wide as though she had seen a vision, her breast rising and falling rapidly with her breathing and her hand nervously fondling the locket that hung around her neck; Blaisedell facing toward the stairs with his bruised face remote and frowning, his round chin set beneath the broad sweep of his fair mustache.

"I guess they are rounding everybody up," Harris said, in a hushed voice. "I am just as glad I'm not a Medusa man today."

"Ben!" Miss Jessie said suddenly. "I want your head bandaged over like Stacey's, and you are to lie down in Stacey's bed. Stacey will have to go down to one of the houses in Medusa Street; he can walk well enough." She spoke to Stacey. "You help him. Quickly, now!"

Tittle said, "Miss Jessie, I'll not have you and Mr. Blaisedell getting in any mess trying to—"

"Hurry!" she snapped. He turned and hobbled painfully back down the hall, Stacey, with his bandaged head, following him. Blaisedell was watching Miss Jessie. The other miners stirred uneasily.

"That was an Orangeman, that sergeant," O'Brien said from the stairs. "I can smell an Orangeman."

"Are you going to try to stop them from coming in here, Miss Jessie?" Bardaman asked. But he was looking at Blaisedell.

Jones laughed shrilly. "You surely scared that bunch off, Marshal!"

Blaisedell shook his head a little, and frowned more deeply. Miss Jessie was looking from face to face with her eyes blazing and the little muscles tugging at the corners of her mouth.

A bearded miner ran heavy-footed in through the dining room from the rear of the General Peach. "Miss Jessie! They have caught Doc and old Heck and Frenchy and Tim Daley and some others down at Tim's house. The deputy's got them there in the jail now. Boys, they are scouring the whole town! They have got wagons coming in and all the strikers are going to be transported out!"

There was an immediate uproar. It was a time before the bearded miner could make himself heard again, "and the general himself's here, Miss Jessie! They are going to shoot us down if we don't—"

He stopped abruptly and all the others were silent as Miss Jessie raised a hand. "They will not bother you here," she said calmly. She looked up at O'Brien, on the stairs. "Will you go up to a front window where you can see them coming? Let us know when you do. The rest of you are to go back to the hospital room." She stood looking from face to face again until they all started down the hall, shuffling their feet but otherwise silent. Then with a glance at Blaisedell she went into her room, and he followed her.

III

There was a disturbance outside the General Peach, a mutter of voices, a crack of boots on the wooden steps and on the porch. A file of townsmen entered, carrying rifles and shotguns, with six-shooters holstered at their sides or thrust into their belts; their faces were set, their eyes excited—Pike and Paul Skinner, Peter Bacon, Sam Brown, Tim French, Owen Parsons, Hasty, Mosbie, Wheeler, Kennon, Egan, Rolfe, Buchanan, Slator. "Marshal!" Pike Skinner called, and immediately the miners reappeared, crowding silently back down the hallway. The door of Miss Jessie's room opened and Blaisedell came out. Miss Jessie stood in the doorway behind him.

"Marshal," the townsmen said, in a scattered greeting, and one or two removed their hats and said, "Miss Jessie."

"Marshal," Pike Skinner said. "It has come time for vigilantes, looks like." His gargoyle's face was earnest. "Marshal, we don't know what to do but we heard you did and there is a bunch of us here that will back any play you want to make. And more coming. We'll not see this thing happen in Warlock."

"Fight if it comes to that," Mosbie said.

"Ought to be a few of you jacks to make a fight of it, too," Hasty said, nodding toward the miners crowded together in the hallway.

"As well as you people!" one of them cried.

"Well, we didn't all come to make a fight," Peter Bacon said. A chew of tobacco worked in his brown, wrinkled cheek. "But we will make a decent enough stand, and I guess fight if we have to do it."

Blaisedell leaned on the door jamb. His intense blue eyes traversed the faces before him. He smiled a little.

Paul Skinner said, "Marshal, it is time folks in this town stood up to things some. You tell us how we're to do, and we'll do it."

"They won't fire when there's a town full of us against them," Kennon said. "It is a pitiful sight; they are stacking miners in my stable there like cordwood."

Blaisedell still said nothing; Pike Skinner looked at Miss Jessie anxiously.

"We are with you, Marshal," Sam Brown said, cracking the butt of his rifle down on the floor. "You lead us on and we'll chase blue breeches right on back to Bright's. We are with you sink or swim."

"Or stuck in the mud," Bacon said, sadly. "Marshal, the sheriff is down here and got Johnny Gannon hobbled. That couldn't do anything anyway. But we are with you, U.S. Cavalry or not."

"It is his place," Miss Jessie said. Their faces all turned toward her. Blaisedell straightened.

Then they were all silent, watching Blaisedell.

All at once he grinned broadly. "Well, boys," he said. "Maybe we can pull some weight here between us."

There was a concerted sigh. "Why, now then!" Mosbie said.

"You want us in here or outside, Marshal?" Oscar Thompson asked.

"I'll make my place on the porch there, if that's all right with you boys. I don't mean to take it on for myself, but it looks like if I can't handle it without going to shooting maybe we all couldn't." His face turned grave again. "For if it came to shooting there'd be dead men and too many cavalry for us, and nothing gained in the end."

"Except by God we fit the sons of bitches!" one of the miners cried in a high, cracked voice.

"You mean to bluff it, Marshal?" Wheeler said worriedly.

Pike Skinner said, "Don't leave us out of it, Marshal!"

"Marshal," Sam Brown said. He sounded embarrassed. "Well, Marshal, no offense, but—well, that time those jacks tramped you at the jail. I mean, a bluff's a bluff, but—"

Blaisedell looked at him coldly. "You asked me how I wanted to do it," he said. "I am telling you how. I am not going to fire on the U.S. Cavalry, or you either. Do you hear?" He gazed from face to face. "I said I will stand by on the porch here. I'll ask the rest of you to do some climbing and get up on the roof of the barn, and the other places on down the street." He grinned again, in a swift flash of teeth. "We will have the U.S. Cavalry surrounded and we'll see if they don't bluff."

Tim French laughed out loud. "Why, if we could call old Espirato up from his grave we could hightail Peach out of here at a run!" The others laughed.

"No shooting!" Blaisedell said sharply. "Now maybe you had better move, boys."

"Squads left!" Paul Skinner said, and limped toward the door. The others started after him.

"General!" someone called back. "Send up chuck now and then, and we will hold out for a month." They tramped out, laughing and talking excitedly.

"Let them have their fun," a miner said bitterly. "They don't want any help from us."

"Looks like we are having it from them, though," Bardaman said. "Marshal, you sure you know what you are doing?"

"No," Blaisedell said, in a strange voice. "No man ever is."

"You had better get your six-shooters, Clay," Miss Jessie said. She said it as though she were the general, after all, and turned back inside her room as Blaisedell started for the stairs. Three miners who stood there glanced at him covertly, each in turn, as he mounted the steps past them.

"I hope MacDonald's black soul rots in hell," a miner in the hallway said. "And General Peach with him."

"Amen."

"This might be a fine show here today," the bitter one said. "But we will get shipped further and harder for it."

"Shut up," Bardaman said. "It's a show worth it, isn't it?"

They were silent again as Blaisedell came back down the stairs. He had taken off his coat, and was bareheaded. The sleeves of his fine linen shirt were gartered on his upper arms, pulling the cuffs free of his wrists. He wore two shell belts, two holstered Colts hung low on his thighs. Their gold handles gleamed in the light as he threw the front door open.

"The best show there is," Bardaman whispered, to the miner next to him. Miss Jessie came to stand behind Blaisedell in the doorway and they watched the men appear on the rooftops across the street.

There was a yell from upstairs. Boots thumped in the upstairs hall; O'Brien yelled from the top of the stairwell, "Marshal! Here they come! It is the whole damned army!"

IV

The troopers made their way down Grant Street with difficulty through the crowd that had collected. There were more than thirty of them, and with these were MacDonald, on a white horse, and Dawson and Newman from the Medusa. At the head of the troop were a major and a young captain. A still younger lieutenant rode beside Dawson. The crowd jeered and cheered as they came through. MacDonald toppled in his saddle as someone pulled on his leg, and there was a burst of laughter. MacDonald lashed out with his quirt, blindly, for his hat had slipped forward over his eyes. His left arm was folded into a black sling.

"Mister Mac!" someone shouted. "You have got yourself a passel of new foremen!"

There was more laughter. The lieutenant grinned sheepishly, the captain looked angry; the major was glancing up at the men on the rooftops along Grant Street, and their weapons. MacDonald spurred the white horse toward the porch of the General Peach, where Blaisedell stood, with Miss Jessie Marlow behind him in the doorway.

"This is the United States Cavalry, Marshal!" he cried. As soon as he spoke the crowd fell silent. "You interfere at your own peril! Major Standley has orders—"

Blaisedell's voice boomed out, drowning MacDonald's. "Can't be the U.S. Cavalry. They would not ride down here to do your blackhearted work for you, MacDonald. Own up, now, boys; what quartermaster wagon did you rob for those blue shirts?"

There was another roar of catcalls and laughter. The major raised his hand and the troopers halted. He said, not loudly, "Mr. Blaisedell, we are here under orders to arrest all the strikers from the Medusa mine, and we propose to search this house for a man named Tittle. You won't be fool enough to try to stop us?" He was a plump man with a half-moon of faded blond mustache and eyelashes that looked white in his dark face.

"Why, yes," Blaisedell said, and laid his hands flat against his holsters. "I am fool enough."

"We have orders to shoot if we have to, Marshal!"

"Why, I can shoot too, Major!"

There was a shout of approbation from the crowd. It ceased immediately as Blaisedell raised a hand for quiet. He pointed a finger at the major. "You will be first, Major. Then you, MacDonald. Then you, Captain. Then I will take those two they couldn't find britches to fit," he said, indicating Dawson and Newman. "And then you, young fellow, if you don't mind waiting your turn."

"You won't get that far!" the captain shouted furiously. He rose in his stirrups. "Major—"

The major motioned to him to be silent and said, "You are now in armed rebellion against the United States government. Do you realize that, sir?"

Blaisedell stood with his arms hanging loosely at his sides, his fair hair gleaming in the sun. Behind and to the right of him Miss Jessie stood straight and proud, with her chin held high.

"Major," Blaisedell said. "The United States government was got in armed rebellion before either of us was born. And got for one thing by people wanting to keep soldiers from busting through the houses they lived in, if I remember my history books right."

"*Hear, hear!*" someone cried hysterically. The captain swung his horse and spurred it toward the crowd. There was a rising clamor. A number of whores from the Row had gathered on the far side of Main Street and now the shouting had a higher pitch to it, as they added their voices to the rest.

"—a woman behind you so no man can shoot!" MacDonald was heard to cry.

"And a troop of cavalry behind you, Mister Mac!" Hasty called, from the roof of the Feed and Grain Barn.

The major said, "You are held in some respect, Marshal; but no man can bluff the army. I advise you to stand aside before this has gone too far!"

"Bluff?" Blaisedell said grimly. "Why, I advise *you* not to find out whether it is a bluff or not."

"*Marshal!*" Pike Skinner bellowed, and instantly there was a flat, echoing crack. A trooper's hat flew off. Blaisedell stood wreathed in smoke, one of his Colts in his hand. In the silence, as the smoke blew apart, he said harshly, "Throw it down, sonny." The trooper, who had raised his carbine, pitched it from him as though it were red hot. He raised a hand to feel his bare head. MacDonald's horse was pitching and side-stepping. The captain cursed. The major backed his horse away from the porch. Miss Jessie had disappeared.

The major shouted to make himself heard. He raised a gauntleted hand and the troopers with one movement brought their carbines to the ready. Blaisedell unholstered his other Colt, aimed one at the major, one at MacDonald. Otherwise he did not move, except to glance quickly around as Miss Jessie reappeared. She had a derringer in her hand; another wild shout went up. Some of the troopers lowered their carbines. The major looked frozen with his hand still raised.

"Major, you will go down like Custer!" Pike Skinner shouted. The men on the rooftops had their weapons pointed down on the troopers in the street. Peter Bacon spat tobacco juice onto the cap of a trooper below him.

"You are surrounded, you blue-leg bastards!" Mosbie bellowed enthusiastically. "We will cut hair today, if you fire on those two."

The major swung his horse around and snapped an order. The lieutenant saluted; with eight of the troopers in line behind him he trotted south down Grant Street, and there dismounted with his men, where they could cover the men on the roofs, some of whom now knelt behind the parapets. The major's face was shining with sweat.

There was a new disturbance in the crowd packed into Main Street. "Shame!" a woman's voice cried shrilly. "Shame on the United States Cavalry! Shame, General Peach! Shame—"

"Peach!" someone yelled.

"Here comes the general!"

He appeared at the corner, with another officer behind him. The crowd gave way before him. "Shame!" the shrill voice cried. "Shame! Shame!" General Peach did not appear to notice. He looked huge on his great gray horse; he rode heavily, slumped in the saddle. His white beard lay against his chest, his blouse was unbuttoned, and an unlit cigar jutted from his mouth like the bowsprit of a sailing ship. His great, black, broad-brimmed hat flapped with the motion of the gray's pace. One side of his hat was pinned to the crown with a silver eagle and there were great yellow eagles on the rear corners of his shabrack. He carried a leather-bound stick in his hand. The townspeople in the street thrust aside, and the gray horse came down the alleyway between them at a slow walk. Behind him rode Colonel Whiteside, a frail, worried-looking man with gray mutton-chop whiskers.

"*Shame!*" the voice continued to cry, increasingly hoarse. "Shame, General Peach! Oh, shame! *Shame!*" There were a few catcalls, a gobbling Apache cry. General Peach did not even move his head.

The captain saluted. The major spurred forward to speak to General Peach, but the general ignored him and the gray horse continued steadily forward, with Whiteside close behind. Peter Bacon spat over the parapet again, while Pike Skinner rose to his feet, with his shotgun over his arm. Blaisedell moved only to replace his six-shooters in their scabbards where one of the golden butt-inserts caught the sun like a flame. Miss Jessie stepped slowly to the far side of the porch, the hand holding the derringer at her side.

General Peach reined to a halt close to the steps of the boardinghouse that bore his name. He spoke in a huge, hollow, reverberating voice. "A long-haired gunman and a pretty woman with a pretty ankle and a pretty little derringer."

Having said it, he sat more erectly in the saddle, blinking sleepily. His eyes looked too small for his broad, squat, fleshy face, his mouth was a pinched dark hole in his beard. He raised his leather-bound stick and scratched behind his ear with its tip. His beard blew and his hat flapped in a gust of wind that ruffled Blaisedell's hair as well.

"All right!" Now there was an edge of anger to the great, blown voice. "You have made your show—" He did not go on, slumping in the saddle again, as though speech had tired him. He sat as though he were waiting for the two on the porch to disappear. There was silence except for the occasional stamp of a hoof or the jingle of harness among the troopers. Blaisedell did not move. Miss Jessie's face looked drawn.

Colonel Whiteside edged his horse forward until he was almost in a line between the general and Blaisedell. "I'm sorry, Miss Marlow!" he said, in his high voice. "We will have to clear the strikers out of your house."

"Have you a warrant, sir?" Miss Jessie said.

"We don't need a warrant, ma'am. We—"

"I say you need a warrant. And I think there can be no warrant for this disgraceful conduct!"

"You stubborn little fool!" MacDonald cried. "This is the military government you are presuming to—"

"Mineowner's government!" a thick Cornish voice shouted, and there was a roar of mocking laughter.

Someone yelled from the rooftops, "Sound the charge, bugler! It is Bull Run all over again." General Peach rose in his stirrups and glanced slowly around him, and up at the roofs.

"We have no government here!" Miss Jessie cried. "Each of us has had to learn to defend his own house!"

"Hear, hear!"

"Shame, General Peach! Oh, *shame* on you!" The clamor began all around. Buck Slavin appeared on the roof of the Feed and Grain Barn. He climbed up on the parapet, waving his arms and shouting for silence.

"When are we going to get a town patent, General?" Slavin shouted. There were cheers. "When do we get a county of our own without the law a day's ride away?" The cheering and whistling swelled and rose, while Slavin waved his arms again. Colonel Whiteside had swung around in his saddle, but General Peach sat staring stolidly at Blaisedell.

"Mineowners' law!" the man with the Cornish accent bellowed, and MacDonald rose in his stirrups to try to see the offender. There was jeering.

Slavin waved his arms for quiet. "People of Warlock!" he cried. "A motion! A motion! That we call our county Peach County in honor of the general. And Warlock the county seat! All in favor!"

There were groans mingled with cheers. "Medusa County!" someone cried, and the groans drowned the cheers. "Blaisedell County!" and the cheers drowned the groans. General Peach looked around as though he had been waked from sleep. The catcalls and the jeering grew louder and louder, there were rebel yells, Apache war cries. The general waved his gauntlet holding the leather-bound stick high above his head, and there was a sudden hush.

"A county of jackasses run by a murdering gunman and his doxy?" he said, in his huge voice. "Call it Espirato County for all of me!" Then, as there were boos, he shouted, "Standley, clear the damned jackasses out of the street!"

The major spurred his horse toward the crowd with obvious reluctance, the captain more eagerly. The troopers swept into line behind them, and, horses sidling forward, they pushed the townspeople back into Main Street. The Apache cry was taken up now throughout the crowd until the street was filled with turkey gobbling. General Peach sat glowering, chewing on his cigar. Whiteside was whispering to him.

He thrust the colonel aside with a motion of his stick. "Madam!" he roared. "You asked a minute ago if I had a warrant to go through your house. I ask you if you have a warrant to keep such a house!" He stopped, and waited; there was silence again. Then he said, "A disorderly house! A brothel for dirty miners complete with pimp and madam!"

He raised his stick and cut it viciously through the air, so that the gray shied. "Madam, you are a vile disgrace!" he shouted hoarsely. "And your *maquereau* with his pistols has killed more decent men than the typhoid. Filth cohabiting with murderous vile filth and prostituting to filth! And time you were stamped out like filth! You are a notorious pair and a public scandal! I will give you and your—"

There was another flat violent crack, and smoke swirled up before Blaisedell again. The general's raised gauntlet no longer contained the leather-bound stick. The troopers swung their horses around as the major shouted a command; a huge sigh rose from the crowd, an aghast and awed intake of breath that blew out instantly in one great cry of approval and triumph. Colonel Whiteside leaned forward in his stirrups with an arm stretched out toward the general and his mouth wide with some inaudible cry. General Peach snapped his fingers and pointed down, and the colonel dismounted and scampered around the gray to find the stick. The cheering grew louder. The general's face was dark red.

Whiteside handed him back the stick, and then hurried to remount. The clamor slackened and died. General Peach continued in the same voice, as though he had not been interrupted at all. "—thirty seconds to get off that porch. And exactly one hour to get out of this town!"

Then he sat motionless and silent, slumped and sleepily blinking once more. He did not heed the colonel's attempts to whisper to him, waving his stick finally as though to brush away a fly. Blaisedell stood facing him with his boots planted apart and his still smoking Colt slanting down in his hand. Slowly he replaced it in its scabbard, and Miss Jessie retreated a little, one hand still gripping the derringer at her side.

Then, all of a sudden, the general sat erect. Laboriously he swung himself out of the saddle. "Sir!" Whiteside whispered. "Sir!" He scrambled from his saddle and tried to intercept the general, who knocked him aside. General Peach tramped through the dust, grunted as he mounted the boardwalk, slapped the leather-bound stick against a black boot. His bootheel struck the first step resoundingly; he mounted the second step.

"Stop right there!" Blaisedell said.

General Peach stopped. He turned, on the step below where Blaisedell stood, to face his troops. He paused there a moment, in the frozen hush, moving his head from side to side as though he were going to speak. Then, with his back to Blaisedell, ponderously, powerfully, but not even swiftly, he swung his arm backhanded, swung the stick in his hand. It struck Blaisedell's skull with a startling crack. Blaisedell staggered back.

General Peach pivoted with the swing of his arm; grunting, he beat the stick down on the six-shooter in Blaisedell's hand. The six-shooter fell. He slashed the stick with a heavier, duller crack across Blaisedell's face. There was a moan from the crowd as Blaisedell fell back again. Miss Jessie screamed.

General Peach moved after Blaisedell with slow, awkward swings of his arm. His tight blouse split down the back and he grunted hugely with every stroke of the leather-bound stick, which flashed through its arc like a brown snake. Blaisedell crumpled and fell. The general straddled his body and brought the stick down again. Miss Jessie flung herself at him, screaming. He slashed at her and she fell back, clutching at her breast.

Then she raised the derringer in both hands and pointed it, as Colonel Whiteside bounded up the steps toward her crying, "No! No!" The hammer fell with the dry snap of a misfire and the colonel caught her in his arms, and wrested the little pistol away. The general slashed his stick down, and down again, unnoticing, "I!" he shouted suddenly, panting. "*I* am! *I am!*"

Then he desisted. He swung around toward the troopers and roared, "What are you men waiting for? Do I have to cut his onions before you will move?"

Major Standley started and called a command. Half the troopers dismounted, and, in single file, followed the major up on the porch, where Colonel Whiteside held Miss Jessie Marlow and General Peach stood astride Clay Blaisedell, mopping his red face with a blue handkerchief, panting. His vacant, small blue eyes watched the troopers enter, almost sleepily. One of them stumbled over one of the gold-handled six-shooters. The next kicked it off the porch. Colonel Whiteside held Miss Jessie's arms, whispering to her; she was not struggling now.

"See that they find that man Tittle, Whiteside," the general said suddenly. "Willingham wants him in particular."

"Yes, sir," Whiteside said.

Peach nodded solemnly. "Then nothing to do but load 'em up, take 'em out; see to it, Whiteside. Load 'em up, take 'em out," he said, nodding again. "Willingham is a power at the convention, Whiteside. Oh, he is a powerful force at the convention. He will be useful to us, Whiteside."

"Yes, sir," the colonel said.

General Peach took off his great hat and wiped his pink bald head. Then he stepped clear of Blaisedell and walked heavily back down the steps. An orderly helped him mount the gray horse. MacDonald sat staring at the porch with his teeth showing in a kind of paralyzed grimace. Troopers began to come out of the door, herding the boarders before them. None of the miners looked at Miss Jessie, or at Blaisedell. The major came out.

"Where is Tittle, ma'am?" he said.

"I won't tell you!"

"Now, ma'am," the colonel said chidingly. "You would do just as well to tell us. We—"

"What will you do if I do not?" Miss Jessie cried. "Turn me over to your men for rape?"

"Now, ma'am!" the colonel groaned. He released her arms. Instantly she ran down the steps toward the general's horse.

She cried, in a hoarse voice, "An army of jackals led by an old boar with a ring in his nose!"

"Hush!" Whiteside said, catching her again. "Hush now, *please*, ma'am! It is bad enough already. Hush, please!"

"Bloody old boar!" she cried. "Crazy old boar!" She began to sob wildly. General Peach stared down at her in silence, frowning. The men on the roof across the street averted their eyes.

Then there was a gasp as Blaisedell rose. He stood clinging to one of the posts that supported the roof of the porch, his face cruelly striped with red welted lines. Again Miss Jessie broke away from the colonel and ran to him, but now her cry was lost in a shout that went up from the corner, and General Peach awoke from his stupor as though galvanized by an electric shock.

"*Espirato!*" someone was shouting, pushing his way through the crowd. "*Espirato!*" He appeared between two of the troopers' horses; it was Deputy Gannon. He ran toward the general.

"Oh, good God!" the colonel cried, as the general slashed the stick across the gray's rump. The gray leaped forward toward the deputy.

"What's that, man?" Peach roared. "What's that you say?"

"Apaches!" the deputy cried. He grasped the gray's bridle, his narrow, crooked-nosed face bent back to peer up into the general's face. The major appeared and ran down the steps, and troopers hurried out of the door behind him. "It's Apaches!" the deputy cried. "Joe Lacey just rode in to say they have killed a bunch of cowboys in Rattlesnake Canyon! He is at the saloon now!"

His further words were lost in shouting. The gray bucked away from his grasp as the general slashed back with the stick again.

"Whiteside!" Peach shouted. "Whiteside! Espirato, d'you hear? Do you *hear*, Whiteside? By the Almighty we will run him to earth this time, Whiteside! Standley, get your men mounted and ready!" The gray started forward through the townspeople. Men crowded around the deputy, shouting questions. No one looked now to see Miss Jessie Marlow helping Blaisedell back inside the General Peach.

The men descended from the rooftops, and the crowd moved away down Main Street. There were a few backward glances, and those made quickly and almost furtively. When they had all gone only Tom Morgan was left, leaning against the adobe wall of the Feed and Grain Barn, still staring at the porch. There was a fixed, contorted grin upon his face that was part a snarl, like that of a stuffed, savage animal, and part expectant, as though he were waiting for something that would change what had happened there.

## 62. *Journals of Henry Holmes Goodpasture*

June 5, 1881

IT WAS a thing I wish I had never seen, a man's downfall and degradation. Poor Blaisedell; should he have pulled that trigger? I have fought the question, pro and con, to exhaustion in my mind. Yet was he not subscribed to it when he made his stand? And was it Miss Jessie's will directing him to that stand? I will not blame her. Poor Blaisedell, we had already seen that incapacity that brought him low today; it was evident too when he was overrun by miners before the jail, that flaw of mercy or humanity, or of a fatal hesitation to be the aggressor at gunplay, or too much awareness of the consequences if he had pulled the trigger, on both occasions—not to himself but to this town.

How would I have him be different? If he had not had this flaw he would have been no more than a hired, calloused killer of men, and we would have turned against him finally for that very heedlessness. Instead, we will turn against him for his failure to be heedless, of consequences or of life, for seeming weakness, for that hesitation that was his ruin; for failure. Now he is pitied, and pity is no more than contempt beribboned and scented.

Pity and shame, a shame for him and for ourselves, who share it. Shame and pain, and pain must savagely turn upon its cause, which is Blaisedell. He should have fired.

Yet how could he have fired upon an old man, an insane old man, but one still to be honored for past deeds and for his position. Ah, but a cunning and treacherous insane old man, who, by the contrivance of turning his back upon Blaisedell, confessed that he knew Blaisedell to be honorable. And must have known that Blaisedell would not fire upon the man who is, after all, the embodiment of law and authority in this place.

Poor devil, he must wish himself dead, honorably dead. That is, perhaps, what should have been. He should have killed General Peach, and been himself instantly, unambiguously, and honorably killed by a volley of carbine fire. We would have crowned him then with laurels for tyrannicide.

Now, too late, I can formulate it: I asked of him only that he not fail. He has failed, yet how can a man be human and not fail? I remember once, before he came, jesting that he would have to be not of flesh and blood to succeed here. He did, until now, succeed, and was human, and is still. I could not grieve for him if he were not. So do most of us grieve; Warlock, for a day, will bleed for those wounds upon his face and spirit, and then, as a man will manage to thrust into oblivion something of which he is mortally ashamed, we will turn away from him.

My first thought, of course, was that Gannon was trying rather ridiculously to create a diversion. It was presently obvious that this was not so. Joe Lacey had indeed arrived in Warlock, with a frightful bullet-furrow across his forehead and a frightful story. It seems that the San Pabloites, including Lacey, Whitby, Cade, Harrison, Mitchell, Hennessey, and others—thirteen in all—were returning empty-handed from Hacienda Puerto, having been driven off by Mexicans, when, yesterday at nightfall, they were ambushed in Rattlesnake Canyon by a band of half-naked Apaches with their bodies horribly daubed with mud. Lacey swears (although this is not given much credence) that he marked Espirato among them, an old man supposedly very tall for an Apache. Any tall Apache immediately becomes Espirato, by which device he was, in the old days, capable of being seen in several places at once. The ambush was carried out with devilish cleverness. The men were riding closely grouped along a narrow and boxlike defile in which the whole group was enclosed at once, when there was a war cry as a signal, whereupon Apaches rose from behind every bush and rock—at least a hundred of them, Lacey says—and began to pour a torrent of hot lead down upon the hapless whites. In a few moments all but Lacey were dead. He saw with his own eyes one brave leap down to cut Whitby's heart from his still living body, and others join to begin the usual disfigurement of the dead.

Lacey himself was in the lead, and miraculously escaped on down the canyon, riding at breakneck speed. He is sure no others escaped their doom.

I was fortunate enough to have entered the Lucky Dollar, where Lacey was steadying his nerves with Taliaferro's whisky, before the rest of the crowd was blocked out by soldiers upon General Peach's entry there. The General, after hearing Lacey's story, announced his intention to depart immediately and with all his troops for the border. Colonel Whiteside interposed that Rattlesnake Canyon is in Mexican Territory, whereupon the General whirled as though he would strike his subordinate. "I will follow Espirato to hell itself, and be damned to the Mexican government!" cried he, to the accompaniment of cheers —for how fickle are men, to whom, a few minutes earlier, Peach had seemed a monster of superhuman powers. Whiteside continued to warn him that if he entered Mexican territory, trouble with that country would result, that he would certainly be court-martialed for it and end his days in disgrace. The General ordered him away contemptuously, and charged Major Standley with the preparation of the cavalry for the ride to the border.

Peach towered over his subordinates like a Titan over pygmies. Hate him as I must, I will admit he was at this moment every inch a general, and an impressive one. He seemed younger. He held himself more erect. His eyes flashed with resolution, and the commands he uttered were clear and terse; he seemed to have recovered himself completely since I had seen him last, in Bright's City.

It was at this time that Willingham entered.* He is a short, rotund man with red whiskers fringing a cold and willful face. He began to seek the General's attention, but Peach rebuffed him and, when Willingham persisted, directed one of his officers to escort the gentleman outside. Peach did this politely enough, but evidently had been holding himself in with some restraint, for when Whiteside again endeavored to make himself heard, Peach bellowed that he would be put under arrest if he uttered another word, and within twenty minutes General Peach and every officer and trooper had departed Warlock for the border.

The position of Willingham, MacDonald, and their henchmen, who have taken refuge in the Western Star Hotel, is perilous indeed, for the Medusa strikers have been released from the livery stable where they were confined, and a great number of them are now standing in Main Street outside the hotel, in ominous silence. Their mood does not seem to be one of violence—although as the day progresses and strong waters are imbibed, agitators listened to, and especially when the miners return this evening from the other mines, the mood may rapidly change, and if I were MacDonald and Willingham I would be shaking in my boots. I understand that Morgan has enlisted himself in Willingham's party, and, with a number of foremen, stands guard at the hotel.

One of Blaikie's hands has arrived, early this afternoon, with more news of the ambush in Rattlesnake Canyon. It now seems that Jack Cade and Mitchell have also escaped, and that their assailants were not Apaches at all, but Mexicans! This version of the ambush has immediately been accepted. For one reason, no doubt, because the possibility of Apaches on the loose and murderously inclined is an extremely unpleasant prospect to contemplate, and, for another, because the rumor has long been that McQuown and most of these same San Pablo men once ambushed Hacienda Puerto riders trailing rustled stock in Rattlesnake Canyon in exactly this same manner, masquerading as Apaches; and so it seems very likely that Don Ignacio's

*Director of a number of mining companies, and president of the board of Porphyrion and Western, "Sunny Will" Willingham was a prominent California politician and a former member of Congress.

vaqueros might have chosen a similar means to vengeance. Horrible though that vengeance seems, there is justice in it, and it is difficult not to wish that men such as Mitchell, and especially Jake Cade, had not been spared.

The Cowboy who brought in this news says he met the cavalry en route, and apprised them of his information—and was summarily brushed aside. It would seem, however, that the marauders will have put many miles between themselves and the border by now, if, indeed, they ever crossed it. And surely General Peach will not cross it himself, in pursuit of what the members of his staff, at least, must come to see are masqueraders.

There is laughter now about his wild, windmill-chasing ride, which, not many hours ago, had a valiant and glorious aspect. But the possibility that he will compound foolishness with idiocy, and lead his force into Mexico, is worrisome. Such an action could easily, in the present state of international relations, lead to reprisals, if not to war. To war in general we are not averse, but we decry it when we are in such an exposed position. Nor is General Peach a military commander in whom it is possible to have much faith.

The crowd of miners before the Western Star seems to have thinned out, and some say that their leaders, who had been let out of jail (the doctor was incarcerated with them!) are now meeting to decide upon a course of action. I fear they may run wild, knowing they have this respite in which to commit whatever arson and destruction they please, before Peach returns and they are rounded up again.

Blaisedell has not been seen. The subject is scrupulously avoided, and gossip is all over General Peach's charge after the nonexistent Apaches. There is a general feeling of the fittingness of the slaughter of the rustlers, and I have heard it said that this ambush took place in exactly the same part of the Canyon as did the previous one, which it avenged. Sheriff Keller I saw in the Lucky Dollar, exceedingly under the influence of strong spirits; with him the judge, equally so. Many Cowboys are coming in from the valley. As usual, the news from Warlock has reached them on the wind, or through the voices of birds. I hope they have not come to gloat over Blaisedell's fall. *They* did not accomplish it. The sight of him dropping mutely beneath General Peach's bludgeon clings to me like an incubus.

## 63. *The Doctor Chooses His Potion*

WORD HAD been sent out that the Medusa strikers were to
meet on the vacant ground next to Robinson's wood yard at
five o'clock, and a little before that time the doctor set out
from Tim Daley's house in company with Fitzsimmons, Daley,
Frenchy Martin, and the others, who, as Fitzsimmons had said,
had been classified as goats rather than sheep by the fact that
they had been incarcerated in the jail rather than in the livery
stable with the rank and file. Old man Heck, in a sulk, had
refused to attend the meeting.

The afternoon had been spent in argument over policy that
had been, by careful indirection, a struggle for power. Old man
Heck's supporters had deserted him one by one, until finally
even Frenchy Martin and Bull Johnson had been won over.
Now the decisions, for better or for worse, lay with the doctor and Fitzsimmons, whom the goats had raised to leadership
over themselves, and so over the sheep.

The doctor had been amazed by his own actions this afternoon. They had been entirely foreign to what he had known
of himself, Dr. David Wagner. The hatred engendered within
the struggle to manipulate words and men just passed, had far
outstripped any felt for the Medusa mine, for MacDonald, and
for the mineowners. He was not even disgusted with himself to
realize that he was as much a subject to this as old man Heck
or Bull Johnson. His jealousy, whenever any man had risen to
challenge him, had been ruthless, his pleasure, when he had
won each separate skirmish, triumphant; he was contemptuous
now of those he had beaten.

Fitzsimmons had clung to his coattails throughout, and
he had been content to have it so, although he knew, too,
that Fitzsimmons was jealous of him, and that he could look
forward to a further struggle for power, one day, with Jimmy
Fitzsimmons. He did look forward to it, to test again this
thing newly discovered in David Wagner against the iron will
and cunning, the pure thrust of ambition in a boy more than
twenty-five years younger than he.

Fitzsimmons glanced sideways at him and winked, solemnly,
and he nodded in reply.

Behind them Daley and Martin were talking in low, excited voices. Several whores peered worriedly from the cribs along the Row, and the dark, wooden faces of Mexican women watched them from the porches of the miners' shacks along Peach Street. Warlock seemed apathetic after an eventful day. Now, the doctor thought, his anger against MacDonald must be regenerated, and yet this done in such a way that he could temper the mood of the strikers at the meeting to the proper course. He began to ponder what he must say to them—different words entirely from those of this afternoon.

"Do you know what, Doc?" Fitzsimmons said, in a low voice. "There is not a miner in this town knows what to do now. They will be so pleased to have us tell them they will wag their tails."

"And do just the opposite," he said, and smiled.

"Not if we tell them what they are going to do is what they *want* to do."

"I think there are more than old Heck who want to burn the Medusa still. Or more than ever."

Fitzsimmons shook his head condescendingly. "They are too scared, Doc. Just so nobody says they are scared. We had just better be damned sure nobody speaks up to say we had better settle quick before the cavalry gets back. That's all we have to watch out for."

"And make sure we show Willingham we think he is in rather a worse position than we are."

"Expect it would be a good idea to get up a torchlight parade tonight?"

"I think it would be very effective, and a good thing for you to turn your energies to. If you are sure you could control it."

"I could control it, all right," Fitzsimmons said stiffly, and glanced at him sideways again.

The little procession passed the wood yard and turned into the vacant property, which had been used for miners' meetings since Lathrop's time. There were a number of miners there already.

The doctor stopped and looked around to meet the eyes that were all fixed upon him. It was as though they knew instinctively that he had been chosen, and deferred without question to the choice. "Doc," Patch said, in grave greeting, and then many of the others took it up. Their tone was different from that of their usual greetings—a pledge of loyalty that had a suspended skepticism in it. They greeted Fitzsimmons by name too, but less deferentially.

"Frenchy," the doctor said, as the rest of the men from Daley's house came up to group around him, "will you see that those planks are set up on the barrels so the speakers will have a place to stand?" Fitzsimmons grinned crookedly as Frenchy went to do it, and the doctor realized why he had spoken so loudly, and to Martin in particular.

"Doc!" Stacey, with his bandaged head, was hurrying toward him. Stacey raised a hand and broke into a trot. "Doc," he panted, as he came up. "You had better come. Miss Jessie needs you at the General Peach."

He felt Fitzsimmons' eyes. "I can't come now," he said curtly. But all at once what had happened at the General Peach, which he had tried to put from his mind as irrelevant, crushed down upon him, and he felt pity for Jessie like a dagger stroke. But not now, he almost groaned; not now. He could not go now.

"It was the marshal sent me," Stacey whispered. Beneath his muslin turban his freckled forehead was creased with worry. "He says she has got the nerves very bad, Doc."

He nodded once. "Get my bag from the Assay Office, will you?" He turned to Fitzsimmons, whose eyebrows rose questioningly in his bland face. "Jimmy, I must go and see about Miss Jessie. You will have to do your best here until I get back."

Fitzsimmons nodded, and then on second thought frowned as though it were a terrible burden and responsibility. "I will do my best, Doc," Fitzsimmons said, massaging the torn knuckles with which he had made sure of his future. "You hurry," he said.

"I will," he replied grimly. He left the lot, ignoring those who called after him; he almost ran down Grant Street to the General Peach. Jessie's door was closed, but he could hear her voice raised shrilly inside her room. Blaisedell opened the door for him.

He stared in shock at Blaisedell's face. It was cross-hatched with great red welts, and his bruised eyes were swollen almost closed. "Thank God you have got here," Blaisedell said, in a low voice. "You had better give her something. She is—"

"David!" Jessie cried, as he entered past Blaisedell. She stood in the center of the room facing him. Her white triangle of a face looked wasted, as though the fire that blazed in her eyes was consuming the flesh around them. Her face contorted into a wild grimace that he realized was meant to be a smile.

Blaisedell closed the door and came up beside him, moving as though he were sore in every fiber. He sounded exhausted. "She wants us to lead the miners up to burn the Medusa mine," he said. "I have been trying to tell her it is—not the right time. I thought if you could give her something to quieten her," he whispered.

"It is the time!" Jessie cried. "It is the time now! David, we will lead them, and we will—"

"Lead the miners, Jessie?" he broke in, and the words seemed a mockery of himself.

"Yes! We will ride up to the Medusa at the head of them, an army of them. How they will cheer and sing! There are barricades there, they say, but that cannot stop us! Oh, Clay!"

"Jessie, Blaisedell is right, I'm afraid. It is not the time."

"It is the time! The cavalry has gone, and—and we have to do *something*!" She had a handkerchief in her hands, which she kept winding around one hand and then the other.

"We don't have to do anything, Jessie," Blaisedell said in a patient voice.

Her sunken, blazing eyes stared at Blaisedell, shifted to stare at the doctor; it was as though she were looking past them both to the Medusa mine, to glory or redemption—he did not know what. She pulled the handkerchief tight between her hands again. "David," she said calmly. "You must help me make him understand."

There was a knock. "That is Stacey with my bag," he said to Blaisedell, who went to open the door. He took Jessie's hands. The handkerchief was wet with perspiration, or with tears. He smiled reassuringly at her and said, "No, Jessie, I'm afraid it really is not the right time. Everything is very confused right now. But maybe tomorrow or the next day you and—"

"Now!" she cried, and her voice was suddenly deep with grief. "Oh, now, *now*!" She swung toward Blaisedell. "Oh, it must be now, before they forget him. Clay, it is for you!"

He took the bag from Blaisedell, and the bottle from it. There was a glass on the bureau and he filled it with water from the pitcher, and stained the water with laudanum. Behind him Jessie said despairingly, "Clay, it is for your sake!"

In the mirror the doctor saw the agony and revulsion written on Blaisedell's cruelly bruised face. Jessie flew to him and pressed her face to his chest, her ringlets flying as she turned her head wildly from side to side, murmuring something to Blaisedell's heart he neither could hear nor wished to hear. Blaisedell stared at him over her brown head as, awkwardly, he patted her back.

The doctor indicated the glass, and Blaisedell said, "Jessie, Doc has got something for you."

Instantly she swung around. Her face darkened with suspicion. "What's that?"

"It is some laudanum to let you rest."

"Rest?" she cried. "Rest! We cannot rest a moment!"

"You had better take it, Jessie," Blaisedell said, in the gentle voice.

The doctor raised the glass with the whisky-colored liquid in it to her, but she lifted a hand as though she would strike it to the floor. "Jessie!" he said sharply.

Her shoulders slumped. She closed her eyes. She began to sob convulsively. She rubbed her knuckles into her closed eyes and swayed, and Blaisedell put an arm around her. The doctor could see the sobs tearing at her frail body. They tore at him as well; with each one he was wrenched with pity for her, and with anger at Clay Blaisedell and the world that had broken her. His hand shook with the glass.

"Drink it, Jessie."

Obediently she drank it down, and he went to turn the coverlet back on the bed. Blaisedell helped her to the bed and she lay down with her hands over her face, her fingers working in her tangled ringlets, her head moving ceaselessly from side to side. The doctor pulled the coverlet up over her as Blaisedell stepped back toward the door.

"I will be going now, Doc," Blaisedell said in his deep voice, and he turned to meet the blue, intense gaze that was almost hidden beneath the swollen lids. Blaisedell said it again, not aloud, but with his lips only, and nodded to him.

"We will do it tomorrow!" Jessie cried suddenly. She raised her head and her eyes swung wildly in search of Blaisedell. "We will lead them to the Medusa tomorrow, Clay. Tomorrow may not be too late!"

"Why, no; tomorrow won't be too late," Blaisedell said, and smiled a little; then he went out, gently closing the door behind him.

The doctor sat down on the bed beside Jessie as she laid her head back again. She closed her eyes, as though she would be glad to rest. As he heard Blaisedell's step upon the stairs he put down the glass and smoothed his hand over her damp, tangled hair.

He glanced up at the mezzotint depicting Cuchulain in his madness, and felt the pain and fury convulse his heart. So Blaisedell would leave, and damned be his soul for ever having come, for having enchanted her, for leaving her forever in the circle of flames and thorns. And the miners and their union? he thought suddenly. There was no choice. He smiled down at her and smoothed his hand over her hair.

"The miners are meeting now, Jessie," he said. "Tomorrow will be time enough."

She nodded and smiled a little, but did not open her eyes. "It would be better today," she said in a small, clear voice. "But he is tired and hurt. I shouldn't have blamed him so. I shouldn't have called him a coward. What a strange thing to say of him!"

"He knew you were disturbed." He looked down at the strong jut of her brows over her sunken, closed eyes, the whitening of her nostrils as she breathed, the determined set to her little chin.

"Oh, I am so glad I thought of it!" she said. "For it will change everything. We will ride, of course, and they will march behind us. We—"

"Tomorrow," he whispered. "Tomorrow, my dear."

He saw her face crumple; she began to sob again, but softly. She said in the small voice, "But you see why I must make him do it, don't you, David? Because what happened here was my fault."

"No, Jessie," he said. "Jessie, you had better try to rest now."

She fell silent, and after a time he thought she must be asleep more from exhaustion than from the effect of the opiate. He left off stroking her hair and gazed at the window, wondering how the miner's meeting was progressing. He felt detached from it now, but there were a few things he would have liked to say. He would have liked to treat with Willingham for them; he thought he would have enjoyed crossing swords with Willingham.

Jessie said sleepily, "He was hurt and sick at heart, and I was so furious— He wanted to leave here tomorrow, he and I. To go somewhere else, and he said he would change his name. It made me so angry that he should think of changing his name! But I should have understood that he was hurt and sick at heart. Oh, dear God, I thought that monster had destroyed him! But it is silly to give in so easily when—"

"Rest," he said. "You must rest."

Again she was silent. He thought of her and Blaisedell leading the miners and wondered if it was any more insane than his trying to lead them himself. He gazed at his world through inward eyes and saw all his ideals and aspirations crumbling gray and ineffectual. He saw himself a fool. Much better, he thought, a torchlight parade than what he would have brought them, if he could have brought them anything; how much finer the flame of the Medusa stope mounting the shafthead frame against the sky, than the gray ashes of reason. He had deluded himself with his ideals of humanity and liberality, but peace came after war, not out of reason. They would have to have fire and blood to make their union. So it had always been, and revolutions were made by men who conquered, or who died, and not by gray thought in gray minds. Peace came with a sword, right with a sword, justice and freedom with swords, and the struggle to them must be led by men with swords rather than by ineffectual men counseling reason and moderation.

He watched the shadows lengthening through the lace curtains. The room was dimmer now, Jessie's pale face shadowed and more peaceful. It was a quiet meeting the miners were having, he thought. He wondered what kind of a showing Fitzsimmons was making, and smiled at these dregs of jealousy in himself. He knew that Fitzsimmons would do well. It was a sad truth that all the masses of men in their causes would be led by ambitious men, by power-hungry, cunningly self-serving men, rather than by the humanists, the idealists; and better led for it, he thought. Fitzsimmons loved neither the miners nor their cause, he loved only himself and the power he might attain through them. Neither did he, David Wagner, love the miners. He loved an ideal, a generality, and hated another. It was more love, and hate, than Fitzsimmons possessed, and yet it had crippled him in the end, because he could see too well how gray and impalpable was a generality, however fine, set against flesh and blood. There was no choice for him between serving an ideal made of straw and serving a single person in unhappiness and pain, whom he loved.

When Jessie spoke again her voice was so blurred he could hardly understand it. "What did Curley Burne matter to him? I cannot understand why Curley Burne mattered to him so, David. He was not good for anything! He was just another rustler. He—" Her voice died, although her lips still moved.

He watched the increasingly slow movement of her lips, and whispered, "Rest." All that is over, he thought; but could not tell her so. There was a knock.

"Doc?" It was Fitzsimmons' voice. He rose quietly, and went to open the door. He put a finger to his lips, and Fitzsimmons glanced past him and nodded. His face was flushed and triumphant. "You and me are to go talk to Willingham!" he whispered excitedly. "We are to work it out somehow. It is up to us!"

"I can't go, Jimmy."

"You can't!" Fitzsimmons avoided his eyes, pouting; but he knew that Fitzsimmons was relieved and pleased.

"My place is here, I'm afraid."

Fitzsimmons made a show of scowling, biting his lip, rubbing a scarred hand over his stubble of beard. "Well—I guess I can't go back and tell them. I guess I will try and go it alone."

"Listen to me. You will have to have something to take back to them. If it looks as though Willingham will give you nothing, tell him they will not go back to work for MacDonald. He will give you that, at least."

Fitzsimmons nodded. "I'll get more than that."

"Good luck, Jimmy." He put out his hand, and took Fitzsimmons' gnarled, scarred hand, shook it once, and released it.

"Thanks, Doc." The other didn't smile. He started away, and then he glanced back, warily, questioningly.

The doctor smiled and said, "No, I won't get in your way. I am a doctor, after all, not a miner. But try to remember that you are serving them, sometimes. Not just yourself, Jimmy."

Fitzsimmons' face flushed more deeply, but his mouth was hard and crookedly set. "Why, it goes together, doesn't it, Doc? Or does sometimes," he said, and grinned and took his leave, his shoulders held very straight, his hands carried before him. No doubt those burned hands would be useful with Willingham, and no doubt Fitzsimmons meant to use them for all they would gain him, and the miners—that went together sometimes. And perhaps, he thought, as he closed the door, it was as much as could be expected in a world of men.

He returned to sit beside Jessie again. As he watched her sleeping face he smiled and felt at rest himself. He thought there was no better vocation he could have asked, had he ever had a choice. Her sleeping face was quite beautiful, but he was worried about her thinness. She was tired, there had been too much strain upon her, but it would be better with Blaisedell gone. He started to touch her hair again, but he was afraid of waking her, so he contented himself with staring at her face as though to memorize it.

He started as there was a shot in Main Street; he frowned as he saw her eyelids move. There were more shots. Her eyes opened.

"What's that?" she whispered.

"Only a cowboy making a little excitement."

Her forehead was wrinkled with worry, her eyes looked troubled. There were more shots, followed by shouting.

"It is just some cowboy," he said soothingly. He took the bottle of laudanum up again and measured ten more drops into her glass, and rose to fill it with water. "Drink this," he said, and she raised her head to drink. The shooting continued, sporadically, and the shouting. Jessie smiled and he saw her relax as Blaisedell's footsteps descended the stairs.

"Clay will stop *that*," she whispered, as she lay back upon the pillow again.

He felt very tense as he listened to Blaisedell's steps in the entryway, and then he too relaxed as they passed Jessie's door and went outside. "I think I will join you, Jessie," he said, smiling down at her. He measured into the glass his usual dosage, in which he had not indulged for some time now, and then added five more drops and poured the water in. He raised the glass ceremoniously. He thought, as he drank the bitter and puckery draught, that it was not too early in the day.

## 64. *Morgan Cashes His Chips*

TOM MORGAN sat on the veranda of the Western Star Hotel and watched the sun's slow descent toward the bright peaks of the Dinosaurs. The crowd of miners had drifted away and now there was no one in the street for whom he had to put on a show of being mineowner-bought, which had made him feel like a fool. Alone now, with the sun going down, he felt at ease.

At the same time he had never felt so excited, nor so pleased with himself. His tongue pried and poked after the tooth he had lost the other night, to Clay, and it seemed to him now that he had played out his life like a kind of bad tooth, merely filling a hole in the jawbone of mankind, to leave, when he had passed on by, a momentary tender spot that not even a blind tongue would remember. But not now; they would remember him.

And now he thought he must have seen the way some time ago. He had told Clay that since he was leaving he might as well be posted out. It was only a step farther, ace over king. He knew what it would do to Clay, clearly he saw that; and yet he knew that it was right, and had to be, for Clay Blaisedell. It would wipe out General Peach, it would do more than that. For after it they could not touch Clay. After it they could make him neither more nor less. Clay would have come the route, and they would have to let him be, for there was no more. And they would remember Tom Morgan.

He felt an urge to crow, like a cock.

But he whispered, "Yes, me too, you poor damned lost son of a bitch!" He glanced to the left where he could see the roof of Miss Jessie Marlow's boardinghouse, where Clay was, and wondered what he was doing now, thinking now, feeling now. He clasped the shotgun that leaned between his legs and banged the butt gently against the planks. "Clay, I am sorry," he whispered. "But it is the only thing." He counted a few more regrets: that he would not be able to beat Peach's head off with his own leather-bound quirt; Taliaferro. He laughed at himself as he realized that there was another regret, too. He wished that someone might know why he was doing this. He wished that Kate, at least, might know. But there was no way, and he supposed that it was fair enough.

He squinted up at the descending sun. Not so fast there! he thought. A miner walked along the far side of the street, and Morgan made a show of scowling and tipping the shotgun forward. Godbold came out of the hotel and down the steps past him, and walked quickly across Broadway.

He watched, in the late afternoon, the slant of sun under the arcades, the bright, shiny brown of a horse's haunch, the colors of the dresses of two whores looking in the window of Good-pasture's store. Sam Brown had not got his sign back up yet, and the yellow rectangle was fading in the sun. The wind blew up a whirl of dust, which traveled a way and died, and sent a dry weed rolling and rustling along the edge of the boardwalk. The light changed as the sun slid down the western slope of the sky, and the shadow line advanced across the dusty street. Now, where the sun struck, it made darker stronger colors that seemed tinged with red. It was getting late, and it was coming time.

He banged the shotgun butt down again and rose. Dawson leaned in the doorway with a rifle under his arm, and looked as though he were putting a lot into wishing he were someplace else. He went inside past Dawson, and propped the shotgun against the counter. The Medusa people were all in the dining room. Newman sat gazing out the window. Willingham was playing a game of solitaire, his black hard-hat seated squarely on top of his head, a hand pulling at his fringe of red beard. MacDonald, seated across from him, was morosely watching the cards.

"The muckers will be in from the other mines pretty quick now," Morgan called into the dining room. "There will be hell busting the door down then."

MacDonald grimaced, and shifted his black-slinged arm around in front of his body. Willingham turned the cards and said, "Mr. Morgan, you enjoy alarming us." He took a gold watch from his vest pocket and consulted it. "I suppose we can't count on that old idiot getting back here tonight, can we?"

"He's forgotten us," MacDonald said, in a hollow voice. Newman, his shoulders hunched, had turned to watch them. Three foremen sat at another table at the far end of the room. None of them looked as though they had anything to be pleased about.

Willingham said, "I told him I would ruin him. I will feel quite put out if he ruins himself by blundering down into Mexico."

"What you big mining men need is a more reliable army. Chasing off after Apaches!"

"I don't believe there are any Apaches," MacDonald said. "Mr. Willingham, I think we ought to get that coach around and—"

"I will not be driven out of here!" Willingham said. He looked down at his cards again. "Well, Mr. Morgan? I thought our bargain was that you were to maintain the battlements. That is out in front, not here."

"Things are slow out there. I can't pick a fight with anybody."

"Good God!" MacDonald said. "We don't want any fights!"

"I thought I was to pick fights and shoot holes in jacks. Run some of them out of town."

"Good God!"

"Mr. Morgan, kindly remove your dubious frontier humor and yourself. Your post is on the veranda."

"I'm going upstairs and change my shirt, and then remove myself for a walk around town."

"Mr. Morgan—"

"I always take a walk around sundown," he said. "I wouldn't miss it for the Medusa mine." He went on upstairs to his room.

There he stripped off his coat, harness, and shirt, and washed himself in the basin. He sat down on the edge of his bed to check the action of his Banker's Special. A thin edge of the sun came in through the window, throwing a watery red light over the bed. There was a beat like that of great slow wings in his head, and he sat with the revolver in his hand staring at the blank wall opposite him for a long time before he rose and put on a new linen shirt. He found that his fingers were shaking as he tried to insert his gold cuff links into the cuffs. "I'll be damned!" he whispered. "Why, Rattlesnake!" He stood before the distorted mirror in his shirt sleeves, regarding his pale face with the slash of black mustache across it. He brushed his hair until it shone silver. He rubbed his hands hard together, stretching and clenching his fingers until they felt limber, and then he poured a little whisky into a glass, raised it, said, "How," bowed to the setting sun, and drank.

Leaving his coat off, he set the Banker's Special inside the buckle of his belt and swaggered back downstairs. Gough stared at him round-eyed. In the dining room a young miner in clean blue pants and shirt, and with disfigured, scarred hands which he held awkwardly before him, was talking to Willingham, while MacDonald stood glaring at him with his face mottled red and white.

"What goes against what's bred into you?" said Willingham, who was still playing solitaire.

"Stope-burning," the boy said.

"Oh, it's stope-burning, is it?" Willingham said caustically.

"Yes, sir," the boy said. "There's most of them feel that way about it now. They figure when Peach gets back he will load us up and ship us out like he was set to do in the first place, so might as well get shipped for goats as sheep. There is some that get satisfaction from a good fire, and knowing how it'll burn a couple-three years. It just goes against what's bred in, with me. And some others."

"Oh, you are talking for some others, are you?"

"I might be," the boy said.

"Blackguarding young—" MacDonald cried, but he stopped as Willingham waved a hand at him.

"How many do you speak for, my boy?"

Leaning in the doorway, Morgan watched Willingham, who had not looked up at the boy yet. Willingham ran out of plays, and picked up the cards and shuffled them.

The boy rubbed his scarred hands together. "Well, I don't know, Mr. Willingham. I guess that would depend. They'd just about all like to go back to work, sure enough. But you know how people get—they don't much like feeling they've got backed down to nothing. That's how come they've stayed out so long. Mr. MacDonald here wouldn't give an inch."

"Hush, Charlie," Willingham said, as MacDonald started to speak. The boy glanced around at Morgan. He had the shadowy beginnings of a beard, and he looked like a card sharp posing as a country bumpkin.

"Not an inch, eh?" Willingham said, shaking his head.

"I guess they wouldn't ever go back to work for Mr. MacDonald. If you'll pardon me for being frank, Mr. Mac."

"Mr. Willingham!" MacDonald cried, in a strangled voice. Willingham only pushed a hand at him, then began to turn the cards once more. He did not look up even now.

"How many do you speak for?" he said again.

"I guess the more I got from you, the more I could speak for."

"I see," Willingham said. "Well, sit down, my boy." The young miner sat down warily, in MacDonald's chair, and Willingham went on. "Let's see if reasonable men cannot work this out amicably. I will warn you in advance that I do not intend to give much more than an inch, but I have always desired to be fair. Sometimes subordinates become over-eager—I recognize that much."

It looked, Morgan thought, as though it would be a good game, with MacDonald first into the pot. He would have liked to stay to watch it, but the sun was going down. He said loudly, "I guess I had better get moving if I expect to run Blaisedell out of town tonight."

The young miner's head swung toward him. MacDonald's mouth gaped open. Willingham rose out of his chair. "Great God!" one of the foremen said.

"I'll be back to collect that thousand dollars pretty quick," Morgan said, and grinned around the room and seated the Banker's Special more firmly in his belt.

"Mr. Morgan!" Willingham cried, but Morgan went on out, past the wide-eyed clerk. Dawson, at the front door, stared at him; as he passed he jerked Dawson's Colt from its scabbard.

Dawson said, "Whuh—"

"Keep out of the street, Fatty," he said. "There's going to be lead flying." He thrust the other's Colt inside his belt, and went down the steps and started west along the boardwalk.

The sun had swelled and deepened in color. It hung like a

red balloon over the sharp-pointed peaks that would soon impale it. It was a sun the equal of which you saw nowhere else, he thought; bigger and brighter than anywhere else, bigger and brighter today. He took his last cigar from his shirt pocket and bit down on it.

He crossed through the dust of Broadway and mounted the boardwalk in the next block. He passed the shell of the Glass Slipper. Men stared at his waist, and he turned his head from side to side to gaze back into their faces. Not one would meet his eyes. Once a cowboy chewing on a cud of tobacco looked back at him for a moment, but he slowed his steps and the cowboy turned quickly aside. No one spoke in his wake. Faces peered out at him over the batwing doors of the Lucky Dollar; six or eight horses were tied to the rail there. He heard whispering behind him now, and he saw Goodpasture watching him from his store window. He glanced up toward the French Palace and tipped his hat in salute. Hearing a movement behind him he turned and grinned to see three cowboys hurriedly getting their horses out of the street.

He went on, under the new sign with the one bullet hole through it, and turned into the jail. Gannon glanced up at him from behind the table, and he brought out Dawson's Colt and leveled it. "Hands up," he said.

Stiff-faced, Gannon rose slowly; his hands continued to rise, shoulder high. "What—" he said, and stopped.

Morgan stepped forward and drew Gannon's Colt and jammed it inside his belt. He motioned Gannon toward the open cell door. Gannon didn't move and he thumbed the hammer back. "Get in there!"

"What the hell do you think you are doing?" Gannon said hoarsely.

"Get in there!" He jammed the muzzle into Gannon's belly and Gannon backed into the cell. He slammed the door and locked it, and tossed the key ring toward the back of the jail. He sneered in at Gannon through the bars. "I promised Kate you wouldn't get hurt," he said, and added, "If this comes wrong you had better tell her if I couldn't do it Pat Cletus couldn't've either."

"What are you going to do?"

"Pistol-whip the spots off this town." With Dawson's Colt in his right hand and Gannon's in his left, he stepped outside.

"Morgan!" Gannon called after him. But he raised his hand and drowned his name in a gunblast; the new sign swung wildly, perforated again.

Now the fuse was lit; he vaulted the tie rail, and his boots sank into the soft dust of the street. The sun sat on the peaks, blood-red, like the yolk of a bad egg. He shivered a little in the wind as he turned his back on the sun. He laughed to see the men scampering along the boardwalks as he swaggered out into the street. He had seen towns shot up before. The best he had ever seen at it was Ben Nicholson, but he could beat that. He spat out his cigar, raised Dawson's Colt, and pulled the trigger again. With the blast rocking in his ears he began to howl like a coyote, an Apache, and a rebel all rolled into one.

"Yah-hoo!" he yelled. "I am the worst man in the West! I am the Black Rattlesnake of Warlock! My mother was a timber wolf and my daddy a mountain lion, and I strangled them both the day I was born!

"Yah-hoo!" he yelled. "I will kill anything that moves, so sit still or die, you sons of bitches; or if you move, crawl! I can spit a man through at fifty yards! I have got lightning in both hands, I comb my hair with wildcats and brush my teeth with barbed wire!" He put a bullet through Taliaferro's sign. A man dived inside the pharmacy, and he fired behind him; a puff of dust rose from the adobe.

"Who wants to die?" he shouted, walking slowly forward. "I am spoiling for a fight! Come on, you sons of bitches—I eat dead cowboys!"

His throat was dry and hoarse from shouting. But he grinned idiotically at the white faces that stared at him. His shirt back felt soaked with sweat. He fired into the air again, and he fired at the yellow patch over the Billiard Parlor. "Come on out and fight!" he yelled. "I have killed forty-five men, half with one shot, and I am going to run some score today!

"Any friends of McQuown's here? I will claw them down with Honest Abe! I am the champeen all-time cowboy killer. Any partners of Brunk's? Come on, you muckering chittle-witted muckers and I will dice your livers for you. Any damned Yankees? No, I can hear them scampering now! Anybody! Come on out, you yellow sons of whores, or I will run this whole town out of itself!"

He raised Dawson's six-shooter and pulled the trigger again;

the hammer snapped down dry. He tossed it and caught it by the barrel, and with a long sweep of his arm slung it through Goodpasture's window with a smash of glass. He raised his left hand and fired Gannon's.

"Come on, I say! Where are those brave possemen? Where is that bunch of jailhouse bummers!" He saw several of them, standing with some cowboys along the wall near the Glass Slipper. "Step up, boys! Come out of your holes! No? Where is that mighty deputy then? He has locked himself in his own jail. Isn't there a man in this town? Any friends of Blaisedell's then? I will warm up on them. Speak up, boys!"

He fired into the air to liven things again. Left-handed, he shot the panes out of the gunshop window. He flung Gannon's used-up Colt toward the pharmacy. A man dodged out of the way, and then snapped stiffly to a standstill as though he were standing at attention.

He drew the Banker's Special from his belt. He laughed and howled, and fired into the air. He saw a movement in the ruin of the Glass Slipper, and he fired and chipped adobe. The dust of the street darkened as the sun went down behind him. The moon was up over the Bucksaws, pale as a cloud. It was time, he thought.

"Yah-hoo!" he screeched. "Where is Clay Blaisedell? Where is that yellow-bellied, hollowed-out, gold-handled, long-haired marshal of Warlock? Whose skirts is he hiding behind? Come on out, Clay Blaisedell! Out of your hole and let's see the color of your plaster guts!"

He had come up even with the Glass Slipper now, and he saw a movement among the townsmen there; he swung the Banker's Special and howled with laughter to see one of them dive to the boardwalk. He saw Mosbie's dark, scarred face twisted with rage. "Come on, Clay," he whispered. "I am starting to feel like a damned fool!"

He walked on down Main Street, laughing and taunting; he swung toward the Billiard Parlor, and the miners there tumbled back inside. "Yah-hoo!" he screamed, with his voice tearing in his throat. "Every man is afraid of me! Where is Clay Blaisedell! He has posted his last man out of this town! Blaisedell! Come out here and play boys' games with me, you yellow Yankee hound. Blaisedell!"

Come on, Clay; come on! I am sick to death of this game already! He walked on across Broadway, and saw Dawson jump back inside the door of the hotel. He saw Clay at the next corner.

"Morgan!" Mosbie yelled, and he spun and squeezed the trigger, and saw through the smoke Mosbie slam back against the wall in the shadow under the arcade, his Colt flying free of his hand. And in his deafened ears he heard Clay call, "Morg!"

Clay stood in the street now with his black hat pulled down to conceal his face, his wide brown leather belt slanting across his hips, the sleeves of his white shirt fluttering in the wind; with a wild relief and jubilation Morgan knew that his luck still held, and, as he jammed the burning barrel of the Banker's Special back into his belt, he knew, with a sudden pride, that he could beat those hands of Clay's if he wished, and knew he could center-shot that white shirt just beneath the black tie-ends, if he wished. He yelled hoarsely, "I can beat you, Blaisedell! You had better hit it fast!"

He cried out once more, wordlessly, in triumph, as his hand swept up with the Banker's Special, beating Clay's hand. Clay's hat flew off. He heard a cry and it was Kate. "*Tom!*" Instantly he was flung staggering back with white-hot death impaling him. He squeezed the trigger once more, unaimed, and the sound was lost in a totality of deafening sound; he sought frenziedly to grin as he staggered forward toward the motionless figure that faced him wreathed in smoke. The Banker's Special was suddenly too heavy. It slipped from his hand. But still he could raise his hand to his breast, slowly up, slowly across and back, while the world blurred into deeper and deeper shadow.

He fell forward into the dust. It received him gently. One arm felt a little cramped and he managed to move it out from under his body. In his eyes there was only dust, which was soft, and strangely wet beneath him. "Tom!" He heard it dimly. "Tom!" He felt a hand upon his back. It caught his shoulder and tried to turn him, Kate's hand, and he heard Kate sobbing through the swell of a vast singing in his ears. He tried to speak to her, but he choked on blood. The dust pulled him away, and he sank through it gratefully; still he could laugh, but now he could weep as well.

## 65. *The Wake at the Lucky Dollar*

### I

MORGAN LAY face down in the dust of Main Street. Kate Dollar bent over him, pulling weakly at his shoulder, her harsh, dry sobbing loud in the silence, her white face turning to stare at Blaisedell, and then at the men who lined the boardwalk. Buck Slavin ducked under the tie rail and came out to join her.

Blaisedell retrieved his hat. His face was invisible beneath its brim in the fading light. Kate Dollar rose as Slavin bent down and turned Morgan over. Morgan's face, caked with white dust, was grinning still. His shirt front was muddy and blood welled through the mud.

"Get your hands off him," Blaisedell said, and Slavin straightened hurriedly, wiping his hands on his trouser legs. Blaisedell's face was a mesh of thick, red welts, his eyes were swollen almost closed.

"You weren't worth it," Kate Dollar said, not loudly, as Blaisedell bent down and picked up Morgan's body. He stood for a moment, staring back at her, and then he carried Morgan slowly back up the street toward the Lucky Dollar. He laid him on the boardwalk, ducked under the rail, and, in the silence, picked him up again. He backed through the batwing doors of the Lucky Dollar, gently maneuvering Morgan's sagging, dusty head past the doors.

Inside, grunting a little now with his burden, Blaisedell moved with heavy steps toward the first faro layout. Men scrambled out of his way, and the dealer and the case keeper retreated. He laid Morgan on the layout amid the chips and counters, and the silver. He straightened Morgan's legs and folded his hands upon his muddy chest, and he stood for a long time in the intense and crowded silence staring down at Morgan. Then he glanced slowly around at the men who watched him, his eyes slanting from face to face white-rimmed like those of a frightened stallion: toward Skinner, Hasty, French, and Bacon, who stood nearby; toward the miners at the bar; toward the sheriff and Judge Holloway, who sat at a table with a whisky bottle between them, the sheriff staring at nothing in frozen concentration, the judge leaning forward with his forehead resting in his hands. Blaisedell glanced up at the sweaty-faced lookout sitting stiffly with his hands held rigid six inches above the shotgun laid across his chair arms.

He took a handkerchief from his pocket and gently brushed the dust from Morgan's face; then he covered the face with the handkerchief and said to the lookout in a jarring voice, "Watch him." His bootheels scuffed loudly as he moved toward the bar. The men edged away before him so that by the time he reached it he had a twenty-foot expanse to himself. He put his hand down flat on the bar. "Whisky," he said, staring into the looking-glass opposite him.

One of the barkeepers brought him a bottle and a glass, and retreated as though on wheels. Blaisedell poured a glassful, raised it and said, "How?" He drank and set the glass down with a sharp clatter.

The sound only intensified the silence. Faces peered in the batwing doors, and men close to the doors began silently to edge toward them, and outside. Those beyond Blaisedell remained in rigid attitudes. Skinner, French, Hasty, and Bacon quietly seated themselves at a table near the judge and the sheriff. A chair scraped and Blaisedell looked around; again his white-rimmed, swollen eyes swung from face to face. They fixed themselves finally upon Taliaferro, who stood down at the far end of the bar, and Taliaferro's mole-spotted dark face turned yellow.

With a slow, hunched motion Blaisedell turned toward him. "Taliaferro!" he said.

Taliaferro screamed, raised his hands high above his head, turned, and fled back through his office doorway as Blaisedell's hand slapped to his side. But he did not draw.

Peter Bacon crossed his hands on the table before him, staring down at them; Pike Skinner was gazing fixedly at Morgan lying on the faro layout with the handkerchief over his face. "Oh my sweet God damn!" the sheriff said, almost inaudibly, his lips barely moving with it. "Don't anybody cross him, for God almighty's sake!"

"Oh Lord, deliver us from evil," the judge said suddenly, loudly, in a drunken voice, and the sheriff flinched.

Blaisedell glanced once at the judge, and then turned back to the bar. "How?" he said, as though to himself; he straightened, staring at his dark reflection in the glass. With a slow, deliberate motion he drew his Colt. The explosion jerked the men around him like puppets on strings; one of the miners cried out shrilly, and the bartenders ducked behind the bar. Sound rocked and echoed through the Lucky Dollar, and, in the smoke, the mirror opposite Blaisedell dissolved into a spider web of cracks. A long shard of glass tipped out and fell, and others crashed down in brittle breakage.

The lookout stood gazing straight ahead of him at nothing, with his hands held out before him like a piano player's. The barkeepers raised their heads. The sheriff rose from his chair and, moving like a sleepwalker, slowly and carefully walked toward the batwing doors, and then, in a rush, fought his way through the men there and outside. Blaisedell stood facing the shattered mirror obscured in gunsmoke still. He thrust the gold-handled six-shooter into its scabbard, grasped the whisky bottle by the neck, and swung around.

He moved back to the layout where Morgan lay. He walked around it, putting the bottle down beside Morgan's head, and stood staring at the men beyond with his swollen eyes in his battered, striped face. No one moved. White-faced, they avoided his gaze, and one another's. He turned toward the judge.

"Say something."

The judge drew his arms in closer to his body, hunching his shoulders, his wrists crossed and his hands held flat against his chest; his head sagged lower.

Blaisedell's mustache twisted contemptuously. He turned back to the others. "Say something."

Peter Bacon looked steadily back at him. Hasty was cleaning his fingernails with minute attention. Tim French, with his back to Blaisedell, stared at Bacon, plucking at his lower lip. Pike Skinner, his ugly, great-eared face flushed beet-red, said, "I guess he would've killed somebody. He broke Mosbie's arm for him. He was after trouble. He—"

"What's Mosbie worth?"

"He was out to kill somebody, Marshal," Hasty said. "He—"

"Kill who? You?"

"Might've been me, I guess," Hasty said, uncomfortably.

"What are you worth?"

Hasty said nothing. French turned slightly, carefully, to glance up at Blaisedell.

"Oh Lord, deliver us!" the judge said.

The whites of Blaisedell's eyes flashed again, his teeth showed briefly beneath his mustache. He hooked his thumb in his shell belt. "Was it what you wanted?" he said to French.

French did not reply.

"What you wanted?" he said to Bacon.

"I guess I never much want to see a man killed, Marshal," Bacon said.

"You are talking to your friends here, Marshal," Skinner said.

"I have got no friends!" Blaisedell's breath leaked steadily, noisily through his half-parted lips. "Don't look at me like that!" he said suddenly.

Peter Bacon, to whom he had spoken, leaned back a little in his chair. His wrinkled face was grayish under the dark tan, his washed blue eyes remained fixed on Blaisedell. Then he rose.

"I'll be going," he said, in a shaky voice. "I don't much like seeing this." He started for the door.

"Come back here," Blaisedell said.

"I guess I won't," Bacon said. His face turned toward Blaisedell as Blaisedell drew the gold-handled Colt, but he said, "I'd never be afraid to turn my back on you, Marshal." He went on outside.

"You've got no cause to turn mean against us here, Marshal," Pike Skinner said.

"I've got cause," Blaisedell said. It was almost dark in the Lucky Dollar now, and his face looked phosphorescent in the dim light. "Judge me," he said. "You judged him. Judge me now." He swung toward Judge Holloway. "Judge me," he said, in the jarring voice.

"What will you do?" the judge cried suddenly. "Kill us all for your pain?" He pulled himself upright, trying to fit his crutch beneath his armpit. With a swift movement Blaisedell skipped forward and kicked the crutch loose. The judge fell heavily, crying out. Blaisedell snatched up the crutch and flung it toward the batwing doors. It fell and slid with a clatter.

"I've had too much of you!" Blaisedell said. "Crawl for it. Crawl past him, that was a man and not all talk!"

Pike Skinner got to his feet, and Tim French half rose;

Blaisedell swung toward them. The judge crawled, awkwardly, sobbing with fear; he crawled past the faro layout, reached the crutch, and pushed it toward the bar, where he pulled himself up, and, sobbing and panting, swung out through the louvre doors. It was silent again. Blaisedell went back to stand beside Morgan's body. He took off his hat and brushed a hand uncertainly over his pale hair. He pointed a finger at one of the barkeepers.

"Bring me four candles over here." He turned slowly, in the dim room. "Take off your damned hats," he said. His voice cracked. "Sing," he said.

There was no sound. One of the barkeepers scurried forward with four white candles. Blaisedell jammed one in the mouth of the whisky bottle, lit it, and placed it beside Morgan's head. He took the bottle from the judge's table and fixed and lit a second, which he placed on the other side of Morgan's head. He handed the other two candles back to the barkeeper and indicated Morgan's feet.

"Sing!" he said again. Someone cleared his throat. Blaisedell began to sing, in the deep, heavy, jarring voice:

"Rock of ages, cleft for me,
Let me hide myself in thee."

The others began to join in, and the hymn rose. The candle flames soared and shivered at Morgan's head and feet.

"Let the water and the blood
From thy side, a healing flood,
Be of sin the double cure,
Save from wrath, and make me pure."

They sang more loudly as Blaisedell's voice led them. They sang the same verse three times, and then the singing abruptly died as Blaisedell's voice ceased. Blaisedell removed the handkerchief with which he had covered Morgan's face.

"You can come past and pay your respects to the dead," he said, quietly now.

Several of the miners came hesitantly forward, and Blaisedell moved to the other side of the layout, so that they had to pass between him and Morgan. He stared into each face as the man passed. The others began to fall into line. There was a scrape of boots upon the floor. One of the miners crossed himself.

"Have you got a cross on?" Blaisedell said. The man's sweating, bearded face paled. He brought from under his shirt a silver crucifix on a greasy cord, which he slipped over his head. Blaisedell took it from him and fixed it upright between Morgan's hands. The men filed on past the faro layout, under Blaisedell's eyes, and each glanced in his turn at Morgan's grinning dead face, and then passed more quickly outside. The candle flames danced, swayed, flickered. Blaisedell beckoned the lookout down from his stand to join the line, and the men at the tables, and the barkeeps. Some, as they went by, crossed themselves, and some nodded with their hats placed awkwardly against their chests, but all in silence and without protest passed by as Blaisedell had directed, and on outside into the crowd that waited in Main Street.

II

"Where's Gannon?" Pike Skinner said, in a stifled voice, when he joined the others outside in the darkness. "Oh hell, oh, God damn it, oh, Jesus Christ," he said helplessly.

"What's he doing now?" someone whispered. They stood crushed together upon the boardwalk, but at a distance from the louvre doors.

"Breaking bottles, it sounds like."

The sound of breaking glass continued, and then they heard furniture being dragged across the floor. There was a wrenching sound of splintering wood. Presently they noticed that there was more light inside.

"Fire," someone said, in a matter-of-fact voice.

"Fire!" another yelled.

Immediately Blaisedell appeared in the doorway, outlined against the strengthening bluish light. He had the lookout's shotgun in his hands. "Get back!" he said, and, because they did not comply rapidly enough, shouted viciously, "Get on back!" and raised the shotgun and cocked it. They fled before him off the boardwalk into the street, and down the boardwalk right and left. Flames rose in great blue tongues inside the doors.

Blaisedell looked huge, black, and two-dimensional standing against them. The fire crackled inside. Soon it coughed and roared, and red and yellow flames were mingled with the blue.

"Fire!" someone shouted. "Fire! It's the Lucky Dollar going!" Others took up the cry. Flames licked out through the louvre doors, and Blaisedell moved aside, and, after a while, walked east along the boardwalk, the men there silently giving way before him, and disappeared into the darkness.

## 66. *Gannon Takes Off His Star*

IN THE jail the flame in the hanging lamp was dim behind the smoky shade. Gannon watched the broad, wide-hatted shadow Pike Skinner made as he moved across before the lamp, pacing toward the names scratched on the wall, and back toward the cell where the judge snored in drunken insensibility upon the prisoners' cot. Peter Bacon sat with his shoulders slumped tiredly in the chair beside the alley door, wiping the sweat and ashes from his face with his bandanna. The fire, at least, was out.

Gannon leaned against the wall and watched Pike and wondered that his legs still held him up. He heard the judge snort in his sleep and the clash of springs as he changed position. The whisky bottle clattered to the floor. He had locked himself in the cell and had the key ring in there with him.

"Well, by Christ," Pike said. "Keller's lit out of here like the fiends was after him and the judge's drunk himself to a coma. What's there for you and me, Pete?"

"Go home and sleep," Peter said.

"Sleep!" Pike cried. "Jesus Christ, sleep! Did you see his eyes?"

"I saw them," Peter said.

Pike rubbed a hand over his dirty face. The back of his hand was black with soot. Then Pike turned to face Gannon. "Johnny, he will kill you!"

"Why, I don't know that it will come to that, Pike," he said.

Pike glared at him with his ugly red face wild with grief and anger; Peter was watching him too, the chew of tobacco moving slowly in his jaw. He felt the skin at the back of his neck crawl. They were looking at him as though he were going to kill himself.

"You didn't see his eyes," Pike said. "Leave him be, for Christ's sake, Johnny! Go home and sleep on it. Maybe he will've come to himself by morning."

Gannon shook his head a little. He could look down through himself as through a hollow tube and see that he was a coward and be neither ashamed of it nor proud that he would do what he had to do. He said, "I guess it doesn't matter much whether he comes to himself or not. You can't go around burning a man's place down. The whole town might've gone."

"And a damned good thing," Pike said. He resumed his pacing. "It's what's wrong," he said. "A town of buildings is more important than a man is." The judge groaned and snorted in the cell, in his troubled sleep.

"I hold it poorly on the judge," Peter said, as bitterly as Gannon had ever heard him speak. "I hold a man should face up to a thing he has got to face up to."

"Shit!" Pike Skinner cried. He halted, facing the names scratched upon the wall, his fists clenched at his sides. "Face up to shit!" he said. He swung around. "Johnny, he is still owed something here!"

"I thought maybe I'd tell him I wouldn't come after him till morning. I thought maybe he might go before, then."

"Johnny, who the hell are you to tell him to go, or arrest him either?"

He felt a stir of anger; he said, stiffly, "I am deputy here, Pike."

"He'll kill you!"

"Maybe he has come to himself already," Peter said.

"Is he still down there?"

"He was just now."

Gannon pushed himself away from the wall. He could smell on himself the stench of ashes and sweat, and fear. "I guess I will be going along, then," he said. Neither Pike nor Peter spoke. The judge snored. He picked up his hat from the table and went on outside into the star-filled dark. The cold wind funneled down the street and he could hear the steady creaking of the sign above his head. He shivered in the cold. The moon was down already in the west, the stars very bright. He walked slowly along the boardwalk, with the hollow pound of his footfalls reverberating in the silence.

A light burned in the window above Goodpasture's store. The French Palace was dark. He crossed Southend Street and stepped carefully past the clutter of boards before the Lucky Dollar where a part of the arcade roof had fallen in. He could smell wet ashes now, and smoke, and the stink of char and whisky, and the sweeter, stomach-convulsing odor with them. Further on there were still a few loiterers standing along the railing. Some of them greeted him as he went by. He passed the burnt-out ruin of the Glass Slipper and crossed Broadway. A lamp burned in a second-story window of the hotel. The rocking chairs were dark, low shapes on the veranda. One of them was occupied, and his heart clenched breathless and painful in his chest for a moment, because it was the chair in which Morgan had always sat. But it would be Blaisedell now.

He heard a faint creak as it rocked. He went to the bottom of the veranda steps and halted there, ten feet away from the chairs. He could make out the faint, pale mass of Blaisedell's face beneath his black hat, the smaller shapes of his pale hands on the chair arms.

"I'm sorry, Blaisedell," he said, and waited. The face turned toward him, and he could see the gleam of Blaisedell's eyes. Blaisedell did not speak.

"It is time, Blaisedell," he said, and he hoped that Blaisedell would remember, but still there was no answer. The rocking chair creaked again. He repeated the words.

Then he took a deep breath and said, "Marshal, I will have to come after you if you are still here by morning. I—"

"Not Marshal," Blaisedell said. "Clay Blaisedell." Blaisedell laughed, and he stepped back, against his will, from that laugh. "Are you running me out of town, Deputy?"

He could see Blaisedell's eyes more clearly now, and more of his face; the welts on it looked like tattoo marks. "No, I am just saying I will have to arrest you in the morning. So I am asking you to go before."

"Nobody tells me that," Blaisedell said. "Or asks me. I will come and go as I please."

"Then I will have to come after you in the morning."

"Come shooting if you do."

"Why, I will do that if I have to, Marshal."

"You'll have to."

He stood there staring at Blaisedell, but Blaisedell was not looking at him any longer. "It is a damned shame, Marshal!" he burst out, but Blaisedell said nothing more, and finally he started on, holding himself carefully and tightly as though, if he did not, he would fall apart like something made of wet straw. He moved on east on Main Street without even being aware where he was going. When he looked back he could no longer see Blaisedell in the darkness.

At the corner of Grant Street he saw a light from the General Peach thrown out onto the dust of the street in a long, dim rectangle. He turned away from it and started up toward Kate's house with the key suddenly a very conscious weight and shape in his pocket. He took it out as he mounted the wooden steps. It rattled against the metal of the lock.

When it entered he turned it and thrust the door open. Inside the floor creaked beneath his weight. He closed the door and stood there waiting for his eyes to accustom themselves to the deeper darkness here. His shoulders ached, and dust and ashes itched upon his face and around his neck. He could make out a shape like a deep coffin on the floor between him and the bedroom door, and there was a flicker of light in the doorway beyond it. Kate's disembodied face appeared, filled with shadows, with a candle flame below it. The box before him was one of her trunks.

"Deputy?" she said, in a calm voice, and he answered yes, nodding, but he did not move, shivering still, though it was warmer here. Kate lowered the candle a little and he saw that she wore a loose robe which she held clasped at the waist with her left hand.

Kate watched him without expression as he removed his hat and started toward her. It was a waxen face above the candle flame, with no paint on it, and a cloud of thick black hair framing it. The beauty spot was missing from her cheek. She looked very slim and boyish in the robe, but a dull point of a breast showed through the silk with the pull of her hand at her waist.

As he approached she moved back with a slight inclination of her head, and, hat in hand, he passed into her bedroom. He watched her place the candle on a box beside her bed. The room was barren now, as he had seen it once before, with only a few clothes hanging upon the wire stretched across one corner, the sad-faced Virgin and her other things evidently packed away for her departure. She sat down on the edge of the bed, stiffly, her eyes raised to him. There were blue-black glints in her hair from the candlelight.

His tongue felt thick in his mouth. "I have told Blaisedell he is to get out of town by morning."

"Have you?" Kate said, tonelessly, and he nodded.

"And did he go?" she said.

He shook his head.

Her full, pale lips opened a little and he could hear the sudden whisper of her breathing. He felt sweaty, foul, and exhausted, and there was a slow, crushing movement in his head, like the laboring of a walking beam. "What do you want of me?" Kate whispered. "Are you afraid?" She unclasped her hand and the robe fell open down her white belly. He averted his eyes.

"Why, I can fix that," she continued. "That is what men come to women for, isn't it?"

"I guess I'm not very much afraid," he said.

"Come to brag? What a man you are?"

He flushed and shook his head.

"Someone to be sorry you are dead?" Kate said. He shook his head again, but she went on. "I have seen all those things. When you have seen everything you still have to watch it over and over—" Her voice broke, but immediately she regained control of it. "And over," she said. "The same things happening and coming on. But I have seen one thing new. I have seen Tom Morgan kill himself, and I know he did it for Clay Blaisedell."

"He has to go," he said. "He is on the prod and mean. He burned Taliaferro's place down, and all but burned the town."

"Oh, he will go. You can make him go by letting him kill you. That is brave, isn't it?"

The candlelight gleamed in her black eyes that were like deep ponds. "But not quite brave enough? Did you come to get the rest from me?" She said it as though it were important to her.

"There is no one else but me to do it," he said hoarsely.

"And—and everything's come to nothing if I don't. It is up to me; do you think I want to do it?"

"Do what? Die? Or kill him?"

"Why, put it to him, even." He wrenched his hat between his hands, and stared down at the swath of her flesh where the robe hung open.

"Tom would kill himself for Blaisedell, but you would do it for a silly star on your chest," Kate said. "Take it off—I will take a man, I won't take a sharp-pointed tin thing like that against me. Take it off!" she said again, as his fingers fumbled the catch loose. He dropped the star in his pocket.

"Not afraid?" Kate said, mockingly; but her face was not mocking. "Wait!" she said. "Tom to pay for Peach, and you for Tom. But I will have my pay too. What for, Johnny? You are not fool enough to think you can beat him?"

"No, I know I can't. That's it, you see."

Her eyes narrowed. With a blunt movement of her hand she pulled the robe further open. "Then why?"

"If I am killed—"

"Give you the rest of your life in a night?" she said. "All of it?" In her face he saw what seemed to him a half-amused contempt, but triumph in it, and increasing triumph, and then pain showed naked there. "Come here then," she said, in a voice he didn't even recognize.

She pulled at her robe again as he dropped to his knees before her. He stifled a sound that welled in his throat, and flung his arms around her and pressed his face into her flesh. She brushed her hand over his head.

"You smell like a horse barn," she said gently. Her hand pressed his face against her. "Johnny, Johnny," she whispered. "Do you think I'd let him kill you?"

He didn't know what she meant. He felt the heavy swell of her breast against his cheek and stared down in the pale dark between them at the gleam of her thighs. Her breast pressed hard against him as she drew a deep breath; she blew it out, and there was darkness. Both her arms held him against her. She smelled very clean, and he was foul. He ran his hands along her body inside her robe, and he had never felt anything so smooth beneath his hands.

She rocked with him, forward and back, and whispered words in his ear that had no sense and were only disconnected sounds, but that were the sounds he had always wanted to hear without ever knowing it before. He was shivering uncontrollably as her hands rose and pressed flat against his cheeks and pulled his face to hers. Her lips were wonderfully warm in the warm darkness and her sharp-pointed fingers pressed into his back with exquisite pain. He twisted his lips from hers once, panting for breath, and she pulled his face into her throat where he could hear her own swift, shivering breath. Her body arched and strained against him, and he cried her name as they fell back and away through darkness, and her flesh enveloped him.

## 67. *Journals of Henry Holmes Goodpasture*

June 5, 1881 (continued)

THE FIRE in the Lucky Dollar has been quenched, and just in time, for a strong wind has come up. Thank God it did not arise earlier, or this town would have burned as swiftly as dry paper—a burnt offering after a man's reputation, or his sanity. A town to form Morgan's funeral pyre, and Blaisedell's parting salute. Or is it of parting? Those who saw him say he was quite insane. Almost, as I write this, I find I wish he had burned us all out: Warlock gone and ourselves scattered, leaving Blaisedell to brood here alone in his madness.

There will be no sleep this night.

The news of the death of General Peach comes as no shock. Neither have I taken it as a sign of New Hope, as Buck Slavin seems to. It is only a meaningless bit of information. Perhaps it is not even true.

I have had a stream of callers. I suppose they have seen my light and sought a fellow human to talk to. Kennon says he has heard that the strike has been settled. Mosbie's arm is broken, but he is not seriously wounded; I had thought he was dead. Kennon says he will resign from the Citizens' Committee; he does not say why. I feel the same. All reason is gone. Egan says that Morgan had got the drop on Gannon and locked him in the jail, which was why our brave deputy was so little in evidence this evening. He did appear during the fire, and helped organize a bucket brigade, the pumper having broken down. Egan says we will have to have a proper fire department; I stare at him stupidly as he says it.

Buck Slavin has come in again and told me the latest news. It is true, evidently, that General Peach is dead at the border. A Lieutenant Avery was here with a detachment—unobtrusively, for I did not see nor hear of them until now—to dispatch back to Bright's City the wagons that had been brought here to transport the miners to the railroad at Welltown. Peach's body is with the main train, which has hastened back up the valley. Whiteside is now presumably acting governor, and Buck is overjoyed. Avery told him, however, that Whiteside seemed a man in a trance. Evidently he was very close to the General when he fell (as he was always protectively close), and was much shocked by the incident, which was, however, a fortunate one. Avery said it was obvious to all but Peach by the time they reached the border that the massacre had been perpetrated by Mexicans in revenge upon the rustlers, and it had taken place, as well, upon Mexican soil. Peach, however, was determined that it was his old antagonist, Espirato, and seemed prepared to pursue him to South America, if necessary. But before he had passed onto Mexican soil, his horse slipped in a narrow defile at the mouth of Rattlesnake Canyon, he fell and died instantly, and mercifully. Whiteside, accompanying him, was the only man to see it. Afterwards his only concern was to get the cavalry and Peach's body back to Bright's City in order to give him a military funeral before decomposition of the remains begins.

Buck has no doubt that Whiteside will now, according to his promise, rectify all our wrongs and wants, and sees Warlock as a future metropolis of the West. Buck is an optimistic and public-minded man. To his mind Blaisedell is only a small and temporary blight upon the body politic; with all else healthy and aright, he will automatically disappear. Like the rest of us, but perhaps for different reasons, he too is no longer interested in the Citizens' Committee. I am apathetic of his ambitions, I am contemptuous of his optimism. The old, corrupt, and

careless god has been replaced in his heaven, and so, he feels,
all will be well with the world, which is, after all, the best of all
possible ones. It is a touching faith, but I am drawn more to
those who wander the night not with excitement for the future
but with dread of it.

I can see many of them through my window, unable to sleep
now that the fire is out. For what fire is out, and what is newly
lighted, and what will burn forever and consume us all? We will
fight fire with futile water or with savage fire to the end of this
earth itself, and never prevail, and we will drown in our water
and burn in our preventive fire. How can men live, and know
that in the end they will merely die?

Pike Skinner, who is frantic, says that Gannon has warned
Blaisedell that he intends to arrest him at sun-up. Skinner says
that Blaisedell will kill him, and I cannot tell whether he feels
more horror that Blaisedell should kill the Deputy, or that the
Deputy, who is Pike's friend, should be killed. Once I would
have stupidly said that the Deputy would not be such a fool.
I have been shown fatuous in my skepticism too many times.
Now I neither believe nor disbelieve, and I feel nothing. There
is nothing left to feel.

It is four in the morning by my watch. Mine is the only
light I can see, the scratching of my pen the only sound. Here
astride the dull and rusty razor's edge between midnight and
morning, I am sick to the bottom of my heart. Where is Buck
Slavin's bright future of faith, hope, and commerce? What is it
even worth, after all? For if men have no worth, there is none
anywhere. I feel very old and I have seen too many things in
my years, which are not so many; no, not even in my years, but
in a few months—in this day.

Outside there is only darkness, pitifully lit by the cold and
disinterested stars, and there is silence through the town, in
which some men sleep and clutch their bedclothes of hope and
optimism to them for warmth. But those I love more do not
sleep, and see no hope, and suffer for those brave ones who
will fall in hopeless effort for us all, whose only gift to us will
be that we will grieve for them a little while; those who see, as
I have come to see, that life is only event and violence without

reason or cause, and that there is no end but the corruption
and the mock of courage and of hope.

Is not the history of the world no more than a record of
violence and death cut in stone? It is a terrible, lonely, love-
less thing to know it, and see—as I realize now the doctor
saw before me—that the only justification is in the attempt,
not in the achievement, for there is no achievement; to know
that each day may dawn fair or fairer than the last, and end as
horribly wretched or more. Can those things that drive men to
their ends be ever stilled, or will they only thrive and grow and
yet more hideously clash one against the other so long as man
himself is not stilled? Can I look out at these cold stars in this
black sky and believe in my heart of hearts that it was this sky
that hung over Bethlehem, and that a star such as these stars
glittered there to raise men's hearts to false hopes forever?

This is the sky of Gethsemane, and that of Bethlehem has
vanished with its star.

## 68. *Gannon Sees the Gold Handles*

I

GANNON CAME awake with a start and stared at the outline
of the window that was emerging gray from the surrounding
darkness. He raised himself carefully on one elbow and looked
down at Kate's sleeping face, with the soft mass of hair beneath
it on the pillow like a heavy shadow, the soft curves of her
lashes on her cheeks, and her lips, which looked carved from
ivory. He watched the rounding and relaxation of her nostrils
as she breathed, and the slow, deep rise and fall of her breast.
One arm was thrown across it and her fingers almost touched
him.

Slowly, watching her face, he began to slide away from
her, stopping when her lips tightened for a moment and then
parted as though she would speak. But she did not waken,
and he eased himself from her bed, and carried his clothing,
shell belt, and boots into the living room to dress. His holstered Colt thumped upon the oilcloth-covered table as he set

it down, and he held his breath for a moment, but there was no sound from the bedroom.

He looked in at her one last time before he put on his boots. Her hand had moved over a little farther, to lie where he had lain. He put the key on the table, went outside, and in the dark gray chill set his boots down and worked his feet into them, and softly closed the door.

The town was empty and out of the grayness buildings and houses came slowly at him like thoughts emerging from the gray edges of his mind, to hang there unattached, two-dimensional, and strange in the silence that was broken only by the hollow clump of his boots upon the boardwalk.

Down Grant Street he could just make out the high bulk of the General Peach, lightless and asleep. He turned right down Main Street. A few stars still showed frail shards of light, but almost as he looked up they were gone. He walked past the hotel and the empty rocking chairs upon the veranda, and across Broadway; he felt a strangely intense sense of possession of the vacant town in the early morning. He passed the ruin of the Glass Slipper, the pharmacy and the gunshop with their shattered windows, and skirted again the charred timbers on the boardwalk before the Lucky Dollar. The sickly sweetish stench, and that of whisky, were dissipated now, but inside the wreckage was still smoking. He crossed Southend and halted for a moment beneath the new sign to gaze into the dim interior of the jail, and felt the adobe breathing the night's chill upon him.

He waited there until he heard the judge stir and snore in the cell, and then he went on to Birch's roominghouse, again removing his boots so he would awaken no one as he climbed the stairs to his room. Upstairs there was a dull concert of snoring, which faded when he closed his door. He lit the lamp and held his hands to its small warmth for a moment, and then he stripped off his clothes and washed himself, soaping and scrubbing his white flesh with a rag and icy water from the crockery pitcher; he shaved his face before the triangle of mirror. He laid out clean clothes and dressed himself with care, his best white shirt, his new striped pants—store pants from the legs of which he tried to rub the creases—and dusted off his new, too-tight star boots, and painfully worked his feet into them. After rubbing his star to a shine he fastened it to his vest, and put that on, and donned his canvas jacket against the cold. He rubbed the dust from each crevice between the cartridge-keepers of his shell belt, frowned at the torn hole at the back, and polished the sharp-edged buckle. He buckled on the belt, cinching it a notch tighter than usual against the crawling cold of his stomach, thrust it down as far as it would go, and knotted the scabbard thong around his thigh tightly too.

Then he produced a whisky bottle half full of oil, and a rag, and sat down at the table to clean his Colt, and oil it, and wipe it dry. He did this over and over again with an intense, rapt attention, rubbing patiently at each small fleck of Main Street dust until the old forty-four-caliber shone dully and richly in the lamplight. He oiled the inside of the holster too, and worked the Colt in and out until it slid to his satisfaction. He replaced the cartridges in the cylinder, let the hammer down upon the empty one, seated the Colt in the holster, scrubbed the oil from his hands, and was ready. Now he could hear some of the miners waking and stirring in their rooms.

He rose and blew out the lamp. As he started out he remembered the spare key to the cell door. He took it with him, on its iron ring, to leave at the jail.

Outside it was lighter, harsher gray now, and down Main Street he could see lights burning among the miners' shacks beyond Grant Street. As he walked toward the jail more of them were lit. The dust of the street was cleanly white, and the slight breeze from the northeast was fresh in his nostrils and no longer cold. The gray above the Bucksaws showed a greenish cast now, a yellow green that faded up and out to darken and merge with the gray world, but higher and brighter almost as he watched, so that he began to walk more rapidly. He turned into the jail, where first he hung the key ring on the peg, and then sat down at the table and placed his hat carefully before him to wait these last few moments. He tried to think only of what he might have left undone.

He glanced toward the cell as the judge groaned and moved, made wet smacking sounds with his lips, groaned, and snored again; he could not see him in the darkness there.

Turning again he watched the whitening dust in the street, and leaned on the scarred table top from which the justice of

Warlock was dispensed, and waited, and wished only that there were some way he could see Warlock's future before him, and wished, with a sudden, terrible pang, that he could hear how they would speak of him.

But he felt, besides a flat and unfocused anxiety that came over him intermittently like a fever, a kind of peace, a certain freedom. He realized that there was no need for self-examination now, no need to question his decisions, no need to reflect upon his guilt, his inadequacy, nor upon himself at all. There were no decisions to be made any more, for there was only responsibility, and it was a freedom of tremendous scope. And he looked once more at the list of the names of the deputies of Warlock upon the whitewashed wall, at his own name scratched last there, but not last, and felt a pride so huge that his eyes filled, and he knew, too, that the pride was worth it all.

A slow tread of bootheels came along the boardwalk, and Pike Skinner turned in the door. There were heavy smudges beneath his eyes, so that they looked like a raccoon's eyes; the flesh of his face was stretched tight over the bone, and two days' growth of beard made his face look dirty. He wore a sheepskin-lined jacket.

"Pike," he said, and Pike nodded to him, and looked in the cell.

"Chicken old son of a bitch," Pike said, with infinite contempt. Then he glanced at the names on the wall, and nodded again as Gannon slid the table drawer open.

He took out the other deputy's star and handed it to Pike, who tossed it up and caught it once, not speaking. He indicated the key ring on its peg. "I brought the other key along. The judge's got one in there with him."

Pike nodded. He tossed the star again; this time he dropped it, and his face reddened as he bent to pick it up.

"Careful of it," Gannon said.

"Shit!" Pike said, and in the word was a grief for which he was grateful. Pike turned away. "There's people out," he said. "Funny how they hear of a thing."

He looked past the other and saw the first light upon the street. "It's close to time, I guess," he said.

"I guess," Pike said.

Peter came in with Tim French. There was a grunting and scraping within the cell; the judge's hands appeared on the bars, then his face between them, heavy with sleep and liquor. The hot, red-veined eyes stared at him unseeing as he put on his hat and nodded, and nodded to Tim and Peter. Peter glanced down at Pike's hand holding the other star.

"Chilly out," Tim said.

He stepped past them, and outside. Down the boardwalk a way Chick Hasty stood, and with him were Wheeler, old Owen Parsons, and Mosbie, with his right arm in a muslin sling and a jacket thrown over his shoulders. There were men along the boardwalks farther down, too, and he saw the miners collecting at the corner of Grant Street, where the wagons from the Medusa and the other mines would pick them up. The first sliver of the sun showed over the Bucksaws, incredibly bright gold and the peak beneath it flaming.

Chick Hasty looked down at him and nodded. Mosbie leaned back and nodded to him past Hasty, sick-eyed. He could hear the increasing bustle of Warlock awakening. Already, with the half-sun showing, the air was warmer. It would be another hot day. He moved farther out upon the boardwalk to lean against the railing and watch the great gold sun slowly climb from its defilade behind the mountains. All at once it was free, and round, and he walked on down the boardwalk past the men leaning against the railing there, and out into the dust of Main Street.

II

Blaisedell came out of the hotel, and immediately the men began moving back off the boardwalks, into doorways and the ruins of the Glass Slipper and the Lucky Dollar. Blaisedell walked slowly out into the street, and then Blaisedell was facing him, a block away, like some mirror-image of himself seen distant and small, but all in black, and Blaisedell began to walk at the same instant that he did. He could see the slant of Blaisedell's shell belt through the opening of his unbuttoned coat, and the gold-handled Colt thrust into his belt there. Blaisedell walked with a slow, long-legged stride, while his own star boots felt heavy in the dust. The boots hurt his feet and his wrist brushed past the butt of his Colt with almost an electric shock. He watched the dust spurting from beneath Blaisedell's boots.

He could see the angry-looking stripes on Blaisedell's face. He felt Blaisedell's eyes, not so much a force now as a kind of meaningless message in a buzzing like that of a depressed telegrapher's key. The sun was very bright in his face, and the figure approaching him began to dance and separate into a number of black-suited advancing figures, and then congeal again into one huge figure that cast a long, oblique shadow.

Then he saw Kate; she stood against the rail before the Glass Slipper, motionless, as though she had been there a long time. She too was dressed all in mourning black, heavily bustled in a black skirt of many folds, a black sacque with lines of fur down the front, her black hat with the cherries on it, black mesh mitts on her hands that gripped the rail. A veil hid her face. He saw her raise her hands to her breast, and he saw Blaisedell glance toward her, and make a curt motion as though he were shaking his head.

Straight down, straight up, Blaisedell had told him; it burst in his mind so there was room for nothing else. He walked steadily on, trying not to limp in his tight boots, and his eyes fixed themselves on Blaisedell's right hand swinging at his side. He felt the muscles in his own arm tighten and strain at every step. He could feel Blaisedell's eyes upon him and now he felt their thrust and still the confused buzzing inside his mind. But he watched Blaisedell's hand; it would be soon. Now, now, now, he thought, at every jolting step; now, now. He felt himself being crushed beneath a black and corrosive despair. Now, he thought; now, now—

It was as though there had been no movement at all. One instant Blaisedell's hand had been swinging at his side, the next it contained the Colt that had been thrust inside his belt. His own hand slammed down—straight down, straight up—but already he was staring into the black hole of Blaisedell's gun muzzle and saw Blaisedell's mouth shaped into a crooked contemptuous half-smile. He steeled himself against the bullet, halting with his feet braced apart and his body tipping forward as though he could brace himself against the shock.

But the shock, the explosion, the tearing pain, did not come.

As he brought his own Colt up level, he hesitated, his finger firm against the trigger, and saw Blaisedell's hand turn with a twisting motion. The gold handle gleamed suddenly as the six-shooter was flung forward and down to disappear in the street with a puff of dust.

Blaisedell's hand moved swiftly again, and the mate of the first Colt appeared. Again his finger tensed against the trigger and again he held it back as Blaisedell flung the other down. The slight contemptuous smile still twisted Blaisedell's lips in his battered face. Blaisedell's arms hung at his sides now, and slowly, uncertainly, he let his own hand drop. His eyes caught another splash of dust, in the street below the railing where Kate stood, her right hand extended and open and her face invisible behind the veil. Blaisedell stood staring at him with his swollen eyes looking shut.

The realization burst in him that all he had to do now was walk the remaining thirty feet and arrest Blaisedell. But he did not move. He would not do it, he thought, in sudden rebellion, as though it were his own thought; but now he was feeling intensely the thrust of all the other eyes that watched this, and it was a force much stronger than that of his own gratitude, his own pity, and he knew all he served that was embodied in the vast weight pinned to his vest, and knew, as he made a slight, not quite peremptory motion with his head, that he spoke not for himself nor even a strict and disinterested code, but for all of them.

Blaisedell started forward again, no longer coming toward him but walking along the track of his shadow toward Good-pasture's corner. He walked with the same, slow, long-legged, stiff-backed stride, not even glancing at Gannon, as he passed him, and turned into Southend and disappeared down toward the Acme Corral.

As Gannon turned to face the corner, he saw, past his shoulder, that the sun seemed not to have moved since he had come out into the street. But now he heard the sounds of hoofs and wagon wheels, and saw the wagons turning into Main Street. He watched the miners climbing into them, and the mules stamping and jerking their heads. More wagons appeared; the Medusa miners were going back to work. Miners appeared all along the boardwalks now, glancing back over their shoulders

at him and at the corner of Southend as they moved toward
the wagons. They made very little noise as they embarked.

Miss Jessie appeared among them, hurrying along the
boardwalk with a dark *rebozo* thrown over her shoulders and
her brown hair tumbling around her head with her steps. She
stopped with one hand braced against one of the arcade posts,
and stared at Kate, and then, blankly, at him.

He heard the pad of hoofs. Blaisedell came out of Southend
Street on a black horse with a white face, white stockings; the
horse pranced and twisted his sleek neck, but Blaisedell's pale,
stone profile did not turn. The black swung around the corner,
and, hindquarters dancing sideways, white stockings brilliant
in the sun, trotted away down Main Street toward the rim.

"Clay!" he heard Miss Jessie call. Blaisedell did not turn, who
must have heard. Gannon heard the running tap of heels upon
the planks. She stopped and leaned against another post before
Goodpasture's store, and then ran out into the street, while the
black danced on away. He saw Pike Skinner and Peter Bacon
watching from the jail doorway, and more men were crowding
out along the boardwalks now, and some into the street.

Miss Jessie ran down Main Street in the dust, holding her
skirts up; she would run swiftly for a time, then decrease her
pace to a walk, then run again. "Clay!" she cried.

Gannon began to move forward with the others, as Miss Jessie ran on. The black horse dropped down over the edge of the
rim, Blaisedell's head and shoulders visible for an instant and
his ruined face turning back to glance once toward the town;
then abruptly he was gone. "*Clay!*" Miss Jessie screamed, with
her voice trailing thinly behind her as she ran. The doctor was
hurrying after her.

Gannon walked with the others down Main Street toward
the rim, where the doctor had caught up with Miss Jessie.
The doctor had an arm around her and was leading her back,
her face dusty and white with huge vacantly staring eyes, her
mouth open and her breast heaving. He saw the wetness at the
corners of her mouth as he passed her and the doctor, and her
eyes glared for a moment at him, vacant no longer, but filled
with tears and hate. He moved on, and heard the doctor whispering to her as he led her back through the groups of men
approaching the rim.

III

From the rim the great, dun sweep of the valley was laid out before them. There were wild flowers on the slopes from the recent rain. The long dead spears of ocotillo were covered with a thin mist of leaves, and from their ends red flaming torches waved and bowed in the breeze. Someone extended an arm to point out Blaisedell, where he guided the black horse among the huge tumbled boulders of the malpais. He was hidden from time to time among the boulders and each time he reappeared it was a smaller figure on a smaller horse, trailing tan clouds of dust that lingered in the air behind him. They watched in silence as he rode on down the stage road toward San Pablo and the Dinosaurs, until they could not be sure they saw him still at all, he was so distant. Yet now and then the tiny black figure on the black horse would stand out clearly against the golden, flower-speckled earth, until, at last, a dust devil rose in a gust of wind. Rising high and leaning across his path, it seemed to envelop him, and, when it had passed and blown itself apart, Blaisedell too was finally lost to sight.

# Afterword:
## A Letter from Henry Holmes Goodpasture

1819 Pringle St.
San Francisco, Calif.
May 14, 1924

My Dear Gavin:*

It has been a long time now, but I am surprised, as I look into the past in order to answer your letter, how easily it all comes back to me. Perhaps I am able to remember it with such immediacy because you and your brother so often asked me to tell and retell stories of my days in Warlock. That must seem a long time ago to you, who are now in your third year at New Haven, but to me, in my eighty-third upon this planet, it is only yesterday.

I am most pleased that you should recall those old stories, and be interested enough to wish to know, now that you are grown, what happened "After."

To begin with, Warlock did not continue to prosper and grow as her citizens had once hoped, and when I departed for San Francisco in 1882, her decline was well under way. The Porphyrion and Western Mining Company had by then bought up the rest of the mines, and struggled for a number of years to cope with the increasing amounts of water met with at the lower levels; but it was a hopeless task, and Porphyrion, faced too with the fall of the silver market, was finally forced to the wall. By 1890 only the Redgold Mine was still in operation. The hamlet of Redgold then flourished briefly but, after the mine closed, became in its turn a ghost like Warlock and so many other mining camps.

In answer to your questions, I shall try to be as succinct as it is possible for a garrulous old man to be. Yes, Warlock did become the county seat of Peach County. Its courthouse still stands (or stood the last time I visited Warlock, seventeen years ago), a fine brick structure that was unfortunately gutted by

*Gavin Sands, Goodpasture's grandson.

a fire soon after the turn of the century. Curiously, its black-ened brick husk seemed to me to have no connection with the adobe husks around it, and even stands near the rim at the southwest corner of the town (where it commands a most striking view of the valley), apart from them. As I say, Warlock was the county seat; but not for long. The county offices were removed to Welltown, I believe in 1891.

Dr. Wagner accompanied Jessie Marlow to Nome, where he died of a heart ailment. Jessie herself operated an establishment there called "The Miners' Rest" for a number of years, and you will find her mentioned in many accounts of the Gold Rush days. I think she married a man named Bogart, or Bogarde, a prospector and saloonkeeper, and himself a figure of minor importance in Nome.

James Fitzsimmons was one of the I.W.W. leaders imprisoned during the Great War. I have heard nothing of him since.

There was never any doubt in Warlock that John Gannon's death was cold-blooded murder. Cade had concealed himself in the alley behind the jail, and the shooting took place in Main Street before my store. I saw the body very shortly after the shooting, and poor Gannon had been clearly shot in the back, nor had his revolver been drawn. I was especially struck by the expression on his face, which was remarkably peaceful; he can-not even have known what struck him down.

Cade took flight, but was apprehended in short order by a posse led by Pike Skinner. His trial was a notorious one, and these stories you have heard stem from his defense, which was based upon the contention that Gannon had not only mur-dered McQuown but had communicated to the Mexican au-thorities information which resulted in the massacre of the Cowboys in Rattlesnake Canyon. As far as I could see, Cade mustered no evidence whatever to support this, but his accusa-tions were then, and probably still are, widely believed. I know that Will Hart, an honest and intelligent man, professed to believe Cade's story. I do not.

Although he was tried in Bright's City, Cade was returned to Warlock for execution, and became the first man legally hanged in Peach County. That was a memorable day.

Pike Skinner was Peach County's first sheriff. Judge Holloway presided briefly over the bench in Warlock's new courthouse.

Buck Slavin was Warlock's first mayor. I am sure you will remember hearing stories of his career in the U.S. Senate. He was a colorful man, a brilliant politician, and had a matchless eye for the main chance.

Arnold Mosbie, who served as a deputy under Skinner, became one of the last of the famous peace officers. He was Marshal in Harrisonburg.

I have heard that the notorious "Big-nose Kate" Williams, of Denver fame, or ill fame, was Warlock's Kate Dollar. I have also heard that Kate Dollar married a wealthy Colorado rancher. One, both, or neither of these stories may be true.

You will notice that I have kept your questions about Blaisedell to the last. No, I cannot say I wish I had been present to hear you and your "know-it-all" friend argue about him. I have heard in my time too many such arguments, and I think you must have held for him as well as I could have done—perhaps better, for I was always chary of making him out a better man than he may have been. What was he? I think in all honesty I must say I do not know, and if *I* do not know in this late year of Our Lord, then I think that no man can. Certainly your opinionated friend cannot.

Nor do I know what became of him. If anyone ever knew, genuinely, it has been a well-kept secret. Of course there have been many rumors, but never one to which I was able to give any credence. The most common has been that Blaisedell was half-blind when he left Warlock, and soon completely lost his sight. Consequently there were a number of tales, variously embroidered, concerning tall, fair, blind men represented as being Blaisedell.

There was at one time an old prospector living in the Dinosaurs, who claimed that Blaisedell had been murdered there by persons unknown, and for a fee he would lead the gullible to view the lonely grave where he swore he had buried Blaisedell's body. Another story has it that Blaisedell changed his name to Blackburn and was town Marshal in Hyattsville, Oklahoma, where he was killed by a man named Petersen in a gun battle over a local belle. Blaisedell has enjoyed a number of sepultures.

Then there were the writings of Caleb Bane, which I suppose many fools have read as gospel. It was Bane, a fabricator of cheap Western fiction, who had given Blaisedell the gold-handled Colts in Fort James, and Bane (who seems to have felt that Blaisedell, because of that gift, belonged to him) continued to write tales about Blaisedell's imaginary continued career long after the subject himself was lost from sight.

I notice in a recent volume of Western memoirs that Blaisedell is spoken of as more a semi-fictional hero than an actual man. But he was a man: I can attest to that, who have seen him eat and drink, and breathe and bleed. And despite the fictions of Bane and his ilk, there have not been many like him, nor like Morgan, nor McQuown, nor John Gannon.

But sometimes I feel as perhaps you may feel, looking back on the stories of these men I told you about when you were a "young 'un"—that I myself was a fictionalizer with an imagination as active as that of Bane, or that in my own mind (as old men will do!) I had gradually stylized and simplified those happenings, that I had fancifully glorified those people, and sought to give them superhuman stature.

I cry out in pain that it is not so, and at the same time come to doubt myself. But I kept a journal through those years, and although the ink is fading on the yellowing pages, it is all still legible. One of these days, if you are interested beyond merely seeking to bulwark your arguments with a classmate, those pages shall be yours.

Now that your letter has caused me to call to memory all those people and those years, I find myself wishing most intensely that I had left to me Time and the powers to flesh out my journals into a True History of Warlock, in all its ramifications, before the man who was Blaisedell, and the other men and women, and the town in which they lived, are totally obscured. . . .

BIOGRAPHICAL NOTES

NOTE ON THE TEXTS

NOTES

# Biographical Notes

**Walter Van Tilburg Clark**  (August 3, 1909–November 10, 1971) was born at his family's summer house near East Orland, Maine, the oldest of four children. His father, Walter Ernest Clark, was an Ohio-born professor of economics and political science who chaired the political science department at the City College of New York, 1907–17. His mother, Euphemia (Abrams) Clark, the daughter of a physician from Hartford, Connecticut, was a Columbia University graduate who had studied piano and composition at college. The family moved from New York City to Reno, Nevada, in 1917, when Walter Ernest Clark accepted a position as president of the University of Nevada. The young Clark, who skipped a grade in elementary school, spent most of his childhood in Reno but summered in La Jolla, California, and lived for a year with an aunt in California's Imperial Valley before matriculating at the University of Nevada in 1927, where he majored in English and was especially interested in poetry. While there he met Barbara Morse, a transfer student from Oberlin whom he married in 1933. He received his B.A. in 1931 and his M.A. from the University of Nevada later that year. He published poems in *Ten Women in Gale's House and Shorter Poems*, a book whose publication costs were paid for by his father, and in *Poetry* magazine. Enrolling in further graduate work at the University of Vermont, he was awarded an M.A. with honors in 1934, having submitted a thesis on the poetry of Robinson Jeffers. In the late 1930s he shifted his literary focus from poetry to fiction, writing at night and on weekends while teaching English during weekdays to middle- and high-school students at a school directed by his wife's brother-in-law in Cazenovia, New York. His daughter Barbara Anne was born in 1937, and his son Robert Morse was born in 1939.

Clark's first published novel, *The Ox-Bow Incident* (1940), met with critical and popular success and was adapted into a film (1943) directed by William Wellman and starring Henry Fonda. In the years that followed, Clark's short stories were frequently published in magazines, with several chosen for the annual O. Henry story prize anthologies. His second novel, *The City of Trembling Leaves*, was published in 1945; *The Track of the Cat* was brought out in 1949 and was the basis for a 1953 film adaptation, also directed by Wellman and starring Robert Mitchum. *The Watchful Gods and Other Stories*, a collection of shorter fiction, appeared in 1950. For health and other reasons, Clark moved west in 1946 and lived in New Mexico (on

Mabel Dodge Luhan's Taos estate), Nevada, Montana, and California, teaching at several universities, including the University of Nevada, Reno; Stanford University; and San Francisco State College.
His last major project was the editing of three volumes of diaries by
the nineteenth-century Nevada journalist Alfred Doten. Clark died of
cancer in Virginia City, Nevada, at the age of sixty-two.

**Jack Schaefer**   (November 19, 1907–January 24, 1991) was born in
Cleveland, Ohio, the third of four children of Carl Schaefer, an attorney, and Minnie (Hively) Schaefer. He spent most of his childhood
in the Cleveland suburb of Lakewood and graduated from Lakewood
High School in 1925. After earning a degree in English from Oberlin
College in 1929 he began graduate work at Columbia University but
abandoned his studies and pursued a career as a journalist, first for
the United Press in New Haven, Connecticut, followed by editorial
positions at several newspapers, including the New Haven *Journal
Courier*, the Baltimore *Sun*, and the Norfolk *Virginian-Pilot*. He also
worked as a teacher in a Connecticut reformatory. In 1931 he married
Eugenia Ives, with whom he had three sons, Carl, Christopher, and
Jonathan, and a daughter, Emily; the couple divorced in 1948. He
married Louisa Dean in 1949. That same year he gave up journalism
to concentrate full-time on fiction writing.
    Schaefer's debut book and the first of his many Westerns, *Shane*,
was written before he had ever been west of Ohio. Published in book
form in 1949, it was the basis for the 1953 film directed by George
Stevens and starring Alan Ladd. After traveling west on a travelogue
assignment for *Holiday* magazine, Schaefer sold his Connecticut farm
and settled in New Mexico, living on a ranch near Cerillos. Within the
Western genre he produced a steady output of stories, novellas, and
novels; among his books are *First Blood* (1953), *The Big Range* (1953),
*The Canyon* (1953), *The Pioneers* (1954), *Company of Cowards* (1957),
*The Kean Land and Other Stories* (1959), *Monte Walsh* (1963), and the
nonfiction collection *Heroes Without Glory: Some Goodmen of the Old
West* (1965). He also wrote the children's books *Old Ramon* (1960)
and *Stubby Pringle's Christmas* (1964).
    Schaefer's final Western novel, *Mavericks*, was published in 1967.
In his later career he focused on nature writing, including *American
Bestiary* (1975) and the dialogues with animals that were collected in
*Conversations with a Pocket Gopher and Other Outspoken Neighbors*
(1978). In 1975, Schaefer was given the Western Literature Association's Distinguished Achievement award, and in 1985 the Western
Writers of America ranked *Shane* as the best Western novel ever written. Schaefer died of congestive heart failure at the age of eighty-three
in Santa Fe, New Mexico.

**Alan Le May**   (June 3, 1899–April 27, 1964) was born in Indianap-
olis, Indiana, the son of John Le May, a metallurgist, and Maude
(Brown) Le May. After the family moved in 1915 to Aurora, Illinois, Le
May attended West Aurora High School, graduating in 1916. He was
a student at Stetson University before enrolling at the University of
Chicago, graduating with a Bachelor of Philosophy degree in 1922; he
also served as an officer in the Illinois National Guard. As early as 1919
he sold and published his stories in *Detective Magazine*. He married
Esther Skinner in 1922, and the couple had a daughter, Joan (Jody),
and a son, Dan; they divorced in 1937. Le May married his second
wife, Arlene, in 1939; they were the adoptive parents of a daughter,
Molly, and a son, Mark.

   In the 1920s Le May worked a variety of jobs, including as a journalist for the Aurora *Beacon News*. His first novel, *Painted Ponies*,
was serialized in *Adventure Magazine* and published in book form
in 1927; it was followed by a novel set in Mississippi, *Pelican Coast*
(1929). He moved in 1929 to San Diego, publishing his stories and
serialized novels frequently in *Collier's* magazine and earning enough
from the sales of his fiction to buy a ranch and begin a short-lived
business raising horses. His fortunes turned and in 1937, because of
debt, difficulties writing, and his divorce, he moved back to Aurora.
Two years later, at the invitation of Cecil B. DeMille, he returned to
Southern California and began his career as a Hollywood screenwriter,
contributing to DeMille projects such as *North West Mounted Police*
(1940), *Reap the Wild Wind* (1942), *The Story of Dr. Wassell* (1944),
and *The Rurales* (never completed). Other Hollywood writing credits
include *The Adventures of Mark Twain* (1944), *High Lonesome* (1950),
which he also directed, *I Dream of Jeannie* (1952), based on the life of
Stephen Foster, and *Blackbeard the Pirate* (1952). He cofounded his
own production company in 1949.

   Le May's novels include *Thunder in the Dust* (1934), *The Smoky
Years* (1935), *Empire for a Lady* (1937), *Useless Cowboy* (1943), *The
Searchers* (1954), *The Unforgiven* (1957), and *By Dim and Flaring
Lamps* (1962). The best known of his novels' film adaptations are the
movie versions of *The Searchers*, directed by John Ford and starring
John Wayne, and *The Unforgiven* (1960), directed by John Huston
and starring Burt Lancaster. Le May died of a brain tumor at home in
Pacific Palisades, California, at the age of sixty-four.

**Oakley Hall**   (July 1, 1920–May 12, 2008) was born in San Diego,
California, the only child of Oakley M. Hall, Sr., an architectural tech-
nician, and Jessie (Sands) Hall, who after separating from her husband
moved to Hawaii with her son and built a greeting-card business out
of her garage in Honolulu. Hall returned to California as a teenager

and graduated from San Diego's Hoover High School. He earned his B.A. with a major in economics from the University of California, Berkeley, in 1943 and was an officer in the Marine Corps during World War II. In 1945 he married Barbara Edinger, who would go on to have a career as a photographer; the couple had three daughters, Sands, Tracy, and Brett, and a son, Oakley III.

After studying for a year in Europe, Hall returned to the United States and sold his first novel, *Murder City* (1949; published under the name O. M. Hall), a crime story written in two weeks. Awarded an M.F.A. by the University of Iowa in 1950, he taught in its Writers' Workshop, 1950–52. His novel *Corpus of Joe Bailey* won the National Book Award for 1953. Hall published four crime novels under the pseudonym Jason Manor in the mid-1950s, as well as *Mardios Beach* (1955) under his own name. *Warlock* (1958) was the first of his many books with the historical West as their setting, which include *The Adelita* (1975), *The Bad Lands* (1978), *The Children of the Sun* (1983), *The Coming of the Kid* (1985), *Apaches* (1986), and *Separations* (1997). *Warlock* was adapted for the screen, as was his novel *The Downhill Racers* (1963).

In 1968 Hall began his long tenure as director of the writing program at the University of California at Irvine, and he cofounded a summer writers' program, the Squaw Valley Community of Writers, in 1969. His insights into the making of fiction were published in the books *The Art and Craft of Novel Writing* (1989) and *How Fiction Works* (2000). He also wrote the libretto for an operatic adaptation of Wallace Stegner's *Angle of Repose*, with music by Andrew Imbrie, which premiered in San Francisco in 1976. Hall's later novels include *Report from Beau Harbor* (1971), *Lullaby* (1982), *Separations* (1997), and *Love and War in California* (2007); toward the end of his career, beginning with *Ambrose Bierce and the Queen of Spades* (1998), he embarked on a series of historical mysteries with the nineteenth-century American writer as their protagonist. Among his honors were his induction into the Cowboy Hall of Fame and a PEN Center West lifetime achievement award. Hall died of cancer and renal failure at the age of eighty-seven at his home in Nevada City, California.

# Note on the Texts

This volume contains the texts of four novels published from 1940 to 1958: *The Ox-Bow Incident* (1940) by Walter Van Tilburg Clark, *Shane* (1949) by Jack Schaefer, *The Searchers* (1954) by Alan Le May, and *Warlock* (1958) by Oakley Hall.

*The Ox-Bow Incident* was the first published novel written by Walter Van Tilburg Clark, though an earlier novel, "Water," had been submitted to publishers in 1937 and rejected. These two novels were among Clark's initial efforts at fiction after he had largely abandoned his ambition to become a poet. Working on the manuscript late at night, on weekends, and during vacation periods, Clark wrote the bulk of *The Ox-Bow Incident* in the first half of 1938 while employed as an English teacher in Cazenovia, New York. The novel was accepted by Random House late in 1938 and was revised by Clark the following year. Random House published *The Ox-Bow Incident* in October 1940 to general critical and commercial success; an edition was published without revision by Victor Gollancz in London in 1941, as well as an edition by the Press of the Readers Club in 1942 with an introduction by Clifton Fadiman. Later American editions, unrevised by Clark, introduced errors; for example, at 30.28–30 in the present volume, the 1960 Signet Classics/New American Library edition and the 2001 Modern Library edition erroneously read "We don't need no trail for this business. We've heard long enough of Tyler and his trails" for "We don't need no trial for this business. We've heard long enough of Tyler and his trials." The 1940 Random House edition of *The Ox-Bow Incident* contains the text printed here.

By his own account, Jack Schaefer began writing fiction "primarily as a means of relaxation" at night after putting in long working days as a newspaper editor. In 1945, while editor of the *Norfolk Virginian-Pilot* in Norfolk, Virginia, he wrote a story about what he deemed "the basic legend of the West" that "kept growing and wound up being a novella." He sent the novella to *Argosy* magazine, where it languished unread for several months before being accepted for publication as a serial. Entitled "Rider from Nowhere," the long tale appeared in *Argosy* in installments in the July, September, and October 1946 issues of the magazine. Schaefer later expanded the story and, after leaving the newspaper business, attempted to sell it to book publishers, at first unsuccessfully but ultimately, after becoming a client of the agent Don Congdon at the Harold Matson Company, contracting with

Houghton Mifflin, who published the novella as *Shane* in October 1949. Because of its appeal to juvenile readers, a number of changes were made in a 1954 illustrated edition also published by Houghton Mifflin in order to expunge instances of mild profanity involving the words "hell" and "damn": for example, at 245.21, "worth a damn" was changed to "worth a hoot"; at 260.37, "Hell, there ain't nobody else" was altered to read "Don't see anybody else." (A complete list of the nineteen passages emended in the 1954 illustrated edition is given in James C. Work's introduction to *Shane: The Critical Edition* [Lincoln: University of Nebraska Press, 1984].) As well as being translated into numerous languages after its successful film version in 1953, an unrevised edition of *Shane* was published in England by Andre Deutsch in 1954. The text of the 1949 Houghton Mifflin edition of *Shane* is printed here.

In 1952, Alan Le May took a sabbatical of several months from his career as a Hollywood screenwriter (and occasionally producer and director) to work on his first novel since *Useless Cowboy* (1944). Under the title "The Avenging Texans," this new novel was bought as a five-part serial by the *Saturday Evening Post*, which published it in November and December 1954, several months after its acceptance. Before its serialization in the *Post* Le May also contracted with Harper & Brothers to publish the novel; for the book, entitled *The Searchers*, he added about one hundred pages of additional material and made other revisions that were completed in the summer of 1954. Published in early November 1954, the first Harper & Brothers edition of *The Searchers* contains the text printed here.

In the mid-1950s Oakley Hall was already an established literary novelist and writer of crime fiction when he turned to the Western and wrote *Warlock*, the first of his several works in the genre and a nominee for the Pulitzer Prize. The novel was published by Viking Press in September 1958. The same typesetting of the text was used for editions published in London by Bodley Hall in 1959 and in New York by New York Review Books Classics in 2005. The present volume prints the text of the 1958 Viking Press edition of *Warlock*.

This volume presents the texts of the original printings chosen for inclusion here, but it does not attempt to reproduce nontextual features of their typographic design. The texts are reprinted without change, except for the correction of typographical errors. Spelling, punctuation, and capitalization are often expressive features and are not altered, even when inconsistent or irregular. The following is a list of typographical errors corrected, cited by page and line number: 39.27–28, him. Out; 56.3, gun-belt; 173.30, asked,; 255.20, of of; 266.8, Wright.; 287.1, that."; 291.23, himself yanked; 296.10, anything.; 366.23, 'em.; 367.10, Amos.; 422.22, yelled,; 446.19,

Harmon,; 448.10, occured; 494.22, Martie,"; 507.18, spoke,; 577.26, capitol;; 581.18, capitol.; 649.37, breath; 666.7, women; 706.31, Marshall; 714.19, Schroeder); 834.28, Marshall; 860.7, Man; 875.39, senilty; 923.19, collander; 951.30, Fitszsimmons'; 958.26, Fitszsimmons; 962.6, his his own cheek; 976.27, "Morgan; 997.10, him "Why?; 998.33, marshall; 1017.2, again "and; 1020.9, stairwall,; 1025.28, *macquereau*; 1033.7, summarially.

# Notes

In the notes below, the reference numbers denote page and line of this volume (the line count includes headings but not blank lines). No note is made for material that is sufficiently explained in context, nor are there notes for material included in standard desk-reference works such as Webster's Eleventh Collegiate, Biographical, and Geographical dictionaries or comparable internet resources such as Merriam-Webster's online dictionary. Foreign words and phrases not in Merriam-Webster's dictionary are translated only if not translated in the text or if words are not evident English cognates. Quotations from Shakespeare are keyed to *The Riverside Shakespeare*, edited by G. Blakemore Evans (Boston: Houghton Mifflin, 1974). Quotations from the Bible are keyed to the King James Version.

## THE OX-BOW INCIDENT

5.31   Virginia City . . . Grant] President Grant visited Virginia City, Nevada, in 1879, during a tour of the West.

72.18   Gladstone] English statesman William Gladstone (1809–1898), four-term prime minister of the United Kingdom.

98.23   feeze] Also spelled "feaze," an obsolete variant of "faze."

103.9   the "Buffalo Gal"] "Buffalo Gals," traditional song often attributed to John "Cool White" Hodges (1821–1891), published author of a version of the song entitled "Lubly Fan Will You Cum Out To Night?" (1844). The song was first published as "Buffalo Gals" (with its author unattributed) in 1848 as sheet music connecting it to the Ethiopian Serenaders, a minstrel blackface troupe.

113.18   "He mahks the sparrow's fall."] See Matthew 10:29: "Are not two sparrows sold for a farthing? and one of them shall not fall on the ground without your Father."

131.38–132.2   the Flying Dutchman . . . forever] The Flying Dutchman is a legendary ghost ship doomed to sail the seas for eternity.

139.7   "No sabbey,"] Don't understand.

## SHANE

254.21–22   blow-up of the Big Horn Mining Association] The Big Horn Mining Association was founded in Cheyenne, Wyoming, in response to reports of gold in the Big Horn mountains in the fall of 1869. Plans to begin searching for gold were delayed because its leaders sought permission from the U.S government to travel through land designated Sioux territory under the terms of the 1858 Fort Laramie Treaty. After petitioning Washington, the association received approval but only for a roundabout approach to the mountain range and with the understanding that the U.S. military in the area would not provide protection or support if the group was attacked. The abortive expedition of about 150 men set out from Cheyenne on May 20, 1870, but was riven by infighting and split into factions. No gold was found, several prospectors were killed by Indians, and only a remnant of the original contingent returned to Cheyenne on August 22.

## THE SEARCHERS

331.18–30  Texas Rangers had just punished . . . bloomed again] The Texas Rangers, first an informal armed group and after 1835 an official law enforcement arm of Texas, fought against the Cherokee, the Comanche, and other Indian tribes in the late 1830s and 1840s. After being deployed during the Mexican-American War, their numbers declined. In 1857–58, with the support of Governors Elisha M. Pease (1812–1883) and his successor Hardin Richard Runnels (1820–1873), the Texas legislature authorized and provided funding for an expansion of the Rangers, which under the command of Captain John Salmon Ford (1815–1897) waged war against the Comanches.

337.24  Hood] Confederate general John Bell Hood (1831–1879).

341.14  a 30–30] Anachronistic reference to a rifle cartridge introduced by Winchester in 1895, so called because its bullet diameter was .30 caliber and it used thirty grains of smokeless powder.

384.29–30  President Grant had given the Society of Friends . . . Agencies] After a delegation of Quakers concerned about the federal government's Indian policies visited the White House in January 1869, President Grant formulated what became known as his "peace policy," appointing members of the Society of Friends as well as representatives from other Christian denominations to lead the Indian Agencies.

412.26  'Bringing home the sheaves,'] "Bringing in the Sheaves" (1874), hymn by Knowles Shaw (1834–1878) often sung to music by George Minor (1845–1904).

416.17–18  on the Washita] An encampment on the Washita River in Oklahoma was the site of an American attack led by Lieutenant Colonel George A. Custer (1839–1876), November 27, 1868, against a group of Cheyenne Indians and their chief Black Kettle (c. 1803–1868), who was fatally shot by U.S. soldiers while trying to escape the battle. The attack resulted in numerous Indian casualties and has often been called a massacre.

440.32  Colonel Mackenzie] The American military officer Ranald S. Mackenzie (1840–1889).

440.33   yellowlegs] Cavalry, so called because of yellow stripes on the legs of their breeches.

468.1   Green grow the rushes, oh] From "Green Grow the Rushes, O," traditional English folk song.

481.18   a *baile*] Spanish: a dance tune.

482.24   *calle*] Spanish: street.

489.21   General Sheridan was in the saddle] Shortly after taking office in 1869 President Grant appointed Lieutenant General Philip H. Sheridan (1813–1888) to be head of the Division of the Missouri, which encompassed much of the territory west of the Mississippi. Sheridan directed the campaign on the Texas panhandle known as the Red River War, 1874–75, against Comanche, Kiowa, Arapaho, and Cheyenne Indians, which led to their forced settlement on reservations.

489.24   Colonel Buell] George P. Buell (1833–1883).

489.27   Colonel Davidson] John Wynn Davidson (1825–1881).

508.26   *reata*] Lariat or lasso, from the Spanish word for rope.

511.37   aparejos] Aparejo, a pack saddle.

## WARLOCK

569.12   Cyprian's cubicle] A prostitute's private room.

583.36   Shiloh] Civil War battle, April 6–7, 1862, a victory for the Union.

591.8   Banker's Special] A type of Colt revolver.

597.25   *pasear*] Spanish: walk.

609.27   Bonnie Prince Charlie] Charles Stuart (1720–1788), grandson of the deposed King James II of England and Ireland, led an insurgent Jacobite rebellion and was defeated at the Battle of Culloden in 1746.

609.28   Cuchulain battling the waves] Cuchulain is the Anglicized name of the legendary Celtic warrior Cú Chilainn, who killed his formidable young son in battle. In one version of Cú Chilainn's life story, the Ulster king Conchobhar, fearing the wrath of his grief, has him enchanted by a spell that compels him to fight the waves of the sea to the point of exhaustion over the course of three days.

609.28   The Grave at St. Helena] Depiction of the first tomb of Napoleon Bonaparte, who was exiled on St. Helena from 1815 until his death in 1821.

610.9–10   Waverley novels] Series of twenty-seven historical novels published by the English writer Sir Walter Scott (1771–1832) from 1814 to 1831, which included *Waverley* (1814), *Rob Roy* (1817), and *Ivanhoe* (1819).

624.20   *Venit, Vidit, Vicit.*] Latin: He came, he saw, he conquered, a variant of the boast attributed to Julius Caesar, "Veni, vidi, vici."

627.34   the Cid] Rodrigo Díaz de Vivar (c. 1043–1099), Spanish hero famous for his military feats, especially the siege of Valencia in 1094.

633.5–7   such favorites as: "She Wore A Wreath of Roses" . . . "A Life on the Ocean Wave,"] "She Wore A Wreath of Roses" (1840), song with words by the English poet, playwright, and novelist Thomas Haynes Bayly (1797–1839) and set to music by the English clergyman and composer Joseph Philip Knight (1812–1887). "Days of Absence," also known as "Rousseau's Dream," hymn based on a melody from the one-act opera *Le Devin du Village* (The Village Soothsayer, 1752) by the Swiss-born philosopher Jean-Jacques Rousseau (1712–1788). "Long, Long Ago," song written by Thomas Haynes Bayly and first published posthumously in 1844. "Tenting Tonight" (1863) by the American songwriter Walter Kittredge (1834–1905), also known as "Tenting on the Old Camp Ground," popular song during the Civil War. "A Life on the Ocean Wave" (1838), musical setting by the English composer Henry Russell (1812–1900) of a poem by the American writer and editor Epes Sargent (1813–1880).

649.5   malapai.] Badlands.

660.12   tommies] Prostitutes.

662.30   hydro-phoby skunk] Rabid skunk.

669.23   *ley fuga*] Spanish *ley de fugas*: lynch law.

686.7   *mozo*] Male servant or handyman.

695.7   *profanum vulgus*] Latin: the common masses.

729.15–17   *Va bien?"* . . . *"Que lástima, joven."*] Spanish: Going well? / Yes, well. / What a pity, young man.

733.32   "The World Turned Upside Down."] Traditional march tune, purportedly played by the British during their surrender at Yorktown during the Revolutionary War.

734.30–31   Excalibur can be drawn from the block] In Arthurian legend, Arthur's ability to extract the sword Excalibur from a stone (or an anvil atop a stone) was proof of his lineage as king.

754.3–6   "What stronger breastplate . . . corrupted."] Shakespeare, *2 Henry VI*, III.ii.232–35.

755.18–20   schoolmen . . . pin.] Opponents of medieval Scholastic philosophers such as Thomas Aquinas (c. 1225–1274) charged that they made tedious arguments about matters as absurd and trivial as the number of angels that could dance on the head of a pin.

761.2–3   St. George . . . dragons.] Legendary accounts and images of the Christian saint depict him slaying a fearsome dragon with a lance.

825.3  *quién sabe*] Spanish: who knows.

829.19  *Suerte.*"] Spanish: (Good) luck.

836.2  sun . . . Bonaparte saw through the mists of Austerlitz] The sun breaking through morning mist on the battlefield became the symbol of Napoleon's victory over the Austrian-Russian army at Austerlitz on December 2, 1805.

837.35–36  thumbs up instead of down, and save the gladiator] The Roman writer Juvenal, in *Satires* 3.36, mentions the *pollice verso* (turned thumb) of spectators watching gladiatorial combats, meant to signify whether or not a defeated gladiator should be killed; it is not clear whether a thumbs-up gesture would have signaled the wish that the gladiator's life be spared. *Pollice Verso* (1872), a widely known painting by the French painter Jean-Léon Gérôme (1824–1904), shows agitated Roman spectators making a thumbs-down gesture while a defeated gladiator pleads for mercy.

839.13–14  poor, bare, forked animals . . . dismal heath] See Lear's speech on the heath in Shakespeare, *King Lear*, III.iv.106–8, before he tears off his clothes: "unaccommodated man is no more but such a poor, bare, fork'd animal as thou art."

944.9–13  The present eye . . . than what not stirs.] Shakespeare, *Troilus and Cressida*, III.iii.180–84.

956.3–4  gnats . . . camels to be swallowed] Cf. Matthew 23:23–24: "Woe unto you, scribes and Pharisees, hypocrites! . . . Ye blind guides, which strain at a gnat, and swallow a camel."

968.2  Philistines] Biblical enemy of the Israelites.

1024.19  Bull Run] First Battle of Bull Run, July 21, 1861, a Confederate victory.

1025.28  *maquereau*] French slang for pimp.

1056.21–28  "Rock of ages . . . pure."] From "Rock of Ages," hymn (1763) by the Anglican priest Augustus Toplady (1740–1778) usually sung to a tune by the American composer Thomas Hastings (1784–1872).

1077.15  I.W.W.] International Workers of the World.

*This book is set in 10 point ITC Galliard Pro, a face designed for digital composition by Matthew Carter and based on the sixteenth-century face Granjon. The paper is acid-free lightweight opaque that will not turn yellow or brittle with age. The binding is sewn, which allows the book to open easily and lie flat. The binding board is covered in Brillianta, a woven rayon cloth made by Van Heek–Scholco Textielfabrieken, Holland. Composition by Dianna Logan, Clearmont, MO. Printing by Sheridan Grand Rapids, Grand Rapids MI. Binding by Dekker Bookbinding, Wyoming MI. Designed by Bruce Campbell.*

# THE LIBRARY OF AMERICA SERIES

Library of America fosters appreciation of America's literary heritage by publishing, and keeping permanently in print, authoritative editions of America's best and most significant writing. An independent nonprofit organization, it was founded in 1979 with seed funding from the National Endowment for the Humanities and the Ford Foundation.

1. Herman Melville: Typee, Omoo, Mardi
2. Nathaniel Hawthorne: Tales & Sketches
3. Walt Whitman: Poetry & Prose
4. Harriet Beecher Stowe: Three Novels
5. Mark Twain: Mississippi Writings
6. Jack London: Novels & Stories
7. Jack London: Novels & Social Writings
8. William Dean Howells: Novels 1875–1886
9. Herman Melville: Redburn, White-Jacket, Moby-Dick
10. Nathaniel Hawthorne: Collected Novels
11 & 12. Francis Parkman: France and England in North America
13. Henry James: Novels 1871–1880
14. Henry Adams: Novels, Mont Saint Michel, The Education
15. Ralph Waldo Emerson: Essays & Lectures
16. Washington Irving: History, Tales & Sketches
17. Thomas Jefferson: Writings
18. Stephen Crane: Prose & Poetry
19. Edgar Allan Poe: Poetry & Tales
20. Edgar Allan Poe: Essays & Reviews
21. Mark Twain: The Innocents Abroad, Roughing It
22 & 23. Henry James: Literary Criticism
24. Herman Melville: Pierre, Israel Potter, The Confidence-Man, Tales & Billy Budd
25. William Faulkner: Novels 1930–1935
26 & 27. James Fenimore Cooper: The Leatherstocking Tales
28. Henry David Thoreau: A Week, Walden, The Maine Woods, Cape Cod
29. Henry James: Novels 1881–1886
30. Edith Wharton: Novels
31 & 32. Henry Adams: History of the U.S. during the Administrations of Jefferson & Madison
33. Frank Norris: Novels & Essays
34. W.E.B. Du Bois: Writings
35. Willa Cather: Early Novels & Stories
36. Theodore Dreiser: Sister Carrie, Jennie Gerhardt, Twelve Men
37. Benjamin Franklin: Writings (2 vols.)
38. William James: Writings 1902–1910
39. Flannery O'Connor: Collected Works
40, 41, & 42. Eugene O'Neill: Complete Plays
43. Henry James: Novels 1886–1890
44. William Dean Howells: Novels 1886–1888
45 & 46. Abraham Lincoln: Speeches & Writings
47. Edith Wharton: Novellas & Other Writings
48. William Faulkner: Novels 1936–1940
49. Willa Cather: Later Novels
50. Ulysses S. Grant: Memoirs & Selected Letters
51. William Tecumseh Sherman: Memoirs
52. Washington Irving: Bracebridge Hall, Tales of a Traveller, The Alhambra
53. Francis Parkman: The Oregon Trail, The Conspiracy of Pontiac
54. James Fenimore Cooper: Sea Tales
55 & 56. Richard Wright: Works
57. Willa Cather: Stories, Poems, & Other Writings
58. William James: Writings 1878–1899
59. Sinclair Lewis: Main Street & Babbitt
60 & 61. Mark Twain: Collected Tales, Sketches, Speeches, & Essays
62 & 63. The Debate on the Constitution
64 & 65. Henry James: Collected Travel Writings
66 & 67. American Poetry: The Nineteenth Century
68. Frederick Douglass: Autobiographies
69. Sarah Orne Jewett: Novels & Stories
70. Ralph Waldo Emerson: Collected Poems & Translations
71. Mark Twain: Historical Romances
72. John Steinbeck: Novels & Stories 1932–1937
73. William Faulkner: Novels 1942–1954
74 & 75. Zora Neale Hurston: Novels, Stories, & Other Writings
76. Thomas Paine: Collected Writings
77 & 78. Reporting World War II: American Journalism
79 & 80. Raymond Chandler: Novels, Stories, & Other Writings

81. Robert Frost: Collected Poems, Prose, & Plays
82 & 83. Henry James: Complete Stories 1892–1910
84. William Bartram: Travels & Other Writings
85. John Dos Passos: U.S.A.
86. John Steinbeck: The Grapes of Wrath & Other Writings 1936–1941
87, 88, & 89. Vladimir Nabokov: Novels & Other Writings
90. James Thurber: Writings & Drawings
91. George Washington: Writings
92. John Muir: Nature Writings
93. Nathanael West: Novels & Other Writings
94 & 95. Crime Novels: American Noir of the 1930s, 40s, & 50s
96. Wallace Stevens: Collected Poetry & Prose
97. James Baldwin: Early Novels & Stories
98. James Baldwin: Collected Essays
99 & 100. Gertrude Stein: Writings
101 & 102. Eudora Welty: Novels, Stories, & Other Writings
103. Charles Brockden Brown: Three Gothic Novels
104 & 105. Reporting Vietnam: American Journalism
106 & 107. Henry James: Complete Stories 1874–1891
108. American Sermons
109. James Madison: Writings
110. Dashiell Hammett: Complete Novels
111. Henry James: Complete Stories 1864–1874
112. William Faulkner: Novels 1957–1962
113. John James Audubon: Writings & Drawings
114. Slave Narratives
115 & 116. American Poetry: The Twentieth Century
117. F. Scott Fitzgerald: Novels & Stories 1920–1922
118. Henry Wadsworth Longfellow: Poems & Other Writings
119 & 120. Tennessee Williams: Collected Plays
121 & 122. Edith Wharton: Collected Stories
123. The American Revolution: Writings from the War of Independence
124. Henry David Thoreau: Collected Essays & Poems
125. Dashiell Hammett: Crime Stories & Other Writings
126 & 127. Dawn Powell: Novels

128. Carson McCullers: Complete Novels
129. Alexander Hamilton: Writings
130. Mark Twain: The Gilded Age & Later Novels
131. Charles W. Chesnutt: Stories, Novels, & Essays
132. John Steinbeck: Novels 1942–1952
133. Sinclair Lewis: Arrowsmith, Elmer Gantry, Dodsworth
134 & 135. Paul Bowles: Novels, Stories, & Other Writings
136. Kate Chopin: Complete Novels & Stories
137 & 138. Reporting Civil Rights: American Journalism
139. Henry James: Novels 1896–1899
140. Theodore Dreiser: An American Tragedy
141. Saul Bellow: Novels 1944–1953
142. John Dos Passos: Novels 1920–1925
143. John Dos Passos: Travel Books & Other Writings
144. Ezra Pound: Poems & Translations
145. James Weldon Johnson: Writings
146. Washington Irving: Three Western Narratives
147. Alexis de Tocqueville: Democracy in America
148. James T. Farrell: Studs Lonigan Trilogy
149, 150, & 151. Isaac Bashevis Singer: Collected Stories
152. Kaufman & Co.: Broadway Comedies
153. Theodore Roosevelt: Rough Riders, An Autobiography
154. Theodore Roosevelt: Letters & Speeches
155. H. P. Lovecraft: Tales
156. Louisa May Alcott: Little Women, Little Men, Jo's Boys
157. Philip Roth: Novels & Stories 1959–1962
158. Philip Roth: Novels 1967–1972
159. James Agee: Let Us Now Praise Famous Men, A Death in the Family, Shorter Fiction
160. James Agee: Film Writing & Selected Journalism
161. Richard Henry Dana Jr.: Two Years Before the Mast & Other Voyages
162. Henry James: Novels 1901–1902
163. Arthur Miller: Plays 1944–1961
164. William Faulkner: Novels 1926–1929
165. Philip Roth: Novels 1973–1977
166 & 167. American Speeches: Political Oratory
168. Hart Crane: Complete Poems & Selected Letters

169. Saul Bellow: Novels 1956–1964
170. John Steinbeck: Travels with Charley & Later Novels
171. Capt. John Smith: Writings with Other Narratives
172. Thornton Wilder: Collected Plays & Writings on Theater
173. Philip K. Dick: Four Novels of the 1960s
174. Jack Kerouac: Road Novels 1957–1960
175. Philip Roth: Zuckerman Bound
176 & 177. Edmund Wilson: Literary Essays & Reviews
178. American Poetry: The 17th & 18th Centuries
179. William Maxwell: Early Novels & Stories
180. Elizabeth Bishop: Poems, Prose, & Letters
181. A. J. Liebling: World War II Writings
182. American Earth: Environmental Writing Since Thoreau
183. Philip K. Dick: Five Novels of the 1960s & 70s
184. William Maxwell: Later Novels & Stories
185. Philip Roth: Novels & Other Narratives 1986–1991
186. Katherine Anne Porter: Collected Stories & Other Writings
187. John Ashbery: Collected Poems 1956–1987
188 & 189. John Cheever: Complete Novels & Collected Stories
190. Lafcadio Hearn: American Writings
191. A. J. Liebling: The Sweet Science & Other Writings
192. The Lincoln Anthology
193. Philip K. Dick: VALIS & Later Novels
194. Thornton Wilder: The Bridge of San Luis Rey & Other Novels 1926–1948
195. Raymond Carver: Collected Stories
196 & 197. American Fantastic Tales
198. John Marshall: Writings
199. The Mark Twain Anthology
200. Mark Twain: A Tramp Abroad, Following the Equator, Other Travels
201 & 202. Ralph Waldo Emerson: Selected Journals
203. The American Stage: Writing on Theater
204. Shirley Jackson: Novels & Stories
205. Philip Roth: Novels 1993–1995
206 & 207. H. L. Mencken: Prejudices
208. John Kenneth Galbraith: The Affluent Society & Other Writings 1952–1967
209. Saul Bellow: Novels 1970–1982
210 & 211. Lynd Ward: Six Novels in Woodcuts
212. The Civil War: The First Year
213 & 214. John Adams: Revolutionary Writings
215. Henry James: Novels 1903–1911
216. Kurt Vonnegut: Novels & Stories 1963–1973
217 & 218. Harlem Renaissance Novels
219. Ambrose Bierce: The Devil's Dictionary, Tales, & Memoirs
220. Philip Roth: The American Trilogy 1997–2000
221. The Civil War: The Second Year
222. Barbara W. Tuchman: The Guns of August, The Proud Tower
223. Arthur Miller: Plays 1964–1982
224. Thornton Wilder: The Eighth Day, Theophilus North, Autobiographical Writings
225. David Goodis: Five Noir Novels of the 1940s & 50s
226. Kurt Vonnegut: Novels & Stories 1950–1962
227 & 228. American Science Fiction: Nine Novels of the 1950s
229 & 230. Laura Ingalls Wilder: The Little House Books
231. Jack Kerouac: Collected Poems
232. The War of 1812
233. American Antislavery Writings
234. The Civil War: The Third Year
235. Sherwood Anderson: Collected Stories
236. Philip Roth: Novels 2001–2007
237. Philip Roth: Nemeses
238. Aldo Leopold: A Sand County Almanac & Other Writings
239. May Swenson: Collected Poems
240 & 241. W. S. Merwin: Collected Poems
242 & 243. John Updike: Collected Stories
244. Ring Lardner: Stories & Other Writings
245. Jonathan Edwards: Writings from the Great Awakening
246. Susan Sontag: Essays of the 1960s & 70s
247. William Wells Brown: Clotel & Other Writings
248 & 249. Bernard Malamud: Novels & Stories of the 1940s, 50s, & 60s
250. The Civil War: The Final Year
251. Shakespeare in America

252. Kurt Vonnegut: Novels 1976–1985

253 & 254. American Musicals 1927–1969

255. Elmore Leonard: Four Novels of the 1970s

256. Louisa May Alcott: Work, Eight Cousins, Rose in Bloom, Stories & Other Writings

257. H. L. Mencken: The Days Trilogy

258. Virgil Thomson: Music Chronicles 1940–1954

259. Art in America 1945–1970

260. Saul Bellow: Novels 1984–2000

261. Arthur Miller: Plays 1987–2004

262. Jack Kerouac: Visions of Cody, Visions of Gerard, Big Sur

263. Reinhold Niebuhr: Major Works on Religion & Politics

264. Ross Macdonald: Four Novels of the 1950s

265 & 266. The American Revolution: Writings from the Pamphlet Debate

267. Elmore Leonard: Four Novels of the 1980s

268 & 269. Women Crime Writers: Suspense Novels of the 1940s & 50s

270. Frederick Law Olmsted: Writings on Landscape, Culture, & Society

271. Edith Wharton: Four Novels of the 1920s

272. James Baldwin: Later Novels

273. Kurt Vonnegut: Novels 1987–1997

274. Henry James: Autobiographies

275. Abigail Adams: Letters

276. John Adams: Writings from the New Nation 1784–1826

277. Virgil Thomson: The State of Music & Other Writings

278. War No More: American Antiwar & Peace Writing

279. Ross Macdonald: Three Novels of the Early 1960s

280. Elmore Leonard: Four Later Novels

281. Ursula K. Le Guin: The Complete Orsinia

282. John O'Hara: Stories

283. The Unknown Kerouac: Rare, Unpublished & Newly Translated Writings

284. Albert Murray: Collected Essays & Memoirs

285 & 286. Loren Eiseley: Collected Essays on Evolution, Nature, & the Cosmos

287. Carson McCullers: Stories, Plays & Other Writings

288. Jane Bowles: Collected Writings

289. World War I and America: Told by the Americans Who Lived It

290 & 291. Mary McCarthy: The Complete Fiction

292. Susan Sontag: Later Essays

293 & 294. John Quincy Adams: Diaries

295. Ross Macdonald: Four Later Novels

296 & 297. Ursula K. Le Guin: The Hainish Novels & Stories

298 & 299. Peter Taylor: The Complete Stories

300. Philip Roth: Why Write? Collected Nonfiction 1960–2014

301. John Ashbery: Collected Poems 1991–2000

302. Wendell Berry: Port William Novels & Stories: The Civil War to World War II

303. Reconstruction: Voices from America's First Great Struggle for Racial Equality

304. Albert Murray: Collected Novels & Poems

305 & 306. Norman Mailer: The Sixties

307. Rachel Carson: Silent Spring & Other Writings on the Environment

308. Elmore Leonard: Westerns

309 & 310. Madeleine L'Engle: The Kairos Novels

311. John Updike: Novels 1959–1965

312. James Fenimore Cooper: Two Novels of the American Revolution

313. John O'Hara: Four Novels of the 1930s

314. Ann Petry: The Street, The Narrows

315. Ursula K. Le Guin: Always Coming Home

316 & 317. Wendell Berry: Collected Essays

318. Cornelius Ryan: The Longest Day, A Bridge Too Far

319. Booth Tarkington: Novels & Stories

320. Herman Melville: Complete Poems

321 & 322. American Science Fiction: Eight Classic Novels of the 1960s

323. Frances Hodgson Burnett: The Secret Garden, A Little Princess, Little Lord Fauntleroy

324. Jean Stafford: Complete Novels

325. Joan Didion: The 1960s & 70s

326. John Updike: Novels 1968–1975

327. Constance Fenimore Woolson: Collected Stories

328. Robert Stone: Dog Soldiers, Flag for Sunrise, Outerbridge Reach

329. Jonathan Schell: The Fate of the Earth, The Abolition, The Unconquerable World

330. Richard Hofstadter: Anti-Intellectualism in American Life, The Paranoid Style in American Politics, Uncollected Essays 1956–1965

# DATE DUE

| | | |
|---|---|---|
| MAY 1 8 2021 | | |
| | | |
| | | |
| | | |
| | | |
| | | |
| | | |
| | | |
| | | |
| | | |
| | | |
| | | |
| | | |
| | | |
| | | |
| | | |
| | | PRINTED IN U.S.A. |

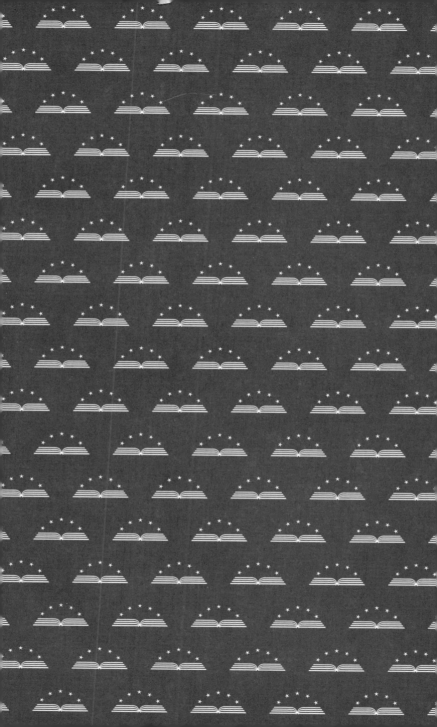